GW01606537

Henry James

The Europeans

Daisy Miller

Washington Square

The Aspern Papers

The Turn of the Screw

The Portrait of a Lady

Heinemann/Octopus

Henry James

The Europeans first published in Great Britain
in 1878 by Macmillan Limited
Daisy Miller first published in Great Britain
in 1880 by Macmillan Limited
Washington Square first published in Great Britain
in 1881 by Macmillan Limited
The Aspern Papers first published in Great Britain
in 1888 by Macmillan Limited
The Turn of the Screw first published in Great Britain
in 1898 by William Heinemann Ltd
The Portrait of a Lady first published in Great Britain
in 1880–2 by Macmillan Limited

This edition first published in Great Britain
in 1981 jointly by

William Heinemann Limited
10 Upper Grosvenor Street
London W1

Martin Secker & Warburg Limited
54 Poland Street
London W1

and

Octopus Books Limited
59 Grosvenor Street
London W1

ISBN 0 905712 55 2

Printed in the United States of America

Contents

The Europeans

Chapter One

A narrow grave-yard in the heart of bustling, indifferent city, seen from the windows of a gloomy-looking inn, is at no time an object of enlivening suggestion; and the spectacle is not at its best when the mouldy tombstones and funereal umbrage have received the ineffectual refreshment of a dull, moist snow-fall. If, while the air is thickened by this frosty drizzle, the calendar should happen to indicate that the blessed vernal season is already six weeks old, it will be admitted that no depressing influence is absent from the scene. This fact was keenly felt on a certain 12th of May, upwards of thirty years since, by a lady who stood looking out of one of the windows of the best hotel in the ancient city of Boston. She had stood there for half an hour – stood there, that is, at intervals; for from time to time she turned back into the room and measured its length with a restless step. In the chimney-place was a red-hot fire, which emitted a small blue flame! and in front of the fire, at a table, sat a young man who was busily plying a pencil. He had a number of sheets of paper, cut into small equal squares, and he was apparently covering them with pictorial designs – strange-looking figures. He worked rapidly and attentively, sometimes threw back his head and held out his drawing at arm's length, and kept up a soft, gay-sounding humming and whistling. The lady brushed past him in her walk; her much-trimmed skirts were voluminous. She never dropped her eyes upon his work; she only turned them, occasionally, as she passed, to a mirror suspended above a toilet-table on the other side of the room. Here she paused a moment, gave a pinch to her waist with her two hands, or raised these members – they were very plump and pretty – to the multifold braids of her hair, with a movement half-caressing, half-corrective. An attentive observer might have fancied that during these periods of desultory self-inspection her face forgot its melancholy; but as soon as she neared the window again it began to proclaim that she was a very ill-pleased woman. And indeed in what met her eyes there was little to be pleased with. The window-panes were battered by the sleet; the head-stones in the grave-yard beneath seemed to be holding themselves askance to keep it out of their faces. A tall iron railing protected them from the street, and on the other side of the railing an assemblage of Bostonians were trampling about in the liquid snow. Many of them were looking up and down; they appeared to be waiting for something. From time to time a strange vehicle drew near to the place where they stood – such a vehicle as the lady at the window, in spite of a considerable acquaintance with human inventions, had never seen before: a huge, low omnibus, painted in brilliant colours, and decorated apparently with jingling bells, attached to a species of groove in the pavement, through which it was dragged, with a great deal of rumbling, bouncing, and scratching, by a couple of remarkably small horses. When it reached a certain point the people in front of the grave-yard, of whom much the greater number were women, carrying satchels and parcels, projected themselves upon it in a compact body – a movement suggesting the scramble for places in a life-boat at sea – and were engulfed in its large interior. Then the life-boat – or the life-car, as the lady at the window of the hotel vaguely designated it – went bumping and jingling away upon its invisible wheels, with the helmsman (the man at the wheel) guiding its course incongruously from the prow. This phenomenon was repeated every three minutes, and the supply of eagerly-moving women in cloaks, bearing reticules and bundles, renewed itself in the most liberal manner. On the other side of the grave-yard was a row of small red-brick houses, showing a series of homely, domestic-looking backs; at the end opposite the hotel, a tall wooden church spire, painted white, rose high into the vagueness of the snow-flakes. The lady at the window looked at it for some time; for reasons of her own she thought it the ugliest thing she had ever seen. She hated it, she despised it; it threw her into a state of irritation that was quite out of proportion to any sensible motive. She had never known herself to care so much about church spires.

She was not pretty; but even when it expressed perplexed irritation her face was most interesting and agreeable. Neither was she in her first youth; yet, though slender, with a great deal of extremely well-fashioned roundness of contour – a suggestion both of maturity and flexibility – she carried her three-and-thirty years as a light-wristed Hebe might have carried a brimming wine-cup. Her complexion was fatigued, as the French say; her mouth was large, her lips too full, her teeth uneven, her chin rather commonly modelled; she has a thick nose, and when she smiled – she was constantly smiling – the lines beside it rose too high, toward her eyes. But these eyes were charming; grey in colour, brilliant, quickly glancing, gently resting, full of intelligence. Her forehead was very low – it was her only handsome feature; and she had a great abundance of crisp dark hair, finely frizzled, which was always braided in a manner that suggested some Southern or Eastern, some remotely foreign, woman. She had a large collection of earrings, and wore them in alternation; and they seemed to give a point to her Oriental or exotic aspect. A compliment had once been paid her which, being repeated to her, gave her greater pleasure than anything she had ever heard. 'A pretty woman?' some one had said, 'Why, her features are very bad.' 'I don't know about her features,' a very discerning observer had answered; 'but she carries her head like a pretty woman.' You may imagine whether, after this, she carried her head less becomingly.

She turned away from the window at last, pressing her hands to her eyes. 'It's too horrible!' she exclaimed. 'I shall go back – I shall go back!' And she flung herself into a chair before the fire.

'Wait a little, dear child,' said the young man softly, sketching away at his little scraps of paper.

The lady put out her foot; it was very small, and there was an immense rosette on her slipper. She fixed her eyes for a while on this ornament, and then she looked at the glowing bed of anthracite coal in the grate. 'Did you ever see anything so hideous as that fire?' she demanded. 'Did you ever see anything so – so *affreux* as – as everything?' She spoke English with perfect purity; but she brought out this French epithet in a manner that indicated that she was accustomed to using French epithets.

'I think the fire is very pretty,' said the young man, glancing at it a moment. 'Those little blue tongues, dancing on top of the crimson embers, are extremely picturesque. They are like a fire in an alchemist's laboratory.'

'You are too good-natured, my dear,' his companion declared.

The young man held out one of his drawings, with his head on one side. His tongue was gently moving along his underlip. 'Good natured – yes. Too good-natured – no.'

'You are irritating,' said the lady, looking at her slipper.

He began to retouch his sketch. 'I think you mean simply that you are irritated.'

'Ah, for that, yes!' said his companion, with a little bitter laugh. 'It's the darkest day of my life – and you know what that means.'

'Wait till tomorrow,' rejoined the young man.

'Yes, we have made a great mistake. If there is any doubt about it today, there certainly will be none tomorrow. *Ce sera clair, au moins!*'

The young man was silent for a few moments, driving his pencil. Then at last, 'There are no such things as mistakes,' he affirmed.

'Very true – for those who are not clever enough to perceive them. Not to recognize one's mistakes – that would be happiness in life,' the lady went on, still looking at her pretty foot.

'My dearest sister,' said the young man, always intent upon his drawing, 'it's the first time you have told me I am not clever.'

'Well, by your own theory I can't call it a mistake,' answered his sister, pertinently enough.

The young man gave a clear, fresh laugh. 'You, at least, are clever enough, dearest sister,' he said.

'I was not so when I proposed this.'

'Was it you who proposed it?' asked her brother.

She turned her head and gave him a little stare. 'Do you desire the credit of it?'

'If you like, I will take the blame,' he said, looking up with a smile.

'Yes,' she rejoined in a moment, 'you make no difference in these things. You have no sense of property.'

The young man gave his joyous laugh again. 'If that means I have no property, you are right!'

'Don't joke about your poverty,' said his sister. 'That is quite as vulgar as to boast about it.'

'My poverty! I have just finished a drawing that will bring me fifty francs!'

'*Voyons!*' said the lady, putting out her hand.

He added a touch or two, and then gave her his sketch. She looked at it, but she went on with her idea of a moment before. 'If a woman were to ask you to marry her you would say, "Certainly, my dear, with pleasure!" And you would marry her, and be ridiculously happy. Then at the end of three months you would say to her, "You know that blissful day when I begged you to be mine!" '

The young man had risen from the table, stretching his arms a little; he walked to the window. 'That is a description of a charming nature,' he said.

'Oh yes, you have a charming nature; I regard that as our capital. If I had not been convinced of that I should never have taken the risk of bringing you to this dreadful country.'

'This comical country, this delightful country!' exclaimed the young man; and he broke into the most animated laughter.

'Is it those women scrambling into the omnibus?' asked his companion. 'What do you suppose is the attraction?'

'I suppose there is a very good-looking man inside,' said the young man.

'In each of them? They come along in hundreds, and the men in this country don't seem at all handsome. As for the women – I have never seen so many at once since I left the convent.'

'The women are very pretty,' her brother declared, 'and the whole affair is very amusing. I must make a sketch of it.' And he came back to the table quickly, and picked up his utensils – a small sketching-board, a sheet of paper, and three or four crayons. He took his place at the window with these things, and stood there glancing out, plying his pencil with an air of easy skill. While he worked he wore a brilliant smile. Brilliant is indeed the word at this moment for his strongly-lighted face. He was eight-and-twenty years old; he had a short, slight, well-made figure. Though he bore a noticeable resemblance to his sister, he was a better-favoured person: fair-haired, clear-faced, witty-looking, with a delicate finish of feature and an expression at once urbane and not at all serious, a warm blue eye, an eyebrow finely drawn and excessively arched – an eyebrow which, if ladies wrote sonnets to those of their lovers, might have made the subject of such a piece of verse – and a light moustache that flourished upwards as if blown that way by the breath of a constant smile. There was something in his physiognomy at once benevolent and picturesque. But, as I have hinted, it was not at all serious. The young man's face was, in this respect, singular; it was not at all serious, and yet it inspired the liveliest confidence.

'Be sure you put in plenty of snow,' said his sister. '*Bontê divine*, what a climate!'

'I shall leave the sketch all white, and I shall put in the little figures in black,' the young man answered, laughing. 'And I shall call it – what is that line in Keats? – Mid-May's Eldest Child!'

'I don't remember,' said the lady, 'that mamma ever told me it was like this.'

'Mamma never told you anything disagreeable. And it's not like this – every day. You will see that tomorrow we shall have a splendid day.'

'*Qu'en savez-vous?* Tomorrow I shall go away.'

'Where shall you go?'

'Anywhere away from here. Back to Silberstadt. I shall write to the Reigning Prince.'

The young man turned a little and looked at her, with his crayon poised. 'My dear Eugenia,' he murmured, 'were you so happy at sea?'

Eugenia got up; she still held in her hand the drawing her brother had given her. It was a bold expressive sketch of a group of miserable people on the deck of a steamer, clinging together and clutching at each other, while the vessel lurched downward, at a terrific angle, into the hollow of a wave. It was extremely clever, and full of a sort of tragi-comical power. Eugenia dropped her eyes upon it and made a sad grimace. 'How can you draw such odious scenes?' she asked. 'I should like to throw it into the fire!' And she tossed the paper away. Her brother watched, quietly, to see where it went. It fluttered down to the floor, where he let it lie. She came toward the window, pinching at her waist. 'Why don't you reproach me – abuse me?' she asked. 'I think I should feel better then. Why don't you tell me that you hate me for bringing you here?'

'Because you would not believe it. I adore you, dear sister! I am delighted to be here, and I am charmed with the prospect.'

'I don't know what had taken possession of me. I had lost my head,' Eugenia went on.

The young man, on his side, went on plying his pencil. 'It is evidently a most curious and interesting country. Here we are, and I mean to enjoy it.'

His companion turned away with an impatient step, but presently came back. 'High spirits are doubtless an excellent thing,' she said; 'but you give one too much of them, and I can't see that they have done you any good.'

The young man stared, with lifted eyebrows, smiling; he tapped his handsome nose with his pencil. 'They have made me happy!'

'That was the least they could do; they have made you nothing else. You have gone through life thanking fortune for such very small favours that she has never put herself to any trouble for you.'

'She must have put herself to a little, I think, to present me with so admirable a sister.'

'Be serious, Felix. You forget that I am your elder.'

'With a sister, then, so elderly!' rejoined Felix, laughing. 'I hoped we had left seriousness in Europe.'

'I fancy you will find it here. Remember that you are nearly thirty years old, and that you are nothing but an obscure Bohemian – a penniless correspondent of an illustrated paper.'

'Obscure as much as you please, but not so much of a Bohemian as you think. And not at all penniless! I have a hundred pounds in my pocket; I have an engagement to make fifty sketches, and I mean to paint the portraits of all our cousins, and of all *their* cousins, at a hundred dollars a head.'

'You are not ambitious,' said Eugenia.

'You are, dear Baroness,' the young man replied.

The Baroness was silent a moment, looking out at the sleet-darkened grave-yard and the bumping horse-cars. 'Yes, I am ambitious,' she said at last. 'And my ambition has brought me to this dreadful place!' She glanced about her – the room had a certain vulgar nudity, the bed and the window were curtainless – and she gave a little passionate sigh. 'Poor old ambition!' she exclaimed. Then she flung herself down upon a sofa which stood near against the wall, and covered her face with her hands.

Her brother went on with his drawing, rapidly and skilfully; and after some moments he sat down beside her and showed her his sketch. 'Now, don't you think that's pretty good for an obscure Bohemian?' he asked. 'I have knocked off another fifty francs.'

Eugenia glanced at the little picture as he laid it on her lap.

'Yes, it is very clever,' she said. And in a moment, she added, 'Do you suppose our cousins do that?'

'Do what?'

'Get into those things, and look like that.'

Felix meditated a while. 'I really can't say. It will be interesting to discover.'

'Oh, the rich people can't!' said the Baroness.

'Are you very sure they are rich?' Felix asked lightly.

His sister slowly turned in her place, looking at him. 'Heavenly powers!' she murmured. 'You have a way of bringing out things!'

'It will certainly be much pleasanter if they are rich,' Felix declared.

'Do you suppose if I had not known they were rich I would ever have come?'

The young man met his sister's somewhat peremptory eye with his bright, contented glance. 'Yes, it certainly will be pleasanter,' he repeated.

'This is all I expect of them,' said the Baroness. 'I don't count upon their being clever or friendly – at first – or elegant or interesting. But I assure you I insist upon their being rich.'

Felix leaned his head upon the back of the sofa and looked a while at the oblong patch of sky to which the window served as frame. The snow was ceasing; it seemed to him that the sky had begun to brighten. 'I count upon their being rich,' he said at last, 'and powerful, and clever, and friendly, and elegant, and interesting, and generallly delightful! *Tu vas voir.*' And he bent forward and kissed his sister. 'Look there!' he went on. 'As a portent, even while I speak, the sky is turning the colour of gold; the day is going to be splendid.'

And indeed, within five minutes the weather had changed. The sun broke out through the snow-clouds and jumped into the Baroness's room. '*Bonté divine*,' exclaimed the lady, 'what a climate!'

'We will go out and see the world,' said Felix.

And after a while they went out. The air had grown warm, as well as brilliant; the sunshine had dried the pavements. They walked about the streets at hazard, looking at the people and the houses, the shops and the vehicles, the blazing blue sky and the muddy crossings, the hurrying men and the slow-strolling maidens, the fresh red bricks and the bright green trees, the extraordinary mixture of smartness and shabbiness. From one hour to another the day had grown vernal; even in the bustling streets there was an odour of earth and blossom. Felix was immensely entertained. He had called it a comical country, and he went about laughing at everything he saw. You would have said that American civilization expressed itself to his sense in a tissue of capital jokes. The jokes were certainly excellent, and the young man's merriment was very joyous and genial. He possessed what is called the pictorial sense, and this first glimpse of democratic manners stirred the same sort of attention that he would have given to the movements of a lively young person with a bright complexion. Such attention would have been demonstrative and complimentary; and in the present case Felix might have passed for the undispirited young exile revisiting the haunts of his childhood. He kept looking at the violet blue sky, at the scintillating air, at the scattered and multiplied patches of colour.

'*Comme c'est bariolé*, eh?' he said to his sister, in that foreign tongue which they both appeared to feel a mysterious prompting occasionally to use.

'Yes, it is *bariolé* indeed,' the Baroness answered. 'I don't like the colouring; it hurts my eyes.'

'It shows how extremes meet,' the young man rejoined. 'Instead of coming to the West we seem to have gone to the East. The way the sky touches the house-tops is just like Cairo; and the red and blue sign-boards patched over the face of everything remind one of Mahometan decoration.'

'The young women are not Mahometan,' said his companion. 'They can't be said to hide their faces. I never saw anything so bold.'

'Thank heaven they don't hide their faces!' cried Felix. 'Their faces are uncommonly pretty.'

'Yes, their faces are often very pretty,' said the Baroness, who was a very clever woman. She was too clever a woman not to be capable of a great deal of just and fine observation. She clung more closely than usual to her brother's arm; she was not exhilarated, as he was; she said very little, but she noted a great many things, and made her reflexions. She was a little excited; she felt that she had indeed come to a strange country, to make her fortune. Superficially, she was conscious of a good deal of irritation and displeasure; the Baroness was a very delicate and fastidious person. Of old, more than once, she had gone, for entertainment's sake and in brilliant company, to a fair in a provincial town. It seemed to her now that she was at an enormous fair – that the entertainment and the *désagrements* were very much the same. She found herself alternately smiling and shrinking; the show was very curious, but it was probable from moment to moment that one would be jostled. The Baroness had never seen so many people walking about before; she had never been so mixed up with people she did not know. But little by little she felt that this fair was a more serious undertaking. She went with her brother into a large public garden, which seemed very pretty, but where she was surprised at seeing no carriages. The afternoon was drawing to a close; the coarse, vivid grass and the slender tree-boles were gilded by the level sunbeams – gilded as with gold that was fresh from the mine. It was the hour at which ladies should come out for an airing and roll past a hedge of pedestrians, holding their parasols askance. Here, however, Eugenia observed no indications of this custom, the absence of which was more anomalous as there was a charming avenue of remarkably graceful arching elms in the most convenient contiguity to a large, cheeful street, in which, evidently, among the more prosperous members of the *bourgeoisie*, a great deal of pedestrianism went forward. Our friends passed out into this well-lighted promenade, and Felix noticed a great many more pretty girls, and called his sister's attention to them. This latter measure, however, was superfluous; for the Baroness had inspected, narrowly, these charming young ladies.

'I feel an intimate conviction that our cousins are like that,' said Felix.

The Baroness hoped so, but this is not what she said. 'They are very pretty,' she said, 'but they are mere little girls. Where are the women – the women of thirty?'

'Of thirty-three, do you mean?' her brother was going to ask; for he understood often both what she said and what she did not say. But he only exclaimed upon the beauty of the sunset, while the Baroness, who had come to seek her fortune, reflected that it would certainly be well for her if the persons against whom she might need to measure herself should all be mere little girls. The sunset was superb; they stopped to look at it; Felix declared that he had never seen such a gorgeous mixture of colours. The Baroness also thought it splendid; and she was perhaps the more easily pleased from the fact that while she stood there she was conscious of much admiring observation on the part of various nice-looking people who passed that way, and to whom a distinguished, strikingly-dressed woman with a foreign air, exclaiming upon the beauties of nature on a Boston street corner in the French tongue, could not be an object of indifference. Eugenia's spirits rose. She surrendered herself to a certain tranquil gaiety. If she had come to seek her fortune, it seemed to her that her fortune would be easy to find. There was a promise of it in the gorgeous purity of the western sky; there was an intimation in the mild unimpertinent gaze of the passers of a certain natural facility in things.

'You will not go back to Silberstadt, eh?' asked Felix.

'Not tomorrow,' said the Baroness.

'Nor write to the Reigning Prince?'

'I shall write to him that they evidently know nothing about him over here.'

'He will not believe you,' said the young man. 'I advise you to let him alone.'

Felix himself continued to be in high good-humour. Brought up among ancient customs and in picturesque cities, he yet found plenty of local colour in the little Puritan metropolis. That evening, after dinner, he told his sister that he would go forth early on the morrow to look up their cousins.

'You are very impatient,' said Eugenia.

'What can be more natural,' he asked, 'after seeing all those pretty girls today? If one's cousins are of that pattern, the sooner one knows them the better.'

'Perhaps they are not,' said Eugenia. 'We ought to have brought some letters – to some other people.'

'The other people would not be our kinsfolk.'

'Possibly they would be none the worse for that,' the Baroness replied.

Her brother looked at her with his eyebrows lifted. 'That was not what you said when you first proposed to me that we should come out here and fraternize with our relatives. You said that it was the prompting of natural affection; and when I suggested some reasons against it you declared that the *voix du sang* should go before everything.'

'You remember all that?' asked the Baroness.

'Vividly! I was greatly moved by it.'

She was walking up and down the room, as she had done in the morning; she stopped in her walk and looked at her brother. She apparently was going to say something, but she checked herself and resumed her walk. Then, in a few moments, she said something different, which had the effect of an explanation of the suppression of her earlier thought. 'You will never be anything but a child, dear brother.'

'One would suppose that you, madam,' answered Felix, laughing, 'were a thousand years old.'

'I am – sometimes,' said the Baroness.

'I will go, then, and announce to our cousins the arrival of a personage so extraordinary. They will immediately come and pay you their respects.'

Eugenia paced the length of the room again, and then she stopped before her brother, laying her hand upon his arm. 'They are not to come and see me,' she said. 'You are not to allow that. That is not the way I shall meet them first.' And in answer to his interrogative glance she went on, 'You will go and examine, and report. You will come back and tell me who they are and what they are; their number, gender, their respective ages – all about them. Be sure you observe everything; be ready to describe to me the locality, the accessories – how shall I say it? – the *mise en scène*. Then, at my own time, I will go to them. I will present myself – I will appear before them!' said the Baroness, this time phrasing her idea with a certain frankness.

'And what message am I to take to them?' asked Felix, who had a lively faith in the justness of his sister's arrangements.

She looked at him a moment – at his expression of agreeable veracity; and, with that justness that he admired, she replied, 'Say what you please. Tell my story in the way that seems to you most – natural.' And she bent her forehead for him to kiss.

Chapter Two

The next day was splendid, as Felix had prophesied; if the winter had suddenly leaped into spring, the spring had for the moment as quickly leaped into summer. This was an observation made by a young girl who came out of a large square house in the country, and strolled about in the spacious garden which separated it from a muddy road. The flowering shrubs and the neatly-disposed plants were basking in the abundant light and warmth; the transparent shade of the great elms – they were magnificent trees – seemed to thicken by the hour; and the intensely habitual stillness offered a submissive medium to the sound of a distant church-bell. The young girl listened to the church-bell; but she was not dressed for church. She was bareheaded; she wore a white muslin waist with an embroidered border, and the skirt of her dress was of coloured muslin. She was a young lady of some two or three and twenty years of age, and though a young person of her sex walking bare-headed in a garden, of a Sunday morning in spring-time, can, in the nature of things, never be a displeasing object, you would not have pronounced this innocent Sabbath-breaker especially pretty. She was tall and pale, thin and a little awkward; her hair was fair and perfectly straight; her eyes were dark, and they had the singularity of seeming at once dull and restless – differing herein, as you see, fatally from the ideal 'fine eyes', which we always imagine to be both brilliant and tranquil. The doors and windows of the large square house were all wide open, to admit the purifying sunshine, which lay in generous patches upon the floor of a wide, high, covered piazza adjusted to two sides of the mansion – a piazza on which several straw-bottomed rocking-chairs and half a dozen of those small cylindrical stools in green and blue porcelain, which suggest an affiliation between the residents and the Eastern trade, were symmetrically disposed.

It was an ancient house – ancient in the sense of being eighty years old; it was built of wood, painted a clean, clear, faded grey, and adorned along the front, at intervals, with flat wooden pilasters, painted white. These pilasters appeared to support a kind of classic pediment, which was decorated in the middle by a large triple window in a boldly-carved frame, and in each of its smaller angles by a glazed circular aperture. A large white door, furnished with a highly-polished brass knocker, presented itself to the rural-looking road, with which it was connected by a spacious pathway, paved with worn and cracked, but very clean, bricks. Behind it there were meadows and orchards, a barn and a pond; and, facing it, a short distance along the road, on the opposite side, stood a smaller house, painted white, with external shutters painted green, a little garden on one hand and an orchard on the other. All this was shining in the morning air, through which the simple details of the picture addressed themselves to the eye as distinctly as the items of a 'sum' in addition.

A second young lady presently came out of the house, across the piazza, descended into the garden and approached the young girl of whom I have spoken. This second young lady was also thin and pale; but she was older than the other; she was shorter; she had dark, smooth hair. Her eyes, unlike the other's, were quick and bright; but they were not at all restless. She wore a straw bonnet with white ribbons; and a long red India scarf, which, on the front of her dress, reached to her feet. In her hand she carried a little key.

'Gertrude,' she said, 'are you very sure you had better not go to church?'

Gertrude looked at her a moment, plucked a small sprig from a lilac-bush, smelled it and threw it away. 'I am not very sure of anything!' she answered.

The other young lady looked straight past her, at the distant pond, which lay shining between the long banks of fir trees. Then she said in a very soft voice, 'This is the key of the dining-room closet. I think you had better have it, if any one should want anything.'

'Who is there to want anything?' Gertrude demanded. 'I shall be all alone in the house.'

'Someone may come,' said her companion.

'Do you mean Mr Brand?'

'Yes, Gertrude. He may like a piece of cake.'

'I don't like men that are always eating cake!' Gertrude declared, giving a pull at the lilac-bush.

Her companion glanced at her, and then looked down on the ground. 'I think father expected you would come to church,' she said. 'What shall I say to him?'

'Say I have a bad headache.'

'Would that be true?' asked the elder lady, looking straight at the pond again.

'No, Charlotte,' said the younger one simply.

Charlotte transferred her quiet eyes to her companion's face. 'I am afraid you are feeling restless.'

'I am feeling as I always feel,' Gertrude replied, in the same tone.

Charlotte turned away; but she stood there a moment. Presently she looked down at the front of her dress. 'Doesn't it seem to you, somehow, as if my scarf were too long?' she asked.

Gertrude walked half round her, looking at the scarf. 'I don't think you wear it right,' she said.

'How should I wear it, dear?'

'I don't know; differently from that. You should draw it differently over your shoulders, round your elbows; you should look differently behind.'

'How should I look?' Charlotte inquired.

'I don't think I can tell you,' said Gertrude, plucking out the scarf a little behind. 'I could do it myself, but I don't think I can explain it.'

Charlotte, by a movement of her elbows, corrected the laxity that had come from her companion's touch. 'Well, some day you must do it for me. It doesn't matter now. Indeed, I don't think it matters,' she added, 'how one looks behind.'

'I should say it mattered more,' said Gertrude. 'Then you don't know who may be observing you. You are not on your guard. You can't try to look pretty.'

Charlotte received this declaration with extreme gravity. 'I don't think one should ever try to look pretty,' she rejoined earnestly.

Her companion was silent. Then she said, 'Well, perhaps it's not of much use.'

Charlotte looked at her a little, and then kissed her. 'I hope you will be better when we come back.'

'My dear sister, I am very well!' said Gertrude.

Charlotte went down the large brick walk to the garden gate; her companion strolled slowly toward the house. At the gate Charlotte met a young man, who was coming in – a tall, fair young man, wearing a high hat and a pair of thread gloves. He was handsome, but rather too stout. He had a pleasant smile. 'Oh, Mr Brand!' exclaimed the young lady.

'I came to see whether your sister was not going to church,' said the young man.

'She says she is not going; but I am very glad you have come. I think if you were to talk to her a little' . . . and Charlotte lowered her voice. 'It seems as if she were restless.'

Mr Brand smiled down on the young lady from his great height. 'I shall be very glad to talk to her. For that I should be willing to absent myself from almost any occasion of worship, however attractive.'

'Well, I suppose you know,' said Charlotte softly, as if positive acceptance of this proposition might be dangerous. 'But I am afraid I shall be late.'

'I hope you will have a pleasant sermon,' said the young man.

'Oh, Mr Gilman is always pleasant,' Charlotte answered. And she went on her way.

Mr Brand went into the garden, where Gertrude, hearing the gate close behind him, turned and looked at him. For a moment she watched him coming; then she turned away. But almost immediately she corrected this movement, and stood still, facing him. He took off his hat and wiped his forehead, as he approached. Then he put on his hat again and held out his hand. His hat being removed, you would have perceived that his forehead was very large and smooth, and his hair abundant but rather colourless. His nose was too large, and his mouth and eyes were too small; but for all this he was, as I have said, a young man of striking appearance. The expression of his little clean-coloured blue eyes was irresistibly gentle and serious; he looked, as the phrase is, as good as gold. The young girl, standing in the garden path, glanced, as he came up, at his thread gloves.

'I hoped you were going to church,' he said. 'I wanted to walk with you.'

'I am very much obliged to you,' Gertrude answered. 'I am not going to church.'

She had shaken hands with him; he held her hand a moment. 'Have you any special reason for not going?'

'Yes, Mr Brand,' said the young girl.

'May I ask what it is?'

She looked at him, smiling; and in her smile, as I have intimated, there was a certain dullness. But mingled with this dullness was something sweet and suggestive. 'Because the sky is so blue!' she said.

He looked at the sky, which was magnificent, and then said, smiling too, 'I have heard of young ladies staying at home for bad weather, but never for good. Your sister, whom I met at the gate, tells me you are depressed,' he added.

'Depressed? I am never depressed.'

'Oh, surely, sometimes,' replied Mr Brand, as if he thought this a regrettable account of one's self.

'I am never depressed,' Gertrude repeated. 'But I am sometimes wicked. When I am wicked I am in high spirits. I was wicked just now to my sister.'

'What did you do to her?'

'I said things that puzzled her – on purpose.'

'Why did you do that, Miss Gertrude?' asked the young man.

She began to smile again. 'Because the sky is so blue!'

'You say things that puzzle me,' Mr Brand declared.

'I always know when I do it,' proceeded Gertrude. 'But people puzzle me more, I think. And they don't seem to know!'

'This is very interesting,' Mr Brand observed, smiling.

'You told me to tell you about my – my struggles,' the young girl went on.

'Let us talk about them. I have so many things to say.'

Gertrude turned away a moment; and then, turning back, 'You had better go to church,' she said.

'You know,' the young man urged, 'that I have always one thing to say.'

Gertrude looked at him a moment. 'Please don't say it now!'

'We are all alone,' he continued, taking off his hat; 'all alone in this beautiful Sunday stillness.'

Gertrude looked around her, at the breaking buds, and shining distance, the blue sky to which she had referred as a pretext for her irregularities. 'That's the reason,' she said, 'why I don't want you to speak. Do me a favour; go to church.'

'May I speak when I come back?' asked Mr Brand.

'If you are still disposed,' she answered.

'I don't know whether you are wicked,' he said, 'but you are certainly puzzling.'

She had turned away; she raised her hands to her ears. He looked at her a moment, and then he slowly walked to church.

She wandered for a while about the garden, vaguely and without purpose. The church-bell had stopped ringing; the stillness was complete. This young lady relished highly, on occasions, the sense of being alone – the absence of the whole family, and the emptiness of the house. Today, apparently, the servants had also gone to church: there was never a figure at the open windows; behind the house there was no stout negress in a red turban, lowering the bucket into the great shingle-hooded well. And the front door of the big, unguarded home stood open, with the trustfulness of the golden age; or, what is more to the purpose, with that of New England's silvery prime. Gertrude slowly passed through it, and went from one of the empty rooms to the other – large, clear-coloured rooms, with white wainscots, ornamented with thin-legged mahogany furniture, and, on the walls, with old-fashioned engravings, chiefly of Scriptural subjects, hung very high. This agreeable sense of solitude, of having the house to herself, of which I have spoken, always excited Gertrude's imagination; she could not have told you why, and neither can her humble historian. It always seemed to her that she must do something particular – that she must honour the occasion; and while she roamed about, wondering what she could do, the occasion usually came to an end. Today she wondered more than ever. At last she took down a book; there was no library in the house, but there were books in all the rooms. None of them were forbidden books, and Gertrude had not stopped at home for the sake of a chance to climb to the inaccessible shelves. She possessed herself of a very obvious volume – one of the series of the *Arabian Nights* – and she brought it out into the portico and sat down with it in her lap. There, for a quarter of an hour, she read the history of the loves of the Prince Camaralzaman and the Princess Badoura. At last, looking up, she beheld, as it seemed to her, the Prince Camaralzaman standing before her. A beautiful young man was making her a very low bow – a magnificent bow, such as she had never seen before. He appeared to have dropped from the clouds; he was wonderfully handsome; he smiled – smiled as if he were smiling on purpose. Extreme surprise, for a moment, kept Gertrude sitting still; then she rose, without even keeping her finger in her book. The young man, with his hat in his hand, still looked at her, smiling and smiling. It was very strange.

'Will you kindly tell me,' said the mysterious visitor at last, 'whether I have the honour of speaking to Miss Wentworth?'

'My name is Gertrude Wentworth,' murmured the young woman.

'Then – then – I have the honour – the pleasure – of being your cousin.'

The young man had so much the character of an apparition that his announcement seemed to complete his unreality. 'What cousin? Who are you?' said Gertrude.

He stepped back a few paces and looked up at the house; then glanced round him at the garden and the distant view. After this he burst out laughing. 'I see it must seem to you very strange,' he said. There was, after all, something substantial in his laughter. Gertrude looked at him from head to foot. Yes, he was remarkably handsome; but his smile was almost a grimace. 'It is very still,' he went on, coming nearer again. And as she only looked at him for reply, he added, 'Are you all alone?'

'Everyone has gone to church,' said Gertrude.

'I was afraid of that!' the young man exclaimed. 'But I hope you are not afraid of me.'

'You ought to tell me who you are,' Gertrude answered.

'I am afraid of you!' said the young man. 'I had a different plan. I expected the servant would take in my card, and that you would put your heads together, before admitting me, and make out my identity.'

Gertrude had been wondering with a quick intensity which brought its result; and the result seemed an answer – a wondrous, delightful answer – to her vague wish that something would befall her. 'I know – I know,' she said. 'You come from Europe.'

'We came two days ago. You have heard of us, then – you believe in us?'

'We have known, vaguely,' said Gertrude, 'that we had relations in France.'

'And have you ever wanted to see us?' asked the young man.

Gertrude was silent for a moment. 'I have wanted to see you.'

'I am glad, then, it is you I have found. We wanted to see you, so we came.'

'On purpose?' asked Gertrude.

The young man looked round him, smiling still. 'Well, yes; on purpose. Does that sound as if we should bore you?' he added. 'I don't think we shall – I really don't think we shall. We are rather fond of wandering, too; and we were glad of a pretext.'

'And you have just arrived?'

'In Boston, two days ago. At the inn I asked for Mr Wentworth. He must be your father. They found out for me where he lived; they seemed often to have heard of him. I determined to come, without ceremony. So, this lovely morning, they set my face in the right direction and told me to walk straight before me, out of town. I came on foot because I wanted to see the country. I walked and walked, and here I am! It's a good many miles.'

'It is seven miles and a half,' said Gertrude softly. Now that this handsome young man was proving himself a reality she found herself vaguely trembling; she was deeply excited. She had never in her life spoken to a foreigner, and she had often thought it would be delightful to do so. Here was one who had suddenly been engendered by the Sabbath stillness for her private use; and such a brilliant, polite, smiling one! She found time and means to compose herself, however; to remind herself that she must exercise a sort of official hospitality. 'We are very – very glad to see you,' she said. 'Won't you come into the house?' And she moved toward the open door.

'You are not afraid of me, then?' asked the young man again, with his light laugh.

She wondered a moment, and then, 'We are not afraid – here,' she said.

'*Ah, comme vous devez avoir raison!*' cried the young man, looking all round him, appreciatively. It was the first time that Gertrude had heard so many words of French spoken. They gave her something of a sensation. Her companion followed her, watching, with a certain excitement of his own, this tall, interesting-looking girl, dressed in her clear, crisp muslin. He paused in the hall, where there was a broad white staircase with a white balustrade. 'What a pleasant house!' he said. 'It's lighter inside than it is out.'

'It's pleasanter here,' said Gertrude, and she led the way into the parlour

– a high, clean, rather empty-looking room. Here they stood looking at each other – the young man smiling more than ever; Gertrude, very serious, trying to smile.

'I don't believe you know my name,' he said. 'I am called Felix Young. Your father is my uncle. My mother was his half-sister, and older than he.'

'Yes,' said Gertrude, 'and she turned Roman Catholic and married in Europe.'

'I see you know,' said the young man. 'She married, and she died. Your father's family didn't like her husband. They called him a foreigner; but he was not. My poor father was born in Sicily, but his parents were American.'

'In Sicily?' Gertrude murmured.

'It is true,' said Felix Young, 'that they had spent their lives in Europe. But they were very patriotic. And so are we.'

'And you are Sicilian,' said Gertrude.

'Sicilian, no! Let's see. I was born at a little place – a dear little place – in France. My sister was born at Vienna.'

'So you are French,' said Gertrude.

'Heaven forbid!' cried the young man. Gertrude's eyes were fixed upon him almost instantly. He began to laugh again. 'I can easily be French, if that will please you.'

'You are a foreigner of some sort,' said Gertrude.

'Of some sort – yes; I suppose so. But who can say of what sort? I don't think we have ever had occasion to settle the question. You know there are people like that. About their country, their religion, their profession, they can't tell.'

Gertrude stood there gazing; she had not asked him to sit down. She had never heard of people like that; she wanted to hear. 'Where do you live?' she asked.

'They can't tell that either!' said Felix. 'I am afraid you will think we are little better than vagabonds. I have lived anywhere – everywhere. I really think I have lived in every city in Europe.' Gertrude gave a little long, soft exhalation. It made the young man smile at her again; and his smile made her blush a little. To take refuge from blushing she asked him if, after his long walk, he was not hungry or thirsty. Her hand was in her pocket; she was fumbling with the little key that her sister had given her. 'Ah, my dear young lady,' he said, clasping his hands a little, 'if you could give me, in charity, a glass of wine!'

Gertrude gave a smile and a little nod, and went quickly out of the room. Presently she came back with a very large decanter in one hand and a plate in the other, on which was placed a big round cake with a frosted top. Gertrude, in taking the cake from the closet, had had a moment of acute consciousness that it composed the refection of which her sister had thought that Mr Brand would like to partake. Her kinsman from across the seas was looking at the pale high-hung engravings. When she came in he turned and smiled at her, as if they had been old friends meeting after a separation. 'You wait upon me yourself?' he asked. 'I am served like the gods!' She had waited upon a great many people, but none of them had ever told her that. The observation added a certain lightness to the step with which she went to a little table where there were some curious red glasses – glasses covered with little gold sprigs, which Charlotte used to dust every morning with her own hands. Gertrude thought the glasses very handsome, and it was a pleasure to her to know that the wine was good; it was her father's famous madeira. Felix Young thought it excellent; he wondered why he had been told that there was no wine in America. She cut him an immense triangle out of the cake, and again she thought of Mr Brand. Felix sat there, with his glass in one hand and his huge morsel of cake in the other – eating, drinking, smiling, talking. 'I am very hungry,' he said. 'I am not at all tired; I am never tired. But I am very hungry.'

'You must stay to dinner,' said Gertrude. 'At two o'clock. They will all have come back from church; you will see the others.'

'Who are the others?' asked the young man. 'Describe them all.'

'You will see for yourself. It is you that must tell me; now, about your sister.'

'My sister is the Baroness Münster,' said Felix.

On hearing that his sister was a Baroness, Gertrude got up and walked about slowly in front of him. She was silent a moment. She was thinking of it. 'Why didn't she come, too?' she asked.

'She did come; she is in Boston, at the hotel.'

'We will go and see her,' said Gertrude, looking at him.

'She begs you will not!' the young man replied. 'She sends you her love; she sent me to announce her. She will come and pay her respects to your father.'

Gertrude felt herself trembling again. A Baroness Münster, who sent a brilliant young man to 'announce' her; who was coming, as the Queen of Sheba came to Solomon, to pay her 'respects' to quiet Mr Wentworth – such a personage presented herself to Gertrude's vision with a most effective unexpectedness. For a moment she hardly knew what to say, 'When will she come?' she asked at last.

'As soon as you will allow her – tomorrow. She is very impatient,' answered Felix, who wished to be agreeable.

'Tomorrow, yes,' said Gertrude. She wished to ask more about her; but she hardly knew what could be predicated of a Baroness Münster. 'Is she – is she – married?'

Felix had finished his cake and wine; he got up, fixing upon the young girl his bright expressive eyes. 'She is married to a German prince – Prince Adolf, of Silberstadt-Schreckenstein. He is not the Reigning Prince; he is a younger brother.'

Gertrude gazed at her informant; her lips were slightly parted. 'Is she a – a *Princess*?' she asked at last.

'Oh no,' said the young man; 'her position is rather a singular one. It's a morganatic marriage.'

'Morganatic?' These were new names and new words to poor Gertrude.

'That's what they call a marriage, you know, contracted between a scion of a ruling house and – and a common mortal. They made Eugenia a Baroness, poor woman; but that was all they could do. Now they want to dissolve the marriage. Prince Adolf, between ourselves, is a ninny; but his brother, who is a clever man, has plans for him. Eugenia, naturally enough, makes difficulties; not, however, that I think she cares much – she's a very clever woman; I'm sure you'll like her – but she wants to bother them. Just now everything is *en l'air*.'

The cheerful off-hand tone in which her visitor related this darkly-romantic tale seemed to Gertrude very strange; but it seemed also to convey a certain flattery to herself, a recognition of her wisdom and dignity. She felt a dozen impressions stirring within her, and presently the one that was uppermost found words. 'They want to dissolve her marriage?' she asked.

'So it appears.'

'And against her will?'

'Against her right.'

'She must be very unhappy!' said Gertrude.

Her visitor looked at her, smiling; he raised his hand to the back of his head and held it there a moment. 'So she says,' he answered. 'That's her story. She told me to tell it you.'

'Tell me more,' said Gertrude.

'No, I will leave that to her; she does it better.'

Gertrude gave a little excited sigh again. 'Well, if she is unhappy,' she said, 'I am glad she has come to us.'

She had been so interested that she failed to notice the sound of a footstep in the portico; and yet it was a footstep that she always recognized. She heard it in the hall, and then she looked out of the window. They were all coming back from church – her father, her sister, and brother, and their cousins, who always came to dinner on Sunday. Mr Brand had come in first; he was in advance of the others, because, apparently, he was still disposed to say what she had not wished him to say an hour before. He came into the parlour, looking for Gertrude. He had two little books in his hand. On seeing Gertrude's companion he slowly stopped, looking at him.

'Is this a cousin?' asked Felix.

Then Gertrude saw that she must introduce him; but her ears, and, by sympathy, her lips, were full of all that he had been telling her. 'This is the Prince,' she said – 'the Prince of Silberstadt-Schreckenstein!'

Felix burst out laughing, and Mr Brand stood staring, while the others, who had passed into the house, appeared behind him in the open doorway.

Chapter Three

That evening, at dinner, Felix Young gave his sister, the Baroness Münster, an account of his impressions. She saw that he had come back in the highest possible spirits; but this fact, to her own mind, was not a reason for rejoicing. She had but a limited confidence in her brother's judgement: his capacity for taking rose-coloured views was such as to vulgarize one of the prettiest of tints. Still, she supposed he could be trusted to give her the mere facts; and she invited him, with some eagerness, to communicate them. 'I suppose, at least, they didn't turn you from the door,' she said. 'You have been away some ten hours.'

'Turn me from the door!' Felix exclaimed. 'They took me to their hearts; they killed the fatted calf.'

'I know what you want to say: they are a collection of angels.'

'Exactly,' said Felix. 'They are a collection of angels – simply.'

'*C'est bien vague*,' remarked the Baroness. 'What are they like?'

'Like nothing you ever saw.'

'I am sure I am obliged; but that is hardly more definite. Seriously, they were glad to see you?'

'Enchanted. It has been the proudest day of my life. Never, never have I been so lionized! I assure you, I was cock of the walk. My dear sister,' said the young man, '*nous n'avons qu'à nous tenir*; we shall be great swells!'

Madame Münster looked at him, and her eye exhibited a slight responsive spark. She touched her lips to a glass of wine, and then she said, 'Describe them. Give me a picture.'

Felix drained his own glass. 'Well, it's in the country, among the meadows and woods; a wild sort of place, and yet not far from here. Only, such a road, my dear! Imagine one of the Alpine glaciers reproduced in mud. But you will not spend much time on it, for they want you to come and stay, once for all.'

'Ah,' said the Baroness, 'they want me to come and stay, once for all? *Bon*.'

'It's intensely rural, tremendously natural; and all overhung with this strange white light, this far-away blue sky. There's a big wooden house – a kind of three storey bungalow; it looks like a magnified Nuremberg toy. There was a gentleman there that made a speech to me about it and called it a "venerable mansion"; but it looks as if it had been built last night.'

'Is it handsome – is it elegant?' asked the Baroness.

Felix looked at her a moment, smiling. 'It's very clean! No splendours, no gilding, no troops of servants; rather straight-backed chairs. But you might eat off the floors, and you can sit down on the stairs.'

'That must be a privilege. And the inhabitants are straight-backed too, of course.'

'My dear sister,' said Felix, 'the inhabitants are charming.'

'In what style?'

'In a style of their own. How shall I describe it? It's primitive; it's patriarchal; it's the *ton* of the golden age.'

'And have they nothing golden but their *ton*? Are there no symptoms of wealth?'

'I should say there was wealth without symptoms. A plain, homely way of life; nothing for show, and very little for – what shall I call it? – for the senses; but a great *aisance*, and a lot of money, out of sight, that comes forward very quietly for subscriptions to institutions, for repairing tenements, for paying doctor's bills; perhaps even for portioning daughters.'

'And the daughters?' Madame Münster demanded. 'How many are there?'

'There are two, Charlotte and Gertrude.'

'Are they pretty?'

'One of them,' said Felix.

'Which is that?'

The young man was silent, looking at his sister. 'Charlotte,' he said at last.

She looked at him in return. 'I see. You are in love with Gertrude. They must be Puritans to their finger-tips; anything but gay!'

'No, they are not gay,' Felix admitted. 'They are sober; they are even severe. They are of a pensive cast; they take things hard. I think there is something the matter with them; they have some melancholy memory or some depressing expectation. It's not the epicurean temperament. My uncle, Mr Wentworth, is a tremendously high-toned old fellow; he looks as if he were undergoing martyrdom, not by fire, but by freezing. But we shall cheer them up; we shall do them good. They will take a good deal of stirring up; but they are wonderfully kind and gentle. And they are appreciative. They think one clever; they think one remarkable!'

'That is very fine, so far as it goes,' said the Baroness. 'But are we to be shut up to these three people, Mr Wentworth and the two young women – what did you say their names were – Deborah and Hephzibah?'

'Oh no; there is another little girl, a cousin of theirs; a very pretty little creature; a thorough little American. And then there is the son of the house.'

'Good,' said the Baroness. 'We are coming to the gentlemen. What of the son of the house?'

'I am afraid he gets tipsy.'

'He, then, has the epicurean temperament! How old is he?'

'He is a boy of twenty; a pretty young fellow, but I am afraid he has vulgar tastes. And then there is Mr Brand – a very tall young man, a sort of lay-priest. They seem to think a good deal of him, but I don't exactly make him out.'

'And is there nothing,' asked the Baroness, 'between these extremes – this mysterious ecclesiastic and that intemperate youth?'

'Oh yes; there is Mr Acton. I think,' said the young man, with a nod at his sister, 'that you will like Mr Acton.'

'Remember that I am very fastidious,' said the Baroness. 'Has he very good manners?'

'He will have them with you. He is a man of the world; he has been to China.'

Madame Münster gave a little laugh. 'A man of the Chinese world! He must be very interesting.'

'I have an idea that he brought home a fortune,' said Felix.

'That is always interesting. Is he young, good-looking, clever?'

'He is less than forty; he has a baldish head; he says witty things. I rather think,' added the young man, 'that he will admire the Baroness Münster.'

'It is very possible,' said this lady. Her brother never knew how she would take things; but shortly afterwards she declared that he had made a very pretty description, and that on the morrow she would go and see for herself.

They mounted, accordingly, into a great barouche – a vehicle as to which the Baroness found nothing to criticize but the price that was asked for it and the fact that the coachman wore a straw hat. (At Silberstadt Madame Münster had had liveries of yellow and crimson.) They drove into the country, and the Baroness, leaning far back and swaying her lace-fringed parasol, looked to right and to left and surveyed the wayside objects. After a while she pronounced them *affreux*. Her brother remarked that it was apparently a country in which the foreground was inferior to the *plans reculés*; and the Baroness rejoined that the landscape seemed to be all foreground. Felix had fixed with his new friends the hour at which he should bring his sister; it was four o'clock in the afternoon. The large clean-faced house wore, to his eyes, as the barouche drove up to it, a very friendly aspect; the high, slender elms made lengthening shadows in front of it. The Baroness descended; her American kinsfolk were stationed in the portico. Felix waved his hat to them, and a tall, lean gentleman, with a high forehead and a clean-shaven face, came forward toward the garden gate. Charlotte Wentworth walked at his side; Gertrude came behind more slowly. Both of these young ladies wore rustling silk dresses. Felix ushered his sister into the gate. 'Be very gracious,' he said to her. But he saw the admonition was superfluous. Eugenia was prepared to be gracious as only Eugenia could be. Felix knew no keener pleasure than to be able to admire his sister unrestrictedly; for if the opportunity was frequent, it was not inveterate. When she desired to please she was to him, as to every one else, the most charming woman in the world. Then he forgot that she was ever anything else; that she was sometimes hard and perverse; that he was occasionally afraid of her. Now, as she took his arm to pass into the garden, he felt that she desired, that she proposed, to please, and this situation made him very happy. Eugenia would please.

The tall gentleman came to meet her, looking very rigid and grave. But it was a rigidity that had no illiberal meaning. Mr Wentworth's manner was pregnant, on the contrary, with a sense of grand responsibility, of the solemnity of the occasion, of its being difficult to show sufficient deference to a lady at once so distinguished and so unhappy. Felix had observed on the day before his characteristic pallor; and now he perceived that there was something almost cadaverous in his uncle's high-featured white face. But so clever were this young man's quick sympathies and perceptions that he had already learned that in these semi-mortuary manifestations there was no cause for alarm. His light imagination had gained a glimpse of Mr Wentworth's spiritual mechanism, and taught him that, the old man being infinitely conscientious, the special operation of conscience within him announced itself by several of the indications of physical faintness.

The Baroness took her uncle's hand, and stood looking at him with her ugly face and her beautiful smile. 'Have I done right to come?' she asked.

'Very right, very right,' said Mr Wentworth, solemnly. He had arranged in his mind a little speech; but now it quite faded away. He felt almost frightened. He had never been looked at in just that way – with just that fixed, intense smile – by any woman; and it perplexed and weighed upon him, now, that the woman who was smiling so, and who had instantly given him a vivid sense of her possessing other unprecedented attributes, was his own niece, the child of his own father's daughter. The idea that his niece should be a German Baroness, married 'morganatically' to a Prince, had already given him much to think about. Was it right, was it just, was it acceptable? He always slept badly, and the night before he had lain awake much more even than usual, asking himself these questions. The strange word 'morganatic' was constantly in his ears; it reminded him of a certain Mrs Morgan whom he had once known, and who had been a bold, unpleasant woman. He had a feeling that it was his duty, so long as the Baroness looked at him, smiling in that way, to meet her glance with his own scrupulously-adjusted, consciously-frigid organs of vision: but on this occasion he failed to perform his duty to the last. He looked away toward his daughters. 'We are very glad to see you,' he had said. 'Allow me to introduce my daughters – Miss Charlotte Wentworth, Miss Gertrude Wentworth.'

The Baroness thought she had never seen people less demonstrative. But Charlotte kissed her and took her hand, looking at her sweetly and solemnly. Gertrude seemed to her most funereal, though Gertrude might have found a source of gaiety in the fact that Felix, with his magnificent smile, had been talking to her; he had greeted her as a very old friend. When she kissed the Baroness she had tears in her eyes. Madame Münster took each of these young women by the hand, and looked at them all over. Charlotte thought her very strange-looking and singularly dressed; she could not have said whether it was well or ill. She was glad, at any rate, that they had put on their silk gowns – especially Gertrude. 'My cousins are very pretty,' said the Baroness, turning her eyes from one to the other. 'Your daughters are very handsome, sir.'

Charlotte blushed quickly; she had never yet heard her personal appearance alluded to in a loud expressive voice. Gertrude looked away – not at Felix; she was extremely pleased. It was not the compliment that pleased her; she did not believe it; she thought herself very plain. She could hardly have told you the source of her satisfaction; it came from something in the way the Baroness spoke, and it was not diminished – it was rather deepened, oddly enough – by the young girl's disbelief. Mr Wentworth was silent; and then he asked, formally, 'Won't you come into the house?'

'These are not all; you have some other children,' said the Baroness.

'I have a son,' Mr Wentworth answered.

'And why doesn't he come to meet me?' Eugenia cried: 'I am afraid he is not so charming as his sisters.'

'I don't know; I will see about it,' the old man declared.

'He is rather afraid of ladies,' Charlotte said softly.

'He is very handsome,' said Gertrude, as loud as she could.

'We will go in and find him. We will draw him out of his *cachette*.' And the Baroness took Mr Wentworth's arm, who was not aware that he had offered it to her, and who, as they walked toward the house, wondered whether he ought to have offered it and whether it was proper for her to take it if it had not been offered. 'I want to know you well,' said the Baroness, interrupting these meditations, 'and I want you to know me.'

'It seems natural that we should know each other,' Mr Wentworth rejoined. 'We are near relatives.'

'Ah, there comes a moment in life when one reverts, irresistibly, to one's natural ties – to one's natural affections. You must have found that!' said Eugenia.

Mr Wentworth had been told the day before by Felix that Eugenia was very clever, very brilliant, and the information had held him in some suspense. This was the cleverness, he supposed; the brilliancy was beginning. 'Yes, the natural affections are very strong,' he murmured.

'In some people,' the Baroness declared. 'Not in all.' Charlotte was walking beside her; she took hold of her hand again, smiling always. 'And you, *cousine*, where did you get that enchanting complexion?' she went on; 'such lilies and roses!' The roses in poor Charlotte's countenance began speedily to predominate over the lilies, and she quickened her step and reached the portico. 'This is the country of complexions,' the Baroness continued, addressing herself to Mr Wentworth. 'I am convinced they are more delicate. There are very good ones in England – in Holland; but they are very apt to be coarse. There is too much red.'

'I think you will find,' said Mr Wentworth, 'that this country is superior in many respects to those you mention. I have been to England and Holland.'

'Ah, you have been to Europe?' cried the Baroness. 'Why didn't you come and see me? But it's better, after all, this way,' she said. They were entering the house; she paused and looked round her. 'I see you have arranged your house – your beautiful house – in the – in the Dutch taste!'

'The house is very old,' remarked Mr Wentworth. 'General Washington once spent a week here.'

'Oh, I have heard of Washington,' cried the Baroness. 'My father used to adore him.'

Mr Wentworth was silent a moment and then, 'I found he was very well known in Europe,' he said.

Felix had lingered in the garden with Gertrude; he was standing before her and smiling, as he had done the day before. What had happened the day before seemed to her a kind of dream. He had been there and he had changed everything; the others had seen him, they had talked with him; but that he should come again, that he should be part of the future, part of her small familiar, much-meditating life – this needed, afresh, the evidence of her senses. The evidence had come to her senses now; and her senses seemed to rejoice in it. 'What do you think of Eugenia?' Felix asked. 'Isn't she charming?'

'She is very brilliant,' said Gertrude. 'But I can't tell yet. She seems to me like a singer singing an air. You can't tell till the song is done.'

'Ah, the song will never be done!' exclaimed the young man, laughing. 'Don't you think her handsome?'

Gertrude had been disappointed in the beauty of the Baroness Münster; she had expected her, for mysterious reasons, to resemble a very pretty portrait of the Empress Josephine, of which there hung an engraving in one of the parlours, and which the younger Miss Wentworth had always greatly admired. But the Baroness was not at all like that – not at all. Though different, however, she was very wonderful, and Gertrude felt herself most suggestively corrected. It was strange, nevertheless, that Felix should speak in that positive way about his sister's beauty. 'I think I *shall* think her handsome,' Gertrude said. 'It must be very interesting to know her. I don't feel as if I ever could.'

'Ah, you will know her well; you will become great friends,' Felix declared, as if this were the easiest thing in the world.

'She is very graceful,' said Gertrude, looking after the Baroness, suspended to her father's arm. It was a pleasure to her to say that any one was graceful.

Felix had been looking about him. 'And your little cousin of yesterday,' he said, 'who was so wonderfully pretty – what has become of her?'

'She is in the parlour,' Gertrude answered. 'Yes, she is very pretty.' She felt as if it were her duty to take him straight into the house, to where he might be near her cousin. But after hesitating a moment she lingered still. 'I didn't believe you would come back,' she said.

'Not come back!' cried Felix, laughing. 'You didn't know, then, the impression made upon this susceptible heart of mine.'

She wondered whether he meant the impression her cousin Lizzie had made. 'Well,' she said, 'I didn't think we should ever see you again.'

'And pray, what did you think would become of me?'

'I don't know. I thought you would melt away.'

'That's a compliment to my solidity! I melt very often,' said Felix, 'but there is always something left of me.'

'I came and waited for you by the door because the others did,' Gertrude went on. 'But if you had never appeared I should not have been surprised.'

'I hope,' declared Felix, looking at her, 'that you would have been disappointed.'

She looked at him a little, and shook her head. 'No – no!'

'*Ah, par exemple!*' cried the young man. 'You deserve that I should never leave you.'

Going into the parlour they found Mr Wentworth performing introductions. A young man was standing before the Baroness, blushing a good deal, laughing a little, and shifting his weight from one foot to the other – a slim, mild-faced young man, with neatly arranged features, like those of Mr Wentworth. Two other gentlemen, behind him, had risen from their seats, and a little apart, near one of the windows, stood a remarkably pretty young girl. The young girl was knitting a stocking; but, while her fingers quickly moved, she looked with wide, brilliant eyes at the Baroness.

'And what is your son's name?' said Eugenia, smiling at the young man.

'My name is Clifford Wentworth, ma'am,' he said in a tremulous voice.

'Why didn't you come out to meet me, Mr Clifford Wentworth?' the Baroness demanded, with her beautiful smile.

'I didn't think you would want me,' said the young man, slowly sidling about.

'One always wants a *beau cousin* – if one has one! But if you are very nice to me in future I won't remember it against you.' And Madame Münster transferred her smile to the other persons present. It rested first upon the candid countenance and long-skirted figure of Mr Brand, whose eyes were intently fixed upon Mr Wentworth, as if to beg him not to prolong an anomalous situation. Mr Wentworth pronounced his name; Eugenia gave him a very charming glance, and then looked at the other gentleman.

This latter personage was a man of rather less than the usual stature and the usual weight, with a quick, observant, agreeable dark eye, a small quantity of thin dark hair, and a small moustache. He had been standing with his hands in his pockets; and when Eugenia looked at him he took them out. But he did not, like Mr Brand, look evasively and urgently at their host. He met Eugenia's eyes; he appeared to appreciate the privilege of meeting them. Madame Münster instantly felt that he was, intrinsically, the most important person present. She was not unconscious that this impression was in some degree manifested in the little sympathetic nod with which she acknowledged Mr Wentworth's announcement, 'My cousin, Mr Acton!'

'Your cousin – not mine?' said the Baroness.

'It only depends upon you,' Mr Acton declared, laughing.

The Baroness looked at him a moment, and noticed that he had very white teeth. 'Let it depend upon your behaviour,' she said. 'I think I had better wait. I have cousins enough. Unless I can also claim relationship,' she added, 'with that charming young lady.' And she pointed to the young girl at the window.

'That's my sister,' said Mr Acton. And Gertrude Wentworth put her arm round the young girl and led her forward. It was not, apparently, that she needed much leading. She came toward the Baroness with a light, quick step, and with perfect self-possession, rolling her stocking round its needles. She had dark blue eyes and dark brown hair; she was wonderfully pretty.

Eugenia kissed her, as she had kissed the other young women, and then held her off a little, looking at her. 'Now this is quite another *type*,' she said; she pronounced the word in the French manner. 'This is a different outline, my uncle, a different character, from that of your own daughters. This, Felix,' she went on, 'is very much more what we have always thought of as the American type.'

The young girl, during this exposition, was smiling askance at every one in turn, and at Felix out of turn. 'I find only one type here!' cried Felix, laughing. 'The type adorable!'

This sally was received in perfect silence, but Felix, who learned all things quickly, had already learned that the silences frequently observed among his new acquaintances were not necessarily restrictive or resentful. It was, as one might say, the silence of expectation, of modesty. They were all standing round his sister, as if they were expecting her to acquit herself of the exhibition of some peculiar faculty, some brilliant talent. Their attitude seemed to imply that she was a kind of conversational mountebank, attired, intellectually, in gauze and spangles. This attitude gave a certain ironical force to Madame Münster's next words. 'Now this is your circle,' she said to her uncle. 'This is your *salon*. These are your regular habitués, eh? I am so glad to see you all together.'

'Oh,' said Mr Wentworth, 'they are always dropping in and out. You must do the same.'

'Father,' interposed Charlotte Wentworth, 'they must do something more.' And she turned her sweet serious face, that seemed at once timid and placid, upon their interesting visitor. 'What is your name?' she asked.

'Eugenia-Camilla-Dolores,' said the Baroness, smiling. 'But you needn't say all that.'

'I will say Eugenia, if you will let me. You must come and stay with us.'

The Baroness laid her hand upon Charlotte's arm very tenderly; but she reserved herself. She was wondering whether it would be possible to 'stay' with these people. 'It would be very charming – very charming,' she said; and her eyes wandered over the company, over the room. She wished to gain time before committing herself. Her glance fell upon young Mr Brand, who stood there with his arms folded and his hand on his chin, looking at her. 'The gentleman, I suppose, is a sort of ecclesiastic,' she added to Mr Wentworth, lowering her voice a little.

'He is a minister,' answered Mr Wentworth.

'A Protestant?' asked Eugenia.

'I am a Unitarian, madam,' replied Mr Brand impressively.

'Ah, I see,' said Eugenia. 'Something new.' She had never heard of this form of worship.

Mr Acton began to laugh, and Gertrude looked anxiously at Mr Brand.

'You have come very far,' said Mr Wentworth.

'Very far – very far,' the Baroness replied, with a graceful shake of her head, a shake that might have meant many different things.

'That's a reason why you ought to settle down with us,' said Mr Wentworth, with that dryness of utterance which, as Eugenia was too intelligent not to feel, took nothing from the delicacy of his meaning.

She looked at him, and for an instant, in his cold, still face, she seemed to see a far-away likeness to the vaguely-remembered image of her mother. Eugenia was a woman of sudden emotions, and now, unexpectedly, she felt one rising in her heart. She kept looking round the circle; she knew that there was admiration in all the eyes that were fixed upon her. She smiled at them all.

'I came to look – to try – to ask,' she said. 'It seems to me I have done well. I am very tired; I want to rest.' There were tears in her eyes. The luminous interior, the gentle, tranquil people, the simple, serious life – the sense of these things pressed upon her with an overmastering force, and she felt herself yielding to one of the most genuine emotions she had ever known. 'I should like to stay here,' she said. 'Pray take me in.'

Though she was smiling, there were tears in her voice as well as in her eyes. 'My dear niece,' said Mr Wentworth softly. And Charlotte put out her arms and drew the Baroness toward her; while Robert Acton turned away, with his hands stealing into his pockets.

Chapter Four

A few days after the Baroness Münster had presented herself to her American kinsfolk she came, with her brother, and took up her abode in that small white house adjacent to Mr Wentworth's own dwelling of which mention has already been made. It was on going with his daughters to return her visit that Mr Wentworth placed this comfortable cottage at her service; the offer being the result of a domestic colloquy, diffused through the ensuing twenty-four hours, in the course of which the two foreign visitors were discussed and analysed with a great deal of earnestness and subtlety. The discussion went forward, as I say, in the family circle; but that circle on the evening following Madame Münster's return to town, as on many other occasions, included Robert Acton and his pretty sister. If you had been present, it would probably not have seemed to you that the advent of these brilliant strangers was treated as an exhilarating occurrence, a pleasure the more in this tranquil household, a prospective source of entertainment. This was not Mr Wentworth's way of treating any human occurrence. The sudden irruption into the well-ordered consciousness of the Wentworths of an element not allowed for in its scheme of usual obligations, required a readjustment of that sense of responsibility which constituted its principal furniture. To consider an event, crudely and baldly, in the light of the pleasure it might bring them, was an intellectual exercise with which Felix Young's American cousins were almost wholly unacquainted, and which they scarcely supposed to be largely pursued in any section of human society. The arrival of Felix and his sister was a satisfaction, but it was a singularly joyless and inelastic satisfaction. It was an extension of duty, of the exercise of the more recondite virtues; but neither Mr Wentworth, nor Charlotte, nor Mr Brand, who, among these excellent people, was a great promoter of reflexion and aspiration, frankly adverted to it as an extension of enjoyment. This function was ultimately assumed by Gertrude Wentworth, who was a peculiar girl, but the full compass of whose peculiarities had not been exhibited before they very ingeniously found their pretext in the presence of these possibly too agreeable foreigners. Gertrude, however, had to struggle with a great accumulation of obstructions, both of the subjective, as the metaphysicians say, and of the objective order; and indeed it is no small part of the purpose of this little history to set forth her struggle. What seemed paramount in this abrupt enlargement of Mr Wentworth's sympathies and those of his daughters was an extension of the field of possible mistakes; and the doctrine, as it may almost be called, of the oppressive gravity of mistakes was one of the most cherished traditions of the Wentworth family.

'I don't believe she wants to come and stay in this house,' said Gertrude; Madame Münster, from this time forward, receiving no other designation than the personal pronoun. Charlotte and Gertrude acquired considerable facility in addressing her, directly, as 'Eugenia'; but in speaking of her to each other they rarely called her anything but 'she'.

'Doesn't she think it good enough for her?' cried little Lizzie Acton, who was always asking unpractical questions that required, in strictness, no answer, and to which indeed she expected no other answer than such as she herself invariably furnished in a small innocently-satirical laugh.

'She certainly expressed a willingness to come,' said Mr Wentworth.

'That was only politeness,' Gertrude rejoined.

'Yes, she is very polite – very polite,' said Mr Wentworth.

'She is too polite,' his son declared, in a softly-growling tone which was habitual to him, but which was an indication of nothing worse than a vaguely humorous intention. 'It is very embarrassing.'

'That is more than can be said of you, sir,' said Lizzie Acton, with her little laugh.

'Well, I don't mean to encourage her,' Clifford went on.

'I'm sure I don't care if you do!' cried Lizzie.

'She will not think of you, Clifford,' said Gertrude gravely.

'I hope not!' Clifford exclaimed.

'She will think of Robert,' Gertrude continued, in the same tone.

Robert Acton began to blush; but there was no occasion for it, for every one was looking at Gertrude – every one, at least, save Lizzie, who, with her pretty head on one side, contemplated her brother.

'Why do you attribute motives, Gertrude?' asked Mr Wentworth.

'I don't attribute motives, father,' said Gertrude. 'I only say she will think of Robert; and she will!'

'Gertrude judges by herself!' Acton exclaimed, laughing. 'Don't you,

Gertrude? Of course the Baroness will think of me. She will think of me from morning till night.'

'She will be very comfortable here,' said Charlotte, with something of a housewife's pride. 'She can have the large north-east room. And the French bedstead,' Charlotte added, with a constant sense of the lady's foreignness.

'She will not like it,' said Gertrude, 'not even if you pin little tidies all over the chairs.'

'Why not, dear?' asked Charlotte, perceiving a touch of irony here, but not resenting it.

Gertrude had left her chair; she was walking about the room; her stiff silk dress, which she had put on in honour of the Baroness, made a sound upon the carpet. 'I don't know,' she replied. 'She will want something more – more private.'

'If she wants to be private she can stay in her room,' Lizzie Acton remarked.

Gertrude paused in her walk, looking at her. 'That would not be pleasant,' she answered. 'She wants privacy and pleasure together.'

Robert Acton began to laugh again. 'My dear cousin, what a picture!'

Charlotte had fixed her serious eyes upon her sister; she wondered whence she had suddenly derived these strange notions. Mr Wentworth also observed his young daughter.

'I don't know what her manner of life may have been,' he said; 'but she certainly never can have enjoyed a more refined and salubrious home.'

Gertrude stood there looking at them all. 'She is the wife of a Prince,' she said.

'We are all princes here,' said Mr Wentworth; 'and I don't know of any palace in this neighbourhood that is to let.'

'Cousin William,' Robert Acton interposed, 'do you want to do something handsome? Make them a present, for three months, of the little house over the way.'

'You are very generous with other people's things!' cried his sister.

'Robert is very generous with his own things,' Mr Wentworth observed dispassionately, and looking in cold meditation at his kinsman.

'Gertrude,' Lizzie went on, 'I had an idea you were so fond of your new cousin.'

'Which new cousin?' asked Gertrude.

'I don't mean the Baroness!' the young girl rejoined, with her laugh. 'I thought you expected to see so much of him.'

'Of Felix? I hope to see a great deal of him,' said Gertrude simply.

'Then why do you want to keep him out of the house?'

Gertrude looked at Lizzie Acton, and then looked away.

'Should you want me to live in the house with you, Lizzie?' asked Clifford.

'I hope you never will. I hate you!' Such was this young lady's reply.

'Father,' said Gertrude, stopping before Mr Wentworth and smiling, with a smile the sweeter, as her smile always was, for its rarity, 'do let them live in the little house over the way. It will be lovely!'

Robert Acton had been watching her. 'Gertrude is right,' he said. 'Gertrude is the cleverest girl in the world. If I might take the liberty, I would strongly recommend their living there.'

'There is nothing there so pretty as the north-east room,' Charlotte urged.

'She will make it pretty. Leave her alone!' Acton exclaimed.

Gertrude, at his compliment, had blushed and looked at him; it was as if some one less familiar had complimented her. 'I am sure she will make it pretty. It will be very interesting. It will be a place to go to. It will be a foreign house.'

'Are we very sure that we need a foreign house?' Mr Wentworth inquired. 'Do you think it desirable to establish a foreign house – in this quiet place?'

'You speak,' said Acton, laughing, 'as if it were a question of the poor Baroness opening a wine-shop or a gaming-table.'

'It would be too lovely!' Gertrude declared again, laying her hand on the back of her father's chair.

'That she should open a gaming-table?' Charlotte asked, with great gravity.

Gertrude looked at her a moment, and then, 'Yes, Charlotte,' she said simply.

'Gertrude is growing pert,' Clifford Wentworth observed, with his humorous young growl. 'That comes of associating with foreigners.'

Mr Wentworth looked up at his daughter, who was standing beside him; he drew her gently forward. 'You must be careful,' he said. 'You must keep watch. Indeed, we must all be careful. This is a great change; we are to be exposed to peculiar influences. I don't say they are bad; I don't judge them in advance. But they may perhaps make it necessary that we should exercise a great deal of wisdom and self-control. It will be a different tone.'

Gertrude was silent a moment, in deference to her father's speech; then she spoke in a manner that was not in the least an answer to it. 'I want to see how they will live. I am sure they will have different hours. She will do all kinds of little things differently. When we go over there it will be like going to Europe. She will have a boudoir. She will invite us to dinner – very late. She will breakfast in her room.'

Charlotte gazed at her sister again. Gertrude's imagination seemed to her to be fairly running riot. She had always known that Gertrude had a great deal of imagination – she had been very proud of it. But at the same time she had always felt that it was a dangerous and irresponsible faculty; and now, to her sense, for the moment, it seemed to threaten to make her sister a strange person who should come in suddenly, as from a journey, talking of the peculiar and possibly unpleasant things she had observed. Charlotte's imagination took no journeys whatever; she kept it, as it were, in her pocket, with the other furniture of this receptacle – a thimble, a little box of peppermint, and a morsel of court-plaster. 'I don't believe she would have any dinner – or any breakfast,' said Miss Wentworth. 'I don't believe she knows how to do anything herself. I should have to get her ever so many servants, and she wouldn't like them'.

'She has a maid,' said Gertrude; 'a French maid. She mentioned her.'

'I wonder if the maid has a little fluted cap and red slippers,' said Lizzie Acton. 'There was a French maid in that play that Robert took me to see. She had pink stockings; she was very wicked.'

'She was a *soubrette*,' Gertrude announced, who had never seen a play in her life. 'They call that a soubrette. It will be a great chance to learn French.' Charlotte gave a little soft, helpless groan. She had a vision of a wicked theatrical person, clad in pink stockings and red shoes, and speaking, with confounding volubility, an incomprehensible tongue, flitting through the sacred penetralia of that large, clean house. 'That is one reason in favour of their coming here,' Gertrude went on. 'But we can make Eugenia speak French to us, and Felix. I mean to begin – the next time.'

Mr Wentworth had kept her standing near him, and he gave her his earnest, thin, unresponsive glance again. 'I want you to make me a promise, Gertrude,' he said.

'What is it?' she asked, smiling.

'Not to get excited. Not to allow these – these occurrences to be an occasion for excitement.'

She looked down at him a moment, and then she shook her head. 'I don't think I can promise that, father. I am excited already.'

Mr Wentworth was silent a while; they all were silent, as if in recognition of something audacious and portentous.

'I think they had better go to the other house,' said Charlotte quietly.

'I shall keep them in the other house,' Mr Wentworth subjoined more pregnantly.

Gertrude turned away; then she looked across at Robert Acton. Her cousin Robert was a great friend of hers; she often looked at him this way instead of saying things. Her glance on this occasion, however, struck him as a substitute for a larger volume of diffident utterance than usual; inviting him to observe, among other things, the inefficiency of her father's design – if design it was – for diminishing, in the interest of quiet nerves, their occasions of contact with their foreign relatives. But Acton immediately complimented Mr Wentworth upon his liberality. 'That's a very nice thing to do,' he said, 'giving them the little house. You will have treated them handsomely, and, whatever happens, you will be glad of it.' Mr Wentworth was liberal, and he knew he was liberal. It gave him pleasure to know it, to feel it, to see it recorded; and this pleasure is the only palpable form of self-indulgence with which the narrator of these incidents will be able to charge him.

'A three days' visit at most, over there, is all I should have found possible,' Madame Münster remarked to her brother, after they had taken possession of the little white house. 'It would have been too *intime* – decidedly too *intime*. Breakfast, dinner, and tea *en famille* – it would have been the end of the world if I could have reached the third day.' And she made the same observation to her maid Augustine, an intelligent person, who enjoyed a liberal share of her confidence. Felix declared that he would willingly spend his life in the bosom of the Wentworth family; that they were the kindest, simplest, most amiable people in the world, and that he had taken a prodigious fancy to them all. The Baroness quite agreed with him that they were simple and kind; they were thoroughly nice people, and she liked them extremely. The girls were perfect ladies; it was impossible to be more of a lady than Charlotte Wentworth, in spite of her little village air. 'But as for thinking them the best company in the world,' said the Baroness, 'that is another thing; and as for wishing to live *porte à porte* with them, I should as soon think of wishing myself back in the convent again, to wear a bombazine apron and sleep in a dormitory.' And yet the Baroness was in high good-humour; she had been very much pleased. With her lively perception and her refined imagination, she was capable of enjoying anything that was characteristic, anything that was good of its kind – the Wentworth household seemed to her very perfect of its kind – wonderfully peaceful and unspotted; pervaded by a sort of dove-coloured freshness that had all the quietude and benevolence of what she deemed to be Quakerism, and yet seemed to be founded upon a degree of material abundance for which, in certain matters of detail, one might have looked in vain at the frugal little court of Silberstadt-Schreckenstein. She perceived immediately that her American relatives thought and talked very little about money; and this of itself made an impression upon Eugenia's imagination. She perceived at the same time that if Charlotte or Gertrude should ask their father for a very considerable sum he would at once place it in their hands; and this made a still greater impression. The greatest impression of all, perhaps, was made by another rapid induction. The Baroness had an immediate conviction that Robert Acton would put his hand into his pocket every day in the week if that rattle-pated little sister of his should bid him. The men in this country, said the Baroness, are evidently very obliging. Her declaration that she was looking for rest and retirement had been by no means wholly untrue; nothing that the Baroness said was wholly untrue. It is but fair to add, perhaps, that nothing that she said was wholly true. She wrote to a friend in Germany that it was a return to nature; it was like drinking new milk, and she was very fond of new milk. She said to herself, of course, that it would be a little dull; but there can be no better proof of her good spirits than the fact that she thought she should not mind its being a little dull. It seemed to her, when from the piazza of her eleemosynary cottage she looked out over the soundless fields, the stony pastures, the clear-faced ponds, the rugged little orchards, that she had never been in the midst of so peculiarly intense a stillness; it was almost a delicate sensual pleasure. It was all very good, very innocent and safe, and out of it something good must come. Augustine, indeed, who had an unbounded faith in her mistress's wisdom and far-sightedness, was a great deal perplexed and depressed. She was always ready to take her cue when she understood it; but she liked to understand it, and on this occasion comprehension failed. What, indeed, was the Baroness doing *dans cette galère*? what fish did she expect to land out of these very stagnant waters? The game was evidently a deep one. Augustine could trust her, but the sense of walking in the dark betrayed itself in the physiognomy of this spare, sober, sallow, middle-aged person, who had nothing in common with Gertrude Wentworth's conception of a soubrette, by the most ironical scowl that had ever rested upon the unpretending tokens of the peace and plenty of the Wentworths. Fortunately, Augustine could quench scepticism in action. She quite agreed with her mistress – or rather she quite outstripped her mistress – in thinking that the little white house was pitifully bare. '*Il faudra,*' said Augustine, '*lui faire un peu de toilette.*' And she began to hang up *portières* in the doorways; to place wax candles, procured after some research, in unexpected situations; to dispose anomalous draperies over the arms of sofas and the backs of chairs. The Baroness had brought with her to the New World a copious provision of the element of costume; and the two Miss Wentworths, when they came over to see her, were somewhat bewildered by the obtrusive distribution of her wardrobe. There were India shawls suspended, curtain-wise, in the parlour door, and curious fabrics, corresponding to Gertrude's metaphysical vision of an opera-cloak, tumbled about in the sitting-places. There were pink silk blinds in the windows, by which the room was peculiarly bedimmed; and along the chimney-piece was disposed a remarkable band of velvet, covered with coarse, dirty-looking lace. 'I have been making myself a little comfortable,' said the Baroness, much to the confusion of Charlotte, who had been on the point of proposing to come and help her put her superfluous draperies away. But what Charlotte mistook for an almost culpably delayed subsidence Gertrude very presently perceived to be the most ingenious, the most interesting, the most romantic intention. 'What is life, indeed, without curtains?' she secretly asked herself; and she appeared to herself to have been leading hitherto an existence singularly garish and totally devoid of festoons.

Felix was not a young man who troubled himself greatly about anything – least of all about the conditions of enjoyment. His faculty of enjoyment was so large, so unconsciously eager, that it may be said of it that it had a permanent advance upon embarrassment and sorrow. His sentient nature was intrinsically joyous, and novelty and change were in themselves a delight to him. As they had come to him with a great deal of frequency, his life had been more agreeable than appeared. Never was a nature more perfectly fortunate. It was not a restless, apprehensive, ambitious spirit, running a race with the tyranny of fate, but a temper so unsuspicious as to put Adversity off her guard, dodging and evading her with the easy, natural motion of a wind-shifted flower. Felix extracted entertainment from all things, and his faculties – his imagination, his intelligence, his affections, his senses – had a hand in the game. It seemed to him that Eugenia and he had been very well treated; there was something absolutely touching in that combination of paternal liberality and social considerateness which marked Mr Wentworth's deportment. It was most uncommonly kind of him, for instance, to have given them a house. Felix was positively amused at having a house of his own; for the little white cottage among the apple trees – the chalet, as Madame Münster always called it – was much more sensibly his own than any domiciliary *quatrième*, looking upon a court, with the rent overdue. Felix had spent a good deal of his life in looking into courts, with a perhaps slightly-tattered pair of elbows resting upon the ledge of a high-perched window, and the thin smoke of a cigarette rising into an atmosphere in which street cries died away and the vibration of chimes from ancient belfries became sensible. He had never known anything so infinitely rural as these New England fields; and he took a great fancy to all their pastoral roughness. He had never had a greater sense of luxurious security; and at the risk of making him seem a rather sordid adventurer I must declare that he found an irresistible charm in the fact that he might dine every day at his uncle's. The charm was irresistible, however, because his fancy flung a rosy light over this homely privilege. He appreciated highly the fare that was set before him. There was a kind of fresh-looking abundance about it which made him think that people must have lived so in the mythological era, when they spread their tables upon the grass, replenished them from cornucopias, and had not particular need of kitchen stoves. But the great thing that Felix enjoyed was having found a family – sitting in the midst of gentle, generous people whom he might call by their first names. He had never known anything more charming than the attention they paid to what he said. It was like a large sheet of clean, fine-grained drawing-paper, all ready to be washed over with effective splashes of water-colour. He had never had any cousins, and he had never before found himself in contact so unrestricted with young unmarried ladies. He was extremely fond of the society of ladies, and it was new to him that it might be enjoyed in just this manner. At first he hardly knew what to make of his state of mind. It seemed to him that he was in love, indiscriminately, with three girls at once. He saw that Lizzie Acton was more brilliantly pretty than Charlotte and Gertrude; but this was scarcely a superiority. His pleasure came from something they had in common – a part of which was, indeed, that physical delicacy which seemed to make it proper that they should always dress in thin materials and clear colours. But they were delicate in other ways, and it was most agreeable to him to feel that these latter delicacies were appreciable by contact, as it were. He had known, fortunately, many virtuous gentlewomen, but it now appeared to him that in his relations with them (especially when they were unmarried) he had been looking at pictures under glass. He perceived at present what a nuisance the glass had been – how it perverted and interfered, how it caught the reflexion of other objects and kept you walking from side to side. He had no need to ask himself whether Charlotte and Gertrude, and Lizzie Acton, were in the right light; they were always in the right light. He liked everything about them; he was, for instance, not at all above liking the fact that they had very slender feet and high insteps. He liked their pretty noses; he liked their surprised eyes and their hesitating, not at all positive, way of speaking; he liked so much knowing that he was perfectly at liberty to be alone for hours, anywhere, with either of them, that preference for one to the other, as a companion of solitude, remained a minor affair. Charlotte Wentworth's sweetly severe features were as agreeable as Lizzie Acton's wonderfully expressive blue eyes; and Gertrude's air of being always ready to walk about and listen was as charming as anything else, especially as she walked very gracefully. After a while Felix began to distinguish; but even then he would often wish, suddenly, that they were not all so sad. Even Lizzie Acton, in spite of her fine little chatter and laughter, appeared sad. Even Clifford Wentworth, who had extreme youth in his favour and kept a buggy with enormous wheels and a little sorrel mare with the prettiest legs in the world – even this fortunate lad was apt to have an averted, uncomfortable glance, and to edge away from you at times, in the manner of a person with a bad conscience. The only person in the circle with no sense of oppression of any kind was, to Felix's perception, Robert Acton.

It might perhaps have been feared that after the completion of those graceful domiciliary embellishments which have been mentioned Madame Münster would have found herself confronted with alarming possibilities of ennui. But as yet she had not taken the alarm. The Baroness was a restless soul, and she projected her restlessness, as it may be said, into any situation that lay before her. Up to a certain point her restlessness might be counted upon to entertain her. She was always expecting something to happen, and, until it was disappointed, expectancy itself was a delicate pleasure. What the Baroness expected just now it would take some ingenuity to set forth; it is enough that while she looked about her she found something to occupy her imagination. She assured herself that she was enchanted with her new relatives; she professed to herself that, like her brother, she felt it a sacred satisfaction to have found a family. It is certain that she enjoyed to the utmost the gentleness of her kinsfolk's deference. She had, first and last, received a great deal of admiration, and her experience of well-turned compliments was very considerable; but she knew that she had never been so real a power, never counted for so much, as now when, for the first time, the standard of comparison of her little circle was a prey to vagueness. The sense, indeed, that the good people about her had, as regards her remarkable self, no standard of comparison at all, gave her a feeling of almost illimitable power. It was true, as she said to herself, that if for this reason they would be able to discover nothing against her, so they would perhaps neglect to perceive some of her superior points; but she always wound up her reflexions by declaring that she would take care of that.

Charlotte and Gertrude were in some perplexity between their desire to show all proper attention to Madame Münster and their fear of being importunate. The little house in the orchard had hitherto been occupied during the summer months by intimate friends of the family, or by poor relations who found in Mr Wentworth a landlord attentive to repairs and oblivious of quarter-day. Under these circumstances the open door of the small house and that of the large one, facing each other across their homely gardens, levied no tax upon hourly visits. But the Misses Wentworth received an impression that Eugenia was no friend to the primitive custom of 'dropping in'; she evidently had no idea of living without a door-keeper. 'One goes into your house as into an inn – except that there are no servants rushing forward,' she said to Charlotte. And she added that that was very charming. Gertrude explained to her sister that she meant just the reverse; she didn't like it at all. Charlotte inquired why she should tell an untruth, and Gertrude answered that there was probably some very good reason for it which they should discover when they knew her better. 'There can surely be no good reason for telling an untruth,' said Charlotte. 'I hope she does not think so.'

They had, of course, desired, from the first, to do everything in the way of helping her to arrange herself. It had seemed to Charlotte that there would be a great many things to talk about; but the Baroness was apparently inclined to talk about nothing.

'Write her a note, asking her leave to come and see her. I think that is what she will like,' said Gertrude.

'Why should I give her the trouble of answering me?' Charlotte asked. 'She will have to write a note and send it over.'

'I don't think she will take any trouble,' said Gertrude profoundly.

'What, then, will she do?'

'That is what I am curious to see,' said Gertrude, leaving her sister with an impression that her curiosity was morbid.

They went to see the Baroness without preliminary correspondence; and in the little salon which she had already created, with its becoming light and its festoons, they found Robert Acton.

Eugenia was intensely gracious, but she accused them of neglecting her cruelly. 'You see Mr Acton has had to take pity upon me,' she said. 'My brother goes off sketching, for hours; I can never depend upon him. So I was to send Mr Acton to beg you to come and give me the benefit of your wisdom.'

Gertrude looked at her sister. She wanted to say, '*That* is what she would have done.' Charlotte said that they hoped the Baroness would always come and dine with them; it would give them so much pleasure; and, in that case, she would spare herself the trouble of having a cook.

'Ah, but I must have a crook!' cried the Baroness. 'An old negress in a yellow turban. I have set my heart upon that. I want to look out of my window and see her sitting there on the grass, against the background of those crooked, dusty little apple trees, pulling the husks off a lapful of Indian corn. That will be local colour, you know. There isn't much of it here – you don't mind my saying that, do you? – so one must make the most of what one can get. I shall be most happy to dine with you whenever you will let me; but I want to be able to ask you sometimes. And I want to be able to ask Mr Acton,' added the Baroness.

'You must come and ask me at home,' said Acton. 'You must come and see me; you must dine with me first. I want to show you my place; I want to introduce you to my mother.' He called again upon Madame Münster, two days later. He was constantly at the other house; he used to walk across the fields from his own place, and he appeared to have fewer scruples than his cousins with regard to dropping in. On this occasion he found that Mr Brand had come to pay his respects to the charming stranger; but after Acton's arrival the young theologian said nothing. He sat in his chair with his two hands clasped, fixing upon his hostess a grave, fascinated stare. The Baroness talked to Robert Acton, but, as she talked, she turned and smiled at Mr Brand, who never took his eyes off her. The two men walked away together; they were going to Mr Wentworth's. Mr Brand still said nothing; but after they had passed into Mr Wentworth's garden he stopped and looked back for some time at the little white house. Then, looking at his companion, with his head bent a little to one side and his eyes somewhat contracted. 'Now, I suppose that's what is called conversation,' he said; 'real conversation.'

'It's what I call a very clever woman,' said Acton, laughing.

'It is most interesting,' Mr Brand continued. 'I only wish she would speak French; it would seem more in keeping. It must be quite the style that we have heard about, that we have read about – the style of conversation of Madame de Staël, of Madame Récamier.'

Acton also looked at Madame Münster's residence among its hollyhocks and apple trees. 'What I should like to know,' he said, smiling, 'is just what has brought Madame Récamier to live in that place!'

Chapter Five

Mr Wentworth, with his cane and his gloves in his hand, went every afternoon to call upon his niece. A couple of hours later she came over to the great house to tea. She had let the proposal that she should regularly dine there fall to the ground; she was in the enjoyment of whatever satisfaction was to be derived from the spectacle of an old negress in a crimson turban shelling peas under the apple trees. Charlotte, who had provided the ancient negress, thought it must be a strange household, Eugenia having told her that Augustine managed everything, the ancient negress included – Augustine, who was naturally devoid of all acquaintance with the expurgatory English tongue. By far the most immoral sentiment which I shall have occasion to attribute to Charlotte Wentworth was a certain emotion of disappointment at finding that in spite of these irregular conditions the domestic arrangements at the small house were apparently not – from Eugenia's peculiar point of view – strikingly offensive. The Baroness found it amusing to go to tea; she dressed as if for dinner. The tea-table offered an anomalous and picturesque repast; and on leaving it they all sat and talked in the large piazza, or wandered about the garden in the starlight, with their ears full of those sounds of strange insects which, though they are supposed to be, all over the world, a part of the magic of summer nights, seemed to the Baroness to have, beneath these western skies, an incomparable resonance.

Mr Wentworth, though, as I say, he went punctiliously to call upon her, was not able to feel that he was getting used to his niece. It taxed his imagination to believe that she was really his half-sister's child. His sister was a figure of his early years; she had been only twenty when she went abroad, never to return, making in foreign parts a wilful and undesirable marriage. His aunt, Mrs Whiteside, who had taken her to Europe for the benefit of the tour, gave, on her return, so lamentable an account of Mr Adolphus Young, to whom the headstrong girl had united her destiny, that it operated as a chill upon family feeling – especially in the case of the half-brothers. Catherine had done nothing subsequently to propitiate her family; she had not even written to them in any way that indicated a lucid appreciation of their suspended sympathy; so that it had become a tradition in Boston circles that the highest charity, as regards this young lady, was to think it well to forget her, and to abstain from conjecture as to the extent to which her aberrations were reproduced in her descendants. Over these young people – a vague report of their existence had come to his ears – Mr Wentworth had not, in the course of years, allowed his imagination to hover. It had plenty of occupation nearer home, and, though he had many cares upon his conscience, the idea that he had been an unnatural uncle was very properly never among the number. Now that his nephew and niece had come before him, he perceived that they were the fruit of influences and circumstances very different from those under which his own familiar progeny had reached a vaguely-qualified maturity. He felt no provocation to say that these influences had been exerted for evil; but he was sometimes afraid that he should not be able to like his distinguished, delicate, lady-like niece. He was paralysed and bewildered by her foreignness. She spoke, somehow, a different language. There was something strange in her words. He had a feeling that another man, in his place, would accommodate himself to her tone; would ask her questions and joke with her, reply to those pleasantries of her own which sometimes seemed startling as addressed to an uncle. But Mr Wentworth could not do these things. He could not even bring himself to attempt to measure her position in the world. She was the wife of a foreign nobleman who desired to repudiate her. This had a singular sound, but the old man felt himself destitute of the materials for a judgement. It seemed to him that he ought to find them in his own experience, as a man of the world and an almost public character; but they were not there, and he was ashamed to confess to himself – much more to reveal to Eugenia by interrogations possibly too innocent – the unfurnished condition of his repository.

It appeared to him that he could get much nearer, as he would have said, to his nephew; though he was not sure that Felix was altogether safe. He was so bright and handsome and talkative that it was impossible not to think well of him; and yet it seemed as if there were something almost impudent, almost vicious – or as if there ought to be – in a young man being at once so joyous and so positive. It was to be observed that while Felix was not at all a serious young man there was somehow more of him – he had more weight and volume and resonance – than a number of young men who were distinctly serious. While Mr Wentworth meditated upon this anomaly his nephew was admiring him unrestrictedly. He thought him a most delicate, generous, high-toned old gentleman, with a very handsome head, of the ascetic type, which he promised himself the profit of sketching. Felix was far from having made a secret of the fact that he wielded the paint-brush, and it was not his own fault if it failed to be generally understood that he was prepared to execute the most striking likenesses on the most reasonable terms. 'He is an artist – my cousin is an artist,' said Gertrude; and she offered this information to every one who would receive it. She offered it to herself, as it were, by way of admonition and reminder; she repeated to herself at odd moments, in lonley places, that Felix was invested with this sacred character. Gertrude had never seen an artist before; she had only read about such people. They seemed to her a romantic and mysterious class, whose life was made up of those agreeable accidents that never happened to other persons. And it merely quickened her meditations on this point that Felix should declare, as he repeatedly did, that he was not really an artist. 'I have never gone into the thing seriously,' he said, 'I have never studied; I have had no training. I do a little of everything, and nothing well. I am only an amateur.'

It pleased Gertrude even more to think that he was an amateur than to think that he was an artist; the former word, to her fancy, had an even subtler connotation. She knew, however, that it was a word to use more soberly. Mr Wentworth used it freely; for though he had not been exactly familiar with it, he found it convenient as a help toward classifying Felix, who, as a young man extremely clever and active and apparently respectable and yet not engaged in any recognized business, was an importunate anomaly. Of course the Baroness and her brother – she was always spoken of first – were a welcome topic of conversation between Mr Wentworth and his daughters and their occasional visitors.

'And the young man, your nephew, what is his profession?' asked an old gentleman – Mr Broderip, of Salem – who had been Mr Wentworth's classmate at Harvard College in the year 1809, and who came into his office in Devonshire Street. (Mr Wentworth, in his later years, used to go but three times a week to his office, where he had a large amount of highly confidential trust-business to transact.)

'Well, he's an amateur,' said Felix's uncle, with folded hands, and with a certain satisfaction in being able to say it. And Mr Broderip had gone back to Salem with a feeling that this was probably a 'European' expression for a broker or a grain-exporter.

'I should like to do your head, sir,' said Felix to his uncle one evening, before them all – Mr Brand and Robert Acton being also present. 'I think I should make a very fine thing of it. It's an interesting head; it's very medieval.'

Mr Wentworth looked grave; he felt awkwardly, as if all the company had come in and found him standing before the looking-glass. 'The Lord made it,' he said. 'I don't think it is for man to make it over again.'

'Certainly the Lord made it,' replied Felix, laughing, 'and He made it very well. But life has been touching up the work. It is a very interesting type of head. It's delightfully wasted and emaciated. The complexion is wonderfully bleached.' And Felix looked round at the circle, as if to call their attention to these interesting points. Mr Wentworth grew visibly paler. 'I should like to do you as an old prelate, an old cardinal, or the prior of an order.'

'A prelate, a cardinal?' murmured Mr Wentworth. 'Do you refer to the Roman Catholic priesthood?'

'I mean an old ecclesiastic who should have led a very pure, abstinent life. Now I take it that has been the case with you, sir; one sees it in your face,' Felix proceeded. 'You have been very – a – very moderate. Don't you think one always sees that in a man's face?'

'You see more in a man's face than I should think of looking for,' said Mr Wentworth coldly.

The Baroness rattled her fan and gave her brilliant laugh. 'It is a risk to look so close!' she exclaimed. 'My uncle has some peccadilloes on his conscience.' Mr Wentworth looked at her, painfully at a loss; and in so far as the signs of a pure and abstinent life were visible in his face they were then probably peculiarly manifest. 'You are a *beau vieillard*, dear uncle,' said Madame Münster, smiling with her foreign eyes.

'I think you are paying me a compliment,' said the old man.

'Surely, I am not first the woman that ever did so!' cried the Baroness.

'I think you are,' said Mr Wentworth gravely. And turning to Felix he added, in the same tone, 'Please don't take my likeness. My children have my daguerreotype. That is quite satisfactory.'

'I won't promise,' said Felix, 'not to work your head into something!'

Mr Wentworth looked at him and then at all the others; and then he got up and slowly walked away.

'Felix,' said Gertrude, in the silence that followed, 'I wish you would paint my portrait.'

Charlotte wondered whether Gertrude was right in wishing this; and she looked at Mr Brand as the most legitimate way of ascertaining. Whatever Gertrude did or said, Charlotte always looked at Mr Brand. It was a standing pretext for looking at Mr Brand – always, as Charlotte thought, in the interest of Gertrude's welfare. It is true that she felt a tremulous interest in Gertrude being right; for Charlotte, in her small way, was an heroic sister.

'We should be glad to have your portrait, Miss Gertrude,' said Mr Brand.

'I should be delighted to paint so charming a model,' Felix declared.

'Do you think you are so lovely, my dear?' asked Lizzie Acton, with her little inoffensive pertness, biting off a knot in her knitting.

'It is not because I think I am beautiful,' said Gertrude, looking all round. 'I don't think I am beautiful at all.' She spoke a sort of conscious deliberateness; and it seemed very strange to Charlotte to hear her discussing this question so publicly. 'It is because I think it would be amusing to sit and be painted. I have always thought that.'

'I am sorry you have not had better things to think about, my daughter,' said Mr Wentworth.

'You are very beautiful, cousin Gertrude,' Felix declared.

'That's a compliment,' said Gertrude. 'I put all the compliments I receive into a little money-jug that has a slit in the side. I shake them up and down, and they rattle. There are not many yet – only two or three.'

'No, it's not a compliment,' Felix rejoined. 'See; I am careful not to give it in the form of a compliment. I did not think you were beautiful at first. But you have come to seem so little by litte.'

'Take care, now, your jug doesn't burst!' exclaimed Lizzie.

'I think sitting for one's portrait is only one of the various forms of idleness,' said Mr Wentworth. 'Their name is legion.'

'My dear sir,' cried Felix, 'you can't be said to idle when you are making a man work so!'

'One might be painted while one is asleep,' suggested Mr Brand, as a contribution to the discussion.

'Ah, do paint me while I am asleep,' said Gertrude to Felix, smiling. And she closed her eyes a little. It had by this time become a matter of almost exciting anxiety to Charlotte what Gertrude would say or would do next.

She began to sit for her portrait on the following day – in the open air, on the north side of the piazza. 'I would you would tell me what you think of us – how we seem to you,' she said to Felix, as he sat before his easel.

'You seem to me the best people in the world,' said Felix.

'You say that,' Gertrude resumed, 'because it saves you the trouble of saying anything else.'

The young man glanced at her over the top of the canvas. 'What else should I say? It would certainly be a great deal of trouble to say anything different.'

'Well,' said Gertrude, 'you have seen people before that you have liked, have you not?'

'Indeed I have, thank Heaven!'

'And they have been very different from us,' Gertrude went on.

'That only proves,' said Felix, 'that there are a thousand different ways of being good company.'

'Do you think us good company?' asked Gertrude.

'Company for a king!'

Gertrude was silent a moment; and then, 'There must be a thousand different ways of being dreary,' she said; 'and sometimes I think we make use of them all.'

Felix stood up quickly, holding up his hand. 'If you could only keep that look on your face for half an hour – while I catch it!' he said. 'It is uncommonly handsome.'

'To look handsome for half an hour – that is a great deal to ask of me,' she answered.

'It would be the portrait of a young woman who has taken some vow, some pledge, that she repents of,' said Felix, 'and who is thinking it over at leisure.'

'I have taken no vow, no pledge,' said Gertrude very gravely. 'I have nothing to repent of.'

'My dear cousin, that was only a figure of speech. I am very sure that no one in your excellent family has anything to repent of.'

'And yet we are always repenting!' Gertrude exclaimed. 'That is what I mean by our being dreary. You know it perfectly well; you only pretend that you don't.'

Felix gave a quick laugh. 'The half-hour is going on, and yet you are handsomer than ever. One must be careful what one says, you see.'

'To me,' said Gertrude, 'you can say anything.'

Felix looked at her, as an artist might, and painted for some time in silence. 'Yes, you seem to me different from your father and sister – from most of the people you have lived with,' he observed.

'To say that one's self,' Gertrude went on, 'is like saying – by implication, at least – that one is better. I am not better; I am much worse. But they say themselves that I am different. It makes them unhappy.'

'Since you accuse me of concealing my real impressions, I may admit that I think the tendency – among you generally – is to be made unhappy too easily.'

'I wish you would tell that to my father,' said Gertrude.

'It might make him more unhappy,' Felix exclaimed, laughing.

'It certainly would. I don't believe you have seen people like that.'

'Ah, my dear cousin, how do you know what I have seen?' Felix demanded. 'How can I tell you?'

'You might tell me a great many things, if you only would. You have seen people like yourself – people who are bright and gay and fond of amusement. We are not fond of amusement.'

'Yes,' said Felix, 'I confess that rather strikes me. You don't seem to me to get all the pleasure out of life that you might. You don't seem to me to enjoy . . . Do you mind my saying this?' he asked, pausing.

'Please go on,' said the girl earnestly.

'You seem to me very well placed, for enjoying. You have money and liberty and what is called in Europe a "position". But you take a painful view of life, as one might say.'

'One ought to think it bright and charming and delightful, eh?' asked Gertrude.

'I should say so – if one can. It is true it all depends upon that,' Felix added.

'You know there is a great deal of misery in the world,' said his model.

'I have seen a little of it,' the young man rejoined. 'But it was all over there – beyond the sea. I don't see any here. This is a paradise.'

Gertrude said nothing; she sat looking at the dahlias and the currant-bushes in the garden, while Felix went on with his work. 'To "enjoy",' she began at last, 'to take life – not painfully, must one do something wrong?'

Felix gave his long light laugh again. 'Seriously, I think not. And for this reason, among others: you strike me as very capable of enjoying, if the chance were given you, and yet at the same time as incapable of wrong-doing.'

'I am sure,' said Gertrude, 'that you are very wrong in telling a person that she is incapable of that. We are never nearer to evil than when we believe that.'

'You are handsomer than ever,' observed Felix irrelevantly.

Gertrude had got used to hearing him say this. There was not so much excitement in it as at first. 'What ought one to do?' she continued. 'To give parties, to go to the theatre, to read novels, to keep late hours?'

'I don't think it's what one does or one doesn't do that promotes enjoyment,' her companion answered. 'It is the general way of looking at life.'

'They look at it as a discipline – that is what they do here. I have often been told that.'

'Well, that's very good. But there is another way,' added Felix, smiling: 'to look at it as an opportunity.'

'An opportunity – yes,' said Gertrude, 'One would get more pleasure that way.'

'I don't attempt to say anything better for it than that it has been my own way – and that is not saying much!' Felix had laid down his palette and brushes; he was leaning back, with his arms folded, to judge the effect of his work. 'And you know,' he said, 'I am a very petty personage.'

'You have a great deal of talent,' said Gertrude.

'No – no,' the young man rejoined, in a tone of cheerful impartiality, 'I have not a great deal of talent. It is nothing at all remarkable. I assure you I should know if it were. I shall always be obscure. The world will never hear of me.' Gertrude looked at him with a strange feeling. She was thinking of the great world which he knew and which she did not, and how full of brilliant talents it must be, since it could afford to make light of his abilities. 'You needn't in general attach much importance to anything I tell you,' he pursued; 'but you may believe me when I say this – that I am little better than a good-natured feather-head.'

'A feather-head?' she repeated.

'I am a species of Bohemian.'

'A Bohemian?' Gertrude had never heard this term before, save as a geographical denomination; and she quite failed to understand the figurative meaning which her companion appeared to attach to it. But it gave her pleasure.

Felix had pushed back his chair and risen to his feet; he slowly came toward her, smiling. 'I am a sort of adventurer,' he said, looking down at her.

She got up, meeting his smile. 'An adventurer?' she repeated. 'I should like to hear your adventures.'

For an instant she believed that he was going to take her hand; but he dropped his own hands suddenly into the pockets of his painting jacket. 'There is no reason why you shouldn't,' he said. 'I have been an adventurer, but my adventures have been very innocent. They have all been happy ones; I don't think there are any I shouldn't tell. They were very pleasant and very pretty; I should like to go over them in memory. Sit down again, and I will begin,' he added in a moment, with his naturally persuasive smile.

Gertrude sat down again on that day, and she sat down on several other days. Felix, while he plied his brush, told her a great many stories, and she listened with charmed avidity. Her eyes rested upon his lips; she was very serious, sometimes, from her air of wondering gravity, he thought she was displeased. But Felix never believed for more than a single moment in any displeasure of his own producing. This would have been fatuity if the optimism it expressed had not been much more a hope than a prejudice. It is beside the matter to say that he had a good conscience; for the best conscience is a sort of self-reproach, and this young man's brilliantly healthy nature spent itself in objective good intentions which were ignorant of any test save exactness in hitting their mark. He told Gertrude how he had walked over France and Italy with a painter's knapsack on his back, paying his way often by knocking off a flattering portrait of his host or hostess. He told her how he had played the violin in a little band of musicians – not of high celebrity – who travelled through foreign lands giving provincial concerts. He told her also how he had been a momentary ornament of a troupe of strolling actors, engaged in the arduous task of interpreting Shakespeare to French and German, Polish and Hungarian audiences.

While this periodical recital was going on Gertrude lived in a fantastic world; she seemed to herself to be reading a romance that came out in daily numbers. She had known nothing so delightful since the perusal of *Nicholas Nickleby*. One afternoon she went to see her cousin, Mrs Acton, Robert's mother, who was a great invalid, never leaving the house. She came back alone, on foot, across the fields – this being a short way which they often used. Felix had gone to Boston with her father, who desired to take the young man to call upon some of his friends, old gentlemen who remembered his mother – remembered her, but said nothing about her – and several of whom, with the gentle ladies their wives, had driven out from town to pay their respects at the little house among the apple trees, in vehicles which reminded the Baroness, who received her visitors with discriminating civility, of the large, light, rattling barouche in which she herself had made her journey to this neighbourhood. The afternoon was waning; in the western sky the great picture of a New England sunset, painted in crimson and silver, was suspended from the zenith; and the stony pastures, as Gertrude traversed them, thinking intently to herself, were covered with a light, clear glow. At the open gate of one of the fields she saw from the distance a man's figure;

he stood there as if he were waiting for her, and as she came nearer she recognized Mr Brand. She had a feeling as of not having seen him for some time; she could not have said for how long, for it yet seemed to her that he had been very lately at the house.

'May I walk back with you?' he asked. And when she said that he might if he wanted, he observed that he had seen her and recognized her half a mile away.

'You must have very good eyes,' said Gertrude.

'Yes, I have very good eyes, Miss Gertrude,' said Mr Brand. She perceived that he meant something; but for a long time past Mr Brand had constantly meant something, and she had almost got used to it. She felt, however, that what he meant had now a renewed power to disturb her, to perplex and agitate her. He walked beside her in silence for a moment, and then he added, 'I have had no trouble in seeing that you are beginning to avoid me. But perhaps,' he went on, 'one needn't have had very good eyes to see that.'

'I have not avoided you,' said Gertrude, without looking at him.

'I think you have been unconscious that you were avoiding me,' Mr Brand replied. 'You have not even known that I was there.'

'Well, you are here now, Mr Brand!' said Gertrude, with a short laugh. 'I know that very well.'

He made no rejoinder. He simply walked beside her, slowly, as they were obliged to walk over the soft grass. Presently they came to another gate, which was closed. Mr Brand laid his hand upon it, but he made no movement to open it; he stood and looked at his companion. 'You are very much interested – very much absorbed,' he said.

Gertrude glanced at him; she saw that he was pale, and that he looked excited. She had never seen Mr Brand excited before, and she felt that the spectacle, if fully carried out, would be impressive, almost painful. 'Absorbed in what?' she asked. Then she looked away, at the illuminated sky. She felt guilty and uncomfortable, and yet she was vexed with herself for feeling so. But Mr Brand, as he stood there looking at her with his small, kind, persistent eyes, represented an immense body of half-obliterated obligations that were rising again into a certain distinctness.

'You have new interests, new occupations,' he went on. 'I don't know that I can say that you have new duties. We have always old ones, Gertrude,' he added.

'Please open the gate, Mr Brand,' she said; and she felt as if, in saying so, she were cowardly and petulant. But he opened the gate, and allowed her to pass; then he closed it behind himself. Before she had time to turn away he put out his hand and held her an instant by the wrist.

'I want to say something to you,' he said.

'I know what you want to say,' she answered. And she was on the point of adding, 'And I know just how you will say it'; but these words she kept back.

'I love you, Gertrude,' he said. 'I love you very much; I love you more than ever.'

He had said the words just as she had known he would; she had heard them before. They had no charm for her; she had said to herself before that it was very strange. It was supposed to be delightful for a woman to listen to such words; but these seemed to her flat and mechanical. 'I wish you would forget that,' she declared.

'How can I – why should I?' he asked.

'I have made you no promise – given you no pledge,' she said, looking at him, with her voice trembling a little.

'You have let me feel that I have an influence over you. You have opened your mind to me.'

'I never opened my mind to you, Mr Brand!' Gertrude cried with some vehemence.

'Then you were not so frank as I thought – as we all thought.'

'I don't see what any one else had to do with it!' cried the girl.

'I mean your father and your sister. You know it makes them happy to think you will listen to me.'

She gave a little laugh. 'It doesn't make them happy,' she said. 'Nothing makes them happy. No one is happy here'.

'I think your cousin is very happy – Mr Young,' rejoined Mr Brand, in a soft, almost timid tone.

'So much the better for him!' And Gertrude gave her little laugh again.

The young man looked at her a moment. 'You are very much changed,' he said.

'I am glad to hear it,' Gertrude declared.

'I am not. I have known you a long time, and I have loved you as you were.'

'I am much obliged to you,' said Gertrude. 'I must be going home.'

He, on his side, gave a little laugh. 'You certainly do avoid me – you see!'

'Avoid me, then,' said the girl.

He looked at her again; and then, very gently, 'No, I will not avoid you,' he replied; 'but I will leave you, for the present, to yourself. I think you will remember – after a while – some of the things you have forgotten. I think you will come back to me; I have great faith in that.'

This time his voice was very touching; there was a strong reproachful force in what he said, and Gertrude could answer nothing. He turned away and stood there, leaning his elbows on the gate and looking at the beautiful sunset. Gertrude left him and took her way home again; but when she reached the middle of the next field she suddenly burst into tears. Her tears seemed to her to have been a long time gathering, and for some moments it was a kind of glee to shed them. But they presently passed away. There was something a little hard in Gertrude; and she never wept again.

Chapter Six

Going of an afternoon to call upon his niece, Mr Wentworth more than once found Robert Acton sitting in her little drawing-room. This was in no degree, to Mr Wentworth, a perturbing fact, for he had no sense of competing with his young kinsman for Eugenia's good graces. Madame Münster's uncle had the highest opinion of Robert Acton, who, indeed, in the family at large, was the object of a great deal of undemonstrative appreciation. They were all proud of him, in so far as the charge of being proud may be brought against people who were, habitually, distinctly guiltless of the misdemeanour known as 'taking credit'. They never boasted of Robert Acton, nor indulged in vainglorious reference to him; they never quoted the clever things he had said, nor mentioned the generous things he had done. But a sort of frigidly-tender faith in his unlimited goodness was a part of their personal sense of right; and there can, perhaps, be no better proof of the high esteem in which he was held than the fact that no explicit judgement was ever passed upon his actions. He was no more praised than he was blamed; but he was tacitly felt to be an ornament to his circle. He was the man of the world of the family. He had been to China and brought home a collection of curiosities; he had made a fortune – or rather he had quintupled a fortune already considerable; he was distinguished by that combination of celibacy, 'property', and good-humour which appeals to even the most subdued imaginations; and it was taken for granted that he would presently place these advantages at the disposal of some well-regulated young woman of his own 'set'. Mr Wentworth was not a man to admit to himself that – his paternal duties apart – he liked any individual much better than all other individuals; but he thought Robert Acton extremely judicious; and this was perhaps as near an approach as he was capable of to the eargerness of preference, which his temperament repudiated as it would have disengaged itself from something slightly unchaste. Acton was, in fact, very judicious – and something more beside; and indeed it must be claimed for Mr Wentworth that in the more illicit parts of his preference there hovered the vague adumbration of a belief that his cousin's final merit was a certain enviable capacity for whistling, rather gallantly, at the sanctions of mere judgement – for showing a larger courage, a finer quality of pluck, than common occasion demanded. Mr Wentworth would never have risked the intimation that Acton was made, in the smallest degree, of the stuff of a hero, but this is small blame to him, for Robert would certainly never have risked it himself. Acton certainly exercised great discretion in all things – beginning with his estimate of himself. He knew that he was by no means so much a man of the world as he was supposed to be in local circles; but it must be added that he knew also that his natural shrewdness had a reach of which he had never quite given local circles the measure. He was addicted to taking the humorous view of things, and he had discovered that even in the narrowest circles such a disposition may find frequent opportunities. Such opportunities had formed for some time – that is, since his return from China, a year and a half before – the most active element in this gentleman's life, which had just now a rather indolent air. He was perfectly willing to get married. He was very fond of books, and he had a handsome library; that is, his books were much more numerous than Mr Wentworth's. He was also very fond of pictures; but it must be confessed, in the fierce light of contemporary criticism, that his walls were adorned with several rather abortive masterpieces. He had got his learning – and there was more of it than commonly appeared – at Harvard College; and he took a pleasure in old associations which made it a part of his daily contentment to live so near this institution that he often passed it in driving to Boston. He was extremely interested in the Baroness Münster.

She was very frank with him; or at least she intended to be. 'I am sure you will find it very strange that I should have settled down in this out-of-the-way part of the world!' she said to him three or four weeks after she had installed herself. 'I am certain you are wondering about my motives. They are very pure.' The Baroness by this time was an old inhabitant; the best society in Boston had called upon her, and Clifford Wentworth had taken her several times to drive in his buggy.

Robert Acton was seated near her, playing with a fan; there were always several fans lying about her drawing-room, with long ribbons of different colours attached to them, and Acton was always playing with one. 'No, I don't find it at all strange,' he said slowly, smiling. 'That a clever woman should turn up in Boston, or its suburbs – that doesn't require so much explanation. Boston is a very nice place.'

'If you wish to make me contradict you,' said the Baroness, '*vous vous y prenez mal*. In certain moods there is nothing I am not capable of agreeing to. Boston is a paradise, and we are in the suburbs of Paradise.'

'Just now I am not at all in the suburbs; I am in the place itself,' rejoined Acton, who was lounging a little in his chair. He was, however, not always lounging; and when he was he was not quite so relaxed as he pretended. To a certain extent, he sought refuge from shyness in this appearance of relaxation; and, like many persons in the same circumstances, he somewhat exaggerated the appearance. Beyond this, the air of being much at his ease was a cover for vigilant observation. He was more than interested in this clever woman, who, whatever he might say, was clever not at all after the Boston fashion; she plunged him into a kind of excitement, held him in vague suspense. He was obliged to admit to himself that he had never yet seen a woman just like this – not even in China. He was ashamed, for inscrutable reasons, of the vivacity of his emotion, and he carried it off, superficially, by taking, still superficially, the humorous view of Madame Münster. It was not at all true that he thought it very natural of her to have made this pious pilgrimage. It might have been said of him in advance that he was too good a Bostonian to regard in the light of an eccentricity the desire of even the remotest alien to visit the New England metropolis. This was an impulse for which, surely, no apology was needed; and Madame Münster was the fortunate possessor of several New England cousins. In fact, however,

Madame Münster struck him as out of keeping with her little circle; she was at the best a very agreeable, a gracefully mystifying, anomaly. He knew very well that it would not do to address these reflexions too crudely to Mr Wentworth; he would never have remarked to the old gentleman that he wondered what the Baroness was up to. And indeed he had no great desire to share his vauge mistrust with any one. There was a personal pleasure in it; the greatest pleasure he had known at least since he had come from China. He would keep the Baroness, for better or worse, to himself; he had a feeling that he deserved to enjoy a monopoly of her, for he was certainly the person who had most adequately gauged her capacity for social intercourse. Before long it became apparent to him that the Baroness was disposed to lay no tax upon such a monopoly.

One day (he was sitting there again and playing with a fan) she asked him to apologize, should the occasion present itself, to certain people in Boston for her not having returned their calls. 'There are half a dozen places,' she said; 'a formidable list. Charlotte Wentworth has written it out for me, in a terrifically distinct hand. There is no ambiguity on the subject; I know perfectly where I must go. Mr Wentworth informs me that the carriage is always at my disposal, and Charlotte offers to go with me, in a pair of tight gloves and a very stiff petticoat. And yet for three days I have been putting it off. They must think me horribly vicious.'

'You ask me to apologize,' said Acton, 'but you don't tell me what excuse I can offer.'

'That is more,' the Baroness declared, 'than I am held to. It would be like my asking you to buy me a bouquet and giving you the money. I have no reason except that – somehow – it's too violent an effort. It is not inspiring. Wouldn't that serve as an excuse, in Boston? I am told they are very sincere; they don't tell fibs. And then Felix ought to go with me, and he is never in readiness. I don't see him. He is always roaming about the fields and sketching old barns, or taking ten-mile walks, or painting someone's portrait, or rowing on the pond, or flirting with Gertrude Wentworth.'

'I should think it would amuse you to go and see a few people,' said Acton. 'You are having a very quiet time of it here. It's a dull life for you.'

'Ah, the quiet – the quiet!' the Baroness exclaimed. 'That's what I like. It's rest. That's what I came here for. Amusement? I have had amusement. And as for seeing people – I have already seen a great many in my life. If it didn't sound ungracious I should say that I wish very humbly your people here would leave me alone!'

Acton looked at her a moment, and she looked at him. She was a woman who took being looked at remarkably well. 'So you have come here for rest?' he asked.

'So I may say. I came for many of those reasons that are no reasons – don't you know? – and yet that are really the best: to come away, to change, to break with everything. When once one comes away one must arrive somewhere, and I asked myself why I shouldn't arrive here.'

'You certainly had time, on the way!' said Acton, laughing.

Madame Münster looked at him again; and then, smiling, 'And I have certainly had time, since I got here, to ask myself why I came. However, I never ask myself idle questions. Here I am, and it seems to me you ought only to thank me.'

'When you go away you will see the difficulties I shall put in your path.'

'You mean to put difficulties in my path?' she asked, rearranging the rosebud in her corsage.

'The greatest of all – that of having been so agreeable—'

'That I shall be unable to depart? Don't be too sure. I have left some very agreeable people over there.'

'Ah,' said Acton, 'but it was to come here, where I am!'

'I didn't know of your existence. Excuse me for saying anything so rude; but, honestly speaking, I did not. No,' the Baroness pursued, 'it was precisely not to see you – such people as you – that I came.'

'Such people as me?' cried Acton.

'I had a sort of longing to come into those natural relations which I knew I should find here. Over there I had only, as I may say, artificial relations. Don't you see the difference?'

'The difference tells against me,' said Acton. 'I suppose I am an artificial relation.'

'Conventional,' declared the Baroness; 'very conventional.'

'Well, there is one way in which the relation of a lady and a gentleman may always become natural,' said Acton.

'You mean by their becoming lovers? That may be natural or not. And at any rate,' rejoined Eugenia, '*nous n'en sommes pas là!*'

They were not, as yet; but a little later, when she began to go with him to drive, it might almost have seemed that they were. He came for her several times, alone, in his high 'wagon', drawn by a pair of charming light-limbed horses. It was different, her having gone with Clifford Wentworth, who was her cousin and so much younger. It was not to be imagined that she should have a flirtation with Clifford, who was a mere shame-faced boy, and whom a large section of Boston society supposed to be 'engaged' to Lizzie Acton. Not indeed that it was to be conceived that the Baroness was a possible party to any flirtation whatever; for she was undoubtedly a married lady. It was generally known that her matrimonial condition was of the 'morganatic' order; but in its natural aversion to suppose that this meant anything less than absolute wedlock, the conscience of the community took refuge in the belief that it implied something even more.

Acton wished her to think highly of American scenery, and he drove her to great distances, picking out the prettiest roads and the largest points of view. If we are good when we are contented, Eugenia's virtues should now certainly have been uppermost; for she found a charm in the rapid movement through a wild country, and in a companion who from time to time made the vehicle dip, with a motion like a swallow's flight, over roads of primitive construction, and who, as she felt, would do a great many things that she might ask him. Sometimes, for a couple of hours together, there were almost no houses; there were nothing but woods and rivers and lakes and horizons adorned with bright-looking mountains. It seemed to the Baroness very wild, as I have said, and lovely; but the impression added something to that sense of the enlargement of opportunity which had been born of her arrival in the New World.

One day – it was late in the afternoon – Acton pulled up his horses on the crest of a hill which commanded a beautiful prospect. He let them stand a long time to rest, while he sat there and talked with Madame Münster.

The prospect was beautiful in spite of there being nothing human within sight. There was a wilderness of woods, and the gleam of a distant river, and a glimpse of half the hill-tops in Massachusetts. The road had a wide, grassy margin, on the farther side of which there flowed a deep, clear brook; there were wild flowers in the grass, and beside the brook lay the trunk of a fallen tree. Acton waited a while; at last a rustic wayfarer came trudging along the road. Acton asked him to hold the horses – a service he consented to render, as a friendly turn to a fellow-citizen. Then he invited the Baroness to descend, and the two wandered away, across the grass, and sat down on the log beside the brook.

'I imagine it doesn't remind you of Silberstadt,' said Acton. It was the first time that he had mentioned Silberstadt to her for particular reasons. He knew she had a husband there, and this was disagreeable to him; and, furthermore, it had been repeated to him that this husband wished to put her away – a state of affairs to which even indirect reference was to be deprecated. It was true, nevertheless, that the Baroness herself had often alluded to Silberstadt; and Acton had often wondered why her husband wished to get rid of her. It was a curious position for a lady – this being known as a repudiated wife; and it is worthy of observation that the Baroness carried it off with exceeding grace and dignity. She had made it felt, from the first, that there were two sides to the question, and that her own side, when she should choose to present it, would be replete with touching interest.

'It does not remind me of the town, of course,' she said; 'of the sculptured gables and the Gothic churches, of the wonderful Schloss, with its moat and its clustering towers. But it has a little look of some other parts of the principality. One might fancy one's self among those grand old German forests, those legendary mountains; the sort of country one sees from the windows at Schreckenstein.'

'What is Schreckenstein?' asked Acton.

'It is a great castle – the summer residence of the Reigning Prince.'

'Have you ever lived there?'

'I have stayed there,' said the Baroness. Acton was silent; he looked a while at the uncastled landscape before him. 'It is the first time you have ever asked me about Silberstadt,' she said. 'I should think you would want to know about my marriage; it must seem to you very strange.'

Acton looked at her a moment. 'Now you wouldn't like me to say that!'

'You Americans have such odd ways!' the Baroness declared. 'You never ask anything outright; there seem to be so many things you can't talk about.'

'We Americans are very polite,' said Acton, whose national consciousness had been complicated by a residence in foreign lands, and who yet disliked to hear Americans abused. 'We don't like to tread upon people's toes,' he said. 'But I should like very much to hear about your marriage. Now tell me how it came about.'

'The Prince fell in love with me,' replied the Baroness simply. 'He pressed his suit very hard. At first he didn't wish me to marry him; on the contrary. But on that basis I refused to listen to him. So he offered me marriage – in so far as he might. I was young, and I confess I was rather flattered. But if it were to be done again now, I certainly should not accept him.'

'How long ago was this?' asked Acton.

'Oh – several years,' said Eugenia. 'You should never ask a woman for dates.'

'Why I should think that when a woman was relating history . . .' Acton answered. 'And now he wants to break it off?'

'They want him to make a political marriage. It is his brother's idea. His brother is very clever.'

'They must be a precious pair!' cried Robert Acton.

The Baroness gave a little philosophic shrug. '*Que voulezvous!* They are princes. They think they are treating me very well. Silberstadt is a perfectly despotic little state, and the Reigning Prince may annul the marriage by a stroke of his pen. But he has promised me, nevertheless, not to do so without my formal consent.'

'And this you have refused?'

'Hitherto. It is an indignity, and I have wished at least to make it difficult for them. But I have a little document in my writing-desk which I have only to sign and send back to the Prince.'

'Then it will be all over?'

The Baroness lifted her hand and dropped it again. 'Of course I shall keep my title; at least, I shall be at liberty to keep it if I choose. And I suppose I shall keep it. One must have a name. And I shall keep my pension. It is very small – it is wretchedly small; but it is what I live on.'

'And you have only to sign that paper?' Acton asked.

The Baroness looked at him a moment. 'Do you urge it?'

He got up slowly, and stood with his hands in his pockets. 'What do you gain by not doing it?'

'I am supposed to gain this advantage – that if I delay, or temporize, the Prince may come back to me, may make a stand against his brother. He is very fond of me, and his brother has pushed him only little by little.'

'If he were to come back to you,' said Acton, 'would you – would you take him back?'

The Baroness met his eyes; she coloured just a little. Then she rose. 'I should have the satisfaction of saying, "Now it is my turn. I break with your Serene Highness!" '

They began to walk toward the carriage. 'Well,' said Robert Acton, 'it's a curious story! How did you make his acquaintance?'

'I was staying with an old lady – an old Countess – in Dresden. She had been a friend of my father's. My father was dead; I was very much alone. My brother was wandering about the world in a theatrical troupe.'

'Your brother ought to have stayed with you.' Acton observed, 'and kept you from putting your trust in princes.'

The Baroness was silent a moment, and then, 'He did what he could,' she said. 'He sent me money. The old Countess encouraged the Prince; she was even pressing. It seems to me,' Madame Münster added gently, 'that – under the circumstances – I behaved very well.'

Acton glanced at her, and made the observation – he had made it before – that a woman looks the prettier for having unfolded her wrongs or her sufferings. 'Well,' he reflected audibly, 'I should like to see you send his Serene Highness – somewhere!'

Madame Münster stooped and picked a daisy from the grass. 'And not sign my renunciation?'

'Well, I don't know – I don't know,' said Acton.

'In one case I should have my revenge; in another case I should have my liberty.'

Acton gave a little laugh as he helped her into the carriage. 'At any rate,' he said, 'take good care of that paper.'

A couple of days afterward he asked her to come and see his house. The visit had already been proposed, but it had been put off in consequence of his mother's illness. She was a constant invalid, and she had passed these recent years, very patiently, in a great flowered arm-chair at her bedroom window. Lately, for some days, she had been unable to see any one; but now she was better, and she sent the Baroness a very civil message. Acton had wished their visitor to come to dinner; but Madame Münster preferred to begin with a simple call. She had reflected that if she should go to dinner Mr Wentworth and his daughters would also be asked, and it had seemed to her that the peculiar character of the occasion would best be preserved in a *tête-à-tête* with her host. Why the occasion should have a peculiar character she explained to no one. As far as any one could see, it was simply very pleasant. Acton came for her and drove her to his door, an operation which was rapidly performed. His house the Baroness mentally pronounced a very good one; more articulately, she declared that it was enchanting. It was large and square and painted brown; it stood in a well-kept shrubbery, and was approached, from the gate, by a short drive. It was, moreover, a much more modern dwelling than Mr Wentworth's, and was more redundantly upholstered and expensively ornamented. The Baroness perceived that her entertainer had analysed material comfort to a sufficiently fine point. And then he possessed the most delightful *chinoiseries* – trophies of his sojourn in the Celestial Empire: pagodas of ebony and cabinets of ivory; sculptured monsters, grinning and leering on chimney-pieces, in front of beautifully-figured hand-screens; porcelain dinner-sets, gleaming behind the glass doors of mahogany buffets; large screens, in corners, covered with tense silk and embroidered with mandarins and dragons. These things were scattered all over the house, and they gave Eugenia a pretext for a complete domiciliary visit. She liked it, she enjoyed it; she thought it a very nice place. It had a mixture of the homely and the liberal, and though it was almost a museum, the large, little-used rooms were as fresh and clean as a well-kept dairy. Lizzie Acton told her that she dusted all the pagodas and other curiosities every day with her own hands; and the Baroness answered that she was evidently a household fairy. Lizzie had not at all the look of a young lady who dusted things; she wore such pretty dresses and had such delicate fingers that it was difficult to imagine her immersed in sordid cares. She came to meet Madame Münster on her arrival, but she said nothing, or almost nothing, and the Baroness again reflected – she had had occasion to do so before – that American girls had no manners. She disliked this little American girl, and she was quite prepared to learn that she had failed to commend herself to Miss Acton. Lizzie struck her as positive and explicit almost to pertness; and the idea of her combining the apparent incongruities of a taste for housework and the wearing of fresh Parisian-looking dresses suggested the possession of a dangerous energy. It was a source of irritation to the Baroness that in this country it should seem to matter whether a little girl were a trifle less or a trifle more of a nonentity; for Eugenia had hitherto been conscious of no moral pressure as regards the appreciation of diminutive virgins. It was perhaps an indication of Lizzie's pertness that she very soon retired and left the Baroness on her brother's hands. Acton talked a great deal about his *chinoiseries*; he knew a good deal about porcelain and bric-à-brac. The Baroness, in her progress through the house, made, as it were, a great many stations. She sat down everywhere, confessed to being a little tired, and asked about the various objects with a curious mixture of alertness and inattention. If there had been any one to say it to, she would have declared that she was positively in love with her host; but she could hardly make this declaration – even in the strictest confidence – to Acton himself. It gave her, nevertheless, a pleasure that had some of the charm of unwontedness to feel, with that admirable keenness with which she was capable of feeling things, that he had a disposition without any edges; that even his humorous irony always expanded toward the point. One's impression of his honesty was almost like carrying a bunch of flowers; the perfume was most agreeable, but they were occasionally an inconvenience. One could trust him, at any rate, round all the corners of the world; and, withal, he was not absolutely simple, which would have been excess; he was only relatively simple, which was quite enough for the Baroness.

Lizzie reappeared, to say that her mother would not be happy to receive Madame Münster; and the Baroness followed her to Mrs Acton's apartment. Eugenia reflected, as she went, that it was not the affectation of impertinence that made her dislike this young lady, for on that ground she could easily have beaten her. It was not an aspiration on the girl's part to rivalry, but a kind of laughing, childishly-mocking indifference to the results of comparison. Mrs Acton was an emaciated, sweet-faced woman of five-and-fifty, sitting with pillows behind her and looking out on a clump of hemlocks. She was very modest, very timid, and very ill; she made Eugenia feel grateful that she herself was not like that – neither so ill, nor, possibly, so modest. On a chair, beside her, lay a volume of Emerson's Essays. It was a great occasion for poor Mrs Acton, in her helpless condition, to be confronted with a clever foreign lady, who had more manner than any lady – any dozen ladies – that she had ever seen.

'I have heard a great deal about you,' she said softly, to the Baroness.

'From your son, eh?' Eugenia asked. 'He has talked to me immensely of you. Oh, he talks of you as you would like,' the Baroness declared; 'as such a son *must* talk of such a mother!'

Mrs Acton sat gazing; this was part of Madame Münster's 'manner'. But Robert Acton was gazing too, in vivid consciousness that he had barely mentioned his mother to their brilliant guest. He never talked of this still maternal presence – a presence refined to such delicacy that it had almost resolved itself, with him, simply into the subjective emotion of gratitude. And Acton rarely talked of his emotions. The Baroness turned her smile toward him, and she instantly felt that she had been observed to be fibbing. She had struck a false note. But who were these people to whom such fibbing was not pleasing? If they were annoyed, the Baroness was equally so; and after the exchange of a few civil inquiries and low-voiced responses she took leave of Mrs Acton. She begged Robert not to come home with her; she would get into the carriage alone; she preferred that. This was imperious, and she thought he looked disappointed. While she stood before the door with him – the carriage was turning in the gravel drive – this thought restored her serenity.

When she had given him her hand in farewell she looked at him a moment. 'I have almost decided to despatch that paper,' she said.

He knew that she alluded to the document that she had called her renunciation; and he assisted her into the carriage without saying anything. But just before the vehicle began to move he said, 'Well, when you have in fact despatched it, I hope you will let me know!'

Chapter Seven

Felix Young finished Gertrude's portrait, and he afterwards transferred to canvas the features of many members of that circle of which it may be said that he had become, for the time, the pivot and the centre. I am afraid it must be confessed that he was a decidedly flattering painter, and that he imparted to his models a romantic grace which seemed easily and cheaply acquired by the payment of a hundred dollars to a young man who made 'sitting' so entertaining. For Felix was paid for his pictures, making, as he did, no secret of the fact that in guiding his steps to the Western world affectionate curiosity had gone hand in hand with a desire to better his condition. He took his uncle's portrait quite as if Mr Wentworth had never averted himself from the experiment; and as he compassed his end only by the exercise of gentle violence it is but fair to add that he allowed the old man to give him nothing but his time. He passed his arm into Mr Wentworth's one summer morning – very few arms, indeed, had ever passed into Mr Wentworth's – and led him across the garden and along the road into the studio which he had extemporized in the little house among the apple trees. The grave gentleman felt himself more and more fascinated by his clever nephew, whose fresh, demonstrative youth seemed a compendium of experiences so strangely numerous. It appeared to him that Felix must know a great deal; he would like to learn what he thought about some of those things as regards which his own conversation had always been formal but his knowledge vague. Felix had a confident, gaily trenchant way of judging human actions which Mr Wentworth grew little by little to envy; it seemed like criticism made easy. Forming an opinion – say on a person's conduct – was with Mr Wentworth a good deal like fumbling in a lock with a key chosen at hazard. He seemed to himself to go about the world with a big bunch of these ineffectual instruments at his girdle. His nephew, on the other hand, with a single turn of the wrist, opened any door as adroitly as a house thief. He felt obliged to keep up the convention that an uncle is always wiser than a nephew, even if he could keep it up no otherwise than by listening in serious silence to Felix's quick, light, constant discourse. But there came a day when he lapsed from consistency and almost asked his nephew's advice.

'Have you ever entertained the idea of settling in the United States?' he asked one morning, while Felix brilliantly plied his brush.

'My dear uncle,' said Felix, 'excuse me if your question makes me smile a little. To begin with, I have never entertained an idea. Ideas often entertain *me;* but I am afraid I have never seriously made a plan. I know what you are going to say; or rather, I know what you think, for I don't think you will say it – that this is very frivolous and loose-minded on my part. So it is; but I am made like that; I take things as they come, and somehow there is always some new thing to follow the last. In the second place, I should never propose to *settle.* I can't settle, my dear uncle; I am not a settler. I know that is what strangers are supposed to do here; they always settle. But I haven't – to answer your question – entertained that idea.'

'You intend to return to Europe and resume your irregular manner of life?' Mr Wentworth inquired.

'I can't say I intend. But it's very likely I shall go back to Europe. After all, I am a European. I feel that, you know. It will depend a good deal upon my sister. She's even more of a European than I, here, you know, she's a picture out of her setting. And as for "resuming", dear uncle, I really have never given up my irregular manner of life. What, for me, could be more irregular than this?'

'Than what?' asked Mr Wentworth, with his pale gravity.

'Well, than everything! Living in the midst of you, this way; this charming, quiet, serious family life; fraternizing with Charlotte and Gertrude; calling upon twenty young ladies, and going out to walk with them; sitting with you in the evening on the piazza and listening to the crickets, and going to bed at ten o'clock.'

'Your description is very animated,' said Mr Wentworth; 'but I see nothing improper in what you describe.'

'Neither do I, dear uncle. It is extremely delightful; I shouldn't like it if it were improper. I assure you I don't like improper things; though I daresay you think I do,' Felix went on, painting away.

'I have never accused you of that.'

'Pray don't,' said Felix; 'because, you see, at bottom I am a terrible Philistine.'

'A Philistine?' repeated Mr Wentworth.

'I mean, as one may say, a plain, God-fearing man.' Mr Wentworth looked at him reservedly, like a mystified sage, and Felix continued, 'I trust I shall enjoy a venerable and venerated old age. I mean to live long. I can hardly call that a plan, perhaps; but it's a keen desire – a rosy vision. I shall be a lively, perhaps even a frivolous, old man!'

'It is natural,' said his uncle sententiously, 'that one should desire to prolong an agreeable life. We have perhaps a selfish indisposition to bring our pleasure to a close. But I presume,' he added, 'that you expect to marry.'

'That too, dear uncle, is a hope, a desire, a vision,' said Felix. It occurred to him for an instant that this was possibly a preface to the offer of the hand of one of Mr Wentworth's admirable daughters. But in the name of decent modesty and a proper sense of the hard realities of this world, Felix banished the thought. His uncle was the incarnation of benevolence, certainly; but from that to accepting – much more postulating – the idea of a union between a young lady with a dowry, presumptively brilliant, and a penniless artist with no prospect of fame, there was a very long way. Felix had lately become conscious of a luxurious preference for the society – if possible, unshared with others – of Gertrude Wentworth; but he had relegated this young lady, for the moment, to the coldly brilliant category of unattainable possessions. She was not the first woman for whom he had entertained an unpractical admiration. He had been in love with duchesses and countesses, and he had made, once or twice, a perilously near approach to cynicism in declaring that the disinterestedness of women had been overrated. On the whole, he had tempered audacity with modesty; and it is but fair to him, now, to say explicitly that he would have been incapable of taking advantage of his present large allowance of familiarity to make love to the younger of his handsome cousins. Felix had grown up among traditions in the light of which such a proceeding looked like a grievous breach of hospitality. I have said that he was always happy, and it may be counted among the present sources of happiness that he had, as regards this matter of his relations with Gertrude, a deliciously good conscience. His own deportment seemed to him suffused with the beauty of virtue – a form of beauty that he admired with the same vivacity with which he admired all other forms.

'I think that if you marry,' said Mr Wentworth presently, 'it will conduce to your happiness.'

'*Sicurissimo!*' Felix exclaimed; and then, arresting his brush, he looked at his uncle with a smile. 'There is something I feel tempted to say to you. May I risk it?'

Mr Wentworth drew himself up a little. 'I am very safe; I don't repeat things.' But he hoped Felix would not risk too much.

Felix was laughing at his answer. 'It's odd to hear you telling me how to be happy. I don't think you know yourself, dear uncle. Now, does that sound brutal?'

The old man was silent a moment, and then, with a dry dignity that suddenly touched his nephew, 'We may sometimes point out a road we are unable to follow.'

'Ah, don't tell me you have had any sorrows,' Felix rejoined. 'I didn't suppose it, and I didn't mean to allude to them. I simply meant that you all don't amuse yourselves.'

'Amuse ourselves? We are not children.'

'Precisely not. You have reached the proper age. I was saying that, the other day, to Gertrude,' Felix added. 'I hope it was not indiscreet.'

'If it was,' said Mr Wentworth, with a keener irony than Felix would have thought him capable of, 'it was but your way of amusing yourself. I am afraid you never had a trouble.'

'Oh yes, I have!' Felix declared, with some spirit; 'before I knew better. But you don't catch me at it again.'

Mr Wentworth maintained for a while a silence more expressive than a deep-drawn sigh. 'You have no children,' he said at last.

'Don't tell me,' Felix exclaimed, 'that your charming young people are a source of grief to you!'

'I don't speak of Charlotte.' And then, after a pause, Mr Wentworth continued, 'I don't speak of Gertrude. But I feel considerable anxiety about Clifford. I will tell you another time.'

The next time he gave Felix a sitting his nephew reminded him that he had taken him into his confidence. 'How is Clifford today?' Felix asked. 'He has always seemed to me a young man of remarkable discretion. Indeed, he is only too discreet; he seems on his guard against me – as if he thought me rather light company. The other day he told his sister – Gertrude repeated it to me – that I was always laughing at him. If I laugh it is simply from the impulse to try and inspire him with confidence. That is the only way I have.'

'Clifford's situation is no laughing matter,' said Mr Wentworth. 'It is very peculiar, as I suppose you have guessed.'

'Ah, you mean his love affair with his cousin?'

Mr Wentworth stared, blushing a little. 'I mean his absence from college. He has been suspended. We have decided not to speak of it unless we are asked.'

'Suspended?' Felix repeated.

'He has been requested by the Harvard authorities to absent himself for six months. Meanwhile he is studying with Mr Brand. We think Mr Brand will help him; at least we hope so.'

'What befell him at college?' Felix asked. 'He was too fond of pleasure? Mr Brand certainly will not teach him any of those secrets!'

'He was too fond of something of which he should not have been fond. I suppose it is considered a pleasure.'

Felix gave a light laugh. 'My dear uncle, is there any doubt about it being a pleasure? *C'est de son âge*, as they say in France.'

'I should have said rather it was a view of later life – of disappointed old age.'

Felix glanced at his uncle, with his lifted eyebrows, and then, 'Of what are you speaking?' he demanded, smiling.

'Of the situation in which Clifford was found.'

'Ah, he was found – he was caught?'

'Necessarily, he was caught. He couldn't walk; he staggered.'

'Oh,' said Felix, 'he drinks! I rather suspected that, from something I observed the first day I came here. I quite agree with you that it is a low taste. It is not a vice for a gentleman. He ought to give it up.'

'We hope for a good deal from Mr Brand's influence,' Mr Wentworth went on. 'He has talked to him from the first. And he never touches anything himself.'

'I will talk to him – I will talk to him!' Felix declared gaily.

'What will you say to him?' asked his uncle, with some apprehension.

Felix for some moments answered nothing. 'Do you mean to marry him to his cousin?' he asked at last.

'Marry him?' echoed Mr Wentworth. 'I shouldn't think his cousin would want to marry him.'

'You have no understanding, then, with Mrs Acton?'

Mr Wentworth stared, almost blankly. 'I have never discussed such subjects with her.'

'I should think it might be time,' said Felix. 'Lizzie Acton is admirably pretty, and if Clifford is dangerous—'

'They are not engaged,' said Mr Wentworth. 'I have no reason to suppose they are engaged.'

'*Par exemple!*' cried Felix. 'A clandestine engagement? Trust me, Clifford, as I say, is a charming boy. He is incapable of that. Lizzie Acton, then, would not be jealous of another woman.'

'I certainly hope not,' said the old man, with a vague sense of jealousy being an even lower vice than a love of liquor.

'The best thing for Clifford, therefore,' Felix propounded, 'is to become interested in some clever, charming woman.' And he paused in his painting, and, with his elbows on his knees, looked with bright communicativeness at his uncle. 'You see, I believe greatly in the influence of women. Living with women helps to make a man a gentleman. It is very true, Clifford has his sisters, who are so charming. But there should be a different sentiment in play from the fraternal, you know. He has Lizzie Acton; but she, perhaps, is rather immature.'

'I suspect Lizzie has talked to him, reasoned with him,' said Mr Wentworth.

'On the impropriety of getting tipsy – on the beauty of temperance? That is dreary work for a pretty young girl. No,' Felix continued; 'Clifford ought to frequent some agreeable woman, who, without ever mentioning such unsavoury subjects, would give him a sense of its being very ridiculous to be fuddled. If he could fall in love with her a little, so much the better. The thing would operate as a cure.'

'Well, now, what lady should you suggest?' asked Mr Wentworth.

'There is a clever woman under your hand. My sister.'

'Your sister – under my hand?' Mr Wentworth repeated.

'Say a word to Clifford. Tell him to be bold. He is well disposed already; he has invited her two or three times to drive. But I don't think he comes to see her. Give him a hint to come – to come often. He will sit there of an afternoon, and they will talk. It will do him good.'

Mr Wentworth meditated. 'You think she will exercise a helpful influence?'

'She will exercise a civilizing – I may call it a sobering – influence. A charming, witty woman always does – especially if she is a little of a coquette. My dear uncle, the society of such women has been half my education. If Clifford is suspended, as you say, from college, let Eugenia be his preceptress.'

Mr Wentworth continued thoughtful. 'You think Eugenia is a coquette?' he asked.

'What pretty woman is not?' Felix demanded in turn. But this, for Mr Wentworth, could at the best have been no answer, for he did not think his niece pretty. 'With Clifford,' the young man pursued, 'Eugenia will simply be enough of a coquette to be a little ironical. That's what he needs. So you recommend him to be nice with her, you know. The suggestion will come best from you.'

'Do I understand,' asked the old man, 'that I am to suggest to my son to make a – a profession of – of affection to Madame Münster?'

'Yes, yes – a profession!' cried Felix sympathetically.

'But, as I understand it, Madame Münster is a married woman.'

'Ah,' said Felix, smiling, 'of course she can't marry him. But she will do what she can.'

Mr Wentworth sat for some time with his eyes on the floor; at last he got up. 'I don't think,' he said, 'that I can undertake to recommend to my son any such course.' And without meeting Felix's surprised glance he broke off his sitting, which was not resumed for a fortnight.

Felix was very fond of the little lake which occupied so many of Mr Wentworth's numerous acres, and of a remarkable grove of pines which lay upon the farther side of it, planted upon a steep embankment and haunted by the summer breeze. The murmur of the air in the far-off tree-tops had a strange distinctness; it was almost articulate. One afternoon the young man came out of his painting-room and passed the open door of Eugenia's little salon. Within, in the cool dimness, he saw his sister, dressed in white, buried in her arm-chair and holding to her face an immense bouquet. Opposite to her sat Clifford Wentworth, twirling his hat. He had evidently just presented the bouquet to the Baroness, whose fine eyes, as she glanced at him over the big roses and geraniums, wore a conversational smile. Felix, standing on the threshold of the cottage, hesitated for a moment as to whether he should retrace his steps and enter the parlour. Then he went his way and passed into Mr Wentworth's garden. That civilizing process to which he had suggested that Clifford should be subjected appeared to have come on of itself. Felix was very sure, at least, that Mr Wentworth had not adopted his ingenious device for stimulating the young man's aesthetic consciousness. 'Doubtless he supposes,' he said to himself, after the conversation that has been narrated, 'that I desire, out of fraternal benevolence, to procure for Eugenia the amusement of a flirtation – or, as he probably calls it, an intrigue – with the too susceptible Clifford. It must be admitted – and I have noticed it before – that nothing exceeds the licence occasionally taken by the imagination of very rigid people.' Felix, on his own side, had of course said nothing to Clifford; but he had observed to Eugenia that Mr Wentworth was much mortified at his son's low tastes. 'We ought to do something to help them, after all their kindness to us,' he had added. 'Encourage Clifford to come to see you, and inspire him with a taste for conversation. That will supplant the other, which only comes from his puerility, from his not taking his position in the world – that of a rich young man of ancient stock – seriously enough. Make him a little more serious. Even if he makes love to you it is no great matter.'

'I am to offer myself as a superior form of intoxication – a substitute for a brandy bottle, eh?' asked the Baroness. 'Truly, in this country one comes to strange uses.'

But she had not positively declined to undertake Clifford's higher education, and Felix, who had not thought of the matter again, being haunted with visions of more personal profit, now reflected that the work of redemption had fairly begun. The idea, in prospect, had seemed of the happiest, but in operation it made him a trifle uneasy. 'What if Eugenia – what if Eugenia – ?' he asked himself softly, the question dying away in his sense of Eugenia's undetermined capacity. But before Felix had time to accept or to reject its admonition, even in this vague form, he saw Robert Acton turn out of Mr Wentworth's enclosure by a distant gate and come toward the cottage in the orchard. Acton had evidently walked from his own house along a shady byway, and he was intending to pay a visit to Madame Münster. Felix watched him for a moment; then he turned away. Acton could be left to play the part of Providence and interrupt – if interruption were needed – Clifford's entanglement with Eugenia.

Felix passed through the garden toward the house and toward a postern gate which opened upon a path leading across the fields, beside a little wood, to the lake. He stopped and looked up at the house; his eyes rested more particularly upon a certain open window, on the shady side. Presently Gertrude appeared there, looking out into the summer light. He took off his hat to her and bade her good-day; he remarked that he was going to row across the pond, and begged that she would do him the honour to accompany him. She looked at him a moment; then, without saying anything, she turned away. But she soon reappeared, below, in one of those quaint and charming Leghorn hats, tied with white satin bows, that were worn at that period; she also carried a green parasol. She went with him to the edge of the lake, where a couple of boats were always moored; they got into one of them, and Felix with gentle strokes propelled it to the opposite shore. The day was the perfection of summer weather; the little lake was the colour of sunshine; the plash of the oars was the only sound, and they found themselves listening to it. They disembarked, and by a winding path ascended the pine-crested mound which overlooked the water, whose white expanse glittered between the trees. The place was delightfully cool, and had the added charm that – in the softly-sounding pine-boughs – you seemed to hear the coolness as well as feel it. Felix and Gertrude sat down on the rust-coloured carpet of pine needles and talked of many things. Felix spoke at last, in the course of talk, of his going away; it was the first time he had alluded to it.

'You are going away?' said Gertrude, looking at him.

'Some day – when the leaves begin to fall. You know I can't stay for ever.'

Gertrude transferred her eyes to the outer prospect, and then, after a pause, she said, 'I shall never see you again.'

'Why not?' asked Felix. 'We shall probably both survive my departure.'

But Gertrude only repeated, 'I shall never see you again. I shall never hear of you,' she went on. 'I shall know nothing about you. I knew nothing about you before, and it will be the same again.'

'I knew nothing about you then, unfortunately,' said Felix. 'But now I shall write to you.'

'Don't write to me. I shall not answer you,' Gertrude declared.

'I should of course burn your letters,' said Felix.

Gertrude looked at him again. 'Burn my letters? You sometimes say strange things.'

'They are not strange in themselves,' the young man answered. 'They are only strange as said to you. You will come to Europe.'

'With whom shall I come?' She asked this question simply; she was very much in earnest. Felix was interested in her earnestness; for some moments he hesitated. 'You can't tell me that,' she pursued. 'You can't say that I shall go with my father and my sister; you don't believe that.'

'I shall keep your letters,' said Felix presently, for all answer.

'I never write. I don't know how to write.' Gertrude, for some time, said nothing more; and her companion, as he looked at her, wished it had not been 'disloyal' to make love to the daughter of an old gentleman who had offered one hospitality. The afternoon waned; the shadows stretched themselves; and the light grew deeper in the western sky. Two persons appeared on the opposite side of the lake, coming from the house and crossing the meadow. 'It is Charlotte and Mr Brand,' said Gertrude. 'They are coming over here.' But Charlotte and Mr Brand only came down to the edge of the water and stood there, looking across; they made no motion to enter the boat that Felix had left at the mooring-place. Felix waved his hat to them; it was too far to call. They made no visible response, and they presently turned away and walked along the shore.

'Mr Brand is not demonstrative,' said Felix. 'He is never demonstrative to me. He sits silent, with his chin in his hand, looking at me. Sometimes he looks away. Your father tells me he is so eloquent; and I should like to hear him talk. He looks like such a noble young man. But with me he will never talk. And yet I am so fond of listening to brilliant imagery!'

'He is very eloquent,' said Gertrude; 'but he has no brilliant imagery. I have heard him talk a great deal. I knew that when they saw us they would not come over here.'

'Ah, he is making *la cour*, as they say, to your sister? They desire to be along?'

'No,' said Gertrude gravely, 'they have no such reason as that for being alone.'

'But why doesn't he make *la cour* to Charlotte?' Felix inquired. 'She is so pretty, so gentle, so good.'

Gertrude glanced at him, and then she looked at the distantly-seen couple they were discussing. Mr Brand and Charlotte were walking side by side. They might have been a pair of lovers, and yet they might not. 'They think I should not be here,' said Gertrude.

'With me? I thought you didn't have those ideas.'

'You don't understand. There are a great many things you don't understand.'

'I understand my stupidity. But why, then, do not Charlotte and Mr Brand, who, as an elder sister and a clergyman, are free to walk about together, come over and make me wiser by breaking up the unlawful interview into which I have lured you?'

'That is the last thing they would do,' said Gertrude.

Felix stared at her a moment, with his lifted eyebrows. '*Je n'y comprends rien!*' he exclaimed; then his eyes followed for a while the retreating figures of this critical pair. 'You may say what you please,' he declared; 'it is evident to me that your sister is not indifferent to her clever companion. It is agreeable to her to be walking there with him. I can see that from here.' And in the excitement of observation Felix rose to his feet.

Gertrude rose also, but she made no attempt to emulate her companion's discovery; she looked rather in another direction. Felix's words had struck her; but a certain delicacy checked her. 'She is certainly not indifferent to Mr Brand; she has the highest opinion of him.'

'One can see it – one can see it,' said Felix in a tone of amused contemplation, with his head on one side. Gertrude turned her back to the opposite shore; it was disagreeable to her to look, but she hoped Felix would say something more. 'Ah, they have wandered away into the wood,' he added.

Gertrude turned round again. 'She is *not* in love with him,' she said; it seemed her duty to say that.

'Then he is in love with her; or if he is not, he ought to be. She is such a perfect little woman of her kind. She reminds me of a pair of old-fashioned silver sugar-tongs; you know I am very fond of sugar. And she is very nice with Mr Brand; I have noticed that; very gentle and gracious.'

Gertrude reflected a moment. Then she took a great resolution. 'She wants him to marry me,' she said. 'So of course she is nice.'

Felix's eyebrows rose higher than ever. 'To marry you! Ah, ah, this is interesting. And you think one must be very nice with a man to induce him to do that?'

Gertrude had turned a little pale, but she went on, 'Mr Brand wants it himself.'

Felix folded his arms and stood looking at her. 'I see – I see,' he said quickly. 'Why did you never tell me this before?'

'It is disagreeable to me to speak of it even now. I wished simply to explain to you about Charlotte.'

'You don't wish to marry Mr Brand, then?'

'No,' said Gertrude gravely.

'And does your father wish it?'

'Very much.'

'And you don't like him – you have refused him?'

'I don't wish to marry him.'

'Your father and sister think you ought to, eh?'

'It is a long story,' said Gertrude. 'They think there are good reasons. I can't explain it. They think I have obligations, and that I have encouraged him.'

Felix smiled at her, as if she had been telling him an amusing story about some one else. 'I can't tell you how this interests me,' he said. 'Now you don't recognize these reasons – these obligations?'

'I am not sure; it is not easy.' And she picked up her parasol and turned away, as if to descend the slope.

'Tell me this,' Felix went on, going with her: 'are you likely to give in – to let them persuade you?'

Gertrude looked at him with the serious face that she had constantly worn in opposition to his almost eager smile.

'I shall never marry Mr Brand,' she said.

'I see!' Felix rejoined. And they slowly descended the hill together, saying nothing till they reached the margin of the pond. 'It is your own affair,' he then resumed; 'but do you know, I am not altogether glad? If it were settled that you were to marry Mr Brand I should take a certain comfort in the arrangement, I should feel more free. I have no right to make love to you myself, eh?' And he paused, lightly pressing his argument upon her.

'None whatever,' replied Gertrude quickly – too quickly.

'Your father would never hear of it; I haven't a penny. Mr Brand, of course, has property of his own, eh?'

'I believe he has some property; but that has nothing to do with it.'

'With you, of course not; but with your father and sister it must have. So, as I say, if this were settled, I should feel more at liberty.'

'More at liberty?' Gertrude repeated. 'Please unfasten the boat.'

Felix untwisted the rope and stood holding it. 'I should be able to say things to you that I can't give myself the pleasure of saying now,' he went on. 'I could tell you how much I admire you, without seeming to pretend to that which I have no right to pretend to. I should make violent love to you,' he added, laughing, 'if I thought you were so placed as not to be offended by it.'

'You mean if I were engaged to another man? That is strange reasoning!' Gertrude exclaimed.

'In that case you would not take me seriously.'

'I take every one seriously!' said Gertrude. And without his help she stepped lightly into the boat.

Felix took up the oars and sent it forward. 'Ah, this is what you have been thinking about? It seemed to me you had something on your mind. I wish very much,' he added, 'that you would tell me some of these so-called reasons – these obligations.'

'They are not real reasons – good reasons,' said Gertrude, looking at the pink and yellow gleams in the water.

'I can't understand that! Because a handsome girl has had a spark of coquetry, that is no reason.'

'If you mean me, it's not that. I have not done that.'

'It is something that troubles you, at any rate,' said Felix.

'Not so much as it used to,' Gertrude rejoined.

He looked at her, smiling always. 'That is not saying much, eh?' But she only rested her eyes, very gravely, on the lighted water. She seemed to him to be trying to hide the signs of the trouble of which she had just told him. Felix felt, at all times, much the same impulse to dissipate visible melancholy that a good housewife feels to brush away dust. There was something he wished to brush away now; suddenly he stopped rowing and poised his oars. 'Why should Mr Brand have addressed himself to you, and not to your sister?' he asked. 'I am sure she would listen to him.'

Gertrude, in her family, was thought capable of a good deal of levity; but her levity had never gone so far as this. It moved her greatly, however, to hear Felix say that he was sure of something; so that, raising her eyes toward him, she tried intently, for some moments, to conjure up this wonderful image of a love affair between her own sister and her own suitor. We know that Gertrude had an imaginative mind; so that it is not impossible that this effort should have been partially successful. But she only murmured, 'Ah, Felix! ah, Felix!'

'Why shouldn't they marry? Try and make them marry!' cried Felix.

'Try and make them?'

'Turn the tables on them. Then they will leave you alone. I will help you as far as I can.'

Gertrude's heart began to beat; she was greatly excited: she had never had anything so interesting proposed to her before. Felix had begun to row again, and now he sent the boat home with long strokes. 'I believe she *does* care for him!' said Gertrude, after they had disembarked.

'Of course she does, and we will marry them off. It will make them happy: it will make every one happy. We shall have a wedding, and I will write an epithalamium.'

'It seems as if it would make *me* happy,' said Gertrude.

'To get rid of Mr Brand, eh? To recover your liberty?'

Gertrude walked on. 'To see my sister married to so good a man.'

Felix gave his light laugh. 'You always put things on those grounds; you will never say anything for yourself. You are all so afraid, here, of being selfish. I don't think you know how,' he went on. 'Let me show you! It will make me happy for myself, and for just the reverse of what I told you a while ago. After that, when I make love to you, you will have to think I mean it.'

'I shall never think you mean anything,' said Gertrude. 'You are too fantastic.'

'Ah,' cried Felix, 'that's a license to say anything! Gertrude, I adore you!'

Chapter Eight

Charlotte and Mr Brand had not returned when they reached the house; but the Baroness had come to tea, and Robert Acton also, who now regularly asked for a place at this generous repast, or made his appearance later in the evening. Clifford Wentworth, with his juvenile growl, remarked upon it.

'You are always coming to tea nowadays, Robert,' he said. 'I should think you had drunk enough tea in China.'

'Since when is Mr Acton more frequent?' asked the Baroness.

'Since you came,' said Clifford. 'It seems as if you were a kind of attraction.'

'I suppose I am a curiosity,' said the Baroness. 'Give me time and I will make you a salon.'

'It would fall to pieces after you go!' exclaimed Acton.

'Don't talk about her going in that familiar way,' Clifford said. 'It makes me feel gloomy.'

Mr Wentworth glanced at his son, and, taking note of these words, wondered if Felix had been teaching him, according to the programme he had sketched out, to make love to the wife of a German prince.

Charlotte came in late with Mr Brand; but Gertrude, to whom, at least, Felix had taught something, looked in vain, in her face, for the traces of a guilty passion. Mr Brand sat down by Gertrude, and she presently asked him why they had not crossed the pond to join Felix and herself.

'It is cruel of you to ask me that,' he answered, very softly. He had a large morsel of cake before him but he fingered it without eating it. 'I sometimes think you are growing cruel,' he added.

Gertrude said nothing; she was afraid to speak. There was a kind of rage in her heart; she felt as if she could easily persuade herself that she was persecuted. She said to herself that it was quite right that she should not allow him to make her believe she was wrong. She thought of what Felix had said to her; she wished, indeed, Mr Brand would marry Charlotte. She looked away from him and spoke no more. Mr Brand ended by eating his cake, while Felix sat opposite, describing to Mr Wentworth the students' duels at Heidelberg. After tea they all dispersed themselves, as usual, upon the piazza and in the garden; and Mr Brand drew near to Gertrude again.

'I didn't come to you this afternoon because you were not alone,' he began; 'because you were with a newer friend.'

'Felix? He is an old friend by this time.'

Mr Brand looked at the ground for some moments. 'I thought I was prepared to hear you speak in that way,' he resumed. 'But I find it very painful.'

'I don't see what else I can say,' said Gertrude.

Mr Brand walked beside her for a while in silence; Gertrude wished he would go away. 'He is certainly very accomplished. But I think I ought to advise you.'

'To advise me?'

'I think I know your nature.'

'I think you don't,' said Gertrude, with a soft laugh.

'You make yourself out worse than you are – to please him,' Mr Brand said sadly.

'Worse – to please him? What do you mean?' asked Gertrude, stopping.

Mr Brand stopped also, and with the same soft straight-forwardness, 'He doesn't care for the things you care for – the great questions of life.'

Gertrude, with her eyes on his, shook her head. 'I don't care for the great questions of life. They are much beyond me.'

'There was a time when you didn't say that,' said Mr Brand.

'Oh,' rejoined Gertrude, 'I think you made me talk a great deal of nonsense. And it depends,' she added, 'upon what you call the great questions of life. There are some things I care for.'

'Are they the things you talk about with your cousin?'

'You should not say things to me against my cousin, Mr Brand,' said Gertrude. 'That is dishonourable.'

He listened to this respectfully; then he answered, with a little vibration of the voice, 'I should be very sorry to do anything dishonourable. But I don't see why it is dishonourable to say that your cousin is frivolous.'

'Go and say it to himself!'

'I think he would admit it,' said Mr Brand. 'That is the tone he would take. He would not be ashamed of it.'

'Then I am not ashamed of it!' Gertrude declared. 'That is probably what I like him for. I am frivolous myself.'

'You are trying, as I said just now, to lower yourself.'

'I am trying for once to be natural!' cried Gertrude passionately. 'I have been pretending, all my life; I have been dishonest; it is you that have made me so!' Mr Brand stood gazing at her, and she went on, 'Why shouldn't I be frivolous, if I want? One has a right to be frivolous, if it's one's nature. No, I don't care for the great questions. I care for pleasure – for amusement. Perhaps I am fond of wicked things; it is very possible!'

Mr Brand remained staring; he was even a little pale, as if he had been frightened. 'I don't think you know what you are saying!' he exclaimed.

'Perhaps not. Perhaps I am talking nonsense. But it is only with you that I talk nonsense. I never do so with my cousin.'

'I will speak to you again, when you are less excited,' said Mr Brand.

'I am always excited when you speak to me. I must tell you that – even if it prevents you altogether, in future. Your speaking to me irritates me. With my cousin it is very different. That seems quiet and natural.'

He looked at her, and then he looked away, with a kind of helpless distress, at the dusky garden and the faint summer stars. After which, suddenly turning back, 'Gertrude, Gertrude!' he softly groaned. 'Am I really losing you?'

She was touched – she was pained; but it had already occurred to her that she might do something better than say so. It would not have alleviated her companion's distress to perceive, just then, whence she had sympathetically borrowed this ingenuity. 'I am not sorry for you,' Gertrude said, 'for in paying so much attention to me you are following a shadow – you are wasting something precious. There is something else you might have that you don't look at – something better than I am. That is a reality!' And then, with intention, she looked at him and tried to smile a little. He thought this smile of hers very strange; but she turned away and left him.

She wandered about alone in the garden wondering what Mr Brand would make of her words, which it had been a singular pleasure for her to utter. Shortly after, passing in front of the house, she saw, at a distance, two persons standing near the garden gate. It was Mr Brand going away and bidding good night to Charlotte, who had walked down with him from the house. Gertrude saw that the parting was prolonged; then she turned her back upon it. She had not gone very far, however, when she heard her sister slowly following her. She neither turned around nor waited for her; she knew what Charlotte was going to say. Charlotte, who at last overtook her, in fact presently began; she had passed her arm into Gertrude's.

'Will you listen to me, dear, if I say something very particular?'

'I know what you are going to say,' said Gertrude. 'Mr Brand feels very badly.'

'Oh, Gertrude, how can you treat him so?' Charlotte demanded. And as her sister made no answer she added, 'After all he has done for you!'

'What has he done for me?'

'I wonder you can ask, Gertrude. He has helped you so. You told me so yourself, a great many times. You told me that he helped you to struggle with your – your peculiarities. You told me that he had taught you how to govern your temper.'

For a moment Gertrude said nothing. Then, 'Was my temper very bad?' she asked.

'I am not accusing you, Gertrude,' said Charlotte.

'What are you doing, then?' her sister demanded, with a little laugh.

'I am pleading for Mr Brand – reminding you of all you owe him.'

'I have given it all back,' said Gertrude, still with her little laugh. 'He can take back the virtue he imparted! I want to be wicked again.'

Her sister made her stop in the path, and fixed upon her in the darkness a sweet reproachful gaze. 'If you talk this way I shall almost believe it. Think of all we owe Mr Brand. Think of how he has always expected something of you. Think how much he has been to us. Think of his beautiful influence upon Clifford.'

'He is very good,' said Gertrude, looking at her sister. 'I know he is very good. But he shouldn't speak against Felix.'

'Felix is good,' Charlotte answered, softly but promptly. 'Felix is very wonderful. Only he is so different. Mr Brand is much nearer to us. I should never think of going to Felix with a trouble – with a question. Mr Brand is much more to us, Gertrude.'

'He is very – very good,' Gertrude repeated. 'He is more to you; yes, much more. Charlotte,' she added suddenly, 'you are in love with him!'

'Oh, Gertrude!' cried poor Charlotte; and her sister saw her blushing in the darkness.

Gertrude put her arm round her. 'I wish he would marry you!' she went on.

Charlotte shook herself free. 'You must not say such things!' she exclaimed, beneath her breath.

'You like him more than you say, and he likes you more than he knows.'

'This is very cruel of you!' Charlotte Wentworth murmured.

But if it was cruel Gertrude continued pitiless. 'Not if it's true,' she answered; 'I wish he would marry you.'

'Please don't say that.'

'I mean to tell him so!' said Gertrude.

'Oh, Gertrude, Gertrude!' her sister almost moaned.

'Yes, if he speaks to me again about myself, I will say, "Why don't you marry Charlotte? She's a thousand times better than I." '

'You *are* wicked; you *are* changed!' cried her sister.

'If you don't like it you can prevent it,' said Gertrude. 'You can prevent it by keeping him from speaking to me!' And with this she walked away, very conscious of what she had done; measuring it and finding a certain joy and a quickened sense of freedom in it.

Mr Wentworth was rather wide of the mark in suspecting that Clifford had begun to pay unscrupulous compliments to his brilliant cousin; for the young man had really more scruples than he received credit for in his family. He had a certain transparent shamefacedness which was in itself a proof that he was not at his ease in dissipation. His collegiate peccadilloes had aroused a domestic murmur as disagreeable to the young man as the creaking of his boots would have been to a house-breaker. Only, as the house-breaker would have simplified matters by removing his *chaussures*, it had seemed to Clifford that the shortest cut to comfortable relations with people – relations which should make him cease to think that when they spoke to him they meant something improving – was to renounce all ambition toward a nefarious development. And, in fact, Clifford's ambition took the most commendable form. He thought of himself in the future as the well-known and much-liked Mr Wentworth, of Boston, who should, in the natural course of prosperity, have married his pretty cousin, Lizzie Acton; should live in a wide-fronted house, in view of the Common; and should drive, behind a light wagon, over the damp autumn roads, a pair of beautifully-matched sorrel horses. Clifford's vision of the coming years was very simple; its most definite features were this element of familiar matrimony and the duplication of his resources for trotting. He had not yet asked his cousin to marry him;

but he meant to do so as soon as he should have taken his degree. Lizzie was serenely conscious of his intention, and she had made up her mind that he would improve. Her brother, who was very fond of this light, quick, competent little Lizzie, saw, on his side, no reason to interpose. It seemed to him a graceful social law that Clifford and his sister should become engaged: he himself was not engaged, but every one else, fortunately, was not such a fool as he. He was fond of Clifford, as well, and had his own way – of which it must be confessed he was a little ashamed – of looking at those aberrations which had led to the young man's compulsory retirement from the neighbouring seat of learning. Acton had seen the world, as he said to himself; he had been to China and had knocked about among men. He had learned the essential difference between a nice young fellow and a mean young fellow, and he was satisfied that there was no harm in Clifford. He believed – although it must be added that he had not quite the courage to declare it – in the doctrine of wild oats, which he thought a useful preventive of superfluous fears. If Mr Wentworth and Charlotte and Mr Brand would only apply it in Clifford's case, they would be happier; and Acton thought it a pity they should not be happier. They took the boy's misdemeanours too much to heart; they talked to him too solemnly; they frightened and bewildered him. Of course there was the great standard of morality, which forbade that a man should get tipsy, play billiards for money, or cultivate his sensual consciousness; but what fear was there that poor Clifford was going to run a tilt at any great standard? It had, however, never occurred to Acton to dedicate the Baroness Münster to the redemption of a refractory collegian. The instrument, here, would have seemed to him quite too complex for the operation. Felix, on the other hand, had spoken in obedience to the belief that the more charming a woman is, the more numerous, literally, are her definite social uses.

Eugenia herself, as we know, had plenty of leisure to enumerate her uses. As I have had the honour of intimating, she had come four thousand miles to seek her fortune; and it is not to be supposed that after this great effort she could neglect any apparent aid to advancement. It is my misfortune that in attempting to describe in a short compass the deportment of this remarkable woman I am obliged to express things rather brutally. I feel this to be the case, for instance, when I say that she had primarily detected such an aid to advancement in the person of Robert Acton, but that she had afterward remembered that a prudent archer has always a second bowstring. Eugenia was a woman of finely-mingled motive, and her intentions were never sensibly gross. She had a sort of aesthetic ideal for Clifford which seemed to her a disinterested reason for taking him in hand. It was very well for a fresh-coloured young gentleman to be ingenuous; but Clifford, really, was crude. With such a pretty face he ought to have prettier manners. She would teach him that, with a beautiful name, the expectation of a large property, and, as they said in Europe, a social position, an only son should know how to carry himself.

Once Clifford had begun to come and see her by himself and for himself, he came very often. He hardly knew why he should come; he saw her almost every evening at his father's house; he had nothing particular to say to her. She was not a young girl, and fellows of his age called only upon young girls. He exaggerated her age; she seemed to him an old woman; it was happy that the Baroness, with all her intelligence, was incapable of guessing this. But gradually it struck Clifford that visiting old women might be, if not natural, at least, as they say of some articles of diet, an acquired taste. The Baroness was certainly a very amusing old woman; she talked to him as no lady – and indeed no gentleman – had ever talked to him before.

'You should go to Europe and make the tour,' she said to him one afternoon. 'Of course, on leaving college, you will go.'

'I don't want to go,' Clifford declared. 'I know some fellows who have been to Europe. They say you can have better fun here.'

'That depends. It depends upon your idea of fun. Your friends probably were not introduced.'

'Introduced?' Clifford demanded.

'They have no opportunity of going into society; they formed no *relations*.' This was one of a certain number of words that the Baroness often pronounced in the French manner.

'They went to a ball, in Paris; I know that,' said Clifford.

'Ah, there are balls and balls; especially in Paris. No, you must go, you know; it is not a thing from which you can dispense yourself. You need it.'

'Oh, I'm very well,' said Clifford. 'I'm not sick.'

'I don't mean for your health, my poor child. I mean for your manners.'

'I haven't got any manners!' growled Clifford.

'Precisely. You don't mind my assenting to that, eh?' asked the Baroness with a smile. 'You must go to Europe and get a few. You can get them better there. It is a pity you might not have come while I was living in – in Germany. I would have introduced you; I had a charming little circle. You would perhaps have been rather young; but the younger one begins, I think, the better. Now, at any rate, you have no time to lose, and when I return you must immediately come to me.'

All this, to Clifford's apprehension, was a great mixture – his beginning young, Eugenia's return to Europe, his being introduced to her charming little circle. What was he to begin, and what was her little circle? His ideas about her marriage had a good deal of vagueness; but they were in so far definite as that he felt it to be a matter not to be freely mentioned. He sat and looked all round the room: he supposed she was alluding in some way to her marriage.

'Oh, I don't want to go to Germany,' he said; it seemed to him the most convenient thing to say.

She looked at him a while, smiling with her lips, but not with her eyes. 'You have scruples?' she asked.

'Scruples?' said Clifford.

'You young people, here, are very singular; one doesn't know where to expect you. When you are not extremely improper you are so terribly proper. I daresay you think that, owing to my irregular marriage, I live with loose people. You were never more mistaken. I have been all the more particular.'

'Oh no,' said Clifford, honestly distressed. 'I never thought such a thing as that.'

'Are you very sure? I am convinced that your father does, and your sisters. They say to each other that, here, I am on my good behaviour, but that over there – married by the left hand – I associate with light women.'

'Oh no,' cried Clifford energetically, 'they don't say such things as that to each other!'

'If they think them they had better say them,' the Baroness rejoined. 'Then they can be contradicted. Please contradict that whenever you hear it, and don't be afraid of coming to see me on account of the company I keep. I have the honour of knowing more distinguished men, my poor child, than you are likely to see in a lifetime. I see very few women; but those are women of rank. So, my dear young Puritan, you needn't be afraid. I am not in the least one of those who think that the society of women who have lost their place in the *vrai monde* is necessary to form a young man. I have never taken that tone. I have kept my place myself, and I think we are a much better school than the others. Trust me, Clifford, and I will prove that to you,' the Baroness continued, while she made the agreeable reflexion that she could not, at least, be accused of perverting her young kinsman. 'So if you ever fall among thieves don't go about saying I sent you to them.'

Clifford thought it so comical that he should know – in spite of her figurative language – what she meant, and that she should mean what he knew, that he could hardly help laughing a little, although he tried hard. 'Oh no! oh no!' he murmured.

'Laugh out, laugh out, if I amuse you!' cried the Baroness. 'I am here for that!' And Clifford thought her a very amusing person indeed. 'But remember,' she said on this occasion, 'that you are coming – next year – to pay me a visit over there.'

About a week afterward she said to him, point-blank, 'Are you seriously making love to your little cousin?'

'Seriously making love' – these words, on Madame Münster's lips, had to Clifford's sense a portentous and embarrassing sound; he hesitated about assenting, lest he should commit himself to more than he understood. 'Well, I shouldn't say it if I was!' he exclaimed.

'Why wouldn't you say it?' the Baroness demanded. 'Those things ought to be known.'

'I don't care whether it is known or not,' Clifford rejoined. 'But I don't want people looking at me.'

'A young man of your importance ought to learn to bear observation – to carry himself as if he were quite indifferent to it. I won't say, exactly, unconscious,' the Baroness explained. 'No, he must seem to know he is observed, and to think it natural he should be; but he must appear perfectly used to it. Now you haven't that, Clifford; you haven't that at all. You must have that, you know. Don't tell me you are not a young man of importance,' Eugenia added. 'Don't say anything so flat as that.'

'Oh no, you don't catch me saying that!' cried Clifford.

'Yes, you must come to Germany,' Madame Münster continued. 'I will show you how people can be talked about and yet not seem to know it. You will be talked about, of course, with me; it will be said you are my lover. I will show you how little one may mind that – how little I shall mind it.'

Clifford sat staring, blushing, and laughing. 'I shall mind it a good deal!' he declared.

'Ah, not too much, you know; that would be uncivil. But I give you leave to mind it a little; especially if you have a passion for Miss Acton. *Voyons*; as regards that, you either have, or you have not. It is very simple to say it.

'You ought to want me to know. If one is arranging a marriage, one tells one's friends.'

'Oh, I'm not arranging anything,' said Clifford.

'You don't intend to marry your cousin?'

'Well, I expect I shall do as I choose!'

The Baroness leaned her head upon the back of her chair and closed her eyes, as if they were tired. Then opening them again, 'Your cousin is very charming,' she said.

'She is the prettiest girl in this place,' Clifford rejoined.

' "In this place" is saying little; she would be charming anywhere. I'm afraid you are entangled.'

'Oh no, I'm not entangled.'

'Are you engaged? At your age that is the same thing.'

Clifford looked at the Baroness with some audacity. 'Will you tell no one?'

'If it's as sacred as that – no.'

'Well, then – we are not!' said Clifford.

'That's the great secret – that you are not, eh?' asked the Baroness, with a quick laugh. 'I am very glad to hear it. You are altogether too young. A young man in your position must choose and compare; he must see the world first. Depend upon it,' she added, 'you should not settle that matter before you have come abroad and paid me that visit. There are several things I should like to call your attention to first.'

'Well, I am rather afraid of that visit,' said Clifford. 'It seems to me it will be rather like going to school again.'

The Baroness looked at him a moment. 'My dear child,' she said, 'there is no agreeable man who has not, at some moment, been to school to a clever woman – probably a little older than himself. And you must be thankful when you get your instruction gratis. With me you would get it gratis.'

The next day Clifford told Lizzie Acton that the Baroness thought her the most charming girl she had ever seen.

Lizzie shook her head. 'No, she doesn't!' she said.

'Do you think everything she says,' asked Clifford, 'is to be taken the opposite way?'

'I think that is!' said Lizzie.

Clifford was going to remark that in this case the Baroness must desire greatly to bring about a marriage between Mr Clifford Wentworth and Miss Elizabeth Acton; but he resolved, on the whole, to suppress this observation.

Chapter Nine

It seemed to Robert Acton, after Eugenia had come to his house, that something had passed between them which made them a good deal more intimate. It was hard to say exactly what, except her telling him that she had taken her resolution with regard to the Prince Adolf; for Madame Münster's visit had made no difference in their relations. He came to see her very often; but he had come to see her very often before. It was agreeable to him to find himself in her little drawing-room; but this was not a new discovery. There was a change, however, in this sense; that if the Baroness had been a great deal in Acton's thoughts before, she was now never out of them. From the first she had been personally fascinating; but the fascination now had become intellectual as well. He was constantly pondering her words and emotions; they were as interesting as the factors in an algebraic problem. This is saying a good deal; for Acton was extremely fond of mathematics. He asked himself whether it could be that he was in love with her, and then hoped he was not; hoped it not so much for his own sake as for that of the amatory passion itself. If this was love, love had been overrated. Love was a poetic impulse, and his own state of feeling with regard to the Baroness was largely characterized by that eminently prosaic sentiment – curiosity. It was true, as Acton with his gently cogitative habit observed to himself, that curiosity, pushed to a given point, might become a romantic passion; and he certainly thought enough about this charming woman to make him restless and even a little melancholy. It puzzled and vexed him at times to feel that he was not more ardent. He was not in the least bent upon remaining a bachelor. In his younger years he had been – or he had tried to be – of the opinion that it would be a good deal 'jollier' not to marry, and he had flattered himself that his single condition was something of a citadel. It was a citadel, at all events, of which he had long since levelled the outworks. He had removed the guns from the ramparts; he had lowered the drawbridge across the moat. The drawbridge had swayed a little under Madame Münster's step; why should he not cause it to be raised again, so that she might be kept a prisoner? He had an idea that she would become – in time at least, and on learning the conveniences of the place for making a lady comfortable – a tolerably patient captive. But the drawbridge was never raised, and Acton's brilliant visitor was as free to depart as she had been to come. It was part of his curiosity to know why the deuce so susceptible a man was *not* in love with so charming a woman. If her various graces were, as I have said, the factors in an algebraic problem, the answer to this question was the indispensable unknown quantity. The pursuit of the unknown quantity was extremely absorbing; for the present it taxed all Acton's faculties.

Toward the middle of August he was obliged to leave home for some days; an old friend, with whom he had been associated in China, had begged him to come to Newport, where he lay extremely ill. His friend got better, and at the end of a week Acton was released. I use the word 'released' advisedly; for in spite of his attachment to his Chinese comrade he had been but a half-hearted visitor. He felt as if he had been called away from the theatre during the progress of a remarkably interesting drama. The curtain was up all this time, and he was losing the fourth act; that fourth act which would be so essential to a just appreciation of the fifth. In other words, he was thinking about the Baroness, who, seen at this distance, seemed a truly distinguished figure. He saw at Newport a great many pretty women, who certainly were figures as distinguished as beautiful light dresses could make them; but though they talked a great deal – and the Baroness's strong point was perhaps also her conversation – Madame Münster appeared to lose nothing by the comparison. He wished she too had come to Newport. Would it not be possible to make up, as they said, a party for visiting the famous watering-place and invite Eugenia to join it? It was true that the complete satisfaction would be to spend a fortnight at Newport with Eugenia alone. It would be a great pleasure to see her, in society, carry everything before her, as he was sure she would do. When Acton caught himself thinking these thoughts he began to walk up and down, with his hands in his pockets, frowning a little and looking at the floor. What did it prove – for it certainly proved something – this lively disposition to be 'off' somewhere with Madame Münster, away from all the rest of them? Such a vision, certainly, seemed a refined implication of matrimony, after the Baroness should have formally got rid of her informal husband. At any rate, Acton, with his characteristic discretion, forebore to give expression to whatever else it might imply, and the narrator of these incidents is not obliged to be more definite.

He returned home rapidly, and, arriving in the afternoon, lost as little time as possible in joining the familiar circle at Mr Wentworth's. On reaching the house, however, he found the piazzas empty. The doors and windows were open, and their emptiness was made clear by the shafts of lamp-light from the parlours. Entering the house, he found Mr Wentworth sitting alone in one of these apartments, engaged in the perusal of the *North American Review*. After they had exchanged greetings and his cousin had made discreet inquiry about his journey, Acton asked what had become of Mr Wentworth's companions.

'They are scattered about, amusing themselves as usual,' said the old man. 'I saw Charlotte, a short time since, seated, with Mr Brand, upon the piazza. They were conversing with their customary animation. I suppose they have joined her sister, who, for the hundredth time, was doing the honours of the garden to her foreign cousin.'

'I suppose you mean Felix,' said Acton. And on Mr Wentworth's assenting, he said, 'And the others?'

'Your sister has not come this evening. You must have seen her at home,' said Mr Wentworth.

'Yes. I proposed to her to come. She declined.'

'Lizzie, I suppose, was expecting a visitor,' said the old man, with a kind of solemn slyness.

'If she was expecting Clifford, he had not turned up.'

Mr Wentworth, at this intelligence, closed the *North American Review* and remarked that he understood Clifford to say that he was going to see his cousin. Privately, he reflected that if Lizzie Acton had had no news of his son, Clifford must have gone to Boston for the evening; an unnatural course of a summer night, especially when accompanied with disingenuous representations.

'You must remember that he has two cousins,' said Acton, laughing. And then, coming to the point, 'If Lizzie is not here,' he added, 'neither apparently is the Baroness.'

Mr Wentworth stared a moment, and remembered that queer proposition of Felix's. For a moment he did not know whether it was not to be wished that Clifford, after all, might have gone to Boston. 'The Baroness has not honoured us tonight,' he said. 'She has not come over for three days.'

'Is she ill?' Acton asked.

'No; I have been to see her.'

'What is the matter with her?'

'Well,' said Mr Wentworth, 'I infer she is tired of us.'

Acton pretended to sit down, but he was restless; he found it impossible to talk with Mr Wentworth. At the end of ten minutes he took up his hat and said that he thought he would 'go off'. It was very late; it was ten o'clock.

His quiet-faced kinsman looked at him a moment. 'Are you going home?' he asked.

Acton hesitated, and then answered that he proposed to go over and take a look at the Baroness.

'Well, *you* are honest, at least,' said Mr Wentworth sadly.

'So are you, if you come to that!' cried Acton, laughing. 'Why shouldn't I be honest?'

The old man opened the *North American* again, and read a few lines. 'If we have ever had any virtue amongst us, we had better keep hold of it now,' he said. He was not quoting.

'We have a Baroness amongst us,' said Acton. 'That's what we must keep hold of!' He was too impatient to see Madame Münster again to wonder what Mr Wentworth was talking about. Nevertheless, after he had passed out of the house and traversed the garden and the little piece of road that separated him for Eugenia's provisional residence, he stopped a moment. He stood in her little garden; the long window of her parlour was open, and he could see the white curtains, with the lamp-light shining through them, swaying softly to and fro in the warm night wind. There was a sort of excitement in the idea of seeing Madame Münster again; he became aware that his heart was beating rather faster than usual. It was this that made him stop, with a half-amused surprise. But in a moment he went along the piazza and, approaching the open window, tapped upon its lintel with his stick. He could see the Baroness within; she was standing in the middle of the room. She came to the window and pulled aside the curtain; then she stood looking at him a moment. She was not smiling; she seemed serious.

'*Mais entrez donc!*' she said at last. Acton passed in across the window-sill; he wondered, for an instant, what was the matter with her. But the next moment she had begun to smile and had put out her hand. 'Better late than never,' she said. 'It is very kind of you to come at this hour.'

'I have just returned from my journey,' said Acton.

'Ah, very kind, very kind,' she repeated, looking about her where to sit.

'I went first to the big house,' Acton continued. 'I expected to find you there.'

She had sunk into her usual chair; but she got up again and began to move about the room. Acton had laid down his hat and stick; he was looking at her, conscious that there was in fact a great charm in seeing her again. 'I don't know whether I ought to tell you to sit down,' she said. 'It is too late to begin a visit.'

'It is too early to end one,' Acton declared; 'and we needn't mind the beginning.'

She looked at him again, and, after a moment, dropped once more into her low chair, while he took a place near her. 'We are in the middle, then?' she asked. 'Was that where we were when you went away? No, I haven't been to the other house.'

'Not yesterday, nor the day before, eh?'

'I don't know how many days it is.'

'You are tired of it,' said Acton.

She leaned back in her chair; her arms were folded. 'That is a terrible accusation, but I have not the courage to defend myself.'

'I am not attacking you,' said Acton. 'I expected something of this kind.'

'It's a proof of extreme intelligence. I hope you enjoyed your journey.'

'Not at all,' Acton declared. 'I would much rather have been here with you.'

'Now you *are* attacking me,' said the Baroness. 'You are contrasting my inconstancy with your own fidelity.'

'I confess I never get tired of people I like.'

'Ah, you are not a poor, wicked, foreign woman, with irritable nerves and a sophisticated mind!'

'Something has happened to you since I went away,' said Acton, changing his place.

'Your going away – that is what has happened to me.'

'Do you mean to say that you have missed me?' he asked.

'If I had meant to say it, it would not be worth your making a note of. I am very dishonest, and my compliments are worthless.'

Acton was silent for some moments. 'You have broken down,' he said at last.

Madame Münster left her chair and began to move about.

'Only for a moment. I shall pull myself together again.'

'You had better not take it too hard. If you are bored, you needn't be afraid to say so – to me at least.'

'You shouldn't say such things as that,' the Baroness answered. 'You should encourage me.'

'I admire your patience; that is encouraging.'

'You shouldn't even say that. When you talk of my patience you are disloyal to your own people. Patience implies suffering; and what have I had to suffer?'

'Oh, not hunger, not unkindness, certainly,' said Acton, laughing. 'Nevertheless, we all admire your patience.'

'You all detest me!' cried the Baroness, with a sudden vehemence, turning her back toward him.

'You make it hard,' said Acton, getting up, 'for a man to say something tender to you.' This evening there was something particularly striking and touching about her; an unwonted softness and a look of suppressed emotion. He felt himself suddenly appreciating the fact that she had behaved very well. She had come to this quiet corner of the world under the weight of a cruel indignity, and she had been so gracefully, modestly thankful for the rest she found there. She had joined that simple circle over the way; she had mingled in its plain provincial talk; she had shared its meagre and savourless pleasures. She had set herself a task, and she had rigidly performed it. She had conformed to the angular conditions of New England life, and she had had the tact and pluck to carry it off as if she liked them. Acton felt a more downright need than he had ever felt before to tell her that he admired her and that she struck him as a very superior woman. All along, hitherto, he had been on his guard with her; he had been cautious, observant, suspicious. But now a certain light tumult in his blood seemed to intimate that a finer degree of confidence in this charming woman would be its own reward. 'We don't detest you,' he went on. 'I don't know what you mean. At any rate, I speak for myself; I don't know anything about the others. Very likely you detest them for the dull life they make you lead. Really, it would give me a sort of pleasure to hear you say so.'

Eugenia had been looking at the door on the other side of the room; now she slowly turned her eyes toward Robert Acton. 'What can be the motive,' she asked, 'of a man like you – an honest man, a *galant homme* – in saying so base a thing as that?'

'Does it sound very base?' asked Acton candidly. 'I suppose it does, and I thank you for telling me so. Of course I don't mean it literally.'

The Baroness stood looking at him. 'How do you mean it?' she asked.

This question was difficult to answer, and Acton, feeling the least bit foolish, walked to the open window and looked out. He stood there, thinking a moment, and then he turned back. 'You know that document that you were to send to Germany,' he said. 'You called it your "renunciation". Did you ever send it?'

Madame Münster's eyes expanded: she looked very grave. 'What a singular answer to my question!'

'Oh, it isn't an answer,' said Acton. 'I have wished to ask you, many times. I thought it probable you would tell me yourself. The question, on my part, seems abrupt now; but it would be abrupt at any time.'

The Baroness was silent a moment; and then, 'I think I have told you too much!' she said.

This declaration appeared to Acton to have a certain force; he had indeed a sense of asking more of her than he offered her. He returned to the window, and watched for a moment, a little star that twinkled through the lattice of the piazza. There were at any rate offers enough he could make; perhaps he had hitherto not been sufficiently explicit in doing so. 'I wish you would ask something of me,' he presently said. 'Is there nothing I can do for you? If you can't stand this dull life any more, let me amuse you!'

The Baroness had sunk once more into a chair, and she had taken up a fan which she held, with both hands, to her mouth. Over the top of the fan her eyes were fixed on him. 'You are very strange tonight,' she said with a laugh.

'I will do anything in the world,' he rejoined, standing in front of her. 'Shouldn't you like to travel about and see something of the country? Won't you go to Niagara? You ought to see Niagara, you know.'

'With you, do you mean?'

'I should be delighted to take you.'

'You alone?'

Acton looked at her, smiling, and yet with a serious air. 'Well, yes; we might go alone,' he said.

'If you were not what you are,' she answered, 'I should feel insulted.'

'How do you mean – what I am?'

'If you were one of the gentlemen I have been used to all my life. If you were not a queer Bostonian.'

'If the gentlemen you have been used to have taught you to expect insults,' said Acton, 'I am glad I am what I am. You had much better come to Niagara.'

'If you wish to "amuse" me,' the Baroness declared, 'you need go to no further expense. You amuse me very effectually.'

He sat down opposite to her; she still held her fan up to her face, with her eyes only showing above it. There was a moment's silence, and then he said, returning to his former question, 'Have you sent that document to Germany?'

Again there was a moment's silence. The expressive eyes of Madame Münster seemed, however, half to break it. 'I will tell you – at Niagara!' she said.

She had hardly spoken when the door at the farther end of the room opened – the door upon which, some minutes previous, Eugenia had fixed her gaze. Clifford Wentworth stood there, blushing and looking rather awkward. The Baroness rose, quickly, and Acton, more slowly, did the same. Clifford gave him no greeting; he was looking at Eugenia.

'Ah, you were here?' exclaimed Acton.

'He was in Felix's studio,' said Madame Münster. 'He wanted to see his sketches.'

Clifford looked at Robert Acton, but he said nothing; he only fanned himself with his hat. 'You chose a bad moment,' said Acton; 'you hadn't much light.'

'I hadn't any!' said Clifford laughing.

'Your candle went out?' Eugenia asked. 'You should have come back here and lighted it again.'

Clifford looked at her a moment. 'So I have – come back. But I have left the candle!'

Eugenia turned away. 'You are very stupid, my poor boy. You had better go home.'

'Well,' said Clifford, 'good night!'

'Haven't you a word to throw to a man when he has safely returned from a dangerous journey?' Acton asked.

'How do you do?' said Clifford. 'I thought – I thought you were—' And he paused, looking at the Baroness again.

'You thought I was at Newport, eh? So I was – this morning.'

'Good night, clever child!' said Madame Münster, over her shoulder.

Clifford stared at her – not at all like a clever child; and then, with one of his little facetious growls, took his departure.

'What is the matter with him?' asked Acton, when he was gone. 'He seemed rather in a muddle.'

Eugenia, who was near the window, glanced out, listening a moment. 'The matter – the matter' – she answered. 'But you don't say such things here.'

'If you mean that he had been drinking a little, you can say that.'

'He doesn't drink any more. I have cured him. And in return he is in love with me.'

It was Acton's turn to stare. He instantly thought of his sister; but he said nothing about her. He began to laugh. 'I don't wonder at his passion! But I wonder at his forsaking your society for that of your brother's paint brushes.'

Eugenia was silent a minute. 'He had not been in the studio. I invented that – at the moment.'

'Invented it? For what purpose?'

'He has an idea of being romantic. He has adopted the habit of coming to see me at midnight – passing only through the orchard and through Felix's painting-room, which has a door opening that way. It seems to amuse him,' added Eugenia, with a little laugh.

Acton felt more surprise than he confessed to, for this was a new view of Clifford, whose irregularities had hitherto been quite without the romantic element. He tried to laugh again, but he felt rather too serious, and after a moment's hesitation his seriousness explained itself. 'I hope you don't encourage him,' he said. 'He must not be inconstant to poor Lizzie.'

'To your sister?'

'You know they are decidedly intimate,' said Acton.

'Ah,' cried Eugenia, smiling, 'has she – has she –'

'I don't know,' Acton interrupted, 'what she has. But I always supposed that Clifford had a desire to make himself agreeable to her.'

'Ah, *par exemple!*' the Baroness went on. 'The little monster! The next time he becomes sentimental I will tell him that he ought to be ashamed of himself.'

Acton was silent a moment. 'You had better say nothing about it.'

'I had told him as much already, on general grounds,' said the Baroness. 'But in this country, you know, the relations of young people are so extraordinary that one is quite at sea. They are not engaged when you would quite say they ought to be. Take Charlotte Wentworth, for instance, and that young ecclesiastic. If I were her father I should insist upon his marrying her; but it appears to be thought there is no urgency. On the other hand, you suddenly learn that a boy of twenty and a little girl who is still with her governess – your sister has no governess? Well, then, who is never away from her mamma – a young couple, in short, between whom you have noticed nothing beyond an exchange of the childish pleasantries characteristic of their age, are on the point of setting up as man and wife.' The Baroness spoke with a certain exaggerated volubility which was in contrast with the languid grace that had characterized her manner before Clifford made his appearance. It seemed to Acton that there was a spark of irritation in her eye – a note of irony (as when she spoke of Lizzie being never away from her mother) in her voice. If Madame Münster was irritated, Robert Acton was vaguely mystified; she began to move about the room again, and he looked at her without saying anything. Presently she took out her watch, and, glancing at it, declared that it was three o'clock in the morning, and that he must go.

'I have not been here an hour,' he said, 'and they are still sitting up at the big house. You can see the lights. Your brother has not come in.'

'Oh, at the big house,' cried Eugenia, 'they are terrible people! I don't know what they may do over there. I am a quiet little humdrum woman; I have rigid rules, and I keep them. One of them is not to have visitors in the small hours – especially clever men like you. So good night!'

Decidedly the Baroness was incisive; and though Acton bade her good night and departed, he was still a good deal mystified.

The next day Clifford Wentworth came to see Lizzie, and Acton, who was at home and saw him pass through the garden, took note of the circumstance. He had a natural desire to make it tally with Madame Münster's account of Clifford's disaffection; but his ingenuity, finding itself unequal to the task, resolved at last to ask help of the young man's candour. He waited till he saw him going away, and then he went out and overtook him in the grounds.

'I wish very much you would answer me a question,' Acton said. 'What were you doing last night at Madame Münster's?'

Clifford began to laugh and to blush, by no means like a young man with a romantic secret. 'What did she tell you?' he asked.

'That is exactly what I don't want to say.'

'Well, I want to tell you the same,' said Clifford; 'and unless I know it perhaps I can't.'

They had stopped in a garden path; Acton looked hard at his rosy young kinsman. 'She said she couldn't fancy what had got into you; you appeared to have taken a violent dislike to her.'

Clifford stared, looking a little alarmed. 'Oh, come,' he growled, 'you don't mean that!'

'And that when – for common civility's sake – you came occasionally to the house, you left her alone and spent your time in Felix's studio, under pretext of looking at his sketches.'

'Oh, come!' growled Clifford, again.

'Did you ever know me to tell an untruth?'

'Yes, lots of them!' said Clifford, seeing an opening out of the discussion for his sarcastic powers. 'Well,' he presently added, 'I thought you were my father.'

'You knew some one was there?'

'We heard you coming in.'

Acton meditated. 'You had been with the Baroness, then?'

'I was in the parlour. We heard your step outside. I thought it was my father.'

'And on that,' asked Acton, 'you ran away?'

'She told me to go – to go out by the studio.'

Acton meditated more intensely; if there had been a chair at hand he would have sat down. 'Why should she wish you not to meet your father?'

'Well,' said Clifford, 'father doesn't like to see me there.'

Acton looked askance at his companion, and forbore to make any comment upon this assertion. 'Has he said so,' he asked, 'to the Baroness?'

'Well, I hope not,' said Clifford. 'He hasn't said so – in so many words – to me. But I know it worries him; and I want to stop worrying him. The Baroness knows it, and she wants me to stop too.'

'To stop coming to see her?'

'I don't know about that; but to stop worrying father. Eugenia knows everything,' Clifford added, with an air of knowingness of his own.

'Ah,' said Acton interrogatively. 'Eugenia knows everything?'

'She knew it was not father coming in.'

'Then why did you go?'

Clifford blushed and laughed afresh. 'Well, I was afraid it was. And besides, she told me to go at any rate.'

'Did she think it was I?' Acton asked.

'She didn't say so.'

Again Robert Acton reflected. 'But you didn't go,' he presently said: 'you came back.'

'I couldn't get out of the studio,' Clifford rejoined. 'The door was locked, and Felix has nailed some planks across the lower half of the confounded windows, to make the light come in from above. So they were no use. I waited there a good while, and then suddenly I felt ashamed. I didn't want to be hiding away from my own father. I couldn't stand it any longer. I bolted out, and when I found it was you I was a little flurried. But Eugenia carried it off, didn't she?' Clifford added, in the tone of a young humorist whose perception had not been permanently clouded by the sense of his own discomfort.

'Beautifully!' said Acton. 'Especially,' he continued, 'when one remembers that you were very imprudent and that she must have been a good deal annoyed.'

'Oh,' cried Clifford, with the indifference of a young man who feels that however he may have failed of felicity in behaviour, he is extremely just in his impressions. 'Eugenia doesn't care for anything!'

Acton hesitated a moment. 'Thank you for telling me this,' he said at last. And then, laying his hand on Clifford's shoulder, he added, 'Tell me one thing more: are you by chance the least bit sweet on the Baroness?'

'No, sir!' said Clifford, almost shaking off his hand.

Chapter Ten

The first Sunday that followed Robert Acton's return from Newport witnessed a change in the brilliant weather that had long prevailed. The rain began to fall and the day was cold and dreary. Mr Wentworth and his daughters put on overshoes and went to church, and Felix Young, without overshoes, went also, holding an umbrella over Gertrude. It is to be feared that, in the whole observance, this was the privilege he most highly valued. The Baroness remained at home; she was in neither a cheerful nor a devotional mood. She had, however, never been, during her residence in the United States, what is called a regular attendant at divine service; and on this particular Sunday morning of which I began with speaking she stood at the window of her little drawing-room, watching the long arm of a rose tree that was attatched to her piazza, but a portion of which had disengaged itself, sway to and fro, shake and gesticulate, against the dusky drizzle of the sky. Every now and then, in a gust of wind, the rose tree scattered a shower of water-drops against the window pane; it appeared to have a kind of human movement – a menacing warning intention. The room was very cold; Madame Münster put on a shawl and walked about.Then she determined to have some fire; and summoning her ancient negress, the contrast of whose polished ebony and whose crimson turban had been at first a source of satisfaction to her, she made arrangements for the production of a crackling flame. This old woman's name was Azarina. The Baroness had begun by thinking that there would be a savoury wildness in her talk, and, for amusement, she had encouraged her to chatter. But Azarina was dry and prim; her conversation was anything but African; she reminded Eugenia of the tiresome old ladies she met in society. She knew, however, how to make a fire; so that after she had laid the logs, Eugenia, who was terribly bored, found a quarter of an hour's entertainment in sitting and watching them blaze and sputter. She had thought it very likely Robert Acton would come and see her; she had not met him since that infelicitous evening. But the morning waned without his coming; several times she thought she heard his step on the piazza, but it was only a window-shutter shaking in a rain-gust. The Baroness, since the beginning of that episode in her career of which a slight sketch has been attempted in these pages, had had many moments of irritation. But today her irritation had a peculiar keenness; it appeared to feed upon itself. It urged her to do something; but it suggested no particularly profitable line of action. If she could have done something at the moment, on the spot, she would have stepped upon a European steamer and turned her back, with a kind of rapture, upon that profoundly mortifying failure, her visit to her American relations. It is not exactly apparent why she should have termed this enterprise a failure, inasmuch as she had been treated with the highest distinction for which allowance had been made in American institutions. Her irritation came, at bottom, from the sense, which, always present, had suddenly grown acute, that the social soil on this big, vague continent was somehow not adapted for growing those plants whose fragrance she especially inclined to inhale, and by which she liked to see herself surrounded – a species of vegetation for which she carried a collection of seedlings, as we may say, in her pocket. She found her chief happiness in the sense of exerting a certain power and making a certain impression; and now she felt the annoyance of a rather wearied swimmer who, on nearing shore, to land, finds a smooth straight wall of rock when he had counted upon a clean firm beach. Her power, in the American air, seemed to have lost its prehensile attributes; the smooth wall of rock was insurmountable. 'Surely *je n'en suis pas là,*' she said to herself, 'that I let it make me uncomfortable that a Mr Robert Acton shouldn't honour me with a visit!' Yet she was vexed that he had not come; and she was vexed at her vexation.

Her brother, at least, came in, stamping in the hall and shaking the wet from his coat. In a moment he entered the room, with a glow in his cheek and half a dozen rain-drops glistening on his moustache. 'Ah, you have a fire,' he said.

'*Les beaux jours sont passés*,' replied the Baroness.

'Never, never! They have only begun,' Felix declared, planting himself before the hearth. He turned his back to the fire, placed his hands behind him, extended his legs and looked away through the window with an expression of face which seemed to denote the perception of rose-colour even in the tints of a wet Sunday.

His sister, from her chair, looked up at him, watching him; and what she saw in his face was not grateful to her present mood. She was not puzzled by many things, but her brother's disposition was a frequent source of wonder to her. I say frequent, and not constant, for there were long periods during which she gave her attention to other problems. Sometimes she had said to herself that his happy temper, his eternal gaiety, was an affectation, a *pose*; but she was vaguely conscious that during the present summer he had been a highly successful comedian. They had never yet had an explanation; she had not known the need for one. Felix was presumably following the bent of his disinterested genius, and she felt that she had no advice to give him that he would understand. With this, there was always a certain element of comfort about Felix – the assurance that he would not interfere. He was very delicate, this pure-minded Felix; in effect, he was her brother, and Madame Münster felt that there was a great propriety, every way, in that. It is true that Felix was delicate; he was not fond of explanations with his sister; this was one of the very few things in the world about which he was uncomfortable. But now he was not thinking of anything uncomfortable.

'Dear brother,' said Eugenia at last, 'do stop making *les yeux doux* at the rain.'

'With pleasure. I will make them at you!' answered Felix.

'How much longer,' asked Eugenia, in a moment, 'do you propose to remain in this lovely spot?'

Felix stared. 'Do you want to go away – already?'

' "Already" is delicious. I am not so happy as you.'

Felix dropped into a chair, looking at the fire. 'The fact is I *am* happy,' he said, in his light, clear tone.

'And do you propose to spend your life in making love to Gertrude Wentworth?'

'Yes!' said Felix, smiling sidewise at his sister.

The Baroness returned his glance, much more gravely; and then, 'Do you like her?' she asked.

'Don't you?' Felix demanded.

The Baroness was silent a moment. 'I will answer you in the words of the gentleman who was asked if he liked music: "Je ne la crains pas!" '

'She admires you immensely,' said Felix.

'I don't care for that. Other women should not admire one.'

'They should dislike you?'

Again Madame Münster hesitated. 'They should hate me! It's a measure of the time I have been losing here that they don't.'

'No time is lost in which one has been happy!' said Felix, with a bright sententiousness which may well have been a little irritating.

'And in which,' rejoined his sister, with a harsher laugh, 'one has secured the affections of a young lady with a fortune!'

Felix explained very candidly and seriously. 'I have secured Gertrude's affection, but I am by no means sure that I have secured her fortune. That may come – or it may not.'

'Ah, well, it may! That's the great point.'

'It depends on her father. He doesn't smile upon our union. You know he wants her to marry Mr Brand.'

"I know nothing about it!' cried the Baroness. 'Please to put on a log.' Felix complied with her request and sat watching the quickening of the flame. Presently his sister added, 'And you propose to elope with mademoiselle?'

'By no means. I don't wish to do anything that's disagreeable to Mr Wentworth. He has been far too kind to us.'

'But you must choose between pleasing yourself and pleasing him.'

'I want to please everyone!' exclaimed Felix joyously. 'I have a good conscience. I made up my mind at the outset that it was not my place to make love to Gertrude.'

'So, to simplify matters, she made love to you?'

Felix looked at his sister with sudden gravity. 'You say you are not afraid of her,' he said. 'But perhaps you ought to be – a little. She's a very clever person.'

'I begin to see it!' cried the Baroness. Her brother, making no rejoinder, leaned back in his chair, and there was a long silence. At last, with an altered accent, Madame Münster put another question, 'You expect, at any rate, to marry?'

'I shall be greatly disappointed if we don't.'

'A disappointment or two will do you good!' the Baroness declared. 'And afterwards, do you mean to turn American?'

'It seems to me I am a very good American already. But we shall go to Europe. Gertrude wants extremely to see the world.'

'Ah, like me, when I came here!' said the Baroness with a little laugh.

'No, not like you,' Felix rejoined, looking at his sister with a certain gentle seriousness. While he looked at her she rose from her chair, and he also got up. 'Gertrude is not at all like you,' he went on; 'but in her own way she is almost as clever.' He paused a moment; his soul was full of an agreeable feeling, and of a lively disposition to express it. His sister, to his spiritual vision, was always like the lunar disk when only a part of it lighted. The shadow on this bright surface seemed to him to expand and to contract; but whatever its proportions, he always appreciated the moonlight. He looked at the Baroness, and then he kissed her. 'I am very much in love with Gertrude,' he said. Eugenia turned away and walked about the room, and Felix continued, 'She is very interesting, and very different from what she seems. She has never had a chance. She is very brilliant. We will go to Europe and amuse ourselves.'

The Baroness had gone to the window, where she stood looking out. The day was drearier than ever; the rain was doggedly falling. 'Yes, to amuse ourselves,' she said at last, 'you had decidely better go to Europe!' Then she turned round, looking at her brother. A chair stood near her; she leaned her hands upon the back of it. 'Don't you think it is very good of me,' she asked, 'to come all this way with you simply to see you properly married – if properly it is?'

'Oh, it will be properly,' cried Felix, with light eagerness.

The Baroness gave a little laugh. 'You are thinking only of yourself, and you don't answer my question. While you are amusing yourself – with the brilliant Gertrude – what shall I be doing?'

'*Vous serez de la partie!*' cried Felix.

'Thank you; I should spoil it.' The Baroness dropped her eyes for some moments. 'Do you propose, however, to leave me here?' she inquired.

Felix smiled at her. 'My dearest sister, where you are concerned I never propose. I execute your commands.'

'I believe,' said Eugenia slowly, 'that you are the most heartless person living. Don't you see that I am in trouble?'

'I saw that you were not cheerful, and I gave you some good news.'

'Well, let me give you some news,' said the Baroness. 'You probably will not have discovered it for yourself. Robert Acton wants to marry me.'

'No, I had not discovered that. But I quite understand it. Why does it make you unhappy?'

'Because I can't decide.'

'Accept him, accept him!' cried Felix joyously. 'He is the best fellow in the world.'

'He is immensely in love with me,' said the Baroness.

'And he has a large fortune. Permit me in turn to remind you of that.'

'Oh, I am perfectly aware of it,' said Eugenia. 'That's a great item in his favour. I am terribly candid.' And she left her place and came nearer her brother, looking at him hard. He was turning over several things; she was wondering in what manner he really understood her.

There were several ways of understanding her: there was what she said, and there was what she meant, and there was something between the two, that was neither. It is probable that, in the last analysis, what she meant was that Felix should spare her the necessity of stating the case more exactly, and should hold himself commissioned to assist her by all honourable means to marry the best fellow in the world. But in all this it was never discovered what Felix understood.

'Once you have your liberty, what are your objections?' he asked.

'Well, I don't particularly like him.'

'Oh, try a little.'

'I am trying now,' said Eugenia. 'I should succeed better if he didn't live here. I could never live here.'

'Make him go to Europe,' Felix suggested.

'Ah, there you speak of happiness based upon violent effort,' the Baroness rejoined. 'That is not what I am looking for. He would never live in Europe.'

'He would live anywhere, with you!' said Felix gallantly.

His sister looked at him still, with a ray of penetration in her charming eyes; then she turned away again. 'You see, at all events,' she presently went on, 'that if it had been said of me that I had come over here to seek my fortune it would have to be added that I have found it!'

'Don't leave it lying!' urged Felix, with smiling solemnity.

'I am much obliged to you for your interest,' his sister declared, after a moment. 'But promise me one thing: *pas de zèle!* If Mr Acton should ask you to plead his cause, excuse yourself.'

'I shall certainly have the excuse,' said Felix, 'that I have a cause of my own to plead.'

'If he should talk of me – favourably,' Eugenia continued, 'warn him against dangerous illusion. I detest importunities; I want to decide at my leisure, with my eyes open.'

'I shall be discreet,' said Felix, 'except to you. To you I will say, Accept him outright.'

She had advanced to the open doorway, and she stood looking at him. 'I will go and dress, and think of it,' she said; and he heard her moving slowly to her apartments.

Late in the afternoon the rain stopped, and just afterward there was a great flaming, flickering, trickling sunset. Felix sat in his painting-room and did some work; but at last, as the light, which had not been brilliant, began to fade, he laid down his brushes and came out to the little piazza of the cottage. Here he walked up and down for some time, looking at the splendid blaze of the western sky, and saying, as he had often said before, that this was certainly the country of sunsets. There was something in these glorious deeps of fire that quickened his imagination; he always found images and promises in the western sky. He thought of a good many things – of roaming about the world with Gertrude Wentworth; he seemed to see their possible adventures, in a glowing frieze, between the cloud-bars; then of what Eugenia had just been telling him. He wished very much that Madame Münster would make a comfortable and honourable marriage. Presently, as the sunset expanded and deepened, the fancy took him of making a note of so magnificent a piece of colouring. He returned to his studio and fetched out a small panel, with his palette and brushes, and, placing the panel against a windowsill, he began to daub with great gusto. While he was so occupied he saw Mr Brand, in the distance, slowly come down from Mr Wentworth's house, nursing a large folded umbrella. He walked with a joyless, meditative tread, and his eyes were bent upon the ground. Felix poised his brush for a moment, watching him; then, by a sudden impulse, as he drew nearer, advanced to the garden gate and signalled to him – the palette and bunch of brushes contributing to this effect.

Mr Brand stopped and started; then he appeared to decide to accept Felix's invitation. He came out of Mr Wentworth's gate and passed along the road; after which he entered the little garden of the cottage. Felix had gone back to his sunset; but he made his visitor welcome while he rapidly brushed it in.

'I wanted so much to speak to you that I thought I would call you,' he said, in the friendliest tone. 'All the more that you have been to see me so little. You have come to see my sister; I know that. But you haven't come to see me – the celebrated artist. Artists are very sensitive, you know; they notice those things.' And Felix turned round, smiling, with a brush in his mouth.

Mr Brand stood there with a certain blank, candid majesty, pulling together the large flaps of his umbrella. 'Why should I come to see you?' he asked. 'I know nothing of Art.'

'It would sound very conceited, I suppose,' said Felix, 'if I were to say that it would be a good little chance for you to learn something. You would ask me why you should learn; and I should have no answer to that. I suppose a minister has no need for Art, eh?'

'He has need for good temper, sir,' said Mr Brand, with decision.

Felix jumped up, with his palette on his thumb and a movement of the liveliest deprecation. 'That's because I keep you standing there while I splash my red paint! I beg a thousand pardons! You see what bad manners Art gives a man; and how right you are to let it alone. I didn't mean you should stand either. The piazza, as you see, is ornamented with rustic chairs; though indeed I ought to warn you that they have nails in the wrong places. I was just making a note of that sunset. I never saw such a blaze of different reds. It looks as if the Celestial City were in flames, eh? If that were really the case I suppose it would be the business of you theologians to put out the fire. Fancy me – an ungodly artist – quietly sitting down to paint it!'

Mr Brand had always credited Felix Young with a certain impudence, but it appeared to him that on this occasion his impudence was so great as to make a special explanation – or even an apology – necessary. And the impression, it must be added, was sufficiently natural. Felix had at all times a brilliant assurance of manner which was simply the vehicle of his good spirits and his good will; but at present he had a special design, and as he would have admitted that the design was audacious, so he was conscious of having summoned all the arts of conversation to his aid. But he was so far from desiring to offend his visitor that he was rapidly asking himself what personal compliment he could pay the young clergyman that would gratify him most. If he could think of it, he was prepared to pay it down. 'Have you been preaching one of your beautiful sermons today?' he suddenly asked, laying down his palette. This was not what Felix had been trying to think of, but it was a tolerable stop-gap.

Mr Brand frowned – as much as a man can frown who has very fair, soft eyebrows, and, beneath them, very gentle, tranquil eyes. 'No, I have not preached any sermon today. Did you bring me over here for the purpose of making that inquiry?'

Felix saw that he was irritated, and he regretted it immensely; but he had no fear of not being, in the end, agreeable to Mr Brand. He looked at him, smiling, and laying his hand on his arm. 'No, no, not for that – not for that. I wanted to ask you something; I wanted to tell you something. I am sure it will interest you very much. Only – as it is something rather private – we had better come into my little studio. I have a western window; we can still see the sunset. *Andiamo!*' And he gave a little pat to his companion's arm.

He led the way in; Mr Brand stiffly and softly followed. The twilight had thickened in the little studio; but the wall opposite the western window was covered with a deep pink flush. There were a great many sketches and half-finished canvases suspended in this rosy glow, and the corners of the room were vague and dusty. Felix begged Mr Brand to sit down; then glancing round him, 'By Jove, how pretty it looks!' he cried. But Mr Brand would not sit down; he went and leaned against the window; he wondered what

Felix wanted of him. In the shadow, on the darker parts of the wall, he saw the gleam of three or four pictures that looked fantastic and surprising. They seemed to represent naked figures. Felix stood there with his head a little bent and his eyes fixed upon his visitor, smiling intensely, pulling his moustache. Mr Brand felt vaguely uneasy. 'It is very delicate – what I want to say,' Felix began. 'But I have been thinking of it for some time.'

'Please say it as quickly as possible,' said Mr Brand.

'It's because you are a clergyman, you know,' Felix went on. 'I don't think I should venture to say it to a common man.'

Mr Brand was silent for a moment. 'If it is a question of yielding to a weakness, of resenting an injury, I am afraid I am a very common man.'

'My dearest friend,' cried Felix, 'this is not an injury; its a benefit – a great service! You will like it extremely. Only it's so delicate!' And, in the dim light, he continued to smile intensely. 'You know I take a great interest in my cousins – in Charlotte and Gertrude Wentworth. That's very evident from my having travelled some five thousand miles to see them.' Mr Brand said nothing, and Felix proceeded. 'Coming into their society as a perfect stranger I received of course a great many new impressions, and my impressions had a great freshnesss, a great keenness. Do you know what I mean?'

'I am not sure that I do; but I should like you to continue.'

'I think my impressions have always had a good deal of freshness,' said Mr Brand's entertainer; 'but on this occasion it was perhaps particularly natural that – coming in, as I say, from outside – I should be struck with things that passed unnoticed among yourselves. And then I had my sister to help me; and she is simply the most observant woman in the world.'

'I am not surprised,' said Mr Brand, 'that in our little circle two intelligent persons should have found food for observation. I am sure that, of late, I have found it myself!'

'Ah, but I shall surprise you yet!' cried Felix, laughing. 'Both my sister and I took a great fancy to my cousin Charlotte.'

'Your cousin Charlotte?' repeated Mr Brand.

'We fell in love with her from the first.'

'You fell in love with Charlotte?' Mr Brand murmured.

'*Dame!*' exclaimed Felix, 'she's a very charming person; and Eugenia was especially smitten.' Mr Brand stood staring, and he pursued, 'Affection, you know, opens one's eyes, and we noticed something. Charlotte is not happy! Charlotte is in love.' And Felix, drawing nearer, laid his hand again upon his companion's arm.

There was something akin to an acknowledgement of fascination in the way Mr Brand looked at him; but the young clergyman retained as yet quite enough self-possession to be able to say, with a good deal of solemnity, 'She is not in love with you.'

Felix gave a light laugh and rejoined with the alacrity of a maritime adventurer who feels a puff of wind in his sail. 'Ah no; if she were in love with me I should know it! I am not so blind as you.'

'As I?'

'My dear sir, you are stone blind. Poor Charlotte is dead in love with *you*!'

Mr Brand said nothing for a moment; he breathed a little heavily. 'Is that what you wanted to say to me?' he asked.

'I have wanted to say it these three weeks. Because of late she has been worse. I told you,' added Felix, 'it was very delicate.'

'Well, sir' – Mr Brand began; 'well, sir—'

'I was sure you didn't know it,' Felix continued. 'But don't you see – as soon as I mention it – how everything is explained?' Mr Brand answered nothing; he looked for a chair and softly sat down. Felix could see that he was blushing; he had looked straight at his host hitherto, but now he looked away. The foremost effect of what he had heard had been a sort of irritation of his modesty. 'Of course,' said Felix, 'I suggest nothing; it would be very presumptuous in me to advise you. But I think there is no doubt about the fact.'

Mr Brand looked hard at the floor for some moments; he was oppressed with a mixture of sensations. Felix, standing there, was very sure that one of them was profound surprise. The innocent young man had been completely unsuspicious of poor Charlotte's hidden flame. This gave Felix great hope; he was sure that Mr Brand would be flattered. Felix thought him very transparent, and indeed he was so; he could neither simulate nor dissimulate. 'I scarcely know what to make of this,' he said at last, without looking up; and Felix was struck with the fact that he offered no protest or contradiction. Evidently Felix had kindled a train of memories – a retrospective illumination. It was making, to Mr Brand's astonished eyes, a very pretty blaze; his second emotion had been a gratification of vanity.

'Thank me for telling you,' Felix rejoined. 'It's a good thing to know.'

'I am not sure of that,' said Mr Brand.

'Ah, don't let her languish!' Felix murmured, lightly and softly.

'You *do* advise me, then?' And Mr Brand looked up.

'I congratulate you!' said Felix, smiling. He had thought at first his visitor was simply appealing; but he saw he was a little ironical.

'It is in your interest; you have interfered with me,' the young clergyman went on.

Felix still stood and smiled. The little room had grown darker, and the crimson glow faded; but Mr Brand could see the brilliant expression of his face. 'I won't pretend not to know what you mean,' said Felix at last. 'But I have not really interfered with you. Of what you had to lose – with another person – you have lost nothing. And think what you have gained!'

'It seems to me I am the proper judge, on each side,' Mr Brand declared. He got up, holding the brim of his hat against his mouth and staring at Felix through the dusk.

'You have lost an illusion!' said Felix.

'What do you call an illusion?'

'The belief that you really know – that you have ever really known – Gertrude Wentworth. Depend upon that,' pursued Felix. 'I don't know her yet; but I have no illusions; I don't pretend to.'

Mr Brand kept gazing, over his hat. 'She has always been a lucid, limpid nature,' he said solemnly.

'She has always been a dormant nature. She was waiting for a touchstone. But now she is beginning to awaken.'

'Don't praise her to me!' said Mr Brand, with a little quaver in his voice. 'If you have the advantage of me that is not generous.'

'My dear sir, I am melting with generosity!' exclaimed Felix. 'And I am not praising my cousin. I am simply attempting a scientific definition of her. She doesn't care for abstractions. Now I think the contrary is what you have always fancied – is the basis on which you have been building. She is extremely preoccupied with the concrete. I care for the concrete too. But Gertrude is stronger than I; she whirls me along.'

Mr Brand looked for a moment into the crown of his hat. 'It's a most interesting nature.'

'So it is,' said Felix. 'But it pulls – it pulls – like a runaway horse. Now, I like the feeling of a runaway horse; and if I am thrown out of the vehicle it is no great matter. But if *you* should be thrown, Mr Brand' – and Felix paused a moment – 'another person also would suffer from the accident.'

'What other person?'

'Charlotte Wentworth?'

Mr Brand looked at Felix for a moment sidewise, mistrustfully; then his eyes slowly wandered over the ceiling. Felix was sure he was secretly struck with the romance of the situation. 'I think this is none of our business,' the young minister murmured.

'None of mine, perhaps; but surely yours!'

Mr Brand lingered still, looking at the ceiling; there was evidently something he wanted to say. 'What do you mean by Miss Gertrude being strong?' he asked abruptly.

'Well,' said Felix meditatively, 'I mean that she has had a great deal of self-possession. She was waiting – for years; even when she seemed, perhaps, to be living in the present. She knew how to wait; she had a purpose. That's what I mean by her being strong.'

'What do you mean by her purpose?'

'Well – the purpose to see the world!'

Mr Brand eyed his strange informant askance again; but he said nothing. At last he turned away, as if to take leave. He seemed bewildered, however; for instead of going to the door he moved toward the opposite corner of the room. Felix stood and watched him for a moment – almost groping about in the dusk; then he led him to the door, with a tender, almost fraternal movement. 'Is that all you have to say?' asked Mr Brand.

'Yes, it's all – but it will bear a good deal of thinking of.'

Felix went with him to the garden gate, and watched him slowly walk away into the thickening twilight with a relaxed rigidity that tried to rectify itself. 'He is offended, excited, bewildered, perplexed – and enchanted!' Felix said to himself. 'That's a capital mixture.'

Chapter Eleven

Since that visit paid by the Baroness Münster to Mrs Acton, of which some account was given at an earlier stage of this narrative, the intercourse between these two ladies had been neither frequent nor intimate. It was not that Mrs Acton had failed to appreciate Madame Münster's charms; on the contrary, her perception of the graces of manner and conversation of her brilliant visitor had been only too acute. Mrs Acton was, as they said in Boston, very 'intense', and her impressions were apt to be too many for her. The state of her health required the restriction of emotion; and this is why, receiving, as she sat in her eternal arm-chair, very few visitors, even of the soberest local type, she had been obliged to limit the number of her interviews with a lady whose costume and manner recalled to her imagination – Mrs Acton's imagination was a marvel – all that she had ever read of the most stirring historical periods. But she had sent the Baroness a great many quaintly-worded messages, and a great many nosegays from her garden, and baskets of beautiful fruit. Felix had eaten the fruit, and the Baroness had arranged the flowers and returned the baskets and the messages. On the day that followed the rainy Sunday of which mention has been made, Eugenia determined to go and pay the beneficent invalid a '*visite d'adieux*'; so it was that, to herself, she qualified her enterprise. It may be noted that neither on the Sunday evening nor on the Monday morning had she received that expected visit from Robert Acton. To his own consciousness, evidently, he was 'keeping away'; and as the Baroness, on her side, was keeping away from her uncle's, whither, for several days, Felix had been the unembarrassed bearer of apologies and regrets for absence, chance had not taken the cards from the hands of design. Mr Wentworth and his daughters had respected Eugenia's seclusion; certain intervals of mysterious retirement appeared to them, vaguely, a natural part of the graceful, rhythmic movement of so remarkable a life. Gertrude especially held these periods in honour; she wondered what Madame Münster did at such times, but she would not have permitted herself to inquire too curiously.

The long rain had freshened the air, and twelve hours' brilliant sunshine had dried the roads; so that the Baroness, in the late afternoon, proposing to walk to Mrs Acton's exposed herself to no great discomfort. As with her charming undulating step she moved along the clean, grassy margin of the road, beneath the thickly-hanging boughs of the orchards, through the quiet of the hour and place, and the rich maturity of the summer, she was even conscious of a sort of luxurious melancholy. The Baroness had the amiable weakness of attaching herself to places – even when she had begun with a little aversion; and now, with the prospect of departure, she felt tenderly toward this well-wooded corner of the Western world, where the sunsets were so beautiful and one's ambitions were so pure. Mrs Acton was able to receive her; but on entering this lady's large, freshly-scented room the Baroness saw that she was looking very ill. She was wonderfully white and transparent, and, in her flowered arm-chair, she made no attempt to move. But she flushed a little – like a young girl, the Baroness thought – and she rested her clear, smiling eyes upon those of her visitor. Her voice was low and monotonous, like a voice that had never expressed any human passions.

'I have come to bid you good-bye,' said Eugenia. 'I shall soon be going away.'

'When are you going away?'

'Very soon – any day.'

'I am very sorry,' said Mrs Acton. 'I hoped you would stay always.'

'Always?' Eugenia demanded.

'Well, I mean a long time,' said Mrs Acton, in her sweet, feeble tone. 'They tell me you are so comfortable – that you have got such a beautiful little house.'

Eugenia stared – that is, she smiled; she thought of her poor little chalet, and she wondered whether her hostess were jesting. 'Yes, my house is exquisite,' she said; 'though not to be compared with yours.'

'And my son is so fond of going to see you,' Mrs Acton added. 'I am afraid my son will miss you.'

'Ah, dear madam,' said Eugenia, with a little laugh, 'I can't stay in America for your son!'

'Don't you like America?'

The Baroness looked at the front of her dress. 'If I liked it – that would not be staying for your son!'

Mrs Acton gazed at her with her grave tender eyes, as if she had not quite understood. The Baroness at last found something irritating in the sweet, soft stare of her hostess; and if one were not bound to be merciful to great invalids she would almost have taken the liberty of pronouncing her, mentally, a fool. 'I am afraid, then, I shall never see you again,' said Mrs Acton. 'You know I am dying.'

'Ah, dear madam,' murmured Eugenia.

'I want to leave my children cheerful and happy. My daughter will probably marry her cousin.'

'Two such interesting young people,' said the Baroness vaguely. She was not thinking of Clifford Wentworth.

'I feel so tranquil about my end,' Mrs Acton went on. 'It is coming so easily, so surely.' And she paused, with her mild gaze always on Eugenia's.

The Baroness hated to be reminded of death; but even in its imminence, so far as Mrs Acton was concerned, she preserved her good manners. 'Ah, madam, you are too charming an invalid,' she rejoined.

But the delicacy of this rejoinder was apparently lost upon her hostes, who went on in her low, reasonable voice. 'I want to leave my children bright and comfortable. You seem to me all so happy here – just as you are. So I wish you could stay. It would be so pleasant for Robert.'

Eugenia wondered what she meant by its being pleasant for Robert; but she felt that she would never know what such a woman as that meant. She got up; she was afraid Mrs Acton would tell her again that she was dying.

'Good-bye, dear madam,' she said. 'I must remember that your strength is precious.'

Mrs Acton took her hand and held it a moment. 'Well, you *have* been happy here, haven't you? And you like us all, don't you? I wish you would stay,' she added, 'in your beautiful little house.'

She had told Eugenia that her waiting-woman would be in the hall, to show her downstairs; but the large landing outside her room was empty, and Eugenia stood there looking about. She felt irritated; the dying lady had not '*la main heureuse*.' She passed slowly downstairs, still looking about. The broad staircase made a great bend, and in the angle was a high window, looking westward, with a deep bench, covered with a row of flowering plants in curious old pots of blue China-ware. The yellow afternoon light came in through the flowers and flickered a little on the white wainscots. Eugenia paused a moment; the house was perfectly still, save for the ticking, somewhere, of a great clock. The lower hall stretched away at the foot of the stairs, half covered over with a large Oriental rug. Eugenia lingered a little, noticing a great many things. '*Comme c'est bien!*' she said to herself; such a large, solid, irreproachable basis for existence the place seemed to her to indicate. And then she reflected that Mrs Acton was soon to withdraw from it. The reflexion accompanied her the rest of the way downstairs, where she paused again, making more observations. The hall was extremely broad, and on either side of the front door was a wide, deeply-set window, which threw the shadows of everything back into the house. There were high-backed chairs along the wall and big Eastern vases upon tables, and, on either side, a large cabinet with a glass front and little curiosities within, dimly gleaming. The doors were open – into the darkened parlour, the library, the dining-room. All these rooms seemed empty. Eugenia passed along, and stopped a moment on the threshold of each. '*Comme c'est bien!*' she murmured again; she had thought of just such a house as this when she decided to come to America. She opened the front door for herself – her light tread had summoned none of the servants – and on the threshold she gave a last look. Outside, she was still in the humour for curious contemplation; so instead of going directly down the little drive, to the gate, she wandered away toward the garden, which lay to the right of the house. She had not gone many yards over the grass before she paused quickly; she perceived a gentleman stretched upon the level verdure, beneath a tree. He had not heard her coming and he lay motionless, flat on his back, with his hands clasped under his head, staring up at the sky; so that the Baroness was able to reflect, at her leisure, upon the question of his identity. It was that of a person who had lately been much in her thoughts; but her first impulse, nevertheless, was to turn away; the last thing she desired was to have the air of coming in quest of Robert Acton. The gentleman on the grass, however, gave her no time to decide; he could not long remain unconscious of so agreeable a presence. He rolled back his eyes, stared, gave an exclamation, and then jumped up. He stood an instant, looking at her.

'Excuse my ridiculous position,' he said.

'I have just now no sense of the ridiculous. But, in case you have, don't imagine I came to see you.'

'Take care,' rejoined Acton, 'how you put it into my head! I was thinking of you.'

'The occupation of extreme leisure!' said the Baroness. 'To think of a woman when you are in that position is no compliment.'

'I didn't say I was thinking well!' Acton affirmed, smiling.

She looked at him, and then she turned away. 'Though I didn't come to see you,' she said, 'remember at least that I am within your gates.'

'I am delighted – I am honoured! Won't you come into the house?'

'I have just come out of it. I have been calling upon your mother. I have been bidding her farewell.'

'Farewell?' Acton demanded.

'I am going away,' said the Baroness. And she turned away again, as if to illustrate her meaning.

'When are you going?' asked Acton, standing a moment in his place. But the Baroness made no answer, and he followed her.

'I came this way to look at your garden,' she said, walking back to the gate, over the grass. 'But I must go.'

'Let me at least go with you.' He went with her, and they said nothing till they reached the gate. It was open, and they looked down the road, which was darkened over with long bosky shadows. 'Must you go straight home?' Acton asked.

But she made no answer. She said, after a moment, 'Why have you not been to see me?' He said nothing, and then she went on. 'Why don't you answer me?'

'I am trying to invent an answer,' Acton confessed.

'Have you none ready?'

'None that I can tell you,' he said. 'But let me walk with you now.'

'You may do as you like.'

She moved slowly along the road, and Acton went with her. Presently he said, 'If I had done as I liked I would have come to see you several times.'

'Is that invented?' asked Eugenia.

'No, that is natural. I stayed away because—'

'Ah, here comes the reason, then!'

'Because I wanted to think about you.'

'Because you wanted to lie down!' said the Baroness. 'I have seen you lie down – almost — in my drawing-room.'

Acton stopped in the road, with a movement which seemed to beg her to linger a little. She paused, and he looked at her a while; he thought her very charming. 'You are jesting,' he said; 'but if you are really going away it is very serious.'

'If I stay,' and she gave a little laugh, 'it is more serious still!'

'When shall you go?'

'As soon as possible.'

'And why?'

'Why should I stay?'

'Because we all admire you so.'

'That is not a reason. I am admired also in Europe.' And she began to walk homeward again.

'What could I say to keep you?' asked Acton. He wanted to keep her, and it was a fact that he had been thinking of her for a week. He was in love with her now; he was conscious of that, or he thought he was; and the only question with him was whether he could trust her.

'What can you say to keep me?' she repeated. 'As I want very much to go it is not in my interest to tell you. Besides, I can't imagine.'

He went on with her in silence; he was much more affected by what she had told him than appeared. Ever since that evening of his return from Newport her image had had a terrible power to trouble him. What Clifford Wentworth had told him – that had affected him, too, in an adverse sense; but it had not liberated him from the discomfort of a charm of which his intelligence was impatient. 'She is not honest, she is not honest,' he kept murmuring to himself. That is what he had been saying to the summer sky, ten minutes before. Unfortunately, he was unble to say it finally, definitively; and now that he was near her it seemed to matter wonderfully little. 'She is a woman who will lie,' he had said to himself. Now, as he went along, he reminded himself of this observation; but it failed to frighten him as it had done before. He almost wished he could make her lie and then convict her of it, so that he might see how he should like that. He kept thinking of this as he walked by her side, while she moved forward with her light, graceful dignity. He had sat with her before; he had driven with her; but he had never walked with her.

'By Jove, how *comme il faut* she is!' he said, as he observed her sidewise. When they reached the cottage in the orchard she passed into the gate without asking him to follow; but she turned round, as he stood there, to bid him good night.

'I asked you a question the other night which you never answered,' he said. 'Have you sent off that document – liberating yourself?'

She hesitated for a single moment – very naturally. Then, 'Yes,' she said simply.

He turned away; he wondered whether that would do for his lie. But he saw her again that evening, for the Baroness reappeared at her uncle's. He had little talk with her, however; two gentlemen had driven out from Boston, in a buggy, to call upon Mr Wentworth and his daughters, and Madame Münster was an object of absorbing interest to both of the visitors. One of them, indeed, said nothing to her; he only sat and watched with intense gravity, and leaned forward solemnly, presenting his ear (a very large one), as if he were deaf, whenever she dropped an observation. He had evidently been impressed with the idea of her misfortunes and reverses; he never smiled. His companion adopted a lighter, easier style; sat as near as possible to Madame Münster; attempted to draw her out, and proposed every few moments a new topic of conversation. Eugenia was less vividly responsive than usual, and had less to say than, from her brilliant reputation, her interlocutor expected, upon the relative merits of European and American institutions; but she was inaccessible to Robert Acton, who roamed about the piazza with his hands in his pockets, listening for the grating sound of the buggy from Boston as it should be brought round to the side door. But he listened in vain, and at last he lost patience. His sister came to him and begged him to take her home, and he presently went off with her. Eugenia observed him leaving the house with Lizzie; in her present mood the fact seemed a contribution to her irritated conviction that he had several precious qualities. 'Even that *mal-élevée* little girl,' she reflected, 'makes him do what she wishes.'

She had been sitting just within one of the long windows that opened upon the piazza; but very soon after Acton had gone away she got up abruptly, just when the talkative gentleman from Boston was asking her what she thought of the 'moral tone' of that city. On the piazza she encountered Clifford Wentworth, coming round from the other side of the house. She stopped him; she told him she wished to speak to him.

'Why didn't you go home with your cousin?' she asked.

Clifford stared. 'Why, Robert has taken her,' he said.

'Exactly so. But you don't usually leave that to him.'

'Oh,' said Clifford, 'I want to see those fellows start off. They don't know how to drive.'

'It is not, then, that you have quarrelled with your cousin?'

Clifford reflected a moment, and then with a simplicity which had, for the Baroness, a singularly baffling quality, 'Oh no; we have made up!' he said.

She looked at him for some moments; but Clifford had begun to be afraid of the Baroness's looks, and he endeavoured, now, to shift himself out of their range. 'Why do you never come to see me any more?' she asked. 'Have I displeased you?'

'Displeased me? Well, I guess not!' said Clifford, with a laugh.

'Why haven't you come, then?'

'Well, because I am afraid of getting shut up in that back room.'

Eugenia kept looking at him. 'I should think you would like that.'

'Like it!' cried Clifford.

'I should, if I were a young man calling upon a charming woman.'

'A charming woman isn't much use to me when I am shut up in that back room!'

'I am afraid I am not of much use to you anywhere!' said Madame Münster. 'And yet you know how I have offered to be.'

'Well,' observed Clifford, by way of response, 'there comes the buggy.'

'Never mind the buggy. Do you know I am going away?'

'Do you mean now?'

'I mean in a few days. I leave this place.'

'You are going back to Europe?'

'To Europe, where you are to come and see me.'

'Oh yes, I'll come out there,' said Clifford.

'But before that,' Eugenia declared, 'you must come and see me here.'

'Well, I shall keep clear of that back room!' rejoined her simple young kinsman.

The Baroness was silent a moment. 'Yes, you must come frankly – boldly. That will be very much better. I see that now.'

'I see it!' said Clifford. And then, in an instant, 'What's the matter with that buggy?' His practised ear had apparently detected an unnatural creak in the wheels of the light vehicle which had been brought to the portico, and he hurried away to investigate so grave an anomaly.

The Baroness walked homeward, alone, in the starlight, asking herself a question. Was she to have gained nothing – was she to have gained nothing?

Gertrude Wentworth had held a silent place in the little circle gathered about the two gentlemen from Boston. She was not interested in the visitors; she was watching Madame Münster, as she constantly watched her. She knew that Eugenia also was not interested – that she was bored; and Gertrude was absorbed in study of the problem how, in spite of her indifference and her absent attention, she managed to have such a charming manner. That was the manner Gertrude would have liked to have; she determined to cultivate it, and she wished that – to give her the charm – she might in future very often be bored. While she was engaged in these researches, Felix Young was looking for Charlotte, to whom he had something to say. For some time now he had had something to say to Charlotte, and this evening his sense of the propriety of holding some special conversation with her had reached the motive point – resolved itself into acute and delightful desire. He wandered through the empty rooms on the large ground-floor of the house, and found her at last in a small apartment denominated, for reasons not immediately apparent, Mr Wentworth's 'office': an extremely neat and well-dusted room, with an array of law-books, in time-darkened sheepskin, on one of the walls; a large map of the United States on the other, flanked on either side by an old steel engraving of one of Raphael's Madonnas, and on the third several glass cases containing specimens of butterflies and beetles. Charlotte was sitting by the lamp, embroidering a slipper. Felix did not ask for whom the slipper was destined; he saw it was very large.

He moved a chair toward her and sat down, smiling as usual, but, at first, not speaking. She watched him with her needle poised, and with a certain shy, fluttered look which she always wore when he approached her. There was something in Felix's manner that quickened her modesty, her self-consciousness; if absolute choice had been given her she would have preferred never to find herself alone with him; and, in fact, though she thought him a most brilliant, distinguished, and well-meaning person, she had exercised a much larger amount of tremulous tact than he had ever suspected to circumvent the accident of *tête-à-tête*. Poor Charlotte could have given no account of the matter that would not have seemed unjust both to herself and to her foreign kinsman; she could only have said – or rather, she would never have said it – that she did not like so much gentleman's society at once. She was not reassured, accordingly, when he began, emphasizing his words with a kind of admiring radiance, 'My dear cousin, I am enchanted at finding you alone.'

'I am very often alone,' Charlotte observed. Then she quickly added, 'I don't mean I am lonely!'

'So clever a woman as you is never lonely,' said Felix. 'You have company in your beautiful work.' And he glanced at the big slipper.

'I like to work,' declared Charlotte simply.

'So do I!' said her companion. 'And I like to idle too. But it is not to idle that I have come in search of you. I want to tell you something very particular.'

'Well,' murmured Charlotte; 'of course, if you must—'

'My dear cousin,' said Felix, 'it's nothing that a young lady may not listen to. At least I suppose it isn't. But *voyons*; you shall judge. I am terribly in love.'

'Well, Felix,' began Miss Wentworth gravely. But her very gravity appeared to check the development of her phrase.

'I am in love with your sister; but in love, Charlotte – in love!' the young man pursued. Charlotte had laid her work in her lap; her hands were tightly folded on top of it; she was staring at the carpet. 'In short, I'm in love, dear lady,' said Felix. 'Now I want you to help me.'

'To help you?' asked Charlotte, with a tremor.

'I don't mean with Gertrude; she and I have a perfect understanding; and oh, how well she understands one! I mean with your father and with the world in general, including Mr Brand.'

'Poor Mr Brand!' said Charlotte slowly, but with a simplicity which made it evident to Felix that the young minister had not repeated to Miss Wentworth the talk that had lately occurred between them.

'Ah, now, don't say "poor" Mr Brand! I don't pity Mr Brand at all. But I pity your father a little, and I don't want to displease him. Therefore, you see, I want you to plead for me. You don't think me very shabby, eh?'

'Shabby?' exclaimed Charlotte softly, for whom Felix represented the most polished and iridescent qualities of mankind.

'I don't mean in my appearance,' rejoined Felix, laughing; for Charlotte was looking at his boots. 'I mean in my conduct. You don't think it's an abuse of hospitality?'

'To – to care for Gertrude?' asked Charlotte.

'To have really expressed one's self. Because I *have* expressed myself, Charlotte; I must tell you the whole truth – I have! Of course I want to marry her – and here is the difficulty. I held off as long as I could; but she is such a terribly fascinating person! She's a strange creature, Charlotte; I don't believe you really know her.' Charlotte took up her tapestry again, and again she laid it down. 'I know your father has had higher views,' Felix continued; 'and I think you have shared them. You have wanted to marry her to Mr Brand.'

'Oh no,' said Charlotte, very earnestly. 'Mr Brand has always admired her. But we did not want anything of that kind.'

Felix stared. 'Surely marriage was what you proposed?'

'Yes; but we didn't wish to force her.'

'*À la bonne heure!* That's very unsafe, you know. With these arranged marriages there is often the deuce to pay.'

'Oh, Felix,' said Charlotte, 'we didn't want to "arrange".'

'I am delighted to hear that. Because in such cases – even when the woman is a thoroughly good creature – she can't help looking for a compensation. A charming fellow comes along – and *voilà*!' Charlotte sat mutely staring at the floor, and Felix presently added, 'Do go on with your slipper. I like to see you work.'

Charlotte took up her variegated canvas, and began to draw vague blue stitches in a big round rose. 'If Gertrude is so – so strange,' she said, 'why do you want to marry her?'

'Ah, that's it, dear Charlotte! I like strange women; I always have liked them. Ask Eugenia! And Gertrude is wonderful; she says the most beautiful things!'

Charlotte looked at him, almost for the first time, as if her meaning required to be severely pointed. 'You have a great influence over her.'

'Yes – and no!' said Felix. 'I had at first, I think; but now it is six of one and half a dozen of the other; it is reciprocal. She affects me strongly – for she *is* so strong. I don't believe you know her; it's a beautiful nature.'

'Oh yes, Felix; I have always thought Gertrude's nature beautiful.'

'Well, if you think so now,' cried the young man, 'wait and see! She's a folded flower. Let me pluck her from the parent tree and you will see her expand. I'm sure you will enjoy it.'

'I don't understand you,' murmured Charlotte. 'I *can't*, Felix.'

'Well, you can understand this – that I beg you to say a good word for me to your father. He regards me, I naturally believe, as a very light fellow, a Bohemian, an irregular character. Tell him I am not all this; if I ever was, I have forgotten it. I am fond of pleasure – yes; but of innocent pleasure. Pain is all one; but in pleasure, you know, there are tremendous distinctions. Say to him that Gertrude is folded flower and that I am a serious man!'

Charlotte got up from her chair, slowly rolling up her work. 'We know you are very kind to every one, Felix,' she said. 'But we are extremely sorry for Mr Brand.'

'Of course you are – you especially! Because,' added Felix hastily, 'you are a woman. But I don't pity him. It ought to be enough for any man that you take an interest in him.'

'It is not enough for Mr Brand,' said Charlotte simply. And she stood there a moment, as if waiting conscientiously for anything more that Felix might have to say.

'Mr Brand is not so keen about his marriage as he was,' he presently said. 'He is afraid of your sister. He begins to think she is wicked.'

Charlotte looked at him now with beautiful appealing eyes – eyes into which he saw the tears rising. 'Oh, Felix, Felix!' she cried, 'what have you done to her?'

'I think she was asleep; I have waked her up!'

But Charlotte, apparently, was really crying; she walked straight out of the room. And Felix, standing there and meditating, had the apparent brutality to take satisfaction in her tears.

Late that night Gertrude, silent and serious, came to him in the garden; it was a kind of appointment. Gertrude seemed to like appointments. She plucked a handful of heliotrope and stuck it in the front of her dress, but she said nothing. They walked together along one of the paths, and Felix looked at the great, square, hospitable house, massing itself vaguely in the starlight, with all its windows darkened.

'I have a little of a bad conscience,' he said. 'I oughtn't to meet you this way till I have got your father's consent.'

Gertrude looked at him for some time. 'I don't understand you.'

'You very often say that,' he said. 'Considering how little we understand each other, it is a wonder how well we get on!'

'We have done nothing but meet since you came here – but meet alone. The first time I ever saw you we were alone,' Gertrude went on. 'What is the difference now? Is it because it is at night?'

'The difference, Gertrude,' said Felix, stepping in the path, 'the difference is that I love you more – more than before!' And then they stood there, talking, in the warm stillness and in front of the closed dark house. 'I have been talking to Charlotte – been trying to bespeak her interest with your father. She has a kind of sublime perversity; was ever a woman so bent upon cutting off her own head?'

'You are too careful,' said Gertrude; 'you are too diplomatic.'

'Well,' cried the young man, 'I didn't come here to make any one unhappy!'

Gertrude looked round her a while in the odorous darkness. 'I will do anything you please,' she said.

'For instance?' said Felix, smiling.

'I will go away. I will do anything you please.'

Felix looked at her in solemn admiration. 'Yes, we will go away,' he said. 'But we will make peace first.'

Gertrude looked about her again, and then she broke out passionately, 'Why do they try to make one feel guilty? Why do they make it so difficult? Why can't they understand?'

'I will make them understand!' said Felix. He drew her hand into his arm, and they wandered about in the garden, talking, for an hour.

Chapter Twelve

Felix allowed Charlotte time to plead his cause; and then, on the third day, he sought an interview with his uncle. It was in the morning; Mr Wentworth was in his office; and, on going in, Felix found that Charlotte was at that moment in conference with he father. She had, in fact, been constantly near him since her interview with Felix! She had made up her mind that it was her duty to repeat very literally her cousin's passionate plea. She had accordingly followed Mr Wentworth about like a shadow, in order to find him at hand when she should have mustered sufficient composure to speak. For poor Charlotte, in this matter, naturally lacked composure; especially when she meditated upon some of Felix's intimations. It was not cheerful work, at the best, to keep giving small hammer-taps to the coffin in which one had laid away, for burial, the poor little unacknowledged offspring of one's own misbehaving heart; and the occupation was not rendered more agreeable by the fact that the ghost of one's stifled dream had been summoned from the shades by the strange, bold words of a talkative young foreigner. What had Felix meant by saying that Mr Brand was not so keen? To herself her sister's justly-depressed suitor had shown no sign of faltering. Charlotte trembled all over when she allowed herself to believe for an instant now and then that, privately, Mr Brand might have faltered; and as it seemed to give more force to Felix's words to repeat them to her father, she was waiting until she should have taught herself to be very calm. But she had now begun to tell Mr Wentworth that she was extremely anxious. She was proceeding to develop this idea, to enumerate the objects of her anxiety, when Felix came in.

Mr Wentworth sat there, with his legs crossed, lifting his dry, pure countenance from the Boston *Advertiser*. Felix entered smiling, as if he had something particular to say, and his uncle looked at him as if he both expected and deprecated this event. Felix vividly expressing himself had come to be a formidable figure to his uncle, who had not yet arrived at definite views as to a proper tone. For the first time in his life, as I have said, Mr Wentworth shirked a responsibility; he earnestly desired that it might not be laid upon him to determine how his nephew's lighter propositions should be treated. He lived under an apprehension that Felix might yet beguile him into assent to doubtful inductions, and his conscience instructed him that the best form of vigilance was the avoidance of discussion. He hoped that the pleasant episode of his nephew's visit would pass away without a further lapse of consistency.

Felix looked at Charlotte with an air of understanding, and then at Mr Wentworth, and then at Charlotte again. Mr Wentworth bent his refined eyebrows upon his nephew and stroked down the first page of the *Advertiser*. 'I ought to have brought a bouquet,' said Felix, laughing. 'In France they always do.'

'We are not in France,' observed Mr Wentworth gravely, while Charlotte earnestly gazed at him.

'No, luckily, we are not in France, where I am afraid I should have a harder time of it. My dear Charlotte, have you rendered me that delightful service?' And Felix bent toward her as if some one had been presenting him.

Charlotte looked at him with almost frightened eyes; and Mr Wentworth thought this might be the beginning of a discussion. 'What is the bouquet for?' he inquired, by way of turning it off.

Felix gazed at him, smiling. '*Pour la demande!*' And then, drawing up a chair, he seated himself, hat in hand, with a kind of conscious solemnity.

Presently he turned to Charlotte again. 'My good Charlotte, my admirable Charlotte,' he murmured, 'you have not played me false – you have not sided against me?'

Charlotte got up, trembling extremely, though imperceptibly. 'You must speak to my father yourself,' she said. 'I think you are clever enough.'

But Felix, rising too, begged her to remain. 'I can speak better to an audience!' he declared.

'I hope it is nothing disagreeable,' said Mr Wentworth.

'It's something delightful, for me!' And Felix, laying down his hat, clasped his hands a little between his knees. 'My dear uncle,' he said, 'I desire, very earnestly, to marry your daughter Gertrude.' Charlotte sank slowly into her chair again, and Mr Wentworth sat staring, with a light in his face that might have been flashed back from an iceberg. He stared and stared; he said nothing. Felix fell back, with his hands still clasped. 'Ah – you don't like it. I was afraid!' He blushed deeply, and Charlotte noticed it – remarking to herself that it was the first time she had ever seen him blush. She began to blush herself, and to reflect that he might be much in love.

'This is very abrupt,' said Mr Wentworth at last.

'Have you never suspected it, dear uncle?' Felix inquired. 'Well, that proves how discreet I have been. Yes, I thought you wouldn't like it.'

'It is very serious, Felix,' said Mr Wentworth.

'You think it's an abuse of hospitality!' exclaimed Felix, smiling again.

'Of hospitality? – an abuse?' his uncle repeated very slowly.

'That is what Felix said to me,' said Charlotte conscientiously.

'Of course you think so; don't defend yourself!' Felix pursued. 'It *is* an abuse, obviously; the most I can claim is that it is perhaps a pardonable one. I simply fell head over heels in love; one can hardly help that. Though you are Gertrude's progenitor I don't believe you know how attractive she is. Dear uncle, she contains the elements of a singularity – I may say a strangely – charming woman!'

'She has always been to me an object of extreme concern,' said Mr Wentworth. 'We have always desired her happiness.'

'Well, here it is!' Felix declared. 'I will make her happy. She believes it, too. Now, hadn't you noticed that?'

'I had noticed that she was much changed,' Mr Wentworth declared, in a tone whose unexpressive, unimpassioned quality appeared to Felix to reveal a profundity of opposition. 'It may be that she is only becoming what you call a charming woman.'

'Gertrude, at heart, is so earnest, so true,' said Charlotte, very softly, fastening her eyes upon her father.

'I delight to hear you praise her!' cried Felix.

'She has a very peculiar temperament,' said Mr Wentworth.

'Eh, even that is praise!' Felix rejoined. 'I know I am not the man you might have looked for. I have no position and no fortune; I can give Gertrude no place in the world. A place in the world – that's what she ought to have; that would bring her out.'

'A place to do her duty!' remarked Mr Wentworth.

'Ah, how charmingly she does it – her duty!' Felix exclaimed, with a radiant face. 'What an exquisite conception she has of it! But she comes honestly by that, dear uncle.' Mr Wentworth and Charlotte both looked at him as if they were watching a greyhound doubling. 'Of course with me she will hide her light under a bushel,' he continued; 'I being the bushel! Now I know you like me – you have certainly proved it: but you think I am frivolous and penniless and shabby! Granted – granted – a thousand times granted. I have been a loose fish – a fiddler, a painter, an actor. But there is this to be said: In the first place, I fancy you exaggerate; you lend me qualities I haven't had. I have been a Bohemian – yes; but in Bohemia I always passed for a gentleman. I wish you could see some of my old *camarades* – they would tell you! It was the liberty I liked, but not the opportunities! My sins were all peccadilloes; I always respected my neighbour's property – my neighbour's wife. Do you see, dear uncle?' Mr Wentworth ought to have seen, his cold blue eyes were intently fixed. 'And then, *c'est fini!* It's all over. *Je me range.* I have settled down to a jog-trot. I find I can earn my living – a very fair one – by going about the world and painting bad portraits. It's not a glorious profession, but it is a perfectly respectable one. You won't deny that, eh? Going about the world, I say? I must not deny that, for that I am afraid I shall always do – in quest of agreeable sitters. When I say agreeable, I mean susceptible of delicate flattery and prompt of payment. Gertrude declares she is willing to share my wanderings and help to pose my models. She even thinks it will be charming; and that brings me to my third point. Gertrude likes me. Encourage her a little and she will tell you so.'

Felix's tongue obviously moved much faster than the imagination of his auditors; his eloquence, like the rocking of a boat in a deep, smooth lake, made long eddies of silence. And he seemed to be pleading and chattering still, with his brightly eager smile, his uplifted eyebrows, his expressive mouth, after he had ceased speaking, and while, with his glance quickly turning from the father to the daughter, he sat waiting for the effect of his appeal. 'It is not your want of means,' said Mr Wentworth, after a period of severe reticence.

'Now it's delightful of you to say that! Only don't say it's my want of character. Because I have a character – I assure you I have; a small one, a little slip of a thing, but still something tangible.'

'Ought you not to tell Felix that it is Mr Brand, father?' Charlotte asked, with infinite mildness.

'It is not only Mr Brand,' Mr Wentworth solemnly declared. And he looked at his knee for a long time. 'It is difficult to explain,' he said. He wished, evidently, to be very just. 'It rests on moral grounds, as Mr Brand says. It is the question whether it is the best thing for Gertrude.'

'What is better – what is better, dear uncle?' Felix rejoined urgently, rising in his urgency and standing before Mr Wentworth. His uncle had been looking at his knee; but when Felix moved he transferred his gaze to the handle of the door which faced him. 'It is usually a fairly good thing for a girl to marry the man she loves!' cried Felix.

While he spoke Mr Wentworth saw the handle of the door begin to turn; the door opened and remained slightly ajar until Felix had delivered himself of the cheerful axiom just quoted. Then it opened altogether, and Gertrude stood there. She looked excited; there was a spark in her sweet dull eyes. She came in slowly, but with an air of resolution, and closing the door softly, looked round at the three persons present. Felix went to her with tender gallantry, holding out his hand, and Charlotte made a place for her on the sofa. But Gertrude put her hands behind her and made no motion to sit down.

'We are talking of you!' said Felix.

'I know it,' she answered. 'That's why I came.' And she fastened her eyes on her father, who returned her gaze very fixedly. In his own cold blue eyes there was a kind of pleading, reasoning light.

'It is better you should be present,' said Mr Wentworth. 'We are discussing your future.'

'Why discuss it?' asked Gertrude. 'Leave it to me.'

'That is, to me!' cried Felix.

'I leave it, in the last resort, to a greater wisdom than ours,' said the old man.

Felix rubbed his forehead gently. 'But *en attendant* the last resort, your father lacks confidence,' he said to Gertrude.

'Haven't you confidence in Felix?' Gertrude was frowning; there was something about her that her father and Charlotte had never seen. Charlotte got up and came to her, as if to put her arm round her; but suddenly, she seemed afraid to touch her.

Mr Wentworth, however, was not afraid. 'I have had more confidence in Felix than in you,' he said.

'Yes, you have never had confidence in me – never, never! I don't know why.'

'Oh sister, sister!' murmured Charlotte.

'You have always needed advice,' Mr Wentworth declared. 'You have had a difficult temperament.'

'Why do you call it difficult? It might have been easy, if you had allowed it. You wouldn't let me be natural. I don't know what you wanted to make of me. Mr Brand was the worst.'

Charlotte at last took hold of her sister. She laid her two hands upon Gertrude's arm. 'He cares so much for you,' she almost whispered.

Gertrude looked at her intently an instant; then kissed her. 'No, he does not,' she said.

'I have never seen you so passionate,' observed Mr Wentworth, with an air of indignation mitigated by high principles.

'I am sorry if I offend you,' said Gertrude.

'You offend me, but I don't think you are sorry.'

'Yes, father, she is sorry,' said Charlotte.

'I would even go further, dear uncle,' Felix interposed. 'I would question whether she really offends you. How can she offend you?'

To this Mr Wentworth made no immediate answer. Then, in a moment, 'She has not profited as we hoped.'

'Profited? *Ah voilà!*' Felix exclaimed.

Gertrude was very pale; she stood looking down. 'I have told Felix I would go away with him,' she presently said.

'Ah, you have said some admirable things!' cried the young man.

'Go away, sister?' asked Charlotte.

'Away – away; to some strange country.'

'That is to frighten you,' said Felix, smiling at Charlotte.

'To – what do you call it?' asked Gertrude, turning an instant to Felix. 'To Bohemia.'

'Do you propose to dispense with preliminaries?' asked Mr Wentworth, getting up.

'Dear uncle, *vous plaisantez*!' cried Felix. 'It seems to me that these are preliminaries.'

Gertrude turned to her father. 'I *have* profited,' she said.'You wanted to form my character. Well, my character is formed – for my age. I know what I want; I have chosen. I am determined to marry this gentleman.'

'You had better consent, sir,' said Felix, very gently.

'Yes, sir, you had better consent,' added a very different voice.

Charlotte gave a little jump, and the others turned to the direction from which it had come. It was the voice of Mr Brand, who had stepped through the long window which stood open to the piazza. He stood patting his forehead with his pocket handkerchief; he was very much flushed; his face wore a singular expression.

'Yes, sir, you had better consent,' Mr Brand repeated, coming forward. 'I know what Miss Gertrude means.'

'My dear friend!' murmured Felix, laying his hand caressingly on the young minister's arm.

Mr Brand looked at him; then at Mr Wentworth; lastly at Gertrude. He did not look at Charlotte. But Charlotte's earnest eyes were fastened to his own countenance; they were asking an immense question of it. The answer to this question could not come all at once; but some of the elements of it were there. It was one of the elements of it that Mr Brand was very red, that he held his head very high, that he had a bright excited eye and an air of embarrassed boldness – the air of a man who has taken a resolve in the execution of which he apprehends the failure, not of his moral, but of his personal, resources. Charlotte thought he looked very grand; and it is incontestable that Mr Brand felt very grand. This, in fact, was the grandest moment of his life; and it was natural that such a moment should contain opportunities of awkwardness for a large, stout, modest young man.

'Come in, sir,' said Mr Wentworth, with an angular wave of his hand. 'It is very proper that you should be present.'

'I know what you are talking about,' Mr Brand rejoined. 'I heard what your nephew said.'

'And he heard what you said!' exclaimed Felix, patting him again on the arm.

'I am not sure that I understood,' said Mr Wentworth, who had angularity in his voice as well as in his gestures.

Gertrude had been looking hard at her former suitor. She had been puzzled, like her sister; but her imagination moved more quickly than Charlotte's. 'Mr Brand asked you to let Felix take me away,' she said to her father.

The young minister gave her a strange look. 'It is not because I don't want to see you any more,' he declared, in a tone intended as it were for publicity.

'I shouldn't think you would want to see me any more,' Gertrude answered gently.

Mr Wentworth stood staring. 'Isn't this rather a change, sir?' he inquired.

'Yes, sir.' And Mr Brand looked everywhere; only still not at Charlotte. 'Yes, sir,' he repeated. And he held his handkerchief a few moments to his lips.

'Where are our moral grounds?' demanded Mr Wentworth, who had always thought Mr Brand would be just the thing for a younger daughter with a peculiar temperament.

'It is sometimes very moral to change, you know,' suggested Felix.

Charlotte had softly left her sister's side. She had edged gently toward her father, and now her hand found its way into his arm. Mr Wentworth had folded up the *Advertiser* into a surprisingly small compass, and, holding the roll with one hand, he earnestly clasped it with the other. Mr Brand was looking at him; and yet, though Charlotte was so near, his eyes failed to meet her own. Gertrude watched her sister.

'It is better not to speak of change,' said Mr Brand. 'In one sense there is no change. There was something I desired – something I asked of you; I desire something still – I ask it of you.' And he paused a moment; Mr Wentworth looked bewildered. 'I should like, in my ministerial capacity, to unite this young couple.'

Gertrude, watching her sister, saw Charlotte flushing intensely, and Mr Wentworth felt her pressing upon his arm. 'Heavenly Powers!' murmured Mr Wentworth. And it was the nearest approach to profanity he had ever made.

'That is very nice; that is very handsome!' Felix exclaimed.

'I don't understand,' said Mr Wentworth; though it was plain that every one else did.

'That is very beautiful, Mr Brand,' said Gertrude, emulating Felix.

'I should like to marry you. It will give me great pleasure.'

'As Gertrude says, it's a beautiful idea,' said Felix.

Felix was smiling, but Mr Brand was not even trying to. He himself treated his proposition very seriously. 'I have thought of it, and I should like to do it,' he affirmed.

Charlotte, meanwhile, was standing with expanded eyes. Her imagination, as I have said, was not so rapid as her sister's, but now it had taken several little jumps. 'Father,' she murmured, 'consent!'

Mr Brand heard her; he looked away. Mr Wentworth, evidently, had no imagination at all. 'I have always thought,' he began slowly, 'that Gertrude's character required a special line of development.'

'Father,' repeated Charlotte, '*consent*.'

Then at last Mr Brand looked at her. Her father felt her leaning more heavily upon his folded arm than she had ever done before; and this, with a certain sweet faintness in her voice, made him wonder what was the matter. He looked down at her and saw the encounter of her gaze with the young theologian's; but even this told him nothing, and he continued to be bewildered. Nevertheless, 'I consent,' he said at last, 'since Mr Brand recommends it.'

'I should like to perform the ceremony very soon,' observed Mr Brand, with a sort of solemn simplicity.

'Come, come, that's charming!' cried Felix profanely.

Mr Wentworth sank into his chair. 'Doubtless, when you understand it,' he said, with a certain judicial asperity.

Gertrude went to her sister and led her away, and Felix having passed his arm into Mr Brand's and stepped out of the long window with him, the old man was left sitting there in unillumined perplexity.

Felix did no work that day. In the afternoon, with Gertrude, he got into one of the boats, and floated about with idly-dipping oars. They talked a good deal of Mr Brand – though not exclusively.

'That was a fine stroke,' said Felix. 'It was really heroic.'

Gertrude sat musing, with her eyes upon the ripples. 'That was what he wanted to be; he wanted to do something fine.'

'He won't be comfortable till he has married us,' said Felix. 'So much the better.'

'He wanted to be magnanimous; he wanted to have a fine moral pleasure. I know him so well,' Gertrude went on. Felix looked at her; she spoke slowly, gazing at the clear water. 'He thought of it a great deal, night and day. He thought it would be beautiful. At last he made up his mind that it was his duty, his duty to do just that – nothing less than that. He felt exalted; he felt sublime. That's how he likes to feel. It is better for him than if I had listened to him.'

'It's better for me,' smiled Felix. 'But do you know, as regards the sacrifice, that I don't believe he admired you when this decision was taken quite so much as he had done a fortnight before?'

'He never admired me. He admires Charlotte; he pitied me. I know him so well.'

'Well, then, he didn't pity you so much.'

Gertrude looked at Felix a little, smiling. 'You shouldn't permit yourself,' she said, 'to diminish the splendour of his action. He admires Charlotte,' she repeated.

'That's capital!' said Felix laughingly, and dipping his oars. I cannot say exactly to which member of Gertrude's phrase he alluded; but he dipped his oars again, and they kept floating about.

Neither Felix nor his sister, on that day, was present at Mr Wentworth's at the evening repast. The two occupants of the chalet dined together, and the young man informed his companion that his marriage was now an assured fact. Eugenia congratulated him, and replied that if he were as reasonable a husband as he had been, on the whole, a brother, his wife would have nothing to complain of.

Felix looked at her a moment, smiling. 'I hope,' he said, 'not to be thrown back on my reason.'

'It is very true,' Eugenia rejoined, 'that one's reason is dismally flat. It's a bed with the mattress removed.'

But the brother and sister, later in the evening, crossed over to the larger house, the Baroness desiring to compliment her prospective sister-in-law. They found the usual circle upon the piazza, with the exception of Clifford Wentworth and Lizzie Acton; and as every one stood up as usual to welcome the Baroness, Eugenia had an admiring audience for her compliment to Gertrude.

Robert Acton stood on the edge of the piazza, leaning against one of the white columns, so that he found himself next to Eugenia, while she acquitted herself of a neat little discourse of congratulation.

'I shall be so glad to know you better,' she said 'I have seen so much less of you than I should have liked. Naturally; now I see the reason why! You will love me a little, won't you? I think I may say I gain on being known.' And terminating these observances with the softest cadence of her voice, the Baroness imprinted a sort of grand official kiss upon Gertrude's forehead.

Increased familiarity had not, to Gertrude's imagination, diminished the mysterious impressiveness of Eugenia's personality, and she felt flattered and transported by this little ceremony. Robert Acton also seemed to admire it, as he admired so many of the gracious manifestations of Madame Münster's wit.

They had the privilege of making him restless, and on this occasion he walked away, suddenly, with his hands in his pockets, and then came back and leaned against his column. Eugenia was now complimenting her uncle upon his daughter's engagement, and Mr Wentworth was listening with his usual plain yet refined politeness. It is to be supposed that by this time his perception of the mutual relations of the young people who surrounded him had become more acute; but he still took the matter very seriously, and he was not at all exhilarated.

'Felix will make her a good husband,' said Eugenia. 'He will be a charming companion; he has a great quality – indestructible gaiety.'

'You think that's a great quality?' asked the old man.

Eugenia meditated, with her eyes upon his. 'You think one gets tired of it, eh?'

'I don't know that I am prepared to say that,' said Mr Wentworth.

'Well, we will say, then, that it is tiresome for others but delightful for one's self. A woman's husband, you know, is supposed to be her second self; so that, for Felix and Gertrude, gaiety will be a common property.'

'Gertrude was always very gay,' said Mr Wentworth. He was trying to follow this argument.

Robert Acton took his hands out of his pockets and came a little nearer to the Baroness. 'You say you gain by being known,' he said. 'One certainly gains by knowing you.'

'What have *you* gained?' asked Eugenia.

'An immense amount of wisdom.'

'That's a questionable advantage for a man who was already so wise!'

Acton shook his head. 'No, I was a great fool before I knew you!'

'And being a fool you made my acquaintance! You are very complimentary.'

'Let me keep it up,' said Acton, laughing. 'I hope, for our pleasure, that your brother's marriage will detain you.'

'Why should I stop for my brother's marriage when I would not stop for my own?' asked the Baroness.

'Why shouldn't you stop in either case, now that, as you say, you have dissolved that mechanical tie that bound you to Europe?'

The Baroness looked at him a moment. 'As I say? You look as if you doubted it.'

'Ah,' said Acton, returning her glance, 'that is a remnant of my old folly! We have other attractions,' he added. 'We are to have another marriage.'

But she seemed not to hear him; she was looking at him still. 'My word was never doubted before,' she said.

'We are to have another marriage,' Acton repeated, smiling.

Then she appeared to understand. 'Another marriage?' And she looked at the others. Felix was chattering to Gertrude; Charlotte, at a distance, was watching them; and Mr Brand, in quite another corner, was turning his back to them and, with his hands under his coat-tails and his large head on one side, was looking at the small, tender crescent of a young moon. 'It ought to be Mr Brand and Charlotte,' said Eugenia, 'but it doesn't look like it.'

'There,' Acton answered, 'you must judge just now by contraries. There is more than there looks to be. I expect that combination one of these days; but that is not what I meant.'

'Well,' said the Baroness, 'I never guess my own lovers; so I can't guess other people's.'

Acton gave a loud laugh, and he was about to add a rejoinder when Mr Wentworth approached his niece. 'You will be interested to hear,' the old man said, with a momentary aspiration toward jocosity, 'of another matrimonial venture in our little circle.'

'I was just telling the Baroness,' Acton observed.

'Mr Acton was apparently about to announce his own engagement,' said Eugenia.

Mr Wentworth's jocosity increased. 'It is not exactly that; but it is in the family. Clifford, hearing this morning that Mr Brand had expressed a desire to tie the nuptial knot for his sister, took it into his head to arrange that, while his hand was in, our good friend should perform a like ceremony for himself and Lizzie Acton.'

The Baroness threw back her head and smiled at her uncle; then turning, with an intenser radiance, to Robert Acton, 'I am certainly very stupid not to have thought of that,' she said. Acton looked down to his boots, as if he thought he had perhaps reached the limits of legitimate experimentation, and for a moment Eugenia said nothing more. It had been, in fact, a sharp knock, and she needed to recover herself. This was done, however, promptly enough. 'Where are the young people?' she asked.

'They are spending the evening with my mother.'

'Is not the thing very sudden?'

Acton looked up. 'Extremely sudden. There had been a tacit understanding; but within a day or two Clifford appears to have received some mysterious impulse to precipitate the affair.'

'The impulse,' said the Baroness, 'was the charms of your very pretty sister.'

'But my sister's charms were an old story; he had always known her.' Acton had begun to experiment again.

Here, however, it was evident the Baroness would not help him. 'Ah, one can't say! Clifford is very young; but he is a nice boy.'

'He's a likeable sort of boy, and he will be a rich man.' This was Acton's last experiment; Madame Münster turned away.

She made but a short visit, and Felix took her home. In her little drawing-room she went almost straight to the mirror over the chimney-piece, and, with a candle uplifted, stood looking into it. 'I shall not wait for your marriage,' she said to her brother. 'Tomorrow my maid shall pack up.'

'My dear sister,' Felix exclaimed, 'we are to be married immediately! Mr Brand is too uncomfortable.'

But Eugenia, turning and still holding her candle aloft, only looked about the little sitting-room at her gimcracks and curtains and cushions. 'My maid shall pack up,' she repeated. '*Bonté divine*, what rubbish! I feel like a strolling actress; these are my "properties".'

'Is the play over, Eugenia?' asked Felix.

She gave him a sharp glance. 'I have spoken my part.'

'With great applause!' said her brother.

'Oh, applause – applause!' she murmured. And she gathered up two or three of her dispersed draperies. She glanced at the beautiful brocade, and then, 'I don't see how I can have endured it!' she said.

'Endure it a little longer. Come to my wedding.'

'Thank you; that's your affair. My affairs are elsewhere.'

'Where are you going?'

'To Germany – by the first ship.'

'You have decided not to marry Mr Acton?'

'I have refused him,' said Eugenia.

Her brother looked at her in silence. 'I am sorry,' he rejoined at last. 'But I was very discreet, as you asked me to be. I said nothing.'

'Please continue, then, not to allude to the matter,' said Eugenia.

Felix inclined himself gravely. 'You shall be obeyed. But your position in Germany?' he pursued.

'Please to make no observations upon it.'

'I was only going to say that I supposed it was altered.'

'You are mistaken.'

'But I thought you had signed—'

'I have not signed!' said the Baroness.

Felix urged her no further, and it was arranged that he should immediately assist her to embark.

Mr Brand was indeed, it appeared, very impatient to consummate his sacrifice and deliver the nuptial benediction which would set it off so handsomely; but Eugenia's impatience to withdraw from a country in which she had not found the fortune she had come to seek was even less to be mistaken. It is true she had not made any very serious exertion; but she appeared to feel justified in generalizing – in deciding that the conditions of action on this provincial continent were not favourable to really superior women. The elder world was, after all, their natural field. The unembarrassed directness with which she proceeded to apply these intelligent conclusions appeared to the little circle of spectators who have figured in our narrative but the supreme exhibition of a character to which the experience of life had imparted an inimitable pliancy. It had a distinct effect upon Robert Acton, who, for the two days preceding her departure, was a very restless and irritated mortal. She passed her last evening at her uncle's, where she had never been more charming; and in parting with Clifford Wentworth's affianced bride she drew from her own finger a curious old ring and presented it to her with the prettiest speech and kiss. Gertrude, who as an affianced bride was also indebted to her gracious bounty, admired this little incident extremely, and Robert Acton almost wondered whether it did not give him the right, as Lizzie's brother and guardian, to offer in return a handsome present to the Baroness. It would have made him extremely happy to be able to offer a handsome present to the Baroness; but he abstained from this expression of his sentiments, and they were in consequence, at the very last, by so much the less comfortable. It was almost at the very last that he saw her – late the night before she went to Boston to embark.

'For myself, I wish you might have stayed,' he said. 'But not for your own sake.'

'I don't make so many differences,' said the Baroness. 'I am simply sorry to be going.'

'That's a much deeper difference than mine,' Acton declared; 'for you mean you are simply glad!'

Felix parted with her on the deck of the ship. 'We shall often meet over there,' he said.

'I don't know,' she answered. 'Europe seems to me much larger than America.'

Mr Brand, of course, in the days that immediately followed, was not the only impatient spirit; but it may be said that of all the young spirits interested in the event none rose more eagerly to the level of the occasion. Gertrude left her father's house with Felix Young; they were imperturbably happy, and they went far away. Clifford and his young wife sought their felicity in a narrower circle, and the latter's influence upon her husband was such as to justify, strikingly, that theory of the elevating effect of easy intercourse with clever women which Felix had propounded to Mr Wentworth. Gertrude was for a good while a distant figure, but she came back when Charlotte married Mr Brand. She was present at the wedding feast, where Felix's gaiety confessed to no change. Then she disappeared, and the echo of a gaiety of her own, mingled with that of her husband, often came back to the home of her earlier years. Mr Wentworth at last found himself listening for it; and Robert Acton, after his mother's death, married a particularly nice young girl.

Daisy Miller

Chapter One

At the little town of Vevey, in Switzerland, there is a particularly comfortable hotel. There are, indeed, many hotels; for the entertainment of tourists is the business of the place, which, as many travellers will remember, is seated upon the edge of a remarkably blue lake – a lake that it behoves every tourist to visit. The shore of the lake presents an unbroken array of establishments of this order, of every category, from the 'grand hotel' of the newest fashion, with a chalk-white front, a hundred balconies, and a dozen flags flying from its roof, to the little Swiss *pension* of an elder day, with its name inscribed in German-looking lettering upon a pink or yellow wall, and an awkward summer-house in the angle of the garden. One of the hotels at Vevey, however, is famous, even classical, being distinguished from many of its upstart neighbours by an air both of luxury and of maturity. In this region, in the month of June, American travellers are extremely numerous; it may be said, indeed, that Vevey assumes at this period some of the characteristics of an American watering-place. There are sights and sounds which evoke a vision, an echo, of Newport and Saratoga. There is a flitting hither and thither of 'stylish' young girls, a rustling of muslin flounces, a rattle of dance-music in the morning hours, a sound of high-pitched voices at all times. You receive an impression of these things at the excellent inn of the Trois Couronnes, and are transported in fancy to the Ocean House or to Congress Hall. But at the Trois Couronnes, it must be added, there are other features that are much at variance with these suggestions: neat German waiters, who look like secretaries of legation; Russian princesses sitting in the garden; little Polish boys walking about, held by the hand, with their governors; a view of the snowy crest of the Dent du Midi and the picturesque towers of the Castle of Chillon.

I hardly know whether it was the analogies or the differences that were uppermost in the mind of a young American, who, two or three years ago, sat in the garden of the Trois Couronnes, looking about him, rather idly, at some of the graceful objects I have mentioned. It was a beautiful summer morning, and in whatever fashion the young American looked at things, they must have seemed to him charming. He had come from Geneva the day before, by the little steamer, to see his aunt, who was staying at the hotel – Geneva having been for a long time his place of residence. But his aunt had a headache – his aunt had almost always a headache – and now she was shut up in her room, smelling camphor, so that he was at liberty to wander about. He was some seven-and-twenty years of age; when his friends spoke of him, they usually said that he was at Geneva, 'studying'. When his enemies spoke of him they said – but, after all, he had no enemies; he was an extremely amiable fellow, and universally liked. What I should say is, simply, that when certain persons spoke of him they affirmed that the reason of his spending so much time at Geneva was that he was extremely devoted to a lady who lived there – a foreign lady – a person older than himself. Very few Americans – indeed I think none – had ever seen this lady, about whom there were some singular stories. But Winterbourne had an old attachment for the little metropolis of Calvinism; he had been put to school there as a boy, and he had afterwards gone to college there – circumstances which had led to his forming a great many youthful friendships. Many of these he had kept, and they were a source of great satisfaction to him.

After knocking at his aunt's door and learning that she was indisposed, he had taken a walk about the town, and then he had come in to his breakfast. He had now finished his breakfast, but he was drinking a small cup of coffee, which had been served to him on a little table in the garden by one of the waiters who looked like an attaché. At last he finished his coffee and lit a cigarette. Presently a small boy came walking along the path – an urchin of nine or ten. The child, who was diminutive for his years, had an aged expression of countenance, a pale complexion, and sharp little features. He was dressed in knickerbockers with red stockings, which displayed his poor little spindleshanks; he also wore a brilliant red cravat. He carried in his hand a long alpenstock, the sharp point of which he thrust into everything that he approached – the flowerbeds, the garden-benches, the trains of the ladies' dresses. In front of Winterbourne he paused, looking at him with a pair of bright, penetrating little eyes.

'Will you give me a lump of sugar?' he asked, in a sharp, hard little voice – a voice immature, and yet, somehow, not young.

Winterbourne glanced at the small table near him, on which his coffee-service rested, and saw that several morsels of sugar remained. 'Yes, you may take one,' he answered; 'but I don't think sugar is good for little boys.'

This little boy stepped forward and carefully selected three of the coveted fragments, two of which he buried in the pocket of his knickerbockers, depositing the other as promptly in another place. He poked his alpenstock, lance-fashion, into Winterbourne's bench, and tried to crack the lump of sugar with his teeth.

'Oh, blazes; it's har-r-d!' he exclaimed, pronouncing the adjective in a peculiar manner.

Winterbourne had immediately perceived that he might have the honour of claiming him as a fellow countryman. 'Take care you don't hurt your teeth,' he said, paternally.

'I haven't got any teeth to hurt. They have all come out. I have only got seven teeth. My mother counted them last night, and one came out right afterwards. She said she'd slap me if any more came out. I can't help it. It's this old Europe. It's the climate that makes them come out. In America they didn't come out. It's these hotels.'

Winterbourne was much amused. 'If you eat three lumps of sugar, your mother will certainly slap you,' he said.

'She's got to give me some candy, then,' rejoined his young interlocutor. 'I can't get any candy here – any American candy. American candy's the best candy.'

'And are American little boys the best little boys?' asked Winterbourne.

'I don't know. I'm an American boy,' said the child.

'I see you are one of the best!' laughed Winterbourne.

'Are you an American man?' pursued this vivacious infant. And then, on Winterbourne's affirmative reply – 'American men are the best,' he declared.

His companion thanked him for the compliment; and the child, who had now got astride of his alpenstock, stood looking about him, while he attacked a second lump of sugar. Winterbourne wondered if he himself had been like this in his infancy, for he had been brought to Europe at about this age.

'Here comes my sister!' cried the child, in a moment. 'She's an American girl.'

Winterbourne looked along the path and saw a beautiful young lady advancing. 'American girls are the best girls,' he said, cheerfully, to his young companion.

'My sister ain't the best!' the child declared. 'She's always blowing at me.'

'I imagine that is your fault, not hers,' said Winterbourne. The young lady meanwhile had drawn near. She was dressed in white muslin, with a hundred frills and flounces, and knots of pale-coloured ribbon. She was bare-headed; but she balanced in her hand a large parasol, with a deep border of embroidery; and she was strikingly, admirably pretty. 'How pretty they are!' thought Winterbourne, straightening himself in his seat, as if he were prepared to rise.

The young lady paused in front of his bench, near the parapet of the garden, which overlooked the lake. The little boy had now converted his alpenstock into a vaulting-pole, by the aid of which he was springing about in the gravel, and kicking it up not a little.

'Randolph,' said the young lady, 'what *are* you doing?'

'I'm going up the Alps,' replied Randolph. 'This is the way!' And he gave another little jump, scattering the pebbles about Winterbourne's ears.

'That's the way they come down,' said Winterbourne.

'He's an American man!' cried Randolph, in his little hard voice.

The young lady gave no heed to this announcement, but looked straight at her brother. 'Well, I guess you had better be quiet,' she simply observed.

It seemed to Winterbourne that he had been in a manner presented. He got up and stepped slowly towards the young girl, throwing away his cigarette. 'This little boy and I have made acquaintance,' he said, with great civility. In Geneva, as he had been perfectly aware, a young man was not at liberty to speak to a young unmarried lady except under certain rarely occurring conditions; but here, at Vevey, what conditions could be better than these? – a pretty American girl coming and standing in front of you in a garden. This pretty American girl, however, on hearing Winterbourne's observation, simply glanced at him; she then turned her head and looked over the parapet, at the lake and the opposite mountains. He wondered whether he had gone too far; but he decided that he must advance farther rather than retreat. While he was thinking of something else to say, the young lady turned to the little boy again.

'I should like to know where you got that pole,' she said.

'I bought it!' responded Randolph.

'You don't mean to say you're going to take it to Italy!'

'Yes, I am going to take it to Italy!' the child declared.

The young girl glanced over the front of her dress, and smoothed out a knot or two of ribbon. Then she rested her eyes upon the prospect again. 'Well, I guess you had better leave it somewhere,' she said, after a moment.

'Are you going to Italy?' Winterbourne inquired, in a tone of great respect.

The young lady glanced at him again. 'Yes, sir,' she replied. And she said nothing more.

'Are you – a – going over the Simplon?' Winterbourne pursued, a little embarrassed.

'I don't know,' she said. 'I suppose it's some mountain. Randolph, what mountain are we going over?'

'Going where?' the child demanded.

'To Italy,' Winterbourne explained.

'I don't know,' said Randolph. 'I don't want to go to Italy. I want to go to America.'

'Oh, Italy is a beautiful place!' rejoined the young man.

'Can you get candy there?' Randolph loudly inquired.

'I hope not,' said his sister. 'I guess you have had enough candy, and mother thinks so too.'

'I haven't had any for ever so long – for a hundred weeks!' cried the boy, still jumping about.

The young lady inspected her flounces and smoothed her ribbons again; and Winterbourne presently risked an observation upon the beauty of the view. He was ceasing to be embarrassed, for he had begun to perceive that she was not in the least embarrassed herself. There had not been the slightest alteration in her charming complexion; she was evidently neither offended nor fluttered. If she looked another way when he spoke to her, and seemed not particularly to hear him, this was simply her habit, her manner. Yet, as he talked a little more, and pointed out some of the objects of interest in the view, with which she appeared quite unacquainted, she gradually gave him more of the benefit of her glance; and then he saw that this glance was perfectly direct and unshrinking. It was not, however, what would have been called an immodest glance, for the young girl's eyes were singularly honest and fresh. They were wonderfully pretty eyes; and, indeed, Winterbourne had not seen for a long time anything prettier than his fair countrywoman's various features – her complexion, her nose, her ears, her teeth. He had a great relish for feminine beauty; he was addicted to observing and analysing it; and as regards this young lady's face he made several observations. It was not at all insipid, but it was not exactly expressive; and though it was eminently delicate, Winterbourne mentally accused it – very forgivingly – of a want of finish. He thought it very possible that Master Randolph's sister was a coquette; he was sure she had a spirit of her own; but in her bright, sweet, superficial little visage there was no mockery, no irony. Before long it became obvious that she was much disposed towards conversation. She told him that they were going to Rome for the winter – she and her mother and Randolph. She asked him if he was a real 'American'; she wouldn't have taken him for one; he seemed more like a German – this was said after a little hesitation, especially when he spoke. Winterbourne, laughing, answered that he had met Germans who spoke like Americans; but that he had not, so far as he remembered, met an American who spoke like a German. Then he asked her if she would not be more comfortable in sitting upon the bench which he had just quitted. She answered that she liked standing up and walking about; but she presently sat down. She told him she was from New York State – 'if you know where that is'. Winterbourne learned more about her by catching hold of her small, slippery brother and making him stand a few minutes by his side.

'Tell me your name, my boy,' he said.

'Randolph C. Miller,' said the boy, sharply. 'And I'll tell you her name'; and he levelled his alpenstock at his sister.

'You had better wait till you are asked!' said this young lady, calmly.

'I should like very much to know your name,' said Winterbourne.

'Her name is Daisy Miller!' cried the child. 'But that isn't her real name; that isn't her name on her cards.'

'It's a pity you haven't got one of my cards!' said Miss Miller.

'Her real name is Annie P. Miller,' the boy went on.

'Ask him *his* name,' said his sister, indicating Winterbourne.

But on this point Randolph seemed perfectly indifferent; he continued to supply information with regard to his own family. 'My father's name is Ezra B. Miller,' he announced. 'My father ain't in Europe; my father's in a better place than Europe.'

Winterbourne imagined for a moment that this was the manner in which the child had been taught to intimate that Mr Miller had been removed to the sphere of celestial rewards. But Randolph immediately added, 'My father's in Schenectady. He's got a big business. My father's rich, you bet.'

'Well!' ejaculated Miss Miller, lowering her parasol and looking at the embroidered border. Winterbourne presently released the child, who departed, dragging his alpenstock along the path. 'He doesn't like Europe,' said the young girl. 'He wants to go back.'

'To Schenectady, you mean?'

'Yes; he wants to go right home. He hasn't got any boys here. There is one boy here, but he always goes round with a teacher; they won't let him play.'

'And your brother hasn't any teacher?' Winterbourne inquired.

'Mother thought of getting him one, to travel round with us. There was a lady told her of a very good teacher; an American lady – perhaps you know her – Mrs Sanders. I think she came from Boston. She told her of this teacher, and we thought of getting him to travel round with us. But Randolph said he didn't want a teacher travelling round with us. He said he wouldn't have lessons when he was in the cars. And we *are* in the cars about half the time. There was an English lady we met in the cars – I think her name was Miss Featherstone; perhaps you know her. She wanted to know why I didn't give Randolph lessons – give him "instructions", she called it. I guess he could give me more instruction than I could give him. He's very smart.'

'Yes,' said Winterbourne; 'he seems very smart.'

'Mother's going to get a teacher for him as soon as we get to Italy. Can you get good teachers in Italy?'

'Very good, I should think,' said Winterbourne.

'Or else she's going to find some school. He ought to learn some more. He's only nine. He's going to college.' And in this way Miss Miller continued to converse upon the affairs of her family, and upon other topics. She sat there with her extremely pretty hands, ornamented with very brilliant rings, folded in her lap, and with her pretty eyes now resting upon those of

Winterbourne, now wandering over the garden, the people who passed by, and the beautiful view. She talked to Winterbourne as if she had known him a long time. He found it very pleasant. It was many years since he had heard a young girl talk so much. It might have been said of this unknown young lady, who had come and sat down beside him upon a bench, that she chattered. She was very quiet, she sat in a charming tranquil attitude; but her lips and her eyes were constantly moving. She had a soft, slender, agreeable voice, and her tone was decidedly sociable. She gave Winterbourne a history of her movements and intentions, and those of her mother and brother, in Europe, and enumerated, in particular, the various hotels at which they had stopped. 'That English lady in the cars,' she said – 'Miss Featherstone – asked me if we didn't all live in hotels in America. I told her I had never been in so many hotels in my life as since I came to Europe. I have never seen so many – it's nothing but hotels.' But Miss Miller did not make this remark with a querulous accent; she appeared to be in the best humour with everything. She declared that the hotels were very good, when once you got used to their ways, and that Europe was perfectly sweet. She was not disappointed – not a bit. Perhaps it was because she had heard so much about it before. She had ever so many intimate friends that had been there ever so many times. And then she had had ever so many dresses and things from Paris. Whenever she put on a Paris dress she felt as if she were in Europe.

'It was a kind of wishing-cap,' said Winterbourne.

'Yes,' said Miss Miller, without examining this analogy; 'it always made me wish I was here. But I needn't have done that for dresses. I am sure they send all the pretty ones to America; you see the most frightful things here. The only thing I don't like,' she proceeded, 'is the society. There isn't any society; or, if there is, I don't know where it keeps itself. Do you? I suppose there is some society somewhere, but I haven't seen anything of it. I'm very fond of society, and I have always had a great deal of it. I don't mean only in Schenectady, but in New York. I used to go to New York every winter. In New York I had lots of society. Last winter I had seventeen dinners given me; and three of them were by gentlemen,' added Daisy Miller. 'I have more friends in New York than in Schenectady – more gentlemen friends; and more young lady friends too,' she resumed in a moment. She paused again for an instant; she was looking at Winterbourne with all her prettiness in her lively eyes and in her light, slightly monotonous smile. 'I have always had,' she said, 'a great deal of gentlemen's society.'

Poor Winterbourne was amused, perplexed, and decidedly charmed. He had never yet heard a young girl express herself in just this fashion; never, at least, save in cases where to say such things seemed a kind of demonstrative evidence of a certain laxity of deportment. And yet was he to accuse Miss Daisy Miller of actual or potential *inconduite*, as they said at Geneva? He felt that he had lived at Geneva so long that he had lost a good deal; he had become dishabituated to the American tone. Never, indeed, since he had grown old enough to appreciate things, had he encountered a young American girl of so pronounced a type as this. Certainly she was very charming; but how deucedly sociable! Was she simply a pretty girl from New York State – were they all like that, the pretty girls who had a good deal of gentlemen's society? Or was she also a designing, an audacious, an unscrupulous young person? Winterbourne had lost his instinct in this matter, and his reason could not help him. Miss Daisy Miller looked extremely innocent. Some people had told him that, after all, American girls were exceedingly innocent; and others had told him that, after all, they were not. He was inclined to think Miss Daisy Miller was a flirt – a pretty American flirt. He had never, as yet, had any relations with young ladies of this category. He had known, here in Europe, two or three women – persons older than Miss Daisy Miller, and provided, for respectability's sake, with husbands – who were great coquettes – dangerous, terrible women, with whom one's relations were liable to take a serious turn. But this young girl was not a coquette in that sense; she was very unsophisticated; she was only a pretty American flirt. Winterbourne was almost grateful for having found the formula that applied to Miss Daisy Miller. He leaned back in his seat; he remarked to himself that she had the most charming nose he had ever seen; he wondered what were the regular conditions and limitations of one's intercourse with a pretty American flirt. It presently became apparent that he was on the way to learn.

'Have you been to that old castle?' asked the young girl, pointing with her parasol to the far-gleaming walls of the Château de Chillon.

'Yes, formerly, more than once,' said Winterbourne. 'You too, I suppose, have seen it?'

'No; we haven't been there. I want to go there dreadfully. Of course I mean to go there. I wouldn't go away from here without having seen that old castle.'

'It's a very pretty excursion,' said Winterbourne, 'and very easy to make. You can drive, you know, or you can go by the little steamer.'

'You can go in the cars,' said Miss Miller.

'Yes; you can go in the cars,' Winterbourne assented.

'Our courier says they take you right up to the castle,' the young girl continued. 'We were going last week; but my mother gave out. She suffers dreadfully from dyspepsia. She said she couldn't go. Randolph wouldn't go either; he says he doesn't think much of old castles. But I guess we'll go this week, if we can get Randolph.'

'Your brother is not interested in ancient monuments?' Winterbourne inquired, smiling.

'He says he don't care much about old castles. He's only nine. He wants to stay at the hotel. Mother's afraid to leave him alone, and the courier won't stay with him; so we haven't been to many places. But it will be too bad if we don't go up there.' And Miss Miller pointed again at the Château de Chillon.

'I should think it might be arranged,' said Winterbourne. 'Couldn't you get someone to stay – for the afternoon – with Randolph?'

Miss Miller looked at him a moment; and then, very placidly – 'I wish *you* would stay with him!' she said.

Winterbourne hesitated a moment. 'I would much rather go to Chillon with you.'

'With me?' asked the young girl, with the same placidity.

She didn't rise, blushing as a young girl at Geneva would have done; and yet Winterbourne, conscious that he had been very bold, thought it possible she was offended. 'With your mother,' he answered very respectfully.

But it seemed that both his audacity and his respect were lost upon Miss Daisy Miller. 'I guess my mother won't go, after all,' she said. 'She don't like to ride round in the afternoon. But did you really mean what you said just now; that you would like to go up there?'

'Most earnestly,' Winterbourne declared.

'Then we may arrange it. If mother will stay with Randolph, I guess Eugenio will.'

'Eugenio?' the young man inquired.

'Eugenio's our courier. He doesn't like to stay with Randolph; he's the most fastidious man I ever saw. But he's a splendid courier. I guess he'll stay at home with Randolph if mother does, and then we can go to the castle.'

Winterbourne reflected for an instant as lucidly as possible – 'we' could only mean Miss Daisy Miller and himself. This programme seemed almost too agreeable for credence; he felt as if he ought to kiss the young lady's hand. Possibly he would have done so – and quite spoiled the project; but at this moment another person – presumably Eugenio – appeared. A tall, handsome man, with superb whiskers, wearing a velvet morning-coat and a brilliant watch-chain, approached Miss Miller, looking sharply at her companion. 'Oh, Eugenio!' said Miss Miller, with the friendliest accent.

Eugenio had looked at Winterbourne from head to foot, he now bowed gravely to the young lady. 'I have the honour to inform mademoiselle that luncheon is upon the table.'

Miss Miller slowly rose. 'See here, Eugenio,' she said. 'I'm going to that old castle, anyway.'

'To the Château de Chillon, mademoiselle?' the courier inquired. 'Mademoiselle has made arrangements?' he added, in a tone which struck Winterbourne as very impertinent.

Eugenio's tone apparently threw, even to Miss Miller's own apprehension, a slightly ironical light upon the young girl's situation. She turned to Winterbourne, blushing a little – a very little. 'You won't back out?' she said.

'I shall not be happy till we go!' he protested.

'And you are staying in this hotel?' she went on. 'And you are really an American?'

The courier stood looking at Winterbourne, offensively. The young man, at least, thought his manner of looking an offence to Miss Miller; it conveyed an imputation that she 'picked up' acquaintances. 'I shall have the honour of presenting you to a person who will tell you all about me,' he said smiling, and referring to his aunt.

'Oh well, we'll go some day,' said Miss Miller. And she gave him a smile and turned away. She put up her parasol and walked back to the inn beside Eugenio. Winterbourne stood looking after her; and as she moved away, drawing her muslin furbelows over the gravel, said to himself that she had the *tournure* of a princess.

Chapter Two

He had, however, engaged to do more than proved feasible, in promising to present his aunt, Mrs Costello, to Miss Daisy Miller. As soon as the former lady had got better of her headache he waited upon her in her apartment; and, after the proper inquiries in regard to her health, he asked her if she had observed, in the hotel, an American family – a mamma, a daughter, and a little boy.

'And a courier?' said Mrs Costello. 'Oh, yes, I have observed them. Seen them – heard them – and kept out of their way.' Mrs Costello was a widow with a fortune; a person of much distinction, who frequently intimated that, if she were not so dreadfully liable to sick-headaches, she would probably have left a deeper impress upon her time. She had a long pale face, a high nose, and a great deal of very striking white hair, which she wore in large puffs and *rouleaux* over the top of her head. She had two sons married in New York, and another who was now in Europe. This young man was amusing himself at Homburg, and, though he was on his travels, was rarely perceived to visit any particular city at the moment selected by his mother for her own appearance there. Her nephew, who had come up to Vevey expressly to see her, was therefore more attentive than those who, as she said, were nearer to her. He had imbibed at Geneva the idea that one must always be attentive to one's aunt. Mrs Costello had not seen him for many years, and she was greatly pleased with him, manifesting her approbation by initiating him into many of the secrets of that social sway which, as she gave him to understand, she exerted in the American capital. She admitted that she was very exclusive; but, if he were acquainted with New York, he would see that one had to be. And her picture of the minutely hierarchical constitution of the society of that city, which she presented to him in many different lights, was, to Winterbourne's imagination, almost oppressively striking.

He immediately perceived, from her tone, that Miss Daisy Miller's place in the social scale was low. 'I am afraid you don't approve of them,' he said.

'They are very common,' Mrs Costello declared. 'They are the sort of Americans that one does one's duty by not – not accepting.'

'Ah, you don't accept them?' said the young man.

'I can't, my dear Frederick. I would if I could, but I can't.'

'The young girl is very pretty,' said Winterbourne, in a moment.

'Of course she's pretty. But she is very common.'

'I see what you mean, of course,' said Winterbourne, after another pause.

'She has that charming look that they all have,' his aunt resumed. 'I can't think where they pick it up; and she dresses in perfection – no, you don't know how well she dresses. I can't think where they get their taste.'

'But, my dear aunt, she is not, after all, a Comanche savage.'

'She is a young lady,' said Mrs Costello, 'who has an intimacy with her mamma's courier?'

'An intimacy with the courier?' the young man demanded.

'Oh, the mother is just as bad! They treat the courier like a familiar friend – like a gentleman. I shouldn't wonder if he dines with them. Very likely they have never seen a man with such good manners, such fine clothes, so like a gentleman. He probably corresponds to the young lady's idea of a Count. He sits with them in the garden, in the evening. I think he smokes.'

Winterbourne listened with interest to these disclosures; they helped him to make up his mind about Miss Daisy. Evidently she was rather wild. 'Well,' he said, 'I am not a courier, and yet she was very charming to me.'

'You had better have said at first,' said Mrs Costello with dignity, 'that you had made her acquaintance.'

'We simply met in the garden, and we talked a bit.'

'*Tout bonnement!* And pray what did you say?'

'I said I should take the liberty of introducing her to my admirable aunt.'

'I am much obliged to you.'

'It was to guarantee my respectability,' said Winterbourne.

'And pray who is to guarantee hers?'

'Ah, you are cruel!' said the young man. 'She's a very nice girl.'

'You don't say that as if you believed it,' Mrs Costello observed.

'She is completely uncultivated,' Winterbourne went on. 'But she is wonderfully pretty, and, in short, she is very nice. To prove that I believe it, I am going to take her to the Château de Chillon.'

'You two are going off there together? I should say it proved just the contrary. How long had you known her, may I ask, when this interesting project was formed. You haven't been twenty-four hours in the house.'

'I had known her half an hour!' said Winterbourne, smiling.

'Dear me!' cried Mrs Costello. 'What a dreadful girl!'

Her nephew was silent for some moments. 'You really think, then,' he began earnestly, and with a desire for trustworthy information – 'you really think that –' But he paused again.

'Think what, sir,' said his aunt.

'That she is the sort of young lady who expects a man – sooner or later – to carry her off?'

'I haven't the least idea what such young ladies expect a man to do. But I really think that you had better not meddle with little American girls that are uncultivated, as you call them. You have lived too long out of the country. You will be sure to make some great mistake. You are too innocent.'

'My dear aunt, I am not so innocent,' said Winterbourne, smiling and curling his moustache.

'You are too guilty, then?'

Winterbourne continued to curl his moustache, meditatively. 'You won't let the poor girl know you then?' he asked at last.

'Is it literally true that she is going to the Château de Chillon with you?'

'I think that she fully intends it.'

'Then, my dear Frederick,' said Mrs Costello, 'I must decline the honour of her acquaintance. I am an old woman, but I am not too old – thank Heaven – to be shocked!'

'But don't they all do these things – the young girls in America?' Winterbourne inquired.

Mrs Costello stared a moment. 'I should like to see my grand-daughters do them!' she declared, grimly.

This seemed to throw some light upon the matter, for Winterbourne remembered to have heard that his pretty cousins in New York were 'tremendous flirts'. If, therefore, Miss Daisy Miller exceeded the liberal licence allowed to these young ladies, it was probable that anything might be expected of her. Winterbourne was impatient to see her again, and he was vexed with himself that, by instinct, he should not appreciate her justly.

Though he was impatient to see her, he hardly knew what he should say to her about his aunt's refusal to become acquainted with her; but he discovered, promptly enough, that with Miss Daisy Miller there was no great need of walking on tiptoe. He found her that evening in the garden, wandering about in the warm starlight, like an indolent sylph, and swinging to and fro the largest fan he had ever beheld. It was ten o'clock. He had dined with his aunt, had been sitting with her since dinner, and had just taken leave of her till the morrow. Miss Daisy Miller seemed very glad to see him; she declared it was the longest evening she had ever passed.

'Have you been all alone?' he asked.

'I have been walking round with mother. But mother gets tired walking round,' she answered.

'Has she gone to bed?'

'No she doesn't like to go to bed,' said the young girl. 'She doesn't sleep – not three hours. She says she doesn't know how she lives. She's dreadfully nervous. I guess she sleeps more than she thinks. She's gone somewhere after Randolph; she wants to try to get him to go to bed. He doesn't like to go to bed.'

'Let us hope she will persuade him,' observed Winterbourne.

'She will talk to him all she can; but he doesn't like her to talk to him,' said Miss Daisy, opening her fan. 'She's going to try to get Eugenio to talk to him. But he isn't afraid of Eugenio. Eugenio's a splendid courier, but he can't make much impression on Randolph! I don't believe he'll go to bed before eleven.' It appeared that Randolph's vigil was in fact triumphantly prolonged, for Winterbourne strolled about with the young girl for some time without meeting her mother. 'I have been looking round for that lady you want to introduce me to,' his companion resumed. 'She's your aunt.' Then, on Winterbourne's admitting the fact, and expressing some curiosity as to how she had learned it, she said she had heard all about Mrs Costello from the chambermaid. She was very quiet and very *comme il faut*; she wore white puffs; she spoke to no one, and she never dined at the *table d'hôte*. Every two days she had a headache. 'I think that's a lovely description, headache and all!' said Miss Daisy, chattering along in her thin, gay voice. 'I want to know her ever so much. I know just what *your* aunt would be; I know I should like her. She would be very exclusive. I like a lady to be exclusive; I'm dying to be exclusive myself. Well, we *are* exclusive, mother and I. We don't speak to everyone – or they don't speak to us. I suppose it's about the same thing. Anyway, I shall be ever so glad to know your aunt.'

Winterbourne was embarrassed. 'She would be most happy,' he said, 'but I am afraid those headaches will interfere.'

The young girl looked at him through the dusk. 'But I suppose she doesn't have a headache every day,' she said, sympathetically.

Winterbourne was silent a moment. 'She tells me she does,' he answered at last – not knowing what to say.

Miss Daisy Miller stopped and stood looking at him. Her prettiness was still visible in the darkness; she was opening and closing her enormous fan. 'She doesn't want to know me!' she said suddenly. 'Why don't you say so? You needn't be afraid. I'm not afraid!' And she gave a little laugh.

Winterbourne fancied there was a tremor in her voice; he was touched, shocked, mortified by it. 'My dear young lady,' he protested, 'she knows no one. It's her wretched health.'

The young girl walked on a few steps, laughing still. 'You needn't be afraid,' she repeated, 'Why should she want to know me?' Then she paused again; she was close to the parapet of the garden, and in front of her was the starlit lake. There was a vague sheen upon its surface, and in the distance were dimly seen mountain forms. Daisy Miller looked out upon the mysterious prospect, and then she gave another little laugh. 'Gracious! she *is* exclusive!' she said. Winterbourne wondered whether she was seriously wounded, and for a moment almost wished that her sense of injury might be such as to make it becoming in him to attempt to reassure and comfort her. He had a pleasant sense that she would be very approachable for consolatory purposes. He felt then, for the instant, quite ready to sacrifice his aunt, conversationally; to admit that she was a proud, rude woman, and to declare that they needn't mind her. But before he had time to commit himself to this perilous mixture of gallantry and impiety, the young lady, resuming her walk, gave an exclamation in quite another tone. 'Well; here's mother! I guess she hasn't got Randolph to go to bed.' The figure of a lady appeared, at a distance, very indistinct in the darkness, and advancing with a slow and wavering movement. Suddenly it seemed to pause.

'Are you sure it is your mother? Can you distinguish her in this thick dusk?' Winterbourne asked.

'Well!' cried Miss Daisy Miller, with a laugh, 'I guess I know my own mother. And when she has got on my shawl, too! She is always wearing my things.'

The lady in question, ceasing to advance, hovered vaguely about the spot at which she had checked her steps.

'I am afraid your mother doesn't see you,' said Winterbourne. 'Or perhaps,' he added – thinking, with Miss Miller, the joke permissible – 'perhaps she feels guilty about your shawl.'

'Oh, it's a fearful old thing!' the young girl replied, serenely. 'I told her she could wear it. She won't come here, because she sees you.'

'Ah, then,' said Winterbourne, 'I had better leave you.'

'Oh, no; come on!' urged Miss Daisy Miller.

'I'm afraid your mother doesn't approve of my walking with you.'

Miss Miller gave him a serious glance. 'It isn't for me; it's for you – that is, it's for *her*. Well; I don't know who it's for! But mother doesn't like any of my gentlemen friends. She's right down timid. She always makes a fuss if I introduce a gentleman. But I *do* introduce them – almost always. If I didn't introduce my gentlemen friends to mother,' the young girl added, in her little soft, flat monotone, 'I shouldn't think I was natural.'

'To introduce me,' said Winterbourne, 'you must know my name.' And he proceeded to pronounce it.

'Oh, dear; I can't say all that!' said his companion, with a laugh. But by this time they had come up to Mrs Miller, who, as they drew near, walked to the parapet of the garden and leaned upon it, looking intently at the lake and turning her back upon them. 'Mother!' said the young girl, in a tone of decision. Upon this the elder lady turned round. 'Mr Winterbourne,' said Miss Daisy Miller, introducing the young man very frankly and prettily. 'Common' she was, as Mrs Costello had pronounced her; yet it was a wonder to Winterbourne that, with her commonness, she had a singularly delicate grace.

Her mother was a small, spare, light person, with a wandering eye, a very exiguous nose, and a large forehead, decorated with a certain amount of thin, much-frizzled hair. Like her daughter, Mrs Miller was dressed with extreme elegance; she had enormous diamonds in her ears. So far as Winterbourne could observe, she gave him no greeting – she certainly was not looking at him. Daisy was near her, pulling her shawl straight. 'What are you doing, poking round here?' this young lady inquired; but by no means with that harshness of accent which her choice of words may imply.

'I don't know,' said her mother, turning towards the lake again.

'I shouldn't think you'd want that shawl!' Daisy exclaimed.

'Well – I do!' her mother answered, with a little laugh.

'Did you get Randolph to go to bed?' asked the young girl.

'No; I couldn't induce him,' said Mrs Miller, very gently. 'He wants to talk to the waiter. He likes to talk to that waiter.'

'I was telling Mr Winterbourne,' the young girl went on; and to the young man's ear her tone might have indicated that she had been uttering his name all her life.

'Oh, yes!' said Winterbourne; 'I have the pleasure of knowing your son.'

Randolph's mamma was silent; she turned her attention to the lake. But at last she spoke. 'Well, I don't see how he lives!'

'Anyhow, it isn't so bad as it was at Dover,' said Daisy Miller.

'And what occurred at Dover?' Winterbourne asked.

'He wouldn't go to bed at all. I guess he sat up all night – in the public parlour. He wasn't in bed at twelve o'clock: I know that.'

'It was half past twelve,' declared Mrs Miller, with mild emphasis.

'Does he sleep much during the day?' Winterbourne demanded.

'I guess he doesn't sleep much,' Daisy rejoined.

'I wish he would!' said her mother. 'It seems as if he couldn't.'

'I think he's real tiresome,' Daisy pursued.

Then, for some moments, there was silence. 'Well, Daisy Miller,' said the elder lady, presently, 'I shouldn't think you'd want to talk against your own brother!'

'Well, he *is* tiresome, mother,' said Daisy, quite without the asperity of a retort.

'He's only nine,' urged Mrs Miller.

'Well, he wouldn't go to that castle,' said the young girl. 'I'm going there with Mr Winterbourne.'

To this announcement, very placidly made, Daisy's mamma offered no response. Winterbourne took for granted that she deeply disapproved of the projected excursion; but he said to himself that she was a simple, easily managed person, and that a few deferential protestations would take the edge from her displeasure. 'Yes,' he began; 'your daughter has kindly allowed me the honour of being her guide.'

Mrs Miller's wandering eyes attached themselves, with a sort of appealing air, to Daisy, who, however, strolled a few steps farther, gently humming to herself. 'I presume you will go in the cars,' said her mother.

'Yes; or in the boat,' said Winterbourne.

'Well, of course, I don't know,' Mrs Miller rejoined. 'I have never been to that castle.'

'It is a pity you shouldn't go,' said Winterbourne, beginning to feel reassured as to her opposition. And yet he was quite prepared to find that, as a matter of course, she meant to accompany her daughter.

'We've been thinking ever so much about going,' she pursued; 'but it seems as if we couldn't. Of course Daisy – she wants to go round. But there's a lady here – I don't know her name – she says she shouldn't think we'd want to go to see castles *here*; she should think we'd want to wait till we got to Italy. It seems as if there would be so many there,' continued Mrs Miller, with an air of increasing confidence. 'Of course, we only want to see the principal ones. We visited several in England,' she presently added.

'Ah, yes! in England there are beautiful castles,' said Winterbourne. 'But Chillon, here, is very well worth seeing.'

'Well, if Daisy feels up to it—' said Mrs Miller, in a tone impregnated with a sense of the magnitude of the enterprise. 'It seems as if there was nothing she wouldn't undertake.'

'Oh, I think she'll enjoy it!' Winterbourne declared. And he desired more and more to make it a certainty that he was to have the privilege of a *tête-à-tête* with the young lady, who was still strolling along in front of them, softly vocalizing. 'You are not disposed, madam,' he inquired, 'to undertake it yourself?'

Daisy's mother looked at him, an instant, askance, and then walked forward in silence. Then – 'I guess she had better go alone,' she said, simply.

Winterbourne observed to himself that this was a very different type of maternity from that of the vigilant matrons who massed themselves in the forefront of social intercourse in the dark old city at the other end of the lake. But his meditations were interrupted by hearing his name very distinctly pronounced by Mrs Miller's unprotected daughter.

'Mr Winterbourne!' murmured Daisy.

'Mademoiselle!' said the young man.

'Don't you want to take me out in a boat?'

'At present?' he asked.

'Of course!' said Daisy.

'Well, Annie Miller!' exclaimed her mother.

'I beg you, madam, to let her go,' said Winterbourne, ardently; for he had never yet enjoyed the sensation of guiding through the summer starlight a skiff freighted with a fresh and beautiful young girl.

'I shouldn't think she'd want to,' said her mother. 'I should think she'd rather go indoors.'

'I'm sure Mr Winterbourne wants to take me,' Daisy declared. 'He's so awfully devoted!'

'I will row you over to Chillon, in the starlight.'

'I don't believe it!' said Daisy.

'Well!' ejaculated the elder lady again.

'You haven't spoken to me for half an hour,' her daughter went on.

'I have been having some very pleasant conversation with your mother,' said Winterbourne.

'Well; I want you to take me out in a boat!' Daisy repeated. They had all stopped, and she turned round and was looking at Winterbourne. Her face wore a charming smile, her pretty eyes were gleaming, she was swinging her great fan about. No; it's impossible to be prettier than that, thought Winterbourne.

'There are half a dozen boats moored at that landing-place,' he said, pointing to certain steps which descended from the garden to the lake. 'If you will do me the honour to accept my arm, we will go and select one of them.'

Daisy stood there smiling; she threw back her head and gave a little light laugh. 'I like a gentleman to be formal!' she declared.

'I assure you it's a formal offer.'

'I was bound I would make you say something,' Daisy went on.

'You see it's not very difficult,' said Winterbourne. 'But I am afraid you are chaffing me.'

'I think not, sir,' remarked Mrs Miller, very gently.

'Do, then, let me give you a row,' he said to the young girl.

'It's quite lovely, the way you say that!' cried Daisy.

'It will be still more lovely to do it.'

'Yes, it would be lovely!' said Daisy. But she made no movement to accompany him; she only stood there laughing.

'I should think you had better find out what time it is,' interposed her mother.

'It is eleven o'clock, madam,' said a voice, with a foreign accent, out of the neighbouring darkness; and Winterbourne, turning, perceived the florid personage who was in attendance upon the two ladies. He had apparently just approached.

'Oh, Eugenio,' said Daisy, 'I am going out in a boat!'

Eugenio bowed. 'At eleven o'clock, mademoiselle?'

'I am going with Mr Winterbourne. This very minute.'

'Do tell her she can't,' said Mrs Miller to the courier.

'I think you had better not go out in a boat, mademoiselle,' Eugenio declared.

Winterbourne wished to Heaven this pretty girl were not so familiar with her courier; but he said nothing.

'I suppose you don't think it's proper!' Daisy exclaimed, 'Eugenio doesn't think anything's proper.'

'I am at your service,' said Winterbourne.

'Does mademoiselle propose to go alone?' asked Eugenio of Mrs Miller.

'Oh, no; with this gentleman!' answered Daisy's mamma.

The courier looked for a moment at Winterbourne – the latter thought he was smiling – and then, solemnly, with a bow, 'As mademoiselle pleases!' he said.

'Oh, I hoped you would make a fuss!' said Daisy. 'I don't care to go now.'

'I myself shall make a fuss if you don't go,' said Winterbourne.

'That's all I want – a little fuss!' And the young girl began to laugh again.

'Mr Randolph has gone to bed!' the courier announced, frigidly.

'Oh, Daisy; now we can go!' said Mrs Miller.

Daisy turned away from Winterbourne, looking at him, smiling and fanning herself. 'Good night,' she said; 'I hope you are disappointed, or disgusted, or something!'

He looked at her, taking the hand she offered him. 'I am puzzled,' he answered.

'Well; I hope it won't keep you awake!' she said, very smartly; and, under the escort of the privileged Eugenio, the two ladies passed towards the house.

Winterbourne stood looking after them; he was indeed puzzled. He lingered beside the lake for a quarter of an hour, turning over the mystery of the young girl's sudden familiarities and caprices. But the only very definite conclusion he came to was that he should enjoy deucedly 'going off' with her somewhere.

Two days afterwards he went off with her to the Castle of Chillon. He waited for her in the large hall of the hotel, where the couriers, the servants, the foreign tourists were lounging about and staring. It was not the place he would have chosen, but she had appointed it. She came tripping downstairs, buttoning her long gloves, squeezing her folded parasol against her pretty figure, dressed in the perfection of a soberly elegant travelling-costume. Winterbourne was a man of imagination and, as our ancestors used to say, of sensibility; as he looked at her dress and, on the great staircase, her little rapid, confiding step, he felt as if there were something romantic going forward. He could have believed he was going to elope with her. He passed out with her among all the idle people that were assembled there; they were all looking at her very hard; she had begun to chatter as soon as she joined him. Winterbourne's preference had been that they should be conveyed to Chillon in a carriage; but she expressed a lively wish to go in the little steamer; she declared that she had a passion for steamboats. There was always such a lovely breeze upon the water, and you saw such lots of people. The sail was not long, but Winterbourne's companion found time to say a great many things. To the young man himself their little excursion was so much of an escapade – an adventure – that, even allowing for her habitual sense of freedom, he had some expectation of seeing her regard it in the same way. But it must be confessed that, in this particular, he was disappointed. Daisy Miller was extremely animated, she was in charming spirits; but she was apparently not at all excited; she was not fluttered; she avoided neither his eyes nor those of anyone else; she blushed neither when she looked at him nor when she saw that people were looking at her. People continued to look at her a great deal, and Winterbourne took much satisfaction in his pretty companion's distinguished air. He had been a little afraid that she would talk loud, laugh overmuch, and even, perhaps, desire to move about the boat a good deal. But he quite forgot his fears; he sat smiling, with his eyes upon her face, while without moving from her place, she delivered herself of a great number of original reflections. It was the most charming garrulity he had ever heard. He had assented to the idea that she was 'common'; but was she so, after all, or was he simply getting used to her commonness? Her conversation was chiefly of what metaphysicians term the objective cast; but every now and then it took a subjective turn.

'What on *earth* are you so grave about?' she suddenly demanded, fixing her agreeable eyes upon Winterbourne's.

'Am I grave?' he asked. 'I had an idea I was grinning from ear to ear.'

'You look as if you were taking me to a funeral. If that's a grin, your ears are very near together.'

'Should you like me to dance a hornpipe on the deck?'

'Pray do, and I'll carry round your hat. It will pay the expenses of our journey.'

'I never was better pleased in my life,' murmured Winterbourne.

She looked at him a moment, and then burst into a little laugh. 'I like to make you say those things! You're a queer mixture!'

In the castle, after they had landed, the subjective element decidedly prevailed. Daisy tripped about the vaulted chambers, rustled her skirts in the corkscrew staircases, flitted back with a pretty little cry and a shudder from the edge of the *oubliettes*, and turned a singularly well-shaped ear to everything that Winterbourne told her about the place. But he saw that she cared very little for feudal antiquities, and that the dusky traditions of Chillon made but a slight impression upon her. They had the good fortune to have been able to walk about without other companionship than that of the custodian; and Winterbourne arranged with this functionary that they should not be hurried – that they should linger and pause wherever they chose. The custodian interpreted the bargain generously – Winterbourne, on his side, had been generous – and ended by leaving them quite to themselves. Miss Miller's observations were not remarkable for logical consistency; for anything she wanted to say she was sure to find a pretext. She found a great many pretexts in the rugged embrasures of Chillon for asking Winterbourne sudden questions about himself – his family, his previous history, his tastes, his habits, his intentions – and for supplying information upon corresponding points in her own personality. Of her own tastes, habits, and intentions Miss Miller was prepared to give the most definite, and indeed the most favourable, account.

'Well; I hope you know enough!' she said to her companion, after he had told her the history of the unhappy Bonivard. 'I never saw a man that knew so much!' The history of Bonivard had evidently, as they say, gone into one ear and out of the other. But Daisy went on to say that she wished Winterbourne would travel with them and 'go round with them'; they might know something, in that case. 'Don't you want to come and teach Randolph?' she asked. Winterbourne said that nothing could possibly please him so much; but that he had unfortunately other occupations. 'Other occupations? I don't believe it!' said Miss Daisy. 'What do you mean? You are not in business.' The young man admitted that he was not in business; but he had engagements which, even within a day or two, would force him to go back to Geneva. 'Oh, bother!' she said, 'I don't believe it!' and she began to talk about something else. But a few moments later, when he was pointing out to her the pretty design of an antique fireplace, she broke out irrelevantly, 'You don't mean to say you are going back to Geneva?'.

'It is a melancholy fact that I shall have to return to Geneva tomorrow.'

'Well, Mr Winterbourne,' said Daisy; 'I think you're horrid!'

'Oh, don't say such dreadful things!' said Winterbourne, 'just at the last.'

'The last!' cried the young girl; 'I call it the first. I have half a mind to leave you here and go straight back to the hotel alone.' And for the next ten minutes she did nothing but call him horrid. Poor Winterbourne was fairly bewildered; no young lady had as yet done him the honour to be so agitated by the announcement of his movements. His companion, after this, ceased to pay any attention to the curiosities of Chillon or the beauties of the lake; she opened fire upon the mysterious charmer in Geneva, whom she appeared to have instantly taken it for granted that he was hurrying back to see. How did Miss Daisy Miller know that there was a charmer in Geneva? Winterbourne, who denied the existence of such a person, was quite unable to discover; and he was divided between amazement at the rapidity of her induction and amusement at the frankness of her *persiflage*. She seemed to him, in all this, an extraordinary mixture of innocence and crudity. 'Does she never allow you more than three days at a time?' asked Daisy, ironically. 'Doesn't she give you a vacation in summer? There's no one so hardworked but they can get leave to go off somewhere at this season. I suppose, if you stay another day, she'll come after you in the boat. Do wait over till Friday, and I will go down to the landing to see her arrive!' Winterbourne began to think he had been wrong to feel disappointed in the temper in which the young lady had embarked. If he had missed the personal accent, the personal accent was now making its appearance. It sounded very distinctly, at last, in her telling him she would stop 'teasing' him if he would promise her solemnly to come down to Rome in the winter.

'That's not a difficult promise to make,' said Winterbourne. 'My aunt has taken an apartment in Rome for the winter, and has already asked me to come and see her.'

'I don't want you to come for your aunt,' said Daisy; 'I want you to come for me.' And this was the only allusion that the young man was ever to hear her make to his invidious kinswoman. He declared that, at any rate, he would certainly come. After this Daisy stopped teasing. Winterbourne took a carriage, and they drove back to Vevey in the dusk; the young girl was very quiet.

In the evening Winterbourne mentiond to Mrs Costello that he had spent the afternoon at Chillon, with Miss Daisy Miller.

'The Americans – of the courier?' asked this lady.

'Ah, happily,' said Winterbourne, 'the courier stayed at home.'

'She went with you all alone?'

'All alone.'

Mrs Costello sniffed a little at her smelling-bottle. 'And that,' she exclaimed, 'is the young person you wanted me to know!'

Chapter Three

Winterbourne, who had returned to Geneva the day after his excursion to Chillon, went to Rome towards the end of January. His aunt had been established there for several weeks, and he had received a couple of letters from her. 'Those people you were so devoted to last summer at Vevey have turned up here, courier and all,' she wrote. 'They seem to have made several acquaintances, but the courier continues to be the most *intime*. The young lady, however, is also very intimate with some third-rate Italians, with whom she rackets about in a way that makes much talk. Bring me that pretty novel of Cherbuliex's – *Paule Mêré* – and don't come later than the 23rd.'

In the natural course of events, Winterbourne, on arriving in Rome, would presently have ascertained Mrs Miller's address at the American banker's and have gone to pay his compliments to Miss Daisy. 'After what happened at Vevey I certainly think I may call upon them,' he said to Mrs Costello.

'If, after what happens – at Vevey and everywhere – you desire to keep up the acquaintance, you are very welcome. Of course a man may know everyone. Men are welcome to the privilege!'

'Pray what is it that happens – here, for instance?' Winterbourne demanded.

'The girl goes about alone with her foreigners. As to what happens further, you must apply elsewhere for information. She has picked up half a dozen of the regular Roman fortune-hunters, and she takes them about to people's houses. When she comes to a party she brings with her a gentleman with a good deal of manner and a wonderful moustache.'

'And where is the mother?'

'I haven't the least idea. They are very dreadful people.'

Winterbourne meditated a moment. 'They are very ignorant – very innocent only. Depend upon it they are not bad.'

'They are hopelessly vulgar,' said Mrs Costello. 'Whether or no being hopelessly vulgar is being "bad" is a question for the metaphysicians. They are bad enough to dislike, at any rate; and for this short life that is quite enough,'

The news that Daisy Miller was surrounded by half a dozen wonderful moustaches checked Winterbourne's impulse to go straightway to see her. He had perhaps not definitely flattered himself that he had made an ineffaceable impression upon her heart, but he was annoyed at hearing of a state of affairs so little in harmony with an image that had lately flitted in and out of his own meditations; the image of a very pretty girl looking out of an old Roman window and asking herself urgently when Mr Winterbourne would arrive. If, however, he determined to wait a little before reminding Miss Miller of his claims to her consideration, he went very soon to call upon two or three other friends. One of these friends was an American lady who had spent several winters at Geneva, where she had placed her children at school. She was a very accomplished woman and she lived in the Via Gregoriana. Winterbourne found her in a little crimson drawing-room, on a third floor; the room was filled with southern sunshine. He had not been there ten minutes when the servant came in, announcing 'Madame Mila!' This announcement was presently followed by the entrance of little Randolph Miller, who stopped in the middle of the room and stood staring at Winterbourne. An instant later his pretty sister crossed the threshold; and then, after a considerable interval, Mrs Miller slowly advanced.

'I know you!' said Randolph.

'I'm sure you know a great many things,' exclaimed Winterbourne, taking him by the hand. 'How is your education coming on?'

Daisy was exchanging greetings very prettily with her hostess; but when she heard Winterbourne's voice she quickly turned her head. 'Well, I declare!' she said.

'I told you I should come, you know,' Winterbourne rejoined, smiling.

'Well – I didn't believe it,' said Miss Daisy.

'I am much obliged to you,' laughed the young man.

'You might have come to see me!' said Daisy.

'I arrived only yesterday.'

'I don't believe that!' the young girl declared.

Winterbourne turned with a protesting smile to her mother; but this lady evaded his glance, and seating herself, fixed her eyes upon her son. 'We've got a bigger place than this,' said Randolph. 'It's all gold on the walls.'

Mrs Miller turned uneasily in her chair. 'I told you if I were to bring you, you would say something!' she murmured.

'I told *you*!' Randolph exclaimed. 'I tell *you*, sir!' he added jocosely, giving Winterbourne a thump on the knee. 'It *is* bigger, too!'

Daisy had entered upon a lively conversation with her hostess; Winterbourne judged it becoming to address a few words to her mother. 'I hope you have been well since we parted at Vevey,' he said.

Mrs Miller now certainly looked at him – at his chin. 'Not very well, sir,' she answered.

'She's got the dyspepsia,' said Randolph. 'I've got it too. Father's got it. I've got it worst!'

This announcement, instead of embarrasing Mrs Miller, seemed to relieve her. 'I suffer from the liver,' she said. 'I think it's this climate; it's less bracing than Schenectady, especially in the winter season. I don't know whether you know we reside at Schenectady. I was saying to Daisy that I certainly hadn't found anyone like Dr Davis, and I didn't believe I should. Oh, at Schenectady, he stands first; they think everything of him. He has so much to do, and yet there was nothing he wouldn't do for me. He said he never saw anything like my dyspepsia, but he was bound to cure it. I'm sure there was nothing he wouldn't try. He was just going to try something new when we came off. Mr Miller wanted Daisy to see Europe for herself. But I wrote to Mr Miller that it seems as if I couldn't get on without Dr Davis. At Schenectady he stands at the very top; and there's a great deal of sickness there, too. It affects my sleep.'

Winterbourne had a good deal of pathological gossip with Dr Davis's patient, during which Daisy chattered unremittingly to her own companion. The young man asked Mrs Miller how she was pleased with Rome. 'Well, I must say I am disappointed,' she answered. 'We had heard so much about it; I suppose we had heard too much. But we couldn't help that. We had been led to expect something different.'

'Ah, wait a little, and you will become very fond of it,' said Winterbourne.

'I hate it worse and worse every day!' cried Randolph.

'You are like the infant Hannibal,' said Winterbourne.

'No, I ain't!' Randolph declared, at a venture.

'You are not much like an infant,' said his mother. 'But we have seen places,' she resumed, 'that I should put a long way before Rome.' And in reply to Winterbourne's interrogation, 'There's Zürich,' she observed; 'I think Zürich is lovely; and we hadn't heard half so much about it.'

'The best place we've seen is the *City of Richmond*!' said Randolph.

'He means the ship,' his mother explained. 'We crossed in that ship. Randolph had a good time on the *City of Richmond*.'

'It's the best place I've seen,' the child repeated. 'Only it was turned the wrong way.'

'Well, we've got to turn the right way some time,' said Mrs Miller, with a little laugh. Winterbourne expressed the hope that her daughter at least found some gratification in Rome, and she declared that Daisy was quite carried away. 'It's on account of the society – the society's splendid. She goes round everywhere; she has made a great number of acquaintances. Of course she goes round more than I do. I must say they have been very sociable; they have taken her right in. And then she knows a great many gentlemen. Oh, she thinks there's nothing like Rome. Of course, it's a great deal pleasanter for a young lady if she knows plenty of gentlemen.'

By this time Daisy had turned her attention again to Winterbourne. 'I've been telling Mrs Walker how mean you were!' the young girl announced.

'And what is the evidence you have offered?' asked Winterbourne, rather annoyed at Miss Miller's want of appreciation of the zeal of an admirer who on his way down to Rome had stopped neither at Bologna nor at Florence, simply because of a certain sentimental impatience. He remembered that a cynical compatriot had once told him that American women – the pretty ones, and this gave a largeness to the axiom – were at once the most exacting in the world and the least endowed with a sense of indebtedness.

'Why, you were awfully mean at Vevey,' said Daisy. 'You wouldn't do anything. You wouldn't stay there when I asked you.'

'My dearest young lady,' cried Winterbourne, with eloquence, 'have I come all the way to Rome to encounter your reproaches?'

'Just hear him say that!' said Daisy to her hostess, giving a twist to a bow on this lady's dress. 'Did you ever hear anything so quaint?'

'So quaint, my dear?' murmured Mrs Walker, in the tone of a partisan of Winterbourne.

'Well, I don't know,' said Daisy, fingering Mrs Walker's ribbons. 'Mrs Walker, I want to tell you something.'

'Mother,' interposed Randolph, with his rough ends to his words, 'I tell you you've got to go. Eugenio'll raise something!'

'I'm not afraid of Eugenio,' said Daisy, with a toss of her head. 'Look here, Mrs Walker,' she went on, 'you know I'm coming to your party.'

'I am delighted to hear it.'

'I've got a lovely dress.'

'I am very sure of that.'

'But I want to ask a favour – permission to bring a friend.'

'I shall be happy to see any of your friends,' said Mrs Walker, turning with a smile to Mrs Miller.

'Oh, they are not my friends,' answered Daisy's mamma, smiling shyly, in her own fashion. 'I never spoke to them!'

'It's an intimate friend of mine – Mr Giovanelli,' said Daisy, without a tremor in her clear little voice or a shadow on her brilliant little face.

Mrs Walker was silent a moment, she gave a rapid glance at Winterbourne. 'I shall be glad to see Mr Giovanelli,' she then said.

'He's an Italian,' Daisy pursued, with the prettiest serenity. 'He's a great friend of mine – he's the handsomest man in the world – except Mr Winterbourne! He knows plenty of Italians, but he wants to know some Americans. He thinks ever so much of Americans. He's tremendously clever. He's perfectly lovely!'

It was settled that this brilliant personage should be brought to Mrs Walker's party, and then Mrs Miller prepared to take her leave. 'I guess we'll go back to the hotel,' she said.

'You may go back to the hotel, mother, but I'm going to take a walk,' said Daisy.

'She's going to walk with Mr Giovanelli,' Randolph proclaimed.

'I am going to the Pincio,' said Daisy, smiling.

'Alone, my dear – at this hour?' Mrs Walker asked. The afternoon was drawing to a close – it was the hour for the throng of carriages and of contemplative pedestrians. 'I don't think it's safe, my dear,' said Mrs Walker.

'Neither do I,' subjoined Mrs Miller. 'You'll get the fever as sure as you live. Remember what Dr Davis told you!'

'Give her some medicine before she goes,' said Randolph.

The company has risen to its feet; Daisy, still showing her pretty teeth, bent over and kissed her hostess. 'Mrs Walker, you are too perfect,' she said. 'I'm not going alone; I am going to meet a friend.'

'Your friend won't keep you from getting the fever,' Mrs Miller observed.

'Is it Mr Giovanelli?' asked the hostess.

Winterbourne was watching the young girl; at this question his attention quickened. She stood there smiling and smoothing her bonnet-ribbons; she glanced at Winterbourne. Then, while she glanced and smiled, she answered without a shade of hesitation, 'Mr Giovanelli – the beautiful Giovanelli.'

'My dear young friend,' said Mrs Walker, taking her hand, pleadingly, 'don't walk off to the Pincio at this hour to meet a beautiful Italian.'

'Well, he speaks English,' said Mrs Miller.

'Gracious me!' Daisy exclaimed, 'I don't want to do anything improper. There's an easy way to settle it.' She continued to glance at Winterbourne. 'The Pincio is only a hundred yards distant, and if Mr Winterbourne were as polite as he pretends he would offer to walk with me!'

Winterbourne's politeness hastened to affirm itself, and the young girl gave him gracious leave to accompany her. They passed downstairs before her mother, and at the door Winterbourne perceived Mrs Miller's carriage drawn up, with the ornamental courier whose acquaintance he had made at Vevey seated within. 'Good-bye, Eugenio!' cried Daisy, 'I'm going to take a walk.' The distance from the Via Gregoriana to the beautiful garden at the other end of the Pincian Hill is, in fact, rapidly traversed. As the day was splendid, however, and the concourse of vehicles, walkers, and loungers numerous, the young Americans found their progress much delayed. This fact was highly agreeable to Winterbourne, in spite of his consciousness of his singular situation. The slow-moving, idly gazing Roman crowd bestowed much attention upon the extremely pretty young foreign lady who was passing through it upon his arm; and he wondered what on earth had been in Daisy's mind when she proposed to expose herself, unattended, to its appreciation. His own mission, to her sense, apparently, was to consign her to the hands of Mr Giovanelli; but Winterbourne, at once annoyed and gratified, resolved that he would do no such thing.

'Why haven't you been to see me?' asked Daisy. 'You can't get out of that.'

'I have had the honour of telling you that I have only just stepped out of the train.'

'You must have stayed in the train a good while after it stopped!' cried the young girl, with her little laugh. 'I suppose you were asleep. You have had time to go to see Mrs Walker.'

'I knew Mrs Walker—' Winterbourne began to explain.

'I knew where you knew her. You knew her at Geneva. She told me so. Well, you knew me at Vevey. That's just as good. So you ought to have come.' She asked him no other question than this; she began to prattle about her own affairs. 'We've got splendid rooms at the hotel; Eugenio says they're the best rooms in Rome. We are going to stay all winter – if we don't die of the fever; and I guess we'll stay then. It's a great deal nicer than I thought; I thought it would be fearfully quiet; I was sure it would be awfully poky. I was sure we should be going round all the time with one of those dreadful old men that explain about the pictures and things. But we only had about a week of that, and now I'm enjoying myself. I know ever so many people, and they are all so charming. The society's extremely select. There are all kinds – English, and Germans, and Italians. I think I like the English best. I like their style of conversation. But there are some lovely Americans. I never saw anything so hospitable. There's something or other every day. There's not much dancing; but I must say I never thought dancing was everything. I was always fond of conversation. I guess I shall have plenty at Mrs Walker's – her rooms are so small.' When they had passed the gate of the Pincian Gardens, Miss Miller began to wonder where Mr Giovanelli might be. 'We had better go straight to that place in front,' she said, 'where you look at the view.'

'I certainly shall not help you to find him,' Winterbourne declared.

'Then I shall find him without you,' said Miss Daisy.

'You certainly won't leave me!' cried Winterbourne.

She burst into her little laugh. 'Are you afraid you'll get lost – or run over? But there's Giovanelli, leaning against that tree. He's staring at the women in the carriages: did you ever see anything so cool?'

Winterbourne perceived at some distance a little man standing with folded arms, nursing his cane. He had a handsome face, an artfully poised hat, a glass in one eye, and a nosegay in his button-hole. Winterbourne looked at him a moment and then said, 'Do you mean to speak to that man?'

'Do I mean to speak to him? Why, you don't suppose I mean to communicate by signs?'

'Pray understand, then,' said Winterbourne, 'that I intend to remain with you.'

Daisy stopped and looked at him, without a sign of troubled consciousness in her face; with nothing but the presence of her charming eyes and her happy dimples. 'Well, she's a cool one!' thought the young man.

'I don't like the way you say that,' said Daisy. 'It's too imperious.'

'I beg your pardon if I say it wrong. The main point is to give you an idea of my meaning.'

The young girl looked at him more gravely, but with eyes that were prettier than ever. 'I have never allowed a gentleman to dictate to me, or to interfere with anything I do.'

'I think you have made a mistake,' said Winterbourne. 'You should sometimes listen to a gentleman – the right one?'

Daisy began to laugh again, 'I do nothing but listen to gentlemen!' she exclaimed. 'Tell me if Mr Giovanelli is the right one?'

The gentleman with the nosegay in his bosom had now perceived our two friends, and was approaching the young girl with obsequious rapidity. He bowed to Winterbourne as well as to the latter's companion; he had a brilliant smile, an intelligent eye; Winterbourne thought him not a bad-looking fellow. But he nevertheless said to Daisy – 'No, he's not the right one.'

Daisy evidently had a natural talent for performing introductions; she mentioned the name of each of her companions to the other. She strolled along with one of them on each side of her; Mr Giovanelli, who spoke English very cleverly – Winterbourne afterwards learned that he had practised the idiom upon a great many American heiresses – addressed her a great deal of very polite nonsense; he was extremely urbane, and the young American, who said nothing, reflected upon that profundity of Italian cleverness which enables people to appear more gracious in proportion as they are more acutely disappointed. Giovanelli, of course, had counted upon something more intimate; he had not bargained for a party of three. But he kept his temper in a manner which suggested far-stretching intentions. Winterbourne flattered himself that he had taken his measure. 'He is not a gentleman,' said the young American; 'he is only a clever imitation of one. He is a music-master, or a penny-a-liner, or a third-rate artist. Damn his good looks!' Mr Giovanelli had certainly a very pretty face; but Winterbourne felt a superior indignation at his own lovely fellow-countrywoman's not knowing the difference between a spurious gentleman and a real one. Giovanelli chattered and jested and made himself wonderfully agreeable. It was true that if he was an imitation the imitation was very skilful. 'Nevertheless,' Winterbourne said to himself, 'a nice girl ought to know!' And then he came back to the question whether this was in fact a nice girl. Would a nice girl – even allowing for her being a little American flirt – make a rendezvous with a presumably low-lived foreigner? The rendezvous in this case, indeed, had been in broad daylight, and in the most crowded corner of Rome; but was it not impossible to regard the choice of these circumstances as a proof of extreme cynicism? Singular though it may seem, Winterbourne was vexed that the young girl, in joining her *amoroso*, should not appear more impatient of his own company, and he was vexed because of his inclination. It was impossible to regard her as a perfectly well-conducted young lady; she was wanting in a certain indispensable delicacy. It would therefore simplify matters greatly to be able to treat her as the object of one of those sentiments which are called by romancers 'lawless passions'. That she should seem to wish to get rid of him would help him to think more lightly of her, and to be able to think more lightly of her would make her much less perplexing. But Daisy, on this occasion, continued to present herself as an inscrutable combination of audacity and innocence.

She had been walking some quarter of an hour, attended by her two cavaliers, and responding in a tone of very childish gaiety, as it seemed to Winterbourne, to the pretty speeches of Mr Giovanelli, when a carriage that had detached itself from the revolving train drew up beside the path. At the same moment Winterbourne perceived that his friend Mrs Walker – the lady whose house he had lately left – was seated in the vehicle and was beckoning to him. Leaving Miss Miller's side, he hastened to obey her summons. Mrs Walker was flushed; she wore an excited air. 'It is really too dreadful,' she said. 'That girl must not do this sort of thing. She must not walk here with you two men. Fifty people have noticed her.'

Winterbourne raised his eyebrows. 'I think it's a pity to make too much fuss about it.'

'It's a pity to let the girl ruin herself!'

'She is very innocent,' said Winterbourne.

'She's very crazy!' cried Mrs Walker. 'Did you ever see anything so imbecile as her mother? After you had all left me, just now, I could not sit still for thinking of it. It seemed too pitiful, not even to attempt to save her. I ordered the carriage and put on my bonnet, and came here as quickly as possible. Thank heaven I have found you!'

'What do you propose to do with us?' asked Winterbourne, smiling.

'To ask her to get in, to drive her about here for half an hour, so that the world may see she is not running absolutely wild, and then to take her safely home.'

'I don't think it's a very happy thought,' said Winterbourne; 'but you can try.'

Mrs Walker tried. The young man went in pursuit of Miss Miller, who had simply nodded and smiled at his interlocutrix in the carriage and had gone her way with her own companion. Daisy, on learning that Mrs Walker wished to speak to her, retraced her steps with a perfect good grace and with Mr Giovanelli at her side. She declared that she was delighted to have a chance to present this gentleman to Mrs Walker. She immediately achieved the introduction, and declared that she had never in her life seen anything so lovely as Mrs Walker's carriage-rug.

'I am glad you admire it,' said this lady, smiling sweetly. 'Will you get in and let me put it over you?'

'Oh, no, thank you,' said Daisy. 'I shall admire it much more as I see you driving round with it.'

'Do get in and drive with me,' said Mrs Walker.

'That would be charming, but it's so enchanting just as I am!' and Daisy gave a brilliant glance at the gentlemen on either side of her.

'It may be enchanting, dear child, but it is not the custom here,' urged Mrs Walker, leaning forward in her victoria with her hands devoutly clasped.

'Well, it ought to be, then!' said Daisy. 'If I didn't walk I should expire.'

'You should walk with your mother, dear,' cried the lady from Geneva, losing patience.

'With my mother dear!' exclaimed the young girl. Winterbourne saw that she scented interference. 'My mother never walked ten steps in her life. And then, you know,' she added with a laugh. 'I am more than five years old.'

'You are old enough to be more reasonable. You are old enough, dear Miss Miller, to be talked about.'

Daisy looked at Mrs Walker, smiling intensely. 'Talked about? What do you mean!'

'Come into my carriage and I will tell you.'

Daisy turned her quickened glance again from one of the gentlemen beside her to the other. Mr Giovanelli was bowing to and fro, rubbing down his gloves and laughing very agreeably; Winterbourne thought it a most unpleasant scene. 'I don't think I want to know what you mean,' said Daisy presently. 'I don't think I should like it.'

Winterbourne wished that Mrs Walker would tuck in her carriage-rug and drive away; but this lady did not enjoy being defied, as she afterwards told him. 'Should you prefer being thought a very reckless girl?' she demanded.

'Gracious me!' exclaimed Daisy. She looked again at Mr Giovanelli, then she turned to Winterbourne. There was a little pink flush in her cheek; she was tremendously pretty. 'Does Mr Winterbourne think,' she asked slowly, smiling, throwing back her head and glancing at him from head to foot, 'that – to save my reputation – I ought to get into the carriage?'

Winterbourne coloured; for an instant he hesitated greatly. It seemed so strange to hear her speak that way of her 'reputation'. But he himself, in fact, must speak in accordance with gallantry. The finest gallantry, here, was simply to tell her the truth; and the truth, for Winterbourne, as the few indications I have been able to give have made him known to the reader, was that Daisy Miller should take Mrs Walker's advice. He looked at her exquisite prettiness; and then he said very gently, 'I think you should get into the carriage.'

Daisy gave a violent laugh. 'I never heard anything so stiff! If this is improper, Mrs Walker,' she pursued, 'then I am all improper, and you must give me up. Goodbye; I hope you'll have a lovely ride!' and, with Mr Giovanelli, who made a triumphantly obsequious salute, she turned away.

Mrs Walker sat looking after her, and there were tears in Mrs Walker's eyes. 'Get in here, sir,' she said to Winterbourne, indicating the place beside her. The young man answered that he felt bound to accompany Miss Miller; whereupon Mrs Walker declared that if he refused her this favour she would never speak to him again. She was evidently in earnest. Winterbourne overtook Daisy and her companion and, offering the young girl his hand, told her that Mrs Walker had made an imperious claim upon his society. He expected that in answer she would say something rather free, something to commit herself still farther to that 'recklessness' from which Mrs Walker had so charitably endeavoured to dissuade her. But she only shook his hand, hardly looking at him, while Mr Giovanelli bade him farewell with a too emphatic flourish of the hat.

Winterbourne was not in the best possible humour as he took his seat in Mrs Walker's victoria. 'That was not clever of you,' he said candidly, while the vehicle mingled again with the throng of carriages.

'In such a case,' his companion answered, 'I don't wish to be clever, I wish to be *earnest*!'

'Well, your earnestness has only offended her and put her off.'

'It has happened very well,' said Mrs Walker. 'If she is so perfectly determined to compromise herself, the sooner one knows it the better; one can act accordingly.'

'I suspect she meant no harm,' Winterourne enjoined.

'So I thought a month ago. But she has been going too far.'

'What has she been doing?'

'Everything that is not done here. Flirting with any man she could pick up; sitting in corners with mysterious Italians; dancing all the evening with the same partners; receiving visits at eleven o'clock at night. Her mother goes away when visitors come.'

'But her brother,' said Winterbourne, laughing, 'sits up till midnight.'

'He must be edified by what he sees. I'm told that at their hotel everyone is talking about her, and that a smile goes round among the servants when a gentleman comes and asks for Miss Miller.'

'The servants be hanged!' said Winterbourne angrily. 'The poor girl's only fault,' he presently added, 'is that she is very uncultivated.'

'She is naturally indelicate,' Mrs Walker declared. 'Take that example this morning. How long had you known her at Vevey?'

'A couple of days.'

'Fancy, then, her making it a personal matter that you should have left the place!'

Winterbourne was silent for some moments; then he said, 'I suspect, Mrs Walker, that you and I have lived too long at Geneva!' And he added a request that she should inform him with what particular design she had made him enter her carriage.

'I wished to beg you to cease your relations with Miss Miller – not to flirt with her – to give her no further opportunity to expose herself – to let her alone, in short.'

'I'm afraid I can't do that,' said Winterbourne. 'I like her extremely.'

'All the more reason that you shouldn't help her to make a scandal.'

'There shall be nothing scandalous in my attentions to her.'

'There certainly will be in the way she takes them. But I have said what I had on my conscience,' Mrs Walker pursued. 'If you wish to rejoin the young lady I will put you down. Here, by the way, you have a chance.'

The carriage was traversing that part of the Pincian Garden which overhangs the wall of Rome and overlooks the beautiful Villa Borghese. It is bordered by a large parapet, near which there are several seats. One of the seats, at a distance, was occupied by a gentleman and a lady, towards whom Mrs Walker gave a toss of her head. At the same moment these persons rose and walked towards the parapet. Winterbourne had asked the coachman to stop; he now descended from the carriage. His companion looked at him a moment in silence; then, while he raised his hat, she drove majestically away. Winterbourne stood there; he had turned his eyes towards Daisy and her cavalier. They evidently saw no one; they were too deeply occupied with each other. When they reached the low garden-wall they stood a moment looking off at the great flat-topped pine-clusters of the Villa Borghese; then Giovanelli seated himself familiarly upon the broad ledge of the wall. The western sun in the opposite sky sent out a brilliant shaft through a couple of cloud-bars; whereupon Daisy's companion took her parasol out of her hands and opened it. She came a little nearer and he held the parasol over her; then, still holding it, he let it rest upon her shoulder, so that both their heads were hidden from Winterbourne. This young man lingered a moment, then he began to walk. But he walked – not towards the couple with the parasol; towards the residence of his aunt, Mrs Costello.

Chapter Four

He flattered himself on the the following day that there was no smiling among the servants when he, at least, asked for Mrs Miller at her hotel. This lady and her daughter, however, were not at home; and on the next day, after repeating his visit, Winterbourne again had the misfortune not to find them. Mrs Walker's party took place on the evening of the third day, and in spite of the frigidity of his last interview with the hostess, Winterbourne was among the guests. Mrs Walker was one of those American ladies who, while residing abroad, make a point, in their own phrase, of studying European society; and she had on this occasion collected several specimens of her diversely born fellow-mortals to serve, as it were, as textbooks. When Winterbourne arrived Daisy Miller was not there; but in a few moments he saw her mother come in alone, very shyly and ruefully. Mrs Miller's hair, above her exposed-looking temples, was more frizzled than ever. As she approached Mrs Walker, Winterbourne also drew near.

'You see I've come all alone,' said poor Mrs Miller. 'I'm so frightened; I don't know what to do; it's the first time I've ever been to a party alone – especially in this country. I wanted to bring Randolph or Eugenio, or someone, but Daisy just pushed me off by myself. I ain't used to going round alone.'

'And does not your daughter intend to favour us with her society?' demanded Mrs Walker, impressively.

'Well, Daisy's all dressed,' said Mrs Miller, with that accent of the dispassionate, if not of the philosophic, historian with which she always recorded the current incidents of her daughter's career. 'She's got dressed on purpose before dinner. But she's got a friend of hers there; that gentleman – the Italian – that she wanted to bring. They've got going at the piano; it seems as if they couldn't leave off. Mr Giovanelli sings splendidly. But I guess they'll come before very long.' concluded Mrs Miller hopefully.

'I'm sorry she should come – in that way,' said Mrs Walker.

'Well, I told her that there was no use in her getting dressed before dinner if she was going to wait three hours,' responded Daisy's mamma. 'I didn't see the use of her putting on such a dress as that to sit round with Mr Giovanelli.'

'This is most horrible!' said Mrs Walker, turning away and addressing herself to Winterbourne. '*Elle s'affiche.* It's her revenge for my having ventured to remonstrate with her. When she comes I shall not speak to her.'

Daisy came after eleven o'clock, but she was not, on such an occasion, a young lady to wait to be spoken to. She rustled forward in radiant loveliness, smiling and chattering, carrying a large bouquet and attended by Mr Giovanelli. Everyone stopped talking and turned and looked at her. She came straight to Mrs Walker. 'I'm afraid you thought I never was coming, so I sent mother off to tell you. I wanted to make Mr Giovanelli practise some things before he came; you know he sings beautifully, and I want you to ask him to sing. This is Mr Giovanelli, you know I introduced him to you; he's got the most lovely voice and he knows the most charming set of songs. I made him go over them this evening, on purpose; we had the greatest time at the hotel.' Of all this Daisy delivered herself with the sweetest, brightest audibleness, looking now at her hostess and now round the room, while she gave a series of little pats, round her shoulders, to the edges of her dress. 'Is there anyone I know?' she asked.

'I think everyone knows you!' said Mrs Walker pregnantly, and she gave a very cursory greeting to Mr Giovanelli. This gentleman bore himself gallantly. He smiled and bowed and showed his white teeth, he curled his moustaches and rolled his eyes, and performed all the proper functions of a handsome Italian at an evening party. He sang, very prettily, half a dozen songs, though Mrs Walker afterwards declared that she had been quite unable to find out who asked him. It was apparently not Daisy who had given him his orders. Daisy sat at a distance from the piano, and though she had publicly, as it were, professed a high admiration for his singing, talked, not inaudibly, while it was going on.

'It's a pity these rooms are so small; we can't dance,' she said to Winterbourne, as if she had seen him five minutes before.

'I am not sorry we can't dance.' Winterbourne answered; 'I don't dance.'

'Of course you don't dance, you're too stiff,' said Miss Daisy. 'I hope you enjoyed your drive with Mrs Walker.'

'No, I didn't enjoy it; I preferred walking with you.'

'We paired off, that was much better,' said Daisy. 'But did you ever hear anything so cool as Mrs Walker's wanting me to get into her carriage and drop poor Mr Giovanelli; and under the pretext that it was proper? People have different ideas! It would have been most unkind; he had been talking about that walk for ten days.'

'He should not have talked about it at all,' said Winterbourne; 'he would never have proposed to a young lady of this country to walk about the streets with him.'

'About the streets?' cried Daisy, with her pretty stare. 'Where then would he have proposed to her to walk? The Pincio is not the streets, either; and

I, thank goodness, am not a young lady of this country. The young ladies of this country have a dreadfully poky time of it, so far as I can learn; I don't see why I should change my habits for *them*.'

'I am afraid your habits are those of a flirt,' said Winterbourne gravely.

'Of course they are,' she cried, giving him her little smiling stare again. 'I'm a fearful, frightful flirt! Did you ever hear of a nice girl that was not? But I suppose you will tell me now that I am not a nice girl.'

'You're a very nice girl, but I wish you would flirt with me, and me only,' said Winterbourne.

'Ah! thank you, thank you very much; you are the last man I should think of flirting with. As I have had the pleasure of informing you, you are too stiff.'

'You say that too often,' said Winterbourne.

Daisy gave a delighted laugh. 'If I could have the sweet hope of making you angry, I would say it again.'

'Don't do that; when I am angry I'm stiffer than ever. But if you won't flirt with me, do cease at least to flirt with your friend at the piano; they don't understand that sort of thing here.'

'I thought they understood nothing else!' exclaimed Daisy.

'Not in young unmarried women.'

'It seems to me much more proper in young unmarried women than in old married ones,' Daisy declared.

'Well,' said Winterbourne, 'when you deal with natives you must go by the custom of the place. Flirting is a purely American custom; it doesn't exist here. So when you show yourself in public with Mr Giovanelli and without your mother—'

'Gracious! Poor mother!' interposed Daisy.

'Though you may be flirting, Mr Giovanelli is not; he means something else.'

'He isn't preaching, at any rate,' said Daisy with vivacity. 'And if you want very much to know, we are neither of us flirting; we are too good friends for that; we are very intimate friends.'

'Ah,' rejoined Winterbourne, 'if you are in love with each other it is another affair.'

She had allowed him up to this point to talk so frankly that he had no expectation of shocking her by this ejaculation; but she immediately got up, blushing visibly, and leaving him to exclaim mentally that little American flirts were the queerest creatures in the world. 'Mr Giovanelli, at least,' she said, giving her interlocutor a single glance, 'never says such very disagreeable things to me.'

Winterbourne was bewildered; he stood staring. Mr Giovanelli had finished singing; he left the piano and came over to Daisy. 'Won't you come into the other room and have some tea?' he asked, bending before her with his decorative smile.

Daisy turned to Winterbourne, beginning to smile again. He was still more perplexed, for this inconsequent smile made nothing clear, though it seemed to prove, indeed, that she had a sweetness and softness that reverted instinctively to the pardon of offences. 'It has never occurred to Mr Winterbourne to offer me any tea,' she said, with her little tormenting manner.

'I have offered you advice,' Winterbourne rejoined.

'I prefer weak tea!' cried Daisy, and she went off with the brilliant Giovanelli. She sat with him in the adjoining room, in the embrasure of the window, for the rest of the evening. There was an interesting performance at the piano, but neither of these young people gave heed to it. When Daisy came to take leave of Mrs Walker, this lady conscientiously repaired the weakness of which she had been guilty at the moment of the young girl's arrival. She turned her back straight upon Miss Miller and left her to depart with what grace she might. Winterbourne was standing near the door; he saw it all. Daisy turned very pale and looked at her mother, but Mrs Miller was humbly unconscious of any violation of the usual social forms. She appeared, indeed, to have felt an incongruous impulse to draw attention to her own striking observance of them. 'Goodnight, Mrs Walker,' she said; 'we've had a beautiful evening. You see if I let Daisy come to parties without me, I don't want her to go away without me.' Daisy turned away, looking with a pale, grave face at the circle near the door; Winterbourne saw that, for the first moment, she was too much shocked and puzzled even for indignation. He on his side was greatly touched.

'That was very cruel,' he said to Mrs Walker.

'She never enters my drawing-room again,' replied his hostess.

Since Winterbourne was not to meet her in Mrs Walker's drawing-room, he went as often as possible to Mrs Miller's hotel. The ladies were rarely at home, but when he found them the devoted Giovanelli was always present. Very often the polished little Roman was in the drawing-room with Daisy alone, Mrs Miller being apparently constantly of the opinion that discretion is the better part of surveillance. Winterbourne noted, at first with surprise, that Daisy on these occasions was never embarrassed or annoyed by his own entrance; but he very presently began to feel that she had no more surprises for him; the unexpected in her behaviour was the only thing to expect. She showed no displeasure at her *tête-à-tête* with Giovanelli being interrupted; she could chatter as freshly and freely with two gentlemen as with one; there was always, in her conversation, the same odd mixture of audacity and puerility. Winterbourne remarked to himself that if she was seriously interested in Giovanelli it was very singular that she should not take more trouble to preserve the sanctity of their interviews, and he liked her the more for her innocent-looking indifference and her apparently inexhaustible good humour. He could hardly have said why, but she seemed to him a girl who would never be jealous. At the risk of exciting a somewhat derisive smile on the reader's part, I may affirm that with regard to the women who had hitherto interested him it very often seemed to Winterbourne among the possibilities that, given certain contingencies, he should be afraid – literally afraid – of these ladies. He had a pleasant sense that he should never be afraid of Daisy Miller. It must be added that this sentiment was not altogether flattering to Daisy; it was part of his conviction, or rather of his apprehension, that she would prove a very light young person.

But she was evidently very much interested in Giovanelli. She looked at him whenever he spoke; she was perpetually telling him to do this and to do that; she was constantly 'chaffing' and abusing him. She appeared completely to have forgotten that Winterbourne had said anything to displease her at Mrs Walker's little party. One Sunday afternoon, having gone to St Peter's with his aunt, Winterbourne perceived Daisy strolling about the great church in company with the inevitable Giovanelli. Presently he pointed out the young girl and her cavalier to Mrs Costello. This lady looked at them a moment through her eyeglass, and then she said:

'That's what makes you so pensive in these days, eh?'

'I had not the least idea I was pensive,' said the young man.

'You are very much preoccupied, you are thinking of something.'

'And what is it,' he asked, 'that you accuse me of thinking of?'

'Of that young lady's, Miss Baker's, Miss Chandler's – what's her name? – Miss Miller's intrigue with that little barber's block.'

'Do you call it an intrigue,' Winterbourne asked – 'an affair that goes on with such peculiar publicity?'

'That's their folly,' said Mrs Costello, 'it's not their merit.'

'No,' rejoined Winterbourne, with something of that pensiveness to which his aunt had alluded. 'I don't believe that there is anything to be called an intrigue.'

'I have heard a dozen people speak of it; they say she is quite carried away by him.'

'They are certainly very intimate,' said Winterbourne.

Mrs Costello inspected the young couple again with her optical instrument. 'He is very handsome. One easily sees how it is. She thinks him the most elegant man in the world, the finest gentleman. She has never seen anything like him; he is better even than the courier. It was the courier probably who introduced him, and if he succeeds in marrying the young lady, the courier will come in for a magnificent commission.'

'I don't believe she thinks of marrying him,' said Winterbourne, 'and I don't believe he hopes to marry her.'

'You may be very sure she thinks of nothing. She goes on from day to day, from hour to hour, as they did in the Golden Age. I can imagine nothing more vulgar. And at the same time,' added Mrs Costello, 'depend upon it that she may tell you any moment that she is "engaged".'

'I think that is more than Giovanelli expects,' said Winterbourne.

'Who is Giovanelli?'

'The little Italian. I have asked questions about him and learned something. He is apparently a perfectly respectable little man. I believe he is in a small way a *cavaliere avvocato*. But he doesn't move in what are called the first circles. I think it is really not absolutely impossible that the courier introduced him. He is evidently immensely charmed with Miss Miller. If she thinks him the finest gentleman in the world, he, on his side, has never found himself in personal contact with such splendour, such opulence, such expensiveness, as this young lady's. And then she must seem to him wonderfully pretty and interesting. I rather doubt whether he dreams of marrying her. That must appear to him too impossible a piece of luck. He has nothing but his handsome face to offer, and there is a substantial Mr Miller in that mysterious land of dollars. Giovanelli knows that he hasn't a title to offer. If he were only a count or a *marchese*! He must wonder at his luck at the way they have taken him up.'

'He accounts for it by his handsome face, and thinks Miss Miller a young lady *qui se passe ses fantaisies*!' said Mrs Costello.

'It is very true,' Winterbourne pursued, 'that Daisy and her mamma have not yet risen to that stage of – what shall I call it? – of culture, at which the idea of catching a count or a *marchese* begins. I believe that they are intellectually incapable of that conception.'

'Ah! but the *cavaliere* can't believe it,' said Mrs Costello.

Of the observation excited by Daisy's 'intrigue', Winterbourne gathered that day at St Peter's sufficient evidence. A dozen of the American colonists in Rome came to talk with Mrs Costello, who sat on a little portable stool at the base of one of the great pilasters. The vesper-service was going forward in splendid chants and organ-tones in the adjacent choir, and meanwhile, between Mrs Costello and her friends, there was a great deal said about poor little Miss Miller's going really 'too far'. Winterbourne was not pleased with what he heard; but when, coming out upon the great steps of the church, he saw Daisy, who had emerged before him, get into an open cab with her accomplice and roll away through the cynical streets of Rome, he could not deny to himself that she was going very far indeed. He felt very sorry for her – not exactly that he believed that she had completely lost her head, but because it was painful to hear so much that was pretty and undefended and natural assigned to a vulgar place among the categories of disorder. He made an attempt after this to give a hint to Mrs Miller. He met one day in the Corso a friend – a tourist like himself – who had just come out of the Doria Palace, where he had been walking through the beautiful gallery. His friend talked for a moment about the superb portrait of Innocent X by Valázquez, which hangs in one of the cabinets of the palace, and then said, 'And in the same cabinet, by the way, I had the pleasure of contemplating a picture of a different kind – that pretty American girl whom you pointed out to me last week.' In answer to Winterbourne's inquiries, his friend narrated that the pretty American girl – prettier than ever – was seated with a companion in the secluded nook in which the great papal portrait is enshrined.

'Who was her companion?' asked Winterbourne.

'A little Italian with a bouquet in his buttonhole. The girl is delightfully pretty, but I thought I understood from you the other day that she was a young lady *du meilleur monde*.'

'So she is!' answered Winterbourne; and having assured himself that his informant had seen Daisy and her companion but five minutes before, he jumped into a cab and went to call on Mrs Miller. She was at home; but she apologized to him for receiving him in Daisy's absence.

'She's gone out somewhere with Mr Giovanelli,' said Mrs Miller. 'She's always going round with Mr Giovanelli.'

'I have noticed that they are very intimate,' Winterbourne observed.

'Oh! it seems as if they couldn't live without each other!' said Mrs Miller. 'Well, he's a real gentleman, anyhow. I keep telling Daisy she's engaged!'

'And what does Daisy say?'

'Oh, she says she isn't engaged. But she might as well be!' this impartial parent resumed. 'She goes on as if she was. But I've made Mr Giovanelli promise to tell me, if *she* doesn't. I should want to write to Mr Miller about it – shouldn't you?'

Winterbourne replied that he certainly should; and the state of mind of Daisy's mamma struck him as so unprecedented in the annals of parental vigilance that he gave up as utterly irrelevant the attempt to place her upon her guard.

After this Daisy was never at home, and Winterbourne ceased to meet her at the houses of their common acquaintances, because, as he perceived, these shrewd people had quite made up their minds that she was going too far. They ceased to invite her, and they intimated that they desired to express to observant Europeans the great truth that, though Miss Daisy Miller was a young American lady, her behaviour was not representative – was regarded by her compatriots as abnormal. Winterbourne wondered how she felt about all the cold shoulders that were turned towards her, and sometimes it annoyed him to suspect that she did not feel at all. He said to himself that she was too light and childish, too uncultivated and unreasoning, too provincial, to have reflected upon her ostracism or even to have perceived it. Then at other moments he believed that she carried about in her elegant and irresponsible little organism a defiant, passionate, perfectly observant consciousness of the impression she produced. He asked himself whether Daisy's defiance came from the consciousness of innocence or from her being, essentially, a young person of the reckless class. It must be admitted that holding oneself to a belief in Daisy's 'innocence' came to seem to Winterbourne more and more a matter of fine-spun gallantry. As I have already had occasion to relate, he was angry at finding himself reduced to chopping logic about this young lady; he was vexed at his want of instinctive certitude as to how far her eccentricities were generic, national, and how far they were personal. From either view of them he had somehow missed her, and now it was too late. She was 'carried away' by Mr Giovanelli.

A few days after his brief interview with her mother, he encountered her in that beautiful abode of flowering desolation known as the Palace of the Caesars. The early Roman spring had filled the air with bloom and perfume, and the rugged surface of the Palantine was muffled with tender verdure. Daisy was strolling along the top of one of those great mounds of ruin that are embanked with mossy marble and paved with monumental inscriptions. It seemed to him that Rome had never been so lovely as just then. He stood looking off at the enchanting harmony of line and colour that remotely encircles the city, inhaling the softly humid odours and feeling the freshness of the year and the antiquity of the place reaffirm themselves in mysterious interfusion. It seemed to him also that Daisy had never looked so pretty; but this had been an observation of his whenever he met her. Giovanelli was at her side, and Giovanelli, too, wore an aspect of even unwonted brilliancy.

'Well,' said Daisy, 'I should think you would be lonesome!'

'Lonesome!' asked Winterbourne.

'You are always going round by yourself. Can't you get anyone to walk with you?'

'I am not so fortunate,' said Winterbourne, 'as your companion.'

Giovanelli, from the first, had treated Winterbourne with distinguished politeness; he listened with a deferential air to his remarks; he laughed, punctiliously, at his pleasantries; he seemed disposed to testify to his belief that Winterbourne was a superior young man. He carried himself in no degree like a jealous wooer; he had obviously a great deal of tact; he had no objection to your expecting a little humility of him. It even seemed to Winterbourne at times that Giovanelli would find a certain mental relief in being able to have a private understanding with him – to say to him, as an intelligent man, that, bless you, *he* knew how extraordinary was this young lady, and didn't flatter himself with delusive – or at least *too* delusive – hopes of matrimony and dollars. On this occasion he strolled away from his companion to pluck a sprig of almond blossom, which he carefully arranged in his buttonhole.

'I know why you say that,' said Daisy, watching Giovanelli. 'Because you think I go round too much with *him*!' And she nodded at her attendant.

'Everyone thinks so – if you care to know,' said Winterbourne.

'Of course I care to know!' Daisy exclaimed seriously. 'But I don't believe it. They are only pretending to be shocked. They don't really care a straw what I do. Besides, I don't go around so much.'

'I think you will find they do care. They will show it – disagreeably.'

Daisy looked at him a moment. 'How – disagreeably?'

'Haven't you noticed anything?' Winterbourne asked.

'I have noticed you. But I noticed you were as stiff as an umbrella the first time I saw you.'

'You will find I am not so stiff as several others,' said Winterbourne, smiling.

'How shall I find it?'

'By going to see the others.'

'What will they do to me?'

'They will give you the cold shoulder. Do you know what that means?'

Daisy was looking at him intently; she began to colour. 'Do you mean as Mrs Walker did the other night?'

'Exactly!' said Winterbourne.

She looked away at Giovanelli, who was decorating himself with his almond blossom. Then looking back at Winterbourne – 'I shouldn't think you would let people be so unkind!' she said.

'How can I help it?' he asked.

'I should think you would say something.'

'I do say something'; and he paused a moment. 'I say that your mother tells me that she believes you are engaged.'

'Well, she does,' said Daisy very simply.

Winterbourne began to laugh. 'And does Randolph believe it?' he asked.

'I guess Randolph doesn't believe anything,' said Daisy. Randolph's scepticism excited Winterbourne to further hilarity, and he observed that Giovanelli was coming back to them. Daisy, observing it too, addressed herself to her countryman. 'Since you have mentioned it,' she said, 'I *am* engaged.' . . . Winterbourne looked at her; he had stopped laughing. 'You don't believe it!' she added.

He was silent a moment; and then, 'Yes, I believe it!' he said.

'Oh, no, you don't,' she answered. 'Well, then – I am not!'

The young girl and her cicerone were on their way to the gate of the enclosure, so that Winterbourne, who had but lately entered, presently took leave of them. A week afterwards he went to dine at a beautiful villa on the Caelian Hill, and, on arriving, dismissed his hired vehicle. The evening was charming, and he promised himself the satisfaction of walking home beneath the Arch of Constantine and past the vaguely lighted monuments of the Forum. There was a waning moon in the sky, and her radiance was not brilliant, but she was veiled in a thin cloud-curtain which seemed to diffuse and equalize it. When, on his return from the villa (it was eleven o'clock),

Winterbourne approached the dusky circle of the Colosseum, it occurred to him, as a lover of the picturesque, that the interior, in the pale moonshine, would be well worth a glance. He turned aside and walked to one of the empty arches, near which, as he observed, an open carriage – one of the little Roman street-cabs – was stationed. Then he passed in among the cavernous shadows of the great structure, and emerged upon the clear and silent arena. The place had never seemed to him more impressive. One half of the gigantic circus was in deep shade; the other was sleeping in the luminous dusk. As he stood there he began to murmur Byron's famous lines out of *Manfred*; but before he had finished his quotation he remembered that if nocturnal meditations in the Colosseum are recommended by the poets, they are deprecated by the doctors. The historic atmosphere was there, certainly; but the historic atmosphere, scientifically considered, was no better than a villainous miasma. Winterbourne walked to the middle of the arena, to take a more general glance, intending thereafter to make a hasty retreat. The great cross in the centre was covered with shadow; it was only as he drew near it that he made it out distinctly. Then he saw that two persons were stationed upon the low steps which formed its base. One of these was a woman, seated; her companion was standing in front of her.

Presently the sound of the woman's voice came to him distinctly in the warm night air. 'Well, he looks at us as one of the old lions or tigers may have looked at the Christian martyrs!' These were the words he heard, in the familiar accent of Miss Daisy Miller.

'Let us hope he is not very hungry,' responded the ingenious Giovanelli. 'He will have to take me first; you will serve for dessert!'

Winterbourne stopped, with a sort of horror; and, it must be added, with a sort of relief. It was as if a sudden illumination had been flashed upon the ambiguity of Daisy's behaviour and the riddle had become easy to read. She was a young lady whom a gentleman need no longer be at pains to respect. He stood there looking at her – looking at her companion, and not reflecting that though he saw them vaguely, he himself must have been more brightly visible. He felt angry with himself that he had bothered so much about the right way of regarding Miss Daisy Miller. Then, as he was going to advance again, he checked himself; not from the fear that he was doing her injustice, but from a sense of the danger of appearing unbecomingly exhilarated by this sudden revulsion from cautious criticism. He turned away towards the entrance of the place; but as he did so he heard Daisy speak again.

'Why, it was Mr Winterbourne! He saw me – and he cuts me!'

What a clever little reprobate she was, and how smartly she played an injured innocence! But he wouldn't cut her. Winterbourne came forward again, and went towards the great cross. Daisy had got up; Giovanelli lifted his hat. Winterbourne had now begun to think simply of the craziness, from a sanitary point of view, of a delicate young girl lounging away the evening in this nest of malaria. What if she *were* a clever little reprobate? That was no reason for her dying of the *perniciosa*. 'How long have you been here?' he asked, almost brutally.

Daisy, lovely in the flattering moonlight, looked at him a moment. Then – 'All the evening,' she answered gently . . . 'I never saw anything so pretty.'

'I am afraid,' said Winterbourne, 'that you will not think Roman fever very pretty. This is the way people catch it. I wonder,' he added, turning to Giovanelli, 'that you, a native Roman, should countenance such a terrible indiscretion.'

'Ah,' said the handsome native, 'for myself, I am not afraid.'

'Neither am I – for you! I am speaking for this young lady.'

Giovanelli lifted his well-shaped eyebrows and showed his brilliant teeth. But he took Winterbourne's rebuke with docility. 'I told the Signorina it was a grave indiscretion; but when was the Signorina ever prudent?'

'I never was sick, and I don't mean to be!' the Signorina declared. 'I don't look like much, but I'm healthy! I was bound to see the Colosseum by moonlight; I shouldn't have wanted to go home without that; and we have had the most beautiful time, haven't we, Mr Giovanelli! If there has been any danger, Eugenio can give me some pills. He has got some splendid pills.'

'I should advise you,' said Winterbourne, 'to drive home as fast as possible and take one!'

'What you say is very wise,' Giovanelli rejoined. 'I will go and make sure the carriage is at hand.' And he went forward rapidly.

Daisy, lovely in the flattering moonlight, looked at him a moment. Then – 'All the evening,' she answered gently . . . 'I never saw anything so pretty.'

'I am afraid,' said Winterbourne, 'that you will not think Roman fever very pretty. This is the way people catch it. I wonder,' he added, turning

Daisy followed with Winterbourne. He kept looking at her; she seemed not in the least embarrassed. Winterbourne said nothing; Daisy chattered about the beauty of the place. 'Well, I *have* seen the Colosseum by moonlight!' she exclaimed. 'That's one good thing.' Then, noticing Winterbourne's silence, she asked him why he didn't speak. He made no answer; he only began to laugh. They passed under one of the dark archways; Giovanelli was in front with the carriage. Here Daisy stopped for a moment, looking at the young American. '*Did* you believe I was engaged the other day?' she asked.

not!'

He felt the young girl's pretty eyes fixed upon him through the thick gloom of the archway; she was apparently going to answer. But Govanelli hurried her forward. 'Quick, quick,' he said; 'if we get in by midnight we are quite safe.'

Daisy took her seat in the carriage, and the fortunate Italian placed himself beside her. 'Don't forget Eugenio's pills!' said Winterbourne, as he lifted his hat.

'I don't care,' said Daisy, in a little strange tone, 'whether I have Roman fever or not!' Upon this the cab-driver cracked his whip, and they rolled away over the desultory patches of the antique pavement.

Winterbourne – to do him justice, as it were – mentioned to no one that he had encountered Miss Miller, at midnight, in the Colosseum with a gentleman; but nevertheless, a couple of days later, the fact of her having been there under these circumstances was known to every member of the little American circle, and commented accordingly. Winterbourne reflected that they had of course known it at the hotel, and that, after Daisy's return, there had been an exchange of jokes between the porter and the cab-driver. But the young man was conscious at the same moment that it had ceased to be a matter of serious regret to him that the little American flirt should be 'talked about' by low-minded menials. These people, a day or two later, had serious information to give: the little American flirt was alarmingly ill. Winterbourne, when the rumour came to him, immediately went to the hotel for more news. He found that two or three charitable friends had preceded him, and that they were being entertained in Mrs Miller's salon by Randolph.

'It's going round at night,' said Randolph – 'that's what made her sick. She's always going round at night. I shouldn't think she'd want to – it's so plaguey dark. You can't see anything here at night, except where there's a moon. In America there's always a moon!' Mrs Miller was invisible; she was now, at least, giving her daughter the advantage of her society. It was evident that Daisy was dangerously ill.

Winterbourne went often to ask for news of her, and once he saw Mrs Miller, who, though deeply alarmed, was – rather to his surprise – perfectly composed, and, as it appeared, a most efficient and judicious nurse. She talked a good deal about Dr Davis, but Winterbourne paid her the compliment of saying to himself that she was not, after all, such a monstrous goose. 'Daisy spoke of you the other day,' she said to him. 'Half the time she doesn't know what she's saying, but that time I think she did. She gave me a message; she told me to tell you. She told me to tell you that she never was engaged to that handsome Italian. I am sure I am very glad; Mr Giovanelli hasn't been near us since she was taken ill. I thought he was so much of a gentleman; but I don't call that very polite! A lady told me that he was afraid I was angry with him for taking Daisy round at night. Well, so I am; but I suppose he knows I'm a lady. I would scorn to scold him. Anyway, she says she's not engaged. I don't know why she wanted you to know; but she said to me three times – "Mind you tell Mr Winterbourne." And then she told me to ask if you remembered the time you went to that castle, in Switzerland. But I said I wouldn't give any such messages as that. Only, if she is not engaged, I'm sure I'm glad to know it.'

But, as Winterbourne had said, it mattered very little. A week after this the poor girl died; it had been a terrible case of the fever. Daisy's grave was in the little Protestant cemetery, in an angle of the wall of imperial Rome, beneath the cypresses and the thick spring flowers. Winterbourne stood there beside it, with a number of other mourners; a number larger than the scandal excited by the young lady's career would have led you to expect. Near him stood Giovanelli, who came nearer still before Winterbourne turned away. Giovanelli was very pale; on this occasion he had no flower in his buttonhole; he seemed to wish to say something. At last he said, 'She was the most beautiful lady I ever saw, and the most amiable.' And then he added in a moment, 'And she was the most innocent.'

Winterbourne looked at him, and presently repeated his words, 'And the most innocent?'

'The most innocent!'

Winterbourne felt sore and angry. 'Why the devil,' he asked, 'did you take her to that fatal place?'

Mr Giovanelli's urbanity was apparently imperturbable. He looked on the ground for a moment, and then he said, 'For myself, I had no fear; and she wanted to go.'

'That was no reason!' Winterbourne declared.

The subtle Roman again dropped his eyes. 'If she had lived, I should have got nothing. She would never have married me, I am sure.'

'She would never have married you?'

'For a moment I hoped so. But no, I am sure.'

Winterbourne listened to him; he stood staring at the raw protuberance among the April daisies. When he turned away again Mr Giovanelli, with his light slow step, had retired.

Winterbourne almost immediately left Rome; but the following summer he again met his aunt, Mrs Costello, at Vevey. Mrs Costello was fond of Vevey. In the interval Winterbourne had often thought of Daisy Miller and her mystifying manners. One day he spoke of her to his aunt – said it was on his conscience that he had done her injustice.

'I am sure I don't know,' said Mrs Costello. 'How did your injustice affect her?'

'She sent me a message before her death which I didn't understand at the time. But I have understood it since. She would have appreciated one's esteem.'

'Is that a modest way,' asked Mrs Costello, 'of saying that she would have reciprocated one's affection?'

Winterbourne offered no answer to this question; but he presently said, 'You were right in that remark that you made last summer. I was booked to make a mistake. I have lived too long in foreign parts.'

Nevertheless, he went back to live at Geneva, whence there continue to come the most contradictory accounts of his motives of sojourn: a report that he is 'studying' hard – an intimation that he is much interested in a very clever foreign lady.

Washington Square

Chapter One

During a portion of the first half of the present century, and more particularly during the latter part of it, there flourished and practised in the city of New York a physician who enjoyed perhaps an exceptional share of the consideration which, in the United States, has always been bestowed upon distinguished members of the medical profession. This profession in America has constantly been held in honour, and more successfully than elsewhere has put forward a claim to the epithet of 'liberal'. In a country in which, to play a social part, you must either earn your income or make believe that you earn it, the healing art has appeared in a high degree to combine two recognized sources of credit. It belongs to the realm of the practical, which in the United States is a great recommendation; and it is touched by the light of science – a merit appreciated in a community in which the love of knowledge has not always been accompanied by leisure and opportunity.

It was an element in Doctor Sloper's reputation that his learning and his skill were very evenly balanced; he was what you might call a scholarly doctor, and yet there was nothing abstract in his remedies – he always ordered you to take something. Though he was felt to be extremely thorough, he was not uncomfortably theoretic; and if he sometimes explained matters rather more minutely than might seem of use to the patient, he never went so far (like some practitioners one had heard of) as to trust to the explanation alone, but always left behind him an inscrutable prescription. There were some doctors that left the prescription without offering any explanation at all; and he did not belong to that class either, which was after all the most vulgar. It will be seen that I am describing a clever man; and this is really the reason why Doctor Sloper had become a local celebrity.

At the time at which we are chiefly concerned with him he was some fifty years of age, and his popularity was at its height. He was very witty, and he passed in the best society of New York for a man of the world – which, indeed, he was, in a very sufficient degree. I hasten to add, to anticipate possible misconception, that he was not the least of a charlatan. He was a thoroughly honest man – honest in a degree of which he had perhaps lacked the opportunity to give the complete measure; and, putting aside the great good nature of the circle in which he practised, which was rather fond of boasting that it possessed the 'brightest' doctor in the country, he daily justified his claim to the talents attributed to him by the popular voice. He was an observer, even a philosopher, and to be bright was so natural to him, and (as the popular voice said) came so easily, that he never aimed at mere effect, and had none of the little tricks and pretensions of second-rate reputations. It must be confessed that fortune had favoured him, and that he had found the path to prosperity very soft to his tread. He had married, at the age of twenty-seven, for love, a very charming girl, Miss Catherine Harrington, of New York, who, in addition to her charms, had brought him a solid dowry. Mrs Sloper was amiable, graceful, accomplished, elegant, and in 1820 she had been one of the pretty girls of the small but promising capital which clustered about the Battery and overlooked the Bay, and of which the uppermost boundary was indicated by the grassy waysides of Canal Street. Even at the age of twenty-seven Austin Sloper had made his mark sufficiently to mitigate the anomaly of his having been chosen among a dozen suitors by a young woman of high fashion, who had ten thousand dollars of income and the most charming eyes in the island of Manhattan. These eyes, and some of their accompaniments, were for about five years a source of extreme satisfaction to the young physician, who was both a devoted and a very happy husband.

The fact of his having married a rich woman made no difference in the line he had traced for himself, and he cultivated his profession with as definite a purpose as if he still had no other resources than his fraction of the modest patrimony which, on his father's death, he had shared with his brothers and sisters. This purpose had not been preponderantly to make money – it had been rather to learn something and to do something. To learn something interesting, and to do something useful – this was, roughly speaking, the programme he had sketched, and of which the accident of his wife having an income appeared to him in no degree to modify the validity. He was fond of his practice, and of exercising a skill of which he was agreeably conscious, and it was so patent a truth that if he were not a doctor there was nothing else he could be, that a doctor he persisted in being, in the best possible conditions. Of course his easy domestic situation saved him a good deal of drudgery, and his wife's affiliation to the 'best people' brought him a good many of those patients whose symptoms are, if not more interesting in themselves than those of the lower orders, at least more consistently displayed. He desired experience, and in the course of twenty years he got a great deal. It must be added that it came to him in some forms which, whatever might have been their intrinsic value, made it the reverse of welcome. His first child, a little boy of extraordinary promise, as the Doctor, who was not addicted to easy enthusiasm, firmly believed, died at three years of age, in spite of everything that the mother's tenderness and the father's science could invent to save him. Two years later Mrs Sloper gave birth to a second infant – an infant of a sex which rendered the poor child, to the Doctor's sense, an inadequate substitute for his lamented first-born, of whom he had promised himself to make an admirable man. The little girl was a disappointment; but this was not the worst. A week after her birth the young mother, who, as the phrase is, had been doing well, suddenly betrayed alarming symptoms, and before another week had elapsed Austin Sloper was a widower.

For a man whose trade was to keep people alive he had certainly done poorly in his own family; and a bright doctor who within three years loses his wife and his little boy should perhaps be prepared to see either his skill or his affection impugned. Our friend, however, escaped criticism; that is, he escaped all criticism but his own, which was much the most competent and most formidable. He walked under the weight of this very private censure for the rest of his days, and bore forever the scars of a castigation to which the strongest hand he knew had treated him on the night that followed his wife's death. The world, which, as I have said, appreciated him, pitied him too much to be ironical; his misfortune made him more interesting, and even helped him to be the fashion. It was observed that even medical families cannot escape the more insidious forms of disease, and that, after all, Doctor Sloper had lost other patients besides the two I have mentioned; which constituted an honourable precedent. His little girl remained to him; and though she was not what he had desired, he proposed to himself to make the best of her. He had on hand a stock of unexpended authority, by which the child, in its early years, profited largely. She had been named, as a matter of course, after her poor mother, and even in her most diminutive babyhood the Doctor never called her anything but Catherine. She grew up a very robust and healthy child, and her father, as he looked at her, often said to himself that, such as she was, he at least need have no fear of losing her. I say 'such as she was', because, to tell the truth – But this is a truth of which will I defer the telling.

Chapter Two

When the child was about ten years old, he invited his sister, Mrs Penniman, to come and stay with him. The Miss Slopers had been but two in number, and both of them had married early in life. The younger, Mrs Almond by name, was the wife of a prosperous merchant and the mother of a blooming family. She bloomed herself, indeed, and was a comely, comfortable, reasonable woman, and a favourite with her clever brother, who, in the matter of women, even when they were nearly related to him, was a man of distinct preferences, He preferred Mrs Almond to his sister Lavinia, who had married a poor clergyman, of a sickly constitution and a flowery style of eloquence, and then, at the age of thirty-three, had been left a widow – without children, without fortune – with nothing but the memory of Mr Penniman's flowers of speech, a certain vague aroma of which hovered about her own conversation. Nevertheless, he had offered her a home under his own roof, which Lavinia accepted with the alacrity of a woman who had spent the ten years of her married life in the town of Poughkeepsie. The Doctor had not proposed to Mrs Penniman to come and live with him indefinitely; he had suggested that she should make an asylum of his house while she looked about for unfurnished lodgings. It is uncertain whether Mrs Penniman ever instituted a search for unfurnished lodgings, but it is beyond dispute that she never found them. She settled herself with her brother and never went away, and, when Catherine was twenty years old, her Aunt Lavinia was still one of the most striking features of her immediate *entourage*. Mrs Penniman's own account of the matter was that she had remained to take charge of her niece's education. She had given this account, at least, to everyone but the Doctor, who never asked for explanations which he could entertain himself any day with inventing. Mrs Penniman, moreover, though she had a good deal of a certain sort of artificial assurance, shrunk, for indefinable reasons, from presenting herself to her brother as a fountain of instruction. She had not a high sense of humour, but she had enough to prevent her from making this mistake; and her brother, on his side, had enough to excuse her, in her situation, for laying him under contribution during a considerable part of a lifetime. He therefore assented tacitly to the proposition which Mrs Penniman had tacitly laid down, that it was of importance that the poor motherless girl should have a brilliant woman near her. His assent could only be tacit, for he had never been dazzled by his sister's intellectual lustre. Save when he fell in love with Catherine Harrington, he had never been dazzled, indeed, by any feminine characteristics whatever; and though he was to a certain extent what is called a ladies' doctor, his private opinion of the more complicated sex was not exalted. He regarded its complications as more curious than edifying, and he had an idea of the beauty of *reason*, which was, on the whole, meagrely gratified by what he observed in his female patients. His wife had been a reasonable woman, but she was a bright exception; among several things that he was sure of, this was perhaps the principal. Such a conviction, of course, did little either to mitigate or to abbreviate his widowhood; and it set a limit to his recognition, at the best, of Catherine's possibilities and of Mrs Penniman's ministrations. He nevertheless, at the end of six months, accepted his sister's permanent presence as an accomplished fact, and as Catherine grew older, perceived that there were in effect good reasons why she should have a companion of her own imperfect sex. He was extremely polite to Lavinia, scrupulously, formally polite; and she had never seen him in anger but once in her life, when he lost his temper in a theological discussion with her late husband. With her he never discussed theology, nor, indeed, discussed anything; he contented himself with making known, very distinctly, in the form of a lucid ultimatum, his wishes with regard to Catherine.

Once, when the girl was about twelve years old, he had said to her:

'Try and make a clever woman of her, Lavinia; I should like her to be a clever woman.'

Mrs Penniman, at this, looked thoughtful a moment. 'My dear Austin,' she then inquired, 'do you think it is better to be clever than to be good?'

'Good for what?' asked the Doctor. 'You are good for nothing unless you are clever.'

From this assertion Mrs Penniman saw no reason to dissent; she possibly reflected that her own great use in the world was owing to her aptitude for many things.

'Of course I wish Catherine to be good,' the Doctor said next day; 'but she won't be any the less virtuous for not being a fool. I am not afraid of her being wicked; she will never have the salt of malice in her character. She is "as good as good bread", as the French say; but six years hence I don't want to have to compare her to good bread-and-butter.'

'Are you afraid she will be insipid? My dear brother, it is I who supply the butter; so you needn't fear!' said Mrs Penniman, who had taken in hand the child's 'accomplishments', overlooking her at the piano, where Catherine displayed a certain talent, and going with her to the dancing-class, where it must be confessed that she made but a modest figure.

Mrs Penniman was a tall, thin, fair, rather faded woman, with a perfectly amiable disposition, a high standard of gentility, a taste for light literature, and a certain foolish indirectness and obliquity of character. She was romantic; she was sentimental; she had a passion for little secrets and mysteries – a very innocent passion, for her secrets had hitherto always been as unpractical as addled eggs. She was not absolutely veracious; but this defect was of no great consequence, for she had never had anything to conceal. She would have liked to have a lover, and to correspond with him under an assumed name, in letters left at a shop. I am bound to say that her imagination never carried the intimacy further than this. Mrs Penniman had never had a lover, but her brother, who was very shrewd, understood her turn of mind. 'When Catherine is about seventeen,' he said to himself, 'Lavinia will try and persuade her that some young man with a moustache is in love with her. It will be quite untrue; no young man, with a moustache or without, will ever be in love with Catherine. But Lavinia will take it up, and talk to her about it; perhaps, even, if her taste for clandestine operations doesn't prevail with her, she will talk to me about it. Catherine won't see it, and won't believe it, fortunately for her peace of mind; poor Catherine isn't romantic.'

She was a healthy, well-grown child, without a trace of her mother's beauty. She was not ugly; she had simply a plain, dull, gentle countenance. The most that had ever been said for her was that she had a 'nice' face; and, though she was an heiress, no one had ever thought of regarding her as a belle. Her father's opinion of her moral purity was abundantly justified; she was excellently, imperturbably good; affectionate, docile, obedient, and much addicted to speaking the truth. In her younger years she was a good deal of a romp, and, though it is an awkward confession to make about one's heroine, I must add that she was something of a glutton. She never, that I know of, stole raisins out of the pantry; but she devoted her pocket-money to the purchase of cream cakes. As regards this, however, a critical attitude would be inconsistent with a candid reference to the early annals of any biographer. Catherine was decidedly not clever; she was not quick with her book, nor, indeed, with anything else. She was not abnormally deficient, and she mustered learning enough to acquit herself respectably in conversation with her contemporaries – among whom it must be avowed, however, that she occupied a secondary place. It is well known that in New York it is possible for a young girl to occupy a primary one. Catherine, who was extremely modest, had no desire to shine, and on most social occasions, as they are called, you would have found her lurking in the background. She was extremely fond of her father, and very much afraid of him; she thought him the cleverest and handsomest and most celebrated of men. The poor girl found her account so completely in the exercise of her affections that the little tremor of fear that mixed itself with her filial passion gave the thing an extra relish rather than blunted its edge. Her deepest desire was to please him, and her conception of happiness was to know that she had succeeded in pleasing him. She had never succeeded beyond a certain point. Though, on the whole, he was very kind to her, she was perfectly aware of this, and to go beyond the point in question seemed to her really something to live for.

What she could not know, of course, was that she disappointed him, though on three or four occasions the Doctor had been almost frank about it. She grew up peacefully and prosperously; but at the age of eighteen Mrs Penniman had not made a clever woman of her. Doctor Sloper would have liked to be proud of his daughter; but there was nothing to be proud of in poor Catherine. There was nothing, of course, to be ashamed of; but this was not enough for the Doctor, who was a proud man, and would have enjoyed being able to think of his daughter as an unusual girl. There would have been a fitness in her being pretty and graceful, intelligent and distinguished – for her mother had been the most charming woman of her little day – and as regards her father, of course he knew his own value. He had moments of irritation at having produced a commonplace child, and he even went so far at times as to take a certain satisfaction in the thought that his wife had not lived to find her out. He was naturally slow in making this discovery himself, and it was not till Catherine had become a young lady grown that he regarded the matter as settled. He gave her the benefit of a great many doubts; he was in no haste to conclude. Mrs Penniman frequently assured him that his daughter had a delightful nature; but he knew how to interpret this assurance. It meant, to his sense, that Catherine was not wise enough to discover that her aunt was a goose – a limitation of mind that could not fail to be agreeable to Mrs Penniman. Both she and her brother, however, exaggerated the young girl's limitations; for Catherine, though she was very fond of her aunt, and conscious of the gratitude she owed her, regarded her without a particle of that gentle dread which gave its stamp to her admiration of her father. To her mind there was nothing of the infinite about Mrs Penniman; Catherine saw her all at once, as it were, and was not dazzled by the apparition; whereas her father's great faculties seemed, as they stretched away, to lose themselves in a sort of luminous vagueness, which indicated, not that they stopped, but that Catherine's own mind ceased to follow them.

It must not be supposed that Doctor Sloper visited his disappointment upon the poor girl, or ever let her suspect that she had played him a trick. On the contrary, for fear of being unjust to her, he did his duty with exemplary zeal, and recognized that she was a faithful and affectionate child. Besides, he was a philosopher: he smoked a good many cigars over his disappointment, and in the fullness of time he got used to it. He satisfied himself that he had expected nothing, though, indeed, with a certain oddity of reasoning. 'I expect nothing,' he said to himself; 'so that, if she gives me a surprise, it will be all clear gain. If she doesn't, it will be no loss.' This was about the time Catherine had reached her eighteenth year; so that it will be seen her father had not been precipitate. At this time she seemed not only incapable of giving surprises; it was almost a question whether she could have received one – she was so quiet and irresponsive. People who expressed themselves roughly called her stolid. But she was irresponsive because she was shy, uncomfortably, painfully shy. This was not always understood, and she sometimes produced an impression of insensibility. In reality, she was the softest creature in the world.

Chapter Three

As a child she had promised to be tall; but when she was sixteen she ceased to grow, and her stature, like most other points in her composition, was not unusual. She was strong, however, and properly made, and, fortunately, her health was excellent. It has been noted that the Doctor was a philosopher, but I would not have answered for his philosophy if the poor girl had proved a sickly and suffering person. Her appearance of health constituted her principal claim to beauty; and her clear, fresh complexion, in which white and red were very equally distributed, was, indeed, an excellent thing to see. Her eye was small and quiet, her features were rather thick, her tresses brown and smooth. A dull, plain girl she was called by rigorous critics – a quiet, lady-like girl, by those of the more imaginative sort, but by neither class was she very elaborately discussed. When it had been duly impressed upon her that she was a young lady – it was a good while before she could believe it – she suddenly developed a lively taste for dress: a lively taste is quite the expression to use. I feel as if I ought to write it very small, her judgement in this matter was by no means infallible; it was liable to confusions and embarrassments. Her great indulgence of it was really the desire of a rather inarticulate nature to manifest itself; she sought to be eloquent in her garments, and to make up for her diffidence of speech by a fine frankness of costume. But if she expressed herself in her clothes, it is certain that people were not to blame for not thinking her a witty person. It must be added that, though she had the expectation of a fortune – Doctor Sloper for a long time had been making twenty thousand dollars a year by his profession, and laying aside the half of it – the amount of money at her disposal was not greater than the allowance made to many poorer girls. In those days, in New York, there were still a few altar-fires flickering in the temple of Republican simplicity, and Doctor Sloper would have been glad to see his daughter present herself, with a classic grace, as a priestess of this mild faith. It made him fairly grimace, in private, to think that a child of his should be both ugly and overdressed. For himself, he was fond of the good things of life, and he made a considerable use of them; but he had a dread of vulgarity, and even a theory that it was increasing in the society that surrounded him. Moreover, the standard of luxury in the United States thirty years ago was carried by no means so high as at present, and Catherine's clever father took the old-fashioned view of the education of young persons. He had no particular theory on the subject; it had scarcely as yet become a necessity of self-defence to have a collection of theories. It simply appeared to him proper and reasonable that a well-bred young woman should not carry half her fortune on her back. Catherine's back was a broad one, and would have carried a good deal; but to the weight of the paternal displeasure she never ventured to expose it, and our heroine was twenty years old before she treated herself, for evening wear, to a red satin gown trimmed with gold fringe; though this was an article which, for many years, she had coveted in secret. It made her look, when she sported it, like a woman of thirty; but oddly enough, in spite of her taste for fine clothes, she had not a grain of coquetry, and her anxiety when she put them on was as to whether they, and not she, would look well. It is a point on which history has not been explicit, but the assumption is warrantable; it was in the royal raiment just mentioned that she presented herself at a little entertainment given by her aunt, Mrs Almond. The girl was at this time in her twenty-first year, and Mrs Almond's party was the beginning of something very important.

Some three or four years before this, Doctor Sloper had moved his household gods up town, as they say in New York. He had been living ever since his marriage in an edifice of red brick, with granite copings and an enormous fan-light over the door, standing in a street within five minutes' walk of the City Hall, which saw its best days (from the social point of view) about 1820. After this, the tide of fashion began to set steadily northward, as, indeed, in New York, thanks to the narrow channel in which it flows, it is obliged to do, and the great hum of traffic rolled farther to the right and left of Broadway. By the time the Doctor changed his residence, the murmur of trade had become a mighty uproar, which was music in the ears of all good citizens interested in the commercial development, as they delighted to call it, of their fortunate isle. Doctor Sloper's interest in this phenomenon was only indirect – though, seeing that, as the years went on, half his patients came to be overworked men of business, it might have been more immediate – and when most of his neighbours' dwellings (also ornamented with granite copings and large fan-lights) had been converted into offices, warehouses, and shipping agencies, and otherwise applied to the base uses of commerce, he determined to look out for a quieter home. The ideal of quiet and of genteel retirement, in 1835, was found in Washington Square, where the Doctor built himself a handsome, modern, wide-fronted house, with a big balcony before the drawing-room windows, and a flight of white marble steps ascending to a portal which was also faced with white marble. This structure, and many of its neighbours, which it exactly resembled, were supposed, forty years ago, to embody the last results of architectural science, and they remain to this day very solid and honourable dwellings. In front of them was the square, containing a considerable quantity of inexpensive vegetation, enclosed by a wooden paling, which increased its rural and accessible appearance; and round the corner was the more august precinct of the Fifth Avenue, taking its origin at this point with a spacious and confident air which already marked it for high destinies. I know not whether it is owing to the tenderness of early associations, but this portion of New York appears to many persons the most delectable. It has a kind of established repose which is not of frequent occurrence in other quarters of the long, shrill city; it has a riper, richer, more honourable look than any of the upper ramifications of the great longitudinal thoroughfare – the look of having had something of a social history. It was here, as you might have been informed on good authority, that you had come into a world which appeared to offer a variety of sources of interest; it was here that your grandmother lived, in venerable solitude, and dispensed a hospitality which commended itself alike to the infant imagination and the infant palate; it was here that you took your first walks abroad, following the nursery-maid with unequal step, and sniffing up the strange odour of the ailanthus-trees which at that time formed the principal umbrage of the Square, and diffused an aroma that you were not yet critical enough to dislike as it deserved; it was here, finally, that your first school, kept by a broad-bosomed, broad-based old lady with a ferule, who was always having tea in a blue cup, with a saucer that didn't match, enlarged the circle both of your observations and your sensations. It was here, at any rate, that my heroine spent many years of her life; which is my excuse for this topographical parenthesis.

Mrs Almond lived much farther up town, in an embryonic street, with a high number – a region where the extension of the city began to assume a theoretic air, where poplars grew beside the pavement (when there was one), and mingled their shade with the steep roofs of desultory Dutch houses, and where pigs and chickens disported themselves in the gutter. These elements of rural picturesqueness have now wholly departed from New York street scenery; but they were to be found within the memory of middle-aged persons in quarters which now would blush to be reminded of them. Catherine had a great many cousins, and with her Aunt Almond's children, who ended by being nine in number, she lived on terms of considerable intimacy. When she was younger they had been rather afraid of her; she was believed, as the phrase is, to be highly educated, and a person who lived in the intimacy of their Aunt Penniman had something of reflected grandeur. Mrs Penniman, among the little Almonds, was an object of more admiration than sympathy. Her manners were strange and formidable, and her mourning robes – she dressed in black for twenty years after her husband's death, and then suddenly appeared, one morning, with pink roses in her cap – were complicated in odd, unexpected places with buckles, bugles, and pins, which discouraged familiarity. She took children too hard, both for good and for evil, and had an oppressive air of expecting subtle things of them; so that going to see her was a good deal like being taken to church and made to sit in a front pew. It was discovered after awhile, however, that Aunt Penniman was but an accident in Catherine's existence, and not a part of its essence, and that when the girl came to spend a Saturday with her cousins, she was available for 'follow-my-master', and even for leap-frog. On this basis an understanding was easily arrived at, and for several years Catherine fraternized with her young kinsmen. I say young kinsmen, because seven of the little Almonds were boys, and Catherine had a preference for those games which are most conveniently played in trousers. By degrees, however, the little Almonds' trousers began to lengthen, and the wearers to disperse and settle themselves in life. The elder children were older than Catherine, and the boys were sent to college or placed in counting-rooms. Of the girls, one married very punctually, and the other as punctually became engaged. It was to celebrate this latter event that Mrs Almond gave the little party I have mentioned. Her daughter was to marry a stout young stockbroker, a boy of twenty: it was thought a very good thing.

Chapter Four

Mrs Penniman, with more buckles and bangles than ever, came, of course, to the entertainment, accompanied by her niece; the Doctor, too, had promised to look in later in the evening. There was to be a good deal of dancing, and before it had gone very far Marian Almond came up to Catherine, in company with a tall young man. She introduced the young man as a person who had a great desire to make our heroine's acquaintance, and as a cousin of Arthur Townsend, her own intended.

Marian Almond was a pretty little person of seventeen, with a very small figure and a very big sash, to the elegance of whose manners matrimony had nothing to add. She already had all the airs of a hostess, receiving the company, shaking her fan, saying that with so many people to attend to she should have no time to dance. She made a long speech about Mr Townsend's cousin, to whom she administered a tap with her fan before turning away to other cares. Catherine had not understood all that she said; her attention was given to enjoying Marian's ease of manner and flow of ideas, and to looking at the young man, who was remarkably handsome. She had succeeded, however, as she often failed to do when people were presented to her, in catching his name, which appeared to be the same as that of Marian's little stockbroker. Catherine was always agitated by an introduction; it seemed a difficult moment, and she wondered that some people – her new acquaintance at this moment, for instance – should mind it so little. She wondered what she ought to say, and what would be the consequences of her saying nothing. The consequences at present were very agreeable. Mr Townsend, leaving her no time for embarrassment, began to talk to her with an easy smile, as if he had known her for a year.

'What a delightful party! What a charming house! What an interesting family! What a pretty girl your cousin is!'

These observations, in themselves of no great profundity, Mr Townsend seemed to offer for what they were worth, and as a contribution to an acquaintance. He looked straight into Catherine's eyes. She answered nothing; she only listened, and looked at him; and he, as if he expected no particular reply, went on to say many other things in the same comfortable and natural manner. Catherine, though she felt tongue-tied, was conscious of no embarrassment; it seemed proper that he should talk, and that she should simply look at him. What made it natural was that he was so handsome, or, rather, as she phrased it to herself, so beautiful. The music had been silent for a while, but it suddenly began again; and then he asked her, with a deeper, intenser smile, if she would do him the honour of dancing with him. Even to this inquiry she gave no audible assent; she simply let him put his arm round her waist – as she did so, it occurred to her more vividly than it had ever done before that this was a singular place for a gentleman's arm to be – and in a moment he was guiding her round the room in the harmonious rotation of the polka. When they paused, she felt that she was red; and then, for some moments, she stopped looking at him. She fanned herself, and looked at the flowers that were painted on her fan. He asked her if she would begin again, and she hesitated to answer, still looking at the flowers.

'Does it make you dizzy?' he asked, in a tone of great kindness.

Then Catherine looked up at him; he was certainly beautiful, and not at all red. 'Yes,' she said; she hardly knew why, for dancing had never made her dizzy.

'Ah, well, in that case,' said Mr Townsend, 'we will sit still and talk. I will find a good place to sit.'

He found a good place – a charming place; a little sofa that seemed meant only for two persons. The rooms by this time were very full; the dancers increased in number, and people stood close in front of them, turning their backs, so that Catherine and her companion seemed secluded and unobserved. '*We* will talk,' the young man had said; but he still did all the talking. Catherine leaned back in her place, with her eyes fixed upon him, smiling, and thinking him very clever. He had features like young men in pictures; Catherine had never seen such features – so delicate, so chiselled and finished – among the young New Yorkers whom she passed in the streets and met at dancing-parties. He was tall and slim, but he looked extremely strong. Catherine thought he looked like a statue. But a statue would not talk like that, and, above all, would not have eyes of so rare a colour. He had never been at Mrs Almond's before; he felt very much like a stranger; and it was very kind of Catherine to take pity on him. He was Arthur Townsend's cousin – not very near; several times removed – and Arthur had brought him to present him to the family. In fact, he was a great stranger in New York. It was his native place; but he had not been there for many years. He had been knocking about the world, and living in queer corners; he had only come back a month or two before. New York was very pleasant, only he felt lonely.

'You see, people forget you,' he said, smiling at Catherine with his delightful gaze, while he leaned forward obliquely, turning towards her, with his elbows on his knees.

It seemed to Catherine that no one who had once seen him would ever forget him; but though she made this reflection she kept it to herself, almost as you would keep something precious.

They sat there for some time. He was very amusing. He asked her about the people that were near them; he tried to guess who some of them were, and he made the most laughable mistakes. He criticized them very freely, in a positive, off-hand way. Catherine had never heard anyone – especially any young man – talk just like that. It was the way a young man might talk in a novel; or, better still, in a play, on the stage, close before the footlights, looking at the audience, and with everyone looking at him, so that you wondered at his presence of mind. And yet Mr Townsend was not like an actor; he seemed so sincere, so natural. This was very interesting; but in the midst of it Marian Almond came pushing through the crowd, with a little ironical cry, when she found these young people still together, which made everyone turn round, and cost Catherine a conscious blush. Marian broke up their talk, and told Mr Townsend – whom she treated as if she were already married, and he had become her cousin – to run away to her mother, who had been wishing for the last half-hour to introduce him to Mr Almond.

'We shall meet again,' he said to Catherine as he left her, and Catherine thought it a very original speech.

Her cousin took her by the arm, and made her walk about. 'I needn't ask you what you think of Morris,' the young girl exclaimed.

'Is that his name?'

'I don't ask you what you think of his name, but what you think of himself,' said Marian.

'Oh, nothing particular,' Catherine answered, dissembling for the first time in her life.

'I have half a mind to tell him that!' cried Marian. 'It will do him good; he's so terribly conceited.'

'Conceited?' said Catherine, staring.

'So Arthur says, and Arthur knows about him.'

'Oh, don't tell him!' Catherine murmured, imploringly.

'Don't tell him he's conceited! I have told him so a dozen times.'

At this profession of audacity Catherine looked down at her little companion in amazement. She supposed it was because Marian was going to be married that she took so much on herself; but she wondered too, whether, when she herself should become engaged, such exploits would be expected of her.

Half an hour later she saw her Aunt Penniman sitting in the embrasure of a window, with her head a little on one side, and her gold eye-glass raised to her eyes, which were wandering about the room. In front of her was a gentleman, bending forward a little, with his back turned to Catherine. She knew his back immediately, though she had never seen it; for when he left her, at Marian's instigation, he had retreated in the best order, without turning round. Morris Townsend – the name had already become very familiar to her, as if someone had been repeating it in her ear for the last half-hour – Morris Townsend was giving his impressions of the company to her aunt, as he had done to herself; he was saying clever things, and Mrs Penniman was smiling, as if she approved of them. As soon as Catherine had perceived this she moved away; she would not have liked him to turn round and see her. But it gave her pleasure – the whole thing. That he should talk with Mrs Penniman, with whom she lived and whom she saw and talked with every day – that seemed to keep him near her, and to make him even easier to contemplate than if she herself had been the object of his civilities; and that Aunt Lavinia should like him, should not be shocked or startled by what he said, this also appeared to the girl a personal gain; for Aunt Lavinia's standard was extremely high, planted as it was over the grave of her late husband, in which, as she had convinced everyone, the very genius of conversation was buried. One of the Almond boys, as Catherine called them, invited our heroine to dance a quadrille, and for a quarter of an hour her feet at least were occupied. This time she was not dizzy; her head was very clear. Just when the dance was over, she found herself in the crowd face to face with her father. Doctor Sloper had usually a little smile, never a very big one, and with this little smile playing in his clear eyes and on his neatly-shaved lips, he looked at his daughter's crimson gown.

'Is it possible that this magnificent person is my child?' he said.

You would have surprised him if you had told him so; but it is a literal fact that he almost never addressed his daughter save in the ironical form. Whenever he addressed her he gave her pleasure; but she had to cut her pleasure out of the piece, as it were. There were portions left over, light remnants and snippets of irony, which she never knew what to do with, which seemed too delicate for her own use; and yet Catherine, lamenting the limitations of her understanding, felt that they were too valuable to waste, and had a belief that if they passed over her head they yet contributed to the general sum of human wisdom.

'I am not magnificent,' she said, mildly, wishing that she had put on another dress.

'You are sumptuous, opulent, expensive,' her father rejoined. 'You look as if you had eighty thousand a year.'

'Well, so long as I haven't—' said Catherine, illogically. Her conception of her prospective wealth was as yet very indefinite.

'So long as you haven't you shouldn't look as if you had. Have you enjoyed your party?'

Catherine hesitated a moment; and then, looking away, 'I am rather tired,' she murmured. I have said that this entertainment was the beginning of something important for Catherine. For the second time in her life she made an indirect answer; and the beginning of a period of dissimulation is certainly a significant date. Catherine was not so easily tired as that.

Nevertheless, in the carriage, as they drove home, she was as quiet as if fatigue had been her portion. Doctor Sloper's manner of addressing his sister Lavinia had a good deal of resemblance to the tone he had adopted towards Catherine.

'Who was the young man that was making love to you?' he presently asked.

'Oh, my good brother!' murmured Mrs Penniman, in deprecation.

'He seemed uncommonly tender. Whenever I looked at you for half an hour, he had the most devoted air.'

'The devotion was not to me,' said Mrs Penniman. 'It was to Catherine; he talked to me of her.'

Catherine had been listening with all her ears. 'Oh, Aunt Penniman!' she exclaimed, faintly.

'He is very handsome; he is very clever; he expressed himself with a great deal – a great deal of felicity,' her aunt went on.

'He is in love with this regal creature, then?' the Doctor inquired, humorously.

'Oh, father!' cried the girl, still more faintly, devoutly thankful the carriage was dark.

'I don't know that; but he admired her dress.'

Catherine did not say to herself in the dark, 'My dress only?' Mrs Penniman's announcement struck her by its richness, not by its meagreness.

'You see,' said her father, 'he thinks you have eighty thousand a year.'

'I don't believe he thinks of that,' said Mrs Penniman; 'he is too refined.'

'He must be tremendously refined not to think of that!'

'Well, he is!' Catherine exclaimed, before she knew it.

'I thought you had gone to sleep,' her father answered. 'The hour has come!' he added to himself. 'Lavinia is going to get up a romance for Catherine. It's a shame to play such tricks on the girl. What is the gentleman's name?' he went on, aloud.

'I didn't catch it, and I didn't like to ask him. He asked to be introduced to me,' said Mrs Penniman, with a certain grandeur; 'but you know how indistinctly Jefferson speaks.' Jefferson was Mr Almond. 'Catherine, dear, what was the gentleman's name?'

For a minute, if it had not been for the rumbling of the carriage, you might have heard a pin drop.

'I don't know, Aunt Lavinia,' said Catherine, very softly. And, with all his irony, her father believed her.

Chapter Five

He learned what he had asked some three or four days later, after Morris Townsend, with his cousin, had called in Washington Square. Mrs Penniman did not tell her brother, on the drive home, that she had intimated to this agreeable young man, whose name she did not know, that, with her niece, she should be very glad to see him; but she was greatly pleased, and even a little flattered, when late on a Sunday afternoon, the two gentlemen made their appearance. His coming with Arthur Townsend made it more natural and easy; the latter young man was on the point of becoming connected with the family, and Mrs Penniman had remarked to Catherine that, as he was going to marry Marian, it would be polite in him to call. These events came to pass late in the autumn, and Catherine and her aunt had been sitting together in the closing dusk, by the firelight, in the high back parlour.

Arthur Townsend fell to Catherine's portion, while his companion placed himself on the sofa beside Mrs Penniman. Catherine had hitherto not been a harsh critic; she was easy to please – she liked to talk with young men. But Marian's betrothed, this evening, made her feel vaguely fastidious; he sat looking at the fire and rubbing his knees with his hands. As for Catherine, she scarcely even pretended to keep up the conversation; her attention had fixed itself on the other side of the room; she was listening to what went on between the other Mr Townsend and her aunt. Every now and then he looked over at Catherine herself and smiled, as if to show that what he said was for her benefit too. Catherine would have liked to change her place, to go and sit near them, where she might see and hear him better. But she was afraid of seeming bold – of looking eager; and, besides, it would not have been polite to Marian's little suitor. She wondered why the other gentleman had picked out her aunt – how he came to have so much to say to Mrs Penniman, to whom, usually, young men were not especially devoted. She was not at all jealous of Aunt Lavinia, but she was a little envious, and, above all, she wondered; for Morris Townsend was an object on which she found that her imagination could exercise itself indefinitely. His cousin had been describing a house that he had taken in view of his union with Marian, and the domestic conveniences he meant to introduce into it; how Marian wanted a larger one, and Mrs Almond recommended a smaller one, and how he himself was convinced that he had got the neatest house in New York.

'It doesn't matter,' he said; 'it's only for three or four years. At the end of three or four years we'll move. That's the way to live in New York – to move every three or four years. Then you always get the last thing. It's because the city's growing so quick – you've got to keep up with it. It's going straight up town – that's where New York's going. If I wasn't afraid Marian would be lonely, I'd go up there – right up to the top – and wait for it. Only have to wait ten years – they'll all come up after you. But Marian says she wants some neighbours – she doesn't want to be a pioneer. She says that if she's got to be the first settler she had better go out to Minnesota. I guess we'll move up little by little; when we get tired of one street we'll go higher. So you see we'll always have a new house; it's a great advantage to have a new house; you get all the latest improvements. They invent everything all over again about every five years, and it's a great thing to keep up with the new things. I always try and keep up with the new things of every kind. Don't you think that's a good motto for a young couple – to keep "going higher"? What's the name of that piece of poetry – what do they call it? – "Excelsior!" '

Catherine bestowed on her junior visitor only just enough attention to feel that this was not the way Mr Morris Townsend had talked the other night, or that he was talking now to her fortunate aunt. But suddenly his aspiring kinsman became more interesting. He seemed to have become conscious that she was affected by his companion's presence, and he thought it proper to explain it.

'My cousin asked me to bring him, or I shouldn't have taken the liberty. He seemed to want very much to come; you know he's awfully sociable. I told him I wanted to ask you first, but he said Mrs Penniman had invited him. He isn't particular what he says when he wants to come somewhere. But Mrs Penniman seems to think it's all right.'

'We are very glad to see him,' said Catherine. And she wished to talk more about him, but she hardly knew what to say. 'I never saw him before,' she went on, presently.

Arthur Townsend stared.

'Why, he told me he talked with you for over half an hour the other night.'

'I mean before the other night. That was the first time.'

'Oh, he has been away from New York – he has been all round the world. He doesn't know many people here, but he's very sociable, and he wants to know everyone.'

'Everyone?' said Catherine.

'Well, I mean all the good ones. All the pretty young ladies – like Mrs Penniman!' And Arthur Townsend gave a private laugh.

'My aunt likes him very much,' said Catherine.

'Most people like him – he's so brilliant.'

'He's more like a foreigner,' Catherine suggested.

'Well, I never knew a foreigner,' said young Townsend, in a tone which seemed to indicate that his ignorance had been optional.

'Neither have I,' Catherine confessed, with more humility. 'They say they are generally brilliant,' she added, vaguely.

'Well, the people of this city are clever enough for me. I know some of them that think they are too clever for me; but they ain't.'

'I suppose you can't be too clever,' said Catherine, still with humility.

'I don't know. I know some people that call my cousin too clever.'

Catherine listened to this statement with extreme interest, and a feeling that if Morris Townsend had a fault it would naturally be that one. But she did not commit herself, and in a moment she asked, 'Now that he has come back, will he stay here always?'

'Ah!' said Arthur, 'if he can get something to do.'

'Something to do?'

'Some place or other; some business.'

'Hasn't he got any?' said Catherine, who had never heard of a young man – of the upper class – in this situation.

'No; he's looking round. But he can't find anything.'

'I am very sorry,' Catherine permitted herself to observe.

'Oh, he doesn't mind,' said young Townsend. 'He takes it easy – he isn't in a hurry. He is very particular.'

Catherine thought he naturally would be, and gave herself up for some moments to the contemplation of this idea, in several of its bearings.

'Won't his father take him into his business – his office?' she at last inquired.

'He hasn't got any father – he has only got a sister. Your sister can't help you much.'

It seemed to Catherine that if she were his sister she would disprove this axiom. 'Is she – is she pleasant?' she asked in a moment.

'I don't know – I believe she's very respectable,' said young Townsend. And then he looked across to his cousin and began to laugh. 'I say, we are talking about you,' he added.

Morris Townsend paused in his conversation with Mrs Penniman, and stared, with a little smile. Then he got up, as if he were going.

'As far as you are concerned, I can't return the compliment,' he said to Catherine's companion. 'But as regards Miss Sloper, it's another affair.'

Catherine thought this little speech wonderfully well turned; but she was embarrassed by it, and she also got up. Morris Townsend stood looking at her and smiling; he put out his hand for farewell. He was going, without having said anything to her; but even on these terms she was glad to have seen him.

'I will tell her what you have said – when you go!' said Mrs Penniman, with a little significant laugh.

Catherine blushed, for she felt almost as if they were making sport of her. What in the world could this beautiful young man have said? He looked at her still, in spite of her blush, but very kindly and respectfully.

'I have had no talk with you,' he said, 'and that was what I came for. But it will be a good reason for coming another time; a little pretext – if I am obliged to give one. I am not afraid of what your aunt will say when I go.'

With this the two young men took their departure; after which Catherine, with her blush still lingering, directed a serious and interrogative eye to Mrs Penniman. She was incapable of elaborate artifice, and she resorted to no jocular device – to no affectation of the belief that she had been maligned – to learn what she desired.

'What did you say you would tell me?' she asked.

Mrs Penniman came up to her, smiling and nodding a little, looked at her all over, and gave a twist to the knot of ribbon in her neck. 'It's a great secret, my dear child; but he is coming a-courting!'

Catherine was serious still. 'Is that what he told you?'

'He didn't say so exactly; but he left me to guess it. I'm a good guesser.'

'Do you mean a-courting me?'

'Not me, certainly, miss; though I must say he is a hundred times more polite to a person who has no longer extreme youth to recommend her than most of the young men. He is thinking of someone else.' And Mrs Penniman gave her niece a delicate little kiss. 'You must be very gracious to him.'

Catherine stared – she was bewildered. 'I don't understand you,' she said; 'he doesn't know me.'

'Oh yes, he does; more than you think. I have told him all about you.'

'Oh, Aunt Penniman!' murmured Catherine, as if this had been a breach of trust. 'He is a perfect stranger – we don't know him.' There was infinite modesty in the poor girl's 'we'.

Aunt Penniman, however, took no account of it; she spoke even with a touch of acrimony. 'My dear Catherine, you know very well that you admire him.'

'Oh, Aunt Penniman!' Catherine could only murmur again. It might very well be that she admired him – though this did not seem to her a thing to talk about. But that this brilliant stranger – this sudden apparition, who had barely heard the sound of her voice – took that sort of interest in her that was expressed by the romantic phrase of which Mrs Penniman had just made use – this could only be a figment of the restless brain of Aunt Lavinia, whom everyone knew to be a woman of powerful imagination.

Chapter Six

Mrs Penniman even took for granted at times that other people had as much imagination as herself; so that when, half an hour later, her brother came in, she addressed him quite on this principle.

'He has just been here, Austin; it's such a pity you missed him.'

'Whom in the world have I missed?' asked the Doctor.

'Mr Morris Townsend; he has made us such a delightful visit.'

'And who in the world is Mr Morris Townsend?'

'Aunt Penniman means the gentleman – the gentleman whose name I couldn't remember,' said Catherine.

'The gentleman at Elizabeth's party who was so struck with Catherine,' Mrs Penniman added.

'Oh, his name is Morris Townsend, is it? And did he come here to propose to you?'

'Oh, father!' murmured the girl for an answer, turning away to the window, where the dusk had deepened to darkness.

'I hope he won't do that without your permission,' said Mrs Penniman, very graciously.

'After all, my dear, he seems to have yours,' her brother answered.

Lavinia simpered, as if this might not be quite enough, and Catherine, with her forehead touching the window-panes, listened to this exchange of epigrams as reservedly as if they had not each been a pin-prick in her own destiny.

'The next time he comes,' the Doctor added, 'you had better call me. He might like to see me.'

Morris Townsend came again some five days afterwards; but Doctor Sloper was not called, as he was absent from home at the time. Catherine was with her aunt when the young man's name was brought in, and Mrs Penniman, effacing herself and protesting, made a great point of her niece's going into the drawing-room alone.

'This time it's for you – for you only,' she said. 'Before, when he talked to me, it was only preliminary – it was to gain my confidence. Literally, my dear, I should not have the *courage* to show myself today.'

And this was perfectly true. Mrs Penniman was not a brave woman, and Morris Townsend had struck her as a young man of great force of character, and of remarkable powers of satire – a keen, resolute, brilliant nature, with which one must exercise a great deal of tact. She said to herself that he was 'imperious', and she liked the word and the idea. She was not the least jealous of her niece, and she had been perfectly happy with Mr Penniman, but in the bottom of her heart she permitted herself the observation, 'That's the sort of husband I should have had!' He was certainly much more imperious – she ended by calling it imperial – than Mr Penniman.

So Catherine saw Mr Townsend alone, and her aunt did not come in even at the end of the visit. The visit was a long one; he sat there, in the front parlour, in the biggest arm-chair, for more than an hour. He seemed more at home this time – more familiar; lounging a little in the chair, slapping a cushion that was near him with his stick, and looking round the room a good deal, and at the objects it contained, as well as at Catherine, whom, however, he also contemplated freely. There was a smile of respectful devotion in his handsome eyes which seemed to Catherine almost solemnly beautiful; it made her think of a young knight in a poem. His talk, however, was not particularly knightly; it was light and easy and friendly; it took a practical turn, and he asked a number of questions about herself – what were her tastes – if she liked this and that – what were her habits. He said to her, with his charming smile, 'Tell me about yourself; give me a little sketch.' Catherine had very little to tell, and she had no talent for sketching; but before he went she had confided to him that she had a secret passion for the theatre, which had been but scantily gratified, and a taste for operatic music – that of Bellini and Donizetti, in especial (it must be remembered, in extenuation of this primitive young woman, that she held these opinions in an age of general darkness) – which she rarely had an occasion to hear, except on the hand organ. She confessed that she was not particularly fond of literature. Morris Townsend agreed with her that books were tiresome things; only, as he said, you had to read a good many before you found it out. He had been to places that people had written books about, and they were not a bit like the descriptions. To see for yourself – that was the great thing; he always tried to see for himself. He had seen all the principal actors – he had been to all the best theatres in London and Paris. But the actors were always like the authors – they always exaggerated. He liked everything to be natural. Suddenly he stopped, looking at Catherine with his smile.

'That's what I like you for; you are so natural. Excuse me,' he added; 'you see I am natural myself.'

And before she had time to think whether she excused him or not – which afterwards, at leisure, she became conscious that she did – he began to talk about music, and to say that it was his greatest pleasure in life. He had heard all the great singers in Paris and London – Pasta and Rubini and Lablache – and when you had done that, you could say that you knew what singing was.

'I sing a little myself,' he said; 'some day I will show you. Not today, but some other time.'

And then he got up to go. He had omitted, by accident, to say that he would sing to her if she would play to him. He thought of this after he got into the street; but he might have spared his compunction, for Catherine had not noticed the lapse. She was thinking only that 'some other time' had a delightful sound; it seemed to spread itself over the future.

This was all the more reason, however, though she was ashamed and uncomfortable, why she should tell her father that Mr Morris Townsend had called again. She announced the fact abruptly, almost violently, as soon as the Doctor came into the house; and having done so – it was her duty – she took measures to leave the room. But she could not leave it fast enough; her father stopped her just as she reached the door.

'Well, my dear, did he propose to you today?' the Doctor asked.

This is just what she had been afraid he would say; and yet she had no answer ready. Of course she would have liked to take it as a joke – as her father must have meant it; and yet she would have liked also, in denying it, to be a little positive, a little sharp, so that he would perhaps not ask the question again. She didn't like it – it made her unhappy. But Catherine could never be sharp; and for a moment she only stood, with her hand on the door-knob, looking at her satiric parent, and giving a little laugh.

'Decidedly,' said the Doctor to himself, 'my daughter is not brilliant!'

But he had no sooner made this reflection than Catherine found something; she had decided, on the whole, to take the thing as a joke.

'Perhaps he will do it the next time,' she exclaimed, with a repetition of her laugh; and she quickly got out of the room.

The Doctor stood staring; he wondered whether his daughter were serious. Catherine went straight to her own room, and by the time she reached it she bethought herself that there was something else – something better – she might have said. She almost wished, now, that her father would ask his question again, so that she might reply, 'Oh yes, Mr Morris Townsend proposed to me, and I refused him.'

The Doctor, however, began to put his questions elsewhere; it naturally having occurred to him that he ought to inform himself properly about this handsome young man, who had formed the habit of running in and out of his house. He addressed himself to the elder of his sisters, Mrs Almond – not going to her for the purpose; there was no such hurry as that; but having made a note of the matter for the first opportunity. The Doctor was never eager, never impatient or nervous; but he made notes of everything, and he regularly consulted his notes. Among them the information he obtained from Mrs Almond about Morris Townsend took its place.

'Lavinia has already been to ask me,' she said. 'Lavinia is most excited; I don't understand it. It's not, after all, Lavinia that the young man is supposed to have designs upon. She is very peculiar.'

'Ah, my dear,' the Doctor replied, 'she has not lived with me these twelve years without my finding it out.'

'She has got such an artificial mind,' said Mrs Almond, who always enjoyed an opportunity to discuss Lavinia's peculiarities with her brother. 'She didn't want me to tell you that she had asked me about Mr Townsend; but I told her I would. She always wants to conceal everything.'

'And yet at moments no one blurts things out with such crudity. She is like a revolving lighthouse – pitch darkness alternating with a dazzling brilliancy! But what did you tell her?' the Doctor asked.

'What I tell you – that I know very little of him.'

'Lavinia must have been disappointed at that,' said the Doctor; 'she would prefer him to have been guilty of some romantic crime. However, we must make the best of people. They tell me our gentleman is the cousin of the little boy to whom you are about to entrust the future of your little girl.'

'Arthur is not a little boy; he is a very old man; you and I will never be so old! He is a distant relation of Lavinia's protégé. The name is the same, but I am given to understand that there are Townsends and Townsends. So Arthur's mother tells me; she talked about branches – younger branches, elder branches, inferior branches – as if it were a royal house. Arthur, it appears, is of the reigning line, but poor Lavinia's young man is not. Beyond this, Arthur's mother knows very little about him; she has only a vague story that he has been "wild". But I know his sister a little, and she is a very nice woman. Her name is Mrs Montgomery; she is a widow, with a little property and five children. She lives in the Second Avenue.'

'What does Mrs Montgomery say about him?'

'That he has talents by which he might distinguish himself.'

'Only he is lazy, eh?'

'She doesn't say so.'

'That's family pride,' said the Doctor. 'What is his profession?'

'He hasn't got any; he is looking for something. I believe he was once in the Navy.'

'Once? What is his age?'

'I suppose he is upward of thirty. He must have gone into the Navy very young. I think Arthur told me that he inherited a small property – which was perhaps the cause of his leaving the Navy – and that he spent it all in a few years. He travelled all over the world, lived abroad, amused himself. I believe it was a kind of system, a theory he had. He has lately come back to America with the intention, as he tells Arthur, of beginning life in earnest.'

Is he in earnest about Catherine, then?'

'I don't see why you should be incredulous,' said Mrs Almond. 'It seems to me that you have never done Catherine justice. You must remember that she has the prospect of thirty thousand a year.'

The Doctor looked at his sister a moment, and then, with lightest touch of bitterness, 'You at least appreciate her,' he said.

Mrs Almond blushed.

'I don't mean that is her only merit; I simply mean that it is a great one. A great many young men think so; and you appear to me never to have been properly aware of that. You have always had a little way of alluding to her as an unmarriageable girl.'

'My allusions are as kind as yours, Elizabeth,' said the Doctor, frankly. 'How many suitors has Catherine had, with all her expectations – how much attention has she ever received? Catherine is not unmarriageable, but she is absolutely unattractive. What other reason is there for Lavinia being so charmed with the idea that there is a lover in the house? There has never been one before, and Lavinia, with her sensitive, sympathetic nature, is not used to the idea. It affects her imagination. I must do the young men of New York the justice to say that they strike me as very disinterested. They prefer pretty girls – lively girls – girls like your own. Catherine is neither pretty nor lively.'

'Catherine does very well; she has a style of her own – which is more than my poor Marian has, who has no style at all,' said Mrs Almond. 'The reason Catherine has received so little attention, is that she seems to all the young men to be older than themselves. She is so large, and she dresses so richly. They are rather afraid of her, I think; she looks as if she had been married already, and you know they don't like married women. And if our young men appear disinterested,' the Doctor's wiser sister went on, 'it is because they marry, as a general thing, so young – before twenty-five, at the age of innocence and sincerity – before the age of calculation. If they only waited a little, Catherine would fare better.'

'As a calculation? Thank you very much,' said the Doctor.

'Wait till some intelligent man of forty comes along, and he will be delighted with Catherine,' Mrs Almond continued.

'Mr Townsend is not old enough, then? His motives may be pure.'

'It is very possible that his motives are pure; I should be very sorry to take the contrary for granted. Lavinia is sure of it; and, as he is a very prepossessing youth, you might give him the benefit of the doubt.'

Doctor Sloper reflected a moment.

'What are his present means of subsistence?'

'I have no idea. He lives, as I say, with his sister.'

'A widow, with five children? Do you mean he lives *upon* her?'

Mrs Almond got up, and with a certain impatience, 'Had you not better ask Mrs Montgomery herself?' she inquired.

'Perhaps I may come to that,' said the Doctor. 'Did you say the Second Avenue?' He made a note of the Second Avenue.

Chapter Seven

He was, however, by no means so much in earnest as this might seem to indicate; and, indeed, he was more than anything else amused with the whole situation. He was not in the least in a state of tension or of vigilance with regard to Catherine's prospects; he was even on his guard against the ridicule that might attach itself to the spectacle of a house thrown into agitation by its daughter and heiress receiving attentions unprecedented in its annals. More than this, he went so far as to promise himself some entertainment from the little drama – if drama it was – of which Mrs Penniman desired to represent the ingenious Mr Townsend as the hero. He had no intention, as yet, of regulating the denouement. He was perfectly willing, as Elizabeth had suggested, to give the young man the benefit of every doubt. There was no great danger in it; for Catherine, at the age of twenty-two, was, after all, a rather mature blossom, such as could be plucked from the stem only by a vigorous jerk. The fact that Morris Townsend was poor, was not of necessity against him; the Doctor had never made up his mind that his daughter should marry a rich man. The fortune she would inherit struck him as a very sufficient provision for two reasonable persons, and if a penniless swain who could give a good account of himself should enter the lists, he should be judged quite upon his personal merits. There were other things besides. The Doctor thought it very vulgar to be precipitate in accusing people of mercenary motives, inasmuch as his door had as yet not been in the least besieged by fortune-hunters; and, lastly, he was very curious to see whether Catherine might really be loved for her moral worth. He smiled as he reflected that poor Mr Townsend had been only twice to the house, and he said to Mrs Penniman that the next time he should come she must ask him to dinner.

He came very soon again, and Mrs Penniman had of course great pleasure in executing this mission. Morris Townsend accepted her invitation with equal good grace, and the dinner took place a few days later. The Doctor had said to himself, justly enough, that they must not have the young man alone; this would partake too much of the nature of encouragement. So two or three other persons were invited; but Morris Townsend, though he was by no means the ostensible, was the real occasion of the feast. There is every reason to suppose that he desired to make a good impression; and if he fell short of this result, it was not for want of a good deal of intelligent effort. The Doctor talked to him very little during dinner; but he observed him attentively, and after the ladies had gone out he pushed him the wine and asked him several questions. Morris was not a young man who needed to be pressed, and he found quite enough encouragement in the superior quality of the claret. The Doctor's wine was admirable, and it may be communicated to the reader that while he sipped it Morris reflected that a cellarful of good liquor – there was evidently a cellarful here – would be a most attractive idiosyncrasy in a father-in-law. The Doctor was struck with his appreciative guest; he saw that he was not a commonplace young man. 'He has ability,' said Catherine's father, 'decided ability; he has a very good head if he chooses to use it. And he is uncommonly well turned out; quite the sort of figure that pleases the ladies; but I don't think I like him.' The Doctor, however, kept his reflections to himself, and talked to his visitors about foreign lands, concerning which Morris offered him more information than he was ready, as he mentally phrased it, to swallow. Doctor Sloper had travelled but little, and he took the liberty of not believing everything that his talkative guest narrated. He prided himself on being something of a physiognomist; and while the young man, chatting with easy assurance, puffed his cigar and filled his glass again, the Doctor sat with his eyes quietly fixed on his bright, expressive face. 'He has the assurance of the devil himself!' said Morris's host; 'I don't think I ever saw such assurance. And his powers of invention are most remarkable. He is very knowing; they were not so knowing as that in my time. And a good head, did I say? I should think so – after a bottle of Madeira, and a bottle and a half of claret!'

After dinner Morris Townsend went and stood before Catherine, who was standing before the fire in her red satin gown.

'He doesn't like me – he doesn't like me at all,' said the young man.

'Who doesn't like you?' asked Catherine.

'Your father; extraordinary man!'

'I don't see how you know,' said Catherine, blushing.

'I feel; I am very quick to feel.'

'Perhaps you are mistaken.'

'Ah, well! you ask him, and you will see.'

'I would rather not ask him, if there is any danger of his saying what you think.'

Morris looked at her with an air of mock melancholy.

'It wouldn't give you any pleasure to contradict him?'

'I never contradict him,' said Catherine.

'Will you hear me abused without opening your lips in my defence?'

'My father won't abuse you. He doesn't know you enough.'

Morris Townsend gave a loud laugh, and Catherine began to blush again.

'I shall never mention you,' she said, to take refuge from her confusion.

'That is very well; but it is not quite what I should have liked you to say. I should have liked you to say, "If my father doesn't think well of you, what does it matter?" '

'Ah, but it would matter; I couldn't say that!' the girl exclaimed.

He looked at her for a moment, smiling a little; and the Doctor, if he had been watching him just then, would have seen a gleam of fine impatience in the sociable softness of his eye. But there was no impatience in his rejoinder – none, at least, save what was expressed in a little appealing sigh. 'Ah, well! then I must not give up the hope of bringing him round.'

He expressed it more frankly to Mrs Penniman later in the evening. But before that he sang two or three songs at Catherine's timid request; not that he flattered himself that this would help to bring her father round. He had a sweet, light tenor voice, and, when he had finished, everyone made some exclamation – everyone, that is, save Catherine, who remained intensely silent. Mrs Penniman declared that his manner of singing was 'most artistic', and Doctor Sloper said it was 'very taking – very taking, indeed'; speaking loudly and distinctly, but with a certain dryness.

'He doesn't like me – he doesn't like me at all,' said Morris Townsend, addressing the aunt in the same manner as he had done the niece. 'He thinks I am all wrong.'

Unlike her niece, Mrs Penniman asked for no explanation. She only smiled very sweetly, as if she understood everything; and, unlike Catherine too, she made no attempt to contradict him. 'Pray, what does it matter?' she murmured, softly.

'Ah, you say the right thing!' said Morris, greatly to the gratification of Mrs Penniman, who prided herself on always saying the right thing.

The Doctor, the next time he saw his sister Elizabeth, let her know that he had made the acquaintance of Lavinia's protégé.

'Physically,' he said, 'he's uncommonly well set up. As an anatomist, it is really a pleasure to me to see such a beautiful structure; although, if people were all like him, I suppose there would be very little need for doctors.'

'Don't you see anything in people but their bones?' Mrs Almond rejoined. 'What do you think of him, as a father?'

'As a father? Thank Heaven, I am not his father!'

'No; but you are Catherine's. Lavinia tells me she is in love.'

'She must get over it. He is not a gentleman.'

'Ah, take care! Remember that he is a branch of the Townsends.'

'He is not what I call a gentleman; he has not the soul of one. He is extremely insinuating; but it's a vulgar nature. I saw through it in a minute. He is altogether too familiar – I hate familiarity. He is a plausible coxcomb.'

'Ah, well,' said Mrs Almond, 'if you make up your mind so easily, it's a great advantage.'

'I don't make up my mind easily. What I tell you is the result of thirty years of observation; and in order to be able to form that judgement in a single evening, I have had to spend a lifetime in study.'

'Very possibly you are right. But the thing is for Catherine to see it.'

'I will present her with a pair of spectacles!' said the Doctor.

Chapter Eight

If it were true that she was in love, she was certainly very quiet about it; but the Doctor was of course prepared to admit that her quietness might mean volumes. She had told Morris Townsend that she would not mention him to her father, and she saw no reason to retract this vow of discretion. It was no more than decently civil, of course, that, after having dined in Washington Square, Morris should call there again; and it was no more than natural that, having been kindly received on this occasion, he should continue to present himself. He had had plenty of leisure on his hands; and thirty years ago, in New York, a young man of leisure had reason to be thankful for aids to self-oblivion. Catherine said nothing to her father about these visits, though they had rapidly become the most important, the most absorbing thing in her life. The girl was very happy. She knew not as yet what would come of it; but the present had suddenly grown rich and solemn. If she had been told she was in love, she would have been a good deal surprised; for she had an idea that love was an eager and exacting passion, and her own heart was filled in these days with the impulse of self-effacement and sacrifice. Whenever Morris Townsend had left the house, her imagination projected itself, with all its strength, into the idea of his soon coming back; but if she had been told at such a moment that he would not return for a year, or even that he would never return, she would not have complained nor rebelled, but would have humbly accepted the decree, and sought for consolation in thinking over the times she had already seen him, the words he had spoken, the sound of his voice, of his tread, the expression of his face. Love demands certain things as a right; but Catherine had no sense of her rights; she had only a consciousness of immense and unexpected favours. Her very gratitude for these things had hushed itself; for it seemed to her that there would be something of impudence in making a festival of her secret. Her father suspected Morris Townsend's visits, and noted her reserve. She seemed to beg pardon for it; she looked at him constantly in silence, as if she meant to say that she said nothing because she was afraid of irritating him. But the poor girl's dumb eloquence irritated him more than anything else would have done, and he caught himself murmuring more than once that it was a grievous pity his only child was a simpleton. His murmurs, however, were inaudible; and for a while he said nothing to anyone. He would have liked to know exactly how often young Townsend came; but he had determined to ask no questions of the girl herself – to say nothing more to her that would show that he watched her. The Doctor had a great idea of being largely just; he wished to leave his daughter her liberty, and interfere only when the danger should be proved. It was not in his manner to obtain information by indirect methods, and it never even occurred to him to question the servants. As for Lavinia, he hated to talk to her about the matter; she annoyed him with her mock romanticism. But he had to come to this. Mrs Penniman's convictions as regards the relations of her niece and the clever young visitor, who saved appearances by coming ostensibly for both the ladies – Mrs Penniman's convictions had passed into a riper and richer phase. There was to be no crudity in Mrs Penniman's treatment of the situation; she had become as uncommunicative as Catherine herself. She was tasting of the sweets of concealment; she had taken up the line of mystery. 'She would be enchanted to be able to prove to herself that she is persecuted,' said the Doctor; and when at last he questioned her, he was sure she would contrive to extract from his words a pretext for this belief.

'Be so good as to let me know what is going on in the house,' he said to her, in a tone which, under the circumstances, he himself deemed genial.

'Going on, Austin?' Mrs Penniman exclaimed. 'Why, I am sure I don't know. I believe that last night the old grey cat had kittens.'

'At her age?' said the Doctor. 'The idea is startling – almost shocking. Be so good as to see that they are all drowned. But what else has happened?'

'Ah, the dear little kittens!' cried Mrs Penniman. 'I wouldn't have them drowned for the world!'

Her brother puffed his cigar a few moments in silence. 'Your sympathy with kittens, Lavinia,' he presently resumed, 'arises from a feline element in your own character.'

'Cats are very graceful, and very clean,' said Mrs Penniman smiling.

'And very stealthy. You are the embodiment both of grace and of neatness; but you are wanting in frankness.'

'You certainly are not, dear brother.'

'I don't pretend to be graceful, though I try to be neat. Why haven't you let me know that Mr Morris Townsend is coming to the house four times a week?'

Mrs Penniman lifted her eyebrows. 'Four times a week!'

'Three times, then, or five times, if you prefer it. I am away all day, and I see nothing. But when such things happen, you should let me know.'

Mrs Penniman, with her eyebrows still raised, reflected intently. 'Dear Austin,' she said at last, 'I am incapable of betraying a confidence. I would rather suffer anything.'

'Never fear; you shall not suffer. To whose confidence is it you allude? Has Catherine made you take a vow of eternal secrecy?'

'By no means. Catherine has not told me as much as she might. She has not been very trustful.'

'It is the young man, then, who has made you his confidante? Allow me to say that it is extremely indiscreet of you to form secret alliances with young men; you don't know where they may lead you.'

'I don't know what you mean by an alliance,' said Mrs Penniman. 'I take a great interest in Mr Townsend; I won't conceal that. But that's all.'

'Under the circumstances, that is quite enough. What is the source of your interest in Mr Townsend?'

'Why,' said Mrs Penniman, musing, and then breaking into her smile, 'that he is so interesting!'

The Doctor felt that he had need of his patience. 'And what makes him interesting? – his good looks?'

'His misfortunes, Austin.'

'Ah, he has had misfortunes? That, of course, is always interesting. Are you at liberty to mention a few of Mr Townsend's?'

I don't know that he would like it,' said Mrs Penniman. 'He has told me a great deal about himself – he has told me, in fact, his whole history. But I don't think I ought to repeat those things. He would tell them to you, I am sure, if he thought you would listen to him kindly. With kindness you may do anything with him.'

The Doctor gave a laugh. 'I shall request him very kindly, then, to leave Catherine alone.'

'Ah!' said Mrs Penniman, shaking her forefinger at her brother, with her little finger turned out, 'Catherine has probably said something to him kinder than that!'

'Said that she loved him? – do you mean that?'

Mrs Penniman fixed her eyes on the floor. 'As I tell you, Austin, she doesn't confide in me.'

'You have an opinion, I suppose, all the same. It is that I ask you for; though I don't conceal from you that I shall not regard it as conclusive.'

Mrs Penniman's gaze continued to rest on the carpet; but at last she lifted it, and then her brother thought it very expressive. 'I think Catherine is very happy; that is all I can say.'

'Townsend is trying to marry her – is that what you mean?'

'He is greatly interested in her.'

'He finds her such an attractive girl?'

'Catherine has a lovely nature, Austin,' said Mrs Penniman, 'and Mr Townsend has had the intelligence to discover that.'

'With a little help from you, I suppose. My dear Lavinia,' cried the Doctor, 'you are an admirable aunt!'

'So Mr Townsend says,' observed Lavinia, smiling.

'Do you think he is sincere?' asked her brother.

'In saying that?'

'No; that's of course. But in his admiration for Catherine?'

'Deeply sincere. He has said to me the most appreciative, the most charming things about her. He would say them to you, if he were sure you would listen to him – gently.'

'I doubt whether I can undertake it. He appears to require a great deal of gentleness.'

'He is a sympathetic, sensitive nature,' said Mrs Penniman.

Her brother puffed his cigar again in silence. 'These delicate qualities have survived his vicissitudes, eh? All this while you haven't told me about his misfortunes.'

'It is a long story,' said Mrs Penniman, 'and I regard it as a sacred trust. But I suppose there is no objection to my saying that he has been wild – he frankly confesses that. But he has paid for it.'

'That's what has impoverished him, eh?'

'I don't mean simply in money. He is very much alone in the world.'

'Do you mean that he has behaved so badly that his friends have given him up?'

'He has had false friends, who have deceived and betrayed him.'

'He seems to have some good ones too. He has a devoted sister, and half a dozen nephews and nieces.'

Mrs Penniman was silent a minute. 'The nephews and nieces are children, and the sister is not a very attractive person.'

'I hope he doesn't abuse her to you,' said the Doctor; 'for I am told he lives upon her.'

'Lives upon her?'

'Lives with her, and does nothing for himself; it is about the same thing.'

'He is looking for a position most earnestly,' said Mrs Penniman. 'He hopes every day to find one.'

'Precisely. He is looking for it here – over there in the front parlour. The position of husband of a weak-minded woman with a large fortune would suit him to perfection!'

Mrs Penniman was truly amiable, but she now gave signs of temper. She rose with much animation, and stood for a moment looking at her brother.

'My dear Austin,' she remarked, 'if you regard Catherine as a weak-minded woman you are particularly mistaken!' And with this she moved majestically away.

Chapter Nine

It was a regular custom with the family in Washington Square to go and spend Sunday evening at Mrs Almond's. On the Sunday after the conversation I have just narrated this custom was not intermitted; and on this occasion, towards the middle of the evening, Doctor Sloper found a reason to withdraw to the library with his brother-in-law, to talk over a matter of business. He was absent some twenty minutes, and when he came back into the circle, which was enlivened by the presence of several friends of the family, he saw that Morris Townsend had come in, and had lost as little time as possible in seating himself on a small sofa beside Catherine. In the large room, where several different groups had been formed, and the hum of voices and of laughter was loud, these two young persons might confabulate, as the Doctor phrased to it himself, without attracting attention. He saw in a moment, however that his daughter was painfully conscious of his own observation. She sat motionless, with her eyes bent down, staring at her open fan, deeply flushed, shrinking together as if to minimize the indiscretion of which she confessed herself guilty.

The Doctor almost pitied her. Poor Catherine was not defiant; she had no genius for bravado, and as she felt that her father viewed her companion's attentions with an unsympathizing eye, there was nothing but discomfort for her in the accident of seeming to challenge him. The Doctor felt, indeed, so sorry for her that he turned away, to spare her the sense of being watched; and he was so intelligent a man that, in his thoughts, he rendered a sort of poetic justice to her situation.

'It must be deucedly pleasant for a plain, inanimate girl like that to have a beautiful young fellow come and sit down beside her, and whisper to her that he is her slave – if that is what this one whispers. No wonder she likes it, and that she thinks me a cruel tyrant; which of course she does, though she is afraid – she hasn't the animation necessary – to admit it to herself. Poor old Catherine!' mused the Doctor; 'I verily believe she is capable of defending me when Townsend abuses me!'

And the force of this reflection, for the moment, was such in making him feel the natural opposition between his point of view and that of an infatuated child, that he said to himself that he was perhaps after all taking things too hard, and crying out before he was hurt. He must not condemn Morris Townsend unheard. He had a great aversion to taking things too hard; he thought that half the discomfort and many of the disappointments of life come from it; and for an instant he asked himself whether, possibly, he did not appear ridiculous to this intelligent young man, whose private perception of incongruities he suspected of being keen. At the end of a quarter of an hour Catherine had got rid of him, and Townsend was now standing before the fireplace in conversation with Mrs Almond.

'We will try him again,' said the Doctor. And he crossed the room and joined his sister and her companion, making her a sign that she should leave the young man to him. She presently did so, while Morris looked at him, smiling, without a sign of evasiveness in his affable eye.

'He's amazingly conceited!' thought the Doctor; and then he said, aloud, 'I am told you are looking out for a position.'

'Oh, a position is more than I should presume to call it,' Morris Townsend answered. 'That sounds so fine. I should like some quiet work – something to turn an honest penny.'

'What sort of thing should you prefer?'

'Do you mean what am I fit for? Very little, I am afraid. I have nothing but my good right arm, as they say in the melodramas.'

'You are too modest,' said the Doctor. 'In addition to your good right arm you have your subtle brain. I know nothing of you but what I see; but I see by your physiognomy that you are extremely intelligent.'

'Ah,' Townsend murmured, 'I don't know what to answer when you say that. You advise me, then, not to despair?'

And he looked at his interlocutor as if the question might have a double meaning. The Doctor caught the look and weighed it a moment before he replied. 'I should be very sorry to admit that a robust and well-disposed young man need ever despair. If he doesn't succeed in one thing, he can try another. Only, I should add, he should choose his line with discretion.'

'Ah, yes, with discretion,' Morris Townsend repeated, sympathetically. 'Well, I have been indiscreet, formerly; but I think I have got over it. I am very steady now.' And he stood a moment, looking down at his remarkably neat shoes. Then at last, 'Were you kindly intending to propose something for my advantage?' he inquired, looking up and smiling.

'D—n his impudence!' the Doctor exclaimed, privately. But in a moment he reflected that he himself had, after all, touched first upon this delicate point, and that his words might have been construed as an offer of assistance. 'I have no particular proposal to make,' he presently said; 'but it occurred to me to let you know that I have you in my mind. Sometimes one hears of opportunities. For instance, should you object of leaving New York – to going to a distance?'

'I am afraid I shouldn't be able to manage that. I must seek my fortune here or nowhere. You see,' added Morris Townsend, 'I have ties – I have responsibilities here. I have a sister, a widow, from whom I have been separated for a long time, and to whom I am almost everything. I shouldn't like to say to her that I must leave her. She rather depends upon me, you see.'

'Ah, that's very proper; family feeling is very proper,' said Doctor Sloper. 'I often think there is not enough of it in our city. I think I have heard of your sister.'

'It is possible, but I rather doubt it; she lives so very quietly.'

'As quietly, you mean,' the Doctor went on, with a short laugh, 'as a lady may do who has several young children.'

'Ah, my little nephews and nieces – that's the very point! I am helping to bring them up,' said Morris Townsend. 'I am a kind of amateur tutor; I give them lessons.'

'That's very proper, as I say; but it is hardly a career.'

'It won't make my fortune,' the young man confessed.

'You must not be too much bent on a fortune,' said the Doctor. 'But I assure you I will keep you in mind; I won't lose sight of you.'

'If my situation becomes desperate I shall perhaps take the liberty of reminding you,' Morris rejoined, raising his voice a little with a brighter smile, as his interlocutor turned away.

Before he left the house the Doctor had a few words with Mrs Almond.

'I should like to see his sister,' he said. 'What do you call her – Mrs Montgomery? I should like to have a little talk with her.'

'I will try and manage it,' Mrs Almond responded. 'I will take the first opportunity of inviting her, and you shall come and meet her; unless, indeed,' Mrs Almond added, 'she first takes it into her head to be sick and to send for you.'

'Ah no, not that; she must have trouble enough without that. But it would have its advantages, for then I should see the children. I should like very much to see the children.'

'You are very thorough. Do you want to catechize them about their uncle?'

'Precisely. Their uncle tells me he has charge of their education, that he saves their mother the expense of school-bills. I should like to ask them a few questions in the commoner branches.'

'He certainly has not the cut of a school-master,' Mrs Almond said to herself a short time afterwards, as she saw Morris Townsend in a corner bending over her niece, who was seated.

And there was, indeed, nothing in the young man's discourse at this moment that savoured of the pedagogue.

'Will you meet me somewhere tomorrow or next day?' he said, in a low tone, to Catherine.

'Meet you?' she asked, lifting her frightened eyes.

'I have something particular to say to you – very particular.'

'Can't you come to the house? Can't you say it there?'

Townsend shook his head gloomily. 'I can't enter your doors again.'

'Oh, Mr Townsend!' murmured Catherine. She trembled as she wondered what had happened – whether her father had forbidden it.

'I can't, in self-respect,' said the young man. 'Your father has insulted me.'

'Insulted you?'

'He has taunted me with my poverty.'

'Oh, you are mistaken – you misunderstood him!' Catherine spoke with energy, getting up from her chair.

'Perhaps I am too proud – too sensitive. But would you have me otherwise?' he asked, tenderly.

'Where my father is concerned, you must not be sure. He is full of goodness,' said Catherine.

'He laughed at me for having no position. I took it quietly; but only because he belongs to you.'

'I don't know,' said Catherine – 'I don't know what he thinks. I am sure he means to be kind. You must not be too proud.'

'I will be proud only of you,' Morris answered. 'Will you meet me in the Square in the afternoon?'

A great blush on Catherine's part had been the answer to the declaration I have just quoted. She turned away, heedless of his question.

'Will you meet me?' he repeated. 'It is very quiet there – no one need see us – towards dusk.'

'It is you who are unkind, it is you who laugh, when you say such things as that.'

'My dear girl!' the young man murmured.

'You know how little there is in me to be proud of. I am ugly and stupid.'

Morris greeted this remark with an ardent murmur, in which she recognized nothing articulate but an assurance that she was his own dearest.

But she went on. 'I am not even – I am not even –' And she paused a moment.

'You are not what?'

'I am not even brave.'

'Ah, then, if you are afraid, what shall we do?'

She hesitated awhile; then at last – 'You must come to the house,' she said; 'I am not afraid of that.'

'I would rather it were in the Square,' the young man urged. 'You know how empty it is, often. No one will see us.'

'I don't care who sees us. But leave me now.'

He left her resignedly; he had got what he wanted. Fortunately he was ignorant that half and hour later, going home with her father, and feeling him near, the poor girl, in spite of her sudden declaration of courage, began to tremble again. Her father said nothing; but she had an idea his eyes were fixed upon her in the darkness. Mrs Penniman also was silent; Morris Townsend had told her that her niece preferred, unromantically, an interview in a chintz-covered parlour to a sentimental tryst beside a fountain sheeted with dead leaves, and she was lost in wonderment at the oddity – almost the perversity – of the choice.

Chapter Ten

Catherine received the young man the next day on the ground she had chosen – amidst the chaste upholstery of a New York drawing-room furnished in the fashion of fifty years ago. Morris had swallowed his pride, and made the effort necessary to cross the threshold of her too derisive parent – an act of magnanimity which could not fail to render him doubly interesting.

'We must settle something – we must take a line,' he declared, passing his hand through his hair and giving a glance at the long, narrow mirror which adorned the space between the two windows, and which had at its base a little gilded bracket covered by a thin slab of white marble, supporting in its turn a backgammon-board folded together in the shape of two volumes – two shining folios inscribed, in greenish-gilt letters, *History of England.* If Morris had been pleased to describe the master of the house as a heartless scoffer, it is because he thought him too much on his guard, and this was the easiest way to express his own dissatisfaction – a dissatisfaction which he had made a point of concealing from the Doctor. It will probably seem to the reader, however, that the Doctor's vigilance was by no means excessive, and that these two young people had an open field. Their intimacy was now considerable, and it may appear that, for a shrinking and retiring person, our heroine had been liberal of her favours. The young man, within a few days, had made her listen to things for which she had not supposed that she was prepared; having a lively foreboding of difficulties, he proceeded to gain as much ground as possible in the present. He remembered that fortune favours the brave, and even if he had forgotten it, Mrs Penniman would have remembered it for him. Mrs Penniman delighted of all things in a drama, and she flattered herself that a drama would now be enacted. Combining as she did the zeal of the prompter with the impatience of the spectator, she had long since done her utmost to pull up the curtain. She, too, expected to figure in the performance – to be the confidante, the Chorus, to speak the epilogue. It may even be said that there were times when she lost sight altogether of the modest heroine of the play in the contemplation of certain great scenes which would naturally occur between the hero and herself.

What Morris had told Catherine at last was simply that he loved her, or rather adored her. Virtually, he had made known as much already – his visits had been a series of eloquent intimations of it. But now he had affirmed it in lover's vows, and, as a memorable sign of it, he had passed his arm round the girl's waist and taken a kiss. This happy certitude had come sooner than Catherine expected, and she had regarded it, very naturally, as a priceless treasure. It may even be doubted whether she had ever definitely expected to possess it; she had not been waiting for it, and she had never said to herself that at a given moment it must come. As I have tried to explain, she was not eager and exacting; she took what was given her from day to day; and if the delightful custom of her lover's visits, which yielded her a happiness in which confidence and timidity were strangely blended, had suddenly come to an end, she would not only not have spoken of herself as one of the forsaken, but she would not have thought of herself as one of the disappointed. After Morris had kissed her, the last time he was with her, as a ripe assurance of his devotion, she begged him to go away, to leave her alone, to let her think. Morris went away, taking another kiss first. But Catherine's meditations had lacked a certain coherence. She felt his kisses on her lips and on her cheeks for a long time afterwards; the sensation was rather an obstacle than an aid to reflection. She would have liked to see her situation all clearly before her, to make up her mind what she should do if, as she feared, her father should tell her that he disapproved of Morris Townsend. But all that she could see with any vividness was that it was terribly strange that anyone should disapprove of him; that there must in that case be some mistake, some mystery, which in a little while would be set at rest. She put off deciding and choosing; before the vision of a conflict with her father she dropped her eyes and sat motionless, holding her breath and waiting. It made her heart beat; it was intensely painful. When Morris kissed her and said these things – that also made her heart beat; but this was worse, and it frightened her. Nevertheless, today, when the young man spoke of settling something, taking a line, she felt that it was the truth, and she answered very simply and without hesitating.

'We must do our duty,' she said; 'we must speak to my father. I will do it tonight; you must do it tomorrow.'

'It is very good of you to do it first,' Morris answered. 'The young man – the happy lover – generally does that. But just as you please.'

It pleased Catherine to think that she should be brave for his sake, and in her satisfaction she even gave a little smile. 'Women have more tact,' she said; 'they ought to do it first. They are more conciliating; they can persuade better.'

'You will need all your powers of persuasion. But, after all,' Morris added, 'you are irresistible.'

'Please don't speak that way – and promise me this: Tomorrow, when you talk with father, you will be very gentle and respectful.'

As much so as possible,' Morris promised. 'It won't be much use, but I shall try. I certainly would rather have you easily than have to fight for you.'

'Don't talk about fighting; we shall not fight.'

'Ah, we must be prepared,' Morris rejoined; 'you especially, because for you it must come hardest. Do you know the first thing your father will say to you?'

'No, Morris; please tell me.'

'He will tell you I am mercenary.'

'Mercenary!'

'It's a big word, but it means a low thing. It means that I am after your money.'

'Oh!' murmured Catherine, softly.

The exclamation was so deprecating and touching that Morris indulged in another little demonstration of affection. 'But he will be sure to say it,' he added.

'It will be easy to be prepared for that,' Catherine said. 'I shall simply say that he is mistaken – that other men may be that way, but that you are not.'

'You must make a great point of that, for it will be his own great point.'

Catherine looked at her lover a minute, and then she said, 'I shall persuade him. But I am glad we shall be rich,' she added.

Morris turned away, looking into the crown of his hat. 'No, it's a misfortune,' he said at last. 'It is from that our difficulty will come.'

'Well, if it is the worst misfortune, we are not so unhappy. Many people would not think it so bad. I will persuade him, and after that we shall be very glad we have money.'

Morris Townsend listened to this robust logic in silence. 'I will leave my defence to you; it's a charge that a man has to stoop to defend himself from.'

Catherine on her side was silent for a while; she was looking at him while he looked, with a good deal of fixedness, out of the window. 'Morris,' she said, abruptly, 'are you very sure you love me?'

He turned round, and in a moment he was bending over her. 'My own dearest, can you doubt it?'

'I have only known it five days,' she said, 'but now it seems to me as if I could never do without it.'

'You will never be called upon to try.' And he gave a little tender, reassuring laugh. Then, in a moment, he added, 'There is something you must tell me, too.' She had closed her eyes after the last words she uttered, and kept them closed; and at this she nodded her head, without opening them. 'You must tell me,' he went on, 'that if your father is dead against me, if he absolutely forbids our marriage, you will still be faithful.'

Catherine opened her eyes, gazing at him, and she could give no better promise than what he read there.

'You will cleave to me?' said Morris. 'You know you are your own mistress – you are of age.'

'Ah, Morris!' she murmured, for all answer; or rather not for all, for she put her hand into his own. He kept it a while, and presently he kissed her again. This is all that need be recorded of their conversation; but Mrs Penniman, if she had been present, would probably have admitted that it was as well it had not taken place beside the fountain in Washington Square.

Chapter Eleven

Catherine listened for her father when he came in that evening, and she heard him go to his study. She sat quiet, though her heart was beating fast, for nearly half an hour; then she went and knocked at his door – a ceremony without which she never crossed the threshold of this apartment. On entering it now, she found him in his chair beside the fire, entertaining himself with a cigar and the evening paper.

'I have something to say to you,' she began very gently; and she sat down in the first place that offered.

'I shall be very happy to hear it, my dear,' said her father. He waited – waited, looking at her – while she stared, in a long silence, at the fire. He was curious and impatient, for he was sure she was going to speak of Morris Townsend; but he let her take her own time, for he was determined to be very mild.

'I am engaged to be married!' Catherine announced at last, still staring at the fire.

The Doctor was startled; the accomplished fact was more than he had expected; but he betrayed no surprise. 'You do right to tell me,' he simply said. 'And who is the happy mortal whom you have honoured with your choice?'

'Mr Morris Townsend.' And as she pronounced her lover's name Catherine looked at him. What she saw was her father's still grey eye and his clear-cut, definite smile. She contemplated these objects for a moment, and then she looked back at the fire; it was much warmer.

'When was this arrangement made?' the Doctor asked.

'This afternoon – two hours ago.'

'Was Mr Townsend here?'

'Yes, father; in the front parlour.' She was very glad that she was not obliged to tell him that the ceremony of their betrothal had taken place out there under the bare ailanthus-trees.

'Is it serious?' said the Doctor.

'Very serious, father.'

Her father was silent a moment. 'Mr Townsend ought to have told me.'

'He means to tell you tomorrow.'

'After I know all about it from you? He ought to have told me before. Does he think I didn't care, because I left you so much liberty?'

'Oh no,' said Catherine; 'he knew you would care. And we have been so much obliged to you for – for the liberty.'

The Doctor gave a short laugh. 'You might have made a better use of it, Catherine.'

'Please don't say that, father!' the girl urged softly, fixing her dull and gentle eyes upon him.

He puffed his cigar awhile, meditatively. 'You have gone very fast,' he said, at last.

'Yes,' Catherine answered, simply; 'I think we have.'

Her father glanced at her an instant, removing his eyes from the fire. 'I don't wonder Mr Townsend likes you; you are so simple and so good.'

'I don't know why it is; but he *does* like me. I am sure of that.'

'And are you very fond of Mr Townsend?'

'I like him very much, of course, or I shouldn't consent to marry him.'

'But you have known him a very short time, my dear.'

'Oh,' said Catherine, with some eagerness, 'it doesn't take long to like a person – when once you begin.'

'You must have begun very quickly. Was it the first time you saw him – that night at your aunt's party?'

'I don't know, father,' the girl answered. 'I can't tell you about that.'

'Of course; that's your own affair. You will have observed that I have acted on that principle. I have not interfered; I have left you your liberty; I have remembered that you are no longer a little girl – that you have arrived at years of discretion.'

'I feel very old – and very wise,' said Catherine, smiling faintly.

'I am afraid that before long you will feel older and wiser yet. I don't like your engagement.'

'Ah!' Catherine exclaimed, softly, getting up from her chair.

'No, my dear. I am sorry to give you pain; but I don't like it. You should have consulted me before you settled it. I have been too easy with you, and I feel as if you had taken advantage of my indulgence. Most decidedly you should have spoken to me first.'

Catherine hesitated a moment, and then – 'It was because I was afraid you wouldn't like it,' she confessed.

'Ah, there it is! You had a bad conscience.'

'No, I have not a bad conscience, father!' the girl cried out, with considerable energy. 'Please don't accuse me of anything so dreadful!' These words, in fact, represented to her imagination something very terrible indeed, something base and cruel, which she associated with malefactors and prisoners. 'It was because I was afraid – afraid—' she went on.

'If you were afraid, it was because you had been foolish.'

'I was afraid you didn't like Mr Townsend.'

'You were quite right. I don't like him.'

'Dear father, you don't know him,' said Catherine, in a voice so timidly argumentative that it might have touched him.

'Very true; I don't know him intimately. But I know him enough; I have my impression of him. You don't know him either.'

She stood before the fire with her hands lightly clasped in front of her; and her father, leaning back in his chair and looking up at her, made this remark with a placidity that might have been irritating.

I doubt, however, whether Catherine was irritated, though she broke into a vehement protest. 'I don't know him?' she cried. 'Why, I know him – better than I have ever known anyone!'

'You know a part of him – what he has chosen to show you. But you don't know the rest.'

'The rest? What is the rest?'

'Whatever it may be, there is sure to be plenty of it.'

'I know what you mean,' said Catherine, remembering how Morris had forewarned her. 'You mean that he is mercenary.'

Her father looked up at her still, with his cold, quiet, reasonable eye. 'If I meant it, my dear, I should say it! But there is an error I wish particularly to avoid – that of rendering Mr Townsend more interesting to you by saying hard things about him.'

'I won't think them hard if they are true,' said Catherine.

'If you don't, you will be a remarkably sensible young woman!'

'They will be your reasons, at any rate, and you will want me to hear your reasons.'

The Doctor smiled a little. 'Very true. You have a perfect right to ask for them.' And he puffed his cigar a few moments. 'Very well, then; without accusing Mr Townsend of being in love only with your fortune – and with the fortune that you justly expect – I will say that there is every reason to suppose that these good things have entered into his calculation more largely than a tender solicitude for your happiness strictly requires. There is, of course, nothing impossible in an intelligent young man entertaining a disinterested affection for you. You are an honest, amiable girl, and an intelligent young man might easily find it out. But the principal thing that we know about this young man – who is, indeed, very intelligent – leads us to suppose that, however much he may value your personal merits, he values your money more. The principal thing we know about him is that he has led a life of dissipation, and has spent a fortune of his own in doing so. That is enough for me, my dear. I wish you to marry a young man with other antecedents – a young man who could give positive guarantees. If Morris Townsend has spent his own fortune in amusing himself, there is every reason to believe that he would spend yours.'

The Doctor delivered himself of these remarks slowly, deliberately, with occasional pauses and prolongations of accent, which made no great allowance for poor Catherine's suspense as to his conclusion. She sat down at last, with her head bent and her eyes still fixed upon him; and strangely enough – I hardly know how to tell it – even while she felt that what he said went so terribly against her, she admired his neatness and nobleness of expression. There was something hopeless and oppressive in having to argue with her father; but she too, on her side, must try to be clear. He was so quiet; he was not at all angry; and she, too, must be quiet. But her very effort to be quiet made her tremble.

'That is not the principal thing we know about him,' she said; and there was a touch of her tremor in her voice. 'There are other things – many other things. He has very high abilities – he wants so much to do something. He is kind, and generous, and true,' said poor Catherine, who had not suspected hitherto the resources of her eloquence. 'And his fortune – his fortune that he spent – was very small.'

'All the more reason he shouldn't have spent it,' cried the Doctor, getting up with a laugh. Then, as Catherine, who had also risen to her feet again, stood there in her rather angular earnestness, wishing so much and expressing so little, he drew her towards him and kissed her. 'You won't think me cruel?' he said, holding her a moment.

This question was not reassuring; it seemed to Catherine, on the contrary, to suggest possibilities which made her feel sick. But she answered coherently enough, 'No, dear father; because if you knew how I feel – and you must know, you know everything – you would be so kind, so gentle.'

'Yes, I think I know how you feel,' the Doctor said. 'I will be very kind – be sure of that. And I will see Mr Townsend tomorrow. Meanwhile, and for the present, be so good as to mention to no one that you are engaged.'

Chapter Twelve

On the morrow, in the afternoon, he stayed at home, awaiting Mr Townsend's call – a proceeding by which it appeared to him (justly perhaps, for he was a very busy man) that he paid Catherine's suitor great honour, and gave both these young people so much the less to complain of. Morris presented himself with a countenance sufficiently serene – he appeared to have forgotten the 'insult' for which he had solicited Catherine's sympathy two evenings before – and Doctor Sloper lost no time in letting him know that he had been prepared for his visit.

'Catherine told me yesterday what has been going on between you,' he said. 'You must allow me to say that it would have been becoming of you to give me notice of your intentions before they had gone so far.'

'I should have done so,' Morris answered, 'if you had not had so much the appearance of leaving your daughter at liberty. She seems to me quite her own mistress.'

'Literally, she is. But she has not emancipated herself morally quite so far, I trust, as to choose a husband without consulting me. I have left her at liberty, but I have not been in the least indifferent. The truth is, that your little affair has come to a head with a rapidity that surprises me. It was only the other day that Catherine made your acquaintance.'

'It was not long ago, certainly,' said Morris, with great gravity. 'I admit that we have not been slow to – to arrive at an understanding. But that was very natural, from the moment we were sure of ourselves – and of each other. My interest in Miss Sloper began the first time I saw her.'

'Did it not by chance precede your first meeting?' the Doctor asked.

Morris looked at him an instant. 'I certainly had already heard that she was a charming girl.'

'A charming girl – that's what you think her?'

'Assuredly. Otherwise I should not be sitting here.'

The Doctor meditated a moment. 'My dear young man,' he said at last, 'you must be very susceptible. As Catherine's father I have, I trust, a just and tender appreciation of her many good qualities; but I don't mind telling you that I have never thought of her as a charming girl, and never expected anyone else to do so.'

Morris Townsend received this statement with a smile that was not wholly devoid of deference. 'I don't know what I might think of her if I were her father. I can't put myself in that place. I speak from my own point of view.'

'You speak very well,' said the Doctor; 'but that is not all that is necessary. I told Catherine yesterday that I disapproved of her engagement.'

'She let me know as much, and I was very sorry to hear it. I am greatly disappointed.' And Morris sat in silence awhile, looking at the floor.

'Did you really expect I would say I was delighted, and throw my daughter into your arms?'

'Oh no; I had an idea you didn't like me.'

'What gave you the idea?'

'The fact that I am poor.'

'That has a harsh sound,' said the Doctor, 'but it is about the truth – speaking of you strictly as a son-in-law. Your absence of means, of a profession, of visible resources or prospects, places you in a category from which it would be imprudent for me to select a husband for my daughter, who is a weak young woman with a large fortune. In any other capacity I am perfectly prepared to like you. As a son-in-law, I abominate you.'

Morris Townsend listened respectfully. 'I don't think Miss Sloper is a weak woman,' he presently said.

'Of course you must defend her – it's the least you can do. But I have known my child twenty years, and you have known her six weeks. Even if she were not weak, however, you would still be a penniless man.'

'Ah, yes; that is *my* weakness! And therefore, you mean, I am mercenary – I only want your daughter's money.'

'I don't say that. I am not obliged to say it; and to say it, save under stress of compulsion, would be very bad taste. I say simply that you belong to the wrong category.'

'But your daughter doesn't marry a category,' Townsend urged, with his handsome smile. 'She marries an individual – an individual whom she is so good as to say she loves.'

'An individual who offers so little in return.'

'Is it possible to offer more than the most tender affection and a life-long devotion?' the young man demanded.

'It depends how we take it. It is possible to offer a few other things besides, and not only is it possible, but it is the custom. A life-long devotion is measured after the fact; and meanwhile it is usual in these cases to give a few material securities. What are yours? A very handsome face and figure, and a very good manner. They are excellent as far as they go, but they don't go far enough.'

'There is one thing you should add to them' said Morris – 'the word of a gentleman.'

'The word of a gentleman that you will always love Catherine? You must be a fine gentleman to be sure of that.'

'The word of a gentleman that I am not mercenary; that my affection for Miss Sloper is as pure and disinterested a sentiment as was ever lodged in a human breast. I care no more for her fortune than for the ashes in that grate.'

'I take note – I take note,' said the Doctor. 'But having done so, I turn to our category again. Even with that solemn vow on your lips, you take your place in it. There is nothing against you but an accident, if you will; but, with my thirty years' medical practice, I have seen that accidents may have far-reaching consequences.'

Morris smoothed his hat – it was already remarkably glossy – and continued to display a self-control which, as the Doctor was obliged to admit, was extremely creditable to him. But his disappointment was evidently keen.

'Is there nothing I can do to make you believe in me?'

'If there were, I should be sorry to suggest it, for – don't you see? – I don't want to believe in you,' said the Doctor, smiling.

'I would go and dig in the fields.'

'That would be foolish.'

'I will take the first work that offers tomorrow.'

'Do so by all means – but for your own sake, not for mine.'

'I see; you think I am an idler!' Morris exclaimed, a little too much in the tone of a man who has made a discovery. But he saw his error immediately, and blushed.

'It doesn't matter what I think, when once I have told you I don't think of you as a son-in-law.'

But Morris persisted: 'You think I would squander her money?'

The Doctor smiled. 'It doesn't matter, as I say; but I plead guilty to that.'

'That's because I spent my own, I suppose,' said Morris. 'I frankly confess that. I have been wild; I have been foolish. I will tell you every crazy thing I ever did, if you like. There were some great follies among the number – I have never concealed that. But I have sown my wild oats. Isn't there some proverb about a reformed rake? I was not a rake, but I assure you I have reformed. It is better to have amused one's self for a while and have done with it. Your daughter would never care for a milksop; and I will take the liberty of saying that you would like one quite as little. Besides, between my money and hers there is a great difference. I spent my own; it was because it was my own that I spent it, and I made no debts; when it was gone I stopped. I don't owe a penny in the world.'

'Allow me to inquire what you are living on now – though I admit,' the Doctor added, 'that the question, on my part, is inconsistent.'

'I am living on the remnants of my property,' said Morris Townsend.

'Thank you,' the Doctor gravely replied.

Yes, certainly, Morris's self-control was laudable. 'Even admitting I attach an undue importance to Miss Sloper's fortune,' he went on, 'would not that be in itself an assurance that I would take good care of it?'

'That you should take too much care would be quite as bad as that you should take too little. Catherine might suffer as much by your economy as by your extravagance.'

'I think you are very unjust!' The young man made this declaration decently, civilly, without violence.

'It is your privilege to think so, and I surrender my reputation to you! I certainly don't flatter myself, I gratify you.'

'Don't you care a little to gratify your daughter? Do you enjoy the idea of making her miserable?'

'I am perfectly resigned to her thinking me a tyrant for a twelvemonth.'

'For a twelvemonth!' exclaimed Morris, with a laugh.

'For a lifetime, then. She may as well be miserable in that way as in the other.'

Here at last Morris lost his temper. 'Ah, you are not polite, sir!' he cried.

'You push me to it – you argue too much.'

'I have a great deal at stake.'

'Well, whatever it is,' said the Doctor, 'you have lost it.'

'Are you sure of that?' asked Morris; 'are you sure your daughter will give me up?'

'I mean, of course, you have lost it as far as I am concerned. As for Catherine's giving you up – no, I am not sure of it. But as I shall strongly recommend it, as I have a great fund of respect and affection in my daughter's mind to draw upon, and as she has the sentiment of duty developed in a very high degree, I think it extremely possible.'

Morris Townsend began to smooth his hat again. 'I, too, have a fund of affection to draw upon,' he observed, at last.

The Doctor at this point showed his own first symptoms of irritation. 'Do you mean to defy me?'

'Call it what you please, sir. I mean not to give your daughter up.'

The Doctor shook his head. 'I haven't the least fear of your pining away your life. You are made to enjoy it.'

Morris gave a laugh. 'Your opposition to my marriage is all the more cruel, then. Do you intend to forbid your daughter to see me again?'

'She is past the age at which people are forbidden, and I am not a father in an old-fashioned novel. But I shall strongly urge her to break with you.'

'I don't think she will,' said Morris Townsend.

'Perhaps not; but I shall have done what I could.'

'She has gone too far—' Morris went on.

'To retreat? Then let her stop where she is.'

'Too far to stop, I mean.'

The Doctor looked at him a moment; Morris had his hand on the door. 'There is a great deal of impertinence in your saying it.'

'I will say no more, sir,' Morris answered; and, making his bow, he left the room.

Chapter Thirteen

It may be thought the Doctor was too positive, and Mrs Almond intimated as much. But, as he said, he had his impression; it seemed to him sufficient, and he had no wish to modify it. He had passed his life in estimating people (it was part of the medical trade), and in nineteen cases out of twenty he was right.

'Perhaps Mr Townsend is the twentieth case,' said Mrs Almond.

'Perhaps he is, though he doesn't look to me at all like a twentieth case. But I will give him the benefit of the doubt, and, to make sure, I will go and talk with Mrs Montgomery. She will almost certainly tell me I have done right; but it is just possible that she will prove to me that I have made the greatest mistake of my life. If she does, I will beg Mr Townsend's pardon. You needn't invite her to meet me, as you kindly proposed; I will write her a frank letter, telling her how matters stand, and asking leave to come and see her.'

'I am afraid the frankness will be chiefly on your side. The poor little woman will stand up for her brother, whatever he may be.'

'Whatever he may be! I doubt that. People are not always so fond of their brothers.'

'Ah,' said Mrs Almond, 'when it's a question of thirty thousand a year coming into a family—'

'If she stands up for him on account of the money, she will be a humbug. If she is a humbug, I shall see it. If I see it, I won't waste time with her.'

'She is not a humbug – she is an exemplary woman. She will not wish to play her brother a trick simply because he is selfish.'

'If she is worth talking to, she will sooner play him a trick than that he should play Catherine one. Has she seen Catherine, by the way – does she know her?'

'Not to my knowledge. Mr Townsend can have had no particular interest in bringing them together.'

'If she is an exemplary woman, no. But we shall see to what extent she answers your description.'

'I shall be curious to hear her description of you,' said Mrs Almond, with a laugh. 'And, meanwhile, how is Catherine taking it?'

'As she takes everything – as a matter of course.'

'Doesn't she make a noise? Hasn't she made a scene?'

'She is not scenic.'

'I thought a lovelorn maiden was always scenic.'

'A ridiculous widow is more so. Lavinia has made me a speech, she thinks me very arbitrary.'

'She has a talent for being in the wrong,' said Mrs Almond. 'But I am very sorry for Catherine, all the same.'

'So am I. But she will get over it.'

'You believe she will give him up?'

'I count upon it. She has such an admiration for her father.'

'Oh, we know all about that. But it only makes me pity her the more. It makes her dilemma the more painful, and the effort of choosing between you and her lover almost impossible.'

'If she can't choose, all the better.'

'Yes; but he will stand there entreating her to choose, and Lavinia will pull on that side.'

'I am glad she is not on my side; she is capable of ruining an excellent cause. The day Lavinia gets in to your boat it capsizes. But she had better be careful,' said the Doctor. 'I will have no treason in my house.'

'I suspect she will be careful; for she is at bottom very much afraid of you.'

'They are both afraid of me, harmless as I am,' the Doctor answered. 'And it is on that that I build – on the salutary terror I inspire.'

Chapter Fourteen

He wrote his frank letter to Mrs Montgomery, who punctually answered it, mentioning an hour at which he might present himself in the Second Avenue. She lived in a neat little house of red brick, which had been freshly painted, with the edges of the bricks very sharply marked out in white. It has now disappeared, with its companions, to make room for a row of structures more majestic. There were green shutters upon the windows without slats, but pierced with little holes, arranged in groups; and before the house was a diminutive 'yard', ornamented with a bush of mysterious character, and surrounded by a low wooden paling, painted in the same green as the shutters. The place looked like a magnified baby-house, and might have been taken down from a shelf in a toy-shop. Doctor Sloper, when he went to call, said to himself, as he glanced at the objects I have enumerated, that Mrs Montgomery was evidently a thrifty and self-respecting little person – the modest proportions of her dwelling seemed to indicate that she was of small stature – who took a virtuous satisfaction in keeping herself tidy, and had resolved that, since she might not be splendid, she would at least be immaculate. She received him in a little parlour, which was precisely the parlour he had expected: a small unspeckled bower, ornamented with a desultory foliage of tissue-paper, and with clusters of glass drops, amidst which – to carry out the analogy – the temperature of the leafy season was maintained by means of a cast-iron stove, emitting a dry blue flame, and smelling strongly of varnish. The walls were embellished with engravings swathed in pink gauze, and the tables ornamented with volumes of extracts from the poets, usually bound in black cloth stamped with florid designs in jaundiced gilt. The Doctor had time to take cognizance of these details; for Mrs Montgomery, whose conduct he pronounced under the circumstances inexcusable, kept him waiting some ten minutes before she appeared. At last, however, she rustled in, smoothing down a stiff poplin dress, with a little frightened flush in a gracefully rounded cheek.

She was a small, plump, fair woman, with a bright, clear eye, and an extraordinary air of neatness and briskness. But these qualities were evidently combined with an unaffected humility, and the Doctor gave her his esteem as soon as he had looked at her. A brave little person, with lively perceptions, and yet a disbelief in her own talent for social, as distinguished from practical, affairs – this was his rapid mental résumé of Mrs Montgomery; who, as he saw, was flattered by what she regarded as the honour of his visit. Mrs Montgomery, in her little red house in the Second Avenue, was a person for whom Doctor Sloper was one of the great men – one of the fine gentlemen of New York; and while she fixed her agitated eyes upon him, while she clasped her mittened hands together in her glossy poplin lap, she had the appearance of saying to herself that he quite answered her idea of what a distinguished guest would naturally be. She apologized for being late; but he interrupted her.

'It doesn't matter,' he said; 'for while I sat here I had time to think over what I wish to say to you, and to make up my mind how to begin.'

'Oh, do begin!' murmured Mrs Montgomery.

'It is not so easy,' said the Doctor, smiling. 'You will have gathered from my letter that I wish to ask you a few questions, and you may not find it very comfortable to answer them.'

'Yes; I have thought what I should say. It is not very easy.'

'But you must understand my situation – my state of mind. Your brother wishes to marry my daughter, and I wish to find out what sort of a young man he is. A good way to do so seemed to be to come and ask you, which I have proceeded to do.'

Mrs Montgomery evidently took the situation very seriously; she was in a state of extreme moral concentration. She kept her pretty eyes, which were illumined by a sort of brilliant modesty, attached to his own countenance, and evidently paid the most earnest attention to each of his words. Her expression indicated that she thought his idea of coming to see her a very superior conception, but that she was really afraid to have opinions on strange subjects.

'I am extremely glad to see you,' she said, in a tone which seemed to admit, at the same time, that this had nothing to do with the question.

The Doctor took advantage of this admission. 'I didn't come to see you for your pleasure; I came to make you say disagreeable things – and you can't like that. What sort of a gentleman is your brother?'

Mrs Montgomery's illuminated gaze grew vague, and began to wander. She smiled a little, and for some time made no answer, so that the Doctor at last became impatient. And her answer, when it came, was not satisfactory. 'It is difficult to talk about one's brother.'

'Not when one is fond of him, and when one has plenty of good to say.'

'Yes, even then, when a good deal depends on it,' said Mrs Montgomery.

'Nothing depends on it for you.'

'I mean for – for—' and she hesitated.

'For your brother himself. I see.'

'I mean for Miss Sloper,' said Mrs Montgomery.

The Doctor liked this; it had the accent of sincerity. 'Exactly; that's the point. If my poor girl should marry your brother, everything – as regards her happiness – would depend on his being a good fellow. She is the best creature in the world, and she could never do him a grain of injury. He, on the other hand, if he should not be all that we desire, might make her very miserable. That is why I want you to throw some light upon his character, you know. Of course, you are not bound to do it. My daughter, whom you have never seen, is nothing to you; and I, possibly, am only an indiscreet and impertinent old man. It is perfectly open to you to tell me that my visit is in very bad taste, and that I had better go about my business. But I don't think you will do this; because I think we shall interest you – my poor girl and I. I am sure that if you were to see Catherine she would interest you very much. I don't mean because she is interesting in the usual sense of the word, but because you would feel sorry for her. She is so soft, so simple-minded, she would be such an easy victim! A bad husband would have remarkable facilities for making her miserable; for she would have neither the intelligence nor the resolution to get the better of him, and yet she would have an exaggerated power of suffering. I see,' added the Doctor, with his most insinuating, his most professional laugh, 'you are already interested.'

'I have been interested from the moment he told me he was engaged,' said Mrs Montgomery.

'Ah! he says that – he calls it an engagement?'

'Oh, he has told me you didn't like it.'

'Did he tell you that I don't like *him*?'

'Yes, he told me that too. I said I couldn't help it,' added Mrs Montgomery.

'Of course you can't. But what you can do is to tell me I am right – to give me an attestation as it were.' And the Doctor accompanied this remark with another professional smile.

Mrs Montgomery, however, smiled not at all; it was obvious that she could not take the humorous view of his appeal. 'That is a good deal to ask,' she said, at last.

'There can be no doubt of that; and I must, in conscience, remind you of the advantages a young man marrying my daughter would enjoy. She has an income of ten thousand dollars in her own right, left her by her mother; if she marries a husband I approve, she will come into almost twice as much more at my death.'

Mrs Montgomery listened in great earnestness to this splendid financial statement; she had never heard thousands of dollars so familiarly talked about. She flushed a little with excitement. 'Your daughter will be immensely rich,' she said, softly.

'Precisely – that's the bother of it.'

'And if Morris should marry her, he – he—' And she hesitated, timidly.

'He would be master of all that money? By no means. He would be master of the ten thousand a year that she has from her mother; but I should leave every penny of my own fortune, earned in the laborious exercise of my profession, to my nephews and nieces.'

Mrs Montgomery dropped her eyes at this, and sat for some time gazing at the straw matting which covered her floor.

'I suppose it seems to you,' said the Doctor, laughing, 'that in so doing I should play your brother a very shabby trick.'

'Not at all. That is too much money to get possession of so easily by marrying. I don't think it would be right.'

'It's right to get all one can. But in this case your brother wouldn't be able. If Catherine marries without my consent, she doesn't get a penny from my own pocket.'

'Is that certain?' asked Mrs Montgomery, looking up.

'As certain as that I sit here.'

'Even if she should pine away?'

'Even if she should pine to a shadow, which isn't probable.'

'Does Morris know this?'

'I shall be most happy to inform him,' the Doctor exclaimed.

Mrs Montgomery resumed her meditations; and her visitor, who was prepared to give time to the affair, asked himself whether, in spite of her little conscientious air, she was not playing into her brother's hands. At the same time he was half-ashamed of the ordeal to which he had subjected her, and was touched by the gentleness with which she bore it. 'If she were a humbug,' he said, 'she would get angry, unless she be very deep indeed. It is not probable that she is as deep as that.'

'What makes you dislike Morris so much?' she presently asked, emerging from her reflections.

'I don't dislike him in the least as a friend, as a companion. He seems to me a charming fellow, and I should think he would be excellent company. I dislike him exclusively as a son-in-law. If the only office of a son-in-law were to dine at the paternal table, I should set a high value upon your brother: he dines capitally. But that is a small part of his function, which, in general, is to be a protector and caretaker of my child, who is singularly ill-adapted to take care of herself. It is there that he doesn't satisfy me. I confess I have nothing but my impression to go by; but I am in the habit of trusting my impression. Of course you are at liberty to contradict it flat. He strikes me as selfish and shallow.'

Mrs Montgomery's eyes expanded a little, and the Doctor fancied he saw the light of admiration in them. 'I wonder you have discovered he is selfish,' she exclaimed.

'Do you think he hides it so well?'

'Very well indeed,' said Mrs Montgomery. 'And I think we are all rather selfish,' she added, quickly.

'I think so too; but I have seen people hide it better than he. You see I am helped by a habit I have of dividing people into classes, into types. I may easily be mistaken about your brother as an individual, but his type is written on his whole person.'

'He is very good-looking,' said Mrs Montgomery.

The Doctor eyed her a moment. 'You women are all the same! But the type to which your brother belongs was made to be the ruin of you, and you were made to be its handmaids and victims. The sign of the type in question is the determination – sometimes terrible in its quiet intensity – to accept nothing of life but its pleasures, and to secure these pleasures chiefly by the aid of your complaisant sex. Young men of this class never do anything for themselves that they can get other people to do for them, and it is the infatuation, the devotion, the superstition of others that keeps them going. These others, in ninety-nine cases out of a hundred, are women. What our young friends chiefly insist upon is that someone else shall suffer for them; and women do that sort of thing, as you must know, wonderfully well.' The Doctor paused a moment, and then he added, abruptly, 'You have suffered immensely for your brother!'

This exclamation was abrupt, as I say, but it was also perfectly calculated. The Doctor had been rather disappointed at not finding his compact and comfortable little hostess surrounded in a more visible degree by the ravages of Morris Townsend's immorality; but he had said to himself that this was not because the young man had spared her, but because she had contrived to plaster up her wounds. They were aching there behind the varnished stove, the festooned engravings, beneath her own neat little poplin bosom; and if he could only touch the tender spot, she would make a movement that would betray her. The words I have just quoted were an attempt to put his finger suddenly upon the place, and they had some of the success that he looked for. The tears sprung for a moment to Mrs Montgomery's eyes, and she indulged in a proud little jerk of the head.

'I don't know how you have found that out!' she exclaimed.

'By a philosophic trick – by what they call induction. You know you have always your option of contradicting me. But kindly answer me a question: Don't you give your brother money? I think you ought to answer that.'

'Yes, I have given him money,' said Mrs Montgomery.

'And you have not had much to give him?'

She was silent a moment. 'If you ask me for a confession of poverty, that is easily made. I am very poor.'

'One would never suppose it from your – your charming house,' said the Doctor. 'I learned from my sister that your income was moderate, and your family numerous.'

'I have five children,' Mrs Montgomery observed; 'but I am happy to say I can bring them up decently.'

'Of course you can – accomplished and devoted as you are. But your brother has counted them over, I suppose?'

'Counted them over?'

'He knows there are five, I mean. He tells me it is he that brings them up.'

Mrs Montgomery stared a moment, and then quickly – 'Oh yes; he teaches them – Spanish.'

The Doctor laughed out. 'That must take a great deal off your hands! Your brother also knows, of course, that you have very little money?'

'I have often told him so,' Mrs Montgomery exclaimed, more unreservedly than she had yet spoken. She was apparently taking some comfort in the Doctor's clairvoyance.

'Which means that you have often occasion to, and that he often sponges on you. Excuse the crudity of my language; I simply express a fact. I don't ask you how much of your money he has had, it is none of my business. I have ascertained what I suspected – what I wished.' And the Doctor got up, gently smoothing his hat. 'Your brother lives on you,' he said, as he stood there.

Mrs Montgomery quickly rose from her chair, following her visitor's movements with a look of fascination. But then, with a certain inconsequence – 'I have never complained of him,' she said.

'You needn't protest – you have not betrayed him. But I advise you not to give him any more money.'

'Don't you see it is in my interest that he should marry a rich person?' she asked. 'If, as you say, he lives on me, I can only wish to get rid of him; and to put obstacles in the way of his marrying is to increase my own difficulties.'

'I wish very much you would come to me with your difficulties,' said the Doctor. 'Certainly, if I throw him back on your hands, the least I can do is to help you to bear the burden. If you will allow me to say so, then, I shall take the liberty of placing in your hands, for the present, a certain fund for your brother's support.'

Mrs Montgomery stared; she evidently thought he was jesting; but she presently saw that he was not, and the complication of her feelings became painful. 'It seems to me that I ought to be very much offended with you,' she murmured.

'Because I have offered you money? That's a superstition,' said the Doctor. 'You must let me come and see you again, and we will talk about these things. I suppose that some of your children are girls?'

'I have two little girls,' said Mrs Montgomery.

'Well, when they grow up, and begin to think of taking husbands, you will see how anxious you will be about the moral character of these husbands. Then you will understand this visit of mine.'

'Ah, you are not to believe that Morris's moral character is bad.'

The Doctor looked at her a little, with folded arms. 'There is something I should greatly like, as a moral satisfaction. I should like to hear you say, "He is abominably selfish." '

The words came out with the grave distinctness of his voice, and they seemed for an instant to create, to poor Mrs Montgomery's troubled vision, a material image. She gazed at it an instant, and then she turned away. 'You distress me, sir!' she exclaimed. 'He is, after all, my brother; and his talents, his talents–' On these last words her voice quavered, and before he knew it she had burst into tears.

'His talents are first-rate,' said the Doctor. 'We must find the proper field for them.' And he assured her most respectfully of his regret at having so greatly discomposed her. 'It's all for my poor Catherine,' he went on. 'You must know her, and you will see.'

Mrs Mongomery brushed away her tears, and blushed at having shed them. 'I should like to know your daughter,' she answered; and then, in an instant – 'Don't let her marry him!'

Doctor Sloper went away with the words gently humming in his ears – 'Don't let her marry him!' They gave him the moral satisfaction of which he had just spoken, and their value was the greater that they had evidently cost a pang to poor little Mrs Montgomery's family pride.

Chapter Fifteen

He had been puzzled by the way that Catherine carried herself; her attitude at this sentimental crisis seemed to him unnaturally passive. She had not spoken to him again after that scene in the library, the day before his interview with Morris: and a week had elapsed without making any change in her manner. There was nothing in it that appealed for pity, and he was even a little disappointed at her not giving him an opportunity to make up for his harshness by some manifestation of liberality which should operate as a compensation. He thought a little of offering to take her for a tour in Europe; but he was determined to do this only in case she should seem mutely to reproach him. He had an idea that she would display a talent for mute reproaches, and he was surprised at not finding himself exposed to these silent batteries. She said nothing, either tacitly or explicitly, and as she was never very talkative, there was now no especial eloquence in her reserve. And poor Catherine was not sulky – a style of behaviour for which she had too little histrionic talent – she was simply very patient. Of course she was thinking over her situation, and she was apparently doing so in a deliberate and unimpassioned manner, with a view of making the best of it.

'She will do as I have bidden her,' said the Doctor; and he made the further reflection that his daughter was not a woman of a great spirit.

I know not whether he had hoped for a little more resistance for the sake of a little more entertainment; but he said to himself, as he had said before, that though it might have its momentary alarms, paternity was, after all, not an exciting vocation.

Catherine meanwhile had made a discovery of a very different sort; it had become vivid to her that there was a great excitement in trying to be a good daughter. She had an entirely new feeling, which may be described as a state of expectant suspense about her own actions. She watched herself as she would have watched another person, and wondered what she would do. It was as if this other person, who was both herself and not herself, had suddenly sprung into being, inspiring her with a natural curiosity as to the performance of untested functions.

'I am glad I have such a good daughter,' said her father, kissing her, after the lapse of several days.

'I am trying to be good,' she answered, turning away, with a conscience not altogether clear.

'If there is anything you would like to say to me, you know you must not hesitate. You needn't feel obliged to be so quiet. I shouldn't care that Mr Townsend should be a frequent topic of conversation, but whenever you have anything particular to say about him I shall be very glad to hear it.'

'Thank you,' said Catherine; 'I have nothing particular at present.'

He never asked her whether she had seen Morris again, because he was sure that if this had been the case she would tell him. She had, in fact, not seen him; she had only written him a long letter. The letter, at least, was long for her; and, it may be added, that it was long for Morris; it consisted of five pages, in a remarkably neat and handsome hand. Catherine's handwriting was beautiful, and she was even a little proud of it: she was extremely fond of copying, and possessed volumes of extracts which testified to this accomplishment; volumes which she had exhibited one day to her lover, when the bliss of feeling that she was important in his eyes was exceptionally keen. She told Morris, in writing, that her father had expressed the wish that she should not see him again, and that she begged he would not come to the house until she should have 'made up her mind'. Morris replied with a passionate epistle, in which he asked to what, in Heaven's name, she wished to make up her mind. Had not her mind been made up two weeks before, and could it be possible that she entertained the idea of throwing him off? Did she mean to break down at the very beginning of their ordeal, after all the promises of fidelity she had both given and extracted? And he gave an account of his own interview with her father – an account not identical at all points with that offered in these pages. 'He was terribly violent,' Morris wrote, 'but you know my self-control. I have need of it all when I remember that I have it in my power to break in upon your cruel captivity.' Catherine sent him, in answer to this, a note of three lines. 'I am in great trouble; do not doubt of my affection, but let me wait a little and think.' The idea of a struggle with her father, of setting up her will against his own, was heavy on her soul, and it kept her quiet, as a great physical weight keeps us motionless. It never entered into her mind to throw her lover off; but from the first she tried to assure herself that there would be a peaceful way out of their difficulty. The assurance was vague, for it contained no element of positive conviction that her father would change his mind. She only had an idea that if she should be very good, the situation would in some mysterious manner improve. To be good she must be patient, outwardly submissive, abstain from judging her father too harshly, and from committing any act of open defiance. He was perhaps right, after all, to think as he did; by which Catherine meant not in the least that his judgement of Morris's motives in seeking to marry her was perhaps a just one, but that it was probably natural and proper that conscientious parents should be suspicious and even unjust. There were probably people in the world as bad as her father supposed Morris to be, and if there were the slightest chance of Morris being one of these sinister persons, the Doctor was right in taking it into account. Of course he could not know what she knew – how the purest love and truth were seated in the young man's eyes; but Heaven, in its time, might appoint a way of bringing him to such knowledge. Catherine expected a good deal of Heaven, and referred to the skies the initiative, as the French say, in dealing with her dilemma. She could not imagine herself imparting any kind of knowledge to her father; there was something superior even in his injustice, and absolute in his mistakes. But she could at least be good, and if she were only good enough, Heaven would invent some way of reconciling all things – the dignity of her father's errors and the sweetness of her own confidence, the strict performance of her filial duties, and the enjoyment of Morris Townsend's affection.

Poor Catherine would have been glad to regard Mrs Penniman as an illuminating agent, a part which this lady herself, indeed, was but imperfectly prepared to play. Mrs Penniman took too much satisfaction in the sentimental shadows of this little drama to have, for the moment, any great interest in dissipating them. She wished the plot to thicken, and the advice that she gave her niece tended, in her own imagination, to produce this result. It was rather incoherent counsel, and from one day to another it contradicted itself; but it was pervaded by an earnest desire that Catherine should do something striking. 'You must *act*, my dear; in your situation the great thing is to act,' said Mrs Penniman, who found her niece altogether beneath her opportunities. Mrs Penniman's real hope was that the girl would make a secret marriage, at which she should officiate as bride's woman or duenna. She had a vision of this ceremony being performed in some subterranean chapel; subterranean chapels in New York were not frequent, but Mrs Penniman's imagination was not chilled by trifles; and of the guilty couple – she liked to think of poor Catherine and her suitor as the guilty couple – being shuffled away in a fast-whirling vehicle to some obscure lodging in the suburbs, where she would pay them (in a thick veil) clandestine visits; where they would endure a period of romantic privation; and when ultimately, after she should have been their earthly providence, their intercessor, their advocate, and their medium of communication with the world, they would be reconciled to her brother in an artistic tableau, in which she herself should be somehow the central figure. She hesitated as yet to recommend this course to Catherine, but she attempted to draw an attractive picture of it to Morris Townsend. She was in daily communication with the young man, whom she kept informed by letters of the state of affairs in Washington Square. As he had been banished, as she said, from the house, she no longer saw him; but she ended by writing to him that she longed for an interview. This interview could take place only on neutral ground, and she bethought herself greatly before selecting a place of meeting. She had an inclination for Greenwood Cemetery, but she gave it up as too distant; she could not absent herself for so long, as she said, without exciting suspicion. Then she thought of the Battery, but that was rather cold and windy, besides one's being exposed to intrusion from the Irish emigrants who at this point alight, with large appetites, in the New World; and at last she fixed upon an oyster saloon in the Seventh Avenue, kept by a Negro – an establishment of which she knew nothing save that she had noticed it in passing. She made an appointment with Morris Townsend to meet him there, and she went to the tryst at dusk, enveloped in an impenetrable veil. He kept her waiting for half an hour – he had almost the whole width of the city to traverse – but she liked to wait, it seemed, to intensify the situation. She ordered a cup of tea, which proved excessively bad, and this gave her a sense that she was suffering in a romantic cause. When Morris at last arrived, they sat together for half an hour in the duskiest corner of the back shop; and it is hardly too much to say that this was the happiest half-hour that Mrs Penniman had known for years. The situation was really thrilling, and it scarcely seemed to her a false note when her companion asked for an oyster stew, and proceeded to consume it before her eyes. Morris, indeed, needed all the satisfaction that stewed oysters could give him, for it may be intimated to the reader that he regarded Mrs Penniman in the light of a fifth wheel to his coach. He was in a state of irritation natural to a gentleman of fine parts who had been snubbed in a benevolent attempt to confer a distinction upon a young woman of inferior characteristics, and the insinuating sympathy of this somewhat desiccated matron appeared to offer him no practical relief. He thought her a humbug, and he judged of humbugs with a good deal of confidence. He had listened and made himself agreeable to her at first, in order to get a footing in Washington Square; and at present he needed all his self-command to be decently civil. It would have gratified him to tell her that she was a fantastic old woman, and that he would like to put her into an omnibus and send her home. We know, however, that Morris possessed the virtue of self-control, and he had moreover the constant habit of seeking to be agreeable; so that, although Mrs Penniman's demeanour only exasperated his already unquiet nerves, he listened to her with a sombre deference in which she found much to admire.

Chapter Sixteen

They had of course immediately spoken of Catherine. 'Did she send me a message, or – or anything?' Morris asked. He appeared to think that she might have sent him a trinket or a lock of her hair.

Mrs Penniman was slightly embarrassed, for she had not told her niece of her intended expedition. 'Not exactly a message,' she said; 'I didn't ask her for one, because I was afraid to – to excite her.'

'I am afraid she is not very excitable.' And Morris gave a smile of some bitterness.

'She is better than that – she is steadfast, she is true.'

'Do you think she will hold fast, then?'

'To the death!'

'Oh, I hope it won't come to that,' said Morris.

'We must be prepared for the worst, and that is what I wish to speak to you about.'

'What do you call the worst?'

'Well,' said Mrs Penniman, 'my brother's hard, intellectual nature.'

'Oh, the devil!'

'He is impervious to pity,' Mrs Penniman added, by way of explanation.

'Do you mean that he won't come round?'

'He will never be vanquished by argument. I have studied him. He will be vanquished only by the accomplished fact.'

'The accomplished fact?'

'He will come round afterwards,' said Mrs Penniman, with extreme significance. 'He cares for nothing but facts – he must be met by facts.'

'Well,' rejoined Morris, 'it is a fact that I wish to marry his daughter. I met him with that the other day, but he was not at all vanquished.'

Mrs Penniman was silent a little, and her smile beneath the shadow of her capacious bonnet, on the edge of which her black veil was arranged curtainwise, fixed itself upon Morris's face with a still more tender brilliancy. 'Marry Catherine first, and meet him afterwards!' she exclaimed.

'Do you recommend that?' asked the young man, frowning heavily.

She was a little frightened, but she went on with considerable boldness. 'That is the way I see it: a private marriage – a private marriage.' She repeated the phrase because she liked it.

'Do you mean that I should carry Catherine off? What do they call it – elope with her?'

'It is not a crime when you are driven to it,' said Mrs Penniman. 'My husband, as I have told you, was a distinguished clergyman – one of the most eloquent men of his day. He once married a young couple that had fled from the house of the young lady's father; he was so interested in their story.

He had no hesitation, and everything came out beautifully. The father was afterwards reconciled, and thought everything of the young man. Mr Penniman married them in the evening, about seven o'clock. The church was so dark you could scarcely see, and Mr Penniman was intensely agitated – he was so sympathetic. I don't believe he could have done it again.'

'Unfortunately, Catherine and I have not Mr Penniman to marry us,' said Morris.

'No, but you have me!' rejoined Mrs Penniman, expressively. 'I can't perform the ceremony, but I can help you; I can watch!'

'The woman's an idiot!' thought Morris, but he was obliged to say something different. It was not, however, materially more civil. 'Was it in order to tell me this that you requested I would meet you here?'

Mrs Penniman had been conscious of a certain vagueness in her errand, and of not being able to offer him any very tangible reward for his long walk. 'I thought perhaps you would like to see one who is so near to Catherine,' she observed, with considerable majesty; 'and also,' she added, 'that you would value an opportunity of sending her something.'

Morris extended his empty hands with a melancholy smile. 'I am greatly obliged to you, but I have nothing to send.'

'Haven't you a *word*?' asked his companion, with her suggestive smile coming back.

Morris frowned again. 'Tell her to hold fast,' he said, rather curtly.

'That is a good word – a noble word: it will make her happy for many days. She is very touching, very brave,' Mrs Penniman went on, arranging her mantle and preparing to depart. While she was so engaged she had an inspiration; she found the phrase that she could boldly offer as a vindication of the step she had taken. 'If you marry Catherine at all risks,' she said, 'you will give my brother a proof of your being what he pretends to doubt.'

'What he pretends to doubt?'

'Don't you know what that is?' Mrs Penniman asked, almost playfully.

'It does not concern me to know,' said Morris, grandly.

'Of course it makes you angry.'

'I despise it,' Morris declared.

'Ah, you know what it is, then?' said Mrs Penniman, shaking her finger at him. 'He pretends that you like – you like the money.'

Morris hesitated a moment; and then, as if he spoke advisedly, 'I *do* like the money!'

'Ah, but not – but not as he means it. You don't like it more than Catherine?'

He leaned his elbows on the table and buried his head in his hands. 'You torture me!' he murmured. And, indeed, this was almost the effect of the poor lady's too importunate interest in his situation.

But she insisted on making her point, 'If you marry her in spite of him, he will take for granted that you expect nothing of him, and are prepared to do without it; and so he will see that you are disinterested.'

Morris raised his head a little, following this argument. 'And what shall I gain by that?'

'Why, that he will see that he has been wrong in thinking that you wished to get his money.'

'And seeing that I wish he would go to the deuce with it, he will leave it to a hospital. Is that what you mean?' asked Morris.

'No, I don't mean that; though that would be very grand,' Mrs Penniman quickly added. 'I mean that, having done you such an injustice, he will think it his duty, at the end, to make some amends.'

Morris shook his head, though it must be confessed he was a little struck with this idea. 'Do you think he is so sentimental?'

'He is not sentimental,' said Mrs Penniman; 'but, to be perfectly fair to him, I think he has, in his own narrow way, a certain sense of duty.'

There passed through Morris Townsend's mind a rapid wonder as to what he might, even under a remote contingency, be indebted to from the action of this principle in Doctor Sloper's breast, and the inquiry exhausted itself in his sense of the ludicrous. 'Your brother has no duties to me,' he said presently, 'and I none to him.'

'Ah, but he has duties to Catherine.'

'Yes; but, you see, on that principle Catherine has duties to him as well.'

Mrs Penniman got up with a melancholy sigh, as if she thought him very unimaginative. 'She has always performed them faithfully; and now do you think she has no duties to *you*?' Mrs Penniman always, even in conversation, italicized her personal pronouns.

'It would sound harsh to say so. I am so grateful for her love,' Morris added.

'I will tell her you said that. And now, remember that if you need me I am there.' And Mrs Penniman, who could think of nothing more to say, nodded vaguely in the direction of Washington Square.

Morris looked some moments at the sanded floor of the shop; he seemed to be disposed to linger a moment. At last, looking up with a certain abruptness, 'It is your belief that if she marries me he will cut her off?' he asked.

Mrs Penniman stared a little, and smiled. 'Why, I have explained to you what I think would happen – that in the end it would be the best thing to do.'

'You mean that, whatever she does, in the long run she will get the money?'

'It doesn't depend upon her, but upon you. Venture to appear as disinterested as you are,' said Mrs Penniman, ingeniously. Morris dropped his eyes on the sanded floor again, pondering this, and she pursued: 'Mr Penniman and I had nothing, and we were very happy. Catherine, moreover, has her mother's fortune, which, at the time my sister-in-law married, was considered a very handsome one.'

'Oh, don't speak of that!' said Morris; and indeed it was quite superfluous, for he had contemplated the fact in all its lights.

'Austin married a wife with money – why shouldn't you?'

'Ah! but your brother was a doctor,' Morris objected.

'Well, all young men can't be doctors.'

'I should think it an extremely loathsome profession,' said Morris, with an air of intellectual independence; then, in a moment, he went on rather inconsequently, 'Do you suppose there is a will already made in Catherine's favour?'

'I suppose so – even doctors must die; and perhaps a little in mine,' Mrs Penniman frankly added.

'And you believe he would certainly change it – as regards Catherine?'

'Yes; and then change it back again.'

'Ah, but one can't depend on that,' said Morris.

'Do you want to *depend* on it?' Mrs Penniman asked.

Morris blushed a little. 'Well, I am certainly afraid of being the cause of an injury to Catherine.'

'Ah! you must not be afraid. Be afraid of nothing, and everything will go well.'

And then Mrs Penniman paid for her cup of tea, and Morris paid for his oyster stew, and they went out together into the dimly lighted wilderness of the Seventh Avenue. The dusk had closed in completely, and the street lamps were separated by wide intervals of a pavement in which cavities and fissures played a disproportionate part. An omnibus, emblazoned with strange pictures, went tumbling over the dislocated cobble-stones.

'How will you go home?' Morris asked, following this vehicle with an interested eye. Mrs Penniman had taken his arm.

She hesitated a moment. 'I think this manner would be pleasant,' she said; and she continued to let him feel the value of his support.

So he walked with her through the devious ways of the west side of the town, and through the bustle of gathering nightfall in populous streets, to the quiet precinct of Washington Square. They lingered a moment at the foot of Doctor Sloper's white marble steps, above which a spotless white door, adorned with a glittering silver plate, seemed to figure for Morris the closed portal of happiness; and then Mrs Penniman's companion rested a melancholy eye upon a lighted window in the upper part of the house.

'That is my room – my dear little room!' Mrs Penniman remarked.

Morris started. 'Then I needn't come walking round the Square to gaze at it.'

'That's as you please. But Catherine's is behind; two noble windows on the second floor. I think you can see them from the other street.'

'I don't want to see them, ma'am.' And Morris turned his back to the house.

'I will tell her you have been *here,* at any rate,' said Mrs Penniman, pointing to the spot where they stood; 'and I will give her your message – that she is to hold fast.'

'Oh yes; of course. You know I write her all that.'

'It seems to say more when it is spoken. And remember, if you need me, that I am *there*,' and Mrs Penniman glanced at the third floor.

On this they separated, and Morris, left to himself, stood looking at the house a moment; after which he turned away, and took a gloomy walk round the Square, on the opposite side, close to the wooden fence. Then he came back, and paused for a minute in front of Doctor Sloper's dwelling. His eyes travelled over it; they even rested on the ruddy windows of Mrs Penniman's apartment. He thought it a devilish comfortable house.

Chapter Seventeen

Mrs Penniman told Catherine that evening – the two ladies were sitting in the back parlour – that she had had an interview with Morris Townsend; and on receiving this news the girl started with a sense of pain. She felt angry for the moment; it was almost the first time she had ever felt angry. It seemed to her that her aunt was meddlesome; and from this came a vague apprehension that she would spoil something.

'I don't see why you should have seen him. I don't think it was right,' Catherine said.

'I was so sorry for him – it seemed to me someone ought to see him.'

'No one but I,' said Catherine, who felt as if she were making the most presumptuous speech of her life, and yet at the same time had an instinct that she was right in doing so.

'But you wouldn't, my dear,' Aunt Lavinia rejoined; 'and I didn't know what might have become of him.'

'I have not seen him because my father has forbidden it,' Catherine said, very simply.

There was a simplicity in this, indeed, which fairly vexed Mrs Penniman. 'If your father forbade you to go to sleep, I suppose you would keep awake!' she commented.

Catherine looked at her. 'I don't understand you. You seem to me very strange.'

'Well, my dear, you will understand me some day!' And Mrs Penniman, who was reading the evening paper, which she perused daily from the first line to the last, resumed her occupation. She wrapped herself in silence; she was determined Catherine should ask her for an account of her interview with Morris. But Catherine was silent for so long that she almost lost patience; and she was on the point of remarking to her that she was very heartless, when the girl at last spoke.

'What did he say?' she asked.

'He said he is ready to marry you any day, in spite of everything.'

Catherine made no answer to this, and Mrs Penniman almost lost patience again; owing to which she at last volunteered the information that Morris looked very handsome, but terribly haggard.

'Did he seem sad?' asked her niece.

'He was dark under the eyes,' said Mrs Penniman. 'So different from when I first saw him; though I am not sure that if I had seen him in this condition the first time, I should not have been even more struck with him. There is something brilliant in his very misery.'

This was, to Catherine's sense, a vivid picture, and though she disapproved, she felt herself gazing at it. 'Where did you see him?' she asked, presently.

'In – in the Bowery; at a confectioner's,' said Mrs Penniman, who had a general idea that she ought to dissemble a little.

'Whereabouts is the place?' Catherine inquired, after another pause.

'Do you wish to go there, my dear?' said her aunt.

'Oh no.' And Catherine got up from her seat and went to the fire, where she stood looking awhile at the glowing coals.

'Why are you so dry, Catherine?' Mrs Penniman said at last.

'So dry?'

'So cold – so irresponsive.'

The girl turned very quickly. 'Did *he* say that?'

Mrs Penniman hesitated a moment. 'I will tell you what he said. He said he feared only one thing – that you would be afraid.'

'Afraid of what?'

'Afraid of your father.'

Catherine turned back to the fire again, and then, after a pause, she said, 'I *am* afraid of my father.'

Mrs Penniman got quickly up from her chair and approached her niece. 'Do you mean to give him up, then?'

Catherine for some time never moved; she kept her eyes on the coals. At last she raised her head and looked at her aunt. 'Why do you push me so?' she asked.

'I don't push you. When have I spoken to you before?'

'It seems to me that you have spoken to me several times.'

'I am afraid it is necessary, then, Catherine,' said Mrs Penniman, with a good deal of solemnity. 'I am afraid you don't feel the importance' – she paused a little; Catherine was looking at her – 'the importance of not disappointing that gallant young heart!' And Mrs Penniman went back to her chair by the lamp, and, with a little jerk, picked up the evening paper again.

Catherine stood there before the fire, with her hands behind her, looking at her aunt, to whom it seemed that the girl had never had just this dark fixedness in her gaze. 'I don't think you understand or that you know me,' she said.

'If I don't, it is not wonderful; you trust me so little.'

Catherine made no attempt to deny this charge, and for some time more nothing was said. But Mrs Penniman's imagination was restless, and the evening paper failed on this occasion to enchain it.

'If you succumb to the dread of your father's wrath,' she said, 'I don't know what will become of us.'

'Did *he* tell you to say these things to me?'

'He told me to use my influence.'

'You must be mistaken,' said Catherine. 'He trusts me.'

'I hope he may never repent of it!' And Mrs Penniman gave a little sharp slap to her newspaper. She knew not what to make of her niece, who had suddenly become stern and contradictious.

This tendency on Catherine's part was presently even more apparent. 'You had much better not make any more appointments with Mr Townsend,' she said. 'I don't think it is right.'

Mrs Penniman rose with considerable majesty. 'My poor child, are you jealous of me?' she inquired.

'Oh, Aunt Lavinia!' murmured Catherine, blushing.

'I don't think it is your place to teach me what is right.'

On this point Catherine made no concession. 'It can't be right to deceive.'

'I certainly have not deceived *you*!'

'Yes; but I promised my father—'

'I have no doubt you promised your father. But I have promised him nothing.'

Catherine had to admit this, and she did so in silence. 'I don't believe Mr Townsend himself likes it,' she said at last.

'Doesn't like meeting me?'

'Not in secret.'

'It was not in secret; the place was full of people.'

'But it was a secret place – away off in the Bowery.'

Mrs Penniman flinched a little. 'Gentlemen enjoy such things,' she remarked, presently. 'I know what gentlemen like.'

'My father wouldn't like it, if he knew.'

'Pray, do you propose to inform him?' Mrs Penniman inquired.

'No, Aunt Lavinia. But please don't do it again.'

'If I do it again you will inform him – is that what you mean? I do not share your dread of my brother; I have always known how to defend my own position. But I shall certainly never again take any step on your behalf; you are much too thankless. I knew you were not a spontaneous nature, but I believed you were firm, and I told your father that he would find you so. I am disappointed, but your father will not be.' And with this Mrs Penniman offered her niece a brief good night, and withdrew to her own apartment.

Chapter Eighteen

Catherine sat alone by the parlour fire – sat there for more than an hour, lost in her meditations. Her aunt seemed to her aggressive and foolish; and to see it so clearly – to judge Mrs Penniman so positively – made her feel old and grave. She did not resent the imputation of weakness; it made no impression on her, for she had not the sense of weakness, and she was not hurt at not being appreciated. She had an immense respect for her father, and she felt that to displease him would be a misdemeanour analogous to an act of profanity in a great temple: but her purpose had slowly ripened, and she believed that her prayers had purified it of its violence. The evening advanced, and the lamp burnt dim without her noticing it; her eyes were fixed upon her terrible plan. She knew her father was in his study – that he had been there all the evening; from time to time she expected to hear him move. She thought he would perhaps come, as he sometimes came, into the parlour. At last the clock struck eleven, and the house was wrapped in silence; the servants had gone to bed. Catherine got up and went slowly to the door of the library, where she waited a moment, motionless. Then she knocked, and then she waited again. Her father had answered her, but she had not the courage to turn the latch. What she had said to her aunt was true enough – she was afraid of him; and in saying that she had no sense of weakness, she meant that she was not afraid of herself. She heard him move within, and he came and opened the door for her.

'What is the matter?' asked the Doctor. 'You are standing there like a ghost!'

She went into the room, but it was some time before she contrived to say what she had come to say. Her father, who was in his dressing-gown and slippers, had been busy at his writing-table, and after looking at her for some moments, and waiting for her to speak, he went and seated himself at his papers again. His back was turned to her – she began to hear the scratching of his pen. She remained near the door, with her heart thumping beneath her bodice; and she was very glad that his back was turned, for it seemed to her that she could more easily address herself to this portion of his person than to his face. At last she began, watching it while she spoke:

'You told me that if I should have anything more to say about Mr Townsend you would be glad to listen to it.'

'Exactly, my dear,' said the Doctor, not turning round, but stopping his pen.

Catherine wished it would go on, but she herself continued: 'I thought I would tell you that I have not seen him again, but that I should like to do so.'

'To bid him good-bye?' asked the Doctor.

The girl hesitated a moment. 'He is not going away.'

The Doctor wheeled slowly round in his chair, with a smile that seemed to accuse her of an epigram; but extremes meet, and Catherine had not intended one. 'It is not to bid him good-bye, then?' her father said.

'No, father, not that; at least not for ever. I have not seen him again, but I should like to see him,' Catherine repeated.

The Doctor slowly rubbed his underlip with the feather of his quill.

'Have you written to him?'

'Yes, four times.'

'You have not dismissed him, then. Once would have done that.'

'No,' said Catherine; 'I have asked him – asked him to wait.'

Her father sat looking at her, and she was afraid he was going to break out into wrath, his eyes were so fine and cold.

'You are a dear, faithful child,' he said, at last. 'Come here to your father.' And he got up, holding out his hands towards her.

The words were a surprise, and they gave her an exquisite joy. She went to him, and he put his arm round her tenderly, soothingly; and then he kissed her. After this he said,

'Do you wish to make me very happy?'

'I should like to – but I am afraid I can't,' Catherine answered.

'You can if you will. It all depends on your will.'

'Is it to give him up?' said Catherine.

'Yes, it is to give him up.'

And he held her still, with the same tenderness, looking into her face and resting his eyes on her averted eyes. There was a long silence; she wished he would release her.

'You are happier than I, father,' she said at last.

'I have no doubt you are unhappy just now. But it is better to be unhappy for three months and get over it, than for many years and never get over it.'

'Yes, if that were so,' said Catherine.

'It would be so; I am sure of that.' She answered nothing, and he went on: 'Have you no faith in my wisdom, in my tenderness, in my solicitude for your future?'

'Oh, father!' murmured the girl.

'Don't you suppose that I know something of men – their vices, their follies, their falsities?'

She detached herself, and turned upon him. 'He is not vicious – he is not false!'

Her father kept looking at her with his sharp, pure eye. 'You make nothing of my judgement, then?'

'I can't believe that!'

'I don't ask you to believe it, but to take it on trust.'

Catherine was far from saying to herself that this was an ingenious sophism; but she met the appeal none the less squarely. 'What has he done – what do you know?'

'He has never done anything – he is a selfish idler.'

'Oh, father, don't abuse him!' she exclaimed, pleadingly.

'I don't mean to abuse him; it would be a great mistake. You may do as you choose,' he added, turning away.

'I may see him again?'

'Just as you choose.'

'Will you forgive me?'

'By no means.'

'It will only be for once.'

'I don't know what you mean by once. You must either give him up or continue the acquaintance.'

'I wish to explain – to tell him to wait.'

'To wait for what?'

'Till you know him better – till you consent.'

'Don't tell him any such nonsense as that. I know him well enough, and I shall never consent.'

'But we can wait a long time,' said poor Catherine, in a tone which was meant to express the humblest conciliation, but which had upon her father's nerves the effect of an iteration not characterized by tact.

The Doctor answered, however, quietly enough: 'Of course; you can wait till I die, if you like.'

Catherine gave a cry of natural horror.

'Your engagement will have one delightful effect upon you; it will make you extremely impatient for that event.'

Catherine stood staring, and the Doctor enjoyed the point he had made. It came to Catherine with the force – or rather with the vague impressiveness – of a logical axiom which it was not in her province to controvert; and yet, though it was a scientific truth, she felt wholly unable to accept it.

'I would rather not marry, if that were true,' she said.

'Give me a proof of it, then; for it is beyond a question that by engaging yourself to Morris Townsend you simply wait for my death.'

She turned away, feeling sick and faint; and the Doctor went on: 'And if you wait for it with impatience, judge, if you please, what *his* eagerness will be.'

Catherine turned it over – her father's words had such an authority for her that her very thoughts were capable of obeying him. There was a dreadful ugliness in it, which seemed to glare at her through the interposing medium of her own feebler reason. Suddenly, however, she had an inspiration – she almost knew it to be an inspiration.

'If I don't marry before your death, I will not after,' she said.

To her father, it must be admitted, this seemed only another epigram; and as obstinacy, in unaccomplished minds, does not usually select such a mode of expression, he was the more surprised at this wanton play of a fixed idea.

'Do you mean that for an impertinence?' he inquired; an inquiry of which, as he made it, he quite perceived the grossness.

'An impertinence? Oh, father, what terrible things you say!'

'If you don't wait for my death, you might as well marry immediately; there is nothing else to wait for.'

For some time Catherine made no answer; but finally she said:

'I think Morris – little by little – might persuade you.'

'I shall never let him speak to me again. I dislike him too much.'

Catherine gave a long, low sigh; she tried to stifle it, for she had made up her mind that it was wrong to make a parade of her trouble, and to endeavour to act upon her father by the meretricious aid of emotion. Indeed, she even thought it wrong – in the sense of being inconsiderate – to attempt to act upon his feelings at all; her part was to effect some gentle, gradual change in his intellectual perception of poor Morris's character. But the means of effecting such a change were at present shrouded in mystery, and she felt miserably helpless and hopeless. She had exhausted all arguments, all replies. Her father might have pitied her and in fact he did so; but he was sure he was right.

'There is one thing you can tell Mr Townsend when you see him again,' he said, 'that if you marry without my consent, I don't leave you a farthing of money. That will interest him more than anything else you can tell him.'

'That would be very right,' Catherine answered. 'I ought not in that case to have a farthing of your money.'

'My dear child,' the Doctor observed, laughing, 'your simplicity is touching. Make that remark, in that tone, and with that expression of countenance, to Mr Townsend, and take a note of his answer. It won't be polite – it will express irritation; and I shall be glad of that, as it will put me in the right; unless, indeed – which is perfectly possible – you should like him the better for being rude to you.'

'He will never be rude to me,' said Catherine, gently.

'Tell him what I say, all the same.'

She looked at her father, and her quiet eyes filled with tears.

'I think I will see him, then,' she murmured, in her timid voice.

'Exactly as you choose.' And he went to the door and opened it for her to go out. The movement gave her a terrible sense of his turning her off.

'It will be only once, for the present,' she added, lingering a moment.

'Exactly as you choose,' he repeated, standing there with his hand on the door. 'I have told you what I think. If you see him, you will be an ungrateful, cruel child; you will have given your old father the greatest pain of his life.'

This was more than the poor girl could bear; her tears overflowed, and she moved towards her grimly consistent parent with a pitiful cry. Her hands were raised in supplication, but he sternly evaded this appeal. Instead of letting her sob out her misery on his shoulder, he simply took her by the arm and directed her course across the threshold, closing the door gently but firmly behind her. After he had done so, he remained listening. For a long time there was no sound; he knew that she was standing outside. He was sorry for her, as I have said; but he was so sure he was right. At last he heard her move away, and then her footstep creaked faintly upon the stairs.

The Doctor took several turns round his study, with his hands in his pockets, and a thin sparkle, possibly of irritation, but partly also of something like humour, in his eye. 'By Jove,' he said to himself, 'I believe she will stick – I believe she will stick!' And this idea of Catherine 'sticking' appeared to have a comical side, and to offer a prospect of entertainment. He determined, as he said to himself, to see it out.

Chapter Nineteen

It was for reasons connected with this determination that on the morrow he sought a few words of private conversation with Mrs Penniman. He sent for her to the library, and he there informed her that he hoped very much that, as regarded this affair of Catherine's, she would mind her p's and q's.

'I don't know what you mean by such an expression,' said his sister. 'You speak as if I were learning the alphabet.'

'The alphabet of common sense is something you will never learn,' the Doctor permitted himself to respond.

'Have you called me here to insult me?' Mrs Penniman inquired.

'Not at all. Simply to advise you. You have taken up young Townsend; that's your own affair. I have nothing to do with your sentiments, your fancies, your affections, your delusions; but what I request of you is that you will keep these things to yourself. I have explained my views to Catherine; she understands them perfectly, and anything that she does further in the way of encouraging Mr Townsend's attentions will be in deliberate opposition to my wishes. Anything that you should do in the way of giving her aid and comfort will be – permit me the expression – distinctly treasonable. You know high treason is a capital offence: take care how you incur the penalty.'

Mrs Penniman threw back her head, with a certain expansion of the eye which she occasionally practised. 'It seems to me that you talk like a great autocrat.'

'I talk like my daughter's father.'

'Not like your sister's brother,' cried Lavinia.

'My dear Lavinia,' said the Doctor. 'I sometimes wonder whether I *am* your brother, we are so extremely different. In spite of differences, however, we can, at a pinch, understand each other; and that is the essential thing just now. Walk straight with regard to Mr Townsend; that's all I ask. It is highly probable you have been corresponding with him for the last three weeks – perhaps even seeing him. I don't ask you – you needn't tell me.' He had a moral conviction that she would contrive to tell a fib about the matter, which it would disgust him to listen to. 'Whatever you have done, stop doing it; that's all I wish.'

'Don't you wish also by chance to murder your child?' Mrs Penniman inquired.

'On the contrary, I wish to make her live and be happy.'

'You will kill her: she passed a dreadful night.'

'She won't die of one dreadful night, nor of a dozen. Remember that I am a distinguished physician.'

Mrs Penniman hesitated a moment; then she risked her retort. 'Your being a distinguished physician has not prevented you from already losing *two members* of your family.'

She had risked it, but her brother gave her such a terribly incisive look – a look so like a surgeon's lancet – that she was frightened at her courage. And he answered her, in words that corresponded to the look, 'It may not prevent me, either, from losing the society of still another.'

Mrs Penniman took herself off with whatever air of depreciated merit was at her command, and repaired to Catherine's room, where the poor girl was closeted. She knew all about her dreadful night, for the two had met again, the evening before, after Catherine left her father. Mrs Penniman was on the landing of the second floor when her niece came upstairs; it was not remarkable that a person of so much subtlety should have discovered that Catherine had been shut up with the Doctor. It was still less remarkable that she should have felt an extreme curiosity to learn the result of this interview, and that this sentiment, combined with her great amiability and generosity, should have prompted her to regret the sharp words lately exchanged between her niece and herself. As the unhappy girl came into sight in the dusky corridor, she made a lively demonstration of sympathy. Catherine's bursting heart was equally oblivious; she only knew that her aunt was taking her into her arms. Mrs Penniman drew her into Catherine's own room, and the two women sat there together far into the small hours, the younger one with her head on the other's lap, sobbing, and sobbing at first in a soundless, stifled manner, and then at last perfectly still. It gratified Mrs Penniman to be able to feel conscientiously that this scene virtually removed the interdict which Catherine had placed upon her indulging in further communion with Morris Townsend. She was not gratified, however, when, in coming back to her niece's room before breakfast, she found that Catherine had risen and was preparing herself for this meal.

'You should not go to breakfast,' she said; 'you are not well enough, after your fearful night.'

'Yes, I am very well, and I am only afraid of being late.'

'I can't understand you,' Mrs Penniman cried. 'You should stay in bed for three days.'

'Oh, I could never do that,' said Catherine, to whom this idea presented no attractions.

Mrs Penniman was in despair; and she noted, with extreme annoyance, that the trace of the night's tears had completely vanished from Catherine's eyes. She had a most impracticable physique. 'What effect do you expect to have upon you father,' her aunt demanded, 'if you come plumping down, without a vestige of any sort of feeling, as if nothing in the world had happened?'

'He would not like me to lie in bed,' said Catherine, simply.

'All the more reason for your doing it. How else do you expect to move him?'

Catherine thought a little. 'I don't know how; but not in that way. I wish to be just as usual.' And she finished dressing – and, according to her aunt's expression, went plumping down into the paternal presence. She was really too modest for consistent pathos.

And yet it was perfectly true that she had had a dreadful night. Even after Mrs Penniman left her she had had no sleep; she lay staring at the uncomforting gloom, with her eyes and ears filled with the movement with which her father had turned her out of his room, and of the words in which he had told her that she was a heartless daughter. Her heart was breaking; she had heart enough for that. At moments it seemed to her that she believed him, and that to do what she was doing a girl must indeed be bad. She *was* bad; but she couldn't help it. She would try to appear good, even if her heart were perverted; and from time to time she had a fancy that she might accomplish something by ingenious concessions to form, though she should persist in caring for Morris. Catherine's ingenuities were indefinite, and we are not called upon to expose their hollowness. The best of them, perhaps, showed itself in that freshness of aspect which was so discouraging to Mrs Penniman, who was amazed at the absence of haggardness in a young woman who for a whole night had lain quivering beneath a father's curse. Poor Catherine was conscious of her freshness; it gave her a feeling about the future which rather added to the weight upon her mind. It seemed a proof that she was strong and solid and dense, and would live to a great age – longer than might be generally convenient; and this idea was pressing, for it appeared to saddle her with a pretension the more, just when the cultivation of any pretension was inconsistent with her doing right. She wrote that day to Morris Townsend, requesting him to come and see her on the morrow, using very few words, and explaining nothing. She would explain everything face to face.

Chapter Twenty

On the morrow, in the afternoon, she heard his voice at the door, and his step in the hall. She received him in the big, bright front parlour, and she instructed the servant that, if anyone should call, she was particularly engaged. She was not afraid of her father's coming in, for at that hour he was always driving about town. When Morris stood there before her, the first thing that she was conscious of was that he was even more beautiful to look at than fond recollection had painted him; the next was that he had pressed her in his arms. When she was free again it appeared to her that she had now indeed thrown herself into the gulf of defiance, and even, for an instant, that she had been married to him.

He told her that she had been very cruel, and had made him very unhappy; and Catherine felt acutely the difficulty of her destiny, which forced her to give pain in such opposite quarters. But she wished that, instead of reproaches, however tender, he would give her help; he was certainly wise enough and clever enough to invent some issue from their troubles. She expressed this belief, and Morris received the assurance as if he thought it natural; but he interrogated at first – as was natural too – rather than committed himself to marking out a course.

'You should not have made me wait so long,' he said. 'I don't know how I have been living; every hour seemed like years. You should have decided sooner.'

'Decided?' Catherine asked.

'Decided whether you would keep me or give me up.'

'Oh, Morris,' she cried, with a long tender murmur, 'I never thought of giving you up!'

'What, then, were you waiting for?' The young man was ardently logical.

'I thought my father might – might—' and she hesitated.

'Might see how unhappy you were?'

'Oh no. But that he might look at it differently.'

'And now you have sent for me to tell me that at last he does so. Is that it?'

This hypothetical optimism gave the poor girl a pang. 'No, Morris,' she said, solemnly, 'he looks at it still in the same way.'

'Then why have you sent for me?'

'Because I wanted to see you,' cried Catherine, piteously.

'That's an excellent reason, surely. But did you want to look at me only? Have you nothing to tell me?'

His beautiful persuasive eyes were fixed upon her face, and she wondered what answer would be noble enough to make to such a gaze as that. For a moment her own eyes took it in, and then – 'I *did* want to look at you,' she said, gently. But after this speech, most inconsistently, she hid her face.

Morris watched her for a moment attentively. 'Will you marry me tomorrow?' he asked, suddenly.

'Tomorrow?'

'Next week, then – any time within a month?'

'Isn't it better to wait?' said Catherine.

'To wait for what?'

She hardly knew for what; but this tremendous leap alarmed her. 'Till we have thought about it a little more.'

He shook his head sadly and reproachfully. 'I thought you had been thinking about it these three weeks. Do you want to turn it over in your mind for five years? You have given me more than time enough. My poor girl,' he added, in a moment, 'you are not sincere.'

Catherine coloured from brow to chin, and her eyes filled with tears. 'Oh, how can you say that?' she murmured.

'Why, you must take me or leave me,' said Morris, very reasonably. 'You can't please your father and me both; you must choose between us.'

'I have chosen you,' she said, passionately.

'Then marry me next week!'

She stood gazing at him. 'Isn't there any other way?'

'None that I know of for arriving at the same result. If there is, I should be happy to hear of it.'

Catherine could think of nothing of the kind, and Morris's luminosity seemed almost pitiless. The only thing she could think of was that her father might, after all, come round; and she articulated, with an awkward sense of her helplessness in doing so, a wish that this miracle might happen.

'Do you think it is in the least degree likely?' Morris asked.

'It would be, if he could only know you.'

'He can know me if he will. What is to prevent it?'

'His ideas, his reasons,' said Catherine. 'They are so – so terribly strong.' She trembled with the recollection of them yet.

'Strong!' cried Morris. 'I would rather you should think them weak.'

'Oh, nothing about my father is weak,' said the girl.

Morris turned away, walking to the window, where he stood looking out. 'You are terribly afraid of him,' he remarked at last.

She felt no impulse to deny it, because she had no shame in it; for, if it was no honour to herself, at least it was an honour to him. 'I suppose I must be,' she said simply.

'Then you don't love me – not as I love you. If you fear your father more than you love me, then your love is not what I hoped it was.'

'Ah, my friend!' she said, going to him.

'Do *I* fear anything?' he demanded, turning round on her. 'For your sake what am I not ready to face?'

'You are noble – you are brave!' she answered, stopping short at a distance that was almost respectful.

'Small good it does me, if you are so timid.'

'I don't think I am – *really*,' said Catherine.

'I don't know what you mean by "really". It is really enough to make us miserable.'

'I should be strong enough to wait – to wait a long time.'

'And suppose after a long time your father should hate me worse than ever?'

'He wouldn't – he couldn't.'

'He would be touched by my fidelity; is that what you mean? If he is so easily touched, then why should you be afraid of him?'

This was much to the point, and Catherine was struck by it. 'I will try not to be,' she said. And she stood there submissively, the image, in advance, of a dutiful and responsible wife. This image could not fail to recommend itself to Morris Townsend, and he continued to give proof of the high estimation in which he held her. It could only have been at the prompting of such a sentiment that he presently mentioned to her that the course recommended by Mrs Penniman was an immediate union, regardless of consequences.

'Yes, Aunt Penniman would like that,' Catherine said, simply, and yet with a certain shrewdness. It must, however, have been in pure simplicity, and from motives quite untouched by sarcasm, that a few moments after she went on to say to Morris that her father had given her a message for him. It was quite on her conscience to deliver this message, and had the mission been ten times more painful, she would have as scrupulously performed it. 'He told me to tell you – to tell you very distinctly, and directly from himself – that if I marry without his consent, I shall not inherit a penny of his fortune. He made a great point of this. He seemed to think – he seemed to think—'

Morris flushed, as any young man of spirit might have flushed at an imputation of baseness. 'What did he seem to think?'

'That it would make a difference.'

'It *will* make a difference – in many things. We shall be by many thousands of dollars the poorer; and that is a great difference. But it will make none in my affection.'

'We shall not want the money,' said Catherine; 'for you know I have a good deal myself.'

'Yes, my dear girl, I know you have something. And he can't touch that.'

'He would never,' said Catherine. 'My mother left it to me.'

Morris was silent awhile. 'He was very positive about this, was he?' he asked at last. 'He thought such a message would annoy me terribly, and make me throw off the mask, eh?'

'I don't know what he thought,' said Catherine sadly.

'Please tell him that I care for his message as much as for that!' and Morris snapped his fingers sonorously.

'I don't think I could tell him that.'

'Do you know you sometimes disappoint me,' said Morris.

'I should think I might. I disappoint everyone – father and Aunt Penniman.'

'Well, it doesn't matter with me, because I am fonder of you than they are.'

'Yes, Morris,' said the girl, with her imagination – what there was of it – swimming in this happy truth, which seemed, after all, invidious to no one.

'Is it your belief that he will stick to it – stick to it for ever – to this idea of disinheriting you? – that your goodness and patience will never wear out his cruelty?'

'The trouble is that if I marry you he will think I am not good. He will think that a proof.'

'Ah, then he will never forgive you!'

This idea, sharply expressed by Morris's handsome lips, renewed for a moment to the poor girl's temporarily pacified conscience all its dreadful vividness. 'Oh, you must love me very much!' she cried.

'There is no doubt of that, my dear,' her lover rejoined. 'You don't like that word "disinherited",' he added, in a moment.

'It isn't the money; it is that he should – that he should feel so.'

'I suppose it seems to you a kind of curse?' said Morris. 'It must be very dismal. But don't you think,' he went on, presently, 'that if you were to try to be very clever, and to set rightly about it, you might in the end conjure it away? Don't you think,' he continued further, in a tone of sympathetic speculation, 'that a really clever woman, in your place, might bring him round at last? Don't you think—'

Here, suddenly, Morris was interrupted; these ingenious inquiries had not reached Catherine's ears. The terrible word disinheritance, with all its impressive moral reprobation, was still ringing there – seemed, indeed, to gather force as it lingered. The mortal chill of her situation struck more deeply into her childlike heart, and she was overwhelmed by a feeling of loneliness and danger. But her refuge was there, close to her, and she put out her hands to grasp it. 'Ah, Morris,' she said, with a shudder, 'I will marry you as soon as you please!' and she surrendered herself, leaning her head on his shoulder.

'My dear good girl!' he exclaimed, looking down at his prize. And then he looked up again, rather vaguely, with parted lips and lifted eyebrows.

Chapter Twenty-one

Doctor Sloper very soon imparted his conviction to Mrs Almond in the same terms in which he had announced it to himself. 'She's going to stick, by Jove! she's going to stick.'

'Do you mean that she is going to marry him?' Mrs Almond inquired.

'I don't know that; but she is not going to break down. She is going to drag out the engagement, in the hope of making me relent.'

'And shall you not relent?'

'Shall a geometrical proposition relent? I am not so superficial.'

'Doesn't geometry treat of surfaces?' asked Mrs Almond, who, as we know, was clever, smiling.

'Yes, but it treats of them profoundly. Catherine and her young man are my surfaces; I have taken their measure.'

'You speak as if it surprised you.'

'It is immense; there will be a great deal to observe.'

'You are shockingly cold-blooded!' said Mrs Almond.

'I need to be, with all this hot blood about me. Young Townsend, indeed, is cool; I must allow him that merit.'

'I can't judge him,' Mrs Almond answered; 'but I am not at all surprised at Catherine.'

'I confess I am a little; she must have been so deucedly divided and bothered.'

'Say it amuses you outright. I don't see why it should be such a joke that your daughter adores you.'

'It is the point where the adoration stops that I find it interesting to fix.'

'It stops where the other sentiment begins.'

'Not at all; that would be simple enough. The two things are extremely mixed up, and the mixture is extremely odd. It will produce some third element, and that's what I'm waiting to see. I wait with suspense – with positive excitement; and that is a sort of emotion that I didn't suppose Catherine would ever provide for me. I am really very much obliged to her.'

'She will cling,' said Mrs Almond; 'she will certainly cling.'

'Yes, as I say, she will stick.'

'Cling is prettier. That's what those very simple natures always do, and nothing could be simpler than Catherine. She doesn't take many impressions; but when she takes one, she keeps it. She is like a copper kettle that receives a dent; you may polish up the kettle, but you can't efface the mark.'

'We must try and polish up Catherine,' said the Doctor. 'I will take her to Europe!'

'She won't forget him in Europe.'

He will forget her, then.'

Mrs Almond looked grave. 'Should you really like that?'

'Extremely,' said the Doctor.

Mrs Penniman, meanwhile, lost little time in putting herself again in communication with Morris Townsend. She requested him to favour her with another interview, but she did not on this occasion select an oyster saloon as the scene of their meeting. She proposed that he should join her at the door of a certain church after service on Sunday afternoon; and she was careful not to appoint the place of worship which she usually visited, and where, as she said, the congregation would have spied upon her. She picked out a less elegant resort, and on issuing from its portal at the hour she had fixed she saw the young man standing apart. She offered him no recognition until she had crossed the street and he had followed her to some distance. Here, with a smile, 'Excuse my apparent want of cordiality,' she said. 'You know what to believe about that. Prudence before everything.' And on his asking her in what direction they should walk, 'Where we shall be least observed,' she murmured.

Morris was not in high good-humour, and his response to this speech was not particularly gallant. 'I don't flatter myself we shall be much observed anywhere.' Then he turned recklessly towards the centre of the town. 'I hope you have come to tell me that he has knocked under,' he went on.

'I am afraid I am not altogether a harbinger of good; and yet, too, I am to a certain extent a messenger of peace. I have been thinking a great deal, Mr Townsend,' said Mrs Penniman.

'You think too much.'

'I suppose I do; but I can't help it, my mind is so terribly active. When I give myself, I give myself. I pay the penalty in my headaches, my famous headaches – a perfect circlet of pain! But I carry it as a queen carries her crown. Would you believe that I have one now? I wouldn't, however, have missed our rendezvous for anything. I have something very important to tell you.'

'Well, let's have it,' said Morris.

'I was perhaps a little headlong the other day in advising you to marry immediately. I have been thinking it over, and now I see it just a little differently.'

'You seem to have a great many different ways of seeing the same object.'

'Their number is infinite!' said Mrs Penniman in a tone which seemed to suggest that this convenient faculty was one of her brightest attributes.

'I recommend you to take one way, and stick to it,' Morris replied.

'Ah, but it isn't easy to choose. My imagination is never quiet, never satisfied. It makes me a bad adviser, perhaps, but it makes me a capital friend.'

'A capital friend who gives bad advice!' said Morris.

'Not intentionally – and who hurries off, at every risk, to make the most humble excuses.'

'Well, what do you advise me now?'

'To be very patient; to watch and wait.'

'And is that bad advice or good?'

'That is not for me to say,' Mrs Penniman rejoined, with some dignity. 'I only claim it is sincere.'

'And will you come to me next week and recommend something different and equally sincere?'

'I may come to you next week, and tell you that I am in the streets.'

'In the streets?'

'I have had a terrible scene with my brother, and he threatens, if anything happens, to turn me out of the house. You know I am a poor woman.'

Morris had a speculative idea that she had a little property; but he naturally did not press this.

'I should be very sorry to see you suffer martyrdom for me,' he said. 'But you make your brother out a regular Turk.'

Mrs Penniman hesitated a little.

'I certainly do not regard Austin as an orthodox Christian.'

'And am I to wait till he is converted?'

'Wait at any rate till he is less violent. Bide your time, Mr Townsend; remember the prize is great.'

Morris walked along some time in silence, tapping the railings and gateposts very sharply with his stick.

'You certainly are devilish inconsistent!' he broke out at last. 'I have already got Catherine to consent to a private marriage.'

Mrs Penniman was indeed inconsistent, for at this news she gave a little jump of gratification.

'Oh, when and where?' she cried. And then she stopped short.

Morris was a little vague about this.

'That isn't fixed; but she consents. It's deuced awkward now to back out.'

Mrs Penniman, as I say, had stopped short; and she stood there with her eyes fixed brilliantly on her companion.

'Mr Townsend,' she proceeded, 'shall I tell you something. Catherine loves you so much that you may do anything.'

This declaration was slightly ambiguous, and Morris opened his eyes.

'I am happy to hear it. But what do you mean by anything?'

'You may postpone – you may change about; she won't think the worse of you.'

Morris stood there still, with his raised eyebrows; then he said, simply and rather dryly, 'Ah!' After this he remarked to Mrs Penniman that if she walked so slowly she would attract notice, and he succeeded, after a fashion, in hurrying her back to the domicile of which her tenure had become so insecure.

Chapter Twenty-two

He had slightly misrepresented the matter in saying that Catherine had consented to take the great step. We left her just now declaring that she would burn her ships behind her; but Morris, after having elicited this declaration, had become conscious of good reasons for not taking it up. He avoided, gracefully enough, fixing a day, though he left her under the impression that he had his eye on one. Catherine may have had her difficulties; but those of her circumspect suitor are also worthy of consideration. The prize was certainly great; but it was only to be won by striking the happy mean between precipitancy and caution. It would be all very well to take one's jump and trust to Providence; Providence was more especially on the side of clever people, and clever people were known by an indisposition to risk their bones.

The ultimate reward of a union with a young woman who was both unattractive and impoverished ought to be connected with immediate disadvantages by some very palpable chain. Between the fear of losing Catherine and her possible fortune altogether, and the fear of taking her too soon and finding this possible fortune as void of actuality as a collection of emptied bottles, it was not comfortable for Morris Townsend to choose – a fact that should be remembered by readers disposed to judge harshly of a young man who may have struck them as making but an indifferently successful use of fine natural parts. He had not forgotten that in any event Catherine had her own ten thousand a year; he had devoted an abundance of meditation to this circumstance. But with his fine parts he rated himself high, and he had a perfectly definite appreciation of his value, which seemed to him inadequately represented by the sum I have mentioned. At the same time he reminded himself that this sum was considerable, that everything is relative, and that if a modest income is less desirable than a large one, the complete absence of revenue is nowhere accounted an advantage.

These reflections gave him plenty of occupation, and made it necessary that he should trim his sail. Doctor Sloper's opposition was the unknown quantity in the problem he had to work out. The natural way to work it out was by marrying Catherine; but in mathematics there are many short cuts, and Morris was not without a hope that he should yet discover one. When Catherine took him at his word, and consented to renounce the attempt to mollify her father, he drew back skilfully enough, as I have said, and kept the wedding-day still an open question. Her faith in his sincerity was so complete that she was incapable of suspecting that he was playing with her; her trouble just now was of another kind. The poor girl had an admirable sense of honour, and from the moment she had brought herself to the point of violating her father's wish, it seemed to her that she had no right to enjoy his protection. It was on her conscience that she ought to live under his roof only so long as she conformed to his wisdom. There was a great deal of glory in such a position, but poor Catherine felt that she had forfeited her claim to it. She had cast her lot with a young man against whom he had solemnly warned her, and broken the contract under which he provided her with a happy home. She could not give up the young man, so she must leave the home; and the sooner the object of her preference offered her another, the sooner her situation would lose its awkward twist. This was close reasoning; but it was commingled with an infinite amount of merely instinctive penitence. Catherine's days, at this time, were dismal, and the weight of some of her hours was almost more than she could bear. Her father never looked at her, never spoke to her. He knew perfectly what he was about, and this was part of a plan. She looked at him as much as she dared (for she was afraid of seeming to offer herself to his observation), and she pitied him for the sorrow she had brought upon him. She held up her head and busied her hands, and went about her daily occupations; and when the state of things in Washington Square seemed intolerable, she closed her eyes and indulged herself with an intellectual vision of the man for whose sake she had broken a sacred law.

Mrs Penniman, of the three persons in Washington Square, had much the most of the manner that belongs to a great crisis. If Catherine was quiet, she was quietly quiet, as I may say, and her pathetic effects, which there was no one to notice, were entirely unstudied and unintended. If the Doctor was stiff and dry, and absolutely indifferent to the presence of his companions, it was so lightly, neatly, easily done, that you would have had to know him well to discover that, on the whole, he rather enjoyed having to be so disagreeable. But Mrs Penniman was elaborately reserved and significantly silent; there was a richer rustle in the very deliberate movements to which she confined herself, and when she occasionally spoke, in connexion with some very trivial event, she had the air of meaning something deeper than what she said. Between Catherine and her father nothing had passed since the evening she went to speak to him in his study. She had something to say to him – it seemed to her she ought to say it – but she kept it back for fear of irritating him. He also had something to say to her; but he was determined not to speak first. He was interested, as we know, in seeing how, if she were left to herself, she would 'stick'. At last she told him she had seen Morris Townsend again, and that their relations remained quite the same.

'I think we shall marry – before very long. And probably, meanwhile, I shall see him rather often; about once a week – not more.'

The Doctor looked at her coldly from head to foot, as if she had been a stranger. It was the first time his eyes had rested on her for a week, which was fortunate, if that was to be their expression. 'Why not three times a day?' he asked. 'What prevents your meeting as often as you choose?'

She turned away a moment; there were tears in her eyes. Then she said, 'It is better once a week.'

'I don't see how it is better. It is as bad as it can be. If you flatter yourself that I care for little modifications of that sort, you are very much mistaken. It is as wrong of you to see him once a week as it would be to see him all day long. Not that it matters to me, however.'

Catherine tried to follow these words, but they seemed to lead towards a vague horror from which she recoiled. 'I think we shall marry pretty soon,' she repeated, at last.

Her father gave her his dreadful look again, as if she were someone else. 'Why do you tell me that? It's no concern of mine.'

'Oh, father,' she broke out, 'don't you care, even if you do feel so?'

'Not a button. Once you marry, it's quite the same to me when, or where, or why you do it; and if you think to compound for your folly by hoisting your fly in this way, you may spare yourself the trouble.'

With this she turned away. But the next day he spoke to her of his own accord, and his manner was somewhat changed. 'Shall you be married within the next four or five months?' he asked.

'I don't know, father,' said Catherine. 'It is not very easy for us to make up our minds.'

'Put it off, then, for six months, and in the meantime I will take you to Europe. I should like you very much to go.'

It gave her such delight, after his words of the day before, to hear that he should 'like' her to do something, and that he still had in his heart any of the tenderness of preference, that she gave a little exclamation of joy. But then she became conscious that Morris was not included in this proposal, and that – as regards really going – she would greatly prefer to remain at home with him. But she blushed none the less more comfortably than she had done of late. 'It would be delightful to go to Europe,' she remarked, with a sense that the idea was not original, and that her tone was not all it might be.

'Very well, then, we will go. Pack up your clothes.'

'I had better tell Mr Townsend,' said Catherine.

Her father fixed his cold eyes upon her. 'If you mean that you had better ask his leave, all that remains to me is to hope he will give it.'

The girl was sharply touched by the pathetic ring of the words; it was the most calculated, the most dramatic little speech the Doctor had ever uttered. She felt that it was a great thing for her, under the circumstances, to have this fine opportunity of showing him her respect; and yet there was something else that she felt as well, and that she presently expressed. 'I sometimes think that if I do what you dislike so much, I ought not to stay with you.'

'To stay with me?'

'If I live with you, I ought to obey you.'

'If that's your theory, it's certainly mine,' said the Doctor, with a dry laugh.

'But if I don't obey you, I ought not to live with you – to enjoy your kindness and protection.'

This striking argument gave the Doctor a sudden sense of having underestimated his daughter; it seemed even more than worthy of a young woman who had revealed the quality of unaggressive obstinacy. But it displeased him – displeased him deeply, and he signified as much. 'That idea is in very bad taste,' he said. 'Did you get it from Mr Townsend?'

'Oh no; it's my own,' said Catherine, eagerly.

'Keep it to yourself, then,' her father answered, more than ever determined she should go to Europe.

Chapter Twenty-three

If Morris Townsend was not to be included in this journey, no more was Mrs Penniman, who would have been thankful for an invitation, but who (to do her justice) bore her disappointment in a perfectly lady-like manner. 'I should enjoy seeing the works of Raphael and the ruins – the ruins of the Pantheon,' she said to Mrs Almond; 'but, on the other hand, I shall not be sorry to be alone and at peace for the next few months in Washington Square. I want rest; I have been through so much in the last four months.' Mrs Almond thought it rather cruel that her brother should not take poor Lavinia abroad; but she easily understood that, if the purpose of his expedition was to make Catherine forget her lover, it was not in his interest to give his daughter this young man's best friend as a companion. 'If Lavinia had not been so foolish, she might visit the ruins of the Pantheon,' she said to herself; and she continued to regret her sister's folly, even though the latter assured her that she had often heard the relics in question most satisfactorily described by Mr Penniman. Mrs Penniman was perfectly aware that her brother's motive in undertaking a foreign tour was to lay a trap for Catherine's constancy; and she imparted this conviction very frankly to her niece.

'He thinks it will make you forget Morris,' she said (she always called the young man 'Morris' now): 'out of sight, out of mind, you know. He thinks that all the things you will see over there will drive him out of your thoughts.'

Catherine looked greatly alarmed. 'If he thinks that, I ought to tell him beforehand.'

Mrs Penniman shook her head. 'Tell him afterwards, my dear –after he has had all the trouble and expense. That's the way to serve him.' And she added, in a softer key, that it must be delightful to think of those who love us among the ruins of the Pantheon.

Her father's displeasure had cost the girl, as we know, a great deal of deep-welling sorrow – sorrow of the purest and most generous kind, without a touch of resentment or rancour; but for the first time, after he had dismissed with such contemptuous brevity her apology for being a charge upon him, there was a spark of anger in her grief. She had felt his contempt; it had scorched her; that speech about her bad taste had made her ears burn for three days. During this period she was less considerate; she had an idea – a rather vague one, but it was agreeable to her sense of injury – that now she was absolved from penance, and might do what she chose. She chose to write to Morris Townsend to meet her in the Square and take her to walk about the town. If she were going to Europe out of respect to her father, she might at least give herself this satisfaction. She felt in every way at present more free and more resolute; there was a force that urged her. Now at last, completely and unreservedly, her passion possessed her.

Morris met her at last, and they took a long walk. She told him immediately what had happened; that her father wished to take her away – it would be for six months – to Europe; she would do absolutely what Morris should think best. She hoped inexpressibly that he would think it best she should stay at home. It was some time before he said what he thought; he asked, as they walked along, a great many questions. There was one that especially struck her; it seemed so incongruous.

'Should you like to see all those celebrated things over there?'

'Oh no, Morris!' said Catherine, quite deprecatingly.

Gracious Heaven, what a dull woman!' Morris exclaimed to himself.

'He thinks I will forget you,' said Catherine; 'that all these things will drive you out of my mind.'

'Well, my dear, perhaps they will.'

'Please don't say that,' Catherine answered, gently, as they walked along. 'Poor father will be disappointed.'

Morris gave a little laugh. 'Yes, I verily believe that your poor father will be disappointed. But you will have seen Europe,' he added, humorously. 'What a take-in!'

'I don't care for seeing Europe,' Catherine said.

'You ought to care, my dear; and it may mollify your father.'

Catherine, conscious of her obstinacy, expected little of this, and could not rid herself of the idea that in going abroad and yet remaining firm, she should play her father a trick. 'Don't you think it would be a kind of deception?' she asked.

'Doesn't he want to deceive you?' cried Morris. 'It will serve him right. I really think you had better go.'

'And not be married for so long?'

'Be married when you come back. You can buy your wedding clothes in Paris.' And then Morris, with great kindness of tone, explained his view of of the matter. It would be a good thing that she should go; it would put them completely in the right. It would show they were reasonable, and willing to wait. Once they were so sure of each other, they could afford to wait – what had they to fear? If there was a particle of chance that her father would be favourably affected by her going, that ought to settle it; for, after all, Morris was very unwilling to be the cause of her being disinherited. It was not for himself, it was for her and for her children. He was willing to wait for her; it would be hard, but he could do it. And over there, among beautiful scenes and noble monuments, perhaps the old gentleman would be softened; such things were supposed to exert a humanizing influence. He might be touched by her gentleness, her patience, her willingness to make any sacrifice but *that* one; and if she should appeal to him some day, in some celebrated spot – in Italy, say, in the evening; in Venice, in a gondola, by moonlight – if she should be a little clever about it, and touch the right chord, perhaps he would fold her in his arms, and tell her that he forgave her. Catherine was immensely struck with this conception of the affair, which seemed eminently worthy of her lover's brilliant intellect, though she viewed it askance in so far as it depended upon her own powers of execution. The idea of being 'clever' in a gondola by moonlight appeared to her to involve elements of which her grasp was not active. But it was settled between them that she should tell her father that she was ready to follow him obediently anywhere, making the mental reservation that she loved Morris Townsend more than ever.

She informed the Doctor she was ready to embark, and he made rapid arrangements for this event. Catherine had many farewells to make, but with only two of them are we actively concerned. Mrs Penniman took a discriminating view of her niece's journey; it seemed to her very proper that Mr Townsend's destined bride should wish to embellish her mind by a foreign tour.

'You leave him in good hands,' she said, pressing her lips to Catherine's forehead. (She was very fond of kissing people's foreheads; it was an involuntary expression of sympathy with the intellectual part.) 'I shall see him often; I shall feel like one of the vestals of old tending the sacred flame.'

'You behave beautifully about not going with us,' Catherine answered, not presuming to examine this analogy.

'It is my pride that keeps me up,' said Mrs Penniman, tapping the body of her dress, which always gave forth a sort of metallic ring.

Catherine's parting with her lover was short, and few words were exchanged.

'Shall I find you just the same when I come back?' she asked; though the question was not the fruit of scepticism.

'The same – only more so,' said Morris, smiling.

It does not enter into our scheme to narrate in detail Doctor Sloper's proceedings in the Eastern hemisphere. He made the grand tour of Europe, travelled in considerable splendour, and (as was to have been expected in a man of his high cultivation) found so much in art and antiquity to interest him, that he remained abroad, not for six months, but for twelve. Mrs Penniman, in Washington Square, accommodated herself to his absence. She enjoyed her uncontested dominion in the empty house, and flattered herself that she made it more attractive to their friends than when her brother was at home. To Morris Townsend at least, it would have appeared that she made it singularly attractive. He was altogether her most frequent visitor, and Mrs Penniman was very fond of asking him to tea. He had his chair – a very easy one – at the fireside in the back parlour (when the great mahogany sliding doors, with silver knobs and hinges, which divided this apartment from its more formal neighbour, were closed), and he used to smoke cigars in the Doctor's study, where he often spent an hour in turning over the curious collections of its absent proprietor. He thought Mrs Penniman a goose, as we know; but he was no goose himself, and, as a young man of luxurious tastes and scanty resources, he found the house a perfect castle of indolence. It became for him a club with a single member. Mrs Penniman saw much less of her sister than while the Doctor was at home; for Mrs Almond had felt moved to tell her that she disapproved of her relations with Mr Townsend. She had no business to be so friendly to a young man of whom their brother thought so meanly, and Mrs Almond was surprised at her levity in foisting a most deplorable engagement upon Catherine.

'Deplorable!' cried Lavinia. 'He will make her a lovely husband.'

'I don't believe in lovely husbands,' said Mrs Almond; 'I only believe in good ones. If he marries her, and she comes into Austin's money, they may get on. He will be an idle, amiable, selfish, and, doubtless, tolerably good-natured fellow. But if she doesn't get the money, and he finds himself tied to her, Heaven have mercy on her! He will have none. He will hate her for his disappointment, and take his revenge; he will be pitiless and cruel. Woe betide poor Catherine! I recommend you to talk a little with his sister; its a pity Catherine can't marry *her*!'

Mrs Penniman had no appetite whatever for conversation with Mrs Montgomery, whose acquaintance she made no trouble to cultivate; and the effect of this alarming forecast of her niece's destiny was to make her think it indeed a thousand pities that Mr Townsend's generous nature should be embittered. Bright enjoyment was his natural element, and how could he be comfortable if there should prove to be nothing to enjoy? It became a fixed idea with Mrs Penniman that he should yet enjoy her brother's fortune, on which she had acuteness enough to perceive that her own claim was small.

'If he doesn't leave it to Catherine, it certainly won't be to leave it to me,' she said.

Chapter Twenty-four

The Doctor, during the first six months he was abroad, never spoke to his daughter of their little difference, partly on system, and partly because he had a great many other things to think about. It was idle to attempt to ascertain the state of her affections without direct inquiry, because if she had not had an expressive manner among the familiar influences of home, she failed to gather animation from the mountains of Switzerland or the monuments of Italy. She was always her father's docile and reasonable associate – going through their sight-seeing in deferential silence, never complaining of fatigue, always ready to start at the hour he had appointed overnight, making no foolish criticisms, and indulging in no refinements of appreciation. 'She is about as intelligent as the bundle of shawls,' the Doctor said, her main superiority being that, while the bundle of shawls sometimes got lost, or tumbled out of the carriage, Catherine was always at her post, and had a firm and ample seat. But her father had expected this, and he was not constrained to set down her intellectual limitations as a tourist to sentimental depression; she had completely divested herself of the characteristics of a victim, and during the whole time that they were abroad she never uttered an audible sigh. He supposed she was in correspondence with Morris Townsend, but he held his peace about it, for he never saw the young man's letters, and Catherine's own missives were always given to the courier to post. She heard from her lover with considerable regularity, but his letters came enclosed in Mrs Penniman's; so that, whenever the Doctor handed her a packet addressed in his sister's hand, he was an involuntary instrument of the passion he condemned. Catherine made this reflection, and six months earlier she would have felt bound to give him warning; but now she deemed herself absolved. There was a sore spot in her heart that his own words had made when once she spoke to him as she thought honour prompted; she would try and please him as far as she could, but she would never speak that way again. She read her lover's letters in secret.

One day, at the end of the summer, the two travellers found themselves in a lonely valley of the Alps. They were crossing one of the passes, and on the long ascent they had got out of the carriage and had wandered much in advance. After a while the Doctor descried a foot-path which, leading through a transverse valley, would bring them out, as he justly supposed, at a much higher point of the ascent. They followed this devious way, and finally lost the path; the valley proved very wild and rough, and their walk became rather a scramble. They were good walkers, however, and they took their adventure easily; from time to time they stopped, that Catherine might rest; and then she sat upon a stone and looked about her at the hard-featured rocks and the glowing sky. It was late in the afternoon, in the last of August; night was coming on, and as they had reached a great elevation, the air was cold and sharp. In the west there was a great suffusion of cold red light, which made the sides of the little valley look only the more rugged and dusky. During one of their pauses her father left her and wandered away to some high place, at a distance, to get a view. He was out of sight; she sat there alone in the stillness, which was just touched by the vague murmur somewhere of a mountain brook. She thought of Morris Townsend, and the place was so desolate and lonely that he seemed very far away. Her father remained absent a long time; she began to wonder what had become of him. But at last he reappeared, coming towards her in the clear twilight, and she got up to go on. He made no motion to proceed, however, but came close to her, as if he had something to say. He stopped in front of her, and stood looking at her with eyes that had kept the light of the flushing snow-summits on which they had just been fixed. Then, abruptly, in a low tone, he asked her an unexpected question,

'Have you given him up?'

The question was unexpected, but Catherine was only superficially unprepared.

'No, father,' she answered.

He looked at her again for some moments without speaking.

'Does he write to you?' he asked.

'Yes, about twice a month.'

The Doctor looked up and down the valley, swinging his stick; then he said to her, in the same low tone,

'I am very angry.'

She wondered what he meant – whether he wished to frighten her. If he did, the place was well chosen: this hard, melancholy dell, abandoned by the summer light, made her feel her loneliness. She looked around her, and her heart grew cold; for a moment her fear was great. But she could think of nothing to say, save to murmur, gently, 'I am sorry.'

'You try my patience,' her father went on, 'and you ought to know what I am. I am not a very good man. Though I am very smooth externally, at bottom I am very passionate; and I assure you I can be very hard,'

She could not think why he told her these things. Had he brought her there on purpose, and was it part of a plan? What was the plan? Catherine asked herself. Was it to startle her suddenly into a retraction – to take an advantage of her by dread? Dread of what? The place was ugly and lonely, but the place could do her no harm. There was a kind of still intensity about her father which made him dangerous, but Catherine hardly went so far as to say to herself that it might be part of his plan to fasten his hand – the neat, fine, supple hand of a distinguished physician – in her throat. Nevertheless, she receded a step. 'I am sure you can be anything you please,' she said; and it was her simple belief.

'I am very angry,' he replied, more sharply.

'Why has it taken you so suddenly?'

'It has not taken me suddenly. I have been raging inwardly for the last six months. But just now this seemed a good place to flare out. It's so quiet, and we are alone.'

'Yes, it's very quiet,' said Catherine, vaguely looking about her. 'Won't you come back to the carriage?'

'In a moment. Do you mean that in all this time you have not yielded an inch?'

'I would if I could, father; but I can't.'

The Doctor looked round him too. 'Should you like to be left in such a place as this, to starve?'

'What do you mean?' cried the girl.

'That will be your fate – that's how he will leave you.'

He would not touch her, but he had touched Morris. The warmth came back to her heart. 'That is not true, father,' she broke out, 'and you ought not to say it. It is not right, and it's not true.'

He shook his head slowly. 'No, it's not right, because you won't believe it. But it *is* true. Come back to the carriage.'

He turned away, and she followed him; he went faster, and was presently much in advance. But from time to time he stopped, without turning round, to let her keep up with him, and she made her way forward with difficulty, her heart beating with the excitement of having for the first time spoken to him in violence. By this time it had grown almost dark, and she ended by losing sight of him. But she kept her course, and after a little, the valley making a sudden turn, she gained the road, where the carriage stood waiting.

In it sat her father, rigid and silent; in silence, too, she took her place beside him.

It seemed to her, later, in looking back upon all this, that for days afterwards not a word had been exchanged between them. The scene had been a strange one, but it had not permanently affected her feeling towards her father, for it was natural, after all, that he should occasionally make a scene of some kind, and he had let her alone for six months. The strangest part of it was that he had said he was not a good man; Catherine wondered a good deal what he had meant by that. The statement failed to appeal to her credence, and it was not grateful to any resentment that she entertained. Even in the utmost bitterness that she might feel, it would give her no satisfaction to think him less complete. Such a saying as that was a part of his great subtlety – men so clever as he might say anything and mean anything; and as to his being hard, that surely, in a man, was a virtue.

He let her alone for six months more – six months during which she accommodated herself without a protest to the extension of their tour. But he spoke again at the end of this time: it was at the very last, the night before they embarked for New York, in the hotel at Liverpool. They had been dining together in a great, dim, musty sitting-room; and then the cloth had been removed, and the Doctor walked slowly up and down. Catherine at last took her candle to go to bed, but her father motioned her to stay.

'What do you mean to do when you get home?' he asked, while she stood there with her candle in her hand.

'Do you mean about Mr Townsend?'

'About Mr Townsend.'

'We shall probably marry.'

The Doctor took several turns again while she waited. 'Do you hear from him as much as ever?'

'Yes, twice a month,' said Catherine, promptly.

'And does he always talk about marriage?'

'Oh yes; that is, he talks about other things too, but he always says something about that.'

'I am glad to hear he varies his subjects; his letters might otherwise be monotonous.'

'He writes beautifully,' said Catherine, who was very glad of a chance to say it.

'They always write beautifully. However, in a given case that doesn't diminish the merit. So, as soon as you arrive, you are going off with him?'

This seemed a rather gross way of putting it, and something that there was of dignity in Catherine resented it. 'I cannot tell you till we arrive,' she said.

'That's reasonable enough,' her father answered. 'That's all I ask of you – that you *do* tell me, that you give me definite notice. When a poor man is to lose his only child, he likes to have an inkling of it beforehand.'

'Oh, father! you will not lose me,' Catherine said, spilling her candle wax.

'Three days before will do,' he went on, 'if you are in a position to be positive then. He ought to be very thankful to me, do you know. I have done a mighty good thing for him in taking you abroad; your value is twice as great, with all the knowledge and taste that you have acquired. A year ago, you were perhaps a little limited – a little rustic; but now you have seen everything, and appreciated everything, and you will be a most entertaining companion. We have fattened the sheep for him before he kills it.' Catherine turned away, and stood staring at the blank door. 'Go to bed,' said her father; 'and as we don't go aboard till noon, you may sleep late. We shall probably have a most uncomfortable voyage.'

Chapter Twenty-five

The voyage was indeed uncomfortable, and Catherine, on arriving in New York, had not the compensation of 'going off', in her father's phrase, with Morris Townsend. She saw him, however, the day after she landed; and in the meantime he formed a natural subject of conversation between our heroine and her Aunt Lavinia, with whom, the night she disembarked, the girl was closeted for a long time before either lady retired to rest.

'I have seen a great deal of him,' said Mrs Penniman. 'He is not very easy to know. I suppose you think you know him; but you don't, my dear. You will some day; but it will only be after you have lived with him. I may almost say *I* have lived with him,' Mrs Penniman proceeded, while Catherine stared. 'I think I know him now; I have had such remarkable opportunities. You will have the same – or, rather, you will have better'; and Aunt Lavinia smiled. 'Then you will see what I mean. It's a wonderful character, full of passion and energy, and just as true.'

Catherine listened with a mixture of interest and apprehension. Aunt Lavinia was intensely sympathetic, and Catherine, for the past year, while she wandered through foreign galleries and churches, and rolled over the smoothness of posting-roads, nursing the thoughts that never passed her lips, had often longed for the company of some intelligent person of her own sex. To tell her story to some kind woman – at moments it seemed to her that this would give her comfort, and she had more than once been on the point of taking the landlady, or the nice young person from the dressmaker's, into her confidence. If a woman had been near her, she would on certain occasions have treated such a companion to a fit of weeping; and she had an apprehension that, on her return, this would form her response to Aunt Lavinia's first embrace. In fact, however, the two ladies had met, in Washington Square, without tears; and when they found themselves alone together a certain dryness fell upon the girl's emotion. It came over her with a greater force that Mrs Penniman had enjoyed a whole year of her lover's society, and it was not a pleasure to her to hear her aunt explain and interpret the young man, speaking of him as if her own knowledge of him were supreme. It was not that Catherine was jealous; but her sense of Mrs Penniman's innocent falsity, which had lain dormant, began to haunt her again, and she was glad that she was safely at home. With this, however, it was a blessing to be able to talk of Morris, to sound his name, to be with a person who was not unjust to him.

'You have been very kind to him,' said Catherine. 'He has written me that, often. I shall never forget that, Aunt Lavinia.'

'I have done what I could; it has been very little. To let him come and talk to me, and give him his cup of tea – that was all. Your Aunt Almond thought it was too much, and used to scold me terribly; but she promised me, at least, not to betray me.'

'To betray you?'

'Not to tell your father. He used to sit in your father's study,' said Mrs Penniman, with a little laugh.

Catherine was silent a moment. This idea was disagreeable to her, and she was reminded again, with pain, of her aunt's secretive habits. Morris, the reader may be informed, had had the tact not to tell her that he sat in her father's study. He had known her but for a few months, and her aunt had known her for fifteen years; and yet he would not have made the mistake of thinking that Catherine would see the joke of the thing. 'I am sorry you made him go into father's room,' she said, after a while.

'I didn't send him; he went himself. He liked to look at the books, and at all those things in the glass cases. He knows all about them; he knows all about everything.'

Catherine was silent again; then, 'I wish he had found some employment,' she said.

'He has found some employment. It's beautiful news, and he told me to tell you as soon as you arrive. He has gone into partnership with a commission merchant. It was all settled, quite suddenly, a week ago.'

This seemed to Catherine indeed beautiful news; it had a fine prosperous air. 'Oh, I'm so glad!' she said; and now, for a moment, she was disposed to throw herself on Aunt Lavinia's neck.

'It's much better than being under someone; and he has never been used to that,' Mrs Penniman went on. 'He is just as good as his partner – they are perfectly equal. You see how right he was to wait. I should like to know what your father can say now! They have got an office in Duane Street, and little printed cards; he brought me one to show me. I have got it in my room, and you shall see it tomorrow. That's what he said to me the last time he was here – "You see how right I was to wait." He has got other people under him instead of being a subordinate. He could never be a subordinate; I have often told him I could never think of him in that way.'

Catherine assented to this proposition, and was very happy to know that Morris was his own master; but she was deprived of the satisfaction of thinking that she might communicate this news in triumph to her father. Her father would care equally little whether Morris were established in business or transported for life. Her trunks had been brought into her room, and further reference to her lover was for a short time suspended, while she opened them and displayed to her aunt some of the spoils of foreign travel. These were rich and abundant; and Catherine had brought home a present to everyone – to everyone save Morris, to whom she had brought simply her indiverted heart. To Mrs Penniman she had been lavishly generous, and Aunt Lavinia spent half an hour in unfolding and folding again, with little ejaculations of gratitude and taste. She marched about for some time in a splendid cashmere shawl, which Catherine had begged her to accept, settling it on her shoulders, and twisting down her head to see how low the point descended behind.

'I shall regard it only as a loan,' she said. 'I will leave it to you again when I die; or, rather,' she added, kissing her niece again, 'I will leave it to your first-born little girl.' And draped in her shawl, she stood there smiling.

'You had better wait till she comes,' said Catherine.

'I don't like the way you say that,' Mrs Penniman rejoined, in a moment. 'Catherine, are you changed?'

'No; I am the same.'

'You have not swerved a line?'

'I am exactly the same,' Catherine repeated, wishing her aunt were a little less sympathetic.

'Well, I am glad'; and Mrs Penniman surveyed her cashmere in the glass. Then, 'How is your father?' she asked, in a moment, with her eyes on her niece. 'Your letters were so meagre – I could never tell.'

'Father is very well.'

'Ah, you know what I mean,' said Mrs Penniman, with a dignity to which the cashmere gave a richer effect. 'Is he still implacable?'

'Oh yes!'

'Quite unchanged?'

'He is, if possible, more firm.'

Mrs Penniman took off her great shawl, and slowly folded it up. 'That is very bad. You had no success with your little project.'

'What little project?'

'Morris told me all about it. The idea of turning the tables on him, in Europe; of watching him, when he was agreeably impressed by some celebrated sight – he pretends to be so artistic, you know – and then just pleading with him and bringing him round.'

'I never tried it. It was Morris's idea; but if he had been with us in Europe, he would have seen that father was never impressed in that way. He *is* artistic – tremendously artistic; but the more celebrated places we visited, and the more he admired them, the less use it would have been to plead with him. They seemed only to make him more determined – more terrible,' said poor Catherine. 'I shall never bring him round, and I expect nothing now.'

'Well, I must say,' Mrs Penniman answered, 'I never supposed you were going to give it up.'

'I have given it up. I don't care now.'

'You have grown very brave,' said Mrs Penniman, with a short laugh. 'I didn't advise you to sacrifice your property.'

'Yes, I am braver than I was. You asked me if I had changed; I have changed in that way. Oh,' the girl went on, 'I have changed very much. And it isn't my property. If *he* doesn't care for it, why should I?'

Mrs Penniman hesitated. 'Perhaps he does care for it.'

'He cares for it for my sake, because he doesn't want to injure me. But he will know – he knows already – how little he need be afraid about that. Besides,' said Catherine, 'I have got plenty of money of my own. We shall be very well off; and now hasn't he got his business? I am delighted about that business.' She went on talking, showing a good deal of excitement as she proceeded. Her aunt had never seen her with just this manner, and Mrs Penniman, observing her, set it down to foreign travel, which had made her more positive, more mature. She thought also that Catherine had improved in appearance; she looked rather handsome. Mrs Penniman wondered whether Morris Townsend would be struck with that. While she was engaged in this speculation, Catherine broke out, with a certain sharpness, 'Why are you so contradictory, Aunt Penniman? You seem to think one thing at one time, and another at another. A year ago, before I went away, you wished me not to mind about displeasing father, and now you seem to recommend me to take another line. You change about so.'

This attack was unexpected, for Mrs Penniman was not used, in any discussion, to seeing the war carried into her own country – possibly because the enemy generally had doubts of finding subsistence there. To her own consciousness, the flowery fields of her reason had rarely been ravaged by a hostile force. It was perhaps on this account that in defending them she was majestic rather than agile.

'I don't know what you accuse me of, save of being too deeply interested in your happiness. It is the first time I have been told I am capricious. That fault is not what I am usually reproached with.'

'You were angry last year that I wouldn't marry immediately, and now you talk about my winning my father over. You told me it would serve him right if he should take me to Europe for nothing. Well, he has taken me for nothing, and you ought to be satisfied. Nothing is changed – nothing but my feeling about father. I don't mind nearly so much now. I have been as good as I could, but he doesn't care. Now I don't care either. I don't know whether I have grown bad; perhaps I have. But I don't care for that. I have come home to be married – that's all I know. That ought to please you, unless you have taken up some new idea; you are so strange. You may do as you please, but you must never speak to me again about pleading with father. I shall never plead with him for anything; that is all over. He has put me off. I am come home to be married.'

This was a more authoritative speech than she had ever heard on her niece's lips, and Mrs Penniman was proportionately startled. She was, indeed, a little awe-struck, and the force of the girl's emotion and resolution left her nothing to reply. She was easily frightened, and she always carried off her discomfiture by a concession – a concession which was often accompanied, as in the present case, by a little nervous laugh.

Chapter Twenty-six

If she had disturbed her niece's temper – she began from this moment forward to talk a good deal about Catherine's temper, an article which up to that time had never been mentioned in connexion with our heroine – Catherine had opportunity on the morrow to recover her serenity. Mrs Penniman had given her a message from Morris Townsend to the effect that he would come and welcome her home on the day after her arrival. He came in the afternoon; but, as may be imagined, he was not on this occasion made free of Doctor Sloper's study. He had been coming and going, for the past year, so comfortably and irresponsibly, that he had a certain sense of being wronged by finding himself reminded that he must now limit his horizon to the front parlour, which was Catherine's particular province.

'I am very glad you have come back,' he said; 'it makes me very happy to see you again.' And he looked at her, smiling, from head to foot, though it did not appear afterwards that he agreed with Mrs Penniman (who, woman-like, went more into details) in thinking her embellished.

To Catherine he appeared resplendent; it was some time before she could believe again that this beautiful young man was her own exclusive property. They had a great deal of characteristic lovers' talk – a soft exchange of inquiries and assurances. In these matters Morris had an excellent grace, which flung a picturesque interest even over the account of his début in the commission business – a subject as to which his companion earnestly questioned him. From time to time he got up from the sofa where they sat together, and walked about the room; after which he came back, smiling and passing his hand through his hair. He was unquiet, as was natural in a young man who had just been reunited to a long-absent mistress, and Catherine made the reflection that she had never seen him so excited. It gave her pleasure, somehow, to note this fact. He asked her questions about her travels, to some of which she was unable to reply, for she had forgotten the names of places and the order of her father's journey. But for the moment she was so happy, so lifted up by the belief that her troubles at last were over, that she forgot to be ashamed of her meagre answers. It seemed to her now that she could marry him without the remnant of a scruple, or a single tremor save those that belonged to joy. Without waiting for him to ask, she told him that her father had come back in exactly the same state of mind – that he had not yielded an inch.

'We must not expect it now,' she said, 'and we must do without it.'

Morris sat looking and smiling. 'My poor, dear girl!' he exclaimed.

'You mustn't pity me,' said Catherine. 'I don't mind it now I am used to it.'

Morris continued to smile, and then he got up and walked about again. 'You had better let me try him.'

'Try to bring him over? You would only make him worse,' Catherine answered, resolutely.

'You say that because I managed it so badly before. But I should manage it differently now. I am much wiser; I have had a year to think of it. I have more tact.'

'Is that what you have been thinking of for a year?'

'Much of the time. You see, the idea sticks in my crop. I don't like to be beaten.'

'How are you beaten if we marry?'

'Of course I am not beaten on the main issue; but I am, don't you see? on all the rest of it – on the question of my reputation, of my relations with your father, of my relations with my own children, if we should have any.'

'We shall have enough for our children; we shall have enough for everything. Don't you expect to succeed in business?'

'Brilliantly, and we shall certainly be very comfortable. But it isn't of the mere material comfort I speak; it is of the moral comfort,' said Morris – 'of the intellectual satisfaction.'

'I have great moral comfort now,' Catherine declared, very simply.

'Of course you have. But with me it is different. I have staked my pride on proving to your father that he is wrong, and now that I am at the head of a flourishing business, I can deal with him as an equal. I have a capital plan – do let me go at him!'

He stood before her with his bright face, his jaunty air, his hands in his pockets; and she got up, with her eyes resting on his own. 'Please don't, Morris; please don't,' she said; and there was a certain mild, sad firmness in her tone which he heard for the first time. 'We must ask no favours of him – we must ask nothing more. He won't relent, and nothing good will come of it. I know it now – I have a very good reason.'

'And pray what is your reason?'

She hesitated to bring it out, but at last it came. 'He is not very fond of me.'

'Oh, bother!' cried Morris, angrily.

'I wouldn't say such a thing without being sure. I saw it, I felt it, in England, just before he came away. He talked to me one night – the last night – and then it came over me. You can tell when a person feels that way. I wouldn't accuse him if he hadn't made me feel that way. I don't accuse him; I just tell you that that's how it is. He can't help it; we can't govern our affections. Do I govern mine? Mightn't he say that to me? It's because he is so fond of my mother, whom we lost so long ago. She was beautiful, and very, very brilliant; he is always thinking of her. I am not at all like her; Aunt Penniman has told me that. Of course it isn't my fault; but neither is it his fault. All I mean is, it's true; and it's a stronger reason for his never being reconciled than simply his dislike for you.'

' "Simply?" ' cried Morris, with a laugh. 'I am much obliged for that.'

'I don't mind about his disliking you now; I mind everything less. I feel differently; I feel separated from my father.'

'Upon my word,' said Morris, 'you are a queer family.'

'Don't say that – don't say anything unkind,' the girl entreated. 'You must be very kind to me now, because, Morris, because' – and she hesitated a moment – 'because I have done a great deal for you.'

'Oh, I know that, my dear.'

She had spoken up to this moment without vehemence or outward sign of emotion, gently, reasoningly, only trying to explain. But her emotion had been ineffectually smothered, and it betrayed itself at last in the trembling of her voice. 'It is a great thing to be separated like that from your father, when you have worshipped him before. It has made me very unhappy; or it would have made me so if I didn't love you. You can tell when a person speaks to you as if – as if—'

'As if what?'

'As if they despised you!' said Catherine, passionately. 'He spoke that way the night before we sailed. It wasn't much, but it was enough, and I thought of it on the voyage all the time. Then I made up my mind. I will never ask him for anything again, or expect anything from him. It would not be natural now. We must be very happy together, and we must not seem to depend upon his forgiveness. And, Morris, Morris, you must never despise me!'

This was an easy promise to make, and Morris made it with fine effect. But for the moment he undertook nothing more onerous.

Chapter Twenty-seven

The doctor, of course, on his return, had a good deal of talk with his sisters. He was at no great pains to narrate his travels or to communicate his impressions of distant lands to Mrs Penniman, upon whom he contented himself with bestowing a memento of his enviable experience in the shape of a velvet gown. But he conversed with her at some length about matters nearer home, and lost no time in assuring her that he was still an inflexible father.

'I have no doubt you have seen a great deal of Mr Townsend, and done your best to console him for Catherine's absence,' he said. 'I don't ask you, and you needn't deny it. I wouldn't put the question to you for the world, and expose you to the inconvenience of having to – a – excogitate an answer. No one has betrayed you, and there has been no spy upon your proceedings. Elizabeth has told no tales, and has never mentioned you except to praise your good looks and good spirits. The thing is simply an inference of my own – an induction, as the philosophers say. It seems to me likely that you would have offered an asylum to an interesting sufferer. Mr Townsend has been a good deal in the house; there is something in the house that tells me so. We doctors, you know, end by acquiring fine perceptions, and it is impressed upon my sensorium that he has sat in these chairs, in a very easy attitude, and warmed himself at that fire. I don't grudge him the comfort of it; it is the only one he will ever enjoy at my expense. It seems likely, indeed, that I shall be able to economize at his own. I don't know what you may have said to him, or what you may say hereafter; but I should like you to know that if you have encouraged him to believe that he will gain anything by hanging on, or that I have budged a hair-breadth from the position I took up a year ago, you have played him a trick for which he may exact reparation. I'm not sure that he may not bring a suit against you. Of course you have done it conscientiously; you have made yourself believe that I can be tired out. This is the most baseless hallucination that ever visited the brain of a genial optimist. I am not in the least tired; I am as fresh as when I started; I am good for fifty years yet. Catherine appears not to have budged an inch either; she is equally fresh; so we are about where we were before. This, however, you know as well as I. What I wish is simply to give you notice of my own state of mind. Take it to heart, dear Lavinia. Beware of the just resentment of a deluded fortune-hunter!'

'I can't say I expected it,' said Mrs Penniman. 'And I had a sort of foolish hope that you would come home without that odious ironical tone with which you treat the most sacred subjects.'

'Don't undervalue irony; it is often of great use. It is not, however, always necessary, and I will show you how gracefully I can lay it aside. I should like to know whether you think Morris Townsend will hang on?'

'I will answer you with your own weapons,' said Mrs Penniman. 'You had better wait and see.'

'Do you call such a speech as that one of my own weapons? I never said anything so rough.'

'He will hang on long enough to make you very uncomfortable, then.'

'My dear Lavinia,' exclaimed the Doctor, 'do you call that irony? I call it pugilism.'

Mrs Penniman, however, in spite of her pugilism, was a good deal frightened, and she took counsel of her fears. Her brother, meanwhile, took counsel, with many reservations, of Mrs Almond, to whom he was no less generous than to Lavinia, and a good deal more communicative.

'I suppose she has had him there all the while,' he said. 'I must look into the state of my wine. You needn't mind telling me now; I have already said all I mean to say to her on the subject.'

'I believe he was in the house a good deal,' Mrs Almond answered. 'But you must admit that your leaving Lavinia quite alone was a great change for her, and that it was natural she should want some society.'

'I do admit that, and that is why I shall make no row about the wine; I shall set it down as compensation to Lavinia. She is capable of telling me that she drank it all herself. Think of the inconceivable bad taste, in the circumstances, of that fellow making free with the house – or coming there at all! If that doesn't describe him, he is indescribable.'

'His plan is to get what he can. Lavinia will have supported him for a year,' said Mrs Almond. 'It's so much gained.'

'She will have to support him for the rest of his life, then,' cried the Doctor; 'but without wine, as they say at the tables d'hôte.'

'Catherine tells me he has set up a business, and is making a great deal of money.'

The Doctor stared. 'She has not told me that – and Lavinia didn't deign.

Ah!' he cried, 'Catherine has given me up. Not that it matters, for all that the business amounts to.'

'She has not given up Mr Townsend,' said Mrs Almond; 'I saw that in the first half-minute. She has come home exactly the same.'

'Exactly the same; not a grain more intelligent. She didn't notice a stick or a stone all the while we were away – not a picture nor a view, not a statue nor a cathedral.'

'How could she notice? She had other things to think of; they are never for an instant out of her mind. She touches me very much.'

'She would touch me if she didn't irritate me. That's the effect she has upon me now. I have tried everything upon her; I really have been quite merciless. But it is of no use whatever; she is absolutely *glued.* I have passed, in consequence, into the exasperated stage. At first I had a good deal of a certain genial curiosity about it; I wanted to see if she really would stick. But, good Lord, one's curiosity is satisfied! I see she is capable of it, and now she can let go.'

'She will never let go,' said Mrs Almond.

'Take care, or you will exasperate me too. If she doesn't let go, she will be shaken off – sent tumbling into the dust. That's a nice position for my daughter. She can't see that if you are going to be pushed, you had better jump. And then she will complain of her bruises.'

'She will never complain,' said Mrs Almond.

'That I shall object to even more. But the deuce will be that I can't prevent anything.'

'If she is to have a fall,' said Mrs Almond, with a gentle laugh, 'we must spread as many carpets as we can.' And she carried out this idea by showing a great deal of motherly kindness to the girl.

Mrs Penniman immediately wrote to Morris Townsend. The intimacy between these two was by this time consummate, but I must content myself with noting but a few of its features. Mrs Penniman's own share in it was a singular sentiment, which might have been misinterpreted, but which in itself was not discreditable to the poor lady. It was a romantic interest in this attractive and unfortunate young man, and yet it was not such an interest as Catherine might have been jealous of. Mrs Penniman had not a particle of jealousy of her niece. For herself, she felt as if she were Morris's mother or sister – a mother or sister of an emotional temperament – and she had an absorbing desire to make him comfortable and happy. She had striven to do so during the year that her brother left her an open field, and her efforts had been attended with the success that has been pointed out. She had never had a child of her own, and Catherine, whom she had done her best to invest with the importance that would naturally belong to a youthful Penniman, had only partly rewarded her zeal. Catherine, as an object of affection and solicitude, had never had that picturesque charm which (as it seemed to her) would have been a natural attribute of her own progeny. Even the maternal passion in Mrs Penniman would have been romantic and factitious, and Catherine was not constituted to inspire a romantic passion. Mrs Penniman was as fond of her as ever, but she had grown to feel that with Catherine she lacked opportunity. Sentimentally speaking, therefore, she had (though she had not disinherited her niece) adopted Morris Townsend, who gave her opportunity in abundance. She would have been very happy to have a handsome and tyrannical son, and would have taken an extreme interest in his love affairs. This was the light in which she had come to regard Morris, who had conciliated her at first, and made his impression by his delicate and calculated deference – a sort of exhibition to which Mrs Penniman was particularly sensitive. He had largely abated his deference afterward, for he economized his resources, but the impression was made, and the young man's very brutality came to have a sort of filial value. If Mrs Penniman had had a son, she would probably have been afraid of him, and at this stage of our narrative she was certainly afraid of Morris Townsend. This was one of the results of his domestication in Washington Square. He took his ease with her – as, for that matter, he would certainly have done with his own mother.

Chapter Twenty-eight

The letter was a word of warning; it informed him that the Doctor had come home more impracticable than ever. She might have reflected that Catherine would supply him with all the information he needed on this point; but we know that Mrs Penniman's reflections were rarely just; and, moreover, she felt that it was not for her to depend on what Catherine might do. She was to do her duty, quite irrespective of Catherine. I have said that her young friend took his ease with her, and it is an illustration of the fact that he made no answer to her letter. He took note of it amply; but he lighted his cigar with it, and he waited, in tranquil confidence that he should receive another. 'His state of mind really freezes my blood,' Mrs Penniman had written, alluding to her brother; and it would have seemed that upon this statement she could hardly improve. Nevertheless, she wrote again, expressing herself with the aid of a different figure. 'His hatred of you burns with a lurid flame – the flame that never dies,' she wrote. 'But it doesn't light up the darkness of your future. If my affection could do so, all the years of your life would be an eternal sunshine. I can extract nothing from C.; she is so terribly secretive, like her father. She seems to expect to be married very soon, and has evidently made preparations in Europe – quantities of clothing, ten pairs of shoes, etc. My dear friend, you cannot set up in married life simply with a few pairs of shoes, can you? Tell me what you think of this. I am intensely anxious to see you, I have so much to say. I miss you dreadfully; the house seems so empty without you. What is the news down town? Is the business extending? – that dear little business: I think it's so brave of you! Couldn't I come to your office? – just for three minutes? I might pass for a customer – is that what you call them? I might come in to buy something – some shares or some railroad things. *Tell me what you think of this plan*. I would carry a little reticule, like a woman of the people.'

In spite of the suggestion about the reticule, Morris appeared to think poorly of the plan, for he gave Mrs Penniman no encouragement whatever to visit his office, which he had already represented to her as a place peculiarly and unnaturally difficult to find. But as she persisted in desiring an interview – up to the last, after months of intimate colloquy, she called these meetings 'interviews' – he agreed that they should take a walk together, and was even kind enough to leave his office for this purpose during the hours at which business might have been supposed to be liveliest. It was no surprise to him, when they met at a street corner, in a region of empty lots and undeveloped pavements (Mrs Penniman being attired as much as possible like a 'woman of the people'), to find that, in spite of her urgency, what she chiefly had to convey to him was the assurance of her sympathy. Of such assurances, however, he had already a voluminous collection, and it would not have been worth his while to foresake a fruitful avocation merely to hear Mrs Penniman say, for the thousandth time, that she had made his cause her own. Morris had something of his own to say. It was not an easy thing to bring out, and, while he turned it over, the difficulty made him acrimonious.

'Oh yes, I know perfectly that he combines the properties of a lump of ice and a red-hot coal,' he observed. 'Catherine has made it thoroughly clear, and you have told me so till I am sick of it. You needn't tell me again; I am perfectly satisfied. He will never give us a penny; I regard that as mathematically proved.'

Mrs Penniman at this point had an inspiration.

'Couldn't you bring a lawsuit against him?' She wondered that this simple expedient had never occurred to her before.

'I will bring a lawsuit against you,' said Morris, 'if you ask me any more such aggravating questions. A man should know when he is beaten,' he added, in a moment. 'I must give her up!'

Mrs Penniman received this declaration in silence, though it made her heart beat a little. It found her by no means unprepared, for she had accustomed herself to the thought that, if Morris should decidedly not be able to get her brother's money, it would not do for him to marry Catherine without it. 'It would not do,' was a vague way of putting the thing; but Mrs Penniman's natural affection completed the idea, which, though it had not as yet been so crudely expressed between them as in the form that Morris had just given it, had nevertheless been implied so often, in certain easy intervals of talk, as he sat stretching his legs in the Doctor's well-stuffed armchairs, that she had grown first to regard it with an emotion which she flattered herself was philosophic, and then to have a secret tenderness for it. The fact that she kept her tenderness secret proves, of course, that she was ashamed of it; but she managed to blink her shame by reminding herself that she was, after all, the official protector of her niece's marriage. Her logic would scarcely have passed muster with the Doctor. In the first place, Morris *must* get the money, and she would help him to it. In the second, it was plain it would never come to him, and it would be a grievous pity he should marry without it – a young man who might so easily find something better. After her brother had delivered himself, on his return from Europe, of that incisive little address that has been quoted, Morris's cause seemed so hopeless that Mrs Penniman fixed her attention exclusively upon the latter branch of her argument. If Morris had been her son, she would certainly have sacrificed Catherine to a superior conception of his future; and to be ready to do so, as the case stood, was therefore even a finer degree of devotion. Nevertheless, it checked her breath a little to have the sacrificial knife, as it were, suddenly thrust into her hand.

Morris walked along a moment, and then he repeated, harshly, 'I must give her up!'

'I think I understand you,' said Mrs Penniman, gently.

'I certainly say it distinctly enough – brutally and vulgarly enough.'

He was ashamed of himself, and his shame was uncomfortable; and as he was extremely intolerant of discomfort, he felt vicious and cruel. He wanted to abuse somebody, and he began, cautiously – for he was always cautious – with himself.

'Couldn't you take her down a little?' he asked.

'Take her down?'

'Prepare her – try and ease me off.'

Mrs Penniman stopped, looking at him very solemnly.

'My poor Morris, do you know how much she loves you?'

'No, I don't. I don't want to know. I have always tried to keep from knowing. It would be too painful.'

'She will suffer much,' said Mrs Penniman.

'You must console her. If you are as good a friend to me as you pretend to be, you will manage it.'

Mrs Penniman shook her head sadly.

'You talk of my "pretending" to like you; but I can't pretend to hate you. I can only tell her I think very highly of you; and how will that console her for losing you?'

'The Doctor will help you. He will be delighted at the thing being broken off; and as he is a knowing fellow, he will invent something to comfort her.'

'He will invent a new torture,' cried Mrs Penniman. 'Heaven deliver her from her father's comfort! It will consist of his crowing over her, and saying, "I always told you so!" '

Morris coloured a most uncomfortable red.

'If you don't console her any better than you console me, you certainly won't be of much use. It's a damned disagreeable necessity; I feel it extremely, and you ought to make it easy for me.'

'I will be your friend for life,' Mrs Penniman declared.

'Be my friend *now*!' and Morris walked on.

She went with him; she was almost trembling.

'Should you like me to tell her?' she asked.

'You mustn't tell her, but you can – you can—' And he hesitated, trying to think what Mrs Penniman could do. 'You can explain to her why it is. It's because I can't bring myself to step in between her and her father – to give him the pretext he grasps at so eagerly (it's a hideous sight!) for depriving her of her rights.'

Mrs Penniman felt with remarkable promptitude the charm of this formula.

'That's so like you,' she said; 'it's so finely felt.'

Morris gave his stick an angry swing.

'Oh damnation!' he exclaimed, perversely.

Mrs Penniman, however, was not discouraged.

'It may turn out better than you think. Catherine is, after all, so very peculiar.' And she thought she might take it upon herself to assure him that, whatever happened, the girl would be very quiet – she wouldn't make a noise. They extended their walk, and while they proceeded Mrs Penniman took upon herself other things besides, and ended by having assumed a considerable burden; Morris being ready enough, as may be imagined, to put everything off upon her. But he was not for a single instant the dupe of her blundering alacrity; he knew that of what she promised she was competent to perform but an insignificant fraction, and the more she professed her willingness to serve him, the greater fool he thought her.

'What will you do if you don't marry her?' she ventured to inquire in the course of this conversation.

'Something brilliant,' said Morris. 'Shouldn't you like me to do something brilliant?'

The idea gave Mrs Penniman exceeding pleasure.

'I shall feel sadly taken in if you don't.'

'I shall have to, to make up for this. This isn't at all brilliant, you know.'

Mrs Penniman mused a little, as if there might be some way of making out that it was; but she had to give up the attempt, and, to carry off the awkwardness of failure, she risked a new inquiry.

'Do you mean – do you mean another marriage?'

Morris greeted this question with a reflection which was hardly the less impudent from being inaudible. 'Surely women are more crude than men!' And then he answered, audibly,

'Never in the world!'

Mrs Penniman felt disappointed and snubbed, and she relieved herself in a little vaguely sarcastic cry. He was certainly perverse.

'I give her up, not for another woman, but for a wider career,' Morris announced.

This was very grand; but still Mrs Penniman, who felt that she had exposed herself, was faintly rancorous.

'Do you mean never to come to see her again?' she asked, with some sharpness.

'Oh no, I shall come again; but what is the use of dragging it out? I have been four times since she came back, and it's terribly awkward work. I can't keep it up indefinitely; she oughtn't to expect that, you know. A woman should never keep a man dangling,' he added, finely.

'Ah, but you must have your last parting!' urged his companion, in whose imagination the idea of last partings occupied a place inferior in dignity only to that of first meetings.

Chapter Twenty-nine

He came again, without managing the last parting; and again and again, without finding that Mrs Penniman had as yet done much to pave the path of retreat with flowers. It was devilish awkward, as he said, and he felt a lively animosity for Catherine's aunt, who, as he had now quite formed the habit of saying to himself, had dragged him into the mess, and was bound in common charity to get him out of it. Mrs Penniman, to tell the truth, had, in the seclusion of her own apartment – and, I may add, amid the suggestiveness of Catherine's, which wore in those days the appearance of that of a young lady laying out her trousseau – Mrs Penniman had measured her responsibilities, and taken fright at their magnitude. The task of preparing Catherine and easing off Morris presented difficulties which increased in the execution, and even led the impulsive Lavinia to ask herself whether the modification of the young man's original project had been conceived in a happy spirit. A brilliant future, a wider career, a conscience exempt from the reproach of interference between a young lady and her natural rights – these excellent things might be too troublesomely purchased. From Catherine herself Mrs Penniman received no assistance whatever; the poor girl was apparently without suspicion of her danger. She looked at her lover with eyes of undiminished trust, and though she had less confidence in her aunt than in a young man with whom she had exchanged so many tender vows, she gave her no handle for explaining or confessing. Mrs Penniman, faltering and wavering, declared Catherine was very stupid, put off the great scene, as she would have called it, from day to day, and wandered about, very uncomfortably, with her unexploded bomb in her hands. Morris's own scenes were very small ones just now; but even these were beyond his strength. He made his visits as brief as possible, and, while he sat with his mistress, found terribly little to talk about. She was waiting for him, in vulgar parlance, to name the day; and so long as he was unprepared to be explicit on this point, it seemed a mockery to pretend to talk about matters more abstract. She had no airs and no arts; she never attempted to disguise her expectancy. She was waiting on his good pleasure, and would wait modestly and patiently; his hanging back at this supreme time might appear strange, but of course he must have a good reason for it. Catherine would have made a wife of the gentle, old-fashioned pattern – regarding reasons as favours and windfalls, but no more expecting one every day than she would have expected a bouquet of camellias. During the period of her engagement, however, a young lady even of the most slender pretensions counts upon more bouquets than at other times; and there was a want of perfume in the air at this moment which at last excited the girl's alarm.

'Are you sick?' she asked of Morris. 'You seem so restless, and you look pale.'

'I am not at all well,' said Morris; and it occurred to him that, if he could only make her pity him enough, he might get off.

'I am afraid you are overworked; you oughtn't to work so much.'

'I must do that.' And then he added, with a sort of calculated brutality, 'I don't want to owe you everything.'

'Ah, how can you say that?'

'I am too proud,' said Morris.

'Yes – you are too proud.'

'Well, you must take me as I am,' he went on; 'you can never change me.'

'I don't want to change you,' she said, gently; 'I will take you as you are.' And she stood looking at him.

'You know people talk tremendously about a man's marrying a rich girl,' Morris remarked. 'It's excessively disagreeable.'

'But I am not rich,' said Catherine.

'You are rich enough to make me talked about.'

'Of course you are talked about. It's an honour.'

'It's an honour I could easily dispense with.'

She was on the point of asking him whether it was not a compensation for this annoyance that the poor girl who had the misfortune to bring it upon him loved him so dearly and believed in him so truly; but she hesitated, thinking that this would perhaps seem an exacting speech, and, while she hesitated, he suddenly left her.

The next time he came, however, she brought it out, and she told him again that he was too proud. He repeated that he couldn't change, and this time she felt the impulse to say that with a little effort he might change.

Sometimes he thought that if he could only make a quarrel with her it might help him; but the question was how to quarrel with a young woman who had such treasures of concession. 'I suppose you think the effort is all on your side,' he broke out. 'Don't you believe that I have my own effort to make?'

'It's all yours now,' she said; 'my effort is finished and done with.'

'Well, mine is not.'

'We must bear things together,' said Catherine. 'That's what we ought to do.'

Morris attempted a natural smile. 'There are some things which we can't very well bear together – for instance, separation.'

'Why do you speak of separation?'

'Ah! you don't like it; I knew you wouldn't.'

'Where are you going, Morris?' she suddenly asked.

He fixed his eye on her a moment, and for a part of that moment she was afraid of it. 'Will you promise not to make a scene?'

'A scene! – do I make scenes?'

'All women do!' said Morris, with the tone of large experience.

'I don't. Where are you going?'

'If I should say I was going away on business, should you think it very strange?'

She wondered a moment, gazing at him. 'Yes – no. Not if you will take me with you.'

'Take you with me – on business?'

'What is your business? Your business is to be with me.'

'I don't earn my living with you,' said Morris. 'Or, rather,' he cried, with a sudden inspiration, 'that's just what I do – or what the world says I do!'

This ought perhaps to have been a great stroke, but it miscarried. 'Where are you going?' Catherine simply repeated.

'To New Orleans – about buying some cotton.'

'I am perfectly willing to go to New Orleans,' Catherine said.

'Do you suppose I would take you to a nest of yellow-fever?' cried Morris. 'Do you suppose I would expose you at such a time as this?'

'If there is yellow-fever, why should you go? Morris, you must not go.'

'It is to make six thousand dollars,' said Morris. 'Do you grudge me that satisfaction?'

'We have no need of six thousand dollars. You think too much about money.'

'You can afford to say that. This is a great chance; we heard of it last night.' And he explained to her in what the chance consisted; and told her a long story, going over more than once several of the details, about the remarkable stroke of business which he and his partner had planned between them.

But Catherine's imagination, for reasons best known to herself, absolutely refused to be fired. 'If you can go to New Orleans, I can go,' she said. 'Why shouldn't you catch yellow-fever quite as easily as I? I am every bit as strong as you, and not in the least afraid of any fever. When we were in Europe we were in very unhealthy places; my father used to make me take some pills. I never caught anything, and I never was nervous. What will be the use of six thousand dollars if you die of a fever? When persons are going to be married they oughtn't to think so much about business. You shouldn't think about cotton; you should think about me. You can go to New Orleans some other time – there will always be plenty of cotton. It isn't the moment to choose: we have waited too long already.' She spoke more forcibly and volubly than he had ever heard her, and she held his arm in her two hands.

'You said you wouldn't make a scene,' cried Morris. 'I call this a scene.'

'It's you that are making it. I have never asked you anything before. We have waited too long already.' And it was a comfort to her to think that she had hitherto asked so little; it seemed to make her right to insist the greater now.

Morris bethought himself a little. 'Very well, then; we won't talk about it any more. I will transact my business by letter.' And he began to smooth his hat, as if to take leave.

'You won't go?' and she stood looking up at him.

He could not give up his idea of provoking a quarrel; it was so much the simplest way. He bent his eyes on her upturned face with the darkest frown he could achieve. 'You are not discreet; you mustn't bully me.'

But, as usual, she conceded everything. 'No, I am not discreet; I know I am too pressing. But isn't it natural? It is only for a moment.'

'In a moment you may do a great deal of harm. Try and be calmer the next time I come.'

'When will you come?'

'Do you want to make conditions?' Morris asked. 'I will come next Saturday.'

'Come tomorrow,' Catherine begged; 'I want you to come tomorrow. I will be very quiet,' she added; and her agitation had by this time become so great that the assurance was not unbecoming. A sudden fear had come over her; it was like the solid conjunction of a dozen disembodied doubts, and her imagination, at a single bound, had traversed an enormous distance. All her being, for the moment, was centred in the wish to keep him in the room.

Morris bent his head and kissed her forehead. 'When you are quiet, you are perfection,' he said; 'but when you are violent, you are not in character.'

It was Catherine's wish that there should be no violence about her save the beating of her heart, which she could not help; and she went on, as gently as possible, 'Will you promise to come tomorrow?'

'I said Saturday!' Morris answered, smiling. He tried a frown at one moment, a smile at another; he was at his wit's end.

'Yes, Saturday too,' she answered, trying to smile. 'But tomorrow first.' He was going to the door, and she went with him quickly. She leaned her shoulder against it; it seemed to her that she would do anything to keep him.

'If I am prevented from coming tomorrow, you will say I have deceived you,' he said.

'How can you be prevented? You can come if you will.'

'I am a busy man – I am not a dangler!' cried Morris, sternly.

His voice was so hard and unnatural that, with a helpless look at him, she turned away; and then he quickly laid his hand on the door knob. He felt as if he were absolutely running away from her. But in an instant she was close to him again, and murmuring in a tone none the less penetrating for being low, 'Morris, you are going to leave me.'

'Yes, for a little while.'

'For how long?'

'Till you are reasonable again.'

'I shall never be reasonable, in that way.' And she tried to keep him longer; it was almost a struggle. 'Think of what I have done!' she broke out. 'Morris, I have given up everything.'

'You shall have everything back.'

'You wouldn't say that if you didn't mean something. What is it? – what has happened? – what have I done? – what has changed you?'

'I will write to you – that is better,' Morris stammered.

'Ah, you won't come back!' she cried, bursting into tears.

'Dear Catherine,' he said, 'don't believe that. I promise you that you shall see me again.' And he managed to get away, and to close the door behind him.

Chapter Thirty

It was almost the last outbreak of passion of her life; at least, she never indulged in another that the world knew anything about. But this one was long and terrible; she flung herself on the sofa and gave herself up to her grief. She hardly knew what had happened; ostensibly she had only had a difference with her lover, as other girls had had before, and the thing was not only not a rupture, but she was under no obligation to regard it even as a menace. Nevertheless, she felt a wound, even if he had not dealt it; it seemed to her that a mask had suddenly fallen from his face. He had wished to get away from her; he had been angry and cruel, and said strange things, with strange looks. She was smothered and stunned; she buried her head in the cushions, sobbing and talking to herself. But at last she raised herself, with the fear that either her father or Mrs Penniman would come in; and then she sat there, staring before her, while the room grew darker. She said to herself that perhaps he would come back to tell her he had not meant what he said; and she listened for his ring at the door, trying to believe that this was probable. A long time passed, but Morris remained absent; the shadows gathered; the evening settled down on the meagre elegance of the light, clear-coloured room; the fire went out. When it had grown dark, Catherine went to the window and looked out; she stood there for half an hour, on the mere chance that he would come up the steps. At last she turned away, for she saw her father come in. He had seen her at the window looking out, and he stopped a moment at the bottom of the white steps, and gravely, with an air of exaggerated courtesy, lifted his hat to her. The gesture was so incongruous to the condition she was in, this stately tribute of respect to a poor girl despised and forsaken was so out of place, that the thing gave her a kind of horror, and she hurried away to her room. It seemed to her that she had given Morris up.

She had to show herself half an hour later, and she was sustained at table by the immensity of her desire that her father should not perceive that anything had happened. This was a great help to her afterwards, and it served her (though never as much as she supposed) from the first. On this occasion Doctor Sloper was rather talkative. He told a great many stories about a wonderful poodle that he had seen at the house of an old lady whom he visited professionally. Catherine not only tried to appear to listen to the anecdotes of the poodle, but she endeavoured to interest herself in them, so as not to think of her scene with Morris. That perhaps was an hallucination; he was mistaken, she was jealous; people didn't change like that from one day to another. Then she knew that she had had doubts before – strange suspicions, that were at once vague and acute – and that he had been different ever since her return from Europe: whereupon she tried again to listen to her father, who told a story so remarkably well. Afterwards she went straight to her own room; it was beyond her strength to undertake to spend the evening with her aunt. All the evening, alone, she questioned herself. Her trouble was terrible; but was it a thing of her imagination, engendered by an extravagant sensibility, or did it represent a clear-cut reality, and had the worst that was possible actually come to pass? Mrs Penniman, with a degree of tact that was as unusual as it was commendable, took the line of leaving her alone. The truth is, that her suspicions having been aroused, she indulged a desire, natural to a timid person, that the explosion should be localized. So long as the air still vibrated she kept out of the way.

She passed and repassed Catherine's door several times in the course of the evening, as if she expected to hear a plaintive moan behind it. But the room remained perfectly still; and accordingly, the last thing before retiring to her own couch, she applied for admittance. Catherine was sitting up, and had a book that she pretended to be reading. She had no wish to go to bed, for she had no expectation of sleeping. After Mrs Penniman had left her she sat up half the night, and she offered her visitor no inducement to remain. Her aunt came stealing in very gently, and approached her with great solemnity.

'I am afraid you are in trouble, my dear. Can I do anything to help you?'

'I am not in any trouble whatever, and do not need any help,' said Catherine, fibbing roundly, and proving thereby that not only our faults, but our most involuntary misfortunes, tend to corrupt our morals.

'Has nothing happened to you?'

'Nothing whatever.'

'Are you very sure, dear?'

'Perfectly sure.'

'And can I really do nothing for you?'

'Nothing, aunt, but kindly leave me alone,' said Catherine.

Mrs Penniman, though she had been afraid of too warm a welcome before, was now disappointed at so cold a one; and in relating afterwards, as she did to many persons, and with considerable variations of detail, the history of the termination of her niece's engagement, she was usually careful to mention that the young lady, on a certain occasion, had 'hustled' her out of the room. It was characteristic of Mrs Penniman that she related this fact, not in the least out of malignity to Catherine, whom she very sufficiently pitied, but simply from a natural disposition to embellish any subject that she touched.

Catherine, as I have said, sat up half the night, as if she still expected to hear Morris Townsend ring at the door. On the morrow this expectation was less unreasonable; but it was not gratified by the reappearance of the young man. Neither had he written; there was not a word of explanation or reassurance. Fortunately for Catherine, she could take refuge from her excitement, which had now become intense, in her determination that her father should see nothing of it. How well she deceived her father we shall have occasion to learn; but her innocent arts were of little avail before a person of the rare perspicacity of Mrs Penniman. This lady easily saw that she was agitated, and if there was any agitation going forward, Mrs Penniman was not a person to forfeit her natural share in it. She returned to the charge the next evening, and requested her niece to confide in her –

to unburden her heart. Perhaps she should be able to explain certain things that now seemed dark, and that she knew more about than Catherine supposed. If Catherine had been frigid the night before, today she was haughty.

'You are completely mistaken, and I have not the least idea what you mean. I don't know what you are trying to fasten on me, and I have never had less need of anyone's explanations in my life.'

In this way the girl delivered herself, and from hour to hour kept her aunt at bay. From hour to hour Mrs Penniman's curiosity grew. She would have given her little finger to know what Morris had said and done, what tone he had taken, what pretext he had found. She wrote to him, naturally, to request an interview; but she received, as naturally, no answer to her petition. Morris was not in a writing mood; for Catherine had addressed him two short notes which met with no acknowledgement. These notes were so brief that I may give them entire. 'Won't you give me some sign that you didn't mean to be so cruel as you seemed on Tuesday?' – that was the first; the other was a little longer. 'If I was unreasonable or suspicious on Tuesday – if I annoyed you or troubled you in any way – I beg your forgiveness, and I promise never again to be so foolish. I am punished enough, and I don't understand. Dear Morris, you are killing me!' These notes were dispatched on the Friday and Saturday; but Saturday and Sunday passed without bringing the poor girl the satisfaction she desired. Her punishment accumulated; she continued to bear it, however, with a good deal of superficial fortitude. On Saturday morning, the Doctor, who had been watching in silence, spoke to his sister Lavinia.

'The thing has happened – the scoundrel has backed out!'

'Never!' cried Mrs Penniman, who had bethought herself what she should say to Catherine, but was not provided with a line of defence against her brother, so that indignant negation was the only weapon in her hands.

'He has begged for a reprieve, then, if you like that better!'

'It seems to make you very happy that your daughter's affections have been trifled with.'

'It does,' said the Doctor; 'for I had foretold it! It's a great pleasure to be in the right.'

'Your pleasures make one shudder!' his sister exclaimed.

Catherine went rigidly through her usual occupations; that is, up to the point of going with her aunt to church on Sunday morning. She generally went to afternoon service as well; but on this occasion her courage faltered, and she begged of Mrs Penniman to go without her.

'I am sure you have a secret,' said Mrs Penniman, with great significance, looking at her rather grimly.

'If I have, I shall keep it!' Catherine answered, turning away.

Mrs Penniman started for church; but before she had arrived, she stopped and turned back, and before twenty minutes had elapsed she re-entered the house, looked into the empty parlours, and then went upstairs and knocked at Catherine's door. She got no answer; Catherine was not in her room, and Mrs Penniman presently ascertained that she was not in the house. 'She has gone to him! she has fled!' Lavinia cried, clasping her hands with admiration and envy. But she soon perceived that Catherine had taken nothing with her – all her personal property in her room was intact – and then she jumped at the hypothesis that the girl had gone forth, not in tenderness, but in resentment. 'She has followed him to his own door! she has burst upon him in his own apartment!' It was in these terms that Mrs Penniman depicted to herself her niece's errand, which, viewed in this light, gratified her sense of the picturesque only a shade less strongly than the idea of a clandestine marriage. To visit one's lover, with tears and reproaches, at his own residence, was an image so agreeable to Mrs Penniman's mind that she felt a sort of aesthetic disappointment at its lacking, in this case, the harmonious accompaniments of darkness and storm. A quiet Sunday afternoon appeared an inadequate setting for it; and, indeed, Mrs Penniman was quite out of humour with the conditions of the time, which passed very slowly as she sat in the front parlour, in her bonnet and her cashmere shawl, awaiting Catherine's return.

This event at last took place. She saw her – at the window – mount the steps, and she went to await her in the hall, where she pounced upon her as soon as she had entered the house, and drew her into the parlour, closing the door with solemnity. Catherine was flushed, and her eye was bright. Mrs Penniman hardly knew what to think.

'May I venture to ask where you have been?' she demanded.

'I have been to take a walk,' said Catherine. 'I thought you had gone to church.'

'I did go to church; but the service was shorter than usual. And pray where did you walk?'

'I don't know!' said Catherine.

'Your ignorance is most extraordinary! Dear Catherine, you can trust me.'

'What am I to trust you with?'

'With your secret – your sorrow.'

'I have no sorrow!' said Catherine, fiercely.

'My poor child,' Mrs Penniman insisted, 'you can't deceive me. I know everything. I have been requested to – a – to converse with you.'

'I don't want to converse!'

'It will relieve you. Don't you know Shakespeare's lines? – "The grief that does not speak!" My dear girl, it is better as it is!'

'What is better?' Catherine asked.

She was really too perverse. A certain amount of perversity was to be allowed for in a young lady whose lover had thrown her over; but not such an amount as would prove inconvenient to his apologists. 'That you should be reasonable,' said Mrs Penniman, with some sternness; 'that you should take counsel of worldly prudence, and submit to practical considerations; that you should agree to – a – separate.'

Catherine had been ice up to this moment, but at this word she flamed up. 'Separate? What do you know about our separating?'

Mrs Penniman shook her head with a sadness in which there was almost a sense of injury. 'Your pride is my pride, and your susceptibilities are mine. I see your side perfectly, but I also' – and she smiled with melancholy suggestiveness – 'I also see the situation as a whole!'

This suggestiveness was lost upon Catherine, who repeated her violent inquiry. 'Why do you talk about separation; what do you know about it?'

'We must study resignation,' said Mrs Penniman, hesitating, but sententious at a venture.

'Resignation to what?'

'To a change of – of our plans.'

'My plans have not changed!' said Catherine, with a little laugh.

'Ah, but Mr Townsend's have,' her aunt answered, very gently.

'What do you mean?'

There was an imperious brevity in the tone of this inquiry, against which Mrs Penniman felt bound to protest; the information with which she had undertaken to supply her niece was after all a favour. She had tried sharpness, and she had tried sternness; but neither would do; she was shocked at the girl's obstinacy. 'Ah well,' she said, 'If he hasn't told you! . . .' and she turned away.

Catherine watched her a moment in silence; then she hurried after her, stopping her before she reached the door. 'Told me what? What do you mean? What are you hinting at and threatening me with?'

'Isn't it broken off?' asked Mrs Penniman.

'My engagement? Not in the least!'

'I beg your pardon in that case. I have spoken too soon!'

'Too soon? Soon or late,' Catherine broke out, 'you speak foolishly and cruelly!'

'What has happened between you then?' asked her aunt, struck by the sincerity of this cry; 'for something certainly has happened.'

'Nothing has happened but that I love him more and more!'

Mrs Penniman was silent an instant. 'I suppose that's the reason you went to see him this afternoon.'

Catherine flushed as if she had been struck. 'Yes, I did go to see him! But that's my own business.'

'Very well, then; we won't talk about it.' And Mrs Penniman moved towards the door again; but she was stopped by a sudden imploring cry from the girl.

'Aunt Lavinia, *where* has he gone?'

'Ah, you admit then that he has gone away! Didn't they know at his house?'

'They said he had left town. I asked no more questions; I was ashamed,' said Catherine, simply enough.

'You needn't have taken so compromising a step if you had had a little more confidence in me,' Mrs Penniman observed, with a good deal of grandeur.

'Is it to New Orleans?' Catherine went on, irrelevantly.

It was the first time Mrs Penniman had heard of New Orleans in this connexion; but she was averse to letting Catherine know that she was in the dark. She attempted to strike an illumination from the instructions she had received from Morris. 'My dear Catherine,' she said, 'when a separation has been agreed upon, the farther he goes away the better.'

'Agreed upon? Has he agreed upon it with you?' A consummate sense of her aunt's meddlesome folly had come over her during the last five minutes, and she was sickened at the thought that Mrs Penniman had been let loose, as it were, upon her happiness.

'He certainly has sometimes advised with me,' said Mrs Penniman.

'Is it you, then, that has changed him and made him so unnatural?' Catherine cried. 'Is it you that have worked on him and taken him from me?

He doesn't belong to you, and I don't see how you have anything to do with what is between us! Is it you that have made this plot, and told him to leave me? How could you be so wicked, so cruel? What have I ever done to you? Why can't you leave me alone? I was afraid you would spoil everything; for you *do* spoil everything you touch! I was afraid of you all the time we were abroad; I had no rest when I thought you were always talking to him.' Catherine went on with growing vehemence, pouring out, in her bitterness and in the clairvoyance of her passion (which suddenly, jumping all processes, made her judge her aunt finally and without appeal), the uneasiness which had lain for so many months was upon her heart.

Mrs Penniman was scared and bewildered; she saw no prospect of introducing her little account of the purity of Morris's motives. 'You are a most ungrateful girl!' she cried. 'Do you scold me for talking with him? I'm sure we never talked of anything but you!'

'Yes; and that was the way you worried him; you made him tired of my very name! I wish you had never spoken of me to him; I never asked your help!'

'I am sure if it hadn't been for me he would never have come to the house, and you would never have known that he thought of you,' Mrs Penniman rejoined, with a good deal of justice.

'I wish he never had come to the house, and that I never had known it! That's better than this,' said poor Catherine.

'You are a very ungrateful girl,' Aunt Lavinia repeated.

Catherine's outbreak of anger and the sense of wrong gave her, while they lasted, the satisfaction that comes from all assertion of force; they hurried her along, and there is always a sort of pleasure in cleaving the air. But at bottom she hated to be violent, and she was conscious of no aptitude for organized resentment. She calmed herself with a great effort, but with great rapidity, and walked about the room a few moments, trying to say to herself that her aunt had meant everything for the best. She did not succeed in saying it with much conviction, but after a little she was able to speak quietly enough.

'I am not ungrateful, but I am very unhappy. It's hard to be grateful for that,' she said. 'Will you please tell me where he is?'

'I haven't the least idea; I am not in secret correspondence with him!' And Mrs Penniman wished, indeed, that she were, so that she might let him know how Catherine abused her, after all she had done.

'Was it a plan of his, then, to break off—?' By this time Catherine had become completely quiet.

Mrs Penniman began again to have a glimpse of her chance for explaining. 'He shrunk – he shrunk,' she said; 'he lacked courage, but it was the courage to injure you! He couldn't bear to bring down on you your father's curse.'

Catherine listened to this with her eyes fixed upon her aunt, and continued to gaze at her for some time afterwards. 'Did he tell you to say that?'

'He told me to say many things – all so delicate, so discriminating; and he told me to tell you he hoped you wouldn't despise him.'

'I don't,' said Catherine; and then she added, 'And will he stay away for ever?'

'Oh, forever is a long time. Your father, perhaps, won't live forever.'

'Perhaps not.'

'I am sure you appreciate – you understand – even though your heart bleeds,' said Mrs Penniman. 'You doubtless think him too scrupulous. So do I, but I respect his scruples. What he asks of you is that you should do the same.'

Catherine was still gazing at her aunt, but she spoke at last as if she had not heard or not understood her. 'It has been a regular plan, then. He has broken it off deliberately; he has given me up.'

'For the present, dear Catherine; he has put it off, only.'

'He has left me alone,' Catherine went on.

'Haven't you *me*?' asked Mrs Penniman, with some solemnity.

Catherine shook her head slowly. 'I don't believe it!' and she left the room.

Chapter Thirty-one

Though she had forced herself to be calm, she preferred practising this virtue in private, and she forbore to show herself at tea – a repast which, on Sundays, at six o'clock, took the place of dinner. Doctor Sloper and his sister sat face to face, but Mrs Penniman never met her brother's eye. Late in the evening she went with him, but without Catherine, to their sister Almond's, where, between the two ladies, Catherine's unhappy situation was discussed with a frankness that was conditioned by a good deal of mysterious reticence on Mrs Penniman's part.

'I am delighted he is not to marry her,' said Mrs Almond, 'but he ought to be horsewhipped all the same.'

Mrs Penniman, who was shocked at her sister's coarseness, replied that he had been actuated by the noblest of motives – the desire not to impoverish Catherine.

'I am very happy that Catherine is not to be impoverished – but I hope he may never have a penny too much! And what does the poor girl say to *you*?' Mrs Almond asked.

'She says I have a genius for consolation,' said Mrs Penniman.

This was the account of the matter that she gave to her sister, and it was perhaps with the consciousness of genius that, on her return that evening to Washington Square, she again presented herself for admittance at Catherine's door. Catherine came and opened it; she was apparently very quiet.

'I only want to give you a little word of advice,' she said. 'If your father asks you, say that everything is going on.'

Catherine stood there, with her hand on the knob, looking at her aunt, but not asking her to come in. 'Do you think he will ask me?'

'I am sure he will. He asked me just now, on our way home from your Aunt Elizabeth's. I explained the whole thing to your Aunt Elizabeth. I said to your father I knew nothing about it.'

'Do you think he will ask me, when he sees – when he sees—?' But here Catherine stopped.

'The more he sees, the more disagreeable he will be,' said her aunt.

'He shall see as little as possible!' Catherine declared.

'Tell him you are to be married.'

'So I am,' said Catherine, softly; and she closed the door upon her aunt.

She could not have said this two days later – for instance, on Tuesday, when she at last received a letter from Morris Townsend. It was an epistle of considerable length, measuring five large square pages, and written at Philadelphia. It was an explanatory document, and it explained a great many things, chief among which were the considerations that had led the writer to take advantage of an urgent 'professional' absence to try and banish from his mind the image of one whose path he had crossed only to scatter it with ruins. He ventured to expect but partial success in this attempt, but he could promise her that, whatever his failure, he would never again interpose between her generous heart and her brilliant prospects and filial duties. He closed with an intimation that his professional pursuits might compel him to travel for some months, and with the hope that when they should each have accommodated themselves to what was sternly involved in their respective positions – even should this result not be reached for years – they should meet as friends, as fellow-sufferers, as innocent but philosophic victims of a great social law. That her life should be peaceful and happy was the dearest wish of him who ventured still to subscribe himself her most obedient servant. The letter was beautifully written, and Catherine, who kept it for many years after this, was able, when her sense of the bitterness of its meaning and the hollowness of its tone had grown less acute, to admire its grace of expression. At present, for a long time after she received it, all she had to help her was the determination, daily more rigid, to make no appeal to the compassion of her father.

He suffered a week to elapse, and then one day, in the morning, at an hour at which she rarely saw him, he strolled into the back parlour. He had watched his time, and he found her alone. She was sitting with some work, and he came and stood in front of her. He was going out; he had on his hat, and was drawing on his gloves.

'It doesn't seem to me that you are treating me just now with all the consideration I deserve,' he said in a moment.

'I don't know what I have done,' Catherine answered, with her eyes on her work.

'You have apparently quite banished from your mind the request I made you at Liverpool before we sailed – the request that you would notify me in advance before leaving my house.'

'I have not left your house,' said Catherine.

'But you intend to leave it, and, by what you gave me to understand, your departure must be impending. In fact, though you are still here in body, you are already absent in spirit. Your mind has taken up its residence with your prospective husband, and you might quite as well be lodged under the conjugal roof for all the benefit we get from your society.'

'I will try and be more cheerful,' said Catherine.

'You certainly ought to be cheerful; you ask a great deal if you are not.

To the pleasure of marrying a charming young man you add that of having your own way; you strike me as a very lucky young lady!'

Catherine got up; she was suffocating. But she folded her work deliberately and correctly, bending her burning face upon it. Her father stood where he had planted himself; she hoped he would go, but he smoothed and buttoned his gloves, and then he rested his hands upon his hips.

'It would be a convenience to me to know when I may expect to have an empty house,' he went on. 'When you go, your aunt marches.'

She looked at him at last, with a long, silent gaze, which, in spite of her pride and her resolution, uttered part of the appeal she had tried not to make. Her father's cold grey eye sounded her own, and he insisted on his point.

'Is it tomorrow? Is it next week, or the week after?'

'I shall not go away!' said Catherine.

The Doctor raised his eyebrows. 'Has he backed out?'

'I have broken off my engagement.'

'Broken it off?'

'I have asked him to leave New York, and he has gone away for a long time.'

The Doctor was both puzzled and disappointed, but he solved his perplexity by saying to himself that his daughter simply misrepresented – justifiably, if one would, but nevertheless, misrepresented – the facts; and he eased off his disappointment, which was that of a man losing a chance for a little triumph that he had rather counted on, by a few words that he uttered aloud.

'How does he take his dismissal?'

'I don't know!' said Catherine, less ingeniously than she had hitherto spoken.

'You mean you don't care? You are rather cruel, after encouraging him and playing with him for so long!'

The Doctor had his revenge, after all.

Chapter Thirty-two

Our story has hitherto moved with very short steps, but as it approaches its termination it must take a long stride. As time went on, it might have appeared to the Doctor that his daughter's account of her rupture with Morris Townsend, mere bravado as he had deemed it, was in some degree justified by the sequel. Morris remained as rigidly and unremittingly absent as if he had died of a broken heart, and Catherine had apparently buried the memory of this fruitless episode as deep as if it had terminated by her own choice. We know that she had been deeply and incurably wounded, but the Doctor had no means of knowing it. He was certainly curious about it, and would have given a good deal to discover the exact truth; but it was his punishment that he never knew – his punishment, I mean, for the abuse of sarcasm in his relations with his daughter. There was a good deal of effective sarcasm in her keeping him in the dark, and the rest of the world conspired with her, in this sense, to be sarcastic. Mrs Penniman told him nothing, partly because he never questioned her – he made too light of Mrs Penniman for that – and partly because she flattered herself that a tormenting reserve, and a serene profession of ignorance, would avenge her for his theory that she had meddled in the matter. He went two or three times to see Mrs Montgomery, but Mrs Montgomery had nothing to impart. She simply knew that her brother's engagement was broken off; and, now that Miss Sloper was out of danger, she preferred not to bear witness in any way against Morris. She had done so before – however unwillingly – because she was sorry for Miss Sloper; but she was not sorry for Miss Sloper now – not at all sorry. Morris had told her nothing about his relations with Miss Sloper at the time, and he had told her nothing since. He was always away, and he very seldom wrote to her; she believed he had gone to California. Mrs Almond had, in her sister's phrase, 'taken up' Catherine violently since the recent catastrophe; but, though the girl was very grateful to her for her kindness, she revealed no secrets, and the good lady could give the Doctor no satisfaction. Even, however, had she been able to narrate to him the private history of his daughter's unhappy love affair, it would have given her a certain comfort to leave him in ignorance; for Mrs Almond was at this time not altogether in sympathy with her brother. She had guessed for herself that Catherine had been cruelly jilted – she knew nothing from Mrs Penniman, for Mrs Penniman had not ventured to lay the famous explanation of Morris's motives before Mrs Almond, though she had thought it good enough for Catherine – and she pronounced her brother too consistently indifferent to what the poor creature must have suffered and must still be suffering. Doctor Sloper had his theory, and he rarely altered his theories. The marriage would have been an abominable one, and the girl had had a blessed escape. She was not to be pitied for that, and to pretend to condole with her would have been to make concessions to the idea that she had ever had a right to think of Morris.

'I put my foot on this idea from the first, and I keep it there now,' said the Doctor. 'I don't see anything cruel in that; one can't keep it there too long.' To this Mrs Almond more than once replied that, if Catherine had got rid of her incongruous lover, she deserved the credit of it, and that to bring herself to her father's enlightened view of the matter must have cost her an effort that he was bound to appreciate.

'I am by no means sure she has got rid of him,' the Doctor said. 'There is not the smallest probability that, after having been as obstinate as a mule for two years, she suddenly became amenable to reason. It is infinitely more probable that he got rid of her.'

'All the more reason you should be gentle with her.'

'I *am* gentle with her. But I can't do the pathetic; I can't pump up tears, to look graceful, over the most fortunate thing that ever happened to her.'

'You have no sympathy,' said Mrs Almond; 'that was never your strong point. You have only to look at her to see that, right or wrong, and whether the rupture came from herself or from him, her poor little heart is grievously bruised.'

'Handling bruises, and even dropping tears on them, doesn't make them any better! My business is to see she gets no more knocks, and that I shall carefully attend to. But I don't at all recognize your description of Catherine. She doesn't strike me in the least as a young woman going about in search of a moral poultice. In fact, she seems to me much better than while the fellow was hanging about. She is perfectly comfortable and blooming; she eats and sleeps, takes her usual exercise, and overloads herself, as usual, with finery. She is always knitting some purse or embroidering some handkerchief, and it seems to me she turns these articles out about as fast as ever. She hasn't much to say; but when had she anything to say? She had her little dance, and now she is sitting down to rest. I suspect that, on the whole, she enjoys it.'

'She enjoys it as people enjoy getting rid of a leg that has been crushed. The state of mind after amputation is doubtless one of comparative repose.'

'If your leg is a metaphor for young Townsend, I can assure you he has never been crushed. Crushed? Not he! He is alive and perfectly intact; and that's why I am not satisfied.'

'Should you have liked to kill him?' asked Mrs Almond.

'Yes, very much. I think it is quite possible that it is all a blind.'

'A blind?'

'An arrangement between them. *Il fait le mort,* as they say in France; but he is looking out of the corner of his eye. You can depend upon it, he has not burnt his ships; he has kept one to come back in. When I am dead, he will set sail again, and then she will marry him.'

'It is interesting to know that you accuse your only daughter of being the vilest of hypocrites,' said Mrs Almond.

'I don't see what difference her being my only daughter makes. It is better to accuse one than a dozen. But I don't accuse anyone. There is not the smallest hypocrisy about Catherine, and I deny that she even pretends to be miserable.'

The Doctor's idea that the thing was a 'blind' had its intermissions and revivals; but it may be said, on the whole, to have increased as he grew older; together with his impressions of Catherine's blooming and comfortable condition. Naturally, if he had not found grounds for viewing her as a lovelorn maiden during the year or two that followed her great trouble, he found none at a time when she had completely recovered her self-possession. He was obliged to recognize the fact that, if the two young people were waiting for him to get out of the way, they were at least waiting very patiently. He had heard from time to time that Morris was in New York; but he never remained there long, and, to the best of the Doctor's belief, had no communication with Catherine. He was sure they never met, and he had reason to suspect that Morris never wrote to her. After the letter that has been mentioned, she heard from him twice again, at considerable intervals; but on none of these occasions did she write herself. On the other hand, as the Doctor observed, she averted herself rigidly from the idea of marrying other people. Her opportunities for doing so were not numerous, but they occurred often enough to test her disposition. She refused a widower, a man with a genial temperament, a handsome fortune, and three little girls (he had heard that she was very fond of children, and he pointed to his own with some confidence); and she turned a deaf ear to the solicitations of a clever young lawyer, who, with the prospect of a great practice, and the reputation of a most agreeable man, had had the shrewdness, when he came to look about him for a wife, to believe that she would suit him better than several younger and prettier girls. Mr Macalister, the widower, had desired to make a marriage of reason, and had chosen Catherine for what he supposed to be her latent matronly qualities; but John Ludlow, who was a year the girl's junior, and spoken of always as a young man who might have his 'pick', was seriously in love with her. Catherine, however, would never look at him; she made it plain to him that she thought he came to see her too often. He afterwards consoled himself, and married a very different person, little Miss Sturtevant, whose attractions were obvious to the dullest comprehension. Catherine, at the time of these events, had left her thirtieth year well behind her, and had quite taken her place as an old maid. Her father would have preferred she should marry, and he once told her that he hoped she would not be too fastidious. 'I should like to see you an honest man's wife before I die,' he said. This was after John Ludlow had been compelled to give it up, though the Doctor had advised him to persevere. The Doctor exercised no further pressure, and had the credit of not 'worrying' at all over his daughter's singleness; in fact, he worried rather more than appeared, and there were considerable periods during which he felt sure that Morris Townsend was hidden behind some door. 'If he is not, why doesn't she marry?' he asked himself. 'Limited as her intelligence may be, she must understand perfectly well that she is made to do the usual thing.' Catherine, however, became an admirable old maid. She formed habits, regulated her days upon a system of her own, interested herself in charitable institutions, asylums, hospitals, and aid societies; and went generally, with an even and noiseless step, about the rigid business of her life. This life had, however, a secret history as well as a public one – if I may talk of the public history of a mature and diffident spinster for whom publicity had always a combination of terrors. From her own point of view the great facts of her career were that Morris Townsend had trifled with her affection, and that her father had broken its spring. Nothing could ever alter these facts; they were always there, like her name, her age, her plain face. Nothing could ever undo the wrong or cure the pain that Morris had inflicted on her, and nothing could ever make her feel towards her father as she felt in her younger years. There was something dead in her life, and her duty was to try and fill the void. Catherine recognized this duty to the utmost; she had a great disapproval of brooding and moping. She had, of course, no faculty for quenching memory in dissipation; but she mingled freely in the usual gaieties of the town, and she became at last an inevitable figure at all respectable entertainments. She was greatly liked, and as time went on she grew to be a sort of kindly maiden-aunt to the younger portion of society. Young girls were apt to confide to her their love affairs (which they never did to Mrs Penniman), and young men to be fond of her without knowing why. She developed a few harmless eccentricities; her habits, once formed, were rather stiffly maintained; her opinions, on all moral and social matters, were extremely conservative; and before she was forty she was regarded as an old-fashioned person, and an authority on customs that had passed away. Mrs

Penniman, in comparison, was quite a girlish figure; she grew younger as she advanced in life. She lost none of her relish for beauty and mystery, but she had little opportunity to exercise it. With Catherine's later wooers she failed to establish relations as intimate as those which had given her so many interesting hours in the society of Morris Townsend. These gentlemen had an indefinable mistrust of her good offices, and they never talked to her about Catherine's charms. Her ringlets, her buckles and bangles glistened more brightly with each succeeding year, and she remained quite the same officious and imaginative Mrs Penniman, and the odd mixture of impetuosity and circumspection, that we have hitherto known. As regards one point, however, her circumspection prevailed, and she must be given due credit for it. For upwards of seventeen years she never mentioned Morris Townsend's name to her niece. Catherine was grateful to her, but this consistent silence, so little in accord with her aunt's character, gave her a certain alarm, and she could never wholly rid herself of a suspicion that Mrs Penniman sometimes had news of him.

Chapter Thirty-three

Little by little Doctor Sloper had retired from his profession; he visited only those patients in whose symptoms he recognized a certain originality. He went again to Europe, and remained two years; Catherine went with him, and on this occasion Mrs Penniman was of the party. Europe apparently had few surprises for Mrs Penniman, who frequently remarked, in the most romantic sites, 'You know I am very familiar with all this.' It should be added that such remarks were usually not addressed to her brother, or yet to her niece, but to fellow-tourists who happened to be at hand, or even to the cicerone or the goatherd in the foreground.

One day, after his return from Europe, the Doctor said something to his daughter that made her start – it seemed to come from so far out of the past.

'I should like you to promise me something before I die.'

'Why do you talk about your dying?' she asked.

'Because I am sixty-eight years old.'

'I hope you will live a long time,' said Catherine.

'I hope I shall! But some day I shall take a bad cold, and then it will not matter much what anyone hopes. That will be the manner of my exit, and when it takes place, remember I told you so. Promise me not to marry Morris Townsend after I am gone.'

This was what made Catherine start, as I have said; but her start was a silent one, and for some moments she said nothing. 'Why do you speak of him?' she asked at last.

'You challenge everything I say. I speak of him because he's a topic, like any other. He's to be seen, like anyone else, and he is still looking for a wife

– having had one and got rid of her, I don't know by what means. He has lately been in New York, and at your cousin Marian's house; your Aunt Elizabeth saw him there.'

'They neither of them told me,' said Catherine.

'That's their merit, it's not yours. He has grown fat and bald, and he has not made his fortune. But I can't trust those facts alone to steel your heart against him, and that's why I ask you to promise.'

'Fat and bald'; these words presented a strange image to Catherine's mind, out of which the memory of the most beautiful young man in the world had never faded. 'I don't think you understand,' she said. 'I very seldom think of Mr Townsend.'

'It will be very easy for you to go on, then. Promise me, after my death, to do the same.'

Again, for some moments, Catherine was silent; her father's request deeply amazed her; it opened an old wound, and made it ache afresh. 'I don't think I can promise that,' she answered.

'It would be a great satisfaction,' said her father.

'You don't understand. I can't promise that.'

The Doctor was silent a minute. 'I ask you for a particular reason. I am altering my will.'

This reason failed to strike Catherine; and indeed she scarcely understood it. All her feelings were merged in the sense that he was trying to treat her as he had treated her years before. She had suffered from it then; and now all her experience, all her acquired tranquillity and rigidity protested. She had been so humble in her youth that she could now afford to have a little pride, and there was something in this request, and in her father's thinking himself so free to make it, that seemed an injury to her dignity. Poor Catherine's dignity was not aggressive; it never sat in state; but if you pushed far enough you could find it. Her father had pushed very far.

'I can't promise,' she simply repeated.

'You are very obstinate,' said the Doctor.

'I don't think you understand.'

'Please explain, then.'

'I can't explain,' said Catherine; 'and I can't promise.'

'Upon my word,' her father exclaimed, 'I had no idea how obstinate you are!'

She knew herself that she was obstinate, and it gave her a certain joy. She was now a middle-aged woman.

About a year after this, the accident that the Doctor had spoken of occurred: he took a violent cold. Driving out to Bloomingdale one April day to see a patient of unsound mind, who was confined in a private asylum for the insane, and whose family greatly desired a medical opinion from an eminent source, he was caught in a spring shower, and being in a buggy, without a hood, he found himself soaked to the skin. He came home with an ominous chill, and on the morrow he was seriously ill. 'It is congestion of the lungs,' he said to Catherine; 'I shall need very good nursing. It will make no difference, for I shall not recover; but I wish everything to be done, to the smallest detail, as if I should. I hate an ill-conducted sick-room, and you will be so good as to nurse me, on the hypothesis that I shall get well.' He told her which of his fellow-physicians to send for, and gave her a multitude of minute directions. It was quite on the optimistic hypothesis that she nursed him. But he had never been wrong in his life, and he was not wrong now. He was touching his seventieth year, and though he had a very well-tempered constitution, his hold upon life had lost its firmness. He died after three weeks' illness, during which Mrs Penniman, as well as his daughter, had been assiduous at his bedside.

On his will being opened, after a decent interval, it was found to consist of two portions. The first of these dated from ten years back, and consisted of a series of dispositions by which he left the great mass of his property to his daughter, with becoming legacies to his two sisters. The second was a codicil, of recent origin, maintaining the annuities to Mrs Penniman and Mrs Almond, but reducing Catherine's share to a fifth of what he had first bequeathed her. 'She is amply provided for from her mother's side,' the document ran, 'never having spent more than a fraction of her income from this source; so that her fortune is already more than sufficient to attract those unscrupulous adventurers whom she has given me reason to believe that she persists in regarding as an interesting class.' The large remainder of his property, therefore, Doctor Sloper had divided into seven unequal parts, which he left, as endowments, to as many different hospitals and schools of medicine in various cities of the Union.

To Mrs Penniman it seemed monstrous that a man should play such tricks with other people's money; for after his death, of course, as she said, it was other people's. 'Of course, you will immediately break the will,' she remarked to Catherine.

'Oh no,' Catherine answered, 'I like it very much. Only I wish it had been expressed a little differently!'

Chapter Thirty-four

It was her habit to remain in town very late in the summer; she preferred the house in Washington Square to any other habitation whatever, and it was under protest that she used to go to the seaside for the month of August. At the sea she spent her month at an hotel. The year that her father died she intermitted this custom altogether, not thinking it consistent with deep mourning; and the year after that she put off her departure till so late that the middle of August found her still in the heated solitude of Washington Square. Mrs Penniman, who was fond of a change, was usually eager for a visit to the country; but this year she appeared quite content with such rural impressions as she could gather at the parlour window from the ailanthus-trees behind the wooden paling. The peculiar fragrance of this vegetation used to diffuse itself in the evening air, and Mrs Penniman, on the warm nights of July, often sat at the open window and inhaled it. This was a happy moment for Mrs Penniman; after the death of her brother she felt more free to obey her impulses. A vague oppression had disappeared from her life, and she enjoyed a sense of freedom of which she had not been conscious since the memorable time, so long ago, when the Doctor went abroad with Catherine and left her at home to entertain Morris Townsend. The year that had elapsed since her brother's death reminded her of that happy time, because, although Catherine, in growing older, had become a person to be reckoned with, yet her society was a very different thing, as Mrs Penniman said, from that of a tank of cold water. The elder lady hardly knew what use to make of this larger margin of her life; she sat and looked at it very much as she had often sat, with her poised needle in her hand, before her tapestry-frame. She had a confident hope, however, that her rich impulses, her talent for embroidery, would still find their application, and this confidence was justified before many months had elapsed.

Catherine continued to live in her father's house, in spite of its being represented to her that a maiden lady of quiet habits might find a more convenient abode in one of the smaller dwellings, with brown stone fronts, which had at this time begun to adorn the transverse thoroughfares in the upper part of the town. She liked the earlier structure – it had begun by this time to be called an 'old house' – and proposed to herself to end her days in it. If it was too large for a pair of unpretending gentlewomen, this was better than the opposite fault; for Catherine had no desire to find herself in closer quarters with her aunt. She expected to spend the rest of her life in Washington Square, and to enjoy Mrs Penniman's society for the whole of this period; as she had a conviction that, long as she might live, her aunt would live at least as long, and always retain her brilliancy and activity. Mrs Penniman suggested to her the idea of a rich vitality.

On one of those warm evenings in July of which mention has been made, the two ladies sat together at an open window, looking out on the quiet square. It was too hot for lighted lamps, for reading, or for work; it might have appeared too hot even for conversation, Mrs Penniman having long been speechless. She sat forward in the window, half on the balcony, humming a little song. Catherine was within the room, in a low rocking-chair, dressed in white, and slowly using a large palmetto fan. It was in this way, at this season, that the aunt and niece, after they had had tea, habitually spent their evenings.

'Catherine,' said Mrs Penniman at last, 'I am going to say something that will surprise you.'

'Pray do,' Catherine answered; 'I like surprises. And it is so quiet now.'

'Well, then, I have seen Morris Townsend.'

If Catherine was surprised, she checked the expression of it; she gave neither a start nor an exclamation. She remained, indeed, for some moments intensely still, and this may very well have been a symptom of emotion. 'I hope he was well,' she said at last.

'I don't know; he is a great deal changed. He would like very much to see you.'

'I would rather not see him,' said Catherine, quickly.

'I was afraid you would say that. But you don't seem surprised!'

'I am – very much.'

'I met him at Marian's,' said Mrs Penniman. 'He goes to Marian's, and they are so afraid you will meet him there. It's my belief that that's why he goes. He wants so much to see you.' Catherine made no response to this, and Mrs Penniman went on, 'I didn't know him at first, he is so remarkably changed; but he knew me in a minute. He says I am not in the least changed. You know how polite he always was. He was coming away when I came, and we walked a little distance together. He is still very handsome, only, of course, he looks older, and he is not so – so animated as he used to be. There was a touch of sadness about him; but there was a touch of sadness about him before, especially when he went away. I am afraid he has not been very successful – that he has never got thoroughly established. I don't suppose he is sufficiently plodding, and that, after all, is what succeeds in this world.' Mrs Penniman had not mentioned Morris Townsend's name to her niece for upwards of the fifth of a century; but now that she had broken the spell, she seemed to wish to make up for lost time, as if there had been a sort of exhilaration in hearing herself talk of him. She proceeded, however, with considerable caution, pausing occasionally to let Catherine give some sign. Catherine gave no other sign than to stop the rocking of her chair and the swaying of her fan; she sat motionless and silent. 'It was on Tuesday last,' said Mrs Penniman, 'and I have been hesitating ever since about telling you. I didn't know how you might like it. At last I thought that it was so long ago that you would probably not have any particular feeling. I saw him again after meeting him at Marian's. I met him in the street, and he went a few steps with me. The first thing he said was about you; he asked ever so many questions. Marian didn't want me to speak to you; she didn't want you to know that they receive him. I told him I was sure that after all these years you couldn't have any feeling about that; you couldn't grudge him the hospitality of his own cousin's house. I said you would be bitter indeed if you did that. Marian has the most extraordinary ideas about what happened between you; she seems to think he behaved in some very unusual manner. I took the liberty of reminding her of the real facts, and placing the story in its true light. *He* has no bitterness, Catherine, I can assure you; and he might be excused for it, for things have not gone well with him. He has been all over the world, and tried to establish himself everywhere; but his evil star was against him. It is most interesting to hear him talk of his evil star. Everything failed; everything but his – you know, you remember – his proud, high spirit. I believe he married some lady somewhere in Europe. You know they marry in such a peculiar matter-of-course way in Europe; a marriage of reason they call it. She died soon afterwards; as he said to me, she only flitted across his life. He has not been in New York for ten years; he came back a few days ago. The first thing he did was to ask me about you. He had heard you had never married; he seemed very much interested about that. He said you had been the real romance of his life.'

Catherine had suffered her companion to proceed from point to point, and pause to pause, without interrupting her; she fixed her eyes on the ground and listened. But the last phrase I have quoted was followed by a pause of peculiar significance, and then, at last, Catherine spoke. It will be observed that before doing so she had received a good deal of information about Morris Townsend. 'Please say no more; please don't follow up that subject.'

'Doesn't it interest you?' asked Mrs Penniman, with a certain timorous archness.

'It pains me,' said Catherine.

'I was afraid you would say that. But don't you think you could get used to it? He wants so much to see you.'

'Please don't, Aunt Lavinia,' said Catherine, getting up from her seat. She moved quickly away, and went to the other window, which stood open to the balcony; and here, in the embrasure, concealed from her aunt by the white curtains, she remained a long time, looking out into the warm darkness. She had had a great shock; it was as if the gulf of the past had suddenly opened, and a spectral figure had risen out of it. There were some things she believed she had got over, some feelings that she had thought of as dead; but apparently there was a certain vitality in them still. Mrs Penniman had made them stir themselves. It was but a momentary agitation, Catherine said to herself; it would presently pass away. She was trembling, and her heart was beating so that she could feel it; but this also would subside. Then suddenly, while she waited for a return of her calmness, she burst into tears. But her tears flowed very silently, so that Mrs Penniman had no observation of them. It was perhaps, however, because Mrs Penniman suspected them that she said no more that evening about Morris Townsend.

Chapter Thirty-five

Her refreshed attention to this gentleman had not those limits of which Catherine desired, for herself, to be conscious; it lasted long enough to enable her to wait another week before speaking of him again. It was under the same circumstances that she once more attacked the subject. She had been sitting with her niece in the evening; only on this occasion, as the night was not so warm, the lamp had been lighted, and Catherine and placed herself near it with a morsel of fancy-work. Mrs Penniman went and sat alone for half and hour on the balcony; then she came in, moving vaguely about the room. At last she sunk into a seat near Catherine, with clasped hands, and a little look of excitement.

'Shall you be angry if I speak to you again about *him*?' she asked.

Catherine looked up at her quietly. 'Who is *he*?'

'He whom you once loved.'

'I shall not be angry, but I shall not like it.'

'He sent you a message,' said Mrs Penniman. 'I promised him to deliver it, and I must keep my promise.'

In all these years Catherine had had time to forget how little she had to thank her aunt for in the season of her misery; she had long ago forgiven Mrs Penniman for taking too much upon herself. But for a moment this attitude of interposition and disinterestedness, this carrying of messages and redeeming of promises, brought back the sense that her companion was a dangerous woman. She had said she would not be angry; but for an instant she felt sore. 'I don't care what you do with your promise!' she answered.

Mrs Penniman, however, with her high conception of the sanctity of pledges, carried her point. 'I have gone too far to retreat,' she said, though precisely what this meant she was not at pains to explain. 'Mr Townsend wishes most particularly to see you, Catherine; he believes that if you knew how much, and why, he wishes it, you would consent to do so.'

'There can be no reason,' said Catherine; 'no good reason.'

'His happiness depends upon it. Is not that a good reason?' asked Mrs Penniman, impressively.

'Not for me. My happiness does not.'

'I think you will be happier after you have seen him. He is going away again – going to resume his wanderings. It is a very lonely, restless, joyless life. Before he goes he wishes to speak to you; it is a fixed idea with him – he is always thinking of it. He has something very important to say to you. He believes that you never understood him – that you never judged him rightly, and the belief has always weighed upon him terribly. He wishes to justify himself; he believes that in a very few words he could do so. He wishes to meet you as a friend.'

Catherine listened to this wonderful speech without pausing in her work; she had now had several days to accustom herself to think of Morris Townsend again as an actuality. When it was over she said simply, 'Please say to Mr Townsend that I wish he would leave me alone.'

She had hardly spoken when a sharp, firm ring at the door vibrated through the summer night. Catherine looked up at the clock; it marked a quarter past nine – a very late hour for visitors, especially in the empty condition of the town. Mrs Penniman at the same moment gave a little start, and then Catherine's eyes turned quickly to her aunt. They met Mrs Penniman's, and sounded them for a moment sharply. Mrs Penniman was blushing; her look was a conscious one; it seemed to confess something. Catherine guessed its meaning, and rose quickly from her chair.

'Aunt Penniman,' she said, in a tone that scared her companion, 'have you taken *the liberty* . . .?'

'My dearest Catherine,' stammered Mrs Penniman, 'just wait till you see him!'

Catherine had frightened her aunt, but she was also frightened herself; she was on the point of rushing to give orders to the servant, who was passing to the door, to admit no one; but the fear of meeting her visitor checked her.

'Mr Morris Townsend.'

This was what she heard, vaguely but recognizably, articulated by the domestic, while she hesitated. She had her back turned to the door of the parlour, and for some moments she kept it turned, feeling that he had come in. He had not spoken, however, and at last she faced about. Then she saw a gentleman standing in the middle of the room, from which her aunt had discreetly retired.

She would never have known him. He was forty-five years old, and his figure was not that of the straight, slim young man she remembered. But it was a very fine presence, and a fair and lustrous beard, spreading itself upon a well-presented chest, contributed to its effect. After a moment Catherine recognized the upper half of the face, which, though her visitor's clustering locks had grown thin, was still remarkably handsome. He stood in a deeply deferential attitude, with his eyes on her face. 'I have ventured – I have ventured'; he said, and then he paused, looking about him, as if he expected her to ask him to sit down. It was the old voice, but it had not the old charm. Catherine, for a minute, was conscious of a distinct determination not to invite him to take a seat. Why had he come? It was wrong for him to come. Morris was embarrassed, but Catherine gave him no help. It was not that she was glad of his embarrassment; on the contrary, it excited all her own liabilities of this kind, and gave her great pain. But how could she welcome him when she felt so vividly that he ought not to have come? 'I wanted so much – I was determined,' Morris went on. But he stopped again; it was not easy. Catherine still said nothing, and he may well have recalled with apprehension her ancient faculty of silence. She continued to look at him, however, and as she did so she made the strangest observation. It seemed to be he, and yet not he; it was the man who had been everything, and yet this person was nothing. How long ago it was – how old she had grown – how much she had lived! She had lived on something that was connected with *him*, and she had consumed it in doing so. This person did not look unhappy. He was fair and well-preserved, perfectly dressed, mature and complete. As Catherine looked at him, the story of his life defined itself in his eyes; he had made himself comfortable, and he had never been caught. But even while her perception opened itself to this, she had no desire to catch him; his presence was painful to her, and she only wished he would go.

'Will you not sit down?' he asked.

'I think we had better not,' said Catherine.

'I offend you by coming?' He was very grave; he spoke in a tone of the richest respect.

'I don't think you ought to have come.'

'Did not Mrs Penniman tell you – did she not give you my message?'

'She told me something, but I did not understand.'

'I wish you would let *me* tell you – let me speak for myself.'

'I don't think it is necessary,' said Catherine.

'Not for you, perhaps, but for me. It would be a great satisfaction – and I have not many.' He seemed to be coming nearer; Catherine turned away. 'Can we not be friends again?' he asked.

'We are not enemies,' said Catherine. 'I have none but friendly feelings to you.'

'Ah, I wonder whether you know the happiness it gives me to hear you say that!' Catherine uttered no intimation that she measured the influence of her words; and he presently went on, 'You have not changed – the years have passed happily for you.'

'They have passed very quietly,' said Catherine.

'They have left no marks; you are admirably young.' This time he succeeded in coming nearer – he was close to her; she saw his glossy perfumed beard, and his eyes above it looking strange and hard. It was very different from his old – from his young – face. If she had first seen him this way she would not have liked him. It seemed to her that he was smiling, or trying to smile. 'Catherine,' he said, lowering his voice, 'I have never ceased to think of you.'

'Please don't say these things,' she answered.

'Do you hate me?'

'Oh no,' said Catherine.

Something in her tone discouraged him, but in a moment he recovered himself. 'Have you still some kindness for me, then?'

'I don't know why you have come here to ask me such things!' Catherine exclaimed.

'Because for many years if has been the desire of my life that we should be friends again.'

'That is impossible.'

'Why so? Not if you will allow it.'

'I will not allow it,' said Catherine.

He looked at her again in silence. 'I see; my presence troubles you and pains you. I will go away; but you must give me leave to come again.'

'Please don't come again,' she said.

'Never? – never?'

She made a great effort; she wished to say something that would make it impossible he should ever again cross her threshold. 'It is wrong of you. There is no propriety in it – no reason for it.'

'Ah, dearest lady, you do me injustice!' cried Morris Townsend. 'We have only waited, and now we are free.'

'You treated me badly,' said Catherine.

'Not if you think of it rightly. You had your quiet life with your father – which was just what I could not make up my mind to rob you of.'

'Yes; I had that.'

Morris felt it to be a considerable damage to his cause that he could not add that she had had something more besides; for it is needless to say that he had learned the contents of Doctor Sloper's will. He was, nevertheless, not at a loss. 'There are worse fates than that!' he exclaimed, with expression; and he might have been supposed to refer to his own unprotected situation. Then he added, with a deeper tenderness, 'Catherine, have you never forgiven me?'

'I forgave you years ago, but it is useless for us to attempt to be friends.'

'Not if we forget the past. We have still a future, thank God!'

'I can't forget – I don't forget,' said Catherine. 'You treated me too badly. I felt it very much; I felt it for years.' And then she went on, with her wish to show him that he must not come to her this way, 'I can't begin again – I can't take it up. Everything is dead and buried. It was too serious; it made a great change in my life. I never expected to see you here.'

'Ah, you are angry!' cried Morris, who wished immensely that he could extort some flash of passion from her calmness. In that case he might hope.

'No, I am not angry. Anger does not last that way for years. But there are other things. Impressions last, when they have been strong. But I can't talk.'

Morris stood stroking his beard, with a clouded eye. 'Why have you never married?' he asked, abruptly. 'You have had opportunities.'

'I didn't wish to marry.'

'Yes, you are rich, you are free; you had nothing to gain.'

'I had nothing to gain,' said Catherine.

Morris looked vaguely round him, and gave a deep sigh. 'Well, I was in hopes that we might still have been friends.'

'I meant to tell you, by my aunt, in answer to your message – if you had waited for an answer – that it was unnecessary for you to come in that hope.'

'Good-bye, then,' said Morris. 'Excuse my indiscretion.'

He bowed, and she turned away – standing there, averted, with her eyes on the ground, for some moments after she had heard him close the door of the room.

In the hall he found Mrs Penniman, fluttered and eager; she appeared to have been hovering there under the irreconcilable promptings of her curiosity and her dignity.

'That was a precious plan of yours!' said Morris, clapping on his hat.

'Is she so hard?' asked Mrs Penniman.

'She doesn't care a button for me – with her confounded little dry manner.'

'Was it very dry?' pursued Mrs Penniman, with solicitude.

Morris took no notice of her question; he stood musing an instant, with his hat on. 'But why the deuce, then, would she never marry?'

'Yes – why indeed?' sighed Mrs Penniman. And then, as if from a sense of the inadequacy of this explanation, 'But you will not despair – you will come back?'

'Come back? Damnation!' And Morris Townsend strode out of the house, leaving Mrs Penniman staring.

Catherine, meanwhile, in the parlour, picking up her morsel of fancy-work, had seated herself with it again – for life, as it were.

The Aspern Papers

Chapter One

I had taken Mrs Prest into my confidence; in truth without her I should have made but little advance, for the fruitful idea in the whole business dropped from her friendly lips. It was she who invented the short cut, who severed the Gordian knot. It is not supposed to be the nature of women to rise as a general thing to the largest and most liberal view – I mean of a practical scheme; but it has struck me that they sometimes throw off a bold conception – such as a man would not have risen to – with singular serenity. 'Simply ask them to take you in on the footing of a lodger' – I don't think that unaided I should have risen to that. I was beating about the bush, trying to be ingenious, wondering by what combination of arts I might become an acquaintance, when she offered this happy suggestion that the way to become an acquaintance was first to become an inmate. Her actual knowledge of the Misses Bordereau was scarcely larger than mine, and indeed I had brought with me from England some definite facts which were new to her. Their name had been mixed up ages before with one of the greatest names of the century, and they lived now in Venice in obscurity, on very small means, unvisited, unapproachable, in a dilapidated old palace on an out-of-the-way canal; this was the substance of my friend's impression of them. She herself had been established in Venice for fifteen years and had done a great deal of good there; but the circle of her benevolence did not include the two shy, mysterious and, as it was somehow supposed, scarcely respectable Americans (they were believed to have lost in their long exile all national quality, besides having had, as their name implied, some French strain in their origin), who asked no favours and desired no attention. In the early years of her residence she had made an attempt to see them, but this had been successful only as regards the little one, as Mrs Prest called the niece; though in reality, as I afterwards learned, she was considerably the bigger of the two. She had heard Miss Bordereau was ill and had a suspicion that she was in want; and she had gone to the house to offer assistance, so that if there were suffering (and American suffering), she should at least not have it on her conscience. The 'little one' received her in the great cold, tarnished Venetian sala, the central hall of the house, paved with marble and roofed with dim cross-beams, and did not even ask her to sit down. This was not encouraging for me, who wished to sit so fast, and I remarked as much to Mrs Prest. She however replied with profundity, 'Ah, but there's all the difference: I went to confer a favour and you will go to ask one. If they are proud you will be on the right side.' And she offered to show me their house to begin with – to row me thither in her gondola. I let her know that I had already been to look at it half a dozen times; but I accepted her invitation, for it charmed me to hover about the place. I had made my way to it the day after my arrival in Venice (it had been described to me in advance by the friend in England to whom I owed definite information as to their possession of the papers), and I had besieged it with my eyes while I considered my plan of campaign. Jeffrey Aspern had never been in it that I knew of; but some note of his voice seemed to abide there by a roundabout implication, a faint reverberation.

Mrs Prest knew nothing about the papers, but she was interested in my curiosity, as she was always interested in the joys and sorrows of her friends. As we went, however, in her gondola, gliding there under the sociable hood with the bright Venetian picture framed on either side by the movable window, I could see that she was amused by my infatuation, the way my interest in the papers had become a fixed idea. 'One would think you expected to find in them the answer to the riddle of the universe,' she said; and I denied the impeachment only by replying that if I had to choose between that precious solution and a bundle of Jeffrey Aspern's letters I knew indeed which would appear to me the greater boon. She pretended to make light of his genius and I took no pains to defend him. One doesn't defend one's god: one's god is in himself a defence. Besides, today, after his long comparative obscuration, he hangs high in the heaven of our literature, for all the world to see; he is a part of the light by which we walk. The most I said was that he was no doubt not a woman's poet: to which she rejoined aptly enough that he had been at least Miss Bordereau's. The strange thing had been for me to discover in England that she was still alive; it was as if I had been told Mrs Siddons was, or Queen Caroline, or the famous Lady Hamilton, for it seemed to me that she belonged to a generation as extinct. 'Why, she must be tremendously old – at least a hundred,' I had said; but on coming to consider dates I saw that it was not strictly necessary that she should have exceeded by very much the common span. None the less she was very far advanced in life and her relations with Jeffrey Aspern had occurred in her early womanhood. 'That is her excuse,' said Mrs Prest, half sententiously and yet also somewhat as if she were ashamed of making a speech so little in the real tone of Venice. As if a woman needed an excuse for having loved the divine poet! He had been not only one of the most brilliant minds of his day (and in those years, when the century was young, there were, as every one knows, many), but one of the most genial men and one of the handsomest.

The niece, according to Mrs Prest, was not so old, and she risked the conjecture that she was only a grand-niece. This was possible; I had nothing but my share in the very limited knowledge of my English fellow-worshipper John Cumnor, who had never seen the couple. The world, as I say, had recognized Jeffrey Aspern, but Cumnor and I had recognized him most. The multitude, today, flocked to his temple, but of that temple he and I regarded ouselves as the ministers. We held, justly, as I think, that we had done more for his memory than anyone else, and we had done it by opening lights into his life. He had nothing to fear from us because he had nothing to fear from the truth, which alone at such a distance of time we could be interested in establishing. His early death had been the only dark spot in his life, unless the papers in Miss Bordereau's hands should perversely bring out others. There had been an impression about 1825 that he had 'treated her badly', just as there had been an impression that he had 'served', as the

London populace says, several other ladies in the same way. Each of these cases Cumnor and I had been able to investigate, and we had never failed to acquit him conscientiously of shabby behaviour. I judged him perhaps more indulgently than my friend; certainly, at any rate, it appeared to me that no man could have walked straighter in the given circumstances. These were almost always awkward. Half the women of his time, to speak liberally, had flung themselves at his head, and out of this pernicious fashion many complications, some of them grave, had not failed to arise. He was not a woman's poet, as I had said to Mrs Prest, in the modern phase of his reputation; but the situation had been different when the man's own voice was mingled with his song. That voice, by every testimony, was one of the sweetest ever heard. 'Orpheus and the Maenads!' was the exclamation that rose to my lips when I first turned over his correspondence. Almost all the Maenads were unreasonable and many of them insupportable; it struck me in short that he was kinder, more considerate than, in his place (if I could imagine myself in such a place!) I should have been.

It was certainly strange beyond all strangeness, and I shall not take up space with attempting to explain it, that whereas in all these other lines of research we had to deal with phantoms and dust, the mere echoes of echoes, the one living source of information that had lingered on into our time had been unheeded by us. Every one of Aspern's contemporaries had, according to our belief, passed away; we had not been able to look into a single pair of eyes into which his had looked or to feel a transmitted contact in any aged hand that his had touched. Most dead of all did poor Miss Bordereau appear, and yet she alone had survived. We exhausted in the course of months our wonder that we had not found her out sooner, and the substance of our explanation was that she had kept so quiet. The poor lady on the whole had had reason for doing so. But it was a revelation to us that it was possible to keep so quiet as that in the latter half of the nineteenth century – the age of newspapers and telegrams and photographs and interviewers. And she had taken no great trouble about it either: she had not hidden herself away in an undiscoverable hole; she had boldly settled down in a city of exhibition. The only secret of her safety that we could perceive was that Venice contained so many curiosities that were greater than she. And then accident had somehow favoured her, as was shown for example in the fact that Mrs Prest had never happened to mention her to me, though I had spent three weeks in Venice – under her nose, as it were – five years before. Mrs Prest had not mentioned this much to anyone; she appeared almost to have forgotten she was there. Of course she had not the responsibilities of an editor. It was no explanation of the old woman's having eluded us to say that she lived abroad, for our researches had again and again taken us (not only by correspondence but by personal inquiry) to France, to Germany, to Italy, in which countries, not counting his important stay in England, so many of the too few years of Aspern's career were spent. We were glad to think at least that in all our publishings (some people consider I believe that we have overdone them), we had only touched in passing and in the most discreet manner on Miss Bordereau's connection. Oddly enough, even if we had had the material (and we often wondered what had become of it), it would have been the most difficult episode to handle.

The gondola stopped, the old palace was there; it was a house of the class which in Venice carries even in extreme dilapidation the dignified name. 'How charming! It's grey and pink!' my companion exclaimed; and that is the most comprehensive description of it. It was not particularly old, only two or three centuries; and it had an air not so much of decay as of quiet discouragement, as if it had rather missed its career. But its wide front, with a stone balcony from end to end of the *piano nobile* or most important floor, was architectural enough, with the aid of various pilasters and arches; and the stucco with which in the intervals it had long ago been endued was rosy in the April afternoon. It overlooked a clean, melancholy, unfrequented canal, which had a narrow *riva* or convenient footway on either side. 'I don't know why – there are no brick gables,' said Mrs Prest, 'but this corner has seemed to me before more Dutch than Italian, more like Amsterdam than like Venice. It's perversely clean, for reasons of its own; and though you can pass on foot scarcely anyone ever thinks of doing so. It has the air of a Protestant Sunday. Perhaps the people are afraid of the Misses Bordereau. I dare say they have the reputation of witches.'

I forget what answer I made to this – I was given up to two other reflections. The first of these was that if the old lady lived in such a big, imposing house she could not be in any sort of misery and therefore would not be tempted by a chance to let a couple of rooms. I expressed this idea to Mrs Prest, who gave me a very logical reply. 'If she didn't live in a big house how could it be a question of her having rooms to spare? If she were not amply lodged herself you would lack ground to approach her. Besides, a big house here, and especially in this *quartier perdu,* proves nothing at all: it is perfectly compatible with a state of penury. Dilapidated old palazzi, if you will go out of the way for them, are to be had for five shillings a year. And as for the people who live in them – no, until you have explored Venice socially as much as I have you can form no idea of their domestic desolation. They live on nothing, for they have nothing to live on.' The other idea that had come into my head was connected with a high blank wall which appeared to confine an expanse of ground on one side of the house. Blank I call it, but it was figured over with the patches that please a painter, repaired breaches, crumblings of plaster, extrusions of brick that had turned pink with time; and a few thin trees, with the poles of certain rickety trellises, were visible over the top. The place was a garden and apparently it belonged to the house. It suddenly occurred to me that if it did belong to the house I had my pretext.

I sat looking out on all this with Mrs Prest (it was covered with the golden glow of Venice) from the shade of our *felze,* and she asked me if I would go in then, while she waited for me, or come back another time. At first I could not decide – it was doubtless very weak of me. I wanted still to think I *might* get a footing, and I was afraid to meet failure, for it would leave me, as I remarked to my companion, without another arrow for my bow. 'Why not another?' she inquired, as I sat there hesitating and thinking it over; and she wished to know why even now and before taking the trouble of becoming an inmate (which might be wretchedly uncomfortable after all, even if it succeeded), I had not the resource of simply offering them a sum of money down. In that way I might obtain the documents without bad nights.

'Dearest lady,' I exclaimed, 'excuse the impatience of my tone when I suggest that you must have forgotten the very fact (surely I communicated it to you) which pushed me to throw myself upon your ingenuity. The old woman won't have the documents spoken of; they are personal, delicate, intimate, and she hasn't modern notions, God bless her! If I should sound that note first I should certainly spoil the game. I can arrive at the papers only by putting her off her guard, and I can put her off her guard only by ingratiating diplomatic practices. Hypocrisy, duplicity are my only chance. I am sorry for it, but for Jeffrey Aspern's sake I would do worse still. First I must take tea with her; then tackle the main job.' And I told over what had happened to John Cumnor when he wrote to her. No notice whatever had been taken of his first letter, and the second had been answered very sharply, in six lines, by the niece. 'Miss Bordereau requested her to say that she could not imagine what he meant by troubling them. They had none of Mr Aspern's papers, and if they had should never think of showing them to any one on any account whatever. She didn't know what he was talking about and begged he would let her alone.' I certainly did not want to be met that way.

'Well,' said Mrs Prest, after a moment, provokingly, 'perhaps after all they haven't any of his things. If they deny it flat how are you sure?'

'John Cumnor is sure, and it would take me long to tell you how his conviction, or his very strong presumption – strong enough to stand against the old lady's not unnatural fib – has built itself up. Besides, he makes much of the internal evidence of the niece's letter.'

'The internal evidence?'

'Her calling him "Mr Aspern".'

'I don't see what that proves.'

'It proves familiarity, and familiarity implies the possession of mementoes, of relics. I can't tell you how that "Mr" touches me – how it bridges over the gulf of time and brings our hero near to me – nor what an edge it gives to my desire to see Juliana. You don't say "Mr" Shakespeare.'

'Would I, any more, if I had a box full of his letters?'

'Yes, if he had been your lover and someone wanted them!' And I added that John Cumnor was so convinced, and so all the more convinced by Miss Bordereau's tone, that he would have come himself to Venice on the business were it not that for him there was the obstacle that it would be difficult to disprove his identity with the person who had written to them, which the old ladies would be sure to suspect in spite of dissimulation and a change of name. If they were to ask him point-blank if he were not their correspondent it would be too awkward for him to lie; whereas I was fortunately not tied in that way. I was a fresh hand and could say no without lying.

'But you will have to change your name,' said Mrs Prest. 'Juliana lives out of the world as much as it is possible to live, but none the less she has probably heard of Mr Aspern's editors; she perhaps possesses what you have published.'

'I have thought of that,' I returned; and I drew out of my pocket-book a visiting-card, neatly engraved with a name that was not my own.

'You are very extravagant; you might have written it,' said my companion.

'This looks more genuine.'

'Certainly, you are prepared to go far! But it will be awkward about your letters; they won't come to you in that mask.'

'My banker will take them in and I will go every day to fetch them. It will give me a little walk.'

'Shall you only depend upon that?' asked Mrs Prest. 'Aren't you coming to see me?'

'Oh, you will have left Venice, for the hot months, long before there are any results. I am prepared to roast all summer – as well as hereafter, perhaps you'll say! Meanwhile, John Cumnor will bombard me with letters addressed, in my feigned name, to the care of the *padrona*.'

'She will recognize his hand,' my companion suggested.

'On the envelope he can disguise it.'

'Well, you're a precious pair! Doesn't it occur to you that even if you are able to say you are not Mr Cumnor in person they may still suspect you of being his emissary?'

'Certainly, and I see only one way to parry that.'

'And what may that be?'

I hesitated a moment. 'To make love to the niece.'

'Ah,' cried Mrs Prest, 'wait till you see her!'

Chapter Two

'I must work the garden – I must work the garden,' I said to myself, five minutes later, as I waited, upstairs, in the long, dusky sala, where the bare scagliola floor gleamed vaguely in a chink of the closed shutters. The place was impressive but it looked cold and cautious. Mrs Prest had floated away, giving me a rendezvous at the end of half an hour by some neighbouring watersteps; and I had been let into the house, after pulling the rusty bell-wire, by a little red-headed, white-faced maid-servant, who was very young and not ugly and wore clicking pattens and a shawl in the fashion of a hood. She had not contented herself with opening the door from above by the usual arrangement of a creaking pulley, though she had looked down at me first from an upper window, dropping the inevitable challenge which in Italy precedes the hospitable act. As a general thing I was irritated by this survival of medieval manners, though as I liked the old I suppose I ought to have liked it; but I was so determined to be genial that I took my false card out of my pocket and held it up to her, smiling as if it were a magic token. It had the effect of one indeed, for it brought her, as I say, all the way down. I begged her to hand it to her mistress, having first written on it in Italian the words, 'Could you very kindly see a gentleman, an American, for a moment?' The little maid was not hostile, and I reflected that even that was perhaps something gained. She coloured, she smiled and looked both frightened and pleased. I could see that my arrival was a great affair, that visits were rare in that house, and that she was a person who would have liked a sociable place. When she pushed forward the heavy door behind me I felt that I had a foot in the citadel. She pattered across the damp, stony lower hall and I followed her up the high staircase – stonier still, as it seemed – without an invitation. I think she had meant I should wait for her below, but such was not my idea, and I took up my station in the sala. She flitted, at the far end of it, into impenetrable regions, and I looked at the place with my heart beating as I had known it to do in the dentist's parlour. It was gloomy and stately, but it owed its character almost entirely to its noble shape and to the fine architectural doors – as high as the doors of houses – which, leading into the various rooms, repeated themselves on either side at intervals. They were surmounted with old faded painted escutcheons, and here and there, in the spaces between them, brown pictures, which I perceived to be bad, in battered frames, were suspended. With the exception of several straw-bottomed chairs with their backs to the wall, the grand obscure vista contained nothing else to minister to effect. It was evidently never used save as a passage, and little even as that. I may add that by the time the door opened again through which the maid-servant had escaped, my eyes had grown used to the want of light.

I had not meant by my private ejaculation that I must myself cultivate the soil of the tangled enclosure which lay beneath the windows, but the lady who came towards me from the distance over the hard, shining floor might have supposed as much from the way in which, as I went rapidly to meet her, I exclaimed, taking care to speak Italian: 'The garden, the garden – do me the pleasure to tell me if it's yours!'

She stopped short, looking at me with wonder; and then, 'Nothing here is mine,' she answered in English, coldly and sadly.

'Oh, you are English; how delightful!' I remarked, ingenuously. 'But surely the garden belongs to the house?'

'Yes, but the house doesn't belong to me.' She was a long, lean, pale person, habited apparently in a dull-coloured dressing-gown, and she spoke with a kind of mild literalness. She did not ask me to sit down, any more than years before (if she were the niece) she had asked Mrs Prest, and we stood face to face in the empty pompous hall.

'Well then, would you kindly tell me to whom I must address myself? I'm afraid you'll think me odiously intrusive, but you know I *must* have a garden – upon my honour I must!'

Her face was not young, but it was simple; it was not fresh, but it was mild. She had large eyes which were not bright, and a great deal of hair which was not 'dressed', and long fine hands which were – possibly – not clean. She clasped these members almost convulsively as, with a confused, alarmed look, she broke out, 'Oh, don't take it away from us; we like it ourselves!'

'You have the use of it then?'

'Oh yes. If it wasn't for that!' And she gave a shy, melancholy smile.

'Isn't it a luxury, precisely? That's why, intending to be in Venice some weeks, possibly all summer, and having some literary work, some reading and writing to do, so that I must be quiet, and yet if possible a great deal in the open air – that's why I have felt that a garden is really indispensable. I appeal to your own experience,' I went on, smiling. 'Now can't I look at yours?'

'I don't know, I don't understand,' the poor woman murmured, planted there and letting her embarrassed eyes wander all over my strangeness.

'I mean only from one of those windows – such grand ones as you have here – if you will let me open the shutters.' And I walked towards the back of the house. When I had advanced half-way I stopped and waited, as if I took it for granted she would accompany me. I had been of necessity very abrupt, but I strove at the same time to give her the impression of extreme courtesy. 'I have been looking at furnished rooms all over the place, and it seems impossible to find any with a garden attached. Naturally in a place like Venice gardens are rare. It's absurd if you like, for a man, but I can't live without flowers.'

'There are none to speak of down there.' She came nearer to me, as if, though she mistrusted me, I had drawn her by an invisible thread. I went on again, and she continued as she followed me: 'We have a few, but they are very common. It costs too much to cultivate them; one has to have a man.'

'Why shouldn't I be the man?' I asked. 'I'll work without wages; or rather I'll put in a gardener. You shall have the sweetest flowers in Venice.'

She protested at this, with a queer little sigh which might also have been a gush of rapture at the picture I presented. Then she observed, 'We don't know you – we don't know you.'

'You know me as much as I know you; that is much more, because you know my name. And if you are English I am almost a countryman.'

'We are not English,' said my companion, watching me helplessly while I threw open the shutters of one of the divisions of the wide high window.

'You speak the language so beautifully: might I ask what you are?' Seen from above the garden was certainly shabby; but I perceived at a glance that it had great capabilities. She made no rejoinder, she was so lost in staring at me, and I exclaimed, 'You don't mean to say you are also by chance American?'

'I don't know; we used to be.'

'Used to be? Surely you haven't changed?'

'It's so many years ago – we are nothing.'

'So many years that you have been living here? Well, I don't wonder at that; it's a grand old house. I suppose you all use the garden,' I went on, 'but I assure you I shouldn't be in your way. I would be very quiet and stay in one corner.'

'We all use it?' she repeated after me, vaguely, not coming close to the window but looking at my shoes. She appeared to think me capable of throwing her out.

'I mean all your family, as many as you are.'

'There is only one other; she is very old – she never goes down.'

'Only one other, in all this great house!' I feigned to be not only amazed but almost scandalized. 'Dear lady, you must have space then to spare!'

'To spare?' she repeated, in the same dazed way.

'Why, you surely don't live (two quiet women – I see *you* are quiet, at any rate) in fifty rooms!' Then with a burst of hope and cheer I demanded: 'Couldn't you let me two or three? That would set me up!'

I had now struck the note that translated my purpose and I need not reproduce the whole of the tune I played. I ended by making my interlocutress believe that I was an honourable person, though of course I did not even attempt to persuade her that I was not an eccentric one. I repeated that I had studies to pursue; that I wanted quiet; that I delighted in a garden and had vainly sought one up and down the city; that I would undertake that before another month was over the dear old house should be smothered in flowers. I think it was the flowers that won my suit, for I afterwards found that Miss Tita (for such the name of this high tremulous spinster proved somewhat incongruously to be) had an insatiable appetite for them. When I speak of my suit as won I mean that before I left her she had promised that she would refer the question to her aunt. I inquired who her aunt might be and she answered, 'Why, Miss Bordereau!' with an air of surprise, as if I might have been expected to know. There were contradictions like this in Tita Bordereau which, as I observed later, contributed to make her an odd and affecting person. It was the study of the two ladies to live so that the world should not touch them, and yet they had never altogether accepted the idea that it never heard of them. In Tita at any rate a grateful susceptibility to human contact had not died out, and contact of a limited order there would be if I should come to live in the house.

'We have never done anything of the sort; we have never had a lodger or any kind of inmate.' So much as this she made a point of saying to me. 'We are very poor, we live very badly. The rooms are very bare – that you might take; they have nothing in them. I don't know how you would sleep, how you would eat.'

'With your permission, I could easily put in a bed and a few tables and chairs. *C'est la moindre des choses* and the affair of an hour or two. I know a little man from whom I can hire what I should want for a few months, for a trifle, and my gondolier can bring the things round in his boat. Of course in this great house you must have a second kitchen, and my servant, who is a wonderfully handy fellow' (this personage was an evocation of the moment), 'can easily cook me a chop there. My tastes and habits are of the simplest; I live on flowers!' And then I ventured to add that if they were very poor it was all the more reason they should let their rooms. They were bad economists – I had never heard of such a waste of material.

I saw in a moment that the good lady had never before been spoken to in that way, with a kind of humorous firmness which did not exclude sympathy but was on the contrary founded on it. She might easily have told me that my sympathy was impertinent, but this by good fortune did not occur to her. I left her with the understanding that she would consider the matter with her aunt and that I might come back the next day for their decision.

'The aunt will refuse; she will think the whole proceeding very *louche*!' Mrs Prest declared shortly after this, when I had resumed my place in her gondola. She had put the idea into my head and now (so little are women to be counted on) she appeared to take a despondent view of it. Her pessimism provoked me and I pretended to have the best hopes; I went so far as to say that I had a distinct presentiment that I should succeed. Upon this Mrs Prest broke out, 'Oh, I see what's in your head! You fancy you have made such an impression in a quarter of an hour that she is dying for you to come and can be depended upon to bring the old one round. If you do get in you'll count it as a triumph.'

I did count it as a triumph, but only for the editor (in the last analysis), not for the man, who had not the tradition of personal conquest. When I went back on the morrow the little maid-servant conducted me straight through the long sala (it opened there as before in perfect perspective and was lighter now, which I thought a good omen) into the apartment from which the recipient of my former visit had emerged on that occasion. It was a large shabby parlour, with a fine old painted ceiling and a strange figure sitting alone at one of the windows. They come back to me now almost with the palpitation they caused, the successive feelings that accompanied my consciousness that as the door of the room closed behind me I was really face to face with the Juliana of some of Aspern's most exquisite and most renowned lyrics. I grew used to her afterwards, though never completely; but as she sat there before me my heart beat as fast as if the miracle of resurrection had taken place for my benefit. Her presence seemed somehow to contain his, and I felt nearer to him at that first moment of seeing her than I ever had been before or ever have been since. Yes, I remember my emotions in their order, even including a curious little tremor that took me when I saw that the niece was not there. With her, the day before, I had become sufficiently familiar, but it almost exceeded my courage (much as I had longed for the event) to be left alone with such a terrible relic as the aunt. She was too strange, too literally resurgent. Then came a check, with the perception that we were not really face to face, inasmuch as she had over her eyes a horrible green shade which, for her, served almost as a mask. I believed for the instant that she had put it on expressly, so that from underneath it she might scrutinize me without being scrutinized herself. At the same time it increased the presumption that there was a ghastly death's-head lurking behind it. The divine Juliana as a grinning skull – the vision hung there until it passed. Then it came to me that she *was* tremendously old – so old that death might take her at any moment, before I had time to get what I wanted from her. The next thought was a correction to that; it lighted up the situation. She would die next week, she would die tomorrow – then I could seize her papers. Meanwhile she sat there neither moving nor speaking. She was very small and shrunken, bent forward, with her hands in her lap. She was dressed in black and her head was wrapped in a piece of old black lace which showed no hair.

My emotion keeping me silent she spoke first, and the remark she made was exactly the most unexpected.

Chapter Three

'Our house is very far from the centre, but the little canal is very *comme il faut.*'

'It's the sweetest corner of Venice and I can imagine nothing more charming,' I hastened to reply. The old lady's voice was very thin and weak, but it had an agreeable, cultivated murmur and there was wonder in the thought that that individual note had been in Jeffrey Aspern's ear.

'Please to sit down there. I hear very well,' she said quietly, as if perhaps I had been shouting at her; and the chair she pointed to was at a certain distance. I took possession of it, telling her that I was perfectly aware that I had intruded, that I had not been properly introduced and could only throw myself upon her indulgence. Perhaps the other lady, the one I had had the honour of seeing the day before, would have explained to her about the garden. That was literally what had given me courage to take a step so unconventional. I had fallen in love at sight with the whole place (she herself probably was so used to it that she did not know the impression it was capable of making on a stranger), and I had felt it was really a case to risk something. Was her own kindness in receiving me a sign that I was not wholly out in my calculation? It would render me extremely happy to think so. I could give her my word of honour that I was a most respectable, inoffensive person and that as an inmate they would be barely conscious of my existence. I would conform to any regulations, any restrictions if they would only let me enjoy the garden. Moreover I should be delighted to give her references, guarantees; they would be of the very best, both in Venice and in England as well as in America.

She listened to me in perfect stillness and I felt that she was looking at me with great attention, though I could see only the lower part of her bleached and shrivelled face. Independently of the refining process of old age it had a delicacy which once must have been great. She had been very fair, she had had a wonderful complexion. She was silent a little after I had ceased speaking; then she inquired, 'If you are so fond of a garden why don't you go to *terra firma,* where there are so many far better than this?'

'Oh, it's the combination!' I answered, smiling; and then, with rather a flight of fancy, 'It's the idea of a garden in the middle of the sea.'

'It's not in the middle of the sea; you can't see the water.'

I stared a moment, wondering whether she wished to convict me of fraud. 'Can't see the water? Why, dear madam, I can come up to the very gate in my boat.'

She appeared inconsequent, for she said vaguely in reply to this, 'Yes, if you have got a boat. I haven't any; it's many years since I have been in one of the gondolas.' She uttered these words as if the gondolas were a curious far-away craft which she knew only by hearsay.

'Let me assure you of the pleasure with which I would put mine at your service!' I exclaimed. I had scarcely said this however before I became aware that the speech was in questionable taste and might also do me the injury of making me appear too eager, too possessed of a hidden motive. But the old woman remained impenetrable and her attitude bothered me by suggesting that she had a fuller vision of me than I had of her. She gave me no thanks for my somewhat extravagant offer but remarked that the lady I had seen the day before was her niece; she would presently come in. She had asked her to stay away a little on purpose, because she herself wished to see me at first alone. She relapsed into silence and I asked myself why she had judged this necessary and what was coming yet; also whether I might venture on some judicious remark in praise of her companion. I went so far as to say that I should be delighted to see her again: she had been so very courteous to me, considering how odd she must have thought me – a declaration which drew from Miss Bordereau another of her whimsical speeches.

'She has very good manners; I bred her up myself!' I was on the point of saying that that accounted for the easy grace of the niece, but I arrested myself in time, and the next moment the old woman went on: 'I don't care who you may be – I don't want to know; it signifies very little today.' This had all the air of being a formula of dismissal, as if her next words would be that I might take myself off now that she had had the amusement of looking on the face of such a monster of indiscretion. Therefore I was all the more surprised when she added, with her soft, venerable quaver, 'You may have as many rooms as you like – if you will pay a good deal of money.'

I hesitated but for a single instant, long enough to ask myself what she meant in particular by this condition. First it struck me that she must have really a large sum in her mind; then I reasoned quickly that her idea of a large sum would probably not correspond to my own. My deliberation, I think, was not so visible as to diminish the promptitude with which I replied, 'I will pay with pleasure and of course in advance whatever you may think it proper to ask me.'

'Well then, a thousand francs a month,' she rejoined instantly, while her baffling green shade continued to cover her attitude.

The figure, as they say, was startling and my logic had been at fault. The sum she had mentioned was, by the Venetian measure of such matters, exceedingly large; there was many an old palace in an out-of-the-way corner that I might on such terms have enjoyed by the year. But so far as my small means allowed I was prepared to spend money, and my decision was quickly taken. I would pay her with a smiling face what she asked, but in that case I would give myself the compensation of extracting the papers from her for nothing. Moreover if she had asked five times as much I should have risen to the occasion; so odious would it have appeared to me to stand chaffering with Aspern's Juliana. It was queer enough to have a question of money with her at all. I assured her that her views perfectly met my own and that on the morrow I should have the pleasure of putting three months' rent into her hand. She received this announcement with serenity and with no apparent sense that after all it would be becoming of her to say that I ought to see the rooms first. This did not occur to her and indeed her serenity was mainly what I wanted. Our little bargain was just concluded when the door opened and the younger lady appeared on the threshold. As soon as Miss Bordereau saw her niece she cried out almost gaily, 'He will give three thousand – three thousand tomorrow!'

Miss Tita stood still, with her patient eyes turning from one of us to the other; then she inquired, scarcely above her breath, 'Do you mean francs?'

'Did you mean francs or dollars?' the old woman asked of me at this.

'I think francs were what you said,' I answered, smiling.

'That is very good,' said Miss Tita, as if she had become conscious that her own question might have looked overreaching.

'What do *you* know? You are ignorant,' Miss Bordereau remarked; not with acerbity but with a strange, soft coldness.

'Yes, of money – certainly of money!' Miss Tita hastened to exclaim.

'I am sure you have your own branches of knowledge,' I took the liberty of saying, genially. There was something painful to me, somehow, in the turn the conversation had taken, in the discussion of the rent.

'She had a very good education when she was young. I looked into that myself,' said Miss Bordereau. Then she added, 'But she has learned nothing since.'

'I have always been with you,' Miss Tita rejoined very mildly, and evidently with no intention of making an epigram.

'Yes, but for that!' her aunt declared, with more satirical force. She evidently meant that but for this her niece would never have got on at all; the point of the observation however being lost on Miss Tita, though she blushed at hearing her history revealed to a stranger. Miss Bordereau went on, addressing herself to me: 'And what time will you come tomorrow with the money?'

'The sooner the better. If it suits you I will come at noon.'

'I am always here but I have my hours,' said the old woman, as if her convenience were not to be taken for granted.

'You mean the times when you receive?'

'I never receive. But I will see you at noon, when you come with the money.'

'Very good, I shall be punctual;' and I added, 'May I shake hands with you, on our contract?' I thought there ought to be some little form, it would make me really feel easier, for I foresaw that there would be no other. Besides, though Miss Bordereau could not today be called personally attractive and there was something even in her wasted antiquity that bade one stand at one's distance, I felt an irresistible desire to hold in my own for a moment the hand that Jeffrey Aspern had pressed.

For a minute she made no answer and I saw that my proposal failed to meet with her approbation. She indulged in no movement of withdrawal, which I half expected; she only said coldly, 'I belong to a time when that was not the custom.'

I felt rather snubbed but I exclaimed good-humouredly to Miss Tita, 'Oh, you will do as well!' I shook hands with her while she replied, with a small flutter, 'Yes, yes, to show it's all arranged!'

'Shall you bring the money in gold?' Miss Bordereau demanded, as I was turning to the door.

I looked at her a moment. 'Aren't you a little afraid, after all, of keeping such a sum as that in the house?' It was not that I was annoyed at her avidity but I was really struck with the disparity between such a treasure and such scanty means of guarding it.

'Whom should I be afraid of if I am not afraid of you?' she asked with her shrunken grimness.

'Ah well,' said I, laughing, 'I shall be in point of fact a protector and I will bring gold if you prefer.'

'Thank you,' the old woman returned with dignity and with an inclination of her head which evidently signified that I might depart. I passed out of the room, reflecting that it would not be easy to circumvent her. As I stood in the sala again I saw that Miss Tita had followed me and I supposed that as her aunt had neglected to suggest that I should take a look at my quarters it was her purpose to repair the omission. But she made no such suggestion; she only stood there with a dim, though not a languid smile, and with an effect of irresponsible, incompetent youth which was almost comically at variance with the faded fact of her person. She was not infirm, like her aunt, but she struck me as still more helpless, because her inefficiency was spiritual, which was not the case with Miss Bordereau's. I waited to see if she would offer to show me the rest of the house, but I did not precipitate the question, inasmuch as my plan was from this moment to spend as much of my time as possible in her society. I only observed at the end of a minute:

'I have had better fortune than I hoped. It was very kind of her to see me. Perhaps you said a good word for me.'

'It was the idea of the money,' said Miss Tita.

'And did you suggest that?'

'I told her that you would perhaps give a good deal.'

'What made you think that?'

'I told her I thought you were rich.'

'And what put that idea into your head?'

'I don't know; the way you talked.'

'Dear me, I must talk differently now,' I declared. 'I'm sorry to say it's not the case.'

'Well,' said Miss Tita, 'I think that in Venice the *forestieri,* in general, often give a great deal for something that after all isn't much,' She appeared to make this remark with a comforting intention, to wish to remind me that if I had been extravagant I was not really foolishly singular. We walked together along the sala, and as I took its magnificent measure I said to her that I was afraid it would not form a part of my *quartiere*. Were my rooms by chance to be among those that opened into it? 'Not if you go above, on the second floor,' she answered with a little startled air, as if she had rather taken for granted I would know my proper place.

'And I infer that that's where your aunt would like me to be.'

'She said your apartments ought to be very distinct.'

'That certainly would be best.' And I listened with respect while she told me that up above I was free to take whatever I liked; that there was another staircase, but only from the floor on which we stood, and that to pass from it to the garden-story or to come up to my lodging I should have in effect to cross the great hall. This was an immense point gained; I foresaw that it would constitute my whole leverage in my relations with the two ladies. When I asked Miss Tita how I was to manage at present to find my way up she replied with an access of that sociable shyness which constantly marked her manner.

'Perhaps you can't. I don't see – unless I should go with you.' She evidently had not thought of this before.

We ascended to the upper floor and visited a long succession of empty rooms. The best of them looked over the garden; some of the others had a view of the blue lagoon, above the opposite rough-tiled housetops. They were all dusty and even a little disfigured with long neglect, but I saw that by spending a few hundred francs I should be able to convert three or four of them into a convenient habitation. My experiment was turning out costly, yet now that I had all but taken possession I ceased to allow this to trouble me. I mentioned to my companion a few of the things that I should put in, but she replied rather more precipitately than usual that I might do exactly what I liked; she seemed to wish to notify me that the Misses Bordereau would take no overt interest in my proceedings. I guessed that her aunt had instructed her to adopt this tone, and I may as well say now that I came afterwards to distinguish perfectly (as I believed) between the speeches she made on her own responsibility and those the old lady imposed upon her. She took no notice of the unswept condition of the rooms and indulged in no explanations nor apologies. I said to myself that this was a sign that Juliana and her niece (disenchanting idea!) were untidy persons, with a low Italian standard; but I afterwards recognized that a lodger who had forced an entrance had no *locus standi* as a critic. We looked out of a good many windows, for there was nothing within the rooms to look at, and still I wanted to linger. I asked her what several different objects in the prospect might be, but in no case did she appear to know. She was evidently not familiar with the view – it was as if she had not looked at it for years – and I presently saw that she was too preoccupied with something else to pretend to care for it. Suddenly she said – the remark was not suggested:

'I don't know whether it will make any difference to you, but the money is for me.'

'The money?'

'The money you are going to bring.'

'Why, you'll make me wish to stay here two or three years.' I spoke as benevolently as possible, though it had begun to act on my nerves that with these women so associated with Aspern the pecuniary question should constantly come back.

'That would be very good for me,' she replied, smiling.

'You put me on my honour!'

She looked as if she failed to understand this, but went on: 'She wants me to have more. She thinks she is going to die.'

'Ah, not soon, I hope!' I exclaimed, with genuine feeling. I had perfectly considered the possibility that she would destroy her papers on the day she should feel her end really approach. I believed that she would cling to them till then and I think I had an idea that she read Aspern's letters over every night or at least pressed them to her withered lips. I would have given a good deal to have a glimpse of the latter spectacle. I asked Miss Tita if the old lady were seriously ill and she replied that she was only very tired – she had lived so very, very long. That was what she said herself – she wanted to die for a change. Besides, all her friends were dead long ago; either they ought to have remained or she ought to have gone. That was another thing her aunt often said – she was not at all content.

'But people don't die when they like, do they?' Miss Tita enquired. I took the liberty of asking why, if there was actually enough money to maintain both of them, there would not be more than enough in case of her being left alone. She considered this difficult problem a moment and then she said, 'Oh, well, you know, she takes care of me. She thinks that when I'm alone I shall be a great fool, I shall not know how to manage.'

'I should have supposed rather that you took care of her. I'm afraid she is very proud.'

'Why, have you discovered that already?' Miss Tita cried, with the glimmer of an illumination in her face.

'I was shut up with her there for a considerable time, and she struck me, she interested me extremely. It didn't take me long to make my discovery. She won't have much to say to me while I'm here.'

'No, I don't think she will,' my companion averred.

'Do you suppose she has some suspicion of me?'

Miss Tita's honest eyes gave me no sign that I had touched a mark. 'I shouldn't think so – letting you in after all so easily.'

'Oh, so easily! she had covered her risk. But where is it that one could take an advantage of her?'

'I oughtn't to tell you if I knew, ought I?' and Miss Tita added, before I had time to reply to this, smiling dolefully, 'Do you think we have any weak points?'

'That's exactly what I'm asking. You would only have to mention them for me to respect them religiously.'

She looked at me, at this, with that air of timid but candid and even gratified curiosity with which she had confronted me from the first; and then she said, 'There is nothing to tell. We are terribly quiet. I don't know how the days pass. We have no life.'

'I wish I might think that I should bring you a little.'

'Oh, we know what we want,' she went on. 'It's all right.'

There were various things I desired to ask her: how in the world they did live; whether they had any friends or visitors, any relations in America or in other countries. But I judged such an inquiry would be premature; I must leave it to a later chance. 'Well, don't *you* be proud,' I contented myself with saying. 'Don't hide from me altogether.'

'Oh, I must stay with my aunt,' she returned, without looking at me. And at the same moment, abruptly, without any ceremony of parting, she quitted me and disappeared, leaving me to make my own way downstairs. I remained a while longer, wandering about the bright desert (the sun was pouring in) of the old house, thinking the situation over on the spot. Not even the pattering little *serva* came to look after me and I reflected that after all this treatment showed confidence.

Chapter Four

Perhaps it did, but all the same, six weeks later, towards the middle of June, the moment when Mrs Prest undertook her annual migration, I had made no measurable advance. I was obliged to confess to her that I had no results to speak of. My first step had been unexpectedly rapid, but there was no appearance that it would be followed by a second. I was a thousand miles from taking tea with my hostesses – that privilege of which, as I reminded Mrs Prest, we both had had a vision. She reproached me with wanting boldness and I answered that even to be bold you must have an opportunity: you may push on through a breach but you can't batter down a dead wall.

She answered that the breach I had already made was big enough to admit any army and accused me of wasting precious hours in whimpering in her salon when I ought to have been carrying on the struggle in the field. It is true that I went to see her very often, on the theory that it would console me (I freely expressed my discouragement) for my want of success on my own premises. But I began to perceive that it did not console me to be perpetually chaffed for my scruples, especially when I was really so vigilant; and I was rather glad when my derisive friend closed her house for the summer. She had expected to gather amusement from the drama of my intercourse with the Misses Bordereau and she was disappointed that the intercourse, and consequently the drama, had not come off. 'They'll lead you on to your ruin,' she said before she left Venice. 'They'll get all your money without showing you a scrap.' I think I settled down to my business with more concentration after she had gone away.

It was a fact that up to that time I had not, save on a single brief occasion, had even a moment's contact with my queer hostesses. The exception had occurred when I carried them according to my promise the terrible three thousand francs. They I found Miss Tita waiting for me in the hall, and she took the money from my hand so that I did not see her aunt. The old lady had promised to receive me, but she apparently thought nothing of breaking that vow. The money was contained in a bag of chamois leather, of respectable dimensions, which my banker had given me, and Miss Tita had to make a big fist to receive it. This she did with extreme solemnity, though I tried to treat the affair a little as a joke. It was in no jocular strain, yet it was with simplicity, that she inquired, weighing the money in her two palms: 'Don't you think it's too much?' To which I replied that that would depend upon the amount of pleasure I should get for it. Hereupon she turned away from me quickly, as she had done the day before, murmuring in a tone different from any she had used hitherto: 'Oh, pleasure, pleasure – there's no pleasure in this house!'

After this, for a long time, I never saw her, and I wondered that the common chances of the day should not have helped us to meet. It could only be evident that she was immensely on her guard against them; and in addition to this the house was so big that for each other we were lost in it. I used to look out for her hopefully as I crossed the sala in my comings and goings, but I was not rewarded with a glimpse of the tail of her dress. It was as if she never peeped out of her aunt's apartment. I used to wonder what she did there week after week and year after year. I had never encountered such a violent *parti pris* of seclusion; it was more than keeping quiet – it was like hunted creatures feigning death. The two ladies appeared to have no visitors whatever and no sort of contact with the world. I judged at least that people could not have come to the house and that Miss Tita could not have gone out without my having some observation of it. I did what I disliked myself for doing (reflecting that it was only once in a way): I questioned my servant about their habits and let him divine that I should be interested in any information he could pick up. But he picked up amazingly little for a knowing Venetian; it must be added that where there is a perpetual fast there are very few crumbs on the floor. His cleverness in other ways was sufficient if it was not quite all that I had attributed to him on the occasion of my first interview with Miss Tita. He had helped my gondolier to bring me round a boat-load of furniture; and when these articles had been carried to the top of the palace and distributed according to our associated wisdom he organized my household with such promptitude as was consistent with the fact that it was composed exclusively of himself. He made me in short as comfortable as I could be with my indifferent prospects. I should have been glad if he had fallen in love with Miss Bordereau's maid or, failing this, had taken her in aversion; either event might have brought about some kind of catastrophe and a catastrophe might have led to some parley. It was my idea that she would have been sociable, and I myself on various occasions saw her flit to and fro on domestic errands, so that I was sure she was accessible. But I tasted of no gossip from that fountain, and I afterwards learned that Pasquale's affections were fixed upon an object that made him heedless of other women. This was a young lady with a powdered face, a yellow cotton gown and much leisure, who used often to come to see him. She practised, at her convenience, the art of a stringer of beads (these ornaments are made in Venice, in profusion; she had her pocket full of them and I used to find them on the floor of my apartment), and kept an eye on the maiden in the house. It was not for me of course to make the domestics tattle, and I never said a word to Miss Bordereau's cook.

It seemed to me a proof of the old lady's determination to have nothing to do with me that she should never have sent me a receipt for my three months' rent. For some days I looked out for it and then, when I had given it up, I wasted a good deal of time in wondering what her reason had been for neglecting so indispensable and familiar a form. At first I was tempted to send her a reminder, after which I relinquished the idea (against my judgement as to what was right in the particular case), on the general ground of wishing to keep quiet. If Miss Bordereau suspected me of ulterior aims, she would suspect me less if I should be businesslike, and yet I consented not to be so. It was possible she intended her omission as an impertinence, a visible irony, to show how she could overreach people who attempted to overreach her. On that hypothesis it was well to let her see that one did not notice her little tricks. The real reading of the matter, I afterwards perceived, was simply the poor old woman's desire to emphasize the fact that I was in the enjoyment of a favour as rigidly limited as it had been liberally bestowed. She had given me part of her house and now she would not give me even a morsel of paper with her name on it. Let me say that even at first this did not make me too miserable, for the whole episode was essentially delightful to me. I foresaw that I should have a summer after my own literary heart, and the sense of holding my opportunity was much greater than the sense of losing it. There could be no Venetian business without patience, and since I adored the place I was much more in the spirit of it for having laid in a large provision. That spirit kept me perpetual company and seemed to look out at me from the revived immortal face – in which all his genius shone – of the great poet who was my prompter. I had invoked him and he had come; he hovered before me half the time; it was as if his bright ghost had returned to earth to tell me that he regarded the affair as his own no less than mine and that we should see it fraternally, cheerfully to a conclusion. It was as if he had said, 'Poor dear, be easy with her; she had some natural prejudices; only give her time. Strange as it may appear to you she was very attractive in 1820. Meanwhile are we not in Venice together, and what better place is there for the meeting of dear friends? See how it glows with the advancing summer; how the sky and the sea and the rosy air and the marble of the palaces all shimmer and melt together.' My eccentric private errand became a part of the general romance and the general glory – I felt even a mystic companionship, a moral fraternity with all those who in the past had been in the service of art. They had worked for beauty, for a devotion; and what else was I doing? That element was in everything that Jeffrey Aspern had written and I was only bringing it to the light.

I lingered in the sala when I went to and fro; I used to watch – as long as I thought decent – the door that led to Miss Bordereau's part of the house. A person observing me might have supposed I was trying to cast a spell upon it or attempting some odd experiment in hypnotism. But I was only praying it would open or thinking what treasure probably lurked behind it. I hold it singular, as I look back, that I should never have doubted for a moment that the sacred relics were there; never have failed to feel a certain joy at being under the same roof with them. After all they were under my hand – they had not escaped me yet; and they made my life continuous, in a fashion, with the illustrious life they had touched at the other end. I lost myself in this satisfaction to the point of assuming – in my quiet extravagance – that poor Miss Tita also went back, went back, as I used to phrase it. She did indeed, the gentle spinster, but not quite so far as Jeffrey Aspern, who was simple hearsay to her, quite as he was to me. Only she had lived for years with Juliana, she had seen and handled the papers and (even though she was stupid) some esoteric knowledge had rubbed off on her. That was what the old woman represented – esoteric knowledge; and this was the idea with which my editorial heart used to thrill. It literally beat faster often, of an evening, when I had been out, as I stopped with my candle in the re-echoing hall on my way up to bed. It was as if at such a moment as that, in the stillness, after the long contradiction of the day, Miss Bordereau's secrets were in the air, the wonder of her survival more palpable. These were the acute impressions. I had them in another form, with more of a certain sort of reciprocity, during the hours that I sat in the garden looking up over the top of my book at the closed windows of my hostess. In these windows no sign of life ever appeared; it was as if, for fear of my catching a glimpse of them, the two ladies passed their days in the dark. But this only proved to me that they had something to conceal; which was what I had wished to demonstrate. Their motionless shutters became as expressive as eyes consciously closed, and I took comfort in thinking that at all events though invisible themselves they saw me between the lashes.

I made a point of spending as much time as possible in the garden, to justify the picture I had originally given of my horticultural passion. And I not only spent time, but (hang it! as I said) I spent money. As soon as I had got my rooms arranged and could give the proper thought to the matter I surveyed the place with a clever expert and made terms for having it put in order. I was sorry to do this, for personally I liked it better as it was, with its weeds and its wild, rough tangle, its sweet, characteristic Venetian shabbiness. I had to be consistent, to keep my promise that I would smother the house in flowers. Moreover I formed this graceful project that by flowers I would make my way – I would succeed by big nosegays. I would batter the old women with lilies – I would bombard their citadel with roses. Their door would have to yield to the pressure when a mountain of carnations should be piled up against it. The place in truth had been brutally neglected. The Venetian capacity for dawdling is of the largest, and for a good many days unlimited litter was all my gardener had to show for his ministrations. There was a great digging of holes and carting about of earth, and after a while I grew so impatient that I had thoughts of sending for my bouquets to the nearest stand. But I reflected that the ladies would see through the chinks of their shutters that they must have been bought and might make up their minds from this that I was a humbug. So I composed myself and finally, though the delay was long, perceived some appearances of bloom. This encouraged me and I waited serenely enough till they multiplied. Meanwhile the real summer days arrived and began to pass, and as I look back upon them they seem to me almost the happiest of my life. I took more and more care to be in the garden whenever it was not too hot. I had an arbour arranged and a low table and an armchair put into it; and I carried out books and portfolios (I had always some business of writing in hand), and worked and waited and mused and hoped, while the golden hours elapsed and the plants drank in the light and the inscrutable old palace turned pale and then, as the day waned, began to flush in it and my papers rustled in the wandering breeze of the Adriatic.

Considering how little satisfaction I got from it at first it is remarkable that I should not have grown more tired of wondering what mystic rites of ennui the Misses Bordereau celebrated in their darkened rooms; whether this had always been the tenor of their life and how in previous years they had escaped elbowing their neigbours. It was clear that they must have had other habits and other circumstances; that they must once have been young or at least middle-aged. There was no end to the questions it was possible to ask about them and no end to the answers it was not possible to frame. I had known many of my country-people in Europe and was familiar with the strange ways they were liable to take up there; but the Misses Bordereau formed altogether a new type of the American absentee. Indeed it was plain that the American name had ceased to have any application to them – I had seen this in the ten minutes I spent in the old woman's room. You could never have said whence they came, from the appearance of either of them; wherever it was they had long ago dropped the local accent and fashion. There was nothing in them that one recognized, and putting the question of speech aside they might have been Norwegians or Spaniards. Miss Bordereau, after all, had been in Europe nearly threequarters of a century; it appeared by some verses addressed to her by Aspern on the occasion of his own second absence from America – verses of which Cumnor and I had after infinite conjecture established solidly enough the date – that she was even then, as a girl of twenty, on the foreign side of the sea. There was an implication in the poem (I hope not just for the phrase) that he had come back for her sake. We had no real light upon her circumstances at that moment, any more than we had upon her origin, which we believed to be of the sort usually spoken of as modest. Cumnor had a theory that she had been a governess in some family in which the poet visited and that, in consequence of her position, there was from the first something unavowed, or rather something positively clandestine, in their relations. I on the other hand had hatched a little romance according to which she was the daughter of an artist, a painter or a sculptor, who had left the western world when the century was fresh, to study in the ancient schools. It was essential to my hypothesis that this amiable man should have lost his wife, should have been poor and unsuccessful and should have had a second daughter, of a disposition quite different from Juliana's. It was also indispensable that he should have been accompanied to Europe by these young ladies and should have established himself there for the remainder of a struggling, saddened life. There was a further implication that Miss Bordereau had had in her youth a perverse and adventurous, albeit a generous and fascinating character, and that she had passed through some singular vicissitudes. By what passions had she been ravaged, by what sufferings had she been blanched, what store of memories had she laid away for the monotonous future?

I asked myself these things as I sat spinning theories about her in my arbour and the bees droned in the flowers. It was incontestable that, whether for right or for wrong, most readers of certain of Aspern's poems (poems not as ambiguous as the sonnets – scarcely more divine, I think – of Shakespeare) had taken for granted that Juliana had not always adhered to the steep footway of renunciation. There hovered about her name a perfume of reckless passion, an intimation that she had not been exactly as the respectable young person in general. Was this a sign that her singer had betrayed her, had given her away, as we say nowadays, to posterity? Certain it is that it would have been difficult to put one's finger on the passage in which her fair fame suffered an imputation. Moreover was not any fame fair enough that was so sure of duration and was associated with works immortal through their beauty? It was a part of my idea that the young lady had had a foreign lover (and an unedifying tragical rupture) before her meeting with Jeffrey Aspern. She had lived with her father and sister in a queer old-fashioned, expatriated, artistic Bohemia, in the days when the aesthetic was only the academic and the painters who knew the best models for a *contadina* and *pifferaro* wore peaked hats and long hair. It was a society less furnished than the coteries of today (in its ignorance of the wonderful chances, the opportunities of the early bird, with which its path was strewn), with tatters of old stuff and fragments of old crockery; so that Miss Bordereau appeared not to have picked up or have inherited many objects of importance. There was no enviable bric-à-brac, with its provoking legend of cheapness, in the room in which I had seen her. Such a fact as that suggested bareness, but none the less it worked happily into the sentimental interest I had always taken in the early movements of my countrymen as visitors to Europe. When Americans went abroad in 1820 there was something romantic, almost heroic in it, as compared with the perpetual ferryings of the present hour, when photography and other conveniences have annihilated surprise. Miss Bordereau sailed with her family on a tossing brig, in the days of long voyages and sharp differences; she had her emotions on the top of yellow diligences, passed the night at inns where she dreamed of travellers' tales, and was struck, on reaching the eternal city, with the elegance of Roman pearls and scarfs. There was something touching to me in all that and my imagination frequently went back to the period. If Miss Bordereau carried it there of course Jeffrey Aspern at other times had done so a great deal more. It was a much more important fact, if one were looking at his genius critically, that he had lived in the days before the general transfusion. It had happened to me to regret that he had known Europe at all; I should have liked to see what he would have written without that experience, by which he had incontestably been enriched. But as his fate had ordered otherwise I went with him – I tried to judge how the old world would have struck him. It was not only there, however, that I watched him; the relations he had entertained with the new had even a livelier interest. His own country after all had had most of his life, and his muse, as they said at that time, was essentially American. That was originally what I had loved him for: that at a period when our native land was nude and crude and provincial, when the famous 'atmosphere' it is supposed to lack was not even missed, when literature was lonely there and art and form almost impossible, he had found means to live and write like one of the first; to be free and general and not at all afraid; to feel, understand and express everything.

Chapter Five

I was seldom at home in the evening, for when I attempted to occupy myself in my apartments the lamplight brought in a swarm of noxious insects, and it was too hot for closed windows. Accordingly I spent the late hours either on the water (the moonlight of Venice is famous), or in the splendid square which serves as a vast forecourt to the strange old basilica of Saint Mark. I sat in front of Florian's *café*, eating ices, listening to music, talking with acquaintances: the traveller will remember how the immense cluster of tables and little chairs stretches like a promontory into the smooth lake of the Piazza. The whole place, of a summer's evening, under the stars and with all the lamps, all the voices and light footsteps on marble (the only sounds of the arcades that enclose it), is like an open-air saloon dedicated to cooling drinks and to a still finer degustation – that of the exquisite impressions received during the day. When I did not prefer to keep mine to myself there was always a stray tourist, disencumbered of his Bädeker, to discuss them with, or some domesticated painter rejoicing in the return of the season of strong effects. The wonderful church, with its low domes and bristling embroideries, the mystery of its mosaic and sculpture, looked ghostly in the tempered gloom, and the sea-breeze passed between the twin columns of the Piazzetta, the lintels of a door no longer guarded, as gently as if a rich curtain were swaying there. I used sometimes on these occasions to think of the Misses Bordereau and of the pity of their being shut up in apartments which in the Venetian July even Venetian vastness did not prevent from being stuffy. Their life seemed miles away from the life of the Piazza, and no doubt it was really too late to make the austere Juliana change her habits. But poor Miss Tita would have enjoyed one of Florian's ices, I was sure; sometimes I even had thoughts of carrying one home to her. Fortunately my patience bore fruit and I was not obliged to do anything so ridiculous.

One evening about the middle of July I came in earlier than usual – I forget what chance had led to this – and instead of going up to my quarters made my way into the garden. The temperature was very high; it was such a night as one would gladly have spent in the open air and I was in no hurry to go to bed. I had floated home in my gondola, listening to the slow splash of the oar in the narrow dark canals, and now the only thought that solicited me was the vague reflection that it would be pleasant to recline at one's length in the fragrant darkness on a garden bench. The odour of the canal was doubtless at the bottom of that aspiration and the breath of the garden, as I entered it, gave consistency to my purpose. It was delicious – just such an air as must have trembled with Romeo's vows when he stood among the flowers and raised his arms to his mistress's balcony. I looked at the windows of the palace to see if by chance the example of Verona (Verona being not far off) had been followed; but everything was dim, as usual, and everything was still. Juliana, on summer nights in her youth, might have murmured down from open windows at Jeffrey Aspern, but Miss Tita was not a poet's mistress any more than I was a poet. This however did not prevent my gratification from being great as I became aware on reaching the end of the garden that Miss Tita was seated in my little bower. At first I only made out an indistinct figure, not in the least counting on such an overture from one of my hostesses; it even occurred to me that some sentimental maid-servant had stolen in to keep a tryst with her sweetheart. I was going to turn away, not to frighten her, when the figure rose to its height and I recognized Miss Bordereau's niece. I must do myself the justice to say that I did not wish to frighten her either, and much as I had longed for some such accident I should have been capable of retreating. It was as if I had laid a trap for her by coming home earlier than usual and adding to that eccentricity by creeping into the garden. As she rose she spoke to me, and then I reflected that perhaps, secure in my almost inveterate absence, it was her nightly practice to take a lonely airing. There was no trap, in truth, because I had had no suspicion. At first I took for granted that the words she uttered expressed discomfiture at my arrival; but as she repeated them – I had not caught them clearly – I had the surprise of hearing her say, 'Oh, dear, I'm so very glad you've come!' She and her aunt had in common the property of unexpected speeches. She came out of the arbour almost as if she were going to throw herself into my arms.

I hasten to add that she did nothing of the kind; she did not even shake hands with me. It was a gratification to her to see me and presently she told my why – because she was nervous when she was out of doors at night alone. The plants and bushes looked so strange in the dark, and there were all sorts of queer sounds she could not tell what they were – like the noises of animals. She stood close to me, looking about her with an air of greater security but without any demonstration of interest in me as an individual. Then I guessed that nocturnal prowlings were not in the least her habit, and I was also reminded (I had been struck with the circumstance in talking with her before I took possession) that it was impossible to over-estimate her simplicity.

'You speak as if you were lost in the backwoods,' I said, laughing. 'How you manage to keep out of this charming place when you have only three steps to take to get into it, is more than I have yet been able to discover. You hide away mighty well so long as I am on the premises, I know; but I had a hope that you peeped out a little at other times. You and your poor aunt are worse off than Carmelite nuns in their cells. Should you mind telling me how you exist without air, without exercise, without any sort of human contact? I don't see how you carry on the common business of life.'

She looked at me as if I were talking some strange tongue and her answer was so little of an answer that I was considerably irritated. 'We go to bed very early – earlier than you would believe.' I was on the point of saying that this only deepened the mystery when she gave me some relief by adding, 'Before you came we were not so private. But I never have been out at night.'

'Never in these fragrant alleys, blooming here under your nose?'

'Ah,' said Miss Tita, 'they were never nice till now!' There was an unmistakable reference in this and a flattering comparison, so that it seemed to me I had gained a small advantage. As it would help me to follow it up to establish a sort of grievance I asked her why, since she thought my garden nice, she had never thanked me in any way for the flowers I had been sending up in such quantities for the previous three weeks. I had not been discouraged – there had been, as she would have observed, a daily armful; but I had been brought up in the common forms and a word of recognition now and then would have touched me in the right place.

'Why I didn't know they were for me!'

'They were for both of you. Why should I make a difference?'

Miss Tita reflected as if she might be thinking of a reason for that, but she failed to produce one. Instead of this she asked abruptly, 'Why in the world do you want to know us?'

'I ought after all to make a difference,' I replied. 'That question is your aunt's; it isn't yours. You wouldn't ask it if you hadn't been put up to it.'

'She didn't tell me to ask you,' Miss Tita replied, without confusion; she was the oddest mixture of the shrinking and the direct.

'Well, she has often wondered about it herself and expressed her wonder to you. She has insisted on it, so that she has put the idea into your head that I am unsufferably pushing. Upon my word I think I have been very discreet. And how completely your aunt must have lost every tradition of sociability, to see anything out of the way in the idea that respectable intelligent people, living as we do under the same roof, should occasionally exchange a remark! What could be more natural? We are of the same country and we have at least some of the same tastes, since, like you, I am intensely fond of Venice.'

My interlocutress appeared incapable of grasping more than one clause in any proposition, and she declared quickly, eagerly, as if she were answering my whole speech: 'I am not in the least fond of Venice. I should like to go far away!'

'Has she always kept you back so?' I went on, to show her that I could be as irrelevant as herself.

'She told me to come out tonight; she has told me very often,' said Miss Tita. 'It is I who wouldn't come. I don't like to leave her.'

'Is she too weak, is she failing?' I demanded, with more emotion, I think, than I intended to show. I judged this by the way her eyes rested upon me in the darkness. It embarrassed me a little, and to turn the matter off I continued genially: 'Do let us sit down together comfortably somewhere and you will tell me all about her.'

Miss Tita made no resistance to this. We found a bench less secluded, less confidential, as it were, than the one in the arbour; and we were still sitting there when I heard midnight ring out from those clear bells of Venice which vibrate with a solemnity of their own over the lagoon and hold the air so much more than the chimes of other places. We were together more than an hour and our interview gave, as it struck me, a great lift to my undertaking. Miss Tita accepted the situation without a protest; she had avoided me for three months, yet now she treated me almost as if these three months had made me an old friend. If I had chosen I might have inferred from this that though she had avoided me she had given a good deal of consideration to doing so. She paid no attention to the flight of time – never worried at my keeping her so long away from her aunt. She talked freely, answering questions and asking them and not even taking advantage of certain longish pauses with which they inevitably alternated to say she thought she had better go in. It was almost as if she were waiting for something – something I might say to her – and intended to give me my opportunity. I was the more struck by this as she told me that her aunt had been less well for a good many days and in a way that was rather new. She was weaker; at moments it seemed as if she had no strength at all; yet more than ever before she wished to be left alone. That was why she had told her to come out – not even to remain in her own room, which was alongside; she said her niece irritated her, made her nervous. She sat still for hours together, as if she were asleep; she had always done that, musing and dozing; but at such times formerly she gave at intervals some small sign of life, of interest, liking her companion to be near her with her work. Miss Tita confided to me that at present her aunt was so motionless that she sometimes feared she was dead; moreover she took hardly any food – one couldn't see what she lived on. The great thing was that she still on most days got up; the serious job was to dress her, to wheel her out of her bedroom. She clung to as many of her old habits as possible and she had always, little company as they had received for years, made a point of sitting in the parlour.

I scarcely knew what to think of all this – of Miss Tita's sudden conversion to sociability and of the strange circumstance that the more the old lady appeared to decline towards her end the less she should desire to be looked after. The story did not hang together, and I even asked myself whether it were not a trap laid for me, the result of a design to make me show my hand. I could not have told why my companions (as they could only by courtesy be called) should have this purpose – why they should try to trip up so lucrative a lodger. At any rate I kept on my guard, so that Miss Tita should not have occasion again to ask me if I had an *arrière-pensée*. Poor woman, before we parted for the night my mind was at rest as to *her* capacity for entertaining one.

She told me more about their affairs than I had hoped; there was no need to be prying, for it evidently drew her out simply to feel that I listened, that I cared. She ceased wondering why I cared, and at last, as she spoke of the brilliant life they had led years before, she almost chattered. It was Miss Tita who judged it brilliant; she said that when they first came to live in Venice, years and years before (I saw that her mind was essentially vague about dates and the order in which events had occurred), there was scarcely a week that they had not some visitor or did not make some delightful *passeggio* in the city. They had seen all the curiosities; they had even been to the Lido in a boat (she spoke as if I might think there was a way on foot); they had had a collation there, brought in three baskets and spread out on the grass. I asked her what people they had known and she said, Oh! very nice ones – the Cavaliere Bombicci and the Contessa Altemura, with whom they had had a great friendship. Also English people – the Churtons and the Goldies and Mrs Stock-Stock, whom they had loved dearly; she was dead and gone, poor dear. That was the case with most of their pleasant circle (this expression was Miss Tita's own), though a few were left, which was a wonder considering how they had neglected them. She mentioned the names of two or three Venetian old women; of a certain doctor, very clever, who was so kind – he came as a friend, he had really given up practice; of the *avvocato* Pochintesta, who wrote beautiful poems and had addressed one to her aunt. These people came to see them without fail every year, usually at the *capo d'anno,* and of old her aunt used to make them some little present – her aunt and she together: small things that she, Miss Tita, made herself, like paper lamp-shades or mats for the decanters of wine at dinner or those woollen things that in cold weather were worn on the wrists. The last few years there had not been many presents; she could not think what to make and her aunt had lost her interest and never suggested. But the people came all the same; if the Venetians liked you once they liked you for ever.

There was something affecting in the good faith of this sketch of former social glories; the picnic at the Lido had remained vivid through the ages and poor Miss Tita evidently was of the impression that she had had a brilliant youth. She had in fact had a glimpse of the Venetian world in its gossiping, home-keeping, parsimonious, professional walks; for I observed for the first time that she had acquired by contact something of the trick of the familiar, soft-sounding, almost infantile speech of the place. I judged that she had imbibed this invertebrate dialect, from the natural way the names of things and people – mostly purely local – rose to her lips. If she knew little of what they represented she knew still less of anything else. Her aunt had drawn in – her failing interest in the table-mats and lamp-shades was a sign of that – and she had not been able to mingle in society or to entertain it alone; so that the matter of her reminiscences struck one as an old world altogether. If she had not been so decent her references would have seemed to carry one back to the queer rococo Venice of Casanova. I found myself falling into the error of thinking of her too as one of Jeffrey Aspern's contemporaries; this came from her having so little in common with my own. It was possible, I said to myself, that she had not even heard of him; it might very well be that Juliana had not cared to lift even for her the veil that covered the temple of her youth. In this case she perhaps would not know of the existence of the papers, and I welcomed that presumption – it made me feel more safe with her – until I remembered that we had believed the letter of disavowal received by Cumnor to be in the handwriting of the niece. If it had been dictated to her she had of course to know what it was about; yet after all the effect of it was to repudiate the idea of any connection with the poet. I held it probable at all events that Miss Tita had not read a word of his poetry. Moreover if, with her companion, she had always escaped the interviewer there was little occasion for her having got it into her head that people were 'after' the letters. People had not been after them, inasmuch as they had not heard of them; and Cumnor's fruitless feeler would have been a solitary accident.

When midnight sounded Miss Tita got up; but she stopped at the door of the house only after she had wandered two or three times with me round the garden. 'When shall I see you again?' I asked, before she went in; to which she replied with promptness that she should like to come out the next night. She added however that she should not come – she was so far from doing everything she liked.

'You might do a few things that *I* like,' I said with a sigh.

'Oh, you – I don't believe you!' she murmured, at this, looking at me with her simple solemnity.

'Why don't you believe me?'

'Because I don't understand you.'

'That is just the sort of occasion to have faith.' I could not say more, though I should have liked to, as I saw that I only mystified her; for I had no wish to have it on my conscience that I might pass for having made love to her. Nothing less should I have seemed to do had I continued to beg a lady to 'believe in me' in an Italian garden on a midsummer night. There was some merit in my scruples, for Miss Tita lingered and lingered: I perceived that she felt that she should not really soon come down again and wished therefore to protract the present. She insisted too on making the talk between us personal to ourselves; and altogether her behaviour was such as would have been possible only to a completely innocent woman.

'I shall like the flowers better now that I know they are also meant for me.'

'How could you have doubted it? If you will tell me the kind you like best I will send a double lot of them.'

'Oh, I like them all best!' Then she went on, familiarly: 'Shall you study – shall you read and write – when you go up to your rooms?'

'I don't do that at night, at this season. The lamplight brings in the animals.'

'You might have known that when you came.'

'I did know it!'

'And in winter do you work at night?'

'I read a good deal, but I don't often write.' She listened as if these details had a rare interest, and suddenly a temptation quite at variance with the prudence I had been teaching myself associated itself with her plain, mild face. Ah yes, she was safe and I could make her safer! It seemed to me from one moment to another that I could not wait longer – that I really must take a sounding. So I went on: 'In general before I go to sleep – very often in bed (it's a bad habit, but I confess to it), I read some great poet. In nine cases out of ten it's a volume of Jeffrey Aspern.'

I watched her well as I pronounced that name but I saw nothing wonderful. Why should I indeed – was not Jeffrey Aspern the property of the human race?

'Oh, we read him – we *have* read him,' she quietly replied.

'He is my poet of poets – I know him almost by heart.'

For an instant Miss Tita hesitated; then her sociability was too much for her.

'Oh, by heart – that's nothing!' she murmured, smiling. 'My aunt used to know him – to know him' – she paused an instant and I wondered what she was going to say – 'to know him as a visitor.'

'As a visitor?' I repeated, staring.

'He used to call on her and take her out.'

I continued to stare. 'My dear lady, he died a hundred years ago!'

'Well,' she said, mirthfully, 'my aunt is a hundred and fifty.'

'Mercy on us!' I exclaimed; 'why didn't you tell me before? I should like so to ask her about him.'

'She wouldn't care for that – she wouldn't tell you,' Miss Tita replied.

'I don't care what she cares for! She *must* tell me – it's not a chance to be lost.'

'Oh, you should have come twenty years ago: then she still talked about him.'

'And what did she say?' I asked, eagerly.

'I don't know – that he liked her immensely.'

'And she – didn't like him?'

'She said he was a god.' Miss Tita gave me this information flatly, without expression; her tone might have made it a piece of trivial gossip. But it stirred me deeply as she dropped the words into the summer night; it seemed such a direct testimony.

'Fancy, fancy!' I murmured. And then, 'Tell me this, please – has she got a portrait of him? They are distressingly rare.'

'A portrait? I don't know,' said Miss Tita; and now there was discomfiture in her face. 'Well, good-night!' she added; and she turned into the house.

I accompanied her into the wide, dusky, stone-paved passage which on the ground floor corresponded with our grand sala. It opened at one end into the garden, at the other upon the canal, and was lighted now only by the small lamp that was always left for me to take up as I went to bed. An extinguished candle which Miss Tita apparently had brought down with her stood on the same table with it. 'Good-night, good-night!' I replied, keeping beside her as she went to get her light. 'Surely you would know, shouldn't you, if she had one?'

'If she had what?' the poor lady asked, looking at me queerly over the flame of her candle.

'A portrait of the god. I don't know what I wouldn't give to see it.'

'I don't know what she has got. She keeps her things locked up.' And Miss Tita went away, towards the staircase, with the sense evidently that she had said too much.

I let her go – I wished not to frighten her – and I contented myself with remarking that Miss Bordereau would not have locked up such a glorious possession as that – a thing a person would be proud of and hang up in a prominent place on the parlour-wall. Therefore of course she had not any portrait. Miss Tita made no direct answer to this and candle in hand, with her back to me, ascended two or three stairs. Then she stopped short and turned round looking at me across the dusky space.

'Do you write – do you write?' There was a shake in her voice – she could scarcely bring out what she wanted to ask.

'Do I write? Oh, don't speak of my writing on the same day with Aspern's!'

'Do you write about *him* – do you pry into his life?'

'Ah, that's your aunt's question; it can't be yours!' I said, in a tone of slightly wounded sensibility.

'All the more reason then that you should answer it. Do you, please?'

I thought I had allowed for the falsehoods I should have to tell; but I found that in fact when it came to the point I had not. Besides, now that I had an opening there was a kind of relief in being frank. Lastly (it was perhaps fanciful, even fatuous), I guessed that Miss Tita personally would not in the last resort be less my friend. So after a moment's hesitation I answered, 'Yes, I have written about him and I am looking for more material. In heaven's name have you got any?'

'Santo Dio!' she exclaimed, without heeding my question; and she hurried upstairs and out of sight. I might count upon her in the last resort, but for the present she was visibly alarmed. The proof of it was that she began to hide again, so that for a fortnight I never beheld her. I found my patience ebbing and after four or five days of this I told the gardener to stop the flowers.

Chapter Six

One afternoon, as I came down from my quarters to go out, I found Miss Tita in the sala: it was our first encounter on that ground since I had come to the house. She put on no air of being there by accident; there was an ignorance of such arts in her angular, diffident directness. That I might be quite sure she was waiting for me she informed me of the fact and told me that Miss Bordereau wished to see me: she would take me into the room at that moment if I had time. If I had been late for a love-tryst I would have stayed for this, and I quickly signified that I should be delighted to wait upon the old lady. 'She wants to talk with you – to know you,' Miss Tita said, smiling as if she herself appreciated that idea; and she led me to the door of her aunt's apartment. I stopped her a moment before she had opened it, looking at her with some curiosity. I told her that this was a great satisfaction to me and a great honour; but all the same I should like to ask what had made Miss Bordereau change so suddenly. It was only the other day that she wouldn't suffer me near her. Miss Tita was not embarrassed by my question; she had as many little unexpected serenities as if she told fibs, but the odd part of them was that they had on the contrary their source in her truthfulness. 'Oh, my aunt changes,' she answered; 'it's so terribly dull – I suppose she's tired.'

'But you told me that she wanted more and more to be alone.'

Poor Miss Tita coloured, as if she found me over-insistent. 'Well, if you don't believe she wants to see you – I haven't invented it! I think people often are capricious when they are very old.'

'That's perfectly true. I only wanted to be clear as to whether you have repeated to her what I told you the other night.'

'What you told me?'

'About Jeffrey Aspern – that I am looking for materials.'

'If I had told her do you think she would have sent for you?'

'That's exactly what I want to know. If she wants to keep him to herself she might have sent for me to tell me so.'

'She won't speak of him,' said Miss Tita. Then as she opened the door she added in a lower tone, 'I have told her nothing.'

The old woman was sitting in the same place in which I had seen her last, in the same position, with the same mystifying bandage over her eyes. Her welcome was to turn her almost invisible face to me and show me that while she sat silent she saw me clearly. I made no motion to shake hands with her; I felt too well on this occasion that that was out of place for ever. It had been sufficiently enjoined upon me that she was too sacred for that sort of reciprocity – too venerable to touch. There was something so grim in her aspect (it was partly the accident of her green shade), as I stood there to be measured, that I ceased on the spot to feel any doubt as to her knowing my secret, though I did not in the least suspect that Miss Tita had not just spoken the truth. She had not betrayed me, but the old woman's brooding instinct had served her; she had turned me over and over in the long, still hours and she had guessed. The worst of it was that she looked terribly like an old woman who at a pinch would burn her papers. Miss Tita pushed a chair forward, saying to me, 'This will be a good place for you to sit.' As I took possession of it I asked after Miss Bordereau's health; expressed the hope that in spite of the very hot weather it was satisfactory. She replied that it was good enough – good enough; that it was a great thing to be alive.

'Oh, as to that, it depends upon what you compare it with!' I exclaimed, laughing.

'I don't compare – I don't compare. If I did that I should have given everything up long ago.'

I liked to think that this was a subtle allusion to the rapture she had known in the society of Jeffrey Aspern – though it was true that such an allusion would have accorded ill with the wish I imputed to her to keep him buried in her soul. What it accorded with was my constant conviction that no human being had ever had a more delightful social gift than his, and what it seemed to convey was that nothing in the world was worth speaking of if one pretended to speak of that. But one did not! Miss Tita sat down beside her aunt, looking as if she had reason to believe some very remarkable conversation would come off between us.

'It's about the beautiful flowers,' said the old lady; 'you sent us so many – I ought to have thanked you for them before. But I don't write letters and I receive only at long intervals.'

She had not thanked me while the flowers continued to come, but she departed from her custom so far as to send for me as soon as she began to fear that they would not come any more. I noted this; I remembered what an acquisitive propensity she had shown when it was a question of extracting gold from me, and I privately rejoiced at the happy thought I had had in suspending my tribute. She had missed it and she was willing to make a concession to bring it back. At the first sign of this concession I could only go to meet her. 'I am afraid you have not had many, of late, but they shall begin again immediately – tomorrow, tonight.'

'Oh, do send us some tonight!' Miss Tita cried, as if it were an immense circumstance.

'What else should you do with them? It isn't a manly taste to make a bower of your room,' the old woman remarked.

'I don't make a bower of my room, but I am exceedingly fond of growing flowers, of watching their ways. There is nothing unmanly in that: it has been the amusement of philosophers, of statesmen in retirement; even I think of great captains.'

'I suppose you know you can sell them – those you don't use,' Miss Bordereau went on. 'I dare say they wouldn't give you much for them; still you could make a bargain.'

'Oh, I have never made a bargain, as you ought to know. My gardener disposes of them and I ask no questions.'

'I would ask a few, I can promise you!' said Miss Bordereau; and it was the first time I had heard her laugh. I could not get used to the idea that this vision of pecuniary profit was what drew out the divine Juliana most.

'Come into the garden yourself and pick them; come as often as you like; come every day. They are all for you,' I pursued, addressing Miss Tita and carrying off this veracious statement by treating it as an innocent joke. 'I can't imagine why she doesn't come down,' I added, for Miss Bordereau's benefit.

'You must make her come; you must come up and fetch her,' said the old woman, to my stupefaction. 'That odd thing you have made in the corner would be a capital place for her to sit.'

The allusion to my arbour was irreverent; it confirmed the impression I had already received that there was a flicker of impertinence in Miss Bordereau's talk, a strange mocking lambency which must have been a part of her adventurous youth and which had outlived passions and faculties. None the less I asked, 'Wouldn't it be possible for you to come down there yourself? Wouldn't it do you good to sit there in the shade, in the sweet air?'

'Oh, sir, when I move out of this it won't be to sit in the air, and I'm afraid that any that may be stirring around me won't be particularly sweet! It will be a very dark shade indeed. But that won't be just yet,' Miss Bordereau continued, cannily, as if to correct any hopes that this courageous allusion to the last receptacle of her mortality might lead me to entertain. 'I have sat here many a day and I have had enough of arbours in my time. But I'm not afraid to wait till I'm called.'

Miss Tita had expected some interesting talk, but perhaps she found it less genial on her aunt's side (considering that I had been sent for with a civil intention) than she had hoped. As if to give the conversation a turn that would put our companion in a light more favourable she said to me, 'Didn't I tell you the other night that she had sent me out? You see that I can do what I like!'

'Do you pity her – do you teach her to pity herself?' Miss Bordereau demanded, before I had time to answer this appeal. 'She has a much easier life than I had when I was her age.'

'You must remember that it has been quite open to me to think you rather inhuman.'

'Inhuman? That's what the poets used to call the women a hundred years ago. Don't try that; you won't do as well as they!' Juliana declared. 'There is no more poetry in the world – that I know of at least. But I won't bandy words with you,' she pursued, and I well remember the old-fashioned, artificial sound she gave to the speech. 'You have made me talk, talk! It isn't good for me at all.' I got up at this and told her I would take no more of her time; but she detained me to ask, 'Do you remember, the day I saw you about the rooms, that you offered us the use of your gondola?' And when I assented, promptly, struck again with her disposition to make a 'good thing' of being there and wondering what she now had in her eye, she broke out, 'Why don't you take that girl out in it and show her the place?'

'Oh dear aunt, what do you want to do with me?' cried the 'girl', with a piteous quaver. 'I know all about the place!'

'Well then, go with him as a cicerone!' said Miss Bordereau, with an effect of something like cruelty in her implacable power of retort – an incongruous suggestion that she was a sarcastic, profane, cynical old woman. 'Haven't we heard that there have been all sorts of changes in all these years? You ought to see them and at your age (I don't mean because you're so young), you ought to take the chances that come. You're old enough, my dear, and this gentleman won't hurt you. He will show you the famous sunsets, if they still go on – *do* they go on? The sun set for me so long ago. But that's not a reason. Besides, I shall never miss you; you think you are too important. Take her to the Piazza; it used to be very pretty,' Miss Bordereau continued, addressing herself to me. 'What have they done with the funny old church? I hope it hasn't tumbled down. Let her look at the shops; she may take some money, she may buy what she likes.'

Poor Miss Tita had got up, discountenanced and helpless, and as we stood there before her aunt it would certainly have seemed to a spectator of the scene that the old woman was amusing herself at our expense. Miss Tita protested, in a confusion of exclamations and murmurs; but I lost no time in saying that if she would do me the honour to accept the hospitality of my boat I would engage that she should not be bored. Or if she did not want so much of my company the boat itself, with the gondolier, was at her service; he was a capital oar and she might have every confidence. Miss Tita, without definitely answering this speech, looked away from me, out of the window, as if she were going to cry; and I remarked that once we had Miss Bordereau's approval we could easily come to an understanding. We would take an hour, whichever she liked, one of the very next days. As I made my obeisance to the old lady I asked her if she would kindly permit me to see her again.

For a moment she said nothing; then she inquired, 'Is it very necessary to your happiness?'

'It diverts me more than I can say.'

'You are wonderfully civil. Don't you know it almost kills *me*?'

'How can I believe that when I see you more animated, more brilliant than when I came in?'

'That is very true, aunt,' said Miss Tita. 'I think it does you good.'

'Isn't it touching, the solicitude we each have that the other shall enjoy herself?' sneered Miss Bordereau. 'If you think me brilliant today you don't know what you are talking about; you have never seen an agreeable woman. Don't try to pay me a compliment; I have been spoiled,' she went on. 'My door is shut, but you may sometimes knock.'

With this she dismissed me and I left the room. The latch closed behind me, but Miss Tita, contrary to my hope, had remained within. I passed slowly across the hall and before taking my way downstairs I waited a little. My hope was answered; after a minute Miss Tita followed me. 'That's a delightful idea about the Piazza,' I said. 'When will you go – tonight, tomorrow?'

She had been disconcerted, as I have mentioned, but I had already perceived and I was to observe again that when Miss Tita was embarrassed she did not (as most women would have done) turn away from you and try to escape, but came closer, as it were, with a deprecating, clinging appeal to be spared, to be protected. Her attitude was perpetually a sort of prayer for assistance, for explanation; and yet no woman in the world could have been less of a comedian. From the moment you were kind to her she depended on you absolutely; her self-consciousness dropped from her and she took the greatest intimacy, the innocent intimacy which was the only thing she could conceive, for granted. She told me she did not know what had got into her aunt; she had changed so quickly, she had got some idea. I replied that she must find out what the idea was and then let me know; we would go and have an ice together at Florian's and she should tell me while we listened to the band.

'Oh, it will take me a long time to find out!' she said, rather ruefully; and she could promise me this satisfaction neither for that night nor for the next. I was patient now, however, for I felt that I had only to wait; and in fact at the end of the week, one lovely evening after dinner, she stepped into my gondola, to which in honour of the occasion I had attached a second oar.

We swept in the course of five minutes into the Grand Canal; whereupon she uttered a murmur of ecstasy as fresh as if she had been a tourist just arrived. She had forgotten how splendid the great water-way looked on a clear, hot summer evening, and how the sense of floating between marble palaces and reflected lights disposed the mind to sympathetic talk. We floated long and far, and though Miss Tita gave no high-pitched voice to her satisfaction I felt that she surrendered herself. She was more than pleased, she was transported; the whole thing was an immense liberation. The gondola moved with slow strokes, to give her time to enjoy it, and she listened to the splash of the oars, which grew louder and more musically liquid as we passed into narrow canals, as if it were a revelation of Venice. When I asked her how long it was since she had been in a boat she answered, 'Oh, I don't know; a long time – not since my aunt began to be ill.' This was not the only example she gave me of her extreme vagueness about the previous years and the line which marked off the period when Miss Bordereau flourished. I was not at liberty to keep her out too long, but we took a considerable *giro* before going to the Piazza. I asked her no questions, keeping the conversation on purpose away from her domestic situation and the things I wanted to know; I poured treasures of information about Venice into her ears, described Florence and Rome, discoursed to her on the charms and advantages of travel. She reclined, receptive, on the deep leather cushions, turned her eyes conscientiously to everything I pointed out to her, and never mentioned to me till some time afterwards that she might be supposed to know Florence better than I, as she had lived there for years with Miss Bordereau. At last she asked, with the shy impatience of a child, 'Are we not really going to the Piazza? That's what I want to see!' I immediatly gave the order that we should go straight; and then we sat silent with the expectation of arrival. As some time still passed, however, she said suddenly, of her own movement, 'I have found out what is the matter with my aunt: she is afraid you will go!'

'What has put that into her head?'

'She has had an idea you have not been happy. That is why she is different now.'

'You mean she wants to make me happier?'

'Well, she wants you not to go; she wants you to stay.'

'I suppose you mean on account of the rent,' I remarked candidly.

Miss Tita's candour showed itself a match for my own. 'Yes, you know; so that I shall have more.'

'How much does she want you to have?' I asked, laughing. 'She ought to fix the sum, so that I may stay till it's made up.'

'Oh, that wouldn't please me,' said Miss Tita. 'It would be unheard of, your taking that trouble.'

'But suppose I should have my own reasons for staying in Venice?'

'Then it would be better for you to stay in some other house.'

'And what would your aunt say to that?'

'She wouldn't like it at all. But I should think you would do well to give up your reasons and go away altogether.'

'Dear Miss Tita,' I said, 'it's not so easy to give them up!'

She made no immediate answer to this, but after a moment she broke out: 'I think I know what your reasons are!'

'I dare say, because the other night I almost told you how I wish you would help me to make them good.'

'I can't do that without being false to my aunt.'

'What do you mean, being false to her?'

'Why, she would never consent to what you want. She has been asked, she has been written to. It made her fearfully angry.'

'Then she *has* got papers of value?' I demanded, quickly.

'Oh, she has got everything!' sighed Miss Tita, with a curious weariness, a sudden lapse into the gloom.

These words caused all my pulses to throb, for I regarded them as precious evidence. For some minutes I was too agitated to speak, and in the interval the gondola approached the Piazzetta. After we had disembarked I asked my companion whether she would rather walk round the square or go and sit at the door of the café; to which she replied that she would do whichever I liked best – I must only remember again how little time she had. I assured her there was plenty to do both, and we made the circuit of the long arcades. Her spirits revived at the sight of the bright shop-windows, and she lingered and stopped, admiring or disapproving of their contents, asking me what I thought of things, theorizing about prices. My attention wandered from her; her words of a while before, 'Oh, she has got everything!' echoed so in my consciousness. We sat down at last in the crowded circle at Florian's, finding an unoccupied table among those that were ranged in the square. It was a splendid night and all the world was out of doors; Miss Tita could not have wished the elements more auspicious for her return to society. I saw that she enjoyed it even more than she told; she was agitated with the multitude of her impressions. She had forgotten what an attractive thing the world is, and it was coming over her that somehow she had for the best years of her life been cheated of it. This did not make her angry; but as she looked all over the charming scene her face had, in spite of its smile of appreciation, the flush of a sort of wounded surprise. She became silent, as if she were thinking with a secret sadness of opportunities, for ever lost, which ought to have been easy; and this gave me a chance to say to her, 'Did you mean a while ago that your aunt has a plan of keeping me on by admitting me occasionally to her presence?'

'She thinks it will make a difference with you if you sometimes see her. She wants you so much to stay that she is willing to make that concession.'

'And what good does she consider that I think it will do me to see her?'

'I don't know; she thinks it's interesting,' said Miss Tita, simply. 'You told her you found it so.'

'So I did; but every one doesn't think so.'

'No, of course not, or more people would try.'

'Well, if she is capable of making that reflection she is capable also of making this further one,' I went on: 'that I must have a particular reason for not doing as others do, in spite of the interest she offers – for not leaving her alone.' Miss Tita looked as if she failed to grasp this rather complicated proposition; so I continued 'If you have not told her what I said to you the other night may she not at least have guessed it?'

'I don't know; she is very suspicious.'

'But she has not been made so by indiscreet curiosity, by persecution?'

'No, no; it isn't that,' said Miss Tita, turning on me a somewhat troubled face. 'I don't know how to say it: it's on account of something – ages ago, before I was born – in her life.'

'Something? What sort of thing?' I asked, as if I myself could have no idea.

'Oh, she has never told me,' Miss Tita answered; and I was sure she was speaking the truth.

Her extreme limpidity was almost provoking, and I felt for the moment that she would have been more satisfactory if she had been less ingenuous. 'Do you suppose it's something to which Jeffrey Aspern's letters and papers – I mean the things in her possession – have reference?'

'I dare say it is!' my companion exclaimed, as if this were a very happy suggestion. 'I have never looked at any of those things.'

'None of them? Then how do you know what they are?'

'I don't,' said Miss Tita, placidly. 'I have never had them in my hands. But I have seen them when she has had them out.'

'Does she have them out often?'

'Not now, but she used to. She is very fond of them.'

'In spite of their being compromising?'

'Compromising?' Miss Tita repeated, as if she was ignorant of the meaning of the word. I felt almost as one who corrupts the innocence of youth.

'I mean their containing painful memories.'

'Oh, I don't think they are painful.'

'You mean you don't think they affect her reputation?'

At this a singular look came into the face of Miss Bordereau's niece – a kind of confession of helplessness, an appeal to me to deal fairly, generously with her. I had brought her to the Piazza, placed her among charming influences, paid her an attention she appreciated, and now I seemed to let her perceive that all this had been a bribe – a bribe to make her turn in some way against her aunt. She was of a yielding nature and capable of doing almost anything to please a person who was kind to her; but the greatest kindness of all would be not to presume too much on this. It was strange enough, as I afterwards thought, that she had not the least air of resenting my want of consideration for her aunt's character, which would have been in the worst possible taste if anything less vital (from my point of view) had been at stake. I don't think she really measured it. 'Do you mean that she did something bad?' she asked in a moment.

'Heaven forbid I should say so, and it's none of my business. Besides, if she did,' I added, laughing, 'it was in other ages, in another world. But why should she not destroy her papers?'

'Oh, she loves them too much.'

'Even now, when she may be near her end?'

'Perhaps when she's sure of that she will.'

'Well, Miss Tita,' I said, 'it's just what I should like you to prevent.'

'How can I prevent it?'

'Couldn't you get them away from her?'

'And give them to you?'

This put the case very crudely, though I am sure there was no irony in her intention. 'Oh, I mean that you might let me see them and look them over. It isn't for myself; there is no personal avidity in my desire. It is simply that they would be of such immense interest to the public, such immeasurable importance as a contribution to Jeffrey Aspern's history.'

She listened to me in her usual manner, as if my speech were full of reference to things she had never heard of, and I felt particularly like the reporter of a newspaper who forces his way into a house of mourning. This was especially the case when after a moment she said, 'There was a gentleman who some time ago wrote to her in very much those words. He also wanted her papers.'

'And did she answer him?' I asked, rather ashamed of myself for not having her rectitude.

'Only when he had written two or three times. He made her very angry.'

'And what did she say?'

'She said he was a devil,' Miss Tita replied, simply.

'She used that expression in her letter?'

'Oh no; she said it to me. She made me write to him.'

'And what did you say?'

'I told him there were no papers at all.'

'Ah, poor gentleman!' I exclaimed.

'I knew there were, but I wrote what she bade me.'

'Of course you had to do that. But I hope I shall not pass for a devil.'

'It will depend upon what you ask me to do for you,' said Miss Tita, smiling.

'Oh, if there is a chance of *your* thinking so my affair is in a bad way! I sha'n't ask you to steal for me, nor even to fib – for you can't fib, unless on paper. But the principal thing is this – to prevent her from destroying the papers.'

'Why, I have no control of her,' said Miss Tita. 'It's she who controls me.'

'But she doesn't control her own arms and legs, does she? The way she would naturally destroy her letters would be to burn them. Now she can't burn them without fire, and she can't get fire unless you give it to her.'

'I have always done everything she has asked,' my companion rejoined. 'Besides, there's Olimpia.'

I was on the point of saying that Olimpia was probably corruptible, but I thought it best not to sound that note. So I simply inquired if that faithful domestic could not be managed.

'Every one can be managed by my aunt,' said Miss Tita. And then she observed that her holiday was over; she must go home.

I laid my hand on her arm, across the table, to stay her a moment. 'What I want of you is a general promise to help me.'

'Oh, how can I – how can I?' she asked, wondering and troubled. She was half surprised, half frightened at my wishing to make her play an active part.

'This is the main thing: to watch her carefully and warn me in time, before she commits that horrible sacrilege.'

'I can't watch her when she makes me go out.'

'That's very true.'

'And when you do too.'

'Mercy on us; do you think she will have done anything tonight?'

'I don't know; she is very cunning.'

'Are you trying to frighten me?' I asked.

I felt this inquiry sufficiently answered when my companion murmured in a musing, almost envious way, 'Oh, but she loves them – she loves them!'

This reflection, repeated with such emphasis, gave me great comfort; but to obtain more of that balm I said, 'If she shouldn't intend to destroy the objects we speak of before her death she will probably have made some disposition by will.'

'By will?'

'Hasn't she made a will for your benefit?'

'Why, she has so little to leave. That's why she likes money,' said Miss Tita.

'Might I ask, since we are really talking things over, what you and she live on?'

'On some money that comes from America, from a lawyer. He sends it every quarter. It isn't much!'

'And won't she have disposed of that?'

My companion hesitated – I saw she was blushing. 'I believe it's mine,' she said; and the look and tone which accompanied these words betrayed so the absence of the habit of thinking of herself that I almost thought her charming. The next instant she added, 'But she had a lawyer once, ever so long ago. And some people came and signed something.'

'They were probably witnesses. And you were not asked to sign? Well then,' I argued, rapidly and hopefully, 'it is because you are the legatee; she has left all her documents to you!'

'If she has it's with very strict conditions,' Miss Tita responded, rising quickly, while the movement gave the words a little character of decision. They seemed to imply that the bequest would be accompanied with a command that the articles bequeathed should remain concealed from every inquisitive eye and that I was very much mistaken if I thought she was the person to depart from an injunction so solemn.

'Oh, of course you will have to abide by the terms,' I said; and she uttered nothing to mitigate the severity of this conclusion. None the less, later, just before we disembarked at her own door, on our return, which had taken place almost in silence, she said to me abruptly, 'I will do what I can to help you.' I was grateful for this – it was very well so far as it went; but it did not keep me from remembering that night in a worried waking hour that I now had her word for it to reinforce my own impression that the old woman was very cunning.

Chapter Seven

The fear of what this side of her character might have led her to do made me nervous for days afterwards. I waited for an intimation from Miss Tita; I almost figured to myself that it was her duty to keep me informed, to let me know definitely whether or no Miss Bordereau had sacrificed her treasures. But as she gave no sign I lost patience and determined to judge so far as was possible with my own senses. I sent late one afternoon to ask if I might pay the ladies a visit, and my servant came back with surprising news. Miss Bordereau could be approached without the least difficulty; she had been moved out into the sala and was sitting by the window that overlooked the garden. I descended and found this picture correct; the old lady had been wheeled forth into the world and had a certain air, which came mainly perhaps from some brighter element in her dress, of being prepared again to have converse with it. It had not yet, however, begun to flock about her; she was perfectly alone and, though the door leading to her own quarters stood open, I had at first no glimpse of Miss Tita. The window at which she sat had the afternoon shade and, one of the shutters having been pushed back, she could see the pleasant garden, where the summer sun had by this time dried up too many of the plants – she could see the yellow light and the long shadows.

'Have you come to tell me that you will take the rooms for six months more?' she asked, as I approached her, startling me by something coarse in her cupidity almost as much as if she had not already given me a specimen of it. Juliana's desire to make our acquaintance lucrative had been, as I have sufficiently indicated, a false note in my image of the woman who had inspired a great poet with immortal lines; but I may say here definitely that I recognized after all that it behoved me to make a large allowance for her. It was I who had kindled the unholy flame; it was I who had put into her head that she had the means of making money. She appeared never to have thought of that; she had been living wastefully for years, in a house five times too big for her, on a footing that I could explain only by the presumption that, excessive as it was, the space she enjoyed cost her next to nothing and that small as were her revenues they left her, for Venice, an appreciable margin. I had descended on her one day and taught her to calculate, and my almost extravagant comedy on the subject of the garden had presented me irresistibly in the light of a victim. Like all persons who achieve the miracle of changing their point of view when they are old she had been intensely converted; she had seized my hint with a desperate, tremulous clutch.

I invited myself to go and get one of the chairs that stood, at a distance, against the wall (she had given herself no concern as to whether I should sit or stand); and while I placed it near her I began, gaily, 'Oh, dear madam, what an imagination you have, what an intellectual sweep! I am a poor devil of a man of letters who lives from day to day. How can I take palaces by the year? My existence is precarious. I don't know whether six months hence I shall have bread to put in my mouth. I have treated myself for once; it has been an immense luxury. But when it comes to going on – !'

'Are your rooms too dear? if they are you can have more for the same money,' Juliana responded. 'We can arrange, we can *combinare*, as they say here.'

'Well yes, since you ask me, they are too dear,' I said. 'Evidently you suppose me richer than I am.'

She looked at me in her barricaded way. 'If you write books don't you sell them?'

'Do you mean don't people buy them? A little – not so much as I could wish. Writing books, unless one be a great genius – and even then! – is the last road to fortune. I think there is no more money to be made by literature.'

'Perhaps you don't choose good subjects. What do you write about?' Miss Bordereau inquired.

'About the books of other people. I'm a critic, an historian, in a small way.' I wondered what she was coming to.

'And what other people, now?'

'Oh, better ones than myself: the great writers mainly – the great philosophers and poets of the past; those who are dead and gone and can't speak for themselves.'

'And what do you say about them?'

'I say they sometimes attached themselves to very clever women!' I answered, laughing. I spoke with great deliberation, but as my words fell upon the air they struck me as imprudent. However, I risked them and I was not sorry, for perhaps after all the old woman would be willing to treat. It seemed to be tolerably obvious that she knew my secret: why therefore drag the matter out? But she did not take what I had said as a confession: she only asked:

'Do you think it's right to rake up the past?'

'I don't know that I know what you mean by raking it up; but how can we get at it unless we dig a little? The present has such a rough way of treading it down.'

'Oh, I like the past, but I don't like critics,' the old woman declared, with her fine tranquillity.

'Neither do I, but I like their discoveries.'

'Aren't they mostly lies?'

'The lies are what they sometimes discover,' I said, smiling at the quiet impertinence of this. 'They often lay bare the truth.'

'The truth is God's, it isn't man's; we had better leave it alone. Who can judge of it – who can say?'

'We are terribly in the dark, I know,' I admitted; 'but if we give up trying what becomes of all the fine things? What becomes of the work I just mentioned, that of the great philosophers and poets? It is all vain words if there is nothing to measure it by.'

'You talk as if you were a tailor,' said Miss Bordereau, whimsically; and then she added quickly, in a different manner, 'This house is very fine; the proportions are magnificent. Today I wanted to look at this place again. I made them bring me out here. When your man came, just now, to learn if I would see you, I was on the point of sending for you, to ask if you didn't mean to go on. I wanted to judge what I'm letting you have. This sala is very grand,' she pursued, like an auctioneer, moving a little, as I guessed, her invisible eyes. 'I don't believe you often have lived in such a house, eh?'

'I can't often afford to!' I said.

'Well then, how much will you give for six months?'

I was on the point of exclaiming – and the air of excruciation in my face would have denoted a moral fact – 'Don't, Juliana; for *his* sake, don't!' But I controlled myself and asked less passionately: 'Why should I remain so long as that?'

'I thought you liked it,' said Miss Bordereau, with her shrivelled dignity.

'So I thought I should.'

For a moment she said nothing more, and I left my own words to suggest to her what they might. I half expected her to say, coldly enough, that if I had been disappointed we need not continue the discussion, and this in spite of the fact that I believed her now to have in her mind (however it had come there), what would have told her that my disappointment was natural. But to my extreme surprise she ended by observing: 'If you don't think we have treated you well enough perhaps we can discover some way of treating you better.' This speech was somehow so incongruous that it made me laugh again, and I excused myself by saying that she talked as if I were a sulky boy, pouting in the corner, to be 'brought round'. I had not a grain of complaint to make; and could anything have exceeded Miss Tita's graciousness in accompanying me a few nights before to the Piazza? At this the old woman went on: 'Well, you brought it on yourself!' And then in a different tone, 'She is a very nice girl.' I assented cordially to this proposition, and she expressed the hope that I did so not merely to be obliging, but that I really liked her. Meanwhile I wondered still more what Miss Bordereau was coming to. 'Except for me, today,' she said, 'she has not a relation in the world.' Did she by describing her niece as amiable and unencumbered wish to represent her as a *parti*?

It was perfectly true that I could not afford to go on with my rooms at a fancy price and that I had already devoted to my undertaking almost all the hard cash I had set apart for it. My patience and my time were by no means exhausted, but I should be able to draw upon them only on a more usual Venetian basis. I was willing to pay the venerable woman with whom my pecuniary dealings were such a discord twice as much as any other *padrona di casa* would have asked, but I was not willing to pay her twenty times as much. I told her so plainly, and my plainness appeared to have some success, for she exclaimed, 'Very good; you have done what I asked – you have made an offer!'

'Yes, but not for half a year. Only by the month.'

'Oh, I must think of that then.' She seemed disappointed that I would not tie myself to a period, and I guessed that she wished both to secure me and to discourage me; to say, severely, 'Do you dream that you can get off with less then six months? Do you dream that even by the end of that time you will be appreciably nearer your victory?' What was more in my mind was that she had a fancy to play me the trick of making me engage myself when in fact she had annihilated the papers. There was a moment when my suspense on this point was so acute that I all but broke out with the question, and what kept it back was but a kind of instinctive recoil (lest it should be a mistake), from the last violence of self-exposure. She was such a subtle old witch that one could never tell where one stood with her. You may imagine whether it cleared up the puzzle when, just after she had said she would think of my proposal and without any formal transition, she drew out of her pocket with an embarrassed hand a small object wrapped in crumpled white paper. She held it there a moment and then she asked, 'Do you know much about curiosities?'

'About curiosities?'

'About antiquities, the old gimcracks that people pay so much for today. Do you know the kind of price they bring?'

I thought I saw what was coming, but I said ingenuously, 'Do you want to buy something?'

'No, I want to sell. What would an amateur give me for that?' She unfolded the white paper and made a motion for me to take from her a small oval portrait. I possessed myself of it with a hand of which I could only hope that she did not perceive the tremor, and she added, 'I would part with it only for a good price.'

At the first glance I recognized Jeffrey Aspern, and I was well aware that I flushed with the act. As she was watching me however I had the consistency to exclaim, 'What a striking face! Do tell me who it is.'

'It's an old friend of mine, a very distinguished man in his day. He gave it to me himself, but I'm afraid to mention his name, lest you never should have heard of him, critic and historian as you are. I know the world goes fast and one generation forgets another. He was all the fashion when I was young.'

She was perhaps amazed at my assurance, but I was surprised at hers; at her having the energy, in her state of health and at her time of life, to wish to sport with me that way simply for her private entertainment – the humour to test me and practise on me. This, at least, was the interpretation that I put upon her production of the portrait, for I could not believe that she really desired to sell it or cared for any information I might give her.

What she wished was to dangle it before my eyes and put a prohibitive price on it. 'The face comes back to me, it torments me,' I said, turning the object this way and that and looking at it very critically. It was a careful but not a supreme work of art, larger than the ordinary miniature and representing a young man with a remarkably handsome face, in a high-collared green coat and a buff waistcoat. I judged the picture to have a valuable quality of resemblance and to have been painted when the model was about twenty-five years old. There are, as all the world knows, three other portraits of the poet in existence, but none of them is of so early a date as this elegant production, 'I have never seen the original but I have seen other likenesses,' I went on. 'You expressed doubt of this generation having heard of the gentleman, but he strikes me for all the world as a celebrity. Now who is he? I can't put my finger on him – I can't give him a label. Wasn't he a writer? Surely he's a poet.' I was determined that it should be she, not I, who should first pronounce Jeffrey Aspern's name.

My resolution was taken in ignorance of Miss Bordereau's extremely resolute character, and her lips never formed in my hearing the syllables that meant so much for her. She neglected to answer my question but raised her hand to take back the picture, with a gesture which though ineffectual was in a high degree peremptory. 'It's only a person who should know for himself that would give me my price,' she said with a certain dryness.

'Oh, then, you have a price?' I did not restore the precious thing; not from any vindictive purpose but because I instinctively clung to it. We looked at each other hard while I retained it.

'I know the least I would take. What it occurred to me to ask you about is the most I shall be able get.'

She made a movement, drawing herself together as if, in a spasm of dread at having lost her treasure, she were going to attempt the immense effort of rising to snatch it from me. I instantly placed it in her hand again, saying as I did so, 'I should like to have it myself, but with your ideas I could never afford it.'

She turned the small oval plate over in her lap, with its face down, and I thought I saw her catch her breath a little, as if she had had a strain or an escape. This however did not prevent her saying in a moment, 'You would buy a likeness of a person you don't know, by an artist who has no reputation?'

'The artist may have no reputation, but that thing is wonderfully well painted,' I replied, to give myself a reason.

'It's lucky you thought of saying that, because the painter was my father.'

'That makes the picture indeed precious!' I exclaimed, laughing; and I may add that a part of my laughter came from my satisfaction in finding that I had been right in my theory of Miss Bordereau's origin. Aspern had of course met the young lady when he went to her father's studio as a sitter. I observed to Miss Bordereau that if she would entrust me with her property for twenty-four hours I should be happy to take advice upon it; but she made no answer to this save to slip it in silence into her pocket. This convinced me still more that she had no sincere intention of selling it during her lifetime, though she may have desired to satisfy herself as to the sum her niece, should she leave it to her, might expect eventually to obtain for it. 'Well, at any rate I hope you will not offer it without giving me notice,' I said, as she remained irresponsive. 'Remember that I am a possible purchaser.'

'I should want your money first!' she returned, with unexpected rudeness; and then, as if she bethought herself that I had just cause to complain of such an insinuation and wished to turn the matter off, asked abruptly what I talked about with her niece when I went out with her that way in the evening.

'You speak as if we had set up the habit,' I replied. 'Certainly I should be very glad if it were to become a habit. But in that case I should feel a still greater scruple at betraying a lady's confidence.'

'Her confidence? Has she got confidence?'

'Here she is – she can tell you herself,' I said; for Miss Tita now appeared on the threshold of the old woman's parlour. 'Have you got confidence, Miss Tita? Your aunt wants very much to know.'

'Not in her, not in her!' the younger lady declared, shaking her head with a dolefulness that was neither jocular nor affected. 'I don't know what to do with her; she has fits of horrid imprudence. She is so easily tired – and yet she has begun to roam – to drag herself about the house.' And she stood looking down at her immemorial companion with a sort of helpless wonder, as if all their years of familiarity had not made her perversities, on occasion, any more easy to follow.

'I know what I'm about. I'm not losing my mind. I dare say you would like to think so,' said Miss Bordereau, with a cynical little sigh.

'I don't suppose you came out here yourself. Miss Tita must have had to lend you a hand,' I interposed, with a pacifying intention.

'Oh, she insisted that we should push her; and when she insists!' said Miss Tita, in the same tone of apprehension; as if there were no knowing what service that she disapproved of her aunt might force her next to render.

'I have always got most things done I wanted, thank God! The people I have lived with have humoured me,' the old woman continued, speaking out of the grey ashes of her vanity.

'I suppose you mean that they have obeyed you.'

'Well, whatever it is, when they like you.'

'It's just because I like you that I want to resist,' said Miss Tita, with a nervous laugh.

'Oh, I suspect you'll bring Miss Bordereau upstairs next, to pay me a visit,' I went on; to which the old lady replied:

'Oh no; I can keep an eye on you from here!'

'You are very tired; you will certainly be ill tonight!' cried Miss Tita.

'Nonsense, my dear; I feel better at this moment than I have done for a month. Tomorrow I shall come out again. I want to be where I can see this clever gentleman.'

'Shouldn't you perhaps see me better in your sitting-room?' I inquired.

'Don't you mean shouldn't you have a better chance at me?' she returned, fixing me a moment with her green shade.

'Ah, I haven't that anywhere! I look at you but I don't see you.'

'You excite her dreadfully – and that is not good,' said Miss Tita, giving me a reproachful, appealing look.

'I want to watch you – I want to watch you!' the old lady went on.

'Well then, let us spend as much of our time together as possible – I don't care where – and that will give you every facility.'

'Oh, I've seen you enough for today. I'm satisfied. Now I'll go home.' Miss Tita laid her hands on the back of her aunt's chair and began to push, but I begged her to let me take her place. 'Oh yes, you may move me this way – you sha'n't in any other!' Miss Bordereau exclaimed, as she felt herself propelled firmly and easily over the smooth, hard floor. Before we reached the door of her own apartment she commanded me to stop, and she took a long, last look up and down the noble sala. 'Oh, it's a magnificent house!' she murmured; after which I pushed her forward. When we had entered the parlour Miss Tita told me that she should now be able to manage, and at the same moment the little red-haired *donna* came to meet her mistress. Miss Tita's idea was evidently to get her aunt immediately back to bed. I confess that in spite of this urgency I was guilty of the indiscretion of lingering; it held me there to think that I was nearer the documents I coveted – that they were probably put away somewhere in the faded, unsociable room. The place had indeed a bareness which did not suggest hidden treasures; there were no dusky nooks nor curtained corners, no massive cabinets nor chests with iron bands. Moreover it was possible, it was perhaps even probable that the old lady had consigned her relics to her bedroom, to some battered box that was shoved under the bed, to the drawer of some lame dressing-table, where they would be in the range of vision by the dim night-lamp. None the less I scrutinized every article of furniture, every conceivable cover for a hoard, and noticed that there were half a dozen things with drawers, and in particular a tall old secretary, with brass ornaments of the style of the Empire – a receptacle somewhat rickety but still capable of keeping a great many secrets. I don't know why this article fascinated me so, inasmuch as I certainly had no definite purpose of breaking into it; but I stared at it so hard that Miss Tita noticed me and changed colour. Her doing this made me think I was right and that wherever they might have been before the Aspern papers at that moment languished behind the peevish little lock of the secretary. It was hard to remove my eyes from the dull mahogany front when I reflected that a simple panel divided me from the goal of my hopes; but I remembered my prudence and with an effort took leave of Miss Bordereau. To make the effort graceful I said to her that I should certainly bring her an opinion about the little picture.

'The little picture?' Miss Tita asked, surprised.

'What do *you* know about it, my dear?' the old woman demanded. 'You needn't mind. I have fixed my price.'

'And what may that be?'

'A thousand pounds.'

'Oh Lord!' cried poor Miss Tita, irrepressibly.

'Is that what she talks to you about?' said Miss Bordereau.

'Imagine your aunt's wanting to know!' I had to separate from Miss Tita with only those words, though I should have liked immensely to add, 'For heaven's sake meet me tonight in the garden!'

Chapter Eight

As it turned out the precaution had not been needed, for three hours later, just as I had finished my dinner, Miss Bordereau's niece appeared, unannounced, in the open doorway of the room in which my simple repasts were served. I remember well that I felt no surprise at seeing her; which is not a proof that I did not believe in her timidity. It was immense, but in a case in which there was a particular reason for boldness it never would have prevented her from running up to my rooms. I saw that she was now quite full of a particular reason; it threw her forward – made her seize me, as I rose to met her, by the arm.

'My aunt is very ill; I think she is dying!'

'Never in the world,' I answered, bitterly. 'Don't you be afraid!'

'Do go for a doctor – do, do! Olimpia is gone for the one we always have, but she doesn't come back; I don't know what has happened to her. I told her that if he was not at home she was to follow him where he had gone; but apparently she is following him all over Venice. I don't know what to do – she looks so as if she were sinking.'

'May I see her, may I judge?' I asked. 'Of course I shall be delighted to bring some one; but hadn't we better send my man instead, so that I may stay with you?'

Miss Tita assented to this and I despatched my servant for the best doctor in the neighbourhood. I hurried downstairs with her, and on the way she told me that an hour after I quitted them in the afternoon Miss Bordereau had had an attack of 'oppression', a terrible difficulty in breathing. This had subsided but had left her so exhausted that she did not come up: she seemed all gone. I repeated that she was not gone, that she would not go yet; whereupon Miss Tita gave me a sharper sidelong glance than she had ever directed at me and said, 'Really, what do you mean? I suppose you don't accuse her of making-believe!' I forget what reply I made to this, but I grant that in my heart I thought the old woman capable of any weird manoeuvre. Miss Tita wanted to know what I had done to her; her aunt had told her that I had made her so angry. I declared I had done nothing – I had been exceedingly careful; to which my companion rejoined that Miss Bordereau had assured her she had had a scene with me – a scene that had upset her. I answered with some resentment that it was a scene of her own making – that I couldn't think what she was angry with me for unless for not seeing my way to give a thousand pounds for the portrait of Jeffrey Aspern. 'And did she show you that? Oh gracious – oh deary me!' groaned Miss Tita, who appeared to feel that the situation was passing out of her control, and that the elements of her fate were thickening around her. I said that I would give anything to possess it, yet that I had not a thousand pounds; but I stopped when we came to the door of Miss Bordereau's room. I had an immense curiosity to pass it, but I thought it my duty to represent to Miss Tita that if I made the invalid angry she ought perhaps to be spared the sight of me. 'The sight of you? Do you think she can *see*?' my companion demanded, almost with indignation. I did think so but forbore to say it, and I softly followed my conductress.

I remember that what I said to her as I stood for a moment beside the old woman's bed was, 'Does she never show you her eyes then? Have you never seen them?' Miss Bordereau had been divested of her green shade, but (it was not my fortune to behold Juliana in her night cap) the upper half of her face was covered by the fall of a piece of dingy lacelike muslin, a sort of extemporized hood which, wound round her head, descended to the end of her nose, leaving nothing visible but her white withered cheeks and puckered mouth, closed tightly and, as it were, consciously. Miss Tita gave me a glance of surprise, evidently not seeing a reason for my impatience. 'You mean that she always wears something? She does it to preserve them.'

'Because they are so fine?'

'Oh, today, today!' And Miss Tita shook her head, speaking very low. 'But they used to be magnificent!'

'Yes indeed, we have Aspern's word for that.' And as I looked again at the old woman's wrappings I could imagine that she had not wished to allow people a reason to say that the great poet had overdone it. But I did not waste time in considering Miss Bordereau, in whom the appearance of respiration was so slight as to suggest that no human attention could ever help her more. I turned my eyes all over the room, rummaging with them the closets, the chests of drawers, the tables. Miss Tita met them quickly and read, I think, what was in them; but she did not answer it, turning away restlessly, anxiously, so that I felt rebuked, with reason, for a preoccupation that was almost profane in the presence of our dying companion. All the same I took another look, endeavouring to pick out mentally the place to try first, for a person who should wish to put his hand on Miss Bordereau's papers directly after her death. The room was a dire confusion; it looked like the room of an old actress. There were clothes hanging over chairs, odd-looking, shabby bundles here and there, and various pasteboard boxes piled together, battered, bulging and discoloured, which might have been fifty years old. Miss Tita after a moment noticed the direction of my eyes again and, as if she guessed how I judged the air of the place (forgetting I had no business to judge it at all), said, perhaps to defend herself from the imputation of complicity in such untidiness:

'She likes it this way; we can't move things. There are old bandboxes she has had most of her life.' Then she added, half taking pity on my real thought, 'Those things were *there*.' And she pointed to a small, low trunk which stood under a sofa where there was just room for it. It appeared to be a queer, superannuated coffer, of painted wood, with elaborate handles and shrivelled straps and with the colour (it had last been endued with a coat of light green) much rubbed off. It evidently had travelled with Juliana in the olden time – in the days of her adventures, which it had shared. It would have made a strange figure arriving at a modern hotel.

'*Were* there – they aren't now?' I asked, startled by Miss Tita's implication.

She was going to answer, but at that moment the doctor came in – the doctor whom the little maid had been sent to fetch and whom she had at last overtaken. My servant, going on his own errand, had met her with her companion in tow, and in the sociable Venetian spirit, retracing his steps with them, had also come up to the threshold of Miss Bordereau's room, where I saw him peeping over the doctor's shoulder. I motioned him away the more instantly that the sight of his prying face reminded me that I myself had almost as little to do there – an admonition confirmed by the sharp way the little doctor looked at me, appearing to take me for a rival who had the field before him. He was a short, fat, brisk gentleman who wore the tall hat of his profession and seemed to look at everything but his patient. He looked particularly at me, as if it struck him that I should be better for a dose, so that I bowed to him and left him with the women, going down to smoke a cigar in the garden. I was nervous; I could not go further; I could not leave the place. I don't know exactly what I thought might happen, but it seemed to me important to be there. I wandered about in the alleys – the warm night had come on – smoking cigar after cigar and looking at the light in Miss Bordereau's windows. They were open now, I could see; the situation was different. Sometimes the light moved, but not quickly; it did not suggest the hurry of a crisis. Was the old woman dying or was she already dead? Had the doctor said that there was nothing to be done at her tremendous age but to let her quietly pass away; or had he simply announced with a look a little more conventional that the end of the end had come? Were the other two women moving about to perform the offices that follow in such a case? It made me uneasy not to be nearer, as if I thought the doctor himself might carry away the papers with him. I bit my cigar hard as it came over me again that perhaps there were now no papers to carry!

I wandered about for an hour – for an hour and a half. I looked out for Miss Tita at one of the windows, having a vague idea that she might come there to give me some sign. Would she not see the red tip of my cigar moving about in the dark and feel that I wanted eminently to know what the doctor had said? I am afraid it is a proof my anxieties had made me gross that I should have taken in some degree for granted that at such an hour, in the midst of the greatest change that could take place in her life, they were uppermost also in poor Miss Tita's mind. My servant came down and spoke to me; he knew nothing save that the doctor had gone after a visit of half an hour. If he had stayed half an hour then Miss Bordereau was still alive: it could not have taken so much time as that to enunciate the contrary. I sent the man out of the house; there were moments when the sense of his curiosity annoyed me and this was one of them. *He* had been watching my cigar-tip from an upper window, if Miss Tita had not; he could not know what I was after and I could not tell him, though I was conscious he had fantastic private theories about me which he thought fine and which I, had I known them, should have thought offensive.

I went upstairs at last but I ascended no higher than the sala. The door of Miss Bordereau's apartment was open showing from the parlour the dimness of a poor candle. I went towards it with a light tread and at the same moment Miss Tita appeared and stood looking at me as I approached. 'She better – she's better,' she said, even before I had asked. 'The doctor has given her something; she woke up, came back to life while he was there. He says there is no immediate danger.'

'No immediate danger? Surely he thinks her condition strange!'

'Yes, because she had been excited. That affects her dreadfully.'

'It will do so again then, because she excites herself. She did so this afternoon.'

'Yes; she mustn't come out any more,' said Miss Tita, with one of her lapses into a deeper placidity.

'What is the use of making such a remark as that if you begin to rattle her about again the first time she bids you?'

'I won't – I won't do it any more.'

'You must learn to resist her,' I went on.

'Oh yes, I shall; I shall do so better if you tell me it's right.'

'You mustn't do it for me; you must do it for yourself. It all comes back to you, if you are frightened.'

'Well, I am not frightened now,' said Miss Tita, cheerfully. 'She is very quiet.'

'Is she conscious again – does she speak?'

'No, she doesn't speak, but she takes my hand. She holds it fast.'

'Yes,' I rejoined, 'I can see what force she still has by the way she grabbed that picture this afternoon. But if she holds you fast how comes it that you are here?'

Miss Tita hesitated a moment; though her face was in deep shadow (she had her back to the light in the parlour and I had put down my own candle far off, near the door of the sala), I thought I saw her smile ingenuously. 'I came on purpose – I heard your step.'

'Why, I came on tiptoe, as inaudibly as possible.'

'Well, I heard you,' said Miss Tita.

'And is your aunt alone now?'

'Oh no; Olimpia is sitting there.'

On my side I hesitated. 'Shall we then step in there?' And I nodded at the parlour; I wanted more and more to be on the spot.

'We can't talk there – she will hear us.'

I was on the point of replying that in that case we would sit silent, but I was too conscious that this would not do, as there was something I desired immensely to ask her. So I proposed that we should walk a little in the sala, keeping more at the other end, where we should not disturb the old lady. Miss Tita assented unconditionally; the doctor was coming again, she said, and she would be there to meet him at the door. We strolled through the fine superfluous hall, where on the marble floor – particularly as at first we said nothing – our footsteps were more audible than I had expected. When we reached the other end – the wide window, inveterately closed, connecting with the balcony that overhung the canal – I suggested that we should remain there, as she would see the doctor arrive still better. I opened the window and we passed out on the balcony. The air of the canal seemed even heavier, hotter than that of the sala. The place was hushed and void; the quiet neighbourhood had gone to sleep. A lamp, here and there, over the narrow black water, glimmered in double; the voice of a man going homeward singing, with his jacket on his shoulder and his hat on his ear, came to us from a distance. This did not prevent the scene from being very *comme il faut,* as Miss Bordereau had called it the first time I saw her. Presently a gondola passed along the canal with its slow rhythmical plash, and as we listened we watched it in silence. It did not stop, it did not carry the doctor; and after it had gone on I said to Miss Tita:

'And where are they now – the things that were in the trunk?'

'In the trunk?'

'That green box you pointed out to me in her room. You said her papers had been there; you seemed to imply that she had transferred them.'

'Oh yes; they are not in the trunk,' said Miss Tita.

'May I ask if you have looked?'

'Yes, I have looked – for you.'

'How for me, dear Miss Tita? Do you mean you would have given them to me if you had found them?' I asked, almost trembling.

She delayed to reply and I waited. Suddenly she broke out, 'I don't know what I would do – what I wouldn't!'

'Would you look again – somewhere else?'

She had spoken with a strange, unexpected emotion, and she went on in the same tone: 'I can't – I can't – while she lies there. It isn't decent.'

'No, it isn't decent,' I replied, gravely. 'Let the poor lady rest in peace.' And the words, on my lips, were not hypocritical, for I felt reprimanded and shamed.

Miss Tita added in a moment, as if she had guessed this and were sorry for me, but at the same time wished to explain that I did drive her on or at least did insist too much: 'I can't deceive her that way. I can't deceive her – perhaps on her deathbed.'

'Heaven forbid I should ask you, though I have been guilty myself!'

'You have been guilty?'

'I have sailed under false colours,' I felt now as if I must tell her that I had given her an invented name, on account of my fear that her aunt would have heard of me and would refuse to take me in. I explained this and also that I had really been a party to the letter written to them by John Cumnor months before.

She listened with great attention, looking at me with parted lips, and when I had made my confession she said, 'Then your real name – what is it?' She repeated it over twice when I had told her, accompanying it with the exclamation 'Gracious, gracious!' Then she added, 'I like your own best.'

'So do I,' I said, laughing. 'Ouf! it's a relief to get rid of the other.'

'So it was a regular plot – a kind of conspiracy?'

'Oh, a conspiracy – we were only two,' I replied, leaving out Mrs Prest of course.

She hesitated; I thought she was perhaps going to say that we had been very base. But she remarked after a moment, in a candid, wondering way, 'How much you must want them!'

'Oh, I do, passionately!' I conceded, smiling. And this chance made me go on, forgetting my compunction of a moment before. 'How can she possibly have changed their place herself? How can she walk? How can she arrive at that sort of muscular exertion? How can she lift and carry things?'

'Oh, when one wants and when one has so much will!' said Miss Tita, as if she had thought over my question already herself and had simply had no choice but that answer – the idea that in the dead of night, or at some moment when the coast was clear, the old woman had been capable of a miraculous effort.

'Have you questioned Olimpia? Hasn't she helped her – hasn't she done it for her?' I asked; to which Miss Tita replied promptly and positively that their servant had had nothing to do with the matter, though without admitting definitely that she had spoken to her. It was as if she were a little shy, a little ashamed now of letting me see how much she had entered into my uneasiness and had me on her mind. Suddenly she said to me, without any immediate relevance:

'I feel as if you were a new person, now that you have got a new name.'

'It isn't a new one; it is a very good old one, thank heaven!'

She looked at me a moment. 'I do like it better.'

'Oh, if you didn't I would almost go on with the other!'

'Would you really?'

I laughed again, but for all answer to this inquiry I said, 'Of course if she can rummage about that way she can perfectly have burnt them.'

'You must wait – you must wait,' Miss Tita moralized mournfully; and her tone ministered little to my patience, for it seemed after all to accept that wretched possibility. I would teach myself to wait, I declared nevertheless; because in the first place I could not do otherwise and in the second I had her promise, given me the other night, that she would help me.

'Of course if the papers are gone that's no use,' she said; not as if she wished to recede, but only to be conscientious.

'Naturally. But if you could only find out!' I groaned, quivering again.

'I thought you said you would wait.'

'Oh, you mean wait even for that?'

'For what then?'

'Oh, nothing,' I replied, rather foolishly, being ashamed to tell her what had been implied in my submission to delay – the idea that she would do more than merely find out. I know not whether she guessed this; at all events she appeared to become aware of the necessity for being a little more rigid.

'I didn't promise to deceive, did I? I don't think I did.'

'It doesn't much matter whether you did or not, for you couldn't!'

I don't think Miss Tita would have contested this even had she not been diverted by our seeing the doctor's gondola shoot into the little canal and approach the house. I noted that he came as fast as if he believed that Miss Bordereau was still in danger. We looked down at him while he disembarked and then went back into the sala to meet him. When he came up however I naturally left Miss Tita to go off with him alone, only asking her leave to come back later for news.

I went out of the house and took a long walk, as far as the Piazza, where my restlessness declined to quit me. I was unable to sit down (it was very late now but there were people still at the little tables in front of the cafés); I could only walk round and round, and I did so half a dozen times. I was uncomfortable, but it gave me a certain pleasure to have told Miss Tita who I really was. At last I took my way home again, slowly getting all but inextricably lost, as I did whenever I went out in Venice: so that it was considerably past midnight when I reached my door. The sala, upstairs, was as dark as usual and my lamp as I crossed it found nothing satisfactory to show me. I was disappointed, for I had notified Miss Tita that I would come back for a report, and I thought she might have left a light there as a sign. The door of the ladies' apartment was closed; which seemed an intimation that my faltering friend had gone to bed, tired of waiting for me. I stood in the middle of the place, considering, hoping she would hear me and perhaps peep out, saying to myself too that she would never go to bed with her aunt in a state so critical; she would sit up and watch – she would be in a chair, in her dressing-gown. I went nearer the door; I stopped there and listened. I heard nothing at all and at last I tapped gently. No answer came and after another minute I turned the handle. There was no light in the room; this ought to have prevented me from going in, but it had no such effect. If I have candidly narrated the importunities, the indelicacies, of which my desire to possess myself of Jeffrey Aspern's papers had rendered me capable I need not shrink from confessing this last indiscretion. I think it was the worst thing I did; yet there were extenuating circumstances. I was deeply though doubtless not disinterestedly anxious for more news of the old lady, and Miss Tita had accepted from me, as it were, a rendezvous which it might have been a point of honour with me to keep. It may be said that her leaving the place dark was a positive sign that she released me, and to this I can only reply that I desired not to be released.

The door of Miss Bordereau's room was open and I could see beyond it the faintness of a taper. There was no sound – my footstep caused no one to stir. I came further into the room; I lingered there with my lamp in my hand. I wanted to give Miss Tita a chance to come to me if she were with her aunt, as she must be. I made no noise to call her; I only waited to see if she would not notice my light. She did not, and I explained this (I found afterwards I was right) by the idea that she had fallen asleep. If she had fallen asleep her aunt was not on her mind, and my explanation ought to have led me to go out as I had come. I must repeat again that it did not, for I found myself at the same moment thinking of something else. I had no definite purpose, no bad intention, but I felt myself held to the spot by an acute, though absurd, sense of opportunity. For what I could not have said, inasmuch as it was not in my mind that I might commit a theft. Even if it had been I was confronted with the evident fact that Miss Bordereau did not leave her secretary, her cupboard and the drawers of her tables gaping. I had no keys, no tools and no ambition to smash her furniture. None the less it came to me that I was now, perhaps alone, unmolested, at the hour of temptation and secrecy, nearer to the tormenting treasure than I had ever been. I held up my lamp, let the light play on the different objects as if it could tell me something. Still there came no movement from the other room. If Miss Tita was sleeping she was sleeping sound. Was she doing so – generous creature – on purpose to leave me the field? Did she know I was there and was she just keeping quiet to see what I would do – what I *could* do? But what could I do, when it came to that? She herself knew even better than I how little.

I stopped in front of the secretary, looking at it very idiotically; for what had it to say to me after all? In the first place it was locked, and in the second it almost surely contained nothing in which I was interested. Ten to one the papers had been destroyed; and even if they had not been destroyed the old woman would not have put them in such a place as that after removing them from the green trunk – would not have transferred them, if she had the idea of their safety on her brain, from the better hiding-place to the worse. The secretary was more conspicuous, more accessible in a room in which she could no longer mount guard. It opened with a key, but there was a little brass handle, like a button, as well; I saw this as I played my lamp over it. I did something more than this at that moment: I caught a glimpse of the possibility that Miss Tita wished me really to understand. If she did not wish me to understand, if she wished me to keep away, why had she not locked the door of communication between the sitting-room and the sala? That would have been a definite sign that I was to leave them alone. If I did not leave them alone she meant me to come for a purpose – a purpose now indicated by the quick, fantastic idea that to oblige me she had unlocked the secretary. She had not left the key, but the lid would probably move if I touched the button. This theory fascinated me, and I bent over very close to judge. I did not propose to do anything, not even – not in the least – to let down the lid; I only wanted to test my theory, to see if the cover *would* move. I touched the button with my hand – a mere touch would tell me; and as I did so (it is embarrassing for me to relate it), I looked over my shoulder. It was a chance, an instinct, for I had not heard anything. I almost let my luminary drop and certainly I stepped back, straightening myself up at what I saw. Miss Bordereau stood there in her night-dress, in the doorway of her room, watching me; her hands were raised, she had lifted the everlasting curtain that covered half her face, and for the first, the last, the only time I beheld her extraordinary eyes. They glared at me, they made me horribly ashamed. I never shall forget her strange little bent white tottering figure, with its lifted head, her attitude, her expression; neither shall I forget the tone in which as I turned, looking at her, she hissed out passionately, furiously:

'Ah, you publishing scoundrel!'

I know not what I stammered, to excuse myself, to explain; but I went towards her, to tell her I meant no harm. She waved me off with her old hands, retreating before me in horror; and the next thing I knew she had fallen back with a quick spasm, as if death had descended on her, into Miss Tita's arms.

Chapter Nine

I left Venice the next morning, as soon as I learnt that the old lady had not succumbed, as I feared at the moment, to the shock I had given her – the shock I may also say she had given me. How in the world could I have supposed her capable of getting out of bed by herself? I failed to see Miss Tita before going; I only saw the *donna,* whom I entrusted with a note for her younger mistress. In this note I mentioned that I should be absent but for a few days. I went to Treviso, to Bassano, to Castelfranco; I took walks and drives and looked at musty old churches with ill-lighted pictures and spent hours seated smoking at the doors of cafés, where there were flies and yellow curtains, on the shady side of sleepy little squares. In spite of these pastimes, which were mechanical and perfunctory, I scantily enjoyed my journey: there was too strong a taste of the disagreeable in my life. It had been devilish awkward, as the young men say, to be found by Miss Bordereau in the dead of night examining the attachment of her bureau; and it had not been less so to have to believe for a good many hours afterwards that it was highly probable I had killed her. In writing to Miss Tita I attempted to minimize these irregularities; but as she gave me no word of answer I could not know what impression I made upon her. It rankled in my mind that I had been called a publishing scoundrel, for certainly I did publish and certainly I had not been very delicate. There was a moment when I stood convinced that the only way to make up for this latter fault was to take myself away altogether on the instant; to sacrifice my hopes and relieve the two poor women for ever of the oppression of my intercourse. Then I reflected that I had better try a short absence first, for I must already have had a sense (unexpressed and dim) that in disappearing completely it would not be merely my own hopes that I should condemn to extinction. It would perhaps be sufficient if I stayed away long enough to give the elder lady time to think she was rid of me. That she would wish to be rid of me after this (if I was not rid of her) was now not to be doubted: that nocturnal scene would have cured her of the disposition to put up with my company for the sake of my dollars. I said to myself that after all I could not abandon Miss Tita, and I continued to say this even while I observed that she quite failed to comply with my earnest request (I had given her two or three addresses, at little towns, *poste restante*) that she would let me know how she was getting on. I would have made my servant write to me but that he was unable to manage a pen. It struck me there was a kind of scorn in Miss Tita's silence (little disdainful as she had ever been), so that I was uncomfortable and sore. I had scruples about going back and yet I had others about not doing so, for I wanted to put myself on a better footing. The end of it was that I did return to Venice on the twelfth day; and as my gondola gently bumped against Miss Bordereau's steps a certain palpitation of suspense told me that I had done myself a violence in holding off so long.

I had faced about so abruptly that I had not telegraphed to my servant. He was therefore not at the station to meet me, but he poked out his head from an upper window when I reached the house. 'They have put her into the earth, *la vecchia*,' he said to me in the lower hall, while he shouldered my valise; and he grinned and almost winked, as if he knew I should be pleased at the news.

'She's dead!' I exclaimed, giving him a very different look.

'So it appears, since they have buried her.'

'It's all over? When was the funeral?'

'The other yesterday. But a funeral you could scarcely call it, signore; it was a dull little passeggio of two gondolas. Poveretta!' the man continued, referring apparently to Miss Tita. His conception of funerals was apparently that they were mainly to amuse the living.

I wanted to know about Miss Tita – how she was and where she was – but I asked him no more questions till we had got upstairs. Now that the fact had met me I took a bad view of it, especially of the idea that poor Miss Tita had had to manage by herself after the end. What did she know about arrangements, about the steps to take in such a case? Poveretta indeed! I could only hope that the doctor had given her assistance and that she had not been neglected by the old friends of whom she had told me, the little band of the faithful whose fidelity consisted in coming to the house once a year. I elicited from my servant that two old ladies and an old gentleman had in fact rallied round Miss Tita and had supported her (they had come for her in a gondola of their own) during the journey to the cemetery, the little red-walled island of tombs which lies to the north of the town, on the way to Murano. It appeared from these circumstances that the Misses Bordereau were Catholics, a discovery I had never made, as the old woman could not go to church and her niece, so far as I perceived, either did not or went only to early mass in the parish, before I was stirring. Certainly even the priests respected their seclusion; I had never caught the whisk of the curato's skirt. That evening, an hour later, I sent my servant down with five words written on a card, to ask Miss Tita if she would see me for a few moments. She was not in the house, where he had sought her, he told me when he came back, but in the garden walking about to refresh herself and gathering flowers. He had found her there and she would be very happy to see me.

I went down and passed half an hour with poor Miss Tita. She had always had a look of musty mourning (as if she were wearing out old robes of sorrow that would not come to an end), and in this respect there was no appreciable change in her appearance. But she evidently had been crying, crying a great deal – simply, satisfying, refreshingly, with a sort primitive, retarded sense of loneliness and violence. But she had none of the formalism or the self-consciousness of grief, and I was almost surprised to see her standing there in the first dusk with her hands full of flowers, smiling at me with her reddened eyes. Her white face, in the frame of her mantilla, looked longer, leaner than usual. I had had an idea that she would be a good deal disgusted with me – would consider that I ought to have been on the spot to advise her, to help her; and, though I was sure there was no rancour in her composition and no great conviction of the importance of her affairs, I had prepared myself for a difference in her manner, for some little injured look, half familiar, half estranged, which should say to my conscience, 'Well, you are a nice person to have professed things!' But historic truth compels me to declare that Tita Bordereau's countenance expressed unqualified pleasure in seeing her late aunt's lodger. That touched him extremely and he thought it simplified his situation until he found it did not. I was as kind to her that evening as I knew how to be, and I walked about the garden with her for half an hour. There was no explanation of any sort between us; I did not ask her why she had not answered my letter. Still less did I repeat what I had said to her in that communication; if she chose to let me suppose that she had forgotten the position in which Miss Bordereau surprised me that night and the effect of the discovery on the old woman I was quite willing to take it that way: I was grateful to her for not treating me as if I had killed her aunt.

We strolled and strolled and really not much passed between us save the recognition of her bereavement, conveyed in my manner and in a visible air that she had of depending on me now, since I let her see that I took an interest in her. Miss Tita had none of the pride that makes a person wish to preserve the look of independence; she did not in the least pretend that she knew at present what would become of her. I forbore to touch particularly on that however, for I certainly was not prepared to say that I would take charge of her. I was cautious; not ignobly, I think, for I felt that her knowledge of life was so small that in her unsophisticated vision there would be no reason why – since I seemed to pity her – I should not look after her. She told me how her aunt had died, very peacefully at the last, and how everything had been done afterwards by the care of her good friends (fortunately, thanks to me, she said, smiling, there was money in the house; and she repeated that when once the Italians like you they are your friends for life); and when we had gone into this she asked me about my *giro*, my impressions, the places I had seen. I told her what I could, making it up partly, I am afraid, as in my depression I had not seen much; and after she had heard me she exclaimed, quite as if she had forgotten her aunt and her sorrow, 'Dear, dear, how much I should like to do such things – to take a little journey!' It came over me for the moment that I ought to propose some tour, say I would take her anywhere she liked; and I remarked at any rate that some excursion to give her a change – might be managed: we would think of it, talk it over. I said never a word to her about the Aspern documents; asked no questions as to what she had ascertained or what had otherwise happened with regard to them before Miss Bordereau's death. It was not that I was not on pins and needles to know, but that I thought it more decent not to betray my anxiety so soon after the catastrophe. I hoped she herself would say something, but she never glanced that way, and I thought this natural at the time. Later, however, that night, it occurred to me that her silence was somewhat strange; for if she had talked of my movements, of anything so detached as the Giorgione at Castelfranco, she might have alluded to what she could easily remember was in my mind. It was not to be supposed that the emotion produced by her aunt's death had blotted out the recollection that I was interested in that lady's relics, and I fidgeted afterwards as it came to me that her reticence might very possibly mean simply that nothing had been found. We separated in the garden (it was she who said she must go in); now that she was alone in the rooms I felt that (judged, at any rate, by Venetian ideas) I was on rather a different footing in regard to visiting her there. As I shook hands with her for good night I asked her if she had any general plan – had thought over what she had better do. 'Oh yes, oh yes, but I haven't settled anything yet,' she replied, quite cheerfully. Was her cheerfulness explained by the impression that I would settle for her?

I was glad the next morning that we had neglected practical questions, for this gave me a pretext for seeing her again immediately. There was a very practical question to be touched upon. I owed it to her to let her know formally that of course I did not expect her to keep me on as a lodger, and also to show some interest in her own tenure, what she might have on her hands in the way of a lease. But I was not destined, as it happened, to converse with her for more than an instant on either of these points. I sent her no message; I simply went down to the sala and walked to and fro there. I knew she would come out; she would very soon discover I was there. Somehow I preferred not to be shut up with her; gardens and big halls seemed better places to talk. It was a splendid morning, with something in the air that told of the waning of the long Venetian summer; a freshness from the sea which stirred the flowers in the garden and made a pleasant draught in the house, less shuttered and darkened now than when the old woman was alive. It was the beginning of autumn, of the end of the golden months. With this it was the end of my experiment – or would be in the course of half an hour, when I should really have learned that the papers had been reduced to ashes. After that there would be nothing left for me but to go to the station; for seriously (and as it struck me in the morning light) I could not linger there to act as guardian to a piece of middle-aged female helplessness. If she had not saved the papers wherein should I be indebted to her? I think I winced a little as I asked myself how much, if she *had* saved them, I should have to recognize and, as it were, to reward such a courtesy. Might not that circumstance after all saddle me with a guardianship? If this idea did not make me more uncomfortable as I walked up and down it was because I was convinced I had nothing to look to. If the old woman had not destroyed everything before she pounced upon me in the parlour she had done so afterwards.

It took Miss Tita rather longer than I had expected to guess that I was there; but when at last she came out she looked at me without surprise. I said to her that I had been waiting for her and she asked why I had not let her know. I was glad the next day that I had checked myself before remarking that I had wished to see if a friendly intuition would not tell her: it became a satisfaction to me that I had not indulged in that rather tender joke. What I did say was virtually the truth – that I was too nervous, since I expected her now to settle my fate.

'Your fate?' said Miss Tita, giving me a queer look; and as she spoke I noticed a rare change in her. She was different from what she had been the evening before – less natural, less quiet. She had been crying the day before and she was not crying now, and yet she struck me as less confident. It was as if something had happened to her during the night, or at least as if she had thought of something that troubled her – something in particular that affected her relations with me, made them more embarrassing and complicated. Had she simply perceived that her aunt's not being there now altered my position?

'I mean about our papers. *Are* there any? You must know now.'

'Yes, there are a great many; more than I supposed.' I was struck with the way her voice trembled as she told me this.

'Do you mean that you have got them in there – and that I may see them?'

'I don't think you can see them,' said Miss Tita, with an extraordinary expression of entreaty in her eyes, as if the dearest hope she had in the world now was that I would not take them from her. But how could she expect me to make such a sacrifice as that after all that had passed between us? What had I come back to Venice for but to see them, to take them? My delight at learning they were still in existence was such that if the poor woman had gone down on her knees to beseech me never to mention them again I would have treated the proceeding as a bad joke. 'I have got them but I can't show them,' she added.

'Not even to me? Ah, Miss Tita!' I groaned, with a voice of infinite remonstrance and reproach.

She coloured and the tears came back to her eyes; I saw that it cost her a kind of anguish to take such a stand but that a dreadful sense of duty had descended upon her. It made me quite sick to find myself confronted with that particular obstacle; all the more that it appeared to me I had been extremely encouraged to leave it out of account. I almost considered that Miss Tita had assured me that if she had no greater hindrance than that –! 'You don't mean to say you made her a deathbed promise? It was precisely against your doing anything of that sort that I thought I was safe. Oh, I would rather she had burned the papers outright than that!'

'No, it isn't a promise,' said Miss Tita.

'Pray what is it then?'

She hesitated and then she said, 'She tried to burn them, but I prevented it. She had hid them in her bed.'

'In her bed?'

'Between the mattresses. That's where she put them when she took them out of the trunk. I can't understand how she did it, because Olimpia didn't help her. She tells me so and I believe her. My aunt only told her afterwards, so that she shouldn't touch the bed – anything but the sheets. So it was badly made,' added Miss Tita, simply.

'I should think so! And how did she try to burn them?'

'She didn't try much; she was too weak, those last days. But she told me – she charged me. Oh, it was terrible! She couldn't speak after that night; she could only make signs.'

'And what did you do?'

'I took them away. I locked them up.'

'In the secretary?'

'Yes, in the secretary,' said Miss Tita, reddening again.

'Did you tell her you would burn them?'

'No, I didn't – on purpose.'

'On purpose to gratify me?'

'Yes, only for that.'

'And what good will you have done me if after all you won't show them?'

'Oh, none; I know that – I know that.'

'And did she believe you had destroyed them?'

'I don't know what she believed at the last. I couldn't tell – she was too far gone.'

'Then if there was no promise and no assurance I can't see what ties you.'

'Oh, she hated it so – she hated it so! She was so jealous. But here's the portrait – you may have that,' Miss Tita announced, taking the little picture, wrapped up in the same manner in which her aunt had wrapped it, out of her pocket.

'I may have it – do you mean you give it to me?' I questioned, staring, as it passed into my hand.

'Oh yes.'

'But it's worth money – a large sum.'

'Well!' said Miss Tita, still with her strange look.

I did not know what to make of it, for it could scarcely mean that she wanted to bargain like her aunt. She spoke as if she wished to make me a present. 'I can't take it from you as a gift,' I said, 'and yet I can't afford to pay you for it according to the ideas Miss Bordereau had of its value. She rated it at a thousand pounds.'

'Couldn't we sell it?' asked Miss Tita.

'God forbid! I prefer the picture to the money.'

'Well then keep it.'

'You are very generous.'

'So are you.'

'I don't know why you should think so,' I replied, and this was a truthful speech, for the singular creature appeared to have some very fine reference in her mind, which I did not in the least seize.

'Well, you have made a great difference for me,' said Miss Tita.

I looked at Jeffrey Aspern's face in the little picture, partly in order not to look at that of my interlocutress, which had begun to trouble me, even to frighten me a little – it was so self-conscious, so unnatural. I made no answer to this last declaration; I only privately consulted Jeffrey Aspern's delightful eyes with my own (they were so young and brilliant, and yet so wise, so full of vision); I asked him what on earth was the matter with Miss Tita. He seemed to smile at me with friendly mockery, as if he were amused at my case. I had got into a pickle for him – as if he needed it! He was unsatisfactory, for the only moment since I had known him. Nevertheless, now that I held the little picture in my hand I felt that it would be a precious possession. 'Is this a bribe to make me give up the papers?' I demanded in a moment, perversely. 'Much as I value it, if I were to be obliged to choose, the papers are what I should prefer. Ah, but ever so much!'

'How can you choose – how can you choose?' Miss Tita asked, slowly, lamentably.

'I see! Of course there is nothing to be said, if you regard the interdiction that rests upon you as quite insurmountable. In this case it must seem to you that to part with them would be an impiety of the worst kind, a simple sacrilege!'

Miss Tita shook her head, full of her dolefulness. 'You would understand if you had known her. I'm afraid,' she quavered suddenly – 'I'm afraid! She was terrible when she was angry.'

'Yes, I saw something of that, that night. She was terrible. Then I saw her eyes. Lord, they were fine!'

'I see them – they stare at me in the dark!' said Miss Tita.

'You are nervous, with all you have been through.'

'Oh yes, very – very!'

'You mustn't mind; that will pass away,' I said, kindly. Then I added, resignedly, for it really seemed to me that I must accept the situation, 'Well, so it is, and it can't be helped. I must renounce.' Miss Tita, at this, looking at me, gave a low, soft moan, and I went on: 'I only wish to heaven she had destroyed them; then there would be nothing more to say. And I can't understand why, with her ideas, she didn't.'

'Oh, she lived on them!' said Miss Tita.

'You can imagine whether that makes me want less to see them,' I answered, smiling. 'But don't let me stand here as if I had it in my soul to tempt you to do anything base. Naturally you will understand I give up my rooms. I leave Venice immediately.' And I took up my hat, which I had placed on a chair. We were still there rather awkwardly, on our feet, in the middle of the sala. She had left the door of the apartments open behind her but she had not led me that way.

A kind of spasm came into her face as she saw me take my hat. 'Immediately – do you mean today?' The tone of the words was tragical – they were a cry of desolation.

'Oh no; not so long as I can be of the least service to you.'

'Well, just a day or two more – just two or three days,' she panted. Then controlling herself she added in another manner, 'She wanted to say something to me – the last day – something very particular, but she couldn't.'

'Something very particular?'

'Something more about the papers.'

'And did you guess – have you any idea?'

'No, I have thought – but I don't know. I have thought all kinds of things.'

'And for instance?'

'Well, that if you were a relation it would be different.'

'If I were a relation?'

'If you were not a stranger. Then it would be the same for you as for me. Anything that is mine – would be yours, and you could do what you like. I couldn't prevent you – and you would have no responsibility.'

She brought out this droll explanation with a little nervous rush, as if she were speaking words she had got by heart. They gave me an impression of subtlety and at first I failed to follow. But after a moment her face helped me to see further, and then a light came into my mind. It was embarrassing, and I bent my head over Jeffrey Aspern's portrait. What an odd expression was in his face! 'Get out of it as you can, my dear fellow!' I put the picture into the pocket of my coat and said to Miss Tita, 'Yes, I'll sell it for you. I sha'n't get a thousand pounds by any means, but I shall get something good.'

She looked at me with tears in her eyes, but she seemed to try to smile as she remarked, 'We can divide the money.'

'No, no, it shall be all yours.' Then I went on, 'I think I know what your poor aunt wanted to say. She wanted to give directions that her papers should be buried with her.'

Miss Tita appeared to consider this suggestion for a moment; after which she declared, with striking decision, 'Oh no, she wouldn't have thought that safe!'

'It seems to me nothing could be safer.'

'She had an idea that when people want to publish they are capable—' And she paused, blushing.

'Of violating a tomb? Mercy on us, what must she have thought of me!'

'She was not just, she was not generous!' Miss Tita cried with sudden passion.

The light that had come into my mind a moment before increased. 'Ah, don't say that, for we *are* a dreadful race.' Then I pursued, 'If she left a will, that may give you some idea.'

'I have found nothing of the sort – she destroyed it. She was very fond of me,' Miss Tita added, incongruously. 'She wanted me to be happy. And if any person should be kind to me – she wanted to speak of that.'

I was almost awestricken at the astuteness with which the good lady found herself inspired, transparent astuteness as it was and sewn, as the phrase is, with white thread. 'Depend upon it she didn't want to make any provision that would be agreeable to me.'

'No, not to you but to me. She knew I should like it if you could carry out your idea. Not because she cared for you but because she did think of me,' Miss Tita went on, with her unexpected, persuasive volubility. 'You could see them – you could use them.' She stopped, seeing that I perceived the sense of that conditional – stopped long enough for me to give some sign which I did not give. She must have been conscious however that though my face showed the greatest embarrassment that was ever painted on a human countenance it was not set as a stone, it was also full of compassion. It was a comfort to me a long time afterwards to consider that she could not have seen in me the smallest symptom of disrespect. 'I don't know what to do; I'm too tormented, I'm too ashamed!' she continued, with vehemence. Then turning away from me and burying her face in her hands she burst into a flood of tears. If she did not know what to do it may be imagined whether I did any better. I stood there dumb, watching her while her sobs resounded in the great empty hall. In a moment she was facing me again, with her streaming eyes. 'I would give you everything – and she would understand, where she is – she would forgive me!'

'Ah, Miss Tita – ah, Miss Tita,' I stammered, for all reply. I did not know what to do, as I say, but at a venture I made a wild, vague movement, in consequence of which I found myself at the door. I remember standing there and saying, 'It wouldn't do – it wouldn't do!' pensively, awkwardly, grotesquely, while I looked away to the opposite end of the sala as if there were a beautiful view there. The next thing I remember is that I was downstairs and out of the house. My gondola was there and my gondolier, reclining on the cushions, sprang up as soon as he saw me. I jumped in and to his usual '*Dove commanda?*' I replied, in a tone that made him stare, 'Anywhere, anywhere; out into the lagoon!'

He rowed me away and I sat there prostrate, groaning softly to myself, with my hat pulled over my face. What in the name of the preposterous did she mean if she did not mean to offer me her hand? That was the price – that was the price! And did she think I wanted it, poor deluded, infatuated, extravagant lady? My gondolier, behind me, must have seen my ears red as I wondered, sitting there under the fluttering *tenda,* with my hidden face, noticing nothing as we passed – wondered whether her delusion, her infatuation had been my own reckless work. Did she think I had made love to her, even to get the papers? I had not, I had not; I repeated that over to myself for an hour, for two hours, till I was wearied if not convinced. I don't know where my gondolier took me; we floated aimlessly about on the lagoon, with slow, rare strokes. At last I became conscious that we were near the Lido, far up, on the right hand, as you turn your back to Venice, and I made him put me ashore. I wanted to walk, to move, to shed some of my bewilderment. I crossed the narrow strip and got to the sea-beach – I took my way towards Malamocco. But presently I flung myself down again on the warm sand, in the breeze, on the coarse dry grass. It took it out of me to think I had been so much at fault, that I had unwittingly but none the less deplorably trifled. But I had not given her cause – distinctly I had not. I had said to Mrs Prest that I would make love to her; but it had been a joke without consequences and I had never said it to Tita Bordereau. I had been as kind as possible, because I really liked her; but since when had that become a crime where a woman of such an age and such an appearance was concerned? I am far from remembering clearly the succession of events and feelings during this long day of confusion, which I spent entirely in wandering about, without going home, until late at night; it only comes back to me that there were moments when I pacified my conscience and others when I lashed it into pain. I did not laugh all day – that I do recollect; the case, however it might have struck others, seemed to me so little amusing. It would have been better perhaps for me to feel the comic side of it. At any rate, whether I had given cause or not it went without saying that I could not pay the price. I could not accept. I could not, for a bundle of tattered papers, marry a ridiculous, pathetic, provincial old woman. It was a proof that she did not think the idea would come to me, her having determined to suggest it herself in that practical, argumentative, heroic way, in which the timidity however had been so much more striking than the boldness that her reasons appeared to come first and her feelings afterwards.

As the day went on I grew to wish that I had never heard of Aspern's relics, and I cursed the extravagant curiosity that had put John Cumnor on the scent of them. We had more than enough material without them and my predicament was the just punishment of that most fatal of human follies, our not having known when to stop. It was very well to say it was no predicament, that the way out was simple, that I had only to leave Venice by the first train in the morning, after writing a note to Miss Tita, to be placed in her hand as soon as I got clear of the house; for it was a strong sign that I was embarrassed that when I tried to make up the note in my mind in advance (I would put it on paper as soon as I got home, before going to bed), I could not think of anything but 'How can I thank you for the rare confidence you have placed in me?' That would never do; it sounded exactly as if an acceptance were to follow. Of course I might go away without writing a word, but that would be brutal and my idea was still to exclude brutal solutions. As my confusion cooled I was lost in wonder at the importance I had attached to Miss Bordereau's crumpled scraps; the thought of them became odious to me and I was as vexed with the old witch for the superstition that had prevented her from destroying them as I was with myself for having already spent more money than I could afford in attempting to control their fate. I forget what I did, where I went after leaving the Lido and at what hour or with what recovery of composure I made my way back to my boat. I only know that in the afternoon, when the air was aglow with the sunset, I was standing before the church of Saints John and Paul and looking up at the small square-jawed face of Bartolommeo Colleoni, the terrible *condottiere* who sits so sturdily astride of his huge bronze horse, on the high pedestal on which Venetian gratitude maintains him. The statue is incomparable, the finest of all mounted figures, unless that of Marcus Aurelius, who rides benignant before the Roman Capitol, be finer: but I was not thinking of that; I only found myself staring at the triumphant captain as if he had an oracle on his lips. The western light shines into all his grimness at that hour and makes it wonderfully personal. But he continued to look far over my head, at the red immersion of another day – he had seen so many go down into the lagoon through the centuries – and if he were thinking of battles and stratagems they were of a different quality from any

I had to tell him of. He could not direct me what to do, gaze up at him as I might. Was it before this or after that I wandered about for an hour in the small canals, to the continued stupefaction of my gondolier, who had never seen me so restless and yet so void of a purpose and could extract from me no order but 'Go anywhere – everywhere – all over the place'? He reminded me that I had not lunched and expressed therefore respectfully the hope that I would dine earlier. He had had long periods of leisure during the day, when I had left the boat and rambled, so that I was not obliged to consider him, and I told him that that day, for a change, I would touch no meat. It was an effect of poor Miss Tita's proposal, not altogether auspicious, that I had quite lost my appetite. I don't know why it happened that on this occasion I was more than ever struck with that queer air of sociability, of cousinship and family life, which makes up half the expression of Venice. Without streets and vehicles, the uproar of wheels, the brutality of horses, and with its little winding ways where people crowd together, where voices sound as in the corridors of a house, where the human step circulates as if it skirted the angles of furniture and shoes never wear out, the place has the character of an immense collective apartment, in which Piazza San Marco is the most ornamented corner and palaces and churches, for the rest, play the part of great divans of repose, tables of entertainment, expanses of decoration. And somehow the splendid common domicile, familiar, domestic and resonant, also resembles a theatre, with actors clicking over bridges and, in straggling processions, tripping along fondamentas. As you sit in your gondola the footways that in certain parts edge the canals assume to the eye the importance of a stage, meeting it at the same angle, and the Venetian figures, moving to and fro against the battered scenery of their little houses of comedy, strike you as members of an endless dramatic troupe.

I went to bed that night very tired, without being able to compose a letter to Miss Tita. Was this failure the reason why I became conscious the next morning as soon as I awoke of a determination to see the poor lady again the first moment she would receive me? That had something to do with it, but what had still more was the fact that during my sleep a very odd revulsion had taken place in my spirit. I found myself aware of this almost as soon as I opened my eyes; it made me jump out of my bed with the movement of a man who remembers that he has left the housedoor ajar or a candle burning under a shelf. Was I still in time to save my goods? That question was in my heart; for what had now come to pass was that in the unconscious cerebration of sleep I had swung back to a passionate appreciation of Miss Bordereau's papers. They were now more precious than ever and a kind of ferocity had come into my desire to possess them. The condition Miss Tita had attached to the possession of them no longer appeared an obstacle worth thinking of, and for an hour, that morning, my repentant imagination brushed it aside. It was absurd that I should be able to invent nothing; absurd to renounce so easily and turn away helpless from the idea that the only way to get hold of the papers was to unite myself to her for life. I would not unite myself and yet I would have them. I must add that by the time I sent down to ask if she would see me I had invented no alternative, though to do so I had had all the time that I was dressing. This failure was humiliating, yet what could the alternative be? Miss Tita sent back word that I might come; and as I descended the stairs and crossed the sala to her door – this time she received me in her aunt's forlorn parlour – I hoped she would not think my errand was to tell her I accepted her hand. She certainly would have made the day before the reflection that I declined it.

As soon as I came into the room I saw that she had drawn this inference, but I also saw something which had not been in my forecast. Poor Miss Tita's sense of her failure had produced an extraordinary alteration in her, but I had been too full of my literary concupiscence to think of that. Now I perceived it; I can scarcely tell how it startled me. She stood in the middle of the room with a face of mildness bent upon me, and her look of forgiveness, of absolution made her angelic. It beautified her; she was younger; she was not a ridiculous old woman. This optical trick gave her a sort of phantasmagoric brightness, and while I was still the victim of it I heard a whisper somewhere in the depths of my conscience: 'Why not, after all – why not?' It seemed to me I was ready to pay the price. Still more distinctly however than the whisper I heard Miss Tita's own voice. I was so struck with the different effect she made upon me that at first I was not clearly aware of what she was saying; then I perceived she had bade me good-bye – she said something about hoping I should be very happy.

'Good-bye – good-bye?' I repeated, with an inflection interrogative and probably foolish.

I saw she did not feel the interrogation, she only heard the words; she had strung herself up to accepting our separation and they fell upon her ear as a proof. 'Are you going today?' she asked. 'But it doesn't matter, for whenever you go I shall not see you again. I don't want to.' And she smiled strangely, with an infinite gentleness. She had never doubted that I had left her the day before in horror. How could she, since I had not come back before night to contradict, even as a simple form, such an idea? And now she had the force of soul – Miss Tita with force of soul was a new conception – to smile at me in her humiliation.

'What shall you do – where shall you go?' I asked.

'Oh, I don't know. I have done the great thing. I have destroyed the papers.'

'Destroyed them?' I faltered.

'Yes; what was I to keep them for? I burnt them last night, one by one, in the kitchen.'

'One by one?' I repeated, mechanically.

'It took a long time – there were so many.' The room seemed to go round me as she said this and a real darkness for a moment descended upon my eyes. When it passed Miss Tita was there still, but the transfiguration was over and she had changed back to a plain, dingy, elderly person. It was in this character she spoke as she said, 'I can't stay with you longer, I can't;' and it was in this character that she turned her back upon me, as I had turned mine upon her twenty-four hours before, and moved to the door of her room. Here she did what I had not done when I quitted her – she paused long enough to give me one look. I have never forgotten it and I sometimes still suffer from it, though it was not resentful. No, there was no resentment, nothing hard or vindictive in poor Miss Tita; for when, later, I sent her in exchange for the portrait of Jeffrey Aspern a larger sum of money than I had hoped to be able to gather for her, writing to her that I had sold the picture, she kept it with thanks; she never sent it back. I wrote to her that I had sold the picture, but I admitted to Mrs Prest, at the time (I met her in London, in the autumn), that it hangs above my writing table. When I look at it my chagrin at the loss of the letters becomes almost intolerable.

The Turn of the Screw

The Turn of the Screw

The story had held us, round the fire, sufficiently breathless, but except the obvious remark that it was gruesome, as, on Christmas eve in an old house, a strange tale should essentially be, I remember no comment uttered till somebody happened to say that it was the only case he had met in which such a visitation had fallen on a child. The case, I may mention, was that of an apparition in just such an old house as had gathered us for the occasion – an appearance, of a dreadful kind, to a little boy sleeping in the room with his mother and waking her up in the terror of it; waking her not to dissipate his dread and soothe him to sleep again, but to encounter also, herself, before she had succeeded in doing so, the same sight that had shaken him. It was this observation that drew from Douglas – not immediately, but later in the evening – a reply that had the interesting consequence to which I call attention. Someone else told a story not particularly effective, which I saw he was not following. This I took for a sign that he had himself something to produce and that we should only have to wait. We waited in fact till two nights later; but that same evening, before we scattered, he brought out what was in his mind.

'I quite agree – in regard to Griffin's ghost, or whatever it was – that its appearing first to the little boy, at so tender an age, adds a particular touch. But it's not the first occurrence of its charming kind that I know to have involved a child. If the child gives the effect another turn of the screw, what do you say to *two* children—?'

'We say, of course,' somebody exclaimed, 'that they give two turns! Also that we want to hear about them.'

I can see Douglas there before the fire, to which he had got up to present his back, looking down at his interlocutor with his hands in his pockets. 'Nobody but me, till now, has ever heard. It's quite too horrible.' This, naturally, was declared by several voices to give the thing the utmost price, and our friend, with quiet art, prepared his triumph by turning his eyes over the rest of us and going on: 'It's beyond everything. Nothing at all that I know touches it.'

'For sheer terror?' I remember asking.

He seemed to say it was not so simple as that; to be really at a loss how to qualify it. He passed his hand over his eyes, made a little wincing grimace. 'For dreadful – dreadfulness!'

'Oh, how delicious!' cried one of the women.

He took no notice of her; he looked at me, but as if, instead of me, he saw what he spoke of. 'For general uncanny ugliness and horror and pain.'

'Well then,' I said, 'just sit right down and begin.'

He turned round to the fire, gave a kick to a log, watched it an instant.

Then as he faced us again: 'I can't begin. I shall have to send to town.' There was a unanimous groan at this, and much reproach; after which, in his preoccupied way, he explained. 'The story's written. It's in a locked drawer – it has not been out for years. I could write to my man and enclose the key; he could send down the packet as he finds it.' It was to me in particular that he appeared to propound this – appeared almost to appeal for aid not to hesitate. He had broken a thickness of ice, the formation of many a winter; had had his reasons for a long silence. The others resented postponement, but it was just his scruples that charmed me. I adjured him to write by the first post and to agree with us for an early hearing; then I asked him if the experience in question had been his own. To this his answer was prompt. 'Oh, thank God, no!'

'And is the record yours? You took the thing down?'

'Nothing but the impression. I took that *here*' – he tapped his heart. 'I've never lost it.'

'Then your manuscript—?'

'Is in old, faded ink, and in the most beautiful hand.' He hung fire again. 'A woman's. She has been dead these twenty years. She sent me the pages in question before she died.' They were all listening now, and of course there was somebody to be arch, or at any rate to draw the inference. But if he put the inference by without a smile it was also without irritation. 'She was a most charming person, but she was ten years older than I. She was my sister's governess,' he quietly said. 'She was the most agreeable woman I've ever known in her position; she would have been worthy of any whatever. It was long ago, and this episode was long before. I was at Trinity, and I found her at home on my coming down the second summer. I was much there that year – it was a beautiful one; and we had, in her off-hours, some strolls and talks in the garden – talks in which she struck me as awfully clever and nice. Oh yes; don't grin: I liked her extremely and am glad to this day to think she liked me too. If she hadn't she wouldn't have told me. She had never told anyone. It wasn't simply that she said so, but that I knew she hadn't. I was sure; I could see. You'll easily judge why when you hear.'

'Because the thing had been such a scare?'

He continued to fix me. 'You'll easily judge,' he repeated: '*you* will.'

I fixed him too. 'I see. She was in love.'

He laughed for the first time. 'You *are* acute. Yes, she was in love. That is she had been. That came out – she couldn't tell her story without it's coming out. I saw it, and she saw I saw it; but neither of us spoke of it. I remember the time and the place – the corner of the lawn, the shade of the great beeches and the long, hot summer afternoon. It wasn't a scene for a shudder; but oh—!' He quitted the fire and dropped back into his chair.

'You'll receive the packet Thursday morning?' I inquired.

'Probably not till the second post.'

'Well then; after dinner—'

'You'll all meet me here?' He looked us round again. 'Isn't anybody going?' It was almost the tone of hope.

'Everybody will stay!'

'*I* will – and *I* will!' cried the ladies whose departure had been fixed. Mrs Griffin, however, expressed the need for a little more light. 'Who was it she was in love with?'

'The story will tell,' I took upon myself to reply.

'Oh, I can't wait for the story!'

'The story *won't* tell,' said Douglas; 'not in any literal, vulgar way.'

'More's the pity then. That's the only way I ever understand.'

'Won't *you* tell, Douglas?' somebody else inquired.

He sprang to his feet again.'Yes – tomorrow. Now I must go to bed. Good night.' And, quickly, catching up a candlestick, he left us slightly bewildered. From our end of the great brown hall we heard his step on the stair; whereupon Mrs Griffin spoke. 'Well, if I don't know who she was in love with, I know who *he* was.'

'She was ten years older,' said her husband.

'*Raison de plus* – at that age! But it's rather nice, his long reticence.'

'Forty years!' Griffin put in.

'With this outbreak at last.'

'The outbreak,' I returned, 'will make a tremendous occasion of Thursday night'; and everyone so agreed with me that, in the light of it, we lost all attention for everything else. The last story, however incomplete and like the mere opening of a serial, had been told; we handshook and 'candle-stuck', as somebody said, and went to bed.

I knew the next day that a letter containing the key had, by the first post, gone off to his London apartments; but in spite of – or perhaps just on account of – the eventual diffusion of this knowledge we quite let him alone till after dinner, till such an hour of the evening, in fact, as might best accord with the kind of emotion on which our hopes were fixed. Then he became as communicative as we could desire and indeed gave us his best reason for being so. We had it from him again before the fire in the hall, as we had had our mild wonders of the previous night. It appeared that the narrative he had promised to read us really required for a proper intelligence a few words of prologue. Let me say here distinctly, to have done with it, that this narrative, from an exact transcript of my own made much later, is what I shall presently give. Poor Douglas, before his death – when it was in sight – committed to me the manuscript that reached him on the third of these days and that, on the same spot, with immense effect, he began to read to our hushed little circle on the night of the fourth. The departing ladies who had said they would stay didn't, of course, thank heaven, stay: they departed, in consequence of arrangements made, in a rage of curiosity, as they professed, produced by the touches with which he had already worked us up. But that only made his little final auditory more compact and select, kept it, round the hearth, subject to a common thrill.

The first of these touches conveyed that the written statement took up the tale at a point after it had, in a manner, begun. The fact to be in possession of was therefore that his old friend, the youngest of several daughters of a poor country parson, had, at the age of twenty, on taking service for the first time in the schoolroom, come up to London, in trepidation, to answer in person an advertisement that had already placed her in brief correspondence with the advertiser. This person proved, on her presenting herself, for judgement, at a house, in Harley Street, that impressed her as vast and imposing – this prospective patron proved a gentleman, a bachelor in the prime of life, such a figure as had never risen, save in a dream or an old novel, before a fluttered, anxious girl out of a Hampshire vicarage. One could easily fix his type; it never, happily, dies out. He was handsome and bold and pleasant, off-hand and gay and kind. He struck her, inevitably, as gallant and splendid, but what took her most of all and gave her the courage she afterwards showed was that he put the whole thing to her as a kind of favour, an obligation he should gratefully incur. She conceived him as rich, but as fearfully extravagant – saw him all in a glow of high fashion, of good looks, of expensive habits, of charming ways with women. He had for his town residence a big house filled with the spoils of travel and the trophies of the chase; but it was to his country home, an old family place in Essex, that he wished her immediately to proceed.

He had been left, by the death of their parents in India, guardian to a small nephew and a small niece, children of a younger, a military brother, whom he had lost two years before. These children were, by the strangest of chances for a man in his position – a lone man without the right sort of experience or a grain of patience – very heavily on his hands. It had all been a great worry and, on his own part doubtless, a series of blunders, but he immensely pitied the poor chicks and had done all he could; had in particular sent them down to his other house, the proper place for them being of course the country, and kept them there, from the first, with the best people he could find to look after them, parting even with his own servants to wait on them and going down himself, whenever he might, to see how they were doing. The awkward thing was that they had practically no other relations and that his own affairs took up all his time. He had put them in possession of Bly, which was healthy and secure, and had placed at the head of their little establishment – but below stairs only – an excellent woman, Mrs Grose, whom he was sure his visitor would like and who had formerly been maid to his mother. She was now housekeeper and was also acting for the time as superintendent to the little girl, of whom, without children of her own, she was, by good luck, extremely fond. There were plenty of people to help, but of course the young lady who should go down as governess would be in supreme authority. She would also have, in holidays, to look after the small boy, who had been for a term at school – young as he was to be sent, but what else could be done? – and who, as the holidays were about to begin, would be back from one day to the other. There had been for the two children at first a young lady whom they had had the misfortune to lose. She had done for them quite beautifully – she was a most respectable person – till her death, the great awkwardness of which had, precisely, left no alternative but the school for little Miles. Mrs Grose, since then, in the way of manners and things, had done as she could for Flora; and there were, further, a cook, a housemaid, a dairywoman, an old pony, an old groom and an old gardener, all likewise thoroughly respectable.

So far had Douglas presented his picture when someone put a question. 'And what did the former governess die of? – of so much respectability?'

Our friend's answer was prompt. 'That will come out. I don't anticipate.'

'Excuse me – I thought that was just what you *are* doing.'

'In her successor's place,' I suggested, 'I should have wished to learn if the office brought with it—'

'Necessary danger to life?' Douglas completed my thought. 'She did wish to learn, and she did learn. You shall hear tomorrow what she learnt. Meanwhile, of course, the prospect struck her as slightly grim. She was young, untried, nervous: it was a vision of serious duties and little company, of really great loneliness. She hesitated – took a couple of days to consult and consider. But the salary offered much exceeded her modest measure, and on a second interview she faced the music, she engaged.' And Douglas, with this, made a pause that, for the benefit of the company, moved me to throw in—

'The moral of which was of course the seduction exercised by the splendid young man. She succumbed to it.'

He got up and, as he had done the night before, went to the fire, gave a stir to a log with his foot, then stood a moment with his back to us. 'She saw him only twice.'

'Yes, but that's just the beauty of her passion.'

A little to my surprise, on this, Douglas turned round to me. 'It *was* the beauty of it. There were others,' he went on, 'who hadn't succumbed. He told her frankly all his difficulty – that for several applicants the conditions had been prohibitive. They were, somehow, simply afraid. It sounded dull – it sounded strange; and all the more so because of his main condition.'

'Which was—?'

'That she should never trouble him – but never, never: neither appeal nor complain nor write about anything; only meet all questions herself, receive all moneys from his solicitor, take the whole thing over and let him alone. She promised to do this, and she mentioned to me that when, for a moment, disburdened, delighted, he held her hand, thanking her for the sacrifice, she already felt rewarded.'

'But was that all her reward?' one of the ladies asked.

'She never saw him again.'

'Oh!' said the lady; which, as our friend immediately left us again, was the only other word of importance contributed to the subject till, the next night, by the corner of the hearth, in the best chair, he opened the faded red cover of a thin old-fashioned gilt-edged album. The whole thing took indeed more nights than one, but on the first occasion the same lady put another question. 'What is your title?'

'I haven't one.'

'Oh, *I* have!' I said. But Douglas, without heeding me, had begun to read with a fine clearness that was like a rendering to the ear of the beauty of his author's hand.

Chapter One

I remember the whole beginning as a succession of flights and drops, a little see-saw of the right throbs and the wrong. After rising, in town, to meet his appeal, I had at all events a couple of very bad days – found myself doubtful again, felt indeed sure I had made a mistake. In this state of mind I spent the long hours of bumping, swinging coach that carried me to the stopping-place at which I was to be met by a vehicle from the house. This convenience, I was told, had been ordered, and I found, towards the close of the June afternoon, a commodious fly in waiting for me. Driving at that hour, on a lovely day, through a country to which the summer sweetness seemed to offer me a friendly welcome, my fortitude mounted afresh and, as we turned into the avenue, encountered a reprieve that was probably but a proof of the point to which it had sunk. I suppose I had expected, or had dreaded, something so melancholy that what greeted me was a good surprise. I remember as a most pleasant impression the broad, clear front, its open windows and fresh curtains and the pair of maids looking out; I remember the lawn and the bright flowers and the crunch of my wheels on the gravel and the clustered tree-tops over which the rooks circled and cawed in the golden sky. The scene had a greatness that made it a different affair from my own scant home, and there immediately appeared at the door, with a little girl in her hand, a civil person who dropped me as decent a curtsey as if I had been the mistress or a distinguished visitor. I had received in Harley Street a narrower notion of the place, and that, as I recalled it, made me think the proprietor still more of a gentleman, suggested that what I was to enjoy might be something beyond his promise.

I had no drop again till the next day, for I was carried triumphantly through the following hours by my introduction to the younger of my pupils. The little girl who accompanied Mrs Grose appeared to me on the spot a creature so charming as to make it a great fortune to have to do with her. She was the most beautiful child I had ever seen, and I afterwards wondered that my employer had not told me more of her. I slept little that night – I was too much excited; and this astonished me too, I recollect, remained with me, adding to my sense of the liberality with which I was treated. The large, impressive room, one of the best in the house, the great state bed, as I almost felt it, the full, figured draperies, the long glasses in which, for the first time, I could see myself from head to foot, all struck me – like the extraordinary charm of my small charge – as so many things thrown in. It was thrown in as well, from the first moment, that I should get on with Mrs Grose in a relation over which, on my way, in the coach, I fear I had rather brooded. The only thing indeed that in this early outlook might have made me shrink again was the clear circumstance of her being so glad to see me. I perceived within half an hour that she was so glad – stout, simple, plain, clean, wholesome woman – as to be positively on her guard against showing it too much. I wondered even then a little why she should wish not to show it and that, with reflection, with suspicion, might of course have made me uneasy.

But it was a comfort that there could be no uneasiness in a connexion with anything so beatific as the radiant image of my little girl, the vision of whose angelic beauty had probably more than anything else to do with the restlessness that, before morning, made me several times rise and wander about my room to take in the whole picture and prospect; to watch, from my open window, the faint summer dawn, to look at such portions of the rest of the house as I could catch, and to listen, while, in the fading dusk, the first birds began to twitter, for the possible recurrence of a sound or two, less natural and not without, but within, that I had fancied I heard. There had been a moment when I believed I recognized, faint and far, the cry of a child; there had been another when I found myself just consciously starting as at the passage, before my door, of a light footstep. But these fancies were not marked enough not to be thrown off, and it is only in the light, or the gloom, I should rather say, of other and subsequent matters that they now come back to me. To watch, teach, 'form' little Flora would too evidently be the making of a happy and useful life. It had been agreed between us downstairs that after this first occasion I should have her as a matter of course at night, her small white bed being already arranged, to that end, in my room. What I had undertaken was the whole care of her, and she had remained, just this last time, with Mrs Grose only as an effect of our consideration for my inevitable strangeness and her natural timidity. In spite of this timidity – which the child herself, in the oddest way in the world, had been perfectly frank and brave about, allowing it, without a sign of uncomfortable consciousness, with the deep, sweet serenity indeed of one of Raphael's holy infants, to be discussed, to be imputed to her and to determine us – I felt quite sure she would presently like me. It was part of what I already liked Mrs Grose herself for, the pleasure I could see her feel in my admiration and wonder as I sat at supper with four tall candles and with my pupil, in a high chair and bib, brightly facing me, between them, over bread and milk. There were naturally things that in Flora's presence could pass between us only as prodigious and gratified looks, obscure and roundabout allusions.

'And the little boy – does he look like her? Is he too so very remarkable?'

One wouldn't flatter a child. 'Oh Miss, *most* remarkable. If you think well of this one!' – and she stood there with a plate in her hand, beaming at our companion, who looked from one of us to the other with placid heavenly eyes that contained nothing to check us.

'Yes; if I do—?'

'You *will* be carried away by the little gentleman!'

'Well, that, I think, is what I came for – to be carried away. I'm afraid, however,' I remember feeling the impulse to add, 'I'm rather easily carried away. I was carried away in London!'

I can still see Mrs Grose's broad face as she took this in. 'In Harley Street?'

'In Harley Street.'

'Well, Miss, you're not the first – and you won't be the last.'

'Oh, I've no pretension,' I could laugh, 'to being the only one. My other pupil, at any rate, as I understand, comes back tomorrow?'

'Not tomorrow – Friday, Miss. He arrives, as you did, by the coach, under care of the guard, and is to be met by the same carriage.'

I forthwith expressed that the proper as well as the pleasant and friendly thing would be therefore that on the arrival of the public conveyance I should be in waiting for him with his little sister; an idea in which Mrs Grose concurred so heartily that I somehow took her manner as a kind of comforting pledge – never falsified, thank heaven! – that we should on every question be quite at one. Oh, she was glad I was there!

What I felt the next day was, I suppose, nothing that could be fairly called a reaction from the cheer of my arrival; it was probably at the most only a slight oppression produced by a fuller measure of the scale, as I walked round them, gazed up at them, took them in, of my new circumstances.

They had, as it were, an extent and mass for which I had not been prepared and in the presence of which I found myself, freshly, a little scared as well as a little proud. Lessons, in this agitation, certainly suffered some delay; I reflected that my first duty was, by the gentlest arts I could contrive, to win the child into the sense of knowing me. I spent the day with her out of doors; I arranged with her, to her great satisfaction, that it should be she, she only, who might show me the place. She showed it step by step and room by room and secret by secret, with droll, delightful, childish talk about it and with the result, in half an hour, of our becoming immense friends. Young as she was, I was struck, throughout our little tour, with her confidence and courage with the way, in empty chambers and dull corridors, on crooked staircases that made me pause and even on the summit of an old machicolated square tower that made me dizzy, her morning music, her disposition to tell me so many more things than she asked, rang out and led me on. I have not seen Bly since the day I left it, and I dare say that to my older and more informed eyes it would now appear sufficiently contracted. But as my little conductress, with her hair of gold and her frock of blue, danced before me round corners and pattered down passages, I had the view of a castle of romance inhabited by a rosy sprite, such a place as would somehow, for diversion of the young idea, take all colour out of storybooks and fairy-tales. Wasn't it just a storybook over which I had fallen a-doze and a-dream? No; it was a big, ugly, antique, but convenient house, embodying a few features of a building still older, half replaced and half utilized, in which I had the fancy of our being almost as lost as a handful of passengers in a great drifting ship. Well, I was, strangely, at the helm!

Chapter Two

This came home to me when, two days later, I drove over with Flora to meet, as Mrs Grose said, the little gentleman; and all the more for an incident that, presenting itself the second evening, had deeply disconcerted me. The first day had been, on the whole, as I have expressed, reassuring; but I was to see it wind up in keen apprehension. The postbag, that evening – it came late – contained a letter for me, which, however, in the hand of my employer, I found to be composed but of a few words enclosing another, addressed to himself, with a seal still unbroken. 'This, I recognize, is from the head-master, and the head-master's an awful bore. Read him, please; deal with him; but mind you don't report. Not a word. I'm off!' I broke the seal with a great effort – so great a one that I was a long time coming to it; took the unopened missive at last up to my room and only attacked it just before going to bed. I had better have let it wait till morning, for it gave me a second sleepless night. With no counsel to take, the next day, I was full of distress; and it finally got so the better of me that I determined to open myself at least to Mrs Grose.

'What does it mean? The child's dismissed his school.'

She gave me a look that I remarked at the moment; then, visibly, with a quick blankness, seemed to try to take it back. 'But aren't they all—?'

'Sent home – yes. But only for the holidays. Miles may never go back at all.'

Consciously, under my attention, she reddened. 'They won't take him?'

'They absolutely decline.'

At this she raised her eyes, which she had turned from me; I saw them fill with good tears. 'What has he done?'

I hesitated; then I judged best simply to hand her my letter – which, however, had the effect of making her, without taking it, simply put her hands behind her. She shook her head sadly. 'Such things are not for me, Miss.'

My counsellor couldn't read! I winced at my mistake, which I attenuated as I could, and opened my letter again to repeat it to her; then, faltering in the act and folding it up once more, I put it back in my pocket. 'Is he really *bad*?'

The tears were still in her eyes. 'Do the gentlemen say so?'

'They go into no particulars. They simply express their regret that it should be impossible to keep him. That can have only one meaning.' Mrs Grose listened with dumb emotion; she forbore to ask me what this meaning might be; so that, presently, to put the thing with some coherence and with the mere aid of her presence to my own mind, I went on: 'That he's an injury to the others.'

At this, with one of the quick turns of simple folk, she suddenly flamed up. 'Master Miles! – *him* an injury?'

There was such a flood of good faith in it that, though I had not yet seen the child, my very fears made me jump to the absurdity of the idea. I found myself, to meet my friend the better, offering it, on the spot, sarcastically. 'To his poor little innocent mates!'

'It's too dreadful,' cried Mrs Grose, 'to say such cruel things! Why, he's scarce ten years old.'

'Yes, yes; it would be incredible.'

She was evidently grateful for such a profession. 'See him, Miss, first. *Then* believe it!' I felt forthwith a new impatience to see him; it was the beginning of a curiosity that, for all the next hours, was to deepen almost to pain. Mrs Grose was aware, I could judge, of what she had produced in me, and she followed it up with assurance. 'You might as well believe it of the little lady. Bless her,' she added the next moment – '*look* at her!'

I turned and saw that Flora, whom, ten minutes before, I had established in the school room with a sheet of white paper, a pencil and a copy of nice 'round O's', now presented herself to view at the open door. She expressed in her little way an extraordinary detachment from disagreeable duties, looking at me, however, with a great childish light that seemed to offer it as a mere result of the affection she had conceived for my person, which had rendered necessary that she should follow me. I needed nothing more than this to feel the full force of Mrs Grose's comparison, and, catching my pupil in my arms, covered her with kisses in which there was a sob of atonement.

None the less, the rest of the day, I watched for further occasion to approach my colleague, especially as, towards evening, I began to fancy she rather sought to avoid me. I overtook her, I remember, on the staircase; we went down together, and at the bottom I detained her, holding her there with a hand on her arm. 'I take what you said to me at noon as a declaration that *you've* never known him to be bad.'

She threw back her head; she had clearly, by this time, and very honestly, adopted an attitude. 'Oh, never known him – I don't pretend *that*!'

I was upset again. 'Then you *have* known him –?'

'Yes indeed, Miss, thank God!'

On reflection I accepted this. 'You mean that a boy who never is –?'

'Is no boy for *me*!'

I held her tighter. 'You like them with the spirit to be naughty?' Then, keeping pace with her answer. 'So do I!' I eagerly brought out. 'But not to the degree to contaminate—'

'To contaminate?' – my big word left her at a loss.

I explained it. 'To corrupt.'

She stared, taking my meaning in; but it produced in her an odd laugh. 'Are you afraid he'll corrupt *you*?' She put the question with such a fine bold humour that, with a laugh, a little silly doubtless, to match her own, I gave way for the time to the apprehension of ridicule.

But the next day, as the hour for my drive approached, I cropped up in another place. 'What was the lady who was here before?'

'The last governess? She was also young and pretty – almost as young and almost as pretty, Miss, even as you.'

'Ah, then, I hope her youth and her beauty helped her!' I recollect throwing off. 'He seems to like us young and pretty!'

'Oh, he *did*,' Mrs Grose assented: 'it was the way he liked everyone!' She had no sooner spoken indeed than she caught herself up. 'I mean that's *his* way – the master's.'

I was struck. 'But of whom did you speak first?'

She looked blank, but she coloured. 'Why, of *him*.'

'Of the master?'

'Of who else?'

There was so obviously no one else that the next moment I had lost my impression of her having accidentally said more than she meant; and I merely asked what I wanted to know. 'Did *she* see anything in the boy—?'

'That wasn't right? She never told me.'

I had a scruple, but I overcame it. 'Was she careful – particular?'

Mrs Grose appeared to try to be conscientious. 'About some things – yes.'

'But not about all?'

Again she considered. 'Well, Miss – she's gone. I won't tell tales.'

'I quite understand your feeling,' I hastened to reply; but I thought it, after an instant, not opposed to this concession to pursue: 'Did she die here?'

'No – she went off.'

I don't know what there was in this brevity of Mrs Grose's that struck me as ambiguous. 'Went off to die?' Mrs Grose looked straight out of the window, but I felt that, hypothetically, I had a right to know what young persons engaged for Bly were expected to do. 'She was taken ill, you mean, and went home?'

'She was not taken ill, so far as appeared, in this house. She left it, at the end of the year, to go home, as she said, for a short holiday, to which the time she had put in had certainly given her a right. We had then a young woman – a nursemaid who had stayed on and who was a good girl and clever; and *she* took the children altogether for the interval. But our young lady never came back, and at the very moment I was expecting her I heard from the master that she was dead.'

I turned this over. 'But of what?'

'He never told me! But please, Miss,' said Mrs Grose, 'I must get to my work.'

Chapter Three

Her thus turning her back on me was fortunately not, for my just preoccupations, a snub that could check the growth of our mutual esteem. We met, after I had brought home little Miles, more intimately than ever on the ground of my stupefaction, my general emotion: so monstrous was I then ready to pronounce it that such a child as had now been revealed to me should be under an interdict. I was a little late on the scene, and I felt, as he stood wistfully looking out for me before the door of the inn at which the coach had put him down, that I had seen him, on the instant, without and within, in the great glow of freshness, the same positive fragrance of purity, in which I had, from the first moment, seen his little sister. He was incredibly beautiful, and Mrs Grose had put her finger on it: everything but a sort of passion of tenderness for him was swept away by his presence. What I then and there took him to my heart for was something divine that I have never found to the same degree in any child – his indescribable little air of knowing nothing in the world but love. It would have been impossible to carry a bad name with a greater sweetness of innocence, and by the time I had got back to Bly with him I remained merely bewildered – so far, that is, as I was not outraged – by the sense of the horrible letter locked up in my room, in a drawer. As soon as I could compass a private word with Mrs Grose I declared to her that it was grotesque.

She promptly understood me. 'You mean the cruel charge—?'

'It doesn't live an instant. My dear woman, *look* at him!'

She smiled at my pretension to have discovered his charm. 'I assure you, Miss, I do nothing else!' What will you say, then?' she immediately added.

'In answer to the letter?' I had made up my mind. 'Nothing.'

'And to his uncle?'

I was incisive. 'Nothing.'

'And to the boy himself?'

I was wonderful. 'Nothing.'

She gave with her apron a great wipe to her mouth. 'Then I'll stand by you. We'll see it out.'

'We'll see it out!' I ardently echoed, giving her my hand to make it a vow.

She held me there a moment, then whisked up her apron again with her detached hand. 'Would you mind, Miss, if I used the freedom—'

'To kiss me? No!' I took the good creature in my arms and, after we had embraced like sisters, felt still more fortified and indignant.

This, at all events, was for the time: a time so full that, as I recall the way it went, it reminds me of all the art I now need to make it a little distinct. What I look back at with amazement is the situation I accepted. I had undertaken, with my companion, to see it out, and I was under a charm, apparently, that could smooth away the extent and the far and difficult connexions of such an effort. I was lifted aloft on a great wave of infatuation and pity. I found it simple, in my ignorance, my confusion, and perhaps my conceit, to assume that I could deal with a boy whose education for the world was all on the point of beginning. I am unable even to remember at this day what proposal I framed for the end of his holidays and the resumption of his studies. Lessons with me indeed, that charming summer, we all had a theory that he was to have; but I now feel that, for weeks, the lessons must have been rather my own. I learnt something – at first certainly – that had not been one of the teachings of my small, smothered life; learnt to be amused, and even amusing, and not to think for the morrow. It was the first time, in a manner, that I had known space and air and freedom, all the music of summer and all the mystery of nature. And then there was consideration – and consideration was sweet. Oh, it was a trap – not designed, but deep – to my imagination, to my delicacy, perhaps to my vanity; to whatever, in me, was most excitable. The best way to picture it all is to say that I was off my guard. They gave me so little trouble – they were of a gentleness so extraordinary. I used to speculate – but even this with a dim disconnectedness – as to how the rough future (for all futures are rough!) would handle them and might bruise them. They had the bloom of health and happiness; and yet, as if I had been in charge of a pair of little grandees, of princes of the blood, for whom everything, to be right, would have to be enclosed and protected, the only form that, in my fancy, the after-years could take for them was that of a romantic, a really royal extension of the garden and the park. It may be, of course, above all, that what suddenly broke into this gives the previous time a charm of stillness – that hush in which something gathers or crouches. The change was actually like the spring of a beast.

In the first weeks the days were long; they often, at their finest, gave me what I used to call my own hour, the hour when, for my pupils, tea-time and bed-time having come and gone, I had, before my final retirement, a small interval alone. Much as I liked my companions, this hour was the thing in the day I liked most; and I liked it best of all when, as the light faded – or rather, I should say, the day lingered and the last calls of the last birds sounded, in a flushed sky, from the old trees – I could take a turn into the grounds and enjoy, almost with a sense of property that amused and flattered me, the beauty and dignity of the place. It was a pleasure at these moments to feel myself tranquil and justified; doubtless, perhaps, also to reflect that by my discretion, my quiet good sense and general high propriety,

I was giving pleasure – if he ever thought of it! – to the person to whose pressure I had responded. What I was doing was what he had earnestly hoped and directly asked of me, and that I *could*, after all, do it proved even a greater joy than I had expected. I dare say I fancied myself, in short, a remarkable young woman and took comfort in the faith that this would more publicly appear. Well, I needed to be remarkable to offer a front to the remarkable things that presently gave their first sign.

It was plump, one afternoon, in the middle of my very hour: the children were tucked away and I had come out for my stroll. One of the thoughts that, as I don't in the least shrink now from noting, used to be with me in these wanderings was that it would be as charming as a charming story suddenly to meet someone. Someone would appear there at the turn of a path and would stand before me and smile and approve. I didn't ask more than that – I only asked that he should *know*; and the only way to be sure he knew would be to see it, and the kind light of it, in his handsome face. That was exactly present to me – by which I mean the face was – when, on the first of these occasions, at the end of a long June day, I stopped short on emerging from one of the plantations and coming into view of the house. What arrested me on the spot – and with a shock much greater than any vision had allowed for – was the sense that my imagination had, in a flash, turned real. He did stand there! – but high up, beyond the lawn and at the very top of the tower to which, on that first morning, little Flora had conducted me. This tower was one of a pair – square, incongruous, crenelated structures – that were distinguished, for some reason, though I could see little difference, as the new and the old. They flanked opposite ends of the house and were probably architectural absurdities, redeemed in a measure indeed by not being wholly disengaged nor of a height too pretentious, dating, in their gingerbread antiquity, from a romantic revival that was already a respectable past. I admired them, had fancies about them, for we could all profit in a degree, especially when they loomed through the dusk, by the grandeur of their actual battlements; yet it was not at such an elevation that the figure I had so often invoked seemed most in place.

It produced in me, this figure, in the clear twilight, I remember, two distinct gasps of emotion, which were, sharply, the shock of my first and that of my second surprise. My second was a violent perception of the mistake of my first: the man who met my eyes was not the person I had precipitately supposed. There came to me thus a bewilderment of vision of which, after these years, there is no living view that I can hope to give. An unknown man in a lonely place is a permitted object of fear to a young woman privately bred; and the figure that faced me was – a few more seconds assured me – as little anyone else I knew as it was the image that had been in my mind. I had not seen it in Harley Street – I had not seen it anywhere. The place, moreover, in the strangest way in the world, had, on the instant, and by the very fact of its appearance, become a solitude. To me at least, making my statement here with a deliberation with which I have never made it, the whole feeling of the moment returns. It was as if, while I took in – what I did take in – all the rest of the scene had been stricken with death. I can hear again, as I write, the intense hush in which the sounds of evening dropped. The rooks stopped cawing in the golden sky and the friendly hour lost, for the minute, all its voice. But there was no other change in nature, unless indeed it were a change that I saw with a stranger sharpness. The gold was still in the sky, the clearness in the air, and the man who looked at me over the battlements was as definite as a picture in a frame. That's how I thought, with extraordinary quickness, of each person that he might have been and that he was not. We were confronted across our distance quite long enough for me to ask myself with intensity who then he was and to feel, as an effect of my inability to say, a wonder that in a few instants more became intense.

The great question, or one of these, is, afterwards, I know, with regard to certain matters, the question of how long they have lasted. Well, this matter of mine, think what you will of it, lasted while I caught at a dozen possibilities, none of which made a difference for the better, that I could see, in there having been in the house – and for how long, above all? – a person of whom I was in ignorance. It lasted while I just bridled a little with the sense that my office demanded that there should be no such ignorance and no such person. It lasted while this visitant, at all events – and there was a touch of the strange freedom, as I remember, in the sign of familiarity of his wearing no hat – seemed to fix me, from his position, with just the question, just the scrutiny through the fading light, that his own presence provoked. We were too far apart to call to each other, but there was a moment at which, at shorter range, some challenge between us, breaking the hush, would have been the right result of our straight mutual stare. He was in one of the angles, the one away from the house, very erect, as it struck me, and with both hands on the ledge. So I saw him as I see the letters I form on this page; then, exactly, after a minute, as if to add to the spectacle, he slowly changed his place – passed, looking at me hard all the while, to the opposite corner of the platform. Yes, I had the sharpest sense that during this transit he never took his eyes from me, and I can see at this moment the way his hand, as he went, passed from one of the crenelations to the next. He stopped at the other corner, but less long, and even as he turned away still markedly fixed me. He turned away; that was all I knew.

Chapter Four

It was not that I didn't wait, on this occasion, for more, for I was rooted as deeply as I was shaken. Was there a 'secret' at Bly – a mystery of Udolpho or an insane, an unmentionable relative kept in unsuspected confinement? I can't say how long I turned it over, or how long, in a confusion of curiosity and dread, I remained where I had had my collision; I only recall that when I re-entered the house darkness had quite closed in. Agitation, in the interval, certainly had held me and driven me, for I must, in circling about the place, have walked three miles; but I was to be, later on, so much more overwhelmed that this mere dawn of alarm was a comparatively human chill. The most singular part of it in fact – singular as the rest had been – was the part I became, in the hall, aware of in meeting Mrs Grose. This picture comes back to me in the general train – the impression, as I received it on my return, of the wide white panelled space, bright in the lamplight and with its portraits and red carpet, and of the good surprised look of my friend, which immediately told me she had missed me. It came to me straightway, under her contact, that, with plain heartiness, mere relieved anxiety at my appearance, she knew nothing whatever that could bear upon the incident I had there ready for her. I had not suspected in advance that her comfortable face would pull me up, and I somehow measured the importance of what I had seen by my thus finding myself hesitate to mention it. Scarce anything in the whole history seems to me so odd as this fact that my real beginning of fear was one, as I may say, with the instinct of sparing my companion. On the spot, accordingly, in the pleasant hall and with her eyes on me, I, for a reason that I couldn't then have phrased, achieved an inward revolution – offered a vague pretext for my lateness and, with the plea of the beauty of the night and of the heavy dew and wet feet, went as soon as possible to my room.

Here it was another affair; here, for many days after, it was a queer affair enough. There were hours, from day to day – or at least there were moments, snatched even from clear duties – when I had to shut myself up to think. It was not so much yet that I was more nervous than I could bear to be as that I was remarkably afraid of becoming so; for the trust I had now to turn over was, simply and clearly, the truth that I could arrive at no account whatever of the visitor with whom I had been so inexplicably and yet, as it seemed to me, so intimately concerned. It took little time to see that I could sound without forms of inquiry and without exciting remark any domestic complication. The shock I had suffered must have sharpened all my senses; I felt sure, at the end of three days and as the result of mere closer attention, that I had not been practised upon by the servants nor made the object of any 'game'. Of whatever it was that I knew nothing was known around me. There was but one sane inference: someone had taken a liberty rather gross. That was what, repeatedly, I dipped into my room and locked the door to say to myself. We had been, collectively, subject to an intrusion; some unscrupulous traveller, curious in old houses, had made his way in unobserved, enjoyed the prospect from the best point of view and then stolen out as he came. If he had given me such a bold hard stare, that was but a part of his indiscretion. The good thing, after all, was that we should surely see no more of him.

This was not so good a thing, I admit, as not to leave me to judge that what, essentially, made nothing else much signify was simply my charming work. My charming work was just my life with Miles and Flora, and through nothing could I so like it as through feeling that I could throw myself into it in trouble. The attraction of my small charges was a constant joy, leading me to wonder afresh at the vanity of my original fears, the distaste I had begun by entertaining for the probable grey prose of my office. There was to be no grey prose, it appeared, and no long grind; so how could work not be charming that presented itself as daily beauty? It was all the romance of the nursery and the poetry of the schoolroom. I don't mean by this, of course, that we studied only fiction and verse; I mean I can express no otherwise the sort of interest my companions inspired. How can I describe that except by saying that instead of growing used to them – and it's a marvel for a governess: I call the sisterhood to witness! – I made constant fresh discoveries. There was one direction, assuredly, in which these discoveries stopped: deep obscurity continued to cover the region of the boy's conduct at school. It had been promptly given me, I have noted, to face that mystery without a pang. Perhaps even it would be nearer the truth to say that – without a word – he himself had cleared it up. He had made the whole charge absurd. My conclusion bloomed there with the real rose-flush of his innocence: he was only too fine and fair for the little horrid, unclean school-world, and he had paid a price for it. I reflected acutely that the sense of such differences, such superiorities of quality, always, on the part of the majority – which could include even stupid, sordid head-masters – turns infallibly to the vindictive.

Both the children had a gentleness (it was their only fault, and it never made Miles a muff) that kept them – how shall I express it? – almost impersonal and certainly quite unpunishable. They were like cherubs of the anecdote, who had – morally at any rate – nothing to whack! I remember feeling with Miles in especial as if he had had, as it were, no history. We expect of a small child a scant one, but there was in this beautiful little boy something extraordinarily sensitive, yet extraordinarily happy, that, more than in any creature of his age I have seen, struck me as beginning anew each day. He had never for a second suffered. I took this as a direct disproof of his having really been chastised. If he had been wicked he would have 'caught' it, and I should have caught it by the rebound – I should have found the trace. I found nothing at all, and he was therefore an angel. He never spoke of his school, never mentioned a comrade or a master; and I, for my part, was quite too much disgusted to allude to them. Of course I was under the spell, and the wonderful part is that, even at the time, I perfectly knew I was. But I gave myself up to it; it was an antidote to any pain, and I had more pains than one. I was in receipt in these days of disturbing letters from home, where things were not going well. But with my children, what things in the world mattered? That was the question I used to put to my scrappy retirements. I was dazzled by their loveliness.

There was a Sunday – to get on – when it rained with such force and for so many hours that there could be no procession to church; in consequence of which, as the day declined, I had arranged with Mrs Grose that, should the evening show improvement, we would attend together the late service. The rain happily stopped, and I prepared for our walk, which, through the park and by the good road to the village, would be a matter of twenty minutes. Coming down stairs to meet my colleague in the hall, I remembered a pair of gloves that had required three stitches and that had received them – with a publicity perhaps not edifying – while I sat with the children at their tea, served on Sundays, by exception, in that cold, clean temple of mahogany and brass, the 'grown-up' dining-room. The gloves had been dropped there, and I turned in to recover them. The day was grey enough, but the afternoon light still lingered, and it enabled me, on crossing the threshold, not only to recognize, on a chair near the wide window, then closed, the articles I wanted, but to become aware of a person on the other side of the window and looking straight in. One step into the room had sufficed; my vision was instantaneous; it was all there. The person looking straight in was the person who had already appeared to me. He appeared thus again with I won't say greater distinctness, for that was impossible, but with a nearness that represented a forward stride in our intercourse and made me, as I met him, catch my breath and turn cold. He was the same – he was the same, and seen, this time, as he had been seen before, from the waist up, the window, though the dining-room was on the ground floor, not going down to the terrace on which he stood. His face was close to the glass, yet the effect of this better view was, strangely, only to show me how intense the former had been. He remained but a few seconds – long enough to convince me he also saw and recognized; but it was as if I had been looking at him for years and had known him always. Something, however, happened this time that had not happened before; his stare into my face, through the glass and across the room, was as deep and hard as then, but it quitted me for a moment during which I could still watch it, see it fix successively several other things. On the spot there came to me the added shock of a certitude that it was not for me he had come there. He had come for someone else.

The flash of this knowledge – for it was knowledge in the midst of dread – produced in me the most extraordinary effect, started, as I stood there, a sudden vibration of duty and courage. I say courage because I was beyond all doubt already far gone. I bounded straight out of the door again, reached that of the house, got, in an instant, upon the drive, and, passing along the terrace as fast as I could rush, turned a corner and came full in sight. But it was in sight of nothing now – my visitor had vanished. I stopped, I almost dropped, with the real relief of this; but I took in the whole scene – I gave him time to reappear. I call it time, but how long was it? I can't speak to the purpose today of the duration of these things. That kind of measure must have left me: they couldn't have lasted as they actually appeared to me to last. The terrace and the whole place, the lawn and the garden beyond it, all I could see of the park, were empty with a great emptiness. There were shrubberies and big trees, but I remember the clear assurance I felt that none of them concealed him. He was there or was not there: not there if I didn't see him. I got hold of this; then, instinctively, instead of returning as I had come, went to the window. It was confusedly present to me that I ought to place myself where he had stood. I did so; I applied my face to the pane and looked, as he had looked, into the room. As if, at this moment, to show me exactly what his range had been, Mrs Grose, as I had done for himself just before, came in from the hall. With this I had the full image of a repetition of what had already occurred. She saw me as I had seen my own visitant; she pulled up short as I had done; I gave her something of the shock that I had received. She turned white, and this made me ask myself if I had blanched as much. She stared, in short, and retreated on just *my* lines, and I knew she had then passed out and come round to me and that I should presently meet her. I remained where I was, and while I waited I thought of more things than one. But there's only one I take space to mention. I wondered why *she* should be scared.

Chapter Five

Oh, she let me know as soon as, round the corner of the house, she loomed again into view. 'What in the name of goodness is the matter—?' She was now flushed and out of breath.

I said nothing till she came quite near. 'With me?' I must have made a wonderful face. 'Do I show it?'

'You're as white as a sheet. You look awful.'

I considered; I could meet on this, without scruple, any innocence. My need to respect the bloom of Mrs Grose's had dropped, without a rustle, from my shoulders, and if I wavered for the instant it was not with what I kept back. I put out my hand to her and she took it; I held her hard a little, liking to feel her close to me. There was a kind of support in the shy heave of her surprise. 'You came for me for church, of course, but I can't go.'

'Has anything happened?'

'Yes. You must know now. Did I look very queer?'

'Through this window? Dreadful!'

'Well,' I said, 'I've been frightened.' Mrs Grose's eyes expressed plainly that *she* had no wish to be, yet also that she knew too well her place not to be ready to share with me any marked inconvenience. Oh, it was quite settled that she *must* share! 'Just what you saw from the dining-room a minute ago was the effect of that. What *I* saw – just before – was much worse.'

Her hand tightened. 'What was it?'

'An extraordinary man. Looking in.'

'What extraordinary man?'

'I haven't the least idea.'

Mrs Grose gazed round us in vain. 'Then where is he gone?'

'I know still less.'

'Have you seen him before?'

'Yes – once. On the old tower.'

She could only look at me harder. 'Do you mean he's a stranger?'

'Oh, very much!'

'Yet you didn't tell me?'

'No – for reasons. But now that you've guessed—'

Mrs Grose's round eyes encountered this charge. 'Ah, I haven't guessed!' she said very simply. 'How can I if *you* don't imagine?'

'I don't in the very least.'

'You've seen him nowhere but on the tower?'

'And on this spot just now.'

Mrs Grose looked round again. 'What was he doing on the tower?'

'Only standing there and looking down at me.'

She thought a minute. 'Was he a gentleman?'

I found I had no need to think. 'No.' She gazed in deeper wonder. 'No.'

'Then nobody about the place? Nobody from the village?'

'Nobody – nobody. I didn't tell you, but I made sure.'

She breathed a vague relief: this was, oddly, so much to the good. It only went indeed a little way. 'But if he isn't a gentleman—'

'What *is* he? He's a horror.'

'A horror?'

'He's – God help me if I know *what* he is!'

Mrs Grose looked round once more; she fixed her eyes on the duskier distance, then, pulling herself together, turned to me with abrupt inconsequence. 'It's time we should be at church.'

'Oh, I'm not fit for church.'

'Won't it do you good?'

'It won't do *them*—!' I nodded at the house.

'The children?'

'I can't leave them now.'

'You're afraid—?'

I spoke boldly. 'I'm afraid of *him*.'

Mrs Grose's large face showed me, at this, for the first time, the far-away faint glimmer of a consciousness more acute: I somehow made out in it the delayed dawn of an idea I myself had not given her and that was as yet quite obscure to me. It comes back to me that I thought instantly of this as something I could get from her; and I felt it to be connected with the desire she presently showed to know more. 'When was it – on the tower?'

'About the middle of the month. At this same hour.'

'Almost at dark,' said Mrs Grose.

'Oh no, not nearly. I saw him as I see you.'

'Then how did he get in?'

'And how did he get out?' I laughed. 'I had no opportunity to ask him! This evening, you see,' I pursued, 'he has not been able to get in.'

'He only peeps?'

'I hope it will be confined to that!' She had now let go my hand; she turned away a little. I waited an instant; then I brought out: 'Go to church. Good-bye. I must watch.'

Slowly she faced me again. 'Do you fear for them?'

We met in another long look. 'Don't *you*?' Instead of answering she came nearer to the window and, for a minute, applied her face to the glass. 'You see how he could see,' I meanwhile went on.

She didn't move. 'How long was he here?'

'Till I came out. I came to meet him.'

Mrs Grose at last turned round, and there was still more in her face. '*I* couldn't have come out.'

'Neither could I!' I laughed again. 'But I did come. I have my duty.'

'So have I mine,' she replied; after which she added: 'What is he like?'

'I've been dying to tell you. But he's like nobody.'

'Nobody?' she echoed.

'He has no hat.' Then seeing in her face that she already, in this, with a deeper dismay, found a touch of picture, I quickly added stroke to stroke. 'He has red hair, very red, close-curling, and a pale face, long in shape, with straight, good features and little, rather queer whiskers that are as red as his hair. His eyebrows are, somehow, darker; they look particularly arched and as if they might move a good deal. His eyes are sharp, strange – awfully; but I only know clearly that they're rather small and very fixed. His mouth's wide, and his lips are thin, and except for his little whiskers he's quite clean-shaven. He gives me a sort of sense of looking like an actor.'

'An actor!' It was impossible to resemble one less, at least, than Mrs Grose at that moment.

'I've never seen one, but so I suppose them. He's tall, active, erect,' I continued, 'but never – no, never! – a gentleman.'

My companion's face had blanched as I went on; her round eyes started and her mild mouth gaped. 'A gentleman?' she gasped, confounded, stupefied: 'a gentleman *he*?'

'You know him then?'

She visibly tried to hold herself. 'But he *is* handsome?'

I saw the way to help her. 'Remarkably!'

And dressed—?'

'In somebody's clothes. They're smart, but they're not his own.'

She broke into a breathless affirmative groan. 'They're the master's!'

I caught it up. 'You *do* know him?'

She faltered but a second. 'Quint!' she cried.

'Quint?'

'Peter Quint – his own man, his valet, when he was here!'

'When the master was?'

Gaping still, but meeting me, she pieced it all together. 'He never wore his hat, but he did wear – well, there were waistcoats missed! They were both here – last year. Then the master went, and Quint was alone.'

I followed, but halting a little. 'Alone?'

'Alone with *us*.' Then, as from a deeper depth, 'In charge,' she added.

'And what became of him?'

She hung fire so long that I was still more mystified. 'He went too,' she brought out at last.

'Went where?'

Her expression, at this, became extraordinary. 'God knows where! He died.'

'Died?' I almost shrieked.

She seemed fairly to square herself, plant herself more firmly to utter the wonder of it. 'Yes. Mr Quint is dead.'

Chapter Six

It took of course more than that particular passage to place us together in presence of what we had now to live with as we could – my dreadful liability to impressions of the order so vividly exemplified, and my companion's knowledge, henceforth – a knowledge half consternation and half compassion – of that liability. There had been, this evening, after the revelation that left me, for an hour, so prostrate – there had been, for either of us, no attendance on any service but a little service of tears and vows, of prayers and promises, a climax to the series of mutual challenges and pledges that had straightway ensued on our retreating together to the schoolroom and shutting ourselves up there to have everything out. The result of our having everything out was simply to reduce our situation to the last rigour of its elements. She herself had seen nothing, not the shadow of a shadow, and nobody in the house but the governess was in the governess's plight; yet she accepted without directly impugning my sanity the truth as I gave it to her, and ended by showing me, on this ground, an awe-stricken tenderness, an expression of the sense of my more than questionable privilege, of which the very breath has remained with me as that of the sweetest of human charities.

What was settled between us, accordingly, that night, was that we thought we might bear things together; and I was not even sure that, in spite of her exemption, it was she who had the best of the burden. I knew at this hour, I think, as well as I knew later what I was capable of meeting to shelter my pupils; but it took me some time to be wholly sure of what my honest ally was prepared for to keep terms with so compromising a contract. I was queer company enough – quite as queer as the company I received; but as I trace over what we went through I see how much common ground we must have found in the one idea that, by good fortune, *could* steady us. It was the idea, the second movement, that led me straight out, as I may say, of the inner chamber of my dread. I could take the air in the court, at least, and there Mrs Grose could join me. Perfectly can I recall now the particular way strength came to me before we separated for the night. We had gone over and over every feature of what I had seen.

'He was looking for someone else, you say – someone who was not you?'

'He was looking for little Miles.' A portentous clearness now possessed me. '*That's* whom he was looking for.'

'But how do you know?'

'I know, I know, I know!' My exaltation grew. 'And *you* know, my dear!'

She didn't deny this, but I required, I felt, not even so much telling as that. She resumed in a moment, at any rate: What if *he* should see him?'

'Little Miles?' That's what he wants!'

She looked immensely scared again. 'The child?'

'Heaven forbid! The man. He wants to appear to *them*.' That he might was an awful conception, and yet, somehow, I could keep at bay; which, moreover, as we lingered there, was what I succeeded in practically proving. I had an absolute certainty that I should see again what I had already seen, but something within me said that by offering myself bravely as the sole subject of such experience, by accepting, by inviting, by surmounting it all, I should serve as an expiatory victim and guard the tranquillity of my companions. The children, in especial, I should thus fence about and absolutely save. I recall one of the last things I said that night to Mrs Grose.

'It does strike me that my pupils have never mentioned—'

She looked at me hard as I musingly pulled up. 'His having been here and the time they were with him?'

'The time they were with him, and his name, his presence, his history, in any way.'

'Oh, the little lady doesn't remember. She never heard or knew.'

'The circumstances of his death?' I thought with some intensity. 'Perhaps not. But Miles would remenber – Miles would know.'

'Ah, don't try him!' broke from Mrs Grose.

I returned her the look she had given me. 'Don't be afraid.' I continued to think. 'It *is* rather odd.'

'That he has never spoken of him?'

'Never by the least allusion. And you tell me they were "great friends"?'

'Oh, it wasn't *him*!' Mrs Grose with emphasis declared. 'It was Quint's own fancy. To play with him, I mean – to spoil him.' She paused a moment; then she added: 'Quint was much too free.'

This gave me, straight from my vision of his face– *such* a face! – a sudden sickness of disgust. 'Too free with *my* boy?'

'Too free with everyone!'

I forebore, for the moment, to analyse this description further than by the reflection that a part of it applied to several of the members of the household, of the half-dozen maids and men who were still of our small colony. But there was everything, for our apprehension, in the lucky fact that no discomfortable legend, no perturbation of scullions, had ever, within anyone's memory, attached to the kind old place. It had neither bad name nor ill fame, and Mrs Grose, most apparently, only desired to cling to me and to quake in silence. I even put her, the very last thing of all, to the test. It was when, at midnight, she had her hand on the schoolroom door to take her leave. 'I have it from you then — for it's of great importance – that he was definitely and admittedly bad?'

'Oh, not admittedly. *I* knew it – but the master didn't.'

'And you never told him?'

'Well, he didn't like tale-bearing – he hated complaints. He was terribly short with anything of that kind, and if people were all right to *him*—'

'He wouldn't be bothered with more?' This squared well enough with my impression of him: he was not a trouble-loving gentleman, nor so very particular perhaps about some of the company *he* kept. All the same, I pressed my interlocutress. 'I promise you *I* would have told!'

She felt my discrimination. 'I dare say I was wrong. But, really, I was afraid.'

'Afraid of what?'

'Of things that man could do. Quint was so clever – he was so deep.'

I took this in still more than, probably, I showed. 'You weren't afraid of anything else? Not of his effect—?'

'His effect?' she repeated with a face of anguish and waiting while I faltered.

'On innocent little precious lives. They were in your charge.'

'No, they were not in mine!' she roundly and distressfully returned. 'The master believed in him and placed him here because he was supposed not to be well and the country air so good for him. So he had everything to say. Yes' – she let me have it – 'even about *them.*'

'Them – that creature?' I had to smother a kind of howl. 'And you could bear it?'

'No. I couldn't – and I can't now!' And the poor woman burst into tears.

A rigid control, from the next day, was, as I have said, to follow them; yet how often and how passionately, for a week, we came back together to the subject! Much as we had discussed it that Sunday night, I was, in the immediate later hours in especial – for it may be imagined whether I slept – still haunted with the shadow of something she had not told me. I myself had kept back nothing, but there was a word Mrs Grose had kept back. I was sure, moreover, by morning, that this was not from a failure of frankness, but because on every side there were fears. It seems to me indeed, in retrospect, that by the time the morrow's sun was high I had restlessly read into the facts before us almost all the meaning they were to receive from subsequent and more cruel occurrences. What they gave me above all was just the sinister figure of the living man – the dead one would keep a while! – and of the months he had continuously passed at Bly, which, added up, made a formidable stretch. The limit of this evil time had arrived only when, on the dawn of a winter's morning, Peter Quint was found, by a labourer going to early work, stone dead on the road from the village: a catastrophe explained – superficially at least – by a visible wound to his head; such a wound as might have been produced – and as, on the final evidence, *had* been – by a fatal slip, in the dark and after leaving the public-house, on the steepish icy slope, a wrong path altogether, at the bottom of which he lay. The icy slope, the turn mistaken at night and in liquor, accounted for much – practically, in the end and after the inquest and boundless chatter, for everything; but there had been matters in his life – strange passages and perils, secret disorders, vices more than suspected – that would have accounted for a good deal more.

I scarce know how to put my story into words that shall be a credible picture of my state of mind; but I was in these days literally able to find a joy in the extraordinary flight of heroism the occasion demanded of me. I now saw that I had been asked for a service admirable and difficult; and there would be a greatness in letting it be seen – oh, in the right quarter! – that I could succeed where many another girl might have failed. It was an immense help to me – I confess I rather applaud myself as I look back! – that I saw my service so strongly and so simply. I was there to protect and defend the little creatures in the world the most bereaved and the most lovable, the appeal of whose helplessness had suddenly become only too explicit, a deep, constant ache of one's own committed heart. We were cut off, really, together; we were united in our danger. They had nothing but me, and I – well, I had *them*. It was in short a magnificent chance. This chance presented itself to me in an image richly material. I was a screen – I was to stand before them. The more I saw, the less they would. I began to watch them in a stifled suspense, a disguised excitement that might well, had it continued too long, have turned to something like madness. What saved me, as I now see, was that it turned to something else altogether. It didn't last as suspense – it was superseded by horrible proofs. Proofs, I say, yes – from the moment I really took hold.

This moment dated from an afternoon hour that I happened to spend in the grounds with the younger of my pupils alone. We had left Miles indoors, on the red cushion of a deep window-seat; he had wished to finish a book, and I had been glad to encourage a purpose so laudable in a young man whose only defect was an occasional excess of the restless. His sister, on the contrary, had been alert to come out, and I strolled with her half an hour, seeking the shade, for the sun was still high and the day exceptionally warm. I was aware afresh, with her, as we went, of how, like her brother, she contrived – it was the charming thing in both children – to let me alone without appearing to drop me and to accompany me without appearing to surround. They were never importunate and yet never listless. My attention to them all really went to seeing them amuse themselves immensely without me: this was a spectacle they seemed actively to prepare and that engaged me as an active admirer. I walked in a world of their invention – they had no occasion whatever to draw upon mine; so that my time was taken only with being, for them, some remarkable person or thing that the game of the moment required and that was merely, thanks to my superior, my exalted stamp, a happy and highly distinguished sinecure. I forget what I was on the present occasion; I only remember that I was something very important and very quiet and that Flora was playing very hard. We were on the edge of the lake, and, as we had lately begun geography, the lake was the Sea of Azof.

Suddenly, in these circumstances, I became aware that, on the other side of the Sea of Azof, we had an interested spectator. The way this knowledge gathered in me was the strangest thing in the world – the strangest, that is, except the very much stranger in which it quickly merged itself. I had sat down with a piece of work – for I was something or other that could sit – on the old stone bench which overlooked the pond; and in this position I began to take in with certitude, and yet without direct vision, the presence, at a distance, of a third person. The old trees, the thick shrubbery, made a great and pleasant shade, but it was all suffused with the brightness of the hot, still hour. There was no ambiguity in anything; none whatever, at least, in the conviction I from one moment to another found myself forming as to what I should see straight before me and across the lake as a consequence of raising my eyes. They were attached at this juncture to the stitching in which I was engaged, and I can feel once more the spasm of my effort not to move them till I should so have steadied myself as to be able to make up my mind what to do. There was an alien object in view – a figure whose right of presence I instantly, passionately questioned. I recollect counting over perfectly the possibilities, reminding myself that nothing was more natural, for instance, than the appearance of one of the men about the place, or even of a messenger, a postman or a tradesman's boy, from the village.

That reminder had as little effect on my practical certitude as I was conscious – still even without looking – of its having upon the character and attitude of our visitor. Nothing was more natural than that these things should be the other things that they absolutely were not.

Of the positive identity of the apparition I would assure myself as soon as the small clock of my courage should have ticked out the right second; meanwhile, with an effort that was already sharp enough, I transferred my eyes straight to little Flora, who, at the moment, was about ten yards away. My heart had stood still for an instant with the wonder and terror of the question whether she too would see; and I held my breath while I waited for what a cry from her, what some sudden innocent sign either of interest or of alarm, would tell me. I waited, but nothing came; then, in the first place – and there is something more dire in this, I feel, than in anything I have too relate – I was determined by a sense that, within a minute, all sounds from her had previously dropped; and, in the second, by the circumstance that, also within the minute, she had, in her play, turned her back to the water. This was her attitude when I at last looked at her – looked with the confirmed conviction that we were still, together, under direct personal notice. She had picked up a small flat piece of wood, which happened to have in it a little hole that had evidently suggested to her the idea of sticking in another fragment that might figure as a mast and make the thing a boat. This second morsel, as I watched her, she was very markedly and intently attempting to tighten in its place. My apprehension of what she was doing sustained me so that after some seconds I felt I was ready for more. Then I again shifted my eyes – I faced what I had to face

Chapter Seven

I got hold of Mrs Grose as soon after this as I could; and I can give no intelligible account of how I fought out the interval. Yet I still hear myself cry as I fairly threw myself into her arms: 'They *know* – it's too monstrous: they know, they know!'

'And what on earth—?' I felt her incredulity as she held me.

'Why, all that *we* know – and heaven knows what else besides!' Then, as she released me, I made it out to her, made it out perhaps only now with full coherency even to myself. 'Two hours ago, in the garden' – I could scarce articulate – 'Flora *saw*!'

Mrs Grose took it as she might have taken a blow in the stomach. 'She has told you?' she panted.

'Not a word – that's the horror. She kept it to herself! The child of eight, *that* child!' Unutterable still, for me, was the stupefaction of it.

Mrs Grose, of course, could only gape the wider. 'Then how do you know?'

'I was there – I saw with my eyes: saw that she was perfectly aware.'

'Do you mean aware of *him*?'

'No – of *her*.' I was conscious as I spoke that I looked prodigious things, for I got the slow reflection of them in my companion's face. 'Another person – this time; but a figure of quite as unmistakable horror and evil: a woman in black, pale and dreadful – with such an air also, and such a face! – on the other side of the lake. I was there with the child – quiet for the hour; and in the midst of it she came.'

'Came how – from where?'

'From where they come from! She just appeared and stood there – but not so near.'

'And without coming nearer?'

'Oh, for the effect and the feeling, she might have been as close as you!'

My friend, with an odd impulse, fell back a step. 'Was she someone you've never seen?'

'Yes. But someone the child has. Someone *you* have.' Then, to show how I had thought it all out: 'My predecessor – the one who died.'

'Miss Jessel?'

'Miss Jessel. You don't believe me?' I pressed.

She turned right and left in her distress. 'How can you be sure?'

This drew from me, in the state of my nerves, a flash of impatience. 'Then ask Flora – *she's* sure!' But I had no sooner spoken than I caught myself up. 'No, for God's sake, *don't*! She'll say she isn't – she'll lie!'

Mrs Grose was not too bewildered instinctively to protest. 'Ah, how *can* you?'

'Because I'm clear. Flora doesn't want me to know.'

'It's only then to spare you.'

'No, no – there are depths, depths! The more I go over it, the more I see in it, and the more I see in it the more I fear. I don't know what I *don't* see – what I *don't* fear!'

Mrs Grose tried to keep up with me. 'You mean you're afraid of seeing her again?'

'Oh no; that's nothing – now!' Then I explained. 'It's of *not* seeing her.'

But my companion only looked wan. 'I don't understand you.'

'Why, it's that the child may keep it up – and that the child assuredly *will* – without my knowing it.'

At the image of this possibility Mrs Grose for a moment collapsed, yet presently to pull herself together again, as if from the positive force of the sense of what, should we yield an inch, there would really be to give way to. 'Dear, dear – we must keep our heads! And after all, if she doesn't mind it—!' She even tried a grim joke. 'Perhaps she likes it!'

'Likes *such* things – a scrap of an infant!'

'Isn't it just a proof of her blessed innocence?' my friend bravely inquired.

She brought me, for the instant, almost round. 'Oh, we must clutch at *that* – we must cling to it! If it isn't a proof of what you say, it's a proof of – God knows what! For the woman's a horror of horrors.'

Mrs Grose, at this, fixed her eyes a minute on the ground; then at last raising them, 'Tell me how you know,' she said.

'Then you admit it's what she was?' I cried.

'Tell me how you know,' my friend simply repeated.

'Know? By seeing her! By the way she looked.'

'At you, do you mean – so wickedly?'

'Dear me, no – I could have borne that. She gave me never a glance. She only fixed the child.'

Mrs Grose tried to see it. 'Fixed her?'

'Ah, with such awful eyes!'

She stared at mine as if they might really have resembled them. 'Do you mean of dislike?'

'God help us, no. Of something much worse.'

'Worse than dislike?' – this left her indeed at a loss.

'With a determination – indescribable. With a kind of fury of intention.'

I made her turn pale. 'Intention?'

'To get hold of her.' Mrs Grose – her eyes just lingering on mine – gave a shudder and walked to the window; and while she stood there looking out I completed my statement. '*That's* what Flora knows.'

After a little she turned round. 'The person was in black, you say?'

'In mourning – rather poor, almost shabby. But – yes – with extraordinary beauty.' I now recognized to what I had at last, stroke by stroke, brought the victim of my confidence, for she quite visibly weighed this. 'Oh, handsome – very, very,' I insisted; 'wonderfully handsome. But infamous.'

She slowly came back to me. 'Miss Jessel – *was* infamous.' She once more took my hand in both her own, holding it as tight as if to fortify me against the increase of alarm I might draw from this disclosure. 'They were both infamous,' she finally said.

So, for a little, we faced it once more together; and I found absolutely a degree of help in seeing it now so straight. 'I appreciate,' I said, 'the great decency of your not having hitherto spoken; but the time has certainly come to give me the whole thing.' She appeared to assent to this, but still only in silence; seeing which I went on: 'I must have it now. Of what did she die? Come, there was something between them.'

'There was everything.'

'In spite of the difference—?'

'Oh, of their rank, their condition' – she brought it woefully out. '*She* was a lady.'

I turned it over; I again saw. 'Yes – she was a lady.'

'And he so dreadfully below,' said Mrs Grose.

I felt that I doubtless needn't press too hard, in such company, on the place of a servant in the scale; but there was nothing to prevent an acceptance of my companion's own measure of my predecessor's abasement. There was a way to deal with that, and I dealt; the more readily for my full vision – on the evidence – of our employer's late clever, good-looking 'own' man; impudent, assured, spoiled, depraved. 'The fellow was a hound.'

Mrs Grose considered as if it were perhaps a little a case for a sense of shades. 'I've never seen one like him. He did what he wished.'

'With *her*?'

'With them all.'

It was as if now in my friend's own eyes Miss Jessel had again appeared. I seemed at any rate, for an instant, to see their evocation of her as distinctly as I had seen her by the pond; and I brought out with decision: 'It must have been also what *she* wished!'

Mrs Grose's face signified that it had been indeed, but she said at the same time: 'Poor woman – she paid for it!'

'Then you do know what she died of?' I asked.

'No – I know nothing. I wanted not to know; I was glad enough I didn't; and I thanked heaven she was well out of this!'

'Yet you had, then, your idea—'

'Of her real reason for leaving? Oh yes – as to that. She couldn't have stayed. Fancy it here – for a governess! And afterwards I imagined – and I still imagine. And what I imagine is dreadful.'

'Not so dreadful as what *I* do,' I replied; on which I must have shown her – as I was indeed but too conscious – a front of miserable defeat. It brought out again all her compassion for me, and at the renewed touch of her kindness my power to resist broke down. I burst, as I had, the other time, made her burst, into tears; she took me to her motherly breast, and my lamentation overflowed. 'I don't do it!' I sobbed in despair; 'I don't save or shield them! It's far worse than I dreamed – they're lost!'

Chapter Eight

What I had said to Mrs Grose was true enough: there were in the matter I had put before her depths and possibilities that I lacked resolution to sound; so that when we met once more in the wonder of it we were of a common mind about the duty of resistance to extravagant fancies. We were to keep our heads if we should keep nothing else – difficult indeed as that might be in the face of what, in our prodigious experience, was least to be questioned. Late that night, while the house slept, we had another talk in my room; when she went all the way with me as to its being beyond doubt that I had seen exactly what I had seen. To hold her perfectly in the pinch of that, I found, I had only to ask her how, if I had 'made it up', I came to be able to give, of each of the persons appearing to me, a picture disclosing, to the last detail, their special marks – a portrait on the exhibition of which she had instantly recognized and named them. She wished, of course – small blame to her! – to sink the whole subject; and I was quick to assure her that my own interest in it had now violently taken the form of a search for the way to escape from it. I encountered her on the ground of a probability that with recurrence – for recurrence we took for granted – I should get used to my danger; distinctly professing that my personal exposure had suddenly become the least of my discomforts. It was my new suspicion that was intolerable; and yet even to this complication the later hours of the day had brought a little ease.

On leaving her, after my first outbreak, I had of course returned to my pupils, associating the right remedy for my dismay with that sense of their charm which I had already found to be a thing I could positively cultivate and which had never failed me yet. I had simply, in other words, plunged afresh into Flora's special society and there become aware – it was almost a luxury! – that she could put her little conscious hand straight upon the spot that ached. She had looked at me in sweet speculation and then had accused me to my face of having 'cried'. I had supposed I had brushed away the ugly signs; but I could literally – for the time, at all events – rejoice, under this fathomless charity, that they had not entirely disappeared. To gaze into the depths of blue of the child's eyes and pronounce their loveliness a trick of premature cunning was to be guilty of a cynicism in preference to which I naturally preferred to abjure my judgement and, so far as might be, my agitation. I couldn't abjure for merely wanting to, but I could repeat to Mrs Grose – as I did there, over and over, in the small hours – that with their voices in the air, their pressure on one's heart and their fragrant faces against one's cheek, everything fell to the ground but their incapacity and their beauty. It was a pity that, somehow, to settle this once for all, I had equally to re-enumerate the signs of subtlety that, in the afternoon, by the lake, had made a miracle of my show of self-possession. It was a pity to be obliged to re-investigate the certitude of the moment itself and repeat how it had come to me as a revelation that the inconceivable communion I then surprised was a matter, for either party, of habit. It was a pity that I should have had to quaver out again the reasons for my not having, in my delusion, so much as questioned that the little girl saw our visitant even as I actually saw Mrs Grose herself, and that she wanted, by just so much as she did thus see, to make me suppose she didn't, and at the same time, without showing anything, arrive at a guess as to whether I myself did! It was a pity that I needed once more to describe the portentous little activity by which she sought to divert my attention – the perceptible increase of movement, the greater intensity of play, the singing, the gabbling, of nonsense and the invitation to romp.

Yet if I had not indulged, to prove there was nothing in it, in this review, I should have missed the two or three dim elements of comfort that still remained to me. I should not for instance have been able to asseverate to my friend that I was certain – which was so much to the good – that *I* at least had not betrayed myself. I should not have been prompted, by stress of need, by desperation of mind – I scarce know what to call it – to invoke such further aid to intelligence as might spring from pushing my colleague fairly to the wall. She had told me, bit by bit, under pressure, a great deal; but a small shifty spot on the wrong side of it all still sometimes brushed my brow like the wing of a bat; and I remember how on this occasion – for the sleeping house and the concentration alike of our danger and our watch seemed to help – I felt the importance of giving the last jerk to the curtain. 'I don't believe anything so horrible,' I recollect saying; 'no, let us put it definitely, my dear, that I don't. But if I did, you know, there's a thing I should require now, just without sparing you the least bit more – oh, not a scrap, come! – to get out of you. What was it you had in mind when, in our distress, before Miles came back, over the letter from his school, you said, under my insistence, that you didn't pretend for him that he had not literally *ever* been "bad"? He has *not* literally "ever", in these weeks that I myself have lived with him and so closely watched him; he has been an imperturbable little prodigy of delightful, loveable goodness. Therefore you might perfectly have made the claim for him if you had not, as it happened, seen an exception to take. What was your exception, and to what passage in your personal observation of him did you refer?'

It was a dreadfully austere inquiry, but levity was not our note, and, at any rate, before the grey dawn admonished us to separate I had got my answer. What my friend had had in mind proved to be immensely to the purpose. It was neither more nor less than the circumstance that for a period of several months Quint and the boy had been perpetually together. It was in fact the very appropriate truth that she had ventured to criticize the propriety, to hint at the incongruity, of so close an alliance, and even to go so far on the subject as a frank overture to Miss Jessel. Miss Jessel had, with a most strange manner, requested her to mind her business, and the good woman had, on this, directly approached little Miles. What she had said to him, since I pressed, was that *she* liked to see young gentlemen not forget their station.

I pressed again, of course, at this. 'You reminded him that Quint was only a base menial?'

'As you might say! And it was his answer, for one thing, that was bad.'

'And for another thing?' I waited. 'He repeated your words to Quint?'

'No, not that. It's just what he *wouldn't*!' she could still impress upon me. 'I was sure, at any rate,' she added, 'that he didn't. But he denied certain occasions.'

'What occasions?'

'When they had been about together quite as if Quint were his tutor – and a very grand one – and Miss Jessel only for the little lady. When he had gone off with the fellow, I mean, and spent hours with him.'

'He then prevaricated about it – he said he hadn't?' Her assent was clear enough to cause me to add in a moment: 'I see. He lied.'

'Oh!' Mrs Grose mumbled. This was a suggestion that it didn't matter; which indeed she backed up by a further remark. 'You see, after all, Miss Jessel didn't mind. She didn't forbid him.'

I considered. 'Did he put that to you as a justification?'

At this she dropped again. 'No, he never spoke of it.'

'Never mentioned her in connexion with Quint?'

She saw, visibly flushing, where I was coming out. 'Well, he didn't show anything. He denied,' she repeated; 'he denied.'

Lord, how I pressed her now! 'So that you could see he knew what was between the two wretches?'

'I don't know – I don't know!' the poor woman groaned.

'You do know, you dear thing,' I replied; 'only you haven't my dreadful boldness of mind, and you keep back, out of timidity and modesty and delicacy, even the impression that, in the past, when you had, without my aid, to flounder about in silence, most of all made you miserable. But I shall get it out of you yet! There was something in the boy that suggested to you,' I continued, 'that he covered and concealed their relation.'

'Oh, he couldn't prevent—'

'Your learning the truth? I dare say! But, heavens,' I fell, with vehemence, a-thinking, 'what it shows that they must, to that extent, have succeeded in making of him!'

'Ah, nothing that's not nice *now*!' Mrs Grose lugubriously pleaded.

'I don't wonder you looked queer,' I persisted, 'when I mentioned to you the letter from his school!'

'I doubt if I looked as queer as you!' she retorted with homely force. 'And if he was so bad then as that comes to, how is he such an angel now?'

'Yes indeed – and if he was a fiend at school! How, how, how? Well,' I said in my torment, 'you must put it to me again, but I shall not be able to tell you for some days. Only, put it to me again!' I cried in a way that made my friend stare. 'There are directions in which I must not for the present let myself go.' Meanwhile I returned to her first example – the one to which she had just previously referred – of the boy's happy capacity for an occasional slip. 'If Quint – on your remonstrance at the time you speak of – was a base menial, one of the things Miles said to you, I find myself guessing, was that you were another.' Again her admission was so adequate that I continued: 'And you forgave him that?'

'Wouldn't *you*?'

'Oh yes!' And we exchanged there, in the stillness, a sound of the oddest amusement. Then I went on: 'At all events, while he was with the man—'

'Miss Flora was with the woman. It suited them all!'

It suited me too, I felt, only too well; by which I mean that it suited exactly the particular deadly view I was in the very act of forbidding myself to entertain. But I so far succeeded in checking the expression of this view that I will throw, just here, no further light on it than may be offered by the mention of my final observation to Mrs Grose. 'His having lied and been impudent are, I confess, less engaging specimens than I had hoped to have from you of the outbreak in him of the little natural man. Still,' I mused, 'they must do, for they make me feel more than ever that I must watch.'

It made me blush, the next minute, to see in my friend's face how much more unreservedly she had forgiven him than her anecdote struck me as presenting to my own tenderness an occasion for doing. This came out when, at the schoolroom door, she quitted me. 'Surely you don't accuse *him*—'

'Of carrying on an intercourse that he conceals from me? Ah, remember that, until further evidence, I now accuse nobody.' Then, before shutting her out to go, by another passage, to her own place, 'I must just wait,' I wound up.

Chapter Nine

I waited and waited, and the days, as they elapsed, took something from my consternation. A very few of them, in fact, passing, in constant sight of my pupils, without a fresh incident, sufficed to give to grievous fancies and even to odious memories a kind of brush of the sponge. I have spoken of the surrender to their extraordinary childish grace as a thing I could actively cultivate, and it may be imagined if I neglected now to address myself to this source for whatever it would yield. Stranger than I can express, certainly, was the effort to struggle against my new lights; it would doubtless have been, however, a greater tension still had it not been so frequently successful. I used to wonder how my little charges could help guessing that I thought strange things about them; and the circumstances that these things only made them more interesting was not by itself a direct aid to keeping them in the dark. I trembled lest they should see that they *were* so immensely more interesting. Putting things at the worst, at all events, as in meditation I so often did, any clouding of their innocence could only be – blameless and foredoomed as they were – a reason the more for taking risks. There were moments when, by an irresistible impulse, I found myself catching them up and pressing them to my heart. As soon as I had done so I used to say to myself: 'What will they think of that? Doesn't it betray too much?' It would have been easy to get into a sad, wild tangle about how much I might betray; but the real account, I feel, of the hours of peace that I could still enjoy was that the immediate charm of my companions was a beguilement still effective even under the shadow of the possibility that it was studied. For if it occurred to me that I might occasionally excite suspicion by the little outbreaks of my sharper passion for them, so too I remember wondering if I mightn't see a queerness in the traceable increase of their own demonstrations.

They were at this period extravagantly and preternaturally fond of me; which, after all, I could reflect, was no more than a graceful response in children perpetually bowed over and hugged. The homage of which they were so lavish succeeded, in truth, for my nerves, quite as well as if I never appeared to myself, as I may say, literally to catch them at a purpose in it. They had never, I think, wanted to do so many things for their poor protectress; I mean – though they got their lessons better and better, which was naturally what would please her most – in the way of diverting, entertaining, surprising her; reading her passages, telling her stories, acting her charades, pouncing out at her, in disguises, as animals and historical characters, and above all astonishing her by the 'pieces' they had secretly got by heart and could interminably recite. I should never get to the bottom – were I to let myself go even now – of the prodigious private commentary, all under still more private correction, with which, in these days, I overscored their full hours. They had shown me from the first a facility for everything, a general faculty which, taking a fresh start, achieved remarkable flights. They got their little tasks as if they loved them, and indulged, from the mere exuberance of the gift, in the most unimposed little miracles of memory. They not only popped out at me as tigers and as Romans, but as Shakespeareans, astronomers and navigators. This was so singularly the case that it had presumably much to do with the fact as to which, at the present day, I am at a loss for a different explanation: I allude to my unnatural composure on the subject of another school for Miles. What I remember is that I was content not, for the time, to open the question, and that contentment must have sprung from the sense of his perpetually striking show of cleverness. He was too clever for a bad governess, for a parson's daughter, to spoil; and the strangest if not the brightest thread in the pensive embroidery I just spoke of was the impression I might have got, if I had dared to work it out, that he was under some influence operating in his small intellectual life as a tremendous incitement.

If it was easy to reflect, however, that such a boy could postpone school, it was at least as marked that for such a boy to have been 'kicked out' by a schoolmaster was a mystification without end. Let me add that in their company now – and I was careful almost never to be out of it – I could follow no scent very far. We lived in a cloud of music and love and success and private theatricals. The musical sense in each of the children was of the quickest, but the elder in especial had a marvellous knack of catching and repeating. The schoolroom piano broke into all gruesome fancies; and when that failed there were confabulations in corners, with a sequel of one of them going out in the highest spirits in order to 'come in' as something new. I had had brothers myself, and it was no revelation to me that little girls could be slavish idolaters of little boys. What surpassed everything was that there was a little boy in the world who could have for the inferior age, sex and intelligence so fine a consideration. They were extraordinarily at one, and to say that they never either quarrelled or complained is to make the note of praise coarse for their quality of sweetness. Sometimes indeed, when I dropped into coarseness, I perhaps came across traces of little understandings between them by which one of them should keep me occupied while the other slipped away. There is a *naïf* side, I suppose, in all diplomacy; but if my pupils practised upon me it was surely with the minimum of grossness. It was all in the other quarter that, after a lull, the grossness broke out.

I find that I really hang back; but I must take my plunge. In going on with the record of what was hideous at Bly I not only challenge the most liberal faith – for which I little care; but – and this is another matter – I renew what I myself suffered, I again push my way through it to the end. There came suddenly an hour after which, as I look back, the affair seems to me to have been all pure suffering; but I have at least reached the heart of it, and the straightest road out is doubtless to advance. One evening – with nothing to lead up or to prepare it – I felt the cold touch of the impression that had breathed on me the night of my arrival and which, much lighter then, as I have mentioned, I should probably have made little of in memory had my subsequent sojourn been less agitated. I had not gone to bed; I sat reading by a couple of candles. There was a roomful of old books at Bly – last-century fiction, some of it, which, to the extent of a distinctly deprecated renown, but never to so much as that of a stray specimen, had reached the sequestered home and appealed to the unavowed curiosity of my youth. I remember that the book I had in my hand was Fielding's *Amelia*; also that I was wholly awake. I recall further both a general conviction that it was horribly late and a particular objection to looking at my watch. I figure, finally, that the white curtain draping, in the fashion of those days, the head of Flora's little bed, shrouded, as I had assured myself long before, the perfection of childish rest. I recollect in short that, though I was deeply interested in my author, I found myself, at the turn of a page and with his spell all scattered, looking straight up from him and hard at the door of my room. There was a moment during which I listened, reminded of the faint sense I had had, the first night, of there being something undefineably astir in the house, and noted the soft breath of the open casement just move the half-drawn blind. Then, with all the marks of a deliberation that must have seemed magnificent had there been anyone to admire it, I laid down my book, rose to my feet and, taking a candle, went straight out of the room and, from the passage, on which my light made little impression, noiselessly closed and locked the door.

I can say now neither what determined nor what guided me, but I went straight along the lobby, holding my candle high, till I came within sight of the tall window that presided over the great turn of the staircase. At this point I precipitately found myself aware of three things. They were practically simultaneous, yet they had flashes of succession. My candle, under a bold flourish, went out, and I perceived, by the uncovered window, that the yielding dusk of earliest morning rendered it unnecessary. Without it, the next instant, I saw that there was someone on the stair. I speak of sequences, but I required no lapse of seconds to stiffen myself for a third encounter with Quint. The apparition had reached the landing half way up and was therefore on the spot nearest the window, where, at sight of me, it stopped short and fixed me exactly as it had fixed me from the tower and from the garden. He knew me as well as I knew him; and so, in the cold, faint twilight, with a glimmer in the high glass and another on the polish of the oak stair below, we faced each other in our common intensity. He was absolutely, on this occasion, a living, detestable, dangerous presence. But that was not the wonder of wonders; I reserve this distinction for quite another circumstance: the circumstance that dread had unmistakably quitted me and that there was nothing in me there that didn't meet and measure him.

I had plenty of anguish after that extraordinary moment, but I had, thank God, no terror. And he knew I had not – I found myself at the end of an instant magnificently aware of this. I felt, in a fierce rigour of confidence, that if I stood my ground a minute I should cease – for the time, at least – to have him to reckon with; and during the minute, accordingly, the thing was as human and hideous as a real interview; hideous just because it *was* human, as human as to have met alone, in the small hours, in a sleeping house, some enemy, some adventurer, some criminal. It was the dead silence of our long gaze at such close quarters that gave the whole horror, huge as it was, its only note of the unnatural. If I had met a murderer in such a place and at such an hour we still at least would have spoken. Something would have passed, in life, between us; if nothing had passed one of us would have moved. The moment was so prolonged that it would have taken but little more to make me doubt if even *I* were in life. I can't express what followed it save by saying that the silence itself – which was indeed in a manner an attestation of my strength – became the element into which I saw the figure disappear; in which I definitely saw it turn, as I might have seen the low wretch to which it had once belonged turn on receipt of an order, and pass, with my eyes on the villainous back that no hunch could have more disfigured, straight down the staircase and into the darkness in which the next bend was lost.

Chapter Ten

I remained a while at the top of the stair, but with the effect presently of understanding that when my visitor had gone, he had gone: then I returned to my room. The foremost thing I saw there by the light of the candle I had left burning was that Flora's little bed was empty; and on this I caught my breath with all the terror that, five minutes before, I had been able to resist. I dashed at the place in which I had left her lying and over which (for the small silk counterpane and the sheets were dissarranged), the white curtains had been deceivingly pulled forward; then my step, to my unutterable relief, produced an answering sound: I perceived an agitation of the window-blind, and the child, ducking down, emerged rosily from the other side of it. She stood there in so much of her candour and so little of her nightgown, with her pink bare feet and the golden glow of her curls. She looked intensely grave, and I had never had such a sense of losing an advantage acquired (the thrill of which had just been so prodigious), as on my consciousness that she addressed me with a reproach. 'You naughty: where *have* you been?' – instead of challenging her own irregularity I found myself arraigned and explaining. She herself explained, for that matter, with the loveliest, eagerest simplicity. She had known suddenly, as she lay there, that I was out of the room, and had jumped up to see what had become of me. I had dropped, with the joy of her reappearance, back into my chair – feeling then, and then only, a little faint; and she had pattered straight over to me, thrown herself upon my knee, given herself to be held with the flame of the candle full in the wonderful little face that was still flushed with sleep. I remember closing my eyes an instant, yieldingly, consciously, as before the excess of something beautiful that shone out of the blue of her own. 'You were looking for me out of the window?' I said. 'You thought I might be walking in the grounds?'

'Well, you know, I thought someone was' – she never blanched as she smiled out that at me.

O, how I looked at her now! 'And did you see anyone?'

'Ah, *no*!' she returned, almost, with the full privilege of childish inconsequence, resentfully, though with a long sweetness in her little drawl of the negative.

At that moment, in the state of my nerves, I absolutely believed she lied; and if I once more closed my eyes it was before the dazzle of the three or four possible ways in which I might take this up. One of these, for a moment, tempted me with such singular intensity that, to withstand it, I must have gripped my little girl with a spasm that, wonderfully, she submitted to without a cry or a sign of fright. Why not break out at her on the spot and have it all over? – give it to her straight in her lovely little lighted face? 'You see, you see, you *know* that you do and that you already quite suspect I believe it; therefore why not frankly confess it to me, so that we may at least live with it together and learn perhaps, in the strangeness of our fate, where we are and what it means?' This solicitation dropped, alas, as it came: if I could immediately have succumbed to it I might have spared myself – well, you'll see what. Instead of succumbing I sprang again to my feet, looked at her bed and took a helpless middle way. 'Why did you pull the curtain over the place to make me think you were still there?'

Flora luminously considered; after which, with her little divine smile: 'Because I don't like to frighten you!'

'But if I had, by your idea, gone out—?'

She absolutely declined to be puzzled; she turned her eyes to the flame of the candle as if the question were as irrelevant, or at any rate as impersonal, as Mrs Marcet or nine-times-nine. 'Oh, but you know,' she quite adequately answered, 'that you might come back, you dear, and that you *have*!' And after a little, when she had got into bed, I had, for a long time, by almost sitting on her to hold her hand, to prove that I recognized the pertinence of my return.

You may imagine the general complexion, from that moment, of my nights. I repeatedly sat up till I didn't know when; I selected moments when my room-mate unmistakably slept, and, stealing out, took noiseless turns in the passage and even pushed as far as to where I had last met Quint. But I never met him there again; and I may as well say at once that I on no other occasion saw him in the house. I just missed, on the staircase, on the other hand, a different adventure. Looking down it from the top I once recognized the presence of a woman seated on one of the lower steps with her back presented to me, her body half bowed and her head, in an attitude of woe, in her hands. I had been there but an instant, however, when she vanished without looking round at me. I knew, none the less, exactly what dreadful face she had to show; and I wondered whether, if instead of being above I had been below, I should have had, for going up, the same nerve I had lately shown Quint. Well, there continued to be plenty of chance for nerve. On the eleventh night after my latest encounter with that gentleman – they were all numbered now – I had an alarm that perilously skirted it and that indeed, from the particular quality of its unexpectedness, proved quite my sharpest shock. It was precisely the first night during this series that, weary with watching, I had felt that I might again without laxity lay myself down at my old hour. I slept immediately and, as I afterwards knew, till about one o'clock; but when I woke it was to sit straight up, as completely roused as if a hand had shook me. I had left a light burning, but it was now out, and I felt an instant certainty that Flora had extinguished it. This brought me to my feet and straight, in the darkness, to her bed, which I found she had left. A glance at the window enlightened me further, and the striking of a match completed the picture.

The child had again got up – this time blowing out the taper, and had again, for some purpose of observation or response, squeezed in behind the blind and was peering out into the night. That she now saw – as she had not, I had satisfied myself, the previous time – was proved to me by the fact that she was disturbed neither by my re-illumination nor by the haste I made to get into slippers and into a wrap. Hidden, protected, absorbed, she evidently rested on the sill – the casement opened forward – and gave herself up. There was a great still moon to help her, and this fact had counted in my quick decision. She was face to face with the apparition we had met at the lake, and could now communicate with it as she had not then been able to do. What I, on my side, had to care for was, without disturbing her, to reach, from the corridor, some other window in the same quarter. I got to the door without her hearing me; I got out of it, closed it and listened, from the other side, for some sound from her. While I stood in the passage I had my eyes on her brother's door, which was but ten steps off and which, indescribably, produced in me a renewal of the strange impulse that I lately spoke of as my temptation. What if I should go straight in and march to *his* window? – what if, by risking to his boyish bewilderment a revelation of my motive, I should throw across the rest of the mystery the long halter of my boldness?

This thought held me sufficiently to make me cross to his threshold and pause again. I preternaturally listened; I figured to myself what might portentously be; I wondered if his bed were also empty and he too were secretly at watch. It was a deep, soundless minute, at the end of which my impulse failed. He was quiet; he might be innocent; the risk was hideous; I turned away. There was a figure in the grounds – a figure prowling for a sight, the visitor with whom Flora was engaged; but it was not the visitor most concerned with my boy. I hesitated afresh, but on other grounds and only a few seconds; then I had made my choice. There were empty rooms at Bly, and it was only a question of choosing the right one. The right one suddenly presented itself to me as the lower one – though high above the gardens – in the solid corner of the house that I have spoken of as the old tower. This was a large, square chamber, arranged with some state as a bedroom, the extravagant size of which made it so inconvenient that it had not for years, though kept by Mrs Grose in exemplary order, been occupied. I had often admired it and I knew my way about in it; I had only, after just faltering at the first chill gloom of its disuse, to pass across it and unbolt as quietly as I could one of the shutters. Achieving this transit, I uncovered the glass without a sound and, applying my face to the pane, was able, the darkness without being much less than within, to see that I commanded the right direction. Then I saw something more. The moon made the night extraordinarily penetrable and showed me on the lawn a person, diminished by distance, who stood there motionless and as if fascinated, looking up to where I had appeared – looking, that is, not so much straight at me as at something that was apparently above me. There was clearly another person above me – there was a person on the tower; but the presence on the lawn was not in the least what I had conceived and had confidently hurried to meet. The presence on the lawn – I felt sick as I made it out – was poor little Miles himself.

Chapter Eleven

It was not till late next day that I spoke to Mrs Grose; the rigour with which I kept my pupils in sight making it often difficult to meet her privately, and the more as we each felt the importance of not provoking – on the part of the servants quite as much as on that of the children – any suspicion of a secret flurry or of a discussion of mysteries. I drew a great security in this particular from her mere smooth aspect. There was nothing in her fresh face to pass on to others my horrible confidences. She believed me, I was sure, absolutely: if she hadn't I don't know what would have become of me, for I couldn't have borne the business alone. But she was a magnificent monument to the blessing of a want of imagination, and if she could see in our little charges nothing but their beauty and amiability, their happiness and cleverness, she had no direct communication with the sources of my trouble. If they had been at all visibly blighted or battered she would doubtless have grown, on tracing it back, haggard enough to match them; as matters stood, however, I could feel her, when she surveyed them with her large white arms folded and the habit of serenity in all her look, thank the Lord's mercy that if they were ruined the pieces would still serve. Flights of fancy gave place, in her mind, to a steady fireside glow, and I had already begun to perceive how, with the development of the conviction that – as time went on without a public accident – our young things could, after all, look out for themselves, she addressed her greatest solicitude to the sad case presented by their instructress. That, for myself, was a sound simplification: I could engage that, to the world, my face should tell no tales, but it would have been, in the conditions, an immense added strain to find myself anxious about hers.

At the hour I now speak of she had joined me, under pressure, on the terrace, where, with the lapse of the season, the afternoon sun was now agreeable; and we sat there together while, before us, at a distance, but within call if we wished, the children strolled to and fro in one of their most manageable moods. They moved slowly, in unison, below us, over the lawn, the boy, as they went, reading aloud from a storybook and passing his arm round his sister to keep her quite in touch. Mrs Grose watched them with positive placidity; then I caught the suppressed intellectual creak with which she conscientiously turned to take from me a view of the back of the tapestry. I had made her a receptacle of lurid things, but there was an odd recognition of my superiority – my accomplishments and my function – in her patience under my pain. She offered her mind to my disclosures as, had I wished to mix a witch's broth and proposed it with assurance, she would have held out a large clean saucepan. This had become thoroughly her attitude by the time that, in my recital of the events of the night, I reached the point of what

Miles had said to me when, after seeing him, at such a monstrous hour, almost on the very spot where he happened now to be, I had gone down to bring him in; choosing then, at the window, with a concentrated need of not alarming the house, rather that method than a signal more resonant. I had left her meanwhile in little doubt of my small hope of representing with success even to her actual sympathy my sense of the real splendour of the little inspiration with which, after I had got him into the house, the boy met my final articulate challenge. As soon as I appeared in the moonlight on the terrace he had come to me as straight as possible; on which I had taken his hand without a word and led him, through the dark spaces, up the staircase where Quint had so hungrily hovered for him, along the lobby where I had listened and trembled, and so to his forsaken room.

Not a sound, on the way, had passed between us, and I had wondered – oh, *how* I had wondered! – if he were groping about in his little mind for something plausible and not too grotesque. It would tax his invention, certainly, and I felt, this time, over his real embarrassment, a curious thrill of triumph. It was a sharp trap for the inscrutable! He couldn't play any longer at innocence; so how the deuce would he get out of it? There beat in me indeed, with the passionate throb of this question, an equal dumb appeal as to how the deuce *I* should. I was confronted at last, as never yet, with all the risk attached even now to sounding my own horrid note. I remember in fact that as we pushed into his little chamber, where the bed had not been slept in at all and the window, uncovered to the moonlight, made the place so clear that there was no need of striking a match – I remember how I suddenly dropped, sank upon the edge of the bed from the force of the idea that he must know how he really, as they say, 'had' me. He could do what he liked, with all his cleverness to help him, so long as I should continue to defer to the old tradition of the criminality of those caretakers of the young who minister to superstitions and fears. He 'had' me indeed, and in a cleft stick; for who would ever absolve me, who would consent that I should go unhung, if, by the faintest tremor of an overture, I were the first to introduce into our perfect intercourse an element so dire? No, no: it was useless to attempt to convey to Mrs Grose, just as it is scarcely less so to attempt to suggest here, how, in our short, stiff brush in the dark, he fairly shook me with admiration. I was of course thoroughly kind and merciful; never, never yet had I placed on his little shoulders hands of such tenderness as those with which, while I rested against the bed, I held him there well under fire. I had no alternative but, in form at least, to put it to him.

'You must tell me now – and all the truth. What did you go out for? What were you doing there?'

I can still see his wonderful smile, the whites of his beautiful eyes and the uncovering of his little teeth, shine to me in the dusk. 'If I tell you why, will you understand?' My heart, at this, leaped into my mouth. *Would* he tell me why? I found no sound on my lips to press it, and I was aware of replying only with a vague, repeated, grimacing nod. He was gentleness itself, and while I wagged my head at him he stood there more than ever a little fairy prince. It was his brightness indeed that gave me a respite. Would it be so great if he were really going to tell me? 'Well,' he said at last, 'just exactly in order that you should do this.'

'Do what?'

'Think me – for a change – *bad*!' I shall never forget the sweetness and gaiety with which he brought out the word, nor how, on top of it, he bent forward and kissed me. It was practically the end of everything. I met his kiss and I had to make, while I folded him for a minute in my arms, the most stupendous effort not to cry. He had given exactly the account of himself that permitted least of my going behind it, and it was only with the effect of confirming my acceptance of it that, as I presently glanced about the room, I could say—

'Then you didn't undress at all?'

He fairly glittered in the gloom. 'Not at all. I sat up and read.'

'And when did you go down?'

'At midnight. When I'm bad I *am* bad!'

'I see, I see – it's charming. But how could you be sure I would know it?'

'Oh, I arranged that with Flora.' His answers rang out with a readiness! 'She was to get up and look out.'

'Which is what she did do.' It was I who fell into the trap!

'So she disturbed you, and, to see what she was looking at, you also looked – you saw.'

'While you,' I concurred, 'caught your death in the night air!'

He literally bloomed so from this exploit that he could afford radiantly to assent. 'How otherwise should I have been bad enough?' he asked. Then, after another embrace, the incident and our interview closed on my recognition of all the reserves of goodness that, for his joke, he had been able to draw upon.

Chapter Twelve

The particular impression I had received proved in the morning light, I repeat, not quite successfully presentable to Mrs Grose, though I reinforced it with the mention of still another remark that he had made before we separated. 'It all lies in half-a-dozen words,' I said to her, 'words that really settle the matter. "Think, you know, what I *might* do!" He threw that off to show me how good he is. He knows down to the ground what he "might" do. That's what he gave them a taste of at school.'

'Lord, you do change!' cried my friend.

'I don't change – I simply make it out. The four, depend upon it, perpetually meet. If on either of these last nights you had been with either child you would clearly have understood. The more I've watched and waited the more I've felt that if there were nothing else to make it sure it would be made so by the systematic silence of each. *Never,* by a slip of the tongue, have they so much as alluded to either of their old friends, any more than Miles has alluded to his expulsion. Oh yes, we may sit here and look at them, and they may show off to us there to their fill; but even while they pretend to be lost in their fairy-tale they're steeped in their vision of the dead restored. He's not reading to her,' I declared; 'they're talking of *them* – they're talking horrors! I go on, I know, as if I were crazy; and it's a wonder I'm not. What I've seen would have made *you* so; but it has only made me more lucid, made me get hold of still other things.'

My lucidity must have seemed awful, but the charming creatures who were victims of it, passing and repassing in their interlocked sweetness, gave my colleague something to hold on by; and I felt how tight she held as, without stirring in the breath of my passion, she covered them still with her eyes. 'Of what other things have you got hold?'

'Why, of the very things that have delighted, fascinated and yet, at bottom, as I now so strangely see, mystified and troubled me. Their more than earthly beauty, their absolutely unnatural goodness. It's a game,' I went on; 'it's a policy and a fraud!'

'On the part of little darlings—?'

'As yet mere lovely babies? Yes, mad as that seems!' The very act of bringing it out really helped me to trace it – follow it all up and piece it all together. 'They haven't been good – they've only been absent. It has been easy to live with them, because they're simply leading a life of their own. They're not mine – they're not ours. They're his and they're hers!'

'Quint's and that woman's?'

'Quint's and that woman's. They want to get to them.'

Oh, how, at this, poor Mrs Grose appeared to study them! 'But for what?'

'For the love of all the evil that, in those dreadful days, the pair put into them. And to ply them with that evil still, to keep up the work of demons, is what brings the others back.'

'Laws!' said my friend under her breath. The exclamation was homely, but it revealed a real acceptance of my further proof of what, in the bad time – for there had been a worse even than this! – must have occurred. There could have been no justification for me as the plain assent of her experience to whatever depth of depravity I found credible in our brace of scoundrels. It was in obvious submission of memory that she brought out after a moment: "They *were* rascals! But what can they now do?' she pursued.

'Do?' I echoed so loud that Miles and Flora, as they passed at their distance, paused an instant in their walk and looked at us. 'Don't they do enough?' I demanded in a lower tone, while the children, having smiled and nodded and kissed hands to us, resumed their exhibition. We were held by it a minute; then I answered: 'They can destroy them!' At this my companion did turn, but the inquiry she launched was a silent one, the effect of which was to make me more explicit. 'They don't know, as yet, quite how – but they're trying hard. They're seen only across, as it were, and beyond – in strange places and on high places, the top of towers, the roof of houses, the outside of windows, the further edge of pools; but there's a deep design, on either side, to shorten the distance and overcome the obstacle; and the success of the tempters is only a question of time. They've only to keep to their suggestions of danger.'

'For the children to come?'

'And perish in the attempt!' Mrs Grose slowly got up, and I scrupulously added: 'Unless, of course, we can prevent!'

Standing there before me while I kept my seat, she visibly turned things over. 'Their uncle must do the preventing. He must take them away.'

'And who's to make him?'

She had been scanning the distance, but she now dropped on me a foolish face. 'You, Miss.'

'By writing to him that his house is poisoned and his little nephew and niece mad?'

'But if they *are*, Miss?'

'And if I am myself, you mean? That's charming news to be sent him by a governess whose prime undertaking was to give him no worry.'

Mrs Grose considered, following the children again. 'Yes, he do hate worry. That was the great reason—'

'Why those fiends took him in so long? No doubt, though his indifference must have been awful. As I'm not a fiend, at any rate, I shouldn't take him in.'

My companion, after an instant and for all answer, sat down again and grasped my arm. 'Make him at any rate come to you.'

I stared. 'To *me*?' I had a sudden fear of what she might do. '"Him"?'

'He ought to *be* here – he ought to help.'

I quickly rose, and I think I must have shown her a queerer face than ever yet. 'You see me asking him for a visit?' No, with her eyes on my face she evidently couldn't. Instead of it even – as a woman reads another – she could see what I myself saw: his derision, his amusement, his contempt for the breakdown of my resignation at being left alone and for the fine machinery I had set in motion to attract his attention to my slighted charms. She didn't know – no one knew – how proud I had been to serve him and to stick to our terms; yet she none the less took the measure, I think, of the warning I now gave her. 'If you should so lose your head as to appeal to him for me—'

She was really frightened. 'Yes, Miss?'

'I would leave, on the spot, both him and you.'

Chapter Thirteen

It was all very well to join them, but speaking to them proved quite as much as ever an effort beyond my strength – offered, in close quarters, difficulties as insurmountable as before. This situation continued a month, and with new aggravations and particular notes, the note above all, sharper and sharper, of the small ironic consciousness on the part of my pupils. It was not, I am as sure today as I was sure then, my mere infernal imagination: it was absolutely traceable that they were aware of my predicament and that this strange relation made, in a manner, for a long time, the air in which we moved. I don't mean that they had their tongues in their cheeks or did anything vulgar, for that was not one of their dangers: I do mean, on the other hand, that the element of the unnamed and untouched became, between us, greater than any other, and that so much avoidance could not have been so successfully effected without a great deal of tacit arrangement. It was as if, at moments, we were perpetually coming into sight of subjects before which we must stop short, turning suddenly out of alleys that we perceived to be blind, closing with a little bang that made us look at each other – for, like all bangs, it was something louder than we had intended – the doors we had indiscreetly opened. All roads lead to Rome, and there were times when it might have struck us that almost every branch of study or subject of conversation skirted forbidden ground. Forbidden ground was the question of the return of the dead in general and of whatever, in especial, might survive, in memory, of the friends little children had lost. There were days when I could have sworn that one of them had, with a small invisible nudge, said to the other: 'She thinks she'll do it this time – but she *won't*!' To 'do it' would have been to indulge for instance – and for once in a way – in some direct reference to the lady who had prepared them for my discipline. They had a delightful endless appetite for passages in my own history, to which I had again and again treated them; they were in possession of everything that had ever happened to me, had had, with every circumstance, the story of my smallest adventures and of those of my brothers and sisters and of the cat and the dog at home, as well as many particulars of the eccentric nature of my father, of the furniture and arrangement of our house and of the conversation of the old women of our village. There were things enough, taking one with another, to chatter about, if one went very fast and knew by instinct when to go round. They pulled with an art of their own the strings of my invention and my memory; and nothing else perhaps, when I thought of such occasions afterwards, gave me so the suspicion of being watched from under cover. It was in any case over *my* life, *my* past and *my* friends alone that we could take anything like our ease; a state of affairs that led them sometimes without the least pertinence to break out into sociable reminders. I was invited – with no visible connexion – to repeat afresh Goody Gosling's celebrated *mot* or to confirm the details already supplied as to the cleverness of the vicarage pony.

It was partly at such junctures as these and partly at quite different ones that, with the turn my matters had now taken, my predicament, as I have called it, grew most sensible. The fact that the days passed for me without another encounter ought, it would have appeared, to have done something towards soothing my nerves. Since the light brush, that second night on the upper landing, of the presence of a woman at the foot of the stair, I had seen nothing, whether in or out of the house, that one had better not have seen. There was many a corner round which I expected to come upon Quint, and many a situation that, in a merely sinister way, would have favoured the appearance of Miss Jessel. The summer had turned, the summer had gone; the autumn had dropped upon Bly and had blown out half our lights. The place, with its grey sky and withered garlands, its bared spaces and scattered dead leaves, was like a theatre after the performance – all strewn with crumpled playbills. They were exactly states of the air, conditions of sound and of stillness, unspeakable impressions of the *kind* of ministering moment, that brought back to me, long enough to catch it, the feeling of the medium in which, that June evening out-of-doors, I had had my first sight of Quint, and in which, too, at those other instants, I had, after seeing him through the window, looked for him in vain in the circle of shrubbery. I recognized the signs, the portents – I recognized the moment, the spot. But they remained unaccompanied and empty, and I continued unmolested; if unmolested one could call a young woman whose sensibility had, in the most extraordinary fashion, not declined but deepened. I had said in my talk with Mrs Grose on that horrid scene of Flora's by the lake – and had perplexed her by so saying – that it would from that moment distress me much more to lose my power than to keep it. I had then expressed what was vividly in my mind: the truth that, whether the children really saw or not – since, that is, it was not yet definitely proved – I greatly preferred, as a safeguard, the fullness of my own exposure. I was ready to know the very worst that was to be known. What I had then had an ugly glimpse of was that my eyes might be sealed just while theirs were most opened. Well, my eyes *were* sealed, it appeared, at present – a consummation for which it seemed blasphemous not to thank God. There was, alas, a difficulty about that: I would have thanked him with all my soul had I not had in a proportionate measure this conviction of the secret of my pupils.

How can I retrace today the strange steps of my obsession? There were times of our being together when I would have been ready to swear that, literally, in my presence, but with my direct sense of it closed, they had visitors who were known and were welcome. Then it was that, had I not been deterred by the very chance that such an injury might prove greater than the injury to be averted, my exaltation would have broken out. 'They're here, they're here, you little wretches,' I would have cried, 'and you can't deny it now!' The little wretches denied it with all the added volume of their sociability and their tenderness, in just the crystal depths of which – like the flash of a fish in a stream – the mockery of their advantage peeped up. The shock, in truth, had sunk into me still deeper than I knew on the night when, looking out to see either Quint or Miss Jessel under the stars, I had beheld the boy over whose rest I watched and who had immediately brought in with him – had straightway, there, turned it on me – the lovely upward look with which, from the battlements above me, the hideous apparition of Quint had played. If it was a question of a scare, my discovery on this occasion had scared me more than any other, and it was in the condition of nerves produced by it that I made my actual inductions. They harassed me so that sometimes, at odd moments, I shut myself up audibly to rehearse – it was at once a fantastic relief and a renewed despair – the manner in which I might come to the point. I approached it from one side and the other while, in my room, I flung myself about, but I always broke down in the monstrous utterance of names. As they died away on my lips I said to myself that I should indeed help them to represent something infamous if, by pronouncing them, I should violate as rare a little case of instinctive delicacy as any schoolroom, probably, had ever known. When I said to myself: '*They* have the manners to be silent, and you, trusted as you are, the baseness to speak!' I felt myself crimson and I covered my face with my hands. After these secret scenes I chattered more than ever, going on volubly enough till one of our prodigious, palpable hushes occurred – I can call them nothing else – the strange, dizzy lift or swim (I try for terms!) into a stillness, a pause of all life, that had nothing to do with the more or less noise that at the moment we might be engaged in making and that I could hear through any deepened exhilaration or quickened recitation or louder strum of the piano. Then it was that the others, the outsiders, were there. Though they were not angels, they 'passed', as the French say, causing me, while they stayed, to tremble with the fear of their addressing to their younger victims some yet more infernal message or more vivid image than they had thought good enough for myself.

What it was most impossible to get rid of was the cruel idea that, whatever I had seen, Miles and Flora saw *more* – things terrible and unguessable and that sprang from dreadful passages of intercourse in the past. Such things naturally left on the surface, for the time, a chill which we vociferously denied that we felt; and we had, all three, with repetition, got into such splendid training that we went, each time, almost automatically, to mark the close of the incident, through the very same movements. It was striking of the children, at all events, to kiss me inveterately with a kind of wild irrelevance and never to fail – one or the other – of the precious question that has helped us through many a peril. 'When do you think he *will* come? Don't you think we *ought* to write?' – there was nothing like that inquiry, we found by experience, for carrying off an awkwardness. 'He' of course was their uncle in Harley Street; and we lived in much profusion of theory that he might at any moment arrive to mingle in our circle. It was impossible to have given less encouragement than he had done to such a doctrine, but if we had not had the doctrine to fall back upon we should have deprived each other of some of our finest exhibitions. He never wrote to them – that may have been selfish, but it was a part of the flattery of his trust of me; for the way in which a man pays his highest tribute to a woman is apt to be but by the more festal celebration of one of the sacred laws of his comfort; and I held that I carried out the spirit of the pledge given not to appeal to him when I let my charges understand that their own letters were but charming literary exercises. They were too beautiful to be posted; I kept them myself; I have them all to this hour. This was a rule indeed which only added to the satiric effect of my being plied with the supposition that he might at any moment be among us. It was exactly as if my charges knew how almost more awkward than anything else that might be for me. There appears to me, moreover, as I look back, no note in all this more extraordinary than the mere fact that, in spite of my tension and of their triumph, I never lost patience with them. Adorable they must in truth have been, I now reflect, that I didn't in these days hate them! Would exasperation, however, if relief had longer been postponed, finally have betrayed me? It little matters, for relief arrived. I call it relief though it was only the relief that a snap brings to a strain or the burst of a thunderstorm to a day of suffocation. It was at least change, and it came with a rush.

Chapter Fourteen

Walking to church a certain Sunday morning, I had little Miles at my side and his sister, in advance of us and at Mrs Grose's, well in sight. It was a crisp, clear day, the first of its order for some time; the night had brought a touch of frost, and the autumn air, bright and sharp, made the church-bells almost gay. It was an odd accident of thought that I should have happened at such a moment to be particularly and very gratefully struck with the obedience of my little charges. Why did they never resent my inexorable, my perpetual society? Something or other had brought nearer home to me that I had all but pinned the boy to my shawl and that, in the way our companions were marshalled before me, I might have appeared to provide against some danger of rebellion. I was like a gaoler with an eye to possible surprises and escapes. But all this belonged – I mean their magnificent little surrender – just to the special array of the facts that were most abysmal. Turned out for Sunday by his uncle's tailor, who had had a free hand and a notion of pretty waistcoats and of his grand little air, Miles's whole title to independence, the rights of his sex and situation, were so stamped upon him that if he had suddenly struck for freedom I should have had nothing to say. I was by the strangest of chances wondering how I should meet him when the revolution unmistakably occurred. I call it a revolution because I now see how, with the word he spoke, the curtain rose on the last act of my dreadful drama and the catastrophe was precipitated. 'Look here, my dear, you know,' he charmingly said, 'when in the world, please, am I going back to school?'

Transcribed here the speech sounds harmless enough, particularly as uttered in the sweet, high, casual pipe with which, at all interlocutors, but above all at his eternal governess, he threw off intonations as if he were tossing roses. There was something in them that always made one 'catch', and I caught, at any rate, now so effectually that I stopped as short as if one of the trees of the park had fallen across the road. There was something new, on the spot, between us, and he was perfectly aware that I recognized it, though, to enable me to do so, he had no need to look a whit less candid and charming than usual. I could feel in him how he already, from my at first finding nothing to reply, perceived the advantage he had gained. I was so slow to find anything that he had plenty of time, after a minute, to continue with his suggestive but inconclusive smile: 'You know, my dear, that for a fellow to be with a lady *always*—!' His 'my dear' was constantly on his lips for me, and nothing could have expressed more the exact shade of the sentiment with which I desired to inspire my pupils than its fond familiarity. It was so respectfully easy.

But, oh, how I felt that at present I must pick my own phrases! I remember that, to gain time, I tried to laugh, and I seemed to see in the beautiful face with which he watched me how ugly and queer I looked. 'And always with the same lady?' I returned.

He neither blenched nor winked. The whole thing was virtually out between us. 'Ah, of course she's a jolly, "perfect" lady; but, after all, I'm a fellow, don't you see? that's – well, getting on.'

I lingered there with him an instant ever so kindly. 'Yes, you're getting on.' Oh, but I felt helpless!

I have kept to this day the heartbreaking little idea of how he seemed to know that and to play with it. 'And you can't say I've not been awfully good, can you?'

I laid my hand on his shoulder, for, though I felt how much better it would have been to walk on, I was not yet quite able. 'No, I can't say that, Miles.'

'Except just that one night, you know—!'

'That one night?' I couldn't look as straight as he.

'Why, when I went down – went out of the house.'

'Oh yes. But I forget what you did it for.'

'You forget?' – he spoke with the sweet extravagance of childish reproach. 'Why, it was to show you I could!'

'Oh yes, you could.'

'And I can again.'

I felt that I might, perhaps, after all, succeed in keeping my wits about me. 'Certainly. But you won't.'

'No, not *that* again. It was nothing.'

'It was nothing,' I said. 'But we must go on.'

He resumed our walk with me, passing his hand into my arm. 'Then when *am* I going back?'

I wore, in turning it over, my most responsible air. 'Were you very happy at school?'

He just considered. 'Oh, I'm happy enough anywhere!'

'Well then,' I quavered, 'if you're just as happy here—!'

'Ah, but that isn't everything! Of course *you* know a lot—'

'But you hint that you know almost as much?' I risked as he paused.

'Not half I want to!' Miles honestly professed. 'But it isn't so much that.'

'What is it then?'

'Well – I want to see more life.'

'I see; I see.' We had arrived within sight of the church and of various persons, including several of the household of Bly, on their way to it and clustered about the door to see us go in. I quickened our step; I wanted to get there before the question between us opened up much further; I reflected hungrily that, for more than an hour, he would have to be silent; and I thought with envy of the comparative dusk of the pew and of the almost spiritual help of the hassock on which I might bend my knees. I seemed literally to be running a race with some confusion to which he was about to reduce me, but I felt that he had got in first when, before we had even entered the churchyard, he threw out—

'I want my own sort!'

It literally made me bound forward. 'There are not many of your own sort, Miles!' I laughed. 'Unless perhaps dear little Flora!'

'You really compare me to a baby girl?'

This found me singularly weak. 'Don't you, then, *love* our sweet Flora?'

'If I didn't – and you too; if I didn't—!' he repeated as if retreating for a jump, yet leaving his thought so unfinished that, after we had come into the gate, another stop, which he imposed on me by the pressure of his arm, had become inevitable. Mrs Grose and Flora had passed into the church, the other worshippers had followed, and we were, for the minute, alone among the old, thick graves. We had paused, on the path from the gate, by a low, oblong, table-like tomb.

'Yes, if you didn't—?'

He looked, while I waited, about at the graves. 'Well, you know what!' But he didn't move, and he presently produced something that made me drop straight down on the stone slab, as if suddenly to rest. 'Does my uncle think what *you* think?'

I markedly rested. 'How do you know what I think?'

'Ah well, of course I don't; for it strikes me you never tell me. But I mean does *he* know?'

'Know what, Miles?'

'Why, the way I'm going on.'

I perceived quickly enough that I could make, to this inquiry, no answer that would not involve something of a sacrifice of my employer. Yet it appeared to me that we were all, at Bly, sufficiently sacrificed to make that venial. 'I don't think your uncle much cares.'

Miles, on this, stood looking at me. 'Then don't you think he can be made to?'

'In what way?'

'Why, by his coming down.'

'But who'll get him to come down?'

'*I* will!' the boy said with extraordinary brightness and emphasis. He gave me another look charged with that expression and then marched off alone into church.

Chapter Fifteen

The business was practically settled from the moment I never followed him. It was a pitiful surrender to agitation, but my being aware of this had somehow no power to restore me. I only sat there on my tomb and read into what my little friend had said to me the fullness of its meaning; by the time I had grasped the whole of which I had also embraced, for absence, the pretext that I was ashamed to offer my pupils and the rest of the congregation such an example of delay. What I said to myself above all was that Miles had got something out of me and that the proof of it, for him, would be just this awkward collapse. He had got out of me that there was something I was much afraid of and that he should probably be able to make use of my fear to gain, for his own purpose, more freedom. My fear was of having to deal with the intolerable question of the grounds of his dismissal from school, for that was really but the question of the horrors gathered behind. That his uncle should arrive to treat with me of these things was a solution that, strictly speaking, I ought now to have desired to bring on; but I could so little face the ugliness and the pain of it that I simply procrastinated and lived from hand to mouth. The boy, to my deep discomposure, was immensely in the right, was in a position to say to me: 'Either you clear up with my guardian the mystery of this interruption of my studies, or you cease to expect me to lead with you a life that's so unnatural for a boy.' What was so unnatural for the particular boy I was concerned with was this sudden revelation of a consciousness and a plan.

That was what really overcame me, what prevented my going in. I walked round the church, hesitating, hovering; I reflected that I had already, with him, hurt myself beyond repair. Therefore I could patch up nothing, and it was too extreme an effort to squeeze beside him into the pew: he would be so much more sure than ever to pass his arm into mine and make me sit there for an hour in close, silent contact with his commentary on our talk. For the first minute since his arrival I wanted to get away from him. As I paused beneath the high east window and listened to the sounds of worship I was taken with an impulse that might master me, I felt, completely should I give it the least encouragement. I might easily put an end to my predicament by getting away altogether. Here was my chance; there was no one to stop me; I could give the whole thing up – turn my back and retreat. It was only a question of hurrying again, for a few preparations, to the house which the attendance at church of so many of the servants would practically have left unoccupied. No one, in short, could blame me if I should just drive desperately off. What was it to get away if I got away only till dinner? That would be in a couple of hours, at the end of which – I had the acute prevision – my little pupils would play at innocent wonder about my non-appearance in their train.

'What *did* you do, you naughty, bad thing? Why in the world, to worry us so – and take our thoughts off too, don't you know? – did you desert us at the very door?' I couldn't meet such questions nor, as they asked them, their false little lovely eyes; yet it was all so exactly what I should have to meet that, as the prospect grew sharp to me, I at last let myself go.

I got, so far as the immediate moment was concerned, away; I came straight out of the churchyard and, thinking hard, retraced my steps through the park. It seemed to me that by the time I reached the house I had made up my mind I would fly. The Sunday stillness both of the approaches and of the interior, in which I met no one, fairly excited me with a sense of opportunity. Were I to get off quickly, this way, I should get off without a scene, without a word. My quickness would have to be remarkable, however, and the question of a conveyance was the great one to settle. Tormented, in the hall, with difficulties and obstacles, I remember sinking down at the foot of the staircase – suddenly collapsing there on the lowest step and then, with a revulsion, recalling that it was exactly where, more than a month before, in the darkness of night and just so bowed with evil things, I had seen the spectre of the most horrible of women. At this I was able to straighten myself; I went the rest of the way up; I made, in my bewilderment, for the schoolroom, where there were objects belonging to me that I should have to take. But I opened the door to find again, in a flash, my eyes unsealed. In the presence of what I saw I reeled straight back upon my resistance.

Seated at my own table in the clear noonday light I saw a person whom, without my previous experience, I should have taken at the first blush for some housemaid who might have stayed at home to look after the place and who, availing herself of rare relief from observation and of the schoolroom table and my pens, ink and paper, had applied herself to the considerable effort of a letter to her sweetheart. There was an effort in the way that, while her arms rested on the table, her hands, with evident weariness, supported her head; but at the moment I took this in I had already become aware that, in spite of my entrance, her attitude strangely persisted. Then it was – with the very act of its announcing itself – that her identity flared up in a change of posture. She rose, not as if she had heard me, but with an indescribable grand melancholy of indifference and detachment, and, within a dozen feet of me, stood there as my vile predecessor. Dishonoured and tragic, she was all before me; but even as I fixed and, for memory, secured it, the awful image passed away. Dark as midnight in her black dress, her haggard beauty and her unutterable woe, she had looked at me long enough to appear to say that her right to sit at my table was as good as mine to sit at hers. While these instants lasted indeed I had the extraordinary chill of a feeling that it was I who was the intruder. It was as a wild protest against it that, actually addressing her – 'You terrible, miserable woman!' – I heard myself break into a sound that, by the open door, rang through the long passage and the empty house. She looked at me as if she heard me, but I had recovered myself and cleared the air. There was nothing in the room the next minute but the sunshine and a sense that I must stay.

Chapter Sixteen

I had so perfectly expected that the return of my pupils would be marked by a demonstration that I was freshly upset at having to take into account that they were dumb about my absence. Instead of gaily denouncing and caressing me they made no allusion to my having failed them, and I was left, for the time, on perceiving that she too said nothing, to study Mrs Grose's odd face. I did this to such purpose that I made sure they had in some way bribed her to silence; a silence that, however, I would engage to break down on the first private opportunity. This opportunity came before tea: I secured five minutes with her in the housekeeper's room, where, in the twilight, amid a smell of lately-baked bread, but with the place all swept and garnished, I found her sitting in pained placidity before the fire. So I see her still, so I see her best: facing the flame from her straight chair in the dusky, shining room, a large clean image of the 'put away' – of drawers closed and locked and rest without a remedy.

'Oh yes, they asked me to say nothing; and to please them – so long as they were there – of course I promised. But what had happened to you?'

'I only went with you for the walk,' I said. 'I had then to come back to meet a friend.'

She showed her surprise. 'A friend – *you*?'

'Oh yes, I have a couple!' I laughed. 'But did the children give you a reason?'

'For not alluding to your leaving us? Yes; they said you would like it better. Do you like it better?'

My face had made her rueful. 'No, I like it worse!' But after an instant I added: 'Did they say why I should like it better?'

'No; Master Miles only said "We must do nothing but what she likes!" '

'I wish indeed he would! And what did Flora say?'

'Miss Flora was too sweet. She said "Oh, of course, of course!" – and I said the same.'

I thought a moment. 'You were too sweet too – I can hear you all. But none the less, between Miles and me, it's now all out.'

'All out?' My companion stared. 'But what, Miss?'

'Everything. It doesn't matter. I've made up my mind. I came home, my dear,' I went on, 'for a talk with Miss Jessel.'

I had by this time formed the habit of having Mrs Grose literally well in hand in advance of my sounding that note; so that even now, as she bravely blinked under the signal of my word, I could keep her comparatively firm. 'A talk! Do you mean she spoke?'

'It came to that. I found her, on my return, in the schoolroom.'

'And what did she say?' I can hear the good woman still, and the candour of her stupefaction.

'That she suffers the torments—!'

It was this, of a truth, that made her, as she filled out my picture, gape. 'Do you mean,' she faltered, '—of the lost?'

'Of the lost. Of the damned. And that's why, to share them—' I faltered myself with the horror of it.

But my companion, with less imagination, kept me up. 'To share them—?'

'She wants Flora.' Mrs Grose might, as I gave it to her, fairly have fallen away from me had I not been prepared. I still held her there, to show I was. 'As I've told you, however, it doesn't matter.'

'Because you've made up your mind? But to what?'

'To everything.'

'And what do you call "everything"?'

'Why, sending for their uncle.'

'Oh Miss, in pity do,' my friend broke out.

'Ah, but I will, I *will*! I see it's the only way. What's "out", as I told you, with Miles is that if he thinks I'm afraid to – and has ideas of what he gains by that – he shall see he's mistaken. Yes, yes; his uncle shall have it here from me on the spot (and before the boy himself if necessary), that if I'm to be reproached with having done nothing again about more school—'

'Yes, Miss—' my companion pressed me.

'Well, there's that awful reason.'

There were now clearly so many of these for my poor colleague that she was excusable for being vague. 'But – a – which?'

'Why, the letter from his old place.'

'You'll show it to the master?'

'I ought to have done so on the instant.'

'Oh no!' said Mrs Grose with decision.

'I'll put it before him,' I went on inexorably, 'that I can't undertake to work the question on behalf of a child who has been expelled—'

'For we've never in the least known what!' Mrs Grose declared.

'For wickedness. For what else – when he's so clever and beautiful and perfect? Is he stupid? Is he untidy? Is he infirm? Is he ill-natured? He's exquisite – so it can be only *that*; and that would open up the whole thing. After all,' I said, 'it's their uncle's fault. If he left here such people—!'

'He didn't really in the least know them. The fault's mine.' She had turned quite pale.

'Well, you shan't suffer,' I answered.

'The children shan't!' she emphatically returned.

I was silent a while; we looked at each other. 'Then what am I to tell him?'

'You needn't tell him anything. *I'll* tell him.'

I measured this. 'Do you mean you'll write—?' Remembering she couldn't, I caught myself up. 'How do you communicate?'

'I tell the bailiff. *He* writes.'

'And should you like him to write our story?'

My question had a sarcastic force that I had not fully intended, and it made her, after a moment, inconsequently break down. The tears were again in her eyes. 'Ah, Miss, *you* write!'

'Well – tonight,' I at last answered; and on this we separated.

Chapter Seventeen

I went so far, in the evening, as to make a beginning. The weather had changed back, a great wind was abroad, and beneath the lamp, in my room, with Flora at peace beside me, I sat for a long time before a blank sheet of paper and listened to the lash of the rain and the batter of the gusts. Finally I went out, taking a candle; I crossed the passage and listened a minute at Miles's door. What, under my endless obsession, I had been impelled to listen for was some betrayal of his not being at rest, and I presently caught one, but not in the form I had expected. His voice tinkled out. 'I say, you there – come in.' It was a gaiety in the gloom!

I went in with my light and found him, in bed, very wide awake, but very much at his ease. 'Well, what are *you* up to?' he asked with a grace of sociability in which it occurred to me that Mrs Grose, had she been present, might have looked in vain for proof that anything was 'out'.

I stood over him with my candle. 'How did you know I was there?'

'Why, of course I heard you. Did you fancy you made no noise? You're like a troop of cavalry!' he beautifully laughed.

'Then you weren't asleep?'

'Not much! I lie awake and think.'

I had put my candle, designedly, a short way off, and then, as he held out his friendly old hand to me, had sat down on the edge of his bed. 'What is it,' I asked, 'that you think of?'

'What in the world, my dear, but *you*?'

'Ah, the pride I take in your appreciation doesn't insist on that! I had so far rather you slept.'

'Well, I think also, you know, of this queer business of ours.'

I marked the coolness of his firm little hand. 'Of what queer business, Miles?'

'Why, the way you bring me up. And all the rest!'

I fairly held my breath a minute, and even from my glimmering taper there was light enough to show how he smiled up at me from his pillow. 'What do you mean by all the rest?'

'Oh, you know, you know!'

I could say nothing for a minute, though I felt, as I held his hand and our eyes continued to meet, that my silence had all the air of admitting his charge and that nothing in the whole world of reality was perhaps at that moment so fabulous as our actual relation. 'Certainly you shall go back to school,' I said, 'if it be that that troubles you. But not to the old place – we must find another, a better. How could I know it did trouble you, this question, when you never told me so, never spoke of it at all?' His clear, listening face, framed in its smooth whiteness, made him for the minute as appealing as some wistful patient in a children's hospital; and I would have given, as the resemblance came to me, all I possessed on earth really to be the nurse or the sister of charity who might have helped to cure him. Well, even as it was, I perhaps might help! 'Do you know you've never said a word to me about your school – I mean the old one; never mentioned it in any way?'

He seemed to wonder; he smiled with the same loveliness. But he clearly gained time; he waited, he called for guidance. 'Haven't I?' It wasn't for *me* to help him – it was for the thing I had met!

Something in his tone and the expression of his face, as I got this from him, set my heart aching with such a pang as it had never yet known; so unutterably touching was it to see his little brain puzzled and his little resources taxed to play, under the spell laid on him, a part of innocence and consistency. 'No, never – from the hour you came back. You've never mentioned to me one of your masters, one of your comrades, nor the least little thing that ever happened to you at school. Never, little Miles – no never – have you given me an inkling of anything that *may* have happened there. Therefore you can fancy how much I'm in the dark. Until you came out, that way, this morning, you had, since the first hour I saw you, scarce even made a reference to anything in your previous life. You seemed so perfectly to accept the present.' It was extraordinary how my absolute conviction of his secret precocity (or whatever I might call the poison of an influence that I dared but half to phrase), made him, in spite of the faint breath of his inward trouble, appear as accessible as an older person – imposed him almost as an intellectual equal. 'I thought you wanted to go on as you are.'

It struck me that at this he just faintly coloured. He gave, at any rate, like a convalescent slightly fatigued, a languid shake of his head. 'I don't – I don't. I want to get away.'

'You're tired of Bly?'

'Oh no, I like Bly.'

'Well, then—?'

'Oh, *you* know what a boy wants!'

I felt that I didn't know so well as Miles, and I took temporary refuge. 'You want to go to your uncle?'

Again, at this, with his sweet ironic face, he made a movement on the pillow. 'Ah, you can't get off with that!'

I was silent a little, and it was I, now, I think, who changed colour. 'My dear, I don't want to get off!'

'You can't, even if you do. You can't, you can't!' – he lay beautifully staring. 'My uncle must come down, and you must completely settle things.'

'If we do,' I returned with some spirit, 'you may be sure it will be to take you quite away.'

'Well, don't you understand that that's exactly what I'm working for? You'll have to tell him – about the way you've let it all drop: you'll have to tell him a tremendous lot!'

The exultation with which he uttered this helped me somehow, for the instant, to meet him rather more. 'And how much will *you*, Miles, have to tell him? There are things he'll ask you!'

He turned it over. 'Very likely. But what things?'

'The things you've never told me. To make up his mind what to do with you. He can't send you back—'

'Oh, I don't want to go back!' he broke in. 'I want a new field.'

He said it with admirable serenity, with positive unimpeachable gaiety; and doubtless it was that very note that most evoked for me the poignancy, the unnatural childish tragedy, of his probable reappearance at the end of three months with all this bravado and still more dishonour. It overwhelmed me now that I should never be able to bear that, and it made me let myself go. I threw myself upon him and in the tenderness of my pity I embraced him. 'Dear little Miles, dear little Miles—!'

My face was close to his, and he let me kiss him, simply taking it with indulgent good humour. 'Well, old lady?'

'Is there nothing – nothing at all that you want to tell me?'

He turned off a little, facing round towards the wall and holding up his hand to look at as one had seen sick children look. 'I've told you – I told you this morning.'

Oh, I was sorry for him! 'That you just want me not to worry you?'

He looked round at me now, as if in recognition of my understanding him; then ever so gently, 'To let me alone,' he replied.

There was even a singular little dignity in it, something that made me release him, yet, when I had slowly risen, linger beside him. God knows I never wished to harass him, but I felt that merely, at this, to turn my back on him was to abandon or, to put it more truly, to lose him. 'I've just begun a letter to your uncle,' I said.

'Well then, finish it!'

I waited a minute. 'What happened before?'

He gazed up at me again. 'Before what?'

'Before you came back. And before you went away.'

For some time he was silent, but he continued to meet my eyes. 'What happened?'

It made me, the sound of the words, in which it seemed to me that I caught for the very first time a small faint quaver of consenting consciousness – it made me drop on my knees beside the bed and seize once more the chance of possessing him. 'Dear little Miles, dear little Miles, if you *knew* how I want to help you! It's only that, it's nothing but that, and I'd rather die than give you a pain or do you a wrong – I'd rather die than hurt a hair of you. Dear little Miles' – oh, I brought it out now even if I *should* go too far – 'I just want you to help me to save you!' But I knew in a moment after this that I had gone too far. The answer to my appeal was instantaneous, but it came in the form of an extraordinary blast and chill, a gust of frozen air and a shake of the room as great as if, in the wild wind, the casement had crashed in. The boy gave a loud, high shriek which, lost in the rest of the shock of sound, might have seemed, indistinctly, though I was so close to him, a note either of jubilation or of terror. I jumped to my feet again and was conscious of darkness. So for a moment we remained, while I stared about me and saw that the drawn curtains were unstirred and the window tight. 'Why, the candle's out!' I then cried.

'It was I who blew it, dear!' said Miles.

Chapter Eighteen

The next day, after lessons, Mrs Grose found a moment to say to me quietly: 'Have you written, Miss?'

'Yes – I've written.' But I didn't add – for the hour – that my letter, sealed and directed, was still in my pocket. There would be time enough to send it before the messenger should go to the village. Meanwhile there had been, on the part of my pupils, no more brilliant, more exemplary morning. It was exactly as if they had both had at heart to gloss over any recent little friction. They performed the dizziest feats of arithmetic, soaring quite out of *my* feeble range, and perpetrated, in higher spirits than ever, geographical and historical jokes. It was conspicuous of course in Miles in particular that he appeared to wish to show how easily he could let me down. This child, to my memory, really lives in a setting of beauty and misery that no words can translate; there was a distinction all his own in every impulse he revealed;

never was a small natural creature, to the uninitiated eye all frankness and freedom, a more ingenious, a more extraordinary little gentleman. I had perpetually to guard against the wonder of contemplation into which my initiated view betrayed me; to check the irrelevant gaze and discouraged sigh in which I constantly both attacked and renounced the enigma of what such a little gentleman could have done that deserved a penalty. Say that, by the dark prodigy I knew, the imagination of all evil *had* been opened up to him: all the justice within me ached for the proof that it could ever have flowered into an act.

He had never, at any rate, been such a little gentleman as when, after our early dinner on this dreadful day, he came round to me and asked if I shouldn't like him, for half an hour, to play to me. David playing to Saul could never have shown a finer sense of the occasion. It was literally a charming exhibition of tact, of magnanimity, and quite tantamount to his saying outright: 'The true knights we love to read about never push an advantage too far. I know what you mean now: you mean that – to be let alone yourself and not followed up – you'll cease to worry and spy upon me, won't keep me so close to you, will let me go and come. Well, I "come", you see – but I don't go! There'll be plenty of time for that. I do really delight in your society, and I only want to show you that I contended for a principle.' It may be imagined whether I resisted this appeal or failed to accompany him again, hand in hand, to the schoolroom. He sat down at the old piano and played as he had never played; and if there are those who think he had better have been kicking a football I can only say that I wholly agree with them. For at the end of a time that under his influence I had quite ceased to measure I started up with a strange sense of having literally slept at my post. It was after luncheon, and by the schoolroom fire, and yet I hadn't really, in the least, slept: I had only done something much worse – I had forgotten. Where, all this time, was Flora? When I put the question to Miles he played on a minute before answering, and then could only say: 'Why, my dear, how do *I* know?' – breaking moreover into a happy laugh which, immediately after, as if it were a vocal accompaniment, he prolonged into incoherent, extravagant song.

I went straight to my room, but his sister was not there; then, before going downstairs, I looked into several others. As she was nowhere about she would surely be with Mrs Grose, whom, in the comfort of that theory, I accordingly proceeded in quest of. I found her where I had found her the evening before, but she met my quick challenge with blank, scared ignorance. She had only supposed that, after the repast, I had carried off both the children; as to which she was quite in her right, for it was the very first time I had allowed the little girl out of my sight without some special provision. Of course now indeed she might be with the maids, so that the immediate thing was to look for her without an air of alarm. This we promptly arranged between us; but when, ten minutes later and in pursuance of our arrangement, we met in the hall, it was only to report on either side that after guarded inquiries we had altogether failed to trace her. For a minute there, apart from observation, we exchanged mute alarms, and I could feel with what high interest my friend returned me all those I had from the first given her.

'She'll be above,' she presently said – 'in one of the rooms you haven't searched.'

'No; she's at a distance.' I had made up my mind. 'She has gone out.'

Mrs Grose stared. 'Without a hat?'

I naturally also looked volumes. 'Isn't that woman always without one?'

'She's with *her*?'

'She's with *her*!' I declared. 'We must find them.'

My hand was on my friend's arm, but she failed for the moment, confronted with such an account of the matter, to respond to my pressure. She communed, on the contrary, on the spot, with her uneasiness. 'And where's Master Miles?'

'Oh, *he's* with Quint. They're in the schoolroom.'

'Lord, Miss!' My view, I was myself aware – and therefore I suppose my tone – had never yet reached so calm an assurance.

'The trick's played,' I went on; 'they've successfully worked their plan. He found the most divine little way to keep me quiet while she went off.'

' "Divine"?' Mrs Grose bewilderedly echoed.

'Infernal, then!' I almost cheerfully rejoined. 'He has provided for himself as well. But come!'

She had helplessly gloomed at the upper regions. 'You leave him—?'

'So long with Quint? Yes – I don't mind that now.'

She always ended, at these moments, by getting possession of my hand, and in this manner she could at present still stay me. But after gasping an instant at my sudden resignation, 'Because of your letter?' she eagerly brought out.

I quickly, by way of answer, felt for my letter, drew it forth, held it up, and then, freeing myself, went and laid it on the great hall-table. 'Luke will take it,' I said as I came back. I reached the house-door and opened it; I was already on the steps.

My companion still demurred: the storm of the night and the early morning had dropped, but the afternoon was damp and grey. I came down to the drive while she stood in the doorway. 'You go with nothing on?'

'What do I care when the child has nothing? I can't wait to dress,' I cried, 'and if you must do so I leave you. Try meanwhile, yourself, upstairs.'

'With *them*?' Oh, on this, the poor woman promptly joined me!

Chapter Nineteen

We went straight to the lake, as it was called at Bly, and I dare say rightly called, though I reflect that it may in fact have been a sheet of water less remarkable than it appeared to my untravelled eyes. My acquaintance with sheets of water was small, and the pool of Bly, at all events on the few occasions of my consenting, under the protection of my pupils, to affront its surface in the old flat-bottomed boat moored there for our use, had impressed me both with its extent and its agitation. The usual place of embarkation was half a mile from the house, but I had an intimate conviction that, wherever Flora might be, she was not near home. She had not given me the slip for any small adventure, and, since the day of the very great one that I had shared with her by the pond, I had been aware, in our walks, of the quarter to which she most inclined. This was why I had now given to Mrs Grose's steps so marked a direction – a direction that made her, when she perceived it, oppose a resistance that showed me she was freshly mystified. 'You're going to the water, Miss? – you think she's *in*—?'

'She may be, though the depth is, I believe, nowhere very great. But what I judge most likely is that she's on the spot from which, the other day, we saw together when I told you.'

'When she pretended not to see—?'

'With that astounding self-possession! I've always been sure she wanted to go back alone. And now her brother has managed it for her.'

Mrs Grose still stood where she had stopped. 'You suppose they really *talk* of them?'

I could meet this with a confidence! 'They say things that, if we heard them, would simply appal us.'

'And if she *is* there—?'

'Yes?'

'Then Miss Jessel is?'

'Beyond a doubt. You shall see.'

'Oh, thank you!' my friend cried, planted so firm that, taking it in, I went straight on without her. By the time I reached the pool, however, she was close behind me, and I knew that, whatever, to her apprehension, might befall me, the exposure of my society struck her as her least danger. She exhaled a moan of relief as we at last came in sight of the greater part of the water without a sight of the child. There was no trace of Flora on that nearer side of the bank where my observation of her had been most startling, and none on the opposite edge, where, save for a margin of some twenty yards, a thick copse came down to the water. The pond, oblong in shape, had a width so scant compared to its length that, with its ends out of view, it might have been taken for a scant river. We looked at the empty expanse, and then I felt the suggestion of my friend's eyes. I knew what she meant and I replied with a negative headshake.

'No, no; wait! She has taken the boat.'

My companion stared at the vacant mooring-place and then again across the lake. 'Then where is it?'

'Our not seeing it is the strongest of proofs. She has used it to go over, and then has managed to hide it.'

'All alone – that child?'

'She's not alone, and at such times she's not a child: she's an old, old woman.' I scanned all the visible shore while Mrs Grose took again, into the queer element I offered her, one of her plunges of submission; then I pointed out that the boat might perfectly be in a small refuge formed by one of the recesses of the pool, an indentation masked, for the hither side, by a projection of the bank and by a clump of trees growing close to the water.

'But if the boat's there, where on earth's *she*?' my colleague anxiously asked.

'That's exactly what we must learn.' And I started to walk further.

'By going all the way round?'

'Certainly, far as it is. It will take us but ten minutes, but it's far enough to have made the child prefer not to walk. She went straight over.'

'Laws!' cried my friend again; the chain of my logic was ever too much for her. It dragged her at my heels even now, and when we had got half way round – a devious, tiresome process, on ground much broken and by a path choked with overgrowth – I paused to give her breath. I sustained her with a grateful arm, assuring her that she might hugely help me; and this started us afresh, so that in the course of but few minutes more we reached a point from which we found the boat to be where I had supposed it. It had been intentionally left as much as possible out of sight and was tied to one of the stakes of a fence that came, just there, down to the brink and that had been an assistance to disembarking. I recognized, as I looked at the pair of short, thick oars, quite safely drawn up, the prodigious character of the feat for a little girl; but I had lived, by this time, too long among wonders and had panted to too many livelier measures. There was a gate in the fence, through which we passed, and that brought us, after a trifling interval, more in the open. Then 'There she is!' we both exclaimed at once.

Flora, a short way off, stood before us on the grass and smiled as if her performance was now complete. The next thing she did, however, was to stoop straight down and pluck – quite as if it were all she was there for – a big, ugly spray of withered fern. I instantly became sure she had just come out of the copse. She waited for us, not herself taking a step, and I was conscious of the rare solemnity with which we presently approached her. She smiled and smiled, and we met; but it was all done in a silence by this time flagrantly ominous. Mrs Grose was the first to break the spell: she threw herself on her knees and, drawing the child to her breast, clasped in a long embrace the little tender, yielding body. While this dumb convulsion lasted I could only watch it – which I did the more intently when I saw Flora's face peep at me over our companion's shoulder. It was serious now – the flicker had left it; but it strengthened the pang with which I at that moment envied Mrs Grose the simplicity of *her* relation. Still, all this while, nothing more passed between us save that Flora had let her foolish fern again drop to the ground. What she and I had virtually said to each other was that pretexts were useless now. When Mrs Grose finally got up she kept the child's hand, so that the two were still before me; and the singular reticence of our communion was even more marked in the frank look she launched me. 'I'll be hanged,' it said, 'if *I'll* speak!'

It was Flora who, gazing all over me in candid wonder, was the first. She was struck with our bareheaded aspect. 'Why, where are your things?'

'Where yours are, my dear!' I promptly returned.

She had already got back her gaiety and appeared to take this as an answer quite sufficient. 'And where's Miles?' she went on.

There was something in the small valour of it that quite finished me: these three words from her were, in a flash like the glitter of a drawn blade, the jostle of the cup that my hand, for weeks and weeks, had held high and full to the brim and that now, even before speaking, I felt overflow in a deluge. I'll tell you if you'll tell *me*—' I heard myself say, then heard the tremor in which it broke.

'Well, what?'

Mrs Grose's suspense blazed at me, but it was too late now, and I brought the thing out handsomely. 'Where, my pet, is Miss Jessel?'

Chapter Twenty

Just as in the churchyard with Miles, the whole thing was upon us. Much as I had made of the fact that this name had never once, between us, been sounded, the quick, smitten glare with which the child's face now received it fairly likened my breach of the silence to the smash of a pane of glass. It added to the interposing cry, as if to stay the blow, that Mrs Grose, at the same instant, uttered over my violence – the shriek of a creature scared, or rather wounded, which, in turn, within a few seconds, was completed by a gasp of my own. I seized my colleague's arm. 'She's there, she's there!'

Miss Jessel stood before us on the opposite bank exactly as she had stood the other time, and I remember, strangely, as the first feeling now produced in me, my thrill of joy at having brought on a proof. She was there, and I was justified; she was there, and I was neither cruel nor mad. She was there for poor scared Mrs Grose, but she was there most for Flora; and no moment of my monstrous time was perhaps so extraordinary as that in which I consciously threw out to her, with the sense that – pale and ravenous demon as she was, she would catch and understand it – an inarticulate message of gratitude. She rose erect on the spot my friend and I had lately quitted, and there was not, in all the long reach of her desire, an inch of her evil that fell short. This first vividness of vision and emotion were things of a few seconds, during which Mrs Grose's dazed blink across to where I pointed struck me as a sovereign sign that she too at last saw, just as it carried my own eyes precipitately to the child. The revelation then of the manner in which Flora was affected startled me, in truth, far more than it would have done to find her also merely agitated, for direct dismay was of course not what I had expected. Prepared and on our guard as our pursuit had actually made her, she would repress every betrayal; and I was therefore shaken, on the spot, by my first glimpse of the particular one for which I had not allowed. To see her, without a convulsion of her small pink face, not even feign to glance in the direction of the prodigy I announced, but only, instead of that, turn at *me* an expression of hard, still gravity, an expression absolutely new and unprecedented and that appeared to read and accuse and judge me – this was a stroke that somehow converted the little girl herself into the very presence that could make me quail. I quailed even though my certitude that she thoroughly saw was never greater than at that instant, and in the immediate need to defend myself I called it passionately to witness. 'She's there, you little unhappy thing – there, there, *there*, and you see her as well as you see me!' I had said shortly before to Mrs Grose that she was not at these times a child, but an old, old woman, and that description of her could not have been more strikingly confirmed than in the way in which, for all answer to this, she simply showed me, without a concession, an admission, of her eyes, a countenance of deeper and deeper, of indeed suddenly quite fixed reprobation. I was by this time – if I can put the whole thing at all together – more appalled at what I may properly call her manner than at anything else, though it was simultaneously with this that I became aware of having Mrs Grose also, and very formidably, to reckon with. My elder companion, the next moment, at any rate, blotted out everything but her own flushed face and her loud, shocked protest, a burst of high disapproval. 'What a dreadful turn, to be sure, Miss! Where on earth do you see anything?'

I could only grasp her more quickly yet, for even while she spoke the hideous plain presence stood undimmed and undaunted. It had already lasted a minute, and it lasted while I continued, seizing my colleague, quite thrusting her at it and presenting her to it, to insist with my pointing hand. 'You don't see her exactly as *we* see? – you mean to say you don't now – *now*? She's as big as a blazing fire! Only look, dearest woman, *look*—!' She looked, even as I did, and gave me, with her deep groan of negation, repulsion, compassion – the mixture with her pity of her relief at her exemption – a sense, touching to me even then, that she would have backed me up if she could. I might well have needed that, for with this hard blow of the proof that her eyes were hopelessly sealed I felt my own situation horribly crumble, I felt – I saw – my livid predecessor press, from her position, on my defeat, and I was conscious, more than all, of what I should have from this instant to deal with in the astounding little attitude of Flora. Into this attitude Mrs Grose immediately and violently entered, breaking, even while there pierced through my sense of ruin a prodigious private triumph, into breathless reassurance.

'She isn't there, little lady, and nobody's there – and you never see nothing, my sweet! How can poor Miss Jessel – when poor Miss Jessel's dead and buried? *We* know, don't we, love?' – and she appealed, blundering in, to the child. 'It's all a mere mistake and a worry and a joke – and we'll go home as fast as we can!'

Our companion, on this, had responded with a strange, quick primness of propriety, and they were again, with Mrs Grose on her feet, united, as it were, in pained opposition to me. Flora continued to fix me with her small mask of reprobation, and even at that minute I prayed God to forgive me for seeming to see that, as she stood there holding tight to our friend's dress, her incomparable childish beauty had suddenly failed, had quite vanished. I've said it already – she was literally, she was hideously hard; she had turned common and almost ugly. 'I don't know what you mean. I see nobody. I see nothing. I never *have*. I think you're cruel. I don't like you!' Then, after this deliverance, which might have been that of a vulgarly pert little girl in the street, she hugged Mrs Grose more closely and buried in her skirts the dreadful little face. In this position she produced an almost furious wail. 'Take me away, take me away – oh, take me away from *her*!'

'From *me*?' I panted.

'From *you* – from you!' she cried.

Even Mrs Grose looked across at me dismayed; while I had nothing to do but communicate again with the figure that, on the opposite bank, without a movement, as rigidly still as if catching, beyond the interval, our voices, was as vividly there for my disaster as it was not there for my service. The wretched child had spoken exactly as if she had got from some outside source each of her stabbing little words, and I could therefore, in the full despair of all I had to accept, but sadly shake my head at her. 'If I had ever doubted, all my doubt would at present have gone. I've been living with the miserable truth, and now it has only too much closed round me. Of course I've lost you: I've interfered, and you've seen – under *her* dictation' – with which I faced, over the pool again, our infernal witness – 'the easy and perfect way to meet it. I've done my best, but I've lost you. Good-bye.' For Mrs Grose I had an imperative, an almost frantic 'Go, go!' before which, in infinite distress, but mutely possessed of the little girl and clearly convinced, in spite of her blindness, that something awful had occurred and some collapse engulfed us, she retreated, by the way we had come, as fast as she could move.

Of what first happened when I was left alone I had no subsequent memory. I only knew that at the end of, I suppose, a quarter of an hour, an odorous dampness and roughness, chilling and piercing my trouble, had made me understand that I must have thrown myself, on my face, on the ground and given way to a wildness of grief. I must have lain there long and cried and sobbed, for when I raised my head the day was almost done. I got up and looked a moment, through the twilight, at the grey pool and its blank, haunted edge, and then I took, back to the house, my dreary and difficult course. When I reached the gate in the fence the boat, to my surprise, was gone, so that I had a fresh reflection to make on Flora's extraordinary command of the situation. She passed that night, by the most tacit, and I should add, were not the word so grotesque a false note, the happiest of arrangements, with Mrs Grose. I saw neither of them on my return, but, on the other hand, as by an ambiguous compensation, I saw a great deal of Miles. I saw – I can use no other phrase – so much of him that it was as if it were more than it had ever been. No evening I had passed at Bly had the portentous quality of this one; in spite of which – and in spite also of the deeper depths of consternation that had opened beneath my feet – there was literally, in the ebbing actual, an extraordinarily sweet sadness. On reaching the house I had never so much as looked for the boy; I had simply gone straight to my room to change what I was wearing and to take in, at a glance, much material testimony to Flora's rupture. Her little belongings had all been removed. When later, by the schoolroom fire, I was served with tea by the usual maid, I indulged, on the article of my other pupil, in no inquiry whatever. He had his freedom now – he might have it to the end! Well, he did have it; and it consisted – in part at least – of his coming in at about eight o'clock and sitting down with me in silence. On the removal of the tea-things I had blown out the candles and drawn my chair closer: I was conscious of a mortal coldness and felt as if I should never again be warm. So, when he appeared, I was sitting in the glow with my thoughts. He paused a moment by the door as if to look at me; then – as if to share them – came to the other side of the hearth and sank into a chair. We sat there in absolute stillness; yet he wanted, I felt, to be with me.

Chapter Twenty-one

Before a new day, in my room, had fully broken, my eyes opened to Mrs Grose, who had come to my bedside with worse news. Flora was so markedly feverish that an illness was perhaps at hand; she had passed a night of extreme unrest, a night agitated above all by fears that had for their subject not in the least her former, but wholly her present governess. It was not against the possible re-entrance of Miss Jessel on the scene that she protested – it was conspicuously and passionately against mine. I was promptly on my feet of course, and with an immense deal to ask; the more that my friend had discernibly now girded her loins to meet me once more. This I felt as soon as I had put to her the question of her sense of the child's sincerity as against my own. 'She persists in denying to you that she saw, or has ever seen, anything?'

My visitor's trouble, truly, was great. 'Ah, Miss, it isn't a matter on which I can push her! Yet it isn't either, I must say, as if I much needed to. It has made her, every inch of her, quite old.'

'Oh, I see her perfectly from here. She resents, for all the world like some high little personage, the imputation on her truthfulness and, as it were, her respectability. "Miss Jessel indeed – *she*!" Ah, she's "respectable", the chit! The impression she gave me there yesterday was, I assure you, the very strangest of all; it was quite beyond any of the others. I *did* put my foot in it! She'll never speak to me again.'

Hideous and obscure as it all was, it held Mrs Grose briefly silent; then she granted my point with a frankness which, I made sure, had more behind it. 'I think indeed, Miss, she never will. She do have a grand manner about it!'

'And that manner' – I summed it up – 'is practically what's the matter with her now.'

Oh, that manner, I could see in my visitor's face, and not a little else besides! 'She asks me every three minutes if I think you're coming in.'

'I see – I see.' I too, on my side, had so much more than worked it out. 'Has she said to you since yesterday – except to repudiate her familiarity with anything so dreadful – a single other word about Miss Jessel?'

'Not one, Miss. And of course you know,' my friend added, 'I took it from her, by the lake that, just then and there at least, there *was* nobody.'

'Rather! And, naturally, you take it from her still.'

'I don't contradict her. What else can I do?'

'Nothing in the world! You've the cleverest little person to deal with. They've made them – their two friends, I mean – still cleverer even than nature did; for it was wondrous material to play on! Flora has now her grievance, and she'll work it to the end.'

'Yes, Miss; but to *what* end?'

'Why, that of dealing with me to her uncle. She'll make me out to him the lowest creature—!'

I winced at the fair show of the scene in Mrs Grose's face; she looked for a minute as if she sharply saw them together. 'And him who thinks so well of you!'

'He has an odd way – it comes over me now,' I laughed, '—of proving it! But that doesn't matter. What Flora wants, of course, is to get rid of me.'

My companion bravely concurred. 'Never again to so much as look at you.'

'So that what you've come to me now for,' I asked, 'is to speed me on my way?' Before she had time to reply, however, I had her in check. 'I've a better idea – the result of my reflections. My going *would* seem the right thing, and on Sunday I was terribly near it. Yet that won't do. It's *you* who must go. You must take Flora.'

My visitor, at this, did speculate. 'But where in the world—?'

'Away from here. Away from *them*. Away, even most of all, now, from me. Straight to her uncle.'

'Only to tell on you—?'

'No, not "only!" To leave me, in addition, with my remedy.'

She was still vague. 'And what *is* your remedy?'

'Your loyalty, to begin with. And then Miles's.'

She looked at me hard. 'Do you think he—?'

'Won't, if he has the chance, turn on me? Yes, I venture still to think it. At all events, I want to try. Get off with his sister as soon as possible and leave me with him alone.' I was amazed, myself, at the spirit I had still in reserve, and therefore perhaps a trifle the more disconcerted at the way in which, in spite of this fine example of it, she hesitated. 'There's one thing, of course,' I went on: 'they mustn't, before she goes, see each other for three seconds.' Then it came over me that, in spite of Flora's presumable sequestration from the instant of her return from the pool, it might already be too late. 'Do you mean,' I anxiously asked, 'that they *have* met?'

At this she quite flushed. 'Ah, Miss, I'm not such a fool as that! If I've been obliged to leave her three or four times, it has been each time with one of the maids, and at present, though she's alone, she's locked in safe. And yet – and yet!' There were too many things.

'And yet what?'

'Well, are you so sure of the little gentleman?'

'I'm not sure of anything but *you*. But I have, since last evening, a new hope. I think he wants to give me an opening. I do believe that – poor little exquisite wretch! – he wants to speak. Last evening, in the firelight and the silence, he sat with me for two hours as if it were just coming.'

Mrs Grose looked hard, through the window, at the grey, gathering day. 'And did it come?'

'No, though I waited and waited, I confess it didn't, and it was without a breach of the silence or so much as a faint allusion to his sister's condition and absence that we at last kissed for good night. All the same,' I continued, 'I can't, if her uncle sees her, consent to his seeing her brother without my having given the boy – and most of all because things have got so bad – a little more time.'

My friend appeared on this ground more reluctant than I could quite understand. 'What do you mean by more time?'

'Well, a day or two – really to bring it out. He'll then be on *my* side – of which you see the importance. If nothing comes, I shall only fail, and you will, at the worst, have helped me by doing, on your arrival in town, whatever you may have found possible.' So I put it before her, but she continued for a little so inscrutably embarrassed that I came again to her aid. 'Unless indeed,' I wound up, 'you really want *not* to go.'

I could see it, in her face, at last clear itself; she put out her hand to me as a pledge. 'I'll go – I'll go. I'll go this morning.'

I wanted to be very just. 'If you *should* wish still to wait, I would engage she shouldn't see me.'

'No, no: it's the place itself. She must leave it.' She held me a moment with heavy eyes, then brought out the rest. 'Your idea's the right one. I myself, Miss—'

'Well?'

'I can't stay.'

The look she gave me with it made me jump at possibilities. 'You mean that, since yesterday, you *have* seen—?'

She shook her head with dignity. 'I've *heard*—!'

'Heard?'

'From that child – horrors! There!' she sighed with tragic relief. 'On my honour, Miss, she says things—!' But at this evocation she broke down; she dropped, with a sudden sob, upon my sofa and, as I had seen her do before, gave way to all the grief of it.

It was quite in another manner that I, for my part, let myself go. 'Oh, thank God!'

She sprang up again at this, drying her eyes with a groan. ' "Thank God?" '

'It so justifies me!'

'It does that, Miss!'

I couldn't have desired more emphasis, but I just hesitated. 'She's so horrible?'

I saw my colleague scarce knew how to put it. 'Really shocking.'

'And about me?'

'About you, Miss – since you must have it. It's beyond everything, for a young lady; and I can't think wherever she must have picked up—'

'The appalling language she applied to me? I can, then!' I broke in with a laugh that was doubtless significant enough.

It only, in truth, left my friend still more grave. 'Well, perhaps I ought to also – since I've heard some of it before! Yet I can't bear it,' the poor woman went on while, with the same movement, she glanced, on my dressing-table, at the face of my watch. 'But I must go back.'

I kept her, however. 'Ah, if you can't bear it—!'

'How can I stop with her, you mean? Why, just *for* that: to get her away. Far from this,' she pursued, 'far from *them*—'

'She may be different? she may be free?' I seized her almost with joy. 'Then, in spite of yesterday, you *believe*—'

'In such doings?' Her simple description of them required, in the light of her expression, to be carried no further, and she gave me the whole thing as she had never done. 'I believe.'

Yes, it was a joy, and we were still shoulder to shoulder: if I might continue sure of that I should care but little what else happened. My support in the presence of disaster would be the same as it had been in my early need of confidence, and if my friend would answer for my honesty I would answer for all the rest. On the point of taking leave of her, none the less, I was to some extent embarrassed. 'There's one thing of course – it occurs to me – to remember. My letter, giving the alarm, will have reached town before you.'

I now perceived still more how she had been beating about the bush and how weary at last it had made her. 'Your letter won't have got there. Your letter never went.'

'What then became of it?'

'Goodness knows! Master Miles—'

'Do you mean *he* took it?' I gasped.

She hung fire, but she overcame her reluctance. 'I mean that I saw yesterday, when I came back with Miss Flora, that it wasn't where you had put it. Later in the evening I had the chance to question Luke, and he declared that he had neither noticed nor touched it.' We could only exchange, on this, one of our deeper mutual soundings, and it was Mrs Grose who first brought up the plumb with an almost elate 'You see!'

'Yes, I see that if Miles took it instead he probably will have read it and destroyed it.'

'And don't you see anything else?'

I faced her a moment with a sad smile. 'It strikes me that by this time your eyes are open even wider than mine.'

They proved to be so indeed, but she could still blush, almost, to show it. 'I make out now what he must have done at school.' And she gave, in her simple sharpness, an almost droll disillusioned nod. 'He stole!'

I turned it over – I tried to be more judicial. 'Well – perhaps.'

She looked as if she found me unexpectedly calm. 'He stole *letters*!'

She couldn't know my reasons for a calmness after all pretty shallow; so I showed them off as I might. 'I hope then it was to more purpose than in this case! The note, at any rate, that I put on the table yesterday,' I pursued, 'will have given him so scant an advantage – for it contained only the bare demand for an interview – that he is already much ashamed of having gone so far for so little, and that what he had on his mind last evening was precisely the need of confession.' I seemed to myself, for the instant, to have mastered it, to see it all. 'Leave us, leave us' – I was already, at the door, hurrying her off. 'I'll get it out of him. He'll meet me – he'll confess. If he confesses, he's saved. And if he's saved—'

'Then *you* are?' The dear woman kissed me on this, and I took her farewell. 'I'll save you without him!' she cried as she went.

Chapter Twenty-two

Yet it was when she had got off – and I missed her on the spot – that the great pinch really came. If I had counted on what it would give me to find myself alone with Miles I speedily perceived, at least, that it would give me a measure. No hour of my stay in fact was so assailed with apprehensions as that of my coming down to learn that the carriage containing Mrs Grose and my younger pupil had already rolled out of the gates. Now I *was*, I said to myself, face to face with the elements, and for much of the rest of the day, while I fought my weakness, I could consider that I had been supremely rash. It was a tighter place still than I had yet turned round in; all the more that, for the first time, I could see in the aspect of others a confused reflection of the crisis. What had happened naturally caused them all to stare; there was too little of the explained, throw out whatever we might, in the suddenness of my colleague's act. The maids and the men looked blank; the effect of which on my nerves was an aggravation until I saw the necessity of making it a positive aid. It was precisely, in short, by just clutching the helm that I avoided total wreck; and I daresay that, to bear up at all, I became, that morning, very grand and very dry. I welcomed the consciousness that I was charged with much to do, and I caused it to be known as well that, left thus to myself, I was quite remarkably firm. I wandered with that manner, for the next hour or two, all over the place and looked, I have no doubt, as if I were ready for any onset. So, for the benefit of whom it might concern, I paraded with a sick heart.

The person it appeared least to concern proved to be, till dinner, little Miles himself. My perambulations had given me, meanwhile, no glimpse of him, but they had tended to make more public the change taking place in our relation as a consequence of his having at the piano, the day before, kept me, in Flora's interest, so beguiled and befooled. The stamp of publicity had of course been fully given by her confinement and departure, and the change itself was now ushered in by our non-observance of the regular custom of the schoolroom. He had already disappeared when, on my way down, I pushed open his door, and I learned below that he had breakfasted – in the presence of a couple of the maids – with Mrs Grose and his sister. He had then gone out, as he said, for a stroll; than which nothing, I reflected, could better have expressed his frank view of the abrupt transformation of my office. What he would now permit this office to consist of was yet to be settled: there was a queer relief, at all events – I mean for myself in especial – in the renouncement of one pretension. If so much had sprung to the surface I scarce put it too strongly in saying that what had perhaps sprung highest was the absurdity of our prolonging the fiction that I had anything more to teach him. It sufficiently stuck out that, by tacit little tricks in which even more than myself he carried out the care of my dignity, I had had to appeal to him to let me off straining to meet him on the ground of his true capacity. He had at any rate his freedom now; I was never to touch it again; as I had amply shown, moreover, when, on his joining me in the schoolroom the previous night, I had uttered, on the subject of the interval just concluded, neither challenge nor hint. I had too much, from this moment, my other ideas. Yet when he at last arrived the difficulty of applying them, the accumulations of my problem, were brought straight home to me by the beautiful little presence on which what had occurred had as yet, for the eye, dropped neither stain nor shadow.

To mark, for the house, the high state I cultivated I decreed that my meals with the boy should be served, as we called it, downstairs; so that I had been awaiting him in the ponderous pomp of the room outside of the window of which I had had from Mrs Grose, that first scared Sunday, my flash of something it would scarce have done to call light. Here at present I felt afresh – for I had felt it again and again – how my equilibrium depended on the success of my rigid will, the will to shut my eyes as tight as possible to thc truth that what I had to deal with was, revoltingly, against nature. I could only get on at all by taking 'nature' into my confidence and my account, by treating my monstrous ordeal as a push in a direction unusual, of course, and unpleasant, but demanding, after all, for a fair front, only another turn of the screw of ordinary human virtue. No attempt, none the less, could well require more tact than just this attempt to supply, one's self, *all* the nature. How could I put even a little of that article into a suppression of reference to what had occurred? How, on the other hand, could I make a reference without a new plunge into the hideous obscure? Well, a sort of answer, after a time, had come to me, and it was so far confirmed as that I was met, incontestably, by the quickened vision of what was rare in my little companion. It was indeed as if he had found even now – as he had so often found at lessons – still some other delicate way to ease me off. Wasn't there light in the fact which, as we shared our solitude, broke out with a specious glitter it had never yet quite worn? – the fact that (opportunity aiding, precious opportunity which had now come), it would be preposterous, with a child so endowed, to forego the help one might wrest from absolute intelligence? What had his intelligence been given him for but to save him? Mightn't one, to reach his mind, risk the stretch of an angular arm over his character? It was as if, when we were face to face in the dining-room, he had literally shown me the way. The roast mutton was on the table, and I had dispensed with attendance. Miles, before he sat down, stood a moment with his hands in his pockets and looked at the joint, on which he seemed on the point of passing some humorous judgement. But what he presently produced was: 'I say, my dear, is she really very awfully ill?'

'Little Flora? Not so bad but that she'll presently be better. London will set her up. Bly had ceased to agree with her. Come here and take your mutton.'

He alertly obeyed me, carried the plate carefully to his seat and, when he was established, went on. 'Did Bly disagree with her so terribly suddenly?'

'Not so suddenly as you might think. One had seen it coming on.'

'Then why didn't you get her off before?'

'Before what?'

'Before she became too ill to travel.'

I found myself prompt. 'She's *not* too ill to travel: she only might have become so if she had stayed. This was just the moment to seize. The journey will dissipate the influence' – oh, I was grand! – 'and carry it off.'

'I see, I see' – Miles, for that matter, was grand too. He settled to his repast with the charming little 'table manner' that, from the day of his arrival, had relieved me of all grossness of admonition. Whatever he had been driven from school for, it was not for ugly feeding. He was irreproachable, as always, today; but he was unmistakably more conscious. He was discernibly trying to take for granted more things than he found, without assistance, quite easy; and he dropped into peaceful silence while he felt his situation. Our meal was of the briefest – mine a vain pretence, and I had the things immediately removed. While this was done Miles stood again with his hands in his little pockets and his back to me – stood and looked out of the wide window through which, that other day, I had seen what pulled me up. We continued silent while the maid was with us – as silent, it whimsically occurred to me, as some young couple who, on their wedding-journey, at the inn, feel shy in the presence of the waiter. He turned round only when the waiter had left us. 'Well – so we're alone!'

Chapter Twenty-three

'Oh, more or less.' I fancy my smile was pale. 'Not absolutely. We shouldn't like that!' I went on.

'No – I suppose we shouldn't. Of course we have the others.'

'We have the others – we have indeed the others,' I concurred.

'Yet even though we have them,' he returned, still with his hands in his pockets and planted there in front of me, 'they don't much count, do they?'

I made the best of it, but I felt wan. 'It depends on what you call "much"!'

'Yes' – with all accommodation – 'everything depends!' On this, however, he faced to the window again and presently reached it with his vague, restless, cogitating step. He remained there a while, with his forehead against the glass, in contemplation of the stupid shrubs I knew and the dull things of November. I had always my hypocrisy of 'work', behind which, now, I gained the sofa. Steadying myself with it there as I had repeatedly done at those moments of torment that I have described as the moments of my knowing the children to be given to something from which I was barred, I sufficiently obeyed my habit of being prepared for the worst. But an extraordinary impression dropped on me as I extracted a meaning from the boy's embarrassed back – none other than the impression that I was not barred now. This inference grew in a few minutes to sharp intensity and seemed bound up with the direct perception that it was positively *he* who was. The frames and squares of the great window were a kind of image, for him, of a kind of failure. I felt that I saw him, at any rate, shut in or shut out. He was admirable, but not comfortable: I took it in with a throb of hope. Wasn't he looking, through the haunted pane, for something he couldn't see? – and wasn't it the first time in the whole business that he had known such a lapse? The first, the very first: I found it a splendid portent. It made him anxious, though he watched himself; he had been anxious all day and, even while in his usual sweet little manner he sat at table, had needed all his small strange genius to give it a gloss. When he at last turned round to meet me it was almost as if this genius had succumbed. 'Well, I think I'm glad Bly agrees with *me*!'

'You would certainly seem to have seen, these twenty-four hours, a good deal more of it than for some time before. I hope,' I went on bravely, 'that you've been enjoying yourself.'

'Oh yes, I've been ever so far; all round about – miles and miles away. I've never been so free.'

He had really a manner of his own, and I could only try to keep up with him. 'Well, do you like it?'

He stood there smiling; then at last he put into two words – 'Do *you*?' – more discrimination than I had ever heard two words contain. Before I had time to deal with that, however, he continued as if with the sense that this was an impertinence to be softened. 'Nothing could be more charming than the way you take it, for of course if we're alone together now it's you that are alone most. But I hope,' he threw in, 'you don't particularly mind!'

'Having to do with you?' I asked. 'My dear child, how can I help minding? Though I've renounced all claim to your company – you're so beyond me – I at least greatly enjoy it. What else should I stay on for?'

He looked at me more directly, and the expression of his face, graver now, struck me as the most beautiful I had ever found in it. 'You stay on just for *that*?'

'Certainly. I stay on as your friend and from the tremendous interest I take in you till something can be done for you that may be more worth your while. That needn't surprise you.' My voice trembled so that I felt it impossible to suppress the shake. 'Don't you remember how I told you, when I came and sat on your bed the night of the storm, that there was nothing in the world I wouldn't do for you?'

'Yes, yes!' He, on his side, more and more visibly nervous, had a tone to master; but he was so much more successful than I that, laughing out through his gravity, he could pretend we were pleasantly jesting. 'Only that, I think, was to get me to do something for *you*!'

'It was partly to get you to do something,' I conceded. 'But, you know, you didn't do it.'

'Oh yes,' he said with the brightest superficial eagerness, 'you wanted me to tell you something.'

'That's it. Out, straight out. What you have on your mind, you know.'

'Ah then, is *that* what you've stayed over for?'

He spoke with a gaiety through which I could still catch the finest little quiver of resentful passion; but I can't begin to express the effect upon me of an implication of surrender even so faint. It was as if what I had yearned for had come at last only to astonish me. 'Well, yes – I may as well make a clean breast of it. It was precisely for that.'

He waited so long that I supposed it for the purpose of repudiating the assumption on which my action had been founded; but what he finally said was: 'Do you mean now – here?'

'There couldn't be a better place or time.' He looked round him uneasily, and I had the rare – oh, the queer! – impression of the very first symptom I had seen in him of the approach of immediate fear. It was as if he were suddenly afraid of me – which struck me indeed as perhaps the best thing to make him. Yet in the very pang of the effort I felt it vain to try sternness, and I heard myself the next instant so gentle as to be almost grotesque. 'You want so to go out again?'

'Awfully!' He smiled at me heroically, and the touching little bravery of it was enhanced by his actually flushing with pain. He had picked up his hat, which he had brought in, and stood twirling it in a way that gave me, even as I was just nearly reaching port, a perverse horror of what I was doing. To do it in *any* way was an act of violence, for what did it consist of but the obtrusion of the idea of grossness and guilt on a small helpless creature who had been for me a revelation of the possibilities of beautiful intercourse? Wasn't it base to create for a being so exquisite a mere alien awkwardness? I suppose I now read into our situation a clearness it couldn't have had at the time, for I seem to see our poor eyes already lighted with some spark of a prevision of the anguish that was to come. So we circled about, with terrors and scruples, like fighters not daring to close. But it was for each other we feared! That kept us a little longer suspended and unbruised. 'I'll tell you everything,' Miles said – 'I mean I'll tell you anything you like. You'll stay on with me, and we shall both be all right and I *will* tell you – I *will*. But not now.'

'Why not now?'

My insistence turned him from me and kept him once more at his window in a silence during which, between us, you might have heard a pin drop. Then he was before me again with the air of a person for whom, outside, someone who had frankly to be reckoned with was waiting. 'I have to see Luke.'

I had not yet reduced him to quite so vulgar a lie, and I felt proportionately ashamed. But, horrible as it was, his lies made up my truth. I achieved thoughtfully a few loops of my knitting. 'Well then, go to Luke, and I'll wait for what you promise. Only, in return for that, satisfy, before you leave me, one very much smaller request.'

He looked as if he felt he had succeeded enough to be able still a little to bargain. 'Very much smaller—?'

'Yes, a mere fraction of the whole. Tell me' – oh, my work preoccupied me, and I was off-hand! – 'if, yesterday afternoon, from the table in the hall, you took, you know, my letter.'

Chapter Twenty-four

My sense of how he received this suffered for a minute from something that I can describe only as a fierce split of my attention – a stroke that at first, as I sprang straight up, reduced me to the mere blind movement of getting hold of him, drawing him close and, while I just fell for support against the nearest piece of furniture, instinctively keeping him with his back to the window. The appearance was full upon us that I had already had to deal with here: Peter Quint had come into view like a sentinel before a prison. The next thing I saw was that, from outside, he had reached the window, and then I knew that, close to the glass and glaring in through it, he offered once more to the room his white face of damnation. It represents but grossly what took place within me at the sight to say that on the second my decision was made; yet I believe that no woman so overwhelmed ever in so short a time recovered her grasp of the *act*. It came to me in the very horror of the immediate presence that the act would be, seeing and facing what I saw and faced, to keep the boy himself unaware. The inspiration – I can call it by no other name – was that I felt how voluntarily, how transcendently, I *might*. It was like fighting with a demon for a human soul, and when I had fairly so appraised it I saw how the human soul – held out, in the tremor of my hands, at arms' length – had a perfect dew of sweat on a lovely childish forehead. The face that was close to mine was as white as the face against the glass, and out of it presently came a sound, not low nor weak, but as if from much farther away, that I drank like a waft of fragrance.

'Yes – I took it.'

At this, with a moan of joy, I enfolded, I drew him close; and while I held him to my breast, where I could feel in the sudden fever of his little body the tremendous pulse of his little heart, I kept my eyes on the thing at the window and saw it move and shift its posture. I have likened it to a sentinel, but its slow wheel, for a moment, was rather the prowl of a baffled beast. My present quickened courage, however, was such that, not too much to let it through, I had to shade, as it were, my flame. Meanwhile the glare of the face was again at the window, the scoundrel fixed as if to watch and wait. It was the very confidence that I might now defy him, as well as the positive certitude, by this time, of the child's unconsciousness, that made me go on. 'What did you take it for?'

'To see what you said about me.'

'You opened the letter?'

'I opened it.'

My eyes were now, as I held him off a little again, on Miles's own face, in which the collapse of mockery showed me how complete was the ravage of uneasiness. What was prodigious was that at last, by my success, his sense was sealed and his communication stopped: he knew that he was in presence, but knew not of what, and knew still less that I also was and that I did know. And what did this strain of trouble matter when my eyes went back to the window only to see that the air was clear again and – by my personal triumph – the influence quenched? There was nothing there. I felt that the cause was mine and that I should surely get *all*. 'And you found nothing!' – I let my elation out.

He gave the most mournful, thoughtful little headshake. 'Nothing.'

'Nothing, nothing!' I almost shouted in my joy.

'Nothing, nothing,' he sadly repeated.

I kissed his forehead; it was drenched. 'So what have you done with it?'

'I've burnt it.'

'Burnt it?' It was now or never. 'Is that what you did at school?'

Oh, what this brought up! 'At school?'

'Did you take letters? – or other things?'

'Other things?' He appeared now to be thinking of something far off and that reached him only through the pressure of his anxiety. Yet it did reach him. 'Did I *steal*?'

I felt myself redden to the roots of my hair as well as wonder if it were more strange to put to a gentleman such a question or to see him take it with allowances that gave the very distance of his fall in the world. 'Was it for that you mightn't go back?'

The only thing he felt was rather a dreary little surprise. 'Did you know I mightn't go back?'

'I know everything.'

He gave me at this the longest and strangest look. 'Everything?'

'Everything. Therefore *did* you –?' But I couldn't say it again.

Miles could, very simply. 'No. I didn't steal.'

My face must have shown him I believed him utterly; yet my hands – but it was for pure tenderness – shook him as if to ask him why, if it was all for nothing, he had condemned me to months of torment. 'What then did you do?'

He looked in vague pain all round the top of the room and drew his breath, two or three times over, as if with difficulty. He might have been standing at the bottom of the sea and raising his eyes to some faint green twilight. 'Well – I said things.'

'Only that?'

'They thought it was enough!'

'To turn you out for?'

Never, truly, had a person 'turned out' shown so little to explain it as this little person! He appeared to weigh my question, but in a manner quite detached and almost helpless. 'Well, I suppose I oughtn't.'

'But to whom did you say them?'

He evidently tried to remember, but it dropped – he had lost it. 'I don't know!'

He almost smiled at me in the desolation of his surrender, which was indeed practically, by this time, so complete that I ought to have left if there. But I was infatuated – I was blind with victory, though even then the very effect that was to have brought him so much nearer was already that of added separation. 'Was it to everyone?' I asked.

'No; it was only to—' But he gave a sick little headshake. 'I don't remember their names.'

'Were they then so many?'

'No – only a few. Those I liked.'

Those he liked? I seemed to float not into clearness, but into a darker obscure, and within a minute there had come to me out of my very pity the appalling alarm of his being perhaps innocent. It was for the instant confounding and bottomless, for if he *were* innocent, what then on earth was *I*? Paralysed, while it lasted, by the mere brush of the question, I let him go a little, so that, with a deep-drawn sigh, he turned away from me again; which, as he faced towards the clear window, I suffered, feeling that I had nothing now there to keep him from. 'And did they repeat what you said?' I went on after a moment.

He was soon at some distance from me, still breathing hard and again with the air, though now without anger for it, of being confined against his will. Once more, as he had done before, he looked up at the dim day as if, of what had hitherto sustained him, nothing was left but an unspeakable anxiety. 'Oh yes,' he nevertheless replied – 'they must have repeated them. To those *they* liked,' he added.

There was, somehow, less of it than I had expected; but I turned it over. 'And these things came round –?'

'To the masters? Oh yes!' he answered very simply. 'But I didn't know they'd tell.'

'The masters? They didn't – they've never told. That's why I ask you.'

He turned to me again his little beautiful fevered face. 'Yes, it was too bad.'

'Too bad?'

'What I suppose I sometimes said. To write home.'

I can't name the exquisite pathos of the contradiction given to such a speech by such a speaker; I only know that the next instant I heard myself throw off with homely force: 'Stuff and nonsense!' But the next after that I must have sounded stern enough. 'What *were* these things?'

My sternness was all for his judge, his executioner; yet it made him avert himself again, and that movement made *me*, with a single bound and an irrepressible cry, spring straight upon him. For there again, against the glass, as if to blight his confession and stay his answer, was the hideous author of our woe – the white face of damnation. I felt a sick swim at the drop of my victory and all the return of my battle, so that the wildness of my veritable leap only served as a great betrayal. I saw him, from the midst of my act, meet it with a divination, and on the perception that even now he only guessed, and that the window was still to his own eyes free, I let the impulse flame up to convert the climax of his dismay into the very proof of his liberation. 'No more, no more, no more!' I shrieked, as I tried to press him against me, to my visitant.

'Is she *here*?' Miles panted as he caught with his sealed eyes the direction of my words. Then as his strange 'she' staggered me and, with a gasp, I echoed it, 'Miss Jessel, Miss Jessel!' he with a sudden fury gave me back.

I seized, stupefied, his supposition – some sequel to what we had done to Flora, but this made me only want to show him that it was better still than that. 'It's not Miss Jessel! But it's at the window – straight before us. It's *there* – the coward horror, there for the last time!'

At this, after a second in which his head made the movement of a baffled dog's on a scent and then gave a frantic little shake for air and light, he was at me in a white rage, bewildered, glaring vainly over the place and missing wholly, though it now, to my sense, filled the room like the taste of poison, the wide, overwhelming presence. 'It's *he*?'

I was so determined to have all my proof that I flashed into ice to challenge him. 'Whom do you mean by "he"?'

'Peter Quint – you devil!' His face gave again, round the room, its convulsed supplication. '*Where?*'

They are in my ears still, his supreme surrender of the name and his tribute to my devotion. 'What does he matter now, my own? – what will he *ever* matter? *I* have you,' I launched at the beast, 'but he has lost you for ever!' Then, for the demonstration of my work, 'There, *there*!' I said to Miles.

But he had already jerked straight round, stared, glared again, and seen but the quiet day. With the stroke of the loss I was so proud of he uttered the cry of a creature hurled over an abyss, and the grasp with which I recovered him might have been that of catching him in his fall. I caught him, yes, I held him – it may be imagined with what a passion; but at the end of a minute I began to feel what it truly was that I held. We were alone with the quiet day, and his little heart, dispossessed, had stopped.

The Portrait of a Lady

Chapter One

Under certain circumstances there are few hours in life more agreeable than the hour dedicated to the ceremony known as afternoon tea. There are circumstances in which, whether you partake of the tea or not – some people of course never do – the situation is in itself delightful. Those that I have in mind in beginning to unfold this simple history offered an admirable setting to an innocent pastime. The implements of the little feast had been disposed upon the lawn of an old English country house in what I should call the perfect middle of a splendid summer afternoon. Part of the afternoon had waned, but much of it was left, and what was left was of the finest and rarest quality. Real dusk would not arrive for many hours; but the flood of summer light had begun to ebb, the air had grown mellow, the shadows were long upon the smooth, dense turf. They lengthened slowly, however, and the scene expressed that sense of leisure still to come which is perhaps the chief source of one's enjoyment of such a scene at such an hour. From five o'clock to eight is on certain occasions a little eternity; but on such an occasion as this the interval could be only an eternity of pleasure. The persons concerned in it were taking their pleasure quietly, and they were not of the sex which is supposed to furnish the regular votaries of the ceremony I have mentioned. The shadows on the perfect lawn were straight and angular; they were the shadows of an old man sitting in a deep wicker-chair near the low table on which the tea had been served, and of two younger men strolling to and fro, in desultory talk, in front of him. The old man had his cup in his hand; it was an unusually large cup, of a different pattern from the rest of the set and painted in brilliant colours. He disposed of its contents with much circumspection, holding it for a long time close to his chin, with his face turned to the house. His companions had either finished their tea or were indifferent to their privilege; they smoked cigarettes as they continued to stroll. One of them, from time to time, as he passed, looked with a certain attention at the elder man, who, unconscious of observation, rested his eyes upon the rich red front of his dwelling. The house that rose beyond the lawn was a structure to repay such consideration and was the most characteristic object in the peculiarly English picture I have attempted to sketch.

It stood upon a low hill, above the river – the river being the Thames at some forty miles from London. A long gabled front of red brick, with the complexion of which time and the weather had played all sorts of pictorial tricks, only, however, to improve and refine it, presented to the lawn its patches of ivy, its clustered chimneys, its windows smothered in creepers. The house had a name and a history; the old gentleman taking his tea would have been delighted to tell you these things: how it had been built under

Edward the Sixth, had offered a night's hospitality to the great Elizabeth (whose august person had extended itself upon a huge, magnificent, and terribly angular bed which still formed the principle honour of the sleeping apartments), had been a good deal bruised and defaced in Cromwell's wars, and then, under the Restoration, repaired and much enlarged; and how, finally, after having been remodelled and disfigured in the eighteenth century, it had passed into the careful keeping of a shrewd American banker, who had bought it originally because (owing to circumstances too complicated to set forth) it was offered at a great bargain: bought it with much grumbling at its ugliness, its antiquity, its incommodity, and who now, at the end of twenty years, had become conscious of a real aesthetic passion for it, so that he knew all its points and would tell you just where to stand to see them in combination and just the hour when the shadows of its various protuberances – which fell so softly upon the warm, weary brickwork – were of the right measure. Besides this, as I have said, he could have counted off most of the successive owners and occupants, several of whom were known to general fame; doing so, however, with an undemonstrative conviction that the latest phase of its destiny was not the least honourable. The front of the house overlooking that portion of lawn with which we are concerned was not the entrance-front; this was in quite another quarter. Privacy here reigned supreme, and the wide carpet of turf that covered the level hill-top seemed but the extension of a luxurious interior. The great still oaks and beeches flung down a shade as dense as that of velvet curtains; and the place was furnished, like a room, with cushioned seats, with rich-coloured rugs, with the books and papers that lay upon the grass. The river was at some distance; where the ground began to slope the lawn, properly speaking, ceased. But it was none the less a charming walk down to the water.

The old gentleman at the tea-table, who had come from America thirty years before, had brought with him, at the top of his baggage, his American physiognomy; and he had not only brought it with him, but he had kept it in the best order, so that, if necessary, he might have taken it back to his own country with perfect confidence. At present, obviously, nevertheless, he was not likely to displace himself; his journeys were over and he was taking the rest that precedes the great rest. He had a narrow, clean-shaven face, with features evenly distributed and an expression of placid acuteness. It was evidently a face in which the range of representation was not large, so that the air of contented shrewdness was all the more of a merit. It seemed to tell that he had been successful in life, yet it seemed to tell also that his success had not been exclusive and invidious, but had had much of the inoffensiveness of failure. He had certainly had a great experience of men, but there was an almost rustic simplicity in the faint smile that played upon his lean, spacious cheek and lighted up his humorous eye as he at last slowly and carefully deposited his big tea-cup upon the table. He was neatly dressed, in well-brushed black; but a shawl was folded upon his knees, and his feet were encased in thick, embroidered slippers. A beautiful collie dog lay upon the grass near his chair, watching the master's face almost as tenderly as the master took in the still more magisterial physiognomy of the house; and a little bristling, bustling terrier bestowed a desultory attendance upon the other gentlemen.

One of these was a remarkably well-made man of five-and-thirty, with a face as English as that of the old gentleman I have just sketched was something else; a noticeably handsome face, fresh-coloured, fair and frank, with firm, straight features, a lively grey eye and the rich adornment of a chestnut beard. This person had a certain fortunate, brilliant, exceptional look – the air of a happy temperament fertilized by a high civilization – which would have made almost any observer envy him at a venture. He was booted and spurred, as if he had dismounted from a long ride; he wore a white hat, which looked too large for him; he held his two hands behind him, and in one of them – a large, white, well-shaped fist – was crumpled a pair of soiled dog-skin gloves.

His companion, measuring the length of the lawn beside him, was a person of quite a different pattern, who, although he might have excited grave curiosity, would not, like the other, have provoked you to wish yourself, almost blindly, in his place. Tall, lean, loosely and feebly put together, he had an ugly, sickly, witty, charming face, furnished, but by no means decorated, with a straggling moustache and whisker. He looked clever and ill – a combination by no means felicitous; and he wore a brown velvet jacket. He carried his hands in his pockets, and there was something in the way he did it that showed the habit was inveterate. His gait had a shambling, wandering quality; he was not very firm on his legs. As I have said, whenever he passed the old man in the chair he rested his eyes upon him; and at this moment, with their faces brought into relation, you would easily have seen they were father and son. The father caught his son's eye at last and gave him a mild, responsive smile.

'I'm getting on very well,' he said.

'Have you drunk your tea?' asked the son.

'Yes, and enjoyed it.'

'Shall I give you some more?'

The old man considered, placidly. 'Well, I guess I'll wait and see.' He had, in speaking, the American tone.

'Are you cold?' the son inquired.

The father slowly rubbed his legs. 'Well, I don't know. I can't tell till I feel.'

'Perhaps someone might feel for you,' said the younger man, laughing.

'Oh, I hope someone will always feel for me! Don't you feel for me, Lord Warburton?'

'Oh yes, immensely,' said the gentleman addressed as Lord Warburton, promptly. 'I'm bound to say you look wonderfully comfortable.'

'Well, I suppose I am, in most respects.' And the old man looked down at his green shawl and smoothed it over his knees. 'The fact is I've been comfortable so many years that I suppose I've got so used to it I don't know it.'

'Yes, that's the bore of comfort,' said Lord Warburton. 'We only know when we're uncomfortable.'

'It strikes me we're rather particular', his companion remarked.

'Oh yes, there's no doubt we're particular,' Lord Warburton murmured. And then the three men remained silent a while; the two younger ones standing looking down at the other, who presently asked for more tea. 'I should think you would be very unhappy with that shawl,' Lord Warburton resumed while his companion filled the old man's cup again.

'Oh no, he must have the shawl!' cried the gentleman in the velvet coat. 'Don't put such ideas as that into his head.'

'It belongs to my wife,' said the old man simply.

'Oh, if it's for sentimental reasons—' And Lord Warburton made a gesture of apology.

'I suppose I must give it to her when she comes,' the old man went on.

'You'll please to do nothing of the kind. You'll keep it to cover your poor old legs.'

'Well, you mustn't abuse my legs,' said the old man. 'I guess they are as good as yours.'

'Oh, you're perfectly free to abuse mine,' his son replied, giving him his tea.

'Well, we're two lame ducks; I don't think there's much difference.'

'I'm much obliged to you for calling me a duck. How's your tea?'

'Well, it's rather hot.'

'That's intended to be a merit.'

'Ah, there's a great deal of merit,' murmured the old man, kindly. 'He's a very good nurse, Lord Warburton.'

'Isn't he a bit clumsy?' asked his lordship.

'Oh no, he's not clumsy – considering that he's an invalid himself. He's a very good nurse – for a sick-nurse. I call him my sick-nurse because he's sick himself.'

'Oh, come, daddy!' the ugly young man exclaimed.

'Well, you are; I wish you weren't. But I suppose you can't help it.'

'I might try: that's an idea,' said the young man.

'Were you ever sick, Lord Warburton?' his father asked.

Lord Warburton considered a moment. 'Yes, sir, once, in the Persian Gulf.'

'He's making light of you, daddy,' said the other young man. 'That's a sort of joke.'

'Well, there seem to be so many sorts now,' daddy replied, serenely. 'You don't look as if you had been sick, anyway, Lord Warburton.'

'He's sick of life; he was just telling me so; going on fearfully about it,' said Lord Warburton's friend.

'Is that true, sir?' asked the old man gravely.

'If it is, your son gave me no consolation. He's a wretched fellow to talk to – a regular cynic. He doesn't seem to believe in anything.'

'That's another sort of joke,' said the person accused of cynicism.

'It's because his health is so poor,' his father explained to Lord Warburton. 'It affects his mind and colours his way of looking at things; he seems to feel as if he had never had a chance. But it's almost entirely theoretical, you know; it doesn't seem to affect his spirits. I've hardly ever seen him when he wasn't cheerful – about as he is at present. He often cheers me up.'

The young man so described looked at Lord Warburton and laughed. 'Is it a glowing eulogy or an accusation of levity? Should you like me to carry out my theories, daddy?'

'By Jove, we should see some queer things!' cried Lord Warburton.

'I hope you haven't taken up that sort of tone,' said the old man.

'Warburton's tone is worse than mine; he pretends to be bored. I'm not in the least bored; I find life only too interesting.'

'Ah, *too* interesting; you shouldn't allow it to be that, you know!'

'I'm never bored when I come here,' said Lord Warburton. 'One gets such uncommonly good talk.'

'Is that another sort of joke?' asked the old man. 'You've no excuse for being bored anywhere. When I was your age I had never heard of such a thing.'

'You must have developed very late.'

'No, I developed very quick; that was just the reason. When I was twenty years old I was very highly developed indeed. I was working tooth and nail. You wouldn't be bored if you had something to do; but all you young men are too idle. You think too much of your pleasure. You're too fastidious, and too indolent, and too rich.'

'Oh, I say,' cried Lord Warburton, 'you're hardly the person to accuse a fellow-creature of being too rich!'

'Do you mean because I'm a banker?' asked the old man.

'Because of that, if you like; and because you have – haven't you? – such unlimited means.'

'He isn't very rich,' the other young man mercifully pleaded. 'He has given away an immense deal of money.'

'Well, I suppose it was his own,' said Lord Warburton; 'and in that case could there be a better proof of wealth? Let not a public benefactor talk of one's being too fond of pleasure.'

'Daddy's very fond of pleasure – of other people's.'

The old man shook his head. 'I don't pretend to have contributed anything to the amusement of my contemporaries.'

'My dear father, you're too modest!'

'That's a kind of joke, sir,' said Lord Warburton.

'You young men have too many jokes. When there are no jokes you've nothing left.'

'Fortunately there are always more jokes,' the ugly young man remarked.

'I don't believe it – I believe things are getting more serious. You young men will find that out.'

'The increasing seriousness of things, then – that's the great opportunity of jokes.'

'They'll have to be grim jokes,' said the old man. 'I'm convinced there will be great changes; and not all for the better.'

'I quite agree with you, sir,' Lord Warburton declared. 'I'm very sure there will be great changes, and that all sorts of queer things will happen. That's why I find so much difficulty in applying your advice; you know you told me the other day that I ought to "take hold" of something. One hesitates to take hold of a thing that may the next moment be knocked sky-high.'

'You ought to take hold of a pretty woman,' said his companion. 'He's trying hard to fall in love,' he added, by way of explanation, to his father.

'The pretty women themselves may be sent flying!' Lord Warburton exclaimed.

'No, no, they'll be firm,' the old man rejoined; 'they'll not be affected by the social and political changes I just referred to.'

'You mean they won't be abolished? Very well, then, I'll lay hands on one as soon as possible and tie her round my neck as a life-preserver.'

'The ladies will save us,' said the old man; 'that is the best of them will

– for I make a difference between them. Make up to a good one and marry her, and your life will become much more interesting.'

A momentary silence marked perhaps on the part of his auditors a sense of the magnanimity of this speech, for it was a secret neither for his son nor for his visitor that his own experiment in matrimony had not been a happy one. As he said, however, he made a difference; and these words may have been intended as a confession of personal error; though of course it was not in place for either of his companions to remark that apparently the lady of his choice had not been one of the best.

'If I marry an interesting woman I shall be interested: is that what you say?' Lord Warburton asked. 'I'm not at all keen about marrying – your son misrepresented me; but there's no knowing what an interesting woman might do with me.'

'I should like to see your idea of an interesting woman,' said his friend.

'My dear fellow, you can't see ideas – especially such highly ethereal ones as mine. If I could only see it myself – that would be a great step in advance.'

'Well, you may fall in love with whomsoever you please; but you mustn't fall in love with my niece,' said the old man.

His son broke into a laugh. 'He'll think you mean that as a provocation! My dear father, you've lived with the English for thirty years, and you've picked up a good many of the things they say. But you've never learned the things they don't say!'

'I say what I please,' the old man returned with all his serenity.

'I haven't the honour of knowing your niece,' Lord Warburton said. 'I think it's the first time I've heard of her.'

'She's a niece of my wife's; Mrs Touchett brings her to England.'

Then young Mr Touchett explained, 'My mother, you know, has been spending the winter in America, and we're expecting her back. She writes that she has discovered a niece and that she has invited her to come out with her.'

'I see – very kind of her,' said Lord Warburton. 'Is the young lady interesting?'

'We hardly know more about her than you; my mother has not gone into details. She chiefly communicates with us by means of telegrams, and her telegrams are rather inscrutable. They say women don't know how to write them, but my mother has thoroughly mastered the art of condensation. "Tired America, hot weather awful, return England with niece, first steamer decent cabin." That's the sort of message we get from her – that was the last that came. But there had been another before, which I think contained the first mention of the niece. "Changed hotel, very bad, impudent clerk, address here. Taken sister's girl, died last year, go to Europe, two sisters, quite independent." Over that my father and I have scarcely stopped puzzling; it seems to admit of so many interpretations.'

'There's one thing very clear in it,' said the old man; 'she has given the hotel clerk a dressing.'

'I'm not sure even of that, since he has driven her from the field. We thought at first that the sister mentioned might be the sister of the clerk; but the subsequent mention of a niece seems to prove that the allusion is to one of my aunts. Then there was a question as to whose the two other sisters were; they are probably two of my late aunt's daughters. But who's "quite independent", and in what sense is the term used? – that point's not yet settled. Does the expression apply more particularly to the young lady my mother has adopted, or does it characterize her sisters equally? – and is it used in a moral or in a financial sense? Does it mean that they've been left well off, or that they wish to be under no obligations? or does it simply mean that they're fond of their own way?'

'Whatever else it means, it's pretty sure to mean that,' Mr Touchett remarked.

'You'll see for yourself,' said Lord Warburton. 'When does Mrs Touchett arrive?'

'We're quite in the dark; as soon as she can find a decent cabin. She may be waiting for it yet; on the other hand she may already have disembarked in England.'

'In that case she would probably have telegraphed to you.'

'She never telegraphs when you would expect it – only when you don't,' said the old man. 'She likes to drop on me suddenly; she thinks she'll find me doing something wrong. She has never done so yet, but she's not discouraged.'

'It's her share of the family trait, the independence she speaks of.' Her son's appreciation of the matter was more favourable. 'Whatever the high spirit of those young ladies may be, her own is a match for it. She likes to do everything for herself and has no belief in anyone's power to help her. She thinks me of no more use than a postage-stamp without gum, and she would never forgive me if I should presume to go to Liverpool to meet her.'

'Will you at least let me know when your cousin arrives?' Lord Warburton asked.

'Only on the condition I've mentioned – that you don't fall in love with her!' Mr Touchett replied.

'That strikes me as hard. Don't you think me good enough?'

'I think you too good – because I shouldn't like her to marry you. She hasn't come here to look for a husband, I hope; so many young ladies are doing that, as if there were no good ones at home. Then she's probably engaged; American girls are usually engaged, I believe. Moreover I'm not sure, after all, that you'd be a remarkable husband.'

'Very likely she's engaged; I've known a good many American girls and they always were; but I could never see that it made any difference, upon my word! As for my being a good husband,' Mr Touchett's visitor pursued, 'I'm not sure of that either. One can but try!'

'Try as much as you please, but don't try on my niece,' smiled the old man, whose opposition to the idea was broadly humorous.

'Ah, well,' said Lord Warburton with a humour broader still, 'perhaps, after all, she's not worth trying on!'

Chapter Two

While this exchange of pleasantries took place between the two Ralph Touchett wandered away a little, with his usual slouching gait, his hands in his pockets, and his little rowdyish terrier at his heels. His face was turned towards the house, but his eyes were bent musingly on the lawn; so that he had been an object of observation to a person who had just made her appearance in the ample doorway for some moments before he perceived her. His attention was called to her by the conduct of his dog, who had suddenly darted forward with a little volley of shrill barks, in which the note of welcome, however, was more sensible than that of defiance. The person in question was a young lady, who seemed immediately to interpret the greeting of the small beast. He advanced with great rapidity and stood at her feet, looking up and barking hard; whereupon, without hesitation, she stooped and caught him in her hands, holding him face to face while he continued his quick chatter. His master now had had time to follow and to see that Bunchie's new friend was a tall girl in a black dress, who at first sight looked pretty. She was bareheaded, as if she were staying in the house – a fact which conveyed perplexity to the son of its master, conscious of that immunity from visitors which had for some time been rendered necessary by the latter's ill-health. Meantime the two other gentlemen had also taken note of the newcomer.

'Dear me, who's that strange woman?' Mr Touchett had asked.

'Perhaps it's Mrs Touchett's niece – the independent young lady,' Lord Warburton suggested. 'I think she must be, from the way she handles the dog.'

The collie, too, had now allowed his attention to be diverted, and he trotted towards the young lady in the doorway, slowly setting his tail in motion as he went.

'But where's my wife then?' murmured the old man.

'I suppose the young lady has left her somewhere: that's a part of the independence.'

The girl spoke to Ralph, smiling, while she still held up the terrier. 'Is this your little dog, sir?'

'He was mine a moment ago; but you've suddenly acquired a remarkable air of property in him.'

'Couldn't we share him?' asked the girl. 'He's such a perfect little darling.'

Ralph looked at her a moment; she was unexpectedly pretty. 'You may have him altogether,' he then replied.

The young lady seemed to have a great deal of confidence, both in herself and in others; but this abrupt generosity made her blush. 'I ought to tell you that I'm probably your cousin,' she brought out, putting down the dog. 'And here's another!' she added quickly, as the collie came up.

'Probably?' the young man exclaimed, laughing. 'I supposed it was quite settled! Have you arrived with my mother?'

'Yes, half an hour ago.'

'And has she deposited you and departed again?'

'No, she went straight to her room, and she told me that, if I should see you, I was to say to you that you must come to her there at a quarter to seven.'

The young man looked at his watch. 'Thank you very much; I shall be punctual.' And then he looked at his cousin. 'You're very welcome here. I'm delighted to see you.'

She was looking at everything, with an eye that denoted clear perception – at her companion, at the two dogs, at the two gentlemen under the trees, at the beautiful scene that surrounded her. 'I've never seen anything so lovely as this place. I've been all over the house; it's too enchanting.'

'I'm sorry you should have been here so long without our knowing it.'

'Your mother told me that in England people arrived very quietly; so I thought it was all right. Is one of those gentlemen your father?'

'Yes, the elder one – the one sitting down,' said Ralph.

The girl gave a laugh. 'I don't suppose it's the other. Who's the other?'

'He's a friend of ours – Lord Warburton.'

'Oh, I hoped there would be a lord; it's just like a novel!' And then, 'Oh, you adorable creature!' she suddenly cried, stooping down and picking up the small dog again.

She remained standing where they had met, making no offer to advance or to speak to Mr Touchett, and while she lingered so near the threshold, slim and charming, her interlocutor wondered if she expected the old man to come and pay her his respects. American girls were used to a great deal of deference, and it had been intimated that this one had a high spirit. Indeed Ralph could see that in her face.

'Won't you come and make acquaintance with my father?' he nevertheless ventured to ask. 'He's old and infirm – he doesn't leave his chair.'

'Ah, poor man, I'm very sorry!' the girl exclaimed, immediately moving forward. 'I got the impression from your mother that he was rather – rather intensely active.'

Ralph Touchett was silent a moment. 'She hasn't seen him for a year.'

'Well, he has a lovely place to sit. Come along, little hound.'

'It's a dear old place,' said the young man, looking sidewise at his neighbour.

'What's his name?' she asked, her attention having again reverted to the terrier.

'My father's name?'

'Yes,' said the young lady with amusement; 'but don't tell him I asked you.'

They had come by this time to where old Mr Touchett was sitting, and he slowly got up from his chair to introduce himself.

'My mother has arrived,' said Ralph, 'and this is Miss Archer.'

The old man placed his two hands on her shoulders, looked at her a moment with extreme benevolence and then gallantly kissed her. 'It's a great pleasure to me to see you here; but I wish you had given us a chance to receive you.'

'Oh, we were received,' said the girl. 'There were about a dozen servants in the hall. And there was an old woman curtsying at the gate.'

'We can do better than that – if we have notice!' And the old man stood there smiling, rubbing his hands, and slowly shaking his head at her. 'But Mrs Touchett doesn't like receptions.'

'She went straight to her room.'

'Yes – and locked herself in. She always does that. Well, I suppose I shall see her next week.' And Mrs Touchett's husband slowly resumed his former posture.

'Before that,' said Miss Archer. 'She's coming down to dinner – at eight o'clock. Don't you forget a quarter to seven,' she added, turning with a smile to Ralph.

'What's to happen at a quarter to seven?'

'I'm to see my mother,' said Ralph.

'Ah, happy boy!' the old man commented. 'You must sit down – you must have some tea,' he observed to his wife's niece.

'They gave me some tea in my room the moment I got there,' this young lady answered. 'I'm sorry you're out of health,' she added, resting her eyes upon her venerable host.

'Oh, I'm an old man, my dear; it's time for me to be old. But I shall be the better for having you here.'

She had been looking all round her again – at the lawn, the great trees, the reedy, silvery Thames, the beautiful old house; and while engaged in this survey she had made room in it for her companions; a comprehensiveness of observation easily conceivable on the part of a young woman who was evidently both intelligent and excited. She had seated herself and had put away the little dog; her white hands, in her lap, were folded upon her black dress; her head was erect, her eye lighted, her flexible figure turned itself easily this way and that, in sympathy with the alertness with which she evidently caught impressions. Her impressions were numerous, and they were all reflected in a clear, still smile. 'I've never seen anything so beautiful as this.'

'It's looking very well,' said Mr Touchett. 'I know the way it strikes you. I've been through all that. But you're very beautiful yourself,' he added with a politeness by no means crudely jocular and with the happy consciousness that his advanced age gave him the privilege of saying such things – even to young persons who might possibly take alarm at them.

What degree of alarm this young person took need not be exactly measured; she instantly rose, however, with a blush which was not a refutation. 'Oh yes, of course I'm lovely!' she returned with a quick laugh. 'How old is your house? Is it Elizabethan?'

'It's early Tudor,' said Ralph Touchett.

She turned towards him, watching his face. 'Early Tudor? How very delightful! And I suppose there are a great many others.'

'There are many much better ones.'

'Don't say that, my son!' the old man protested. 'There's nothing better than this.'

'I've got a very good one; I think in some respects it's rather better,' said

Lord Warburton, who as yet had not spoken, but who had kept an attentive eye upon Miss Archer. He slightly inclined himself, smiling; he had an excellent manner with women. The girl appreciated it in an instant; she had not forgotten that this was Lord Warburton. 'I should like very much to show it to you,' he added.

'Don't believe him,' cried the old man; 'don't look at it! It's a wretched old barrack – not to be compared with this.'

'I don't know – I can't judge,' said the girl, smiling at Lord Warburton.

In this discussion Ralph Touchett took no interest whatever; he stood with his hands in his pockets, looking greatly as if he should like to renew his conversation with his new-found cousin. 'Are you very fond of dogs?' he inquired by the way of beginning. He seemed to recognize that it was an awkward beginning for a clever man.

'Very fond of them indeed.'

'You must keep the terrier, you know,' he went on, still awkwardly.

'I'll keep him while I'm here, with pleasure.'

'That will be for a long time, I hope.'

'You're very kind. I hardly know. My aunt must settle that.'

'I'll settle it with her – at a quarter to seven.' And Ralph looked at his watch again.

'I'm glad to be here at all,' said the girl.

'I don't believe you allow things to be settled for you.'

'Oh yes; if they're settled as I like them.'

'I shall settle this as I like it,' said Ralph. 'It's most unaccountable that we should never have known you.'

'I was there – you had only to come and see me.'

'There? Where do you mean?'

'In the United States: in New York and Albany and other American places.'

'I've been there – all over, but I never saw you. I can't make it out.'

Miss Archer just hesitated. 'It was because there had been some disagreement between your mother and my father, after my mother's death, which took place when I was a child. In consequence of it we never expected to see you.'

'Ah, but I don't embrace all my mother's quarrels – heaven forbid!' the young man cried. 'You've lately lost your father?' he went on more gravely.

'Yes; more than a year ago. After that my aunt was very kind to me; she came to see me and proposed that I should come with her to Europe.'

'I see,' said Ralph. 'She has adopted you.'

'Adopted me?' The girl stared, and her blush came back to her, together with a momentary look of pain which gave her interlocutor some alarm. He had underestimated the effect of his words. Lord Warburton, who appeared constantly desirous of a nearer view of Miss Archer, strolled towards the two cousins at the moment, and as he did so she rested her wider eyes on him. 'Oh no; she has not adopted me. I'm not a candidate for adoption.'

'I beg a thousand pardons,' Ralph murmured. 'I meant – I meant—' He hardly knew what he meant.

'You meant she has taken me up. Yes; she likes to take people up. She has been very kind to me; but,' she added with a certain visible eagerness of desire to be explicit, 'I'm very fond of my liberty.'

'Are you talking about Mrs Touchett?' the old man called out from his chair. 'Come here, my dear, and tell me about her. I'm always thankful for information.'

The girl hesitated again, smiling. 'She's really very benevolent,' she answered; after which she went over to her uncle, whose mirth was excited by her words.

Lord Warburton was left standing with Ralph Touchett, to whom in a moment he said: 'You wished a while ago to see my idea of an interesting woman. There it is!'

Chapter Three

Mrs Touchett was certainly a person of many oddities, of which her behaviour on returning to her husband's house after many months was a noticeable specimen. She had her own way of doing all that she did, and this is the simplest description of a character which, although by no means without liberal motions, rarely succeeded in giving an impression of suavity. Mrs Touchett might do a great deal of good, but she never pleased. This way of her own, of which she was so fond, was not intrinsically offensive – it was just unmistakably distinguished from the ways of others. The edges of her conduct were so very clear-cut that for susceptible persons it sometimes had a knife-like effect. That hard fineness came out in her deportment during the first hours of her return from America, under circumstances in which it might have seemed that her first act would have been to exchange greetings with her husband and son. Mrs Touchett, for reasons which she deemed excellent, always retired on such occasions into impenetrable seclusion, postponing the more sentimental ceremony until she had repaired the disorder of dress with a completeness which had the less reason to be of high importance as neither beauty nor vanity were concerned in it. She was a plain-faced old woman, without graces and without any great elegance, but with an extreme respect for her own motives. She was usually prepared to explain these – when the explanation was asked as a favour; and in such a case they proved totally different from those that had been attributed to her. She was virtually separated from her husband, but she appeared to perceive nothing irregular in the situation. It had become clear, at an early stage of their community, that they should never desire the same thing at the same moment, and this appearance had prompted her to rescue disagreement from the vulgar realm of accident. She did what she could to erect it into a law – a much more edifying aspect of it – by going to live in Florence, where she bought a house and established herself; and by leaving her husband to take care of the English branch of his bank. This arrangement greatly pleased her; it was so felicitously definite. It struck her husband in the same light, in a foggy square in London, where it was at times the most definite fact he discerned; but he would have preferred that such unnatural things should have a greater vagueness. To agree to disagree had cost him an effort; he was ready to agree to almost anything but that, and saw no reason why either assent or dissent should be so terribly consistent. Mrs Touchett indulged in no regrets nor speculations, and usually came once a year to spend a month with her husband, a period during which she apparently took pains to convince him that she had adopted the right system. She was not fond of the English style of life, and had three or four reasons for it to which she currently alluded; they bore upon minor points of that ancient order, but for Mrs Touchett they amply justified non-residence. She detested bread-sauce, which, as she said, looked like a poultice and tasted like soap; she objected to the consumption of beer by her maid-servants; and she affirmed that the British laundress (Mrs Touchett was very particular about the appearance of her linen) was not a mistress of her art. At fixed intervals she paid a visit to her own country; but this last had been longer than any of its predecessors.

She had taken up her niece – there was little doubt of that. One wet afternoon, some four months earlier than the occurrence lately narrated, this young lady had been seated alone with a book. To say she was so occupied is to say that her solitude did not press upon her; for her love of knowledge had a fertilizing quality and her imagination was strong. There was at this time, however, a want of fresh taste in her situation which the arrival of an unexpected visitor did much to correct. The visitor had not been announced; the girl heard her at last walking about the adjoining room. It was in an old house at Albany, a large, square, double house, with a notice of sale in the windows of one of the lower apartments. There were two entrances, one of which had long been out of use but had never been removed. They were exactly alike – large white doors, with an arched frame and wide side-lights, perched upon little 'stoops' of red stone, which descended sidewise to the brick pavement of the street. The two houses together formed a single dwelling, the party-wall having been removed and the rooms placed in communication. These rooms, above-stairs, were extremely numerous, and were painted all over exactly alike, in a yellowish white which had grown sallow with time. On the third floor there was a sort of arched passage, connecting the two sides of the house, which Isabel and her sisters used in their childhood to call the tunnel and which, though it was short and well-lighted, always seemed to the girl to be strange and lonely, especially on winter afternoons. She had been in the house, at different periods, as a child; in those days her grandmother lived there. Then there had been an absence of ten years, followed by a return to Albany before her father's death. Her grandmother, old Mrs Archer, had exercised, chiefly within the limits of the family, a large hospitality in the early period, and the little girls often spent weeks under her roof – weeks of which Isabel had the happiest memory. The manner of life was different from that of her own home – larger, more plentiful, practically more festal; the discipline of the nursery was delightfully vague and the opportunity of listening to the conversation of one's elders (which with Isabel was a highly valued pleasure) almost unbounded. There was a constant coming and going; her grandmother's sons and daughters and their children appeared to be in the enjoyment of standing invitations to arrive and remain, so that the house offered to a certain extent the appearance of a bustling provincial inn kept by a gentle old landlady who sighed a great deal and never presented a bill. Isabel of course knew nothing about bills; but even as a child she thought her grandmother's home romantic. There was a covered piazza behind it, furnished with a swing which was a source of tremulous interest; and beyond this was a long garden, sloping down to the stable and containing peach trees of barely credible familiarity. Isabel had stayed with her grandmother at various seasons, but somehow all her visits had a flavour of peaches. On the other side, across the street, was an old house that was called the Dutch House – a peculiar structure dating from the earliest colonial time, composed of bricks that had been painted yellow, crowned with a gable that was pointed out to strangers, defended by a rickety wooden paling and standing sidewise to the street. It was occupied by a primary school for children of both sexes, kept or rather let go, by a demonstrative lady of whom Isabel's chief recollection was that her hair was fastened with strange bedroomy combs at the temples and that she was the widow of someone of consequence. The little girl had been offered the opportunity of laying a foundation of knowledge in this establishment; but having spent a single day in it, she had protested against its laws and had been allowed to stay at home, where, in the September days, when the windows of the Dutch House were open, she used to hear the hum of childish voices repeating the multiplication table – an incident in which the elation of liberty and the pain of exclusion were indistinguishably mingled. The foundation of her knowledge was really laid in the idleness of her grandmother's house, where, as most of the other inmates were not reading people, she had uncontrolled use of a library full of books with frontispieces, which she used to climb upon a chair to take down. When she had found one to her taste – she was guided in the selection chiefly by the frontispiece – she carried it into a mysterious apartment which lay beyond the library and which was called, traditionally, no one knew why, the office. Whose office it had been and at what period it had flourished, she never learned; it was enough for her that it contained an echo and a pleasant musty smell and that it was a chamber of disgrace for old pieces of furniture whose infirmities were not always apparent (so that the disgrace seemed unmerited and rendered them victims of injustice) and with which, in the manner of children, she had established relations almost human, certainly dramatic. There was an old hair-cloth sofa in especial, to which she had confided a hundred childish sorrows. The place owed much of its mysterious melancholy to the fact that it was properly entered from the second door of the house, the door that had been condemned, and that it was secured by bolts which a particularly slender little girl found it impossible to slide. She knew that this silent, motionless portal opened into the street; if the sidelights had not been filled with green paper she might have looked out upon the little brown stoop and the well-worn brick pavement. But she had no wish to look out, for this would have interfered with her theory that there was a strange, unseen place on the other side – a place which became to the child's imagination, according to its different moods, a region of delight or of terror.

It was in the 'office' still that Isabel was sitting on that melancholy afternoon of early spring which I have just mentioned. At this time she might have had the whole house to choose from, and the room she had selected was the most depressed of its scenes. She had never opened the bolted door nor removed the green paper (renewed by other hands) from its sidelights; she had never assured herself that the vulgar street lay beyond. A crude, cold rain fell heavily; the spring-time was indeed an appeal – and it seemed a cynical, insincere appeal – to patience. Isabel, however, gave as little heed as possible to cosmic treacheries; she kept her eyes on her book and tried to fix her mind. It had lately occurred to her that her mind was a good deal of a vagabond, and she had spent much ingenuity in training it to a military step and teaching it to advance, to halt, to retreat, to perform even more complicated manoeuvres at the word of command. Just now she had given it marching orders and it had been trudging over the sandy plains of a history of German Thought. Suddenly she became aware of a step very different from her own intellectual pace; she listened a little and perceived that someone was moving in the library, which communicated with the office. It struck her first as the step of a person from whom she was looking for a visit, then almost immediately announced itself as the tread of a woman and a stranger – her possible visitor being neither. It had an inquisitive, experimental quality which suggested that it would not stop short of the threshold of the office; and in fact the doorway of this apartment was presently occupied by a lady who paused there and looked very hard at our heroine. She was a plain, elderly woman, dressed in a comprehensive waterproof mantle; she had a face with a good deal of rather violent point.

'Oh,' she began, 'is that where you usually sit?' She looked about at the heterogeneous chairs and tables.

'Not when I have visitors,' said Isabel, getting up to receive the intruder.

She directed their course back to the library while the visitor continued to look about her. 'You seem to have plenty of other rooms; they're in rather better condition. But everything's immensely worn.'

'Have you come to look at the house?' Isabel asked. 'The servant will show it to you.'

'Send her away; I don't want to buy it. She has probably gone to look for you and is wandering about upstairs; she didn't seem at all intelligent. You had better tell her it's no matter.' And then, since the girl stood there hesitating and wondering, this unexpected critic said to her abruptly: 'I suppose you're one of the daughters?'

Isabel thought she had very strange manners. 'It depends upon whose daughters you mean.'

'The late Mr Archer's – and my poor sister's.'

'Ah,' said Isabel slowly, 'you must be our crazy Aunt Lydia!'

'Is that what your father told you to call me? I'm your Aunt Lydia, but I'm not at all crazy: I haven't a delusion! And which of the daughters are you?'

'I'm the youngest of the three, and my name's Isabel.'

'Yes; the others are Lilian and Edith. And are you the prettiest?'

'I haven't the least idea,' said the girl.

'I think you must be.' And in this way the aunt and the niece made friends. The aunt had quarrelled years before with her brother-in-law, after the death of her sister, taking him to task for the manner in which he brought up his three girls. Being a high-tempered man he had requested her to mind her own business, and she had taken him at his word. For many years she held no communication with him and after his death had addressed not a word to his daughters, who had been bred in that disrespectful view of her which we have just seen Isabel betray. Mrs Touchett's behaviour was, as usual, perfectly deliberate. She intended to go to America to look after her investments (with which her husband, in spite of his financial position, had nothing to do) and would take advantage of this opportunity to inquire into the condition of her nieces. There was no need of writing, for she should attach no importance to any account of them she should elicit by letter; she believed, always, in seeing for one's self. Isabel found, however, that she knew a good deal about them, and knew about the marriage of the two elder girls; knew that their poor father had left very little money, but that the house in Albany, which had passed into his hands, was to be sold for their benefit; knew, finally, that Edmund Ludlow, Lilian's husband, had taken upon himself to attend to this matter, in consideration of which the young couple, who had come to Albany during Mr Archer's illness, were remaining there for the present and, as well as Isabel herself, occupying the old place.

'How much money do you expect for it?' Mrs Touchett asked of her companion, who had brought her to sit in the front parlour, which she had inspected without enthusiasm.

'I haven't the least idea,' said the girl.

'That's the second time you have said that to me,' her aunt rejoined. 'And yet you don't look at all stupid.'

'I'm not stupid; but I don't know anything about money.'

'Yes, that's the way you were brought up – as if you were to inherit a million. What have you in point of fact inherited?'

'I really can't tell you. You must ask Edmund and Lilian; they'll be back in half an hour.'

'In Florence we should call it a very bad house,' said Mrs Touchett; 'but here, I dare say, it will bring a high price. It ought to make a considerable sum for each of you. In addition to that you *must* have something else; it's most extraordinary your not knowing. The position's of value, and they'll probably pull it down and make a row of shops. I wonder you don't do that yourself; you might let the shops to great advantage.'

Isabel stared; the idea of letting shops was new to her. 'I hope they won't pull it down,' she said; 'I'm extremely fond of it.'

'I don't see what makes you fond of it; your father died here.'

'Yes; but I don't dislike it for that,' the girl rather strangely returned. 'I like places in which things have happened – even if they're sad things. A great many people have died here; the place has been full of life.'

'Is that what you call being full of life?'

'I mean full of experience – of people's feelings and sorrows. And not of their sorrows only, for I've been very happy here as a child.'

'You should go to Florence if you like houses in which things have happened – especially deaths. I live in an old palace in which three people have been murdered; three that were known and I don't know how many more besides.'

'In an old palace?' Isabel repeated.

'Yes, my dear; a very different affair from this. This is very bourgeois.'

Isabel felt some emotion, for she had always thought highly of her grandmother's house. But the emotion was of a kind which led her to say: 'I should like very much to go to Florence.'

'Well, if you'll be very good, and do everything I tell you, I'll take you there,' Mrs Touchett declared.

Our young woman's emotion deepened; she flushed a little and smiled at her aunt in silence. 'Do everything you tell me? I don't think I can promise that.'

'No, you don't look like a person of that sort. You're fond of your own way; but it's not for me to blame you.'

'And yet, to go to Florence,' the girl exclaimed in a moment, 'I'd promise almost anything!'

Edmund and Lilian were slow to return, and Mrs Touchett had an hour's uninterrupted talk with her niece, who found her a strange and interesting figure: a figure essentially – almost the first she had ever met. She was as eccentric as Isabel had always supposed; and hitherto, whenever the girl had heard people described as eccentric, she had thought of them as offensive or alarming. The term had always suggested to her something grotesque and even sinister. But her aunt made it a matter of high but easy irony, or comedy and led her to ask herself if the common tone, which was all she had known, had ever been as interesting. No one certainly had on any occasion so held her as this little thin-lipped, bright-eyed foreign-looking woman, who retrieved an insignificant appearance by a distinguished manner and, sitting there in a well-worn waterproof, talked with striking familiarity of the courts of Europe. There was nothing flighty about Mrs Touchett, but she recognized no social superiors, and, judging the great ones of the earth in a way that spoke of this, enjoyed the consciousness of making an impression on a candid and susceptible mind. Isabel at first had answered a good many questions, and it was from her answers apparently that Mrs Touchett derived a high opinion of her intelligence. But after this she had asked a good many, and her aunt's answers, whatever turn they took, struck her as food for deep reflection. Mrs Touchett waited for the return of her other niece as long as she thought reasonable, but as at six o'clock Mrs Ludlow had not come in she prepared to take her departure.

'Your sister must be a great gossip. Is she accustomed to staying out so many hours?'

'You've been out almost as long as she,' Isabel replied; 'she can have left the house but a short time before you came in.'

Mrs Touchett looked at the girl without resentment; she appeared to enjoy a bold retort and to be disposed to be gracious. 'Perhaps she hasn't had so good an excuse as I. Tell her at any rate that she must come and see me this evening at that horrid hotel. She may bring her husband if she likes, but she needn't bring you. I shall see plenty of you later.'

Chapter Four

Mrs Ludlow was the eldest of the three sisters, and was usually thought the most sensible; the classification being in general that Lilian was the practical one, Edith the beauty, and Isabel the 'intellectual' superior. Mrs Keyes, the second of the group, was the wife of an officer of the United States Engineers, and as our history is not further concerned with her it will suffice that she was indeed very pretty and that she formed the ornament of those various military stations, chiefly in the unfashionable West, to which, to her deep chagrin, her husband was successively relegated. Lilian had married a New York lawyer, a young man with a loud voice and an enthusiasm for his profession; the match was not brilliant, any more than Edith's, but Lilian had occasionally been spoken of as a young woman who might be thankful to marry at all – she was so much plainer than her sisters. She was, however, very happy, and now, as the mother of two peremptory little boys and the mistress of a wedge of brown stone violently driven into Fifty-third Street, seemed to exult in her condition as in a bold escape. She was short and solid, and her claim to figure was questioned, but she was conceded presence, though not majesty; she had moreover, as people said, improved since her marriage, and the two things in life of which she was most distinctly conscious were her husband's force in argument and her sister Isabel's originality. 'I've never kept up with Isabel – it would have taken *all* my time,' she had often remarked; in spite of which, however, she held her rather wistfully in sight; watching her as a motherly spaniel might watch a free greyhound. 'I want to see her safely married – that's what I want to see,' she frequently noted to her husband.

'Well, I must say I should have no particular desire to marry her,' Edmund Ludlow was accustomed to answer in an extremely audible tone.

'I know you say that for argument; you always take the opposite ground. I don't see what you've against her except that she's so original.'

'Well, I don't like originals; I like translations,' Mr Ludlow had more than once replied. 'Isabel's written in a foreign tongue. I can't make her out. She ought to marry an Armenian or a Portuguese.'

'That's just what I'm afraid she'll do!' cried Lilian, who thought Isabel capable of anything.

She listened with great interest to the girl's account of Mrs Touchett's appearance and in the evening prepared to comply with their aunt's commands. Of what Isabel then said no report has remained, but her sister's words had doubtless prompted a word spoken to her husband as the two were making ready for their visit. 'I do hope immensely she'll do something handsome for Isabel; she has evidently taken a great fancy to her.'

'What is it you wish her to do?' Edmund Ludlow asked. 'Make her a big present?'

'No indeed; nothing of the sort. But take an interest in her – sympathize with her. She's evidently just the sort of person to appreciate her. She has lived so much in foreign society; she told Isabel all about it. You know you've always thought Isabel rather foreign.'

'You want her to give her a little foreign sympathy, eh? Don't you think she gets enough at home?'

'Well, she ought to go abroad,' said Mrs Ludlow. 'She's just the person to go abroad.'

'And you want the old lady to take her, is that it?'

'She has offered to take her – she's dying to have Isabel go. But what I want her to do when she gets there is to give her all the advantages. I'm sure all we've got to do,' said Mrs Ludlow, 'is to give her a chance.'

'A chance for what?'

'A chance to develop.'

'Oh Moses!' Edmund Ludlow exclaimed. 'I hope she isn't going to develop any more!'

'If I were not sure you only said that for argument I should feel very badly,' his wife replied. 'But you know you love her.'

'*Do* you know I love you?' the young man said, jocosely, to Isabel a little later, while he brushed his hat.

'I'm sure I don't care whether you do or not!' exclaimed the girl; whose voice and smile, however, were less haughty than her words.

'Oh, she feels so grand since Mrs Touchett's visit,' said her sister.

But Isabel challenged this assertion with a good deal of seriousness. 'You must not say that, Lily. I don't feel grand at all.'

'I'm sure there's no harm,' said the conciliatory Lily.

'Ah, but there's nothing in Mrs Touchett's visit to make one feel grand.'

'Oh,' exclaimed Ludlow, 'she's grander than ever!'

'Whenever I feel grand,' said the girl, 'it will be for a better reason.'

Whether she felt grand or no, she at any rate felt different, felt as if something had happened to her. Left to herself for the evening she sat a while under the lamp, her hands empty, her usual avocations unheeded. Then she rose and moved about the room, and from one room to another, preferring the places where the vague lamplight expired. She was restless and even agitated; at moments she trembled a little. The importance of what had happened was out of proportion to its appearance; there had really been a change in her life. What it would bring with it was as yet extremely indefinite; but Isabel was in a situation that gave a value to any change. She had a desire to leave the past behind her and, as she said to herself, to begin afresh. This desire indeed was not a birth of the present occasion; it was as familiar as the sound of the rain upon the window and it had led to her beginning afresh a great many times. She closed her eyes as she sat in one of the dusky corners of the quiet parlour; but it was not with a desire for dozing forgetfulness. It was on the contrary because she felt too wide-eyed and wished to check the sense of seeing too many things at once. Her imagination was by habit ridiculously active; when the door was not open it jumped out of the window. She was not accustomed indeed to keep it behind bolts; and at important moments, when she would have been thankful to make use of her judgement alone, she paid the penalty of having given undue encouragement to the faculty of seeing without judging. At present, with her sense that the note of change had been struck, came gradually a host of images of the things she was leaving behind her. The years and hours of her life came back to her, and for a long time, in a stillness broken only by the ticking of the big bronze clock, she passed them in review. It had been a very happy life and she had been a very fortunate person – this was the truth that seemed to emerge most vividly. She had had the best of everything, and in a world in which the circumstances of so many people made them unenviable it was an advantage never to have known anything particularly unpleasant. It appeared to Isabel that the unpleasant had been even too absent from her knowledge, for she had gathered from her acquaintance with literature that it was often a source of interest and even of instruction. Her father had kept it away from her – her handsome, much-loved father, who always had such an aversion to it. It was a great felicity to have been his daughter; Isabel rose even to pride in her parentage. Since his death she had seemed to see him as turning his braver side to his children and as not having managed to ignore the ugly quite so much in practice as in aspiration. But this only made her tenderness for him greater; it was scarcely even painful to have to suppose him too generous, too good-natured, too indifferent to sordid considerations. Many persons had held that he carried this indifference too far, especially the large number of those to whom he owed money. Of their opinions Isabel was never very definitely informed; but it may interest the reader to know that, while they had recognized in the late Mr Archer a remarkably handsome head and a very taking manner (indeed, as one of them had said, he was always taking something), they had declared that he was making a very poor use of his life. He had squandered a substantial fortune, he had been deplorably convivial, he was known to have gambled freely. A few very harsh critics went so far as to say that he had not even brought up his daughters. They had had no regular education and no permanent home; they had been at once spoiled and neglected; they had lived with nursemaids and governesses (usually very bad ones) or had been sent to superficial schools, kept by the French, from which, at the end of a month, they had been removed in tears. This view of the matter would have excited Isabel's indignation, for to her own sense her opportunities had been large. Even when her father had left his daughters for three months at Neufchâtel with a French *bonne* who had eloped with a Russian nobleman staying at the same hotel – even in this irregular situation (an incident of the girl's eleventh year) she had been neither frightened nor ashamed, but had thought it a romantic episode in a liberal education. Her father had a large way of looking at life, of which his restlessness and even his occasional incoherency of conduct had been only a proof. He wished his daughters, even as children, to see as much of the world as possible; and it was for this purpose that, before Isabel was fourteen, he had transported them three times across the Atlantic, giving them on each occasion, however, but a few months' view of the subject proposed: a course which had whetted our heroine's curiosity without enabling her to satisfy it. She ought to have been a partisan of her father, for she was the member of his trio who most 'made up' to him for the disagreeables he didn't mention. In his last days his general willingness to take leave of a world in which the difficulty of doing as one liked appeared to increase as one grew older had been sensibly modified by the pain of separation from his clever, his superior, his remarkable girl. Later, when the journeys to Europe ceased, he still had shown his children all sorts of indulgence, and if he had been troubled about money-matters nothing ever disturbed their irreflective consciousness of many possessions. Isabel, though she danced very well, had not the recollection of having been in New York a successful member of the choreographic circle; her sister Edith was, as everyone said, so very much more fetching. Edith was so striking an example of success that Isabel could have no illusions as to what constituted this advantage, or as to the limits of her own power to frisk and jump and shriek – above all with rightness of effect. Nineteen persons out of twenty (including the younger sister herself) pronounced Edith infinitely the prettier of the two; but the twentieth, besides reversing this judgement, had the entertainment of thinking all the others aesthetic vulgarians. Isabel had in the depths of her nature an even more unquenchable desire to please Edith; but the depths of this young lady's nature were a very out-of-the-way place, between which and the surface communication was interrupted by a dozen capricious forces. She saw the young men who came in large numbers to see her sister; but as a general thing they were afraid of her; they had a belief that some special preparation was required for talking with her. Her reputation of reading a great deal hung about her like the cloudy envelope of a goddess in an epic; it was supposed to engender difficult questions and to keep the conversation at a low temperature. The poor girl liked to be thought clever, but she hated to be thought bookish; she used to read in secret and, though her memory was excellent, to abstain from showy reference. She had a great desire for knowledge, but she really preferred almost any source of information to the printed page; she had an immense curiosity about life and was constantly staring and wondering. She carried within herself a great fund of life, and her deepest enjoyment was to feel the continuity between the movements of her own soul and the agitations of the world. For this reason she was fond of seeing great crowds and large stretches of country, of reading about revolutions and wars, of looking at historical pictures – a class of efforts as to which she had often committed the conscious solecism of forgiving them much bad painting for the sake of the subject. While the Civil War went on she was still a very young girl; but she passed months of this long period in a state of almost passionate excitement, in which she felt herself at times (to her extreme confusion) stirred almost indiscriminately by the valour of either army. Of course the circumspection of suspicious swains had never gone the length of making her a social proscript; for the number of those whose hearts, as they approached her, beat only just fast enough to remind them they had heads as well, had kept her unacquainted with the supreme disciplines of her sex and age. She had had everything a girl could have: kindness, admiration, bonbons, bouquets, the sense of exclusion from none of the privileges of the world she lived in, abundant opportunity for dancing, plenty of new dresses, the London *Spectator*, the latest publications, the music of Gounod, the poetry of Browning, the prose of George Eliot.

These things now, as memory played over them, resolved themselves into a multitude of scenes and figures. Forgotten things came back to her; many others, which she had lately thought of great moment, dropped out of sight.

The result was kaleidoscopic, but the movement of the instrument was checked at last by the servant's coming in with the name of a gentleman. The name of the gentleman was Caspar Goodwood; he was a straight young man from Boston, who had known Miss Archer for the last twelve-month and who, thinking her the most beautiful young woman of her time, had pronounced the time, according to the rule I have hinted at, a foolish period of history. He sometimes wrote to her and had within a week or two written from New York. She had thought it very possible he would come in – had indeed all the rainy day been vaguely expecting him. Now that she learned he was there, nevertheless, she felt no eagerness to receive him. He was the finest young man she had ever seen, was indeed quite a splendid young man; he inspired her with a sentiment of high, of rare respect. She had never felt equally moved to it by any other person. He was supposed by the world in general to wish to marry her, but this of course was between themselves. It at least may be affirmed that he had travelled from New York to Albany expressly to see her; having learned in the former city, where he was spending a few days and where he had hoped to find her, that she was still at the State capital. Isabel delayed for some minutes to go to him; she moved about the room with a new sense of complications. But at last she presented herself and found him standing near the lamp. He was tall, strong, and somewhat stiff; he was also lean and brown. He was not romantically, he was much rather obscurely, handsome; but his physiognomy had an air of requesting your attention, which it rewarded according to the charm you found in blue eyes of remarkable fixedness, the eyes of a complexion other than his own, and a jaw of the somewhat angular mould which is supposed to bespeak resolution. Isabel said to herself that it bespoke resolution tonight; in spite of which, in half an hour, Caspar Goodwood, who had arrived hopeful as well as resolute, took his way back to his lodging with the feeling of a man defeated. He was not, it may be added, a man weakly to accept defeat.

Chapter Five

Ralph Touchett was a philosopher, but nevertheless he knocked at his mother's door (at a quarter to seven) with a good deal of eagerness. Even philosophers have their preferences, and it must be admitted that of his progenitors his father ministered most to his sense of the sweetness to filial dependence. His father, as he had often said to himself, was the more motherly; his mother, on the other hand, was paternal, and even, according to the slang of the day, gubernatorial. She was nevertheless very fond of her only child and had always insisted on his spending three months of the year with her. Ralph rendered perfect justice to her affection and knew that in her thoughts and her thoroughly arranged and servanted life his turn always came after the other nearest subjects of her solicitude, the various punctualities of performance of the workers of her will. He found her completely dressed for dinner, but she embraced her boy with her gloved hands and made him sit on the sofa beside her. She inquired scrupulously about her husband's health and about the young man's own, and, receiving no very brilliant account of either, remarked that she was more than ever convinced of her wisdom in not exposing herself to the English climate. In this case she also might have given way. Ralph smiled at the idea of his mother's giving way, but made no point of reminding her that his own infirmity was not the result of the English climate, from which he absented himself for a considerable part of each year.

He had been a very small boy when his father, Daniel Tracy Touchett, a native of Rutland, in the State of Vermont, came to England as subordinate partner in a banking-house where some ten years later he gained preponderant control. Daniel Touchett saw before him a life-long residence in his adopted country, of which, from the first, he took a simple, sane, and accommodating view. But, as he said to himself, he had no intention of disamericanizing, nor had he a desire to teach his only son any such subtle art. It had been for himself so very soluble a problem to live in England assimilated yet unconverted that it seemed to him equally simple his lawful heir should after his death carry on the grey old bank in the white American light. He was at pains to intensify this light, however, by sending the boy home for his education. Ralph spent several terms at an American school and took a degree at an American university, after which, as he struck his father on his return as even redundantly native, he was placed for some three years in residence at Oxford. Oxford swallowed up Harvard, and Ralph became at last English enough. His outward conformity to the manners that surrounded him was none the less the mask of a mind that greatly enjoyed its independence, on which nothing long imposed itself, and which, naturally inclined to adventure and irony, indulged in a boundless liberty of appreciation. He began with being a young man of promise; at Oxford he distinguished himself, to his father's ineffable satisfaction, and the people about him said it was a thousand pities so clever a fellow should be shut out from a career. He might have had a career by returning to his own country (though this point is shrouded in uncertainty) and even if Mr Touchett had been willing to part with him (which was not the case) it would have gone hard with him to put a watery waste permanently between himself and the old man whom he regarded as his best friend. Ralph was not only fond of his father, he admired him – he enjoyed the opportunity of observing him. Daniel Touchett, to his perception, was a man of genius, and though he himself had no aptitude for the banking mystery he made a point of learning enough of it to measure the great figure his father had played. It was not this, however, he mainly relished; it was the fine ivory surface, polished as by the English air, that the old man had opposed to possibilities of penetration. Daniel Touchett had been neither at Harvard nor at Oxford, and it was his own fault if he had placed in his son's hands the key to modern criticism. Ralph, whose head was full of ideas which his father had never guessed, had a high esteem for the latter's originality. Americans, rightly or wrongly, are commended for the ease with which they adapt themselves to foreign conditions; but Mr Touchett had made of the very limits of his pliancy half the ground of his general success. He had retained in their freshness most of his marks of primary pressure; his tone, as his son always noted with pleasure, was that of the more luxuriant parts of New England. At the end of his life he had become, on his own ground, as mellow as he was rich; he combined consummate shrewdness with the disposition superficially to fraternize, and his 'social position', on which he had never wasted a care, had the firm perfection of an unthumbed fruit. It was perhaps his want of imagination and of what is called the historic consciousness; but to many of the impressions usually made by English life upon the cultivated stranger his sense was completely closed. There were certain differences he had never perceived, certain habits he had never formed, certain obscurities he had never sounded. As regards these latter, on the day he *had* sounded them his son would have thought less well of him.

Ralph, on leaving Oxford, had spent a couple of years in travelling; after which he had found himself perched on a high stool in his father's bank. The responsibility and honour of such positions is not, I believe, measured by the height of the stool, which depends upon other considerations: Ralph, indeed, who had very long legs, was fond of standing, and even of walking about, at his work. To this exercise, however, he was obliged to devote but a limited period, for at the end of some eighteen months he had become aware of his being seriously out of health. He had caught a violent cold, which fixed itself on his lungs and threw them into dire confusion. He had to give up work and apply, to the letter, the sorry injunction to take care of himself. At first he slighted the task; it appeared to him it was not himself in the least he was taking care of, but an uninteresting and uninterested person with whom he had nothing in common. This person, however, improved on acquaintance, and Ralph grew at last to have a certain grudging tolerance, even an undemonstrative respect, for him. Misfortune makes strange bedfellows, and our young man, feeling that he had something at stake in the matter – it usually struck him as his reputation for ordinary wit – devoted to his graceless charge an amount of attention of which note was duly taken and which had at least the effect of keeping the poor fellow alive. One of his lungs began to heal, the other promised to follow its example, and he was assured he might outweather a dozen winters if he would betake himself to those climates in which consumptives chiefly congregate. As he had grown extremely fond of London, he cursed the flatness of exile: but at the same time that he cursed he conformed, and gradually, when he found his sensitive organ grateful even for grim favours, he conferred them with a lighter hand. He wintered abroad, as the phrase is; basked in the sun, stopped at home when the wind blew, went to bed when it rained, and once or twice, when it had snowed overnight, almost never got up again.

A secret hoard of indifference – like a thick cake a fond old nurse might have slipped into his first school outfit – came to his aid and helped to reconcile him to sacrifice; since at the best he was too ill for aught but that arduous game. As he said to himself, there was really nothing he had wanted very much to do, so that he had at least not renounced the field of valour. At present, however, the fragrance of forbidden fruit seemed occasionally to float past him and remind him that the finest of pleasures is the rush of action. Living as he now lived was like reading a good book in a poor translation – a meagre entertainment for a young man who felt that he might have been an excellent linguist. He had good winters and poor winters, and while the former lasted he was sometimes the sport of a vision of virtual recovery. But this vision was dispelled some three years before the occurrence of the incidents with which this history opens: he had on that occasion remained later than usual in England and had been overtaken by bad weather before reaching Algiers. He arrived more dead than alive and lay there for several weeks between life and death. His convalescence was a miracle, but the first use he had made of it was to assure himself that such miracles happened but once. He said to himself that his hour was in sight and that it behoved him to keep his eyes upon it, yet that it was also open to him to spend the interval as agreeably as might be consistent with such a preoccupation. With the prospect of losing them the simple use of his faculties became an exquisite pleasure; it seemed to him the joys of contemplation had never been sounded. He was far from the time when he had found it hard that he should be obliged to give up the idea of distinguishing himself; an idea none the less importunate for being vague and none the less delightful for having had to struggle in the same breast with bursts of inspiring self-criticism. His friends at present judged him more cheerful, and attributed it to a theory, over which they shook their heads knowingly, that he would recover his health. His serenity was but the array of wild flowers niched in his ruin.

It was very probably this sweet-tasting property of the observed thing in itself that was mainly concerned in Ralph's quickly-stirred interest in the advent of a young lady who was evidently not insipid. If he was consideringly disposed, something told him, here was occupation enough for a succession of days. It may be added, in summary fashion, that the imagination of loving – as distinguished from that of being loved – had still a place in his reduced sketch. He had only forbidden himself the riot of expression. However, he shouldn't inspire his cousin with a passion, nor would she be able, even should she try, to help him to one. 'And now tell me about the young lady,' he said to his mother. 'What do you mean to do with her?'

Mrs Touchett was prompt, 'I mean to ask your father to invite her to stay three or four weeks at Gardencourt.'

'You needn't stand on any such ceremony as that,' said Ralph. 'My father will ask her as a matter of course.'

'I don't know about that. She's my niece; she's not his.'

'Good Lord, dear mother; what a sense of property! That's all the more reason for his asking her. But after that – I mean after three months (for it's absurd asking the poor girl to remain but for three or four paltry weeks) – what do you mean to do with her?'

'I mean to take her to Paris. I mean to get her clothing.'

'Ah yes, that's of course. But independently of that?'

'I shall invite her to spend the autumn with me in Florence.'

'You don't rise above detail, dear mother,' said Ralph. 'I should like to know what you mean to do with her in a general way.'

'My duty!' Mrs Touchett declared. 'I suppose you pity her very much,' she added.

'No, I don't think I pity her. She doesn't strike me as inviting compassion. I think I envy her. Before being sure, however, give me a hint of where you see your duty.'

'In showing her four European countries – I shall leave her the choice of two of them – and in giving her the opportunity of perfecting herself in French, which she already knows very well.'

Ralph frowned a little. 'That sounds rather dry – even allowing her the choice of two of the countries.'

'If it's dry,' said his mother with a laugh, 'you can leave Isabel alone to water it! She is as good as a summer rain, any day.'

'Do you mean she's a gifted being?'

'I don't know whether she's a gifted being, but she's a clever girl – with a strong will and a high temper. She has no idea of being bored.'

'I can imagine that,' said Ralph; and then he added abruptly: 'How do you two get on?'

'Do you mean by that that I'm a bore? I don't think she finds me one. Some girls might, I know; but Isabel's too clever for that. I think I greatly amuse her. We get on because I understand her; I know the sort of girl she is. She's very frank, and I'm very frank: we know just what to expect of each other.'

'Ah, dear mother,' Ralph exclaimed, 'one always knows what to expect of *you*! You've never surprised me but once, and that's today – in presenting me with a pretty cousin whose existence I had never suspected.'

'Do you think her so very pretty?'

'Very pretty indeed; but I don't insist upon that. It's her general air of being someone in particular that strikes me. Who is this rare creature, and what is she? Where did you find her, and how did you make her acquaintance?'

'I found her in an old house at Albany, sitting in a dreary room on a rainy day, reading a heavy book and boring herself to death. She didn't know she was bored, but when I left her no doubt of it she seemed very grateful for the service. You may say I shouldn't have enlightened her – I should have let her alone. There's a good deal in that, but I acted conscientiously; I thought she was meant for something better. It occurred to me that it would be a kindness to take her about and introduce her to the world. She thinks she knows a great deal of it – like most American girls; but like most American girls she's ridiculously mistaken. If you want to know, I thought she would do me credit. I like to be well thought of, and for a woman of my age there's no greater convenience, in some ways, than an attractive niece. You know I had seen nothing of my sister's children for years; I disapproved entirely of the father. But I always meant to do something for them when he should have gone to his reward. I ascertained where they were to be found and, without any preliminaries, went and introduced myself. There are two others of them, both of whom are married; but I saw only the elder, who has, by the way, a very uncivil husband. The wife, whose name is Lily, jumped at the idea of my taking an interest in Isabel; she said it was just what her sister needed – that someone should take an interest in her. She spoke of her as you might speak of some young person of genius – in want of encouragement and patronage. It may be that Isabel's a genius; but in that case I've not yet learned her special line. Mrs Ludlow was especially keen about my taking her to Europe; they all regard Europe over there as a land of emigration, of rescue, a refuge for their superfluous population. Isabel herself seemed very glad to come, and the thing was easily arranged.

There was a little difficulty about the money-question, as she seemed averse to being under pecuniary obligations. But she has a small income and she supposes herself to be travelling at her own expense.'

Ralph had listened attentively to this judicious report, by which his interest in the subject of it was not impaired. 'Ah, if she's a genius,' he said, 'we must find out her special line. Is it by chance for flirting?'

'I don't think so. You may suspect that at first, but you'll be wrong. You won't, I think, in any way, be easily right about her.'

'Warburton's wrong then!' Ralph rejoicingly exclaimed. 'He flatters himself he has made that discovery.'

His mother shook her head. 'Lord Warburton won't understand her. He needn't try.'

'He's very intelligent,' said Ralph; 'but it's right he should be puzzled once in a while.'

'Isabel will enjoy puzzling a lord,' Mrs Touchett remarked.

Her son frowned a little. 'What does she know about lords?'

'Nothing at all: that will puzzle him all the more.'

Ralph greeted these words with a laugh and looked out of the window. Then, 'Are you not going down to see my father?' he asked.

'At a quarter to eight,' said Mrs Touchett.

Her son looked at his watch. 'You've another quarter of an hour then. Tell me some more about Isabel.' After which, as Mrs Touchett declined his invitation, declaring that he must find out for himself, 'Well,' he pursued, 'she'll certainly do you credit. But won't she also give you trouble?'

'I hope not; but if she does I shall not shrink from it. I never do that.'

'She strikes me as very natural,' said Ralph.

'Natural people are not the most trouble.'

'No,' said Ralph; 'you yourself are a proof of that. You're extremely natural, and I'm sure you have never troubled anyone. It *takes* trouble to do that. But tell me this; it just occurs to me. Is Isabel capable of making herself disagreeable?'

'Ah,' cried his mother, 'you ask too many questions! Find that out for yourself.'

His questions, however, were not exhausted. 'All this time,' he said, 'you've not told me what you intend to do with her.'

'Do with her? You talk as if she were a yard of calico. I shall do absolutely nothing with her, and she herself will do everything she chooses. She gave me notice of that.'

'What you meant then, in your telegram, was that her character's independent.'

'I never know what I mean in my telegrams – especially those I send from America. Clearness is too expensive. Come down to your father.'

'It's not yet a quarter to eight,' said Ralph.

'I must allow for his impatience,' Mrs Touchett answered.

Ralph knew what to think of his father's impatience; but, making no rejoinder, he offered his mother his arm. This put it in his power, as they descended together, to stop her a moment on the middle landing of the staircase – the broad, low, wide-armed staircase of time-blackened oak which was one of the most striking features of Gardencourt. 'You've no plan of marrying her?' he smiled.

'Marrying her? I should be sorry to play her such a trick! But apart from that, she's perfectly able to marry herself. She has every facility.'

'Do you mean to say she has a husband picked out?'

'I don't know about a husband, but there's a young man in Boston—!'

Ralph went on; he had no desire to hear about the young man in Boston. 'As my father says, they're always engaged!'

His mother had told him that he must satisfy his curiosity at the source, and it soon became evident he should not want for occasion. He had a good deal of talk with his young kinswoman when the two had been left together in the drawing-room. Lord Warburton, who had ridden over from his own house, some ten miles distant, remounted and took his departure before dinner; and an hour after this meal was ended Mr and Mrs Touchett, who appeared to have quite emptied the measure of their forms, withdrew, under the valid pretext of fatigue, to their respective apartments. The young man spent an hour with his cousin; though she had been travelling half the day she appeared in no degree spent. She was really tired; she knew it, and knew she should pay for it on the morrow; but it was her habit at this period to carry exhaustion to the furthest point and confess to it only when dissimulation broke down. A fine hypocrisy was for the present possible; she was interested; she was, as she said to herself, floated. She asked Ralph to show her the pictures; there were a great many in the house, most of them of his own choosing. The best were arranged in an oaken gallery, of charming proportions, which had a sitting-room at either end of it and which in the evening was usually lighted. The light was insufficient to show the pictures to advantage, and the visit might have stood over to the morrow. This suggestion Ralph had ventured to make; but Isabel looked disappointed – smiling still, however – and said: 'If you please I should like to see them just a little.' She was eager, she knew she was eager and now seemed so; she couldn't help it. 'She doesn't take suggestions,' Ralph said to himself; but he said it without irritation; her pressure amused and even pleased him. The lamps were on brackets, at intervals, and if the light was imperfect it was genial. It fell upon the vague squares of rich colour and on the faded gilding of heavy frames; it made a sheen on the polished floor of the gallery. Ralph took a candlestick and moved about, pointing out the things he liked; Isabel, inclining to one picture after another, indulged in little exclamations and murmurs. She was evidently a judge; she had a natural taste; he was struck with that. She took a candlestick herself and held it slowly here and there; she lifted it high, and as she did so he found himself pausing in the middle of the place and bending his eyes much less upon the pictures than on her presence. He lost nothing, in truth, by these wandering glances, for she was better worth looking at than most works of art. She was undeniably spare, and ponderably light, and provably tall; when people had wished to distinguish her from the other two Miss Archers they had always called her the willowy one. Her hair, which was dark even to blackness, had been an object of envy to many women; her light grey eyes, a little too firm perhaps in her graver moments, had an enchanting range of concession. They walked slowly up one side of the gallery and down the other, and then she said: 'Well, now I know more than I did when I began!'

'You apparently have a great passion for knowledge,' her cousin returned.

'I think I have; most girls are horridly ignorant.'

'You strike me as different from most girls.'

'Ah, some of them *would* – but the way they're talked to!' murmured Isabel, who preferred not to dilate just yet on herself. Then in a moment, to change the subject, 'Please tell me – isn't there a ghost?' she went on.

'A ghost?'

'A castle-spectre, a thing that appears. We call them ghosts in America.'

'So we do here, when we see them.'

'You do see them then? You ought to, in this romantic old house.'

'It's not a romantic old house,' said Ralph. 'You'll be disappointed if you count on that. It's a dismally prosaic one; there's no romance here but what you may have brought with you.'

'I've brought a great deal; but it seems to me I've brought it to the right place.'

'To keep it out of harm, certainly; nothing will ever happen to it here, between my father and me.'

Isabel looked at him a moment. 'Is there never anyone here but your father and you?'

'My mother, of course.'

'Oh, I know your mother; she's not romantic. Haven't you other people?'

'Very few.'

'I'm sorry for that; I like so much to see people.'

'Oh, we'll invite all the county to amuse you,' said Ralph.

'Now you're making fun of me,' the girl answered rather gravely. 'Who was the gentleman on the lawn when I arrived?'

'A county neighbour; he doesn't come very often.'

'I'm sorry for that; I liked him,' said Isabel.

'Why, it seemed to me that you barely spoke to him,' Ralph objected.

'Never mind, I like him all the same. I like your father too, immensely.'

'You can't do better than that. He's the dearest of the dear.'

'I'm so sorry he is ill,' said Isabel.

'You must help me to nurse him; you ought to be a good nurse.'

'I don't think I am; I've been told I'm not; I'm said to have too many theories. But you haven't told me about the ghost,' she added.

Ralph, however, gave no heed to this observation. 'You like my father and you like Lord Warburton. I infer also that you like my mother.'

'I like your mother very much, because – because—' And Isabel found herself attempting to assign a reason for her affection for Mrs Touchett.

'Ah, we never know why!' said her companion, laughing.

'I always know why,' the girl answered. 'It's because she doesn't expect one to like her. She doesn't care whether one does or not.'

'So you adore her – out of perversity? Well, I take greatly after my mother,' said Ralph.

'I don't believe you do at all. You wish people to like you, and you try to make them do it.'

'Good heavens, how you see through one!' he cried with a dismay that was not altogether jocular.

'But I like you all the same,' his cousin went on. 'The way to clinch the matter will be to show me the ghost.'

Ralph shook his head sadly. 'I might show it to you, but you'd never see it. The privilege isn't given to everyone; it's not enviable. It has never been seen by a young, happy, innocent person like you. You must have suffered first, have suffered greatly, have gained some miserable knowledge. In that way your eyes are opened to it. I saw it long ago,' said Ralph.

'I told you just now I'm very fond of knowledge,' Isabel answered.

'Yes, of happy knowledge – of pleasant knowledge. But you haven't suffered, and you're not made to suffer. I hope you'll never see the ghost!'

She had listened to him attentively, with a smile on her lips, but with a certain gravity in her eyes. Charming as he found her, she had struck him as rather presumptuous – indeed it was a part of her charm; and he wondered what she would say. 'I'm not afraid, you know,' she said: which seemed quite presumptuous enough.

'You're not afraid of suffering?'

'Yes, I'm afraid of suffering. But I'm not afraid of ghosts. And I think people suffer too easily,' she added.

'I don't believe *you* do,' said Ralph, looking at her with his hands in his pockets.

'I don't think that's a fault,' she answered. 'It's not absolutely necessary to suffer; we were not made for that.'

'You were not, certainly.'

'I'm not speaking of myself.' And she wandered off a little.

'No, it isn't a fault,' said her cousin. 'It's a merit to be strong.'

'Only, if you don't suffer they call you hard,' Isabel remarked.

They passed out of the smaller drawing-room, into which they had returned from the gallery, and paused in the hall, at the foot of the staircase. Here Ralph presented his companion with her bedroom candle, which he had taken from a niche. 'Never mind what they call you. When you do suffer they call you an idiot. The great point's to be as happy as possible.'

She looked at him a little; she had taken her candle and placed her foot on the oaken stair. 'Well,' she said, 'that's what I came to Europe for, to be as happy as possible. Good night.'

'Good night! I wish you all success, and shall be very glad to contribute to it!'

She turned away, and he watched her as she slowly ascended. Then, with his hands always in his pockets, he went back to the empty drawing-room.

Chapter Six

Isabel Archer was a young person of many theories; her imagination was remarkably active. It had been her fortune to possess a finer mind than most of the persons among whom her lot was cast; to have a larger perception of surrounding facts and to care for knowledge that was tinged with the unfamiliar. It is true that among her contemporaries she passed for a young woman of extraordinary profundity; for these excellent people never withheld their admiration from a reach of intellect of which they themselves were not conscious, and spoke of Isabel as a prodigy of learning, a creature reported to have read the classic authors – in translations. Her paternal aunt, Mrs Varian, once spread the rumour that Isabel was writing a book – Mrs Varian having a reverence for books – and averred that the girl would distinguish herself in print. Mrs Varian thought highly of literature, for which she entertained that esteem that is connected with a sense of privation. Her own large house, remarkable for its assortment of mosaic tables and decorated ceilings, was unfurnished with a library, and in the way of printed volumes contained nothing but half a dozen novels in paper on a shelf in the apartment of one of the Miss Varians. Practically, Mrs Varian's acquaintance with literature was confined to the New York *Interviewer*; as she very justly said, after you had read the *Interviewer* you had lost all faith in culture. Her tendency, with this, was rather to keep the *Interviewer* out of the way of her daughters; she was determined to bring them up properly, and they read nothing at all. Her impression with regard to Isabel's labours was quite illusory; the girl had never attempted to write a book and had no desire for the laurels of authorship. She had no talent for expression and too little of the consciousness of genius; she only had a general idea that people were right when they treated her as if she were rather superior. Whether or not she were superior, people were right in admiring her if they thought her so; for it seemed to her often that her mind moved more quickly than theirs, and this encouraged an impatience they might easily be confounded with superiority. It may be affirmed without delay that Isabel was probably very liable to the sin of self-esteem; she often surveyed with complacency the field of her own nature; she was in the habit of taking for granted, on scanty evidence, that she was right; she treated herself to occasions of homage. Meanwhile her errors and delusions were frequently such as a biographer interested in preserving the dignity of his subject must shrink from specifying. Her thoughts were a tangle of vague outlines which had never been corrected by the judgement of people speaking with authority. In matters of opinion she had had her own way, and it had led her into a thousand ridiculous zigzags. At moments she discovered she was grotesquely wrong, and then she treated herself to a week of passionate humility. After this she held her head higher than ever again; for it was of no use, she had an unquenchable desire to think well of herself. She had a theory that it was only under this provision life was worth living; that one should be one of the best, should be conscious of a fine organization (she couldn't help knowing her organization was fine), should move in a realm of light, of natural wisdom, of happy impulse, of inspiration gracefully chronic. It was almost as unnecessary to cultivate doubt of one's self as to cultivate doubt of one's best friend: one should try to be one's own best friend and to give one's self, in this manner, distinguished company. The girl had a certain nobleness of imagination which rendered her a good many services and played her a great many tricks. She spent half her time in thinking of beauty and bravery and magnanimity; she had a fixed determination to regard the world as a place of brightness, of free expansion, of irresistible action: she held it must be detestable to be afraid or ashamed. She had an infinite hope that she should never do anything wrong. She had resented so strongly, after discovering them, her mere errors of feeling (the discovery always made her tremble as if she had escaped from a trap which might have caught her and smothered her) that the chance of inflicting a sensible injury upon another person, presented only as a contingency, caused her at moments to hold her breath. That always struck her as the worst thing that could happen to her. On the whole, reflectively, she was in no uncertainty about the things that were wrong. She had no love of their look, but when she fixed them hard she recognized them. It was wrong to be mean, to be jealous, to be false, to be cruel; she had seen very little of the evil of the world, but she had seen women who lied and who tried to hurt each other. Seeing such things had quickened her high spirit; it seemed indecent not to scorn them. Of course the danger of a high spirit was the danger of inconsistency – the danger of keeping up the flag after the place has surrendered; a sort of behaviour so crooked as to be almost a dishonour to the flag. But Isabel, who knew little of the sorts of artillery to which young women are exposed, flattered herself that such contradictions would never be noted in her own conduct. Her life should always be in harmony with the most pleasing impression she should produce; she would be what she appeared, and she would appear what she was. Sometimes she went so far as to wish that she might find herself some day in a difficult position, so that she should have the pleasure of being as heroic as the occasion demanded. Altogether, with her meagre knowledge, her inflated ideals, her confidence at once innocent and dogmatic, her temper at once exacting and indulgent, her mixture of curiosity and fastidiousness, of vivacity and indifference, her desire to look very well and to be if possible even better, her determination to see, to try, to know, her combination of the delicate, desultory, flame-like spirit and the eager and personal creature of conditions: she would be an easy victim of scientific criticism if she were not intended to awaken on the reader's part an impulse more tender and more purely expectant.

It was one of her theories that Isabel Archer was very fortunate in being independent, and that she ought to make some very enlightened use of that state. She never called it the state of solitude, much less of singleness; she thought such descriptions weak, and, besides, her sister Lily constantly urged her to come and abide. She had a friend whose acquaintance she had made shortly before her father's death, who offered so high an example of useful activity that Isabel always thought of her as a model. Henrietta Stackpole had the advantage of an admired ability; she was thoroughly launched in journalism, and her letters to the *Interviewer*, from Washington, Newport, the White Mountains, and other places, were universally quoted. Isabel pronounced them with confidence 'ephemeral', but she esteemed the courage, energy and good-humour of the writer, who, without parents and without property, had adopted three of the children of an infirm and widowed sister and was paying their school-bills out of the proceeds of her literary labour. Henrietta was in the van of progress and had clear-cut views on most subjects; her cherished desire had long been to come to Europe and write a series of letters to the *Interviewer* from the radical point of view – an enterprise the less difficult as she knew perfectly in advance what her opinions would be and to how many objections most European institutions lay open. When she heard that Isabel was coming she wished to start at once; thinking, naturally, that it would be delightful the two should travel together. She had been obliged, however, to postpone this enterprise. She thought Isabel a glorious creature, and had spoken of her covertly in some of her letters, though she never mentioned the fact to her friend, who would not have taken pleasure in it and was not a regular student of the *Interviewer*. Henrietta, for Isabel, was chiefly a proof that a woman might suffice to herself and be happy. Her resources were of the obvious kind; but even if one had not the journalistic talent and a genius for guessing, as Henrietta said, what the public was going to want, one was not therefore to conclude that one had no vocation, no beneficent aptitude of any sort, and resign one's self to being frivolous and hollow. Isabel was stoutly determined not to be hollow. If one should wait with the right patience one would find some happy work to one's hand. Of course, among her theories, this young lady was not without a collection of views on the subject of marriage. The first on the list was a conviction of the vulgarity of thinking too much of it. From lapsing into eagerness on this point she earnestly prayed she might be delivered; she held that a woman ought to be able to live to herself, in the absence of exceptional flimsiness, and that it was perfectly possible to be happy without the society of a more or less coarse-minded person of another sex. The girl's prayer was very sufficiently answered; something pure and proud that there was in her – something cold and dry an unappreciated suitor with a taste for analysis might have called it – had hitherto kept her from any great vanity of conjecture on the article of possible husbands. Few of the men she saw seemed worth a ruinous expenditure, and it made her smile to think that one of them should present himself as an incentive to hope and a reward of patience. Deep in her soul – it was the deepest thing there – lay a belief that if a certain light should dawn she could give herself completely; but this image, on the whole, was too formidable to be attractive. Isabel's thoughts hovered about it, but they seldom rested on it long; after a little it ended in alarms. It often seemed to her that she thought too much about herself; you could have made her colour, any day in the year, by calling her a rank egoist. She was always planning out her development, desiring her perfection, observing her progress. Her nature had, in her conceit, a certain garden-like quality, a suggestion of perfume and murmuring boughs, of shady bowers and lengthening vistas, which made her feel that introspection was, after all, an exercise in the open air, and that a visit to the recesses of one's spirit was harmless when one returned from it with a lapful of roses. But she was often reminded that there were other gardens in the world than those of her remarkable soul, and that there were moreover a great many places which were not gardens at all – only dusky pestiferous tracts, planted thick with ugliness and misery. In the current of that repaid curiosity on which she had lately been floating, which had conveyed her to this beautiful old England and might carry her much further still, she often checked herself with the thought of the thousands of people who were less happy than herself – a thought which for the moment made her fine, full consciousness appear a kind of immodesty. What should one do with the misery of the world in a scheme of the agreeable for one's self? It must be confessed that this question never held her long. She was too young, too impatient to live, too unacquainted with pain. She always returned to her theory that a young woman whom after all everyone thought clever should begin by getting a general impression of life. This impression was necessary to prevent mistakes, and after it should be secured she might make the unfortunate condition of others a subject of special attention.

England was a revelation to her, and she found herself as diverted as a child at a pantomime. In her infantine excursions to Europe she had seen only the Continent, and seen it from the nursery window; Paris, not London, was her father's Mecca, and into many of his interests there his children had naturally not entered. The images of that time moreover had grown faint and remote, and the old-world quality in everything that she now saw had all the charm of strangeness. Her uncle's house seemed a picture made real; no refinement of the agreeable was lost upon Isabel; the rich perfection of Gardencourt at once revealed a world and gratified a need. The large, low rooms, with brown ceilings and dusky corners, the deep embrasures and curious casements, the quiet light on dark, polished panels, the deep greenness outside, that seemed always peeping in, the sense of well-ordered privacy in the centre of a 'property' – a place where sounds were felicitously accidental, where the tread was muffled by the earth itself and in the thick mild air all friction dropped out of contact and all shrillness out of talk – these things were much to the taste of our young lady, whose taste played a considerable part in her emotions. She formed a fast friendship with her uncle, and often sat by his chair when he had had it moved out to the lawn. He passed hours in the open air, sitting with folded hands like a placid, homely, household god, a god of service, who had done his work and received his wages and was trying to grow used to weeks and months made up only of off-days. Isabel amused him more than she suspected – the effect she produced upon people was often different from what she supposed – and he frequently gave himself the pleasure of making her chatter. It was by this term that he qualified her conversation, which had much of the 'point' observable in that of the young ladies of her country, to whom the ear of the world is more directly presented than to their sisters in other lands. Like the mass of American girls Isabel had been encouraged to express herself; her remarks had been attended to; she had been expected to have emotions and opinions. Many of her opinions had doubtless but a slender value, many of her emotions passed away in the utterance; but they had left a trace in giving her the habit of seeming at least to feel and think, and in imparting moreover to her words when she was really moved that prompt vividness which so many people had regarded as a sign of superiority. Mr Touchett used to think that she reminded him of his wife when his wife was in her teens. It was because she was fresh and natural and quick to understand, to speak – so many characteristics of her niece – that he had fallen in love with Mrs Touchett. He never expressed this analogy to the girl herself, however; for if Mrs Touchett had once been like Isabel, Isabel was not at all like Mrs Touchett. The old man was full of kindness for her; it was a long time, as he said, since they had had any young life in the house; and our rustling, quickly-moving, clear-voiced heroine was as agreeable to his sense as the sound of flowing water. He wanted to do something for her and wished she would ask it of him. She would ask nothing but questions; it is true that of these she asked a quantity. Her uncle had a great fund of answers, though her pressure sometimes came in forms that puzzled him. She questioned him immensely about England, about the British constitution, the English character, the state of politics, the manners and customs of the royal family, the peculiarities of the aristocracy, the way of living and thinking of his neighbours; and in begging to be enlightened on these points she usually inquired whether they corresponded with the descriptions in the books. The old man always looked at her a little with his fine dry smile while he smoothed down the shawl spread across his legs.

'The books?' he once said; 'well, I don't know much about the books. You must ask Ralph about that. I've always ascertained for myself – got my information in the natural form. I never asked many questions even; I just kept quiet and took notice. Of course I've had very good opportunities – better than what a young lady would naturally have. I'm of an inquisitive disposition, though you mightn't think it if you were to watch me: however much you might watch me I should be watching you more. I've been watching these people for upwards of thirty-five years, and I don't hesitate to say that I've acquired considerable information. It's a very fine country on the whole – finer perhaps than what we give it credit for on the other side. There are several improvements I should like to see introduced; but the necessity of them doesn't seem to be generally felt as yet. When the necessity of a thing is generally felt they usually manage to accomplish it; but they seem to feel pretty comfortable about waiting till then. I certainly feel more at home among them than I expected to when I first came over; I suppose it's because I've had a considerable degree of success. When you're successful you naturally feel more at home.'

'Do you suppose that if I'm successful I shall feel at home?' Isabel asked.

'I should think it very probable, and you certainly will be successful. They like American young ladies very much over here; they show them a great deal of kindness. But you mustn't feel too much at home, you know.'

'Oh, I'm by no means sure it will *satisfy* me,' Isabel judicially emphasized. 'I like the place very much, but I'm not sure I shall like the people.'

'The people are very good people; especially if you like them.'

'I've no doubt they're good,' Isabel rejoined; 'but are they pleasant in society? They won't rob me or beat me; but will they make themselves agreeable to me? That's what I like people to do. I don't hesitate to say so, because I always appreciate it. I don't believe they're very nice to girls; they're not nice to them in the novels.'

'I don't know about the novels,' said Mr Touchett. 'I believe the novels have a great deal of ability, but I don't suppose they're very accurate. We once had a lady who wrote novels staying here; she was a friend of Ralph's and he asked her down. She was very positive, quite up to everything; but she was not the sort of person you could depend on for evidence. Too free a fancy – I suppose that was it. She afterwards published a work of fiction in which she was understood to have given a representation – something in the nature of a caricature, as you might say – of my unworthy self. I didn't read it, but Ralph just handed me the book with the principal passages marked. It was understood to be a description of my conversation; American peculiarities, nasal twang, Yankee notions, stars and stripes. Well, it was not at all accurate; she couldn't have listened very attentively. I had no objection to her giving a report of my conversation, if she liked; but I didn't like the idea that she hadn't taken the trouble to listen to it. Of course I talk like an American – I can't talk like a Hottentot. However I talk, I've made them understand me pretty well over here. But I don't talk like the old gentleman in that lady's novel. He wasn't an American; we wouldn't have him over there at any price. I just mention the fact to show you that they're not always accurate. Of course, as I've no daughters, and as Mrs Touchett resides in Florence, I haven't had much chance to notice about the young ladies. It sometimes appears as if the young women in the lower class were not very well treated; but I guess their position is better in the upper and even to some extent in the middle.'

'Gracious,' Isabel exclaimed; 'how many classes have they? About fifty, I suppose.'

'Well, I don't know that I ever counted them. I never took much notice of the classes. That's the advantage of being an American here; you don't belong to any class.'

'I hope so,' said Isabel. 'Imagine one's belonging to an English class!'

'Well, I guess some of them are pretty comfortable – especially towards the top. But for me there are only two classes: the people I trust and the people I don't. Of those two, my dear Isabel, you belong to the first.'

'I'm much obliged to you,' said the girl quickly. Her way of taking compliments seemed sometimes rather dry; she got rid of them as rapidly as possible. But as regards this she was sometimes misjudged, she was thought insensible to them, whereas in fact she was simply unwilling to show how infinitely they pleased her. To show that was to show too much. 'I'm sure the English are very conventional,' she added.

'They've got everything pretty well fixed,' Mr Touchett admitted. 'It's all settled beforehand – they don't leave it to the last moment.'

'I don't like to have everything settled beforehand,' said the girl. 'I like more unexpectedness.'

Her uncle seemed amused at her distinctness of preference. 'Well, it's settled beforehand that you'll have great success,' he rejoined. 'I suppose you'll like that.'

'I shall not have success if they're too stupidly conventional. I'm not in the least stupidly conventional. I'm just the contrary. That's what they won't like.'

'No, no, you're all wrong,' said the old man. 'You can't tell what they'll like. They're very inconsistent; that's their principal interest.'

'Ah well,' said Isabel, standing before her uncle with her hands clasped about the belt of her black dress and looking up and down the lawn – 'that will suit me perfectly!'

Chapter Seven

The two amused themselves, time and again, with talking of the attitude of the British public as if the young lady had been in a position to appeal to it; but in fact the British public remained for the present profoundly indifferent to Miss Isabel Archer, whose fortune had dropped her, as her cousin said, into the dullest house in England. Her gouty uncle received very little company, and Mrs Touchett, not having cultivated relations with her husband's neighbours, was not warranted in expecting visits from them. She had, however, a peculiar taste; she liked to receive cards. For what is usually called social intercourse she had very little relish; but nothing pleased her more than to find her hall table whitened with oblong morsels of symbolic pasteboard. She flattered herself that she was a very just woman, and had mastered the sovereign truth that nothing in this world is got for nothing. She had played no social part as mistress of Gardencourt, and it was not to be supposed that, in the surrounding country, a minute account should be kept of her comings and goings. But it is by no means certain that she did not feel it to be wrong that so little notice was taken of them and that her failure (really very gratuitous) to make herself important in the neighbourhood had not much to do with the acrimony of her allusions to her husband's adopted country. Isabel presently found herself in the singular situation of defending the British constitution against her aunt; Mrs Touchett having formed the habit of sticking pins into this venerable instrument. Isabel always felt an impulse to pull out the pins; not that she imagined they inflicted any damage on the tough old parchment, but because it seemed to her her aunt might make better use of her sharpness. She was very critical herself – it was incidental to her age, her sex, and her nationality; but she was very sentimental as well, and there was something in Mrs Touchett's dryness that set her own moral fountains flowing.

'Now what's your point of view?' she asked of her aunt. 'When you criticize everything here you should have a point of view. Yours doesn't seem to be American – you thought everything over there so disagreeable. When I criticize I have mine; it's thoroughly American!'

'My dear young lady,' said Mrs Touchett, 'there are as many points of view in the world as there are people of sense to take them. You may say that doesn't make them very numerous! American? Never in the world; that's shockingly narrow. My point of view, thank God, is personal!'

Isabel thought this a better answer than she admitted; it was a tolerable description of her own manner of judging, but it would not have sounded well for her to say so. On the lips of a person less advanced in life and less enlightened by experience than Mrs Touchett such a declaration would savour of immodesty, even of arrogance. She risked it nevertheless in talking with Ralph, with whom she talked a great deal and with whom her conversation was of a sort that gave a large licence to extravagance. Her cousin used, as the phrase is, to chaff her; he very soon established with her a reputation for treating everything as a joke, and he was not a man to neglect the privileges such a reputation conferred. She accused him of an odious want of seriousness, of laughing at all things, beginning with himself. Such slender faculty of reverence as he possessed centred wholly upon his father; for the rest, he exercised his wit indifferently upon his father's son, this gentleman's weak lungs, his useless life, his fantastic mother, his friends (Lord Warburton in especial), his adopted, and his native country, his charming new-found cousin. 'I keep a band of music in my ante-room,' he said once to her. 'It has orders to play without stopping; it renders me two excellent services. It keeps the sounds of the world from reaching the private apartments, and it makes the world think that dancing's going on within.' It was dance-music indeed that you usually heard when you came within ear-shot of Ralph's band; the liveliest waltzes seemed to float upon the air. Isabel often found herself irritated by this perpetual fiddling; she would have liked to pass through the ante-room, as her cousin called it, and enter the private apartments. It mattered little that he had assured her they were a very dismal place; she would have been glad to undertake to sweep them and set them in order. It was but half-hospitality to let her remain outside; to punish him for which Isabel administered innumerable taps with the ferule of her straight young wit. It must be said that her wit was exercised to a large extent in self-defence, for her cousin amused himself with calling her 'Columbia' and accusing her of a patriotism so heated that it scorched. He drew a caricature of her in which she was represented as a very pretty young woman dressed, on the lines of the prevailing fashion, in the folds of the national banner. Isabel's chief dread in life at this period of her development was that she should appear narrow-minded; what she feared next afterwards was that she should really be so. But she nevertheless made no scruple of abounding in her cousin's sense and pretending to sigh for the charms of her native land. She would be as American as it pleased him to regard her, and if he chose to laugh at her she would give him plenty of occupation. She defended England against his mother, but when Ralph sang its praises on purpose, as she said, to work her up, she found herself able to differ from him on a variety of points. In fact, the quality of this small ripe country seemed as sweet to her as the taste of an October pear; and her satisfaction was at the root of the good spirits which enabled her to take her cousin's chaff and return it in kind. If her good humour flagged at moments it was not because she thought herself ill-used, but because she suddenly felt sorry for Ralph. It seemed to her he was talking as a blind and had little heart in what he said.

'I don't know what's the matter with you,' she observed to him once; 'but I suspect you're a great humbug.'

'That's your privilege,' Ralph answered, who had not been used to being so crudely addressed.

'I don't know what you care for; I don't think you care for anything. You don't really care for England when you praise it; you don't care for America even when you pretend to abuse it.'

'I care for nothing but you, dear cousin,' said Ralph.

'If I could believe even that, I should be very glad.'

'Ah well, I should hope so!' the young man exclaimed.

Isabel might have believed it and not have been far from the truth. He thought a great deal about her; she was constantly present to his mind. At a time when his thoughts had been a good deal of a burden to him her sudden arrival, which promised nothing and was an open-handed gift of fate, had refreshed and quickened them, given them wings and something to fly for. Poor Ralph had been for many weeks steeped in melancholy; his outlook, habitually sombre, lay under the shadow of a deeper cloud. He had grown anxious about his father, whose gout, hitherto confined to his legs, had begun to ascend into regions more vital. The old man had been gravely ill in the spring, and the doctors had whispered to Ralph that another attack would be less easy to deal with. Just now he appeared disburdened of pain, but Ralph could not rid himself of a suspicion that this was a subterfuge of the enemy, who was waiting to take him off his guard. If the manoeuvre should succeed there would be little hope of any great resistance. Ralph had always taken for granted that his father would survive him – that his own name would be the first grimly called. The father and son had been close companions, and the idea of being left alone with the remnant of a tasteless life on his hands was not gratifying to the young man, who had always and tacitly counted upon his elder's help in making the best of a poor business. At the prospect of losing his great motive Ralph lost indeed his one inspiration. If they might die at the same time it would be all very well; but without the encouragement of his father's society he should barely have patience to await his own turn. He had not the incentive of feeling that he was indispensable to his mother; it was a rule with his mother to have no regrets. He bethought himself of course that it had been a small kindness to his father to wish that, of the two, the active rather than the passive party should know the felt wound; he remembered that the old man had always treated his own forecast of an early end as a clever fallacy, which he should be delighted to discredit so far as he might by dying first. But of the two triumphs, that of refuting a sophistical son and that of holding on a while longer to a state of being which, with all abatements, he enjoyed, Ralph deemed it no sin to hope the latter might be vouchsafed to Mr Touchett.

These were nice questions, but Isabel's arrival put a stop to his puzzling over them. It even suggested there might be a compensation for the intolerable ennui of surviving his genial sire. He wondered whether he were harbouring 'love' for this spontaneous young woman from Albany; but he judged that on the whole he was not. After he had known her for a week he quite made up his mind to this, and every day he felt a little more sure. Lord Warburton had been right about her; she was a really interesting little figure. Ralph wondered how their neighbour had found it out so soon; and then he said it was only another proof of his friend's high abilities, which he had always greatly admired. If his cousin were to be nothing more than an entertainment to him, Ralph was conscious she was an entertainment of a high order. 'A character like that,' he said to himself – 'a real little passionate force to see at play is the finest thing in nature. It's finer than the finest work of art – than a Greek bas-relief, than a great Titian, than a Gothic cathedral. It's very pleasant to be so well treated where one had least looked for it. I had never been more blue, more bored, than for a week before she came; I had never expected less that anything pleasant would happen. Suddenly I receive a Titian, by the post, to hang on my wall – a Greek bas-relief to stick over my chimney-piece. The key of a beautiful edifice is thrust into my hand, and I'm told to walk in and admire. My poor boy, you've been sadly ungrateful, and now you had better keep very quiet and never grumble again.' The sentiment of these reflections was very just; but it was not exactly true that Ralph Touchett had had a key put into his hand. His cousin was a very brilliant girl, who would take, as he said, a good deal of knowing; but she needed the knowing, and his attitude with regard to her, though it was contemplative and critical, was not judicial. He surveyed the edifice from the outside and admired it greatly; he looked in at the windows and received an impression of proportions equally fair. But he felt that he saw it only by glimpses and that he had not yet stood under the roof. The door was fastened, and though he had keys in his pocket he had a conviction that none of them would fit. She was intelligent and generous; it was a fine free nature; but what was she going to do with herself? This question was irregular, for with most women one had no occasion to ask it. Most women did with themselves nothing at all; they waited, in attitudes more or less gracefully passive, for a man to come that way and furnish them with a destiny. Isabel's originality was that she gave one an impression of having intentions of her own. 'Whenever she executes them,' said Ralph, 'may I be there to see!'

It devolved upon him of course to do the honours of the place. Mr Touchett was confined to his chair, and his wife's position was that of rather a grim visitor; so that in the line of conduct that opened itself to Ralph duty and inclination were harmoniously mixed. He was not a great walker, but he strolled about the grounds with his cousin – a pastime for which the weather remained favourable with a persistency not allowed for in Isabel's somewhat lugubrious prevision of the climate; and in the long afternoons, of which the length was but the measure of her gratified eagerness, they took a boat on the river, the dear little river, as Isabel called it, where the opposite shore seemed still a part of the foreground of the landscape; or drove over the country in a phaeton – a low, capacious, thick-wheeled phaeton formerly much used by Mr Touchett, but which he had now ceased to enjoy. Isabel enjoyed it largely and, handling the reins in a manner which approved itself to the groom as 'knowing', was never weary of driving her uncle's capital horses through winding lanes and byways full of the rural incidents she had confidently expected to find; past cottages thatched and timbered, past ale-houses latticed and sanded, past patches of an ancient common and glimpses of empty parks, between hedgerows made thick by midsummer. When they reached home they usually found tea had been served on the lawn and that Mrs Touchett had not shrunk from the extremity of handing her husband his cup. But the two for the most part sat silent; the old man with his head back and his eyes closed, his wife occupied with her knitting and wearing that appearance of rare profundity with which some ladies consider the movement of their needles.

One day, however, a visitor had arrived. The two young persons, after spending an hour on the river, strolled back to the house and perceived Lord Warburton sitting under the trees and engaged in conversation, of which even at a distance the desultory character was appreciable, with Mrs Touchett. He had driven over from his own place with a portmanteau and had asked, as the father and son often invited him to do, for a dinner and a lodging. Isabel, seeing him for half an hour on the day of her arrival, had discovered in this brief space that she liked him; he had indeed rather sharply registered himself on her fine sense and she had thought of him several times. She had hoped she should see him again – hoped too that she should see a few others. Gardencourt was not dull; the place itself was sovereign, her uncle was more and more a sort of golden grandfather, and Ralph was unlike any cousin she had ever encountered – her idea of cousins having tended to gloom. Then her impressions were still so fresh and so quickly renewed that there was as yet hardly a hint of vacancy in the view. But Isabel had need to remind herself that she was interested in human nature and that her foremost hope in coming abroad had been that she should see a great many people. When Ralph said to her, as he had done several times, 'I wonder you find this endurable; you ought to see some of the neighbours and some of our friends, because we have really got a few, though you would never suppose it' – when he offered to invite what he called a 'lot of people' and make her acquainted with English society, she encouraged the hospitable impulse and promised in advance to hurl herself into the fray. Little however, for the present, had come of his offers, and it may be confided to the reader that if the young man delayed to carry them out it was because he found the labour of providing for his companion by no means so severe as to require extraneous help. Isabel had spoken to him very often about 'specimens', it was a word that played a considerable part in her vocabulary; she had given him to understand that she wished to see English society illustrated by eminent cases.

'Well now, there's a specimen,' he said to her as they walked up from the riverside and he recognized Lord Warburton.

'A specimen of what?' asked the girl.

'A specimen of an English gentleman.'

'Do you mean they're all like him?'

'Oh no; they're not all like him.'

'He's a favourable specimen then,' said Isabel; 'because I'm sure he's nice.'

'Yes, he's very nice. And he's very fortunate.'

The fortunate Lord Warburton exchanged a handshake with our heroine and hoped she was very well. 'But I needn't ask that,' he said, 'since you've been handling the oars.'

'I've been rowing a little,' Isabel answered; 'but how should you know it?'

'Oh, I know *he* doesn't row; he's too lazy,' said his lordship, indicating Ralph Touchett with a laugh.

'He has a good excuse for his laziness,' Isabel rejoined, lowering her voice a little.

'Ah, he has a good excuse for everything!' cried Lord Warburton, still with his sonorous mirth.

'My excuse for not rowing is that my cousin rows so well,' said Ralph. 'She does everything well. She touches nothing that she doesn't adorn!'

'It makes one want to be touched, Miss Archer,' Lord Warburton declared.

'Be touched in the right sense and you'll never look the worse for it,' said Isabel, who, if it pleased her to hear it said that her accomplishments were numerous, was happily able to reflect that such complacency was not the indication of a feeble mind, inasmuch as there were several things in which she excelled. Her desire to think well of herself had at least the element of humility that it always needed to be supported by proof.

Lord Warburton not only spent the night at Gardencourt, but he was persuaded to remain over the second day; and when the second day was ended he determined to postpone his departure till the morrow. During this period he addressed many of his remarks to Isabel, who accepted this evidence of his esteem with a very good grace. She found herself liking him extremely; the first impression he had made on her had had weight, but at the end of an evening spent in his society she scarce fell short of seeing him – though quite without luridity – as a hero of romance. She retired to rest with a sense of good fortune, with a quickened consciousness of possible felicities. 'It's very nice to know two such charming people as those,' she said, meaning by 'those' her cousin and her cousin's friend. It must be added moreover that an incident had occurred which might have seemed to put her good humour to the test. Mr Touchett went to bed at half past nine o'clock, but his wife remained in the drawing-room with the other members of the party. She prolonged her vigil for something less than an hour, and then, rising, observed to Isabel that it was time they should bid the gentlemen good night. Isabel had as yet no desire to go to bed; the occasion wore, to her sense, a festive character, and feasts were not in the habit of terminating so early. So, without further thought, she replied, very simply:

'Need I go, dear aunt? I'll come up in half an hour.'

'It's impossible I should wait for you,' Mrs Touchett answered.

'Ah, you needn't wait! Ralph will light my candle,' Isabel gaily engaged.

'I'll light your candle; do let me light your candle, Miss Archer!' Lord Warburton exclaimed. 'Only I beg it shall not be before midnight.'

Mrs Touchett fixed her bright little eyes upon him a moment and transferred them coldly to her niece. 'You can't stay alone with the gentlemen. You're not – you're not at your blest Albany, my dear.'

Isabel rose, blushing. 'I wish I were,' she said.

'Oh, I say, mother!' Ralph broke out.

'My dear Mrs Touchett!' Lord Warburton murmured.

'I didn't make your country, my lord,' Mrs Touchett said majestically. 'I must take it as I find it.'

'Can't I stay with my own cousin?' Isabel inquired.

'I'm not aware that Lord Warburton is your cousin.'

'Perhaps *I* had better go to bed!' the visitor suggested. 'That will arrange it.'

Mrs Touchett gave a little look of despair and sat down again. 'Oh, if it's necessary I'll stay up till midnight.'

Ralph meanwhile handed Isabel her candlestick. He had been watching her; it had seemed to him her temper was involved – an accident that might be interesting. But if he had expected anything of a flare he was disappointed, for the girl simply laughed a little, nodded good night, and withdrew accompanied by her aunt. For himself he was annoyed at his mother, though he thought she was right. Above-stairs the two ladies separated at Mrs Touchett's door. Isabel had said nothing on her way up.

'Of course you're vexed at my interfering with you,' said Mrs Touchett.

Isabel considered. 'I'm not vexed, but I'm surprised – and a good deal mystified. Wasn't it proper I should remain in the drawing-room?'

'Not in the least. Young girls here – in decent houses – don't sit alone with the gentlemen late at night.'

'You were very right to tell me then,' said Isabel. 'I don't understand it, but I'm very glad to know it.'

'I shall always tell you,' her aunt answered, 'whenever I see you taking what seems to me too much liberty.'

'Pray do; but I don't say I shall always think your remonstrance just.'

'Very likely not. You're too fond of your own ways.'

'Yes, I think I'm very fond of them. But I always want to know the things one shouldn't do.'

'So as to do them?' asked her aunt.

'So as to choose,' said Isabel.

Chapter Eight

As she was devoted to romantic effects Lord Warburton ventured to express a hope that she would come some day and see his house, a very curious old place. He extracted from Mrs Touchett a promise that she would bring her niece to Lockleigh, and Ralph signified his willingness to attend the ladies if his father should be able to spare him. Lord Warburton assured our heroine that in the meantime his sisters would come and see her. She knew something about his sisters, having sounded him, during the hours they spent together while he was at Gardencourt, on many points connected with his family. When Isabel was interested she asked a great many questions, and as her companion was a copious talker she urged him on this occasion by no means in vain. He told her he had four sisters and two brothers and had lost both his parents. The brothers and sisters were very good people – 'not particularly clever, you know,' he said, 'but very decent and pleasant'; and he was so good as to hope Miss Archer might know them well. One of the brothers was in the Church, settled in the family living, that of Lockleigh, which was a heavy, sprawling parish, and was an excellent fellow in spite of his thinking differently from himself on every conceivable topic. And then Lord Warburton mentioned some of the opinions held by his brother, which were opinions Isabel had often heard expressed and that she supposed to be entertained by a considerable portion of the human family. Many of them indeed she supposed she had held herself, till he assured her she was quite mistaken, that it was really impossible, that she had doubtless imagined she entertained them, but that she might depend that, if she thought them over a little, she would find there was nothing in them. When she answered that she had already thought several of the questions involved over very attentively he declared that she was only another example of what he had often been struck with – the fact that, of all the people in the world, the Americans were the most grossly superstitious. They were rank Tories and bigots, every one of them; there were no conservatives like American conservatives. Her uncle and her cousin were there to prove it; nothing could be more medieval than many of their views; they had ideas that people in England nowadays were ashamed to confess to; and they had the impudence moreover, said his lordship, laughing, to pretend they knew more about the needs and dangers of this poor dear stupid old England than he who was born in it and owned a considerable slice of it – the more shame to him! From all of which Isabel gathered that Lord Warburton was a nobleman of the newest pattern, a reformer, a radical, a contemner of ancient ways. His other brother, who was in the army in India, was rather wild and pig-headed and had not been of much use as yet but to make debts for Warburton to pay – one of the most precious privileges of an elder brother. 'I don't think I shall pay any more,' said her friend; 'he lives a monstrous deal better than I do, enjoys unheard-of-luxuries and thinks himself a much finer gentleman than I. As I'm a consistent radical I go in only for equality; I don't go in for the superiority of the younger brothers.' Two of his four sisters, the second and fourth, were married, one of them having done very well, as they said, the other only so-so. The husband of the elder, Lord Haycock, was a very good fellow, but unfortunately a horrid Tory; and his wife, like all good English wives, was worse than her husband. The other had espoused a smallish squire in Norfolk and, though married but the other day, had already five children. This information and much more Lord Warburton imparted to his young American listener, taking pains to make many things clear and to lay bare to her apprehension the peculiarities of English life. Isabel was often amused at his explicitness and at the small allowance he seemed to make either for her own experience or for her imagination. 'He thinks I'm a barbarian,' she said, 'and that I've never seen forks and spoons; and she used to ask him artless questions for the pleasure of hearing him answer seriously. Then when he had fallen into the trap, 'It's a pity you can't see me in my war-paint and feathers,' she remarked; 'if I had known how kind you are to the poor savages I would have brought over my native costume!' Lord Warburton had travelled through the United States and knew much more about them than Isabel; he was so good as to say that America was the most charming country in the world, but his recollections of it appeared to encourage the idea that Americans in England would need to have a great many things explained to them. 'If I had only had you to explain things to me in America!' he said. 'I was rather puzzled in your country; in fact I was quite bewildered, and the trouble was that the explanations only puzzled me more. You know I think they often gave me the wrong ones on purpose; they're rather clever about that over there. But when I explain you can trust me; about what I tell you there's no mistake.' There was no mistake at least about his being very intelligent and cultivated and knowing almost everything in the world. Although he gave the most interesting and thrilling glimpses Isabel felt he never did it to exhibit himself, and though he had had rare chances and had tumbled in, as she put it, for high prizes, he was as far as possible from making a merit of it. He had enjoyed the best things of life, but they had not spoiled his sense of proportion. His quality was a mixture of the effect of rich experience – oh, so easily come by! – with a modesty at times almost boyish; the sweet and wholesome savour of which – it was as agreeable as something tasted – lost nothing from the addition of a tone of responsible kindness.

'I like your specimen English gentleman very much,' Isabel said to Ralph after Lord Warburton had gone.

'I like him too – I love him well,' Ralph returned. 'But I pity him more.'

Isabel looked at him askance. 'Why, that seems to me his only fault – that one can't pity him a little. He appears to have everything, to know everything, to *be* everything.'

'Oh, he's in a bad way!' Ralph insisted.

'I suppose you don't mean in health?'

'No, as to that he's detestably sound. What I mean is that he's a man with a great position who's playing all sorts of tricks with it. He doesn't take himself seriously.'

'Does he regard himself as a joke?'

'Much worse, he regards himself as an imposition – as an abuse.'

'Well, perhaps he is,' said Isabel.

'Perhaps he is – though on the whole I don't think so. But in that case what's more pitiable than a sentient, self-conscious abuse planted by other hands, deeply rooted but aching with a sense of its injustice? For me, in his place, I could be as solemn as a statue of Buddha. He occupies a position that appeals to my imagination. Great responsibilities, great opportunities, great consideration, great wealth, great power, a natural share in the public affairs of a great country. But he's all in a muddle about himself, his position, his power, and indeed about everything in the world. He's the victim of a critical age; he has ceased to believe in himself and he doesn't know what to believe in. When I attempt to tell him (because if I were he I know very well what I should believe in) he calls me a pampered bigot. I believe he seriously thinks me an awful Philistine; he says I don't understand my time. I understand it certainly better than he, who can neither abolish himself as a nuisance nor maintain himself as an institution.'

'He doesn't look very wretched,' Isabel observed.

'Possibly not; though, being a man of a good deal of charming taste, I think he often has uncomfortable hours. But what is it to say of a being of his opportunities that he's not miserable? Besides, I believe he is.'

'I don't,' said Isabel.

'Well,' her cousin rejoined, 'if he isn't he ought to be!'

In the afternoon she spent an hour with her uncle on the lawn, where the old man sat, as usual, with his shawl over his legs and his large cup of diluted tea in his hands. In the course of conversation he asked her what she thought of their late visitor.

Isabel was prompt. 'I think he's charming.'

'He's a nice person,' said Mr Touchett, 'but I don't recommend you to fall in love with him.'

'I shall not do it then; I shall never fall in love but on your recommendation. Moreover,' Isabel added, 'my cousin gives me rather a sad account of Lord Warburton.'

'Oh, indeed? I don't know what there may be to say, but you must remember that Ralph *must* talk.'

'He thinks your friend's too subversive – or not subversive enough! I don't quite understand which,' said Isabel.

The old man shook his head slowly, smiled and put down his cup. 'I don't know which either. He goes very far, but it's quite possible he doesn't go far enough. He seems to want to do away with a good many things, but he seems to want to remain himself. I suppose that's natural, but it's rather inconsistent.'

'Oh, I hope he'll remain himself,' said Isabel. 'If he were to be done away with his friends would miss him sadly.'

'Well,' said the old man, 'I guess he'll stay and amuse his friends. I should certainly miss him very much here at Gardencourt. He always amuses me when he comes over, and I think he amuses himself as well. There's a considerable number like him, round in society; they're very fashionable just now. I don't know what they're trying to do – whether they're trying to get up a revolution. I hope at any rate they'll put it off till after I'm gone. You see they want to disestablish everything; but I'm a pretty big landowner here, and I don't want to be disestablished. I wouldn't have come over if I had thought they were going to behave like that,' Mr Touchett went on with expanding hilarity. 'I came over because I thought England was a safe country. I call it a regular fraud if they are going to introduce any considerable changes; there'll be a large number disappointed in that case.'

'Oh, I do hope they'll make a revolution!' Isabel exclaimed. 'I should delight in seeing a revolution.'

'Let me see,' said her uncle, with a humorous intention; 'I forget whether you're on the side of the old or on the side of the new. I've heard you take such opposite views.'

'I'm on the side of both. I guess I'm a little on the side of everything. In a revolution – after it was well begun – I think I should be a high, proud loyalist. One sympathizes more with them, and they've a chance to behave so exquisitely. I mean so picturesquely.'

'I don't know that I understand what you mean by behaving picturesquely, but it seems to me that you do that always, my dear.'

'Oh, you lovely man, if I could believe that!' the girl interrupted.

'I'm afraid, after all, you won't have the pleasure of going gracefully to the guillotine here just now,' Mr Touchett went on. 'If you want to see a big outbreak you must pay us a long visit. You see, when you come to the point it wouldn't suit them to be taken at their word.'

'Of whom are you speaking?'

'Well, I mean Lord Warburton and his friends – the radicals of the upper class. Of course I only know the way it strikes me. They talk about the changes, but I don't think they quite realize. You and I, you know, we know what it is to have lived under democratic institutions: I always thought them very comfortable, but I was used to them from the first. And then I ain't a lord; you're a lady, my dear, but I ain't a lord. Now over here I don't think it quite comes home to them. It's a matter of every day and every hour, and I don't think many of them would find it as pleasant as what they've got. Of course if they want to try, it's their own business; but I expect they won't try very hard.'

'Don't you think they're sincere?' Isabel asked.

'Well, they want to *feel* earnest,' Mr Touchett allowed; 'but it seems as if they took it out in theories mostly. Their radical views are a kind of amusement; they've got to have some amusement, and they might have coarser tastes than that. You see they're very luxurious, and these progressive ideas are about their biggest luxury. They make them feel moral and yet don't damage their position. They think a great deal of their position; don't let one of them ever persuade you he doesn't, for if you were to proceed on that basis you'd be pulled up very short.'

Isabel followed her uncle's argument, which he unfolded with his quaint distinctness, most attentively, and though she was unacquainted with the British aristocracy she found it in harmony with her general impressions of human nature. But she felt moved to put in a protest on Lord Warburton's behalf. 'I don't believe Lord Warburton's a humbug; I don't care what the others are. I should like to see Lord Warburton put to the test.'

'Heaven deliver me from my friends!' Mr Touchett answered. 'Lord Warburton's a very amiable young man – a very fine young man. He has a hundred thousand a year. He owns fifty thousand acres of the soil of this little island and ever so many things besides. He has half a dozen houses to live in. He has a seat in Parliament as I have one at my own dinner table. He has elegant tastes – cares for literature, for art, for science, for charming young ladies. The most elegant is his taste for the new views. It affords him a great deal of pleasure – more perhaps than anything else, except the young ladies. His old house over there – what does he call it, Lockleigh? – is very attractive; but I don't think it's as pleasant as this. That doesn't matter, however – he has so many others. His views don't hurt anyone as far as I can see; they certainly don't hurt himself. And if there were to be a revolution he would come off very easily. They wouldn't touch him, they'd leave him as he is: he's too much liked.'

'Ah, he couldn't be a martyr even if he wished!' Isabel sighed. 'That's a very poor position.'

'He'll never be a martyr unless you make him one,' said the old man.

Isabel shook her head; there might have been something laughable in the fact that she did it with a touch of melancholy. 'I shall never make anyone a martyr.'

'You'll never be one, I hope.'

'I hope not. But you don't pity Lord Warburton then as Ralph does?'

Her uncle looked at her a while with genial acuteness. 'Yes, I do, after all!'

Chapter Nine

The two Misses Molyneux, this nobleman's sisters, came presently to call upon her, and Isabel took a fancy to the young ladies, who appeared to her to show a most original stamp. It is true that when she described them to her cousin by that term he declared that no epithet could be less applicable than this to the two Misses Molyneux, since there were fifty thousand young women in England who exactly resembled them. Deprived of this advantage, however, Isabel's visitors retained that of an extreme sweetness and shyness of demeanour, and of having, as she thought, eyes like the balanced basins, the circles of 'ornamental water', set, in parterres, among the geraniums.

'They're not morbid, at any rate, whatever they are,' our heroine said to herself; and she deemed this a great charm, for two or three of the friends of her girlhood had been regrettably open to the charge (they would have been so nice without it), to say nothing of Isabel's having occasionally suspected it as a tendency of her own. The Misses Molyneux were not in their first youth, but they had bright, fresh complexions and something of the smile of childhood. Yes, their eyes, which Isabel admired, were round, quiet, and contented, and their figures, also of a generous roundness, were encased in sealskin jackets. Their friendliness was great, so great that they were almost embarrassed to show it; they seemed somewhat afraid of the young lady from the other side of the world and rather looked than spoke their good wishes. But they made it clear to her that they hoped she would come to luncheon at Lockleigh, where they lived with their brother, and then they might see her very, very often. They wondered if she wouldn't come over some day and sleep: they were expecting some people on the twenty-ninth, so perhaps she would come while the people were there.

'I'm afraid it isn't anyone very remarkable,' said the elder sister; 'but I dare say you'll take us as you find us.'

'I shall find you delightful; I think you're enchanting just as you are,' replied Isabel, who often praised profusely.

Her visitors flushed, and her cousin told her, after they were gone, that if she said such things to those poor girls they would think she was in some wild, free manner practising on them: he was sure it was the first time they had been called enchanting.

'I can't help it,' Isabel answered. 'I think it's lovely to be so quiet and reasonable and satisfied. I should like to be like that.'

'Heaven forbid!' cried Ralph with ardour.

'I mean to try and imitate them,' said Isabel. 'I want very much to see them at home.'

She had this pleasure a few days later, when, with Ralph and his mother, she drove over to Lockleigh. She found the Misses Molyneux sitting in a vast drawing-room (she perceived afterwards it was one of several) in a wilderness of faded chintz; they were dressed on this occasion in black velveteen. Isabel liked them even better at home than she had done at Gardencourt, and was more than ever struck with the fact that they were not morbid. It had seemed to her before that if they had a fault it was a want of play of mind; but she presently saw they were capable of deep emotion. Before luncheon she was alone with them for some time, on one side of the room, while Lord Warburton, at a distance, talked to Mrs Touchett.

'Is it true your brother's such a great radical?' Isabel asked. She knew it was true, but we have seen that her interest in human nature was keen, and she had a desire to draw the Misses Molyneux out.

'Oh dear, yes; he's immensely advanced,' said Mildred, the younger sister.

'At the same time Warburton's very reasonable,' Miss Molyneux observed.

Isabel watched him a moment at the other side of the room; he was clearly trying hard to make himself agreeable to Mrs Touchett. Ralph had met the frank advances of one of the dogs before the fire that the temperature of an English August, in the ancient expanses, had not made an impertinence. 'Do you suppose your brother's sincere?' Isabel inquired with a smile.

'Oh, he must be, you know!' Mildred exclaimed quickly, while the elder sister gazed at our heroine in silence.

'Do you think he would stand the test?'

'The test?'

'I mean for instance having to give up all this.'

'Having to give up Lockleigh?' said Miss Molyneux, finding her voice.

'Yes, and the other places; what are they called?'

The two sisters exchanged an almost frightened glance. 'Do you mean – do you mean on account of the expense?' the younger one asked.

'I dare say he might let one or two of his houses,' said the other.

'Let them for nothing?' Isabel demanded.

'I can't fancy his giving up his property,' said Miss Molyneux.

'Ah, I'm afraid he is an impostor!' Isabel returned. 'Don't you think it's a false position?'

Her companions, evidently, had lost themselves. 'My brother's position?' Miss Molyneux inquired.

'It's thought a very good position,' said the younger sister. 'It's the first position in this part of the county.'

'I dare say you think me very irreverent,' Isabel took occasion to remark. 'I suppose you revere your brother and are rather afraid of him.'

'Of course one looks up to one's brother,' said Miss Molyneux simply.

'If you do that he must be very good – because you, evidently, are beautifully good.'

'He's most kind. It will never be known, the good he does.'

'His ability is known,' Mildred added; 'everyone thinks it's immense.'

'Oh, I can see that,' said Isabel. 'But if I were he I should wish to fight to the death: I mean for the heritage of the past. I should hold it tight.'

'I think one ought to be liberal,' Mildred argued gently. 'We've always been so, even from the earliest times.'

'Ah well,' said Isabel, 'you've made a great success of it; I don't wonder you like it. I see you're very fond of crewels.'

When Lord Warburton showed her the house, after luncheon, it seemed to her a matter of course that it should be a noble picture. Within, it had been a good deal modernized – some of its best points had lost their purity; but as they saw it from the gardens, a stout grey pile, of the softest, deepest, most weather-fretted hue, rising from a broad, still moat, it affected the young visitor as a castle in a legend. The day was cool and rather lustreless; the first note of autumn had been struck, and the watery sunshine rested on the walls in blurred and desultory gleams, washing them, as it were, in places tenderly chosen, where the ache of antiquity was keenest. Her host's brother, the Vicar, had come to luncheon, and Isabel had had five minutes' talk with him – time enough to institute a search for a rich ecclesiasticism and give it up as vain. The marks of the Vicar of Lockleigh were a big, athletic figure, a candid, natural countenance, a capacious appetite, and a tendency to indiscriminate laughter. Isabel learned afterwards from her cousin that before taking orders he had been a mighty wrestler and that he was still, on occasion – in the privacy of the family circle as it were – quite capable of flooring his man. Isabel liked him – she was in the mood for liking everything; but her imagination was a good deal taxed to think of him as a source of spiritual aid. The whole party, on leaving lunch, went to walk in the grounds; but Lord Warburton exercised some ingenuity in engaging his least familiar guest in a stroll apart from the others.

'I wish you to see the place properly, seriously,' he said. 'You can't do so if your attention is distracted by irrelevant gossip.' His own conversation (though he told Isabel a good deal about the house, which had a very curious history) was not purely archaeological; he reverted at intervals to matters more personal – matters personal to the young lady as well as to himself. But at last, after a pause of some duration, returning for a moment to their ostensible theme, 'Ah, well,' he said, 'I'm very glad indeed you like the old barrack. I wish you could see more of it – that you could stay here a while. My sisters have taken an immense fancy to you – if that would be any inducement.'

'There's no want of inducements,' Isabel answered; 'but I'm afraid I can't make engagements. I'm quite in my aunt's hands.'

'Ah, pardon me if I say I don't exactly believe that. I'm pretty sure you can do whatever you want.'

'I'm sorry if I make that impression on you; I don't think it's a nice impression to make.'

'It has the merit of permitting me to hope.' And Lord Warburton paused a moment.

'To hope what?'

'That in future I may see you often.'

'Ah,' said Isabel, 'to enjoy that pleasure I needn't be so terribly emancipated.'

'Doubtless not; and yet, at the same time, I don't think your uncle likes me.'

'You're very much mistaken. I've heard him speak very highly of you.'

'I'm glad you have talked about me,' said Lord Warburton. 'But, I nevertheless don't think he'd like me to keep coming to Gardencourt.'

'I can't answer for my uncle's tastes,' the girl rejoined, 'though I ought as far as possible to take them into account. But for myself I shall be very glad to see you.'

'Now that's what I like to hear you say. I'm charmed when you say that.'

'You're easily charmed, my lord,' said Isabel.

'No, I'm not easily charmed!' And then he stopped a moment. 'But you've charmed me, Miss Archer.'

These words were uttered with an indefinable sound which startled the girl; it struck her as the prelude to something grave: she had heard the sound before and she recognized it. She had no wish, however, that for the moment such a prelude should have a sequel, and she said as gaily as possible and as quickly as an appreciable degree of agitation would allow her: 'I'm afraid there's no prospect of my being able to come here again.'

'Never?' said Lord Warburton.

'I won't say "never"; I should feel very melodramatic.'

'May I come and see you then some day next week?'

'Most assuredly. What is there to prevent it?'

'Nothing tangible. But with you I never feel safe. I've a sort of sense that you're always summing people up.'

'You don't of necessity lose by that.'

'It's very kind of you to say so; but, even if I gain, stern justice is not what I most love. Is Mrs Touchett going to take you abroad?'

'I hope so.'

'Is England not good enough for you?'

'That's a very Machiavellian speech; it doesn't deserve an answer. I want to see as many countries as I can.'

'Then you'll go on judging, I suppose.'

'Enjoying, I hope too.'

'Yes, that's what you enjoy most; I can't make out what you're up to,' said Lord Warburton. 'You strike me as having mysterious purposes – vast designs.'

'You're so good as to have a theory about me which I don't at all fill out. Is there anything mysterious in a purpose entertained and executed every year, in the most public manner, by fifty thousand of my fellow-countrymen – the purpose of improving one's mind by foreign travel?'

'You can't improve your mind, Miss Archer,' her companion declared. 'It's already a most formidable instrument. It looks down on us all; it despises us.'

'Despises you? You're making fun of me,' said Isabel seriously.

'Well, you think us "quaint" – that's the same thing. I won't be thought "quaint", to begin with; I'm not so in the least. I protest.'

'That protest is one of the quaintest things I've ever heard,' Isabel answered with a smile.

Lord Warburton was briefly silent. 'You judge only from the outside – you don't care,' he said presently. 'You only care to amuse yourself.' The note she had heard in his voice a moment before reappeared, and mixed with it now was an audible strain of bitterness – a bitterness so abrupt and inconsequent that the girl was afraid she had hurt him. She had often heard that the English are a highly eccentric people, and she had even read in some ingenious author that they are at bottom the most romantic of races. Was Lord Warburton suddenly turning romantic – was he going to make her a scene, in his own house, only the third time they had met? She was reassured quickly enough by her sense of his great good manners, which was not impaired by the fact that he had already touched the furthest limit of good taste in expressing his admiration of a young lady who had confided in his hospitality. She was right in trusting to his good manners, for he presently went on, laughing a little and without a trace of the accent that had discomposed her: 'I don't mean of course that you amuse yourself with trifles. You select great materials; the foibles, the afflictions of human nature, the peculiarities of nations!'

'As regards that,' said Isabel, 'I should find in my own nation entertainment for a lifetime. But we've a long drive, and my aunt will soon wish to start.' She turned back towards the others and Lord Warburton walked beside her in silence. But before they reached the others, 'I shall come and see you next week,' he said.

She had received an appreciable shock, but as it died away she felt that she couldn't pretend to herself that it was altogether a painful one. Nevertheless she made answer to his declaration, coldly enough, 'Just as you please.' And her coldness was not the calculation of her effect – a game she played in a much smaller degree than would have seemed probable to many critics. It came from a certain fear.

Chapter Ten

The day after her visit to Lockleigh she received a note from her friend Miss Stackpole – a note of which the envelope, exhibiting in conjunction the postmark of Liverpool and the neat calligraphy of the quick-fingered Henrietta, caused her some liveliness of emotion. 'Here I am, my lovely friend,' Miss Stackpole wrote; 'I managed to get off at last. I decided only the night before I left New York – the *Interviewer* having come round to my figure. I put a few things into a bag, like a veteran journalist, and came down to the steamer in a street-car. Where are you and where can we meet? I suppose you're visiting at some castle or other and have already acquired the correct accent. Perhaps even you have married a lord; I almost hope you have, for I want some introductions to the first people and shall count on you for a few. The *Interviewer* wants some light on the nobility. My first impressions (of the people at large) are not rose-coloured; but I wish to talk them over with you, and you know that, whatever I am, at least I'm not superficial. I've also something very particular to tell you. Do appoint a meeting as quickly as you can; come to London (I should like so much to visit the sights with you) or else let me come to you, *wherever you are*. I will do so with pleasure; for you know everything interests me and I wish to see as much as possible of the inner life.'

Isabel judged best not to show this letter to her uncle; but she acquainted him with its purport, and, as she expected, he begged her instantly to assure Miss Stackpole, in his name, that he should be delighted to receive her at Gardencourt. 'Though she's a literary lady,' he said, 'I suppose that, being an American, she won't show me up, as that other one did. She has seen others like me.'

'She has seen no other so delightful!' Isabel answered; but she was not altogether at ease about Henrietta's reproductive instincts, which belonged to that side of her friend's character which she regarded with least complacency. She wrote to Miss Stackpole, however, that she would be very welcome under Mr Touchett's roof; and this alert young woman lost no time in announcing her prompt approach. She had gone up to London, and it was from that centre that she took the train for the station nearest to Gardencourt, where Isabel and Ralph were in waiting to receive her.

'Shall I love her or shall I hate her?' Ralph asked while they moved along the platform.

'Whichever you do will matter very little to her,' said Isabel. 'She doesn't care a straw what men think of her.'

'As a man I'm bound to dislike her then. She must be a kind of monster. Is she very ugly?'

'No, she's decidedly pretty.'

'A female interviewer – a reporter in petticoats? I'm very curious to see her,' Ralph conceded.

'It's very easy to laugh at her but it is not easy to be as brave as she.'

'I should think not; crimes of violence and attacks on the person require more or less pluck. Do you suppose she'll interview *me*?'

'Never in the world. She'll not think you of enough importance.'

'You'll see,' said Ralph. 'She'll send a description of us all, including Bunchie, to her newspaper.'

'I shall ask her not to,' Isabel answered.

'You think she's capable of it then?'

'Perfectly.'

'And yet you've made her your bosom-friend?'

'I've not made her my bosom-friend; but I like her in spite of her faults.'

'Ah well,' said Ralph, 'I'm afraid I shall dislike her in spite of her merits.'

'You'll probably fall in love with her at the end of three days.'

'And have my love-letters published in the *Interviewer*? Never!' cried the young man.

The train presently arrived, and Miss Stackpole, promptly descending, proved, as Isabel had promised, quite delicately, even though rather provincially fair. She was a neat, plump person, of medium stature, with a round face, a small mouth, a delicate complexion, a bunch of light brown ringlets at the back of her head and a peculiarly open, surprised-looking eye. The most striking point in her appearance was the remarkable fixedness of this organ, which rested without impudence or defiance, but as if in conscientious exercise of a natural right, upon every object it happened to encounter. It rested in this manner upon Ralph himself, a little arrested by Miss Stackpole's gracious and comfortable aspect, which hinted that it wouldn't be so easy as he had assumed to disapprove of her. She rustled, she shimmered, in fresh, dove-coloured draperies, and Ralph saw at a glance that she was as crisp and new and comprehensive as a first issue before the folding. From top to toe she had probably no misprint. She spoke in a clear, high voice – a voice not rich but loud; yet after she had taken her place with her companions in Mr Touchett's carriage she struck him as not all in the large type, the type of horrid 'headings', that he had expected. She answered the inquiries made of her by Isabel, however, and in which the young man ventured to join, with copious lucidity; and later, in the library at Gardencourt, when she had made the acquaintance of Mr Touchett (his wife not having thought it necessary to appear) did more to give the measure of her confidence in her powers.

'Well, I should like to know whether you consider yourselves American or English,' she broke out. 'If once I knew I could talk to you accordingly.'

'Talk to us anyhow and we shall be thankful,' Ralph liberally answered.

She fixed her eyes on him, and there was something in their character that reminded him of large polished buttons – buttons that might have fixed the elastic loops of some tense receptacle: he seemed to see the reflection of surrounding objects on the pupil. The expression of a button is not usually deemed human, but there was something in Miss Stackpole's gaze that made him, as a very modest man, feel vaguely embarrassed – less inviolate, more dishonoured, than he liked. This sensation, it must be added, after he had spent a day or two in her company, sensibly diminished, though it never wholly lapsed. 'I don't suppose that you're going to undertake to persuade me that *you're* an American,' she said.

'To please you I'll be an Englishman, I'll be a Turk!'

'Well, if you can change about that way you're very welcome,' Miss Stackpole returned.

'I'm sure you understand everything and that differences of nationality are no barrier to you,' Ralph went on.

Miss Stackpole gazed at him still. 'Do you mean the foreign languages?'

'The languages are nothing. I mean the spirit – the genius.'

'I'm not sure that I understand you,' said the correspondent of the *Interviewer*; 'but I expect I shall before I leave.'

'He's what's called a cosmopolite,' Isabel suggested.

'That means he's a little of everything and not much of any. I must say I think patriotism is like charity – it begins at home.'

'Ah, but where does home begin, Miss Stackpole?' Ralph inquired.

'I don't know where it begins, but I know where it ends. It ended a long time before I got here.'

'Don't you like it over here?' asked Mr Touchett with his aged, innocent voice.

'Well, sir, I haven't quite made up my mind what ground I shall take. I feel a good deal crammed. I felt it on the journey from Liverpool to London.'

'Perhaps you were in a crowded carriage,' Ralph suggested.

'Yes, but it was crowded with friends – a party of Americans whose acquaintance I had made upon the steamer; a lovely group from Little Rock, Arkansas. In spite of that I felt cramped – I felt something pressing upon me; I couldn't tell what it was. I felt at the very commencement as if I were not going to accord with the atmosphere. But I suppose I shall make my own atmosphere. That's the true way – then you can breathe. Your surroundings seem very attractive.'

'Ah, we too are a lovely group!' said Ralph, 'Wait a little and you'll see.'

Miss Stackpole showed every disposition to wait and evidently was prepared to make a considerable stay at Gardencourt. She occupied herself in the mornings with literary labour; but in spite of this Isabel spent many hours with her friend, who, once her daily task performed, deprecated, in fact defied, isolation. Isabel speedily found occasion to desire her to desist from celebrating the charms of their common sojourn in print, having discovered, on the second morning of Miss Stackpole's visit, that she was engaged on a letter to the *Interviewer*, of which the title, in her exquisitely neat and legible hand (exactly that of the copybooks which our heroine remembered at school) was 'Americans and Tudors – Glimpses of Gardencourt'. Miss Stackpole, with the best conscience in the world, offered to read her letter to Isabel, who immediately put in her protest.

'I don't think you ought to do that. I don't think you ought to describe the place.'

Henrietta gazed at her as usual. 'Why, it's just what the people want, and it's a lovely place.'

'It's too lovely to be put in the newspapers, and it's not what my uncle wants.'

'Don't you believe that!' cried Henrietta. 'They're always delighted afterwards.'

'My uncle won't be delighted – nor my cousin either. They'll consider it a breach of hospitality.'

Miss Stackpole showed no sense of confusion; she simply wiped her pen, very neatly, upon an elegant little implement which she kept for the purpose, and put away her manuscript. 'Of course if you don't approve I won't do it; but I sacrifice a beautiful subject.'

'There are plenty of other subjects, there are subjects all round you. We'll take some drives; I'll show you some charming scenery.'

'Scenery's not my department; I always need a human interest. You know I'm deeply human, Isabel; I always was,' Miss Stackpole rejoined. 'I was going to bring in your cousin – the alienated American. There's a great demand just now for the alienated American, and your cousin's a beautiful specimen. I should have handled him severely.'

'He would have died of it!' Isabel exclaimed. 'Not of the severity, but of the publicity.'

'Well, I should have liked to kill him a little. And I should have delighted to do your uncle, who seems to me a much nobler type – the American faithful still. He's a grand old man; I don't see how he can object to my paying him honour.'

Isabel looked at her companion in much wonderment; it struck her as strange that a nature in which she found so much to esteem should break down so in spots. 'My poor Henrietta,' she said, 'you've no sense of privacy.'

Henrietta coloured deeply, and for a moment her brilliant eyes were suffused, while Isabel found her more than ever inconsequent. 'You do me great injustice,' said Miss Stackpole with dignity. 'I've never written a word about myself!'

'I'm very sure of that; but it seems to me one should be modest for others also!'

'Ah, that's very good!' cried Henrietta, seizing her pen again. 'Just let me make a note of it and I'll put it in somewhere.' She was a thoroughly good-natured woman, and half an hour later she was in as cheerful a mood as should have been looked for in a newspaper-lady in want of matter. 'I've promised to do the social side,' she said to Isabel, 'and how can I do it unless I get ideas? If I can't describe this place don't you know some place I can describe?' Isabel promised she would bethink herself, and the next day, in conversation with her friend, she happened to mention her visit to Lord Warburton's ancient house. 'Ah, you must take me there – that's just the place for me!' Miss Stackpole cried. 'I must get a glimpse of the nobility.'

'I can't take you,' said Isabel; 'but Lord Warburton's coming here, and you'll have a chance to see him and observe him. Only if you intend to repeat his conversation I shall certainly give him warning.'

'Don't do that,' her companion pleaded; 'I want him to be natural.'

'An Englishman's never so natural as when he's holding his tongue,' Isabel declared.

It was not apparent, at the end of three days, that her cousin had, according to her prophecy, lost his heart to their visitor, though he had spent a good deal of time in her society. They strolled about the park together and sat under the trees, and in the afternoon, when it was delightful to float along the Thames, Miss Stackpole occupied a place in the boat in which hitherto Ralph had had but a single companion. Her presence proved somehow less irreducible to soft particles than Ralph had expected in the natural perturbation of his sense of the perfect solubility of that of his cousin; for the correspondent of the *Interviewer* prompted mirth in him, and he had long since decided that the *crescendo* of mirth should be the flower of his declining days. Henrietta, on her side, failed a little to justify Isabel's declaration with regard to her indifference to masculine opinion; for poor Ralph appeared to have presented himself to her as an irritating problem, which it would be almost immoral not to work out.

'What does he do for a living?' she asked of Isabel the evening of her arrival. 'Does he go round all day with his hands in his pockets?'

'He does nothing,' smiled Isabel; 'he's a gentleman of large leisure.'

'Well, I call that a shame – when I have to work like a car-conductor,' Miss Stackpole replied. 'I should like to show him up.'

'He's in wretched health; he's quite unfit for work,' Isabel urged.

'Pshaw! don't you believe it. I work when I'm sick,' cried her friend. Later, when she stepped into the boat on joining the water-party, she remarked to Ralph that she supposed he hated her and would like to drown her.

'Ah no,' said Ralph, 'I keep my victims for a slower torture. And you'd be such an interesting one!'

'Well, you do torture me; I may say that. But I shock all your prejudices; that's one comfort.'

'My prejudices? I haven't a prejudice to bless myself with. There's intellectual poverty for you.'

'The more shame to you; I've some delicious ones. Of course I spoil your flirtation, or whatever it is you call it, with your cousin; but I don't care for that, as I render her the service of drawing you out. She'll see how thin you are.'

'Ah, do draw me out!' Ralph exclaimed. 'So few people will take the trouble.'

Miss Stackpole, in this undertaking appeared to shrink from no effort; resorting largely, whenever the opportunity offered, to the natural expedient of interrogation. On the following day the weather was bad, and in the afternoon the young man, by way of providing indoor amusement, offered to show her the pictures. Henrietta strolled through the long gallery in his society, while he pointed out its principal ornaments and mentioned the painters and subjects. Miss Stackpole looked at the pictures in perfect silence, committing herself to no opinion, and Ralph was gratified by the fact that she delivered herself of none of the little ready-made ejaculations of delight of which the visitors to Gardencourt were so frequently lavish. This young lady indeed, to do her justice, was but little addicted to the use of conventional terms; there was something earnest and inventive in her tone, which at times, in its strained deliberation, suggested a person of high culture speaking a foreign language. Ralph Touchett subsequently learned that she had at one time officiated as art-critic to a journal of the other world; but she appeared, in spite of this fact, to carry in her pocket none of the small change of admiration. Suddenly, just after he had called her attention to a charming Constable, she turned and looked at him as if he himself had been a picture.

'Do you always spend your time like this?' she demanded.

'I seldom spend it so agreeably.'

'Well, you know what I mean – without any regular occupation.'

'Ah,' said Ralph, 'I'm the idlest man living.'

Miss Stackpole directed her gaze to the Constable again, and Ralph bespoke her attention for a small Lancret hanging near it, which represented a gentleman in a pink doublet and hose and a ruff, leaning against the pedestal of the statue of a nymph in a garden and playing the guitar to two ladies seated on the grass. 'That's my ideal of a regular occupation,' he said.

Miss Stackpole turned to him again, and, though her eyes had rested upon the picture, he saw she had missed the subject. She was thinking of something much more serious. 'I don't see how you can reconcile it to your conscience.'

'My dear lady, I *have* no conscience!'

'Well, I advise you to cultivate one. You'll need it the next time you go to America.'

'I shall probably never go again.'

'Are you ashamed to show yourself?'

Ralph meditated with a mild smile. 'I suppose that if one has no conscience one has no shame.'

'Well, you've got plenty of assurance,' Henrietta declared. 'Do you consider it right to give up your country?'

'Ah, one doesn't give up one's country any more than one gives up one's grandmother. They're both antecedent to choice – elements of one's composition that are not to be eliminated.'

'I suppose that means that you've tried and been worsted. What do they think of you over here?'

'They delight in me.'

'That's because you truckle to them.'

'Ah, set it down a little to my natural charm!' Ralph sighed.

'I don't know anything about your natural charm. If you've got any charm it's quite unnatural. It's wholly acquired – or at least you've tried hard to acquire it, living over here. I don't say you've succeeded. It's a charm that I don't appreciate, anyway. Make yourself useful in some way, and then we'll talk about it.'

'Well, now, tell me what I shall do,' said Ralph.

'Go right home, to begin with.'

'Yes, I see. And then?'

'Take right hold of something.'

'Well, now, what sort of thing?'

'Anything you please, so long as you take hold. Some new idea, some big work.'

'Is it very difficult to take hold?' Ralph inquired.

'Not if you put your heart into it.'

'Ah, my heart,' said Ralph. 'If it depends upon my heart—!'

'Haven't you got a heart?'

'I had one a few days ago, but I've lost it since.'

'You're not serious,' Miss Stackpole remarked; 'that's what's the matter with you.' But for all this, in a day or two, she again permitted him to fix her attention and on the later occasion assigned a different cause to his mysterious perversity. 'I know what's the matter with you, Mr Touchett,' she said. 'You think you're too good to get married.'

'I thought so till I knew you, Miss Stackpole,' Ralph answered; 'and then I suddenly changed my mind.'

'Oh pshaw!' Henrietta groaned.

'Then it seemed to me,' said Ralph, 'that I was not good enough.'

'It would improve you. Besides, it's your duty.'

'Ah,' cried the young man, 'one has so many duties! Is that a duty too?'

'Of course it is – did you never know that before? It's everyone's duty to get married.'

Ralph meditated a moment; he was disappointed. There was something in Miss Stackpole he had begun to like; it seemed to him that if she was not a charming woman she was at least a very good 'sort'. She was wanting in distinction, but, as Isabel had said, she was brave: she went into cages, she flourished lashes, like a spangled lion-tamer. He had not supposed her to be capable of vulgar arts, but these last words struck him as a false note. When a marriageable young woman urges matrimony on an unencumbered young man the most obvious explanation of her conduct is not the altruistic impulse.

'Ah, well now, there's a good deal to be said about that,' Ralph rejoined.

'There may be, but that's the principal thing. I must say I think it looks very exclusive, going round all alone, as if you thought no woman was good enough for you. Do you think you're better than any one else in the world? In America it's usual for people to marry.'

'If it's my duty,' Ralph asked, 'is it not, by analogy, yours as well?'

Miss Stackpole's ocular surfaces unwinkingly caught the sun. 'Have you the fond hope of finding a flaw in my reasoning? Of course I've as good a right to marry as anyone else.'

'Well then,' said Ralph, 'I won't say it vexes me to see you single. It delights me rather.'

'You're not serious yet. You never will be.'

'Shall you not believe me to be so on the day I tell you I desire to give up the practice of going round alone?'

Miss Stackpole looked at him for a moment in a manner which seemed to announce a reply that might technically be called encouraging. But to his great surprise this expression suddenly resolved itself into an appearance of alarm and even of resentment. 'No, not even then,' she answered dryly. After which she walked away.

'I've not conceived a passion for your friend,' Ralph said that evening to Isabel, 'though we talked some time this morning about it.'

'And you said something she didn't like,' the girl replied.

Ralph stared. 'Has she complained of me?'

'She told me she thinks there's something very low in the tone of Europeans towards women.'

'Does she call me a European?'

'One of the worst. She told me you had said to her something that an American never would have said. But she didn't repeat it.'

Ralph treated himself to a luxury of laughter. 'She's an extraordinary combination. Did she think I was making love to her?'

'No; I believe even Americans do that. But she apparently thought you mistook the intention of something she had said, and put an unkind construction on it.'

'I thought she was proposing marriage to me and I accepted her. Was that unkind?'

Isabel smiled. 'It was unkind to *me*. I don't want you to marry.'

'My dear cousin, what's one to do among you all?' Ralph demanded. 'Miss Stackpole tells me it's my bounden duty, and that it's hers, in general, to see I do mine!'

'She has a great sense of duty,' said Isabel gravely. 'She has indeed, and it's the motive of everything she says. That's what I like her for. She thinks it's unworthy of you to keep so many things to yourself. That's what she wanted to express. If you thought she was trying to – to attract you, you were very wrong.'

'It's true it was an odd way, but I did think she was trying to attract me. Forgive my depravity.'

'You're very conceited. She had no interested views, and never supposed you would think she had.'

'One must be very modest then to talk with such women,' Ralph said humbly. 'But it's a very strange type. She's too personal – considering that she expects other people not to be. She walks in without knocking at the door.'

'Yes,' Isabel admitted, 'she doesn't sufficiently recognize the existence of knockers; and indeed I'm not sure that she doesn't think them rather a pretentious ornament. She thinks one's door should stand ajar. But I persist in liking her.'

'I persist in thinking her too familiar,' Ralph rejoined, naturally somewhat uncomfortable under the sense of having been doubly deceived in Miss Stackpole.

'Well,' said Isabel, smiling, 'I'm afraid it's because she's rather vulgar that I like her.'

'She would be flattered by your reason!'

'If I should tell her I wouldn't express it in that way. I should say it's because there's something of the "people" in her.'

'What do you know about the people? and what does she, for that matter?'

'She knows a great deal, and I know enough to feel that she's a kind of emanation of the great democracy – of the continent, the country, the nation. I don't say that she sums it all up, that would be too much to ask of her. But she suggests it; she vividly figures it.'

'You like her then for patriotic reasons. I'm afraid it is on those very grounds I object to her.'

'Ah,' said Isabel with a kind of joyous sigh, 'I like so many things! If a thing strikes me with a certain intensity I accept it. I don't want to swagger, but I suppose I'm rather versatile. I like people to be totally different from Henrietta – in the style of Lord Warburton's sisters for instance. So long as I look at the Misses Molyneux they seem to me to answer a kind of ideal. Then Henrietta presents herself, and I'm straightaway convinced by *her*; not so much in respect to herself as in respect to what masses behind her.'

'Ah, you mean the back view of her,' Ralph suggested.

'What she says is true,' his cousin answered; 'you'll never be serious. I like the great country stretching away beyond the rivers and across the prairies, blooming and smiling and spreading till it stops at the green Pacific! A strong, sweet, fresh odour seems to rise from it, and Henrietta – pardon my simile – has something of that odour in her garments.'

Isabel blushed a little as she concluded this speech, and the blush, together with the momentary ardour she had thrown into it, was so becoming to her that Ralph stood smiling at her for a moment after she had ceased speaking. 'I'm not sure the Pacific's so green as that,' he said; 'but you're a young woman of imagination. Henrietta, however, does smell of the Future – it almost knocks one down!'

Chapter Eleven

He took a resolve after this not to misinterpret her words even when Miss Stackpole appeared to strike the personal note most strongly. He bethought himself that persons, in her view, were simple and homogeneous organisms, and that he, for his own part, was too perverted a representative of the nature of man to have a right to deal with her in strict reciprocity. He carried out his resolve with a great deal of tact, and the young lady found in renewed contact with him no obstacle to the exercise of her genius for unshrinking inquiry, the general application of her confidence. Her situation at Gardencourt therefore, appreciated as we have seen her to be by Isabel and full of appreciation herself of that free play of intelligence which, to her sense, rendered Isabel's character a sister-spirit, and of the easy venerableness of Mr Touchett, whose noble tone, as she said, met with her full approval – her situation at Gardencourt would have been perfectly comfortable had she not conceived an irresistible mistrust of the little lady for whom she had at first supposed herself obliged to 'allow' as mistress of the house. She presently discovered, in truth, that this obligation was of the lightest and that Mrs Touchett cared very little how Miss Stackpole behaved. Mrs Touchett had defined her to Isabel as both an adventuress and a bore – adventuresses usually giving one more of a thrill; she had expressed some surprise at her niece's having selected such a friend, yet had immediately added that she knew Isabel's friends were her own affair and that she had never undertaken to like them all or to restrict the girl to those she liked.

'If you could see none but the people I like, my dear, you'd have a very small society,' Mrs Touchett frankly admitted; 'and I don't think I like any man or woman well enough to recommend them to you. When it comes to recommending it's a serious affair. I don't like Miss Stackpole – everything about her displeases me; she talks so much too loud and looks at one as if one wanted to look at *her* – which one doesn't. I'm sure she has lived all her life in a boarding-house, and I detest the manners and the liberties of such places. If you ask me if I prefer my own manners, which you doubtless think very bad, I'll tell you that I prefer them immensely. Miss Stackpole knows I detest boarding-house civilization, and she detests me for detesting it, because she thinks it the highest in the world. She'd like Gardencourt a great deal better if it were a boarding-house. For me, I find it almost too much of one! We shall never get on together therefore, and there's no use trying.'

Mrs Touchett was right in guessing that Henrietta disapproved of her, but she had not quite put her finger on the reason. A day or two after Miss Stackpole's arrival she had made some invidious reflections on American hotels, which excited a vein of counter-argument on the part of the correspondent of the *Interviewer*, who in the exercise of her profession had acquainted herself, in the western world, with every form of caravansary. Henrietta expressed the opinion that American hotels were the best in the world, and Mrs Touchett, fresh from a renewed struggle with them, recorded a conviction that they were the worst. Ralph, with his experimental geniality, suggested, by way of healing the breach, that the truth lay between the two extremes and that the establishments in question ought to be described as fair middling. This contribution to the discussion, however, Miss Stackpole rejected with scorn. Middling indeed! If they were not the best in the world they were the worst, but there was nothing middling about an American hotel.

'We judge from different points of view, evidently,' said Mrs Touchett. 'I like to be treated as an individual; you like to be treated as a "party".'

'I don't know what you mean,' Henrietta replied. 'I like to be treated as an American lady.'

'Poor American ladies!' cried Mrs Touchett with a laugh. 'They're the slaves of slaves.'

'They're the companions of freemen,' Henrietta retorted.

'They're the companions of their servants – the Irish chambermaid and the Negro waiter. They share their work.'

'Do you call the domestics in an American household "slaves"?' Miss Stackpole inquired. 'If that's the way you desire to treat them, no wonder you don't like America.'

'If you've not good servants you're miserable,' Mrs Touchett serenely said: 'They're very bad in America, but I've five perfect ones in Florence.'

'I don't see what you want with five,' Henrietta couldn't help observing. 'I don't think I should like to see five persons surrounding me in that menial position.'

'I like them in that position better than in some others,' proclaimed Mrs Touchett with much meaning.

'Should you like me better if I were your butler, dear?' her husband asked.

'I don't think I should: you wouldn't at all have the *tenue*.'

'The companions of freemen – I like that, Miss Stackpole,' said Ralph. 'It's a beautiful description.'

'When I said freemen I didn't mean you, sir!'

And this was the only reward that Ralph got for his compliment. Miss Stackpole was baffled; she evidently thought there was something treasonable in Mrs Touchett's appreciation of a class which she privately judged to be a mysterious survival of feudalism. It was perhaps because her mind was oppressed with this image that she suffered some days to elapse before she took occasion to say to Isabel: 'My dear friend, I wonder if you're growing faithless.'

'Faithless? Faithless to you, Henrietta?'

'No, that would be a great pain; but it's not that.'

'Faithless to my country then?'

'Ah, that I hope will never be. When I wrote to you from Liverpool I said I had something particular to tell you. You've never asked me what it is. Is it because you've suspected?'

'Suspected what? As a rule I don't think I suspect,' said Isabel. 'I remember now that phrase in your letter, but I confess I had forgotten it. What have you to tell me?'

Henrietta looked disappointed, and her steady gaze betrayed it. 'You don't ask that right – as if you thought it important. You're changed – you're thinking of other things.'

'Tell me what you mean, and I'll think of that.'

'Will you really think of it? That's what I wish to be sure of.'

'I've not much control of my thoughts, but I'll do my best,' said Isabel, Henrietta gazed at her, in silence, for a period which tried Isabel's patience, so that our heroine added at last: 'Do you mean that you're going to be married?'

'Not till I've seen Europe!' said Miss Stackpole. 'What are you laughing at?' she went on. 'What I mean is that Mr Goodwood came out in the steamer with me.'

'Ah!' Isabel responded.

'You say *that* right. I had a good deal of talk with him; he has come after you.'

'Did he tell you so?'

'No, he told me nothing; that's how I knew it,' said Henrietta cleverly. 'He said very little about you, but I spoke of you a good deal.'

Isabel waited. At the mention of Mr Goodwood's name she had turned a little pale. 'I'm very sorry you did that,' she observed at last.

'It was a pleasure to me, and I liked the way he listened. I could have talked a long time to such a listener; he was so quiet, so intense; he drank it all in.'

'What did you say about me?' Isabel asked.

'I said you were on the whole the finest creature I know.'

'I'm very sorry for that. He thinks too well of me already; he oughtn't to be encouraged.'

'He's dying for a little encouragement. I see his face now, and his earnest absorbed look while I talked. I never saw an ugly man look so handsome.'

'He's very simple minded,' said Isabel. 'And he's not so ugly.'

'There's nothing so simplifying as a grand passion.'

'It's not a grand passion; I'm very sure it's not that.'

'You don't say that as if you were sure.'

Isabel gave rather a cold smile. 'I shall say it better to Mr Goodwood himself.'

'He'll soon give you a chance,' said Henrietta. Isabel offered no answer to this assertion, which her companion made with an air of great confidence.

'He'll find you changed,' the latter pursued. 'You've been affected by your new surroundings.'

'Very likely. I'm affected by everything.'

'By everything but Mr Goodwood!' Miss Stackpole exclaimed with a slightly harsh hilarity.

Isabel failed even to smile back and in a moment she said: 'Did he ask you to speak to me?'

'Not in so many words. But his eyes asked it – and his handshake, when he bade me good-bye.'

'Thank you for doing so.' And Isabel turned away.

'Yes, you're changed; you've got new ideas over here,' her friend continued.

'I hope so,' said Isabel; 'one should get as many new ideas as possible.'

'Yes; but they shouldn't interfere with the old ones when the old ones have been the right ones.'

Isabel turned about again. 'If you mean that I had any idea with regard to Mr Goodwood—!' But she faltered before her friend's implacable glitter.

'My dear child, you certainly encouraged him.'

Isabel made for the moment as if to deny this charge; instead of which, however, she presently answered: 'It's very true. I did encourage him.' And then she asked if her companion had learned from Mr Goodwood what he intended to do. It was a concession to her curiosity, for she disliked discussing the subject and found Henrietta wanting in delicacy.

'I asked him, and he said he meant to do nothing,' Miss Stackpole answered. 'But I don't believe that; he's not a man to do nothing. He is a man of high, bold action. Whatever happens to him he'll always do something, and whatever he does will always be right.'

'I quite believe that.' Henrietta might be wanting in delicacy, but it touched the girl, all the same, to hear this declaration.

'Ah, you *do* care for him!' her visitor rang out.

'Whatever he does will always be right,' Isabel repeated. 'When a man's of that infallible mould what does it matter to him what one feels?'

'It may not matter to him, but it matters to one's self.'

'Ah, what it matters to me – that's not what we're discussing,' said Isabel with a cold smile.

This time her companion was grave. 'Well, I don't care; you *have* changed. You're not the girl you were a few short weeks ago, and Mr Goodwood will see it. I expect him here any day.'

'I hope he'll hate me then,' said Isabel.

'I believe you hope it about as much as I believe him capable of it.'

To this observation our heroine made no return; she was absorbed in the alarm given her by Henrietta's intimation that Caspar Goodwood would present himself at Gardencourt. She pretended to herself, however, that she thought the event impossible, and, later, she communicated her disbelief to her friend. For the next forty-eight hours, nevertheless, she stood prepared to hear the young man's name announced. The feeling pressed upon her; it made the air sultry, as if there were to be a change of weather; and the weather, socially speaking, had been so agreeable during Isabel's stay at Gardencourt that any change would be for the worse. Her suspense indeed was dissipated the second day. She had walked into the park in company with the sociable Bunchie, and after strolling about for some time, in a manner at once listless and restless, had seated herself on a garden bench, within sight of the house, beneath a spreading beech, where, in a white dress ornamented with black ribbons, she formed among the flickering shadows a graceful and harmonious image. She entertained herself for some moments with talking to the little terrier, as to whom the proposal of an ownership divided with her cousin had been applied as impartially as possible – as impartially as Bunchie's own somewhat fickle and inconstant sympathies would allow. But she was notified for the first time, on this occasion, of the finite character of Bunchie's intellect; hitherto she had been mainly struck with its extent. It seemed to her at last that she would do well to take a book; formerly, when heavy-hearted, she had been able, with the help of some well-chosen volume, to transfer the seat of consciousness to the organ of pure reason. Of late, it was not to be denied, literature had seemed a fading light, and even after she had reminded herself that her uncle's library was provided with a complete set of those authors which no gentlemen's collection should be without, she sat motionless and empty-handed, her eyes bent on the cool green turf of the lawn. Her meditations were presently interrupted by the arrival of a servant who handed her a letter. The letter bore the London postmark and was addressed in a hand she knew – that came into her vision, already so held by him, with the vividness of the writer's voice or his face. This document proved short and may be given entire.

MY DEAR MISS ARCHER – I don't know whether you will have heard of my coming to England, but even if you have not it will scarcely be a surprise to you. You will remember that when you gave me my dismissal at Albany, three months ago, I did not accept it. I protested against it. You in fact appeared to accept my protest and to admit that I had the right on my side. I had come to see you with the hope that you would let me bring you over to my conviction; my reasons for entertaining this hope had been of the best. But you disappointed it; I found you changed, and you were able to give me no reason for the change. You admitted that you were unreasonable, and it was the only concession you would make; but it was a very cheap one, because that's not your character. No, you are not, and you never will be, arbitrary or capricious. Therefore it is that I believe you will let me see you again. You told me that I'm not disagreeable to you, and I believe it; for I don't see why that should be. I shall always think of you; I shall never think of anyone else. I came to England simply because you are here; I couldn't stay at home after you had gone; I hated the country because you were not in it. If I like this country at present it is only because it holds you. I have been to England before, but have never enjoyed it much. May I not come and see you for half an hour? This at present is the dearest wish of yours faithfully

CASPAR GOODWOOD

Isabel read this missive with such deep attention that she had not perceived an approaching tread on the soft grass. Looking up, however, as she mechanically folded it she saw Lord Warburton standing before her.

Chapter Twelve

She put the letter into her pocket and offered her visitor a smile of welcome, exhibiting no trace of discomposure and half surprised at her coolness.

'They told me you were out here,' said Lord Warburton; 'and as there was no one in the drawing-room and it's really you that I wish to see, I came out with no more ado.'

Isabel had got up; she felt a wish, for the moment, that he should not sit down beside her. 'I was just going indoors.'

'Please don't do that; it's much jollier here; I've ridden over from Lockleigh; it's a lovely day.' His smile was peculiarly friendly and pleasing, and his whole person seemed to emit that radiance of good feeling and good fare which had formed the charm of the girl's first impression of him. It surrounded him like a zone of fine June weather.

'We'll walk about a little then,' said Isabel, who could not divest herself of the sense of an intention on the part of her visitor and who wished both to elude the intention and to satisfy her curiosity about it. It had flashed upon her vision once before, and it had given her on that occasion, as we know, a certain alarm. This alarm was composed of several elements, not all of which were disagreeable; she had indeed spent some days in analysing them and had succeeded in separating the pleasant part of the idea of Lord Warburton's 'making up' to her from the painful. It may appear to some readers that the young lady was both precipitate and unduly fastidious; but the latter of these facts, if the charge be true, may serve to exonerate her from the discredit of the former. She was not eager to convince herself that a territorial magnate, as she had heard Lord Warburton called, was smitten with her charms; the fact of a declaration from such a source carrying with it really more questions than it would answer. She had received a strong impression of his being a 'personage', and she had occupied herself in examining the image so conveyed. At the risk of adding to the evidence of her self-sufficiency it must be said that there had been moments when this possibility of admiration by a personage represented to her an aggression almost to the degree of an affront, quite to the degree of an inconvenience. She had never yet known a personage; there had been no personages, in this sense, in her life; there were probably none such at all in her native land. When she had thought of individual eminence she had thought of it on the basis of character and wit – of what one might like in a gentleman's mind and in his talk. She herself was a character – she couldn't help being aware of that; and hitherto her visions of a completed consciousness had concerned themselves largely with moral images – things as to which the question would be whether they pleased her sublime soul. Lord Warburton loomed up before her, largely and brightly, as a collection of attributes and powers which were not to be measured by this simple rule, but which demanded a different sort of appreciation – an appreciation that the girl with her habit of judging quickly and freely, felt she lacked patience to bestow. He appeared to demand of her something that no one else, as it were, had presumed to do. What she felt was that a territorial, a political, a social magnate had conceived the design of drawing her into the system in which he rather invidiously lived and moved. A certain instinct, not imperious, but persuasive, told her to resist – murmured to her that virtually she had a system and an orbit of her own. It told her other things besides – things which both contradicted and confirmed each other; that a girl might do much worse than trust herself to such a man and that it would be very interesting to see something of his system from his own point of view; that on the other hand, however, there was evidently a great deal of it which she should regard only as a complication of every hour, and that even in the whole there was something stiff and stupid which would make it a burden. Furthermore there was a young man lately come from America who had no system at all, but who had a character of which it was useless for her to try to persuade herself that the impression on her mind had been light. The letter she carried in her pocket all sufficiently reminded her of the contrary. Smile not, however, I venture to repeat, at this simple young woman from Albany who debated whether she should accept an English peer before he had offered himself and who was disposed to believe that on the whole she could do better. She was a person of great good faith, and if there was a great deal of folly in her wisdom those who judge her severely may have the satisfaction of finding that, later, she became consistently wise only at the cost of an amount of folly which will constitute almost a direct appeal to charity.

Lord Warburton seemed quite ready to walk, to sit, or to do anything that Isabel should propose, and he gave her this assurance with his usual air of being particularly pleased to exercise a social virtue. But he was, nevertheless, not in command of his emotions, and as he strolled beside her for a moment, in silence, looking at her without letting her know it, there was something embarrassed in his glance and his misdirected laughter. Yes, assuredly – as we have touched on the point, we may return to it for a moment again – the English are the most romantic people in the world and Lord Warburton was about to give an example of it. He was about to take a step which would astonish all his friends and displease a great many of them, and which had superficially nothing to recommend it. The young lady who trod the turf beside him had come from a queer country across the sea which he knew a good deal about; her antecedents, her associations were very vague to his mind except in so far as they were generic, and in this sense they showed as distinct and unimportant. Miss Archer had neither a fortune nor the sort of beauty that justifies a man to the multitude, and he calculated that he had spent about twenty-six hours in her company. He had summed up all this – the perversity of the impulse, which had declined to avail itself of the most liberal opportunities to subside, and the judgement of mankind, as exemplified particularly in the more quickly-judging half of it: he had looked these things well in the face and then had dismissed them from his thoughts. He cared no more for them than for the rosebud in his buttonhole. It is the good fortune of a man who for the greater part of a lifetime has abstained without effort from making himself disagreeable to his friends, that when the need comes for such a course it is not discredited by irritating associations.

'I hope you had a pleasant ride,' said Isabel, who observed her companion's hesitancy.

'It would have been pleasant if for nothing else than that it brought me here.'

'Are you so fond of Gardencourt?' the girl asked, more and more sure that he meant to make some appeal to her; wishing not to challenge him if he hesitated, and yet to keep all the quietness of her reason if he proceeded. It suddenly came upon her that her situation was one which a few weeks ago she would have deemed deeply romantic: the park of an old English country house, with the foreground embellished by a 'great' (as she supposed) nobleman in the act of making love to a young lady who, on careful inspection, should be found to present remarkable analogies with herself. But if she was now the heroine of the situation she succeeded scarcely the less in looking at it from the outside.

'I care nothing for Gardencourt,' said her companion. 'I care only for you.'

'You've known me too short a time to have a right to say that, and I can't believe you're serious.'

These words of Isabel's were not perfectly sincere, for she had no doubt whatever that he himself was. They were simply a tribute to the fact, of which she was perfectly aware, that those he had just uttered would have excited surprise on the part of a vulgar world. And, moreover, if anything beside the sense she had already acquired that Lord Warburton was not a loose thinker had been needed to convince her, the tone in which he replied would quite have served the purpose.

'One's right in such a matter is not measured by the time, Miss Archer; it's measured by the feeling itself. If I were to wait three months it would make no difference; I shall not be more sure of what I mean than I am today. Of course I've seen you very little, but my impression dates from the very first hour we met. I lost no time, I fell in love with you then. It was at first sight, as the novels say; I know now that's not a fancy-phrase, and I shall think better of novels for evermore. Those two days I spent here settled it; I don't know whether you suspected I was doing so, but I paid – mentally speaking I mean – the greatest possible attention to you. Nothing you said, nothing you did, was lost upon me. When you came to Lockleigh the other day – or rather when you went away – I was perfectly sure. Nevertheless I made up my mind to think it over and to question myself narrowly. I've done so; all these days I've done nothing else. I don't make mistakes about such things; I'm a very judicious animal. I don't go off easily, but when I'm touched, it's for life. It's for life, Miss Archer, it's for life,' Lord Warburton repeated in the kindest, tenderest, pleasantest voice Isabel had ever heard, and looking at her with eyes charged with the light of a passion that had sifted itself clear of the baser parts of emotion – the heat, the violence, the unreason – and that burned as steadily as a lamp in a windless place.

By tacit consent, as he talked, they had walked more and more slowly, and at last they stopped and he took her hand. 'Ah, Lord Warburton, how little you know me!' Isabel said very gently. Gently too she drew her hand away.

'Don't taunt me with that, that I don't know you better makes me unhappy enough already; it's all my loss. But that's what I want, and it seems to me I'm taking the best way. If you'll be my wife, then I shall know you, and when I tell you all the good I think of you you'll not be able to say it's from ignorance.'

'If you know me little I know you even less,' said Isabel.

'You mean that, unlike yourself, I may not improve on acquaintance? Ah, of course that's very possible. But think, to speak to you as I do, how determined I must be to try and give satisfaction! You do like me rather, don't you?'

'I like you very much, Lord Warburton,' she answered; and at this moment she liked him immensely.

'I thank you for saying that; it shows you don't regard me as a stranger. I really believe I've filled all the other relations of life very creditably, and I don't see why I shouldn't fill this one – in which I offer myself to you – seeing that I care so much more about it. Ask the people who know me well; I've friends who'll speak for me.'

'I don't need the recommendation of your friends,' said Isabel.

'Ah now, that's delightful of you. You believe in me yourself.'

'Completely,' Isabel declared. She quite glowed there, inwardly, with the pleasure of feeling she did.

The light in her companion's eyes turned into a smile, and he gave a long exhaltation of joy. 'If you're mistaken, Miss Archer, let me lose all I possess!'

She wondered whether he meant this for a reminder that he was rich, and, on the instant, felt sure that he didn't. He was sinking that, as he would have said himself; and indeed he might safely leave it to the memory of any interlocutor, especially of one to whom he was offering his hand. Isabel had prayed that she might not be agitated, and her mind was tranquil enough, even while she listened and asked herself what it was best she should say, to indulge in this incidental criticism. What she should say, had she asked herself? Her foremost wish was to say something if possible not less kind than what he had said to her. His words had carried perfect conviction with them; she felt she did, all so mysteriously, matter to him. 'I thank you more than I can say for your offer,' she returned at last. 'It does me great honour.'

'Ah, don't say that!' he broke out. 'I was afraid you'd say something like that. I don't see what you've to do with that sort of thing. I don't see why you should thank me – it's I who ought to thank you for listening to me: a man you know so little coming down on you with such a thumper! Of course it's a great question; I must tell you that I'd rather ask it than have it to answer myself. But the way you've listened – or at least your having listened at all – gives me some hope.'

'Don't hope too much,' Isabel said.

'Oh Miss Archer!' her companion murmured, smiling again, in his seriousness, as if such a warning might perhaps be taken but as the play of high spirits, the exuberance of elation.

'Should you be greatly surprised if I were to beg you not to hope at all?' Isabel asked.

'Surprised? I don't know what you mean by surprise. It wouldn't be that; it would be a feeling very much worse.'

Isabel walked on again; she was silent for some minutes. 'I'm very sure that, highly as I already think of you, my opinion of you, if I should know you well, would only rise. But I'm by no means sure that you wouldn't be disappointed. And I say that not in the least out of conventional modesty; it's perfectly sincere.'

'I'm willing to risk it, Miss Archer,' her companion replied.

'It's a great question, as you say. It's a very difficult question.'

'I don't expect you of course to answer it outright. Think it over as long as may be necessary. If I can gain by waiting I'll gladly wait a long time. Only remember that in the end my dearest happiness depends on your answer.'

'I should be very sorry to keep you in suspense,' said Isabel.

'Oh, don't mind. I'd much rather have a good answer six months hence than a bad one today.'

'But it's very probable that even six months hence I shouldn't be able to give you one that you'd think good.'

'Why not, since you really like me?'

'Ah, you must never doubt that,' said Isabel.

'Well then, I don't see what more you ask!'

'It's not what I ask; it's what I can give. I don't think I should suit you; I really don't think I should.'

'You needn't worry about that. That's my affair. You needn't be a better royalist than the king.'

'It's not only that,' said Isabel; 'but I'm not sure I wish to marry anyone.'

'Very likely you don't. I've no doubt a great many women began that way,' said his lordship, who, be it averred, did not in the least believe in the axiom he thus beguiled his anxiety by uttering. 'But they're frequently persuaded.'

'Ah, that's because they want to be!' And Isabel lightly laughed.

Her suitor's countenance fell, and he looked at her for a while in silence. 'I'm afraid it's my being an Englishman that makes you hesitate,' he said presently. 'I know your uncle thinks you ought to marry in your own country.'

Isabel listened to this assertion with some interest; it had never occurred to her that Mr Touchett was likely to discuss her matrimonial prospects with Lord Warburton. 'Has he told you that?'

'I remember his making the remark. He spoke perhaps of Americans generally.'

'He appears himself to have found it very pleasant to live in England.' Isabel spoke in a manner that might have seemed a little perverse, but which expressed both her constant perception of her uncle's outward felicity and her general disposition to elude any obligation to take a restricted view.

It gave her companion hope, and he immediately cried with warmth: 'Ah, my dear Miss Archer, old England's a very good sort of country, you know! And it will be still better when we've furbished it up a little.'

'Oh, don't furbish it, Lord Warburton; leave it alone. I like it this way.'

'Well then, if you like it, I'm more and more unable to see your objection to what I propose.'

'I'm afraid I can't make you understand.'

'You ought at least to try. I've a fair intelligence. Are you afraid – afraid of the climate? We can easily live elsewhere, you know. You can pick out your climate, the whole world over.'

These words were uttered with a breadth of candour that was like the embrace of strong arms – that was like the fragrance straight in her face, and by his clean, breathing lips, of she knew not what strange gardens, what charged airs. She would have given her little finger at that moment to feel strongly and simply the impulse to answer: 'Lord Warburton, it's impossible for me to do better in this wonderful world, I think, than commit myself, very gratefully, to your loyalty.' But though she was lost in admiration of her opportunity she managed to move back into the deepest shade of it, even as some wild, caught creature in a vast cage. The 'splendid' security so offered her was *not* the greatest she could conceive. What she finally bethought herself of saying was something very different – something that deferred the need of really facing her crisis. 'Don't think me unkind if I ask you to say no more about this today.'

'Certainly, certainly!' her companion cried. 'I wouldn't bore you for the world.'

'You've given me a great deal to think about, and I promise you to do it justice.'

'That's all I ask of you, of course – and that you'll remember how absolutely my happiness is in your hands.'

Isabel listened with extreme respect to this admonition, but she said after a minute: 'I must tell you that what I shall think about is some way of letting you know that what you ask is impossible – letting you know it without making you miserable.'

'There's no way to do that, Miss Archer. I won't say that if you refuse me you'll kill me; I shall not die of it. But I shall do worse; I shall live to• no purpose.'

'You'll live to marry a better woman than I.'

'Don't say that, please,' said Lord Warburton very gravely. 'That's fair to neither of us.'

'To marry a worse one then.'

'If there are better women than you I prefer the bad ones. That's all I can say,' he went on with the same earnestness. 'There's no accounting for tastes.'

His gravity made her feel equally grave, and she showed it by again requesting him to drop the subject for the present. 'I'll speak to you myself – very soon. Perhaps I shall write to you.'

'At your convenience, yes,' he replied. 'Whatever time you take, it must seem to me long, and I suppose I must make the best of that.'

'I shall not keep you in suspense; I only want to collect my mind a little.'

He gave a melancholy sigh and stood looking at her a moment, with his hands behind him, giving short nervous shakes to his hunting-crop. 'Do you know I'm very much afraid of it – of that remarkable mind of yours?'

Our heroine's biographer can scarcely tell why, but the question made her start and brought a conscious blush to her cheek. She returned his look a moment, and then with a note in her voice that might almost have appealed to his compassion, 'So am I, my lord!' she oddly exclaimed.

His compassion was not stirred, however; all he possessed of the faculty of pity was needed at home. 'Ah! be merciful, be merciful,' he murmured.

'I think you had better go,' said Isabel. 'I'll write to you'

'Very good; but whatever you write I'll come and see you, you know.' And then he stood reflecting, his eyes fixed on the observant countenance of Bunchie, who had the air of having understood all that had been said and pretending to carry off the indiscretion by a simulated fit of curiosity as to the roots of an ancient oak. 'There's one thing more,' he went on. 'You know, if you don't like Lockleigh – if you think it's damp or anything of that sort – you need never go within fifty miles of it. It's not damp, by the way; I've had the house thoroughly examined; it's perfectly safe and right. But if you shouldn't fancy it you needn't dream of living in it. There's no difficulty whatever about that; there are plenty of houses. I thought I'd just mention it; some people don't like a moat, you know. Good-bye.'

'I adore a moat,' said Isabel. 'Good-bye.'

He held out his hand, and she gave him hers a moment – a moment long enough for him to bend his handsome bared head and kiss it. Then, still agitating, in his mastered emotion, his implement of the chase, he walked rapidly away. He was evidently much upset.

Isabel herself was upset, but she had not been affected as she would have imagined. What she felt was not a great responsibility, a great difficulty of choice; it appeared to her there had been no choice in the question. She couldn't marry Lord Warburton; the idea failed to support any enlightened prejudice in favour of the free exploration of life that she had hitherto entertained or was now capable of entertaining. She must write this to him, she must convince him, and that duty was comparatively simple. But what disturbed her, in the sense that it struck her with wonderment, was this very fact that it cost her so little to refuse a magnificent 'chance'. With whatever qualifications one would, Lord Warburton had offered her a great opportunity; the situation might have discomforts, might contain oppressive, might contain narrowing elements, might prove really but a stupefying anodyne; but she did her sex no injustice in believing that nineteen women out of twenty would have accommodated themselves to it without a pang. Why then upon her also should it not irresistibly impose itself? Who was she, what was she, that she should hold herself superior? What view of life, what design upon fate, what conception of happiness, had she that pretended to be larger than these large, these fabulous occasions? If she wouldn't do such a thing as that then she must do great things, she must do something greater. Poor Isabel found ground to remind herself from time to time that she must not be too proud, and nothing could be more sincere than her prayer to be delivered from such a danger: the isolation and loneliness of pride had for her mind the horror of a desert place. If it had been pride that interfered with her accepting Lord Warburton such a *bêtise* was singularly misplaced; and she was so conscious of liking him that she ventured to assure herself it was the very softness, and the fine intelligence, of sympathy. She liked him too much to marry him, that was the truth; something assured her there was a fallacy somewhere in the glowing logic of the proposition – as *he* saw it – even though she mightn't put her very finest finger-point on it; and to inflict upon a man who offered so much a wife with a tendency to criticize would be a peculiarly discreditable act. She had promised him she would consider his question, and when, after he had left her, she wandered back to the bench where he had found her and lost herself in meditation, it might have seemed that she was keeping her vow. But this was not the case; she was wondering if she were not a cold, hard, priggish person, and, on her at last getting up and going rather quickly back to the house, felt, as she had said to her friend, really frightened at herself.

Chapter Thirteen

It was this feeling and not the wish to ask advice – she had no desire whatever for that – that led her to speak to her uncle of what had taken place. She wished to speak to someone; she should feel more natural, more human, and her uncle, for this purpose, presented himself in a more attractive light than either her aunt or her friend Henrietta. Her cousin of course was a possible confidant; but she would have had to do herself violence to air this special secret to Ralph. So the next day, after breakfast, she sought her occasion. Her uncle never left his apartment till the afternoon, but he received his cronies, as he said, in his dressing-room. Isabel had quite taken her place in the class so designated, which, for the rest, included the old man's son, his physician, his personal servant, and even Miss Stackpole. Mrs Touchett did not figure in the list, and this was an obstacle the less to Isabel's finding her host alone. He sat in a complicated mechanical chair, at the open window of his room, looking westward over the park and the river, with his newspapers and letters piled up beside him, his toilet freshly and minutely made, and his smooth, speculative face composed to benevolent expectation.

She approached her point directly. 'I think I ought to let you know that Lord Warburton has asked me to marry him. I suppose I ought to tell my aunt; but it seems best to tell you first.'

The old man expressed no surprise, but thanked her for the confidence she showed him. 'Do you mind telling me whether you accepted him?' he then inquired.

'I've not answered him definitely yet; I've taken a little time to think of it, because that seems more respectful. But I shall not accept him.'

Mr Touchett made no comment upon this; he had the air of thinking that, whatever interest he might take in the matter from the point of view of sociability, he had no active voice in it. 'Well, I told you you'd be a success over here. Americans are highly appreciated.'

'Very highly indeed,' said Isabel. 'But at the cost of seeming both tasteless and ungrateful, I don't think I can marry Lord Warburton.'

'Well,' her uncle went on, 'of course an old man can't judge for a young lady. I'm glad you didn't ask me before you made up your mind. I suppose

I ought to tell you,' he added slowly, but as if it were not of much consequence, 'that I've known all about it these three days.'

'About Lord Warburton's state of mind?'

'About his intentions, as they say here. He wrote me a very pleasant letter, telling me all about them. Should you like to see his letter?' the old man obligingly asked.

'Thank you; I don't think I care about that. But I'm glad he wrote to you; it was right that he should, and he would be certain to do what was right.'

'Ah well, I guess you do like him!' Mr Touchett declared. 'You needn't pretend you don't.'

'I like him extremely; I'm very free to admit that. But I don't wish to marry anyone just now.'

'You think someone may come along whom you may like better. Well, that's very likely,' said Mr Touchett, who appeared to wish to show his kindness to the girl by easing off her decision, as it were, and finding cheerful reasons for it.

'I don't care if I don't meet anyone else. I like Lord Warburton quite well enough.' She fell into that appearance of a sudden change of point of view with which she sometimes startled and even displeased her interlocutors.

Her uncle, however, seemed proof against either of these impressions. 'He's a very fine man,' he resumed in a tone which might have passed for that of encouragement. 'His letter was one of the pleasantest I've received for some weeks. I suppose one of the reasons I liked it was that it was all about you; that is all except the part that was about himself. I suppose he told you all that.'

'He would have told me everything I wished to ask him,' Isabel said.

'But you didn't feel curious?'

'My curiosity would have been idle – once I had determined to decline his offer.'

'You didn't find it sufficiently attractive?' Mr Touchett inquired.

She was silent a little. 'I suppose it was that,' she presently admitted. 'But I don't know why.'

'Fortunately ladies are not obliged to give reasons,' said her uncle. 'There's a great deal that's attractive about such an idea; but I don't see why the English should want to entice us away from our native land. I know that we try to attract them over there, but that's because our population is insufficient. Here, you know, they're rather crowded. However, I presume there's room for charming young ladies everywhere.'

'There seems to have been room here for you,' said Isabel, whose eyes had been wandering over the large pleasure-spaces of the park.

Mr Touchett gave a shrewd, conscious smile. 'There's room everywhere, my dear, if you'll pay for it. I sometimes think I've paid too much for this. Perhaps you also might have to pay too much.'

'Perhaps I might,' the girl replied.

That suggestion gave her something more definite to rest on than she had found in her own thoughts, and the fact of this association of her uncle's mild acuteness with her dilemma seemed to prove that she was concerned with the natural and reasonable emotions of life and not altogether a victim to intellectual eagerness and vague ambitions – ambitions reaching beyond Lord Warburton's beautiful appeal, reaching to something indefinable and possibly not commendable. In so far as the indefinable had an influence upon Isabel's behaviour at this juncture, it was not the conception, even unformulated, of a union with Caspar Goodwood; for however she might have resisted conquest at her English suitor's large quiet hands she was at least as far removed from the disposition to let the young man from Boston take positive possession of her. The sentiment in which she sought refuge after reading his letter was a critical view of his having come abroad; for it was part of the influence he had upon her that he seemed to deprive her of the sense of freedom. There was a disagreeably strong push, a kind of hardness of presence, in his way of rising before her. She had been haunted at moments by the image, by the danger, of his disapproval and had wondered – a consideration she had never paid in equal degree to anyone else – whether he would like what she did. The difficulty was that more than any man she had ever known, more than poor Lord Warburton (she had begun now to give his lordship the benefit of this epithet), Caspar Goodwood expressed for her an energy – and she had already felt it as a power – that was of his very nature. It was in no degree a matter of his 'advantages' – it was a matter of the spirit that sat in his clear-burning eyes like some tireless watcher at a window. She might like it or not, but he insisted, ever, with his whole weight and force: even in one's usual contact with him one had to reckon with that. The idea of a diminished liberty was particularly disagreeable to her at present, since she had just given a sort of personal accent to her independence by looking so straight at Lord Warburton's big bribe and yet turning away from it. Sometimes Caspar Goodwood had seemed to range himself on the side of her destiny, to be the stubbornest fact she knew; she said to herself at such moments that she might evade him for a time, but that she must make terms with him at last – terms which would be certain to be favourable to himself. Her impulse had been to avail herself of the things that helped her to resist such an obligation; and this impulse had been much concerned in her eager acceptance of her aunt's invitation, which had come to her at an hour when she expected from day to day to see Mr Goodwood and when she was glad to have an answer ready for something she was sure he would say to her. When she had told him at Albany, on the evening of Mrs Touchett's visit, that she couldn't then discuss difficult questions, dazzled as she was by the great immediate opening of her aunt's offer of 'Europe', he declared that this was no answer at all; and it was now to obtain a better one that he was following her across the sea. To say to herself that he was a kind of grim fate was well enough for a fanciful young woman who was able to take much for granted in him: but the reader has a right to a nearer and a clearer view.

He was the son of a proprietor of well-known cotton-mills in Massachusetts – a gentleman who had accumulated a considerable fortune in the exercise of this industry. Caspar at present managed the works, and with a judgement and a temper which, in spite of keen competition and languid years, had kept their prosperity from dwindling. He had received the better part of his education at Harvard College, where, however, he had gained renown rather as a gymnast and an oarsman than as a gleaner of more dispersed knowledge. Later on he had learned that the finer intelligence too could vault and pull and strain – might even, breaking the record, treat itself to rare exploits. He had thus discovered in himself a sharp eye for the mystery of mechanics, and had invented an improvement in the cotton-spinning process which was now largely used and was known by his name. You might have seen it in the newspapers in connexion with this fruitful contrivance; assurance of which he had given to Isabel by showing her in the columns of the New York *Interviewer* an exhaustive article on the Goodwood patent – an article not prepared by Miss Stackpole, friendly as she had proved herself to his more sentimental interests. There were intricate, bristling things he rejoiced in; he liked to organize, to contend, to administer; he could make people work his will, believe in him, march before him and justify him. This was the art, as they said, of managing men – which rested, in him, further, on a bold though brooding ambition. It struck those who knew him well that he might do greater things than carry on a cotton factory; there was nothing cottony about Caspar Goodwood, and his friends took for granted that he would somehow and somewhere write himself in bigger letters. But it was as if something large and confused, something dark and ugly, would have to call upon him: he was not after all in harmony with mere smug peace and greed and gain, an order of things of which the vital breath was ubiquitous advertisement. It pleased Isabel to believe that he might have ridden, on a plunging steed, the whirlwind of a great war – a war like the Civil strife that had over-darkened her conscious childhood and his ripening youth.

She liked at any rate this idea of his being by character and in fact a mover of men – liked it much better than some other points in his nature and aspect. She cared nothing for his cotton mill – the Goodwood patent left her imagination absolutely cold. She wished him no ounce less of his manhood, but she sometimes thought he would be rather nicer if he looked, for instance, a little differently. His jaw was too square and set and his figure too straight and stiff: these things suggested a want of easy consonance with the deeper rhythms of life. Then she viewed with reserve a habit he had of dressing always in the same manner; it was not apparently that he wore the same clothes continually, for, on the contrary, his garments had a way of looking rather too new. But they all seemed of the same piece; the figure, the stuff, was so drearily usual. She had reminded herself more than once that this was a frivolous objection to a person of his importance; and then she had amended the rebuke by saying that it would be a frivolous objection only if she were in love with him. She was not in love with him and therefore might criticize his small defects as well as his great – which latter consisted in the collective reproach of his being too serious, or, rather, not of his being so, since one could never be, but certainly of his seeming so. He showed his appetites and designs too simply and artlessly; when one was alone with him he talked too much about the same subject, and when other people were present he talked too little about anything. And yet he was of supremely strong, clean make – which was so much: she saw the different fitted parts of him as she had seen, in museums and portraits, the different fitted parts of armoured warriors – in plates of steel handsomely inlaid with gold. It was very strange: where, ever, was any tangible link between her impression and her act? Caspar Goodwood had never corresponded to her idea of a delightful person, and she supposed that this was why he left her so harshly critical. When, however, Lord Warburton, who not only did correspond with it, but gave an extension to the term, appealed to her approval, she found herself still unsatisfied. It was certainly strange.

The sense of her incoherence was not a help to answering Mr Goodwood's letter, and Isabel determined to leave it a while unhonoured. If he had determined to persecute her he must take the consequences; foremost among which was his being left to perceive how little it charmed her that he should come down to Gardencourt. She was already liable to the incursions of one suitor at this place, and though it might be pleasant to be appreciated in opposite quarters there was a kind of grossness in entertaining two such passionate pleaders at once, even in a case where the entertainment should consist of dismissing them. She made no reply to Mr Goodwood; but at the end of three days she wrote to Lord Warburton, and the letter belongs to our history.

DEAR LORD WARBURTON – A great deal of earnest thought has not led me to change my mind about the suggestion you were so kind as to make me the other day. I am not, I am really and truly not, able to regard you in the light of a companion for life; or to think of your home – your various homes – as the settled seat of my existence. These things cannot be reasoned about, and I very earnestly entreat you not to return to the subject we discussed so exhaustively. We see our lives from our own point of view; that is the privilege of the weakest and humblest of us; and I shall never be able to see mine in the manner you proposed. Kindly let this suffice you, and do me the justice to believe that I have given your proposal the deeply respectful consideration it deserves. It is with this very great regard that I remain sincerely yours,

ISABEL ARCHER

While the author of this missive was making up her mind to dispatch it Henrietta Stackpole formed a resolve which was accompanied by no demur. She invited Ralph Touchett to take a walk with her in the garden, and when he had assented with that alacrity which seemed constantly to testify to his high expectations, she informed him that she had a favour to ask of him. It may be admitted that at this information the young man flinched; for we know that Miss Stackpole had struck him as apt to push an advantage. The alarm was unreasoned, however; for he was clear about the area of her indiscretion as little as advised of its vertical depth, and he made a very civil profession of the desire to serve her. He was afraid of her and presently told her so. 'When you look at me in a certain way my knees knock together, my faculties desert me; I'm filled with trepidation and I ask only for strength to execute your commands. You've an address that I've never encountered in any woman.'

'Well,' Henrietta replied good-humouredly, 'if I had not known before that you were trying somehow to abash me I should know it now. Of course I'm easy game – I was brought up with such different customs and ideas. I'm not used to your arbitrary standards, and I've never been spoken to in America as you have spoken to me. If a gentleman conversing with me over there were to speak to me like that I shouldn't know what to make of it. We take everything more naturally over there, and, after all, we're a great deal more simple. I admit that; I'm very simple myself. Of course if you choose to laugh at me for it you're very welcome; but I think on the whole I would rather be myself than you. I'm quite content to be myself; I don't want to change. There are plenty of people that appreciate me just as I am. It's true they're nice fresh free-born Americans!' Henrietta had lately taken up the tone of helpless innocence and large concession. 'I want you to assist me a little,' she went on. 'I don't care in the least whether I amuse you while you do so; or, rather, I'm perfectly willing your amusement should be your reward. I want you to help me about Isabel.'

'Has she injured you?' Ralph asked.

'If she had I shouldn't mind, and I should never tell you. What I'm afraid of is that she'll injure herself.'

'I think that's very possible,' said Ralph.

His companion stopped in the garden-walk, fixing on him perhaps the very gaze that unnerved him. 'That too would amuse you, I suppose. The way you do say things! I never heard anyone so indifferent.'

'To Isabel? Ah, not that!'

'Well, you're not in love with her, I hope.'

'How can that be, when I'm in love with Another?'

'You're in love with yourself, that's the Other!' Miss Stackpole declared. 'Much good may it do you! But if you wish to be serious once in your life here's a chance; and if you really care for your cousin here's an opportunity to prove it. I don't expect you to understand her; that's too much to ask. But you needn't do that to grant my favour. I'll supply the necessary intelligence.'

'I shall enjoy that immensely!' Ralph exclaimed. 'I'll be Caliban and you shall be Ariel.'

'You're not at all like Caliban, because you're sophisticated, and Caliban was not. But I'm not talking about imaginary characters; I'm talking about Isabel. Isabel's intensely real. What I wish to tell you is that I find her fearfully changed.'

'Since you came, do you mean?'

'Since I came and before I came. She's not the same as she once so beautifully was.'

'As she was in America?'

'Yes, in America. I suppose you know she comes from there. She can't help it, but she does.'

'Do you want to change her back again?'

'Of course I do, and I want you to help me.'

'Ah,' said Ralph, 'I'm only Caliban; I'm not Prospero.'

'You were Prospero enough to make her what she has become. You've acted on Isabel Archer since she came here, Mr Touchett.'

'I, my dear Miss Stackpole? Never in the world. Isabel Archer has acted on me – yes; she acts on everyone. But I've been absolutely passive.'

'You're too passive then. You had better stir yourself and be careful. Isabel's changing every day; she's drifting away – right out to sea. I've watched her and I can see it. She's not the bright American girl she was. She's taking different views, a different colour, and turning away from her old ideals. I want to save those ideals, Mr Touchett, and that's where you come in.'

'Not surely as an ideal?'

'Well, I hope not,' Henrietta replied promptly. 'I've got a fear in my heart that she's going to marry one of these fell Europeans, and I want to prevent it.'

'Ah, I see,' cried Ralph; 'and to prevent it you want me to step in and marry her?'

'Not quite; that remedy would be as bad as the disease, for you're the typical, the fell European from whom I wish to rescue her. No; I wish you to take an interest in another person – a young man to whom she once gave great encouragement and whom she now doesn't seem to think good enough. He's a thoroughly grand man and a very dear friend of mine, and I wish very much you would invite him to pay a visit here.'

Ralph was much puzzled by this appeal, and it is perhaps not to the credit of his purity of mind that he failed to look at it at first in the simplest light. It wore, to his eyes, a tortuous air, and his fault was that he was not quite sure that anything in the world could really be as candid as this request of Miss Stackpole's appeared. That a young woman should demand that a gentleman whom she described as her very dear friend should be furnished with an opportunity to make himself agreeable to another young woman, a young woman whose attention had wandered and whose charms were greater – this was an anomaly which for the moment challenged all his ingenuity of interpretation. To read between the lines was easier than to follow the text, and to suppose that Miss Stackpole wished the gentleman invited to Gardencourt on her own account was the sign not so much of a vulgar as of an embarrassed mind. Even from this venial act of vulgarity, however, Ralph was saved, and saved by a force that I can only speak of as inspiration. With no more outward light on the subject than he already possessed he suddenly acquired the conviction that it would be a sovereign injustice to the correspondent of the *Interviewer* to assign a dishonourable motive to any act of hers. This conviction passed into his mind with extreme rapidity; it was perhaps kindled by the pure radiance of the young lady's imperturbable gaze. He returned this challenge a moment, consciously, resisting an inclination to frown as one frowns in the presence of larger luminaries. 'Who's the gentleman you speak of?'

'Mr Caspar Goodwood – of Boston. He has been extremely attentive to Isabel – just as devoted to her as he can live. He has followed her out here and he's at present in London. I don't know his address, but I guess I can obtain it.'

'I've never heard of him,' said Ralph.

'Well, I suppose you haven't heard of everyone. I don't believe he has ever heard of you; but that's no reason why Isabel shouldn't marry him.'

Ralph gave a mild ambiguous laugh. 'What a rage you have for marrying people! Do you remember how you wanted to marry *me* the other day?'

'I've got over that. You don't know how to take such ideas. Mr Goodwood does, however; and that's what I like about him. He's a splendid man and a perfect gentleman, and Isabel knows it.'

'Is she very fond of him?'

'If she isn't she ought to be. He's simply wrapped up in her.'

'And you wish me to ask him here,' said Ralph reflectively.

'It would be an act of true hospitality.'

'Caspar Goodwood,' Ralph continued – 'it's rather a striking name.'

'I don't care anything about his name. It might be Ezekiel Jenkins, and I should say the same. He's the only man I have ever seen whom I think worthy of Isabel.'

'You're a very devoted friend,' said Ralph.

'Of course I am. If you say that to pour scorn on me I don't care.'

'I don't say it to pour scorn on you; I'm very much struck with it.'

'You're more satiric than ever, but I advise you not to laugh at Mr Goodwood.'

'I assure you I'm very serious; you ought to understand that,' said Ralph.

In a moment his companion understood it. 'I believe you are; now you're too serious.'

'You're difficult to please.'

'Oh, you're very serious indeed. You won't invite Mr Goodwood.'

'I don't know,' said Ralph. 'I'm capable of strange things. Tell me a little about Mr Goodwood. What's he like?'

'He's just the opposite of you. He's at the head of a cotton factory; a very fine one.'

'Has he pleasant manners?' asked Ralph.

'Splendid manners – in the American style.'

'Would he be an agreeable member of our little circle?'

'I don't think he'd care much about our little circle. He'd concentrate on Isabel.'

'And how would my cousin like that?'

'Very possibly not at all. But it will be good for her. It will call back her thoughts.'

'Call them back – from where?'

'From foreign parts and other unnatural places. Three months ago she gave Mr Goodwood every reason to suppose he was acceptable to her, and it's not worthy of Isabel to go back on a real friend simply because she has changed the scene. I've changed the scene too, and the effect of it has been to make me care more for my old associations than ever. It's my belief that the sooner Isabel changes it back again the better. I know her well enough to know that she would never be truly happy over here, and I wish her to form some strong American tie that will act as a preservative.'

'Aren't you perhaps a little too much in a hurry?' Ralph inquired. 'Don't you think you ought to give her more of a chance in poor old England?'

'A chance to ruin her bright young life? One's never too much in a hurry to save a precious human creature from drowning.'

'As I understand it then,' said Ralph, 'you wish me to push Mr Goodwood overboard after her. Do you know,' he added, 'that I've never heard her mention his name?'

Henrietta gave a brilliant smile. 'I'm delighted to hear that; it proves how much she thinks of him.'

Ralph appeared to allow that there was a good deal in this, and he surrendered to thought while his companion watched him askance. 'If I should invite Mr Goodwood,' he finally said, 'it would be to quarrel with him.'

'Don't do that; he'd prove the better man.'

'You certainly are doing your best to make me hate him! I really don't think I can ask him. I should be afraid of being rude to him.'

'It's just as you please,' Henrietta returned. 'I had no idea you were in love with her yourself.'

'Do you really believe that?' the young man asked with lifted eyebrows.

'That's the most natural speech I've ever heard you make! Of course I believe it,' Miss Stackpole ingeniously said.

'Well,' Ralph concluded, 'to prove to you that you're wrong I'll invite him. It must be of course as a friend of yours.'

'It will not be as a friend of mine that he'll come; and it will not be to prove to me that I'm wrong that you'll ask him – but to prove it to yourself!'

These last words of Miss Stackpole's (on which the two presently separated) contained an amount of truth which Ralph Touchett was obliged to recognize; but it so far took the edge from too sharp a recognition that, in spite of his suspecting it would be rather more indiscreet to keep than to break his promise, he wrote Mr Goodwood a note of six lines, expressing the pleasure it would give Mr Touchett the elder that he should join a little party at Gardencourt, of which Miss Stackpole was a valued member. Having sent his letter (to the care of a banker whom Henrietta suggested) he waited in some suspense. He had heard this fresh formidable figure named for the first time; for when his mother had mentioned on her arrival that there was a story about the girl's having an 'admirer' at home, the idea had seemed deficient in reality and he had taken no pains to ask questions the answers to which would involve only the vague or the disagreeable. Now, however, the native admiration of which his cousin was the object had become more concrete; it took the form of a young man who had followed her to London, who was interested in a cotton mill and had manners in the most splendid of the American styles. Ralph had two theories about this intervener. Either his passion was a sentimental fiction of Miss Stackpole's (there was always a sort of tacit understanding among women, born of the solidarity of the sex, that they should discover or invent lovers for each other), in which case he was not to be feared and would probably not accept the invitation; or else he would accept the invitation and in this event prove himself a creature too irrational to demand further consideration. The latter clause of Ralph's argument might have seemed incoherent; but it embodied his conviction that if Mr Goodwood were interested in Isabel in the serious manner described by Miss Stackpole he would not care to present himself at Gardencourt on a summons from the latter lady. 'On this supposition,' said Ralph, 'he must regard her as a thorn on the stem of his rose; as an intercessor he must find her wanting in tact.'

Two days after he had sent his invitation he received a very short note from Caspar Goodwood, thanking him for it, regretting that other engagements made a visit to Gardencourt impossible and presenting many compliments to Miss Stackpole. Ralph handed the note to Henrietta, who, when she had read it, exclaimed: 'Well, I never have heard of anything so stiff!'

'I'm afraid he doesn't care so much about my cousin as you suppose,' Ralph observed.

'No, it's not that; it's some subtler motive. His nature's very deep. But I'm determined to fathom it, and I shall write to him to know what he means.'

His refusal of Ralph's overtures was vaguely disconcerting; from the moment he declined to come to Gardencourt our friend began to think him of importance. He asked himself what it signified to him whether Isabel's admirers should be desperadoes or laggards; they were not rivals of his and were perfectly welcome to act out their genius. Nevertheless he felt much curiosity as to the result of Miss Stackpole's promised inquiry into the causes of Mr Goodwood's stiffness – a curiosity for the present ungratified, inasmuch as when he asked her three days later if she had written to London she was obliged to confess she had written in vain. Mr Goodwood had not replied.

'I suppose he's thinking it over,' she said; 'he thinks everything over; he's not *really* at all impetuous. But I'm accustomed to having my letters answered the same day.' She presently proposed to Isabel, at all events that they should make an excursion to London together. 'If I must tell the truth,' she observed, 'I'm not seeing much at this place, and I shouldn't think you were either. I've not even seen that aristocrat – what's his name? – Lord Washburton. He seems to let you severely alone.'

'Lord Warburton's coming tomorrow, I happen to know,' replied her friend, who had received a note from the master of Lockleigh in answer to her own letter. 'You'll have every opportunity of turning him inside out.'

'Well, he may do for one letter, but what's one letter when you want to write fifty? I've described all the scenery in this vicinity and raved about all the old women and donkeys. You may say what you please, scenery doesn't make a vital letter. I must go back to London and get some impressions of real life. I was there but three days before I came away, and that's hardly time to get in touch.'

As Isabel, on her journey from New York to Gardencourt, had seen even less of the British capital than this, it appeared a happy suggestion of Henrietta's that the two should go thither on a visit of pleasure. The idea struck Isabel as charming; she was curious of the thick detail of London, which had always loomed large and rich to her. They turned over their schemes together and indulged in visions of romantic hours. They would stay at some picturesque old inn – one of the inns described by Dickens – and drive over the town in those delightful hansoms. Henrietta was a literary woman, and the great advantage of being a literary woman was that you could go everywhere and do everything. They would dine at a coffee house and go afterwards to the play; they would frequent the Abbey and the British Museum and find out where Doctor Johnson had lived, and Goldsmith and Addison. Isabel grew eager and presently unveiled the bright vision to Ralph, who burst into a fit of laughter which scarce expressed the sympathy she had desired.

'It's a delightful plan,' he said. 'I advise you to go to the Duke's Head in Covent Garden, an easy, informal, old-fashioned place, and I'll have you put down at my club.'

'Do you mean it's improper?' Isabel asked. 'Dear me, isn't anything proper here? With Henrietta surely I may go anywhere; she isn't hampered in that way. She has travelled over the whole American continent and can at least find her way about this minute island.'

'Ah then,' said Ralph, 'let me take advantage of her protection to go up to town as well. I may never have a chance to travel so safely!'

Chapter Fourteen

Miss Stackpole would have prepared to start immediately; but Isabel, as we have seen, had been notified that Lord Warburton would come again to Gardencourt, and she believed it her duty to remain there and see him. For four or five days he had made no response to her letter; then he had written, very briefly, to say he would come to luncheon two days later. There was something in these delays and postponements that touched the girl and renewed her sense of his desire to be considerate and patient, not to appear to urge her too grossly; a consideration the more studied that she was so sure he 'really liked' her. Isabel told her uncle she had written to him, mentioning also his intention of coming; and the old man, in consequence, left his room earlier than usual and made his appearance at the two o'clock repast. This was by no means an act of vigilance on his part, but the fruit of a benevolent belief that his being of the company might help to cover any conjoined straying away in case Isabel should give their noble visitor another hearing. That personage drove over from Lockleigh and brought the elder of his sisters with him, a measure presumably dictated by reflections of the same order as Mr Touchett's. The two visitors were introduced to Miss Stackpole, who, at luncheon, occupied a seat adjoining Lord Warburton's. Isabel, who was nervous and had no relish for the prospect of again arguing the question he had so prematurely opened, could not help admiring his good-humoured self-possession, which quite disguised the symptoms of that preoccupation with her presence it was natural she should suppose him to feel. He neither looked at her nor spoke to her, and the only sign of emotion was that he avoided meeting her eyes. He had plenty of talk for the others, however, and he appeared to eat his luncheon with discrimination and appetite. Miss Molyneux, who had a smooth, nunlike forehead and wore a large silver cross suspended from her neck, was evidently preoccupied with Henrietta Stackpole, upon whom her eyes constantly rested in a manner suggesting a conflict between deep alienation and yearning wonder. Of the two ladies from Lockleigh she was the one Isabel had liked best; there was such a world of hereditary quiet in her. Isabel was sure moreover that her mild forehead and silver cross referred to some weird Anglican mystery – some delightful reinstitution perhaps of the quaint office of the canoness. She wondered what Miss Molyneux would think of her if she knew Miss Archer had refused her brother: and then she felt sure that Miss Molyneux would never know – that Lord Warburton never told her such things. He was fond of her and kind to her, but on the whole he told her little. Such, at least, was Isabel's theory; when, at table, she was not occupied in conversation she was usually occupied in forming theories about her neighbours. According to Isabel, if Miss Molyneux should ever learn what had passed between Miss

Archer and Lord Warburton she would probably be shocked at such a girl's failure to rise; or no, rather (this was our heroine's last position) she would impute to the young American but a due consciousness of inequality.

Whatever Isabel might have made of her opportunities, at all events, Henrietta Stackpole was by no means disposed to neglect those in which she now found herself immersed. 'Do you know you're the first lord I've ever seen?' she said very promptly to her neighbour. 'I suppose you think I'm awfully benighted.'

'You've escaped seeing some very ugly men,' Lord Warburton answered, looking a trifle absently about the table.

'Are they very ugly? They try to make us believe in America that they're all handsome and magnificent and that they wear wonderful robes and crowns.'

'Ah, the robes and crowns are gone out of fashion,' said Lord Warburton, 'like your tomahawks and revolvers.'

'I'm sorry for that; I think an aristocracy ought to be splendid,' Henrietta declared. 'If it's not that, what is it?'

'Oh, you know, it isn't much, at the best,' her neighbour allowed. 'Won't you have a potato?'

'I don't care much for these European potatoes. I shouldn't know you from an ordinary American gentleman.'

'Do talk to me as if I *were* one,' said Lord Warburton. 'I don't see how you manage to get on without potatoes; you must find so few things to eat over here.'

Henrietta was silent a little; there was a chance he was not sincere. 'I've had hardly any appetite since I've been here,' she went on at last; 'so it doesn't much matter. I don't approve of *you*, you know; I feel as if I ought to tell you that.'

'Don't approve of me?'

'Yes; I don't suppose anyone ever said such a thing to you before did they? I don't approve of lords as an institution. I think the world has got beyond them – far beyond.'

'Oh, so do I. I don't approve of myself in the least. Sometimes it comes over me – how I should object to myself if I were not myself, don't you know? But that's rather good, by the way – not to be vain-glorious.'

'Why don't you give it up then?' Miss Stackpole inquired.

'Give up – a—?' asked Lord Warburton, meeting her harsh inflexion with a very mellow one.

'Give up being a lord.'

'Oh, I'm so little of one! One would really forget all about it if you wretched Americans were not constantly reminding one. However, I do think of giving it up, the little there is left of it, one of these days.'

'I should like to see you do it!' Henrietta exclaimed rather grimly.

'I'll invite you to the ceremony; we'll have a supper and a dance.'

'Well,' said Miss Stackpole, 'I like to see all sides. I don't approve of a privileged class, but I like to hear what they have to say for themselves.'

'Mighty little, as you see!'

'I should like to draw you out a little more,' Henrietta continued. 'But you're always looking away. You're afraid of meeting my eye. I see you want to escape me.'

'No, I'm only looking for those despised potatoes.'

'Please explain about that young lady – your sister – then. I don't understand about her. Is she a Lady?'

'She's a capital good girl.'

'I don't like the way you say that – as if you wanted to change the subject. Is her position inferior to yours?'

'We neither of us have any position to speak of; but she's better off than I, because she has none of the bother.'

'Yes, she doesn't look as if she had much bother. I wish I had as little bother as that. You do produce quiet people over here, whatever else you may do.'

'Ah, you see one takes life easily, on the whole,' said Lord Warburton. 'And then you know we're very dull. Ah, we can be dull when we try!'

'I should advise you to try something else. I shouldn't know what to talk to your sister about; she looks so different. Is that silver cross a badge?'

'A badge?'

'A sign of rank.'

Lord Warburton's glance had wandered a good deal but at this it met the gaze of his neighbour. 'Oh yes,' he answered in a moment; 'the women go in for those things. The silver cross is worn by the eldest daughters of Viscounts.' Which was his harmless revenge for having occasionally had his credulity too easily engaged in America. After luncheon he proposed to Isabel to come into the gallery and look at the pictures; and though she knew he had seen the pictures twenty times she complied without criticizing this pretext. Her conscience now was very easy; ever since she sent him her letter she had felt particularly light of spirit. He walked slowly to the end of the gallery, staring at its contents and saying nothing; and then he suddenly broke out: 'I hoped you wouldn't write to me that way.'

'It was the only way, Lord Warburton,' said the girl. 'Do try and believe that.'

'If I could believe it of course I should let you alone. But we can't believe by willing it; and I confess I don't understand. I could understand your disliking me; that I could understand well. But that you should admit you do—'

'What have I admitted?' Isabel interrupted, turning slightly pale.

'That you think me a good fellow; isn't that it?' She said nothing, and he went on: 'You don't seem to have any reason, and that gives me a sense of injustice.'

'I have a reason, Lord Warburton.' She said it in a tone that made his heart contract.

'I should like very much to know it.'

'I'll tell you some day when there's more to show for it.'

'Excuse my saying that in the meantime I must doubt of it.'

'You make me very unhappy,' said Isabel.

'I'm not sorry for that; it may help you to know how I feel. Will you kindly answer me a question?' Isabel made no audible assent, but he apparently saw in her eyes something that gave him courage to go on. 'Do you prefer someone else?'

'That's a question I'd rather not answer.'

'Ah, you *do* then!' her suitor murmured with bitterness.

The bitterness touched her, and she cried out: 'You're mistaken! I don't.'

He sat down on a bench, unceremoniously, doggedly, like a man in trouble; leaning his elbows on his knees and staring at the floor. 'I can't even be glad of that,' he said at last, throwing himself back against the wall; 'for that would be an excuse.'

She raised her eyebrows in surprise. 'An excuse? Must I excuse myself?'

He paid, however, no answer to the question. Another idea had come into his head. 'Is it my political opinions? Do you think I go too far?'

'I can't object to your political opinions, because I don't understand them.'

'You don't care what I think!' he cried, getting up. 'It's all the same to you.'

Isabel walked to the other side of the gallery and stood there showing him her charming back, her light slim figure, the length of her white neck as she bent her head, and the density of her dark braids. She stopped in front of a small picture as if for the purpose of examining it; and there was something so young and free in her movement that her very pliancy seemed to mock at him. Her eyes, however, saw nothing; they had suddenly been suffused with tears. In a moment he followed her, and by this time she had brushed her tears away; but when she turned round her face was pale and the expression of her eyes strange. 'That reason that I wouldn't tell you – I'll tell it you after all. It's that I can't escape my fate.'

'Your fate?'

'I should try to escape it if I were to marry you.'

'I don't understand. Why should not *that* be your fate as well as anything else?'

'Because it's not,' said Isabel femininely. 'I know it's not. It's not my fate to give up – I know it can't be.'

Poor Lord Warburton stared, an interrogative point in either eye. 'Do you call marrying *me* giving up?'

'Not in the usual sense. It's getting – getting – getting a great deal. But it's giving up other chances.'

'Other chances for what?'

'I don't mean chances to marry,' said Isabel, her colour quickly coming back to her. And then she stopped, looking down with a deep frown, as if it were hopeless to attempt to make her meaning clear.

'I don't think it presumptuous in me to suggest that you'll gain more than you'll lose,' her companion observed.

'I can't escape unhappiness,' said Isabel. 'In marrying you I shall be trying to.'

'I don't know whether you'd try to, but you certainly would: that I must in candour admit!' he exclaimed with an anxious laugh.

'I mustn't – I can't!' cried the girl.

'Well, if you're bent on being miserable I don't see why you should make *me* so. Whatever charms a life of misery may have for you, it has none for me.'

'I'm not bent on a life of misery,' said Isabel. 'I've always been intensely determined to be happy, and I've often believed I should be. I've told people that; you can ask them. But it comes over me every now and then that I can never be happy in any extraordinary way; not by turning away, by separating myself.'

'By separating yourself from what?'

'From life. From the usual chances and dangers, from what most people know and suffer.'

Lord Warburton broke into a smile that almost denoted hope. 'Why, my dear Miss Archer,' he began to explain with the most considerable eagerness, 'I don't offer you any exoneration from life or from any chances or dangers whatever. I wish I could; depend upon it I would! For what do you take me, pray? Heaven help me, I'm not the Emperor of China! All I offer you is the chance of taking the common lot in a comfortable sort of way. The common lot? Why, I'm devoted to the common lot! Strike an alliance with me, and I promise you that you shall have plenty of it. You shall separate from nothing whatever – not even from your friend Miss Stackpole.'

'She'd never approve of it,' said Isabel, trying to smile and take advantage of this side-issue; despising herself too, not a little, for doing so.

'Are we speaking of Miss Stackpole?' his lordship asked impatiently. 'I never saw a person judge things on such theoretic grounds.'

'Now I suppose you're speaking of me,' said Isabel with humility; and she turned away again, for she saw Miss Molyneux enter the gallery, accompanied by Henrietta and by Ralph.

Lord Warburton's sister addressed him with a certain timidity and reminded him she ought to return home in time for tea, as she was expecting company to partake of it. He made no answer – apparently not having heard her; he was preoccupied, and with good reason. Miss Molyneux – as if he had been Royalty – stood like a lady-in-waiting.

'Well, I never, Miss Molyneux!' said Henrietta Stackpole. 'If I wanted to go he'd have to go. If I wanted my brother to do a thing he'd have to do it.'

'Oh, Warburton does everything one wants,' Miss Molyneux answered with a quick, shy laugh. 'How very many pictures you have!' she went on, turning to Ralph.

'They look a good many, because they're all put together,' said Ralph. 'But it's really a bad way.'

'Oh, I think it's so nice. I wish we had a gallery at Lockleigh. I'm so very fond of pictures,' Miss Molyneux went on, persistently, to Ralph, as if she were afraid Miss Stackpole would address her again. Henrietta appeared at once to fascinate and to frighten her.

'Ah yes, pictures are very convenient,' said Ralph, who appeared to know better what style of reflection was acceptable to her.

'They're so very pleasant when it rains,' the young lady continued. 'It has rained of late so very often.'

'I'm sorry you're going away, Lord Warburton,' said Henrietta. 'I wanted to get a great deal more out of you.'

'I'm not going away,' Lord Warburton answered.

'Your sister says you must. In America the gentlemen obey the ladies.'

'I'm afraid we have some people to tea,' said Miss Molyneux, looking at her brother.

'Very good, my dear. We'll go.'

'I hoped you would resist!' Henrietta exclaimed. 'I wanted to see what Miss Molyneux would do.'

'I never do anything,' said this young lady.

'I suppose in your position it's sufficient for you to exist!' Miss Stackpole returned. 'I should like very much to see you at home.'

'You must come to Lockleigh again,' said Miss Molyneux, very sweetly, to Isabel, ignoring this remark of Isabel's friend.

Isabel looked into her quiet eyes a moment, and for that moment seemed to see in their grey depths the reflection of everything she had rejected in rejecting Lord Warburton – the peace, the kindness, the honour, the possessions, a deep security and a great exclusion. She kissed Miss Molyneux and then she said: 'I'm afraid I can never come again.'

'Never again?'

'I'm afraid I'm going away.'

'Oh, I'm so very sorry,' said Miss Molyneux. 'I think that's so very wrong of you.'

Lord Warburton watched this little passage; then he turned away and stared at a picture. Ralph, leaning against the rail before the picture with his hands in his pockets, had for the moment been watching him.

'I should like to see you at home,' said Henrietta, whom Lord Warburton found beside him. 'I should like an hour's talk with you; there are a great many questions I wish to ask you.'

'I shall be delighted to see you,' the proprietor of Lockleigh answered; 'but I'm certain not to be able to answer many of your questions. When will you come?'

'Whenever Miss Archer will take me. We're thinking of going to London, but we'll go and see you first. I'm determined to get some satisfaction out of you.'

'If it depends upon Miss Archer I'm afraid you won't get much. She won't come to Lockleigh; she doesn't like the place.'

'She told me it was lovely!' said Henrietta.

Lord Warburton hesitated. 'She won't come, all the same. You had better come alone,' he added.

Henrietta straightened herself, and her large eyes expanded. 'Would you make that remark to an English lady?' she inquired with soft asperity.

Lord Warburton stared. 'Yes, if I liked her enough.'

'You'd be careful not to like her enough. If Miss Archer won't visit your place again it's because she doesn't want to take me. I know what she thinks of me, and I suppose you think the same – that I oughtn't to bring in individuals.' Lord Warburton was at a loss; he had not been made acquainted with Miss Stackpole's professional character and failed to catch her allusion. 'Miss Archer has been warning you!' she therefore went on.

'Warning me?'

'Isn't that why she came off alone with you here – to put you on your guard?'

'Oh dear, no,' said Lord Warburton brazenly; 'our talk had no such solemn character as that.'

'Well, you've been on your guard – intensely. I suppose it's natural to you; that's just what I wanted to observe. And so, too, Miss Molyneux – she wouldn't commit herself. *You* have been warned, anyway,' Henrietta continued, addressing this young lady; 'but for you it wasn't necessary.'

'I hope not,' said Miss Molyneux vaguely.

'Miss Stackpole takes notes,' Ralph soothingly explained. 'She's a great satirist; she sees through us all and she works us up.'

'Well, I must say I never have had such a collection of bad material!' Henrietta declared, looking from Isabel to Lord Warburton and from this nobleman to his sister and to Ralph. 'There's something the matter with you all; you're as dismal as if you had got a bad cable.'

'You do see through us, Miss Stackpole,' said Ralph in a low tone, giving her a little intelligent nod as he led the party out of the gallery. 'There's something the matter with us all.'

Isabel came behind these two; Miss Molyneux, who decidedly liked her immensely, had taken her arm, to walk beside her over the polished floor. Lord Warburton strolled on the other side with his hands behind him and his eyes lowered. For some moments he said nothing; and then, 'Is it true you're going to London?' he asked.

'I believe it has been arranged.'

'And when shall you come back?'

'In a few days; but probably for a very short time. I'm going to Paris with my aunt.'

'When, then, shall I see you again?'

'Not for a good while,' said Isabel. 'But some day or other, I hope.'

'Do you really hope it?'

'Very much.'

He went a few steps in silence; then he stopped and put out his hand. 'Good-bye.'

'Good-bye,' said Isabel.

Miss Molyneux kissed her again, and she let the two depart. After it, without rejoining Henrietta and Ralph, she retreated to her own room; in which apartment, before dinner, she was found by Mrs Touchett, who had stopped on her way to the saloon. 'I may as well tell you,' said that lady, 'that your uncle has informed me of your relations with Lord Warburton.'

Isabel considered. 'Relations? They're hardly relations. That's the strange part of it: he has seen me but three or four times.'

'Why did you tell your uncle rather than me?' Mrs Touchett dispassionately asked.

Again the girl hesitated. 'Because he knows Lord Warburton better.'

'Yes, but I know you better.'

'I'm not sure of that,' said Isabel, smiling.

'Neither am I, after all; especially when you give me that rather conceited look. One would think you were awfully pleased with yourself and had carried off a prize! I suppose that when you refuse an offer like Lord Warburton's it's because you expect to do something better.'

'Ah, my uncle didn't say that!' cried Isabel, smiling still.

Chapter Fifteen

It had been arranged that the two young ladies should proceed to London under Ralph's escort, though Mrs Touchett looked with little favour on the plan. It was just the sort of plan, she said, that Miss Stackpole would be sure to suggest, and she inquired if the correspondent of the *Interviewer* was to take the party to stay at her favourite boarding-house.

'I don't care where she takes us to stay, so long as there's local colour,' said Isabel. 'That's what we're going to London for.'

'I suppose that after a girl had refused an English lord she may do anything,' her aunt rejoined. 'After that one needn't stand on trifles.'

'Should you have liked me to marry Lord Warburton?' Isabel inquired.

'Of course I should.'

'I thought you disliked the English so much.'

'So I do; but it's all the greater reason for making use of them.'

'Is that your idea of marriage?' And Isabel ventured to add that her aunt appeared to her to have made very little use of Mr Touchett.

'Your uncle's not an English nobleman,' said Mrs Touchett, 'though even if he had been I should still probably have taken up my residence in Florence.'

'Do you think Lord Warburton could make me any better than I am?' the girl asked with some animation. 'I don't mean I'm too good to improve. I mean – I mean that I don't love Lord Warburton enough to marry him.'

'You did right to refuse him then,' said Mrs Touchett in her smallest, sparest voice. 'Only, the next great offer you get, I hope you'll manage to come up to your standard.'

'We had better wait till the offer comes before we talk about it. I hope very much I may have no more offers for the present. They upset me completely.'

'You probably won't be troubled with them if you adopt permanently the Bohemian manner of life. However, I've promised Ralph not to criticize.'

'I'll do whatever Ralph says is right,' Isabel returned. 'I've unbounded confidence in Ralph.'

'His mother's much obliged to you!' this lady dryly laughed.

'It seems to me indeed she ought to feel it!' Isabel irrepressibly answered.

Ralph had assured her that there would be no violation of decency in their paying a visit – the little party of three – to the sights of the metropolis; but Mrs Touchett took a different view. Like many ladies of her country who had lived a long time in Europe, she had completely lost her native tact on such points, and in her reaction, not in itself deplorable, against the liberty allowed to young persons beyond the seas, had fallen into gratuitous and exaggerated scruples. Ralph accompanied their visitors to town and established them at a quiet inn in a street that ran at right angles to Piccadilly. His first idea had been to take them to his father's house in Winchester Square, a large, dull mansion which at this period of the year was shrouded in silence and brown holland; but he bethought himself that, the cook being at Gardencourt, there was no one in the house to get them their meals, and Pratt's Hotel accordingly became their resting-place. Ralph, on his side, found quarters in Winchester Square, having a 'den' there of which he was very fond and being familiar with deeper fears than that of a cold kitchen. He availed himself largely indeed of the resources of Pratt's Hotel, beginning his day with an early visit to his fellow travellers, who had Mr Pratt in person, in a large bulging white waistcoat, to remove their dish-covers. Ralph turned up, as he said, after breakfast, and the little party made out a scheme of entertainment for the day. As London wears in the month of September a face blank but for its smears of prior service, the young man, who occasionally took an apologetic tone, was obliged to remind his companion, to Miss Stackpole's high derision, that there wasn't a creature in town.

'I suppose you mean the aristocracy are absent,' Henrietta answered; 'but I don't think you could have a better proof that if they were absent altogether they wouldn't be missed. It seems to me the place is about as full as it can be. There's no one here, of course, but three or four millions of people. What is it you call them – the lower-middle class? They're only the population of London, and that's of no consequence.'

Ralph declared that for him the aristocracy left no void that Miss Stackpole herself didn't fill, and that a more contented man was nowhere at that moment to be found. In this he spoke the truth, for the stale September days, in the huge half-empty town, had a charm wrapped in them as a coloured gem might be wrapped in a dusty cloth. When he went home at night to the empty house in Winchester Square, after a chain of hours with his comparatively ardent friends, he wandered into the big dusky dining-room, where the candle he took from the hall table, after letting himself in, constituted the only illumination. The square was still, the house was still; when he raised one of the windows of the dining-room to let in the air he heard the slow creak of the boots of a lone constable. His own step, in the empty place, seemed loud and sonorous; some of the carpets had been raised, and whenever he moved he roused a melancholy echo. He sat down in one of the armchairs; the big dark dining-table twinkled here and there in the small candle-light; the pictures on the wall, all of them very brown, looked vague and incoherent. There was a ghostly presence as of dinners long since digested, of table-talk that had lost its actuality. This hint of the supernatural perhaps had something to do with the fact that his imagination took a flight and that he remained in his chair a long time beyond the hour at which he should have been in bed; doing nothing, not even reading the evening paper. I say he did nothing, and I maintain the phrase in the face of the fact that he thought at these moments of Isabel. To think of Isabel could only be for him an idle pursuit, leading to nothing and profiting little to anyone. His cousin had not yet seemed to him so charming as during these days spent in sounding, tourist-fashion, the deeps and shallows of the metropolitan element. Isabel was full of premises, conclusions, emotions; if she had come in search of local colour she found it everywhere. She asked more questions than he could answer, and launched brave theories, as to historic cause and social effect, that he was equally unable to accept or to refute. The party went more than once to the British Museum and to that brighter palace of art which reclaims for antique variety so large an area of a monotonous suburb; they spent a morning in the Abbey and went on a penny-steamer to the Tower; they looked at pictures both in public and private collections and sat on various occasions beneath the great trees in Kensington Gardens. Henrietta proved an indestructible sightseer and a more lenient judge than Ralph had ventured to hope. She had indeed many disappointments, and London at large suffered from her vivid remembrance of the strong points of the American civic ideas; but she made the best of its dingy dignities and only heaved an occasional sigh and uttered a desultory 'Well!' which led no further and lost itself in retrospect. The truth was that, as she said herself, she was not in her element. 'I've not a sympathy with inanimate objects,' she remarked to Isabel at the National Gallery; and she continued to suffer from the meagreness of the glimpse that had as yet been vouchsafed to her of the inner life. Landscapes by Turner and Assyrian bulls were a poor substitute for the literary dinner-parties at which she had hoped to meet the genius and renown of Great Britain.

'Where are your public men, where are your men and women of intellect?' she inquired of Ralph, standing in the middle of Trafalgar Square as if she had supposed this to be a place where she would naturally meet a few. 'That's one of them on the top of the column, you say – Lord Nelson? Was he a lord too? Wasn't he high enough, that they had to stick him a hundred feet in the air? That's the past – I don't care about the past; I want to see some of the leading minds of the present. I won't say of the future, because I don't believe much in your future.' Poor Ralph had few leading minds among his acquaintance and rarely enjoyed the pleasure of button-holing a celebrity; a state of things which appeared to Miss Stackpole to indicate a deplorable want of enterprise. 'If I were on the other side I should call,' she said, 'and tell the gentleman, whoever he might be, that I had heard a great deal about him and had come to see for myself. But I gather from what you say that this is not the custom here. You seem to have plenty of meaningless customs, but none of those that would help along. We *are* in advance, certainly. I suppose I shall have to give up the social side altogether'; and Henrietta, though she went about with her guidebook and pencil and wrote a letter to the *Interviewer* about the Tower (in which she described the execution of Lady Jane Grey), had a sad sense of falling below her mission.

The incident that had preceded Isabel's departure from Gardencourt left a painful trace in our young woman's mind: when she felt again in her face, as from a recurrent wave, the cold breath of her last suitor's surprise, she could only muffle her head till the air cleared. She could not have done less than what she did; this was certainly true. But her necessity, all the same, had been as graceless as some physical act in a strained attitude, and she felt no desire to take credit for her conduct. Mixed with this imperfect pride, nevertheless, was a feeling of freedom which in itself was sweet and which, as she wandered through the great city with her ill-matched companions, occasionally throbbed into odd demonstrations. When she walked in Kensington Gardens she stopped the children (mainly of the poorer sort) whom she saw playing on the grass; she asked them their names and gave them sixpence and, when they were pretty, kissed them. Ralph noticed these quaint charities; he noticed everything she did. One afternoon, that his companions might pass the time, he invited them to tea in Winchester Square, and he had the house set in order as much as possible for their visit. There was another guest to meet them, an amiable bachelor, an old friend of Ralph's who happened to be in town and for whom prompt commerce with Miss Stackpole appeared to have neither difficulty nor dread. Mr Bantling, a stout, sleek, smiling man of forty, wonderfully dressed, universally informed, and incoherently amused, laughed immoderately at everything Henrietta said, gave her several cups of tea, examined in her society the bric-à-brac, of which Ralph had a considerable collection, and afterwards, when the host proposed they should go out into the square and pretend it was a *fête-champêtre,* walked round the limited enclosure several times with her and, at a dozen turns of their talk, bounded responsive – as with a positive passion for argument – to her remarks upon the inner life.

'Oh, I see; I dare say you found it very quiet at Gardencourt. Naturally there's not much going on there when there's such a lot of illness about. Touchett's very bad, you know; the doctors have forbidden his being in England at all, and he has only come back to take care of his father. The old man, I believe, has half a dozen things the matter with him. They call it gout, but to my certain knowledge he has organic disease so developed that you may depend upon it he'll go, some day soon, quite quickly. Of course that sort of thing makes a dreadfully dull house; I wonder they have people when they can do so little for them. Then I believe Mr Touchett's always squabbling with his wife; she lives away from her husband, you know, in that extraordinary American way of yours. If you want a house where there's always something going on, I recommend you to go down and stay with my sister, Lady Pensil, in Bedfordshire. I'll write to her tomorrow and I'm sure she'll be delighted to ask you. I know just what you want – you want a house where they go in for theatricals and picnics and that sort of thing. My sister's just that sort of woman; she's always getting up something or other and she's always glad to have the sort of people who help her. I'm sure she'll ask you down by return post: she's tremendously fond of distinguished people and writers. She writes herself, you know; but I haven't read everything she has written. It's usually poetry, and I don't go in much for poetry – unless it's Byron. I suppose you think a great deal of Byron in America,' Mr Bantling continued expanding in the stimulating air of Miss Stackpole's attention, bringing up his sequences promptly and changing his topic with an easy turn of hand. Yet he none the less gracefully kept in sight of the idea, dazzling to Henrietta, of her going to stay with Lady Pensil in Bedfordshire. 'I understand what you want: you want to see some genuine English sport. The Touchett's aren't English at all, you know; they have their own habits, their own language, their own food – some odd religion even, I believe, of their own. The old man thinks it's wicked to hunt, I'm told. You must get down to my sister's in time for the theatricals, and I'm sure she'll be glad to give you a part. I'm sure you act well; I know you're very clever. My sister's forty years old and has seven children, but she's going to play the principal part. Plain as she is she makes up awfully well – I *will* say for her. Of course you needn't act if you don't want to.'

In this manner Mr Bantling delivered himself while they strolled over the grass in Winchester Square, which, although it had been peppered by the London soot, invited the tread to linger. Henrietta thought her blooming, easy-voiced bachelor, with his impressibility to feminine merit and his splendid range of suggestion, a very agreeable man, and she valued the opportunity he offered her. 'I don't know but I *would* go, if your sister should ask me. I think it would be my duty. What do you call her name?'

'Pensil. It's an odd name, but it isn't a bad one.'

'I think one name's as good as another. But what's her rank?'

'Oh, she's a baron's wife; a convenient sort of rank. You're fine enough and you're not too fine.'

'I don't know but what she'd be too fine for me. What do you call the place she lives in – Bedfordshire?'

'She lives away in the northern corner of it. It's a tiresome country, but I dare say you won't mind it. I'll try and run down while you're there.'

All this was very pleasant to Miss Stackpole, and she was sorry to be obliged to separate from Lady Pensil's obliging brother. But it happened that she had met the day before, in Piccadilly, some friends whom she had not seen for a year: the Miss Climbers, two ladies from Wilmington, Delaware, who had been travelling on the Continent and were now preparing to re-embark. Henrietta had had a long interview with them on the Piccadilly pavement, and though the three ladies all talked at once they had not exhausted their store. It had been agreed therefore that Henrietta should come and dine with them in their lodgings in Jermyn Street at six o'clock on the morrow, and she now bethought herself of this engagement. She prepared to start for Jermyn Street, taking leave first of Ralph Touchett and Isabel, who, seated on garden chairs in another part of the enclosure, were occupied – if the term may be used – with an exchange of amenities less pointed than the practical colloquy of Miss Stackpole and Mr Bantling. When it had been settled between Isabel and her friend that they should be reunited at some reputable hour at Pratt's Hotel, Ralph remarked that the latter must have a cab. She couldn't walk all the way to Jermyn Street.

'I suppose you mean it's improper for me to walk alone!' Henrietta exclaimed. 'Merciful powers, have I come to this?'

'There's not the slightest need of your walking alone,' Mr Bantling gaily interposed. 'I should be greatly pleased to go with you.'

'I simply meant that you'd be late for dinner,' Ralph returned. 'Those poor ladies may easily believe that we refuse, at the last, to spare you.'

'You had better have a hansom, Henrietta,' said Isabel.

'I'll get you a hansom if you'll trust me,' Mr Bantling went on. 'We might walk a little till we meet one.'

'I don't see why I shouldn't trust him, do *you*?' Henrietta inquired of Isabel.

'I don't see what Mr Bantling could do to you,' Isabel obligingly answered; 'but, if you like, we'll walk with you till you find your cab.'

'Never mind; we'll go alone. Come on, Mr Bantling, and take care you get me a good one.'

Mr Bantling promised to do his best, and the two took their departure, leaving the girl and her cousin together in the square, over which a clear September twilight had now begun to gather. It was perfectly still; the wide quadrangle of dusky houses showed lights in none of the windows, where the shutters and blinds were closed; the pavements were a vacant expanse, and, putting aside two small children from a neighbouring slum, who, attracted by symptoms of abnormal animation in the interior, poked their faces between the rusty rails of the enclosure, the most vivid object within sight was the big red pillar-post on the south-east corner.

'Henrietta will ask him to get into the cab and go with her to Jermyn Street,' Ralph observed. He always spoke of Miss Stackpole as Henrietta.

'Very possibly,' said his companion.

'Or rather, no, she won't,' he went on. 'But Bantling will ask leave to get in.'

'Very likely again. I'm very glad they're such good friends.'

'She has made a conquest. He thinks her a brilliant woman. It may go far,' said Ralph.

Isabel was briefly silent. 'I call Henrietta a very brilliant woman, but I don't think it will go far. They would never really know each other. He has not the least idea what she really is, and she has no just comprehension of Mr Bantling.'

'There's no more usual basis of union than a mutual misunderstanding. But it ought not to be so difficult to understand Bob Bantling,' Ralph added. 'He is a very simple organism.'

'Yes, but Henrietta's a simpler one still. And, pray, what am I to do?' Isabel asked, looking about her through the fading light, in which the limited landscape-gardening of the square took on a large and effective appearance. 'I don't imagine that you'll propose that you and I, for our amusement, shall drive about London in a hansom.'

'There's no reason we shouldn't stay here – if you don't dislike it. It's very warm; there will be half an hour yet before dark; and if you permit it I'll light a cigarette.'

'You may do what you please,' said Isabel, 'if you'll amuse me till seven o'clock. I propose at that hour to go back and partake of a simple and solitary repast – two poached eggs and a muffin – at Pratt's Hotel.'

'Mayn't I dine with you?' Ralph asked.

'No, you'll dine at your club.'

They had wandered back to their chairs in the centre of the square again, and Ralph had lighted his cigarette. It would have given him extreme pleasure to be present in person at the modest little feast she had sketched; but in default of this he liked even being forbidden. For the moment, however, he liked immensely being alone with her, in the thickening dusk, in the centre of the multitudinous town; it made her seem to depend upon him and to be in his power. This power he could exert but vaguely; the best exercise of it was to accept her decision submissively – which indeed there was already an emotion in doing. 'Why won't you let me dine with you?' he demanded after a pause.

'Because I don't care for it.'

'I suppose you're tired of me.'

'I shall be an hour hence. You see I have the gift of foreknowledge.'

'Oh, I shall be delightful meanwhile,' said Ralph. But he said nothing more, and as she made no rejoinder they sat some time in a stillness which seemed to contradict his promise of entertainment. It seemed to him she was preoccupied, and he wondered what she was thinking about; there were two or three very possible subjects. At last he spoke again. 'Is your objection to my society this evening caused by your expectation of another visitor?'

'She turned her head with a glance of her clear, fair eyes. 'Another visitor? What visitor should I have?'

He had none to suggest; which made his question seem to himself silly as well as brutal. 'You've a great many friends that I don't know. You've a whole past from which I was perversely excluded.'

'You were reserved for my future. You must remember that my past is over there across the water. There's none of it here in London.'

'Very good, then, since your future is seated beside you. Capital thing to have your future so handy.' And Ralph lighted another cigarette and reflected that Isabel probably meant she had received news that Mr Caspar Goodwood had crossed to Paris. After he had lighted his cigarette he puffed it a while, and then he resumed. 'I promised just now to be very amusing; but you see I don't come up to the mark, and the fact is there's a good deal of temerity in one's undertaking to amuse a person like you. What do you care for my feeble attempts? You've grand ideas – you've a high standard in such matters. I ought at least to bring in a band of music or a company of mountebanks.'

'One mountebank's enough, and you do very well. Pray go on, and in another ten minutes I shall begin to laugh.'

'I assure you I'm very serious,' said Ralph. 'You do really ask a great deal.'

'I don't know what you mean. I ask nothing!'

'You accept nothing,' said Ralph. She coloured, and now suddenly it seemed to her that she guessed his meaning. But why should he speak to her of such things? He hesitated a little and then he continued: 'There's something I should like very much to say to you. It's a question I wish to ask. It seems to me I've a right to ask it, because I've a kind of interest in the answer.'

'Ask what you will,' Isabel replied gently, 'and I'll try to satisfy you.'

'Well then, I hope you won't mind my saying that Warburton has told me of something that has passed between you.'

Isabel suppressed a start; she sat looking at her open fan. 'Very good; I suppose it was natural he should tell you.'

'I have his leave to let you know he has done so. He has some hope still,' said Ralph.

'Still?'

'He had it a few days ago.'

'I don't believe he has any now,' said the girl.

'I'm very sorry for him then; he's such an honest man.'

'Pray, did he ask you to talk to me?'

'No, not that. But he told me because he couldn't help it. We're old friends, and he was greatly disappointed. He sent me a line asking me to come and see him, and I drove over to Lockleigh the day before he and his sister lunched with us. He was very heavy-hearted; he had just got a letter from you.'

'Did he show you the letter?' asked Isabel with momentary loftiness.

'By no means. But he told me it was a neat refusal. I was very sorry for him,' Ralph repeated.

For some moments Isabel said nothing; then at last, 'Do you know how often he had seen me?' she inquired. 'Five or six times.'

'That's to your glory.'

'It's not for that I say it.'

'What then do you say it for? Not to prove that poor Warburton's state of mind's superficial, because I'm pretty sure you don't think that.'

Isabel certainly was unable to say she thought it; but presently she said something else. 'If you've not been requested by Lord Warburton to argue with me, then you're doing it disinterestedly – or for the love of argument.'

'I've no wish to argue with you at all. I only wish to leave you alone. I'm simply greatly interested in your own sentiments.'

'I'm greatly obliged to you!' cried Isabel with a slightly nervous laugh.

'Of course you mean that I'm meddling in what doesn't concern me. But why shouldn't I speak to you of this matter without annoying you or embarrassing myself? What's the use of being your cousin if I can't have a few privileges? What's the use of adoring you without hope of a reward if I can't have a few compensations? What's the use of being ill and disabled and restricted to mere spectatorship at the game of life if I really can't see the show when I've paid so much for my ticket? Tell me this,' Ralph went on while she listened to him with quickened attention. 'What had you in mind when you refused Lord Warburton?'

'What had I in mind?'

'What was the logic – the view of your situation – that dictated so remarkable an act?'

'I didn't wish to marry him – if that's logic.'

'No, that's not logic – and I knew that before. It's really nothing, you know. What was it you *said* to yourself? You certainly said more than that.'

Isabel reflected a moment, then answered with a question of her own. 'Why do you call it a remarkable act? That's what your mother thinks too.'

'Warburton's such a thorough good sort; as a man, I consider he has hardly a fault. And then he's what they call here no end of a swell. He has immense possessions, and his wife would be thought a superior being. He unites the intrinsic and the extrinsic advantages.'

Isabel watched her cousin as to see how far he would go. 'I refused him because he was too perfect then. I'm not perfect myself, and he's too good for me. Besides, his perfection would irritate me.'

'That's ingenious rather than candid,' said Ralph. 'As a fact you think nothing in the world too perfect for you.'

'Do you think I'm so good?'

'No, but you're exacting, all the same, without the excuse of thinking yourself good. Nineteen women out of twenty, however, even of the most exacting sort, would have managed to do with Warburton. Perhaps you don't know how he has been stalked.'

'I don't wish to know. But it seems to me,' said Isabel, 'that one day when we talked to him you mentioned odd things in him.'

Ralph smokingly considered. 'I hope that what I said then had no weight with you; for they were not faults, the things I spoke of: they were simply peculiarities of his position. If I had known he wished to marry you I'd never have alluded to them. I think I said that as regards that position he was rather a sceptic. It would have been in your power to make him a believer.'

'I think not. I don't understand the matter, and I'm not conscious of any mission of that sort. You're evidently disappointed,' Isabel added, looking at her cousin with rueful gentleness. 'You'd have liked me to make such a marriage.'

'Not in the least. I'm absolutely without a wish on the subject. I don't pretend to advise you, and I content myself with watching you – with the deepest interest.'

She gave rather a conscious sigh. 'I wish I could be as interesting to myself as I am to you!'

'There you're not candid again; you're extremely interesting to yourself. Do you know, however,' said Ralph, 'that if you've really given Warburton his final answer I'm rather glad it has been what it was. I don't mean I'm glad for you, and still less of course for him. I'm glad for myself.'

'Are *you* thinking of proposing to me?'

'By no means. From the point of view I speak of that would be fatal; I should kill the goose that supplies me with the material of my inimitable omelettes. I use that animal as the symbol of my insane illusions. What I mean is that I shall have the thrill of seeing what a young lady does who won't marry Lord Warburton.'

'That's what your mother counts upon too,' said Isabel.

'Ah, there will be plenty of spectators! We shall hang on the rest of your career. I shall not see all of it, but I shall probably see the most interesting years. Of course if you were to marry our friend you'd still have a career – a very decent, in fact a very brilliant one. But relatively speaking it would be a little prosaic. It would be definitely marked out in advance; it would be wanting in the unexpected. You know I'm extremely fond of the unexpected, and now that you've kept the game in your hands I depend on your giving us some grand example of it.'

'I don't understand you very well,' said Isabel, 'but I do so well enough to be able to say that if you look for grand examples of anything from me I shall disappoint you.'

'You'll do so only by disappointing yourself – and that will go hard with you!'

To this she made no direct reply; there was an amount of truth in it that would bear consideration. At last she said abruptly: 'I don't see what harm there is in my wishing not to tie myself. I don't want to begin life by marrying. There are other things a woman can do.'

'There's nothing she can do so well. But you're of course so many-sided.'

'If one's two-sided it's enough,' said Isabel.

'You're the most charming of polygons!' her companion broke out. At a glance from his companion, however, he became grave, and to prove it went on: 'You want to see life – you'll be hanged if you don't, as the young men say.'

'I don't think I want to see it as the young men want to see it. But I do want to look about me.'

'You want to drain the cup of experience.'

'No, I don't wish to touch the cup of experience. It's a poisoned drink! I only want to see for myself.'

'You want to see, but not to feel,' Ralph remarked.

'I don't think that if one's a sentient being one can make the distinction. I'm a good deal like Henrietta. The other day when I asked her if she wished to marry she said: "Not till I've seen Europe!" I too don't wish to marry till I've seen Europe.'

'You evidently expect a crowned head will be struck with you.'

'No, that would be worse than marrying Lord Warburton. But it's getting very dark,' Isabel continued, 'and I must go home.' She rose from her place, but Ralph only sat still and looked at her. As he remained there she stopped, and they exchanged a gaze that was full on either side, but especially on Ralph's, of utterances too vague for words.

'You've answered my question,' he said at last. 'You've told me what I wanted. I'm greatly obliged to you.'

'It seems to me I've told you very little.'

'You've told me the great thing: that the world interests you and that you want to throw yourself into it.'

Her silvery eyes shone a moment in the dusk. 'I never said that.'

'I think you meant it. Don't repudiate it. It's so fine!'

'I don't know what you're trying to fasten upon me, for I'm not in the least an adventurous spirit. Women are not like men.'

Ralph slowly rose from his seat and they walked together to the gate of the square. 'No,' he said; 'women rarely boast of their courage. Men do so with a certain frequency.'

'Men have it to boast of!'

'Women have it too. You've a great deal.'

'Enough to go home in a cab to Pratt's Hotel, but not more.'

Ralph unlocked the gate, and after they had passed out he fastened it. 'We'll find your cab,' he said; and as they turned towards a neighbouring street in which this quest might avail he asked her again if he mightn't see her safely to the inn.

'By no means,' she answered; 'you're very tired; you must go home and go to bed.'

The cab was found, and he helped her into it, standing a moment at the door. 'When people forget I'm a poor creature I'm often incommoded,' he said. 'But it's worse when they remember it!'

Chapter Sixteen

She had had no hidden motive in wishing him not to take her home; it simply struck her that for some days past she had consumed an inordinate quantity of his time, and the independent spirit of the American girl whom extravagance of aid places in an attitude that she ends by finding 'affected' had made her decide that for these few hours she must suffice to herself. She had moreover a great fondness for intervals of solitude, which since her arrival in England had been but meagrely met. It was a luxury she could always command at home and she had wittingly missed it. That evening, however, an incident occurred which – had there been a critic to note it – would have taken all colour from the theory that the wish to be quite by herself had caused her to dispense with her cousin's attendance. Seated towards nine o'clock in the dim illumination of Pratt's Hotel and trying with the aid of two tall candles to lose herself in a volume she had brought from Gardencourt, she succeeded only to the extent of reading other words than those printed on the page – words that Ralph had spoken to her that afternoon. Suddenly the well-muffled knuckle of the waiter was applied to the door, which presently gave way to his exhibition, even as a glorious trophy, of the card of a visitor. When this memento had offered to her fixed sight the name of Mr Caspar Goodwood she let the man stand before her without signifying her wishes.

'Shall I show the gentleman up, ma'am?' he asked with a slightly encouraging inflexion.

Isabel hesitated still and while she hesitated glanced at the mirror. 'He may come in,' she said at last; and waited for him not so much smoothing her hair as girding her spirit.

Caspar Goodwood was accordingly the next moment shaking hands with her, but saying nothing till the servant had left the room. 'Why didn't you answer my letter?' he then asked in a quick, full, slightly peremptory tone – the tone of a man whose questions were habitually pointed and who was capable of much insistence.

She answered by a ready question, 'How did you know I was here?'

'Miss Stackpole let me know,' said Caspar Goodwood. 'She told me you would probably be at home alone this evening and would be willing to see me.'

'Where did she see you – to tell you that?'

'She didn't see me; she wrote to me.'

Isabel was silent; neither had sat down; they stood there with an air of defiance, or at least of contention. 'Henrietta never told me she was writing to you,' she said at last. 'This is not kind of her.'

'Is it so disagreeable to you to see me?' asked the young man.

'I didn't expect it. I don't like such surprises.'

'But you knew I was in town; it was natural we should meet.'

'Do you call this meeting? I hoped I shouldn't see you. In so big a place as London it seemed very possible.'

'It was apparently repugnant to you even to write to me,' her visitor went on.

Isabel made no reply; the sense of Henrietta Stackpole's treachery, as she momentarily qualified it, was strong within her. 'Henrietta's certainly not a model of all the delicacies!' she exclaimed with bitterness. 'It was a great liberty to take.'

'I suppose I'm not a model either – of those virtues or of any others. The fault's mine as much as hers.'

As Isabel looked at him it seemed to her that his jaw had never been more square. This might have displeased her, but she took a different turn. 'No, it's not your fault so much as hers. What you've done was inevitable, I suppose, for *you*.'

'It was indeed!' cried Caspar Goodwood with a voluntary laugh. 'And now that I've come, at any rate, mayn't I stay?'

'You may sit down, certainly.'

She went back to her chair again, while her visitor took the first place that offered, in the manner of a man accustomed to pay little thought to that sort of furtherance. 'I've been hoping every day for an answer to my letter. You might have written me a few lines.'

'It wasn't the trouble of writing that prevented me; I could as easily have written you four pages as one. But my silence was an intention,' Isabel said. 'I thought it the best thing.'

He sat with his eyes fixed on hers while she spoke; then he lowered them and attached them to a spot in the carpet as if he were making a strong effort to say nothing but what he ought. He was a strong man in the wrong, and he was acute enough to see that an uncompromising exhibition of his strength would only throw the falsity of his position into relief. Isabel was not incapable of tasting any advantage of position over a person of this quality, and though little desirous to flaunt it in his face she could enjoy being able to say 'You know you oughtn't to have written to me yourself!' and to say it with an air of triumph.

Caspar Goodwood raised his eyes to her own again; they seemed to shine through the vizard of a helmet. He had a strong sense of justice and was ready any day in the year – over and above this – to argue the question of his rights. 'You said you hoped never to hear from me again; I know that. But I never accepted any such rule as my own. I warned you that you should hear very soon.'

'I didn't say I hoped *never* to hear from you,' said Isabel.

'Not for five years then; for ten years; twenty years. It's the same thing.'

'Do you find it so? It seems to me there's a great difference. I can imagine that at the end of ten years we might have a very pleasant correspondence. I shall have matured my epistolary style.'

She looked away while she spoke these words, knowing them of so much less earnest a cast than the countenance of her listener. Her eyes, however, at last came back to him, just as he said very irrelevantly. 'Are you enjoying your visit to your uncle?'

'Very much indeed.' She dropped, but then she broke out. 'What good do you expect to get by insisting?'

'The good of not losing you.'

'You've no right to talk of losing what's not yours. And even from your own point of view,' Isabel added, 'you ought to know when to let one alone.'

'I disgust you very much,' said Caspar Goodwood gloomily; not as if to provoke her to compassion for a man conscious of this blighting fact, but as if to set it well before himself, so that he might endeavour to act with his eyes on it.

'Yes, you don't at all delight me, you don't fit in, not in any way, just now, and the worst is that your putting it to the proof in this manner is quite unnecessary.' It wasn't certainly as if his nature had been soft, so that pin-pricks would draw blood from it; and from the first of her acquaintance with him, and of her having to defend herself against a certain air that he had of knowing better what was good for her than she knew herself, she had recognized the fact that perfect frankness was her best weapon. To attempt to spare his sensibility or to escape from him edgewise, as one might do from a man who had barred the way less sturdily – this, in dealing with Caspar Goodwood, who would grasp at everything of every sort that one might give him, was wasted agility. It was not that he had not susceptibilities, but his passive surface, as well as his active, was large and hard, and he might always be trusted to dress his wounds, so far as they required it, himself. She came back, even for her measure of possible pangs and aches in him, to her old sense that he was naturally plated and steeled, armed essentially for aggression.

'I can't reconcile myself to that,' he simply said. There was a dangerous liberality about it; for she felt how open it was to make the point that he had not always disgusted her.

'I can't reconcile myself to it either, and it's not the state of things that ought to exist between us. If you'd only try to banish me from your mind for a few months we should be on good terms again.'

'I see. If I should cease to think of you at all for a prescribed time, I should find I could keep it up indefinitely.'

'Indefinitely is more than I ask. It's more even than I should like.'

'You know that what you ask is impossible,' said the young man, taking his adjective for granted in a manner she found irritating.

'Aren't you capable of making a calculated effort?' she demanded. 'You're strong for everything else; why shouldn't you be strong for that?'

'An effort calculated for what?' And then as she hung fire, 'I'm capable of nothing with regard to you,' he went on, 'but just of being infernally in love with you. If one's strong one loves only the more strongly.'

'There's a good deal in that'; and indeed our young lady felt the force of it – felt it thrown off, into the vast of truth and poetry, as practically a bait to her imagination. But she promptly came round. 'Think of me or not, as you find most possible; only leave me alone.'

'Until when?'

'Well, for a year or two.'

'Which do you mean? Between one year and two there's all the difference in the world.'

'Call it two then,' said Isabel with a studied effect of eagerness.

'And what shall I gain by that?' her friend asked with no sign of wincing.

'You'll have obliged me greatly.'

'And what will be my reward?'

'Do you need a reward for an act of generosity?'

'Yes, when it involves a great sacrifice.'

'There's no generosity without some sacrifice. Men don't understand such things. If you make the sacrifice you'll have all my admiration.'

'I don't care a cent for your admiration – not one straw, with nothing to show for it. When will you marry me? That's the only question.'

'Never – if you go on making me feel only as I feel at present.'

'What do I gain then by not trying to make you feel otherwise?'

'You'll gain quite as much as by worrying me to death!' Caspar Goodwood bent his eyes again and gazed a while into the crown of his hat. A deep flush overspread his face; she could see her sharpness had at last penetrated. This immediately had a value – classic, romantic, redeeming, what did she know? – for her; 'the strong man in pain' was one of the categories of the human appeal, little charm as he might exert in the given case. 'Why do you make me say such things to you?' she cried in a trembling voice. 'I only want to be gentle – to be thoroughly kind. It's not delightful to me to feel people care for me and yet to have to try and reason them out of it. I think others also ought to be considerate; we have each to judge for ourselves. I know you're considerate, as much as you can be; you've good reasons for what you do. But I really don't want to marry, or to talk about it at all now. I shall probably never do it – no, never. I've a perfect right to feel that way, and it's no kindness to a woman to press her so hard, to urge her against her will. If I give you pain I can only say I'm very sorry. It's not my fault; I can't marry you simply to please you. I won't say that I shall always remain your friend, because when women say that, in these situations, it passes, I believe, for a sort of mockery. But try me some day.'

Caspar Goodwood, during this speech, had kept his eyes fixed upon the name of his hatter, and it was not until some time after she had ceased speaking that he raised them. When he did so the sight of a rosy, lovely eagerness in Isabel's face threw some confusion into his attempt to analyse her words. 'I'll go home – I'll go tomorrow – I'll leave you alone,' he brought out at last. 'Only,' he heavily said, 'I hate to lose sight of you!'

'Never fear. I shall do no harm.'

'You'll marry someone else, as sure as I sit here,' Caspar Goodwood declared.

'Do you think that a generous charge?'

'Why not? Plenty of men will try to make you.'

'I told you just now that I don't wish to marry and that I almost certainly never shall.'

'I know you did, and I like your "almost certainly"! I put no faith in what you say.'

'Thank you very much. Do you accuse me of lying to shake you off? You say very delicate things.'

'Why should I not say that? You've given me no pledge of anything at all.'

'No, that's all that would be wanting!'

'You may perhaps even believe you're safe – from wishing to be. But you're not,' the young man went on as if preparing himself for the worst.

'Very well then. We'll put it that I'm not safe. Have it as you please.'

'I don't know, however,' said Caspar Goodwood, 'that my keeping you in sight would prevent it.'

'Don't you indeed? I'm after all very much afraid of you. Do you think I'm so very easily pleased?' she asked suddenly, changing her tone.

'No – I don't; I shall try to console myself with that. But there are a certain number of very dazzling men in the world, no doubt; and if there were only one it would be enough. The most dazzling of all will make straight for you. You'll be sure to take no one who isn't dazzling.'

'If you mean by dazzling brilliantly clever,' Isabel said' '—and I can't imagine what else you mean – I don't need the aid of a clever man to teach me how to live. I can find it out for myself.'

'Find out how to live alone? I wish that, when you have, you'd teach *me*!'

She looked at him a moment; then with a quick smile, 'Oh, *you* ought to marry!' she said.

He might be pardoned if for an instant this exclamation seemed to him to sound the infernal note, and it is not on record that her motive for discharging such a shaft had been of the clearest. He oughtn't to stride about lean and hungry, however – she certainly felt *that* for him. 'God forgive you!' he murmured between his teeth as he turned away.

Her accent had put her slightly in the wrong, and after a moment she felt the need to right herself. The easiest way to do it was to place him where she had been. 'You do me great injustice – you say what you don't know!' she broke out. 'I shouldn't be an easy victim – I've proved it.'

'Oh, to me, perfectly.'

'I've proved it to others as well.' And she paused a moment. 'I refused a proposal of marriage last week; what they call – no doubt – a dazzling one.'

'I'm very glad to hear it,' said the young man gravely.

'It was a proposal many girls would have accepted; it had everything to recommend it.' Isabel had not proposed to herself to tell this story, but, now she had begun, the satisfaction of speaking it out and doing herself justice took possession of her. 'I was offered a great position and a great fortune – by a person whom I like extremely.'

Caspar watched her with intense interest. 'Is he an Englishman?'

'He's an English nobleman,' said Isabel.

Her visitor received this announcement at first in silence, but at last said: 'I'm glad he's disappointed.'

'Well then, as you have companions in misfortune, make the best of it.'

'I don't call him a companion,' said Caspar grimly.

'Why not – since I declined his offer absolutely?'

'That doesn't make him my companion. Besides, he's an Englishman.'

'And pray isn't an Englishman a human being?' Isabel asked.

'Oh, those people? They're not of *my* humanity, and I don't care what becomes of them.'

'You're very angry,' said the girl. 'We've discussed this matter quite enough.'

'Oh yes, I'm very angry. I plead guilty to that!'

She turned away from him, walked to the open window and stood a moment looking into the dusky void of the street, where a turbid gaslight alone represented social animation. For some time neither of these young persons spoke; Caspar lingered near the chimney-piece with eyes gloomily attached. She had virtually requested him to go – he knew that; but at the risk of making himself odious he kept his ground. She was too nursed a need to be easily renounced, and he had crossed the sea all to wring from her some scrap of a vow. Presently she left the window and stood again before him. 'You do me very little justice – after my telling you what I told you just now. I'm sorry I told you – since it matters so little to you.'

'Ah,' cried the young man, 'if you were thinking of *me* when you did it!' And then he paused with the fear that she might contradict so happy a thought.

'I was thinking of you a little,' said Isabel.

'A little? I don't understand. If the knowledge of what I feel for you had any weight with you at all, calling it a "little" is a poor account of it.'

Isabel shook her head as if to carry off a blunder. 'I've refused a most kind, noble gentleman. Make the most of that.'

'I thank you then,' said Caspar Goodwood gravely. 'I thank you immensely.'

'And now you had better go home.'

'May I not see you again?' he asked.

'I think it's better not. You'll be sure to talk of this, and you see it leads to nothing.'

'I promise you not to say a word that will annoy you.'

Isabel reflected and then answered: 'I return in a day or two to my uncle's, and I can't propose to you to come there. It would be too inconsistent.'

Caspar Goodwood, on his side, considered. 'You must do me justice too. I received an invitation to your uncle's more than a week ago, and I declined it.'

She betrayed surprise. 'From whom was your invitation?'

'From Mr Ralph Touchett, whom I suppose to be your cousin. I declined it because I had not your authorization to accept it. The suggestion that Mr Touchett should invite me appeared to have come from Miss Stackpole.'

'It certainly never did from me. Henrietta really goes very far,' Isabel added.

'Don't be too hard on her – that touches *me*.'

'No; if you declined you did quite right, and I thank you for it.' And she gave a little shudder of dismay at the thought that Lord Warburton and Mr Goodwood might have met at Gardencourt: it would have been so awkward for Lord Warburton.

'When you leave your uncle where do you go?' her companion asked.

'I go abroad with my aunt – to Florence and other places.'

The serenity of this announcement struck a chill to the young man's heart; he seemed to see her whirled away into circles from which he was inexorably excluded. Nevertheless he went on quickly with his questions. 'And when shall you come back to America?'

'Perhaps not for a long time. I'm very happy here.'

'Do you mean to give up your country?'

'Don't be an infant!'

'Well, you'll be out of my sight indeed!' said Caspar Goodwood.

'I don't know,' she answered rather grandly. 'The world – with all these places so arranged and so touching each other – comes to strike one as rather small.'

'It's a sight too big for *me*!' Caspar exclaimed with a simplicity our young lady might have found touching if her face had not been set against concessions.

This attitude was part of a system, a theory, that she had lately embraced, and to be thorough she said after a moment: 'Don't think me unkind if I say it's just *that* – being out of your sight – that I like. If you were in the same place I should feel you were watching me, and I don't like that – I like my liberty too much. If there's a thing in the world I'm fond of,' she went on with a slight recurrence of grandeur, 'it's my personal independence.'

But whatever there might be of the too superior in this speech moved Caspar Goodwood's admiration; there was nothing he winced at in the large air of it. He had never supposed she hadn't wings and the need of beautiful free movements – he wasn't, with his own long arms and strides, afraid of any force in her. Isabel's words, if they had been meant to shock him, failed of the mark and only made him smile with the sense that here was common ground. 'Who would wish less to curtail your liberty than I? What can give me greater pleasure than to see you perfectly independent – doing whatever you like? It's to make you independent that I want to marry you.'

'That's a beautiful sophism,' said the girl with a smile more beautiful still.

'An unmarried woman – a girl of your age – isn't independent. There are all sorts of things she can't do. She's hampered at every step.'

'That's as she looks at the question,' Isabel answered with much spirit. 'I'm not in my first youth – I can do what I choose – I belong quite to the independent class. I've neither father nor mother; I'm poor and of a serious disposition; I'm not pretty. I therefore am not bound to be timid and conventional; indeed I can't afford such luxuries. Besides, I try to judge things for myself; to judge wrong, I think, is more honourable than not to judge at all. I don't wish to be a mere sheep in the flock; I wish to choose my fate and know something of human affairs beyond what other people think is compatible with propriety to tell me.' She paused a moment, but not long enough for her companion to reply. He was apparently on the point of doing so when she went on: 'Let me say this to you, Mr Goodwood. You're so kind as to speak of being afraid of my marrying. If you should hear a rumour that I'm on the point of doing so – girls are liable to have such things said about them – remember what I have told you about my love of liberty and venture to doubt it.'

There was something passionately positive in the tone in which she gave him this advice, and he saw a shining candour in her eyes that helped him to believe her. On the whole he felt reassured, and you might have perceived it by the manner in which he said, quite eagerly: 'You want simply to travel for two years? I'm quite willing to wait two years, and you may do what you like in the interval. If that's all you want, pray say so. I don't want you to be conventional; do I strike you as conventional myself? Do you want to improve your mind? Your mind's quite good enough for me; but if it interests you to wander about a while and see different countries I shall be delighted to help you in any way in my power.'

'You're very generous; that's nothing new to me. The best way to help me will be to put as many hundred miles of sea between us as possible.'

'One would think you were going to commit some atrocity!' said Caspar Goodwood.

'Perhaps I am. I wish to be free even to do that if the fancy takes me.'

'Well then,' he said slowly, 'I'll go home.' And he put out his hand, trying to look contented and confident.

Isabel's confidence in him, however, was greater than any he could feel in her. Not that he thought her capable of committing an atrocity; but, turn it over as he would there was something ominous in the way she reserved her option. As she took his hand she felt a great respect for him; she knew how much he cared for her and she thought him magnanimous. They stood so for a moment, looking at each other, united by a hand-clasp which was not merely passive on her side. 'That's right,' she said very kindly, almost tenderly. 'You'll lose nothing by being a reasonable man.'

'But I'll come back, wherever you are, two years hence,' he returned with characteristic grimness.

We have seen that our young lady was inconsequent, and at this she suddenly changed her note. 'Ah, remember. I promise nothing – absolutely nothing!' Then more softly, as if to help him to leave her: 'And remember too that I shall not be an easy victim!'

'You'll get very sick of your independence.'

'Perhaps I shall; it's even very probable. When that day comes I shall be very glad to see you.'

She had laid her hand on the knob of the door that led into her room, and she waited a moment to see whether her visitor would not take his departure. But he appeared unable to move; there was still an immense unwillingness in his attitude and a sore remonstrance in his eyes. 'I must leave you now,' said Isabel; and she opened the door and passed into the other room.

This apartment was dark, but the darkness was tempered by a vague radiance sent up through the window from the court of the hotel, and Isabel could make out the masses of the furniture, the dim shining of the mirror and the looming of the big four-posted bed. She stood still a moment, listening, and at last she heard Caspar Goodwood walk out of the sitting-room and close the door behind him. She stood still a little longer, and then, by an irresistible impulse, dropped on her knees before her bed and hid her face on her arms.

Chapter Seventeen

She was not praying; she was trembling – trembling all over. Vibration was easy to her, was in fact too constant with her, and she found herself now humming like a smitten harp. She only asked, however, to put on the cover, to case herself again in brown holland, but she wished to resist her excitement, and the attitude of devotion, which she kept for some time, seemed to help her to be still. She intensely rejoiced that Caspar Goodwood was gone; there was something in having thus got rid of him that was like the payment, for a stamped receipt, of some debt too long on her mind. As she felt the glad relief she bowed her head a little lower; the sense was there, throbbing in her heart, it was part of her emotion, but it was a thing to be ashamed of – it was profane and out of place. It was not for some ten minutes that she rose from her knees, and even when she came back to the sitting-room her tremor had not quite subsided. It had had, verily, two causes: part of it was to be accounted for by her long discussion with Mr Goodwood, but it might be feared that the rest was simply the enjoyment she found in the exercise of her power. She sat down in the same chair again and took up her book, but without going through the form of opening the volume. She leaned back, with that low, soft, aspiring murmur with which she often uttered her response to accidents of which the brighter side was not superficially obvious, and yielded to the satisfaction of having refused two ardent suitors in a fortnight. That love of liberty of which she had given Caspar Goodwood so bold a sketch was as yet almost exclusively theoretic; she had not been able to indulge it on a large scale. But it appeared to her she had done something; she had tasted of the delight, if not of battle, at least of victory; she had done what was truest to her plan. In the glow of this consciousness the image of Mr Goodwood taking his sad walk homeward through the dingy town presented itself with a certain reproachful force; so that, as at the same moment the door of the room was opened, she rose with an apprehension that he had come back. But it was only Henrietta Stackpole returning from her dinner.

Miss Stackpole immediately saw that our young lady had been 'through' something, and indeed the discovery demanded no great penetration. She went straight up to her friend who received her without a greeting. Isabel's elation in having sent Caspar Goodwood back to America presupposed her being in a manner glad he had come to see her; but at the same time she perfectly remembered Henrietta had had no right to set a trap for her. 'Has he been here, dear?' the latter yearningly asked.

Isabel turned away and for some moments answered nothing. 'You acted very wrongly,' she declared at last.

'I acted for the best. I only hope you acted as well.'

'You're not the judge. I can't trust you,' said Isabel.

This declaration was unflattering, but Henrietta was much too unselfish to heed the charge it conveyed; she cared only for what it intimated with regard to her friend. 'Isabel Archer,' she observed with equal abruptness and solemnity, 'if you marry one of these people I'll never speak to you again!'

'Before making so terrible a threat you had better wait till I'm asked,' Isabel replied. Never having said a word to Miss Stackpole about Lord Warburton's overtures, she had now no impulse whatever to justify herself to Henrietta by telling her that she had refused that nobleman.

'Oh, you'll be asked quick enough, once you get off on the Continent. Annie Climber was asked three times in Italy – poor plain little Annie.'

'Well, if Annie Climber wasn't captured why should I be?'

'I don't believe Annie was pressed; but you'll be.'

'That's a flattering conviction,' said Isabel without alarm.

'I don't flatter you, Isabel, I tell you the truth!' cried her friend. 'I hope you don't mean to tell me that you didn't give Mr Goodwood some hope.'

'I don't see why I should tell you anything; as I said to you just now, I can't trust you. But since you're so much interested in Mr Goodwood I won't conceal from you that he returns immediately to America.'

'You don't mean to say you've sent him off?' Henrietta almost shrieked.

'I asked him to leave me alone; and I ask you the same, Henrietta.' Miss Stackpole glittered for an instant with dismay and then passed to the mirror over the chimney-piece and took off her bonnet. 'I hope you've enjoyed your dinner,' Isabel went on.

But her companion was not to be diverted by frivolous propositions. 'Do you know where you're going, Isabel Archer?'

'Just now I'm going to bed,' said Isabel with persistent frivolity.

'Do you know where you're drifting?' Henrietta pursued, holding out her bonnet delicately.

'No, I haven't the least idea, and I find it very pleasant not to know. A swift carriage, of a dark night, rattling with four horses over roads that one can't see – that's my idea of happiness.'

'Mr Goodwood certainly didn't teach you to say such things as that – like the heroine of an immoral novel,' said Miss Stackpole. 'You're drifting to some great mistake.'

Isabel was irritated by her friend's interference, yet she still tried to think what truth this declaration could represent. She could think of nothing that diverted her from saying: 'You must be very fond of me, Henrietta, to be willing to be so aggressive.'

'I love you intensely, Isabel,' said Miss Stackpole with feeling.

'Well, if you love me intensely let me as intensely alone. I asked that of Mr Goodwood, and I must also ask it of you.'

'Take care you're not let alone too much.'

'That's what Mr Goodwood said to me. I told him I must take the risks.'

'You're a creature of risks – you make me shudder!' cried Henrietta. 'When does Mr Goodwood return to America?'

'I don't know – he didn't tell me.'

'Perhaps you didn't inquire,' said Henrietta with the note of righteous irony.

'I gave him too little satisfaction to have the right to ask questions of him.'

This assertion seemed to Miss Stackpole for a moment to bid defiance to comment; but at last she exclaimed: 'Well, Isabel, if I didn't know you I might think you were heartless!'

'Take care,' said Isabel; 'you're spoiling me.'

'I'm afraid I've done that already. I hope, at least,' Miss Stackpole added, 'that he may cross with Annie Climber!'

Isabel learned from her the next morning that she had determined not to return to Gardencourt (where old Mr Touchett had promised her a renewed welcome), but to wait in London the arrival of the invitation that Mr Bantling had promised her from his sister Lady Pensil. Miss Stackpole related very freely her conversation with Ralph Touchett's sociable friend and declared to Isabel that she really believed she had now got hold of something that would lead to something. On the receipt of Lady Pensil's letter – Mr Bantling had virtually guaranteed the arrival of this document – she would immediately depart for Bedfordshire, and if Isabel cared to look out for her impressions in the *Interviewer* she would certainly find them. Henrietta was evidently going to see something of the inner life this time.

'Do you know where you're drifting, Henrietta Stackpole?' Isabel asked, imitating the tone in which her friend had spoken the night before.

'I'm drifting to a big position – that of the Queen of American Journalism. If my next letter isn't copied all over the West I'll swallow my penwiper!'

She had arranged with her friend Miss Annie Climber, the young lady of the continental offers, that they should go together to make those purchases which were to constitute Miss Climber's farewell to a hemisphere in which she at least had been appreciated; and she presently repaired to Jermyn Street to pick up her companion. Shortly after her departure Ralph Touchett was announced, and as soon as he came in Isabel saw he had something on his mind. He very soon took his cousin into his confidence. He had received from his mother a telegram to the effect that his father had had a sharp attack of his old malady, that she was much alarmed and that she begged he would instantly return to Gardencourt. On this occasion at least Mrs Touchett's devotion to the electric wire was not open to criticism.

'I've judged it best to see the great doctor, Sir Matthew Hope, first,' Ralph said; 'by great good luck he's in town. He's to see me at half past twelve, and I shall make sure of his coming down to Gardencourt – which he will do the more readily as he has already seen my father several times, both there and in London. There's an express at two-forty-five, which I shall take; and you'll come back with me or remain here a few days longer, exactly as you prefer.'

'I shall certainly go with you,' Isabel returned. 'I don't suppose I can be of any use to my uncle, but if he's ill I shall like to be near him.'

'I think you're fond of him,' said Ralph with a certain shy pleasure in his face. 'You appreciate him, which all the world hasn't done. The quality's too fine.'

'I quite adore him,' Isabel after a moment said.

'That's very well. After his son he's your greatest admirer.'

She welcomed this assurance, but she gave secretly a small sigh of relief at the thought that Mr Touchett was one of those admirers who couldn't propose to marry her. This, however, was not what she spoke; she went on to inform Ralph that there were other reasons for her not remaining in London. She was tired of it and wished to leave it; and then Henrietta was going away – going to stay in Bedfordshire.

'In Bedfordshire?'

'With Lady Pensil, the sister of Mr Bantling, who has answered for an invitation.'

Ralph was feeling anxious, but at this he broke into a laugh. Suddenly, none the less, his gravity returned. 'Bantling's a man of courage. But if the invitation should get lost on the way?'

'I thought the British post office was impeccable.'

'The good Homer sometimes nods,' said Ralph. 'However,' he went on more brightly, 'the good Bantling never does, and, whatever happens, he'll take care of Henrietta.'

Ralph went to keep his appointment with Sir Matthew Hope, and Isabel made her arrangements for quitting Pratt's Hotel. Her uncle's danger touched her nearly, and while she stood before her open trunk, looking about her vaguely for what she should put into it, the tears suddenly rose to her eyes. It was perhaps for this reason that when Ralph came back at two o'clock to take her to the station she was not yet ready. He found Miss Stackpole, however, in the sitting-room, where she had just risen from her luncheon, and this lady immediately expressed her regret at his father's illness.

'He's a grand old man,' she said; 'he's faithful to the last. If it's really to be the last – pardon my alluding to it, but you must often have thought of the possibility – I'm sorry that I shall not be at Gardencourt.'

'You'll amuse yourself much more in Bedfordshire.'

'I shall be sorry to amuse myself at such a time,' said Henrietta with much propriety. But she immediately added: 'I should like so to commemorate the closing scene.'

'My father may live a long time,' said Ralph simply. Then, adverting to topics more cheerful, he interrogated Miss Stackpole as to her own future.

Now that Ralph was in trouble she addressed him in a tone of larger allowance and told him that she was much indebted to him for having made her acquainted with Mr Bantling. 'He has told me just the things I want to know,' she said; 'all the society items and all about the royal family. I can't make out that what he tells me about the royal family is much to their credit; but he says that's only my peculiar way of looking at it. Well, all I want is that he should give me the facts; I can put them together quick enough, once I've got them.' And she added that Mr Bantling had been so good as to promise to come and take her out that afternoon.

'To take you where?' Ralph ventured to inquire.

'To Buckingham Palace. He's going to show me over it, so that I may get some idea how they live.'

'Ah,' said Ralph, 'we leave you in good hands. The first thing we shall hear is that you're invited to Windsor Castle.'

'If they ask me, I shall certainly go. Once I get started I'm not afraid. But for all that,' Henrietta added in a moment, 'I'm not satisfied; I'm not at peace about Isabel.'

'What is her last misdemeanour?'

'Well, I've told you before, and I suppose there's no harm in my going on. I always finish a subject that I take up. Mr Goodwood was here last night.'

Ralph opened his eyes; he even blushed a little – his blush being the sign of an emotion somewhat acute. He remembered that Isabel, in separating from him in Winchester Square, had repudiated his suggestion that her motive in doing so was the expectation of a visitor at Pratt's Hotel, and it was a new pang to him to have to suspect her of duplicity. On the other hand, he quickly said to himself, what concern was it of his that she should have made an appointment with a lover? Had it not been thought graceful in every age that young ladies should make a mystery of such appointments? Ralph gave Miss Stackpole a diplomatic answer. 'I should have thought that, with the views you expressed to me the other day, this would satisfy you perfectly.'

'That he should come to see her? That was very well, as far as it went. It was a little plot of mine; I let him know that we were in London, and when it had been arranged that I should spend the evening out I sent him a word – the word we just utter to the "wise". I hoped he would find her alone; I won't pretend I didn't hope that you'd be out of the way. He came to see her, but he might as well have stayed away.'

'Isabel was cruel?' – and Ralph's face lighted with the relief of his cousin's not having shown duplicity.

'I don't exactly know what passed between them. But she gave him no satisfaction – she sent him back to America.'

'Poor Mr Goodwood!' Ralph sighed.

'Her only idea seems to be to get rid of him,' Henrietta went on.

'Poor Mr Goodwood!' Ralph repeated. The exclamation, it must be confessed, was automatic; it failed exactly to express his thoughts, which were taking another line.

'You don't say that as if you felt it. I don't believe you care.'

'Ah,' said Ralph, 'you must remember that I don't know this interesting young man – that I've never seen him.'

'Well, I shall see him, and I shall tell him not to give up. If I didn't believe Isabel would come round,' Miss Stackpole added – 'well, I'd give up myself. I mean I'd give *her* up!'

Chapter Eighteen

It had occurred to Ralph that, in the conditions, Isabel's parting with her friend might be of a slightly embarrassed nature, and he went down to the door of the hotel in advance of his cousin, who, after a slight delay, followed with the traces of an unaccepted remonstrance, as he thought, in her eyes. The two made the journey to Gardencourt in almost unbroken silence, and the servant who met them at the station had no better news to give them of Mr Touchett – a fact which caused Ralph to congratulate himself afresh on Sir Matthew Hope's having promised to come down in the five o'clock train and spend the night. Mrs Touchett, he learned, on reaching home, had been constantly with the old man and was with him at that moment; and this fact made Ralph say to himself that, after all, what his mother wanted was just easy occasion. The finer natures were those that shone at the larger times. Isabel went to her own room, noting throughout the house that perceptible hush which precedes a crisis. At the end of an hour, however, she came downstairs in search of her aunt, whom she wished to ask about Mr Touchett. She went into the library, but Mrs Touchett was not there, and as the weather, which had been damp and chill, was now altogether spoiled, it was not probable she had gone for her usual walk in the grounds. Isabel was on the point of ringing to send a question to her room, when this purpose quickly yielded to an unexpected sound – the sound of low music proceeding apparently from the saloon. She knew her aunt never touched the piano, and the musician was therefore probably Ralph, who played for his own amusement. That he should have resorted to this recreation at the present time indicated apparently that his anxiety about his father had been relieved; so that the girl took her way, almost with restored cheer, towards the source of the harmony. The drawing-room at Gardencourt was an apartment of great distances, and, as the piano was placed at the end of it farthest removed from the door at which she entered, her arrival was not noticed by the person seated before the instrument. This person was neither Ralph nor his mother; it was a lady whom Isabel immediately saw to be a stranger to herself, though her back was presented to the door. This back – an ample and well-dressed one – Isabel viewed for some moments with surprise. The lady was of course a visitor who had arrived during her absence and who had not been mentioned by either of the servants – one of them her aunt's maid – of whom she had had speech since her return. Isabel had already learned, however, with what treasures of reserve the function of receiving orders may be accompanied, and she was particularly conscious of having been treated with dryness by her aunt's maid, through whose hands she had slipped perhaps a little too mistrustfully and with an effect of plumage but the more lustrous. The advent of a guest was in itself far from disconcerting; she had not yet divested herself of a young faith that each new acquaintance would exert some momentous influence on her life. By the time she had made these reflections she became aware that the lady at the piano played remarkably well. She was playing something of Schubert's – Isabel knew not what, but recognized Schubert – and she touched the piano with a discretion of her own. It showed skill, it showed feeling; Isabel sat down noiselessly on the nearest chair and waited till the end of the piece. When it was finished she felt a strong desire to thank the player, and rose from her seat to do so, while at the same time the stranger turned quickly round, as if but just aware of her presence.

'That's very beautiful, and your playing makes it more beautiful still,' said Isabel with all the young radiance with which she usually uttered a truthful rapture.

'You don't think I disturbed Mr Touchett then?' the musician answered as sweetly as this compliment deserved. 'The house is so large and his room so far away that I thought I might venture, especially as I played just – just *du bout des doigts*.'

'She's a Frenchwoman,' Isabel said to herself; 'she says that as if she were French.' And this supposition made the visitor more interesting to our speculative heroine. 'I hope my uncle's doing well,' Isabel added. 'I should think that to hear such lovely music as that would really make him feel better.'

The lady smiled and discriminated. 'I'm afraid there are moments in life when even Schubert has nothing to say to us. We must admit, however, that they are our worst.'

'I'm not in that state now then,' said Isabel. 'On the contrary I should be so glad if you would play something more.'

'If it will give you pleasure – delighted.' And this obliging person took her place again and struck a few chords, while Isabel sat down nearer the instrument. Suddenly the newcomer stopped with her hands on the keys, half-turning and looking over her shoulder. She was forty years old and not pretty, though her expression charmed. 'Pardon me,' she said; 'but are you the niece – the young American?'

'I'm my aunt's niece,' Isabel replied with simplicity.

The lady at the piano sat still a moment longer, casting her air of interest over her shoulder. 'That's very well; we're compatriots.' And then she began to play.

'Ah then she's not French,' Isabel murmured; and as the opposite supposition had made her romantic it might have seemed that this revelation would have marked a drop. But such was not the fact; rarer even than to be French seemed it to be American on such interesting terms.

The lady played in the same manner as before, softly and solemnly, and while she played the shadows deepened in the room. The autumn twilight gathered in, and from her place Isabel could see the rain, which had now begun in earnest, washing the cold-looking lawn and the wind shaking the great trees. At last, when the music had ceased, her companion got up and, coming nearer with a smile, before Isabel had time to thank her again, said: 'I'm very glad you've come back; I've heard a great deal about you.'

Isabel thought her a very attractive person, but nevertheless spoke with a certain abruptness in reply to this speech. 'From whom have you heard about me?'

The stranger hesitated a single moment and then, 'From your uncle,' she answered. 'I've been here three days, and the first day he let me come and pay him a visit in his room. Then he talked constantly of you.'

'As you didn't know me that must rather have bored you.'

'It made me want to know you. All the more that since then – your aunt being so much with Mr Touchett – I've been quite alone and have got rather tired of my own society. I've not chosen a good moment for my visit.'

A servant had come in with lamps and was presently followed by another bearing the tea-tray. On the appearance of this repast Mrs Touchett had apparently been notified, for she now arrived and addressed herself to the tea-pot. Her greeting to her niece did not differ materially from her manner of raising the lid of this receptacle in order to glance at the contents: in neither act was it becoming to make a show of avidity. Questioned about her husband she was unable to say he was better; but the local doctor was with him, and much light was expected from this gentleman's consultation with Sir Matthew Hope.

'I suppose you two ladies have made acquaintance,' she pursued. 'If you haven't I recommend you to do so; for so long as we continue – Ralph and I – to cluster about Mr Touchett's bed you're not likely to have much society but each other.'

'I know nothing about you but that you're a great musician,' Isabel said to the visitor.

'There's a good deal more than that to know,' Mrs Touchett affirmed in her little dry tone.

'A very little of it, I am sure, will content Miss Archer!' the lady exclaimed with a light laugh. 'I'm an old friend of your aunt's. I've lived much in Florence. I'm Madame Merle.' She made this last announcement as if she were referring to a person of tolerably distinct identity. For Isabel, however, it represented little; she could only continue to feel that Madame Merle had as charming a manner as any she had ever encountered.

'She's not a foreigner in spite of her name,' said Mrs Touchett. 'She was born – I always forget where you were born.'

'It's hardly worth while then I should tell you.'

'On the contrary,' said Mrs Touchett, who rarely missed a logical point; 'if I remembered your telling me would be quite superfluous.'

Madame Merle glanced at Isabel with a sort of worldwide smile, a thing that over-reached frontiers. 'I was born under the shadow of the national banner.'

'She's too fond of mystery,' said Mrs Touchett; 'that's her great fault.'

'Ah,' exclaimed Madame Merle, 'I've great faults, but I don't think that's one of them; it certainly isn't the greatest. I came into the world in the

Brooklyn navy-yard. My father was a high officer in the United States Navy, and had a post – a post of responsibility – in that establishment at the time. I suppose I ought to love the sea, but I hate it. That's why I don't return to America. I love the land; the great thing is to love something.'

Isabel, as a dispassionate witness, had not been struck with the force of Mrs Touchett's characterization of her visitor, who had an expressive, communicative, responsive face, by no means of the sort which, to Isabel's mind, suggested a secretive disposition. It was a face that told of an amplitude of nature and of quick and free motions and though it had no regular beauty, was in the highest degree engaging and attaching. Madame Merle was a tall, fair, smooth woman; everything in her person was round and replete, though without those accumulations which suggest heaviness. Her features were thick but in perfect proportion and harmony, and her complexion had a healthy clearness. Her grey eyes were small but full of light and incapable of stupidity – incapable, according to some people, even of tears; she had a liberal, full-rimmed mouth which when she smiled drew itself upward to the left side in a manner that most people thought very odd, some very affected and a few very graceful. Isabel inclined to range herself in the last category. Madame Merle had thick, fair hair, arranged somehow 'classically' and as if she were a Bust, Isabel judged – a Juno or a Niobe; and large white hands, of a perfect shape, a shape so perfect that their possessor, preferring to leave them unadorned, wore no jewelled rings. Isabel had taken her at first, as we have seen, for a Frenchwoman; but extended observation might have ranked her as a German – a German of high degree, perhaps an Austrian, a baroness, a countess, a princess. It would never have been supposed she had come into the world in Brooklyn – though one could doubtless not have carried through any argument that the air of distinction marking her in so eminent a degree was inconsistent with such a birth. It was true that the national banner had floated immediately over her cradle, and the breezy freedom of the stars and stripes might have shed an influence upon the attitude she there took towards life. And yet she had evidently nothing of the fluttered, flapping quality of a morsel of bunting in the wind; her manner expressed the repose and confidence which come from a large experience. Experience, however, had not quenched her youth; it had simply made her sympathetic and supple. She was in a word a woman of strong impulses kept in admirable order. This commended itself to Isabel as an ideal combination.

The girl made these reflexions while the three ladies sat at their tea, but that ceremony was interrupted before long by the arrival of the great doctor from London, who had been immediately ushered into the drawing-room. Mrs Touchett took him off to the library for a private talk; and then Madame Merle and Isabel parted, to meet again at dinner. The idea of seeing more of this interesting woman did much to mitigate Isabel's sense of the sadness now settling on Gardencourt.

When she came into the drawing-room before dinner she found the place empty; but in the course of a moment Ralph arrived. His anxiety about his father had been lightened; Sir Matthew Hope's view of his condition was less depressed than his own had been. The doctor recommended that the nurse alone should remain with the old man for the next three or four hours; so that Ralph, his mother and the great physician himself were free to dine at table. Mrs Touchett and Sir Matthew appeared; Madame Merle was the last.

Before she came Isabel spoke of her to Ralph, who was standing before the fireplace. 'Pray who is this Madame Merle?'

'The cleverest woman I know, not excepting yourself,' said Ralph.

'I thought she seemed very pleasant.'

'I was sure you'd think her very pleasant.'

'Is that why you invited her?'

'I didn't invite her, and when we came back from London I didn't know she was here. No one invited her. She's a friend of my mother's, and just after you and I went to town my mother got a note from her. She had arrived in England (she usually lives abroad, though she has first and last spent a good deal of time here), and asked leave to come down for a few days. She's a woman who can make such proposals with perfect confidence; she's so welcome wherever she goes. And with my mother there could be no question of hesitating; she's the one person in the world whom my mother very much admires. If she were not herself (which she after all much prefers), she would like to be Madame Merle. It would indeed be a great change.'

'Well, she's very charming,' said Isabel. 'And she plays beautifully.'

'She does everything beautifully. She's complete.'

Isabel looked at her cousin a moment. 'You don't like her.'

'On the contrary, I was once in love with her.'

'And she didn't care for you, and that's why you don't like her.'

'How can we have discussed such things? Monsieur Merle was then living.'

'Is he dead now?'

'So she says.'

'Don't you believe her?'

'Yes, because the statement agrees with the probabilities. The husband of Madame Merle would be likely to pass away.'

Isabel gazed at her cousin again. 'I don't know what you mean. You mean something – that you don't mean. What was Monsieur Merle?'

'The husband of Madame.'

'You're very odious. Has she any children?'

'Not the least little child – fortunately.'

'Fortunately?'

'I mean fortunately for the child. She'd be sure to spoil it.'

Isabel was apparently on the point of assuring her cousin for the third time that he was odious; but the discussion was interrupted by the arrival of the lady who was the topic of it. She came rustling in quickly, apologizing for being late, fastening a bracelet, dressed in dark blue satin, which exposed a white bosom that was ineffectually covered by a curious silver necklace. Ralph offered her his arm with the exaggerated alertness of a man who was no longer a lover.

Even if this had still been his condition, however, Ralph had other things to think about. The great doctor spent the night at Gardencourt and, returning to London on the morrow, after another consultation with Mr Touchett's own medical adviser, concurred in Ralph's desire that he should see the patient again on the day following. On the day following Sir Matthew Hope reappeared at Gardencourt, and now took a less encouraging view of the old man, who had grown worse in the twenty-four hours. His feebleness was extreme, and to his son, who constantly sat by his bedside, it often seemed that his end must be at hand. The local doctor, a very sagacious man, in whom Ralph had secretly more confidence than in his distinguished colleague, was constantly in attendance, and Sir Matthew Hope came back several times. Mr Touchett was much of the time unconscious; he slept a great deal; he rarely spoke. Isabel had a great desire to be useful to him and was allowed to watch with him at hours when his other attendants (of whom Mrs Touchett was not the least regular) went to take rest. He never seemed to know her, and she always said to herself 'Suppose he should die while I'm sitting here'; an idea which excited her and kept her awake. Once he opened his eyes for a while and fixed them upon her intelligently, but when she went to him, hoping he would recognize her, he closed them and relapsed into stupor. The day after this, however, he revived for a longer time; but on this occasion Ralph only was with him. The old man began to talk, much to his son's satisfaction, who assured him that they should presently have him sitting up.

'No, my boy,' said Mr Touchett, 'not unless you bury me in a sitting posture, as some of the ancients – was it the ancients? – used to do.'

'Ah, daddy, don't talk about that,' Ralph murmured. 'You mustn't deny that you're getting better.'

'There will be no need of my denying it if you don't say it,' the old man answered. 'Why should we prevaricate just at the last? We never prevaricated before. I've got to die some time, and it's better to die when one's sick than when one's well. I'm very sick – as sick as I shall ever be. I hope you don't want to prove that I shall ever be worse than this? That would be too bad. You don't? Well then.'

Having made this excellent point he became quiet; but the next time that Ralph was with him he again addressed himself to conversation. The nurse had gone to her supper and Ralph was alone in charge, having just relieved Mrs Touchett, who had been on guard since dinner. The room was lighted only by the flickering fire, which of late had become necessary, and Ralph's tall shadow was projected over wall and ceiling with an outline constantly varying but always grotesque.

'Who's that with me – is it my son?' the old man asked.

'Yes, it's your son, daddy.'

'And is there no one else?'

'No one else.'

Mr Touchett said nothing for a while; and then, 'I want to talk a little,' he went on.

'Won't it tire you?' Ralph demurred.

'It won't matter if it does. I shall have a long rest. I want to talk about *you*.'

Ralph had drawn nearer to the bed; he sat leaning forward with his hand on his father's. 'You had better select a brighter topic.'

'You were always bright; I used to be proud of your brightness. I should like so much to think you'd do something.'

'If you leave us,' said Ralph, 'I shall do nothing but miss you.'

'That's just what I don't want; it's what I want to talk about. You must get a new interest.'

'I don't want a new interest, daddy. I have more old ones than I know what to do with.'

The old man lay there looking at his son; his face was the face of the dying, but his eyes were the eyes of Daniel Touchett. He seemed to be reckoning over Ralph's interests. 'Of course you have your mother,' he said at last 'You'll take care of her.'

'My mother will always take care of herself,' Ralph returned.

'Well,' said his father, 'perhaps as she grows older she'll need a little help.'

'I shall not see that. She'll outlive me.'

'Very likely she will; but that's no reason—!' Mr Touchett let his phrase die away in a helpless but not quite querulous sigh and remained silent again.

'Don't trouble yourself about us,' said his son. 'My mother and I get on very well together, you know.'

'You get on by always being apart; that's not natural.'

'If you leave us we shall probably see more of each other.'

'Well,' the old man observed with wandering irrelevance, 'it can't be said that my death will make much difference in your mother's life.'

'It will probably make more than you think.'

'Well, she'll have more money,' said Mr Touchett. 'I've left her a good wife's portion, just as if she had been a good wife.'

'She has been one, daddy, according to her own theory. She has never troubled you.'

'Ah, some troubles are pleasant,' Mr Touchett murmured. 'Those you've given me for instance. But your mother has been less – less – what shall I call it? less out of the way since I've been ill. I presume she knows I've noticed it.'

'I shall certainly tell her so; I'm so glad you mention it.'

'It won't make any difference to her; she doesn't do it to please me. She does it to please – to please—' And he lay a while trying to think why she did it. 'She does it because it suits her. But that's not what I want to talk about,' he added. 'It's about *you*. You'll be very well off.'

'Yes,' said Ralph, 'I know that. But I hope you've not forgotten the talk we had a year ago – when I told you exactly what money I should need and begged you to make some good use of the rest.'

'Yes, yes, I remember. I made a new will – in a few days. I suppose it was the first time such a thing had happened – a young man trying to get a will made against him.'

'It is not against me,' said Ralph. 'It would be against me to have a large property to take care of. It's impossible for a man in my state of health to spend much money, and enough is as good as a feast.'

'Well, you'll have enough – and something over. There will be more than enough for one – there will be enough for two.'

'That's too much,' said Ralph.

'Ah, don't say that. The best thing you can do, when I'm gone, will be to marry.'

Ralph had foreseen what his father was coming to, and this suggestion was by no means fresh. It had long been Mr Touchett's most ingenious way of taking the cheerful view of his son's possible duration. Ralph had usually treated it facetiously; but present circumstances proscribed the facetious. He simply fell back in his chair and returned his father's appealing gaze.

'If I, with a wife who hasn't been very fond of me, have had a very happy life,' said the old man, carrying his ingenuity further still, 'what a life mightn't you have if you should marry a person different from Mrs Touchett. There are more different from her than there are like her.' Ralph still said nothing; and after a pause his father resumed softly: 'What do you think of your cousin?'

At this Ralph started, meeting the question with a strained smile. 'Do I understand you to propose that I should marry Isabel?'

'Well, that's what it comes to in the end. Don't you like Isabel?'

'Yes, very much.' And Ralph got up from his chair and wandered over to the fire. He stood before it an instant and then he stopped and stirred it mechanically. 'I like Isabel very much,' he repeated.

'Well,' said his father, 'I know she likes you. She has told me how much she likes you.'

'Did she remark that she would like to marry me?'

'No, but she can't have anything against you. And she's the most charming young lady I've ever seen. And she would be good to you. I have thought a great deal about it.'

'So have I,' said Ralph, coming back to the bedside again. 'I don't mind telling you that.'

'You *are* in love with her then? I should think you would be. It's as if she came over on purpose.'

'No, I'm not in love with her; but I should be if – if certain things were different.'

'Ah, things are always different from what they might be,' said the old man. 'If you wait for them to change you'll never do anything. I don't know whether you know,' he went on; 'but I suppose there's no harm in my alluding to it at such an hour as this: there was someone wanted to marry Isabel the other day, and she wouldn't have him.'

'I know she refused Warburton: he told me himself.'

'Well, that proves there's a chance for somebody else.'

'Somebody else took his chance the other day in London – and got nothing by it.'

'Was it you?' Mr Touchett eagerly asked.

'No, it was an older friend; a poor gentleman who came over from America to see about it.'

'Well, I'm sorry for him, whoever he was. But it only proves what I say – that the way's open to you.'

'If it is, dear father, it's all the greater pity that I'm unable to tread it. I haven't many convictions; but I have three or four that I hold strongly. One is that people, on the whole, had better not marry their cousins. Another is that people in an advanced stage of pulmonary disorder had better not marry at all.'

The old man raised his weak hand and moved it to and fro before his face. 'What do you mean by that? You look at things in a way that would make everything wrong. What sort of a cousin is a cousin that you had never seen for more than twenty years of her life? We're all each other's cousins, and if we stopped at that the human race would die out. It's just the same with your bad lung. You're a great deal better than you used to be. All you want is to lead a natural life. It is a great deal more natural to marry a pretty young lady that you're in love with than it is to remain single on false principles.'

'I'm not in love with Isabel,' said Ralph.

'You said just now that you would if you didn't think it wrong. I want to prove to you that it isn't wrong.'

'It will only tire you, dear daddy,' said Ralph, who marvelled at his father's tenacity and at his finding strength to insist. 'Then where shall we all be?'

'Where shall you be if I don't provide for you? You won't have anything to do with the bank, and you won't have me to take care of. You say you've so many interests; but I can't make them out.'

Ralph leaned back in his chair with folded arms; his eyes were fixed for some time in meditation. At last, with the air of a man fairly mustering courage, 'I take a great interest in my cousin,' he said, 'but not the sort of interest you desire. I shall not live many years; but I hope I shall live long enough to see what she does with herself. She's entirely independent of me; I can exercise very little influence upon her life. But I should like to do something for her.'

'What should you like to do?'

'I should like to put a little wind in her sails.'

'What do you mean by that?'

'I should like to put it into her power to do some of the things she wants. She wants to see the world for instance. I should like to put money in her purse.'

'Ah, I'm glad you've thought of that,' said the old man. 'But I've thought of it too. I've left her a legacy – five thousand pounds.'

'That's capital; it's very kind of you. But I should like to do a little more.'

Something of that veiled acuteness with which it had been on Daniel Touchett's part the habit of a lifetime to listen to a financial proposition still lingered in the face in which the invalid had not obliterated the man of business. 'I shall be happy to consider it,' he said softly.

'Isabel's poor then. My mother tells me that she has but a few hundred dollars a year. I should like to make her rich.'

'What do you mean by rich?'

'I call people rich when they're able to meet the requirements of their imagination. Isabel has a great deal of imagination.'

'So have you, my son,' said Mr Touchett, listening very attentively but a little confusedly.

'You tell me I shall have money enough for two. What I want is that you should kindly relieve me of my superfluity and make it over to Isabel. Divide my inheritance into two equal halves and give her the second.'

'To do what she likes with?'

'Absolutely what she likes.'

'And without an equivalent?'

'What equivalent could there be?'

'The one I've already mentioned.'

'Her marrying – someone or other? It's just to do away with anything of that sort that I make my suggestion. If she has an easy income she'll never have to marry for a support. That's what I want cannily to prevent. She wishes to be free, and your bequest will make her free.'

'Well, you seem to have thought it out,' said Mr Touchett. 'But I don't see why you appeal to me. The money will be yours, and you can easily give it to her yourself.'

Ralph openly stared. 'Ah, dear father, *I* can't offer Isabel money!'

The old man gave a groan. 'Don't tell me you're not in love with her! Do you want *me* to have the credit of it?'

'Entirely. I should like it simply to be a clause in your will without the slightest reference to me.'

'Do you want me to make a new will then?'

'A few words will do it; you can attend to it the next time you feel a little lively.'

'You must telegraph to Mr Hilary then. I'll do nothing without my solicitor.'

'You shall see Mr Hilary tomorrow.'

'He'll think we've quarrelled, you and I,' said the old man.

'Very probably; I shall like him to think it,' said Ralph, smiling; 'and, to carry out the idea, I give you notice that I shall be very sharp, quite horrid and strange, with you.'

The humour of this appeared to touch his father, who lay a little while taking it in. 'I'll do anything you like,' Mr Touchett said at last; 'but I'm not sure it's right. You say you want to put wind in her sails; but aren't you afraid of putting too much?'

'I should like to see her going before the breeze!' Ralph answered.

'You speak as if it were for your mere amusement.'

'So it is, a good deal.'

'Well, I don't think I understand,' said Mr Touchett with a sigh. 'Young men are very different from what I was. When I cared for a girl – when I was young – I wanted to do more than look at her. You've scruples that I shouldn't have had, and you've ideas that I shouldn't have had either. You say Isabel wants to be free, and that her being rich will keep her from marrying for money. Do you think that she's a girl to do that?'

'By no means. But she has less money than she has ever had before. Her father then gave her everything, because he used to spend his capital. She has nothing but the crumbs of that feast to live on, and she doesn't really know how meagre they are – she has yet to learn it. My mother has told me all about it. Isabel will learn it when she's really thrown upon the world, and it would be very painful to me to think of her coming to the consciousness of a lot of wants she should be unable to satisfy.'

'I've left her five thousand pounds. She can satisfy a good many wants with that.'

'She can indeed. But she would probably spend it in two or three years.'

'You think she'd be extravagant then?'

'Most certainly,' said Ralph, smiling serenely.

Poor Mr Touchett's acuteness was rapidly giving place to pure confusion. 'It would merely be a question of time then, her spending the larger sum?'

'No – though at first I think she'd plunge into that pretty freely: she'd probably make over a part of it to each of her sisters. But after that she'd come to her senses, remember she has still a lifetime before her, and live within her means.'

'Well, you *have* worked it out,' said the old man helplessly. 'You do take an interest in her, certainly.'

'You can't consistently say I go too far. You wished me to go farther.'

'Well, I don't know,' Mr Touchett answered. 'I don't think I enter into your spirit. It seems to me immoral.'

'Immoral, dear daddy?'

'Well, I don't know that it's right to make everything so easy for a person.'

'It surely depends upon the person. When the person's good, your making things easy is all to the credit of virtue. To facilitate the execution of good impulses, what can be a nobler act?'

This was a little difficult to follow, and Mr Touchett considered it for a while. At last he said: 'Isabel's a sweet young thing; but do you think she's so good as that?'

'She's as good as her best opportunities,' Ralph returned.

'Well,' Mr Touchett declared, 'she ought to get a great many opportunities for sixty thousand pounds.'

'I've no doubt she will.'

'Of course I'll do what you want,' said the old man. 'I only want to understand it a little.'

'Well, dear daddy, don't you understand it now?' his son caressingly asked. 'If you don't we won't take any more trouble about it. We'll leave it alone.'

Mr Touchett lay a long time still. Ralph supposed he had given up the attempt to follow. But at last, quite lucidly, he began again. 'Tell me this first. Doesn't it occur to you that a young lady with sixty thousand pounds may fall a victim to the fortune-hunters?'

'She'll hardly fall a victim to more than one.'

'Well, one's too many.'

'Decidedly. That's a risk, and it has entered into my calculation. I think it appreciable, but I think it's small, and I'm prepared to take it.'

Poor Mr Touchett's acuteness had passed into perplexity, and his perplexity now passed into admiration. 'Well, you *have* gone into it!' he repeated. 'But I don't see what good you're to get of it.'

Ralph leaned over his father's pillows and gently smoothed them; he was aware their talk had been unduly prolonged. 'I shall get just the good I said a few moments ago I wished to put into Isabel's reach – that of having met the requirements of my imagination. But it's scandalous, the way I've taken advantage of you!'

Chapter Nineteen

As Mrs Touchett had foretold, Isabel and Madame Merle were thrown much together during the illness of their host, so that if they had not become intimate it would have been almost a breach of good manners. Their manners were of the best, but in addition to this they happened to please each other. It is perhaps too much to say that they swore an eternal friendship, but tacitly at least they called the future to witness. Isabel did so with a perfectly good conscience, though she would have hesitated to admit she was intimate with her new friend in the high sense she privately attached to this term. She often wondered indeed if she ever had been, or ever could be, intimate with anyone. She had an ideal of friendship as well as of several other sentiments, which it failed to seem to her in this case – it had not seemed to her in other cases – that the actual completely expressed. But she often reminded herself that there were essential reasons why one's ideal could never become concrete. It was a thing to believe in, not to see – a matter of faith, not of experience. Experience, however, might supply us with very creditable imitations of it, and the part of wisdom was to make the best of these. Certainly, on the whole, Isabel had never encountered a more agreeable and interesting figure than Madame Merle; she had never met a person having less of that fault which is the principal obstacle to friendship – the air of reproducing the more tiresome, the stale, the too-familiar parts of one's own character. The gates of the girl's confidence were opened wider than they had ever been; she said things to this amiable auditress that she had not yet said to anyone. Sometimes she took alarm at her candour: it was as if she had given to a comparative stranger the key to her cabinet of jewels. These spirtual gems were the only ones of any magnitude that Isabel possessed, but there was all the greater reason for their being carefully guarded. Afterwards, however, she always remembered that one should never regret a generous error and that if Madame Merle had not the merits she attributed to her, so much the worse for Madame Merle. There was no doubt she had great merits – she was charming, sympathetic, intelligent, cultivated. More than this (for it had not been Isabel's ill-fortune to go through life without meeting in her own sex several persons of whom no less could fairly be said), she was rare, superior, and pre-eminent. There are many amiable people in the world, and Madame Merle was far from being vulgarly good-natured and restlessly witty. She knew how to think – an accomplishment rare in women; and she had thought to very good purpose. Of course, too, she knew how to feel; Isabel couldn't have spent a week with her without being sure of that. This was indeed Madame Merle's great talent, her most perfect gift. Life had told upon her; she had felt it strongly, and it was part of the satisfaction to be taken in her society that when the girl talked of what she was pleased to call serious matters this lady understood her so easily and quickly. Emotion, it is true, had become with her rather historic; she made no secret of the fact that the fount of passion, thanks to having been rather violently tapped at one period, didn't flow quite so freely as of yore. She proposed moreover, as well as expected, to cease feeling; she freely admitted that of old she had been a little mad, and now she pretended to be perfectly sane.

'I judge more than I used to,' she said to Isabel, 'but it seems to me one has earned the right. One can't judge till one's forty; before that we're too eager, too hard, too cruel, and in addition much too ignorant. I'm sorry for you; it *will* be a long time before you're forty. But every gain's a loss of some kind; I often think that after forty one *can't* really feel. The freshness, the quickness have certainly gone. You'll keep them longer than most people; it will be a great satisfaction to me to see you some years hence. I want to see what life makes of you. One thing's certain – it can't spoil you. It may pull you about horribly, but I defy it to break you up.'

Isabel received this assurance as a young soldier, still panting from a slight skirmish in which he has come off with honour, might receive a pat on the shoulder from his colonel. Like such a recognition of merit it seemed to come with authority. How could the lightest word do less on the part of a person who was prepared to say, of almost everything Isabel told her, 'Oh, I've been in that, my dear; it passes, like everything else.' On many of her interlocutors Madame Merle might have produced an irritating effect; it was disconcertingly difficult to surprise her. But Isabel, though by no means incapable of desiring to be effective, had not at present this impulse. She was too sincere, too interested in her judicious companion. And then moreover Madame Merle never said such things in the tone of triumph or of boastfulness; they dropped from her like cold confessions.

A period of bad weather had settled upon Gardencourt; the days grew shorter and there was an end to the pretty tea-parties on the lawn. But our young woman had long indoor conversations with her fellow visitor, and in spite of the rain the two ladies often sallied forth for a walk, equipped with the defensive apparatus which the English climate and the English genius have between them brought to such perfection. Madame Merle liked almost everything, including the English rain. 'There's always a little of it and never too much at once,' she said; 'and it never wets you and it always smells good.' She declared that in England the pleasures of smell were great – that in this inimitable island there was a certain mixture of fog and beer and soot which, however odd it might sound, was the national aroma, and was most agreeable to the nostril; and she used to lift the sleeve of her British overcoat and bury her nose in it, inhaling the clear, fine scent of the wool. Poor Ralph Touchett, as soon as the autumn had begun to define itself, became almost a prisoner; in bad weather he was unable to step out of the house, and he used sometimes to stand at one of the windows with his hands in his pockets and, from a countenance half-rueful, half-critical, watch Isabel and Madame Merle as they walked down the avenue under a pair of umbrellas. The roads about Gardencourt were so firm, even in the worst weather, that the two ladies always came back with a healthy glow in their cheeks, looking at the soles of their neat, stout boots and declaring that their walk had done them inexpressible good. Before luncheon, always, Madame Merle was engaged; Isabel admired and envied her rigid possession of her morning. Our heroine had always passed for a person of resources and had taken a certain pride in being one; but she wandered, as by the wrong side of the wall of a private garden, round the enclosed talents, accomplishments, aptitudes of Madame Merle. She found herself desiring to emulate them, and in twenty such ways this lady presented herself as a model. 'I should like awfully to be *so*!' Isabel secretly exclaimed, more than once, as one after another of her friend's fine aspects caught the light, and before long she knew that she had learned a lesson from a high authority. It took no great time indeed for her to feel herself, as the phrase is, under an influence. 'What's the harm,' she wondered, 'so long as it's a good one? The more one's under a good influence the better. The only thing is to see our steps as we take them – to understand them as we go. That, no doubt, I shall always do. I needn't be afraid of becoming too pliable; isn't it my fault that I'm not pliable enough?' It is said that imitation is the sincerest flattery; and if Isabel was sometimes moved to gape at her friend aspiringly and despairingly it was not so much because she desired herself to shine as because she wished to hold up the lamp for Madame Merle. She liked her extremely, but was even more dazzled than attracted. She sometimes asked herself what Henrietta Stackpole would say to her thinking so much of this perverted product of their common soil, and had a conviction that it would be severely judged. Henrietta would not at all subscribe to Madame Merle; for reasons she could not have defined this truth came home to the girl. On the other hand she was equally sure that, should the occasion offer, her new friend would strike off some happy view of her old: Madame Merle was too humorous, too observant, not to do justice to Henrietta, and on becoming acquainted with her would probably give the measure of a tact which Miss Stackpole couldn't hope to emulate. She appeared to have in her experience a touchstone for everything, and somewhere in the capacious pocket of her genial memory she would find the key to Henrietta's value. 'That's the great thing,' Isabel solemnly pondered; 'that's the supreme good fortune; to be in a better position for appreciating people than they are for appreciating you.' And she added that such, when one considered it, was simply the essence of the aristocratic situation. In this light, if in none other, one should aim at the aristocratic situation.

I may not count over all the links in the chain which led Isabel to think of Madame Merle's situation as aristocratic – a view of it never expressed in any reference made to it by that lady herself. She had known great things and great people, but she had never played a great part. She was one of the small ones of the earth; she had not been born to honours, she knew the world too well to nourish fatuous illusions on the article of her own place in it. She had encountered many of the fortunate few and was perfectly aware of those points at which their fortune differed from hers. But if by her informed measure she was no figure for a high scene, she had yet to Isabel's imagination a sort of greatness. To be so cultivated and civilized, so wise and so easy, and still make so light of it – that was really to be a great lady, especially when one so carried and presented one's self. It was as if somehow she had all society under contribution, and all the arts and graces it practised – or was the effect rather that of charming uses found *for* her, even from a distance, subtle service rendered by her to a clamorous world wherever she might be? After breakfast she wrote a succession of letters, as those arriving for her appeared innumerable: her correspondence was a source of surprise to Isabel when they sometimes walked together to the village post office to deposit Madame Merle's offering to the mail. She knew more people, as she told Isabel, than she knew what to do with, and something was always turning up to be written about. Of painting she was devotedly fond, and made no more of brushing in a sketch than of pulling off her gloves. At Gardencourt she was perpetually taking advantage of an hour's sunshine to go out with a camp-stool and a box of water-colours. That she was a brave musician we have already perceived, and it was evidence of the fact that when she seated herself at the piano, as she always did in the evening, her listeners resigned themselves without a murmur to losing the grace of her talk. Isabel, since she had known her, felt ashamed of her own facility, which she now looked upon as basely inferior; and indeed, though she had been thought rather a prodigy at home, the loss to society when, in taking her place upon the music-stool, she turned her back to the room, was usually deemed greater than the gain. When Madame Merle was neither writing, nor painting, nor touching the piano, she was usually employed upon wonderful tasks of rich embroidery, cushions, curtains, decorations for the chimney-piece; an art in which her bold, free invention was as noted as the agility of her needle. She was never idle, for when engaged in none of the ways I have mentioned she was either reading (she appeared to Isabel to read 'everything important'), or walking out, or playing patience with the cards, or talking with her fellow inmates. And with all this she had always the social quality, was never rudely absent and yet never too seated. She laid down her pastimes as easily as she took them up; she worked and talked at the same time and appeared to impute scant worth to anything she did. She gave away her sketches and tapestries; she rose from the piano or remained there, according to the convenience of her auditors, which she always unerringly divined. She was in short the most comfortable, profitable, amenabe person to live with. If for Isabel she had a fault it was that she was not natural; by which the girl meant, not that she was either affected or pretentious, since from these vulgar vices no woman could have been more exempt, but that her nature had been too much overlaid by custom and her angles too much rubbed away. She had become too flexible, too useful, was too ripe and too final. She was in a word too perfectly the social animal that man and woman are supposed to have been intended to be; and she had rid herself of every remnant of that tonic wildness which we may assume to have belonged even to the most amiable persons in the ages before country-house life was the fashion. Isabel found it difficult to think of her in any detachment or privacy, she existed only in her relations, direct or indirect, with her fellow mortals. One might wonder what commerce she could possibly hold with her own spirit. One always ended, however, by feeling that a charming surface doesn't necessarily prove one superficial; this was an illusion in which, in one's youth, one had but just escaped being nourished. Madame Merle was not superficial – not she. She was deep, and her nature spoke none the less in her behaviour because it spoke a conventional tongue. 'What's language at all but a convention?' said Isabel. 'She has the good taste not to pretend, like some people I've met, to express herself by original signs.'

'I'm afraid you've suffered much,' she once found occasion to say to her friend in response to some allusion that had appeared to reach far.

'What makes you think that?' Madame Merle asked with the amused smile of a person seated at a game of guesses. 'I hope I haven't too much the droop of the misunderstood.'

'No; but you sometimes say things that I think people who have always been happy wouldn't have found out.'

'I haven't always been happy,' said Madame Merle, smiling still but with a mock gravity, as if she were telling a child a secret. 'Such a wonderful thing!'

But Isabel rose to the irony. 'A great many people give me the impression of never having for a moment felt anything.'

'It's very true; there are many more iron pots certainly than porcelain. But you may depend on it that every one bears some mark; even the hardest iron pots have a little bruise, a little hole somewhere. I flatter myself that I'm rather stout, but if I must tell you the truth I've been shockingly chipped and cracked. I do very well for service yet, because I've been cleverly mended; and I try to remain in the cupboard – the quiet, dusky cupboard where there's an odour of stale spices – as much as I can. But when I've to come out and into a strong light – then, my dear, I'm a horror!'

I know not whether it was on this occasion or on some other that when the conversation had taken the turn I have just indicated she said to Isabel that she would some day a tale unfold. Isabel assured her she should delight to listen to one, and reminded her more than once of this engagement. Madame Merle, however, begged repeatedly for a respite, and at last frankly told her young companion that they must wait till they knew each other better. This would be sure to happen; a long friendship so visibly lay before them. Isabel assented, but at the same time inquired if she mightn't be trusted – if she appeared capable of a betrayal of confidence.

'It's not that I'm afraid of your repeating what I say,' her fellow visitor answered; 'I'm afraid, on the contrary, of your taking it too much to yourself. You'd judge me too harshly; you're of the cruel age.' She preferred for the present to talk to Isabel of Isabel, and exhibited the greatest interest in our heroine's history, sentiments, opinions, prospects. She made her chatter and listened to her chatter with infinite good nature. This flattered and quickened the girl, who was struck with all the distinguished people her friend had known and with her having lived, as Mrs Touchett said, in the best company in Europe. Isabel thought the better of herself for enjoying the favour of a person who had so large a field of comparison; and it was perhaps partly to gratify the sense of profiting by comparison that she often appealed to these stores of reminiscence. Madame Merle had been a dweller in many lands and had social ties in a dozen different countries. 'I don't pretend to be educated,' she would say, 'but I think I know my Europe', and she spoke one day of going to Sweden to stay with an old friend, and another of proceeding to Malta to follow up a new acquaintance. With England, where she had often dwelt, she was thoroughly familiar, and for Isabel's benefit threw a great deal of light upon the customs of the country and the character of the people, who 'after all', as she was fond of saying, were the most convenient in the world to live with.

'You mustn't think it strange her remaining here at such a time as this, when Mr Touchett's passing away,' that gentleman's wife remarked to her niece. 'She is incapable of a mistake; she's the most tactful woman I know. It's a favour to me that she stays; she's putting off a lot of visits at great houses,' said Mrs Touchett, who never forgot that when she herself was in England her social value sank two or three degrees in the scale. 'She has her pick of places; she's not in want of a shelter. But I've asked her to put in this time because I wish you to know her. I think it will be a good thing for you. Serena Merle hasn't a fault.'

'If I didn't already like her very much that description might alarm me,' Isabel returned.

'She's never the least little bit "off". I've brought you out here and I wish to do the best for you. Your sister Lily told me she hoped I would give you plenty of oportunities. I give you one in putting you in relation with Madame Merle. She's one of the most brilliant women in Europe.'

'I like her better than I like your description of her,' Isabel persisted in saying.

'Do you flatter yourself that you'll ever feel her open to criticism? I hope you'll let me know when you do.'

'That will be cruel – to you,' said Isabel.

'You needn't mind me. You won't discover a fault in her.'

'Perhaps not. But I dare say I shan't miss it.'

'She knows absolutely everything on earth there is to know,' said Mrs Touchett.

Isabel after this observed to their companion that she hoped she knew Mrs Touchett considered she hadn't a speck on her perfection. On which, 'I'm obliged to you,' Madame Merle replied, 'but I'm afraid your aunt imagines, or at least alludes to, no aberrations that the clock-face doesn't register.'

'So that you mean you've a wild side that's unknown to her?'

'Ah no, I fear my darkest sides are my tamest. I mean that having no faults, for your aunt, means that one's never late for dinner – that is for *her* dinner. I was not late, by the way, the other day, when you came back from London; the clock was just at eight when I came into the drawing-room: it was the rest of you that were before the time. It means that one answers a letter the day one gets it and that when one comes to stay with her one doesn't bring too much luggage and is careful not to be taken ill. For Mrs Touchett those things constitute virtue; it's a blessing to be able to reduce it to its elements.'

Madame Merle's own conversation, it will be perceived, was enriched with bold, free touches of criticism, which, even when they had a restrictive effect, never struck Isabel as ill-natured. It couldn't occur to the girl for instance that Mrs Touchett's accomplished guest was abusing her; and this for very good reasons. In the first place Isabel rose eagerly to the sense of her shades; in the second Madame Merle implied that there was a great deal more to say; and it was clear in the third that for a person to speak to one without ceremony of one's near relations was an agreeable sign of that person's intimacy with one's self. These signs of deep communion multiplied as the days elapsed, and there was none of which Isabel was more sensible than of her companion's preference for making Miss Archer herself a topic. Though she referred frequently to the incidents of her own career she never lingered upon them; she was as little of a gross egotist as she was of a flat gossip.

'I'm old and stale and faded,' she said more than once; 'I'm of no more interest than last week's newspaper. You're young and fresh and of today; you've the great thing – you've actuality. I once had it – we all have it for an hour. You, however, will have it for longer. Let us talk about you then; you can say nothing I shall not care to hear. It's a sign that I'm growing old – that I like to talk with younger people. I think it's a very pretty compensation. If we can't have youth within us we can have it outside, and I really think we see it and feel it better that way. Of course we must be in sympathy with it – that I shall always be. I don't know that I shall ever be ill-natured with old people – I hope not; there are certainly some old people I adore. But I shall never be anything but abject with the young; they touch me and appeal to me too much. I give you *carte blanche* then; you can even be impertinent if you like; I shall let it pass and horribly spoil you. I speak as if I were a hundred years old, you say? Well, I am, if you please; I was born before the French Revolution. Ah, my dear, *je viens de loin*; I belong to the old, old world. But it's not of that I want to talk; I want to talk about the new. You must tell me more about America; you never tell me enough. Here I've been since I was brought here as a helpless child, and it's ridiculous, or rather it's scandalous, how little I know about that splendid, dreadful, funny country – surely the greatest and drollest of them all. There are a great many of us like that in these parts, and I must say I think we're a wretched set of people. You should live in your own land; whatever it may be you have your natural place there. If we're not good Americans we're certainly poor Europeans; we've no natural place here. We're mere parasites crawling over the surface; we haven't our feet in the soil. At least one can know it and not have illusions. A woman perhaps can get on; a woman, it seems to me, has no natural place anywhere; wherever she finds herself she has to remain on the surface and, more or less, to crawl. You protest, my dear? you're horrified? you declare you'll never crawl? It's very true that I don't see you crawling; you stand more upright than a good many poor creatures. Very good; on the whole, I don't think you'll crawl. But the men, the Americans; *je vous demande un peu*, what do they make of it over here? I don't envy them trying to arrange themselves. Look at poor Ralph Touchett: what sort of a figure do you call that? Fortunately he has a consumption; I say fortunately because it gives him something to do. His consumption's his *carrière*; it's a kind of position. You can say: "Oh, Mr Touchett, he takes care of his lungs, he knows a great deal about climates." But without that who would he be, what would he represent? "Mr Ralph Touchett: an American who lives in Europe." That signifies absolutely nothing – it's impossible anything should signify less. "He's very cultivated," they say: "he has a very pretty collection of old snuff-boxes." The collection is all that's wanted to make it pitiful. I'm tired of the sound of the word; I think it's grotesque. With the poor old father it's different; he has his identity, and it's rather a massive one. He represents a great financial house, and that, in our day, is as good as anything else. For an American, at any rate, that will do very well. But I persist in thinking your cousin very lucky to have a chronic malady so long as he doesn't die of it. It's much better than the snuff-boxes. If he weren't ill, you say he'd do something? – he'd take his father's place in the house. My poor child, I doubt it; I don't think he's at all fond of the house. However, you know him better than I, though I used to know him rather well, and he may have the benefit of the doubt. The worst case, I think, is a friend of mine, a countryman of ours, who lives in Italy (where he also was brought before he knew better), and who is one of the most delightful men I know. Some day you must know him. I'll bring you together and then you'll see what I mean. He's Gilbert Osmond – he lives in Italy; that's all one can say about him or make of him. He's exceedingly clever, a man made to be distinguished; but, as I tell you, you exhaust the description when you say he's Mr Osmond who lives *tout bêtement* in Italy. No career, no name, no position, no fortune, no past, no future, no anything. Oh yes, he paints, if you please – paints in water-colours, like me, only better than I. His painting's pretty bad; on the whole I'm rather glad of that. Fortunately he's very indolent, so indolent that it amounts to a sort of position. He can say, "Oh, I do nothing; I'm too deadly lazy. You can do nothing today unless you get up at five o'clock in the morning." In that way he becomes a sort of exception; you feel he might do something if he'd only rise early. He never speaks of his painting – to people at large; he's too clever for that. But he has a little girl – a dear little girl; he does speak of *her*. He's devoted to her, and if it were a career to be an excellent father he'd be very distinguished. But I'm afraid that's no better than the snuff-boxes; perhaps not even so good. Tell me what they do in America,' pursued Madame Merle, who, it must be observed parenthetically, did not deliver herself all at once of these reflections, which are presented in a cluster for the convenience of the reader. She talked of Florence, where Mr Osmond lived and where Mrs Touchett occupied a medieval palace; she talked of Rome, where she herself had a little *pied-à-terre* with some rather good old damask. She talked of places, of people and even, as the phrase is, of 'subjects'; and from time to time she talked of their kind old host and of the prospect of his recovery. From the first she had thought this prospect small, and Isabel had been struck with the positive, discriminating, competent way in which she took the measure of his remainder of life. One evening she announced definitely that he wouldn't live.

'Sir Matthew Hope told me so as plainly as was proper,' she said; 'standing there, near the fire, before dinner. He makes himself very agreeable, the great doctor. I don't mean his saying that has anything to do with it. But he says such things with great tact. I had told him I felt ill at my ease, staying here at such a time; it seemed to me so indiscreet – it wasn't as if I could nurse. "You must remain, you must remain," he answered; "your office will come later." Wasn't that a very delicate way of saying both that poor Mr Touchett would go and that I might be of some use as a consoler? In fact, however, I shall not be of the slightest use. Your aunt will console herself; she, and she alone, knows just how much consolation she'll require. It would be a very delicate matter for another person to undertake to administer the dose. With your cousin it will be different; he'll miss his father immensely. But I should never presume to condole with Mr Ralph; we're not on those terms.' Madame Merle had alluded more than once to some undefined incongruity in her relations with Ralph Touchett; so Isabel took this occasion of asking her if they were not good friends.

'Perfectly, but he doesn't like me.'

'What have you done to him?'

'Nothing whatever. But one has no need of a reason for that.'

'For not liking you? I think one has need of a very good reason.'

'You're very kind. Be sure you have one ready for the day you begin.'

'Begin to dislike you? I shall never begin.'

'I hope not; because if you do you'll never end. That's the way with your cousin; he doesn't get over it. It's an antipathy of nature – if I can call it that when it's all on his side. I've nothing whatever against him and don't bear him the least little grudge for not doing me justice. Justice is all I want. However, one feels that he's a gentleman and would never say anything underhand about me. *Cartes sur table,' Madame* Merle subjoined in a moment, 'I'm not afraid of him.'

'I hope not indeed,' said Isabel, who added something about his being the kindest creature living. She remembered, however, that on her first asking him about Madame Merle he had answered her in a manner which this lady might have thought injurious without being explicit. There was something between them, Isabel said to herself, but she said nothing more than this. If it were something of importance it should inspire respect; if it were not it was not worth her curiosity. With all her love of knowledge she had a natural shrinking from raising curtains and looking into unlighted corners. The love of knowledge coexisted in her mind with the finest capacity for ignorance.

But Madame Merle sometimes said things that startled her, made her raise her clear eyebrows at the time and think of the words afterwards. 'I'd give a great deal to be your age again,' she broke out once with a bitterness which, though diluted in her customary amplitude of ease, was imperfectly disguised by it. 'If I could only begin again – if I could have my life before me!'

'Your life's before you yet,' Isabel answered gently, for she was vaguely awe-struck.

'No; the best part's gone, and gone for nothing.'

'Surely not for nothing,' said Isabel.

'Why not – what have I got? Neither husband, nor child, nor fortune, nor position, nor the traces of a beauty that I never had.'

'You have many friends, dear lady.'

'I'm not so sure!' cried Madame Merle.

'Ah, you're wrong. You have memories, graces, talents—'

But Madame Merle interrupted her. 'What have my talents brought me? Nothing but the need of using them still, to get through the hours, the years, to cheat myself with some pretence of movement, of unconsciousness. As for my graces and memories the less said about them the better. You'll be my friend till you find a better use for your friendship.'

'It will be for you to see that I don't then,' said Isabel.

'Yes; I would make an effort to keep you.' And her companion looked at her gravely. 'When I say I should like to be your age I mean with your qualities – frank, generous, sincere like you. In that case I should have made something better of my life.'

'What should you have liked to do that you've not done?'

Madame Merle took a sheet of music – she was seated at the piano and had abruptly wheeled about on the stool when she first spoke – and mechanically turned the leaves. 'I'm very ambitious!' she at last replied.

'And your ambitions have not been satisfied? They must have been great.'

'They *were* great. I should make myself ridiculous by talking of them.'

Isabel wondered what they could have been – whether Madame Merle had aspired to wear a crown. 'I don't know what your idea of success may be, but you seem to me to have been successful. To me indeed you're a vivid image of success.'

Madame Merle tossed away the music with a smile. 'What's *your* idea of success?'

'You evidently think it must be a very tame one. It's to see some dream of one's youth come true.'

'Ah,' Madame Merle exclaimed, 'that I've never seen! But my dreams were so great – so preposterous. Heaven forgive me, I'm dreaming now!' And she turned back to the piano and began grandly to play. On the morrow she said to Isabel that her definition of success had been very pretty, yet frightfully sad. Measured in that way, who had ever succeeded? The dreams of one's youth, why they were enchanting, they were divine! Who had ever seen such things come to pass?

'I myself – a few of them,' Isabel ventured to answer.

'Already? They must have been dreams of yesterday.'

'I began to dream very young,' Isabel smiled.

'Ah, if you mean the aspirations of your childhood – that of having a pink sash and a doll that could close her eyes.'

'No, I don't mean that.'

'Or a young man with a fine moustache going down on his knees to you.'

'No, nor that either,' Isabel declared with still more emphasis.

Madame Merle appeared to note this eagerness. 'I suspect that's what you do mean. We've all had the young man with the moustache. He's the inevitable young man; he doesn't count.'

Isabel was silent a little but then spoke with extreme and characteristic inconsequence. 'Why shouldn't he count? There are young men and young men'

'And yours was a paragon – is that what you mean?' asked her friend with a laugh. 'If you've had the identical young man you dreamed of, then that was success, and I congratulate you with all my heart. Only in that case why didn't you fly with him to his castle in the Apennines?'

'He has no castle in the Apennines.'

'What has he? An ugly brick house in Fortieth Street? Don't tell me that; I refuse to recognize that as an ideal.'

'I don't care anything about his house,' said Isabel.

'That's very crude of you. When you've lived as long as I you'll see that every human being has his shell and that you must take the shell into account. By the shell I mean the whole envelope of circumstances. There's no such thing as an isolated man or woman; we're each of us made up of some cluster of appurtenances. What shall we call our "self"? Where does it begin? where does it end? It overflows into everything that belongs to us – and then it flows back again. I know a large part of myself is in the clothes I choose to wear. I've a great respect for *things*! One's self – for other people – is one's expression of one's self; and one's house, one's furniture, one's garments, the books one reads, the company one keeps – these things are all expressive.'

This was very metaphysical; not more so, however, than several observations Madame Merle had already made. Isabel was fond of metaphysics, but was unable to accompany her friend into this bold analysis of the human personality. 'I don't agree with you. I think just the other way. I don't know whether I succeed in expressing myself, but I know that nothing else expresses me. Nothing that belongs to me is any measure of me; everything's on the contrary a limit, a barrier, and a perfectly arbitrary one. Certainly the clothes which, as you say, I choose to wear, don't express me; and heaven forbid they should!'

'You dress very well,' Madame Merle lightly interposed.

'Possibly; but I don't care to be judged by that. My clothes may express the dressmaker, but they don't express me. To begin with it's not my own choice that I wear them; they're imposed upon me by society.'

'Should you prefer to go without them?' Madame Merle inquired in a tone which virtually terminated the discussion.

I am bound to confess, though it may cast some discredit on the sketch I have given of the youthful loyalty practised by our heroine towards this accomplished woman, that Isabel had said nothing whatever to her about Lord Warburton and had been equally reticent on the subject of Caspar Goodwood. She had not, however, concealed the fact that she had had opportunities of marrying and had even let her friend know of how advantageous a kind they had been. Lord Warburton had left Lockleigh and was gone to Scotland, taking his sisters with him; and though he had written to Ralph more than once to ask about Mr Touchett's health the girl was not liable to the embarrassment of such inquiries as, had he still been in the neighbourhood, he would probably have felt bound to make in person. He had excellent ways, but she felt sure that if he had come to Gardencourt he would have seen Madame Merle, and that if he had seen her he would have liked her and betrayed to her that he was in love with her young friend. It so happened that during this lady's previous visits to Gardencourt – each of them much shorter than the present – he had either not been at Lockleigh or had not called at Mr Touchett's. Therefore, though she knew him by name as the great man of that county, she had no cause to suspect him as a suitor of Mrs Touchett's freshly-imported niece.

'You've plenty of time,' she had said to Isabel in return for the mutilated confidences which our young woman made her and which didn't pretend to be perfect, though we have seen that at moments the girl had compunctions at having said so much. 'I'm glad you've done nothing yet – that you have it still to do. It's a very good thing for a girl to have refused a few good offers – so long of course as they are not the best she's likely to have. Pardon me if my tone seems horribly corrupt; one must take the worldly view sometimes. Only don't keep on refusing for the sake of refusing. It's a pleasant exercise of power; but accepting's after all an exercise of power as well. There's always the danger of refusing once too often. It was not the one I fell into – I didn't refuse often enough. You're an exquisite creature and I should like to see you married to a prime minister. But speaking strictly, you know, you're not what is technically called a *parti*. You're extremely good-looking and extremely clever; in yourself you're quite exceptional. You appear to have the vaguest ideas about your earthly possessions; but from what I can make out you're not embarrassed with an income. I wish you had a little money.'

'I wish I had!' said Isabel, simply, apparently forgetting for the moment that her poverty had been a venial fault for two gallant gentlemen.

In spite of Sir Matthew Hope's benevolent recommendation Madame Merle did not remain to the end, as the issue of poor Mr Touchett's malady had now come frankly to be designated. She was under pledges to other people which had at last to be redeemed, and she left Gardencourt with the understanding that she should in any event see Mrs Touchett there again, or else in town, before quitting England. Her parting with Isabel was even more like the beginning of a friendship than their meeting had been. 'I'm going to six places in succession, but I shall see no one I like so well as you. They'll all be old friends, however; one doesn't make new friends at my age. I've made a great exception for you. You must remember that and must think as well of me as possible. You must reward me by believing in me.'

By way of answer Isabel kissed her, and, though some women kiss with facility, there are kisses and kisses, and this embrace was satisfactory to Madame Merle. Our young lady, after this, was much alone; she saw her aunt and cousin only at meals, and discovered that of the hours during which Mrs Touchett was invisible only a minor portion was now devoted to nursing her husband. She spent the rest in her own apartments, to which access was not allowed even to her niece, apparently occupied there with mysterious and inscrutable exercises. At table she was grave and silent; but her solemnity was not an attitude – Isabel could see it was a conviction. She wondered if her aunt repented of having taken her own way so much; but there was no visible evidence of this – no tears, no sighs, no exaggeration of a zeal always to its own sense adequate. Mrs Touchett seemed simply to feel the need of thinking things over and summing them up; she had a little moral account-book – with columns unerringly ruled and a sharp steel clasp – which she kept with exemplary neatness. Uttered reflection had with her ever, at any rate, a practical ring. 'If I had foreseen this I'd not have proposed your coming abroad now,' she said to Isabel after Madame Merle had left the house. 'I'd have waited and sent for you next year.'

'So that perhaps I should never have known my uncle? It's a great happiness to me to have come now.'

'That's very well. But it was not that you might know your uncle that I brought you to Europe.' A perfectly veracious speech; but, as Isabel thought, not as perfectly timed. She had leisure to think of this and other matters. She took a solitary walk every day and spent vague hours in turning over books in the library. Among the subjects that engaged her attention were the adventures of her friend Miss Stackpole, with whom she was in regular correspondence. Isabel liked her friend's private epistolary style better than her public; that is she felt her public letters would have been excellent if they had not been printed. Henrietta's career, however, was not so successful as might have been wished even in the interest of her private felicity; that view of the inner life of Great Britain which she was so eager to take appeared to dance before her like an *ignis fatuus*. The invitation from Lady Pensil, for mysterious reasons, had never arrived; and poor Mr Bantling himself, with all his friendly ingenuity, had been unable to explain so grave a dereliction on the part of a missive that had obviously been sent. He had evidently taken Henrietta's affairs much to heart, and believed that he owed her a set-off to this illusory visit to Bedfordshire. 'He says he should think I would go to the Continent,' Henrietta wrote; 'and as he thinks of going there himself I suppose his advice is sincere. He wants to know why I don't take a view of French life; and it's a fact that I want very much to see the new Republic. Mr Bantling doesn't care much about the Republic, but he thinks of going over to Paris anyway. I must say he's quite as attentive as I could wish, and at least I shall have seen one polite Englishman. I keep telling Mr Bantling that he ought to have been an American, and you should see how that pleases him. Whenever I say so he always breaks out with the same exclamation – "Ah, but really, come now!" ' A few days later she wrote that she had decided to go to Paris at the end of the week and that Mr Bantling had promised to see her off – perhaps even would go as far as Dover with her. She would wait in Paris till Isabel should arrive, Henrietta added; speaking quite as if Isabel were to start on her continental journey alone and making no allusion to Mrs Touchett. Bearing in mind his interest in their late companion, our heroine communicated several passages from this correspondence to Ralph, who followed with an emotion akin to suspense the career of the representative of the *Interviewer*.

'It seems to me she's doing very well,' he said, 'going over to Paris with an ex-Lancer! If she wants something to write about she has only to describe that episode.'

'It's not conventional, certainly,' Isabel answered; 'but if you mean that – as far as Henrietta is concerned – it's not perfectly innocent, you're very much mistaken. You'll never understand Henrietta.'

'Pardon me, I understand her perfectly. I didn't at all at first, but now I've the point of view. I'm afraid, however, that Bantling hasn't; he may have some surprises. Oh, I understand Henrietta as well as if I had made her!'

Isabel was by no means sure of this, but she abstained from expressing further doubt, for she was disposed in these days to extend a great charity to her cousin. One afternoon less than a week after Madame Merle's departure she was seated in the library with a volume to which her attention was not fastened. She had placed herself in a deep window-bench, from which she looked out into the dull, damp park; and as the library stood at right angles to the entrance-front of the house she could see the doctor's brougham, which had been waiting for the last two hours before the door. She was struck with his remaining so long, but at last she saw him appear in the portico, stand a moment slowly drawing on his gloves and looking at the knees of his horse, and then get into the vehicle and roll away. Isabel kept her place for half an hour; there was a great stillness in the house. It was so great that when she at least heard a soft, slow step on the deep carpet of the room she was almost startled by the sound. She turned quickly away from the window and saw Ralph Touchett standing there with his hands still in his pockets, but with a face absolutely void of its usual latent smile. She got up and her movement and glance were a question.

'It's all over,' said Ralph.

'Do you mean that my uncle—?' And Isabel stopped.

'My dear father died an hour ago.'

'Ah, my poor Ralph!' she gently waited, putting out her two hands to him.

Chapter Twenty

Some fortnight after this Madame Merle drove up in a hansom cab to the house in Winchester Square. As she descended from her vehicle she observed, suspended between the dining-room windows, a large, neat, wooden tablet, on whose fresh black ground were inscribed in white paint the words – 'This noble freehold mansion to be sold'; with the name of the agent to whom application should be made. 'They certainly lose no time,' said the visitor as, after sounding the big brass knocker, she waited to be admitted; 'it's a practical country!' And within the house, as she ascended to the drawing-room, she perceived numerous signs of abdication; pictures removed from the walls and placed upon sofas, windows undraped and floors laid bare. Mrs Touchett presently received her and intimated in a few words that condolences might be taken for granted.

'I know what you're going to say – he was a very good man. But I know it better than any one, because I gave him more chance to show it. In that I think I was a good wife.' Mrs Touchett added that at the end her husband apparently recognized this fact. 'He has treated me most liberally,' she said; 'I won't say more liberally than I expected, because I didn't expect. You know that as a general thing I don't expect. But he chose, I presume, to recognize the fact that though I lived much abroad and mingled – you may say freely – in foreign life, I never exhibited the smallest preference for anyone else.'

'For anyone but yourself,' Madame Merle mentally observed; but the reflection was perfectly inaudible.

'I never sacrificed my husband to another,' Mrs Touchett continued with her stout curtness.

'Oh no,' thought Madame Merle; 'you never did anything for another!'

There was a certain cynicism in these mute comments which demands an explanation; the more so as they are not in accord either with the view – somewhat superficial perhaps – that we have hitherto enjoyed of Madame Merle's character or with the literal facts of Mrs Touchett's history; the more so, too, as Madame Merle had a well-founded conviction that her friend's last remark was not in the least to be construed as a side-thrust at herself. The truth is that the moment she had crossed the threshold she received an impression that Mr Touchett's death had had subtle consequences and that these consequences had been profitable to a little circle of persons among whom she was not numbered. Of course it was an event which would naturally have consequences; her imagination had more than once rested upon this fact during her stay at Gardencourt. But it had been one thing to foresee such a matter mentally and another to stand among its massive records. The idea of a distribution of property – she would almost have said of spoils – just now pressed upon her senses and irritated her with a sense of exclusion. I am far from wishing to picture her as one of the hungry mouths or envious hearts of the general herd, but we have already learned of her having desires that had never been satisfied. If she had been questioned, she would of course have admitted – with a fine proud smile – that she had not the faintest claim to a share in Mr Touchett's relics. 'There was never anything in the world between us,' she would have said. 'There was never that, poor man!' – with a fillip of her thumb and her third finger. I hasten to add, moreover, that if she couldn't at the present moment keep from quite perversely yearning she was careful not to betray herself. She had after all as much sympathy for Mrs Touchett's gains as for her losses.

'He has left me this house,' the newly-made widow said; 'but of course I shall not live in it; I've a much better one in Florence. The will was opened only three days since, but I've already offered the house for sale. I've also a share in the bank; but I don't yet understand if I'm obliged to leave it there. If not I shall certainly take it out. Ralph, of course, has Gardencourt; but I'm not sure that he'll have means to keep up the place. He's naturally left very well off, but his father has given away an immense deal of money; there are bequests to a string of third cousins in Vermont. Ralph, however, is very fond of Gardencourt and would be quite capable of living there – in summer – with a maid-of-all-work and a gardener's boy. There's one remarkable clause in my husband's will,' Mrs Touchett added. 'He has left my niece a fortune.'

'A fortune!' Madame Merle softly repeated.

'Isabel steps into something like seventy thousand pounds.'

Madame Merle's hands were clasped in her lap; at this she raised them, still clasped, and held them a moment against her bosom while her eyes, a little dilated, fixed themselves on those of her friend, 'Ah,' she cried, 'the clever creature!'

Mrs Touchett gave her a quick look. 'What do you mean by that?'

For an instant Madame Merle's colour rose and she dropped her eyes. 'It certainly is clever to achieve such results – without an effort!'

'There assuredly was no effort. Don't call it an achievement.'

Madame Merle was seldom guilty of the awkwardness of retracting what she had said; her wisdom was shown rather in maintaining it and placing it in a favourable light. 'My dear friend Isabel would certainly not have had seventy thousand pounds left her if she had not been the most charming girl in the world. Her charm includes great cleverness.'

'She never dreamed, I'm sure, of my husband's doing anything for her; and I never dreamed of it either, for he never spoke to me of his intention,' Mrs Touchett said. 'She had no claim upon him whatever; it was no great recommendation to him that she was my niece. Whatever she achieved she achieved unconsciously.'

'Ah,' rejoined Madame Merle, 'those are the greatest strokes!'

Mrs Touchett reserved her opinion. 'The girl's fortunate; I don't deny that. But for the present she's simply stupefied.'

'Do you mean that she doesn't know what to do with the money?'

'That, I think, she has hardly considered. She doesn't know what to think about the matter at all. It has been as if a big gun were suddenly fired off behind her; she's feeling herself to see if she be hurt. It's but three days since she received a visit from the principal executor, who came in person, very gallantly, to notify her. He told me afterwards that when he had made his little speech she suddenly burst into tears. The money's to remain in the affairs of the bank, and she's to draw the interest.'

Madame Merle shook her head with a wise and now quite benignant smile. 'How very delicious! After she has done that two or three times she'll get used to it.' Then after a silence, 'What does your son think of it?' she abruptly asked.

'He left England before the will was read – used up by his fatigue and anxiety and hurrying off to the south. He's on his way to the Riviera and I've not yet heard from him. But it's not likely he'll ever object to anything done by his father.'

'Didn't you say his own share had been cut down?'

'Only at his wish. I know that he urged his father to do something for the people of America. He's not in the least addicted to looking after number one.'

'It depends upon whom he regards as number one!' said Madame Merle. And she remained thoughtful a moment, her eyes bent on the floor. 'Am I not to see your happy niece?' she asked at last as she raised them.

'You may see her; but you'll not be struck with her being happy. She has looked as solemn, these three days, as a Cimabue Madonna!' And Mrs Touchett rang for a servant.

Isabel came in shortly after the footman had been sent to call her; and Madame Merle thought, as she appeared, that Mrs Touchett's comparison had its force. The girl was pale and grave – an effect not mitigated by her deeper mourning; but the smile of her brightest moments came into her face as she saw Madame Merle, who went forward, laid her hand on our heroine's shoulder and, after looking at her a moment, kissed her as if she were returning the kiss she had received from her at Gardencourt. This was the only allusion the visitor, in her great good taste, made for the present to her young friend's inheritance.

Mrs Touchett had no purpose of awaiting in London the sale of her house. After selecting from among its furniture the objects she wished to transport to her other abode, she left the rest of its contents to be disposed of by the auctioneer and took her departure for the Continent. She was of course accompanied on this journey by her niece, who now had plenty of leisure to measure and weigh and otherwise handle the windfall on which Madame Merle had covertly congratulated her. Isabel thought very often of the fact of her accession of means, looking at it in a dozen different lights; but we shall not now attempt to follow her train of thought or to explain exactly why her new consciousness was at first oppressive. This failure to rise to immediate joy was indeed but brief; the girl presently made up her mind that to be rich was a virtue because it was to be able to *do*, and that to do could only be sweet. It was the graceful contrary of the stupid side of weakness – especially the feminine variety. To be weak was, for a delicate young person, rather graceful, but, after all, as Isabel said to herself, there was a larger grace than that. Just now, it is true, there was not much to do – once she had sent off a cheque to Lily and another to poor Edith; but she was thankful for the quiet months which her mourning robes and her aunt's fresh widowhood compelled them to spend together. The acquisition of power made her serious; she scrutinized her power with a kind of tender ferocity, but was not eager to exercise it. She began to do so during a stay of some weeks which she eventually made with her aunt in Paris, though in ways that will inevitably present themselves as trivial. They were the ways most naturally imposed in a city in which the shops are the admiration of the world, and that were prescribed unreservedly by the guidance of Mrs Touchett, who took a rigidly practical view of the transformation of her niece from a poor girl to a rich one. 'Now that you're a young woman of fortune you must know how to play the part – I mean to play it well,' she said to Isabel once for all; and she added that the girl's first duty was to have everything handsome. 'You don't know how to take care of your things, but you must learn,' she went on; this was Isabel's second duty. Isabel submitted, but for the present her imagination was not kindled; she longed for opportunities, but these were not the opportunities she meant.

Mrs Touchett rarely changed her plans, and, having intended before her husband's death to spend a part of the winter in Paris, saw no reason to deprive herself – still less to deprive her companion – of this advantage. Though they would live in great retirement she might still present her niece, informally, to the little circle of her fellow countrymen dwelling upon the skirts of the Champs-Élysées. With many of these amiable colonists Mrs Touchett was intimate; she shared their expatriation, their convictions, their pastimes, their ennui. Isabel saw them arrive with a good deal of assiduity at her aunt's hotel, and pronounced on them with a trenchancy doubtless to be accounted for by the temporary exaltation of her sense of human duty. She made up her mind that their lives were, though luxurious, inane, and incurred some disfavour by expressing this view on bright Sunday afternoons, when the American absentees were engaged in calling on each other. Though her listeners passed for people kept exemplarily genial by their cooks and dressmakers, two or three of them thought her cleverness, which was generally admitted, inferior to that of the new theatrical pieces. 'You all live here this way, but what does it lead to?' she was pleased to ask. 'It doesn't seem to lead to anything, and I should think you'd get very tired of it.'

Mrs Touchett thought the question worthy of Henrietta Stackpole. The two ladies had found Henrietta in Paris, and Isabel constantly saw her; so that Mrs Touchett had some reason for saying to herself that if her niece were not clever enough to originate almost anything, she might be suspected of having borrowed that style of remark from her journalistic friend. The first occasion on which Isabel had spoken was that of a visit paid by the two ladies to Mrs Luce, an old friend of Mrs Touchett's and the only person in Paris she now went to see. Mrs Luce had been living in Paris since the days of Louis Philippe; she used to say jocosely that she was one of the generation of 1830 – a joke of which the point was not always taken. When it failed Mrs Luce used to explain – 'Oh yes, I'm one of the romantics'; her French had never become quite perfect. She was always at home on Sunday afternoons and surrounded by sympathetic compatriots, usually the same. In fact she was at home at all times, and reproduced with wondrous truth in her well-cushioned little corner of the brilliant city, the domestic tone of her native Baltimore. This reduced Mr Luce, her worthy husband, a tall, lean, grizzled, well-brushed gentleman who wore a gold eye-glass and carried his hat a little too much on the back of his head, to mere platonic praise of the 'distractions' of Paris – they were his great word – since you would never have guessed from what cares he escaped to them. One of them was that he went every day to the American banker's, where he found a post office that was almost as sociable and colloquial an institution as in an American country town. He passed an hour (in fine weather) in a chair in the Champs-Élysées, and he dined uncommonly well at his own table, seated above a waxed floor which it was Mrs Luce's happiness to believe had a finer polish than any other in the French capital. Occasionally he dined with a friend or two at the Café Anglais, where his talent for ordering a dinner was a source of felicity to his companions and an object of admiration even to the head-waiter of the establishment. These were his only known pastimes, but they had beguiled his hours for upwards of half a century, and they doubtless justified his frequent declaration that there was no place like Paris. In no other place, on these terms, could Mr Luce flatter himself that he was enjoying life. There was nothing like Paris, but it must be confessed that Mr Luce thought less highly of this scene of his dissipations than in earlier days. In the list of his resources his political reflections should not be omitted, for they were doubtless the animating principle of many hours that superficially seemed vacant. Like many of his fellow colonists Mr Luce was a high – or rather a deep – conservative, and gave no countenance to the government lately established in France. He had no faith in its duration and would assure you from year to year that its end was close at hand. 'They want to be kept down, sir, to be kept down; nothing but the strong hand – the iron heel – will do for them,' he would frequently say of the French people; and his ideal of a fine showy clever rule was that of the superseded Empire. 'Paris is much less attractive than in the days of the Emperor; *he* knew how to make a city pleasant,' Mr Luce had often remarked to Mrs Touchett, who was quite of his own way of thinking and wished to know what one had crossed that odious Atlantic for but to get away from republics.

'Why, madam, sitting in the Champs-Élysées, opposite to the Palace of Industry, I've seen the court-carriages from the Tuileries pass up and down as many as seven times a day. I remember one occasion when they went as high as nine. What do you see now? It's no use talking, the style's all gone. Napoleon knew what the French people want, and there'll be a dark cloud over Paris, *our* Paris, till they get the Empire back again.'

Among Mrs Luce's visitors on Sunday afternoons was a young man with whom Isabel had had a good deal of conversation and whom she found full of valuable knowledge. Mr Edward Rosier – Ned Rosier as he was called – was native to New York and had been brought up in Paris, living there under the eye of his father who, as it happened, had been an early and intimate friend of the late Mr Archer. Edward Rosier remembered Isabel as a little girl; it had been his father who came to the rescue of the small Archers at the inn at Neufchâtel (he was travelling that way with the boy and had stopped at the hotel by chance), after their *bonne* had gone off with the Russian prince and when Mr Archer's whereabouts remained for some days a mystery. Isabel remembered perfectly the neat little male child whose hair smelt of a delicious cosmetic and who had a *bonne* all his own, warranted to lose sight of him under no provocation. Isabel took a walk with the pair beside the lake and thought little Edward as pretty as an angel – a comparison by no means conventional in her mind, for she had a very definite conception of a type of features which she supposed to be angelic and which her new friend perfectly illustrated. A small pink face surmounted by a blue velvet bonnet and set off by a stiff embroidered collar had become the countenance of her childish dreams; and she had firmly believed for some time afterwards that the heavenly hosts conversed among themselves in a queer little dialect of French-English, expressing the properest sentiments, as when Edward told her that he was 'defended' by his *bonne* to go near the edge of the lake, and that one must always obey to one's *bonne*. Ned Rosier's English had improved; at least it exhibited in a less degree the French variation. His father was dead and his *bonne* dismissed, but the young man still conformed to the spirit of their teaching – he never went to the edge of the lake. There was still something agreeable to the nostrils about him and something not offensive to nobler organs. He was a very gentle and gracious youth, with what are called cultivated tastes – an acquaintance with old china, with good wine, with the bindings of books, with the *Almanach de Gotha*, with the best shops, the best hotels, the hours of railway trains. He could order a dinner almost as well as Mr Luce, and it was probable that as his experience accumulated he would be a worthy successor to that gentleman, whose rather grim politics he also advocated in a soft and innocent voice. He had some charming rooms in Paris, decorated with old Spanish altar-lace, the envy of his female friends, who declared that his chimney-piece was better draped than the high shoulders of many a duchess. He usually, however, spent a part of every winter at Pau, and had once passed a couple of months in the United States.

He took a great interest in Isabel and remembered perfectly the walk at Neufchâtel, when she would persist in going so near the edge. He seemed to recognize this same tendency in the subversive inquiry that I quoted a moment ago, and set himself to answer our heroine's question with greater urbanity than it perhaps deserved. 'What does it lead to, Miss Archer? Why Paris leads everywhere. You can't go anywhere unless you come here first. Everyone that comes to Europe has got to pass through. You don't mean it in that sense so much! You mean what good it does you? Well, how can you penetrate futurity? How can you tell what lies ahead? If it's a pleasant road I don't care where it leads. I like the road, Miss Archer; I like the dear old asphalt. You can't get tired of it – you can't if you try. You think you would, but you wouldn't; there's always something new and fresh. Take the Hôtel Drouot, now; they sometimes have three and four sales a week. Where can you get such things as you can here? In spite of all they say I maintain they're cheaper too, if you know the right places. I know plenty of places, but I keep them to myself. I'll tell you, if you like, as a particular favour; only you mustn't tell anyone else. Don't you go anywhere without asking me first; I want you to promise me that. As a general thing avoid the Boulevards; there's very little to be done on the Boulevards. Speaking conscientiously – *sans blague* – I don't believe anyone knows Paris better than I. You and Mrs Touchett must come and breakfast with me some day, and I'll show you my things; *je ne vous dis que ça!* There has been a great deal of talk about London of late; it's the fashion to cry up London. But there's nothing in it – you can't do anything in London. No Louis-Quinze – nothing of the First Empire; nothing but their eternal Queen Anne. It's good for one's bedroom, Queen Anne – for one's washing-room; but it isn't proper for a *salon*. Do I spend my life at the auctioneer's?' Mr Rosier pursued in answer to another question of Isabel's. 'Oh no; I haven't the means. I wish I had. You think I'm a mere trifler; I can tell by the expression of your face – you've got a wonderfully expressive face. I hope you don't mind my saying that; I mean it as a kind of warning. You think I ought to do something, and so do I, so long as you leave it vague. But when you come to the point you see you have to stop. I can't go home and be a shopkeeper. You think I'm very well fitted? Ah, Miss Archer, you overrate me. I can buy very well, but I can't sell; you should see when I sometimes try to get rid of my things. It takes much more ability to make other people buy than to buy yourself. When I think how clever they must be, the people who make *me* buy! Ah no; I couldn't be a shopkeeper; I can't be a doctor; it's a repulsive business. I can't be a clergyman; I haven't got convictions. And then I can't pronounce the names right in the Bible. They're very difficult, in the Old Testament particularly. I can't be a lawyer; I don't understand – how do you call it? – the American *procēdure*. Is there anything else? There's nothing for a gentleman in America. I should like to be a diplomatist; but American diplomacy – that's not for gentlemen either. I'm sure if you had seen the last min—'

Henrietta Stackpole, who was often with her friend when Mr Rosier, coming to pay his compliments late in the afternoon, expressed himself after the fashion I have sketched, usually interrupted the young man at this point and read him a lecture on the duties of the American citizen. She thought him most unnatural; he was worse than poor Ralph Touchett. Henrietta, however, was at this time more than ever addicted to fine criticism, for her conscience had been freshly alarmed as regards Isabel. She had not congratulated this young lady on her augmentations and begged to be excused from doing so.

'If Mr Touchett had consulted me about leaving you the money,' she frankly asserted, 'I'd have said to him "Never!" '

'I see,' Isabel had answered. 'You think it will prove a curse in disguise. Perhaps it will.'

'Leave it to someone you care less for – that's what I should have said.'

'To yourself for instance?' Isabel suggested jocosely. And then, 'Do you really believe it will ruin me?' she asked in quite another tone.

'I hope it won't ruin you; but it will certainly confirm your dangerous tendencies.'

'Do you mean the love of luxury – of extravagance?'

'No, no,' said Henrietta; 'I mean your exposure on the moral side. I approve of luxury; I think we ought to be as elegant as possible. Look at the luxury of our western cities; I've seen nothing over here to compare with it. I hope you'll never become grossly sensual; but I'm not afraid of that. The peril for you is that you live too much in the world of your own dreams. You're not enough in contact with reality – with the toiling, striving, suffering, I may even say sinning, world that surrounds you. You're too fastidious; you've too many graceful illusions. Your newly acquired thousands will shut you up more and more to the society of a few selfish and heartless people who will be interested in keeping them up.'

Isabel's eyes expanded as she gazed at this lurid scene. 'What are my illusions?' she asked. 'I try so hard not to have any.'

'Well,' said Henrietta, 'you think you can lead a romantic life, that you can live by pleasing yourself and pleasing others. You'll find you're mistaken. Whatever life you lead you must put your soul in it – to make any sort of success of it; and from the moment you do that it ceases to be romance, I assure you; it becomes grim reality! And you can't always please yourself; you must sometimes please other people. That, I admit, you're very ready to do; but there's another thing that's still more important – you must often *dis*please others. You must always be ready for that – you must never shrink from it. That doesn't suit you at all – you're too fond of admiration, you like to be thought well of. You think we can escape disagreeable duties by taking romantic views – that's your great illusion, my dear. But we can't. You must be prepared on many occasions in life to please no one at all – not even yourself.'

Isabel shook her head sadly; she looked troubled and frightened. 'This, for you, Henrietta,' she said, 'must be one of those occasions!'

It was certainly true that Miss Stackpole, during her visit to Paris, which had been professionally more remunerative than her English sojourn, had not been living in the world of dreams. Mr Bantling, who had now returned to England, was her companion for the first four weeks of her stay; and about Mr Bantling there was nothing dreamy. Isabel learned from her friend that the two had led a life of great personal intimacy and that this had been a peculiar advantage to Henrietta, owing to the gentleman's remarkable knowledge of Paris. He had explained everything, shown her everything, been her constant guide and interpreter. They had breakfasted together, dined together, gone to the theatre together, supped together, really in a manner quite lived together. He was a true friend, Henrietta more than once assured our heroine; and she had never supposed that she could like any Englishman so well. Isabel could not have told you why, but she found something that ministered to mirth in the alliance the correspondent of the *Interviewer* had struck with Lady Pensil's brother; her amusement moreover subsisted in face of the fact that she thought it a credit to each of them. Isabel couldn't rid herself of a suspicion that they were playing somehow at cross-purposes – that the simplicity of each had been entrapped. But this simplicity was on either side none the less honourable. It was as graceful on Henrietta's part to believe that Mr Bantling took an interest in the diffusion of lively journalism and in consolidating the position of lady correspondents as it was on the part of his companion to suppose that the cause of the *Interviewer* – a periodical of which we never formed a very definite conception – was, if subtly analysed (a task to which Mr Bantling felt himself quite equal), but the cause of Miss Stackpole's need of demonstrative affection. Each of these groping celibates supplied at any rate a want of which the other was impatiently conscious. Mr Bantling, who was of rather a slow and a discursive habit, relished a prompt, keen, positive woman, who charmed him by the influence of a shining, challenging eye and a kind of bandbox freshness, and who kindled a perception of raciness in a mind to which the usual fare of life seemed unsalted. Henrietta, on the other hand, enjoyed the society of a gentleman who appeared somehow, in his way, made, by expensive, roundabout, almost 'quaint' processes, for her use, and whose leisured state, though generally indefensible, was a decided boon to a breathless mate, and who was furnished with an easy, traditional, though by no means exhaustive, answer to almost any social or practical question that could come up. She often found Mr Bantling's answers very convenient, and in the press of catching the American post would largely and showily address them to publicity. It was to be feared that she was indeed drifting towards those abysses of sophistication as to which Isabel, wishing for a good-humoured retort, had warned her. There might be danger in store for Isabel; but it was scarcely to be hoped that Miss Stackpole, on her side, would find permanent rest in any adoption of the views of a class pledged to all the old abuses. Isabel continued to warn her good-humouredly; Lady Pensil's obliging brother was sometimes, on our heroine's lips, an object of irreverent and facetious allusion. Nothing, however, could exceed Henrietta's amiability on this point; she used to abound in the sense of Isabel's irony and to enumerate with elation the hours she had spent with this perfect man of the world – a term that had ceased to make with her, as previously, for opprobrium. Then, a few moments later, she would forget that they had been talking jocosely and would mention with impulsive earnestness some expedition she had enjoyed in his company. She would say: 'Oh, I know all about Versailles; I went there with Mr Bantling. I was bound to see it thoroughly – I warned him when we went out there that I was thorough: so we spent three days at the hotel and wandered all over the place. It was lovely weather – a kind of Indian summer, only not so good. We just lived in that park. Oh yes; you can't tell me anything about Versailles.' Henrietta appeared to have made arrangements to meet her gallant friend during the spring in Italy.

Chapter Twenty-one

Mrs Touchett, before arriving in Paris, had fixed the day for her departure and by the middle of February had begun to travel southward. She interrupted her journey to pay a visit to her son, who at San Remo, on the Italian shore of the Mediterranean, had been spending a dull, bright winter beneath a slow-moving white umbrella. Isabel went with her aunt as a matter of course, though Mrs Touchett, with homely, customary logic, had laid before her a pair of alternatives.

'Now, of course, you're completely your own mistress and are as free as the bird on the bough. I don't mean you were not so before, but you're at present on a different footing – property erects a kind of barrier. You can do a great many things if you're rich which would be severely criticized if you were poor. You can go and come, you can travel alone, you can have your own establishment: I mean of course if you'll take a companion – some decayed gentlewoman, with a darned cashmere and dyed hair, who paints on velvet. You don't think you'd like that? Of course you can do as you please; I only want you to understand how much you're at liberty. You might take Miss Stackpole as your *dame de compagnie*; she'd keep people off very well. I think, however, that it's a great deal better you should remain with me, in spite of there being no obligation. It's better for several reasons, quite apart from your liking it. I shouldn't think you'd like it, but I recommend you to make the sacrifice. Of course whatever novelty there may have been at first in my society has quite passed away, and you see me as I am – a dull, obstinate, narrow-minded old woman.'

'I don't think you're at all dull,' Isabel had replied to this.

'But you do think I'm obstinate and narrow-minded? I told you so!' said Mrs Touchett with much elation at being justified.

Isabel remained for the present with her aunt, because, in spite of eccentric impulses, she had a great regard for what was usually deemed decent, and a young gentlewoman without visible relations had always struck her as a flower without foliage. It was true that Mrs Touchett's conversation had never again appeared so brilliant as that first afternoon in Albany, when she sat in her damp waterproof and sketched the opportunities that Europe would offer to a young person of taste. This, however, was in a great measure the girl's own fault; she had got a glimpse of her aunt's experience, and her imagination constantly anticipated the judgements and emotions of a woman who had very little of the same faculty. Apart from this, Mrs Touchett had a great merit; she was as honest as a pair of compasses. There was a comfort in her stiffness and firmness; you knew exactly where to find her and were never liable to chance encounters and concussions. On her own ground she was perfectly present, but was never overinquisitive as regards the territory of her neighbour. Isabel came at last to have a kind of undemonstrable pity for her; there seemed something so dreary in the condition of a person whose nature had, as it were, so little surface – offered so limited a face to the accretions of human contact. Nothing tender, nothing sympathetic, had ever had a chance to fasten upon it – no wind-sown blossom, no familiar softening moss. Her offered, her passive extent, in other words, was about that of a knife-edge. Isabel had reason to believe none the less that as she advanced in life she made more of those concessions to the sense of something obscurely distinct from convenience – more of them than she independently exacted. She was learning to sacrifice consistency to considerations of that inferior order for which the excuse must be found in the particular case. It was not to the credit of her absolute rectitude that she should have gone the longest way round to Florence in order to spend a few weeks with her invalid son; since in former years it had been one of her most definite convictions that when Ralph wished to see her he was at liberty to remember that Palazzo Crescentini contained a large apartment known as the quarter of the signorino.

'I want to ask you something,' Isabel said to this young man the day after her arrival at San Remo – 'something I've thought more than once of asking you by letter, but that I've hesitated on the whole to write about. Face to face, nevertheless, my question seems easy enough. Did you know your father intended to leave me so much money?'

Ralph stretched his legs a little farther than usual and gazed a little more fixedly at the Mediterranean. 'What does it matter, my dear Isabel, whether I knew? My father was very obstinate.'

'So,' said the girl, 'you did know.'

'Yes; he told me. We even talked it over a little.'

'What did he do it for?' asked Isabel abruptly.

'Why, as a kind of compliment.'

'A compliment on what?'

'On your so beautifully existing.'

'He liked me too much,' she presently declared.

'That's a way we all have.'

'If I believed that I should be very unhappy. Fortunately I don't believe it. I want to be treated with justice; I want nothing but that.'

'Very good. But you must remember that justice to a lovely being is after all a florid sort of sentiment.'

'I'm not a lovely being. How can you say that, at the very moment when I'm asking such odious questions? I must seem to you delicate!'

'You seem to me troubled,' said Ralph.

'I am troubled.'

'About what?'

For a moment she answered nothing; then she broke out: 'Do you think it good for me suddenly to be made so rich? Henrietta doesn't.'

'Oh, hang Henrietta!' said Ralph coarsely. 'If you ask *me* I'm delighted at it.'

'Is that why your father did it – for your amusement?'

'I differ with Miss Stackpole,' Ralph went on more gravely. 'I think it very good for you to have means.'

Isabel looked at him with serious eyes. 'I wonder whether you know what's good for me – or whether you care.'

'If I know depend upon it I care. Shall I tell you what it is? Not to torment yourself.'

'Not to torment you, I suppose you mean.'

'You can't do that; I'm proof. Take things more easily. Don't ask yourself so much whether this or that is good for you. Don't question your conscience so much – it will get out of tune like a strummed piano. Keep it for great occasions. Don't try so much to form your character – it's like trying to pull open a tight, tender young rose. Live as you like best, and your character will take care of itself. Most things are good for you; the exceptions are very rare, and a comfortable income's not one of them.' Ralph paused, smiling; Isabel had listened quickly. 'You've too much power of thought – above all too much conscience,' Ralph added. 'It's out of all reason, the number of things you think wrong. Put back your watch. Diet your fever. Spread your wings; rise above the ground. It's never wrong to do that.'

She had listened eagerly, as I say; and it was her nature to understand quickly. 'I wonder if you appreciate what you say. If you do, you take a great responsibility.'

'You frighten me a little, but I think I'm right,' said Ralph, persisting in cheer.

'All the same what you say is very true,' Isabel pursued. 'You could say nothing more true. I'm absorbed in myself – I look at life too much as a doctor's prescription. Why indeed should we perpetually be thinking whether things are good for us, as if we were patients lying in a hospital? Why should I be so afraid of not doing right? As if it mattered to the world whether I do right or wrong!'

'You're a capital person to advise,' said Ralph; 'you take the wind out of *my* sails!'

She looked at him as if she had not heard him – though she was following out the train of reflection which he himself had kindled. 'I try to care more about the world than about myself – but I always come back to myself. It's because I'm afraid.' She stopped; her voice had trembled a little. 'Yes, I'm afraid; I can't tell you. A large fortune means freedom, and I'm afraid of that. It's such a fine thing, and one should make such a good use of it. If one shouldn't one would be ashamed. And one must keep thinking; it's a constant effort. I'm not sure it's not a greater happiness to be powerless.'

'For weak people I've no doubt it's a greater happiness. For weak people the effort not to be contemptible must be great.'

'And how do you know I'm not weak?' Isabel asked.

'Ah,' Ralph answered with a flush that the girl noticed, 'if you are I'm awfully sold!'

The charm of the Mediterranean coast only deepened for our heroine on acquaintance, for it was the threshold of Italy, the gate of admirations. Italy, as yet imperfectly seen and felt, stretched before her as a land of promise, a land in which a love of the beautiful might be comforted by endless knowledge. Whenever she strolled upon the shore with her cousin – and she was the companion of his daily walk – she looked across the sea, with longing eyes, to where she knew that Genoa lay. She was glad to pause, however, on the edge of this larger adventure; there was such a thrill even in the preliminary hovering. It affected her moreover as a peaceful interlude, as a hush of the drum and fife in a career which she had little warrant as yet for regarding as agitated, but which nevertheless she was constantly picturing to herself by the light of her hopes, her fears, her fancies, her ambitions, her predilections, and which reflected these subjective accidents in a manner sufficiently dramatic. Madame Merle had predicted to Mrs Touchett that after their young friend had put her hand into her pocket half a dozen times she would be reconciled to the idea that it had been filled by a munificent uncle; and the event justified, as it had so often justified before, that lady's perspicacity. Ralph Touchett had praised his cousin for being morally inflammable, that is for being quick to take a hint that was meant as good advice. His advice had perhaps helped the matter; she had at any rate before leaving San Remo grown used to feeling rich. The consciousness in question found a proper place in rather a dense little group of ideas that she had about herself, and often it was by no means the least agreeable. It took perpetually for granted a thousand good intentions. She lost herself in a maze of visions; the fine things to be done by a rich, independent, generous girl who took a large human view of occasions and obligations were sublime in the mass. Her fortune therefore became to her mind a part of her better self; it gave her importance, gave her even, to her own imagination, a certain ideal beauty. What it did for her in the imagination of others is another affair, and on this point we must also touch in time. The visions I have just spoken of were mixed with other debates. Isabel liked better to think of the future than of the past; but at times, as she listened to the murmur of the Mediterranean waves, her glance took a backward flight. It rested upon two figures which, in spite of increasing distance, were still sufficiently salient; they were recognizable without difficulty as those of Caspar Goodwood and Lord Warburton. It was strange how quickly these images of energy had fallen into the background of our young lady's life. It was in her disposition at all times to lose faith in the reality of absent things; she could summon back her faith, in case of need, with an effort, but the effort was often painful even when the reality had been pleasant. The past was apt to look dead and its revival rather to show the livid light of a judgement-day. The girl moreover was not prone to take for granted that she herself lived in the mind of others – she had not the fatuity to believe she left indelible traces. She was capable of being wounded by the discovery that she had been forgotten; but of all liberties the one she herself found sweetest was the liberty to forget. She had not given her last shilling, sentimentally speaking, either to Caspar Goodwood or to Lord Warburton, and yet couldn't but feel them appreciably in debt to her. She had of course reminded herself that she was to hear from Mr Goodwood again; but this was not to be for another year and a half, and in that time a great many things might happen. She had indeed failed to say to herself that her American suitor might find some other girl more comfortable to woo; because, though it was certain many other girls would prove so, she had not the smallest belief that this merit would attract him. But she reflected that she herself might know the humiliation of change, might really, for that matter, come to the end of the things that were not Caspar (even though there appeared so many of them), and find rest in those very elements of his presence which struck her now as impediments to the finer respiration. It was conceivable that these impediments should some day prove a sort of blessing in disguise – a clear and quiet harbour enclosed by a brave granite breakwater. But that day could only come in its order, and she couldn't wait for it with folded hands. That Lord Warburton should continue to cherish her image seemed to her more than a noble humility or an enlightened pride ought to wish to reckon with. She had so definitely undertaken to preserve no record of what had passed between them that a corresponding effort on his own part would be eminently just. This was not, as it may seem, merely a theory tinged with sarcasm. Isabel candidly believed that his lordship would, in the usual phrase, get over his disappointment. He had been deeply affected – this she believed, and she was still capable of deriving pleasure from the belief; but it was absurd that a man both so intelligent and so honourably dealt with should cultivate a scar out of proportion to any wound. Englishmen liked moreover to be comfortable, said Isabel, and there could be little comfort for Lord Warburton, in the long run, in brooding over a self-sufficient American girl who had been but a casual acquaintance. She flattered herself that, should she hear from one day to another that he had married some young woman of his own country who had done more to deserve him, she should receive the news without a pang even of surprise. It would have proved that he believed she was firm – which was what she wished to seem to him. That alone was grateful to her pride.

Chapter Twenty-two

On one of the first days of May, some six months after old Mr Touchett's death, a small group that might have been described by a painter as composing well was gathered in one of the many rooms of an ancient villa crowning an olive-muffled hill outside of the Roman gate of Florence. The villa was a long, rather blank-looking structure, with the far-projecting roof which Tuscany loves and which, on the hills that encircle Florence, when considered from a distance, makes so harmonious a rectangle with the straight, dark, definite cypresses that usually rise in groups of three or four beside it. The house had a front upon a little grassy, empty, rural piazza which occupied a part of the hill-top; and this front, pierced with a few windows in irregular relations and furnished with a stone bench lengthily adjusted to the base of the structure and useful as a lounging-place to one or two persons wearing more or less of that air of undervalued merit which in Italy, for some reason or other, always gracefully invests anyone who confidently assumes a perfectly passive attitude – this antique, solid, weather-worn, yet imposing front had a somewhat incommunicative character. It was the mask, not the face of the house. It had heavy lids, but no eyes; the house in reality looked another way – looked off behind, into splendid openness and the range of the afternoon light. In that quarter the villa overhung the slope of its hill and the long valley of the Arno, hazy with Italian colour. It had a narrow garden, in the manner of a terrace, productive chiefly of tangles of wild roses and other old stone benches, mossy and sun-warmed. The parapet of the terrace was just the height to lean upon, and beneath it the ground declined into the vagueness of olive-crops and vineyards. It is not, however, with the outside of the place that we are concerned; on this bright morning of ripened spring its tenants had reason to prefer the shady side of the wall. The windows of the ground floor, as you saw them from the piazza, were, in their noble proportions, extremely architectural; but their function seemed less to offer communication with the world than to defy the world to look in. They were massively crossbarred, and placed at such a height that curiosity, even on tiptoe, expired before it reached them. In an apartment lighted by a row of three of these jealous apertures – one of the several distinct apartments into which the villa was divided and which were mainly occupied by foreigners of random race long resident in Florence – a gentleman was seated in company with a young girl and two good sisters from a religious house. The room was, however, less sombre than our indications may have represented, for it had a wide, high door, which now stood open into the tangled garden behind; and the tall lattices admitted on occasion more than enough of the Italian sunshine. It was moreover a seat of ease, indeed of luxury, telling of arrangements subtly studied and refinements frankly proclaimed, and containing a variety of those faded hangings of damask and tapestry, those chests and cabinets of carved and time-polished oak, those angular specimens of pictorial art in frames as pedantically primitive, those perverse-looking relics of medieval brass and pottery, of which Italy has long been the not-quite-exhausted storehouse. These things kept terms with articles of modern furniture in which large allowance had been made for a lounging generation; it was to be noticed that all the chairs were deep and well padded and that much space was occupied by a writing table of which the ingenious perfection bore the stamp of London and the nineteenth century. There were books in profusion and magazines and newspapers, and a few small, odd, elaborate pictures, chiefly in water-colour. One of these productions stood on a drawing-room easel before which at the moment we begin to be concerned with her, the young girl I have mentioned had placed herself. She was looking at the picture in silence.

Silence – absolute silence – had not fallen upon her companions; but their talk had an appearance of embarrassed continuity. The two good sisters had not settled themselves in their respective chairs; their attitude expressed a final reserve and their faces showed the glaze of prudence. They were plain, ample, mild-featured women, with a kind of business-like modesty to which the impersonal aspect of their stiffened linen and of the serge that draped them as if nailed on frames gave an advantage. One of them, a person of a certain age, in spectacles, with a fresh complexion and a full cheek, had a more discriminating manner than her colleague, as well as the responsibility of their errand, which apparently related to the young girl. This object of interest wore her hat – an ornament of extreme simplicity and not at variance with her plain muslin gown, too short for her years, though it must already have been 'let out'. The gentleman who might have been supposed to be entertaining the two nuns was perhaps conscious of the difficulties of his function, it being in its way as arduous to converse with the very meek as with the very mighty. At the same time he was clearly much occupied with their quiet charge, and while she turned her back to him his eyes rested gravely on her slim, small figure. He was a man of forty, with a high but well-shaped head, on which the hair, still dense, but prematurely grizzled, had been cropped close. He had a fine, narrow, extremely modelled and composed face, of which the only fault was just this effect of it running a trifle too much to points; an appearance to which the shape of the beard contributed not a little. This beard, cut in the manner of the portraits of the sixteenth century and surmounted by a fair moustache, of which the ends had a romantic upward flourish, gave its wearer a foreign, traditionary look and suggested that he was a gentleman who studied style. His conscious, curious eyes, however, eyes at once vague and penetrating, intelligent and hard, expressive of the observer as well as of the dreamer, would have assured you that he studied it only within well-chosen limits, and that in so far as he sought it he found it. You would have been much at a loss to determine his original clime and country; he had none of the superficial signs that usually render the answer to this question an insipidly easy one. If he had English blood in his veins it had probably received some French or Italian commixture; but he suggested, fine gold coin as he was, no stamp nor emblem of the common mintage that provides for general circulation; he was the elegant complicated medal struck off for a special occasion. He had a light, lean, rather languid-looking figure, and was apparently neither tall nor short. He was dressed as a man dresses who takes little other trouble about it than to have no vulgar things.

'Well, my dear, what do you think of it?' he asked of the young girl. He used the Italian tongue, and used it with perfect ease; but this would not have convinced you he was Italian.

The child turned her head earnestly to one side and the other. 'It's very pretty, papa. Did you make it yourself?'

'Certainly I made it. Don't you think I'm clever?'

'Yes, papa, very clever; I also have learned to make pictures.' And she turned round and showed a small, fair face painted with a fixed and intensely sweet smile.

'You should have brought me a specimen of your powers.'

'I've brought a great many; they're in my trunk.'

'She draws very – very carefully,' the elder of the nuns remarked, speaking in French.

'I'm glad to hear it. Is it you who have instructed her?'

'Happily no,' said the good sister, blushing a little. '*Ce n'est pas ma partie*. I teach nothing; I leave that to those who are wiser. We've an excellent drawing-master, Mr – Mr – what is his name?' she asked of her companion.

Her companion looked about at the carpet. 'It's a German name,' she said in Italian, as if it needed to be translated.

'Yes,' the other went on, 'he's a German and we've had him many years.'

The young girl, who was not heeding the conversation, had wandered away to the open door of the large room and stood looking into the garden.

'And you, my sister, are French,' said the gentleman.

'Yes, sir,' the visitor gently replied. 'I speak to the pupils in my own tongue. I know no other. But we have sisters of other countries – English, German, Irish. They all speak their proper language.'

The gentleman gave a smile. 'Has my daughter been under the care of one of the Irish ladies?' And then, as he saw that his visitors suspected a joke, though failing to understand it, 'You're very complete,' he instantly added.

'Oh, yes, we're complete. We've everything, and everything's of the best.'

'We have gymnastics,' the Italian sister ventured to remark. 'But not dangerous.'

'I hope not. Is that *your* branch?' A question which provoked much candid hilarity on the part of the two ladies; on the subsidence of which their entertainer, glancing at his daughter, remarked that she had grown.

'Yes, but I think she has finished. She'll remain – not big,' said the French sister.

'I'm not sorry. I prefer women like books – very good and not too long. But I know,' the gentleman said, 'no particular reason why my child should be short.'

The nun gave a temperate shrug, as if to intimate that such things might be beyond our knowledge. 'She's in very good health; that's the best thing.'

'Yes, she looks sound.' And the young girl's father watched her a moment. 'What do you see in the garden?' he asked in French.

'I see many flowers,' she replied in a sweet, small voice and with an accent as good as his own.

'Yes, but not many good ones. However, such as they are, go out and gather some for *ces dames*.'

The child turned to him with her smile heightened by pleasure. 'May I, truly?'

'Ah, when I tell you,' said her father.

The girl glanced at the elder of the nuns. 'May I, truly, *ma mère*?'

'Obey monsieur your father, my child,' said the sister blushing again.

The child, satisfied with this authorization, descended from the threshold and was presently lost to sight. 'You don't spoil them,' said her father gaily.

'For everything they must ask leave. That's our system. Leave is freely granted, but they must ask it.'

'Oh, I don't quarrel with your system; I've no doubt it's excellent. I sent you my daughter to see what you'd make of her. I had faith.'

'One must have faith,' the sister blandly rejoined, gazing through her spectacles.

'Well, has my faith been rewarded? What have you made of her?'

The sister dropped her eyes a moment. 'A good Christian, monsieur.'

Her host dropped his eyes as well; but it was probable that the movement had in each case a different spring. 'Yes, and what else?'

He watched the lady from the convent, probably thinking she would say that a good Christian was everything; but for all her simplicity she was not so crude as that. 'A charming young lady – a real little woman – a daughter in whom you will have nothing but contentment.'

'She seems to me very *gentille*,' said the father. 'She's really pretty.'

'She's perfect. She has no faults.'

'She never had any as a child, and I'm glad you have given her none.'

'We love her too much,' said the spectacled sister with dignity. 'And as for faults, how can we give what we have not? *Le couvent n'est pas comme le monde, monsieur*. She's our daughter, as you may say. We've had her since she was so small.'

'Of all those we shall lose this year she's the one we shall miss most,' the younger woman murmured deferentially.

'Ah, yes, we shall talk long of her,' said the other. 'We shall hold her up to the new ones.' And at this the good sister appeared to find her spectacles dim; while her companion, after fumbling a moment, presently drew forth a pocket-handkerchief of durable texture.

'It's not certain you'll lose her; nothing's settled yet,' their host rejoined quickly; not as if to anticipate their tears, but in the tone of a man saying what was most agreeable to himself.

'We should be very happy to believe that. Fifteen is very young to leave us.'

'Oh,' exclaimed the gentleman with more vivacity than he had yet used, 'it is not I who wish to take her away. I wish you could keep her always!'

'Ah, monsieur,' said the elder sister, smiling and getting up, 'good as she is, she's made for the world. *Le monde y gagnera*.'

'If all the good people were hidden away in convents how would the world get on?' her companion softly inquired, rising also.

This was a question of a wider bearing that the good woman apparently supposed; and the lady in spectacles took a harmonizing view by saying comfortably: 'Fortunately there are good people everywhere.'

'If you're going there will be two less here,' her host remarked gallantly.

For this extravagant sally his simple visitors had no answer, and they simply looked at each other in decent depreciation; but their confusion was speedily covered by the return of the young girl with two large bunches of roses – one of them all white, the other red.

'I give you your choice, maman Catherine,' said the child. 'It's only the colour that's different, maman Justine; there are just as many roses in one bunch as in the other.'

The two sisters turned to each other, smiling and hesitating, with 'Which will you take?' and 'No, it's for you to choose.'

'I'll take the red, thank you,' said mother Catherine in the spectacles. 'I'm so red myself. They'll comfort us on our way back to Rome.'

'Ah, they won't last,' cried the young girl. 'I wish I could give you something that would last!'

'You've given us a good memory of yourself, my daughter. That will last!'

'I wish nuns could wear pretty things. I would give you my blue beads,' the child went on.

'And do you go back to Rome tonight?' her father inquired.

'Yes, we take the train again. We've so much to do *là-bas*.'

'Are you not tired?'

'We are never tired.'

'Ah, my sister, sometimes,' murmured the junior votaress.

'Not today, at any rate. We have rested too well here. *Que Dieu vous garde, ma fille*.'

Their host, while they exchanged kisses with his daughter, went forward to open the door through which they were to pass; but as he did so he gave a slight exclamation, and stood looking beyond. The door opened into a vaulted ante-chamber, as high as a chapel and paved with red tiles; and into this ante-chamber a lady had just been admitted by a servant, a lad in shabby livery, who was now ushering her towards the apartment in which our friends were grouped. The gentleman at the door, after dropping his exclamation, remained silent; in silence too the lady advanced. He gave her no further audible greeting and offered her no hand, but stood aside to let her pass into the saloon. At the threshold she hesitated. 'Is there anyone?' she asked.

'Someone you may see.'

She went in and found herself confronted with the two nuns and their pupil, who was coming forward, between them, with a hand in the arm of each. At the sight of the new visitor they all paused, and the lady, who had also stopped, stood looking at them. The young girl gave a little soft cry: 'Ah, Madame Merle!'

The visitor had been slightly startled, but her manner the next instant was none the less gracious. 'Yes, it's Madame Merle, come to welcome you home.' And she held out two hands to the girl, who immediately came up to her, presenting her forehead to be kissed. Madame Merle saluted this portion of her charming little person and then stood smiling at the two nuns. They acknowledged her smile with a decent obeisance, but permitted themselves no direct scrutiny of this imposing, brilliant woman, who seemed to bring in with her something of the radiance of the outer world.

'These ladies have brought my daughter home, and now they return to the convent,' the gentleman explained.

'Ah, you go back to Rome? I've lately come from there. It's very lovely now,' said Madame Merle.

The good sisters, standing with their hands folded into their sleeves, accepted this statement uncritically; and the master of the house asked his new visitor how long it was since she had left Rome. 'She came to see me at the convent,' said the younger girl before the lady addressed had time to reply.

'I've been more than once, Pansy,' Madame Merle declared. 'Am I not your great friend in Rome?'

'I remember the last time best,' said Pansy, 'because you told me I should come away.'

'Did you tell her that?' the child's father asked.

'I hardly remember. I told her what I thought would please her. I've been in Florence a week. I hoped you would come to see me.'

'I should have done so if I had known you were there. One doesn't know such things by inspiration – thought I suppose one ought. You had better sit down.'

These two speeches were made in a particular tone of voice – a tone half-lowered and carefully quiet, but as from habit rather than from any definite need. Madame Merle looked about her, choosing her seat. 'You're going to the door with these women? Let me of course not interrupt the ceremony. *Je vous salue, mesdames*,' she added, in French, to the nuns, as if to dismiss them.

'This lady's a great friend of ours; you will have seen her at the convent,' said their entertainer. 'We've much faith in her judgement, and she'll help me to decide whether my daughter shall return to you at the end of the holidays.'

'I hope you'll decide in our favour, madame,' the sister in spectacles ventured to remark.

'That's Mr Osmond's pleasantry; I decide nothing,' said Madame Merle, but also as in pleasantry. 'I believe you've a very good school, but Miss Osmond's friends must remember that she's very naturally meant for the world.'

'That's what I've told monsieur,' sister Catherine answered. 'It's precisely to fit her for the world,' she murmured, glancing at Pansy, who stood, at a little distance, attentive to Madame Merle's elegant apparel.

'Do you hear that, Pansy? You're very naturally meant for the world,' said Pansy's father.

The child fixed him an instant with her pure young eyes. 'Am I not meant for you, papa?'

Papa gave a quick, light laugh. 'That doesn't prevent it! I'm of the world, Pansy.'

'Kindly permit us to retire,' said sister Catherine. 'Be good and wise and happy in any case, my daughter.'

'I shall certainly come back and see you,' Pansy returned, recommencing her embraces, which were presently interrupted by Madame Merle.

'Stay with me, dear child,' she said, 'while your father takes the good ladies to the door.'

Pansy stared, disappointed, yet not protesting. She was evidently impregnated with the idea of submission, which was due to anyone who took the tone of authority; and she was a passive spectator of the operation of her fate. 'May I not see maman Catherine get into the carriage?' she nevertheless asked very gently.

'It would please me better if you'd remain with me,' said Madame Merle, while Mr Osmond and his companions, who had bowed low again to the other visitor, passed into the ante-chamber.

'Oh yes, I'll stay,' Pansy answered; and she stood near Madame Merle, surrendering her little hand, which this lady took. She stared out of the window; her eyes had filled with tears.

'I'm glad they've taught you to obey,' said Madame Merle. 'That's what good little girls should do.'

'Oh yes, I obey very well,' cried Pansy with soft eagerness, almost with boastfulness, as if she had been speaking of her piano-playing. And then she gave a faint, just audible sigh.

Madame Merle, holding her hand, drew it across her own fine palm and looked at it. The gaze was critical, but it found nothing to deprecate; the child's small hand was delicate and fair. 'I hope they always see that you wear gloves,' she said in a moment. 'Little girls usually dislike them.'

'I used to dislike them, but I like them now,' the child made answer.

'Very good, I'll make you a present of a dozen.'

'I thank you very much. What colours will they be?' Pansy demanded with interest.

Madame Merle meditated. 'Useful colours.'

'But very pretty?'

'Are you very fond of pretty things?'

'Yes; but – but not too fond,' said Pansy with a trace of asceticism.

'Well, they won't be too pretty,' Madame Merle returned with a laugh. She took the child's other hand and drew her nearer; after which, looking at her a moment. 'Shall you miss your mother Catherine?' she went on.

'Yes – when I think of her.'

'Try then not to think of her. Perhaps some day,' added Madame Merle, 'you'll have another mother.'

'I don't think that's necessary,' Pansy said, repeating her little soft conciliatory sigh. 'I had more than thirty mothers at the convent.'

Her father's step sounded again in the ante-chamber, and Madame Merle got up, releasing the child. Mr Osmond came in and closed the door; then, without looking at Madame Merle, he pushed one or two chairs back into their places. His visitor waited a moment for him to speak, watching him as he moved about. Then at last she said: 'I hoped you'd have come to Rome. I thought it possible you'd have wished yourself to fetch Pansy away.'

'That was a natural supposition; but I'm afraid it's not the first time I've acted in defiance of your calculations.'

'Yes,' said Madame Merle, 'I think you very perverse.'

Mr Osmond busied himself for a moment in the room – there was plenty of space in it to move about – in the fashion of a man mechanically seeking pretexts for not giving an attention which may be embarrassing. Presently, however, he had exhausted his pretexts; there was nothing left for him – unless he took up a book – but to stand with his hands behind him looking at Pansy. 'Why didn't you come and see the last of maman Catherine?' he asked of her abruptly in French.

Pansy hesitated a moment, glancing at Madame Merle. 'I asked her to stay with me,' said this lady, who had seated herself again in another place.

'Ah, that was better,' Osmond conceded. With which he dropped into a chair and sat looking at Madame Merle; bent forward a little, his elbows on the edge of the arms and his hands interlocked.

'She's going to give me some gloves,' said Pansy.

'You needn't tell that to everyone, my dear,' Madame Merle observed.

'You're very kind to her,' said Osmond. 'She's supposed to have everything she needs.'

'I should think she had had enough of the nuns.'

'If we're going to discuss that matter she had better go out of the room.'

'Let her stay,' said Madame Merle. 'We'll talk of something else.'

'If you like I won't listen,' Pansy suggested with an appearance of candour which imposed conviction.

'You may listen, charming child, because you won't understand,' her father replied. The child sat down, deferentially, near the open door, within sight of the garden, into which she directed her innocent, wistful eyes; and Mr Osmond went on irrelevently, addressing himself to his other companion. 'You're looking particularly well.'

'I think I always look the same,' said Madame Merle.

'You always *are* the same. You don't vary. You're a wonderful woman.'

'Yes, I think I am.'

'You sometimes change your mind, however. You told me on your return from England that you wouldn't leave Rome again for the present.'

'I'm pleased that you remember so well what I say. That was my intention. But I've come to Florence to meet some friends who have lately arrived and as to whose movements I was at that time uncertain.'

'That reason's characteristic. You're always doing something for your friends.'

Madame Merle smiled straight at her host. 'It's less characteristic than your comment upon it – which is perfectly insincere. I don't however, make a crime of that,' she added, 'because if you don't believe what you say there's no reason *why* you should. I don't ruin myself for my friends; I don't deserve your praise. I care greatly for myself.'

'Exactly; but yourself includes so many other selves – so much of everyone else and of everything. I never knew a person whose life touched so many other lives.'

'What do you call one's life?' asked Madame Merle. 'One's appearance, one's movements, one's engagements, one's society?'

'I call *your* life your ambitions,' said Osmond.

Madame Merle looked a moment at Pansy. 'I wonder if she understands that,' she murmured.

'You see she can't stay with us!' And Pansy's father gave rather a joyless smile. 'Go into the garden, *mignonne*, and pluck a flower or two for Madame Merle,' he went on in French.

'That's just what I wanted to do,' Pansy exclaimed, rising with promptness and noiselessly departing. Her father followed her to the open door, stood a moment watching her, and then came back, but remained standing, or rather strolling to and fro, as if to cultivate a sense of freedom which in another attitude might be wanting.

'My ambitions are principally for you,' said Madame Merle, looking up at him with a certain courage.

'That comes back to what I say. I'm part of your life – I and a thousand others. You're not selfish – I can't admit that. If you were selfish, what should I be? What epithet would properly describe me?'

'You're indolent. For me that's your worst fault.'

'I'm afraid it's really my best.'

'You don't care,' said Madame Merle gravely.

'No; I don't think I care much. What sort of a fault do you call that? My indolence, at any rate, was one of the reasons I didn't go to Rome. But it was only one of them.'

'It's not of importance – to me at least – that you didn't go; though I should have been glad to see you. I'm glad you're not in Rome now – which you might be, would probably be, if you had gone there a month ago. There's something I should like you to do at present in Florence.'

'Please remember my indolence,' said Osmond.

'I do remember it; but I beg you to forget it. In that way you'll have both the virtue and the reward. This is not a great labour, and it may prove a real interest. How long is it since you made a new acquaintance?'

'I don't think I've made any since I made yours.'

'It's time then you should make another. There's a friend of mine I want you to know.'

Mr Osmond, in his walk, had gone back to the open door again and was looking at his daughter as she moved about in the intense sunshine. 'What good will it do me?' he asked with a sort of genial crudity.'

Madame Merle waited. 'It will amuse you.' There was nothing crude in this rejoinder; it had been thoroughly well considered.

'If you say that, you know, I believe it,' said Osmond coming towards her. 'There are some points in which my confidence in you is complete. I'm perfectly aware, for instance, that you know good society from bad.'

'Society is all bad.'

'Pardon me. That isn't – the knowledge I impute to you – a common sort of wisdom. You've gained it in the right way – experimentally; you've compared an immense number of more or less impossible people with each other.'

'Well, I invite you to profit by my knowledge.'

'To profit? Are you very sure that I shall?'

'It's what I hope. It will depend on yourself. If I could only induce you to make an effort!'

'Ah, there you are! I knew something tiresome was coming. What in the world – that's likely to turn up here – is worth an effort?'

Madame Merle flushed as with a wounded intention. 'Don't be foolish, Osmond. No one knows better than you what *is* worth an effort. Haven't *I* seen you in old days?'

'I recognize some things. But they're none of them probable in this poor life.'

'It's the effort that makes them probable,' said Madame Merle.

'There's something in that. Who then is your friend?'

'The person I came to Florence to see. She's a niece of Mrs Touchett, whom you'll not have forgotten.'

'A niece? The word niece suggests youth and ignorance. I see what you're coming to.'

'Yes, she's young – twenty-three years old. She's a great friend of mine. I met her for the first time in England, several months ago, and we struck up a grand alliance. I like her immensely, and I do what I don't do every day – I admire her. You'll do the same.'

'Not if I can help it.'

'Precisely. But you won't be able to help it.'

'Is she beautiful, clever, rich, splendid, universally intelligent, and unprecedentedly virtuous? It's only on those conditions that I care to make her acquaintance. You know I asked you some time ago never to speak to me of a creature who shouldn't correspond to that description. I know plenty of dingy people; I don't want to know any more.'

'Miss Archer isn't dingy; she's as bright as the morning. She corresponds to your description; it's for that I wish you to know her. She fills all your requirements.'

'More or less of course.'

'No; quite literally. She's beautiful, accomplished, generous, and, for an American, well-born. She's also very clever and very amiable, and she has a handsome fortune.'

Mr Osmond listened to this in silence, appearing to turn it over in his mind with his eyes on his informant. 'What do you want to do with her?' he asked at last.

'What you see. Put her in your way.'

'Isn't she meant for something better than that?'

'I don't pretend to know what people are meant for,' said Madame Merle. 'I only know what I can do with them.'

'I'm sorry for Miss Archer!' Osmond declared.

Madame Merle got up. 'If that's a beginning of interest in her I take note of it.'

The two stood there face to face; she settled her mantilla, looking down at it as she did so. 'You're looking very well,' Osmond repeated still less relevantly than before. 'You have some idea. You're never so well as when you've got an idea; they're always becoming to you.'

In the manner and tone of these two persons, on first meeting at any juncture, and especially when they met in the presence of others, was something indirect and circumspect, as if they had approached each other obliquely and addressed each other by implication. The effect of each appeared to be to intensify to an appreciable degree the self-consciousness of the other. Madame Merle of course carried off any embarrassment better than her friend; but even Madame Merle had not on this occasion the form she would have liked to have – the perfect self-possession she would have wished to wear for her host. The point to be made is, however, that at a certain moment the element between them, whatever it was, always levelled itself and left them more closely face to face than either ever was with anyone else. This was what had happened now. They stood there knowing each other well and each on the whole willing to accept the satisfaction of knowing as a compensation for the inconvenience – whatever it might be – of being known. 'I wish very much you were not so heartless,' Madame Merle quietly said. 'It has always been against you, and it will be against you now.'

'I'm not so heartless as you think. Every now and then something touches me – as for instance your saying just now that your ambitions are for me. I don't understand it; I don't see how or why they should be. But it touches me, all the same.'

'You'll probably understand it even less as time goes on. There are some things you'll never understand. There's no particular need you should.'

'You, after all, are the most remarkable of women,' said Osmond. 'You have more in you than almost anyone. I don't see why you think Mrs Touchett's niece should matter very much to me, when – when—' But he paused a moment.

'When I myself have mattered so little?'

'That of course is not what I meant to say. When I've known and appreciated such a woman as you.'

'Isabel Archer's better than I,' said Madame Merle.

Her companion gave a laugh. 'How little you must think of her to say that!'

'Do you suppose I'm capable of jealousy? Please answer me that.'

'With regard to me? No; on the whole I don't.'

'Come and see me then, two days hence. I'm staying at Mrs Touchett's – Palazzo Crescentini – and the girl will be there.'

'Why didn't you ask me that at first simply, without speaking of the girl?' said Osmond. 'You could have had her there at any rate.'

Madame Merle looked at him in the manner of a woman whom no question he could ever put would find unprepared. 'Do you wish to know why? Because I've spoken of you to her.'

Osmond frowned and turned away. 'I'd rather not know that.' Then in a moment he pointed out the easel supporting the little water-colour drawing. 'Have you seen what's there – my last?'

Madame Merle drew near and considered. 'Is it the Venetian Alps – one of your last year's sketches?'

'Yes – but how you guess everything!'

She looked a moment longer, then turned away. 'You know I don't care for your drawings.'

'I know it, yet I'm always surprised at it. They're really so much better than most people's.'

'That may very well be. But as the only thing you do – well, it's so little. I should have liked you to do so many other things: those were my ambitions.'

'Yes; you've told me many times – things that were impossible.'

'Things that were impossible,' said Madame Merle. And then in quite a different tone: 'In itself your little picture's very good.' She looked about the room – at the old cabinets, pictures, tapestries, surfaces of faded silk. 'Your rooms at least are perfect. I'm struck with that afresh whenever I come back; I know none better anywhere. You understand this sort of thing as nobody anywhere does. You've such adorable taste.'

'I'm sick of my adorable taste,' said Gilbert Osmond.

'You must nevertheless let Miss Archer come and see it. I've told her about it.'

'I don't object to showing my things – when people are not idiots.'

'You do it delightfully. As cicerone of your museum you appear to particular advantage.'

Mr Osmond, in return for this compliment, simply looked at once colder and more attentive. 'Did you say she was rich?'

'She has seventy thousand pounds.'

'*En écus bien comptés?*'

'There's no doubt whatever about her fortune. I've seen it, as I may say.'

'Satisfactory woman! – I mean *you*. And if I go to see her shall I see the mother?'

'The mother? She has none – nor the father either.'

'The aunt then – whom did you say? – Mrs Touchett.'

'I can easily keep her out of the way.'

'I don't object to her,' said Osmond; 'I rather like Mrs Touchett. She has a sort of old-fashioned character that's passing away – a vivid identity. But that long jackanapes the son – is he about the place?'

'He's there, but he won't trouble you.'

'He's a good deal of a donkey.'

'I think you're mistaken. He's a very clever man. But he's not fond of being about when I'm there, because he doesn't like me.'

'What could be more asinine than that? Did you say she has looks?' Osmond went on.

'Yes; but I won't say it again, lest you should be disappointed in them. Come and make a beginning; that's all I ask of you.'

'A beginning of what?'

Madame Merle was silent a little. 'I want you of course to marry her.'

'The beginning of the end? Well, I'll see for myself. Have you told her that?'

'For what do you take me? She's not so coarse a piece of machinery – nor am I.'

'Really,' said Osmond after some meditation, 'I don't understand your ambitions.'

'I think you'll understand this one after you've seen Miss Archer. Suspend your judgement.' Madame Merle, as she spoke, had drawn near the open door of the garden, where she stood a moment looking out. 'Pansy has really grown pretty,' she presently added.

'So it seemed to me.'

'But she has had enough of the convent.'

'I don't know,' said Osmond. 'I like what they've made of her. It's very charming.'

'That's not the convent. It's the child's nature.'

'It's the combination, I think. She's as pure as a pearl.'

'Why doesn't she come back with my flowers then?' Madame Merle asked. 'She's not in a hurry.'

'We'll go and get them.'

'She doesn't like me,' the visitor murmured as she raised her parasol and they passed into the garden.

Chapter Twenty-three

Madame Merle, who had come to Florence on Mrs Touchett's arrival at the invitation of this lady – Mrs Touchett offering her for a month the hospitality of Palazzo Crescentini – the judicious Madame Merle spoke to Isabel afresh about Gilbert Osmond and expressed the hope she might know him; making, however, no such point of the matter as we have seen her do in recommending the girl herself to Mr Osmond's attention. The reason of this was perhaps that Isabel offered no resistance whatever to Madame Merle's proposal. In Italy, as in England, the lady had a multitude of friends, both among the natives of the country and its heterogeneous visitors. She had mentioned to Isabel most of the people the girl would find it well to 'meet' – of course, she said, Isabel could know whomever in the wide world she would – and had placed Mr Osmond near the top of the list. He was an old friend of her own; she had known him these dozen years; he was one of the cleverest and most agreeable men– well, in Europe simply. He was altogether above the respectable average; quite another affair. He wasn't a professional charmer – far from it, and the effect he produced depended a good deal on the state of his nerves and his spirits. When not in the right mood he could fall as low as anyone, saved only by his looking at such hours rather like a demoralized prince in exile. But if he cared or was interested or rightly challenged – just exactly rightly it had to be – then one felt his cleverness and his distinction. Those qualities didn't depend, in him, as in so many people, on his not committing or exposing himself. He had his perversities – which indeed Isabel would find to be the case with all the men really worth knowing – and didn't cause his light to shine equally for all persons. Madame Merle, however, thought she could undertake that for Isabel he would be brilliant. He was easily bored, too easily, and dull people always put him out; but a quick and cultivated girl like Isabel would give him a stimulus which was too absent from his life. At any rate he was a person not to miss. One shouldn't attempt to live in Italy without making a friend of Gilbert Osmond, who knew more about the country than anyone except two or three German professors. And if they had more knowledge than he it was he who had most perception and taste – being artistic through and through. Isabel remembered that her friend had spoken of him during their plunge, at Gardencourt, into the deeps of talk, and wondered a little what was the nature of the tie binding these superior spirits. She felt that Madame Merle's ties always somehow had histories, and such an impression was part of the interest created by this inordinate woman. As regards her relations with Mr Osmond, however, she hinted at nothing but a long-established calm friendship. Isabel said she should be happy to know a person who had enjoyed so high a confidence for so many years. 'You ought to see a great many men,' Madame

Merle remarked; 'you ought to see as many as possible, so as to get used to them.'

'Used to them?' Isabel repeated with that solemn stare which sometimes seemed to proclaim her deficient in the sense of comedy. 'Why, I'm not afraid of them – I'm as used to them as the cook to the butcher-boys.'

'Used to them, I mean, so as to despise them. That's what one comes to with most of them. You'll pick out, for your society, the few whom you don't despise.'

This was a note of cynicism that Madame Merle didn't often allow herself to sound; but Isabel was not alarmed, for she had never supposed that as one saw more of the world the sentiment of respect became the most active of one's emotions. It was excited, none the less, by the beautiful city of Florence, which pleased her not less than Madame Merle had promised; and if her unassisted perception had not been able to gauge its charms she had clever companions as priests to the mystery. She was in no want indeed of aesthetic illumination, for Ralph found it a joy that renewed his own early passion to act as cicerone to his eager young kinswoman. Madame Merle remained at home; she had seen the treasures of Florence again and again and had always something else to do. But she talked of all things with remarkable vividness of memory – she recalled the right-hand corner of the large Perugino and the position of the hands of the Saint Elizabeth in the picture next to it. She had her opinions as to the character of many famous works of art, differing often from Ralph with great sharpness and defending her interpretations with as much ingenuity as good-humour. Isabel listened to the discussions taking place between the two with a sense that she might derive much benefit from them and that they were among the advantages she couldn't have enjoyed for instance in Albany. In the clear May mornings before the formal breakfast – this repast at Mrs Touchett's was served at twelve o'clock – she wandered with her cousin through the narrow and sombre Florentine streets, resting a while in the thicker dusk of some historic church or the vaulted chambers of some dispeopled convent. She went to the galleries and palaces; she looked at the pictures and statues that had hitherto been great names to her, and exchanged for a knowledge which was sometimes a limitation a presentiment which proved usually to have been a blank. She performed all those acts of mental prostration in which, on a first visit to Italy, youth and enthusiasm so freely indulge; she felt her heart beat in the presence of immortal genius and knew the sweetness of rising tears in eyes to which faded fresco and darkened marble grew dim. But the return, every day, was even pleasanter than the going forth: the return into the wide, monumental court of the great house in which Mrs Touchett, many years before, had established herself, and into the high, cool rooms where the carven rafters and pompous frescoes of the sixteenth century looked down on the familiar commodities of the age of advertisement. Mrs Touchett inhabited an historic building in a narrow street whose very name recalled the strife of medieval factions; and found compensation for the darkness of her frontage in the modicity of her rent and the brightness of a garden where nature itself looked as archaic as the rugged architecture of the palace and which cleared and scented the rooms in regular use. To live in such a place was, for Isabel, to hold to her ear all day a shell of the sea of the past. This vague eternal rumour kept her imagination awake.

Gilbert Osmond came to see Madame Merle, who presented him to the young lady lurking at the other side of the room. Isabel took on this occasion little part in the talk; she scarcely even smiled when the others turned to her invitingly; she sat there as if she had been at the play and had paid even a large sum for her place. Mrs Touchett was not present, and these two had it, for the effect of brilliancy, all their own way. They talked of the Florentine, the Roman, the cosmopolite world, and might have been distinguished performers figuring for a charity. It all had the rich readiness that would have come from rehearsal. Madame Merle appealed to her as if she had been on the stage, but she could ignore any learnt cue without spoiling the scene; although of course she thus put dreadfully in the wrong the friend who had told Mr Osmond she could be depended on. This was no matter for once; even if more had been involved she could have made no attempt to shine. There was something in the visitor that checked her and held her in suspense – made it more important she should get an impression of him than that she should produce one herself. Besides, she had little skill in producing an impression which she knew to be expected: nothing could be happier, in general, than to seem dazzling, but she had a perverse unwillingness to glitter by arrangement. Mr Osmond, to do him justice, had a well-bred air of expecting nothing, a quiet ease that covered everything, even the first show of his own wit. This was the more grateful as his face, his head, was sensitive; he was not handsome, but he was fine, as fine as one of the drawings in the long gallery above the bridge of the Uffizi. And his very voice was fine – the more strangely that, with its clearness, it yet somehow wasn't sweet. This had had really to do with making her abstain from interference. His utterance was the vibration of glass, and if she had put out her finger she might have changed the pitch and spoiled the concert. Yet before he went she had to speak.

'Madame Merle,' he said, 'consents to come up to my hill-top some day next week and drink tea in my garden. It would give me much pleasure if you would come with her. It's thought rather pretty – there's what they call a general view. My daughter too would be so glad – or rather, for she's too young to have strong emotions, *I* should be so glad – so very glad.' And Mr Osmond paused with a slight air of embarrassment, leaving his sentence unfinished. 'I should be so happy if you could know my daughter,' he went on a moment afterwards.

Isabel replied that she should be delighted to see Miss Osmond and that if Madame Merle would show her the way to the hill-top she should be very grateful. Upon this assurance the visitor took his leave; after which Isabel fully expected her friend would scold her for having been so stupid. But to her surprise that lady, who indeed never fell into the mere matter-of-course, said to her in a few moments: 'You were charming, my dear; you were just as one would have wished you. You're never disappointing.'

A rebuke might possibly have been irritating, though it is much more probable that Isabel would have taken it in good part; but, strange to say, the words that Madame Merle actually used caused her the first feeling of displeasure she had known this ally to excite. 'That's more than I intended,' she answered coldly. 'I'm under no obligation that I know of to charm Mr Osmond.'

Madame Merle perceptibly flushed, but we know it was not her habit to retract. 'My dear child, I didn't speak for him, poor man; I spoke for yourself. It's not of course a question as to his liking you; it matters little whether he likes you or not! But I thought you liked *him*.'

'I did,' said Isabel honestly. 'But I don't see what that matters either.'

'Everything that concerns you matters to me,' Madame Merle returned with her weary nobleness; 'especially when at the same time another old friend's concerned.'

Whatever Isabel's obligations may have been to Mr Osmond, it must be admitted that she found them sufficient to lead her to put to Ralph sundry questions about him. She thought Ralph's judgements distorted by his trials, but she flattered herself she had learned to make allowance for that.

'Do I know him?' said her cousin. 'Oh, yes, I "know" him; not well, but on the whole enough. I've never cultivated his society, and he apparently has never found mine indispensable to his happiness. Who is he, what is he? He's a vague, unexplained American who has been living these thirty years, or less, in Italy. Why do I call him unexplained? Only as a cover for my ignorance; I don't know his antecedents, his family, his origin. For all I do know he may be a prince in disguise; he rather looks like one, by the way – like a prince who has abdicated in a fit of fastidiousness and has been in a state of disgust ever since. He used to live in Rome; but of late years he has taken up his abode here; I remember hearing him say that Rome has grown vulgar. He has a great dread of vulgarity; that's his special line; he hasn't any other that I know of. He lives on his income, which I suspect of not being vulgarly large. He's a poor but honest gentleman – that's what he calls himself. He married young and lost his wife, and I believe he has a daughter. He also has a sister, who's married to some small Count or other, of these parts; I remember meeting her of old. She's nicer than he, I should think, but rather impossible. I remember there used to be some stories about her. I don't think I recommend you to know her. But why don't you ask Madame Merle about these people? She knows them all much better than I.'

'I ask you because I want your opinion as well as hers,' said Isabel.

'A fig for my opinion! If you fall in love with Mr Osmond what will you care for that?'

'Not much, probably. But meanwhile it has a certain importance. The more information one has about one's dangers the better.'

'I don't agree to that – it may make them dangers. We know too much about people in these days; we hear too much. Our ears, our minds, our mouths, are stuffed with personalities. Don't mind anything anyone tells you about anyone else. Judge everyone and everything for yourself.'

'That's what I try to do,' said Isabel; 'but when you do that people call you conceited.'

'You're not to mind them – that's precisely my argument; not to mind what they say about yourself any more than what they say about your friend or your enemy.'

Isabel considered. 'I think you're right; but there are some things I can't help minding: for instance when my friend's attacked or when I myself am praised.'

'Of course you're always at liberty to judge the critic. Judge people as critics, however,' Ralph added, 'and you'll condemn them all!'

'I shall see Mr Osmond for myself,' said Isabel. 'I've promised to pay him a visit.'

'To pay him a visit?'

'To go and see his view, his pictures, his daughter – I don't know exactly what. Madame Merle's to take me; she tells me a great many ladies call on him.'

'Ah, with Madame Merle you may go anywhere, *de confiance*,' said Ralph. 'She knows none but the best people.'

Isabel said no more about Mr Osmond, but she presently remarked to her cousin that she was not satisfied with his tone about Madame Merle. 'It seems to me you insinuate things about her. I don't know what you mean, but if you've any grounds for disliking her I think you should either mention them frankly or else say nothing at all.'

Ralph, however, resented this charge with more apparent earnestness than he commonly used. 'I speak of Madame Merle exactly as I speak *to* her: with an even exaggerated respect.'

'Exaggerated, precisely. That's what I complain of.'

'I do so because Madame Merle's merits are exaggerated.'

'By whom, pray? By me? If so I do her a poor service.'

'No, no; by herself.'

'Ah, I protest!' Isabel earnestly cried. 'If ever there was a woman who made small claims—!'

'You put your finger on it,' Ralph interrupted. 'Her modesty's exaggerated. She has no business with small claims – she has a perfect right to make large ones.'

'Her merits are large then. You contradict yourself.'

'Her merits are immense,' said Ralph. 'She's indescribably blameless; a pathless desert of virtue; the only woman I know who never gives one a chance.'

'A chance for what?'

'Well, say to call her a fool! She's the only woman I know who has but that one little fault.'

Isabel turned away with impatience. 'I don't understand you; you're too paradoxical for my plain mind.'

'Let me explain. When I say she exaggerates I don't mean it in the vulgar sense – that she boasts, overstates, gives too fine an account of herself. I mean literally that she pushes the search for perfection too far – that her merits are in themselves overstrained. She's too good, too kind, too clever, too learned, too accomplished, too everything. She's too complete, in a word. I confess to you that she acts on my nerves and that I feel about her a good deal as that intensely human Athenian felt about Aristides the Just.'

Isabel looked hard at her cousin; but the mocking spirit, if it lurked in his words, failed on this occasion to peep from his face. 'Do you wish Madame Merle to be banished?'

'By no means. She's much too good company. I delight in Madame Merle,' said Ralph Touchett simply.

'You're very odious, sir!' Isabel exclaimed. And then she asked him if he knew anything that was not to the honour of her brilliant friend.

'Nothing whatever. Don't you see that's just what I mean? On the character of everyone else you may find some little black speck; if I were to take half an hour to it, some day, I've no doubt I should be able to find one on yours. For my own, of course, I'm spotted like a leopard. But on Madame Merle's nothing, nothing, nothing!'

'That's just what I think!' said Isabel with a toss of her head. 'That is why I like her so much.'

'She's a capital person for you to know. Since you wish to see the world you couldn't have a better guide.'

'I suppose you mean by that that she's worldly?'

'Worldly? No,' said Ralph, 'she's the great round world itself!'

It had certainly not, as Isabel for the moment took it into her head to believe, been a refinement of malice in him to say that he delighted in Madame Merle. Ralph Touchett took his refreshment wherever he could find it, and he would not have forgiven himself if he had been left wholly unbeguiled by such a mistress of the social art. There are deep-lying sympathies and antipathies, and it may have been that, in spite of the administered justice she enjoyed at his hands, her absence from his mother's house would not have made life barren to him. But Ralph Touchett had learned more or less inscrutably to attend, and there could have been nothing so 'sustained' to attend to as the general performance of Madame Merle. He tasted her in sips, he let her stand, with an opportuneness she herself could not have surpassed. There were moments when he felt almost sorry for her; and these, oddly enough, were the moments when his kindness was least demonstrative. He was sure she had been yearningly ambitious and that what she had visibly accomplished was far below her secret measure. She had got herself into perfect training, but had won none of the prizes. She was always plain Madame Merle, the widow of a Swiss *négociant*, with a small income and a large acquaintance, who stayed with people a great deal and was almost as universally 'liked' as some new volume of smooth twaddle. The contrast between this position and any one of some half-dozen others that he supposed to have at various moments engaged her hope had an element of the tragical. His mother thought he got on beautifully with their genial guest; to Mrs Touchett's sense two persons who dealt so largely in too-ingenious theories of conduct – that is of their own – would have much in common. He had given due consideration to Isabel's intimacy with her eminent friend, having long since made up his mind that he could not, without opposition, keep his cousin to himself; and he made the best of it, as he had done of worse things. He believed it would take care of itself; it wouldn't last forever. Neither of these two superior persons knew the other as well as she supposed, and when each had made an important discovery or two there would be, if not a rupture, at least a relaxation. Meanwhile he was quite willing to admit that the conversation of the elder lady was an advantage to the younger, who had a great deal to learn and would doubtless learn it better from Madame Merle than from some other instructors of the young. It was not probable that Isabel would be injured.

Chapter Twenty-four

It would certainly have been hard to see what injury could arise to her from the visit she presently paid to Mr Osmond's hill-top. Nothing could have been more charming than this occasion – a soft afternoon in the full maturity of the Tuscan spring. The companions drove out of the Roman Gate, beneath the enormous blank superstructure which crowns the fine clear arch of that portal and makes it nakedly impressive, and wound between high-walled lanes into which the wealth of blossoming orchards over-drooped and flung a fragrance, until they reached the small superurban piazza, of crooked shape, where the long brown wall of the villa occupied in part by Mr Osmond formed a principal, or at least a very imposing, object. Isabel went with her friend through a wide, high court, where a clear shadow rested below and a pair of light-arched galleries, facing each other above, caught the upper sunshine upon their slim columns and the flowering plants in which they were dressed. There was something grave and strong in the place; it looked somehow as if, once you were in, you would need an act of energy to get out. For Isabel, however, there was of course as yet no thought of getting out, but only of advancing. Mr Osmond met her in the cold antechamber – it was cold even in the month of May – and ushered her, with her conductress, into the apartment to which we have already been introduced. Madame Merle was in front, and while Isabel lingered a little, talking with him, she went forward familiarly and greeted two persons who were seated in the saloon. One of these was little Pansy, on whom she bestowed a kiss; the other was a lady whom Mr Osmond indicated to Isabel as his sister, the Countess Gemini. 'And that's my little girl,' he said, 'who has just come out of her convent.'

Pansy had on a scant white dress, and her fair hair was neatly arranged in a net; she wore her small shoes tied sandal-fashion about her ankles. She made Isabel a little conventual curtsey and then came to be kissed. The Countess Gemini simply nodded without getting up: Isabel could see she was a woman of high fashion. She was thin and dark and not at all pretty, having features that suggested some tropical bird – a long beaklike nose, small, quickly-moving eyes, and a mouth and chin that receded extremely. Her expression, however, thanks to various intensities of emphasis and wonder, of horror and joy, was not inhuman, and, as regards her appearance, it was plain she understood herself and made the most of her points. Her attire, voluminous and delicate, bristling with elegance, had the look of shimmering plumage, and her attitudes were as light and sudden as those of a creature who perched upon twigs. She had a great deal of manner; Isabel, who had never known anyone with so much manner, immediately classed her as the most affected of women. She remembered that Ralph had not recommended her as an acquaintance; but she was ready to acknowledge that to a casual view the Countess Gemini revealed no depths. Her demonstrations suggested the violent waving of some flag of general truce – white silk with fluttering streamers.

'You'll believe I'm glad to see you when I tell you it's only because I knew you were to be here that I came myself. I don't come and see my brother – I make him come and see me. This hill of his is impossible – I don't see what possesses him. Really, Osmond, you'll be the ruin of my horses some day, and if it hurts them you'll have to give me another pair. I heard them wheezing today; I assure you I did. It's very disagreeable to hear one's horses wheezing when one's sitting in the carriage; it sounds too as if they weren't what they should be. But I've always had good horses; whatever else I may have lacked I've always managed that. My husband doesn't know much, but I think he knows a good horse. In general Italians don't, but my husband goes in, according to his poor light, for everything English. My horses are English – so it's all the greater pity they should be ruined. I must tell you,' she went on, directly addressing Isabel, 'that Osmond doesn't often invite me; I don't think he likes to have me. It was quite my own idea, coming today. I like to see new people, and I'm sure you're very new. But don't sit there; that chair's not what it looks. There are some very good seats here, but there are also some horrors.'

These remarks were delivered with a series of little jerks and pecks, of roulades of shrillness, and in an accent that was as some fond recall of good English, or rather of good American, in adversity.

'I don't like to have you, my dear?' said her brother. 'I'm sure you're invaluable.'

'I don't see any horrors anywhere,' Isabel returned, looking about her. 'Everything seems to me beautiful and precious.'

'I've a few good things,' Mr Osmond allowed; 'indeed I've nothing very bad. But I've not what I should have liked.'

He stood there a little awkwardly, smiling and glancing about; his manner was an odd mixture of the detached and the involved. He seemed to hint that nothing but the right 'values' was of any consequence. Isabel made a rapid induction: perfect simplicity was not the badge of his family. Even the little girl from the convent, who, in her prim white dress, with her small submissive face and her hands locked before her, stood there as if she were about to partake of her first communion, even Mr Osmond's diminutive daughter had a kind of finish that was not entirely artless.

'You'd have liked a few things from the Uffizi and the Pitti – that's what you'd have liked,' said Madame Merle.

'Poor Osmond, with his old curtains and crucifixes!' the Countess Gemini exclaimed: she appeared to call her brother only by his family name. Her ejaculation had no particular object; she smiled at Isabel as she made it and looked at her from head to foot.

Her brother had not heard her; he seemed to be thinking what he could say to Isabel. 'Won't you have some tea? – you must be very tired,' he at last bethought himself of remarking.

'No indeed, I'm not tired; what have I done to tire me?' Isabel felt a certain need of being very direct, of pretending to nothing; there was something in the air, in her general impression of things – she could hardly have said what it was – that deprived her of all disposition to put herself forward. The place, the occasion, the combination of people, signified more than lay on the surface; she would try to understand – she would not simply utter graceful platitudes. Poor Isabel was doubtless not aware that many women would have uttered graceful platitudes to cover the working of their observation. It must be confessed that her pride was a trifle alarmed. A man she had heard spoken of in terms that excited interest and who was evidently capable of distinguishing himself, had invited her, a young lady not lavish of her favours, to come to his house. Now that she had done so the burden of the entertainment rested naturally on his wit. Isabel was not rendered less observant, and for the moment, we judge, she was not rendered more indulgent, by perceiving that Mr Osmond carried his burden less complacently than might have been expected. 'What a fool I was to have let myself so needlessly in—!' she could fancy his exclaiming to himself.

'You'll be tired when you go home, if he shows you all his bibelots and gives you a lecture on each,' said the Countess Gemini.

'I'm not afraid of that; but if I'm tired I shall at least have learned something.'

'Very little, I suspect. But my sister's dreadfully afraid of learning anything,' said Mr Osmond.

'Oh, I confess to that; I don't want to know anything more – I know too much already. The more you know the more unhappy you are.'

'You should not undervalue knowledge before Pansy who has not finished her education,' Madame Merle interposed with a smile.

'Pansy will never know any harm,' said the child's father. 'Pansy's a little convent-flower.'

'Oh, the convents, the convents!' cried the Countess with a flutter of her ruffles. 'Speak to me of the convents! You may learn anything there; I'm a convent-flower myself. I don't pretend to be good, but the nuns do. Don't you see what I mean?' she went on, appealing to Isabel.

Isabel was not sure she saw, and she answered that she was very bad at following arguments. The Countess then declared that she herself detested arguments, but that this was her brother's taste – he would always discuss. 'For me,' she said, 'one should like a thing or one shouldn't; one can't like everything, of course. But one shouldn't attempt to reason it out – you never know where it may lead you. There are some very good feelings that may have bad reasons, don't you know? And then there are very bad feelings, sometimes, that have good reasons. Don't you see what I mean? I don't care anything about reasons, but I know what I like.'

'Ah, that's the great thing,' said Isabel, smiling and suspecting that her acquaintance with this lightly flitting personage would not lead to intellectual repose. If the Countess objected to argument Isabel at this moment had as little taste for it, and she put out her hand to Pansy with a pleasant sense that such a gesture committed her to nothing that would admit of a divergence of views. Gilbert Osmond apparently took a rather hopeless view of his sister's tone; he turned the conversation to another topic. He presently sat down on the other side of his daughter, who had shyly brushed Isabel's fingers with her own; but he ended by drawing her out of her chair and making her stand between his knees, leaning against him while he passed his arm round her slimness. The child fixed her eyes on Isabel with a still, disinterested gaze which seemed void of an intention, yet conscious of an attraction. Mr Osmond talked of many things; Madame Merle had said he could be agreeable when he chose, and today, after a little, he appeared not only to have chosen but to have determined. Madame Merle and Countess Gemini sat a little apart, conversing in the effortless manner of persons who knew each other well enough to take their ease; but every now and then Isabel heard the Countess, at something said by her companion, plunge into the latter's lucidity as a poodle splashes after a thrown stick. It was as if Madame Merle were seeing how far she would go. Mr Osmond talked of Florence, of Italy, of the pleasure of living in that country and of the abatements to the pleasure. There were both satisfactions and drawbacks; the drawbacks were numerous; strangers were too apt to see such a world as all romantic. It met the case soothingly for the human, for the social failure – by which he meant the people who couldn't 'realize', as they said, on their sensibility; they could keep it about them there, in their poverty, without ridicule, as you might keep an heirloom or an inconvenient entailed place that brought you in nothing. Thus there were advantages in living in the country which contained the greatest sum of beauty. Certain impressions you could get only there. Others favourable to life, you never got, and you got some that were very bad. But from time to time you got one of a quality that made up for everything. Italy, all the same, had spoiled a great many people; he was even fatuous enough to believe at times that he himself might have been a better man if he had spent less of his life there. It made one idle and dilettantish and second-rate; it had no discipline for the character, didn't cultivate in you, otherwise expressed, the successful social and other 'cheek' that flourished in Paris and London. 'We're sweetly provincial,' said Mr Osmond, 'and I'm perfectly aware that I myself am as rusty as a key that has no lock to fit it. It polishes me up a little to talk with you – not that I venture to pretend I can turn that very complicated lock I suspect your intellect of being! But you'll be going away before I've seen you three times, and I shall perhaps never see you after that. That's what it is to live in a country that people come to. When they're disagreeable here it's bad enough; when they're agreeable it's still worse. As soon as you like them they're off again! I've been deceived too often; I've ceased to form attachments, to permit myself to feel attractions. You mean to stay – to settle? That would be really comfortable. Ah yes, your aunt's a sort of guarantee; I believe she may be depended on. Oh, she's an old Florentine; I mean literally an old one; not a modern outsider. She's a contemporary of the Medici; she must have been present at the burning of Savonarola, and I'm not sure she didn't throw a handful of chips into the flame. Her face is very much like some faces in the early pictures; little, dry, definite faces that must have had a good deal of expression, but almost always the same one. Indeed I can show you her portrait in a fresco of Ghirlandaio's. I hope you don't object to my speaking that way of your aunt, eh? I've an idea you don't. Perhaps you think that's even worse. I assure you there's no want of respect in it, to either of you. You know I'm a particular admirer of Mrs Touchett.'

While Isabel's host exerted himself to entertain her in this somewhat confidential fashion she looked occasionally at Madame Merle, who met her eyes with an inattentive smile in which, on this occasion, there was no infelicitous intimation that our heroine appeared to advantage. Madame

Merle eventually proposed to the Countess Gemini that they should go into the garden, and the Countess, rising and shaking out her feathers, began to rustle towards the door. 'Poor Miss Archer!' she exclaimed, surveying the other group with expressive compassion. 'She has been brought quite into the family.'

'Miss Archer can certainly have nothing but sympathy for a family to which you belong,' Mr Osmond answered, with a laugh which, though it had something of a mocking ring, had also a finer patience.

'I don't know what you mean by that! I'm sure she'll see no harm in me but what you tell her. I'm better than he says, Miss Archer,' the Countess went on. 'I'm only rather an idiot and a bore. Is that all he has said? Ah then, you keep him in good-humour. Has he opened on one of his favourite subjects? I give you notice that there are two or three that he treats *à fond*. In that case you had better take off your bonnet.'

'I don't think I know what Mr Osmond's favourite subjects are,' said Isabel, who had risen to her feet.

The Countess assumed for an instant an attitude of intense meditation, pressing one of her hands, with the finger-tips gathered together, to her forehead. 'I'll tell you in a moment. One's Machiavelli; the other's Vittoria Colonna; the next is Metastasio.'

'Ah, with me,' said Madame Merle, passing her arm into the Countess Gemini's as if to guide her course to the garden, 'Mr Osmond's never so historical.'

'Oh you,' the Countess answered as they moved away, 'you yourself are Machiavelli! – you yourself are Vittoria Colonna!'

'We shall hear next that poor Madame Merle is Metastasio!' Gilbert Osmond resignedly sighed.

Isabel had got up on the assumption that they too were to go into the garden; but her host stood there with no apparent inclination to leave the room, his hands in the pockets of his jacket and his daughter, who had now locked her arm into one of his own, clinging to him and looking up while her eyes moved from his own face to Isabel's. Isabel waited, with a certain unuttered contentedness, to have her movements directed; she liked Mr Osmond's talk, his company: she had what always gave her a very private thrill, the consciousness of a new relation. Through the open doors of the great room she saw Madame Merle and the Countess stroll across the fine grass of the garden; then she turned, and her eyes wandered over the things scattered about her. The understanding had been that Mr Osmond should show her his treasures; his pictures and cabinets all looked like treasures. Isabel after a moment went towards one of the pictures to see it better; but just as she had done so he said to her abruptly: 'Miss Archer, what do you think of my sister?'

She faced him with some surprise. 'Ah, don't ask me that – I've seen your sister too little.'

'Yes, you've seen her very little; but you must have observed that there is not a great deal of her to see. What do you think of our family tone?' he went on with his cool smile. 'I should like to know how it strikes a fresh, unprejudiced mind. I know what you're going to say – you've had almost no observation of it. Of course this is only a glimpse. But just take notice, in future, if you have a chance. I sometimes think we've got into a rather bad way, living off here among things and people not our own, without responsibilities or attachments, with nothing to hold us together or keep us up; marrying foreigners, forming artificial tastes, playing tricks with our natural mission. Let me add, though, that I say that much more for myself than for my sister. She's a very honest lady – more so than she seems. She's rather unhappy, and as she's not of a serious turn she doesn't tend to show it tragically: she shows it comically instead. She has got a horrid husband, though I'm not sure she makes the best of him. Of course, however, a horrid husband's an awkward thing. Madame Merle gives her excellent advice, but it's a good deal like giving a child a dictionary to learn a language with. He can look out the words, but he can't put them together. My sister needs a grammar, but unfortunately she's not grammatical. Pardon my troubling you with these details; my sister was very right in saying you've been taken into the family. Let me take down that picture; you want more light.'

He took down the picture, carried it towards the window, related some curious facts about it. She looked at the other works of art, and he gave her such further information as might appear most acceptable to a young lady making a call on a summer afternoon. His pictures, his medallions and tapestries were interesting; but after a while Isabel felt the owner much more so, and independently of them, thickly as they seemed to overhang him. He resembled no one she had ever seen; most of the people she knew might be divided into groups of half a dozen specimens. There were one or two exceptions to this; she could think for instance of no group that would contain her aunt Lydia. There were other people who were, relatively speaking, original – original, as one might say, by courtesy – such as Mr Goodwood, as her cousin Ralph, as Henrietta Stackpole, as Lord Warburton, as Madame Merle. But in essentials, when one came to look at them, these individuals belonged to types already present to her mind. Her mind contained no class offering a natural place to Mr Osmond – he was a specimen apart. It was not that she recognized all these truths at the hour, but they were falling into order before her. For the moment she only said to herself that this 'new relation' would perhaps prove her very most distinguished. Madame Merle had had that note of rarity, but what quite other power it immediately gained when sounded by a man! It was not so much what he said and did but rather what he withheld, that marked him for her as by one of those signs as the highly curious that he was showing her on the underside of old plates and in the corner of sixteenth-century drawings: he indulged in no striking deflections from common usage, he was an original without being an eccentric. She had never met a person of so fine a grain. The peculiarity was physical, to begin with, and it extended to impalpabilities. His dense, delicate hair, his overdrawn, retouched features, his clear complexion, ripe without being coarse, the very evenness of the growth of his beard, and that light, smooth slenderness of structure which made the movement of a single one of his fingers produce the effect of an expressive gesture – these personal points struck our sensitive young woman as signs of quality, of intensity, somehow as promises of interest. He was certainly fastidious and critical; he was probably irritable. His sensibility had governed him – possibly governed him too much; it had made him impatient of vulgar troubles and had led him to live by himself, in a sorted, sifted, arranged world, thinking about art and beauty and history. He had consulted his taste in everything – his taste alone perhaps, as a sick man consciously incurable consults at last only his lawyer: that was what made him so different from everyone else. Ralph had something of this same quality, this appearance of thinking that life was a matter of connoisseurship; but in Ralph it was an anomaly, a kind of humorous excrescence, whereas in Mr Osmond it was the keynote, and everything was in harmony with it. She was certainly far from understanding him completely; his meaning was not at all times obvious. It was hard to see what he meant for instance by speaking of his provincial side – which was exactly the side she would have taken him most to lack. Was it a harmless paradox, intended to puzzle her? or was it the last refinement of high culture? She trusted she should learn in time; it would be very interesting to learn. If it was provincial to have that harmony, what then was the finish of the capital? And she could put this question in spite of so feeling her host a shy personage; since such shyness as his – the shyness of ticklish nerves and fine perceptions – was perfectly consistent with the best breeding. Indeed it was almost a proof of standards and touchstones other than the vulgar: he must be so sure the vulgar would be first on the ground. He wasn't a man of easy assurance, who chatted and gossiped with the fluency of a superficial nature he was critical of himself as well as of others, and, exacting a good deal of others, to think them agreeable, probably took a rather ironical view of what he himself offered: a proof into the bargain that he was not grossly conceited. If he had not been shy he wouldn't have effected that gradual, subtle, successful conversion of it to which she owed both what pleased her in him and what mystified her. If he had suddenly asked her what she thought of the Countess Gemini, that was doubtless a proof that he was interested in her; it could scarcely be as a help to knowledge of his own sister. That he should be so interested showed an inquiring mind; but it was a little singular he should sacrifice his fraternal feeling to his curiosity. This was the most eccentric thing he had done.

There were two other rooms, beyond the one in which she had been received, equally full of romantic objects, and in these apartments Isabel spent a quarter of an hour. Everything was in the last degree curious and precious, and Mr Osmond continued to be the kindest of ciceroni as he led her from one fine piece to another and still held his little girl by the hand. His kindness almost surprised our young friend, who wondered why he should take so much trouble for her; and she was oppressed at last with the accumulation of beauty and knowledge to which she found herself introduced. There was enough for the present; she had ceased to attend to what he said; she listened to him with attentive eyes, but was not thinking of what he told her. He probably thought her quicker, cleverer in every way, more prepared, than she was. Madame Merle would have pleasantly exaggerated; which was a pity, because in the end he would be sure to find out, and then perhaps even her real intelligence wouldn't reconcile him to his mistake. A part of Isabel's fatigue came from the effort to appear as intelligent as she believed Madame Merle had described her, and from the fear (very unusual with her) of exposing – not her ignorance; for that she cared comparatively little – but her possible grossness of perception. It would have annoyed her to express a liking for something he, in his superior enlightenment, would think she oughtn't to like; or to pass by something at which the truly initiated mind would arrest itself. She had no wish to fall into that grotesqueness – in which she had seen women (and it was a warning) serenely, yet ignobly, flounder. She was very careful therefore as to what she said, as to what she noticed or failed to notice; more careful than she had ever been before.

They came back into the first of the rooms, where the tea had been served; but as the two other ladies were still on the terrace, and as Isabel had not yet been made acquainted with the view, the paramount distinction of the place, Mr Osmond directed her steps into the garden without more delay. Madame Merle and the Countess had had chairs brought out, and as the afternoon was lovely the Countess proposed that they should take their tea in the open air. Pansy therefore was sent to bid the servant bring out the preparations. The sun had got low, the golden light took a deeper tone, and on the mountains and the plain that stretched beneath them the masses of purple shadow glowed as richly as the places that were still exposed. The scene had an extraordinary charm. The air was almost solemnly still, and the large expanse of the landscape, with its gardenlike culture and nobleness of outline, its teeming valley and delicately-fretted hills, its peculiarly human-looking touches of habitation, lay there in splendid harmony and classic grace. 'You seem so well pleased that I think you can be trusted to come back,' Osmond said as he led his companion to one of the angles of the terrace.

'I shall certainly come back,' she returned, 'in spite of what you say about its being bad to live in Italy. What was that you said about one's natural mission? I wonder if I should forsake my natural mission if I were to settle in Florence.'

'A woman's natural mission is to be where she's most appreciated.'

'The point's to find out where that is.'

'Very true – she often wastes a great deal of time in the inquiry. People ought to make it very plain to her.'

'Such a matter would have to be made very plain to me,' smiled Isabel.

'I'm glad, at any rate, to hear you talk of settling. Madame Merle had given me an idea that you were of a rather roving disposition. I thought she spoke of your having some plan of going round the world.'

'I'm rather ashamed of my plans; I make a new one every day.'

'I don't see why you should be ashamed; it's the greatest of pleasures.'

'It seems frivolous, I think,' said Isabel. 'One ought to choose something very deliberately, and be faithful to that.'

'By that rule then, I've not been frivolous.'

'Have you never made plans?'

'Yes, I made one years ago, and I'm acting on it today.'

'It must have been a very pleasant one,' Isabel permitted herself to observe.

'It was very simple. It was to be as quiet as possible.'

'As quiet?' the girl repeated.

'Not to worry – not to strive nor struggle. To resign myself. To be content with little.' He spoke these sentences slowly, with short pauses between, and his intelligent regard was fixed on his visitor's with the conscious air of a man who has brought himself to confess something.

'Do you call that simple?' she asked with mild irony.

'Yes, because it's negative.'

'Has your life been negative?'

'Call it affirmative if you like. Only it has affirmed my indifference. Mind you, not my natural indifference – I *had* none. But my studied, my wilful renunciation.'

She scarcely understood him; it seemed a question whether he were joking or not. Why should a man who struck her as having a great fund of reserve suddenly bring himself to be so confidential? This was his affair, however, and his confidences were interesting. 'I don't see why you should have renounced,' she said in a moment.

'Because I could do nothing. I had no prospects, I was poor, and I was not a man of genius. I had no talents even; I took my measure early in life. I was simply the most fastidious young gentleman living. There were two or three people in the world I envied – the Emperor of Russia, for instance, and the Sultan of Turkey! There were even moments when I envied the Pope of Rome – for the consideration he enjoys. I should have been delighted to be considered to that extent; but since that couldn't be I didn't care for anything less, and I made up my mind not to go in for honours. The leanest gentleman can always consider himself, and fortunately I *was*, though lean, a gentleman. I could do nothing in Italy – I couldn't even be an Italian patriot. To do that I should have had to get out of the country; and I was too fond of it to leave it, to say nothing of my being too well satisfied with it, on the whole, as it then was, to wish it altered. So I've passed a great many years here on that quiet plan I spoke of. I've not been at all unhappy. I don't mean to say I've cared for nothing; but the things I've cared for have been definite – limited. The events of my life have been absolutely unperceived by any one save myself; getting an old silver crucifix at a bargain (I've never bought anything dear, of course), or discovering, as I once did, a sketch by Correggio on a panel daubed over by some inspired idiot.'

This would have been rather a dry account of Mr Osmond's career if Isabel had fully believed it; but her imagination supplied the human element which she was sure had not been wanting. His life had been mingled with other lives more than he admitted; naturally she couldn't expect him to enter into this. For the present she abstained from provoking further revelations; to intimate that he had not told her everything would be more familiar and less considerate than she now desired to be – would in fact be uproariously vulgar. He had certainly told her quite enough. It was her present inclination, however, to express a measured sympathy for the success with which he had preserved his independence. 'That's a very pleasant life,' she said, 'to renounce everything but Correggio!'

'Oh, I've made in my way a good thing of it. Don't imagine I'm whining about it. It's one's own fault if one isn't happy.'

This was large; she kept down to something smaller. 'Have you lived here always?'

'No, not always. I lived a long time at Naples, and many years in Rome. But I've been here a good while. Perhaps I shall have to change, however; to do something else. I've no longer myself to think of. My daughter's growing up and may very possibly not care so much for the Correggios and crucifixes as I. I shall have to do what's best for Pansy.'

'Yes, do that,' said Isabel. 'She's such a dear little girl.'

'Ah,' cried Gilbert Osmond beautifully, 'she's a little saint of heaven! She is my great happiness!'

Chapter Twenty-five

While this sufficiently intimate colloquy (prolonged for some time after we cease to follow it) went forward Madame Merle and her companion, breaking a silence of some duration, had begun to exchange remarks. They were sitting in an attitude of unexpressed expectancy; an attitude especially marked on the part of the Countess Gemini, who, being of a more nervous temperament than her friend, practised with less success the art of disguising impatience. What these ladies were waiting for would not have been apparent and was perhaps not very definite to their own minds. Madame Merle waited for Osmond to release their young friend from her *tête-à-tête*, and the Countess waited because Madame Merle did. The Countess, moreover, by waiting, found the time ripe for one of her pretty perversities. She might have desired for some minutes to place it. Her brother wandered with Isabel to the end of the garden, to which point her eyes followed them.

'My dear,' she then observed to her companion, 'you'll excuse me if I don't congratulate you!'

'Very willingly, for I don't in the least know why you should.'

'Haven't you a little plan that you think rather well of?' And the Countess nodded at the sequestered couple.

Madame Merle's eyes took the same direction; then she looked serenely at her neighbour. 'You know I never understand you very well,' she smiled.

'No one can understand better than you when you wish. I see that just now you *don't* wish.'

'You say things to me that no one else does,' said Madame Merle gravely, yet without bitterness.

'You mean things you don't like? Doesn't Osmond sometimes say such things?'

'What your brother says has a point.'

'Yes, a poisoned one sometimes. If you mean that I'm not so clever as he you mustn't think I shall suffer from your sense of our difference. But it will be much better that you should understand me.'

'Why so?' asked Madame Merle. 'To what will it conduce?'

'If I don't approve of your plan you ought to know it in order to appreciate the danger of my interfering with it.'

Madame Merle looked as if she were ready to admit that there might be something in this; but in a moment she said quietly: 'You think me more calculating than I am.'

'It's not your calculating I think ill of; it's your calculating wrong. You've done so in this case.'

'You must have made extensive calculations yourself to discover that.'

'No, I've not had time. I've seen the girl but this once,' said the Countess, 'and the conviction has suddenly come to me. I like her very much.'

'So do I,' Madame Merle mentioned.

'You've a strange way of showing it.'

'Surely I've given her the advantage of making your acquaintance.'

'That indeed,' piped the Countess, 'is perhaps the best thing that could happen to her!'

Madame Merle said nothing for some time. The Countess's manner was odious, was really low; but it was an old story, and with her eyes upon the violet slope of Monte Morello she gave herself up to reflection. 'My dear lady,' she finally resumed, 'I advise you not to agitate yourself. The matter you allude to concerns three persons much stronger of purpose than yourself.'

'Three persons? You and Osmond of course. But is Miss Archer also very strong of purpose?'

'Quite as much so as we.'

'Ah then,' said the Countess radiantly, 'if I convince her it's her interest to resist you she'll do so successfully!'

'Resist us? Why do you express yourself so coarsely? She's not exposed to compulsion or deception.'

'I'm not sure of that. You're capable of anything, you and Osmond. I don't mean Osmond by himself, and I don't mean you by yourself. But together you're dangerous – like some chemical combination.'

'You had better leave us alone then,' smiled Madame Merle.

'I don't mean to touch you – but I shall talk to that girl.'

'My poor Amy,' Madame Merle murmured, 'I don't see what has got into your head.'

'I take an interest in her – that's what has got into my head. I like her.'

Madame Merle hesitated a moment. 'I don't think she likes you.'

The Countess's bright little eyes expanded and her face was set in a grimace. 'Ah, you *are* dangerous – even by yourself!'

'If you want her to like you don't abuse your brother to her,' said Madame Merle.

'I don't suppose you pretend she has fallen in love with him in two interviews.'

Madame Merle looked a moment at Isabel and at the master of the house. He was leaning against the parapet, facing her, his arms folded; and she at present was evidently not lost in the mere impersonal view, persistently as she gazed at it. As Madame Merle watched her she lowered her eyes; she was listening, possibly with a certain embarrassment, while she pressed the point of her parasol into the path. Madame Merle rose from her chair. 'Yes, I think so!' she pronounced.

The shabby footboy, summoned by Pansy – he might, tarnished as to livery and quaint as to type, have issued from some stray sketch of old-time manners, been 'put in' by the brush of a Longhi or a Goya – had come out with a small table and placed it on the grass, and then had gone back and fetched the tea-tray; after which he had again disappeared, to return with a couple of chairs. Pansy had watched these proceedings with the deepest interest, standing with her small hands folded together upon the front of her scanty frock; but she had not presumed to offer assistance. When the tea-table had been arranged, however, she gently approached her aunt.

'Do you think papa would object to my making the tea?'

The Countess looked at her with a deliberately critical gaze and without answering her question. 'My poor niece,' she said, 'is that your best frock?'

'Ah no,' Pansy answered, 'it's just a little *toilette* for common occasions.'

'Do you call it a common occasion when I come to see you? – to say nothing of Madame Merle and the pretty lady yonder.'

Pansy reflected for a moment, turning gravely from one of the persons mentioned to the other. Then her face broke into its perfect smile. 'I have a pretty dress, but even that one's very simple. Why should I expose it beside your beautiful things?'

'Because it's the prettiest you have; for me you must always wear the prettiest. Please put it on the next time. It seems to me they don't dress you so well as they might.'

The child sparingly stroked down her antiquated skirt. 'It's a good little dress to make tea – don't you think? Don't you believe papa would allow me?'

'Impossible for me to say, my child,' said the Countess. 'For me, your father's ideas are unfathomable. Madame Merle understands them better. Ask *her*.'

Madame Merle smiled with her usual grace. 'It's a weighty question – let me think. It seems to me it would please your father to see a careful little daughter making his tea. It's the proper duty of the daughter of the house – when she grows up.'

'So it seems to me, Madame Merle!' Pansy cried. 'You shall see how well I'll make it. A spoonful for each.' And she began to busy herself at the table.

'Two spoonfuls for me,' said the Countess, who, with Madame Merle, remained for some moments watching her. 'Listen to me, Pansy,' the Countess resumed at last. 'I should like to know what you think of your visitor.'

'Ah, she's not mine – she's papa's,' Pansy objected.

'Miss Archer came to see you as well,' said Madame Merle.

'I'm very happy to hear that. She has been very polite to me.'

'Do you like her then?' the Countess asked.

'She's charming – charming,' Pansy repeated in her little neat conversational tone. 'She pleases me thoroughly.'

'And how do you think she pleases your father?'

'Ah really, Countess!' murmured Madame Merle dissuasively. 'Go and call them to tea,' she went on to the child.

'You'll see if they don't like it!' Pansy declared; and departed to summon the others, who had still lingered at the end of the terrace.

'If Miss Archer's to become her mother it's surely interesting to know if the child likes her,' said the Countess.

'If your brother marries again it won't be for Pansy's sake,' Madame Merle replied. 'She'll soon be sixteen, and after that she'll begin to need a husband rather than a stepmother.'

'And will you provide the husband as well?'

'I shall certainly take an interest in her marrying fortunately. I imagine you'll do the same.'

'Indeed I shan't!' cried the Countess. 'Why should I, of all women, set such a price on a husband?'

'You didn't marry fortunately; that's what I'm speaking of. When I say a husband I mean a good one.'

'There are no good ones. Osmond won't be a good one.'

Madame Merle closed her eyes a moment. 'You're irritated just now; I don't know why,' she presently said. 'I don't think you'll really object either to your brother's or to your niece's marrying, when the time comes for them to do so; and as regards Pansy I'm confident that we shall some day have the pleasure of looking for a husband for her together. Your large acquaintance will be a great help.'

'Yes, I'm irritated,' the Countess answered. 'You often irritate me. Your own coolness is fabulous. You're a strange woman.'

'It's much better that we should always act together,' Madame Merle went on.

'Do you mean that as a threat?' asked the Countess rising.

Madame Merle shook her head as for quiet amusement. 'No indeed, you've not my coolness!'

Isabel and Mr Osmond were now slowly coming towards them and Isabel had taken Pansy by the hand. 'Do you pretend to believe he'd make her happy?' the Countess demanded.

'If he should marry Miss Archer I suppose he'd behave like a gentleman.'

The Countess jerked herself into a succession of attitudes. 'Do you mean as most gentlemen behave? That would be much to be thankful for! Of course Osmond's a gentleman; his own sister needn't be reminded of that. But does he think he can marry any girl he happens to pick out? Osmond's a gentleman, of course; but I must say I've *never*, no, no, never, seen anyone of Osmond's pretensions! What they're all founded on is more than I can say. I'm his own sister; I might be supposed to know. Who is he, if you please? What has he ever done? If there had been anything particularly grand in his origin – if he were made of some superior clay – I presume I should have got some inkling of it. If there had been any great honours or splendours in the family I should certainly have made the most of them: they would have been quite in my line. But there's nothing, nothing, nothing. One's parents were charming people of course; but so were yours, I've no doubt. Everyone's a charming person nowadays. Even I'm a charming person; don't laugh, it has literally been said. As for Osmond, he has always appeared to believe that he's descended from the gods.'

'You may say what you please,' said Madame Merle, who had listened to this quick outbreak none the less attentively, we may believe, because her eye wandered away from the speaker and her hands busied themselves with adjusting the knots of ribbon on her dress. 'You Osmonds are a fine race – your blood must flow from some very pure source. Your brother, like an intelligent man, has had the conviction of it if he has not had the proofs. You're modest about it, but you yourself are extremely distinguished. What do you say about your niece? The child's a little princess. Nevertheless,' Madame Merle added, 'it won't be an easy matter for Osmond to marry Miss Archer. Yet he can try.'

'I hope she'll refuse him. It will take him down a little.'

'We mustn't forget that he is one of the cleverest of men.'

'I've heard you say that before, but I haven't yet discovered what he has done.'

'What he has done? He has done nothing that has had to be undone. And he has known how to wait.'

'To wait for Miss Archer's money? How much of it is there?'

'That's not what I mean,' said Madame Merle. 'Miss Archer has seventy thousand pounds.'

'Well, it's a pity she's so charming,' the Countess declared. 'To be sacrificed, any girl would do. She needn't be superior.'

'If she weren't superior your brother would never look at her. He must have the best.'

'Yes,' returned the Countess as they went forward a little to meet the others, 'he's very hard to satisfy. That makes me tremble for her happiness!'

Chapter Twenty-six

Gilbert Osmond came to see Isabel again; that is he came to Palazzo Crescentini. He had other friends there as well, and to Mrs Touchett and Madame Merle he was always impartially civil; but the former of these ladies noted the fact that in the course of a fortnight he called five times, and compared it with another fact that she found no difficulty in remembering. Two visits a year had hitherto constituted his regular tribute to Mrs Touchett's worth, and she had never observed him select for such visits those moments, of almost periodical recurrence, when Madame Merle was under her roof. It was not for Madame Merle that he came; these two were old friends and he never put himself out for her. He was not fond of Ralph – Ralph had told her so – and it was not supposable that Mr Osmond had suddenly taken a fancy to her son. Ralph was imperturbable – Ralph had a kind of loose-fitting urbanity that wrapped him about like an ill-made overcoat, but of which he never divested himself; he thought Mr Osmond very good company and was willing at any time to look at him in the light of hospitality. But he didn't flatter himself that the desire to repair a past injustice was the motive of their visitor's calls; he read the situation more clearly. Isabel was the attraction, and in all conscience a sufficient one. Osmond was a critic, a student of the exquisite, and it was natural he should be curious of so rare an apparition. So when his mother observed to him that it was plain what Mr Osmond was thinking of, Ralph replied that he was quite of her opinion. Mrs Touchett had from far back found a place on her scant list for this gentleman, though wondering dimly by what art and what process – so negative and so wise as they were – he had everywhere effectively imposed himself. As he had never been an importunate visitor he had had no chance to be offensive, and he was recommended to her by his appearance of being as well able to do without her as she was to do without him – a quality that always, oddly enough, affected her as providing ground for a relation with her. It gave her no satisfaction, however, to think that he had taken it into his head to marry her niece. Such an alliance, on Isabel's part, would have an air of almost morbid perversity. Mrs Touchett easily remembered that the girl had refused an English peer; and that a young lady with whom Lord Warburton had not successfully wrestled should content herself with an obscure American dilettante, a middle-aged widower with an uncanny child and an ambiguous income, this answered to nothing in Mrs Touchett's conception of success. She took, it will be observed, not the sentimental, but the political, view of matrimony – a view which has always had much to recommend it. 'I trust she won't have the folly to listen to him,' she said to her son; to which Ralph replied that Isabel's listening was one thing and Isabel's answering quite another. He knew she had listened to several parties, as his father would have said, but had made them listen in return; and he found much entertainment in the idea that in these few months of his knowing her he should observe a fresh suitor at her gate. She had wanted to see life, and fortune was serving her to her taste; a succession of fine gentlemen going down on their knees to her would do as well as anything else. Ralph looked forward to a fourth, a fifth, a tenth besieger; he had no conviction she would stop at a third. She would keep the gate ajar and open a parley; she would certainly not allow number three to come in. He expressed this view, somewhat after this fashion, to his mother, who looked at him as if he had been dancing a jig. He had such a fanciful, pictorial way of saying things that he might as well address her in the deaf-mute's alphabet.

'I don't think I know what you mean,' she said; 'you use too many figures of speech; I could never understand allegories. The two words in the language I most respect are Yes and No. If Isabel wants to marry Mr Osmond she'll do so in spite of all your comparisons. Let her alone to find a fine one herself for anything she undertakes. I know very little about the young man in America; I don't think she spends much of her time in thinking of him, and I suspect he has got tired of waiting for her. There's nothing in life to prevent her marrying Mr Osmond if she only looks at him in a certain way. That's all very well; no one approves more than I of one's pleasing one's self. But she takes her pleasure in such odd things; she's capable of marrying Mr Osmond for the beauty of his opinions or for his autograph of Michelangelo. She wants to be disinterested: as if she were the only person who's in danger of not being so! Will *he* be so disinterested when he has the spending of her money? That was her idea before your father's death, and it has acquired new charms for her since. She ought to marry someone of whose disinterestedness she shall herself be sure; and there would be no such proof of that as his having a fortune of his own.'

'My dear mother, I'm not afraid,' Ralph answered. 'She's making fools of us all. She'll please herself, of course; but she'll do so by studying human nature at close quarters and yet retaining her liberty. She had started on an exploring exhibition, and I don't think she'll change her course, at the outset, at a signal from Gilbert Osmond. She may have slackened speed for an hour, but before we know it she'll be steaming away again. Excuse another metaphor.'

Mrs Touchett excused it perhaps, but was not so much reassured as to withhold from Madame Merle the expression of her fears. 'You who know everything,' she said, 'you must know this: whether that curious creature's really making love to my niece.'

'Gilbert Osmond?' Madame Merle widened her clear eyes and, with a full intelligence, 'Heaven help us,' she exclaimed, 'that's an idea!'

'Hadn't it occurred to you?'

'You make me feel an idiot, but I confess it hadn't. I wonder,' she added, 'if it has occurred to Isabel.'

'Oh, I shall now ask her,' said Mrs Touchett.

Madame Merle reflected. 'Don't put it into her head. The thing would be to ask Mr Osmond.'

'I can't do that,' said Mrs Touchett. 'I won't have him inquire of me – as he perfectly may with that air of his, given Isabel's situation – what business it is of mine.'

'I'll ask him myself,' Madame Merle bravely declared.

'But what business – for *him* – is it of yours?'

'It's being none whatever is just why I can afford to speak. It's so much less my business than any one's else that he can put me off with anything he chooses. But it will be by the way he does this that I shall know.'

'Pray let me hear then,' said Mrs Touchett, 'of the fruits of your penetration. If I can't speak to him, however, at least I can speak to Isabel.'

Her companion sounded at this the note of warning. 'Don't be too quick with her. Don't inflame her imagination.'

'I never did anything in life to anyone's imagination. But I'm always sure of her doing something – well, not of *my* kind.'

'No, you wouldn't like this,' Madame Merle observed without the point of interrogation.

'Why in the world should I, pray? Mr Osmond has nothing the least solid to offer.'

Again Madame Merle was silent while her thoughtful smile drew up her mouth even more charmingly than usual towards the left corner. 'Let us distinguish. Gilbert Osmond's certainly not the first comer. He's a man who in favourable conditions might very well make a great impression. He has made a great impression, to my knowledge, more than once.'

'Don't tell me about his probably quite cold-blooded love-affairs; they're nothing to me!' Mrs Touchett cried. 'What you say's precisely why I wish he would cease his visits. He has nothing in the world that I know of but a dozen or two of early masters and a more or less pert little daughter.'

'The early masters are now worth a good deal of money,' said Madame Merle, 'and the daughter's a very young and very innocent and very harmless person.'

'In other words she's an insipid little chit. Is that what you mean? Having no fortune she can't hope to marry as they marry here; so that Isabel will have to furnish her either with a maintenance or with a dowry.'

'Isabel probably wouldn't object to being kind to her. I think she likes the poor child.'

'Another reason then for Mr Osmond's stopping at home! Otherwise, a week hence, we shall have my niece arriving at the conviction that her mission in life's to prove that a stepmother may sacrifice herself – and that, to prove it, she must first become one.'

'She would make a charming stepmother,' smiled Madame Merle; 'but

I quite agree with you that she had better not decide upon her mission too hastily. Changing the form of one's mission's almost as difficult as changing the shape of one's nose: there they are, each, in the middle of one's face and one's character – one has to begin too far back. But I'll investigate and report to you.'

All this went on quite over Isabel's head; she had no suspicions that her relations with Mr Osmond were being discussed. Madame Merle had said nothing to put her on her guard; she alluded no more pointedly to him than to the other gentlemen of Florence, native and foreign, who now arrived in considerable numbers to pay their respects to Miss Archer's aunt. Isabel thought him interesting – she came back to that; she liked so to think of him. She had carried away an image from her visit to his hill-top which her subsequent knowledge of him did nothing to efface and which put on for her a particular harmony with other supposed and divined things, histories within histories: the image of a quiet, clever, sensitive, distinguished man, strolling on a moss-grown terrace above the sweet Val d'Arno and holding by the hand a little girl whose bell-like clearness gave a new grace to childhood. The picture had no flourishes, but she liked its lowness of tone and the atmosphere of summer twilight that pervaded it. It spoke of the kind of personal issue that touched her most nearly; of the choice between objects, subjects, contacts – what might she call them? – of a thin and those of a rich association; of a lonely, studious life in a lovely land; of an old sorrow that sometimes ached today; of a feeling of pride that was perhaps exaggerated, but that had an element of nobleness; of a care for beauty and perfection so natural and so cultivated together that the career appeared to stretch beneath it in the disposed vistas and with the ranges of steps and terraces and fountains of a formal Italian garden – allowing only for arid places freshened by the natural dews of a quaint half-anxious, half-helpless fatherhood. At Palazzo Crescentini Mr Osmond's manner remained the same; diffident at first – oh self-conscious beyond doubt! and full of the effort (visible only to a sympathetic eye) to overcome this disadvantage; an effort which usually resulted in a great deal of easy, lively, very positive, rather aggressive, always suggestive talk. Mr Osmond's talk was not injured by the indication of an eagerness to shine; Isabel found no difficulty in believing that a person was sincere who had so many of the signs of strong conviction – as for instance an explicit and graceful appreciation of anything that might be said on his own side of the question, said perhaps by Miss Archer in especial. What continued to please this young woman was that while he talked so for amusement he didn't talk, as she had heard people, for 'effect'. He uttered his ideas as if, odd as they often appeared, he were used to them and had lived with them; old polished knobs and heads and handles, of precious substance, that could be fitted if necessary to new walking-sticks – not switches plucked in destitution from the common tree and then too elegantly waved about. One day he brought his small daughter with him, and she rejoiced to renew acquaintance with the child, who, as she presented her forehead to be kissed by every member of the circle, reminded her vividly of an *ingénue* in a French play. Isabel had never seen a little person of this pattern; American girls were very different – different too were the maidens of England. Pansy was so formed and finished for her tiny place in the world, and yet in imagination, as one could see, so innocent and infantine.

She sat on the sofa by Isabel; she wore a small grenadine mantle and a pair of the useful gloves that Madame Merle had given her – little grey gloves with a single button. She was like a sheet of blank paper – the ideal *jeune fille* of foreign fiction. Isabel hoped that so fair and smooth a page would be covered with an edifying text.

The Countess Gemini also came to call upon her, but the Countess was quite another affair. She was by no means a blank sheet; she had been written over in a variety of hands, and Mrs Touchett, who felt by no means honoured by her visit, pronounced that a number of unmistakable blots were to be seen upon her surface. The Countess gave rise indeed to some discussion between the mistress of the house and the visitor from Rome, in which Madame Merle (who was not such a fool as to irritate people by always agreeing with them) availed herself felicitously enough of that large licence of dissent which her hostess permitted as freely as she practised it. Mrs Touchett had declared it a piece of audacity that this highly compromised character should have presented herself at such a time of day at the door of a house in which she was esteemed so little as she must long have known herself to be at Palazzo Crescentini. Isabel had been made acquainted with the estimate prevailing under that roof: it represented Mr Osmond's sister as a lady who had so mismanaged her improprieties that they had ceased to hang together at all – which was at the least what one asked of such matters – and had become the mere floating fragments of a wrecked renown, incommoding social circulation. She had been married by her mother – a more administrative person, with an appreciation of foreign titles which the daughter, to do her justice, had probably by this time thrown off – to an Italian nobleman who had perhaps given her some excuse for attempting to quench the consciousness of outrage. The Countess, however, had consoled herself outrageously, and the list of her excuses had now lost itself in the labyrinth of her adventures. Mrs Touchett had never consented to receive her, though the Countess had made overtures of old. Florence was not an austere city; but, as Mrs Touchett said, she had to draw the line somewhere.

Madame Merle defended the luckless lady with a great deal of zeal and wit. She couldn't see why Mrs Touchett should make a scapegoat of a woman who had really done no harm, who had only done good in the wrong way. One must certainly draw the line, but while one was about it one should draw it straight: it was a very crooked chalk-mark that would exclude the Countess Gemini. In that case Mrs Touchett had better shut up her house; this perhaps would be the best course so long as she remained in Florence. One must be fair and not make arbitrary differences: the Countess had doubtless been imprudent, she had not been so clever as other women. She was a good creature, not clever at all; but since when had that been a ground of exclusion from the best society? For ever so long now one had heard nothing about her, and there could be no better proof of her having renounced the error of her ways than her desire to become a member of Mrs Touchett's circle. Isabel could contribute nothing to this interesting dispute, not even a patient attention; she contented herself with having given a friendly welcome to the unfortunate lady, who, whatever her defects, had at least the merit of being Mr Osmond's sister. As she liked the brother Isabel thought it proper to try and like the sister: in spite of the growing complexity of things she was still capable of these primitive sequences. She had not received the happiest impression of the Countess on meeting her at the villa, but was thankful for an opportunity to repair the accident. Had not Mr Osmond remarked that she was a respectable person? To have proceeded from Gilbert Osmond this was a crude proposition, but Madame Merle bestowed upon it a certain improving polish. She told Isabel more about the poor Countess than Mr Osmond had done, and related the history of her marriage and its consequences. The Count was a member of an ancient Tuscan family, but of such small estate that he had been glad to accept Amy Osmond, in spite of the questionable beauty which had yet not hampered her career, with the modest dowry her mother was able to offer – a sum about equivalent to that which had already formed her brother's share of their patrimony. Count Gemini since then, however, had inherited money, and now they were well enough off, as Italians went, though Amy was horribly extravagant. The Count was a low-lived brute; he had given his wife every pretext. She had no children; she had lost three within a year of their birth. Her mother, who had bristled with pretensions to elegant learning and published descriptive poems and corresponded on Italian subjects with the English weekly journals, her mother had died three years after the Countess's marriage, the father, lost in the grey American dawn of the situation, but reputed originally rich and wild, having died much earlier. One could see this in Gilbert Osmond, Madame Merle held – see that he had been brought up by a woman; though, to do him justice, one would suppose it had been by a more sensible woman than the American Corinne, as Mrs Osmond had liked to be called. She had brought her children to Italy after her husband's death, and Mrs Touchett remembered her during the year that followed her arrival. She thought her a horrible snob; but this was an irregularity of judgement on Mrs Touchett's part, for she, like Mrs Osmond, approved of political marriages. The Countess was very good company and not really the featherhead she seemed; all one had to do with her was to observe the simple condition of not believing a word she said. Madame Merle had always made the best of her for her brother's sake; he appreciated any kindness shown to Amy, because (if it had to be confessed for him) he rather felt she let down their common name. Naturally he couldn't like her style, her shrillness, her egotism, her violations of taste and above all of truth: she acted badly on his nerves, she was not *his* sort of woman. What was his sort of woman? Oh, the very opposite of the Countess, a woman to whom the truth should be habitually sacred. Isabel was unable to estimate the number of times her visitor had, in half an hour, profaned it: the Countess indeed had given her an impression of rather silly sincerity. She had talked almost exclusively about herself; how much she should like to know Miss Archer; how thankful she should be for a real friend; how base the people in Florence were; how tired she was of the place; how much she should like to live somewhere else – in Paris, in London, in Washington; how impossible it was to get anything nice to wear in Italy except a little old lace; how dear the world was growing everywhere; what a life of suffering and privation she had led. Madame Merle listened with interest to Isabel's account of this passage, but she had not needed it to feel exempt from anxiety. On the whole she was not afraid of the Countess, and she could afford to do what was altogether best – not to appear so.

Isabel had meanwhile another visitor, whom it was not, even behind her back, so easy a matter to patronize. Henrietta Stackpole, who had left Paris after Mrs Touchett's departure for San Remo and had worked her way down, as she said, through the cities of North Italy, reached the banks of the Arno about the middle of May. Madame Merle surveyed her with a single glance, took her in from head to foot, and after a pang of despair determined to endure her. She determined indeed to delight in her. She mightn't be inhaled as a rose, but she might be grasped as a nettle. Madame Merle genially squeezed her into insignificance, and Isabel felt that in foreseeing this liberality she had done justice to her friend's intelligence. Henrietta's arrival had been announced by Mr Bantling, who, coming down from Nice while she was at Venice, and expecting to find her in Florence, which she had not yet reached, called at Palazzo Crescentini to express his disappointment. Henrietta's own advent occurred two days later and produced in Mr Bantling an emotion amply accounted for by the fact that he had not seen her since the termination of the episode at Versailles. The humorous view of his situation was generally taken, but it was uttered only by Ralph Touchett, who, in the privacy of his own apartment, when Bantling smoked a cigar there, indulged in goodness knew what strong comedy on the subject of the all-judging one and her British backer. This gentleman took the joke in perfectly good part and candidly confessed that he regarded the affair as a positive intellectual adventure. He liked Miss Stackpole extremely; he thought she had a wonderful head on her shoulders, and found great comfort in the society of a woman who was not perpetually thinking about what would be said and how what she did, how what *they* did – and they had done things! – would look. Miss Stackpole never cared how anything looked, and, if she didn't care, pray why should he? But his curiosity had been roused; he wanted awfully to see if she ever *would* care. He was prepared to go as far as she – he didn't see why he should break down first.

Henrietta showed no signs of breaking down. Her prospects had brightened on her leaving England, and she was now in the full enjoyment of her copious resources. She had indeed been obliged to sacrifice her hopes with regard to the inner life; the social question, on the Continent, bristled with difficulties even more numerous than those she had encountered in England. But on the Continent there was the outer life, which was palpable and visible at every turn, and more easily convertible to literary uses than the customs of those opaque islanders. Out of doors in foreign lands, as she ingeniously remarked, one seemed to see the right side of the tapestry; out of doors in England one seemed to see the wrong side, which gave one no notion of the figure. The admission costs her historian a pang, but Henrietta, despairing of more occult things, was not paying much attention to the outer life. She had been studying it for two months at Venice, from which city she sent to the *Interviewer* a conscientious account of the gondolas, the Piazza, the Bridge of Sighs, the pigeons, and the young boatman who chanted Tasso. The *Interviewer* was perhaps disappointed, but Henrietta was at least seeing Europe. Her present purpose was to get down to Rome before the malaria should come on – she apparently supposed that it began on a fixed day; and with this design she was to spend at present but few days in Florence. Mr Bantling was to go with her to Rome, and she pointed out to Isabel that as he had been there before, as he was a military man and as he had had a classical education – he had been bred at Eton, where they study nothing but Latin and Whyte-Melville, said Miss Stackpole – he would be a most useful companion in the city of the Caesars. At this juncture Ralph had the happy idea of proposing to Isabel that she also, under his own escort, should make a pilgrimage to Rome. She expected to pass a portion of the next winter there – that was very well; but meantime there was no harm in surveying the field. There were ten days left of the beautiful month of May – the most precious month of all to the true Rome-lover. Isabel would become a Rome-lover; that was a foregone conclusion. She was provided with a trusty companion of her own sex, whose society, thanks to the fact of other calls on this lady's attention, would probably not be oppressive. Madame Merle would remain with Mrs Touchett; she had left Rome for the summer and wouldn't care to return. She professed herself delighted to be left at peace in Florence; she had locked up her apartment and sent her cook home to Palestrina. She urged Isabel, however, to assent to Ralph's proposal, and assured her that a good introduction to Rome was not a thing to be despised. Isabel in truth needed no urging, and the party of four arranged its little journey. Mrs Touchett, on this occasion, had resigned herself to the absence of a duenna; we have seen that she now inclined to the belief that her niece should stand alone. One of Isabel's preparations consisted of her seeing Gilbert Osmond before she started and mentioning her intention to him.

'I should like to be in Rome with you,' he commented. 'I should like to see you on that wonderful ground.'

She scarcely faltered. 'You might come then.'

'But you'll have a lot of people with you.'

'Ah,' Isabel admitted, 'of course I shall not be alone.'

For a moment he said nothing more. 'You'll like it,' he went on at last. 'They've spoiled it, but you'll rave about it.'

'Ought I to dislike it because, poor old dear – the Niobe of Nations, you know – it has been spoiled?' she asked.

'No, I think not. It has been spoiled so often,' he smiled. 'If I were to go, what should I do with my little girl?'

'Can't you leave her at the villa?'

'I don't know that I like that – though there's a very good old woman who looks after her. I can't afford a governess.'

'Bring her with you then,' said Isabel promptly.

Mr Osmond looked grave. 'She has been in Rome all winter, at her convent; and she's too young to make journeys of pleasure.'

'You don't like bringing her forward?' Isabel inquired.

'No, I think young girls should be kept out of the world.'

'I was brought up on a different system.'

'You? Oh, with you it succeeded, because you – you were exceptional.'

'I don't see why,' said Isabel, who, however, was not sure there was not some truth in the speech.

Mr Osmond didn't explain; he simply went on; 'If I thought it would make her resemble you to join a social group in Rome I'd take her there tomorrow.'

'Don't make her resemble me,' said Isabel. 'Keep her like herself.'

'I might send her to my sister,' Mr Osmond observed. He had almost the air of asking advice; he seemed to like to talk over his domestic matters with Miss Archer.

'Yes,' she concurred; 'I think that wouldn't do much towards making her resemble me!'

After she had left Florence Gilbert Osmond met Madame Merle at the Countess Gemini's. There were other people present; the Countess's drawing-room was usually well filled, and the talk had been general, but after a while Osmond left his place and came and sat on an ottoman half-behind, half-besides Madame Merle's chair. 'She wants me to go to Rome with her,' he remarked in a low voice.

'To go with her?'

'To be there while she's there. She proposed it.'

'I suppose you mean that you proposed it and she assented.'

'Of course I gave her a chance. But she's encouraging – she's very encouraging.'

'I rejoice to hear it – but don't cry victory too soon. Of course you'll go to Rome.'

'Ah,' said Osmond, 'it makes one work, this idea of yours!'

'Don't pretend you don't enjoy it – you're very ungrateful. You've not been so well occupied these many years.'

'The way you talk it's beautiful,' said Osmond. 'I ought to be grateful for that.'

'Not too much so, however,' Madame Merle answered. She talked with her usual smile, leaning back in her chair and looking round the room. 'You've made a very good impression, and I've seen for myself that you've received one. You've not come to Mrs Touchett's seven times to oblige me.'

'The girl's not disagreeable,' Osmond quietly conceded.

Madame Merle dropped her eye on him a moment, during which her lips closed with a certain firmness. 'Is that all you can find to say about that fine creature?'

'All? Isn't it enough? Of how many people have you heard me say more?'

She made no answer to this, but still presented her talkative grace to the room. 'You're unfathomable,' she murmured at last. 'I'm frightened at the abyss into which I shall have cast her.'

He took it almost gaily. 'You can't draw back – you've gone too far.'

'Very good; but you must do the rest yourself.'

'I shall do it,' said Gilbert Osmond.

Madam Merle remained silent and he changed his place again; but when she rose to go he also took leave. Mrs Touchett's victoria was awaiting her guest in the court, and after he had helped his friend into it he stood there detaining her. 'You're very indiscreet,' she said rather wearily; 'you shouldn't have moved when I did.'

He had taken off his hat; he passed his hand over his forehead. 'I always forget; I'm out of the habit.'

'You're quite unfathomable,' she repeated, glancing up at the windows of the house, a modern structure in the new part of the town.

He paid no heed to this remark, but spoke in his own sense. 'She's really very charming. I've scarcely known anyone more graceful.'

'It does me good to hear you say that. The better you like her the better for me.'

'I like her very much. She's all you described her, and into the bargain capable, I feel, of great devotion. She has only one fault.'

'What's that?'

'Too many ideas.'

'I warned you she was clever.'

'Fortunately they're very bad ones,' said Osmond.

'Why is that fortunate?'

'*Dame*, if they must be sacrificed!'

Madame Merle leaned back, looking straight before her; then she spoke to the coachman. But her friend again detained her. 'If I go to Rome what shall I do with Pansy?'

'I'll go and see her,' said Madame Merle.

Chapter Twenty-seven

I may not attempt to report in it fulness our young woman's response to the deep appeal of Rome, to analyse her feelings as she trod the pavement of the Forum or to number her pulsations as she crossed the threshold of Saint Peter's. It is enough to say that her impression was such as might have been expected of a person of her freshness and her eagerness. She had always been fond of history, and here was history in the stones of the street and the atoms of the sunshine. She had an imagination that kindled at the mention of great deeds, and wherever she turned some great deed had been acted. These things strongly moved her, but moved her all inwardly. It seemed to her companions that she talked less than usual, and Ralph Touchett, when he appeared to be looking listlessly and awkwardly over her head, was really dropping on her an intensity of observation. By her own measure she was very happy; she would even have been willing to take these hours for the happiest she was ever to know. The sense of the terrible human past was heavy to her, but that of something altogether contemporary would suddenly give it wings that it could wave in the blue. Her consciousness was so mixed that she scarcely knew where the different parts of it would lead her, and she went about in a repressed ecstasy of contemplation, seeing often in the things she looked at a great deal more than was there, and yet not seeing many of the items enumerated in her Murray. Rome, as Ralph said confessed to the psychological moment. The herd of re-echoing tourists had departed and most of the solemn places had relapsed into solemnity. The sky was a blaze of blue, and the plash of the fountains in their mossy niches had lost its chill and doubled its music. On the corners of the warm, bright streets one stumbled on bundles of flowers. Our friends had gone one afternoon – it was the third of their stay – to look at the latest excavations in the Forum, these labours having been for some time previous largely extended. They had descended from the modern street to the level of the

Sacred Way, along which they wandered with a reverence of step which was not the same on the part of each. Henrietta Stackpole was struck with the fact that ancient Rome had been paved a good deal like New York, and even found an analogy between the deep chariot-ruts traceable in the antique street and the overjangled iron grooves which express the intensity of American life. The sun had begun to sink, the air was a golden haze, and the long shadows of broken column and vague pedestal leaned across the field of ruin. Henrietta wandered away with Mr Bantling, whom it was apparently delightful to her to hear speak of Julius Caesar as a 'cheeky old boy', and Ralph addressed such elucidations as he was prepared to offer to the attentive ear of our heroine. One of the humble archaeologists who hover about the place had put himself at the disposal of the two, and repeated his lesson with a fluency which the decline of the season had done nothing to impair. A process of digging was on view in a remote corner of the Forum, and he presently remarked that if it should please the *signori* to go and watch it a little they might see something of interest. The proposal commended itself more to Ralph than to Isabel, weary with much wandering; so that she admonished her companion to satisfy his curiosity while she patiently awaited his return. The hour and the place were much to her taste – she should enjoy being briefly alone. Ralph accordingly went off with the cicerone while Isabel sat down on a prostrate column near the foundations of the Capitol. She wanted a short solitude, but she was not long to enjoy it. Keen as was her interest in the rugged relics of the Roman past that lay scattered about her and in which the corrosion of centuries had still left so much of individual life, her thoughts, after resting a while on these things, had wandered, by a concatenation of stages it might require some subtlety to trace, to regions and objects charged with a more active appeal. From the Roman past to Isabel Archer's future was a long stride, but her imagination had taken it in a single flight and now hovered in slow circles over the nearer and richer field. She was so absorbed in her thoughts, as she bent her eyes upon a row of cracked but not dislocated slabs covering the ground at her feet, that she had not heard the sound of approaching footsteps before a shadow was thrown across the line of her vision. She looked up and saw a gentleman – a gentleman who was not Ralph come back to say that the excavations were a bore. This personage was startled as she was startled; he stood there baring his head to her perceptibly pale surprise.

'Lord Warburton!' Isabel exclaimed as she rose.

'I had no idea it was you. I turned that corner and came upon you.'

She looked about her to explain. 'I'm alone, but my companions have just left me. My cousin's gone to look at the work over there.'

'Ah yes; I see.' And Lord Warburton's eyes wandered vaguely in the direction she had indicated. He stood firmly before her now; he had recovered his balance and seemed to wish to show it, though very kindly. 'Don't let me disturb you,' he went on, looking at her dejected pillar. 'I'm afraid you're tired.'

'Yes, I'm rather tired.' She hesitated a moment, but sat down again. 'Don't let me interrupt *you*,' she added.

'Oh dear, I'm quite alone, I've nothing on earth to do. I had no idea you were in Rome. I've just come from the East. I'm only passing through.'

'You've been making a long journey,' said Isabel, who had learned from Ralph that Lord Warburton was absent from England.

'Yes, I came abroad for six months – soon after I saw you last. I've been in Turkey and Asia Minor; I came the other day from Athens.' He managed not to be awkward, but he wasn't easy, and after a longer look at the girl he came down to nature. 'Do you wish me to leave you, or will you let me stay a little?'

She took it all humanely. 'I don't wish you to leave me, Lord Warburton; I'm very glad to see you.'

'Thank you for saying that. May I sit down?'

The fluted shaft on which she had taken her seat would have afforded a resting-place to several persons, and there was plenty of room even for a highly developed Englishman. This fine specimen of that great class seated himself near our young lady, and in the course of five minutes he had asked her several questions, taken rather at random and to which, as he put some of them twice over, he apparently somewhat missed catching the answer; had given her too some information about himself which was not wasted upon her calmer feminine sense. He repeated more than once that he had not expected to meet her, and it was evident that the encounter touched him in a way that would have made preparation advisable. He began abruptly to pass from the impunity of things to their solemnity, and from their being delightful to their being impossible. He was splendidly sunburnt; even his multitudinous beard had been burnished by the fire of Asia. He was dressed in the loose-fitting, heterogeneous garments in which the English traveller in foreign lands is wont to consult his comfort and affirm his nationality; and with his pleasant steady eyes, his bronzed complexion, fresh beneath its seasoning, his manly figure, his minimizing manner and his general air of being a gentleman and an explorer, he was such a representative of the British race as need not in any clime have been disavowed by those who have a kindness for it. Isabel noted these things and was glad she had always liked him. He had kept, evidently in spite of shocks, every one of his merits – properties these partaking of the essence of great decent houses, as one might put it; resembling their innermost fixtures and ornaments, not subject to vulgar shifting and removable only by some whole break-up. They talked of the matters naturally in order; her uncle's death, Ralph's state of health, the way she had passed her winter, her visit to Rome, her return to Florence, her plans for the summer, the hotel she was staying at; and then of Lord Warburton's own adventures, movements, intentions, impressions, and present domicile. At last there was a silence, and it said so much more than either had said that it scarce needed his final words. 'I've written to you several times.'

'Written to me? I've never had your letters.'

'I never sent them. I burned them up.'

'Ah,' laughed Isabel, 'it was better that you should do that than I!'

'I thought you wouldn't care for them,' he went on with a simplicity that touched her. 'It seemed to me that after all I had no right to trouble you with letters.'

'I should have been very glad to have news of you. You know how I hoped that – that—' But she stopped; there would be such a flatness in the utterance of her thought.

'I know what you're going to say. You hoped we should always remain good friends.' This formula, as Lord Warburton uttered it, was certainly flat enough; but then he was interested in making it appear so.

She found herself reduced simply to 'Please don't talk of all that'; a speech which hardly struck her as improvement on the other.

'It's a small consolation to allow me!' her companion exclaimed with force.

'I can't pretend to console you,' said the girl, who, all still as she sat there, threw herself back with a sort of inward triumph on the answer that had satisfied him so little six months before. He was pleasant, he was powerful, he was gallant; there was no better man than he. But her answer remained.

'It's very well you don't try to console me; it wouldn't be in your power,' she heard him say through the medium of her strange elation.

'I hoped we should meet again, because I had no fear you would attempt to make me feel I had wronged you. But when you do that – the pain's greater than the pleasure.' And she got up with a small conscious majesty, looking for her companions.

'I don't want to make you feel that; of course I can't say that. I only just want you to know one or two things – in fairness to myself, as it were. I won't return to the subject again. I felt very strongly what I expressed to you last year; I couldn't think of anything else. I tried to forget – energetically, systematically. I tried to take an interest in somebody else. I tell you this because I want you to know I did my duty. I didn't succeed. It was for the same purpose I went abroad – as far away as possible. They say travelling distracts the mind, but it didn't distract mine. I've thought of you perpetually, ever since I last saw you. I'm exactly the same. I love you just as much, and everything I said to you then is just as true. This instant at which I speak to you shows me again exactly how, to my great misfortune, you just insuperably *charm* me. There – I can't say less. I don't mean, however, to insist; it's only for a moment. I may add that when I came upon you a few minutes since, without the smallest idea of seeing you, I was, upon my honour, in the very act of wishing I knew where you were.' He had recovered his self-control, and while he spoke it became complete. He might have been addressing a small committee – making all quietly and clearly a statement of importance; aided by an occasional look at a paper of notes concealed in his hat, which he had not again put on. And the committee, assuredly, would have felt the point proved.

'I've often thought of you, Lord Warburton,' Isabel answered. 'You may be sure I shall always do that.' And she added in a tone of which she tried to keep up the kindness and keep down the meaning: 'There's no harm in that on either side.'

They walked along together, and she was prompt to ask about his sisters and request him to let them know she had done so. He made for the moment no further reference to their great question, but dipped again into shallower and safer waters. But he wished to know when she was to leave Rome, and on her mentioning the limit of her stay declared he was glad it was still so distant.

'Why do you say that if you yourself are only passing through?' she inquired with some anxiety.

'Ah, when I said I was passing through I didn't mean that one would treat Rome as if it were Clapham Junction. To pass through Rome is to stop a week or two.'

'Say frankly that you mean to stay as long as I do!'

His flushed smile, for a little, seemed to sound her. 'You won't like that. You're afraid you'll see too much of me.'

'It doesn't matter what I like. I certainly can't expect you to leave this delightful place on my account. But I confess I'm afraid of you.'

'Afraid I'll begin again? I promise to be very careful.'

They had gradually stopped and they stood a moment face to face. 'Poor Lord Warburton!' she said with a compassion intended to be good for both of them.

'Poor Lord Warburton indeed! But I'll be careful.'

'You may be unhappy, but you shall not make *me* so. That I can't allow.'

'If I believed I could make you unhappy I think I should try it.' At this she walked in advance and he also proceeded. 'I'll never say a word to displease you.'

'Very good. If you do, our friendship's at an end.'

'Perhaps some day – after a while – you'll give me leave.'

'Give you leave to make me unhappy?'

He hesitated. 'To tell you again—' But he checked himself. 'I'll keep it down. I'll keep it down always.'

Ralph Touchett had been joined in his visit to the excavation by Miss Stackpole and her attendant, and these three now emerged from among the mounds of earth and stone collected round the aperture and came into sight of Isabel and her companion. Poor Ralph hailed his friend with joy qualified by wonder, and Henrietta exclaimed in a high voice 'Gracious, there's that lord!' Ralph and his English neighbour greeted with the austerity with which, after long separations, English neighbours greet, and Miss Stackpole rested her large intellectual gaze upon the sunburnt traveller. But she soon established her relation to the crisis. 'I don't suppose you remember me, sir.'

'Indeed I do remember you,' said Lord Warburton. 'I asked you to come and see me, and you never came.'

'I don't go everywhere I'm asked,' Miss Stackpole answered coldly.

'Ah well, I won't ask you again,' laughed the master of Lockleigh.

'If you do I'll go; so be sure!'

Lord Warburton, for all his hilarity, seemed sure enough. Mr Bantling had stood by without claiming a recognition, but he now took occasion to nod to his lordship, who answered him with a friendly 'Oh, you here, Bantling?' and a handshake.

'Well,' said Henrietta, 'I didn't know you knew him!'

'I guess you don't know everyone I know,' Mr Bantling rejoined facetiously.

'I thought that when an Englishman knew a lord he always told you.'

'Ah, I'm afraid Bantling was ashamed of me,' Lord Warburton laughed again. Isabel took pleasure in that note; she gave a small sigh of relief as they kept their course homeward.

The next day was Sunday; she spent her morning over two long letters – one to her sister Lily, the other to Madame Merle; but in neither of these epistles did she mention the fact that a rejected suitor had threatened her with another appeal. Of a Sunday afternoon all good Romans (and the best

Romans are often the northern barbarians) follow the custom of going to vespers at Saint Peter's; and it had been agreed among our friends that they would drive together to the great church. After lunch, an hour before the carriage came, Lord Warburton presented himself at the Hôtel de Paris and paid a visit to the two ladies, Ralph Touchett and Mr Bantling having gone out together. The visitor seemed to have wished to give Isabel a proof of his intention to keep the promise made her the evening before; he was both discreet and frank – not even dumbly importunate or remotely intense. He thus left her to judge what a mere good friend he could be. He talked about his travels, about Persia, about Turkey, and when Miss Stackpole asked him whether it would 'pay' for her to visit those countries assured her they offered a great field to female enterprise. Isabel did him justice, but she wondered what his purpose was and what he expected to gain even by proving the superior strain of his sincerity. If he expected to melt her by showing what a good fellow he was, he might spare himself the trouble. She knew the superior strain of everything about him, and nothing he could now do was required to light the view. Moreover his being in Rome at all affected her as a complication of the wrong sort – she liked so complications of the right. Nevertheless, when, on bringing his call to a close, he said he too should be at Saint Peter's and should look out for her and her friends, she was obliged to reply that he must follow his convenience.

In the church, as she strolled over its tesselated acres, he was the first person she encountered. She had not been one of the superior tourists who are 'disappointed' in Saint Peter's and find it smaller than its fame; the first time she passed beneath the huge leathern curtain that strains and bangs at the entrance, the first time she found herself beneath the far-arching dome and saw the light drizzle down through the air thickened with incense and with the reflections of marble and gilt, of mosaic and bronze, her conception of greatness rose and dizzily rose. After this it never lacked space to soar. She gazed and wondered like a child or a peasant, she paid her silent tribute to the seated sublime. Lord Warburton walked beside her and talked of Saint Sophia of Constantinople; she feared for instance that he would end by calling attention to his exemplary conduct. The service had not yet begun, but at Saint Peter's there is much to observe, and as there is something almost profane in the vastness of the place, which seems meant as much for physical as for spiritual exercise, the different figures and groups, the mingled worshippers and spectators, may follow their various intentions without conflict or scandal. In that splendid immensity individual indiscretion carries but a short distance. Isabel and her companions, however, were guilty of none; for though Henrietta was obliged in candour to declare that Michelangelo's dome suffered by comparison with that of the Capitol at Washington, she addressed her protest chiefly to Mr Bantling's ear and reserved it in its more accentuated form for the columns of the *Interviewer*. Isabel made the circuit of the church with his lordship, and as they drew near the choir on the left of the entrance the voices of the Pope's singers were borne to them over the heads of the large number of persons clustered outside the doors. They paused a while on the skirts of this crowd, composed in equal measure of Roman cockneys and inquisitive strangers, and while they stood there the sacred concert went forward. Ralph, with Henrietta and Mr Bantling, was apparently within, where Isabel, looking beyond the dense group in front of her, saw the afternoon light silvered by clouds of incense that seemed to mingle with the splendid chant, slope through the embossed recesses of high windows. After a while the singing stopped and then Lord Warburton seemed disposed to move off with her. Isabel could only accompany him; whereupon she found herself confronted with Gilbert Osmond, who appeared to have been standing at a short distance behind her. He now approached with all the forms – he appeared to have multiplied them on this occasion to suit the place.

'So you decided to come?' she said as she put out her hand.

'Yes, I came last night and called this afternoon at your hotel. They told me you had come here, and I looked about for you.'

'The others are inside,' she decided to say.

'I didn't come for the others,' he promptly returned.

She looked away; Lord Warburton was watching them; perhaps he had heard this. Suddenly she remembered it to be just what he had said to her the morning he came to Gardencourt to ask her to marry him. Mr Osmond's words had brought the colour to her cheek, and this reminiscence had not the effect of dispelling it. She repaired any betrayal by mentioning to each companion the name of the other, and fortunately at this moment Mr Bantling emerged from the choir, cleaving the crowd with British valour and followed by Miss Stackpole and Ralph Touchett. I say fortunately, but this is perhaps a superficial view of the matter; since on perceiving the gentleman from Florence Ralph Touchett appeared to take the case as not committing him to joy. He didn't hang back, however, from civility, and presently observed to Isabel, with due benevolence, that she would soon have all her friends about her. Miss Stackpole had met Mr Osmond in Florence, but she had already found occasion to say to Isabel that she liked him no better than her other admirers – than Mr Touchett and Lord Warburton, and even than little Mr Rosier in Paris. 'I don't know what it's in you,' she had been pleased to remark, 'but for a nice girl you do attract the most unnatural people. Mr Goodwood's the only one I've any respect for, and he's just the one you don't appreciate.'

'What's your opinion of Saint Peter's?' Mr Osmond was meanwhile inquiring of our young lady.

'It's very large and very bright,' she contented herself with replying.

'It's too large; it makes one feel like an atom.'

'Isn't that the right way to feel in the greatest of human temples?' she asked with rather a liking for her phrase.

'I suppose it's the right way to feel everywhere, when one *is* nobody. But I like it in a church as little as anywhere else.'

'You ought indeed to be a Pope!' Isabel exclaimed, remembering something he had referred to in Florence.

'Ah, I should have enjoyed that!' said Gilbert Osmond.

Lord Warburton meanwhile had joined Ralph Touchett, and the two strolled away together. 'Who's the fellow speaking to Miss Archer?' his lordship demanded.

'His name's Gilbert Osmond – he lives in Florence,' Ralph said.

'What is he besides?'

'Nothing at all. Oh yes, he's an American, but one forget that – he's so little of one.'

'Has he known Miss Archer long?'

'Three or four weeks.'

'Does she like him?'

'She's trying to find out.'

'And will she?'

'Find out—?' Ralph asked.

'Will she like him?'

'Do you mean will she accept him?'

'Yes,' said Lord Warburton after an instant; 'I suppose that's what I horribly mean.'

'Perhaps not if one does nothing to prevent it,' Ralph replied.

His lordship stared a moment, but apprehended. 'Then we must be perfectly quiet?'

'As quiet as the grave. And only on the chance!' Ralph added.

'The chance she may?'

'The chance she may not?'

Lord Warburton took this at first in silence, but he spoke again. 'Is he awfully clever?'

'Awfully,' said Ralph.

His companion thought. 'And what else?'

'What more do you want?' Ralph groaned.

'Do you mean what more does *she*?'

Ralph took him by the arm to turn him: they had to rejoin the others. 'She wants nothing that *we* can give her.'

'Ah well, if she won't have You—!' said his lordship handsomely as they went.

Chapter Twenty-eight

On the morrow, in the evening, Lord Warburton went again to see his friends at their hotel, and at this establishment he learned that they had gone to the opera. He drove to the opera with the idea of paying them a visit in their box after the easy Italian fashion; and when he had obtained his admittance – it was one of the secondary theatres – looked about the large, bare, ill-lighted house. An act had just terminated and he was at liberty to pursue his quest. After scanning two or three tiers of boxes he perceived in one of the largest of these receptacles a lady whom he easily recognized. Miss Archer was seated facing the stage and partly screened by the curtain of the box; and beside her, leaning back in his chair, was Mr Gilbert Osmond. They appeared to have the place to themselves, and Warburton supposed their companions had taken advantage of the recess to enjoy the relative coolness of the lobby. He stood a while with his eyes on the interesting pair; he asked himself if he should go up and interrupt the harmony. At last he judged that Isabel had seen him, and this accident determined him. There should be no marked holding off. He took his way to the upper regions and on the staircase met Ralph Touchett slowly descending, his hat at the inclination of ennui and his hands where they usually were.

'I saw you below a moment since and was going down to you. I feel lonely and want company,' was Ralph's greeting.

'You've some that's very good which you've yet deserted.'

'Do you mean my cousin? Oh, she has a visitor and doesn't want me. Then Miss Stackpole and Bantling have gone out to a café to eat an ice – Miss Stackpole delights in an ice. I didn't think *they* wanted me either. The opera's very bad: the women look like laundresses and sing like peacocks. I felt very low.'

'You had better go home,' Lord Warburton said without affectation.

'And leave my young lady in this sad place? Ah no, I must watch over her.'

'She seems to have plenty of friends.'

'Yes, that's why I must watch,' said Ralph with the same large mock-melancholy.

'If she doesn't want you it's probable she doesn't want me.'

'No, you're different. Go to the box and stay there while I walk about.'

Lord Warburton went to the box, where Isabel's welcome was as to a friend so honourably old that he vaguely asked himself what queer temporal province she was annexing. He exchanged greetings with Mr Osmond, to whom he had been introduced the day before and who, after he came in, sat blandly apart and silent, as if repudiating competence in the subjects of allusion now probable. It struck her second visitor that Miss Archer had, in operatic conditions, a radiance, even a slight exaltation; as she was, however, at all times a keenly glancing quickly moving, completely animated young woman, he may have been mistaken on this point. Her talk with him moreover pointed to presence of mind; it expressed a kindness so ingenious and deliberate as to indicate that she was in undisturbed possession of her faculties. Poor Lord Warburton had moments of bewilderment. She had discouraged him, formally, as much as a woman could; what business had she then with such arts and such felicities, above all with such tones of reparation – preparation? Her voice had tricks of sweetness, but why play them on *him*? The others came back; the bare, familiar, trivial opera began again. The box was large, and there was room for him to remain if he would sit a little behind and in the dark. He did so for half an hour, while Mr Osmond remained in front, leaning forward, his elbows on his knees, just behind Isabel. Lord Warburton heard nothing, and from his gloomy corner saw nothing but the clear profile of this young lady defined against the dim illumination of the house. When there was another interval no one moved. Mr Osmond talked to Isabel, and Lord Warburton kept his corner. He did so but for a short time, however; after which he got up and bade good night to the ladies. Isabel said nothing to detain him, but it didn't prevent his being puzzled again. Why should she mark so one of his values – quite the wrong one – when she would have nothing to do with another, which was quite right? He was angry with himself for being puzzled, and then angry for being angry, Verdi's music did little to comfort him, and he left the theatre and walked homeward, without knowing his way, through the tortuous, tragic streets of Rome, where heavier sorrows than his had been carried under the stars.

'What's the character of that gentleman?' Osmond asked of Isabel after he had retired.

'Irreproachable – don't you see it?'

'He owns about half England; that's his character,' Henrietta remarked. 'That's what they call a free country!'

'Ah, he's a great proprietor? Happy man!' said Gilbert Osmond.

'Do you call that happiness – the ownership of wretched human beings?' cried Miss Stackpole. 'He owns his tenants and has thousands of them. It's pleasant to own something, but inanimate objects are enough for me. I don't insist on flesh and blood and minds and consciences.'

'It seems to me you own a human being or two,' Mr Bantling suggested jocosely. 'I wonder if Warburton orders his tenants about as you do me.'

'Lord Warburton's a great radical,' Isabel said. 'He has very advanced opinions.'

'He has very advanced stone walls. His park's enclosed by a gigantic iron fence, some thirty miles round,' Henrietta announced for the information of Mr Osmond. 'I should like him to converse with a few of our Boston radicals.'

'Don't they approve of iron fences?' asked Mr Bantling.

'Only to shut up wicked conservatives. I always feel as if I were talking to *you* over something with a neat top-finish of broken glass.'

'Do you know him well, this unreformed reformer?' Osmond went on questioning Isabel.

'Well enough for all the use I have for him.'

'And how much of a use is that?'

'Well, I like to like him.'

' "Liking to like" – why, it makes a passion!' said Osmond.

'No' – she considered – 'keep that for liking to *dis*like.'

'Do you wish to provoke me then,' Osmond laughed, 'to a passion for *him*?'

She said nothing for a moment, but then met the light question with a disproportionate gravity. 'No, Mr Osmond; I don't think I should ever dare to provoke you. Lord Warburton, at any rate,' she more easily added, 'is a very nice man.'

'Of great ability?' her friend inquired.

'Of excellent ability, and as good as he looks.'

'As good as he's good-looking do you mean? He's very good-looking. How detestably fortunate! – to be a great English magnate, to be clever and handsome into the bargain, and, by way of finishing off, to enjoy your high favour! That's a man I could envy.'

Isabel considered him with interest. 'You seem to me to be always envying someone. Yesterday it was the Pope; today it's poor Lord Warburton.'

'My envy's not dangerous; it wouldn't hurt a mouse. I don't want to destroy the people – I only want to *be* them. You see it would destroy only myself.'

'You'd like to be the Pope?' said Isabel.

'I should love it – but I should have gone in for it earlier. But why' – Osmond reverted – 'do you speak of your friend as poor?'

'Women – when they are very, very good – sometimes pity men after they've hurt them; that's their great way of showing kindness,' said Ralph, joining in the conversation for the first time and with a cynicism so transparently ingenious as to be virtually innocent.

'Pray, have I hurt Lord Warburton?' Isabel asked, raising her eyebrows as if the idea were perfectly fresh.

'It serves him right if you have,' said Henrietta while the curtain rose for the ballet.

Isabel saw no more of her attributive victim for the next twenty-four hours, but on the second day after the visit to the opera she encountered him in the gallery of the Capitol, where he stood before the lion of the collection, the statue of the Dying Gladiator. She had come in with her companions, among whom, on this occasion again, Gilbert Osmond had his place, and the party, having ascended the staircase, entered the first and finest of the rooms. Lord Warburton addressed her alertly enough, but said in a moment that he was leaving the gallery. 'And I'm leaving Rome,' he added. 'I must bid you good-bye.' Isabel, inconsequently enough, was now sorry to hear it. This was perhaps because she had ceased to be afraid of his renewing his suit; she was thinking of something else. She was on the point of naming her regret, but she checked herself and simply wished him a happy journey; which made him look at her rather unlightedly. 'I'm afraid you'll think me very "volatile". I told you the other day I wanted so much to stop.'

'Oh no; you could easily change your mind.'

'That's what I have done.'

'*Bon voyage* then.'

'You're in a great hurry to get rid of me,' said his lordship quite dismally.

'Not in the least. But I hate partings.'

'You don't care what I do,' he went on pitifully.

Isabel looked at him a moment. 'Ah,' she said, 'you're not keeping your promise!'

He coloured like a boy of fifteen. 'If I'm not, then it's because I can't; and that's why I'm going.'

'Good-bye then.'

'Good-bye.' He lingered still, however. 'When shall I see you again?'

Isabel hesitated, but soon, as if she had had a happy inspiration: 'Some day after you're married.'

'That will never be. It will be after you are.'

'That will do as well,' she smiled.

'Yes, quite as well. Good-bye.'

They shook hands, and he left her alone in the glorious room, among the shining antique marbles. She sat down in the centre of the circle of these presences, regarding them vaguely, resting her eyes on their beautiful blank faces; listening, as it were, to their eternal silence. It is impossible, in Rome at least, to look long at a great company of Greek sculptures without feeling the effect of their noble quietude; which, as with a high door closed for the ceremony, slowly drops on the spirit the large white mantle of peace. I say in Rome especially, because the Roman air is an exquisite medium for such impressions. The golden sunshine mingles with them, the deep stillness of the past, so vivid yet, though it is nothing but a void full of names, seems to throw a solemn spell upon them. The blinds were partly closed in the windows of the Capitol, and a clear, warm shadow rested on the figures and made them more mildly human. Isabel sat there a long time, under the charm of their motionless grace, wondering to what, of their experience, their absent eyes were open, and how, to our ears, their alien lips would sound. The dark red walls of the room threw them into relief; the polished marble floor reflected their beauty. She had seen them all before, but her enjoyment repeated itself, and it was all the greater because she was glad again, for the time, to be alone. At last, however, her attention lapsed, drawn off by a deeper tide of life. An occasional tourist came in, stopped and stared a moment at the Dying Gladiator, and then passed out of the other door, creaking over the smooth pavement. At the end of half an hour Gilbert Osmond reappeared, apparently in advance of his companions. He strolled towards her slowly, with his hands behind him and his usual inquiring, yet not quite appealing smile. 'I'm surprised to find you alone, I thought you had company.'

'So I have – the best.' And she glanced at the Antinous and the Faun.

'Do you call them better company than an English peer?'

'Ah, my English peer left me some time ago.' She got up, speaking with intention a little dryly.

Mr Osmond noted her dryness, which contributed for him to the interest of his question. 'I'm afraid that what I heard the other evening is true: you're rather cruel to that nobleman.'

Isabel looked a moment at the vanquished Gladiator. 'It's not true. I'm scrupulously kind.'

'That's exactly what I mean!' Gilbert Osmond returned, and with such happy hilarity that his joke needs to be explained. We know that he was fond of originals, of rarities, of the superior and the exquisite; and now that he had seen Lord Warburton, whom he thought a very fine example of his race and order, he perceived a new attraction in the idea of taking to himself a young lady who had qualified herself to figure in his collection of choice objects by declining so noble a hand. Gilbert Osmond had a high appreciation of this particular patriciate; not so much for its distinction, which he thought easily surpassable, as for its solid actuality. He had never forgiven his star for not appointing him to an English dukedom, and he could measure the unexpectedness of such conduct as Isabel's. It would be proper that the woman he might marry should have done something of that sort.

Chapter Twenty-nine

Ralph Touchett, in talk with his excellent friend, had rather markedly qualified, as we know, his recognition of Gilbert Osmond's personal merits; but he might really have felt himself illiberal in the light of that gentleman's conduct during the rest of the visit to Rome. Osmond spent a portion of each day with Isabel and her companions, and ended by affecting them as the easiest of men to live with. Who wouldn't have seen that he could command, as it were, both tact and gaiety? – which perhaps was exactly why Ralph had made his old-time look of superficial sociability a reproach to him. Even Isabel's invidious kinsman was obliged to admit that he was just now a delightful associate. His good-humour was imperturbable, his knowledge of the right fact, his production of the right word, as convenient as the friendly flicker of a match for your cigarette. Clearly he was amused – as amused as a man could be who was so little ever surprised, and that made him almost applausive. It was not that his spirits were visibly high – he would never, in the concert of pleasure, touch the big drum by so much as a knuckle: he had a mortal dislike to the high, ragged note, to what he called random ravings. He thought Miss Archer sometimes of too precipitate a readiness. It was pity she had that fault, because if she had not had it she would really have had none; she would have been as smooth to his general need of her as handled ivory to the palm. If he was not personally loud, however, he was deep, and during these closing days of the Roman May he knew a complacency that matched with slow irregular walks under the pines of the Villa Borghese, among the small sweet meadow-flowers and the mossy marbles. He was pleased with everything; he had never before been pleased with so many things at once. Old impressions, old enjoyments, renewed themselves; one evening, going home to his room at the inn, he wrote down a little sonnet to which he prefixed the title of 'Rome Revisited'. A day or two later he showed this piece of correct and ingenious verse to Isabel, explaining to her that it was an Italian fashion to commemorate the occasions of life by a tribute to the muse.

He took his pleasures in general singly; he was too often – he would have admitted that – too sorely aware of something wrong, something ugly; the fertilizing dew of a conceivable felicity too seldom descended on his spirit. But at present he was happy – happier than he had perhaps ever been in his life, and the feeling had a large foundation. This was simply the sense of success – the most agreeable emotion of the human heart. Osmond had never had too much of it; in this respect he had the irritation of satiety, as he knew perfectly well and often reminded himself. 'Ah no, I've not been spoiled; certainly I've not been spoiled,' he used inwardly to repeat. 'If I do succeed before I die I shall thoroughly have earned it.' He was too apt to reason as if 'earning' this boon consisted above all of covertly aching for it and might be confined to that exercise. Absolutely void of it, also, his career had not been; he might indeed have suggested to a spectator here and there that he was resting on vague laurels. But his triumphs were, some of them, now too old; others had been too easy. The present one had been less arduous than might have been expected, but had been easy – that is had been rapid – only because he had made an altogether exceptional effort, a greater effort than he had believed it in him to make. The desire to have something or other to show for his 'parts' – to show somehow or other – had been the dream of his youth; but as the years went on the conditions attached to any marked proof of rarity had affected him more and more as gross and detestable; like the swallowing of mugs of beer to advertise what one could 'stand'. If an anonymous drawing on a museum wall had been conscious and watchful it might have known this peculiar pleasure of being at last and all of a sudden identified – as from the hand of a great master – by the so high and so unnoticed fact of style. His 'style' was what the girl discovered with a little help; and now, beside herself enjoying it, she should publish it to the world without his having any of the trouble. She should do the thing *for* him, and he would not have waited in vain.

Shortly before the time fixed in advance for her departure this young lady received from Mrs Touchett a telegram running as follows: 'Leave Florence 4th June for Bellaggio, and take you if you have not other views. But can't wait if you dawdle in Rome.' The dawdling in Rome was very pleasant, but Isabel had different views, and she let her aunt know she would immediately join her. She told Gilbert Osmond that she had done so, and he replied that, spending many of his summers as well as his winters in Italy, he himself would loiter a little longer in the cool shadow of Saint Peter's. He would not return to Florence for ten days more, and in that time she would have started for Bellaggio. It might be months in this case before he should see her again. This exchange took place in the large decorated sitting-room occupied by our friends at the hotel; it was late in the evening and Ralph Touchett was to take his cousin back to Florence on the morrow. Osmond had found the girl alone; Miss Stackpole had contracted a friendship with a delightful American family on the fourth floor and had mounted the interminable staircase to pay them a visit. Henrietta contracted friendships, in travelling, with great freedom, and had formed in railway carriages several that were among her most valued ties. Ralph was making arrangements for the morrow's journey, and Isabel sat alone in a wilderness of yellow upholstery. The chairs and sofas were orange; the walls and windows were draped in purple and gilt. The mirrors, the pictures had great flamboyant frames; the ceiling was deeply vaulted and painted over with naked muses and cherubs. For Osmond the place was ugly to distress; the false colours, the sham splendour were like vulgar, bragging, lying talk. Isabel had taken in hand a volume of Ampère, presented, on their arrival in Rome, by Ralph; but though she held it in her lap with her finger vaguely kept in the place she was not impatient to pursue her study. A lamp covered with a drooping veil of pink tissue-paper burned on the table beside her and diffused a strange pale rosiness over the scene.

'You say you'll come back; but who knows?' Gilbert Osmond said. 'I think you're more likely to start on your voyage round the world. You're under no obligation to come back; you can do exactly what you choose; you can roam through space.'

'Well, Italy's a part of space,' Isabel answered. 'I can take it on the way.'

'On the way round the world? No, don't do that. Don't put us in a parenthesis – give us a chapter to ourselves. I don't want to see you on your travels. I'd rather see you when they're over. I should like to see you when you're tired and satiated,' Osmond added in a moment. 'I shall prefer you in that state.'

Isabel, with her eyes bent, fingered the pages of M. Ampère. 'You turn things into ridicule without seeming to do it, though not, I think, without intending it. You've no respect for my travels – you think them ridiculous.'

'Where do you find that?'

She went on in the same tone, fretting the edge of her book with the paper-knife. 'You see my ignorance, my blunders, the way I wander about as if the world belonged to me, simply because – because it has been put into my power to do so. You don't think a woman ought to do that. You think it bold and ungraceful.'

'I think it beautiful,' said Osmond. 'You know my opinions – I've treated you to enough of them. Don't you remember my telling you that one ought to make one's life a work of art? You looked rather shocked at first; but then I told you that it was exactly what you seemed to me to be trying to do with your own.'

She looked up from her book. 'What you despise most in the world is bad, is stupid art.'

'Possibly. But yours seem to me very clear and very good.'

'If I were to go to Japan next winter you would laugh at me,' she went on.

Osmond gave a smile – a keen one, but not a laugh, for the tone of their conversation was not jocose. Isabel had in fact her solemnity; he had seen it before. 'You have an imagination that startles one!'

'That's exactly what I say. You think such an idea absurd.'

'I would give my little finger to go to Japan; it's one of the countries I want most to see. Can't you believe that, with my taste for old lacquer?'

'I haven't a taste for old lacquer to excuse me,' said Isabel.

'You've a better excuse – the means of going. You're quite wrong in your theory that I laugh at you. I don't know what has put it into your head.'

'It wouldn't be remarkable if you did think it ridiculous that I should have the means to travel when you've not; for you know everything, and I know nothing.'

'The more reason why you should travel and learn,' smiled Osmond. 'Besides,' he added as if it were a point to be made, 'I don't know everything.'

Isabel was not struck with the oddity of his saying this gravely; she was thinking that the pleasantest incident of her life – so it pleased her to qualify these too few days in Rome, which she might musingly have likened to the figure of some small princess of one of the ages of dress over-muffled in a mantle of state and dragging a train that it took pages or historians to hold up – that this felicity was coming to an end. That most of the interest of the time had been owing to Mr Osmond was a reflection she was not just now at pains to make; she had already done the point abundant justice. But she said to herself that if there were a danger they should never meet again, perhaps after all it would be as well. Happy things don't repeat themselves, and her adventure wore already the changed, the seaward face of some romantic island from which, after feasting on purple grapes, she was putting off while the breeze rose. She might come back to Italy and find him different – this strange man who pleased her just as he was; and it would be better not to come than run the risk of that. But if she was not to come the greater the pity that the chapter was closed; she felt for a moment a pang that touched the source of tears. The sensation kept her silent, and Gilbert Osmond was silent too; he was looking at her. 'Go everywhere,' he said at last, in a low, kind voice; 'do everything; get everything out of life. Be happy – be triumphant.'

'What do you mean by being triumphant?'

'Well, doing what you like.'

'To triumph, then, it seems to me, is to fail! Doing all the vain things one likes is often very tiresome.'

'Exactly,' said Osmond with his quiet quickness. 'As I intimated just now, you'll be tired some day.' He paused a moment and then he went on: 'I don't know whether I had better not wait till then for something I want to say to you.'

'Ah, I can't advise you without knowing what it is. But I'm horrid when I'm tired,' Isabel added with due inconsequence.

'I don't believe that. You're angry, sometimes – that I can believe, though I've never seen it. But I'm sure you're never "cross".'

'Not even when I lose my temper?'

'You don't lose it – you find it, and that must be beautiful.' Osmond spoke with a noble earnestness. 'They must be great moments to see.'

'If I could only find it now!' Isabel nervously cried.

'I'm not afraid; I should fold my arms and admire you. I'm speaking very seriously.' He leaned forward, a hand on each knee; for some moments he bent his eyes on the floor. 'What I wish to say to you,' he went on at last, looking up, 'is that I find I'm in love with you.'

She instantly rose. 'Ah, keep that till I *am* tired!'

'Tired of hearing it from others?' He sat there raising his eyes to her. 'No, you may heed it now or never, as you please. But after all I must say it now.' She had turned away, but in the movement she had stopped herself and dropped her gaze upon him. The two remained a while in this situation, exchanging a long look – the large conscious look of the critical hours of life. Then he got up and came near her, deeply respectful, as if he were afraid he had been too familiar. 'I'm absolutely in love with you.'

He had repeated the announcement in a tone of almost impersonal discretion, like a man who expected very little from it but who spoke for his own needed relief. The tears came into her eyes: this time they obeyed the sharpness of the pang that suggested to her somehow the slipping of a fine bolt – backward, forward, she couldn't have said which. The words he had uttered made him, as he stood there, beautiful and generous, invested him as with the golden air of early autumn; but, morally speaking, she retreated before them – facing him still – as she had retreated in the other cases before a like encounter. 'Oh don't say that, please,' she answered with an intensity that expressed the dread of having, in this case too, to choose and decide. What made her dread great was precisely the force which, as it would seem, ought to have banished all dread – the sense of something within herself, deep down, that she supposed to be inspired and trustful passion. It was there like a large sum stored in a bank – which there was a terror in having to begin to spend. If she touched it, it would all come out.

'I haven't the idea that it will matter much to you,' said Osmond. 'I've too little to offer you. What I have – it's enough for me; but it's not enough for you. I've neither fortune, nor fame, nor extrinsic advantages of any kind. So I offer nothing. I only tell you because I think it can't offend you, and some day or other it may give you pleasure. It gives me pleasure, I assure you,' he went on, standing there before her, considerately inclined to her, turning his hat, which he had taken up, slowly round with a movement which had all the decent tremor of awkwardness and none of its oddity, and presenting to her his firm, refined, slightly ravaged face. 'It gives me no pain, because it's perfectly simple. For me you'll always be the most important woman in the world.'

Isabel looked at herself in this character – looked intently, thinking she filled it with a certain grace. But what she said was not an expression of any such complacency. 'You don't offend me; but you ought to remember that, without being offended; one may be incommoded, troubled.' 'Incommoded': she heard herself saying that, and it struck her as a ridiculous word. But it was what stupidly came to her.

'I remember perfectly. Of course you're surprised and startled. But if it's nothing but that, it will pass away. And it will perhaps leave something that I may not be ashamed of.'

'I don't know what it may leave. You see at all events that I'm not overwhelmed,' said Isabel with rather a pale smile. 'I'm not too troubled to think. And I think that I'm glad we're separating – that I leave Rome tomorrow.'

'Of course I don't agree with you there.'

'I don't at all *know* you,' she added abruptly; and then she coloured as she heard herself saying what she had said almost a year before to Lord Warburton.

'If you were not going away you'd know me better.'

'I shall do that some other time.'

'I hope so. I'm very easy to know.'

'No, no,' she emphatically answered – 'there you're not sincere. You're not easy to know; no one could be less so.'

'Well,' he laughed, 'I said that because I know myself. It may be a boast, but I do.'

'Very likely; but you're very wise.'

'So are you, Miss Archer!' Osmond exclaimed.

'I don't feel so just now. Still, I'm wise enough to think you had better go. Good night.'

'God bless you!' said Gilbert Osmond, taking the hand which she failed to surrender. After which he added, 'If we meet again you'll find me as you leave me. If we don't I shall be so all the same.'

'Thank you very much. Good-bye.'

There was something quietly firm about Isabel's visitor; he might go of his own movement, but wouldn't be dismissed. 'There's one thing more. I haven't asked anything of you – not even a thought in the future; you must do me that justice. But there's a little service I should like to ask. I shall not return home for several days; Rome's delightful, and it's a good place for a man in my state of mind. Oh, I know you're sorry to leave it; but you're right to do what your aunt wishes.'

'She doesn't even wish it!' Isabel broke out strangely.

Osmond was apparently on the point of saying something that would match these words, but he changed his mind and rejoined simply: 'Ah well, it's proper you should go with her, very proper. Do everything that's proper; I go in for that. Excuse my being so patronizing. You say you don't know me, but when you do you'll discover what a worship I have for propriety.'

'You're not conventional?' Isabel gravely asked.

'I like the way you utter that word! No, I'm not conventional: I'm convention itself. You don't understand that?' And he paused a moment, smiling. 'I should like to explain it.' Then with a sudden, quick, bright naturalness, 'Do come back again,' he pleaded. 'There are so many things we might talk about.'

She stood there with lowered eyes. 'What service did you speak of just now?'

'Go and see my little daughter before you leave Florence. She's alone at the villa; I decided not to send her to my sister, who hasn't at all my ideas. Tell her she must love her poor father very much,' said Gilbert Osmond gently.

'It will be a great pleasure to me to go,' Isabel answered. 'I'll tell her what you say. Once more good-bye.'

On this he took a rapid, respectful leave. When he had gone she stood a moment looking about her and seated herself slowly and with an air of deliberation. She sat there till her companions came back, with folded hands, gazing at the ugly carpet. Her agitation – for it had not diminished – was very still, very deep. What had happened was something that for a week past her imagination had been going forward to meet; but here, when it came, she stopped – that sublime principle somehow broke down. The working of this young lady's spirit was strange, and I can only give it to you as I see it, not hoping to make it seem altogether natural. Her imagination, as I say, now hung back; there was a last vague space it couldn't cross – a dusky, uncertain tract which looked ambiguous and even slightly treacherous, like a moorland seen in the winter twilight. But she was to cross it yet.

Chapter Thirty

She returned on the morrow to Florence, under her cousin's escort, and Ralph Touchett, though usually restive under railway discipline, thought very well of the successive hours passed in the train that hurried his companion away from the city now distinguished by Gilbert Osmond's preference – hours that were to form the first stage in a larger scheme of travel. Miss Stackpole had remained behind; she was planning a little trip to Naples, to be carried out with Mr Bantling's aid. Isabel was to have three days in Florence before 4 June, the date of Mrs Touchett's departure, and she determined to devote the last of these to her promise to call on Pansy Osmond. Her plan, however, seemed for a moment likely to modify itself in deference to an idea of Madame Merle's. This lady was still at Casa Touchett; but she too was on the point of leaving Florence, her next station being an ancient castle in the mountains of Tuscany, the residence of a noble family of that country, whose acquaintance (she had known them, as she said, 'forever') seemed to Isabel, in the light of certain photographs of their immense crenellated dwelling which her friend was able to show her, a precious privilege. She mentioned to this fortunate woman that Mr Osmond had asked her to take a look at his daughter, but didn't mention that he had also made her a declaration of love.

'*Ah, comme cela se trouve!*' Madame Merle exclaimed. 'I myself have been thinking it would be a kindness to pay the child a little visit before I go off.'

'We can go together then,' Isabel reasonably said: 'reasonably' because the proposal was not uttered in the spirit of enthusiasm. She had prefigured her small pilgrimage as made in solitude; she should like it better so. She was nevertheless prepared to sacrifice this mystic sentiment to her great consideration for her friend.

That personage finely meditated. 'After all, why should we both go; having, each of us, so much to do during these last hours?'

'Very good; I can easily go alone.'

'I don't know about your going alone – to the house of a handsome bachelor. He has been married – but so long ago!'

Isabel stared. 'When Mr Osmond's away what does it matter?'

'They don't know he's away, you see.'

'They? Whom do you mean?'

'Everyone. But perhaps it doesn't signify.'

'If you were going why shouldn't I?' Isabel asked.

'Because I'm an old frump and you're a beautiful young woman.'

'Granting all that, you're not promised.'

'How much you think of your promises!' said the elder woman in mild mockery.

'I think a great deal of my promises. Does that surprise you?'

'You're right,' Madame Merle audibly reflected. 'I really think you wish to be kind to the child.'

'I wish very much to be kind to her.'

'Go and see her then; no one will be the wiser. And tell her I'd have come if you hadn't. Or rather,' Madame Merle added, '*don't* tell her. She won't care.'

As Isabel drove, in the publicity of an open vehicle, along the winding way which led to Mr Osmond's hill-top, she wondered what her friend had meant by no one's being the wiser. Once in a while, at large intervals, this lady whose voyaging discretion, as a general thing, was rather of the open sea than of the risky channel, dropped a remark of ambiguous quality, struck a note that sounded false. What cared Isabel Archer for the vulgar judgements of obscure people? and did Madame Merle suppose that she was capable of doing a thing at all if it had to be sneakingly done? Of course not: she must have meant something else – something which in the press of the hours that preceded her departure she had not had time to explain. Isabel would return to this some day; there were sorts of things as to which she liked to be clear. She heard Pansy strumming at the piano in another place as she herself was ushered into Mr Osmond's drawing-room; the little girl was 'practising', and Isabel was pleased to think she performed this duty with rigour. She immediately came in, smoothing down her frock, and did the honours of her father's house with a wide-eyed earnestness of courtesy. Isabel sat there half an hour, and Pansy rose to the occasion as the small, winged fairy in the pantomime soars by the aid of the dissimulated wire – not chattering, but conversing, and showing the same respectful interest in

Isabel's affairs that Isabel was so good as to take in hers. Isabel wondered at her; she had never had so directly presented to her nose the white flower of cultivated sweetness. How well the child had been taught, said our admiring young woman; how prettily she had been directed and fashioned; and yet how simple, how natural, how innocent she had been kept! Isabel was fond, ever, of the question of character and quality, of sounding, as who should say, the deep personal mystery, and it had pleased her, up to this time, to be in doubt as to whether this tender slip were not really all-knowing. Was the extremity of her candour but the perfection of self-consciousness? Was it put on to please her father's visitor, or was it the direct expression of an unspotted nature? The hour that Isabel spent in Mr Osmond's beautiful empty, dusky rooms – the windows had been half-darkened, to keep out the heat, and here and there, through an easy crevice, the splendid summer day peeped in, lighting a gleam of faded colour or tarnished gilt in the rich gloom – her interview with the daughter of the house, I say, effectually settled this question. Pansy was really a blank page, a pure white surface, successfully kept so; she had neither art, nor guile, nor temper, nor talent – only two or three small exquisite instincts: for knowing a friend, for avoiding a mistake, for taking care of an old toy or a new frock. Yet to be so tender was to be touching withal, and she could be felt as an easy victim of fate. She would have no will, no power to resist, no sense of her own importance; she would easily be mystified, easily crushed: her force would be all in knowing when and where to cling. She moved about the place with her visitor, who had asked leave to walk through the other rooms again, where Pansy gave her judgement on several works of art. She spoke of her prospects, her occupations, her father's intentions; she was not egotistical, but felt the propriety of supplying the information so distinguished a guest would naturally expect.

'Please tell me,' she said, 'did papa, in Rome, go to see Madame Catherine? He told me he would if he had time. Perhaps he had not time. Papa likes a great deal of time. He wished to speak about my education; it isn't finished yet, you know. I don't know what they can do with me more; but it appears it's far from finished. Papa told me one day he thought he would finish it himself; for the last year or two, at the convent, the masters that teach the tall girls are so very dear. Papa's not rich, and I should be very sorry if he were to pay much money for me, because I don't think I'm worth it. I don't learn quickly enough, and I have no memory. For what I'm told, yes – especially when it's pleasant; but not for what I learn in a book. There was a young girl who was my best friend, and they took her away from the convent, when she was fourteen, to make – how do you say it in English? – to make a *dot*. You don't say it in English? I hope it isn't wrong; I only mean they wished to keep the money to marry her. I don't know whether it is for that that papa wishes to keep the money – to marry *me*. It costs so much to marry!' Pansy went on with a sigh; 'I think papa might make that economy. At any rate I'm too young to think about it yet, and I don't care for any gentleman; I mean for any but him. If he were not my papa I should like to marry him; I would rather be his daughter than the wife of – of some strange person. I miss him very much, but not so much as you might think, for I've been so much away from him. Papa has always been principally for holidays. I miss Madame Catherine almost more; but you must not tell him that. You shall not see him again? I'm very sorry, and he'll be sorry too. Of everyone who comes here I like you the best. That's not a great compliment, for there are not many people. It was very kind of you to come today – so far from your house; for I'm really as yet only a child. Oh, yes, I've only the occupations of a child. When did *you* give them up, the occupations of a child? I should like to know how old you are, but I don't know whether it's right to ask. At the convent they told us that we must never ask the age. I don't like to do anything that's not expected; it looks as if one had not been properly taught. I myself – I should never like to be taken by surprise. Papa left directions for everything. I go to bed very early. When the sun goes off that side I go into the garden. Papa left strict orders that I was not to get scorched. I always enjoy the view; the mountains are so graceful. In Rome, from the convent, we saw nothing but roofs and bell-towers. I practise three hours. I don't play very well. You play yourself? I wish very much you'd play something for me; papa has the idea that I should hear good music. Madame Merle has played for me several times; that's what I like best about Madame Merle; she has great facility. I shall never have facility. And I've no voice – just a small sound like the squeak of a slate-pencil making flourishes.'

Isabel gratified this respectful wish, drew off her gloves and sat down to the piano, while Pansy, standing beside her, watched her white hands move quickly over the keys. When she stopped she kissed the child good-bye, held her close, looked at her long. 'Be very good,' she said; 'give pleasure to your father.'

'I think that's what I live for,' Pansy answered. 'He has not much pleasure; he's rather a sad man.'

Isabel listened to this assertion with an interest which she felt it almost a torment to be obliged to conceal. It was her pride that obliged her, and a certain sense of decency; there were still other things in her head which she felt a strong impulse, instantly checked, to say to Pansy about her father; there were things it would have given her pleasure to hear the child, to make the child say. But she no sooner became conscious of these things than her imagination was hushed with horror at the idea of taking advantage of the little girl – it was of this she would have accused herself – and of exhaling into that air where he might still have a subtle sense for it any breath of her charmed state. She had come – she had come, but she had stayed only an hour. She rose quickly from the music-stool; even then, however, she lingered a moment, still holding her small companion, drawing the child's sweet slimness closer and looking down at her almost in envy. She was obliged to confess it to herself – she would have taken a passionate pleasure in talking of Gilbert Osmond to this innocent, diminutive creature who was so near him. But she said no other word; she only kissed Pansy once again. They went together through the vestibule, to the door that opened on the court; and there her young hostess stopped, looking rather wistfully beyond. 'I may go no farther. I've promised papa not to pass this door.'

'You're right to obey him; he'll never ask you anything unreasonable.'

'I shall always obey him. But when will you come again?'

'Not for a long time, I'm afraid.'

'As soon as you can, I hope. I'm only a little girl,' said Pansy, 'but I shall always expect you.' And the small figure stood in the high, dark doorway, watching Isabel cross the clear, grey court and disappear into the brightness beyond the big *portone*, which gave a wider dazzle as it opened.

Chapter Thirty-one

Isabel came back to Florence, but only after several months; an interval sufficiently replete with incident. It is not, however, during this interval that we are closely concerned with her; our attention is engaged again on a certain day in the late spring-time, shortly after her return to Palazzo Crescentini and a year from the date of the incidents just narrated. She was alone on this occasion, in one of the smaller of the numerous rooms devoted by Mrs Touchett to social uses, and there was that in her expression and attitude which would have suggested that she was expecting a visitor. The tall window was open, and though its green shutters were partly drawn the bright air of the garden had come in through a broad interstice and filled the room with warmth and perfume. Our young woman stood near it for some time, her hands clasped behind her; she gazed abroad with the vagueness of unrest. Too troubled for attention she moved in a vain circle. Yet it could not be in her thought to catch a glimpse of her visitor before he should pass into the house, since the entrance to the palace was not through the garden, in which stillness and privacy always reigned. She wished rather to forestall his arrival by a process of conjecture, and to judge by the expression of her face this attempt gave her plenty to do. Grave she found herself, and positively more weighted, as by the experience of the lapse of the year she had spent in seeing the world. She had ranged, she would have said, through space and surveyed much of mankind, and was therefore now, in her own eyes, a very different person from the frivolous young woman from Albany who had begun to take the measure of Europe on the lawn at Gardencourt a couple of years before. She flattered herself she had harvested wisdom and learned a great deal more of life than this light-minded creature had even suspected. If her thoughts just now had inclined themselves to retrospect, instead of fluttering their wings nervously about the present, they would have evoked a multitude of interesting pictures. These pictures would have been both landscapes and figure-pieces; the latter, however, would have been the more numerous. With several of the images that might have been projected on such a field we are already acquainted. There would be for instance the conciliatory Lily, our heroine's sister and Edmund Ludlow's wife, who had come out from New York to spend five months with her relative. She had left her husband behind her, but had brought her children, to whom Isabel now played with equal munificence and tenderness the part of maiden aunt. Mr Ludlow, towards the last, had been able to snatch a few weeks from his forensic triumphs and, crossing the ocean with extreme rapidity, had spent a month with the two ladies in Paris before taking his wife home. The little Ludlows had not yet, even from the American point of view, reached the proper tourist-age; so that while her sister was with her Isabel had confined her movements to a narrow circle. Lily and the babies had joined her in Switzerland in the month of July, and they had spent a summer of fine weather in an Alpine valley where the flowers were thick in the meadows, and the shade of great chestnuts made a resting-place for such upward wanderings as might be undertaken by ladies and children on warm afternoons. They had afterwards reached the French capital, which was worshipped, and with costly ceremonies, by Lily, but thought of as noisily vacant by Isabel, who in these days made use of her memory of Rome as she might have done, in a hot and crowded room, of a phial of something pungent hidden in her handkerchief.

Mrs Ludlow sacrificed, as I say, to Paris, yet had doubts and wonderments not allayed at that altar; and after her husband had joined her found further chagrin in his failure to throw himself into these speculations. They all had Isabel for subject; but Edmund Ludlow, as he had always done before, declined to be surprised, or distressed, or mystified, or elated, at anything his sister-in-law might have done or have failed to do. Mrs Ludlow's mental motions were sufficiently various. At one moment she thought it would be so natural for that young woman to come home and take a house in New York – the Rossiters', for instance, which had an elegant conservatory and was just round the corner from her own; at another she couldn't conceal her surprise at the girl's not marrying some member of one of the great aristocracies. On the whole, as I have said, she had fallen from high communion with the probabilities. She had taken more satisfaction in Isabel's accession of fortune than if the money had been left to herself; it had seemed to her to offer just the proper setting for her sister's slightly meagre, but scarce the less eminent figure. Isabel had developed less, however, than Lily had thought likely – development, to Lily's understanding, being somehow mysteriously connected with morning calls and evening parties. Intellectually, doubtless, she had made immense strides; but she appeared to have achieved few of those social conquests of which Mrs Ludlow had expected to admire the trophies. Lily's conception of such achievements was extremely vague; but this was exactly what she had expected of Isabel – to give it form and body. Isabel could have done as well as she had done in New York; and Mrs Ludlow appealed to her husband to know whether there was any privilege she enjoyed in Europe which the society of that city might not offer her. We know ourselves that Isabel had made conquests – whether inferior or not to those she might have effected in her native land it would be a delicate matter to decide; and it is not altogether with a feeling of complacency that I again mention that she had not rendered these honourable victories public. She had not told her sister the history of Lord Warburton, nor had she given her a hint of Mr Osmond's state of mind; and she had had no better reason for her silence than that she didn't wish to speak. It was more romantic to say nothing, and, drinking deep, in secret, of romance, she was as little disposed to ask poor Lily's advice as she would have been to close that rare volume for ever. But Lily knew nothing of these discriminations, and could only pronounce her sister's career a strange anti-climax – an impression confirmed by the fact that Isabel's silence about Mr Osmond, for instance, was in direct proportion to the frequency with which he occupied her thoughts. As this happened very often it sometimes appeared to Mrs Ludlow that she had lost her courage. So uncanny a result of so exhilarating an incident as inheriting a fortune was of course perplexing to the cheerful Lily; it added to her general sense that Isabel was not at all like other people.

Our young lady's courage, however, might have been taken as reaching its height after her relations had gone home. She could imagine braver things than spending the winter in Paris – Paris had sides by which it so resembled New York, Paris was like smart, neat prose – and her close correspondence with Madame Merle did much to stimulate such flights. She had never had a keener sense of freedom, of the absolute boldness and wantonness of liberty, than when she turned away from the platform at the Euston Station on one of the last days of November, after the departure of the train that was to convey poor Lily, her husband and her children to their ship at Liverpool. It had been good for her to regale; she was very conscious of that; she was very observant, as we know, of what was good for her, and her effort was constantly to find something that was good enough. To profit by the present advantage till the latest moment she had made the journey from Paris with the unenvied travellers. She would have accompanied them to Liverpool as well, only Edmund Ludlow had asked her, as a favour, not to do so; it made Lily so fidgety and she asked such impossible questions. Isabel watched the train move away; she kissed her hand to the elder of her small nephews, a demonstrative child who leaned dangerously far out of the window of the carriage and made separation an occasion of violent hilarity, and then she walked back into the foggy London street. The world lay before her – she could do whatever she chose. There was a deep thrill in it all, but for the present her choice was tolerably discreet; she chose simply to walk back from Euston Square to her hotel. The early dusk of a November afternoon had already closed in; the streetlamps, in the thick, brown air, looked weak and red; our heroine was unattended and Euston Square was a long way from Piccadilly. But Isabel performed the journey with a positive enjoyment of its dangers and lost her way almost on purpose, in order to get more sensations, so that she was disappointed when an obliging policeman easily set her right again. She was so fond of the spectacle of human life that she enjoyed even the aspect of gathering dusk in the London streets – the moving crowds, the hurrying cabs, the lighted shops, the flaring stalls, the dark, shining dampness of everything. That evening, at her hotel, she wrote to Madam Merle that she should start in a day or two for Rome. She made her way down to Rome without touching at Florence – having gone first to Venice and then proceeded southward by Ancona. She accomplished this journey without other assistance than that of her servant, for her natural protectors were not now on the ground. Ralph Touchett was spending the winter at Corfu, and Miss Stackpole, in the September previous, had been recalled to America by a telegram from the *Interviewer*. This journal offered its brilliant correspondent a fresher field for her genius than the mouldering cities of Europe, and Henrietta was cheered on her way by a promise from Mr Bantling that he would soon come over to see her. Isabel wrote to Mrs Touchett to apologize for not presenting herself just yet in Florence, and her aunt replied characteristically enough. Apologies, Mrs Touchett intimated, were of no more use to her than bubbles, and she herself never dealt in such articles. One either did the thing or one didn't, and what one 'would' have done belonged to the sphere of the irrelevant, like the idea of a future life or of the origin of things. Her letter was frank, but (a rare case with Mrs Touchett) not so frank as it pretended. She easily forgave her niece for not stopping at Florence, because she took it for a sign that Gilbert Osmond was less in question there than formerly. She watched of course to see if he would now find a pretext for going to Rome, and derived some comfort from learning that he had not been guilty of an absence.

Isabel, on her side, had not been a fortnight in Rome before she proposed to Madame Merle that they should make a little pilgrimage to the East. Madame Merle remarked that her friend was restless, but she added that she herself had always been consumed with the desire to visit Athens and Constantinople. The two ladies accordingly embarked on this expedition, and spent three months in Greece, in Turkey, in Egypt. Isabel found much to interest her in these countries, though Madame Merle continued to remark that even among the most classic sites, the scenes most calculated to suggest repose and reflection, a certain incoherence prevailed in her. Isabel travelled rapidly and recklessly; she was like a thirsty person draining cup after cup. Madame Merle meanwhile, as lady-in-waiting to a princess circulating *incognita*, panted a little in her rear. It was on Isabel's invitation she had come, and she imparted all due dignity to the girl's uncountenanced state. She played her part with the tact that might have been expected of her, effacing herself and accepting the position of a companion whose expenses were profusely paid. The situation, however, had no hardships, and people who met this reserved though striking pair on their travels would not have been able to tell you which was patroness and which client. To say that Madame Merle improved on acquaintance states meagrely the impression she made on her friend, who had found her from the first so ample and so easy. At the end of an intimacy of three months Isabel felt she knew her better; her character had revealed itself, and the admirable woman had also at last redeemed her promise of relating her history from her own point of view – a consummation the more desirable as Isabel had already heard it related from the point of view of others. This history was so sad a one (in so far as it concerned the late M. Merle, a positive adventurer, she might say, though originally so plausible, who had taken advantage, years before, of her youth and of an inexperience in which doubtless those who knew her only now would find it difficult to believe); it abounded so in startling and lamentable incidents that her companion wondered a person so *éprouvée* could have kept so much of her freshness, her interest in life. Into this freshness of Madame Merle's she obtained a considerable insight; she seemed to see it as professional, as slightly mechanical, carried about in its case like the fiddle of the virtuoso, or blanketed and bridled like the 'favourite' of the jockey. She liked her as much as ever, but there was a corner of the curtain that never was lifted; it was as if she had remained after all something of a public performer, condemned to emerge only in character and in costume. She had once said that she came from a distance, that she belonged to the 'old, old' world, and Isabel never lost the impression that she was the product of a different moral or social clime from her own, that she had grown up under other stars.

She believed then that at bottom she had a different morality. Of course the morality of civilized persons has always much in common; but our young woman had a sense in her values gone wrong or, as they said at the shops, marked down. She considered, with the presumption of youth, that a morality differing from her own must be inferior to it; and this conviction was an aid to detecting an occasional flash of cruelty, an occasional lapse from candour, in the conversation of a person who had raised delicate kindness to an art and whose pride was too high for the narrow ways of deception. Her conception of human motives might, in certain lights, have been acquired at the court of some kingdom in decadence, and there were several in her list of which our heroine had not even heard. She had not heard of everything, that was very plain; and there were evidently things in the world of which it was not advantageous to hear. She had once or twice had a positive scare; since it so affected her to have to exclaim, of her friend, 'Heaven forgive her, she doesn't understand me!' Absurd as it may seem this discovery operated as a shock, left her with a vague dismay in which there was even an element of foreboding. The dismay of course subsided, in the light of some sudden proof of Madame Merle's remarkable intelligence; but it stood for a high-water-mark in the ebb and flow of confidence. Madame Merle had once declared her belief that when a friendship ceases to grow it immediately begins to decline – there being no point of equilibrium between liking more and liking less. A stationary affection, in other words, was impossible – it must move one way or the other. However that might be, the girl had in these days a thousand uses for her sense of the romantic, which was more active than it had ever been. I do not allude to the impulse it received as she gazed at the Pyramids in the course of an excursion from Cairo, or as she stood among the broken columns of the Acropolis and fixed her eyes upon the point designated to her as the Strait of Salamis; deep and memorable as these emotions had remained. She came back by the last of March from Egypt and Greece and made another stay in Rome. A few days after her arrival Gilbert Osmond descended from Florence and remained three weeks, during which the fact of her being with his old friend Madame Merle, in whose house she had gone to lodge, made it virtually inevitable that he should see her every day. When the last of April came she wrote to Mrs Touchett that she should now rejoice to accept an invitation given long before, and went to pay a visit at Palazzo Crescentini, Madame Merle on this occasion remaining in Rome. She found her aunt alone; her cousin was still at Corfu. Ralph, however, was expected in Florence from day to day, and Isabel, who had not seen him for upwards of a year, was prepared to give him the most affectionate welcome.

Chapter Thirty-two

It was not of him, nevertheless, that she was thinking while she stood at the window near which we found her a while ago, and it was not of any of the matters I have rapidly sketched. She was not turned to the past, but to the immediate, impending hour. She had reason to expect a scene, and she was not fond of scenes. She was not asking herself what she should say to her visitor; this question had already been answered. What he would say to her – that was the interesting issue. It could be nothing in the least soothing – she had warrant for this, and the conviction doubtless showed in the cloud on her brow. For the rest, however, all clearness reigned in her; she had put away her mourning and she walked in no small shimmering splendour. She only felt older – ever so much, and as if she were 'worth more' for it, like some curious piece in an antiquary's collection. She was not at any rate left indefinitely to her apprehensions, for a servant at last stood before her with a card on his tray. 'Let the gentleman come in,' she said, and continued to gaze out of the window after the footman had retired. It was only when she had heard the door close behind the person who presently entered that she looked round.

Caspar Goodwood stood there – stood and received a moment, from head to foot, the bright, dry gaze with which she rather withheld than offered a greeting. Whether his sense of maturity had kept pace with Isabel's we shall perhaps presently ascertain; let me say meanwhile that to her critical glance he showed nothing of the injury of time. Straight, strong, and hard, there was nothing in his appearance that spoke positively either of youth or of age; if he had neither innocence nor weakness, so he had no practical philosophy. His jaw showed the same voluntary cast as in earlier days; but a crisis like the present had in it of course something grim. He had the air of a man who had travelled hard; he said nothing at first, as if he had been out of breath. This gave Isabel time to make a reflection: 'Poor fellow, what great things he's capable of, and what a pity he should waste so dreadfully his splendid force! What a pity too that one can't satisfy everybody!' It gave her time to do more – to say at the end of a minute: 'I can't tell you how I hoped you wouldn't come!'

'I've no doubt of that.' And he looked about him for a seat. Not only had he come, but he meant to settle.

'You must be very tired,' said Isabel, seating herself, and generously, as she thought, to give him his opportunity.

'No, I'm not at all tired. Did you ever know me to be tired?'

'Never; I wish I had! When did you arrive?'

'Last night, very late; in a kind of snail-train they call the express. These Italian trains go at about the rate of an American funeral.'

'That's in keeping – you must have felt as if you were coming to bury me!' And she forced a smile of encouragement to an easy view of their situation. She had reasoned the matter well out, making it perfectly clear that she broke no faith and falsified no contract; but for all this she was afraid of her visitor. She was ashamed of her fear; but she was devoutly thankful there was nothing else to be ashamed of. He looked at her with his stiff insistence, an insistence in which there was such a want of tact; especially when the dull dark beam in his eye rested on her as a physical weight.

'No, I didn't feel that; I couldn't think of you as dead. I wish I could!' he candidly declared.

'I thank you immensely.'

'I'd rather think of you as dead than as married to another man.'

'That's very selfish of you!' she returned with the ardour of a real conviction. 'If you're not happy yourself others have yet a right to be.'

'Very likely it's selfish; but I don't in the least mind your saying so. I don't mind anything you can say now – I don't feel it. The cruellest things you could think of would be mere pin-pricks. After what you've done I shall never feel anything – I mean anything but that. That I shall feel all my life.'

Mr Goodwood made these detached assertions with dry deliberateness, in his hard, slow American tone, which flung no atmospheric colour over propositions intrinsically crude. The tone made Isabel angry rather than touched her; but her anger perhaps was fortunate, inasmuch as it gave her a further reason for controlling herself. It was under the pressure of this control that she became, after a little, irrelevant. 'When did you leave New York?'

He threw up his head as if calculating. 'Seventeen days ago.'

'You must have travelled fast in spite of your slow trains.'

'I came as fast as I could. I'd have come five days ago if I had been able.'

'It wouldn't have made any difference, Mr Goodwood,' she coldly smiled.

'Not to you – no. But to me.'

'You gain nothing that I see.'

'That's for me to judge!'

'Of course. To me it seems that you only torment yourself.' And then, to change the subject, she asked him if he had seen Henrietta Stackpole. He looked as if he had not come from Boston to Florence to talk of Henrietta Stackpole; but he answered, distinctly enough, that this young lady had been with him just before he left America. 'She came to see you?' Isabel then demanded.

'Yes, she was in Boston, and she called at my office. It was the day I had got your letter.'

'Did you tell her?' Isabel asked with a certain anxiety.

'Oh, no,' said Caspar Goodwood simply; 'I didn't want to do that. She'll hear it quick enough; she hears everything.'

'I shall write to her, and then she'll write to me and scold me,' Isabel declared, trying to smile again.

Caspar, however, remained sternly grave. 'I guess she'll come right out,' he said.

'On purpose to scold me?'

'I don't know. She seemed to think she had not seen Europe thoroughly.'

'I'm glad you tell me that,' Isabel said. 'I must prepare for her.'

Mr Goodwood fixed his eyes for a moment on the floor; then at last, raising them, 'Does she know Mr Osmond?' he inquired.

'A little. And she doesn't like him. But of course I don't marry to please Henrietta,' she added. It would have been better for poor Caspar if she had tried a little more to gratify Miss Stackpole; but he didn't say so; he only asked, presently, when her marriage would take place. To which she made answer that she didn't know yet. 'I can only say it will be soon. I've told no one but yourself and one other person – an old friend of Mr Osmond's.

'Is it a marriage your friends won't like?' he demanded.

'I really haven't an idea. As I say, I don't marry for my friends.'

He went on, making no exclamation, no comment, only asking questions, doing it quite without delicacy. 'Who and what then is Mr Gilbert Osmond?'

'Who and what? Nobody and nothing but a very good and very honourable man. He's not in business,' said Isabel. 'He's not rich; he's not known for anything in particular.'

She disliked Mr Goodwood's questions, but she said to herself that she owed it to him to satisfy him as far as possible. The satisfaction poor Caspar exhibited was, however, small; he sat very upright, gazing at her. 'Where does he come from? Where does he belong?'

She had never been so little pleased with the way he said 'belawng'. 'He comes from nowhere. He has spent most of his life in Italy.'

'You said in your letter he was American. Hasn't he a native place?'

'Yes, but he has forgotten it. He left it as a small boy.'

'Has he never gone back?'

'Why should he go back?' Isabel asked, flushing all defensively. 'He has no profession.'

'He might have gone back for his pleasure. Doesn't he like the United States?'

'He doesn't know them. Then he's very quiet and very simple – he contents himself with Italy.'

'With Italy and with you,' said Mr Goodwood with gloomy plainness and no appearance of trying to make an epigram. 'What has he ever done?' he added abruptly.

'That I should marry him? Nothing at all,' Isabel replied while her patience helped itself by turning a little to hardness. 'If he had done great things would you forgive me any better? Give me up, Mr Goodwood; I'm marrying a perfect nonentity. Don't try to take an interest in him. You can't.'

'I can't appreciate him; that's what you mean. And you don't mean in the least that he's a perfect nonentity. You think he's grand, you think he's great, though no one else thinks so.'

Isabel's colour deepened; she felt this really acute of her companion, and it was certainly a proof of the aid that passion might render perceptions she had never taken for fine. 'Why do you always come back to what others think? I can't discuss Mr Osmond with you.'

'Of course not,' said Caspar reasonably. And he sat there with his air of stiff helplessness, as if not only this were true, but there was nothing else that they might discuss.

'You see how little you gain,' she accordingly broke out – 'how little comfort or satisfaction I can give you.'

'I didn't expect you to give me much.'

'I don't understand then why you came.'

'I came because I wanted to see you once more – even just as you are.'

'I appreciate that; but if you had waited a while, sooner or later we should have been sure to meet, and our meeting would have been pleasanter for each of us than this.'

'Waited till after you're married? That's just what I didn't want to do. You'll be different then.'

'Not very. I shall still be a great friend of yours. You'll see.'

'That will make it all the worse,' said Mr Goodwood grimly.

'Ah, you're unaccommodating! I can't promise to dislike you in order to help you to resign yourself.'

'I shouldn't care if you did!'

Isabel got up with movement of repressed impatience and walked to the window, where she remained a moment looking out. When she turned round her visitor was still motionless in his place. She came towards him again and stopped, resting her hand on the back of the chair she had just quitted. 'Do you mean you came simply to look at me? That's better for you perhaps than for me.'

'I wished to hear the sound of your voice,' he said.

'You've heard it, and you see it says nothing very sweet.'

'It gives me pleasure, all the same.' And with this he got up.

She had felt pain and displeasure on receiving early that day the news he was in Florence and by her leave would come within an hour to see her. She had been vexed and distressed, though she had sent back word by his messenger that he might come when he would. She had not been better pleased when she saw him; his being there at all was so full of heavy implications. It implied things she could never assent to – rights, reproaches, remonstrance, rebuke, the expectation of making her change her purpose. These things, however, if implied, had not been expressed; and now our young lady, strangely enough, began to resent her visitor's remarkable self-control. There was a dumb misery about him that irritated her; there was a manly staying of his hand that made her heart beat faster. She felt her agitation rising, and she said to herself that she was angry in the way a woman is angry when she has been in the wrong. She was not in the wrong; she had fortunately not that bitterness to swallow; but, all the same, she wished he would denounce her a little. She had wished his visit would be short; it had no purpose, no propriety; yet now that he seemed to be turning away she felt a sudden horror of his leaving her without uttering a word that would give her an opportunity to defend herself more than she had done in writing to him a month before, in a few carefully chosen words, to announce her engagement. If she were not in the wrong, however, why should she desire to defend herself? It was an excess of generosity on Isabel's part to desire that Mr Goodwood should be angry. And if he had not meanwhile held himself hard it might have made him so to hear the tone in which she suddenly exclaimed, as if she were accusing him of having accused her: 'I've not deceived you! I was perfectly free!'

'Yes, I know that,' said Caspar.

'I gave you full warning that I'd do as I chose.'

'You said you'd probably never marry, and you said it with such a manner that I pretty well believed it.'

She considered this an instant. 'No one can be more surprised than myself at my present intention.'

'You told me that if I heard you were engaged I was not to believe it,' Caspar went on. 'I heard it twenty days ago from yourself, but I remembered what you had said. I thought there might be some mistake, and that's partly why I came.'

'If you wish me to repeat it by word of mouth, that's soon done. There's no mistake whatever.'

'I saw that as soon as I came into the room.'

'What good would it do you that I shouldn't marry?' she asked with a certain fierceness.

'I should like it better than this.'

'You're very selfish, as I said before.'

'I know that. I'm selfish as iron.'

'Even iron sometimes melts! If you'll be reasonable I'll see you again.'

'Don't you call me reasonable now?'

'I don't know what to say to you,' she answered with sudden humility.

'I shan't trouble you for a long time,' the young man went on. He made a step towards the door, but he stopped. 'Another reason why I came was that I wanted to hear what you would say in explanation of your having changed your mind.'

Her humbleness as suddenly deserted her. 'In explanation? Do you think I'm bound to explain?'

He gave her one of his long dumb looks. 'You were very positive. I did believe it.'

'So did I. Do you think I could explain if I would?'

'No, I suppose not. Well,' he added, 'I've done what I wished. I've seen you.'

'How little you make of these terrible journeys,' she felt the poverty of her presently replying.

'If you're afraid I'm knocked up – in any such way as that – you may be at your ease about it.' He turned away, this time in earnest, and no handshake, no sign of parting, was exchanged between them. At the door he stopped with his hand on the knob. 'I shall leave Florence tomorrow,' he said without a quaver.

'I'm delighted to hear it!' she answered passionately. Five minutes after he had gone out she burst into tears.

Chapter Thirty-three

Her fit of weeping, however, was soon smothered, and the signs of it had vanished when, an hour later, she broke the news to her aunt. I use this expression because she had been sure Mrs Touchett would not be pleased; Isabel had only waited to tell her till she had seen Mr Goodwood. She had an odd impression that it would not be honourable to make the fact public before she should have heard what Mr Goodwood would say about it. He had said rather less than she expected, and she now had a somewhat angry sense of having lost time. But she would lose no more; she waited till Mrs Touchett came into the drawing-room before the midday breakfast, and then she began. 'Aunt Lydia, I've something to tell you.'

Mrs Touchett gave a little jump and looked at her almost fiercely. 'You needn't tell me; I know what it is.'

'I don't know how you know.'

'The same way that I know when the window's open – by feeling a draught. You're going to marry that man.'

'What man do you mean?' Isabel inquired with great dignity.

'Madame Merle's friend – Mr Osmond.'

'I don't know why you call him Madame Merle's friend. Is that the principal thing he's known by?'

'If he's not her friend he ought to be – after what she has done for him!' cried Mrs Touchett. 'I shouldn't have expected it of her; I'm disappointed.'

'If you mean that Madame Merle has had anything to do with my engagement you're greatly mistaken,' Isabel declared with a sort of ardent coldness.

'You mean that your attractions were sufficient, without the gentleman's having had to be lashed up? You're quite right. They're immense, your attractions, and he would never have presumed to think of you if she hadn't put him up to it. He has a very good opinion of himself, but he was not a man to take trouble. Madame Merle took the trouble *for* him.'

'He has taken a great deal for himself!' cried Isabel with a voluntary laugh.

Mrs Touchett gave a sharp nod. 'I think he must, after all, to have made you like him so much.'

'I thought he even pleased *you*.'

'He did, at one time; and that's why I'm angry with him.'

'Be angry with me, not with him,' said the girl.

'Oh, I'm always angry with you; that's no satisfaction! Was it for this that you refused Lord Warburton?'

'Please don't go back to that. Why shouldn't I like Mr Osmond, since others have done so?'

'Others, at their wildest moments, never wanted to marry him. There's nothing *of* him,' Mrs Touchett explained.

'Then he can't hurt me,' said Isabel.

'Do you think you're going to be happy? No one's happy, in such doing, you should know.'

'I shall set the fashion then. What does one marry for?'

'What *you* will marry for, heaven only knows. People usually marry as they go into partnership – to set up a house. But in your partnership you'll bring everything.'

'Is it that Mr Osmond isn't rich? Is that what you're talking about?' Isabel asked.

'He has no money; he has no name; he has no importance. I value such things and I have the courage to say it; I think they're very precious. Many other people think the same, and they show it. But they give some other reason.'

Isabel hesitated a little. 'I think I value everything that's valuable. I care very much for money, and that's why I wish Mr Osmond to have a little.'

'Give it to him then; but marry someone else.'

'His name's good enough for me,' the girl went on. 'It's a very pretty name. Have I such a fine one myself?'

'All the more reason you should improve on it. There are only a dozen American names. Do you marry him out of charity?'

'It was my duty to tell you, Aunt Lydia, but I don't think it's my duty to explain to you. Even if it were I shouldn't be able. So please don't remonstrate; in talking about it you have me at a disadvantage. I can't talk about it.'

'I don't remonstrate, I simply answer you: I must give some sign of intelligence. I saw it coming, and I said nothing. I never meddle.'

'You never do, and I'm greatly obliged to you. You've been very considerate.'

'It was not considerate – it was convenient,' said Mrs Touchett. 'But I shall talk to Madame Merle.'

'I don't see why you keep bringing her in. She has been a very good friend to me.'

'Possibly; but she has been a poor one to me.'

'What has she done to you?'

'She has deceived me. She had as good as promised me to prevent your engagement.'

'She couldn't have prevented it.'

'She can do anything; that's what I've always liked her for. I knew she could play any part; but I understood that she played them one by one. I didn't understand that she would play two at the same time.'

'I don't know what part she may have played to you,' Isabel said; 'that's between yourselves. To me she has been honest and kind and devoted.'

'Devoted, of course; she wished you to marry her candidate. She told me she was watching you only in order to interpose.'

'She said that to please you,' the girl answered; conscious, however, of the inadequacy of the explanation.

'To please me by deceiving me? She knows me better. Am I pleased today?'

'I don't think you're ever much pleased,' Isabel was obliged to reply. 'If

Madame Merle knew you would learn the truth what had she to gain by insincerity?'

'She gained time, as you see. While I waited for her to interfere you were marching away, and she was really beating the drum.'

'That's very well. But by your own admission you saw I was marching, and even if she had given the alarm you wouldn't have tried to stop me.'

'No, but someone else would.'

'Whom do you mean?' Isabel asked, looking very hard at her aunt.

Mrs Touchett's little bright eyes, active as they usually were, sustained her gaze rather than returned it. 'Would you have listened to Ralph?'

'Not if he had abused Mr Osmond.'

'Ralph doesn't abuse people; you know that perfectly. He cares very much for you.'

'I know he does,' said Isabel; 'and I shall feel the value of it now, for he knows that whatever I do I do with reason.'

'He never believed you would do this. I told him you were capable of it, and he argued the other way.'

'He did it for the sake of argument,' the girl smiled. 'You don't accuse him of having deceived you; why should you accuse Madame Merle?'

'He never pretended he'd prevent it.'

'I'm glad of that!' cried Isabel gaily. 'I wish very much,' she presently added, 'that when he comes you'd tell him first of my engagement.'

'Of course I'll mention it,' said Mrs Touchett. 'I shall say nothing more to you about it, but I give you notice I shall talk to others.'

'That's as you please. I only meant that it's rather better the announcement should come from you than from me.'

'I quite agree with you; it's much more proper!' And on this the aunt and the niece went to breakfast, where Mrs Touchett, as good as her word, made no allusion to Gilbert Osmond. After an interval of silence, however, she asked her companion from whom she had received a visit an hour before.

'From an old friend – an American gentleman,' Isabel said with a colour in her cheek.

'An American gentleman of course. It's only an American gentleman who calls at ten o'clock in the morning.'

'It was half past ten; he was in a great hurry; he goes away this evening.'

'Couldn't he have come yesterday, at the usual time?'

'He only arrived last night.'

'He spends but twenty-four hours in Florence?' Mrs Touchett cried. 'He's an American gentleman truly.'

'He is indeed,' said Isabel, thinking with perverse admiration of what Caspar Goodwood had done for her.

Two days afterwards Ralph arrived; but though Isabel was sure that Mrs Touchett had lost no time in imparting to him the great fact, he showed at first no open knowledge of it. Their prompted talk was naturally of his health; Isabel had many questions to ask about Corfu. She had been shocked by his appearance when he came into the room; she had forgotten how ill he looked. In spite of Corfu he looked very ill today, and she wondered if he were really worse or if she were simply disaccustomed to living with an invalid. Poor Ralph made no nearer approach to conventional beauty as he advanced in life, and the now apparently complete loss of his health had done little to mitigate the natural oddity of his person. Blighted and battered, but still responsive and still ironic, his face was like a lighted lantern patched with paper and unsteadily held; his thin whisker languished upon a lean cheek; the exorbitant curve of his nose defined itself more sharply. Lean he was altogether, lean and long and loosely-jointed; an accidental cohesion of relaxed angles. His brown velvet jacket had become perennial; his hands had fixed themselves in his pockets; he shambled and stumbled and shuffled in a manner that denoted great physical helplessness. It was perhaps this whimsical gait that helped to mark his character more than ever as that of the humorous invalid – the invalid for whom even his own disabilities are part of the general joke. They might well indeed with Ralph have been the chief cause of the want of seriousness marking his view of a world in which the reason for his own continued presence was past finding out. Isabel had grown fond of his ugliness; his awkwardness had become dear to her. They had been sweetened by association; they struck her as the very terms on which it had been given him to be charming. He was so charming that her sense of his being ill had hitherto had a sort of comfort in it; the state of his health had seemed not a limitation, but a kind of intellectual advantage; it absolved him from all professional and official emotions and left him the luxury of being exclusively personal. The personality so resulting was delightful; he had remained proof against the staleness of disease; he had had to consent to be deplorably ill, yet had somehow escaped being formally sick. Such had been the girl's impression of her cousin; and when she had pitied him it was only on reflection. As she reflected a good deal she had allowed him a certain amount of compassion; but she always had a dread of wasting that essence – a precious article, worth more to the giver than to anyone else. Now, however, it took no great sensibility to feel that poor Ralph's tenure of life was less elastic than it should be. He was a bright, free, generous spirit, he had all the illumination of wisdom and none of its pedantry, and yet he was distressfully dying.

Isabel noted afresh that life was certainly hard for some people, and she felt a delicate glow of shame as she thought how easy it now promised to become for herself. She was prepared to learn that Ralph was not pleased with her engagement; but she was not prepared, in spite of her affection for him, to let this fact spoil the situation. She was not even prepared, or so she thought, to resent his want of sympathy; for it would be his privilege – it would be indeed his natural line – to find fault with any step she might take towards marriage. One's cousin always pretended to hate one's husband; that was traditional, classical; it was a part of one's cousin's always pretending to adore one. Ralph was nothing if not critical; and though she would certainly, other things being equal, have been as glad to marry to please him as to please anyone, it would be absurd to regard as important that her choice should square with his views. What were his views after all? He had pretended to believe she had better have married Lord Warburton; but this was only because she had refused that excellent man. If she had accepted him Ralph would certainly have taken another tone; he always took the opposite. You could criticize any marriage; it was the essence of a marriage to be open to criticism. How well she herself, should she only give her mind to it, might criticize this union of her own! She had other employment, however, and Ralph was welcome to relieve her of the care. Isabel was prepared to be most patient and most indulgent. He must have seen that, and this made it the more odd he should say nothing. After three days had elapsed without his speaking our young woman wearied of waiting; dislike it as he would, he might at least go through the form. We, who know more about poor Ralph than his cousin, may easily believe that during the hours that followed his arrival at Palazzo Crescentini he had privately gone through many forms. His mother had literally greeted him with the great news, which had been even more sensibly chilling than Mrs Touchett's maternal kiss. Ralph was shocked and humiliated; his calculations had been false and the person in the world in whom he was most interested was lost. He drifted about the house like a rudderless vessel in a rocky stream, or sat in the garden of the palace on a great cane chair, his long legs extended, his head thrown back and his hat pulled over his eyes. He felt cold about the heart; he had never liked anything less. What could he do, what could he say? If the girl were irreclaimable could he pretend to like it? To attempt to reclaim her was permissible only if the attempt should succeed. To try to persuade her of anything sordid or sinister in the man to whose deep art she had succumbed would be decently discreet only in the event of her being persuaded. Otherwise he should simply have damned himself. It cost him an equal effort to speak his thought and to dissemble; he could neither assent with sincerity nor protest with hope. Meanwhile he knew – or rather he supposed – that the affinanced pair were daily renewing their mutual vows. Osmond at this moment showed himself little at Palazzo Crescentini; but Isabel met him every day elsewhere, as she was free to do after their engagement had been made public. She had taken a carriage by the month, so as not to be indebted to her aunt for the means of pursuing a course of which Mrs Touchett disapproved, and she drove in the morning to the Cascine. This suburban wilderness, during the early hours, was void of all intruders, and our young lady, joined by her lover in its quietest part, strolled with him a while through the grey Italian shade and listened to the nightingales.

Chapter Thirty-four

One morning, on her return from her drive, some half-hour before luncheon, she quitted her vehicle in the court of the palace and, instead of ascending the great staircase, crossed the court, passed beneath another archway and entered the garden. A sweeter spot at this moment could not have been imagined. The stillness of noontide hung over it, and the warm shade, enclosed and still, made bowers like spacious caves. Ralph was sitting there in the clear gloom, at the base of a statue of Terpsichore – a dancing nymph with taper fingers and inflated draperies in the manner of Bernini; the extreme relaxation of his attitude suggested at first to Isabel that he was asleep. Her light footstep on the grass had not roused him, and before turning away she stood for a moment looking at him. During this instant he opened his eyes; upon which she sat down on a rustic chair that matched with his own. Though in her irritation she had accused him of indifference she was not blind to the fact that he had visibly had something to brood over. But she had explained his air of absence partly by the languor of his increased weakness, partly by worries connected with the property inherited from his father – the fruit of eccentric arrangements of which Mrs Touchett disapproved and which, as she had told Isabel, now encountered opposition from the other partners in the bank. He ought to have gone to England, his mother said instead of coming to Florence; he had not been there for months, and took no more interest in the bank than in the state of Patagonia.

'I'm sorry I waked you,' Isabel said; 'you look too tired.'

'I feel too tired. But I was not asleep. I was thinking of you.'

'Are you tired of that?'

'Very much so. It leads to nothing. The road's long and I never arrive.'

'What do you wish to arrive at?' she put to him, closing her parasol.

'At the point of expressing to myself properly what I think of your engagement.'

'Don't think too much of it,' she lightly returned.

'Do you mean that it's none of my business?'

'Beyond a certain point, yes.'

'That's the point I want to fix. I had an idea you may have found me wanting in good manners. I've never congratulated you.'

'Of course I've noticed that. I wondered why you were silent.'

'There have been a good many reasons. I'll tell you now,' Ralph said. He pulled off his hat and laid it on the ground; then he sat looking at her. He leaned back under the protection of Bernini, his head against his marble pedestal, his arms dropped on either side of him, his hands laid upon the rests of his wide chair. He looked awkward, uncomfortable; he hesitated long. Isabel said nothing; when people were embarrassed she was usually sorry for them, but she seemed determined not to help Ralph to utter a word that should not be to the honour of her high decision. 'I think I've hardly got over my surprise,' he went on at last. 'You were the last person I expected to see caught.'

'I don't know why you call it caught.'

'Because you're going to be put into a cage.'

'If I like my cage, that needn't trouble you,' she answered.

'That's what I wonder at; that's what I've been thinking of.'

'If you've been thinking you may imagine how I've thought! I'm satisfied that I'm doing well.'

'You must have changed immensely. A year ago you valued your liberty beyond everything. You wanted only to see life.'

'I've seen it,' said Isabel. 'It doesn't look to me now, I admit, such an inviting expanse.'

'I don't pretend it is; only I had an idea that you took a genial view of it and wanted to survey the whole field.'

'I've seen that one can't do anything so general. One must choose a corner and cultivate that.'

'That's what I think. And one must choose as good a corner as possible.

I had no idea, all winter, while I read your delightful letters, that you were choosing. You said nothing about it, and your silence put me off my guard.'

'It was not a matter I was likely to write to you about. Besides, I knew nothing of the future. It has all come lately. If you had been on your guard, however,' Isabel asked, 'what would you have done?'

'I should have said "Wait a little longer".'

'Wait for what?'

'Well, for a little more light,' said Ralph with rather an absurd smile, while his hands found their way into his pockets.

'Where should my light have come from? From you?'

'I might have struck a spark or two.'

Isabel had drawn off her gloves; she smoothed them out as they lay upon her knee. The mildness of this movement was accidental, for her expression was not conciliatory. 'You're beating about the bush, Ralph. You wish to say you don't like Mr Osmond, and yet you're afraid.'

'Willing to wound and yet afraid to strike? I'm willing to wound *him*, yes – but not to wound you. I'm afraid of you, not of him. If you marry him it won't be a fortunate way for me to have spoken.'

'*If* I marry him! Have you had any expectation of dissuading me?'

'Of course that seems to you too fatuous.'

'No,' said Isabel after a little; 'it seems to me too touching.'

'That's the same thing. It makes me so ridiculous that you pity me.'

She stroked out her long gloves again. 'I know you've a great affection for me. I can't get rid of that.'

'For heaven's sake don't try. Keep that well in sight. It will convince you how intensely I want you to do well.'

'And how little you trust me!'

There was a moment's silence; the warm noontide seemed to listen. 'I trust you, but I don't trust him,' said Ralph.

She raised her eyes and gave him a wide, deep look. 'You've said it now, and I'm glad you've made it so clear. But you'll suffer by it.'

'Not if you're just.'

'I'm very just,' said Isabel. 'What better proof of it can there be than that I'm not angry with you? I don't know what's the matter with me, but I'm not. I was when you began, but it has passed away. Perhaps I ought to be angry, but Mr Osmond wouldn't think so. He wants me to know everything; that's what I like him for. You've nothing to gain, I know that. I've never been so nice to you, as a girl, that you should have much reason for wishing me to remain one. You give very good advice; you've often done so. No, I'm very quiet; I've always believed in your wisdom,' she went on, boasting of her quietness, yet speaking with a kind of contained exaltation. It was her passionate desire to be just; it touched Ralph to the heart, affected him like a caress from a creature he had injured. He wished to interrupt, to reassure her; for a moment he was absurdly inconsistent; he would have retracted what he had said. But she gave him no chance; she went on, having caught a glimpse, as she thought, of the heroic line and desiring to advance in that direction. 'I see you've some special idea; I should like very much to hear it. I'm sure it's disinterested; I feel that. It seems a strange thing to argue about, and of course I ought to tell you definitely that if you expect to dissuade me you may give it up. You'll not move me an inch; it's too late.

As you say, I'm caught. Certainly it won't be pleasant for you to remember this, but your pain will be in your own thoughts. I shall never reproach you.'

'I don't think you ever will,' said Ralph. 'It's not in the least the sort of marriage I thought you'd make.'

'What sort of marriage was that, pray?'

'Well, I can hardly say. I hadn't exactly a positive view of it, but I had a negative. I didn't think you'd decide for – well, for *that* type.'

'What's the matter with Mr Osmond's type, if it be one? His being so independent, so individual, is what *I* most see in him,' the girl declared. 'What do you know against him? You know him scarcely at all.'

'Yes,' Ralph said, 'I know him very little, and I confess I haven't the facts and items to prove him a villain. But all the same I can't help feeling that you're running a grave risk.'

'Marriage is always a grave risk, and his risk's as grave as mine.'

'That's his affair! If he's afraid, let him back out. I wish to God he would.'

Isabel reclined in her chair, folding her arms and gazing a while at her cousin. 'I don't think I understand you,' she said at last coldly. 'I don't know what you're talking about.'

'I believed you'd marry a man of more importance.'

Cold, I say, her tone had been, but at this a colour like a flame leaped into her face. 'Of more importance to whom? It seems to me enough that one's husband should be of importance to one's self!'

Ralph blushed as well; his attitude embarrassed him. Physically speaking he proceeded to change it; he straightened himself, then leaned forward, resting a hand on each knee. He fixed his eyes on the ground; he had an air of the most respectful deliberation. 'I'll tell you in a moment what I mean,' he presently said. He felt agitated, intensely eager; now that he had opened the discussion he wished to discharge his mind. But he wished also to be superlatively gentle.

Isabel waited a little – then she went on with majesty. 'In everything that makes one care for people Mr Osmond is pre-eminent. There may be nobler natures, but I've never had the pleasure of meeting one. Mr Osmond's is the finest I know; he's good enough for me, and interesting enough, and clever enough. I'm far more struck with what he has and what he represents than with what he may lack.'

'I had treated myself to a charming vision of your future,' Ralph observed without answering this: 'I had amused myself with planning out a high destiny for you. There was to be nothing of this sort in it. You were not to come down so easily or so soon.'

'Come down, you say?'

'Well, that renders my sense of what has happened to you. You seemed to me to be soaring far up in the blue – to be sailing in the bright light, over the heads of men. Suddenly someone tosses up a faded rosebud – a missile that should never have reached you – and straight you drop to the ground. It hurts me,' said Ralph audaciously, 'hurts me as if I had fallen myself!'

The look of pain and bewilderment deepened in his companion's face. 'I don't understand you in the least,' she repeated. 'You say you amused yourself with a project for my career – I don't understand that. Don't amuse yourself too much, or I shall think you're doing it at my expense.'

Ralph shook his head. 'I'm not afraid of your not believing that I've had great ideas for you.'

'What do you mean by my soaring and sailing?' she pursued. 'I've never moved on a higher plane than I'm moving on now. There's nothing higher for a girl than to marry a – a person she likes,' said poor Isabel, wandering into the didactic.

'It's your liking the person we speak of that I venture to criticize, my dear cousin. I should have said that the man for you would have been a more active, larger, freer sort of nature.' Ralph hesitated, then added: 'I can't get over the sense that Osmond is somehow – well, small.' He had uttered the last word with no great assurance; he was afraid she would flash out again. But to his surprise she was quiet; she had the air of considering.

'Small?' She made it sound immense.

'I think he's narrow, selfish. He takes himself so seriously!'

'He has a great respect for himself; I don't blame him for that,' said Isabel. 'It makes one more sure to respect others.'

Ralph for a moment felt almost reassured by her reasonable tone. 'Yes, but everything is relative; one ought to feel one's relation to things – to others. I don't think Mr Osmond does that.'

'I've chiefly to do with his relation to me. In that he's excellent.'

'He's the incarnation of taste,' Ralph went on, thinking hard how he could best express Gilbert Osmond's sinister attributes without putting himself in the wrong by seeming to describe him coarsely. He wished to describe him impersonally, scientifically. 'He judges and measures, approves and condemns, altogether by that.'

'It's a happy thing then that his taste should be exquisite.'

'It's exquisite, indeed, since it has led him to select you as his bridge. But have you ever seen such a taste – a really exquisite one – ruffled?'

'I hope it may never be my fortune to fail to gratify my husband's.'

At these words a sudden passion leaped to Ralph's lips. 'Ah, that's wilful, that's unworthy of you! You were not meant to be measured in that way – you were meant for something better than to keep guard over the sensibilities of a sterile dilettante!

Isabel rose quickly and he did the same, so that they stood for a moment looking at each other as if he had flung down a defiance or an insult. But 'You go too far', she simply breathed.

'I've said what I had on my mind – and I've said it because I love you!'

Isabel turned pale: was he too on that tiresome list? She had a sudden wish to strike him off. 'Ah, then, you're not disinterested!'

'I love you, but I love without hope,' said Ralph quickly, forcing a smile and feeling that in that last declaration he had expressed more than he intended.

Isabel moved away and stood looking into the sunny stillness of the garden; but after a little she turned back to him. 'I'm afraid your talk then is the wildness of despair! I don't understand it – but it doesn't matter. I'm not arguing with you; it's impossible I should; I've only tried to listen to you. I'm much obliged to you for attempting to explain,' she said gently, as if the anger with which she had just sprung up had already subsided. 'It's very good of you to try to warn me, if you're really alarmed; but I won't promise to think of what you've said: I shall forget it as soon as possible. Try and forget it yourself; you've done your duty, and no man can do more. I can't explain to you what I feel, what I believe, and I wouldn't if I could.' She paused a moment and then went on with an inconsequence that Ralph observed even in the midst of his eagerness to discover some symptom of concession. 'I can't enter into your idea of Mr Osmond; I can't do it justice, because I see him in another way. He's not important – no, he's not important; he's a man to whom importance is supremely indifferent. If that's what you mean when you call him "small", then he's as small as you please. I call that large – it's the largest thing I know. I won't pretend to argue with you about a person I'm going to marry,' Isabel repeated. 'I'm not in the least concerned to defend Mr Osmond; he's not so weak as to need my defence. I should think it would seem strange even to yourself that I should talk of him so quietly and coldly, as if he were anyone else. I wouldn't talk of him at all to anyone but you; and you, after what you've said – I may just answer you once for all. Pray, would you wish me to make a mercenary marriage – what they call a marriage of ambition? I've only one ambition – to be free to follow out a good feeling. I had others once, but they've passed away. Do you complain of Mr Osmond because he's not rich? That's just what I like him for. I've fortunately money enough; I've never felt so thankful for it as today. There have been moments when I should like to go and kneel down by your father's grave: he did perhaps a better thing than he knew when he put it into my power to marry a poor man – a man who has borne his poverty with such dignity, with such indifference. Mr Osmond has never scrambled nor struggled – as he cared for no worldly prize. If that's to be narrow, if that's to be selfish, then it's very well. I'm not frightened by such words, I'm not even displeased; I'm only sorry that you should make a mistake. Others might have done so, but I'm surprised that *you* should. You might know a gentleman when you see one – you might know a fine mind. Mr Osmond makes no mistakes! He knows everything, he understands everything, he has the kindest, gentlest, highest spirit. You've got hold of some false idea. It's a pity, but I can't help it; it regards you more than me.' Isabel paused a moment, looking at her cousin with an eye illumined by a sentiment which contradicted the careful calmness of her manner – mingled sentiment, to which the angry pain excited by his words and the wounded pride of having needed to justify a choice of which she felt only the nobleness and purity, equally contributed. Though she paused Ralph said nothing; he saw she had more to say. She was grand, but she was highly solicitous; she was indifferent, but she was all in a passion. 'What sort of a person should you have liked me to marry?' she asked suddenly. 'You talk about one's soaring and sailing, but if one marries at all one touches the earth. One has human feelings and needs, one has a heart in one's bosom, and one must marry a particular individual. Your mother has never forgiven me for not having come to a better understanding with Lord Warburton, and she's horrified at my contenting myself with a person who has none of his great advantages – no property, no title, no honours, no houses, no lands, nor position, nor reputation, nor brilliant belongings of any sort. It's the total absence of all these things that please me. Mr Osmond's simply a very lonely, a very cultivated and a very honest man – he's not a prodigious proprietor.'

Ralph had listened with great attention, as if everything she said merited deep consideration; but in truth he was only half-thinking of the things she said, he was for the rest simply accommodating himself to the weight of his total impression – the impression of her ardent good faith. She was wrong, but she believed; she was deluded, but she was dismally consistent. It was wonderfully characteristic of her that, having invented a fine theory about Gilbert Osmond, she loved him not for what he really possessed, but for his very poverties dressed out as honours. Ralph remembered what he had said to his father about wishing to put it into her power to meet the requirements of her imagination. He had done so, and the girl had taken full advantage of the luxury. Poor Ralph felt sick; he felt ashamed. Isabel had uttered her last words with a low solemnity of conviction which virtually terminated the discussion and she closed it formally by turning away and walking back to the house. Ralph walked beside her, and they passed into the court together and reached the big staircase. Here he stopped and Isabel paused, turning on him a face of elation – absolutely and perversely of gratitude. His opposition had made her own conception of her conduct clearer to her. 'Shall you not come up to breakfast?' she asked.

'No; I want no breakfast; I'm not hungry.'

'You ought to eat,' said the girl; 'you live on air.'

'I do, very much, and I shall go back into the garden and take another mouthful. I came thus far simply to say this. I told you last year that if you were to get into trouble I should feel terribly sold. That's how I feel today.'

'Do you think I'm in trouble?'

'One's in trouble when one's in error.'

'Very well,' said Isabel; 'I shall never complain of my trouble to you!' And she moved up the staircase.

Ralph, standing there with his hands in his pockets, followed her with his eyes; then the lurking chill of the high-walled court struck him and made him shiver, so that he returned to the garden to breakfast on the Florentine sunshine.

Chapter Thirty-five

Isabel, when she strolled in the Cascine with her lover, felt no impulse to tell him how little he was approved at Palazzo Crescentini. The discreet opposition offered to her marriage by her aunt and her cousin made on the whole no great impression upon her; the moral of it was simply that they disliked Gilbert Osmond. This dislike was not alarming to Isabel; she scarcely even regretted it; for it served mainly to throw into higher relief the fact, in every way so honourable, that she married to please herself. One did other things to please other people; one did this for a more personal satisfaction; and Isabel's satisfaction was confirmed by her lover's admirable good conduct. Gilbert Osmond was in love, and he had never deserved less than during these still, bright days, each of them numbered, which preceded the fulfilment of his hopes, the harsh criticism passed upon him by Ralph Touchett. The chief impression produced on Isabel's spirit by this criticism was that the passion of love separated its victim terribly from everyone but the loved object. She felt herself disjoined from everyone she had ever known before – from her two sisters, who wrote to express a dutiful hope that she would be happy, and a surprise, somewhat more vague, at her not having chosen a consort who was the hero of a richer accumulation of anecdote; from Henrietta, who, she was sure, would come out, too late, on purpose to remonstrate; from Lord Warburton, who would certainly console himself, and from Caspar Goodwood, who perhaps would not; from her aunt, who had cold, shallow ideas about marriage, for which she was not sorry to display her contempt; and from Ralph, whose talk about having great views for her was surely but a whimsical cover for a personal disappointment. Ralph apparently wished her not to marry at all – that was what it really meant – because he was amused with the spectacle of her adventures as a single woman. His disappointment made him say angry things about the man she preferred even to him: Isabel flattered herself that she believed Ralph had been angry. It was the more easy for her to believe this because, as I say, she had now little free or unemployed emotion for minor needs, and accepted as an incident, in fact quite as an ornament, of her lot the idea that to prefer Gilbert Osmond as she preferred him was perforce to break all other ties. She tasted of the sweets of this preference, and they made her conscious, almost with awe, of the invidious and remorseless tide of the charmed and possessed condition, great as was the traditional honour and imputed virtue of being in love. It was the tragic part of happiness; one's right was always made of the wrong of someone else.

The elation of success, which surely now flamed high in Osmond, emitted meanwhile very little smoke for so brilliant a blaze. Contentment, on his part, took no vulgar form; excitement, in the most self-conscious of men, was a kind of ecstasy of self-control. This disposition, however, made him an admirable lover; it gave him a constant view of the smitten and dedicated state. He never forgot himself, as I say; and so he never forgot to be graceful and tender, to wear the appearance – which presented indeed no difficulty – of stirred senses and deep intentions. He was immensely pleased with his young lady; Madame Merle had made him a present of incalculable value. What could be a finer thing to live with than a high spirit attuned to softness? For would not the softness be all for one's self, and the strenuousness for society, which admired the air of superiority? What could be a happier gift in a companion than a quick, fanciful mind which saved one repetitions and reflected one's thought on a polished, elegant surface? Osmond hated to see his thought reproduced literally – that made it look stale and stupid; he preferred it to be freshened in the reproduction even as 'words' by music. His egotism had never taken the crude form of desiring a dull wife; this lady's intelligence was to be a silver plate, not an earthen one – a plate that he might heap up with ripe fruits, to which it would give a decorative value, so that talk might become for him a sort of served dessert. He found the silver quality in this perfection in Isabel; he could tap her imagination with his knuckle and make it ring. He knew perfectly, though he had not been told, that their union enjoyed little favour with the girl's relations; but he had always treated her so completely as an independent person that it hardly seemed necessary to express regret for the attitude of her family. Nevertheless, one morning, he made an abrupt allusion to it. 'It's the difference in our fortune they don't like,' he said. 'They think I'm in love with your money.'

'Are you speaking of my aunt – of my cousin?' Isabel asked. 'How do you know what they think?'

'You've not told me they're pleased, and when I wrote to Mrs Touchett the other day she never answered my note. If they had been delighted I should have had some sign of it, and the fact of my being poor and you rich is the most obvious explanation of their reserve. But of course when a poor man marries a rich girl he must be prepared for imputations. I don't mind them; I only care for one thing – for your not having the shadow of a doubt. I don't care what people of whom I ask nothing think – I'm not even capable perhaps of wanting to know. I've never so concerned myself, God forgive me, and why should I begin today, when I have taken to myself a compensation for everything? I won't pretend I'm sorry you're rich; I'm delighted. I delight in everything that's yours – whether it be money or virtue. Money's a horrid thing to follow, but a charming thing to meet. It seems to me, however, that I've sufficiently proved the limits of my itch for it: I never in my life tried to earn a penny, and I ought to be less subject to suspicion than most of the people one sees grubbing and grabbing. I suppose it's their business to suspect – that of your family; it's proper on the whole they should. They'll like me better some day; so will you, for that matter. Meanwhile my business is not to make myself bad blood, but simply to be thankful for life and love.' 'It has made me better, loving you,' he said on another occasion; 'it has made me wiser and easier and – I won't pretend to deny – brighter and nicer and even stronger. I used to want a great many things before and to be angry I didn't have them. Theoretically I was satisfied, as I once told you. I flattered myself I had limited my wants. But I was subject to irritation; I used to have morbid, sterile, hateful fits of hunger, of desire. Now I'm really satisfied, because I can't think of anything better. It's just as when one has been trying to spell out a book in the twilight and suddenly the lamp comes in. I had been putting out my eyes over the book of life and finding nothing to reward me for my pains; but now that I can read it properly I see it's a delightful story. My dear girl, I can't tell you how life seems to stretch there before us – what a long summer afternoon awaits us. It's the latter half of an Italian day – with a golden haze, and the shadows just lengthening, and that divine delicacy in the light, the air, the landscape, which I have loved all my life and which you love today. Upon my honour, I don't see why we shouldn't get on. We've got what we like – to say nothing of having each other. We've the faculty of admiration and several capital convictions. We're not stupid, we're not mean, we're not under bonds to any kind of ignorance or dreariness. You're remarkably fresh, and I'm remarkably well-seasoned. We've my poor child to amuse me; we'll try and make up some little life for her. It's all soft and mellow – it has the Italian colouring.'

They made a good many plans, but they left themselves also a good deal of latitude; it was a matter of course, however, that they should live for the present in Italy. It was in Italy that they had met, Italy had been a party to their first impressions of each other, and Italy should be a party to their happiness. Osmond had the attachment of old acquaintance and Isabel the stimulus of new, which seemed to assure her a future at a high level of consciousness of the beautiful. The desire for unlimited expansion had been succeeded in her soul by the sense that life was vacant without some private duty that might gather one's energies to a point. She had told Ralph she had 'seen life' in a year or two and that she was already tired, not of the act of living, but of that of observing. What had become of all her ardours, her aspirations, her theories, her high estimate of her independence and her incipient conviction that she should never marry? These things had been absorbed in a more primitive need – a need the answer to which brushed away numberless questions, yet gratified infinite desires. It simplified the situation at a stroke, it came down from above like the light of the stars, and it needed no explanation. There was explanation enough in the fact that he was her lover, her own, and that she should be able to be of use to him. She could surrender to him with a kind of humility, she could marry him with a kind of pride; she was not only taking, she was giving.

He brought Pansy with him two or three times to the Cascine – Pansy who was very little taller than a year before, and not much older. That she would always be a child was the conviction expressed by her father, who held her by the hand when she was in her sixteenth year and told her to go and play while he sat down a little with the pretty lady. Pansy wore a short dress and a long coat; her hat always seemed too big for her. She found pleasure in walking off, with quick, short steps, to the end of the alley, and then in walking back with a smile that seemed an appeal for approbation. Isabel approved in abundance, and the abundance had the personal touch that the child's affectionate nature craved. She watched her indications as if for herself also much depended on them – Pansy already so represented part of the service she could render, part of the responsibility she could face. Her father took so the childish view of her that he had not yet explained to her the new relation in which he stood to the elegant Miss Archer. 'She doesn't know,' he said to Isabel; 'she doesn't guess; she thinks it perfectly natural that you and I should come and walk here together simply as good friends. There seems to me something enchantingly innocent in that; it's the way I like her to be. No, I'm not a failure, as I used to think; I've succeeded in two things. I'm to marry the woman I adore, and I've brought up my child, as I wished, in the old way.'

He was very fond, in all things, of the 'old way'; that had struck Isabel as one of his fine, quiet, sincere notes. 'It occurs to me that you'll not know whether you've succeeded until you've told her,' she said. 'You must see how she takes your news. She may be horrified – she may be jealous.'

'I'm not afraid of that; she's too fond of you on her own account. I should like to leave her in the dark a little longer – to see if it will come into her head that if we're not engaged we ought to be.'

Isabel was impressed by Osmond's artistic, the plastic view, as it somehow appeared, of Pansy's innocence – her own appreciation of it being more anxiously moral. She was perhaps not the less pleased when he told her a few days later that he had communicated the fact to his daughter, who had made such a pretty little speech – 'Oh, then I shall have a beautiful sister!' She was neither surprised nor alarmed; she had not cried, as he expected.

'Perhaps she had guessed it,' said Isabel.

'Don't say that; I should be disgusted if I believed that. I thought it would be just a little shock; but the way she took it proves that her good manners are paramount. That's also what I wished. You shall see for yourself; tomorrow she shall make you her congratulations in person.'

The meeting, on the morrow, took place at the Countess Gemini's, whither Pansy had been conducted by her father, who knew that Isabel was to come in the afternoon to return a visit made her by the Countess on learning that they were to become sisters-in-law. Calling at Casa Touchett the visitor had not found Isabel at home; but after our young woman had been ushered into the Countess's drawing-room Pansy arrived to say that her aunt would presently appear. Pansy was spending the day with that lady, who thought her of an age to begin to learn how to carry herself in company. It was Isabel's view that the little girl might have given lessons on deportment to her relative, and nothing could have justified this conviction more than the manner in which Pansy acquitted herself while they waited together for the Countess. Her father's decision, the year before, had finally been to send her back to the convent to receive the last graces, and Madame Catherine had evidently carried out her theory that Pansy was to be fitted for the great world.

'Papa has told me that you've kindly consented to marry him,' said this excellent woman's pupil. 'It's very delightful; I think you'll suit very well.'

'You think I shall suit *you*?'

'You'll suit me beautifully; but what I mean is that you and papa will suit each other. You're both so quiet and so serious. You're not so quiet as he – or even as Madame Merle; but you're more quiet than many others. He should not for instance have a wife like my aunt. She's always in motion, in agitation – today especially; you'll see when she comes in. They told us at the convent it was wrong to judge our elders, but I suppose there's no harm if we judge them favourably. You'll be a delightful companion for papa.'

'For you too, I hope,' Isabel said.

'I speak first of him on purpose. I've told you already what I myself think of you; I liked you from the first. I admire you so much that I think it will be a good fortune to have you always before me. You'll be my model; I shall try to imitate you though I'm afraid it will be very feeble. I'm very glad for papa – he needed something more than me. Without you I don't see how he could have got it. You'll be my stepmother, but we mustn't use that word. They're always said to be cruel; but I don't think you'll ever so much as pinch or even push me. I'm not afraid at all.'

'My good little Pansy,' said Isabel gently. 'I shall be ever so kind to you.' A vague, inconsequent vision of her coming in some odd way to need it had intervened with the effect of a chill.

'Very well then, I've nothing to fear,' the child returned with her note of prepared promptitude. What teaching she had, it seemed to suggest – or what penalties for non-performance she dreaded!

Her description of her aunt had not been incorrect; the Countess Gemini was further than ever from having folded her wings. She entered the room with a flutter through the air and kissed Isabel first on the forehead and then on each cheek as if according to some ancient prescribed rite. She drew the visitor to a sofa and, looking at her with a variety of turns of the head, began to talk very much as if, seated brush in hand before an easel, she was applying a series of considered touches to a composition of figures already sketched in. 'If you expect me to congratulate you I must beg you to excuse me. I don't suppose you care if I do or not; I believe you're supposed not to care – through being so clever – for all sorts of ordinary things. But I care myself if I tell fibs; I never tell them unless there's something rather good to be gained. I don't see what's to be gained with you – especially as you wouldn't believe me. I don't make professions any more than I make paper flowers or flouncey lampshades – I don't know how. My lampshades would be sure to take fire, my roses and my fibs to be larger than life. I'm very glad for my own sake that you're to marry Osmond; but I won't pretend I'm glad for yours. You're very brilliant – you know that's the way you're always spoken of; you're an heiress and very good-looking and original, not *banal*; so it's a good thing to have you in the family. Our family's very good, you know; Osmond will have told you that; and my mother was rather distinguished – she was called the American Corinne. But we're dreadfully fallen, I think, and perhaps you'll pick us up. I've great confidence in you; there are ever so many things I want to talk to you about. I never congratulate any girl on marrying; I think they ought to make it somehow not quite so awful a steel trap. I suppose Pansy oughtn't to hear all this; but that's what she has come to me for – to acquire the tone of society. There's no harm in her knowing what horrors she may be in for. When first I got an idea that my brother had designs on you I thought of writing to you, to recommend you, in the strongest terms, not to listen to him. Then I thought it would be disloyal, and I hate anything of that kind. Besides, as I say, I was enchanted for myself; and after all I'm very selfish. By the way, you won't respect me, not one little mite, and we shall never be intimate. I should like it, but you won't. Some day, all the same, we shall be better friends than you will believe at first. My husband will come and see you, though, as you probably know, he's on no sort of terms with Osmond. He's very fond of going to see pretty women, but I'm not afraid of you. In the first place I don't care what he does. In the second, you won't care a straw for him; he won't be a bit, at any time, your affair, and, stupid as he is, he'll see you're not his. Some day, if you can stand it, I'll tell you all about him. Do you think my niece ought to go out of the room? Pansy, go and practise a little in my boudoir.'

'Let her stay, please,' said Isabel. 'I would rather hear nothing that Pansy may not!'

Chapter Thirty-six

One afternoon of the autumn of 1876, towards dusk, a young man of pleasing appearance rang at the door of a small apartment on the third floor of an old Roman house. On its being opened he inquired for Madame Merle; whereupon the servant, a neat, plain woman, with a French face and a lady's maid's manner, ushered him into a diminutive drawing-room and requested the favour of his name. 'Mr Edward Rosier,' said the young man, who sat down to wait till his hostess should appear.

The reader will perhaps not have forgotten that Mr Rosier was an ornament of the American circle in Paris, but it may also be remembered that he sometimes vanished from its horizon. He had spent a portion of several winters at Pau, and as he was a gentleman of constituted habits he might have continued for years to pay his annual visit to this charming resort. In the summer of 1876, however, an incident befell him which changed the current not only of his thoughts, but of his customary sequences. He passed a month in the Upper Engadine and encountered at Saint Moritz a charming young girl. To this little person he began to pay, on the spot, particular attention: she struck him as exactly the household angel he had long been looking for. He was never precipitate, he was nothing if not discreet, so he forebore for the present to declare his passion; but it seemed to him when they parted – the young lady to go down into Italy and her admirer to proceed to Geneva, where he was under bonds to join other friends – that he should be romantically wretched if he were not to see her again. The simplest way to do so was to go in the autumn to Rome, where Miss Osmond was domiciled with her family. Mr Rosier started on his pilgrimage to the Italian capital and reached it on the first of November. It was a pleasant thing to do, but for the young man there was a strain of the heroic in the enterprise. He might expose himself, unseasoned, to the poison of the Roman air, which in November lay, notoriously, much in wait. Fortune, however, favours the brave; and this adventurer, who took three grains of quinine a day, had at the end of a month no cause to deplore his temerity. He had made to a certain extent good use of his time; he had devoted it in vain to finding a flaw in Pansy Osmond's composition. She was admirably finished; she had had the last touch; she was really a consummate piece. He thought of her in amorous meditation a good deal as he might have thought of a Dresden-china shepherdess. Miss Osmond, indeed, in the bloom of her juvenility, had a hint of the rococo which Rosier, whose taste was predominantly for that manner, could not fail to appreciate. That he esteemed the productions of comparatively frivolous periods would have been apparent from the attention he bestowed upon Madame Merle's drawing-room, which, although furnished with specimens of every style, was especially rich in articles of the last two centuries. He had immediately put a glass into one eye and looked round; and then 'By jove, she has some jolly good things!' he had yearningly murmured. The room was small and densely filled with furniture; it gave an impression of faded silk and little statuettes which might totter if one moved. Rosier got up and wandered about with his careful tread, bending over the tables charged with knick-knacks and the cushions embossed with princely arms. When Madame Merle came in she found him standing before the fireplace with his nose very close to the great lace flounce attached to the damask cover of the mantel. He lifted it delicately, as if he were smelling it.

'It's old Venetian,' she said; 'it's rather good.'

'It's too good for this; you ought to wear it.'

'They tell me you have some better in Paris, in the same situation.'

'Ah, but I can't wear mine,' smiled the visitor.

'I don't see why you shouldn't! I've better lace than that to wear.'

His eyes wandered, lingeringly, round the room again. 'You've some very good things.'

'Yes, but I hate them.'

'Do you want to get rid of them?' the young man quickly asked.

'No, it's good to have something to hate: one works it off!'

'I love my things,' said Mr Rosier as he sat there flushed with all his recognitions. 'But it's not about them, nor about yours, that I came to talk to you.' He paused a moment and then, with greater softness: 'I care more for Miss Osmond than for all the *bibelots* in Europe!'

Madame Merle opened wide eyes. 'Did you come to tell me that?'

'I came to ask your advice.'

She looked at him with a friendly frown, stroking her chin with her large white hand. 'A man in love, you know, doesn't ask advice.'

'Why not, if he's in a difficult position? That's often the case with a man in love. I've been in love before, and I know. But never so much as this time – really never so much. I should like particularly to know what you think of my prospects. I'm afraid that for Mr Osmond I'm not – well, a real collector's piece.'

'Do you wish me to intercede?' Madame Merle asked with her fine arms folded and her handsome mouth drawn up to the left.

'If you could say a good word for me I should be greatly obliged. There will be no use in my troubling Miss Osmond unless I have good reason to believe her father will consent.'

'You're very considerate; that's in your favour. But you assume in rather an off-hand way that *I* think you a prize.'

'You've been very kind to me,' said the young man. 'That's why I came.'

'I'm always kind to people who have good Louis Quatorze. It's very rare now, and there's no telling what one may get by it.' With which the left-hand corner of Madame Merle's mouth gave expression to the joke.

But he looked, in spite of it, literally apprehensive and consistently strenuous. 'Ah, I thought you liked me for myself!'

'I like you very much; but, if you please, we won't analyse. Pardon me if I seem patronizing, but I think you a perfect little gentleman. I must tell you, however, that I've not the marrying of Pansy Osmond.'

'I didn't suppose that. But you've seemed to me intimate with her family, and I thought you might have influence.'

Madame Merle considered. 'Whom do you call her family?'

'Why, her father; and – how do you say it in English? – her *belle-mère*.'

'Mr Osmond's her father, certainly; but his wife can scarcely be termed a member of her family. Mrs Osmond has nothing to do with marrying her.'

'I'm sorry for that,' said Rosier with an amiable sigh of good faith. 'I think Mrs Osmond would favour me.'

'Very likely – if her husband doesn't.'

He raised his eyebrows. 'Does she take the opposite line from him?'

'In everything. They think quite differently.'

'Well,' said Rosier, 'I'm sorry for that; but it's none of my business. She's very fond of Pansy.'

'Yes, she's very fond of Pansy.'

'And Pansy has a great affection for her. She has told me how she loves her as if she were her own mother.'

'You must, after all, have had some very intimate talk with the poor child,' said Madame Merle. 'Have you declared your sentiments?'

'Never!' cried Rosier, lifting his neatly gloved hand. 'Never till I've assured myself of those of the parents.'

'You always wait for that? You've excellent principles; you observe the proprieties.'

'I think you're laughing at me,' the young man murmured, dropping back in his chair and feeling his small moustache. 'I didn't expect that of you, Madame Merle.'

She shook her head calmly, like a person who saw things as she saw them. 'You don't do me justice. I think your conduct in excellent taste and the best you could adopt. Yes, that's what I think.'

'I wouldn't agitate her – only to agitate her; I love her too much for that,' said Ned Rosier.

'I'm glad, after all, that you've told me,' Madame Merle went on. 'Leave it to me a little; I think I can help you.'

'I said you were the person to come to!' her visitor cried with prompt elation.

'You were very clever,' Madame Merle returned more dryly. 'When I say I can help you I mean once assuming your cause to be good. Let us think a little if it is.'

'I'm awfully decent, you know,' said Rosier earnestly. 'I won't say I've no faults, but I'll say I've no vices.'

'All that's negative, and it always depends, also, on what people call vices. What's the positive side? What's the virtuous? What have you got besides your Spanish lace and your Dresden teacups?'

'I've a comfortable little fortune – about forty thousand francs a year. With the talent I have for arranging, we can live beautifully on such an income.'

'Beautifully, no. Sufficiently, yes. Even that depends on where you live.'

'Well, in Paris. I would undertake it in Paris.'

Madame Merle's mouth rose to the left. 'It wouldn't be famous; you'd have to make use of the teacups, and they'd get broken.'

'We don't want to be famous. If Miss Osmond should have everything pretty it would be enough. When one's as pretty as she one can afford – well, quite cheap *faïence*. She ought never to wear anything but muslin – without the sprig,' said Rosier reflectively.

'Wouldn't you even allow her the sprig? She'd be much obliged to you at any rate for that theory.'

'It's the correct one, I assure you; and I'm sure she'd enter into it. She understands all that; that's why I love her.'

'She's a very good little girl, and most tidy – also extremely graceful. But her father, to the best of my belief, can give her nothing.'

Rosier scarce demurred. 'I don't in the least desire that he should. But I may remark, all the same, that he lives like a rich man.'

'The money's his wife's; she brought him a large fortune.'

'Mrs Osmond then is very fond of her stepdaughter; she may do something.'

'For a love-sick swain you have your eyes about you!' Madame Merle exclaimed with a laugh.

'I esteem a *dot* very much. I can do without it, but I esteem it.'

'Mrs Osmond,' Madame Merle went on, 'will probably prefer to keep her money for her own children.'

'Her own children? Surely she has none.'

'She may have yet. She had a poor little boy, who died two years ago, six months after his birth. Others therefore may come.'

'I hope they will, if it will make her happy. She's a splendid woman.'

Madame Merle failed to burst into speech. 'Ah, about her there's much to be said. Splendid as you like! We've not exactly made out that you're a *parti*. The absence of vices is hardly a source of income.'

'Pardon me, I think it may be,' said Rosier quite lucidly.

'You'll be a touching couple, living on your innocence!'

'I think you underrate me.'

'You're not so innocent as that? Seriously,' said Madame Merle, 'of course forty thousand francs a year and a nice character are a combination to be considered. I don't say it's to be jumped at, but there might be a worse offer. Mr Osmond, however, will probably incline to believe he can do better.'

'*He* can do so perhaps; but what can his daughter do? She can't do better than marry the man she loves. For she does, you know,' Rosier added eagerly.

'She does – I know it.'

'Ah,' cried the young man, 'I said you were the person to come to.'

'But I don't know how *you* know it, if you haven't asked her,' Madame Merle went on.

'In such a case there's no need of asking and telling; as you say, we're an innocent couple. How did *you* know it?'

'I who am not innocent? By being very crafty. Leave it to me; I'll find out for you.'

Rosier got up and stood smoothing his hat. 'You say that rather coldly. Don't simply find out how it is, but try to make it as it should be.'

'I'll do my best. I'll try to make the most of your advantages.'

'Thank you so very much. Meanwhile then I'll say a word to Mrs Osmond.'

'*Gardez-vous-en bien!*' And Madame Merle was on her feet. 'Don't set her going, or you'll spoil everything.'

Rosier gazed into his hat; he wondered whether his hostess *had* been after all the right person to come to. 'I don't think I understand you. I'm an old friend of Mrs Osmond, and I think she would like me to succeed.'

'Be an old friend as much as you like; the more old friends she has the better, for she doesn't get on very well with some of her new. But don't for the present try to make her take up the cudgels for you. Her husband may have other views, and, as a person who wishes her well, I advise you not to multiply points of difference between them.'

Poor Rosier's face assumed an expression of alarm; a suit for the hand of Pansy Osmond was even a more complicated business than his taste for proper transitions had allowed. But the extreme good sense which he concealed under a surface suggesting that of a careful owner's 'best set' came to his assistance. 'I don't see that I'm bound to consider Mr Osmond so very much!' he exclaimed.

'No, but you should consider *her*. You say you're an old friend. Would you make her suffer?'

'Not for the world.'

'Then be very careful, and let the matter alone till I've taken a few soundings.'

'Let the matter alone, dear Madame Merle? Remember that I'm in love.'

'Oh, you won't burn up! Why did you come to me, if you're not to heed what I say?'

'You're very kind; I'll be very good,' the young man promised. 'But I'm afraid Mr Osmond's pretty hard,' he added in his mild voice as he went to the door.

Madame Merle gave a short laugh. 'It has been said before. But his wife isn't easy either.'

'Ah, she's a splendid woman!' Ned Rosier repeated, for departure.

He resolved that his conduct should be worthy of an aspirant who was already a model of discretion; but he saw nothing in any pledge he had given Madame Merle that made it improper he should keep himself in spirits by an occasional visit to Miss Osmond's home. He reflected constantly on what his adviser had said to him, and turned over in his mind the impression of her rather circumspect tone. He had gone to her *de confiance*, as they put it in Paris; but it was possible he had been precipitate. He found difficulty in thinking of himself as rash – he had incurred this reproach so rarely; but it certainly was true that he had known Madame Merle only for the last month, and that his thinking her a delightful woman was not, when one came to look into it, a reason for assuming that she would be eager to push Pansy Osmond into his arms, gracefully arranged as these members might be to receive her. She had indeed shown him benevolence, and she was a person of consideration among the girl's people, where she had a rather striking appearance (Rosier had more than once wondered how she managed it) of being intimate without being familiar. But possibly he had exaggerated these advantages. There was no particular reason why she should take trouble for him; a charming woman was charming to everyone, and Rosier felt rather a fool when he thought of his having appealed to her on the ground that she had distinguished him. Very likely – though she had appeared to say it in joke – she was really only thinking of his *bibelots*. Had it come into her head that he might offer her two or three of the gems of his collection? If she would only help him to marry Miss Osmond he would present her with his whole museum. He could hardly say so to her outright; it would seem too gross a bribe. But he should like her to believe it.

It was with these thoughts that he went again to Mrs Osmond's, Mrs Osmond having an 'evening' – she had taken the Thursday of each week – when his presence could be accounted for on general principles of civility. The object of Mr Rosier's well-regulated affection dwelt in a high house in the very heart of Rome; a dark and massive structure overlooking a sunny *piazzetta* in the neighbourhood of the Farnese Palace. In a palace, too, little Pansy lived – a palace by Roman measure, but a dungeon to poor Rosier's apprehensive mind. It seemed to him of evil omen that the young lady he wished to marry, and whose fastidious father he doubted of his ability to conciliate, should be immured in a kind of domestic fortress, a pile which bore a stern old Roman name, which smelt of historic deed, of crime and craft and violence, which was mentioned in 'Murray' and visited by tourists who looked, on a vague survey, disappointed and depressed, and which had frescoes by Caravaggio in the *piano nobile* and a row of mutilated statues and dusty urns in the wide, nobly-arched loggia overhanging the damp court where a fountain gushed out of a mossy niche. In a less preoccupied frame of mind he could have done justice to the Palazzo Roccanera; he could have entered into the sentiment of Mrs Osmond, who had once told him that on settling themselves in Rome she and her husband had chosen this habitation for the love of local colour. It had local colour enough, and though he knew less about architecture than about Limoges enamels he could see that the proportions of the windows and even the details of the cornice had quite the grand air. But Rosier was haunted by the conviction that at picturesque periods young girls had been shut up there to keep them from their true loves, and then, under the threat of being thrown into convents, had been forced into unholy marriages. There was one point, however, to which he always did justice when once he found himself in Mrs Osmond's warm, rich-looking reception-rooms, which were on the second floor. He acknowledged that these people were very strong in 'good things'. It was a taste of Osmond's own – not at all of hers; this she had told him the first time he came to the house, when, after asking himself for a quarter of an hour whether they had even better 'French' than he in Paris, he was obliged on the spot to admit that they had, very much, and vanquished his envy, as a gentleman should, to the point of expressing to his hostess his pure admiration of her treasures. He learned from Mrs Osmond that her husband had made a large collection before their marriage and that, though he had annexed a number of fine pieces within the last three years, he had achieved his greatest finds at a time when he had not the advantage of her advice. Rosier interpreted this information according to principles of his own. For 'advice' read 'cash', he said to himself; and the fact that Gilbert Osmond had landed his highest prizes during his impecunious season confirmed his most cherished doctrine – the doctrine that a collector may freely be poor if he be only patient. In general, when Rosier presented himself on a Thursday evening, his first recognition was for the walls of the saloon; there were three or four objects his eyes really yearned for. But after his talk with Madame Merle he felt the extreme seriousness of his position; and now, when he came in, he looked about for the daughter of the house with such eagerness as might be permitted a gentleman whose smile, as he crossed a threshold, always took everything comfortable for granted.

Chapter Thirty-seven

Pansy was not in the first of the rooms, a large apartment with a concave ceiling and walls covered with old red damask; it was here Mrs Osmond usually sat – though she was not in her most customary place tonight – and that a circle of more especial intimates gathered about the fire. The room was flushed with subdued, diffused brightness; it contained the larger things and – almost always – an odour of flowers. Pansy on this occasion was presumably in the next of the series, the resort of younger visitors, where tea was served. Osmond stood before the chimney, leaning back with his hands behind him; he had one foot up and was warming the sole. Half a dozen persons, scattered near him, were talking together; but he was not in the conversation; his eyes had an expression, frequent with them, that seemed to represent them as engaged with objects more worth their while than the appearances actually thrust upon them. Rosier, coming in unannounced, failed to attract his attention; but the young man, who was very punctilious, though he was even exceptionally conscious that it was the wife, not the husband, he had come to see, went up to shake hands with him. Osmond put out his left hand, without changing his attitude.

'How d'ye do? My wife's somewhere about.'

'Never fear; I shall find her,' said Rosier cheerfully.

Osmond, however, took him in; he had never in his life felt himself so efficiently looked at. 'Madame Merle has told him, and he doesn't like it,' he privately reasoned. He had hoped Madame Merle would be there, but she was not in sight; perhaps she was in one of the other rooms or would come later. He had never especially delighted in Gilbert Osmond, having a fancy he gave himself airs. But Rosier was not quickly resentful, and where politeness was concerned had ever a strong need of being quite in the right. He looked round him and smiled, all without help, and then in a moment, 'I saw a jolly good piece of Capo di Monte today,' he said.

Osmond answered nothing at first; but presently, while he warmed his boot-sole, 'I don't care a fig for Capo di Monte!' he returned.

'I hope you're not losing your interest?'

'In old pots and plates? Yes, I'm losing my interest.'

Rosier for an instant forgot the delicacy of his position. 'You're not thinking of parting with a – a piece or two?'

'No, I'm not thinking of parting with anything at all, Mr Rosier,' said Osmond, with his eyes still on the eyes of his visitor.

'Ah, you want to keep, but not to add,' Rosier remarked brightly.

'Exactly. I've nothing I wish to match.'

Poor Rosier was aware he had blushed; he was distressed at his want of assurance. 'Ah well, *I* have!' was all he could murmur; and he knew his murmur was partly lost as he turned away. He took his course to the adjoining room and met Mrs Osmond coming out of the deep doorway. She was dressed in black velvet; she looked high and splendid, as he had said, and yet oh so radiantly gentle! We know what Mr Rosier thought of her and the terms in which, to Madame Merle, he had expressed his admiration. Like his appreciation of her dear little stepdaughter it was based partly on his eye for decorative character, his instinct for authenticity; but also on a sense for uncatalogued values, for that secret of a 'lustre' beyond any recorded losing or rediscovering, which his devotion to brittle wares had still not disqualified him to recognize. Mrs Osmond, at present, might well have gratified such tastes. The years had touched her only to enrich her; the flower of her youth had not faded, it only hung more quietly on its stem. She had lost something of that quick eagerness to which her husband had privately taken exception – she had more the air of being able to wait. Now, at all events, framed in the gilded doorway, she struck our young man as the picture of a gracious lady. 'You see I'm very regular,' he said. 'But who should be if I'm not?'

'Yes, I've known you longer than anyone here. But we mustn't indulge in tender reminiscenes. I want to introduce you to a young lady.'

'Ah, please, what young lady?' Rosier was immensely obliging; but this was not what he had come for.

'She sits there by the fire in pink and has no one to speak to.'

Rosier hesitated a moment. 'Can't Mr Osmond speak to her? He's within six feet of her.'

Mrs Osmond also hesitated. 'She's not very lively, and he doesn't like dull people.'

'But she's good enough for me? Ah, now, that's hard!'

'I only mean that you've ideas for two. And then you're so obliging.'

'So is your husband.'

'No, he's not – to me.' And Mrs Osmond vaguely smiled.

'That's a sign he should be doubly so to other women.'

'So I tell him,' she said, still smiling.

'You see I want some tea,' Rosier went on, looking wistfully beyond.

'That's perfect. Go and give some to my young lady.'

'Very good; but after that I'll abandon her to her fate. The simple truth is I'm dying to have a little talk with Miss Osmond.'

'Ah,' said Isabel, turning away, 'I can't help you there!'

Five minutes later, while he handed a tea-cup to the damsel in pink, whom he had conducted into the other room, he wondered whether, in making to Mrs Osmond the profession I have just quoted, he had broken the spirit of his promise to Madame Merle. Such a question was capable of occupying this young man's mind for a considerable time. At last, however, he became – comparatively speaking – reckless; he cared little what promises he might break. The fate to which he had threatened to abandon the damsel in pink proved to be none so terrible; for Pansy Osmond, who had given him the tea for his companion – Pansy was as fond as ever of making tea – presently came and talked to her. Into this mild colloquy Edward Rosier entered little; he sat by moodily, watching his small sweetheart. If we look at her now through his eyes we shall at first not see much to remind us of the obedient little girl who, at Florence, three years before, was sent to walk short distances in the Cascine while her father and Miss Archer talked together of matters sacred to elder people. But after a moment we shall perceive that if at nineteen Pansy has become a young lady she doesn't really fill out the part; that if she has grown very pretty she lacks in a deplorable degree the quality known and esteemed in the appearance of females as style; and that if she is dressed with great freshness she wears her smart attire with an undisguised appearance of saving it – very much as if it were lent her for the occasion. Edward Rosier, it would seem, would have been just the man to note these defects; and in point of fact there was not a quality of this young lady, of any sort, that he had not noted. Only he called her qualities by names of his own – some of which indeed were happy enough. 'No, she's unique – she's absolutely unique,' he used to say to himself; and you may be sure that not for an instant would he have admitted to you that she was wanting in style. Style? Why, she had the style of a little princess; if you couldn't see it you had no eye. It was not modern, it was not conscious, it would produce no impression in Broadway; the small, serious damsel, in her stiff little dress, only looked like an Infanta of Velazquez. This was enough for Edward Rosier, who thought her delightfully old-fashioned. Her anxious eyes, her charming lips, her slip of a figure, were as touching as a childish prayer. He had now an acute desire to know just to what point she liked him – a desire which made him fidget as he sat in his chair. It made him feel hot, so that he had to pat his forehead with his handkerchief; he had never been so uncomfortable. She was such a perfect *jeune fille*, and one couldn't make of a *jeune fille* the inquiry requisite for throwing light on such a point. A *jeune fille* was what Rosier had always dreamed of – a *jeune fille* who should yet not be French, for he had felt that this nationality would complicate the question. He was sure Pansy had never looked at a newspaper and that, in the way of novels, if she had read Sir Walter Scott it was the very most. An American *jeune fille* – what could be better than that? She would be frank and gay, and yet would not have walked alone, nor have received letters from men, nor have been taken to the theatre to see the comedy of manners. Rosier could not deny that, as the matter stood, it would be a breach of hospitality to appeal directly to this unsophisticated creature; but he was now in imminent danger of asking himself if hospitality were the most sacred thing in the world. Was not the sentiment that he entertained for Miss Osmond of infinitely greater importance? Of greater importance to him – yes; but not probably to the master of the house. There was one comfort; even if this gentleman had been placed on his guard by Madame Merle he would not have extended the warning to Pansy; it would not have been part of his policy to let her know that a prepossessing young man was in love with her. But he *was* in love with her, the prepossessing young man; and all these restrictions of circumstance had ended by irritating him. What had Gilbert Osmond meant by giving him two fingers of his left hand? If Osmond was rude, surely he himself might be bold. He felt extremely bold after the dull girl in so vain a disguise of rose-colour had responded to the call of her mother, who came in to say, with a significant simper at Rosier, that she must carry her off to other triumphs. The mother and daughter departed together, and now it depended only upon him that he should be virtually alone with Pansy. He had never been alone with her before; he had never been alone with a *jeune fille*. It was a great moment; poor Rosier began to pat his forehead again. There was another room beyond the one in which they stood – a small room that had been thrown open and lighted, but that, the company not being numerous, had remained empty all the evening. It was empty yet; it was upholstered in pale yellow; there were several lamps; through the open door it looked the very temple of authorized love. Rosier gazed a moment through this aperture; he was afraid that Pansy would run away, and felt almost capable of stretching out a hand to detain her. But she lingered where the other maiden had left them, making no motion to join a knot of visitors on the far side of the room. For a little it occurred to him that she was frightened – too frightened perhaps to move; but a second glance assured him she was not, and he then reflected that she was too innocent indeed for that. After a supreme hesitation he asked if he might go and look at the yellow room, which seemed so attractive yet so virginal. He had been there already with Osmond, to inspect the furniture, which was of the First French Empire, and especially to admire the clock (which he didn't really admire), an immense classic structure of that period. He therefore felt that he had now begun to manoeuvre.

'Certainly, you may go,' said Pansy; 'and if you like I'll show you.' She was not in the least frightened.

'That's just what I hoped you'd say; you're so very kind.' Rosier murmured.

They went in together; Rosier really thought the room very ugly, and it seemed cold. The same idea appeared to have struck Pansy. 'It's not for winter evenings; it's more for summer,' she said. 'It's papa's taste; he has so much.'

He had a good deal, Rosier thought; but some of it was very bad. He looked about him; he hardly knew what to say in such a situation. 'Doesn't Mrs Osmond care how her rooms are done? Has she no taste?' he asked.

'Oh, yes, a great deal; but it's more for literature,' said Pansy – 'and for conversation. But papa cares also for those things. I think he knows everything.'

Rosier was silent a little. 'There's one thing I'm sure he knows!' he broke out presently. 'He knows that when I come here it's, with all respect to him, with all respect to Mrs Osmond, who's so charming – it's really,' said the young man, 'to see you!'

'To see me?' And Pansy raised her vaguely troubled eyes.

'To see you; that's what I come for,' Rosier repeated, feeling the intoxication of a rupture with authority.

Pansy stood looking at him, simply, intently, openly; a blush was not needed to make her face more modest. 'I thought it was for that.'

'And it was not disagreeable to you?'

'I couldn't tell; I didn't know. You never told me,' said Pansy.

'I was afraid of offending you.'

'You don't offend me,' the young girl murmured, smiling as if an angel had kissed her.

'You like me then, Pansy?' Rosier asked very gently, feeling very happy.

'Yes – I like you.'

They had walked to the chimney-piece where the big cold Empire clock was perched; they were well within the room and beyond observation from without. The tone in which she had said these four words seemed to him the very breath of nature, and his only answer could be to take her hand and hold it a moment. Then he raised it to his lips. She submitted, still with her pure, trusting smile, in which there was something ineffably passive. She liked him – she had liked him all the while; now anything might happen! She was ready – she had been ready always waiting for him to speak. If he had not spoken she would have waited for ever; but when the word came she dropped like the peach from the shaken tree. Rosier felt that if he should draw her towards him and hold her to his heart she would submit without a murmur, would rest there without a question. It was true that this would be a rash experiment in a yellow Empire *salottino*. She had known it was for her he came, and yet like what a perfect little lady she had carried it off!

'You're very dear to me,' he murmured, trying to believe that there was after all such a thing as hospitality.

She looked a moment at her hand, where he had kissed it. 'Did you say papa knows?'

'You told me just now he knows everything.'

'I think you must make sure,' said Pansy.

'Ah, my dear, when once I'm sure of *you*!' Rosier murmured in her ear; whereupon she turned back to the other rooms with a little air of consistency which seemed to imply that their appeal should be immediate.

The other rooms meanwhile had become conscious of the arrival of Madame Merle, who, wherever she went, produced an impression when she entered. How she did it the most attentive spectator could not have told you, for she neither spoke loud, nor laughed profusely, nor moved rapidly, nor dressed with splendour, nor appealed in any appreciable manner to the audience. Large, fair, smiling, serene, there was something in her very tranquillity that diffused itself, and when people looked round it was because of a sudden quiet. On this occasion she had done the quietest thing she could do; after embracing Mrs Osmond, which was more striking, she had sat down on a small sofa to commune with the master of the house. There was a brief exchange of commonplaces between these two – they always paid, in public, a certain formal tribute to the commonplace – and then Madame Merle, whose eyes had been wandering, asked if little Mr Rosier had come this evening.

'He came nearly an hour ago – but he has disappeared,' Osmond said.

'And where's Pansy?'

'In the other room. There are several people there.'

'He's probably among them,' said Madame Merle.

'Do you wish to see him?' Osmond asked in a provokingly pointless tone.

Madame Merle looked at him a moment; she knew each of his tones to the eighth of a note. 'Yes, I should like to say to him that I've told you what he wants, and that it interests you but feebly.'

'Don't tell him that. He'll try to interest me more – which is exactly what I don't want. Tell him I hate his proposal.'

'But you don't hate it.'

'It doesn't signify; I don't love it. I let him see that, myself, this evening, I was rude to him on purpose. That sort of thing's a great bore. There's no hurry.'

'I'll tell him that you'll take time and think it over.'

'No, don't do that. He'll hang on.'

'If I discourage him he'll do the same.'

'Yes, but in the one case he'll try to talk and explain – which would be exceedingly tiresome. In the other he'll probably hold his tongue and go in for some deeper game. That will leave me quiet. I hate talking with a donkey.'

'Is that what you call poor Mr Rosier?'

'Oh, he's a nuisance – with his eternal majolica.'

Madame Merle dropped her eyes; she had a faint smile. 'He's a gentleman, he has a charming temper; and, after all, an income of forty thousand francs!'

'It's misery – "genteel" misery,' Osmond broke in. 'It's not what I've dreamed of for Pansy.'

'Very good then. He has promised me not to speak to her.'

'Do you believe him?' Osmond asked absent-mindedly.

'Perfectly. Pansy has thought a great deal about him; but I don't suppose you consider that that matters.'

'I don't consider it matters at all; but neither do I believe she has thought of him.'

'That opinion's more convenient,' said Madame Merle quietly.

'Has she told you she's in love with him?'

'For what do you take her? And for what do you take me?' Madame Merle added in a moment.

Osmond had raised his foot and was resting his slim ankle on the other knee: he clasped his ankle in his hand familiarly – his long, fine forefinger and thumb could make a ring for it – and gazed a while before him. 'This kind of thing doesn't find me unprepared. It's what I educated her for. It was all for this – that when such a case should come up she should do what I prefer.'

'I'm not afraid that she'll not do it.'

'Well then, where's the hitch?'

'I don't see any. But, all the same, I recommend you not to get rid of Mr Rosier. Keep him on hand; he may be useful.'

'I can't keep him. Keep him yourself.'

'Very good; I'll put him into a corner and allow him so much a day.' Madame Merle had, for the most part, while they talked, been glancing about her; it was her habit in this situation, just as it was her habit to interpose a good many blank-looking pauses. A long drop followed the last words I have quoted; and before it had ended she saw Pansy come out of the adjoining room, followed by Edward Rosier. The girl advanced a few steps and then stopped and stood looking at Madame Merle and at her father.

'He has spoken to her,' Madame Merle went on to Osmond.

Her companion never turned his head. 'So much for your belief in his promises. He ought to be horsewhipped.'

'He intends to confess, poor little man!'

Osmond got up; he had now taken a sharp look at his daughter. 'It doesn't matter,' he murmured, turning away.

Pansy after a moment came up to Madame Merle with her little manner of unfamiliar politeness. This lady's reception of her was not more intimate; she simply, as she rose from the sofa, gave her a friendly smile.

'You're very late,' the young creature gently said.

'My dear child, I'm never later than I intend to be.'

Madame Merle had not got up to be gracious to Pansy; she moved towards Edward Rosier. He came to meet her and, very quickly, as if to get it off his mind, 'I've spoken to her!' he whispered.

'I know it, Mr Rosier.'

'Did she tell you?'

'Yes, she told me. Behave properly for the rest of the evening, and come and see me tomorrow at a quarter past five.' She was severe, and in the manner in which she turned her back to him there was a degree of contempt which caused him to mutter a decent imprecation.

He had no intention of speaking to Osmond; it was neither the time nor the place. But he instinctively wandered towards Isabel, who sat talking with an old lady. He sat down on the other side of her; the old lady was Italian, and Rosier took for granted she understood no English. 'You said just now you wouldn't help me,' he began to Mrs Osmond. 'Perhaps you'll feel differently when you know – when you know—!'

Isabel met his hesitation. 'When I know what?'

'That she's all right.'

'What do you mean by that?'

'Well, that we've come to an understanding.'

'She's all wrong,' said Isabel. 'It won't do.'

Poor Rosier gazed at her half-pleadingly, half-angrily; a sudden flush testified to his sense of injury. 'I've never been treated so,' he said. 'What is there against me, after all? That's not the way I'm usually considered. I could have married twenty times.'

'It's a pity you didn't. I don't mean twenty times, but once, comfortably,' Isabel added, smiling kindly. 'You're not rich enough for Pansy.'

'She doesn't care a straw for one's money.'

'No, but her father does.'

'Ah yes, he has proved that!' cried the young man.

Isabel got up, turning away from him, leaving her old lady without ceremony; and he occupied himself for the next ten minutes in pretending to look at Gilbert Osmond's collection of miniatures, which were neatly arranged on a series of small velvet screens. But he looked without seeing; his cheek burned; he was too full of his sense of injury. It was certain that he had never been treated that way before; he was not used to being thought not good enough. He knew how good he was, and if such a fallacy had not been so pernicious he could have laughed at it. He searched again for Pansy, but she had disappeared, and his main desire was now to get out of the house. Before doing so he spoke once more to Isabel; it was not agreeable to him to reflect that he had just said a rude thing to her – the only point that would now justify a low view of him.

'I referred to Mr Osmond as I shouldn't have done, a while ago,' he began. 'But you must remember my situation.'

'I don't remember what you said,' she answered coldly.

'Ah, you're offended, and now you'll never help me.'

She was silent an instant, and then with a change of tone: 'It's not that I won't; I simply can't!' Her manner was almost passionate.

'If you *could*, just a little, I'd never again speak of your husband save as an angel.'

'The inducement's great,' said Isabel gravely – inscrutably, as he afterwards, to himself, called it; and she gave him, straight in the eyes, a look which was also inscrutable. It made him remember somehow that he had known her as a child; and yet it was keener than he liked, and he took himself off.

Chapter Thirty-eight

He went to see Madame Merle on the morrow, and to his surprise she let him off rather easily. But she made him promise that he would stop there till something should have been decided. Mr Osmond had had higher expectations; it was very true that as he had no intention of giving his daughter a portion such expectations were open to criticism or even, if one would, to ridicule. But she would advise Mr Rosier not to take that tone; if he would possess his soul in patience he might arrive at his felicity. Mr Osmond was not favourable to his suit, but it wouldn't be a miracle if he should gradually come round. Pansy would never defy her father, he might depend on that; so nothing was to be gained by precipitation. Mr Osmond needed to accustom his mind to an offer of a sort that he had not hitherto entertained, and this result must come of itself – it was useless to try to force it. Rosier remarked that his own situation would be in the meanwhile the most uncomfortable in the world, and Madame Merle assured him that she felt for him. But, as she justly declared, one couldn't have everything one wanted; she had learned that lesson for herself. There would be no use in his writing to Gilbert Osmond, who had charged her to tell him as much. He wished the matter dropped for a few weeks and would himself write when he should have anything to communicate that it might please Mr Rosier to hear.

'He doen't like your having spoken to Pansy. Ah, he doesn't like it all,' said Madame Merle.

'I'm perfectly willing to give him a chance to tell me so!'

'If you do that he'll tell you more than you care to hear. Go to the house, for the next month, as little as possible, and leave the rest to me.'

'As little as possible? Who's to measure the possibility?'

'Let me measure it. Go on Thursday evenings with the rest of the world, but don't go at all at odd times, and don't fret about Pansy. I'll see that she understands everything. She's a calm little nature; she'll take it quietly.'

Edward Rosier fretted about Pansy a good deal, but he did as he was advised, and awaited another Thursday evening before returning to Palazzo Roccanera. There had been a party at dinner, so that though he went early the company was already tolerably numerous. Osmond, as usual, was in the first room, near the fire, staring straight at the door, so that, not to be distinctly uncivil, Rosier had to go and speak to him.

'I'm glad that you can take a hint,' Pansy's father said, slightly closing his keen, conscious eyes.

'I take no hints. But I took a message, as I supposed it to be.'

'You took it? Where did you take it?'

It seemed to poor Rosier he was being insulted, and he waited a moment, asking himself how much a true lover ought to submit to. 'Madame Merle gave me, as I understood it, a message from you – to the effect that you declined to give me the opportunity I desire, the opportunity to explain my wishes to you.' And he flattered himself he spoke rather sternly.

'I don't see what Madame Merle has to do with it. Why did you apply to Madame Merle?'

'I asked her for an opinion – for nothing more. I did so because she had seemed to me to know you very well.'

'She doesn't know me so well as she thinks,' said Osmond.

'I'm sorry for that, because she has given me some little ground for hope.'

Osmond stared into the fire a moment. 'I set a great price on my daughter.'

'You can't set a higher one than I do. Don't I prove it by wishing to marry her?'

'I wish to marry her very well,' Osmond went on with a dry impertinence which, in another mood, poor Rosier would have admired.

'Of course I pretend she'd marry well in marrying me. She couldn't marry a man who loves her more – or whom, I may venture to add, she loves more.'

'I'm not bound to accept your theories as to whom my daughter loves' – and Osmond looked up with a quick, cold smile.

'I'm not theorizing. Your daughter has spoken.'

'Not to me,' Osmond continued, now bending forward a little and dropping his eyes to his boot-toes.

'I have her promise, sir!' cried Rosier with the sharpness of exasperation.

As their voices had been pitched very low before, such a note attracted some attention from the company. Osmond waited till this little movement had subsided; then he said, all undisturbed: 'I think she has no recollection of having given it.'

They had been standing with their faces to the fire, and after he had uttered these last words the master of the house turned round again to the room. Before Rosier had time to reply he perceived that a gentleman – a stranger – had just come in, unannounced, according to the Roman custom, and was about to present himself to his host. The latter smiled blandly, but somewhat blankly; the visitor had a handsome face and a large, fair beard, and was evidently an Englishman.

'You apparently don't recognize me,' he said with a smile that expressed more than Osmond's.

'Ah yes, now I do. I expected so little to see you.'

Rosier departed and went in direct pursuit of Pansy. He sought her, as usual, in the neighbouring room, but again encountered Mrs Osmond in his path. He gave his hostess no greeting – he was too righteously indignant, but said to her crudely: 'Your husband's awfully cold-blooded.'

She gave the same mystical smile he had noticed before. 'You can't expect everyone to be as hot as yourself.'

'I don't pretend to be cold, but I'm cool. What has he been doing to his daughter?'

'I've no idea.'

'Don't you take any interest?' Rosier demanded with his sense that she too was irritating.

For a moment she answered nothing; then, 'No!' she said abruptly and with a quickened light in her eyes which directly contradicted the word.

'Pardon me if I don't believe that. Where's Miss Osmond?'

'In the corner, making tea. Please leave her there.'

Rosier instantly discovered his friend, who had been hidden by intervening groups. He watched her, but her own attention was entirely given to her occupation. 'What on earth has he done to her?' he asked again imploringly. 'He declares to me she has given me up.'

'She has not given you up,' Isabel said in a low tone and without looking at him.

'Ah, thank you for that! Now I'll leave her alone as long as you think proper!'

He had hardly spoken when he saw her change colour, and became aware that Osmond was coming towards her accompanied by the gentleman who had just entered. He judged the latter, in spite of the advantage of good looks and evident social experience, a little embarrassed. 'Isabel,' said her husband, 'I bring you an old friend.'

Mrs Osmond's face, though it wore a smile, was, like her old friend's not perfectly confident. 'I'm very happy to see Lord Warburton,' she said. Rosier turned away and, now that his talk with her had been interrupted, felt absolved from the little pledge he had just taken. He had a quick impression that Mrs Osmond wouldn't notice what he did.

Isabel in fact, to do him justice, for some time quite ceased to observe him. She had been startled; she hardly knew if she felt a pleasure or a pain. Lord Warburton, however, now that he was face to face with her, was plainly quite sure of his own sense of the matter; though his grey eyes had still their fine original property of keeping recognition and attestation strictly sincere. He was 'heavier' than of yore and looked older; he stood there very solidly and sensibly.

'I suppose you didn't expect to see me,' he said; 'I've but just arrived. Literally, I only got here this evening. You see I've lost no time in coming to pay you my respects. I knew you were at home on Thursdays.'

'You see the fame of your Thursdays has spread to England,' Osmond remarked to his wife.

'It's very kind of Lord Warburton to come so soon; we're greatly flattered,' Isabel said.

'Ah well, it's better than stopping in one of those horrible inns,' Osmond went on.

'The hotel seems very good; I think it's the same at which I saw you four years since. You know it was here in Rome that we first met; it's a long time ago. Do you remember where I bade you good-bye?' his lordship asked of his hostess. 'It was in the Capitol, in the first room.'

'I remember that myself,' said Osmond. 'I was there at the time.'

'Yes, I remember you there. I was very sorry to leave Rome – so sorry that, somehow or other, it became almost a dismal memory, and I've never cared to come back till today. But I knew you were living here,' her old friend went on to Isabel, 'and I assure you I've often thought of you. It must be a charming place to live in,' he added with a look, round him, at her established home, in which she might have caught the dim ghost of his old ruefulness.

'We should have been glad to see you at any time,' Osmond observed with propriety.

'Thank you very much. I haven't been out of England since then. Till a month ago I really supposed my travels over.'

'I've heard of you from time to time,' said Isabel, who had already, with her rare capacity for such inward fears, taken the measure of what meeting him again meant for her.

'I hope you've heard no harm. My life has been a remarkably complete blank.'

'Like the good reigns in history,' Osmond suggested. He appeared to think his duties as a host now terminated – he had performed them so conscientiously. Nothing could have been more adequate, more nicely measured, than his courtesy to his wife's old friend. It was punctilious, it was explicit, it was everything but natural – a deficiency which Lord Warburton, who, himself, had on the whole a good deal of nature, may be supposed to have perceived. 'I'll leave you and Mrs Osmond together,' he added. 'You have reminiscences into which I don't enter.'

'I'm afraid you lose a good deal!' Lord Warburton called after him, as he moved away, in a tone which perhaps betrayed overmuch an appreciation of his generosity. Then the visitor turned on Isabel the deeper, the deepest, consciousness of his look, which gradually became more serious. 'I'm really very glad to see you.'

'It's very pleasant. You're very kind.'

'Do you know that you're changed – a little?'

She just hesitated. 'Yes – a good deal.'

'I don't mean for the worse, of course; and yet how can I say for the better?'

'I think I shall have no scruple in saying that to *you*,' she bravely returned.

'Ah well, for me – it's a long time. It would be a pity there shouldn't be something to show for it.' They sat down and she asked him about his sisters, with other inquiries of a somewhat perfunctory kind. He answered her questions as if they interested him, and in a few moments she saw – or believed she saw – that he would press with less of his whole weight than of yore. Time had breathed upon his heart and, without chilling it, given it a relieved sense of having taken the air. Isabel felt her usual esteem for Time rise at a bound. Her friend's manner was certainly that of a contented man, one who would rather like people, or like her at least, to know him for such. 'There's something I must tell you without more delay,' he resumed. 'I've brought Ralph Touchett with me.'

'Brought him with you?' Isabel's surprise was great.

'He's at the hotel; he was too tired to come out and has gone to bed.'

'I'll go to see him,' she immediately said.

'That's exactly what I hoped you'd do. I had an idea you hadn't seen much of him since your marriage, that in fact your relations were a – a little more formal. That's why I hesitated – like an awkward Briton.'

'I'm as fond of Ralph as ever,' Isabel answered. 'But why has he come to Rome?' The declaration was very gentle, the question a little sharp.

'Because he's very far gone, Mrs Osmond.'

'Rome then is no place for him. I heard from him that he had determined to give up his custom of wintering abroad and to remain in England, indoors, in what he called an artificial climate.'

'Poor fellow, he doesn't succeed with the artificial! I went to see him three weeks ago, at Gardencourt, and found him thoroughly ill. He has been getting worse every year, and now he has no strength left. He smokes no more cigarettes! He had got up an artificial climate indeed; the house was as hot as Calcutta. Nevertheless he had suddenly taken it into his head to start for Sicily. I didn't believe in it – neither did the doctors, nor any of his friends. His mother, as I suppose you know, is in America, so there was no one to prevent him. He stuck to his idea that it would be the saving of him to spend the winter at Catania. He said he could take servants and furniture, could make himself comfortable, but in point of fact he hasn't brought anything. I wanted him at least to go by sea, to save fatigue; but he said he hated the sea and wished to stop at Rome. After that, though I thought it all rubbish, I made up my mind to come with him. I'm acting as – what do you call it in America? – as a kind of moderator. Poor Ralph's very moderate now. We left England a fortnight ago, and he has been very bad on the way. He can't keep warm, and the farther south we come the more he feels the cold. He has got rather a good man, but I'm afraid he's beyond human help. I wanted him to take with him some clever fellow – I mean some sharp young doctor; but he wouldn't hear of it. If you don't mind my saying so, I think it was a most extraordinary time for Mrs Touchett to decide on going to America.'

Isabel had listened eagerly; her face was full of pain and wonder. 'My aunt does that at fixed periods and lets nothing turn her aside. When the date comes round she starts; I think she'd have started if Ralph had been dying.'

'I sometimes think he *is* dying,' Lord Warburton said.

Isabel sprang up. 'I'll go to him then now.'

He checked her; he was a little disconcerted at the quick effect of his words. 'I don't mean I thought so tonight. On the contrary, today, in the train, he seemed particularly well; the idea of our reaching Rome – he's very fond of Rome, you know – gave him strength. An hour ago, when I bade him good night, he told me he was very tired, but very happy. Go to him in the morning; that's all I mean. I didn't tell him I was coming here; I didn't decide to till after we had separated. Then I remembered he had told me you had an evening, and that it was this very Thursday. It occurred to me to come in and tell you he's here, and let you know you had perhaps better not wait for him to call. I think he said he hadn't written to you.' There was no need of Isabel's declaring that she would act upon Lord Warburton's information; she looked, as she sat there, like a winged creature held back. 'Let alone that I wanted to see you for myself,' her visitor gallantly added.

'I don't understand Ralph's plan; it seems to me very wild,' she said. 'I was glad to think of him between those thick walls at Gardencourt.'

'He was completely alone there; the thick walls were his only company.'

'You went to see him; you've been extremely kind '

'Oh dear, I had nothing to do,' said Lord Warburton.

'We hear, on the contrary, that you're doing great things. Everyone speaks of you as a great statesman, and I'm perpetually seeing your name in *The Times*, which, by the way, doesn't appear to hold it in reverence. You're apparently as wild a radical as ever.'

'I don't feel nearly so wild; you know the world has come round to me. Touchett and I have kept up a sort of parliamentary debate all the way from London. I tell him he's the last of the Tories, and he calls me the King of the Goths – says I have, down to the details of my personal appearance, every sign of the brute. So you see there's life in him yet.'

Isabel had many questions to ask about Ralph, but she abstained from asking them all. She would see for herself on the morrow. She perceived that after a little Lord Warburton would tire of that subject – he had a conception of other possible topics. She was more and more able to say to herself that he had recovered, and, what is more to the point, she was able to say it without bitterness. He had been for her, of old, such an image of urgency, of insistence, of something to be resisted and reasoned with, that his reappearance at first menaced her with a new trouble. But she was now reassured; she could see he only wished to live with her on good terms, that she was to understand he had forgiven her and was incapable of the bad taste of making pointed allusions. This was not a form of revenge, of course; she had no suspicion of his wishing to punish her by an exhibition of disillusionment; she did him the justice to believe it had simply occurred to him that she would now take a good-natured interest in knowing he was resigned. It was the resignation of a healthy, manly nature, in which sentimental wounds could never fester. British politics had cured him; she had known they would. She gave an envious thought to the happier lot of men, who are always free to plunge into the healing waters of action. Lord Warburton of course spoke of the past, but he spoke of it without implications; he even went so far as to allude to their former meeting in Rome as a very jolly time. And he told her he had been immensely interested in hearing of her marriage and that it was a great pleasure for him to make Mr Osmond's acquaintance – since he could hardly be said to have made it on the other occasion. He had not written to her at the time of that passage in her history, but he didn't apologize to her for this. The only thing he implied was that they were old friends, intimate friends. It was very much as an intimate friend that he said to her, suddenly, after a short pause which he had occupied in smiling, as he looked about him, like a person amused, at a provincial entertainment, by some innocent game of guesses—

'Well now, I suppose you're very happy and all that sort of thing?'

Isabel answered with a quick laugh; the tone of his remark struck her almost as the accent of comedy. 'Do you suppose if I were not I'd tell you?'

'Well, I don't know. I don't see why not.'

'I do then. Fortunately, however, I'm very happy.'

'You've got an awfully good house.'

'Yes, it's very pleasant. But that's not my merit – it's my husband's.'

'You mean he has arranged it?'

'Yes, it was nothing when we came.'

'He must be very clever.'

'He has a genius for upholstery,' said Isabel.

'There's a great rage for that sort of thing now. But you must have a taste of your own.'

'I enjoy things when they're done, but I've no ideas. I can never propose anything.'

'Do you mean you accept what others propose?'

'Very willingly, for the most part.'

'That's a good thing to know. I shall propose to you something.'

'It will be very kind. I must say, however, that I've in a few small ways a certain initiative. I should like for instance to introduce you to some of these people.'

'Oh, please don't; I prefer sitting here. Unless it be to that young lady in the blue dress. She has a charming face.'

'The one talking to the rosy young man? That's my husband's daughter.'

'Lucky man, your husband. What a dear little maid!'

'You must make her acquaintance.'

'In a moment – with pleasure. I like looking at her from here.' He ceased to look at her, however, very soon; his eyes constantly reverted to Mrs Osmond. 'Do you know I was wrong just now in saying you had changed?' he presently went on. 'You seem to me, after all, very much the same.'

'And yet I find it a great change to be married,' said Isabel with mild gaiety.

'It affects most people more than it has affected you. You see I haven't gone in for that.'

'It rather surprises me.'

'You ought to understand it, Mrs Osmond. But I do want to marry,' he added more simply.

'It ought to be very easy,' Isabel said, rising – after which she reflected, with a pang perhaps too visible, that she was hardly the person to say this. It was perhaps because Lord Warburton divined the pang that he generously forbore to call her attention to her not having contributed then to the facility.

Edward Rosier had meanwhile seated himself on an ottoman beside Pansy's tea-table. He pretended at first to talk to her about trifles, and she asked him who was the new gentleman conversing with her stepmother.

'He's an English lord,' said Rosier. 'I don't know more.'

'I wonder if he'll have some tea. The English are so fond of tea.'

'Never mind that; I've something particular to say to you.'

'Don't speak so loud – everyone will hear,' said Pansy.

'They won't hear if you continue to look that way: as if your only thought in life was the wish the kettle would boil.'

'It has just been filled; the servants never know!' – and she sighed with the weight of her responsibility.

'Do you know what your father said to me just now? That you didn't mean what you said a week ago.'

'I don't mean everything I say. How can a young girl do that? But I mean what I say to *you*.'

'He told me you had forgotten me.'

'Ah no, I don't forget,' said Pansy, showing her pretty teeth in a fixed smile.

'Then everything's just the very same?'

'Ah no, not the very same. Papa has been terribly severe.'

'What has he done to you?'

'He asked me what *you* had done to me, and I told him everything. Then he forbade me to marry you.'

'You needn't mind that.'

'Oh yes, I must indeed. I can't disobey papa.'

'Not for one who loves you as I do, and whom you pretend to love?'

She raised the lid of the teapot, gazing into this vessel for a moment; then she dropped six words into its aromatic depths. 'I love you just as much.'

'What good will that do me?'

'Ah,' said Pansy, raising her sweet, vague eyes, 'I don't know that.'

'You disappoint me,' groaned poor Rosier.

She was silent a little; she handed a teacup to a servant. 'Please don't talk any more.'

'Is this to be all my satisfaction?'

'Papa said I was not to talk with you.'

'Do you sacrifice me like that? Ah, it's too much!'

'I wish you'd wait a little,' said the girl in a voice just distinct enough to betray a quaver.

'Of course I'll wait if you'll give me hope. But you take my life away.'

'I'll not give you up – oh no!' Pansy went on.

'He'll try and make you marry someone else.'

'I'll never do that.'

'What then are we to wait for?'

She hesitated again. 'I'll speak to Mrs Osmond and she'll help us.' It was in this manner that she for the most part designated her stepmother.

'She won't help us much. She's afraid.'

'Afraid of what?'

'Of your father, I suppose.'

Pansy shook her little head. 'She's not afraid of anyone. We must have patience.'

'Ah, that's an awful word,' Rosier groaned; he was deeply disconcerted. Oblivious of the customs of good society, he dropped his head into his hand and, supporting it with a melancholy grace, sat staring at the carpet. Presently he became aware of a good deal of movement about him and, as he looked up, saw Pansy making a curtsy – it was still her little curtsy of the convent – to the English lord whom Mrs Osmond had introduced.

Chapter Thirty-nine

It will probably not surprise the reflective reader that Ralph Touchett should have seen less of his cousin since her marriage than he had done before that event – an event of which he took such a view as could hardly prove a confirmation of intimacy. He had uttered his thought, as we know, and after this had held his peace, Isabel not having invited him to resume a discussion which marked an era in their relations. That discussion had made a difference – the difference he feared rather than the one he hoped. It had not chilled the girl's zeal in carrying out her engagement, but it had come dangerously near to spoiling a friendship. No reference was ever again made between them to Ralph's opinion of Gilbert Osmond, and by surrounding this topic with a sacred silence they managed to preserve a semblance of reciprocal frankness. But there was a difference, as Ralph often said to himself – there was a difference. She had not forgiven him, she never would forgive him: that was all he had gained. She thought she had forgiven him; she believed she didn't care; and as she was both very generous and very proud these convictions represented a certain reality. But whether or no the event should justify him he would virtually have done her a wrong, and the wrong was of the sort that women remember best. As Osmond's wife she could never again be his friend. If in this character she should enjoy the felicity she expected, she would have nothing but contempt for the man who had attempted, in advance, to undermine a blessing so dear; and if on the other hand his warning should be justified the vow she had taken that he should never know it would lay upon her spirit such a burden as to make her hate him. So dismal had been, during the year that followed his cousin's marriage, Ralph's prevision of the future; and if his meditations appear morbid we must remember he was not in the bloom of health. He consoled himself as he might by behaving (as he deemed) beautifully, and was present at the ceremony by which Isabel was united to Mr Osmond, and which was performed in Florence in the month of June. He learned from his mother that Isabel at first had thought of celebrating her nuptials in her native land, but that as simplicity was what she chiefly desired to secure she had finally decided, in spite of Osmond's professed willingness to make a journey of any length, that this characteristic would be best embodied in their being married by the nearest clergyman in the shortest time. The thing was done therefore at the little American chapel, on a very hot day, in the presence only of Mrs Touchett and her son, of Pansy Osmond and the Countess Gemini. That severity in the proceedings of which I just spoke was in part the result of the absence of two persons who might have been looked for on the occasion and who would have lent it a certain richness. Madame Merle had been invited, but Madame Merle, who was unable to leave Rome, had written a gracious letter of excuses. Henrietta Stackpole had not been invited, as her departure from America announced to Isabel by Mr Goodwood, was in fact frustrated by the duties of her profession; but she had sent a letter, less gracious than Madame Merle's, intimating that, had she been able to cross the Atlantic, she would have been present not only as a witness but as a critic. Her return to Europe had taken place somewhat later, and she had effected a meeting with Isabel in the autumn, in Paris, when she had indulged – perhaps a trifle too freely – her critical genius. Poor Osmond, who was chiefly the subject of it, had protested so sharply that Henrietta was obliged to declare to Isabel that she had taken a step which put a barrier between them. 'It isn't in the least that you've married – it is that you have married *him*,' she had deemed it her duty to remark; agreeing, it will be seen, much more with Ralph Touchett than she suspected, though she had few of his hesitations and compunctions. Henrietta's second visit to Europe, however, was not apparently to have been made in vain; for just at the moment when Osmond had declared to Isabel that he really must object to that newspaper-woman, and Isabel had answered that it seemed to her he took Henrietta too hard, the good Mr Bantling had appeared upon the scene and proposed that they should take a run down to Spain. Henrietta's letters from Spain had proved the most acceptable she had yet published, and there had been one in especial, dated from the Alhambra and entitled 'Moors and Moonlight', which generally passed for her masterpiece. Isabel had been secretly disappointed at her husband's not seeing his way simply to take the poor girl for funny. She even wondered if his sense of fun, or of the funny – which would be his sense of humour, wouldn't it? – were by chance defective. Of course she herself looked at the matter as a person whose present happiness had nothing to grudge to Henrietta's violated conscience. Osmond had thought their alliance a kind of monstrosity; he couldn't imagine what they had in common. For him, Mr Bantling's fellow tourist was simply the most vulgar of women, and he had also pronounced her the most abandoned. Against this latter clause of the verdict Isabel had appealed with an ardour that had made him wonder afresh at the oddity of some of his wife's tastes. Isabel could explain it only by saying that she liked to know people who were as different as possible from herself. 'Why then don't you make the acquaintance of your washerwoman?' Osmond had inquired; to which Isabel had answered that she was afraid her washerwoman wouldn't care for her. Now Henrietta cared so much.

Ralph had seen nothing of her for the greater part of the two years that had followed her marriage; the winter that formed the beginning of her residence in Rome he had spent again at San Remo, where he had been joined in the spring by his mother, who afterwards had gone with him to England, to see what they were doing at the bank – an operation she couldn't induce him to perform. Ralph had taken a lease of his house at San Remo, a small villa which he had occupied still another winter; but late in the month of April of this second year he had come down to Rome. It was the first time since her marriage that he had stood face to face with Isabel; his desire to see her again was then of the keenest. She had written to him from time to time, but her letters told him nothing he wanted to know. He had asked his mother what she was making of her life, and his mother had simply answered that she supposed she was making the best of it. Mrs Touchett had not the imagination that communes with the unseen, and she now pretended to no intimacy with her niece, whom she rarely encountered. This young woman appeared to be living in a sufficiently honourable way, but Mrs Touchett still remained of the opinion that her marriage had been a shabby affair. It had given her no pleasure to think of Isabel's establishment, which she was sure was a very lame business. From time to time, in Florence, she rubbed against the Countess Gemini, doing her best always to minimize the contact; and the Countess reminded her of Osmond, who made her think of Isabel. The Countess was less talked of in these days; but Mrs Touchett augured no good of that: it only proved how she had been talked of before. There was a more direct suggestion of Isabel in the person of Madame Merle; but Madame Merle's relations with Mrs Touchett had undergone a perceptible change. Isabel's aunt had told her, without circumlocution, that she had played too ingenious a part; and Madame Merle, who never quarrelled with anyone, who appeared to think no one worth it, and who had performed the miracle of living, more or less, for several years with Mrs Touchett and showing no symptom of irritation – Madame Merle now took a very high tone and declared that this was an accusation from which she couldn't stoop to defend herself. She added, however (without stooping), that her behaviour had been only too simple, that she had believed only what she saw, that she saw Isabel was not eager to marry and Osmond not eager to please (his repeated visits had been nothing; he was boring himself to death on his hill-top and he came merely for amusement). Isabel had kept her sentiments to herself, and her journey to Greece and Egypt had effectually thrown dust in her companion's eyes. Madame Merle accepted the event – she was unprepared to think of it as a scandal; but that she had played any part in it, double or single, was an imputation against which she proudly protested. It was doubtless in consequence of Mrs Touchett's attitude, and of the injury it offered to habits consecrated by many charming seasons, that Madame Merle had, after this, chosen to pass many months in England, where her credit was quite unimpaired. Mrs Touchett had done her a wrong; there are some things that can't be forgiven. But Madame Merle suffered in silence; there was always something exquisite in her dignity.

Ralph, as I say, had wished to see for himself; but while engaged in this pursuit he had yet felt afresh what a fool he had been to put the girl on her guard. He had played the wrong card, and now he had lost the game. He should see nothing, he should learn nothing; for him she would always wear a mask. His true line would have been to profess delight in her union, so that later, when, as Ralph phrased it, the bottom should fall out of it, she might have the pleasure of saying to him that he had been a goose. He would gladly have consented to pass for a goose in order to know Isabel's real situation. At present, however, she neither taunted him with his fallacies nor pretended that her own confidence was justified; if she wore a mask it completely covered her face. There was something fixed and mechanical in the serenity painted on it; this was not an expression, Ralph said – it was a representation, it was even an advertisement. She had lost her child; that was a sorrow, but it was a sorrow she scarcely spoke of; there was more to say about it than she could say to Ralph. It belonged to the past, moreover; it had occurred six months before and she had already laid aside the tokens of mourning. She appeared to be leading the life of the world; Ralph heard her spoken of as having a 'charming position'. He observed that she produced the impression of being peculiarly enviable, that it was supposed, among many people, to be a privilege even to know her. Her house was not open to everyone, and she had an evening in the week to which people were not invited as a matter of course. She lived with a certain magnificence, but you needed to be a member of her circle to perceive it; for there was nothing to gape at, nothing to criticize, nothing even to admire, in the daily proceedings of Mr and Mrs Osmond. Ralph, in all this, recognized the hand of the master; for he knew that Isabel had no faculty for producing studied impressions. She struck him as having a great love of movement, of gaiety, of late hours, of long rides, of fatigue; an eagerness to be entertained, to be interested, even to be bored, to make acquaintances, to see people who were talked about, to explore the neighbourhood of Rome, to enter into relation with certain of the mustiest relics of its old society. In all this there was much less discrimination than in that desire for comprehensiveness of development on which he had been used to exercise his wit. There was a kind of violence in some of her impulses, of crudity in some of her experiments, which took him by surprise: it seemed to him that she even spoke faster, moved faster, breathed faster, than before her marriage. Certainly she had fallen into exaggerations – she who used to care so much for the pure truth; and whereas of old she had a great delight in good-humoured argument, in intellectual play (she never looked so charming as when in the genial heat of discussion she received a crushing blow full in the face and brushed it away as a feather), she appeared now to think there was nothing worth people's either differing about or agreeing upon. Of old she had been curious, and now she was indifferent, and yet in spite of her indifference her activity was greater than ever. Slender still, but lovelier than before, she had gained no great maturity of aspect; yet there was an amplitude and a brilliancy in her personal arrangements that gave a touch of insolence to her beauty. Poor human-hearted Isabel, what perversity had bitten her? Her light step drew a mass of drapery behind it; her intelligent head sustained a majesty of ornament. The free, keen girl had become quite another person; what he saw was the fine lady who was supposed to represent something. What did Isabel represent? Ralph asked himself; and he could only answer by saying that she represented Gilbert Osmond. 'Good heavens, what a function!' he then woefully exclaimed. He was lost in wonder at the mystery of things.

He recognized Osmond, as I say; he recognized him at every turn. He saw how he kept all things within limits; how he adjusted, regulated, animated their manner of life. Osmond was in his element; at last he had material to work with. He always had an eye to effect, and his effects were deeply calculated. They were produced by no vulgar means, but the motive was as vulgar as the art was great. To surround his interior with a sort of invidious sanctity, to tantalize society with a sense of exclusion, to make people believe his house was different from every other, to impart to the face that he presented to the world a cold originality – this was the ingenious effort of the personage to whom Isabel had attributed a superior morality. 'He works with superior material,' Ralph said to himself; 'it's rich abundance compared with his former resources.' Ralph was a clever man; but Ralph had never – to his own sense – been so clever as when he observed, *in petto*, that under the guise of caring only for intrinsic values Osmond lived exclusively for the world. Far from being its master as he pretended to be, he was its very humble servant, and the degree of its attention was his only measure of success. He lived with his eye on it from morning till night, and the world was so stupid it never suspected the trick. Everything he did was *pose* – *pose* so subtly considered that if one were not on the lookout one mistook it for impulse. Ralph had never met a man who lived so much in the land of consideration. His tastes, his studies, his accomplishments, his collections, were all for a purpose. His life on his hill-top at Florence had been the conscious attitude of years. His solitude, his ennui, his love for his daughter, his good manners, his bad manners, were so many features of a mental image constantly present to him as a model of impertinence and mystification. His ambition was not to please the world, but to please himself by exciting the world's curiosity and then declining to satisfy it. It had made him feel great, ever, to play the world a trick. The thing he had done in his life most directly to please himself was his marrying Miss Archer; though in this case indeed the gullible world was in a manner embodied in poor Isabel, who had been mystified to the top of her bent. Ralph of course found a fitness in being consistent; he had embraced a creed, and as he had suffered for it he could not in honour forsake it. I give this little sketch of its articles for what they may at the time have been worth. It was certain that he was very skilful in fitting the facts to his theory – even the fact that during the month he spent in Rome at this period the husband of the woman he loved appeared to regard him not in the least as an enemy.

For Gilbert Osmond Ralph had not now that importance. It was not that he had the importance of a friend; it was rather that he had none at all. He was Isabel's cousin and he was rather unpleasantly ill – it was on this basis that Osmond treated with him. He made the proper inquiries, asked about his health, about Mrs Touchett, about his opinion of winter climates, whether he were comfortable at his hotel. He addressed him, on the few occasions of their meeting, not a word that was not necessary; but his manner had always the urbanity proper to conscious success in the presence of conscious failure. For all this, Ralph had had towards the end, a sharp inward vision of Osmond's making it of small ease to his wife that she should continue to receive Mr Touchett. He was not jealous – he had not that excuse; no one could be jealous of Ralph. But he made Isabel pay for her old-time kindness, of which so much was still left; and as Ralph had no idea of her paying too much, so when his suspicion had become sharp, he had taken himself off. In doing so he had deprived Isabel of a very interesting occupation: she had been constantly wondering what fine principle was keeping him alive. She had decided that it was his love of conversation; his conversation had been better than ever. He had given up walking; he was no longer a humorous stroller. He sat all day in a chair – almost any chair would serve, and was so dependent on what you would do for him that, had not his talk been highly contemplative, you might have thought he was blind. The reader already knows more about him than Isabel was ever to know, and the reader may therefore be given the key to the mystery. What kept Ralph alive was simply the fact that he had not yet seen enough of the person in the world in whom he was most interested: he was not yet satisfied. There was more to come; he couldn't make up his mind to lose that. He wanted to see what she would make of her husband – or what her husband would make of her. This was only the first act of the drama, and he was determined to sit out the performance. His determination had held good; it had kept him going some eighteen months more, till the time of his return to Rome with Lord Warburton. It had given him indeed such an air of intending to live indefinitely that Mrs Touchett, though more accessible to confusions of thought in the manner of this strange, unremunerative – and unremunerated – son of hers than she had ever been before, had, as we have learned, not scrupled to embark for a distant land. If Ralph had been kept alive by suspense it was with a good deal of the same emotion – the excitement of wondering in what state she should find him – that Isabel mounted to his apartment the day after Lord Warburton had notified her of his arrival in Rome.

She spent an hour with him; it was the first of several visits. Gilbert Osmond called on him punctually, and on their sending their carriage for him Ralph came more than once to Palazzo Roccanera. A fortnight elapsed, at the end of which Ralph announced to Lord Warburton that he thought after all he wouldn't go to Sicily. The two men had been dining together after a day spent by the latter in ranging about the Campagna. They had left the table, and Warburton, before the chimney, was lighting a cigar, which he instantly removed from his lips.

'Won't go to Sicily? Where then will you go?'

'Well, I guess I won't go anywhere,' said Ralph, from the sofa, all shamelessly.

'Do you mean you'll return to England?'

'Oh dear no; I'll stay in Rome.'

'Rome won't do for you. Rome's not warm enough.'

'It will have to do. I'll make it do. See how well I've been.'

Lord Warburton looked at him a while, puffing a cigar and as if trying to see it. 'You've been better than you were on the journey, certainly. I wonder how you lived through that. But I don't understand your condition. I recommend you to try Sicily.'

'I can't try,' said poor Ralph. 'I've done trying. I can't move farther. I can't face that journey. Fancy me between Scylla and Charybdis! I don't want to die on the Sicilian plains – to be snatched away, like Proserpine in the same locality, to the Plutonian shades.'

'What the deuce then did you come for?' his lordship inquired.

'Because the idea took me. I see it won't do. It really doesn't matter where I am now. I've exhausted all remedies. I've swallowed all climates. As I'm here I'll stay. I haven't a single cousin in Sicily – much less a married one.'

'Your cousin's certainly an inducement. But what does the doctor say?'

'I haven't asked him, and I don't care a fig. If I die here Mrs Osmond will bury me. But I shall not die here.'

'I hope not.' Lord Warburton continued to smoke reflectively. 'Well, I must say,' he resumed, 'for myself I'm very glad you don't insist on Sicily. I had a horror of that journey.'

'Ah, but for you it needn't have mattered. I had no idea of dragging you in my train.'

'I certainly didn't mean to let you go alone.'

'My dear Warburton, I never expected you to come farther than this,' Ralph cried.

'I should have gone with you and seen you settled,' said Lord Warburton.

'You're a very good Christian. You're a very kind man.'

'Then I should have come back here.'

'And then you'd have gone to England.'

'No, no; I should have stayed.'

'Well,' said Ralph, 'if that's what we are both up to, I don't see where Sicily comes in!'

His companion was silent; he sat staring at the fire. At last, looking up, 'I say, tell me this,' he broke out; 'did you really mean to go to Sicily when we started?'

'*Ah, vous m'en demandez trop!* Let me put a question first. Did you come with me quite – platonically?'

'I don't know what you mean by that. I wanted to come abroad.'

'I suspect we've each been playing our little game.'

'Speak for yourself. I made no secret whatever of my desiring to be here a while.'

'Yes, I remember you said you wished to see the Minister of Foreign Affairs.'

'I've seen him three times. He's very amusing.'

'I think you've forgotten what you came for,' said Ralph.

'Perhaps I have,' his companion answered rather gravely.

These two were gentlemen of a race which is not distinguished by the absence of reserve, and they had travelled together from London to Rome without an allusion to matters that were uppermost in the mind of each. There was an old subject they had once discussed, but it had lost its recognized place in their attention, and even after their arrival in Rome, where many things led back to it, they had kept the same half-diffident, half-confident silence.

'I recommend you to get the doctor's consent, all the same,' Lord Warburton went on, abruptly, after an interval.

'The doctor's consent will spoil it. I never have it when I can help it.'

'What then does Mrs Osmond think?' Ralph's friend demanded.

'I've not told her. She'll probably say that Rome's too cold and even offer to go with me to Catania. She's capable of that.'

'In your place I should like it.'

'Her husband won't like it.'

'Ah, well, I can fancy that; though it seems to me you're not bound to mind his likings. They're his affair.'

'I don't want to make any more trouble between them,' said Ralph.

'Is there so much already?'

'There's complete preparation for it. Her going off with me would make the explosion. Osmond isn't fond of his wife's cousin.'

'Then of course he'd make a row. But won't he make a row if you stop here?'

'That's what I want to see. He made one the last time I was in Rome, and then I thought it my duty to disappear. Now I think it's my duty to stop and defend her.'

'My dear Touchett, your defensive powers—!' Lord Warburton began with a smile. But he saw something in his companion's face that checked him. 'Your duty, in these premises, seems to me rather a nice question,' he observed instead.

Ralph for a short time answered nothing. 'It's true that my defensive powers are small,' he returned at last; 'but as my aggressive ones are still smaller Osmond may after all not think me worth his gunpowder. At any rate,' he added, 'there are things I'm curious to see.'

'You're sacrificing your health to your curiosity then?'

'I'm not much interested in my health, and I'm deeply interested in Mrs Osmond.'

'So am I. But not as I once was,' Lord Warburton added quickly. This was one of the allusions he had not hitherto found occasion to make.

'Does she strike you as very happy?' Ralph inquired, emboldened by this confidence.

'Well, I don't know; I've hardly thought. She told me the other night she was happy.'

'Ah, she told *you*, of course,' Ralph exclaimed, smiling.

'I don't know that. It seems to me I was rather the sort of person she might have complained to.'

'Complained? She'll never complain. She has done it – what she *has* done – and she knows it. She'll complain to you least of all. She's very careful.'

'She needn't be. I don't mean to make love to her again.'

'I'm delighted to hear it. There can be no doubt at least of *your* duty.'

'Ah no,' said Lord Warburton gravely; 'none!'

'Permit me to ask,' Ralph went on, 'whether it's to bring out the fact that you don't mean to make love to her that you're so very civil to the little girl?'

Lord Warburton gave a slight start; he got up and stood before the fire, looking at it hard. 'Does that strike you as very ridiculous?'

'Ridiculous? Not in the least, if you really like her.'

'I think her a delightful little person. I don't know when a girl of that age has pleased me more.'

'She's a charming creature. Ah, she at least is genuine.'

'Of course there's the difference in our ages – more than twenty years.'

'My dear Warburton,' said Ralph, 'are you serious?'

'Perfectly serious – as far as I've got.'

'I'm very glad. And, heaven help us,' cried Ralph, 'how cheered-up old Osmond will be!'

His companion frowned. 'I say, don't spoil it. I shouldn't propose for his daughter to please *him*.'

'He'll have the perversity to be pleased all the same.'

'He's not so fond of me as that,' said his lordship.

'As that? My dear Warburton, the drawback of your position is that people needn't be fond of you at all to wish to be connected with you. Now, with me in such a case, I should have the happy confidence that they loved me.'

Lord Warburton seemed scarcely in the mood for doing justice to general axioms – he was thinking of a special case. 'Do you judge she'll be pleased?'

'The girl herself? Delighted, surely.'

'No, no; I mean Mrs Osmond.'

Ralph looked at him a moment. 'My dear fellow, what has she to do with it?'

'Whatever she chooses. She's very fond of Pansy.'

'Very true – very true.' And Ralph slowly got up. 'It's an interesting question – how far her fondness for Pansy will carry her.' He stood there a moment with his hands in his pockets and rather a clouded brow. 'I hope, you know, that you're very – very sure. The deuce!' he broke off. 'I don't know how to say it.'

'Yes, you do; you know how to say everything.'

'Well, it's awkward. I hope you're sure that among Miss Osmond's merits her being – a – so near her stepmother isn't a leading one?'

'Good heavens, Touchett!' cried Lord Warburton angrily, 'for what do you take me?'

Chapter Forty

Isabel had not seen much of Madame Merle since her marriage, this lady having indulged in frequent absences from Rome. At one time she had spent six months in England; at another she had passed a portion of a winter in Paris. She had made numerous visits to distant friends and gave countenance to the idea that for the future she should be a less inveterate Roman than in the past. As she had been inveterate in the past only in the sense of constantly having an apartment in one of the sunniest niches of the Pincian – an apartment which often stood empty – this suggested a prospect of almost constant absence; a danger which Isabel at one period had been much inclined to deplore. Familiarity had modified in some degree her first impression of Madame Merle, but it had not essentially altered it; there was still much wonder of admiration in it. That personage was armed at all points; it was a pleasure to see a character so completely equipped for the social battle. She carried her flag discreetly, but her weapons were polished steel, and she used them with a skill which struck Isabel as more and more that of a veteran. She was never weary, never overcome with disgust; she never appeared to need rest or consolation. She had her own ideas; she had of old exposed a great many of them to Isabel, who knew also that under an appearance of extreme self-control her highly-cultivated friend concealed a rich sensibility. But her will was mistress of her life; there was something gallant in the way she kept going. It was as if she had learned the secret of it – as if the art of life were some clever trick she had guessed. Isabel, as she herself grew older, became acquainted with revulsions, with disgusts; there were days when the world looked black and she asked herself with some sharpness what it was that she was pretending to live for. Her old habit had been to live by enthusiasm, to fall in love with suddenly perceived possibilities, with the idea of some new adventure. As a younger person she had been used to proceed from one little exaltation to the other: there were scarcely any dull places between. But Madame Merle had suppressed enthusiasm; she fell in love nowadays with nothing; she lived entirely by reason and by wisdom. There were hours when Isabel would have given anything for lessons in this art; if her brilliant friend had been near she would have made an appeal to her. She had become aware more than before of the advantage of being like that – of having made one's self a firm surface, a sort of corselet of silver.

But, as I say, it was not till the winter during which we lately renewed acquaintance with our heroine that the personage in question made again a continuous stay in Rome. Isabel now saw more of her than she had done since her marriage; but by this time Isabel's needs and inclinations had considerably changed. It was not at present to Madame Merle that she would have applied for instruction; she had lost the desire to know this lady's clever trick. If she had troubles she must keep them to herself, and if life was difficult it would not make it easier to confess herself beaten. Madame Merle was doubtless of great use to herself and an ornament to any circle; but was she – would she be – of use to others in periods of refined embarrassment? The best way to profit by her friend – this indeed Isabel had always thought – was to imitate her, to be as firm and bright as she. She recognized no embarrassments, and Isabel, considering this fact, determined for the fiftieth time to brush aside her own. It seemed to her too, on the renewal of an intercourse which had virtually been interrupted, that her old ally was different, was almost detached – pushing to the extreme a certain rather artificial fear of being indiscreet. Ralph Touchett, we know, had been of the opinion that she was prone to exaggeration, to forcing the note – was apt, in the vulgar phrase, to overdo it. Isabel had never admitted this charge – had never indeed quite understood it; Madame Merle's conduct, to her perception, always bore the stamp of good taste, was always 'quiet'. But in this matter of not wishing to intrude upon the inner life of the Osmond family it at last occurred to our young woman that she overdid a little. That of course was not the best taste; that was rather violent. She remembered too much that Isabel was married; that she had now other interests; that though she, Madame Merle, had known Gilbert Osmond and his little Pansy very well, better almost than anyone, she was not after all of the inner circle. She was on her guard; she never spoke of their affairs till she was asked, even pressed – as when her opinion was wanted; she had a dread of seeming to meddle. Madame Merle was as candid as we know, and one day she candidly expressed this dread to Isabel.

'I *must* be on my guard,' she said; 'I might so easily, without suspecting it, offend you. You would be right to be offended, even if my intention should have been of the purest. I must not forget that I knew your husband long before you did; I must not let that betray me. If you were a silly woman you might be jealous. You're not a silly woman; I know that perfectly. But neither am I; therefore I'm determined not to get into trouble. A little harm's very soon done; a mistake's made before one knows it. Of course if I had wished to make love to your husband I had ten years to do it in, and nothing to prevent; so it isn't likely I shall begin today, when I'm so much less attractive than I was. But if I were to annoy you by seeming to take a place that doesn't belong to me, you wouldn't make that reflection; you'd simply say I was forgetting certain differences. I'm determined not to forget them. Certainly a good friend isn't always thinking of that; one doesn't suspect one's friends of injustice. I don't suspect you, my dear, in the least; but I suspect human nature. Don't think I make myself uncomfortable; I'm not always watching myself. I think I sufficiently prove it in talking to you as I do now. All I wish to say is, however, that if you were to be jealous – that's the form it would take – I shouldn't be sure to think it was a little my fault. It certainly wouldn't be your husband's.'

Isabel had had three years to think over Mrs Touchett's theory that Madame Merle had made Gilbert Osmond's marriage. We know how she had at first received it. Madame Merle might have made Gilbert Osmond's marriage, but she certainly had not made Isabel Archer's. That was the work of – Isabel scarcely knew what: of nature, providence, fortune, of the eternal mystery of things. It was true her aunt's complaint had been not so much of Madame Merle's activity as of her duplicity; she had brought about the strange event and then she had denied her guilt. Such guilt would not have been great, to Isabel's mind; she couldn't make a crime of Madame Merle's having been the producing cause of the most important friendship she had ever formed. This had occurred to her just before her marriage, after her little discussion with her aunt and at a time when she was still capable of that large inward reference, the tone almost of the philosophic historian, to her scant young annals. If Madame Merle had desired her change of state she could only say it had been a very happy thought. With her, moreover, she had been perfectly straightforward; she had never concealed her high opinion of Gilbert Osmond. After their union Isabel discovered that her husband took a less convenient view of the matter; he seldom consented to finger, in talk, this roundest and smoothest bead of their social rosary.

'Don't you like Madame Merle?' Isabel had once said to him. 'She thinks a great deal of you.'

'I'll tell you once for all,' Osmond had answered. 'I liked her once better than I do today. I'm tired of her, and I'm rather ashamed of it. She's so almost unnaturally good! I'm glad she's not in Italy, it makes for relaxation – for a sort of moral *détente*. Don't talk of her too much; it seems to bring her back. She'll come back in plenty of time.'

Madame Merle, in fact, had come back before it was too late – too late, I mean, to recover whatever advantage she might have lost. But meantime, if, as I have said, she was sensibly different, Isabel's feelings were also not quite the same. Her consciousness of the situation was as acute as of old, but it was much less satisfying. A dissatisfied mind, whatever else it may miss, is rarely in want of reasons; they bloom as thick as buttercups in June. The fact of Madame Merle's having had a hand in Gilbert Osmond's marriage ceased to be one of her titles to consideration; it might have been written, after all, that there was not so much to thank her for. As time went on there was less and less, and Isabel once said to herself that perhaps without her these things would not have been. That reflection indeed was instantly stifled; she knew an immediate horror at having made it. 'Whatever happens to me let me not be unjust,' she said; 'let me bear my burdens myself and not shift them upon others!' This disposition was tested, eventually, by that ingenious apology for her present conduct which Madame Merle saw fit to make and of which I have given a sketch; for there was something irritating – there was almost an air of mockery – in her neat discriminations and clear convictions. In Isabel's mind today there was nothing clear; there was a confusion of regrets, a complication of fears. She felt helpless as she turned away from her friend, who had just made the statements I have quoted: Madame Merle knew so little what she was thinking of! She was herself moreover so unable to explain. Jealous of her – jealous of her with Gilbert? The idea just then suggested no near reality. She almost wished jealousy had been possible; it would have made in a manner for refreshment. Wasn't it in manner one of the symptoms of happiness? Madame Merle, however, was wise, so wise that she might have been pretending to know Isabel better than Isabel knew herself. This young woman had always been fertile in resolutions – many of them of an elevated character; but at no period had they flourished (in the privacy of her heart) more richly than today. It is true that they all had a family likeness; they might have been summed up in the determination that if she was to be unhappy it should not be by a fault of her own. Her poor winged spirit had always had a great desire to do its best, and it had not as yet been seriously discouraged. It wished, therefore, to hold fast to justice – not to pay itself by petty revenges. To associate Madame Merle with its disappointment would be a petty revenge – especially as the pleasure to be derived from that would be perfectly insincere. It might feed her sense of bitterness, but it would not loosen her bonds. It was impossible to pretend that she had not acted with her eyes open; if ever a girl was a free agent she had been. A girl in love was doubtless not a free agent; but the sole source of her mistake had been within herself. There had been no plot, no snare; she had looked and considered and chosen. When a woman had made such a mistake, there was only one way to repair it – just immensely (oh, with the highest grandeur!) to accept it. One folly was enough, especially when it was to last for ever; a second one would not much set it off. In this vow of reticence there was a certain nobleness which kept Isabel going; but Madame Merle had been right, for all that, in taking her precautions.

One day about a month after Ralph Touchett's arrival in Rome Isabel came back from a walk with Pansy. It was not only part of her general determination to be just that she was at present very thankful for Pansy – it was also a part of her tenderness for things that were pure and weak. Pansy was dear to her, and there was nothing else in her life that had the rightness of the young creature's attachment or the sweetness of her own clearness about it. It was like a soft presence – like a small hand in her own; on Pansy's part it was more than an affection – it was a kind of ardent coercive faith. On her own side her sense of the girl's dependence was more than a pleasure; it operated as a definite reason when motives threatened to fail her. She had said to herself that we must take our duty where we find it, and that we must look for it as much as possible. Pansy's sympathy was a direct admonition; it seemed to say that here was an opportunity, not eminent perhaps, but unmistakable. Yet an opportunity for what Isabel could hardly have said; in general, to be more for the child than the child was able to be for herself. Isabel could have smiled, in these days, to remember that her little companion had once been ambiguous, for she now perceived that Pansy's ambiguities were simply her own grossness of vision.

She had been unable to believe any one could care so much – so extraordinarily much – to please. But since then she had seen this delicate faculty in operation, and now she knew what to think of it. It was the whole creature – it was a sort of genius. Pansy had no pride to interfere with it, and though she was constantly extending her conquests she took no credit for them. The two were constantly together; Mrs Osmond was rarely seen without her stepdaughter. Isabel liked her company; it had the effect of one's carrying a nosegay composed all of the same flower. And then not to neglect Pansy, not under any provocation to neglect her – this she had made an article of religion. The young girl had every appearance of being happier in Isabel's society than in that of anyone save her father, whom she admired with an intensity justified by the fact that, as paternity was an exquisite pleasure to Gilbert Osmond, he had always been luxuriously mild. Isabel knew how Pansy liked to be with her and how she studied the means of pleasing her. She had decided that the best way of pleasing her was negative, and consisted in not giving her trouble – a conviction which certainly could have had no reference to trouble already existing. She was therefore ingeniously passive and almost imaginatively docile; she was careful even to moderate the eagerness with which she assented to Isabel's propositions and which might have implied that she could have thought otherwise. She never interrupted, never asked social questions, and though she delighted in approbation, to the point of turning pale when it came to her, never held out her hand for it. She only looked towards it wistfully – an attitude which, as she grew older, made her eyes the prettiest in the world. When during the second winter at Palazzo Roccanera she began to go to parties, to dances, she always, at a reasonable hour, lest Mrs Osmond should be tired, was the first to propose departure. Isabel appreciated the sacrifice of the late dances, for she knew her little companion had a passionate pleasure in this exercise, taking her steps to the music like a conscientious fairy. Society, moreover, had no drawbacks for her; she liked even the tiresome parts – the heat of ballrooms, the dullness of dinners, the crush at the door, the awkward waiting for the carriage. During the day, in this vehicle, beside her stepmother, she sat in a small fixed, appreciative posture, bending forward and faintly smiling, as if she had been taken to drive for the first time.

On the day I speak of they had driven out of one of the gates of the city and at the end of half an hour had left the carriage to await then by the roadside while they walked away over the short grass of the Campagna, which even in the winter months is sprinkled with delicate flowers. This was almost a daily habit with Isabel, who was fond of a walk and had a swift length of step, though not so swift a one as on her first coming to Europe. It was not the form of exercise that Pansy loved best, but she liked it, because she liked everything; and she moved with a shorter undulation beside her father's wife, who afterwards, on their return to Rome, paid a tribute to her preferences by making the circuit of the Pincian or the Villa Borghese. She had gathered a handful of flowers in a sunny hollow, far from the walls of Rome, and on reaching Palazzo Roccanera she went straight to her room, to put them into water. Isabel passed into the drawing-room, the one she herself usually occupied, the second in order from the large ante-chamber which was entered from the staircase and in which even Gilbert Osmond's rich devices had not been able to correct a look of rather grand nudity. Just beyond the threshold of the drawing-room she stopped short, the reason for her doing so being that she had received an impression. The impression had, in strictness, nothing unprecedented; but she felt it as something new, and the soundlessness of her step gave her time to take in the scene before she interrupted it. Madame Merle was there in her bonnet, and Gilbert Osmond was talking to her; for a minute they were unaware she had come in. Isabel had often seen that before, certainly; but what she had not seen, or at least had not noticed, was that their colloquy had for the moment converted itself into a sort of familiar silence from which she instantly perceived that her entrance would startle them. Madame Merle was standing on the rug, a little way from the fire; Osmond was in a deep chair, leaning back and looking at her. Her head was erect, as usual, but her eyes were bent on his. What struck Isabel first was that he was sitting while Madame Merle stood; there was an anomaly in this that arrested her. Then she perceived that they had arrived at a desultory pause in their exchange of ideas and were musing, face to face, with the freedom of old friends who sometimes exchange ideas without uttering them. There was nothing to shock in this; they were old friends in fact. But the thing made an image, lasting only a moment, like a sudden flicker of light. Their relative positions, their absorbed mutual gaze, struck her as something detected. But it was all over by the time she had fairly seen it. Madame Merle had seen her and had welcomed her without moving; her husband, on the other hand, had instantly jumped up. He presently murmured something about wanting a walk and, after having asked their visitor to excuse him, left the room.

'I came to see you, thinking you would have come in; and as you hadn't I waited for you,' Madame Merle said.

'Didn't he ask you to sit down?' Isabel asked with a smile.

Madame Merle looked about her. 'Ah, it's very true; I was going away.'

'You must stay now.'

'Certainly. I came for a reason; I've something on my mind.'

'I've told you that before,' Isabel said – 'that it takes something extraordinary to bring you to this house.'

'And you know what I've told *you*; that whether I come or whether I stay away, I've always the same motive – the affection I bear you.'

'Yes, you've told me that.'

'You look just now as if you didn't believe it,' said Madame Merle.

'Ah,' Isabel answered, 'the profundity of your motives, that's the last thing I doubt!'

'You doubt sooner of the sincerity of my words.'

Isabel shook her head gravely. 'I know you've always been kind to me.'

'As often as you would let me. You don't always take it; then one has to let you alone. It's not to do you a kindness, however, that I've come today; it's quite another affair. I've come to get rid of a trouble of my own – to make it over to you. I've been talking to your husband about it.'

'I'm surprised at that; he doesn't like troubles.'

'Especially other people's; I know very well. But neither do you, I suppose. At any rate, whether you do or not, you must help me. It's about poor Mr Rosier.'

'Ah,' said Isabel reflectively, 'it's his trouble then, not yours.'

'He has succeeded in saddling me with it. He comes to see me ten times a week, to talk about Pansy.'

'Yes, he wants to marry her. I know all about it.'

Madame Merle hesitated. 'I gathered from your husband that perhaps you didn't.'

'How should he know what I know? He has never spoken to me of the matter.'

'It's probably because he doesn't know how to speak of it.'

'It's nevertheless the sort of question in which he's rarely at fault.'

'Yes, because as a general thing he knows perfectly well what to think. Today he doesn't.'

'Haven't you been telling him?' Isabel asked.

Madame Merle gave a bright, voluntary smile. 'Do you know you're a little dry?'

'Yes; I can't help it. Mr Rosier has also talked to me.'

'In that there's some reason. You're so near the child.'

'Ah,' said Isabel, 'for all the comfort I've given him! If you think me dry. I wonder what *he* thinks.'

'I believe he thinks you can do more than you have done.'

'I can do nothing.'

'You can do more at least than I. I don't know what mysterious connexion he may have discovered between me and Pansy; but he came to me from the first, as if I held his fortune in my hand. Now he keeps coming back, to spur me up, to know what hope there is, to pour out his feelings.'

'He's very much in love,' said Isabel.

'Very much – for him.'

'Very much for Pansy, you might say as well.'

Madame Merle dropped her eyes a moment. 'Don't you think she's attractive?'

'The dearest little person possible – but very limited.'

'She ought to be all the easier for Mr Rosier to love. Mr Rosier's not unlimited.'

'No,' said Isabel, 'he has about the extent of one's pocket-handkerchief – the small ones with lace borders.' Her humour had lately turned a good deal to sarcasm, but in a moment she was ashamed of exercising it on so innocent an object as Pansy's suitor. 'He's very kind, very honest,' she presently added; 'and he's not such a fool as he seems.'

'He assures me that she delights in him,' said Madame Merle.

'I don't know; I've not asked her.'

'You've never sounded her a little.'

'It's not my place; it's her father's.'

'Ah, you're too literal!' said Madame Merle.

'I must judge for myself.'

Madame Merle gave her smile again. 'It isn't easy to help you.'

'To help me?' said Isabel very seriously. 'What do you mean?'

'It's easy to displease you. Don't you see how wise I am to be careful? I notify you, at any rate, as I notified Osmond, that I wash my hands of the love-affairs of Miss Pansy and Mr Edward Rosier. *Je n'y peux rien, moi!* I can't talk to Pansy about him. Especially,' added Madame Merle, 'as I don't think him a paragon of husbands.'

Isabel reflected a little; after which, with a smile, 'You don't wash your hands then!' she said. After which again she added in another tone: 'You can't – you're too much interested.'

Madame Merle slowly rose; she had given Isabel a look as rapid as the intimation that had gleamed before our heroine a few moments before. Only this time the latter saw nothing. 'Ask him the next time, and you'll see.'

'I can't ask him; he has ceased to come to the house. Gilbert has let him know that he's not welcome.'

'Ah yes,' said Madame Merle, 'I forgot that – though it's the burden of his lamentation. He says Osmond has insulted him. All the same,' she went on, 'Osmond doesn't dislike him so much as he thinks.' She had got up as if to close the conversation, but she lingered, looking about her, and had evidently more to say. Isabel perceived this and even saw the point she had in view; but Isabel also had her own reasons for not opening the way.

'That must have pleased him, if you've told him,' she answered, smiling.

'Certainly I've told him; as far as that goes I've encouraged him. I've preached patience, have said that his case isn't desperate if he'll only hold his tongue and be quiet. Unfortunately he has taken it into his head to be jealous.'

'Jealous?'

'Jealous of Lord Warburton, who, he says, is always here.'

Isabel, who was tired, had remained sitting; but at this she also rose. 'Ah!' she exclaimed simply, moving slowly to the fireplace. Madame Merle observed her as she passed and while she stood a moment before the mantelglass and pushed into its place a wandering tress of hair.

'Poor Mr Rosier keeps saying there's nothing impossible in Lord Warburton's falling in love with Pansy,' Madame Merle went on.

Isabel was silent a little; she turned away from the glass. 'It's true – there's nothing impossible,' she returned at last, gravely and more gently.

'So I've had to admit to Mr Rosier. So, too, your husband thinks.'

'That I don't know.'

'Ask him and you'll see.'

'I shall not ask him,' said Isabel.

'Pardon me; I forgot you had pointed that out. Of course,' Madame Merle added, 'you've had infinitely more observation of Lord Warburton's behaviour than I.'

'I see no reason why I shouldn't tell you that he likes my stepdaughter very much.'

Madame Merle gave one of her quick looks again. 'Likes her, you mean – as Mr Rosier means?'

'I don't know how Mr Rosier means; but Lord Warburton has let me know that he's charmed with Pansy.'

'And you've never told Osmond?' This observation was immediate, precipitate; it almost burst from Madame Merle's lips.

Isabel's eyes rested on her. 'I suppose he'll know in time; Lord Warburton has a tongue and knows how to express himself.'

Madame Merle instantly became conscious that she had spoken more quickly than usual, and the reflection brought the colour to her cheek. She gave the treacherous impulse time to subside and then said as if she had been thinking it over a little: 'That would be better than marrying poor Mr Rosier.'

'Much better, I think.'

'It would be very delightful; it would be a great marriage. It's really very kind of him.'

'Very kind of him?'

'To drop his eyes on a simple little girl.'

'I don't see that.'

'It's very good of you. But after all, Pansy Osmond—'

'After all, Pansy Osmond's the most attractive person he has ever known!' Isabel exclaimed.

Madame Merle stared, and indeed she was justly bewildered. 'Ah, a moment ago I thought you seemed rather to disparage her.'

'I said she was limited. And so she is. And so's Lord Warburton.'

'So are we all, if you come to that. If it's no more than Pansy deserves, all the better. But if she fixes her affections on Mr Rosier I won't admit that she deserves it. That will be too perverse.'

'Mr Rosier's a nuisance!' Isabel cried abruptly.

'I quite agree with you, and I'm delighted to know that I'm not expected to feed his flame. For the future, when he calls on me, my door shall be closed to him.' And gathering her mantle together Madame Merle prepared to depart. She was checked, however, on her progress to the door, by an inconsequent request from Isabel.

'All the same, you know, be kind to him.'

She lifted her shoulders and eyebrows and stood looking at her friend. 'I don't understand your contradictions! Decidedly I shan't be kind to him, for it will be a false kindness. I want to see her married to Lord Warburton.'

'You had better wait till he asks her.'

'If what you say's true, he'll ask her. Especially,' said Madame Merle in a moment, 'if you make him.'

'If I make him?'

'It's quite in your power. You've great influence with him.'

Isabel frowned a little. 'Where did you learn that?'

'Mrs Touchett told me. Not you – never!' said Madame Merle, smiling.

'I certainly never told you anything of the sort.'

'You might have done so – so far as opportunity went – when we were by way of being confidential with each other. But you really told me very little; I've often thought so since.'

Isabel had thought so too, and sometimes with a certain satisfaction. But she didn't admit it now – perhaps because she wished not to appear to exult in it. 'You seem to have had an excellent informant in my aunt,' she simply returned.

'She let me know you had declined an offer of marriage from Lord Warburton, because she was greatly vexed and was full of the subject. Of course I think you've done better in doing as you did. But if you wouldn't marry Lord Warburton yourself, make him the reparation of helping him to marry someone else.'

Isabel listened to this with a face that persisted in not reflecting the bright expressiveness of Madame Merle's. But in a moment she said, reasonably and gently enough: 'I should be very glad indeed if, as regards Pansy, it could be arranged.' Upon which her companion, who seemed to regard this as a speech of good omen, embraced her more tenderly than might have been expected and triumphantly withdrew.

Chapter Forty-one

Osmond touched on this matter that evening for the first time; coming very late into the drawing-room, where she was sitting alone. They had spent the evening at home, and Pansy had gone to bed; he himself had been sitting since dinner in a small apartment in which he had arranged his books and which he called his study. At ten o'clock Lord Warburton had come in, as he always did when he knew from Isabel that she was to be at home; he was going somewhere else and he sat for half an hour. Isabel after asking him for news of Ralph, said very little to him, on purpose; she wished him to talk with her stepdaughter. She pretended to read; she even went after a little to the piano; she asked herself if she mightn't leave the room. She had come little by little to think well of the idea of Pansy's becoming the wife of the master of beautiful Lockleigh, though at first it had not presented itself in a manner to excite her enthusiasm. Madame Merle, that afternoon, had applied the match to an accumulation of inflammable material. When Isabel was unhappy she always looked about her – partly from impulse and partly by theory – for some form of positive exertion. She could never rid herself of the sense that unhappiness was a state of disease – of suffering as opposed to doing. To 'do' – it hardly mattered what – would therefore be an escape, perhaps in some degree a remedy. Besides, she wished to convince herself that she had done everything possible to content her husband; she was determined not be be haunted by visions of his wife's limpness under appeal. It would please him greatly to see Pansy married to an English nobleman, and justly please him, since this nobleman was so sound a character. It seemed to Isabel that if she could make it her duty to bring about such an event she should play the part of a good wife. She wanted to be that; she wanted to be able to believe sincerely, and with proof of it, that she had been that. Then such an undertaking had other recommendations. It would occupy her, and she desired occupation. It would even amuse her, and if she could really amuse herself she perhaps might be saved. Lastly, it would be a service to Lord Warburton, who evidently pleased himself greatly with the charming girl. It was a little 'weird' he should – being what he was; but there was no accounting for such impressions. Pansy might captivate anyone – anyone at least but Lord Warburton. Isabel would have thought her too small, too slight, perhaps even too artificial for that. There was always a little of the doll about her, and that was not what he had been looking for. Still, who could say what men ever were looking for? They looked for what they found; they knew what pleased them only when they saw it. No theory was valid in such matters, and nothing was more unaccountable or more natural than anything else. If he had cared for *her* it might seem odd he should care for Pansy, who was so different; but he had not cared for her so much as he had supposed. Or if he had, he had completely got over it, and it was natural that, as that affair had failed, he should think something of quite another sort might succeed. Enthusiasm, as I say, had not come at first to Isabel, but it came today and made her feel almost happy. It was astonishing what happiness she could still find in the idea of procuring a pleasure for her husband. It was a pity, however, that Edward Rosier had crossed their path.

At this reflection the light that had suddenly gleamed upon that path lost something of its brightness. Isabel was unfortunately as sure that Pansy thought Mr Rosier the nicest of all the young men – as sure as if she had held an interview with her on the subject. It was very tiresome she should be so sure, when she had carefully abstained from informing herself; almost as tiresome as that poor Mr Rosier should have taken it into his own head. He was certainly very inferior to Lord Warburton. It was not the difference in fortune so much as the difference in the men; the young American was really so light a weight. He was much more of the type of the useless fine gentleman than the English nobleman. It was true that there was no particular reason why Pansy should marry a statesman; still, if a statesman admired her, that was his affair, and she would make a perfect little pearl of a peeress.

It may seem to the reader that Mrs Osmond had grown of a sudden strangely cynical, for she ended by saying to herself that this difficulty could probably be arranged. An impediment that was embodied in poor Rosier could not anyhow present itself as a dangerous one; there were always means of levelling secondary obstacles. Isabel was perfectly aware that she had not taken the measure of Pansy's tenacity, which might prove to be inconveniently great; but she inclined to see her as rather letting go, under suggestion, than as clutching under deprecation – since she had certainly the faculty of assent developed in a very much higher degree than that of protest. She would cling, yes, she would cling; but it really mattered to her very little what she clung to. Lord Warburton would do as well as Mr Rosier – especially as she seemed quite to like him; she had expressed this sentiment to Isabel without a single reservation; she had said she thought his conversation most interesting – he had told her all about India. His manner to Pansy had been of the rightest and easiest – Isabel noticed that for herself, as she also observed that he talked to her not in the least in a patronizing way, reminding himself of her youth and simplicity, but quite as if she understood his subjects with that sufficiency with which she followed those of the fashionable operas. This went far enough for attention to the music and the baritone. He was careful only to be kind – he was as kind as he had been to another fluttered young chit at Gardencourt. A girl might well be touched by that; she remembered how she herself had been touched, and said to herself that if she had been as simple as Pansy the impression would have been deeper still. She had not been simple when she refused him; that operation had been as complicated as, later, her acceptance of Osmond had been. Pansy, however, in spite of *her* simplicity, really did understand, and was glad that Lord Warburton should talk to her, not about her partners and bouquets, but about the state of Italy, the condition of the peasantry, the famous grist-tax, the *pellagra*, his impressions of Roman society. She looked at him, as she drew her needle through her tapestry, with sweet submissive eyes, and when she lowered them she gave little quiet oblique glances at his person, his hands, his feet, his clothes, as if she were considering him. Even his person, Isabel might have reminded her, was better than Mr Rosier's. But Isabel contented herself at such moments with wondering where this gentleman was; he came no more at all to Palazzo Roccanera. It was surprising, as I say, the hold it had taken of her – the idea of assisting her husband to be pleased.

It was surprising for a variety of reasons which I shall presently touch upon. On the evening I speak of, while Lord Warburton sat there, she had been on the point of taking the great step of going out of the room and leaving her companions alone. I say the great step, because it was in this light that Gilbert Osmond would have regarded it, and Isabel was trying as much as possible to take her husband's view. She succeeded after a fashion, but she fell short of the point I mention. After all she couldn't rise to it; something held her and made this impossible. It was not exactly that it would be base or insidious; for women as a general thing practise such manoeuvres with a perfectly good conscience, and Isabel was instinctively much more true than false to the common genius of her sex. There was a vague doubt that interposed – a sense that she was not quite sure. So she remained in the drawing-room, and after a while Lord Warburton went off to his party, of which he promised to give Pansy a full account on the morrow. After he had gone she wondered if she had prevented something which would have happened is she had absented herself for a quarter of an hour; and then she pronounced – always mentally – that when their distinguished visitor should wish her to go away he would easily find means to let her know it. Pansy said nothing whatever about him after he had gone, and Isabel studiously said nothing, as she had taken a vow of reserve until after he should have declared himself. He was a little longer in coming to this than might seem to accord with the description he had given Isabel of his feelings. Pansy went to bed, and Isabel had to admit that she could not now guess what her stepdaughter was thinking of. Her transparent little companion was for the moment not to be seen through.

She remained alone, looking at the fire, until, at the end of half an hour, her husband came in. He moved about a while in silence and then sat down; he looked at the fire like herself. But she now had transferred her eyes from the flickering flame in the chimney to Osmond's face, and she watched him while he kept his silence. Covert observation had become a habit with her; an instinct, of which it is not an exaggeration to say that it was allied to that of self-defence, had made it habitual. She wished as much as possible to know his thoughts, to know what he would say, beforehand, so that she might prepare her answer. Preparing answers had not been her strong point of old; she had rarely in this respect got further than thinking afterwards of clever things she might have said. But she had learned caution – learned it in a measure from her husband's very countenance. It was the same face she had looked into with eyes equally earnest perhaps, but less penetrating, on the terrace of a Florentine villa; except that Osmond had grown slightly stouter since his marriage. He still, however, might strike one as very distinguished.

'Has Lord Warburton been here?' he presently asked.

'Yes, he stayed half an hour.'

'Did he see Pansy?'

'Yes; he sat on the sofa beside her.'

'Did he talk to her much?'

'He talked almost only to her.'

'It seems to me he's attentive. Isn't that what you call it?'

'I don't call it anything,' said Isabel; 'I've waited for you to give it a name.'

'That's a consideration you don't always show,' Osmond answered after a moment.

'I've determined, this time, to try and act as you'd like. I've so often failed of that.'

Osmond turned his head slowly, looking at her. 'Are you trying to quarrel with me?'

'No, I'm trying to live at peace.'

'Nothing's more easy; you know I don't quarrel myself.'

'What do you call it when you try to make me angry?' Isabel asked.

'I don't try; if I've done so it has been the most natural thing in the world. Moreover I'm not in the least trying now.'

Isabel smiled. 'It doesn't matter. I've determined never to be angry again.'

'That's an excellent resolve. Your temper isn't good.'

'No – it's not good.' She pushed away the book she had been reading and took up the band of tapestry Pansy had left on the table.

'That's partly why I've not spoken to you about this business of my daughter's,' Osmond said, designating Pansy in the manner that was not frequent with him. 'I was afraid I should encounter opposition – that you too would have views on the subject. I've sent little Rosier about his business.'

'You were afraid I'd plead for Mr Rosier? Haven't you noticed that I've never spoken to you of him?'

'I've never given you a chance. We've so little conversation in these days. I know he was an old friend of yours.'

'Yes; he's an old friend of mine.' Isabel cared little more for him than for the tapestry that she held in her hand; but it was true that he was an old friend and that with her husband she felt a desire not to extenuate such ties. He had a way of expressing contempt for them which fortified her loyalty to them, even when, as in the present case, they were in themselves insignificant. She sometimes felt a sort of passion of tenderness for memories which had no other merit than that they belonged to her unmarried life. 'But as regards Pansy,' she added in a moment, 'I've given him no encouragement.'

'That's fortunate,' Osmond observed.

'Fortunate for me, I suppose you mean. For him it matters little.'

'There's no use talking of him,' Osmond said. 'As I tell you, I've turned him out,'

'Yes; but a lover outside's always a lover. He's sometimes even more of one. Mr Rosier still has hope.'

'He's welcome to the comfort of it! My daughter has only to sit perfectly quiet to become Lady Warburton.'

'Should you like that?' Isabel asked with a simplicity which was not so affected as it may appear. She was resolved to assume nothing, for Osmond had a way of unexpectedly turning her assumptions against her. The intensity with which he would like his daughter to become Lady Warburton had been the very basis of her own recent reflections. But that was for herself; she would recognize nothing until Osmond should have put it into words; she would not take for granted with him that he thought Lord Warburton a prize worth an amount of effort that was unusual among the Osmonds. It was Gilbert's constant intimation that for him nothing in life was a prize; that he treated as from equal to equal with the most distinguished people in the world, and that his daughter had only to look about her to pick out a prince. It cost him therefore a lapse from consistency to say explicitly that he yearned for Lord Warburton and that if this nobleman should escape his equivalent might not be found; with which moreover it was another of his customary implications that he was never inconsistent. He would have liked his wife to glide over the point. But strangely enough, now that she was face to face with him and although an hour before she had almost invented a scheme for pleasing him, Isabel was not accommodating, would not glide. And yet she knew exactly the effect on his mind of her question: it would operate as an humiliation. Never mind; he was terribly capable of humiliating *her* – all the more so that he was also capable of waiting for great opportunities and of showing sometimes an almost unaccountable indifference to small ones. Isabel perhaps took a small opportunity because she would not have availed herself of a great one.

Osmond at present acquitted himself very honourably. 'I should like it extremely; it would be a great marriage. And then Lord Warburton has another advantage: he's an old friend of yours. It would be pleasant for him to come into the family. It's very odd Pansy's admirers should all be your old friends.'

'It's natural that they should come to see me. In coming to see me they see Pansy. Seeing her it's natural they should fall in love with her.'

'So I think. But you're not bound to do so.'

'If she should marry Lord Warburton I should be very glad,' Isabel went on frankly. 'He's an excellent man. You say, however, that she has only to sit perfectly still. Perhaps she won't sit perfectly still. If she loses Mr Rosier she may jump up!'

Osmond appeared to give no heed to this; he sat gazing at the fire. 'Pansy would like to be a great lady,' he remarked in a moment with a certain tenderness of tone. 'She wishes above all to please,' he added.

'To please Mr Rosier, perhaps.'

'No, to please me.'

'Me too a little, I think,' said Isabel.

'Yes, she has a great opinion of you. But she'll do what I like.'

'If you're sure of that, it's very well,' she went on.

'Meantime,' said Osmond, 'I should like our distinguished visitor to speak.'

'He has spoken – to me. He has told me it would be a great pleasure to him to believe she could care for him.'

Osmond turned his head quickly, but at first he said nothing. Then, 'Why didn't you tell me that?' he asked sharply.

'There was no opportunity. You know how we live. I've taken the first chance that has offered.'

'Did you speak to him of Rosier?'

'Oh yes, a little.'

'That was hardly necessary.'

'I though it best he should know, so that, so that—' And Isabel paused.

'So that what?'

'So that he might act accordingly.'

'So that he might back out, do you mean?'

'No, so that he might advance while there's yet time.'

'That's not the effect it seems to have had.'

'You should have patience,' said Isabel. 'You know Englishmen are shy.'

'This one's not. He was not when he made love to *you*.'

She had been afraid Osmond would speak of that; it was disagreeable to her. 'I beg your pardon; he was extremely so,' she returned.

He answered nothing for some time; he took up a book and fingered the pages while she sat silent and occupied herself with Pansy's tapestry. 'You must have a great deal of influence with him,' Osmond went on at last. 'The moment you really wish it you can bring him to the point.'

This was more offensive still; but she felt the great naturalness of his saying it, and it was after all extremely like what she had said to herself. 'Why should I have influence?' she asked. 'What have I ever done to put him under an obligation to me?'

'You refused to marry him,' said Osmond with his eyes on his book.

'I must not presume too much on that,' she replied.

He threw down the book presently and got up, standing before the fire with his hands behind him. 'Well, I hold that it lies in your hands. I shall leave it there. With a little goodwill you may manage it. Think that over and remember how much I count on you.' He waited a little, to give her time to answer; but she answered nothing, and he presently strolled out of the room.

Chapter Forty-two

She had answered nothing because his words had put the situation before her and she was absorbed in looking at it. There was something in them that suddenly made vibrations deep, so that she had been afraid to trust herself to speak. After he had gone she leaned back in her chair and closed her eyes; and for a long time, far into the night and still farther, she sat in the still drawing-room, given up to her meditation. A servant came in to attend to the fire, and she bade him bring fresh candles and then go to bed. Osmond had told her to think of what he had said; and she did so indeed, and of many other things. The suggestion from another that she had a definite influence on Lord Warburton – this had given her the start that accompanies unexpected recognition. Was it true that there was something still between them that might be a handle to make him declare himself to Pansy – a susceptibility, on his part, to approval, a desire to do what would please her? Isabel had hitherto not asked herself the question, because she had not been forced; but now that it was directly presented to her she saw the answer, and the answer frightened her. Yes, there was something – something on Lord Warburton's part. When he had first come to Rome she believed the link that united them to be completely snapped; but little by little she had been reminded that it had yet a palpable existence. It was as thin as a hair, but there were moments when she seemed to hear it vibrate. For herself nothing was changed; what she once thought of him she always thought; it was needless this feeling should change; it seemed to her in fact a better feeling than ever. But he? had he still the idea that she might be more to him than other women? Had he the wish to profit by the memory of the few moments of intimacy through which they had once passed? Isabel knew she had read some of the signs of such a disposition. But what were his hopes, his pretensions, and in what strange way were they mingled with his evidently very sincere appreciation of poor Pansy? Was he in love with Gilbert Osmond's wife, and if so what comfort did he expect to derive from it? If he was in love with Pansy he was not in love with her stepmother, and if he was in love with her stepmother he was not in love with Pansy. Was she to cultivate the advantage she possessed in order to make him commit himself to Pansy, knowing he would do so for her sake and not for the small creature's own – was this the service her husband had asked of her? This at any rate was the duty with which she found herself confronted – from the moment she admitted to herself that her old friend had still an uneradicated predilection for her society. It was not an agreeable task; it was in fact a repulsive one. She asked herself with dismay whether Lord Warburton were pretending to be in love with Pansy in order to cultivate another satisfaction and what might be called other chances. Of this refinement of duplicity she presently acquitted him; she preferred to believe him in perfect good faith. But if his admiration for Pansy were a delusion this was scarcely better than its being an affection. Isabel wandered among these ugly possibilities until she had completely lost her way; some of them, as she suddenly encountered them, seemed ugly enough. Then she broke out of the labyrinth, rubbing her eyes, and declared that her imagination surely did her little honour and that her husband's did him even less. Lord Warburton was as disinterested as he need be, and she was no more to him than she need wish. She would rest upon this till the contrary should be proved; proved more effectually than by a cynical intimation of Osmond's.

Such a resolution, however, brought her this evening but little peace, for her soul was haunted with terrors which crowded to the foreground of thought as quickly as a place was made for them. What had suddenly set them into livelier motion she hardly knew, unless it were the strange impression she had received in the afternoon of her husband's being in more direct communication with Madame Merle than she suspected. That impression came back to her from time to time, and now she wondered it had never come before. Besides this, her short interview with Osmond half an hour ago was a striking example of his faculty for making everything wither that he touched, spoiling everything for her that he looked at. It was very well to undertake to give him a proof of loyalty; the real fact was that the knowledge of his expecting a thing raised a presumption against it. It was as if he had had the evil eye; as if his presence were a blight and his favour a misfortune. Was the fault in himself, or only in the deep mistrust she had conceived for him? This mistrust was now the clearest result of their short married life; a gulf had opened between them over which they looked at each other with eyes that were on either side a declaration of the deception suffered. It was a strange opposition, of the like of which she had never dreamed – an opposition in which the vital principle of the one was a thing of contempt to the other. It was not her fault – she had practised no deception; she had only admired and believed. She had taken all the first steps in the purest confidence, and then she had suddenly found the infinite vista of a multiplied life to be a dark, narrow alley with a dead wall at the end. Instead of leading to the high places of happiness, from which the world would seem to lie below one, so that one could look down with a sense of exaltation and advantage, and judge and choose and pity, it led rather downward and earthward, into realms of restriction and depression where the sound of other lives, easier and freer, was heard as from above, and where it served to deepen the feeling of failure. It was her deep distrust of her husband – this was what darkened the world. That is a sentiment easily indicated, but not so easily explained, and so composite in its character that much time and still more suffering had been needed to bring it to its actual perfection. Suffering, with Isabel, was an active condition; it was not a chill, a stupor, a despair; it was a passion of thought, of speculation, of response to every pressure. She flattered herself that she had kept her failing faith to herself, however – that no one suspected it but Osmond. Oh, he knew it, and there were times when she thought he enjoyed it. It had come gradually – it was not till the first year of their life together, so admirably intimate at first, had closed that she had taken the alarm. Then the shadows had begun to gather; it was as if Osmond deliberately, almost malignantly, had put the lights out one by one. The dusk at first was vague and thin, and she could still see her way in it. But it steadily deepened, and if now and again it had occasionally lifted there were certain corners of her prospect that were impenetrably black. These shadows were not an emanation from her own mind; she was very sure of that; she had done her best to be just and temperate, to see only the truth. They were a part, they were a kind of creation and consequence, of her husband's very presence. They were not his misdeeds, his turpitudes; she accused him of nothing – that is but of one thing, which was *not* a crime. She knew of no wrong he had done; he was not violent, he was not cruel: she simply believed he hated her. That was all she accused him of, and the miserable part of it was precisely that it was not a crime, for against a crime she might have found redress. He had discovered that she was so different, that she was not what he had believed she would prove to be. He had thought at first he could change her, and she had done her best to be what he would like. But she was, after all, herself – she couldn't help that; and now there was no use pretending, wearing a mask or a dress, for he knew her and had made up his mind. She was not afraid of him; she had no apprehension he would hurt her; for the ill-will he bore her was not of that sort. He would if possible never give her a pretext, never put himself in the wrong. Isabel, scanning the future with dry, fixed eyes, saw that he would have the better of her there. She would give him many pretexts, she would often put herself in the wrong. There were times when she almost pitied him; for if she had not deceived him in intention she understood how completely she must have done so in fact. She had effaced herself when he first knew her; she had made herself small, pretending there was less of her than there really was. It was because she had been under the extraordinary charm that he, on his side, had taken pains to put forth. He was not changed; he had not disguised himself, during the year of his courtship, any more than she. But she had seen only half his nature then, as one saw the disk of the moon when it was partly masked by the shadow of the earth. She saw the full moon now – she saw the whole man. She kept still, as it were, so that he should have a free field, and yet in spite of this she had mistaken a part for the whole.

Ah, she had been immensely under the charm! It had not passed away; it was there still: she still knew perfectly what it was that made Osmond delightful when he chose to be. He had wished to be when he made love to her, and as she had wished to be charmed it was not wonderful he had succeeded. He had succeeded because he had been sincere; it never occurred to her now to deny him that. He admired her – he had told her why: because she was the most imaginative woman he had known. It might very well have been true; for during those months she had imagined a world of things that had no substance. She had had a more wondrous vision of him, fed through charmed senses and oh such stirred fancy! – she had not read him right. A certain combination of features had touched her, and in them she had seen the most striking of figures. That he was poor and lonely and yet that somehow he was noble – that was what had interested her and seemed to give her her opportunity. There had been an indefinable beauty about him – in his situation, in his mind, in his face. She had felt at the same time that he was helpless and ineffectual, but the feeling had taken the form of a tenderness which was the very flower of respect. He was like a sceptical voyager strolling on the beach while he waited for the tide, looking seaward yet not putting to sea. It was in all this she had found her occasion. She would launch his boat for him; she would be his providence; it would be a good thing to love him. And she had loved him, she had so anxiously and yet so ardently given herself – a good deal for what she found in him, but a good deal also for what she brought him and what might enrich the gift. As she looked back at the passion of those full weeks she perceived in it a kind of maternal strain – the happiness of a woman who felt that she was a contributor, that she came with charged hands. But for her money, as she saw today, she would never have done it. And then her mind wandered off to poor Mr Touchett, sleeping under English turf, the beneficent author of infinite woe! For this was the fantastic fact. At bottom her money had been a burden, had been on her mind, which was filled with the desire to transfer the weight of it to some other conscience, to some more prepared receptacle. What would lighten her own conscience more effectually than to make it over to the man with the best taste in the world? Unless she should have given it to a hospital there would have been nothing better she could do with it; and there was no charitable institution in which she had been as much interested as in Gilbert Osmond. He would use her fortune in a way that would make her think better of it and rub off a certain grossness attaching to the good luck of an unexpected inheritance. There had been nothing very delicate in inheriting seventy thousand pounds; the delicacy had been all in Mr Touchett's leaving them to her. But to marry Gilbert Osmond and bring him such a portion – in that there would be delicacy for her as well. There would be less for him – that was true; but that was his affair, and if he loved her he wouldn't object to her being rich. Had he not had the courage to say he was glad she was rich?

Isabel's cheek burned when she asked herself if she had really married on a factitious theory, in order to do something finely appreciable with her money. But she was able to answer quickly enough that this was only half the story. It was because a certain ardour took possession of her – a sense of the earnestness of his affection and a delight in his personal qualities. He was better than anyone else. This supreme conviction had filled her life for months, and enough of it still remained to prove to her that she could not have done otherwise. The finest – in the sense of being the subtlest – manly organism she had ever known had become her property, and the recognition of her having but to put out her hands and take it had been originally a sort of act of devotion. She had not been mistaken about the beauty of his mind; she knew that organ perfectly now. She had lived with it, she had lived *in* it almost – it appeared to have become her habitation. If she had been captured it had taken a firm hand to seize her; that reflection perhaps had some worth. A mind more ingenious, more pliant, more cultivated, more trained to admirable exercises, she had not encountered; and it was this exquisite instrument she had now to reckon with. She lost herself in infinite dismay when she thought of the magnitude of *his* deception. It was a wonder, perhaps, in view of this, that he didn't hate her more. She remembered perfectly the first sign he had given of it – it had been like the bell that was to ring up the curtain upon the real drama of their life. He said to her one day that she had too many ideas and that she must get rid of them. He had told her that already, before their marriage; but then she had not noticed it: it had come to her only afterwards. This time she might well have noticed it, because he had really meant it. The words had been nothing superficially, but when in the light of deepening experience she had looked into them they had then appeared portentous. He had really meant it – he would have liked her to have nothing of her own but her pretty appearance. She had known she had too many ideas; she had more even than he had supposed, many more than she had expressed to him when he had asked her to marry him. Yes, she *had* been hypocritical; she had liked him so much. She had too many ideas for herself; but that was just what one married for, to share them with someone else. One couldn't pluck them up by the roots, though of course one might suppress them, be careful not to utter them. It had not been this, however, his objecting to her opinions; this had been nothing. She had no opinions – none that she would not have been eager to sacrifice in the satisfaction of feeling herself loved for it. What he had meant had been the whole thing – her character, the way she felt, the way she judged. This was what she had kept in reserve; this was what he had not known until he had found himself – with the door closed behind, as it were – set down face to face with it. She had a certain way of looking at life which he took as a personal offence. Heaven knew that now at least it was a very humble, accommodating way! The strange thing was that she should not have suspected from the first that his own had been so different. She had thought it so large, so enlightened, so perfectly that of an honest man and a gentleman. Hadn't he assured her that he had no superstitions, no dull limitations, no prejudices that had lost their freshness? Hadn't he all the appearance of a man living in the open air of the world, indifferent to small considerations, caring only for truth and knowledge and believing that two intelligent people ought to look for them together and, whether they found them or not, find at least some happiness in the search? He had told her he loved the conventional; but there was a sense in which this seemed a noble declaration. In that sense, that of the love of harmony and order and decency and of all the stately offices of life, she went with him freely, and his warning had contained nothing ominous. But when, as the months had elapsed, she had followed him farther and he had led her into the mansion of his own habitation, then, *then* she had seen where she really was.

She could live it over again, the incredulous terror with which she had taken the measure of her dwelling. Between those four walls she had lived ever since; they were to surround her for the rest of her life. It was the house of darkness, the house of dumbness, the house of suffocation. Osmond's beautiful mind gave it neither light nor air; Osmond's beautiful mind indeed seemed to peep down from a small high window and mock at her. Of course it had not been physical suffering; for physical suffering there might have been a remedy. She could come and go; she had her liberty; her husband was perfectly polite. He took himself so seriously; it was something appalling. Under all his culture, his cleverness, his amenity, under his good-nature, his facility, his knowledge of life, his egotism lay hidden like a serpent in a bank of flowers. She had taken him seriously, but she had not taken him so seriously as that. How could she – especially when she had known him better? She was to think of him as he thought of himself – as the first gentleman in Europe. So it was that she had thought of him at first, and that indeed was the reason she had married him. But when she began to see what it implied she drew back; there was more in the bond than she had meant to put her name to. It implied a sovereign contempt for everyone but some three or four very exalted people whom he envied, and for everything in the world but half a dozen ideas of his own. That was very well; she would have gone with him even there a long distance: for he pointed out to her so much of the baseness and shabbiness of life, opened her eyes so wide to the stupidity, the depravity, the ignorance of mankind, that she had been properly impressed with the infinite vulgarity of things and of the virtue of keeping one's self unspotted by it. But this base, ignoble world, it appeared, was after all what one was to live for; one was to keep for ever in one's eye, in order not to enlighten or convert or redeem it, but to extract from it some recognition of one's own superiority. On the one hand it was despicable, bu on the other it afforded a standard. Osmond had talked to Isabel about his renunciation, his indifference, the ease with which he dispensed with the usual aids to success; and all this had seemed to her admirable. She had thought it a grand indifference, an exquisite independence. But indifference was really the last of his qualities; she had never seen any one who thought so much of others. For herself, avowedly, the world had always interested her and the study of her fellow creatures been her constant passion. She would have been willing, however, to renounce all her curiosities and sympathies for the sake of a personal life, if the person concerned had only been able to make her believe it was a gain! This at least was her present conviction; and the thing certainly would have been easier than to care for society as Osmond cared for it.

He was unable to live without it, and she saw that he had never really done so; he had looked at it out of his window even when he appeared to be most detached from it. He had his ideal, just as she had tried to have hers; only it was strange that people should seek for justice in such different quarters. His ideal was a conception of high prosperity and propriety, of the aristocratic life, which she now saw that he deemed himself always, in essence at least, to have led. He had never lapsed from it for an hour; he would never have recovered from the shame of doing so. That again was very well; here too she would have agreed; but they attached such different ideas, such different associations and desires, to the same formulas. Her notion of the aristocratic life was simply the union of great knowledge with great liberty; the knowledge would give one a sense of duty and the liberty a sense of enjoyment. But for Osmond it was altogether a thing of forms, a conscious, calculated attitude. He was fond of the old, the consecrated, the transmitted; so was she, but she pretended to do what she chose with it. He had an immense esteem for tradition; he had told her once that the best thing in the world was to have it, but that if one was so unfortunate as not to have it one must immediately proceed to make it. She knew that he meant by this that she hadn't it, but that he was better off; though from what source he had derived his traditions she never learned. He had a very large collection of them, however; that was very certain, and after a little she began to see. The great thing was to act in accordance with them; the great thing not only for him but for her. Isabel had an undefined conviction that to serve for another person than their proprietor traditions must be of a thoroughly superior kind; but she nevertheless assented to this intimation that she too must march to the stately music that floated down from unknown periods in her husband's past; she who of old had been so free of step, so desultory, so devious, so much the reverse of processional. There were certain things they must do, a certain posture they must take, certain people they must know and not know. When she saw this rigid system close about her, draped though it was in pictured tapestries, that sense of darkness and suffocation of which I have spoken took possession of her; she seemed shut up with an odour of mould and decay. She had resisted of course; at first very humorously, ironically, tenderly; then, as the situation grew more serious, eagerly, passionately, pleadingly. She had pleaded the cause of freedom, of doing as they chose, of not caring for the aspect and denomination of their life – the cause of other instincts and longings, of quite another ideal.

Then it was that her husband's personality, touched as it never had been, stepped forth and stood erect. The things she had said were answered only by his scorn, and she could see he was ineffably ashamed of her. What did he think of her – that she was base, vulgar, ignoble? He at least knew now that she had no traditions! It had not been in his prevision of things that she should reveal such flatness; her sentiments were worthy of a radical newspaper or a Unitarian preacher. The real offence, as she ultimately perceived, was her having a mind of her own at all. Her mind was to be his – attached to his own like a small garden-plot to a deer-park. He would rake the soil gently and water the flowers; he would weed the beds and gather an occasional nose-gay. It would be a pretty piece of property for a proprietor already far-reaching. He didn't wish her to be stupid. On the contrary, it was because she was clever that she had pleased him. But he expected her intelligence to operate altogether in his favour, and so far from desiring her mind to be a blank he had flattered himself that it would be richly receptive. He had expected his wife to feel with him and for him, to enter into his opinions, his ambitions, his preferences; and Isabel was obliged to confess that this was no great insolence on the part of a man so accomplished and a husband originally at least so tender. But there were certain things she could never take in. To begin with, they were hideously unclean. She was not a daughter of the Puritans, but for all that she believed in such a thing as chastity and even as decency. It would appear that Osmond was far from doing anything of the sort; some of his traditions made her push back her skirts. Did all women have lovers? Did they all lie and even the best have their price? Were there only three or four that didn't deceive their husbands? When Isabel heard such things she felt a greater scorn for them than for the gossip of a village parlour – a scorn that kept its freshness in a very tainted air. There was the taint of her sister-in-law: did her husband judge only by the Countess Gemini? This lady very often lied, and she had practised deceptions that were not simply verbal. It was enough to find these facts assumed among Osmond's traditions – it was enough without giving them such a general extension. It was her scorn of his assumptions, it was this that made him draw himself up. He had plenty of contempt, and it was proper his wife should be as well furnished; but that she should turn the hot light of her disdain upon his own conception of things – this was a danger he had not allowed for. He believed he should have regulated her emotions before she came to it; and Isabel could easily imagine how his ears had scorched on his discovering he had been too confident. When one had a wife who gave one that sensation there was nothing left but to hate her.

She was morally certain now that this feeling of hatred, which at first had been a refuge and a refreshment, had become the occupation and comfort of his life. The feeling was deep, because it was sincere; he had had the revelation that she could after all dispense with him. If to herself the idea was startling, if it presented itself at first as a kind of infidelity, a capacity for pollution, what infinite effect might it not be expected to have had upon *him*? It was very simple; he despised her; she had no traditions and the moral horizon of a Unitarian minister. Poor Isabel, who had never been able to understand Unitarianism! This was the certitude she had been living with now for a time that she had ceased to measure. What was coming – what was before them? That was her constant question. What would he do – what ought *she* to do? When a man hated his wife what did it lead to? She didn't hate him, that she was sure of, for every little while she felt a passionate wish to give him a pleasant surprise. Very often, however, she felt afraid, and it used to come over her, as I have intimated, that she had deceived him at the very first. They were strangely married, at all events, and it was a horrible life. Until that morning he had scarcely spoken to her for a week; his manner was as dry as a burned-out fire. She knew there was a special reason; he was displeased at Ralph Touchett's staying on in Rome. He thought she saw too much of her cousin – he had told her a week before it was indecent she should go to him at his hotel. He would have said more than this if Ralph's invalid state had not appeared to make it brutal to denounce him; but having had to contain himself had only deepened his disgust. Isabel read all this as she would have read the hour on the clock-face; she was as perfectly aware that the sight of her interest in her cousin stirred her husband's rage as if Osmond had locked her into her room – which she was sure was what he wanted to do. It was her honest belief that on the whole she was not defiant, but she certainly couldn't pretend to be indifferent to Ralph. She believed he was dying at last and that she should never see him again, and this gave her a tenderness for him that she had never known before. Nothing was a pleasure to her now; how could anything be a pleasure to a woman who knew that she had thrown away her life? There was an everlasting weight on her heart – there was a livid light on everything. But Ralph's little visit was a lamp in the darkness; for the hour that she sat with him her ache for herself became somehow her ache for *him*. She felt today as if he had been her brother. She had never had a brother, but if she had and she were in trouble and he was dying, he would be dear to her as Ralph was. Ah yes, if Gilbert was jealous of her there was perhaps some reason; it didn't make Gilbert look better to sit for half an hour with Ralph. It was not that they talked of him – it was not that she complained. His name was never uttered between them. It was simply that Ralph was generous and that her husband was not. There was something in Ralph's talk, in his smile, in the mere fact of his being in Rome, that made the blasted circle round which she walked more spacious. He made her feel the good of the world; he made her feel what might have been. He was after all as intelligent as Osmond – quite apart from his being better. And thus it seemed to her an act of devotion to conceal her misery from him. She concealed it elaborately; she was perpetually, in their talk, hanging out curtains and arranging screens. It lived before her again – it had never had time to die – that morning in the garden at Florence when he had warned her against Osmond. She had only to close her eyes to see the place, to hear his voice, to feel the warm, sweet air. How could he have known? What a mystery, what a wonder of wisdom! As intelligent as Gilbert? He was much more intelligent – to arrive at such a judgement as that. Gilbert had never been so deep, so just. She had told him then that from her at least he should never know if he was right; and this was what she was taking care of now. It gave her plenty to do; there was passion, exaltation, religion in it. Women find their religion sometimes in strange exercises, and Isabel at present, in playing a part before her cousin, had an idea that she was doing him a kindness. It would have been a kindness perhaps if he had been for a single instant a dupe. As it was, the kindness consisted mainly in trying to make him believe that he had once wounded her greatly and that the event had put him to shame, but that, as she was very generous and he was so ill, she bore him no grudge and even considerately forbore to flaunt her happiness in his face. Ralph smiled to himself, as he lay on his sofa, at this extraordinary form of consideration; but he forgave her for having forgiven him. She didn't wish him to have the pain of knowing she was unhappy: that was the great thing, and it didn't matter that such knowledge would rather have righted him.

For herself, she lingered in the soundless saloon long after the fire had gone out. There was no danger of her feeling the cold; she was in a fever. She heard the small hours strike, and then the great ones, but her vigil took no heed of time. Her mind, assailed by visions, was in a state of extraordinary activity, and her visions might as well come to her there, where she sat up to meet them, as on her pillow, to make a mockery of rest. As I have said, she believed she was not defiant, and what could be a better proof of it than that she should linger there half the night, trying to persuade herself that there was no reason why Pansy shouldn't be married as you would put a letter in the post office? When the clock struck four she got up; she was going to bed at last, for the lamp had long since gone out and the candles burned down to their sockets. But even then she stopped again in the middle of the room and stood there gazing at a remembered vision – that of her husband and Madame Merle unconsciously and familiarly associated.

Chapter Forty-three

Three nights after this she took Pansy to a great party, to which Osmond, who never went to dances, did not accompany them. Pansy was as ready for a dance as ever; she was not of a generalizing turn and had not extended to other pleasures the interdict she had seen placed on those of love. If she was biding her time or hoping to circumvent her father she must have had a prevision of success. Isabel thought this unlikely; it was much more likely that Pansy had simply determined to be a good girl. She had never had such a chance, and she had a proper esteem for chances. She carried herself no less attentively than usual and kept no less anxious an eye upon her vaporous skirts; she held her bouquet very tight and counted over the flowers for the twentieth time. She made Isabel feel old; it seemed so long since she had been in a flutter about a ball. Pansy, who was greatly admired, was never in want of partners, and very soon after their arrival she gave Isabel, who was not dancing, her bouquet to hold. Isabel had rendered her this service for some minutes when she became aware of the near presence of Edward Rosier. He stood before her; he had lost his affable smile and wore a look of almost military resolution. The change in his appearance would have made Isabel smile if she had not felt his case to be at bottom a hard one: he had always smelt so much more of heliotrope than of gunpowder. He looked at her a moment somewhat fiercely, as if to notify her he was dangerous, and then dropped his eyes on her bouquet. After he had inspected it his glance softened and he said quickly: 'It's all pansies; it must be hers!'

Isabel smiled kindly. 'Yes, it's hers; she gave it to me to hold.'

'May I hold it a little, Mrs Osmond?' the poor young man asked.

'No, I can't trust you; I'm afraid you wouldn't give it back.'

'I'm not sure that I should; I should leave the house with it instantly. But may I not at least have a single flower?'

Isabel hesitated a moment, and then, smiling still, held out the bouquet. 'Choose one yourself. It's frightful what I'm doing for you.'

'Ah, if you do no more than this, Mrs Osmond!' Rosier exclaimed with his glass in one eye, carefully choosing his flower.

'Don't put it in your button-hole,' she said. 'Don't for the world!'

'I should like her to see it. She has refused to dance with me, but I wish to show her that I believe in her still.'

'It's very well to show it to her, but it's out of place to show it to others. Her father has told her not to dance with you.'

'And is that all *you* can do for me? I expected more from you, Mrs Osmond,' said the young man in a tone of fine general reference. 'You know our acquaintance goes back very far – quite into the days of our innocent childhood.'

'Don't make me out too old,' Isabel patiently answered. 'You come back to that very often, and I've never denied it. But I must tell you that, old friends as we are, if you had done me the honour to ask me to marry you I should have refused you on the spot.'

'Ah, you don't esteem me then. Say at once that you think me a mere Parisian trifler!'

'I esteem you very much, but I'm not in love with you. What I mean by that, of course, is that I'm not in love with you for Pansy.'

'Very good; I see. You pity me – that's all.' And Edward Rosier looked all round, inconsequently, with his single glass. It was a revelation to him that people shouldn't be more pleased; but he was at least too proud to show that the deficiency struck him as general.

Isabel for a moment said nothing. His manner and appearance had not the dignity of the deepest tragedy; his little glass, among other things, was against that. But she suddenly felt touched; her own unhappiness, after all, had something in common with his, and it came over her, more than before, that here, in recognizable, if not in romantic form, was the most affecting thing in the world – young love struggling with adversity. 'Would you really be very kind to her?' she finally asked in a low tone.

He dropped his eyes devoutly and raised the little flower that he held in his fingers to his lips. Then he looked at her. 'You pity me; but don't you pity *her* a little?'

'I don't know; I'm not sure. She'll always enjoy life.'

'It will depend on what you call life!' Mr Rosier effectively said. 'She won't enjoy being tortured.'

'There'll be nothing of that.'

'I'm glad to hear it. She knows what she's about. You'll see.'

'I think she does, and she'll never disobey her father. But she's coming back to me,' Isabel added, 'and I must beg you to go away.'

Rosier lingered a moment till Pansy came in sight on the arm of her cavalier; he stood just long enough to look her in the face. Then he walked away, holding up his head; and the manner in which he achieved this sacrifice to expediency convinced Isabel he was very much in love.

Pansy, who seldom got disarranged in dancing, looking perfectly fresh and cool after this exercise, waited a moment and then took back her bouquet. Isabel watched her and saw she was counting the flowers; whereupon she said to herself that decidedly there were deeper forces at play than she had recognized. Pansy had seen Rosier turn away, but she said nothing to Isabel about him; she talked only of her partner, after he had made his bow and retired; of the music, the floor, the rare misfortune of having already torn her dress. Isabel was sure, however, she had discovered her lover to have abstracted a flower; though this knowledge was not needed to account for the dutiful grace with which she responded to the appeal of her next partner. That perfect amenity under acute constraint was part of a larger system. She was again led forth by a flushed young man, this time carrying her bouquet; and she had not been absent many minutes when Isabel saw Lord Warburton advancing through the crowd. He presently drew near and bade her good evening; she had not seen him since the day before. He looked about him, and then 'Where's the little maid?' he asked. It was in this manner that he had formed the harmless habit of alluding to Miss Osmond.

'She's dancing,' said Isabel. 'You'll see her somewhere.'

He looked among the dancers and at last caught Pansy's eye. 'She sees me, but she won't notice me,' he then remarked. 'Are you not dancing?'

'As you see, I'm a wall-flower.'

'Won't you dance with me?'

'Thank you; I'd rather you should dance with the little maid.'

'One needn't prevent the other – especially as she's engaged.'

'She's not engaged for everything, and you can reserve yourself. She dances very hard, and you'll be the fresher.'

'She dances beautifully,' said Lord Warburton, following her with his eyes. 'Ah, at last,' he added, 'she has given me a smile.' He stood there with his handsome, easy, important physiognomy; and as Isabel observed him it came over her, as it had done before, that it was strange a man of his mettle should take an interest in a little maid. It struck her as a great incongruity; neither Pansy's small fascinations, nor his own kindness, his good-nature, not even his need for amusement, which was extreme and constant, were sufficient to account for it. 'I should like to dance with you,' he went on in a moment, turning back to Isabel; 'but I think I like even better to talk with you.'

'Yes, it's better, and it's more worthy of your dignity. Great statesmen oughtn't to waltz.'

'Don't be cruel. Why do you recommend me then to dance with Miss Osmond?'

'Ah, that's different. If you danced with her it would look simply like a piece of kindness – as if you were doing it for her amusement. If you dance with me you'll look as if you were doing it for your own.'

'And pray haven't I a right to amuse myself?'

'No, not with the affairs of the British Empire on your hands.'

'The British Empire be hanged! You're always laughing at it.'

'Amuse yourself with talking to me,' said Isabel.

'I'm not sure it's really a recreation. You're too pointed; I've always to be defending myself. And you strike me as more than usually dangerous tonight. Will you absolutely not dance?'

'I can't leave my place. Pansy must find me here.'

He was silent a little. 'You're wonderfully good to her,' he said suddenly.

Isabel stared a little and smiled. 'Can you imagine one's not being?'

'No indeed. I know how one is charmed with her. But you must have done a great deal for her.'

'I've taken her out with me,' said Isabel, smiling still. 'And I've seen that she has proper clothes.'

'Your society must have been a great benefit to her. You've talked to her, advised her, helped her develop.'

'Ah yes, if she isn't the rose she has lived near it.'

She laughed, and her companion did as much; but there was a certain visible preoccupation in his face which interfered with complete hilarity. 'We all try to live as near it as we can,' he said after a moment's hesitation.

Isabel turned away; Pansy was about to be restored to her, and she welcomed the diversion. We know how much she liked Lord Warburton; she thought him pleasanter even than the sum of his merits warranted; there was something in his friendship that appeared a kind of resource in case of indefinite need; it was like having a large balance at the bank. She felt happier when he was in the room; there was something reassuring in his approach; the sound of his voice reminded her of the beneficence of nature. Yet for all that it didn't suit her that he should be too near her, that he should take too much of her good-will for granted. She was afraid of that; she averted herself from it; she wished he wouldn't. She felt that if he should come too near, as it were, it might be in her to flash out and bid him keep his distance. Pansy came back to Isabel with another rent in her skirt, which was the inevitable consequence of the first and which she displayed to Isabel with serious eyes. There were too many gentlemen in uniform; they wore those dreadful spurs, which were fatal to the dresses of little maids. It hereupon became apparent that the resources of women are innumerable. Isabel devoted herself to Pansy's desecrated drapery; she fumbled for a pin and repaired the injury; she smiled and listened to her account of her adventures. Her attention, her sympathy were immediate and active; and they were in direct proportion to a sentiment with which they were in no way connected – a lively conjecture as to whether Lord Warburton might be trying to make love to her. It was not simply his words just then; it was others as well; it was the reference and the continuity. This was what she thought about while she pinned up Pansy's dress. If it were so, as she feared, he was of course unwitting; he himself had not taken account of his attention. But this made it none the more auspicious, made the situation none the less impossible. The sooner he should get back into right relations with things the better. He immediately began to talk to Pansy – on whom it was certainly mystifying to see that he dropped a smile of chastened devotion. Pansy replied, as usual, with a little air of conscientious aspiration; he had to bend towards her a good deal in conversation, and her eyes, as usual, wandered up and down his robust person as if he had offered it to her for exhibition. She always seemed a little frightened; yet her fright was not of the painful character that suggests dislike; on the contrary, she looked as if she knew that he knew she liked him. Isabel left them together a little and wandered towards a friend whom she saw near and with whom she talked till the music of the following dance began, for which she knew Pansy to be also engaged. The girl joined her presently, with a little fluttered flush, and Isabel, who scrupulously took Osmond's view of his daughter's complete dependence, consigned her, as a precious and momentary loan, to her appointed partner. About all this matter she had her own imaginations, her own reserves; there were moments when Pansy's extreme adhesiveness made each of them, to her sense, look foolish. But Osmond had given her a sort of tableau of her position as his daughter's duenna, which consisted of gracious alternations of concession and contraction; and there were directions of his which she liked to think she obeyed to the letter. Perhaps, as regards some of them, it was because her doing so appeared to reduce them to the absurd.

After Pansy had been led away, she found Lord Warburton drawing near her again. She rested her eyes on him steadily; she wished she could sound his thoughts. But he had no appearance of confusion. 'She has promised to dance with me later,' he said.

'I'm glad of that. I suppose you've engaged her for the cotillion.'

At this he looked a little awkward. 'No, I didn't ask her for that. It's a quadrille.'

'Ah, you're not clever!' said Isabel almost angrily. 'I told her to keep the cotillion in case you should ask for it.'

'Poor little maid, fancy that!' And Lord Warburton laughed frankly. 'Of course I will if you like.'

'If I like? Oh, if you dance with her only because I like it—!'

'I'm afraid I bore her. She seems to have a lot of young fellows on her book.'

Isabel dropped her eyes, reflecting rapidly; Lord Warburton stood there looking at her and she felt his eyes on her face. She felt much inclined to ask him to remove them. She didn't do so, however; she only said to him, after a minute, with her own raised: 'Please let me understand.'

'Understand what?'

'You told me ten days ago that you'd like to marry my stepdaughter. You've not forgotten it!'

'Forgotten it? I wrote to Mr Osmond about it this morning.'

'Ah,' said Isabel, 'he didn't mention to me that he had heard from you.'

Lord Warburton stammered a little. 'I – I didn't send my letter.'

'Perhaps you forgot *that*.'

'No, I wasn't satisfied with it. It's an awkward sort of letter to write, you know. But I shall send it tonight.'

'At three o'clock in the morning?'

'I mean later, in the course of the day.'

'Very good. You still wish then to marry her?'

'Very much indeed.'

'Aren't you afraid that you'll bore her?' And as her companion stared at this inquiry Isabel added: 'If she can't dance with you for half an hour how will she be able to dance with you for life?'

'Ah,' said Lord Warburton readily, 'I'll let her dance with other people! About the cotillion, the fact is I thought that you – that you—'

'That I would do it with you? I told you I'd do nothing.'

'Exactly; so that while it's going on I might find some quiet corner where we may sit down and talk.'

'Oh,' said Isabel gravely, 'you're much too considerate of me.'

When the cotillion came Pansy was found to have engaged herself, thinking, in perfect humility, that Lord Warburton had no intentions. Isabel recommended him to seek another partner, but he assured her that he would dance with no one but herself. As, however, she had, in spite of the remonstrances of her hostess, declined other invitations on the ground that she was not dancing at all, it was not possible for her to make an exception in Lord Warburton's favour.

'After all I don't care to dance,' he said; 'it's a barbarous amusement: I'd much rather talk.' And he intimated that he had discovered exactly the corner he had been looking for – a quiet nook in one of the smaller rooms, where the music would come to them faintly and not interfere with conversation: Isabel had decided to let him carry out his idea; she wished to be satisfied. She wandered away from the ballroom with him, though she knew her husband desired she should not lose sight of his daughter. It was with his daughter's *prêtendant*, however; that would make it right for Osmond. On her way out of the ballroom she came upon Edward Rosier, who was standing in a doorway, with folded arms, looking at the dance in the attitude of a young man without illusions. She stopped a moment and asked him if he were not dancing.

'Certainly not, if I can't dance with *her*!' he answered.

'You had better go away then,' said Isabel with the manner of good counsel.

'I shall not go till she does!' And he let Lord Warburton pass without giving him a look.

The nobleman, however, had noticed the melancholy youth, and he asked Isabel who her dismal friend was, remarking that he had seen him somewhere before.

'It's the young man I've told you about, who's in love with Pansy.'

'Ah yes, I remember. He looks rather bad.'

'He has reason. My husband won't listen to him.'

'What's the matter with him?' Lord Warburton inquired. 'He seems very harmless.'

'He hasn't money enough, and he isn't very clever.'

Lord Warburton listened with interest; he seemed struck with this account of Edward Rosier. 'Dear me; he looked a well-set-up young fellow.'

'So he is, but my husband's very particular.'

'Oh, I see.' And Lord Warburton paused a moment. 'How much money has he got?' he then ventured to ask.

'Some forty thousand francs a year.'

'Sixteen hundred pounds? Ah, but that's very good, you know.'

'So I think. My husband, however, has larger ideas.'

'Yes; I've noticed that your husband has very large ideas. Is he really an idiot, the young man?'

'An idiot? Not in the least; he's charming. When he was twelve years old I myself was in love with him.'

'He doesn't look much more than twelve today,' Lord Warburton rejoined vaguely, looking about him. Then with more point, 'Don't you think we might sit here?' he asked.

'Wherever you please.' The room was a sort of boudoir, pervaded by a subdued, rose-coloured light; a lady and gentleman moved out of it as our friends came in. 'It's very kind of you to take such an interest in Mr Rosier,' Isabel said.

'He seems to me rather ill-treated. He had a face a yard long. I wondered what ailed him.'

'You're a just man,' said Isabel. 'You've a kind thought even for a rival.'

Lord Warburton suddenly turned with a stare. 'A rival! Do you call him my rival?'

'Surely – if you both wish to marry the same person.'

'Yes – but since he has no chance!'

'I like you, however that may be, for putting yourself in his place. It shows imagination.'

'You like me for it?' Lord Warburton looked at her with an uncertain eye. 'I think you mean you're laughing at me for it.'

'Yes, I'm laughing at you a little. But I like you as somebody to laugh at.'

'Ah well, then, let me enter into his situation a little more. What do you suppose one could do for him?'

'Since I have been praising your imagination I'll leave you to imagine that yourself,' Isabel said. 'Pansy too would like you for that.'

'Miss Osmond? Ah, she, I flatter myself, likes me already.'

'Very much, I think.'

He waited a little; he was still questioning her face. 'Well then, I don't understand you. You don't mean that she cares for him?'

'Surely I've told you I thought she did.'

A quick blush sprang to his brow. 'You told me she would have no wish apart from her father's, and as I've gathered that he would favour me—!' He paused a little and then suggested 'Don't you see?' through his blush.

'Yes, I told you she has an immense wish to please her father, and that it would probably take her very far.'

'That seems to me a very proper feeling,' said Lord Warburton.

'Certainly; it's a very proper feeling.' Isabel remained silent for some moments; the room continued empty; the sound of the music reached them with its richness softened by the interposing apartments. Then at last she said: 'But it hardly strikes me as the sort of feeling to which a man would wish to be indebted for a wife.'

'I don't know; if the wife's a good one and he thinks she does well!'

'Yes, of course you must think that.'

'I do; I can't help it. You call that very British, of course.'

'No, I don't. I think Pansy would do wonderfully well to marry you, and I don't know who should know it better than you. But you're not in love.'

'Ah, yes I am, Mrs Osmond!'

Isabel shook her head. 'You like to think you are while you sit here with me. But that's not how you strike me.'

'I'm not like the young man in the doorway. I admit that. But what makes it so unnatural? Could any one in the world be more loveable than Miss Osmond?'

'No one, possibly. But love has nothing to do with good reasons.'

'I don't agree with you. I'm delighted to have good reasons.'

'Of course you are. If you were really in love you wouldn't care a straw for them.'

'Ah, really in love – really in love!' Lord Warburton exclaimed, folding his arms, leaning back his head and stretching himself a little. 'You must remember that I'm forty-two years old. I won't pretend I'm as I once was.'

'Well, if you're sure,' said Isabel, 'it's all right.'

He answered nothing; he sat there, with his head back, looking before him. Abruptly, however, he changed his positon; he turned quickly to his friend. 'Why are you so unwilling, so sceptical?'

She met his eyes, and for a moment they looked straight at each other. If she wished to be satisfied she saw something that satisfied her; she saw in his expression the gleam of an idea that she was uneasy on her own account – that she was perhaps even in fear. It showed a suspicion, not a hope, but such as it was it told her what she wanted to know. Not for an instant should he suspect her of detecting in his proposal of marrying her step-daughter an implication of increased nearness to herself, or of thinking it, on such a betrayal, ominous. In that brief, extremely personal gaze, however, deeper meanings passed between them than they were conscious of at the moment.

'My dear Lord Warburton,' she said, smiling, 'you may do, so far as I'm concerned, whatever comes into your head.'

And with this she got up and wandered into the adjoining room, where, within her companion's view, she was immediately addressed by a pair of gentlemen, high personages in the Roman world, who met her as if they had been looking for her. While she talked with them she found herself regretting she had moved; it looked a little like running away – all the more as Lord Warburton didn't follow her. She was glad of this, however, and at any rate she was satisfied. She was so well satisfied that when, in passing back into the ballroom, she found Edward Rosier still planted in the doorway, she stopped and spoke to him again. 'You did right not to go away. I've some comfort for you.'

'I need it,' the young man softly wailed, 'when I see you so awfully thick with *him*!'

'Don't speak of him; I'll do what I can for you. I'm afraid it won't be much, but what I can I'll do.'

He looked at her with gloomy obliqueness. 'What has suddenly brought you round?'

'The sense that you are an inconvenience in doorways!' she answered, smiling as she passed him. Half an hour later she took leave, with Pansy, and at the foot of the staircase the two ladies, with many other departing guests, waited a while for their carriage. Just as it approached Lord Warburton came out of the house and assisted them to reach their vehicle. He stood a moment at the door, asking Pansy if she had amused herself; and she, having answered him, fell back with a little air of fatigue. Then Isabel, at the window, detaining him by a movement of her finger, murmured gently: 'Don't forget to send your letter to her father!'

Chapter Forty-four

The Countess Gemini was often extremely bored – bored, in her own phrase, to extinction. She had not been extinguished, however, and she struggled bravely enough with her destiny, which had been to marry an unaccommodating Florentine who insisted upon living in his native town, where he enjoyed such consideration as might attach to a gentleman whose talent for losing at cards had not the merit of being incidental to an obliging disposition. The Count Gemini was not liked even by those who won from him; and he bore a name which, having a measurable value in Florence, was, like the local coin of the old Italian states, without currency in other parts of the peninsula. In Rome he was simply a very dull Florentine, and it is not remarkable that he should not have cared to pay frequent visits to a place where to carry it off, his dullness needed more explanation than was convenient. The Countess lived with her eyes upon Rome, and it was the constant grievance of her life that she had not an habitation there. She was ashamed to say how seldom she had been allowed to visit that city; it scarcely made the matter better that there were other members of the Florentine nobility who never had been there at all. She went whenever she could; that was all she could say. Or rather not all, but all she said she could say. In fact she had much more to say about it, and had often set forth the reasons why she hated Florence and wished to end her days in the shadow of Saint Peter's. They are reasons, however, that do not closely concern us, and were usually summed up in the declaration that Rome, in short, was the Eternal City and that Florence was simply a pretty little place like any other. The Countess apparently needed to connect the idea of eternity with her amusements. She was convinced that society was infinitely more interesting in Rome, where you met celebrities all winter at evening parties. At Florence there were no celebrities; none at least that one had heard of. Since her brother's marriage her impatience had greatly increased; she was so sure his wife had a more brilliant life than herself. She was not so intellectual as Isabel, but she was intellectual enough to do justice to Rome – not to the ruins and the catacombs, not even perhaps to the monuments and museums, the church ceremonies and the scenery; but certainly to all the rest. She heard a great deal about her sister-in-law and knew perfectly that Isabel was having a beautiful time. She had indeed seen it for herself on the only occasion on which she had enjoyed the hospitality of Palazzo Roccanera. She had spent a week there during the first winter of her brother's marriage, but she had not been encouraged to renew this satisfaction. Osmond didn't want her – that she was perfectly aware of; but she would have gone all the same, for after all she didn't care two straws about Osmond. It was her husband who wouldn't let her, and the money question was always a trouble.

Isabel had been very nice; the Countess, who had liked her sister-in-law from the first, had not been blinded by envy to Isabel's personal merits. She had always observed that she got on better with clever women than with silly ones like herself; the silly ones could never understand her wisdom, whereas the clever ones – the really clever ones – always understood her silliness. It appeared to her that, different as they were in appearance and general style, Isabel and she had somewhere a patch of common ground that they would set their feet upon at last. It was not very large, but it was firm, and they should both know it when once they had really touched it. And then she lived, with Mrs Osmond, under the influence of a pleasant surprise; she was constantly expecting that Isabel would 'look down' on her, and she as constantly saw this operation postponed. She asked herself when it would begin, like fireworks, or Lent, or the opera season; not that she cared much, but she wondered what kept it in abeyance. Her sister-in-law regarded her with none but level glances and expressed for the poor Countess as little contempt as admiration. In reality Isabel would as soon have thought of despising her as of passing a moral judgement on a grasshopper. She was not indifferent to her husband's sister, however; she was rather a little afraid of her. She wondered at her; she thought her very extraordinary. The Countess seemed to her to have no soul; she was like a bright rare shell, with a polished surface and a remarkably pink lip, in which something would rattle when you shook it. This rattle was apparently the Countess's spiritual principle, a little loose nut that tumbled about inside of her. She was too odd for disdain, too anomalous for comparisons. Isabel would have invited her again (there was no question of inviting the Count); but Osmond, after his marriage, had not scrupled to say frankly that Amy was a fool of the worst species – a fool whose folly had the irrepressibility of genius. He said at another time that she had no heart; and he added in a moment that she had given it all away – in small pieces, like a frosted wedding-cake. The fact of not having been asked was of course another obstacle to the Countess's going again to Rome; but at the period with which this history has now to deal she was in receipt of an invitation to spend several weeks at Palazzo Roccanera. The proposal had come from Osmond himself, who wrote to his sister that she must be prepared to be very quiet. Whether or no she found in this phrase all the meaning he had put into it I am unable to say; but she accepted the invitation on any terms. She was curious, moreover; for one of the impressions of her former visit had been that her brother had found his match. Before the marriage she had been sorry for Isabel, so sorry as to have had serious thoughts – if any of the Countess's thoughts were serious – of putting her on her guard. But she had let that pass, and after a little she was reassured. Osmond was as lofty as ever, but his wife would not be an easy victim. The Countess was not very exact at measurements, but it seemed to her that if Isabel should draw herself up she would be the taller spirit of the two. What she wanted to learn now was whether Isabel had drawn herself up; it would give her immense pleasure to see Osmond overtopped.

Several days before she was to start for Rome a servant brought her the card of a visitor – a card with the simple superscription 'Henrietta C. Stackpole'. The Countess pressed her finger-tips to her forehead; she didn't remember to have known any such Henrietta as that. The servant then remarked that the lady had requested him to say that if the Countess should not recognize her name she would know her well enough on seeing her. By the time she appeared before her visitor she had in fact reminded herself that there was once a literary lady at Mrs Touchett's; the only woman of letters she had ever encountered – that is the only modern one, since she was the daughter of a defunct poetess. She recognized Miss Stackpole immediately, the more so that Miss Stackpole seemed perfectly unchanged; and the Countess, who was thoroughly good-natured, thought it rather fine to be called on by a person of that sort of distinction. She wondered if Miss Stackpole had come on account of her mother – whether she had heard of the American Corinne. Her mother was not at all like Isabel's friend; the Countess could see at a glance that this lady was much more contemporary; and she received an impression of the improvements that were taking place – chiefly in distant countries – in the character (the professional character) of literary ladies. Her mother had been used to wear a Roman scarf thrown over a pair of shoulders timorously bared of their tight black velvet (oh the old clothes!) and a gold laurel-wreath set upon a multitude of glossy ringlets. She had spoken softly and vaguely, with the accent of her 'Creole' ancestors, as she always confessed; she sighed a great deal and was not at all enterprising. But Henrietta, the Countess could see, was always closely buttoned and compactly braided; there was something brisk and business-like in her appearance; her manner was almost conscientiously familiar. It was as impossible to imagine her ever vaguely sighing as to imagine a letter posted without its address. The Countess could not but feel that the correspondent of the *Interviewer* was much more in the movement than the American Corinne. She explained that she had called on the Countess because she was the only person she knew in Florence, and that when she visited a foreign city she liked to see something more than superficial travellers. She knew Mrs Touchett, but Mrs Touchett was in America, and even if she had been in Florence Henrietta would not have put herself out for her, since Mrs Touchett was not one of her admirations.

'Do you mean by that that I am?' the Countess graciously asked.

'Well, I like you better than I do her,' said Miss Stackpole. 'I seem to remember that when I saw you before you were very interesting. I don't know whether it was an accident or whether it's your usual style. At any rate I was a good deal struck with what you said. I made use of it afterwards in print.'

'Dear me!' cried the Countess, staring and half-alarmed; 'I had no idea I ever said anything remarkable! I wish I had known it at the time.'

'It was about the position of woman in this city,' Miss Stackpole remarked. 'You threw a good deal of light upon it.'

'The position of woman's very uncomfortable. Is that what you mean? And you wrote it down and published it?' the Countess went on. 'Ah, do let me see it!'

'I'll write to them to send you the paper if you like,' Henrietta said. 'I didn't mention your name; I only said a lady of high rank. And then I quoted your views.'

The Countess threw herself hastily backward, tossing up her clasped hands. 'Do you know I'm rather sorry you didn't mention my name? I should have rather liked to see my name in the papers. I forget what my views were; I have so many! But I'm not ashamed of them. I'm not at all like my brother – I suppose you know my brother? He thinks it a kind of scandal to be put in the papers; if you were to quote him he'd never forgive you.'

'He needn't be afraid; I shall never refer to him,' said Miss Stackpole with bland dryness. 'That's another reason,' she added, 'why I wanted to come to see you. You know Mr Osmond married my dearest friend.'

'Ah, yes; you were a friend of Isabel's. I was trying to think what I knew about you.'

'I'm quite willing to be known by that,' Henrietta declared. 'But that isn't what your brother likes to know me by. He has tried to break up my relations with Isabel.'

'Don't permit it,' said the Countess.

'That's what I want to talk about. I'm going to Rome.'

'So am I!' the Countess cried. 'We'll go together.'

'With great pleasure. And when I write about my journey I'll mention you by name as my companion.'

The Countess sprang from her chair and came and sat on the sofa beside her visitor. 'Ah, you must send me the paper! My husband won't like it, but he need never see it. Besides, he doesn't know how to read.'

Henrietta's large eyes became immense. 'Doesn't know how to read? May I put that into my letter?'

'Into your letter?'

'In the *Interviewer*. That's my paper.'

'Oh yes, if you like; with his name. Are you going to stay with Isabel?'

Henrietta held up her head, gazing a little in silence at her hostess. 'She has not asked me. I wrote to her I was coming, and she answered that she would engage a room for me at a *pension*. She gave no reason.'

The Countess listened with extreme interest. 'The reason's Osmond,' she pregnantly remarked.

'Isabel ought to make a stand,' said Miss Stackpole. 'I'm afraid she has changed a great deal. I told her she would.'

'I'm sorry to hear it; I hoped she would have her own way. Why doesn't my brother like you?' the Countess ingenuously added.

'I don't know and I don't care. He's perfectly welcome not to like me; I don't want everyone to like me; I should think less of myself if some people did. A journalist can't hope to do much good unless he gets a good deal hated; that's the way he knows how his work goes on. And it's just the same for a lady. But I didn't expect it of Isabel.'

'Do you mean that she hates you?' the Countess inquired.

'I don't know; I want to see. That's what I'm going to Rome for.'

'Dear me, what a tiresome errand!' the Countess exclaimed.

'She doesn't write to me in the same way; it's easy to see there's a difference. If you know anything,' Miss Stackpole went on, 'I should like to hear it beforehand, so as to decide on the line I shall take.'

The Countess thrust out her under lip and gave a gradual shrug. 'I know very little; I see and hear very little of Osmond. He doesn't like me any better than he appears to like you.'

'Yet you're not a lady correspondent,' said Henrietta pensively.

'Oh, he has plenty of reasons. Nevertheless they've invited me – I'm to stay in the house!' And the Countess smiled almost fiercely; her exultation, for the moment, took little account of Miss Stackpole's disappointment.

This lady, however, regarded it very placidly. 'I shouldn't have gone if she *had* asked me. That is I think I shouldn't; and I'm glad I hadn't to make up my mind. It would have been a very difficult question. I shouldn't have liked to turn away from her, and yet I shouldn't have been happy under her roof. A *pension* will suit me very well. But that's not all.'

'Rome's very good just now,' said the Countess; 'there are all sorts of brilliant people. Did you ever hear of Lord Warburton?'

'Hear of him? I know him very well. Do you consider him very brilliant?' Henrietta inquired.

'I don't know him, but I'm told he's extremely *grand seigneur*. He's making love to Isabel.'

'Making love to her?'

'So I'm told; I don't know the details,' said the Countess lightly. 'But Isabel's pretty safe.'

Henrietta gazed earnestly at her companion; for a moment she said nothing. 'When do you go to Rome?' she inquired abruptly.

'Not for a week, I'm afraid.'

'I shall go tomorrow,' Henrietta said. 'I think I had better not wait.'

'Dear me, I'm sorry; I'm having some dresses made. I'm told Isabel receives immensely. But I shall see you there; I shall call on you at your *pension*.' Henrietta sat still – she was lost in thought; and suddenly the Countess cried: 'Ah, but if you don't go with me you can't describe our journey!'

Miss Stackpole seemed unmoved by this consideration; she was thinking of something else and presently expressed it. 'I'm not sure that I understand you about Lord Warburton.'

'Understand me? I mean he's very nice, that's all.'

'Do you consider it nice to make love to married women?' Henrietta inquired with unprecedented distinctness.

The Countess stared, and then with a little violent laugh: 'It's certain all the nice men do it. Get married and you'll see!' she added.

'That idea would be enough to prevent me,' said Miss Stackpole. 'I should want my own husband; I shouldn't want anyone else's. Do you mean that Isabel's guilty – guilty—?' And she paused a little, choosing her expression.

'Do you mean she's guilty? Oh dear no, not yet, I hope. I only mean that Osmond's very tiresome and that Lord Warburton, as I hear, is a great deal at the house. I'm afraid you're scandalized.'

'No, I'm just anxious,' Henrietta said.

'Ah, you're not very complimentary to Isabel! You should have more confidence. I'll tell you,' the Countess added quickly: 'if it will be a comfort to you I engage to draw him off.'

Miss Stackpole answered at first only with the deeper solemnity of her gaze. 'You don't understand me,' she said after a while. 'I haven't the idea you seem to suppose. I'm not afraid for Isabel – in that way. I'm only afraid she's unhappy – that's what I want to get at.'

The Countess gave a dozen turns of the head; she looked impatient and sarcastic. 'That may very well be; for my part I should like to know whether Osmond is.' Miss Stackpole had begun a little to bore her.

'If she's really changed that must be at the bottom of it,' Henrietta went on.

'You'll see; she'll tell you,' said the Countess.

'Ah, she may *not* tell me – that's what I'm afraid of!'

'Well, if Osmond isn't amusing himself – in his own old way – I flatter myself I shall discover it,' the Countess rejoined.

'I don't care for that,' said Henrietta.

'I do immensely! If Isabel's unhappy I'm very sorry for her, but I can't help it. I might tell her something that would make her worse, but I can't tell her anything that would console her. What did she go and marry him for? If she had listened to me she'd have got rid of him. I'll forgive her, however, if I find she has made things hot for him! If she has simply allowed him to trample upon her I don't know that I shall even pity her. But I don't think that's very likely. I count upon finding that if she's miserable she has at least made *him* so.'

Henrietta got up; these seemed to her, naturally, very dreadful expectations. She honestly believed she had no desire to see Mr Osmond unhappy; and indeed he could not be for her the subject of a flight of fancy. She was on the whole rather disappointed in the Countess, whose mind moved in a narrower circle than she had imagined, though with a capacity for coarseness even there. 'It will be better if they love each other,' she said for edification.

'They can't. He can't love anyone.'

'I presumed that was the case. But it only aggravates my fear for Isabel. I shall positively start tomorrow.'

'Isabel certainly has devotees,' said the Countess, smiling very vividly. 'I declare I don't pity her.'

'It may be I can't assist her,' Miss Stackpole pursued, as if it were well not to have illusions.

'You can have wanted to, at any rate; that's something. I believe that's what you came from America for,' the Countess suddenly added.

'Yes, I wanted to look after her,' Henrietta said serenely.

Her hostess stood there smiling at her with small bright eyes and an eager-looking nose; with cheeks into each of which a flush had come. 'Ah, that's very pretty – *c'est bien gentil*! Isn't it what they call friendship?'

'I don't know what they call it. I thought I had better come.'

'She's very happy – she's very fortunate,' the Countess went on. 'She has others besides.' And then she broke out passionately. 'She's more fortunate than I! I'm as unhappy as she – I've a very bad husband; he's a great deal worse than Osmond. And I've no friends. I thought I had, but they're gone. No one, man or woman, would do for me what you've done for her.'

Henrietta was touched; there was nature in this bitter effusion. She gazed at her companion a moment, and then: 'Look here, Countess, I'll do anything for you that you like. I'll wait over and travel with you.'

'Never mind,' the Countess answered with a quick change of tone: 'only describe me in the newspaper!'

Henrietta, before leaving her, however, was obliged to make her understand that she could give no fictitious representation of her journey to Rome. Miss Stackpole was a strictly veracious reporter. On quitting her she took the way to the Lung' Arno, the sunny quay beside the yellow river where the bright-faced inns familiar to tourists stand all in a row. She had learned her way before this through the streets of Florence (she was very quick in such matters), and was therefore able to turn with great decision of step out of the little square which forms the approach to the bridge of the Holy Trinity. She proceeded to the left, towards the Ponte Vecchio, and stopped in front of one of the hotels which overlook that delightful structure. Here she drew forth a small pocket-book, took from it a card and a pencil and, after meditating a moment, wrote a few words. It is our privilege to look over her shoulder, and if we exercise it we may read the brief query: 'Could I see you this evening for a few moments on a very important matter?' Henrietta added that she should start on the morrow for Rome. Armed with this document she approached the porter, who now had taken up his station in the doorway, and asked if Mr Goodwood were at home. The porter replied, as porters always reply, that he had gone out about twenty minutes before; whereupon Henrietta presented her card and begged it might be handed him on his return. She left the inn and pursued her course along the quay to the severe portico of the Uffizi, through which she presently reached the entrance of the famous gallery of paintings. Making her way in, she ascended the high staircase which leads to the upper chambers. The long corridor, glazed on one side and decorated with antique busts, which gives admission to these apartments, presented an empty vista in which the bright winter light twinkled upon the marble floor. The gallery is very cold and during the midwinter weeks but scantily visited. Miss Stackpole may appear more ardent in her quest of artistic beauty than she has hitherto struck us as being, but she had after all her preferences and admirations. One of the latter was the little Correggio of the Tribune – the Virgin kneeling down before the sacred infant, who lies in a litter of straw, and clapping her hands to him while he delightedly laughs and crows. Henrietta had a special devotion to this intimate scene – she thought it the most beautiful picture in the world. On her way, at present, from New York to Rome, she was spending but three days in Florence, and yet reminded herself that they must not elapse without her paying another visit to her favourite work of art. She had a great sense of beauty in all ways, and it involved a good many intellectual obligations. She was about to turn into the Tribune when a gentleman came out of it; whereupon she gave a little exclamation and stood before Caspar Goodwood.

'I've just been at your hotel,' she said. 'I left a card for you.'

'I'm very much honoured,' Caspar Goodwood answered as if he really meant it.

'It was not to honour you I did it; I've called on you before and I know you don't like it. It was to talk to you a little about something.'

He looked for a moment at the buckle in her hat. 'I shall be very glad to hear what you wish to say.'

'You don't like to talk with me,' said Henrietta. 'But I don't care for that; I don't talk for your amusement. I wrote a word to ask you to come and see me; but since I've met you here this will do as well.'

'I was just going away,' Goodwood stated; 'but of course I'll stop.' He was civil, but not enthusiastic.

Henrietta, however, never looked for great professions, and she was so much in earnest that she was thankful he would listen to her on any terms. She asked him first, none the less, if he had seen all the pictures.

'All I want to. I've been here an hour.'

'I wonder if you've seen my Correggio,' said Henrietta. 'I came up on purpose to have a look at it.' She went into the Tribune and he slowly accompanied her.

'I suppose I've seen it, but I didn't know it was yours. I don't remember pictures – especially that sort.' She had pointed out her favourite work, and he asked her if it was about Correggio she wished to talk with him.

'No,' said Henrietta, 'it's about something less harmonious!' They had the small, brilliant room, a splendid cabinet of treasures, to themselves; there was only a custode hovering about the Medicean Venus. 'I want you to do me a favour,' Miss Stackpole went on.

Caspar Goodwood frowned a little, but he expressed no embarrassment at the sense of not looking eager. His face was that of a much older man than our earlier friend. 'I'm sure it's something I shan't like,' he said rather loudly.

'No, I don't think you'll like it. If you did it would be no favour.'

'Well, let's hear it,' he went on in the tone of a man quite conscious of his patience.

'You may say there's no particular reason why you should do me a favour. Indeed I only know of one: the fact that if you'd let me I'd gladly do *you* one.' Her soft, exact tone, in which there was no attempt at effect, had an extreme sincerity; and her companion, though he presented rather a hard surface, couldn't help being touched by it. When he was touched he rarely showed it, however, by the usual signs; he neither blushed, nor looked away, nor looked conscious. He only fixed his attention more directly; he seemed to consider with added firmness. Henrietta continued therefore disinterestedly, without the sense of an advantage. 'I may say now, indeed – it seems a good time – that if I've ever annoyed you (and I think sometimes I have) it's because I knew I was willing to suffer annoyance for you. I've troubled you – doubtless. But I'd *take* trouble for you.'

Goodwood hesitated. 'You're taking trouble now.'

'Yes, I am – some. I want you to consider whether it's better on the whole that you should go to Rome.'

'I thought you were going to say that!' he answered rather artlessly.

'You *have* considered it then?'

'Of course I have, very carefully. I've looked all round it. Otherwise I shouldn't have come so far as this. That's what I stayed in Paris two months for. I was thinking it over.'

'I'm afraid you decided as you liked. You decided it was best because you were so much attracted.'

'Best for whom, do you mean?' Goodwood demanded.

'Well, for yourself first. For Mrs Osmond next.'

'Oh, it won't do *her* any good! I don't flatter myself that.'

'Won't it do her some harm? – that's the question.'

'I don't see what it will matter to her. I'm nothing to Mrs Osmond. But if you want to know, I do want to see her myself.'

'Yes, and that's why you go.'

'Of course it is. Could there be a better reason?'

'How will it help you? – that's what I want to know,' said Miss Stackpole.

'That's just what I can't tell you. It's just what I was thinking about in Paris.'

'It will make you more discontented.'

'Why do you say "more" so?' Goodwood asked rather sternly. 'How do you know I'm discontented?'

'Well,' said Henrietta, hesitating a little, 'you seem never to have cared for another.'

'How do you know what I care for?' he cried with a big blush. 'Just now I care to go to Rome.'

Henrietta looked at him in silence, with a sad yet luminous expression. 'Well,' she observed at last, 'I only wanted to tell you what I think; I had it on my mind. Of course you think it's none of my business. But nothing is anyone's business on that principle.'

'It's very kind of you; I'm greatly obliged to you for your interest,' said Caspar Goodwood. 'I shall go to Rome and I shan't hurt Mrs Osmond.'

'You won't hurt her, perhaps. But will you help her? – that's the real issue.'

'Is she in need of help?' he asked slowly, with a penetrating look.

'Most women always are,' said Henrietta, with conscientious evasiveness and generalizing less hopefully than usual. 'If you go to Rome,' she added, 'I hope you'll be a true friend – not a selfish one!' And she turned off and began to look at the pictures.

Caspar Goodwood let her go and stood watching her while she wandered round the room; but after a moment he rejoined her. 'You've heard something about her here,' he then resumed. 'I should like to know what you've heard.'

Henrietta had never prevaricated in her life, and, though on this occasion there might have been a fitness in doing so, she decided, after thinking some minutes, to make no superficial exception. 'Yes, I've heard,' she answered; 'but as I don't want you to go to Rome I won't tell you.'

'Just as you please. I shall see for myself,' he said. Then inconsistently, for him, 'You've heard she's unhappy!' he added.

'Oh, you won't see that!' Henrietta exclaimed.

'I hope not. When do you start?'

'Tomorrow, by the evening train. And you?'

Goodwood hung back; he had no desire to make his journey to Rome in Miss Stackpole's company. His indifference to this advantage was not of the same character as Gilbert Osmond's, but it had at this moment an equal distinctness. It was rather a tribute to Miss Stackpole's virtues than a reference to her faults. He thought her very remarkable, very brilliant, and he had, in theory, no objection to the class to which she belonged. Lady correspondents appeared to him a part of the natural scheme of things in a progressive country, and though he never read their letters he supposed that they ministered somehow to social prosperity. But it was this very eminence of their position that made him wish Miss Stackpole didn't take so much for granted. She took for granted that he was always ready for some allusion to Mrs Osmond; she had done so when they met in Paris, six weeks after his arrival in Europe, and she had repeated the assumption with every successive opportunity. He had no wish whatever to allude to Mrs Osmond; he was *not* always thinking of her; he was perfectly sure of that. He was the most reserved, the least colloquial of men, and this inquiring authoress was constantly flashing her lantern into the quiet darkness of his soul. He wished she didn't care so much; he even wished, though it might seem rather brutal of him, that she would leave him alone. In spite of this, however, he just now made other reflections – which show how widely different, in effect, his ill-humour was from Gilbert Osmond's. He desired to go immediately to Rome; he would have liked to go alone, in the night-train. He hated the European railway-carriages, in which one sat for hours in a vice, knee to knee and nose to nose with a foreigner to whom one presently found one's self objecting with all the added vehemence of one's wish to have the window open; and if they were worse at night even than by day, at least at night one could sleep and dream of an American saloon-car. But he couldn't take a night-train when Miss Stackpole was starting in the morning; it struck him that this would be an insult to an unprotected woman. Nor could he wait until after she had gone unless he should wait longer than he had patience for. It wouldn't do to start the next day. She worried him; she oppressed him; the idea of spending the day in a European railway-carriage with her offered a complication of irritations. Still, she was a lady travelling alone; it was his duty to put himself out for her. There could be no two questions about that; it was a perfectly clear necessity. He looked extremely grave for some moments and then said, wholly without the flourish of gallantry but in a tone of extreme distinctness, 'Of course if you're going tomorrow I'll go too, as I may be of assistance to you.'

'Well, Mr Goodwood, I should hope so!' Henrietta returned imperturbably.

Chapter Forty-five

I have already had reason to say that Isabel knew her husband to be displeased by the continuance of Ralph's visit to Rome. That knowledge was very present to her as she went to her cousin's hotel the day after she had invited Lord Warburton to give a tangible proof of his sincerity; and at this moment, as at others, she had a sufficient perception of the sources of Osmond's opposition. He wished her to have no freedom of mind, and he knew perfectly well that Ralph was an apostle of freedom. It was just because he was this, Isabel said to herself, that it was a refreshment to go and see him. It will be perceived that she partook of this refreshment in spite of her husband's aversion to it, that is partook of it, as she flattered herself, discreetly. She had not as yet undertaken to act in direct opposition to his wishes; he was her appointed and inscribed master; she gazed at moments with a sort of incredulous blankness at this fact. It weighed upon her imagination, however; constantly present to her mind were all the traditionary decencies and sanctities of marriage. The idea of violating them filled her with shame as well as with dread, for on giving herself away she had lost sight of this contingency in the perfect belief that her husband's intentions were as generous as her own. She seemed to see, none the less, the rapid approach of the day when she should have to take back something she had solemnly bestown. Such a ceremony would be odious and monstrous; she tried to shut her eyes to it meanwhile. Osmond would do nothing to help it by beginning first; he would put that burden upon her to the end. He had not yet formally forbidden her to call upon Ralph; but she felt sure that unless Ralph should very soon depart this prohibition would come. How could poor Ralph depart? The weather as yet made it impossible. She could perfectly understand her husband's wish for the event; she didn't, to be just, see how he *could* like her to be with her cousin. Ralph never said a word against him, but Osmond's sore, mute protest was none the less founded. If he should positively interpose, if he should put forth his authority, she would have to decide, and that wouldn't be easy. The prospect made her heart beat and her cheeks burn, as I say, in advance; there were moments when, in her wish to avoid an open rupture, she found herself wishing Ralph would start even at a risk. And it was of no use that, when catching herself in this state of mind, she called herself a feeble spirit, a coward. It was not that she loved Ralph less, but that almost anything seemed preferable to repudiating the most serious act – the single sacred act – of her life. That appeared to make the whole future hideous. To break with Osmond once would be to break for ever; any open acknowledgement of irreconcilable needs would be an admission that their whole attempt had proved a failure. For them there could be no condonement, no compromise, no easy forgetfulness, no formal readjustment. They had attempted only one thing, but that one thing was to have been exquisite. Once they missed it nothing else would do; there was no conceivable substitute for that success. For the moment, Isabel went to the Hôtel de Paris as often as she thought well; the measure of propriety was in the canon of taste, and there couldn't have been a better proof that morality was, so to speak, a matter of earnest appreciation. Isabel's application of that measure had been particularly free today, for in addition to the general truth that she couldn't leave Ralph to die alone she had something important to ask of him. This indeed was Gilbert's business as well as her own.

She came very soon to what she wished to speak of. 'I want you to answer me a question. It's about Lord Warburton.'

'I think I guess your question,' Ralph answered from his armchair, out of which his thin legs protruded at greater length than ever.

'Very possibly you guess it. Please then answer it.'

'Oh, I don't say I can do that.'

'You're intimate with him,' she said; 'you've a great deal of observation of him.'

'Very true. But think how he must dissimulate!'

'Why should he dissimulate? That's not his nature.'

'Ah, you must remember that the circumstances are peculiar,' said Ralph with an air of private amusement.

'To a certain extent – yes. But is he really in love?'

'Very much, I think. I can make that out.'

'Ah!' said Isabel with a certain dryness.

Ralph looked at her as if his mild hilarity had been touched with mystification. 'You say that as if you were disappointed.'

Isabel got up, slowly smoothing her gloves and eyeing them thoughtfully. 'It's after all no business of mine.'

'You're very philosophic,' said her cousin. And then in a moment: 'May I inquire what you're talking about?'

Isabel stared. 'I thought you knew. Lord Warburton tells me he wants, of all things in the world, to marry Pansy. I've told you that before, without eliciting a comment from you. You might risk one this morning, I think. Is it your belief that he really cares for her?'

'Ah, for Pansy, no!' cried Ralph very positively.

'But you said just now he did.'

Ralph waited a moment. 'That he cared for you, Mrs Osmond.'

Isabel shook her head gravely. 'That's nonsense, you know.'

'Of course it is. But the nonsense is Warburton's, not mine.'

'That would be very tiresome.' She spoke, as she flattered herself, with much subtlety.

'I ought to tell you indeed,' Ralph went on, 'that to me he has denied it.'

'It's very good of you to talk about it together! Has he also told you that he's in love with Pansy?'

'He has spoken very well of her – very properly. He has let me know, of course, that he thinks she would do very well at Lockleigh.'

'Does he really think it?'

'Ah, what Warburton really thinks—!' said Ralph.

Isabel fell to smoothing her gloves again; they were long, loose gloves on which she could freely expend herself. Soon, however, she looked up, and then, 'Ah, Ralph, you give me no help!' she cried abruptly and passionately.

It was the first time she had alluded to the need for help, and the words shook her cousin with their violence. He gave a long murmur of relief, of pity, of tenderness; it seemed to him that at last the gulf between them had been bridged. It was this that made him exclaim in a moment: 'How unhappy you must be!'

He had no sooner spoken than she recovered her self-possession, and the first use she made of it was to pretend she had not heard him. 'When I talk of your helping me I talk great nonsense,' she said with quick smile. 'The idea of my troubling you with my domestic embarrassments! The matter's very simple; Lord Warburton must get on by himself. I can't undertake to see him through.'

'He ought to succeed easily,' said Ralph.

Isabel debated. 'Yes – but he has not always succeeded.'

'Very true. You know, however, how that always surprised me. Is Miss Osmond capable of giving us a surprise?'

'It will come from him, rather. I seem to see that after all he'll let the matter drop.'

'He'll do nothing dishonourable,' said Ralph.

'I'm very sure of that. Nothing can be more honourable than for him to leave the poor child alone. She cares for another person, and it's cruel to attempt to bribe her by magnificent offers to give him up.'

'Cruel to the other person perhaps – the one she cares for. But Warburton isn't obliged to mind that.'

'No, cruel to her,' said Isabel. 'She would be very unhappy if she were to allow herself to be persuaded to desert poor Mr Rosier. That idea seems to amuse you; of course you're not in love with him. He has the merit – for Pansy – of being in love with Pansy. She can see at a glance that Lord Warburton isn't.'

'He'd be very good to her,' said Ralph.

'He has been good to her already. Fortunately, however, he has not said a word to disturb her. He could come and bid her good-bye tomorrow with perfect propriety.'

'How would your husband like that?'

'Not at all; and he may be right in not liking it. Only he must obtain satisfaction himself.'

'Has he commissioned you to obtain it?' Ralph ventured to ask.

'It was natural that as an old friend of Lord Warburton's – an older friend, that is, than Gilbert – I should take an interest in his intentions.'

'Take an interest in his renouncing them, you mean?'

Isabel hesitated, frowning a little. 'Let me understand. Are you pleading his cause?'

'Not in the least. I'm very glad he shouldn't become your stepdaughter's husband. It makes such a very queer relation to you!' said Ralph, smiling. 'But I'm rather nervous lest your husband should think you haven't pushed him enough.'

Isabel found herself able to smile as well as he. 'He knows me well enough not to have expected me to push. He himself has no intention of pushing, I presume. I'm not afraid I shall not be able to justify myself!' she said lightly.

Her mask had dropped for an instant, but she had put it on again, to Ralph's infinite disappointment. He had caught a glimpse of her natural face and he wished immensely to look into it. He had an almost savage desire to hear her complain of her husband – hear her say that she should be held accountable for Lord Warburton's defection. Ralph was certain that this was her situation; he knew by instinct, in advance, the form that in such an event Osmond's displeasure would take. It could only take the meanest and cruellest. He would have liked to warn Isabel of it – to let her see at least how he judged for her and how he knew. It little mattered that Isabel would know much better; it was for his own satisfaction more than for hers that he longed to show her he was not deceived. He tried and tried again to make her betray Osmond; he felt cold-blooded, cruel, dishonourable almost, in doing so. But it scarcely mattered, for he only failed. What had she come for then, and why did she seem almost to offer him a chance to violate their tacit convention? Why did she ask him his advice if she gave him no liberty to answer her? How could they talk of her domestic embarrassments, as it pleased her humourously to designate them, if the principal factor was not to be mentioned? These contradictions were themselves but an indication of her trouble, and her cry for help, just before, was the only thing he was bound to consider. 'You'll be decidedly at variance, all the same,' he said in a moment. And as she answered nothing, looking as if she scare understood. 'You'll find yourselves thinking very differently,' he continued.

'That may easily happen, among the most united couples!' She took up her parasol; he saw she was nervous, afraid of what he might say. 'It's a matter we can hardly quarrel about, however,' she added; 'for almost all the interest is on his side. That's very natural. Pansy's after all his daughter – not mine.' And she put out her hand to wish him good-bye.

Ralph took an inward resolution that she shouldn't leave him without his letting her know that he knew everything: it seemed too great an opportunity to lose. 'Do you know what his interest will make him say?' he asked as he took her hand. She shook her head, rather dryly – not discouragingly – and he went on. 'It will make him say that your want of zeal is owing to jealousy.' He stopped a moment; her face made him afraid.

'To jealousy?'

'To jealousy of his daughter.'

She blushed red and threw back her head. 'You're not kind,' she said in a voice that he had never heard on her lips.

'Be frank with me and you'll see,' he answered.

But she made no reply; she only pulled her hand out of his own, which he tried still to hold, and rapidly withdrew from the room. She made up her mind to speak to Pansy, and she took an occasion on the same day, going to the girl's room before dinner. Pansy was already dressed; she was always in advance of the time: it seemed to illustrate her pretty patience and the graceful stillness with which she could sit and wait. At present she was seated, in her fresh array, before the bedroom fire; she had blown out her candles on the completion of her toilet, in accordance with the economical habits in which she had been brought up and which she was now more careful than ever to observe; so that the room was lighted only by a couple of logs. The rooms in Palazzo Roccanera were as spacious as they were numerous, and Pansy's virginal bower was an immense chamber with a dark, heavily-timbered ceiling. Its diminutive mistress, in the midst of it, appeared but a speck of humanity, and as she got up, with quick deference, to welcome Isabel, the latter was more than ever struck with her shy sincerity. Isabel had a difficult task – the only thing was to perform it as simply as possible. She felt bitter and angry, but she warned herself against betraying this heat. She was afraid even of looking too grave, or at least too stern; she was afraid of causing alarm. But Pansy seemed to have guessed she had come more or less as a confessor; for after she had moved the chair in which she had been sitting a little nearer to the fire and Isabel had taken her place in it, she kneeled down on a cushion in front of her, looking up and resting her clasped hands on her stepmother's knees. What Isabel wished to do was to hear from her own lips that her mind was not occupied with Lord Warburton; but if she desired the assurance she felt herself by no means at liberty to provoke it. The girl's father would have qualified this as rank treachery; and indeed Isabel knew that if Pansy should display the smallest germ of a disposition to encourage Lord Warburton her own duty was to hold her tongue. It was difficult to interrogate without appearing to suggest; Pansy's supreme simplicity, an innocence even more complete than Isabel had yet judged it, gave to the most tentative inquiry something of the effect of an admonition. As she knelt there in the vague firelight, with her pretty dress dimly shining, her hands folded half in appeal and half in submission, her soft eyes, raised and fixed, full of the seriousness of the situation, she looked to Isabel like a childish martyr decked out for sacrifice and scarcely presuming even to hope to avert it. When Isabel said to her that she had never yet spoken to her of what might have been going on in relation to her getting married, but that her silence had not been indifference or ignorance, had only been the desire to leave her at liberty, Pansy bent forward, raised her face nearer and nearer, and with a little murmur which evidently expressed a deep longing, answered that she had greatly wished her to speak and that she begged her to advise her now.

'It's difficult for me to advise you,' Isabel returned. 'I don't know how I can undertake that. That's for your father; you must get his advice and, above all, you must act on it.'

At this Pansy dropped her eyes; for a moment she said nothing. 'I think I should like your advice better than papa's,' she presently remarked.

'That's not as it should be,' said Isabel coldly. 'I love you very much, but your father loves you better.'

'It isn't because you love me – it's because you're a lady,' Pansy answered with the air of saying something very reasonable. 'A lady can advise a young girl better than a man.'

'I advise you then to pay the greatest respect to your father's wishes.'

'Ah yes,' said the child eagerly, 'I must do that.'

'But if I speak to you now about your getting married it's not for your own sake, it's for mine,' Isabel went on. 'If I try to learn from you what you expect, what you desire, it's only that I may act accordingly.'

Pansy stared, and then very quickly, 'Will you do everything I want?' she asked.

'Before I say yes I must know what such things are.'

Pansy presently told her that the only thing she wanted in life was to marry Mr Rosier. He had asked her and she had told him she would do so if her papa would allow it. Now her papa wouldn't allow it.

'Very well then, it's impossible,' Isabel pronounced.

'Yes, it's impossible,' said Pansy without a sigh and with the same extreme attention in her clear little face.

'You must think of something else then,' Isabel went on; but Pansy, sighing at this, told her that she had attempted that feat without the least success.

'You think of those who think of you,' she said with a faint smile. 'I know Mr Rosier thinks of me.'

'He ought not to,' said Isabel loftily. 'Your father has expressly requested he shouldn't.'

'He can't help it, because he knows I think of *him*.'

'You shouldn't think of him. There's some excuse for him, perhaps; but there's none for you.'

'I wish you would try to find one,' the girl exclaimed as if she were praying to the Madonna.

'I should be very sorry to attempt it,' said the Madonna with unusual frigidity. 'If you knew someone else was thinking of you, would you think of him?'

'No one can think of me as Mr Rosier does; no one has the right.'

'Ah, but I don't admit Mr Rosier's right!' Isabel hypocritically cried.

Pansy only gazed at her, evidently much puzzled; and Isabel, taking advantage of it, began to represent to her the wretched consequences of disobeying her father. At this Pansy stopped her with the assurance that she would never disobey him, would never marry without his consent. And she announced, in the serenest, simplest tone, that, though she might never marry Mr Rosier, she would never cease to think of him. She appeared to have accepted the idea of eternal singleness; but Isabel of course was free to reflect that she had no conception of its meaning. She was perfectly sincere; she was prepared to give up her lover. This might seem an important step towards taking another, but for Pansy, evidently, it failed to lead in that direction. She felt no bitterness towards her father; there was no bitterness in her heart; there was only the sweetness of fidelity to Edward Rosier, and a strange, exquisite intimation that she could prove it better by remaining single than even by marrying him.

'Your father would like you to make a better marriage,' said Isabel. 'Mr Rosier's fortune is not at all large.'

'How do you mean better – if that would be good enough? And I have myself so little money; why should I look for a fortune?'

'Your having so little is a reason for looking for more.' With which Isabel was grateful for the dimness of the room; she felt as if her face were hideously insincere. It was what she was doing for Osmond; it was what one had to do for Osmond! Pansy's solemn eyes, fixed on her own, almost embarrassed her; she was ashamed to think she had made so light of the girl's preference.

'What should you like me to do?' her companion softly demanded.

The question was a terrible one, and Isabel took refuge in timorous vagueness. 'To remember all the pleasure it's in your power to give your father.'

'To marry someone else, you mean – if he should ask me?'

For a moment Isabel's answer caused itself to be waited for; then she heard herself utter it in the stillness that Pansy's attention seemed to make. 'Yes – to marry someone else.'

The child's eyes grew more penetrating; Isabel believed she was doubting her sincerity, and the impression took force from her slowly getting up from her cushion. She stood there a moment with her small hands unclasped and then quavered out: 'Well, I hope no one will ask me!'

'There has been a question of that. Someone else would have been ready to ask you.'

'I don't think he can have been ready,' said Pansy.

'It would appear so – if he had been sure he'd succeed.'

'If he had been sure? Then he wasn't ready!'

Isabel thought this rather sharp; she also got up and stood a moment looking into the fire. 'Lord Warburton has shown you great attention,' she resumed; 'of course you know it's of him I speak.' She found herself, against her expectation, almost placed in the position of justifying herself; which led her to introduce this nobleman more crudely than she had intended.

'He has been very kind to me, and I like him very much. But if you mean that he'll propose for me I think you're mistaken.'

'Perhaps I am. But your father would like it extremely.'

Pansy shook her head with a little wise smile. 'Lord Warburton won't propose simply to please papa.'

'Your father would like you to encourage him,' Isabel went on mechanically.

'How can I encourage him?'

'I don't know. Your father must tell you that.'

Pansy said nothing for a moment; she only continued to smile as if she were in possession of a bright assurance. 'There's no danger – no danger!' she declared at last.

There was a conviction in the way she said this, and a felicity in her believing it, which conducted to Isabel's awkwardness. She felt accused of dishonesty, and the idea was disgusting. To repair her self-respect she was on the point of saying that Lord Warburton had let her know that there *was* a danger. But she didn't; she only said – in her embarrassment rather wide of the mark – that he surely had been most kind, most friendly.

'Yes, he has been very kind,' Pansy answered. 'That's what I like him for.'

'Why then is the difficulty so great?'

'I've always felt sure of his knowing that I don't want – what did you say I should do? – to encourage him. He knows I don't want to marry, and he wants me to know that he therefore won't trouble me. That's the meaning of his kindness. It's as if he said to me: "I like you very much, but if it doesn't please you I'll never say it again." I think that's very kind, very noble,' Pansy went on with deepening positiveness. 'That is all we've said to each other. And he doesn't care for me either. Ah no, there's no danger.'

Isabel was touched with wonder at the depths of perception of which this submissive little person was capable; she felt afraid of Pansy's wisdom – began almost to retreat before it. 'You must tell your father that,' she remarked reservedly.

'I think I'd rather not,' Pansy unreservedly answered.

'You oughtn't to let him have false hopes.'

'Perhaps not; but it will be good for me that he should. So long as he believes that Lord Warburton intends anything of the kind you say, papa won't propose anyone else. And that will be an advantage for me,' said the child very lucidly.

There was something brilliant in her lucidity, and it made her companion draw a long breath. It relieved this friend of a heavy responsibility. Pansy had a sufficient illumination of her own, and Isabel felt that she herself just now had no light to spare from her small stock. Nevertheless it still clung to her that she must be loyal to Osmond, that she was on her honour in dealing with his daughter. Under the influence of this sentiment she threw out another suggestion before she retired – a suggestion with which it seemed to her that she should have done her utmost. 'Your father takes for granted at least that you would like to marry a nobleman.'

Pansy stood in the open doorway; she had drawn back the curtain for Isabel to pass. 'I think Mr Rosier looks like one!' she remarked very gravely.

Chapter Forty-six

Lord Warburton was not seen in Mrs Osmond's drawing-room for several days, and Isabel couldn't fail to observe that her husband said nothing to her about having received a letter from him. She couldn't fail to observe, either, that Osmond was in a state of expectancy and that, though it was not agreeable to him to betray it, he thought their distinguished friend kept him waiting quite too long. At the end of four days he alluded to his absence.

'What has become of Warburton? What does he mean by treating one like a tradesman with a bill?'

'I know nothing about him,' Isabel said. 'I saw him last Friday at the German ball. He told me then that he meant to write to you.'

'He has never written to me.'

'So I supposed, from your not having told me.'

'He's an odd fish,' said Osmond comprehensively. And on Isabel's making no rejoinder he went on to inquire whether it took his lordship five days to indite a letter. 'Does he form his words with such difficulty?'

'I don't know,' Isabel was reduced to replying. 'I've never had a letter from him.'

'Never had a letter? I had an idea that you were at one time in intimate correspondence.'

She answered that this had not been the case, and let the conversation drop. On the morrow, however, coming into the drawing-room late in the afternoon, her husband took it up again.

'When Lord Warburton told you of his intention of writing what did you say to him?' he asked.

She just faltered. 'I think I told him not to forget it.'

'Did you believe there was a danger of that?'

'As you say, he's an odd fish.'

'Apparently he has forgotten it,' said Osmond. 'Be so good as to remind him.'

'Should you like me to write to him?' she demanded.

'I've no objection whatever.'

'You expect too much of me.'

'Ah yes, I expect a great deal of you.'

'I'm afraid I shall disappoint you,' said Isabel.

'My expectations have survived a good deal of disappointment.'

'Of course I know that. Think how I must have disappointed myself! If you really wish hands laid on Lord Warburton you must lay them yourself.'

For a couple of minutes Osmond answered nothing; then he said: 'That won't be easy, with you working against me.'

Isabel started; she felt herself beginning to tremble. He had a way of looking at her through half-closed eyelids, as if he were thinking of her but scarcely saw her, which seemed to her to have a wonderfully cruel intention. It appeared to recognize her as a disagreeable necessity of thought, but to ignore her for the time as a presence. That effect had never been so marked as now. 'I think you accuse me of something very base,' she returned.

'I accuse you of not being trustworthy. If he doesn't after all come forward it will be because you've kept him off. I don't know that it's base: it is the kind of thing a woman always thinks she may do. I've no doubt you've the finest ideas about it.'

'I told you I would do what I could,' she went on.

'Yes, that gained you time.'

It came over her, after he had said this, that she had once thought him beautiful. 'How much you must want to make sure of him!' she exclaimed in a moment.

She had no sooner spoken than she perceived the full reach of her words, of which she had not been conscious in uttering them. They made a comparison between Osmond and herself, recalled the fact that she had once held this coveted treasure in her hand and felt herself rich enough to let it fall. A momentary exultation took possession of her – a horrible delight in having wounded him; for his face instantly told her that none of the force of her exclamation was lost. He expressed nothing otherwise, however; he only said quickly: 'Yes, I want it immensely.'

At this moment a servant came in to usher a visitor, and he was followed the next by Lord Warburton, who received a visible check on seeing Osmond. He looked rapidly from the master of the house to the mistress; a movement that seemed to denote a reluctance to interrupt or even a perception of ominous conditions. Then he advanced, with his English address, in which a vague shyness seemed to offer itself as an element of good breeding; in which the only defect was a difficulty in achieving transitions. Osmond was embarrassed; he found nothing to say; but Isabel remarked promptly enough, that they had been in the act of talking about their visitor. Upon this her husband added that they hadn't known what was become of him – they had been afraid he had gone away. 'No,' he explained, smiling and looking at Osmond; 'I'm only on the point of going.' And then he mentioned that he found himself suddenly recalled to England: he should start on the morrow or the day after. 'I'm awfully sorry to leave poor Touchett!' he ended by exclaiming.

For a moment neither of his companions spoke; Osmond only leaned back in his chair, listening. Isabel didn't look at him; she could only fancy how he looked. Her eyes were on their visitor's face, where they were the more free to rest that those of his lordship carefully avoided them. Yet Isabel was sure that had she met his glance she would have found it expressive. 'You had better take poor Touchett with you,' she heard her husband say, lightly enough, in a moment.

'He had better wait for warmer weather,' Lord Warburton answered. 'I shouldn't advise him to travel just now.'

He sat there a quarter of an hour, talking as if he might not soon see them again – unless indeed they should come to England, a course he strongly recommended. Why shouldn't they come to England in the autumn? – that struck him as a very happy thought. It would give him such pleasure to do what he could for them – to have them come and spend a month with him. Osmond, by his own admission, had been to England but once; which was an absurd state of things for a man of his leisure and intelligence. It was just the country for him – he would be sure to get on well there. Then Lord Warburton asked Isabel if she remembered what a good time she had had there and if she didn't want to try it again. Didn't she want to see Gardencourt once more? Gardencourt was really very good. Touchett didn't take proper care of it, but it was the sort of place you could hardly spoil by letting it alone. Why didn't they come and pay Touchett a visit? He surely must have asked them. Hadn't asked them? What an ill-mannered wretch! – and Lord Warburton promised to give the master of Gardencourt a piece of his mind. Of course it was a mere accident; he would be delighted to have them. Spending a month with Touchett and a month with himself, and seeing all the rest of the people they must know there, they really wouldn't find it half bad. Lord Warburton added that it would amuse Miss Osmond as well, who had told him that she had never been to England and whom he had assured it was a country she deserved to see. Of course she didn't need to go to England to be admired – that was her fate everywhere; but she would be an immense success there, she certainly would, if that was any inducement. He asked if she were not at home: couldn't he say good-bye? Not that he liked good-byes – he always funked them. When he left England the other day he hadn't said good-bye to a two-legged creature. He had half a mind to leave Rome without troubling Mrs Osmond for a final interview. What could be more dreary than final interviews? One never said the things one wanted – one remembered them all an hour afterwards. On the other hand one usually said a lot of things one shouldn't, simply from a sense that one had to say something. Such a sense was upsetting; it muddled one's wits. He had it at present, and that was the effect it produced on him. If Mrs Osmond didn't think he spoke as he ought she must set it down to agitation; it was no light thing to part with Mrs Osmond. He was really very sorry to be going. He had thought of writing to her instead of calling – but he would write to her at any rate, to tell her a lot of things that would be sure to occur to him as soon as he had left the house. They must think seriously about coming to Lockleigh.

If there was anything awkward in the conditions of his visit or in the announcement of his departure it failed to come to the surface. Lord Warburton talked about his agitation; but he showed it in no other manner, and Isabel saw that since he had determined on a retreat he was capable of executing it gallantly. She was very glad for him; she liked him quite well enough to wish him to appear to carry a thing off. He would do that on any occasion – not from impudence but simply from the habit of success; and Isabel felt it out of her husband's power to frustrate this faculty. A complex operation, as she sat there, went on in her mind. On one side she listened to their visitor; said what was proper to him: read, more or less, between the lines of what he said to himself; and wondered how he would have spoken if he had found her alone. On the other she had a perfect consciousness of Osmond's emotion. She felt almost sorry for him; he was condemned to the sharp pain of loss without the relief of cursing. He had had a great hope, and now, as he saw it vanish into smoke, he was obliged to sit and smile and twirl his thumbs. Not that he troubled himself to smile very brightly; he treated their friend on the whole to as vacant a countenance as so clever a man could very well wear. It was indeed a part of Osmond's cleverness that he could look consummately uncompromised. His present appearance, however, was not a confession of disappointment; it was simply a part of Osmond's habitual system, which was to be inexpressive exactly in proportion as he was really intent. He had been intent on this prize from the first; but he had never allowed his eagerness to irradiate his refined face. He had treated his possible son-in-law as he treated everyone – with an air of being interested in him only for his own advantage, not for any profit to a person already so generally, so perfectly provided as Gilbert Osmond. He would give no sign now of an inward rage which was the result of a vanished prospect of gain – not the faintest or subtlest. Isabel could be sure of that, if it was any satisfaction to her. Strangely, very strangely, it was a satisfaction; she wished Lord Warburton to triumph before her husband, and at the same time she wished her husband to be very superior before Lord Warburton. Osmond, in his way, was admirable; he had, like their visitor, the advantage of an acquired habit. It was not that of succeeding, but it was something almost as good – that of not attempting. As he leaned back in his place, listening but vaguely to the other's friendly offers and suppressed explanations – as if it were only proper to assume that they were addressed essentially to his wife – he had at least (since so little else was left him) the comfort of thinking how well he personally had kept out of it, and how the air of indifference, which he was now able to wear, had the added beauty of consistency. It was something to be able to look as if the leavetaker's movements had no relation to his own mind. The latter did well, certainly; but Osmond's performance was in its very nature more finished. Lord Warburton's position was after all an easy one; there was no reason in the world why he shouldn't leave Rome. He had had beneficent inclinations, but they had stopped short of fruition; he had never committed himself, and his honour was safe. Osmond appeared to take but a moderate interest in the proposal that they should go and stay with him and in his allusion to the success Pansy might extract from their visit. He murmured a recognition, but left Isabel to say that it was a matter requiring grave consideration. Isabel, even while she made this remark, could see the great vista which had suddenly opened out in her husband's mind with Pansy's little figure marching up the middle of it.

Lord Warburton had asked leave to bid good-bye to Pansy, but neither Isabel nor Osmond had made any motion to send for her. He had the air of giving out that his visit must be short; he sat on a small chair, as if it were only for a moment, keeping his hat in his hand. But he stayed and stayed; Isabel wondered what he was waiting for. She believed it was not to see Pansy; she had an impression that on the whole he would rather not see Pansy. It was of course to see herself alone – he had something to say to her. Isabel had no great wish to hear it, for she was afraid it would be an explanation, and she could perfectly dispense with explanations. Osmond, however, presently got up, like a man of good taste to whom it had occurred that so inveterate a visitor might wish to say just the last word of all to the ladies. 'I've a letter to write before dinner,' he said; 'you must excuse me. I'll see if my daughter's disengaged, and if she is she shall know you're here.

Of course when you come to Rome you'll always look us up. Mrs Osmond will talk to you about the English expedition: she decides all those things.'

The nod with which, instead of a handshake, he wound up this little speech was perhaps rather a meagre form of salutation; but on the whole it was all the occasion demanded. Isabel reflected that after he left the room Lord Warburton would have no pretext for saying, 'Your husband's very angry'; which would have been extremely disagreeable to her. Nevertheless, if he had done so, she would have said: 'Oh, don't be anxious. He doesn't hate *you*; it's me that he hates!'

It was only when they had been left alone together that her friend showed a certain vague awkwardness – sitting down in another chair, handling two of three of the objects that were near him. 'I hope he'll make Miss Osmond come,' he presently remarked. 'I want very much to see her.'

'I'm glad it's the last time,' said Isabel.

'So am I. She doesn't care for me.'

'No, she doesn't care for you.'

'I don't wonder at it,' he returned. Then he added with inconsequence: 'You'll come to England, won't you?'

'I think we had better not.'

'Ah, you owe me a visit. Don't you remember that you were to have come to Lockleigh once, and you never did?'

'Everything's changed since then,' said Isabel.

'Not changed for the worse, surely – as far as we're concerned. To see you under my roof' – and he hung fire but an instant – 'would be a great satisfaction.'

She had feared an explanation; but that was the only one that occurred. They talked a little of Ralph, and in another moment Pansy came in, already dressed for dinner and with a little red spot in either cheek. She shook hands with Lord Warburton and stood looking up into his face with a fixed smile – a smile that Isabel knew, though his lordship probably never suspected it, to be near akin to a burst of tears.

'I'm going away,' he said. 'I want to bid you good-bye.'

'Good-bye, Lord Warburton.' Her voice perceptibly trembled.

'And I want to tell you how much I wish you may be very happy.'

'Thank you, Lord Warburton,' Pansy answered.

He lingered a moment and gave a glance at Isabel. 'You ought to be very happy – you've got a guardian angel.'

'I'm sure I shall be happy,' said Pansy in the tone of a person whose certainties were always cheerful.

'Such a conviction as that will take you a great way. But if it should ever fail you, remember – remember—' And her interlocutor stammered a little. 'Think of me sometimes, you know!' he said with a vague laugh. Then he shook hands with Isabel in silence, and presently he was gone.

When he had left the room she expected an effusion of tears from her stepdaughter; but Pansy in fact treated her to something very different.

'I think you *are* my guardian angel!' she exclaimed very sweetly.

Isabel shook her head. 'I'm not an angel of any kind. I'm at the most your good friend.'

'You're a very good friend then – to have asked papa to be gentle with me.'

'I've asked your father nothing,' said Isabel, wondering.

'He told me just now to come to the drawing-room and then he gave me a very kind kiss.'

'Ah,' said Isabel, 'that was quite his own idea!'

She recognized the idea perfectly; it was very characteristic, and she was to see a great deal more of it. Even with Pansy he couldn't put himself the least in the wrong. They were dining out that day, and after their dinner they went to another entertainment; so that it was not till late in the evening that Isabel saw him alone. When Pansy kissed him before going to bed he returned her embrace with even more than his usual munificence, and Isabel wondered if he meant it as a hint that his daughter had been injured by the machinations of her stepmother. It was a partial expression, at any rate, of what he continued to expect of his wife. She was about to follow Pansy, but he remarked that he wished she would remain; he had something to say to her. Then he walked about the drawing-room a little, while she stood waiting in her cloak.

'I don't understand what you wish to do,' he said in a moment. 'I should like to know – so that I may know how to act.'

'Just now I wish to go to bed. I'm very tired.'

'Sit down and rest; I shall not keep you long. Not there – take a comfortable place.' And he arranged a multitude of cushions that were scattered in picturesque disorder upon a vast divan. This was not, however, where she seated herself; she dropped into the nearest chair. The fire had gone out; the lights in the great room were few. She drew her cloak about her; she felt mortally cold. 'I think you're trying to humiliate me,' Osmond went on. 'It's a most absurd undertaking.'

'I haven't the least idea what you mean,' she returned.

'You've played a very deep game; you've managed it beautifully.'

'What is it that I've managed?'

'You've not quite settled it, however; we shall see him again.' And he stopped in front of her, with his hands in his pockets, looking down at her thoughtfully, in his usual way, which seemed meant to let her know that she was not an object, but only a rather disagreeable incident, of thought.

'If you mean that Lord Warburton's under an obligation to come back you're wrong,' Isabel said. 'He's under none whatever.'

'That's just what I complain of. But when I say he'll come back I don't mean he'll come from a sense of duty.'

'There's nothing else to make him. I think he has quite exhausted Rome.'

'Ah no, that's a shallow judgement. Rome's inexhaustible.' And Osmond began to walk about again. 'However, about that perhaps there's no hurry,' he added. 'It's rather a good idea of his that we should go to England. If it were not for the fear of finding your cousin there I think I should try to persuade you.'

'It may be that you'll not find my cousin,' said Isabel.

'I should like to be sure of it. However, I shall be as sure as possible. At the same time I should like to see his house, that you told me so much about at one time: what do you call it? – Gardencourt. It must be a charming thing. And then, you know, I've a devotion to the memory of your uncle: you made me take a great fancy to him. I should like to see where he lived and died. That indeed is a detail. Your friend was right. Pansy ought to see England.'

'I've no doubt she would enjoy it,' said Isabel.

'But that's a long time hence; next autumn's far off,' Osmond continued; 'and meantime there are things that more nearly interest us. Do you think me so very proud?' he suddenly asked.

'I think you very strange.'

'You don't understand me.'

'No, not even when you insult me.'

'I don't insult you; I'm incapable of it. I merely speak of certain facts, and if the allusion's an injury to you the fault's not mine. It's surely a fact that you have kept all this matter quite in your own hands.'

'Are you going back to Lord Warburton?' Isabel asked. 'I'm very tired of his name.'

'You shall hear it again before we've done with it.'

She had spoken of his insulting her, but it suddenly seemed to her that this ceased to be a pain. He was going down – down; the vision of such a fall made her almost giddy: that was the only pain. He was too strange, too different; he didn't touch her. Still, the working of his morbid passion was extraordinary, and she felt a rising curiosity to know in what light he saw himself justified. 'I might say to you that I judge you've nothing to say to me that's worth hearing,' she returned in a moment. 'But I should perhaps be wrong. There's a thing that would be worth my hearing – to know in the plainest words of what it is you accuse me.'

'Of having prevented Pansy's marriage to Warburton. Are those words plain enough?'

'On the contrary, I took a great interest in it. I told you so; and when you told me that you counted on me – that I think was what you said – I accepted the obligation. I was a fool to do so, but I did it.'

'You pretended to do it, and you even pretended reluctance to make me more willing to trust you. Then you began to use your ingenuity to get him out of the way.'

'I think I see what you mean,' said Isabel.

'Where's the letter you told me he had written me?' her husband demanded.

'I haven't the least idea; I haven't asked him.'

'You stopped it on the way,' said Osmond.

Isabel slowly got up; standing there in her white cloak, which covered her to her feet, she might have represented the angel of disdain, first cousin to that of pity. 'Oh, Gilbert, for a man who was so fine—!' she exclaimed in a long murmur.

'I was never so fine as you. You've done everything you wanted. You've got him out of the way without appearing to do so, and you've placed me in the position in which you wished to see me – that of a man who has tried to marry his daughter to a lord, but has grotesquely failed.'

'Pansy doesn't care for him. She's very glad he's gone,' Isabel said.

'That has nothing to do with the matter.'

'And he doesn't care for Pansy.'

'That won't do; you told me he did. I don't know why you wanted this particular satisfaction,' Osmond continued; 'you might have taken some other. It doesn't seem to me that I've been presumptuous – that I have taken too much for granted. I've been very modest about it, very quiet. The idea didn't originate with me. He began to show that he liked her before I ever thought of it. I left it all to you.'

'Yes, you were very glad to leave it to me. After this you must attend to such things yourself.'

He looked at her a moment; then he turned away. 'I thought you were very fond of my daughter.'

'I've never been more so than today.'

'Your affection is attended with immense limitations. However, that perhaps is natural.'

'Is this all you wished to say to me?' Isabel asked, taking a candle that stood on one of the tables.

'Are you satisfied? Am I sufficiently disappointed?'

'I don't think that on the whole you're disappointed. You've had another opportunity to try to stupefy me.'

'It's not that. It's proved that Pansy can aim high.'

'Poor little Pansy!' said Isabel as she turned away with her candle.

Chapter Forty-seven

It was from Henrietta Stackpole that she learned how Caspar Goodwood had come to Rome; an event that took place three days after Lord Warburton's departure. This latter fact had been preceded by an incident of some importance to Isabel – the temporary absence, once again, of Madame Merle, who had gone to Naples to stay with a friend, the happy possessor of a villa at Posillippo. Madame Merle had ceased to minister to Isabel's happiness, who found herself wondering whether the most discreet of women might not also by chance be the most dangerous. Sometimes, at night, she had strange visions; she seemed to see her husband and her friend – his friend – in dim, indistinguishable combination. It seemed to her that she had not done with her; this lady had something in reserve. Isabel's imagination applied itself actively to this elusive point, but every now and then it was checked by a nameless dread, so that when the charming woman was away from Rome she had almost a consciousness of respite. She had already learned from Miss Stackpole that Caspar Goodwood was in Europe, Henrietta having written to make it known to her immediately after meeting him in Paris. He himself never wrote to Isabel, and though he was in Europe she thought it very possible he might not desire to see her. Their last interview, before her marriage, had had quite the character of a complete rupture; if she remembered rightly he had said he wished to take his last look at her. Since then he had been the most discordant survival of her earlier time – the only one in fact with which a permanent pain was associated. He had left her that morning with a sense of the most superfluous of shocks: it was like a collision between vessels in broad daylight. There had been no mist, no hidden current to excuse it, and she herself had only wished to steer wide. He had bumped against her prow, however, while her hand was on the tiller, and – to complete the metaphor – had given the lighter vessel a strain which still occasionally betrayed itself in a faint creaking. It had been horrid to see him, because he represented the only serious harm that (to her belief) she had ever done in the world: he was the only person with an unsatisfied claim on her. She had made him unhappy, she couldn't help it; and his unhappiness was a grim reality. She had cried with rage, after he had left her, at – she hardly knew what: she tried to think it had been at his want of consideration. He had come to her with his unhappiness when her own bliss was so perfect; he had done his best to darken the brightness of those pure rays. He had not been violent, and yet there had been a violence in the impression. There had been a violence at any rate in something somewhere; perhaps it was only in her own fit of weeping and in that after-sense of the same which had lasted three or four days.

The effect of his final appeal had in short faded away, and all the first year of her marriage he had dropped out of her books. He was a thankless subject of reference; it was disagreeable to have to think of a person who was sore and sombre about you and whom you could yet do nothing to relieve. It would have been different if she had been able to doubt, even a little, of his unreconciled state, as she doubted of Lord Warburton's; unfortunately it was beyond question, and this aggressive, uncompromising look of it was just what made it unattractive. She could never say to herself that here was a sufferer who had compensations, as she was able to say in the case of her English suitor. She had no faith in Mr Goodwood's compensations and no esteem for them. A cotton-factory was not a compensation for anything – least of all for having failed to marry Isabel Archer. And yet, beyond that, she hardly knew what he had – save of course his intrinsic qualities. Oh, he was intrinsic enough; she never thought of his even looking for artificial aids. If he extended his business – that, to the best of her belief, was the only form exertion could take with him – it would be because it was an enterprising thing, or good for the business; not in the least because he might hope it would overlay the past. This gave his figure a kind of bareness and bleakness which made the accident of meeting it in memory or in apprehension a peculiar concussion; it was deficient in the social drapery commonly muffling, in an overcivilized age, the sharpness of human contacts. His perfect silence, moreover, the fact that she never heard from him and very seldom heard any mention of him, deepened this impression of his loneliness. She asked Lily for news of him, from time to time; but Lily knew nothing of Boston – her imagination was all bounded on the east by Madison Avenue. As time went on Isabel had thought of him oftener, and with fewer restrictions; she had had more than once the idea of writing to him. She had never told her husband about him – never let Osmond know of his visits to her in Florence, a reserve not dictated in the early period by a want of confidence in Osmond, but simply by the consideration that the young man's disappointment was not her secret but his own. It would be wrong of her, she had believed, to convey it to another, and Mr Goodwood's affairs could have, after all, little interest for Gilbert. When it had come to the point she had never written to him; it seemed to her that, considering his grievance, the least she could do was to let him alone. Nevertheless she would have been glad to be in some way nearer to him. It was not that it ever occurred to her that she might have married him; even after the consequences of her actual union had grown vivid to her that particular reflection, though she indulged in so many, had not had the assurance to present itself. But on finding herself in trouble he had become a member of that circle of things with which she wished to set herself right. I have mentioned how passionately she needed to feel that her unhappiness should not have come to her through her own fault. She had no near prospect of dying, and yet she wished to make her peace with the world – to put her spiritual affairs in order. It came back to her from time to time that there was an account still to be settled with Caspar, and she saw herself disposed or able to settle it today on terms easier for him than ever before. Still, when she learned he was coming to Rome she felt all afraid; it would be more disagreeable for him than for anyone else to make out – since he *would* make it out, as over a falsified balance-sheet or something of that sort – the intimate disarray of her affairs. Deep in her breast she believed that he had invested his all in her happiness, while the others had invested only a part. He was one more person from whom she should have to conceal her stress. She was reassured, however, after he arrived in Rome, for he spent several days without coming to see her.

Henrietta Stackpole, it may well be imagined, was much more punctual, and Isabel was largely favoured with the society of her friend. She threw herself into it, for now that she had made such a point of keeping her conscience clear, that was one way of proving she had not been superficial – the more so as the years, in their flight, had rather enriched than blighted those peculiarities which had been humorously criticized by persons less interested than Isabel, and which were still marked enough to give loyalty a spice of heroism. Henrietta was as keen and quick and fresh as ever, and as neat and bright and fair. Her remarkably open eyes, lighted like great glazed railway stations, had put up no shutters; her attire had lost none of its crispness, her opinions none of their national reference. She was by no means quite unchanged, however; it struck Isabel she had grown vague. Of old she had never been vague; though undertaking many inquiries at once, she had managed to be entire and pointed about each. She had a reason for everything she did; she fairly bristled with motives. Formerly, when she came to Europe it was because she wished to see it, but now, having already seen it, she had no such excuse. She didn't for a moment pretend that the desire to examine decaying civilizations had anything to do with her present enterprise; her journey was rather an expression of her independence of the old world than of a sense of further obligations to it. 'It's nothing to come to Europe,' she said to Isabel; 'it doesn't seem to me one needs so many reasons for that. It is something to stay at home; this is much more important.' It was not therefore with a sense of doing anything very important that she treated herself to another pilgrimage to Rome; she had seen the place before and carefully inspected it; her present act was simply a sign of familiarity, of her knowing all about it, of her having as good a right as any one else to be there. This was all very well, and Henrietta was restless; she had a perfect right to be restless too, if one came to that. But she had after all a better reason for coming to Rome than that she cared for it so little. Her friend easily recognized it, and with it the worth of the other's fidelity. She had crossed the stormy ocean in midwinter because she had guessed that Isabel was sad. Henrietta guessed a great deal, but she had never guessed so happily as that. Isabel's satisfactions just now were few, but even if they had been more numerous there would still have been something of individual joy in her sense of being justified in having always thought highly of Henrietta. She had made large concessions with regard to her, and had yet insisted that, with all abatements, she was very valuable. It was not her own triumph, however, that she found good; it was simply the relief of confessing to this confidant, the first person to whom she had owned it, that she was not in the least at her ease. Henrietta had herself approached this point with the smallest possible delay, and had accused her to her face of being wretched. She was a woman, she was a sister; she was not Ralph, nor Lord Warburton, nor Caspar Goodwood, and Isabel could speak.

'Yes, I'm wretched,' she said very mildly. She hated to hear herself say it; she tried to say it as judicially as possible.

'What does he do to you?' Henrietta asked, frowning as if she were inquiring into the operations of a quack doctor.

'He does nothing. But he doesn't like me.'

'He's very hard to please!' cried Miss Stackpole. 'Why don't you leave him?'

'I can't change that way,' Isabel said.

'Why not, I should like to know? You won't confess that you've made a mistake. You're too proud.'

'I don't know whether I'm too proud. But I can't publish my mistake. I don't think that's decent. I'd much rather die.'

'You won't think so always,' said Henrietta.

'I don't know what great unhappiness might bring me to; but it seems to me I shall always be ashamed. One must accept one's deeds. I married him before all the world; I was perfectly free; it was impossible to do anything more deliberate. One can't change that way,' Isabel repeated.

'You *have* changed, in spite of the impossibility. I hope you don't mean to say you like him.'

Isabel debated. 'No, I don't like him. I can tell you, because I'm weary of my secret. But that's enough; I can't announce it on the housetops.'

Henrietta gave a laugh. 'Don't you think you're rather too considerate?'

'It's not of him that I'm considerate – it's of myself!' Isabel answered.

It was not surprising Gilbert Osmond should not have taken comfort in Miss Stackpole; his instinct had naturally set him in opposition to a young lady capable of advising his wife to withdraw from the conjugal roof. When she arrived in Rome he had said to Isabel that he hoped she would leave her friend the interviewer alone; and Isabel had answered that he at least had nothing to fear from her. She said to Henrietta that as Osmond didn't like her she couldn't invite her to dine, but they could easily see each other in other ways. Isabel received Miss Stackpole freely in her own sitting-room, and took her repeatedly to drive, face to face with Pansy, who, bending a little forward, on the opposite seat of the carriage, gazed at the celebrated authoress with a respectful attention which Henrietta occasionally found irritating. She complained to Isabel that Miss Osmond had a little look as if she should remember everything one said. 'I don't want to be remembered that way,' Miss Stackpole declared; 'I consider that my conversation refers only to the moment, like the morning papers. Your stepdaughter, as she sits there, looks as if she kept all the back numbers and would bring them out some day against me.' She could not teach herself to think favourably of Pansy, whose absence of initiative, of conversation, of personal claims, seemed to her, in a girl of twenty, unnatural and even uncanny. Isabel presently saw that Osmond would have liked her to urge a little the cause of her friend, insist a little upon his receiving her, so that he might appear to suffer for good manners' sake. Her immediate acceptance of his objections put him too much in the wrong – it being in effect one of the disadvantages of expressing contempt that you cannot enjoy at the same time the credit of expressing sympathy. Osmond held to his credit, and yet he held to his objections – all of which were elements difficult to reconcile. The right thing would have been that Miss Stackpole should come to dine at Palazzo Roccanera once or twice, so that (in spite of his superficial civility, always so great) she might judge for herself how little pleasure it gave him. From the moment, however, that both the ladies were so unaccommodating, there was nothing for Osmond but to wish the lady from New York would take herself off. It was surprising how little satisfaction he got from his wife's friends; he took occasion to call Isabel's attention to it.

'You're certainly not fortunate in your intimates; I wish you might make a new collection,' he said to her one morning in reference to nothing visible at the moment, but in a tone of ripe reflection which deprived the remark of all brutal abruptness. 'It's as if you had taken the trouble to pick out the people in the world that I have least in common with. Your cousin I have always thought a conceited ass – besides his being the most ill-favoured animal I know. Then it's insufferably tiresome that one can't tell him so; one must spare him on account of his health. His health seems to me the best part of him; it gives him privileges enjoyed by no one else. If he's so desperately ill there's only one way to prove it; but he seems to have no mind for that. I can't say much more for the great Warburton. When one really thinks of it, the cool insolence of that performance was something rare! He comes and looks at one's daughter as if she were a suite of apartments; he tries the door-handles and looks out of the windows, raps on the walls and almost thinks he'll take the place. Will you be so good as to draw up a lease? Then, on the whole, he decides that the rooms are too small; he doesn't think he could live on a third floor; he must look out for a *piano nobile*. And he goes away after having got a month's lodging in the poor little apartment for nothing. Miss Stackpole, however, is your most wonderful invention. She strikes me as a kind of monster. One hasn't a nerve in one's body that she doesn't set quivering. You know I never have admitted that she's a woman. Do you know what she reminds me of? Of a new steel pen – the most odious thing in nature. She talks as a steel pen writes; aren't her letters, by the way, on ruled paper? She thinks and moves and walks and looks exactly as she talks. You may say that she doesn't hurt me, inasmuch as I don't see her. I don't see her, but I hear her; I hear her all day long. Her voice is in my ears; I can't get rid of it. I know exactly what she says, and every inflexion of the tone in which she says it. She says charming things about me, and they give you great comfort. I don't like at all to think she talks about me – I feel as I should feel if I knew the footman were wearing my hat.'

Henrietta talked about Gilbert Osmond, as his wife assured him, rather less than he suspected. She had plenty of other subjects, in two of which the reader may be supposed to be especially interested. She let her friend know that Caspar Goodwood had discovered for himself that she was unhappy, though indeed her ingenuity was unable to suggest what comfort he hoped to give her by coming to Rome and yet not calling on her. They met him twice in the street, but he had no appearance of seeing them; they were driving, and he had a habit of looking straight in front of him, as if he proposed to take in but one object at a time. Isabel could have fancied she had seen him the day before; it must have been with just that face and step that he had walked out of Mrs Touchett's door at the close of their last interview. He was dressed just as he had been dressed on that day, Isabel remembered the colour of his cravat; and yet in spite of this familiar look there was a strangeness in his figure too, something that made her feel it afresh to be rather terrible he should have come to Rome. He looked bigger and more overtopping than of old, and in those days he certainly reached high enough. She noticed that the people whom he passed looked back after him; but he went straight forward, lifting above them a face like a February sky.

Miss Stackpole's other topic was very different; she gave Isabel the latest news about Mr Bantling. He had been out in the United States the year before, and she was happy to say she had been able to show him considerable attention. She didn't know how much he had enjoyed it, but she would undertake to say it had done him good; he wasn't the same man when he left as he had been when he came. It had opened his eyes and shown him that England wasn't everything. He had been very much liked in most places, and thought extremely simple – more simple than the English were commonly supposed to be. There were people who had thought him affected; she didn't know whether they meant that his simplicity was an affectation. Some of his questions were too discouraging; he thought all the chambermaids were farmers' daughters – or all the farmers' daughters were chambermaids – she couldn't exactly remember which. He hadn't seemed able to grasp the great school system; it had been really too much for him. On the whole he had behaved as if there were too much of everything – as if he could only take in a small part. The part he had chosen was the hotel system and the river navigation. He had seemed really fascinated with the hotels; he had a photograph of every one he had visited. But the river steamers were his principal interest; he wanted to do nothing but sail on the big boats. They had travelled together from New York to Milwaukee, stopping at the most interesting cities on the route; and whenever they started afresh he had wanted to know if they could go by the steamer. He seemed to have no idea of geography – had an impression that Baltimore was a Western city and was perpetually expecting to arrive at the Mississippi. He appeared never to have heard of any river in America but the Mississippi and was unprepared to recognize the existence of the Hudson, though obliged to confess at last that it was fully equal to the Rhine. They had spent some pleasant hours in the palace-cars; he was always ordering ice-cream from the coloured man. He could never get used to that idea – that you could get ice-cream in the cars. Of course you couldn't, nor fans, nor candy, nor anything in the English cars! He found the heat quite overwhelming, and she had told him she indeed expected it was the biggest he had ever experienced. He was now in England, hunting – 'hunting round' Henrietta called it. These amusements were those of the American red men; we had left that behind long ago, the pleasures of the chase. It seemed to be generally believed in England that we wore tomahawks and feathers; but such a costume was more in keeping with English habits. Mr Bantling would not have time to join her in Italy, but when she should go to Paris again he expected to come over. He wanted very much to see Versailles again; he was very fond of the ancient *régime*. They didn't agree about that, but that was what she liked Versailles for, that you could see the ancient *régime* had been swept away. There were no dukes and marquises there now; she remembered on the contrary one day when there were five American families, walking all round. Mr Bantling was very anxious that she should take up the subject of England again, and he thought she might get on better with it now; England had changed a good deal within two or three years. He was determined that if she went there he should go to see his sister, Lady Pensil, and that this time the invitation should come to her straight. The mystery about that other one had never been explained.

Caspar Goodwood came at last to Palazzo Roccanera; he had written Isabel a note beforehand, to ask leave. This was promptly granted; she would be at home at six o'clock that afternoon. She spent the day wondering what he was coming for – what good he expected to get of it. He had presented himself hitherto as a person destitute of the faculty of compromise, who would take what he had asked for or take nothing. Isabel's hospitality, however, raised no questions, and she found no great difficulty in appearing happy enough to deceive him. It was her conviction at least that she deceived him, made him say to himself that he had been misinformed. But she also saw, so she believed, that he was not disappointed, as some other men, she was sure, would have been; he had not come to Rome to look for an opportunity. She never found out what he had come for; he offered her no explanation; there could be none but the very simple one that he wanted to see her. In other words he had come for his amusement. Isabel followed up this induction with a good deal of eagerness, and was delighted to have found a formula that would lay the ghost of this gentleman's ancient grievance. If he had come to Rome for his amusement this was exactly what she wanted; for if he cared for amusement he had got over his heartache. If he had got over his heartache everything was as it should be and her responsibilities were at an end. It was true that he took his recreation a little stiffly, but he had never been loose and easy and she had every reason to believe he was satisfied with what he saw. Henrietta was not in his confidence, though he was in hers, and Isabel consequently received no side-light upon his state of mind. He was open to little conversation on general topics; it came back to her that she had said of him once, years before, 'Mr Goodwood speaks a good deal, but he doesn't talk.' He spoke a good deal now, but he talked perhaps as little as ever; considering, that is, how much there was in Rome to talk about. His arrival was not calculated to simplify her relations with her husband, for if Mr Osmond didn't like her friends Mr Goodwood had no claim upon his attention save as having been one of the first of them. There was nothing for her to say of him but that he was the very oldest; this rather meagre synthesis exhausted the facts. She had been obliged to introduce him to Gilbert; it was impossible she should not ask him to dinner, to her Thursday evenings, of which she had grown very weary, but to which her husband still held for the sake not so much of inviting people as of not inviting them.

To the Thursdays Mr Goodwood came regularly, solemnly, rather early; he appeared to regard them with a good deal of gravity. Isabel every now and then had a moment of anger; there was something so literal about him; she thought he might know that she didn't know what to do with him. But she couldn't call him stupid; he was not that in the least; he was only extraordinarily honest. To be as honest as that made a man very different from most people; one had to be almost equally honest with *him*. She made this latter reflection at the very time she was flattering herself she had persuaded him that she was the most light-hearted of women. He never threw any doubt on this point, never asked her any personal questions. He got on much better with Osmond than had seemed probable. Osmond had a great dislike to being counted on; in such a case he had an irresistible need of disappointing you. It was in virtue of this principle that he gave himself the entertainment of taking a fancy to a perpendicular Bostonian whom he had been depended upon to treat with coldness. He asked Isabel if Mr Goodwood also had wanted to marry her, and expressed surprise at her not having accepted him. It would have been an excellent thing, like living under some tall belfry which would strike all the hours and make a queer vibration in the upper air. He declared he liked to talk with the great Goodwood; it wasn't easy at first, you had to climb up an interminable steep staircase, up to the top of the tower; but when you got there you had a big view and felt a little fresh breeze. Osmond, as we know, had delightful qualities, and he gave Caspar Goodwood the benefit of them all. Isabel could see that Mr Goodwood thought better of her husband than he had ever wished to; he had given her the impression that morning in Florence of being inaccessible to a good impression. Gilbert asked him repeatedly to dinner, and Mr Goodwood smoked a cigar with him afterwards and even desired to be shown his collections. Gilbert said to Isabel that he was very original; he was as strong and of as good a style as an English portmanteau, – he had plenty of straps and buckles which would never wear out, and a capital patent lock. Caspar Goodwood took to riding on the Campagna and devoted much time to this exercise; it was therefore mainly in the evening that Isabel saw him. She bethought herself of saying to him one day that if he were willing he could render her a service And then she added smiling:

'I don't know, however, what right I have to ask a service of you.'

'You're the person in the world who has most right,' he answered. 'I've given you assurances that I've never given anyone else.'

The service was that he should go and see her cousin Ralph, who was ill at the Hôtel de Paris, alone, and be as kind to him as possible. Mr Goodwood had never seen him, but he would know who the poor fellow was; if she was not mistaken Ralph had once invited him to Gardencourt. Caspar remembered the invitation perfectly, and, though he was not supposed to be a man of imagination, had enough to put himself in the place of a poor gentleman who lay dying at a Roman inn. He called at the Hôtel de Paris and, on being shown into the presence of the master of Gardencourt, found Miss Stackpole sitting beside his sofa. A singular change had in fact occurred in this lady's relations with Ralph Touchett. She had not been asked by Isabel to go and see him, but on hearing that he was too ill to come out had immediately gone of her own motion. After this she had paid him a daily visit – always under the conviction that they were great enemies. 'Oh yes, we're intimate enemies,' Ralph used to say; and he accused her freely – as freely as the humour of it would allow – of coming to worry him to death. In reality they became excellent friends, Henrietta much wondering that she should never have liked him before. Ralph liked her exactly as much as he had always done; he had never doubted for a moment that she was an excellent fellow. They talked about everything and always differed; about everything, that is, but Isabel – a topic as to which Ralph always had a thin forefinger on his lips. Mr Bantling on the other hand proved a great resource; Ralph was capable of discussing Mr Bantling with Henrietta for hours. Discussion was stimulated of course by their inevitable difference of view – Ralph having amused himself with taking the ground that the genial ex-guardsman was a regular Machiavelli. Caspar Goodwood could contribute nothing to such a debate; but after he had been left alone with his host he found there were various other matters they could take up. It must be admitted that the lady who had just gone out was not one of these; Caspar granted all Miss Stackpole's merits in advance, but had no further remark to make about her. Neither, after the first allusions, did the two men expatiate upon Mrs Osmond – a theme in which Goodwood perceived as many dangers as Ralph. He felt very sorry for that unclassable personage; he couldn't bear to see a pleasant man, so pleasant for all his queerness, so beyond anything to be done. There was always something to be done, for Goodwood, and he did it in this case by repeating several times his visit to the Hôtel de Paris. It seemed to Isabel that she had been very clever; she had artfully disposed of the superfluous Caspar. She had given him an occupation; she had converted him into a caretaker of Ralph. She had a plan of making him travel northward with her cousin as soon as the first mild weather should allow it. Lord Warburton had brought Ralph to Rome and Mr Goodwood should take him away. There seemed a happy symmetry in this, and she was now intensely eager that Ralph should depart. She had a constant fear he would die there before her eyes and a horror of the occurrence of this event at an inn, by her door, which he had so rarely entered. Ralph must sink to his last rest in his own dear house, in one of those deep, dim chambers of Gardencourt where the dark ivy would cluster round the edges of the glimmering window. There seemed to Isabel in these days something sacred in Gardencourt; no chapter of the past was more perfectly irrecoverable. When she thought of the months she had spent there the tears rose to her eyes. She flattered herself, as I say, upon her ingenuity, but she had need of all she could muster; for several events occurred which seemed to confront and defy her. The Countess Gemini arrived from Florence – arrived with her trunks, her dresses, her chatter, her falsehoods, her frivolity, the strange, the unholy legend of the number of her lovers. Edward Rosier, who had been away somewhere – no one, not even Pansy, knew where – reappeared in Rome and began to write her long letters, which she never answered. Madame Merle returned from Naples and said to her with a strange smile: 'What on earth did you do with Lord Warburton?' As if it were any business of hers!

Chapter Forty-eight

One day, towards the end of February, Ralph Touchett made up his mind to return to England. He had his own reasons for this decision, which he was not bound to communicate; but Henrietta Stackpole, to whom he mentioned his intention, flattered herself that she guessed them. She forbore to express them, however; she only said, after a moment, as she sat by his sofa: 'I suppose you know you can't go alone?'

'I've no idea of doing that,' Ralph answered. 'I shall have people with me.'

'What do you mean by "people"? Servants whom you pay?'

'Ah,' said Ralph jocosely, 'after all, they're human beings.'

'Are there any women among them?' Miss Stackpole desired to know.

'You speak as if I had a dozen! No, I confess I haven't a soubrette in my employment.'

'Well,' said Henrietta calmly, 'you can't go to England that way. You must have a woman's care.'

'I've had so much of yours for the past fortnight that it will last me a good while.'

'You've not had enough of it yet. I guess I'll go with you,' said Henrietta.

'Go with me?' Ralph slowly raised himself from his sofa.

'Yes, I know you don't like me, but I'll go with you all the same. It would be better for your health to lie down again.'

Ralph looked at her a little; then he slowly relapsed. 'I like you very much,' he said in a moment.

Miss Stackpole gave one of her infrequent laughs. 'You needn't think that by saying that you can buy me off. I'll go with you, and what is more I'll take care of you.'

'You're a very good woman,' said Ralph.

'Wait till I get you safely home before you say that. It won't be easy. But you had better go, all the same.'

Before she left him, Ralph said to her: 'Do you really mean to take care of me?'

'Well, I mean to try.'

'I notify you then that I submit. Oh, I submit!' And it was perhaps a sign of submission that a few minutes after she had left him alone he burst into a loud fit of laughter. It seemed to him so inconsequent, such a conclusive proof of his having abdicated all functions and renounced all exercise, that he should start on a journey across Europe under the supervision of Miss Stackpole. And the great oddity was that the prospect pleased him; he was gratefully, luxuriously passive. He felt even impatient to start; and indeed he had an immense longing to see his own house again. The end of everything was at hand; it seemed to him he could stretch out his arm and touch the goal. But he wanted to die at home; it was the only wish he had left – to extend himself in the large quiet room where he had last seen his father lie, and close his eyes upon the summer dawn.

That same day Caspar Goodwood came to see him, and he informed his visitor that Miss Stackpole had taken him up and was to conduct him back to England. 'Ah then,' said Caspar, 'I'm afraid I shall be a fifth wheel to the coach. Mrs Osmond has made *me* promise to go with you.'

'Good heavens – it's the golden age! You're all too kind.'

'The kindness of my part is to her; it's hardly to you.'

'Granting that, *she's* kind,' smiled Ralph.

'To get people to go with you? Yes, that's a sort of kindness,' Goodwood answered without lending himself to the joke. 'For myself, however,' he added, 'I'll go so far as to say that I would rather travel with you and Miss Stackpole than with Miss Stackpole alone.'

'And you'd rather stay here than do either,' said Ralph. 'There's really no need of your coming. Henrietta's extraordinarily efficient.'

'I'm sure of that. But I've promised Mrs Osmond.'

'You can easily get her to let you off.'

'She wouldn't let me off for the world. She wants me to look after you, but that isn't the principal thing. The principal thing is that she wants me to leave Rome.'

'Ah, you see too much in it,' Ralph suggested.

'I bore her,' Goodwood went on; 'she has nothing to say to me, so she invented that.'

'Oh then, if it's a convenience to her I certainly will take you with me. Though I don't see why it should be a convenience,' Ralph added in a moment.

'Well,' said Caspar Goodwood simply, 'she thinks I'm watching her.'

'Watching her?'

'Trying to make out if she's happy.'

'That's easy to make out,' said Ralph. 'She's the most visibly happy woman I know.'

'Exactly so; I'm satisfied,' Goodwood answered dryly. For all his dryness, however, he had more to say. 'I've been watching her; I was an old friend and it seemed to me I had the right. She pretends to be happy; that was what she undertook to be; and I thought I should like to see for myself what it amounts to. I've seen,' he continued with a harsh ring in his voice, 'and I don't want to see any more. I'm now quite ready to go.'

'Do you know it strikes me as about time you should?' Ralph rejoined. And this was the only conversation these gentlemen had about Isabel Osmond.

Henrietta made her preparations for departure, and among them she found it proper to say a few words to the Countess Gemini, who returned at Miss Stackpole's *pension* the visit which this lady had paid her in Florence.

'You were very wrong about Lord Warburton,' she remarked to the Countess. 'I think it right you should know that.'

'About his making love to Isabel? My poor lady, he was at her house three times a day. He has left traces of his passage!' the Countess cried.

'He wished to marry your niece; that's why he came to the house.'

The Countess started, and then with an inconsiderate laugh: 'Is that the story that Isabel tells? It isn't bad, as such things go. If he wishes to marry my niece, pray why doesn't he do it? Perhaps he has gone to buy the wedding ring and will come back with it next month, after I'm gone.'

'No, he'll not come back. Miss Osmond doesn't wish to marry him.'

'She's very accommodating! I knew she was fond of Isabel, but I didn't know she carried it so far.'

'I don't understand you,' said Henrietta coldly, and reflecting that the Countess was unpleasantly perverse. 'I really must stick to my point – that Isabel never encouraged the attentions of Lord Warburton.'

'My dear friend, what do you and I know about it? All we know is that my brother's capable of everything.'

'I don't know what your brother's capable of,' said Henrietta with dignity.

'It's not her encouraging Warburton that I complain of; it's her sending him away. I want particularly to see him. Do you suppose she thought I would make him faithless?' the Countess continued with audacious insistence. 'However, she's only keeping him, one can feel that. The house is full of him there; he's quite in the air. Oh yes, he has left traces; I'm sure I shall see him yet.'

'Well,' said Henrietta after a little, with one of those inspirations which had made the fortune of her letters to the *Interviewer*, 'perhaps he'll be more successful with you than with Isabel!'

When she told her friend of the offer she had made Ralph Isabel replied that she could have done nothing that would have pleased her more. It had always been her faith that at bottom Ralph and this young woman were made to understand each other. 'I don't care whether he understands me or not,' Henrietta declared. 'The great thing is that he shouldn't die in the cars.'

'He won't do that,' Isabel said, shaking her head with an extension of faith.

'He won't if I can help it. I see you want us all to go. I don't know what you want do do.'

'I want to be alone,' said Isabel.

'You won't be that so long as you've so much company at home.'

'Ah, they're part of the comedy. You others are spectators.'

'Do you call it a comedy, Isabel Archer?' Henrietta rather grimly asked.

'The tragedy then if you like. You're all looking at me; it makes me uncomfortable.'

Henrietta engaged in this act for a while. 'You're like the stricken deer, seeking the innermost shade. Oh, you do give me such a sense of helplessness?' she broke out.

'I'm not at all helpless. There are many things I mean to do.'

'It's not you I'm speaking of: it's myself. It's too much, having come on purpose, to leave you just as I find you.'

'You don't do that; you leave me much refreshed,' Isabel said.

'Very mild refreshment – sour lemonade! I want you to promise me something.'

'I can't do that. I shall never make another promise. I made such a solemn one four years ago, and I've succeeded so ill in keeping it.'

'You've had no encouragement. In this case I should give you the greatest.

Leave your husband before the worst comes; that's what I want you to promise.'

'The worst? What do you call the worst?'

'Before your character gets spoiled.'

'Do you mean my disposition? It won't get spoiled,' Isabel answered, smiling. 'I'm taking very good care of it. I'm extremely struck,' she added, turning away, 'with the off-hand way in which you speak of a woman's leaving her husband. It's easy to see you've never had one!'

'Well,' said Henrietta as if she were beginning an argument, 'nothing is more common in our Western cities, and it's to them, after all, that we must look in the future.' Her argument, however, does not concern this history, which has too many other threads to unwind. She announced to Ralph Touchett that she was ready to leave Rome by any train he might designate, and Ralph immediately pulled himself together for departure. Isabel went to see him at the last, and he made the same remark that Henrietta had made. It struck him that Isabel was uncommonly glad to get rid of them all.

For all answer to this she gently laid her hand on his and said in a low tone, with a quick smile: 'My dear Ralph !'

It was answer enough, and he was quite contented. But he went on in the same way, jocosely, ingenuously: 'I've seen less of you than I might, but it's better than nothing. And then I've heard a great deal about you.'

'I don't know from whom, leading the life you've done.'

'From the voices of the air! Oh, from no one else; I never let other people speak of you. They always say you're "charming", and that's so flat.'

'I might have seen more of you certainly,' Isabel said. 'But when one's married one has so much occupation.'

'Fortunately I'm not married. When you come to see me in England I shall be able to entertain you with all the freedom of a bachelor.' He continued to talk as if they should certainly meet again, and succeeded in making the assumption appear almost just. He made no allusion to his term being near, to the probability that he should not outlast the summer. If he preferred it so, Isabel was willing enough; the reality was sufficiently distinct without their erecting finger-posts in conversation. That had been well enough for the earlier time, though about this, as about his other affairs, Ralph had never been egotistic. Isabel spoke of his journey, of the stages into which he should divide it, of the precautions he should take. 'Henrietta's my greatest precaution,' he went on. 'The conscience of that woman's sublime.'

'Certainly she'll be very conscientious.'

'Will be? She has been! It's only because she thinks it's her duty that she goes with me. There's a conception of duty for you.'

'Yes, it's a generous one,' said Isabel, 'and it makes me deeply ashamed. I ought to go with you, you know.'

'Your husband wouldn't like that.'

'No, he wouldn't like it. But I might go, all the same.'

'I'm startled by the boldness of your imagination. Fancy my being a cause of disagreement between a lady and her husband!'

'That's why I don't go,' said Isabel simply – yet not very lucidly.

Ralph understood well enough, however. 'I should think so, with all those occupations you speak of.'

'It isn't that. I'm afraid,' said Isabel. After a pause she repeated, as if to make herself, rather than him, hear the words: 'I'm afraid.'

Ralph could hardly tell what her tone meant; it was so strangely deliberate – apparently so void of emotion. Did she wish to do public penance for a fault of which she had not been convicted? or were her words simply an attempt at enlightened self-analysis? However this might be, Ralph could not resist so easy an opportunity. 'Afraid of your husband?'

'Afraid of myself!' she said, getting up. She stood there a moment and then added: 'If I were afraid of my husband that would be simply my duty. That's what women are expected to be.'

'Ah yes,' laughed Ralph; 'but to make up for it there's always some man awfully afraid of some woman!'

She gave no heed to this pleasantry, but suddenly took a different turn. 'With Henrietta at the head of your little band,' she exclaimed abruptly, 'there will be nothing left for Mr Goodwood!'

'Ah, my dear Isabel,' Ralph answered, 'he's used to that. There *is* nothing left for Mr Goodwood.'

She coloured and then observed, quickly, that she must leave him. They stood together a moment; both her hands were in both of his. 'You've been my best friend,' she said.

'It was for you that I wanted – that I wanted to live. But I'm of no use to you.'

Then it came over her more poignantly that she should not see him again. She could not accept that; she could not part with him that way. 'If you should send for me I'd come,' she said at last.

'Your husband won't consent to that.'

'Oh yes, I can arrange it.'

'I shall keep that for my last pleasure!' said Ralph.

In answer to which she simply kissed him. It was a Thursday, and that evening Caspar Goodwood came to Palazzo Roccanera. He was among the first to arrive, and he spent some time in conversation with Gilbert Osmond, who almost always was present when his wife received. They sat down together, and Osmond, talkative, communicative, expansive, seemed possessed with a kind of intellectual gaiety. He leaned back with his legs crossed, lounging and chatting, while Goodwood, more restless, but not at all lively, shifted his position, played with his hat, made the little sofa creak beneath him. Osmond's face wore a sharp, aggressive smile; he was as a man whose perceptions have been quickened by good news. He remarked to Goodwood that he was sorry they were to lose him; he himself should particularly miss him. He saw so few intelligent men – they were surprisingly scarce in Rome. He must be sure to come back; there was something very refreshing, to an inveterate Italian like himself, in talking with a genuine outsider.

'I'm very fond of Rome, you know,' Osmond said; 'but there's nothing I like better than to meet people who haven't that superstition. The modern world's after all very fine. Now you're thoroughly modern and yet are not at all common. So many of the moderns we see are such very poor stuff. If they're the children of the future we're willing to die young. Of course the ancients too are often very tiresome. My wife and I like everything that's really new – not the mere pretence of it. There's nothing new, unfortunately, in ignorance and stupidity. We see plenty of that in forms that offer themselves as a revelation of progress, of light. A revelation of vulgarity! There's a certain kind of vulgarity which I believe is really new; I don't think there ever was anything like it before. Indeed I don't find vulgarity, at all, before the present century. You see a faint menace of it here and there in the last, but today the air has grown so dense that delicate things are literally not recognized. Now, we've *liked you*—!' With which he hesitated a moment, laying his hand gently on Goodwood's knee and smiling with a mixture of assurance and embarrassment. 'I'm going to say something extremely offensive and patronizing, but you must let me have the satisfaction of it. We've liked you because – because you've reconciled us a little to the future. If there are to be a certain number of people like you – *à la bonne heure*! I'm talking for my wife as well as for myself, you see. She speaks for me, my wife; why shouldn't I speak for her? We're as united, you know, as the candlestick and the snuffers. Am I assuming too much when I say that I think I've understood from you that your occupations have been – a – commercial? There's a danger in that, you know; but it's the way you have escaped that strikes us. Excuse me if my little compliment seems in execrable taste; fortunately my wife doesn't hear me. What I mean is that you *might have been* – a – what I was mentioning just now. The whole American world was in a conspiracy to make you so. But you resisted, you've something about you that saved you. And yet you're so modern, so modern; the most modern man we know! We shall always be delighted to see you again.'

I have said that Osmond was in good humour, and these remarks will give ample evidence of the fact. They were infinitely more personal than he usually cared to be, and if Caspar Goodwood had attended to them more closely he might have thought that the defence of delicacy was in rather odd hands. We may believe, however, that Osmond knew very well what he was about, and that if he chose to use the tone of patronage with a grossness not in his habits he had an excellent reason for the escapade. Goodwood had only a vague sense that he was laying it on somehow; he scarcely knew where the mixture was applied. Indeed he scarcely knew what Osmond was talking about; he wanted to be alone with Isabel, and that idea spoke louder to him than her husband's perfectly-pitched voice. He watched her talking with other people and wondered when she would be at liberty and whether he might ask her to go into one of the other rooms. His humour was not, like Osmond's, of the best; there was an element of dull rage in his consciousness of things. Up to this time he had not disliked Osmond personally; he had only thought him very well-informed and obliging and more than he had supposed like the person whom Isabel Archer would naturally marry. His host had won in the open field a great advantage over him, and Goodwood had too strong a sense of fair play to have been moved to underrate him on that account. He had not tried positively to think well of him; this was a flight of sentimental benevolence of which, even in the days when he came nearest to reconciling himself to what had happened, Goodwood was quite incapable. He accepted him as rather a brilliant personage of the amateurish kind, afflicted with a redundancy of leisure which it amused him to work off in little refinements of conversation. But he only half trusted him; he could never make out why the deuce Osmond should lavish refinements of any sort upon *him*. It made him suspect that he found some private entertainment in it, and it ministered to a general impression that his triumphant rival had in his composition a streak of perversity. He knew indeed that Osmond could have no reason to wish him evil; he had nothing to fear from him. He had carried off a supreme advantage and could afford to be kind to a man who had lost everything. It was true that Goodwood had at times grimly wished he were dead and would have liked to kill him; but Osmond had no means of knowing this, for practice had made the younger man perfect in the art of appearing inaccessible today to any violent emotion. He cultivated this art in order to deceive himself, but it was others that he deceived first. He cultivated it, moreover, with very limited success; of which there could be no better proof than the deep, dumb irritation that reigned in his soul when he heard Osmond speak of his wife's feelings as if he were commissioned to answer for them.

That was all he had had an ear for in what his host said to him this evening; he had been conscious that Osmond made more of a point even than usual of referring to the conjugal harmony prevailing at Palazzo Roccanera. He had been more careful than ever to speak as if he and his wife had all things in sweet community and it were as natural to each of them to say 'we' as to say 'I'. In all this there was an air of intention that had puzzled and angered our poor Bostonian, who could only reflect for his comfort that Mrs Osmond's relations with her husband were none of his business. He had no proof whatever that her husband misrepresented her, and if he judged her by the surface of things was bound to believe that she liked her life. She had never given him the faintest sign of discontent. Miss Stackpole had told him that she had lost her illusions, but writing for the papers had made Miss Stackpole sensational. She was too fond of early news. Moreover, since her arrival in Rome she had been much on her guard; she had pretty well ceased to flash her lantern at him. This indeed, it may be said for her, would have been quite against her conscience. She had now seen the reality of Isabel's situation, and it had inspired her with a just reserve. Whatever could be done to improve it the most useful form of assistance would not be to inflame her former lovers with a sense of her wrongs. Miss Stackpole continued to take a deep interest in the state of Mr Goodwood's feelings, but she showed it at present only by sending him choice extracts, humorous and other, from the American journals, of which she received several by every post and which she always perused with a pair of scissors in her hand. The articles she cut out she placed in an envelope addressed to Mr Goodwood, which she left with her own hand at his hotel. He never asked her a question about Isabel: hadn't he come five thousand miles to see for himself? He was thus not in the least authorized to think Mrs Osmond unhappy; but the very absence of authorization operated as an irritant, ministered to the harshness with which, in spite of his theory that he had ceased to care, he now recognized that, so far as she was concerned, the future had nothing more for him. He had not even the satisfaction of knowing the truth; apparently he could not even be trusted to respect her if she *were* unhappy. He was hopeless, helpless, useless. To this last character she had called his attention by her ingenious plan for making him leave Rome. He had no objection whatever to doing what he could for her cousin, but it made him grind his teeth to think that of all the services she might have asked of him this was the one she had been eager to select. There had been no danger of her choosing one that would have kept him in Rome.

Tonight what he was chiefly thinking of was that he was to leave her tomorrow and that he had gained nothing by coming but the knowledge that he was as little wanted as ever. About herself he had gained no knowledge; she was imperturbable, inscrutable, impenetrable. He felt the old bitterness, which he had tried so hard to swallow, rise again in his throat, and he knew there are disappointments that last as long as life. Osmond went on talking; Goodwood was vaguely aware that he was touching again upon his perfect intimacy with his wife. It seemed to him for a moment that the man had a kind of demonic imagination; it was impossible that without malice he should have selected so unusual a topic. But what did it matter, after all, whether he were demonic or not, and whether she loved him or hated him? She might hate him to the death without one's gaining a straw one's self. 'You travel, by the by, with Ralph Touchett,' Osmond said. 'I suppose that means you'll move slowly?'

'I don't know. I shall do just as he likes.'

'You're very accommodating. We're immensely obliged to you; you must really let me say it. My wife has probably expressed to you what we feel. Touchett has been on our minds all winter; it has looked more than once as if he would never leave Rome. He ought never to have come; it's worse than an imprudence for people in that state to travel; it's a kind of indelicacy. I wouldn't for the world be under such an obligation to Touchett as he has been to – to my wife and me. Other people inevitably have to look after him, and everyone isn't so generous as you.'

'I've nothing else to do,' Caspar said dryly.

Osmond looked at him a moment askance. 'You ought to marry, and then you'd have plenty to do! It's true that in that case you wouldn't be quite so available for deeds of mercy.'

'Do you find that as a married man you're so much occupied?' the young man mechanically asked.

'Ah, you see, being married's in itself an occupation. It isn't always active; it's often passive; but that takes even more attention. Then my wife and I do so many things together. We read, we study, we make music, we walk, we drive – we talk even, as when we first knew each other. I delight, to this hour, in my wife's conversation. If you're ever bored take my advice and get married. Your wife indeed may bore you, in that case; but you'll never bore yourself. You'll always have something to say to yourself – always have a subject of reflection.'

'I'm not bored,' said Goodwood. 'I've plenty to think about and to say to myself.'

'More than to say to others!' Osmond exclaimed with a light laugh. 'Where shall you go next? I mean after you've consigned Touchett to his natural caretakers – I believe his mother's at last coming back to look after him. That little lady's superb; she neglects her duties with a finish—! Perhaps you'll spend the summer in England?'

'I don't know. I've no plans.'

'Happy man! That's a little bleak, but it's very free.'

'Oh yes, I'm very free.'

'Free to come back to Rome I hope,' said Osmond as he saw a group of new visitors enter the room. 'Remember that when you do come we count on you!'

Goodwood had meant to go away early, but the evening elapsed without his having a chance to speak to Isabel otherwise than as one of several associated interlocutors. There was something perverse in the inveteracy with which she avoided him; his unquenchable rancour discovered an intention where there was certainly no appearance of one. There was absolutely no appearance of one. She met his eyes with her clear hospitable smile, which seemed almost to ask that he would come and help her to entertain some of her visitors. To such suggestions, however, he opposed but a stiff impatience. He wandered about and waited; he talked to the few people he knew, who found him for the first time rather self-contradictory. This was indeed rare with Caspar Goodwood, though he often contradicted others. There was often music at Palazzo Roccanera, and it was usually very good. Under cover of the music he managed to contain himself; but towards the end, when he saw the people beginning to go, he drew near to Isabel and asked her in a low tone if he might not speak to her in one of the other rooms, which he had just assured himself was empty. She smiled as if she wished to oblige him but found herself absolutely prevented. 'I'm afraid it's impossible. People are saying good night, and I must be where they can see me.'

'I shall wait till they are all gone then.'

She hesitated a moment. 'Ah, that will be delightful!' she exclaimed.

And he waited, though it took a long time yet. There were several people, at the end, who seemed tethered to the carpet. The Countess Gemini, who was never herself till midnight, as she said, displayed no consciousness that the entertainment was over; she had still a little circle of gentlemen in front of the fire, who every now and then broke into a united laugh. Osmond had disappeared – he never bade good-bye to people; and as the Countess was extending her range, according to her custom at this period of the evening, Isabel had sent Pansy to bed. Isabel sat a little apart; she too appeared to wish her sister-in-law would sound a lower note and let the last loiterers depart in peace.

'May I not say a word to you now?' Goodwood presently asked her.

She got up immediately, smiling. 'Certainly, we'll go somewhere else if you like.' They went together, leaving the Countess with her little circle, and for a moment after they had crossed the threshold neither of them spoke. Isabel would not sit down; she stood in the middle of the room slowly fanning herself; she had for him the same familiar grace. She seemed to wait for him to speak. Now that he was alone with her all the passion he had never stifled surged into his senses; it hummed in his eyes and made things swim round him. The bright, empty room grew dim and blurred, and through the heaving veil he felt her hover before him with gleaming eyes and parted lips. If he had seen more distinctly he would have perceived her smile was fixed and a trifle forced – that she was frightened at what she saw in his own face. 'I suppose you wish to bid me good-bye?' she said.

'Yes – but I don't like it. I don't want to leave Rome,' he answered with almost plaintive honesty.

'I can well imagine. It's wonderfully good of you. I can't tell you how kind I think you.'

For a moment more he said nothing. 'With a few words like that you make me go.'

'You must come back some day,' she brightly returned.

'Some day? You mean as long a time hence as possible.'

'Oh no; I don't mean all that.'

'What *do* you mean? I don't understand! But I said I'd go, and I'll go,' Goodwood added.

'Come back whenever you like,' said Isabel with attempted lightness.

'I don't care a straw for your cousin!' Caspar broke out.

'Is that what you wished to tell me?'

'No, no; I didn't want to tell you anything: I wanted to ask you—' he paused a moment, and then – 'what have you really made of your life?' he said, in a low, quick tone. He paused again, as if for an answer; but she said nothing, and he went on: 'I can't understand, I can't penetrate you! What am I to believe – what do you want me to think?' Still she said nothing; she only stood looking at him, now quite without pretending to ease. 'I'm told you're unhappy, and if you are I should like to know it. That would be something for me. But you yourself say you're happy, and you're somehow so still, so smooth, so hard. You're completely changed. You conceal everything; I haven't really come near you.'

'You come very near,' Isabel said gently, but in a tone of warning.

'And yet I don't touch you! I want to know the truth. Have you done well?'

'You ask a great deal.'

'Yes – I've always asked a great deal. Of course you won't tell me. I shall never know if you can help it. And then it's none of my business.' He had spoken with a visible effort to control himself, to give a considerate form to an inconsiderate state of mind. But the sense that it was his last chance, that he loved her and had lost her, that she would think him a fool whatever he should say, suddenly gave him a lash and added a deep vibration to his low voice. 'You're perfectly inscrutable, and that's what makes me think you've something to hide. I tell you I don't care a straw for your cousin, but I don't mean that I don't like him. I mean that it isn't because I like him that I go away with him. I'd go if he were an idiot and you should have asked me. If you should ask me I'd go to Siberia tomorrow. Why do you want me to leave the place? You must have some reason for that; if you were as contented as you pretend you are you wouldn't care. I'd rather know the truth about you, even if it's damnable, than have come here for nothing. That isn't what I came for. I thought I shouldn't care. I came because I wanted to assure myself that I needn't think of you any more. I haven't thought of anything else, and you're quite right to wish me to go away. But if I must go, there's no harm in my letting myself out for a single moment, is there? If you're really hurt – if *he* hurts you – nothing *I* say will hurt you. When I tell you I love you it's simply what I came for. I thought it was for something else; but it was for that. I shouldn't say it if I didn't believe I should never see you again. It's the last time – let me pluck a single flower! I've no right to say that, I know; and you've no right to listen. But you don't listen; you never listen, you're always thinking of something else. After this I must go, of course; so I shall at least have a reason. Your asking me is no reason, not a real one. I can't judge by your husband,' he went on irrelevantly, almost incoherently; I don't understand him; he tells me you adore each other. Why does he tell me that? What business is it of mine? When I say that to you, you look strange. But you always look strange. Yes, you've something to hide. It's none of my business – very true. But I love you,' said Caspar Goodwood.

As he said, she looked strange. She turned her eyes to the door by which they had entered and raised her fan as if in warning. 'You've behaved so well; don't spoil it,' she uttered softly.

'No one hears me. It's wonderful what you tried to put me off with. I love you as I've never loved you.'

'I know it. I knew it as soon as you consented to go.'

'You can't help it – of course not. You would if you could, but you can't, unfortunately. Unfortunately for me, I mean. I ask nothing – nothing, that is, I shouldn't. But I do ask one sole satisfaction: – that you tell me – that you tell me—!'

'That I tell you what?'

'Whether I may pity you.'

'Should you like that?' Isabel asked, trying to smile again.

'To pity you? Most assuredly! That at least would be doing something. I'd give my life to it.'

She raised her fan to her face, which it covered all except her eyes. They rested a moment on his. 'Don't give your life to it; but give a thought to it every now and then.' And with that she went back to the Countess Gemini.

Chapter Forty-nine

Madame Merle had not made her appearance at Palazzo Roccanera on the evening of that Thursday of which I have narrated some of the incidents, and Isabel, though she observed her absence, was not surprised by it. Things had passed between them which added no stimulus to sociability, and to appreciate which we must glance a little backward. It has been mentioned that Madame Merle returned from Naples shortly after Lord Warburton had left Rome, and that on her first meeting with Isabel (whom, to do her justice, she came immediately to see) her first utterance had been an inquiry as to the whereabouts of this nobleman for whom she appeared to hold her dear friend accountable.

'Please don't talk of him,' said Isabel for answer; 'we've heard so much of him of late.'

Madame Merle bent her head on one side a little, protestingly, and smiled at the left corner of her mouth. 'You've heard, yes. But you must remember that I've not, in Naples. I hoped to find him here and to be able to congratulate Pansy.'

'You may congratulate Pansy still; but not on marrying Lord Warburton.'

'How you say that! Don't you know I had set my heart on it?' Madame Merle asked with a great deal of spirit, but still with the intonation of good humour.

Isabel was discomposed, but she was determined to be good humoured too. 'You shouldn't have gone to Naples then. You should have stayed here to watch the affair.'

'I had too much confidence in you. But do you think it's too late?'

'You had better ask Pansy,' said Isabel.

'I shall ask her what you've said to her.'

These words seemed to justify the impulse of self-defence aroused on Isabel's part by her perceiving that her visitor's attitude was a critical one. Madame Merle, as we know, had been very discreet hitherto; she had never criticized; she had been markedly afraid of intermeddling. But apparently she had only reserved herself for this occasion, since she now had a dangerous quickness in her eye and an air of irritation which even her admirable ease was not able to transmute. She had suffered a disappointment which excited Isabel's surprise – our heroine having no knowledge of her zealous interest in Pansy's marriage; and she betrayed it in a manner which quickened Mrs Osmond's alarm. More clearly than ever before Isabel heard a cold, mocking voice proceed from she knew not where, in the dim void that surrounded her, and declare that this bright, strong, definite, worldly woman, this incarnation of the practical, the personal, the immediate, was a powerful agent in her destiny. She was nearer to her than Isabel had yet discovered, and her nearness was not the charming accident she had so long supposed. The sense of accident indeed had died within her that day when she happened to be struck with the manner in which the wonderful lady and her own husband sat together in private. No definite suspicion had as yet taken its place; but it was enough to make her view this friend with a different eye, to have been led to reflect that there was more intention in her past behaviour than she had allowed for at the time. Ah yes, there had been intention, there had been intention, Isabel said to herself; and she seemed to wake from a long pernicious dream. What was it that brought home to her that Madame Merle's intention had not been good? Nothing but the mistrust which had lately taken body and which married itself now to the fruitful wonder produced by her visitor's challenge on behalf of poor Pansy. There was something in this challenge which had at the very outset excited an answering defiance; a nameless vitality which she could see to have been absent from her friend's professions of delicacy and caution. Madame Merle had been unwilling to interfere, certainly, but only so long as there was nothing to interfere with. It will perhaps seem to the reader that Isabel went fast in casting doubt, on mere suspicion, on a sincerity proved by several years of good offices. She moved quickly indeed, and with reason, for a strange truth was filtering into her soul. Madame Merle's interest was identical with Osmond's: that was enough. 'I think Pansy will tell you nothing that will make you more angry,' she said in answer to her companion's last remark.

'I'm not in the least angry. I've only a great desire to retrieve the situation. Do you consider that Warburton has left us for ever?'

'I can't tell you; I don't understand you. It's all over; please let it rest. Osmond has talked to me a greal deal about it, and I've nothing more to say or to hear. I've no doubt,' Isabel added, 'that he'll be very happy to discuss the subject with you.'

'I know what he thinks; he came to see me last evening.'

'As soon as you had arrived? Then you know all about it and you needn't apply to me for information.'

'It isn't information I want. At bottom it's sympathy. I had set my heart on that marriage; the idea did what so few things do – it satisfied the imagination.'

'Your imagination, yes. But not that of the persons concerned.'

'You mean by that of course that I'm not concerned. Of course not directly. But when one's such an old friend one can't help having something at stake. You forget how long I've known Pansy. You mean, of course,' Madame Merle added, 'that *you* are one of the persons concerned.'

'No; that's the last thing I mean. I'm very weary of it all.'

Madame Merle hesitated a little. 'Ah yes, your work's done.'

'Take care what you say,' said Isabel very gravely.

'Oh, I take care; never perhaps more than when it appears least. Your husband judges you severely.'

Isabel made for a moment no answer to this; she felt choked with bitterness. It was not the insolence of Madame Merle's informing her that Osmond had been taking her into his confidence as against his wife that struck her most; for she was not quick to believe that this was meant for insolence. Madame Merle was very rarely insolent, and only when it was exactly right. It was not right now, or at least it was not right yet. What touched Isabel like a drop of corrosive acid upon an open wound was the knowledge that Osmond dishonoured her in his words as well as in his thoughts. 'Should you like to know how I judge *him*?' she asked at last.

'No, because you'd never tell me. And it would be painful for me to know.'

There was a pause, and for the first time since she had known her Isabel thought Madame Merle disagreeable. She wished she would leave her. 'Remember how attractive Pansy is, and don't despair,' she said abruptly, with a desire that this should close their interview.

But Madame Merle's expansive presence underwent no contraction. She only gathered her mantle about her and, with the movement scattered upon the air a faint, agreeable fragrance. 'I don't despair; I feel encouraged. And I didn't come to scold you; I came if possible to learn the truth. I know you'll tell it if I ask you. It's an immense blessing with you that one can count upon that. No, you won't believe what a comfort I take in it.'

'What truth do you speak of?' Isabel asked, wondering.

'Just this: whether Lord Warburton changed his mind quite of his own movement or because you recommended it. To please himself I mean, or to please you. Think of the confidence I must still have in you, in spite of having lost a little of it,' Madame Merle continued with a smile, 'to ask such a question as that!' She sat looking at her friend, to judge the effect of her words, and then went on: 'Now don't be heroic, don't be unreasonable, don't take offence. It seems to me I do you an honour in speaking so. I don't know another woman to whom I would do it. I haven't the least idea that any other woman would tell me the truth. And don't you see how well it is that your husband should know it? It's true that he doesn't appear to have had any tact whatever in trying to extract it; he has indulged in gratuitous suppositions. But that doesn't alter the fact that it would make a difference in his view of his daughter's prospects to know distinctly what really occurred. Lord Warburton simply got tired of the poor child, that's one thing, and it's a pity. If he gave her up to please you it's another. That's a pity too, but in a different way. Then, in the latter case you'd perhaps resign yourself to not being pleased – to simply seeing your stepdaughter married. Let him off – let us have him!'

Madame Merle had proceeded very deliberately, watching her companion and apparently thinking she could proceed safely. As she went on Isabel grew pale; she clasped her hands more tightly in her lap. It was not that her visitor had at last thought it the right time to be insolent; for this was not what was most apparent. It was a worse horror than that. 'Who are you – what are you?' Isabel murmured. 'What have you to do with my husband?' It was strange that for the moment she drew as near to him as if she had loved him.

'Ah then, you take it heroically! I'm very sorry. Don't think, however, that I shall do so.'

'What have you to do with me?' Isabel went on.

Madame Merle slowly got up, stroking her muff, but not removing her eyes from Isabel's face. 'Everything!' she answered.

Isabel sat there looking up at her, without rising; her face was almost a prayer to be enlightened. But the light of this woman's eyes seemed only a darkness. 'Oh misery!' she murmured at last; and she fell back, covering her face with her hands. It had come over her like a high-surging wave that Mrs Touchett was right. Madame Merle had married her. Before she uncovered her face again that lady had left the room.

Isabel took a drive alone that afternoon; she wished to be far away, under the sky, where she could descend from her carriage and tread upon the daisies. She had long before this taken old Rome into her confidence, for in a world of ruins the ruin of her happiness seemed a less unnatural catastrophe. She rested her weariness upon things that had crumbled for centuries and yet still were upright; she dropped her secret sadness into the silence of lonely places, where its very modern quality detached itself and grew objective, so that as she sat in a sun-warmed angle on a winter's day, or stood in a mouldy church to which no one came, she could almost smile at it and think of its smallness. Small it was, in the large Roman record, and her haunting sense of the continuity of the human lot easily carried her from the less to the greater. She had become deeply, tenderly acquainted with Rome: it interfused and moderated her passion. But she had grown to think of it chiefly as the place where people had suffered. This was what came to her in the starved churches, where the marble columns, transferred from pagan ruins, seemed to offer her a companionship in endurance and the musty incense to be a compound of long-unanswered prayers. There was no gentler nor less consistent heretic than Isabel; the firmest of worshippers, gazing at dark altar-pictures or clustered candles, could not have felt more intimately the suggestiveness of these objects nor have been more liable at such moments to a spiritual visitation. Pansy as we know, was almost always her companion, and of late the Countess Gemini, balancing a pink parasol, had lent brilliancy to their equipage; but she still occasionally found herself alone when it suited her mood and where it suited the place. On such occasions she had several resorts; the most accessible of which perhaps was a seat on the low parapet which edges the wide grassy space before the high, cold front of Saint John Lateran, whence you look across the Campagna at the far-trailing outline of the Alban Mount and at that mighty plain between, which is still so full of all that has passed from it. After the departure of her cousin and his companions she roamed more than usual; she carried her sombre spirit from one familiar shrine to the other. Even when Pansy and the Countess were with her she felt the touch of a vanished world. The carriage, leaving the walls of Rome behind, rolled through narrow lanes where the wild honey-suckle had begun to tangle itself in the hedges, or waited for her in quiet places where the fields lay near, while she strolled farther and farther over the flower-freckled turf, or sat on a stone that had once had a use and gazed through the veil of her personal sadness at the splendid sadness of the scene – at the dense, warm light, the far gradations and soft confusion of colour, the motionless shepherds in lonely attitudes, the hills where the cloud-shadows had the lightness of a blush.

On the afternoon I began with speaking of, she had taken a resolution not to think of Madame Merle; but the resolution proved vain, and this lady's image hovered constantly before her. She asked herself, with an almost childlike horror of the supposition, whether to this intimate friend of several years the great historical epithet of *wicked* were to be applied. She knew the idea only by the Bible and other literary works; to the best of her belief she had had no personal acquaintance with wickedness. She had desired a large acquaintance with human life, and in spite of her having flattered herself that she cultivated it with some success this elementary privilege had been denied her. Perhaps it was not wicked – in the historic sense – to be even deeply false; for that was what Madame Merle had been – deeply, deeply, deeply. Isabel's Aunt Lydia had made this discovery long before, and had mentioned it to her niece; but Isabel had flattered herself at this time that she had a much richer view of things, especially of the spontaneity of her own career and the nobleness of her own interpretations, than poor stiffly reasoning Mrs Touchett. Madame Merle had done what she wanted; she had brought about the union of her two friends; a reflection which could not fail to make it a matter of wonder that she should so much have desired such an event. There were people who had the match-making passion, like the votaries of art; but Madame Merle, great artist as she was, was scarcely one of these. She thought too ill of marriage, too ill even of life; she had desired that particular marriage but had not desired others. She had therefore had a conception of gain, and Isabel asked herself where she had found her profit. It took her naturally a long time to discover, and even then her discovery was imperfect. It came back to her that Madame Merle, though she had seemed to like her from their first meeting at Gardencourt, had been doubly affectionate after Mr Touchett's death and after learning that her young friend had been subject to the good old man's charity. She had found her profit not in the gross device of borrowing money, but in the more refined idea of introducing one of her intimates to the young woman's fresh and ingenuous fortunes. She had naturally chosen her closest intimate, and it was already vivid enough to Isabel that Gilbert occupied this position. She found herself confronted in this manner with the conviction that the man in the world whom she had supposed to be the least sordid had married her, like a vulgar adventurer, for her money. Strange to say, it had never before occurred to her; if she had thought a good deal of harm of Osmond she had not done him this particular injury. This was the worst she could think of, and she had been saying to herself that the worst was still to come. A man might marry a woman for her money perfectly well; the thing was often done. But at least he should let her know. She wondered whether, since he had wanted her money, her money would now satisfy him. Would he take her money and let her go? Ah, if Mr Touchett's great charity would but help her today it would be blessed indeed! It was not slow to occur to her that if Madame Merle had wished to do Gilbert a service his recognition to her of the boon must have lost its warmth. What must be his feelings today in regard to his too zealous benefactress, and what expression must they have found on the part of such a master of irony? It is a singular, but a characteristic, fact that before Isabel returned from her silent drive she had broken its silence by the soft exclamation: 'Poor, poor Madame Merle!'

Her compassion would perhaps have been justified if on this same afternoon she had been concealed behind one of the valuable curtains of time-softened damask which dressed the interesting little *salon* of the lady to whom it referred; the carefully-arranged apartment to which we once paid a visit in company with the discreet Mr Rosier. In that apartment, towards six o'clock, Gilbert Osmond was seated, and his hostess stood before him as Isabel had seen her stand on an occasion commemorated in this history with an emphasis appropriate not so much to its apparent as to its real importance.

'I don't believe you're unhappy; I believe you like it,' said Madame Merle.

'Did I say I was unhappy?' Osmond asked with a face grave enough to suggest that he might have been.

'No, but you don't say the contrary, as you ought in common gratitude.'

'Don't talk about gratitude,' he returned dryly. 'And don't aggravate me,' he added in a moment.

Madame Merle slowly seated herself, with her arms folded and her white hands arranged as a support to one of them and an ornament, as it were, to the other. She looked exquisitely calm but impressively sad. 'On your side, don't try to frighten me. I wonder if you guess some of my thoughts.'

'I trouble about them no more than I can help. I've quite enough of my own.'

'That's because they're so delightful.'

Osmond rested his head against the back of his chair and looked at his companion with a cynical directness which seemed also partly an expression of fatigue. 'You do aggravate me,' he remarked in a moment. 'I'm very tired.'

'*Eh moi donc?*' cried Madame Merle.

'With you it's because you fatigue yourself. With me it's not my own fault.'

'When I fatigue myself it's for you. I've given you an interest. That's a great gift.'

'Do you call it an interest?' Osmond inquired with detachment.

'Certainly, since it helps you to pass your time.'

'The time has never seemed longer to me than this winter.'

'You've never looked better; you've never been so agreeable, so brilliant.'

'Damn my brilliancy!' he thoughtfully murmured. 'How little, after all, you know me!'

'If I don't know you I know nothing,' smiled Madame Merle. 'You've the feeling of complete success.'

'No, I shall not have that till I've made you stop judging me.'

'I did that long ago. I speak from old knowledge. But you express yourself more too.'

Osmond just hung fire. 'I wish you'd express yourself less!'

'You wish to condemn me to silence? Remember that I've never been a chatterbox. At any rate there are three or four things I should like to say to you first. Your wife doesn't know what to do with herself,' she went on with a change of tone.

'Pardon me; she knows perfectly. She has a line sharply drawn. She means to carry out her ideas.'

'Her ideas today must be remarkable.'

'Certainly they are. She has more of them than ever.'

'She was unable to show me any this morning,' said Madame Merle. 'She seemed in a very simple, almost in a stupid, state of mind. She was completely bewildered.'

'You had better say at once that she was pathetic.'

'Ah no, I don't want to encourage you too much.'

He still had his head against the cushion behind him; the ankle of one foot rested on the other knee. So he sat for a while. 'I should like to know what's the matter with you,' he said at last.

'The matter – the matter—!' And here Madame Merle stopped. Then she went on with a sudden outbreak of passion, a burst of summer thunder in a clear sky: 'The matter is that I would give my right hand to be able to weep, and that I can't!'

'What good would it do you to weep?'

'It would make me feel as I felt before I knew you.'

'If I've dried your tears, that's something. But I've seen you shed them.'

'Oh, I believe you'll make me cry still. I mean make me howl like a wolf. I've a great hope, I've a great need, of that. I was vile this morning; I was horrid,' she said.

'If Isabel was in the stupid state of mind you mention she probably didn't perceive it,' Osmond answered.

'It was precisely my deviltry that stupefied her. I couldn't help it; I was full of something bad. Perhaps it was something good; I don't know. You've not only dried up my tears; you've dried up my soul.'

'It's not I then that am responsible for my wife's condition,' Osmond said. 'It's pleasant to think that I shall get the benefit of your influence upon her. Don't you know the soul is an immortal principle? How can it suffer alteration?'

'I don't believe at all that it's an immortal principle. I believe it can perfectly be destroyed. That's what has happened to mine, which was a very good one to start with; and it's you I have to thank for it. You're *very* bad,' she added with gravity in her emphasis.

'Is this the way we're to end?' Osmond asked with the same studied coldness.

'I don't know how we're to end. I wish I did! How do bad people end?

– especially as to their *common* crimes. You have made me as bad as yourself.'

'I don't understand you. You seem to me quite good enough,' said Osmond, his conscious indifference giving an extreme effect to the words.

Madame Merle's self-possession tended on the contrary to diminish, and she was nearer losing it than on any occasion on which we have had the pleasure of meeting her. The glow of her eye turned sombre; her smile betrayed a painful effort. 'Good enough for anything that I've done with myself? I suppose that's what you mean.'

'Good enough to be always charming!' Osmond exclaimed, smiling too.

'Oh God!' his companion murmured; and, sitting there in her ripe freshness, she had recourse to the same gesture she had provoked on Isabel's part in the morning: she bent her face and covered it with her hands.

'Are you going to weep after all?' Osmond asked; and on her remaining motionless he went on: 'Have I ever complained to you?'

She dropped her hands quickly. 'No, you've taken your revenge otherwise – you have taken it on *her*.'

Osmond threw back his head farther; he looked a while at the ceiling and might have been supposed to be appealing, in an informal way, to the heavenly powers. 'Oh, the imagination of women! It's always vulgar, at bottom. You talk of revenge like a third-rate novelist.'

'Of course you haven't complained. You've enjoyed your triumph too much.'

'I'm rather curious to know what you call my triumph.'

'You've made your wife afraid of you.'

Osmond changed his position; he leaned forward, resting his elbows on his knees and looking a while at a beautiful old Persian rug, at his feet. He had an air of refusing to accept anyone's valuation of anything, even of time, and of preferring to abide by his own; a peculiarity which made him at moments an irritating person to converse with. 'Isabel's not afraid of me, and it's not what I wish,' he said at last. 'To what do you want to provoke me when you say such things as that?'

'I've thought over all the harm you can do me,' Madame Merle answered. 'Your wife was afraid of me this morning, but in me it was really you she feared.'

'You may have said things that were in very bad taste; I'm not responsible for that. I didn't see the use of your going to see her at all: you're capable of acting without her. I've not made *you* afraid of me that I can see,' he went on; 'how then should I have made her? You're at least as brave. I can't think where you've picked up such rubbish; one might suppose you knew me by this time.' He got up as he spoke and walked to the chimney, where he stood a moment bending his eye, as if he had seen them for the first time, on the delicate specimens of rare porcelain with which it was covered. He took up a small cup and held it in his hand; then, still holding it and leaning his arm on the mantel, he pursued: 'You always see too much in everything; you overdo it; you lose sight of the real. I'm much simpler than you think.'

'I think you're very simple.' And Madame Merle kept her eye on her cup. 'I've come to that with time. I judged you, as I say, of old; but it's only since your marriage that I've understood you. I've seen better what you have been to your wife than I ever saw what you were for me. Please be very careful of that precious object.'

'It already has a wee bit of a tiny crack,' said Osmond dryly as he put it down. 'If you didn't understand me before I married it was cruelly rash of you to put me into such a box. However, I took a fancy to my box myself; I thought it would be a comfortable fit. I asked very little; I only asked that she should like me.'

'That she should like you so much!'

'So much, of course; in such a case one asks the maximum. That she should adore me, if you will. Oh yes, I wanted that.'

'I never adored you,' said Madame Merle.

'Ah, but you pretended to!'

'It's true that you never accused me of being a comfortable fit,' Madame Merle went on.

'My wife has declined – declined to do anything of the sort,' said Osmond. 'If you're determined to make a tragedy of that, the tragedy's hardly for her.'

'The tragedy's for me!' Madame Merle exclaimed, rising with a long low sigh but having a glance at the same time for the contents of her mantelshelf. 'It appears that I'm to be severely taught the disadvantages of a false position.'

'You express yourself like a sentence in a copybook. We must look for our comfort where we can find it. If my wife doesn't like me, at least my child does. I shall look for compensations in Pansy. Fortunately I haven't a fault to find with her.'

'Ah,' she said softly, 'if I had a child—!'

Osmond waited, and then, with a little formal air, 'The children of others may be a great interest!' he announced.

'You're more like a copybook than I. There's something after all that holds us together.'

'Is it the idea of the harm I may do you?' Osmond asked.

'No; it's the idea of the good I may do for you. It's that,' Madame Merle pursued, 'that made me so jealous of Isabel. I want it to be *my* work,' she added, with her face, which had grown hard and bitter, relaxing to its habit of smoothness.

Her friend took up his hat and his umbrella, and after giving the former article two or three strokes with his coat-cuff, 'On the whole, I think,' he said, 'you had better leave it to me.'

After he had left her she went, the first thing, and lifted from the mantelshelf the attenuated coffee-cup in which he had mentioned the existence of a crack; but she looked at it rather abstractedly. 'Have I been so vile all for nothing?' she vaguely wailed.

Chapter Fifty

As the Countess Gemini was not acquainted with the ancient monuments Isabel occasionally offered to introduce her to these interesting relics and to give their afternoon drive an antiquarian aim. The Countess, who professed to think her sister-in-law a prodigy of learning, never made an objection, and gazed at masses of Roman brickwork as patiently as if they had been mounds of modern drapery. She had not the historic sense, though she had in some directions the anecdotic, and as regards herself the apologetic, but she was so delighted to be in Rome that she only desired to float with the current. She would gladly have passed an hour every day in the damp darkness of the Baths of Titus if it had been a condition of her remaining at Palazzo Roccanera. Isabel, however, was not a severe cicerone; she used to visit the ruins chiefly because they offered an excuse for talking about other matters than the love-affairs of the ladies of Florence, as to which her companion was never weary of offering information. It must be added that during these visits the Countess forbade herself every form of active research; her preference was to sit in the carriage and exclaim that everything was most interesting. It was in this manner that she had hitherto examined the Coliseum, to the infinite regret of her niece, who – with all the respect that she owed her – could not see why she should not descend from the vehicle and enter the building. Pansy had so little chance to ramble that her view of the case was not wholly disinterested; it may be divined that she had a secret hope that, once inside, her parents' guest might be induced to climb to the upper tiers. There came a day when the Countess announced her willingness to undertake this feat – a mild afternoon in March when the windy month expressed itself in occasional puffs of spring. The three ladies went into the Coliseum together, but Isabel left her companions to wander over the place. She had often ascended to those desolate ledges from which the Roman crowd used to bellow applause and where now the wild flowers (when they are allowed) bloom in the deep crevices; and today she felt weary and disposed to sit in the despoiled arena. It made an intermission too, for the Countess often asked more from one's attention than she gave in return; and Isabel believed that when she was alone with her niece she let the dust gather for a moment on the ancient scandals of the Arnide. She so remained below therefore, while Pansy guided her undiscriminating aunt to the steep brick staircase at the foot of which the custodian unlocks the tall wooden gate. The great enclosure was half in shadow; the western sun brought out the pale red tone of the great blocks of travertine – the latent colour that is the only living element in the immense ruin. Here and there wandered a peasant or a tourist, looking up at the far sky-line where, in the clear stillness, a multitude of swallows kept circling and plunging. Isabel presently became aware that one of the other visitors, planted in the middle of the arena, had turned his attention to her own person and was looking at her with a certain little poise of the head which she had some weeks before perceived to be characteristic of baffled but indestructible purpose. Such an attitude, today, could belong only to Mr Edward Rosier; and this gentleman proved in fact to have been considering the question of speaking to her. When he had assured himself that she was unaccompanied he drew near, remarking that though she would not answer his letters she would perhaps not wholly close her ears to his spoken eloquence. She replied that her stepdaughter was close at hand and that she could only give him five minutes; whereupon he took out his watch and sat down upon a broken block.

'It's very soon told,' said Edward Rosier. 'I've sold all my bibelots!' Isabel gave instinctively an exclamation of horror; it was as if he had told her he had had all his teeth drawn. 'I've sold them by auction at the Hôtel Drouot,' he went on. 'The sale took place three days ago, and they've telegraphed me the result. It's magnificent.'

'I'm glad to hear it; but I wish you had kept your pretty things.'

'I have the money instead – fifty thousand dollars. Will Mr Osmond think me rich enough now?'

'Is it for that you did it?' Isabel asked gently.

'For what else in the world could it be? That's the only thing I think of. I went to Paris and made my arrangements. I couldn't stop for the sale; I couldn't have seen them going off; I think it would have killed me. But I put them into good hands, and they brought high prices. I should tell you I have kept my enamels. Now I have the money in my pocket, and he can't say I'm poor!' the young man exclaimed defiantly.

'He'll say now that you're not wise,' said Isabel, as if Gilbert Osmond had never said this before.

Rosier gave her a sharp look. 'Do you mean that without my bibelots I'm nothing? Do you mean they were the best thing about me? That's what they told me in Paris; oh they were very frank about it. But they hadn't seen *her*!'

'My dear friend, you deserve to succeed,' said Isabel very kindly.

'You say that so sadly that it's the same as if you said I shouldn't.' And he questioned her eyes with the clear trepidation of his own. He had the air of a man who knows he has been the talk of Paris for a week and is full half a head taller in consequence, but who also has a painful suspicion that in spite of this increase of stature one or two persons still have the perversity to think him diminutive. 'I know what happened here while I was away,' he went on. 'What does Mr Osmond expect after she has refused Lord Warburton?'

Isabel debated. 'That she'll marry another nobleman.'

'What other nobleman?'

'One that he'll pick out.'

Rosier slowly got up, putting his watch into his waistcoat-pocket. 'You're laughing at someone, but this time I don't think it's at me.'

'I didn't mean to laugh,' said Isabel. 'I laugh very seldom. Now you had better go away.'

'I feel very safe!' Rosier declared without moving. This might be; but it evidently made him feel more so to make the announcement in rather a loud voice, balancing himself a little complacently on his toes and looking all round the Coliseum as if it were filled with an audience. Suddenly Isabel saw him change colour; there was more of an audience than he had suspected. She turned and perceived that her two companions had returned from their excursion. 'You must really go away,' she said quickly.

'Ah, my dear lady, pity me!' Edward Rosier murmured in a voice strangely at variance with the announcement I have just quoted. And then he added eagerly, like a man who in the midst of his misery is seized by a happy thought: 'Is that lady the Countess Gemini? I've a great desire to be presented to her.'

Isabel looked at him a moment. 'She has no influence with her brother.'

'Ah, what a monster you make him out!' And Rosier faced the Countess, who advanced, in front of Pansy, with an animation partly due perhaps to the fact that she perceived her sister-in-law to be engaged in conversation with a very pretty young man.

'I'm glad you've kept your enamels!' Isabel called as she left him. She went straight to Pansy, who, on seeing Edward Rosier, had stopped short, with lowered eyes. 'We'll go back to the carriage,' she said gently.

'Yes, it's getting late,' Pansy returned more gently still. And she went on without a murmur, without faltering or glancing back.

Isabel, however, allowing herself this last liberty, saw that a meeting had immediately taken place between the Countess and Mr Rosier. He had removed his hat and was bowing and smiling; he had evidently introduced himself while the Countess's expressive back displayed to Isabel's eye a gracious inclination. These facts, none the less, were presently lost to sight, for Isabel and Pansy took their places again in the carriage. Pansy, who faced her stepmother, at first kept her eyes fixed on her lap; then she raised them and rested them on Isabel's. There shone out of each of them a little melancholy ray – a spark of timid passion which touched Isabel to the heart. At the same time a wave of envy passed over her soul, as she compared the tremulous longing, the definite ideal of the child with her own dry despair. 'Poor little Pansy!' she affectionately said.

'Oh never mind!' Pansy answered in the tone of eager apology.

And then there was a silence; the Countess was a long time coming. 'Did you show your aunt everything, and did she enjoy it?' Isabel asked at last.

'Yes, I showed her everything. I think she was very much pleased.'

'And you're not tired, I hope.'

'Oh no, thank you, I'm not tired.'

The Countess still remained behind, so that Isabel requested the footman to go into the Coliseum and tell her they were waiting. He presently returned with the announcement that the Signora Countessa begged them not to wait – she would come home in a cab!

About a week after this lady's quick sympathies had enlisted themselves with Mr Rosier, Isabel, going rather late to dress for dinner, found Pansy sitting in her room. The girl seemed to have been awaiting her; she got up from her low chair. 'Pardon my taking the liberty,' she said in a small voice. 'It will be the last – for some time.'

Her voice was strange, and her eyes, widely opened, had an excited, frightened look. 'You're not going away!' Isabel exclaimed.

'I'm going to the convent.'

'To the convent?'

Pansy drew nearer, till she was near enough to put her arms round Isabel and rest her head on her shoulder. She stood this way a moment, perfectly still; but her companion could feel her tremble. The quiver of her little body expressed everything she was unable to say. Isabel nevertheless pressed her. 'Why are you going to the convent?'

'Because papa thinks it best. He says a young girl's better, every now and then, for making a little retreat. He says the world, always the world, is very bad for a young girl. This is just a chance for a little seclusion – a little reflection.' Pansy spoke in short detached sentences, as if she could scarce trust herself; and then she added with a triumph of self-control: 'I think papa's right; I've been so much in the world this winter.'

Her announcement had a strange effect on Isabel; it seemed to carry a larger meaning than the girl herself knew. 'When was this decided?' she asked. 'I've heard nothing of it.'

'Papa told me half an hour ago; he thought it better it shouldn't be too much talked about in advance. Madame Catherine's to come for me at a quarter past seven, and I'm only to take two frocks. It's only for a few weeks; I'm sure it will be very good. I shall find all those ladies who used to be so kind to me, and I shall see the little girls who are being educated. I'm very fond of little girls,' said Pansy with an effect of diminutive grandeur. 'And I'm also very fond of Mother Catherine. I shall be very quiet and think a great deal.'

Isabel listened to her, holding her breath; she was almost awe-struck. 'Think of *me* sometimes.'

'Ah, come and see me soon!' cried Pansy; and the cry was very different from the heroic remarks of which she had just delivered herself.

Isabel could say nothing more; she understood nothing; she only felt how little she yet knew her husband. Her answer to his daughter was a long, tender kiss.

Half an hour later she learned from her maid that Madame Catherine had arrived in a cab and had departed again with the signorina. On going to the drawing-room before dinner she found the Countess Gemini alone, and this lady characterized the incident by exclaiming, with a wonderful toss of the head, '*En voilà, ma chère, une pose!*' But if it was an affectation she was at a loss to see what her husband affected. She could only dimly perceive that he had more traditions than she supposed. It had become her habit to be so careful as to what she said to him that, strange as it may appear, she hesitated, for several minutes after he had come in, to allude to his daughter's sudden departure: she spoke of it only after they were seated at table. But she had forbidden herself ever to ask Osmond a question. All she could do was to make a declaration, and there was one that came very naturally. 'I shall miss Pansy very much.'

He looked a while, with his head inclined a little, at the basket of flowers in the middle of the table. 'Ah yes,' he said at last, 'I had thought of that. You must go and see her, you know; but not too often. I dare say you wonder why I sent her to the good sisters; but I doubt if I can make you understand. It doesn't matter; don't trouble yourself about it. That's why I had not spoken of it. I didn't believe you would enter into it. But I've always had the idea; I've always thought it a part of the education of one's daughter. One's daughter should be fresh and fair; she should be innocent and gentle.

With the manners of the present time she is liable to become so dusty and crumpled. Pansy's a little dusty, a little dishevelled; she has knocked about too much. This bustling, pushing rabble that calls itself society – one should take her out of it occasionally. Convents are very quiet, very convenient, very salutary. I like to think of her there, in the old garden, under the arcade, among those tranquil virtuous women. Many of them are gentlewomen born; several of them are noble. She will have her books and her drawing, she will have her piano. I've made the most liberal arrangements. There is to be nothing ascetic; there's just to be a certain little sense of sequestration. She'll have time to think, and there's something I want her to think about.' Osmond spoke deliberately, reasonably, still with his head on one side, as if he were looking at the basket of flowers. His tone, however, was that of a man not so much offering an explanation as putting a thing into words – almost into pictures – to see, himself, how it would look. He considered a while the picture he had evoked and seemed greatly pleased with it. And then he went on: 'The Catholics are very wise after all. The convent is a great institution; we can't do without it; it corresponds to an essential need in families, in society. It's a school of good manners; it's a school of repose. Oh, I don't want to detach my daughter from the world,' he added; 'I don't want to make her fix her thoughts on any other. This one's very well, as *she* should take it, and she may think of it as much as she likes. Only she must think of it in the right way.'

Isabel gave an extreme attention to this little sketch; she found it indeed intensely interesting. It seemed to show her how far her husband's desire to be effective was capable of going – to the point of playing theoretic tricks on the delicate organism of his daughter. She could not understand his purpose, no – not wholly; but she understood it better than he supposed or desired, inasmuch as she was convinced that the whole proceeding was an elaborate mystification, addressed to herself and destined to act upon her imagination. He had wanted to do something sudden and arbitrary, something unexpected and refined; to mark the difference between his sympathies and her own, and show that if he regarded his daughter as a precious work of art it was natural he should be more and more careful about the finishing touches. If he wished to be effective he had succeeded; the incident struck a chill into Isabel's heart. Pansy had known the convent in her childhood and had found a happy home there; she was fond of the good sisters, who were very fond of her, and there was therefore for the moment no definite hardship in her lot. But all the same the girl had taken fright; the impression her father desired to make would evidently be sharp enough. The old Protestant tradition had never faded from Isabel's imagination, and as her thoughts attached themselves to this striking example of her husband's genius – she sat looking, like him, at the basket of flowers – poor little Pansy became the heroine of a tragedy. Osmond wished it to be known that he shrank from nothing, and his wife found it hard to pretend to eat her dinner. There was a certain relief presently, in hearing the high, strained voice of her sister-in-law. The Countess too, apparently, had been thinking the thing out, but had arrived at a different conclusion from Isabel.

'It's very absurd, my dear Osmond,' she said, 'to invent so many pretty reasons for poor Pansy's banishment. Why don't you say at once that you want to get her out of my way? Haven't you discovered that I think very well of Mr Rosier? I do indeed; he seems to me *simpaticissimo*. He has made me believe in true love; I never did before! Of course you've made up your mind that with those convictions I'm dreadful company for Pansy.'

Osmond took a sip of a glass of wine; he looked perfectly good-humoured. 'My dear Amy,' he answered, smiling as if he were uttering a piece of gallantry, 'I don't know anything about your convictions, but if I suspected that they interfere with mine it would be much simpler to banish *you*.'

Chapter Fifty-one

The Countess was not banished; but she felt the insecurity of her tenure of her brother's hospitality. A week after this incident Isabel received a telegram from England, dated from Gardencourt and bearing the stamp of Mrs Touchett's authorship. 'Ralph cannot last many days,' it ran, 'and if convenient would like to see you. Wishes me to say that you must come only if you've not other duties. Say, for myself, that you used to talk a good deal about your duty and to wonder what it was; shall be curious to see whether you've found it out. Ralph is really dying, and there's no other company.' Isabel was prepared for this news, having received from Henrietta Stackpole a detailed account of her journey to England with her appreciative patient. Ralph had arrived more dead than alive, but she had managed to convey him to Gardencourt, where he had taken to his bed, which, as Miss Stackpole wrote, he evidently would never leave again. She added that she had really had two patients on her hands instead of one, inasmuch as Mr Goodwood, who had been of no earthly use, was quite as ailing, in a different way, as Mr Touchett. Afterwards she wrote that she had been obliged to surrender the field to Mrs Touchett, who had just returned from America and had promptly given her to understand that she didn't wish any interviewing at Gardencourt. Isabel had written to her aunt shortly after Ralph came to Rome, letting her know of his critical condition and suggesting that she should lose no time in returning to Europe. Mrs Touchett had telegraphed an acknowledgement of this admonition, and the only further news Isabel received from her was the second telegram I have just quoted.

Isabel stood a moment looking at the latter missive; then, thrusting it into her pocket, she went straight to the door of her husband's study. Here she again paused an instant, after which she opened the door and went in. Osmond was seated at the table near the window with a folio volume before him, propped against a pile of books. This volume was open at a page of small coloured plates, and Isabel presently saw that he had been copying from it the drawing of an antique coin. A box of water-colours and fine brushes lay before him, and he had already transferred to a sheet of immaculate paper the delicate, finely tinted disk. His back was turned towards the door, but he recognized his wife without looking round.

'Excuse me for disturbing you,' she said.

'When I come to your room I always knock,' he answered, going on with his work.

'I forgot; I had something else to think of. My cousin's dying.'

'Ah, I don't believe that,' said Osmond, looking at his drawing through a magnifying glass. 'He was dying when we married; he'll outlive us all.'

Isabel gave herself no time, no thought, to appreciate the careful cynicism of this declaration; she simply went on quickly, full of her own intention: 'My aunt has telegraphed for me; I must go to Gardencourt.'

'Why must you go to Gardencourt?' Osmond asked in the tone of impartial curiosity.

'To see Ralph before he dies.'

To this, for some time, he made no rejoinder; he continued to give his chief attention to his work, which was of a sort that would brook no negligence. 'I don't see the need of it,' he said at last. 'He came to see you here. I didn't like that; I thought his being in Rome a great mistake. But I tolerated it because it was to be the last time you should see him. Now you tell me it's not to have been the last. Ah, you're not grateful!'

'What am I to be grateful for?'

Gilbert Osmond laid down his little implements, blew a speck of dust from his drawing, slowly got up, and for the first time looked at his wife. 'For my not having interfered while he was here.'

'Oh yes, I am. I remember perfectly how distinctly you let me know you didn't like it. I was very glad when he went away.'

'Leave him alone then. Don't run after him.'

Isabel turned her eyes away from him; they rested upon his little drawing. 'I must go to England,' she said, with a full consciousness that her tone might strike an irritable man of taste as stupidly obstinate.

'I shall not like it if you do,' Osmond remarked.

'Why should I mind that? You won't like it if I don't. You like nothing I do or don't do. You pretend to think I lie.'

Osmond turned slightly pale; he gave a cold smile. 'That's why you must go then? Not to see your cousin, but to take a revenge on me.'

'I know nothing about revenge.'

'I do,' said Osmond. 'Don't give me an occasion.'

'You're only too eager to take one. You wish immensely that I would commit some folly.'

'I should be gratified in that case if you disobeyed me.'

'If I disobeyed you?' said Isabel in a low tone which had the effect of mildness.

'Let it be clear. If you leave Rome today it will be a piece of the most deliberate, the most calculated, opposition.'

'How can you call it calculated? I received my aunt's telegram but three minutes ago.'

'You calculate rapidly; it's a great accomplishment. I don't see why we should prolong our discussion; you know my wish.' And he stood there as if he expected to see her withdraw.

But she never moved; she couldn't move, strange as it may seem; she still wished to justify herself; he had the power, in an extraordinary degree, of making her feel this need. There was something in her imagination he could always appeal to against her judgement. 'You've no reason for such a wish,' said Isabel, 'and I've every reason for going. I can't tell you how unjust you seem to me. But I think you know. It's your own opposition that's calculated. It's malignant.'

She had never uttered her worst thought to her husband before, and the sensation of hearing it was evidently new to Osmond. But he showed no surprise, and his coolness was apparently a proof that he had believed his wife would in fact be unable to resist for ever his ingenious endeavour to draw her out. 'It's all the more intense then,' he answered. And he added almost as if he were giving her a friendly counsel: 'This is a very important matter.' She recognized that; she was fully conscious of the weight of the occasion; she knew that between them they had arrived at a crisis. Its gravity made her careful; she said nothing, and he went on. 'You say I've no reason? I have the very best. I dislike, from the bottom of my soul, what you intend to do. It's dishonourable; it's indelicate; it's indecent. Your cousin is nothing whatever to me, and I'm under no obligation to make concessions to him. I've already made the very handsomest. Your relations with him, while he was here, kept me on pins and needles; but I let that pass, because from week to week I expected him to go. I've never liked him and he has never liked me. That's why you like him – because he hates me,' said Osmond with a quick, barely audible tremor in his voice. 'I've an ideal of what my wife should do and should not do. She should not travel across Europe alone, in defiance of my deepest desire, to sit at the bedside of other men. Your cousin's nothing to you; he's nothing to us. You smile most expressively when I talk about *us*, but I assure you that *we*, *we*, Mrs Osmond, is all I know. I take our marriage seriously; you appear to have found a way of not doing so. I'm not aware that we're divorced or separated; for me we're indissolubly united. You are nearer to me than any human creature, and I'm nearer to you. It may be a disagreeable proximity; it's one, at any rate of our own deliberate making. You don't like to be reminded of that, I know; but I'm perfectly willing, because – because—' And he paused a moment, looking as if he had something to say which would be very much to the point. 'Because I think we should accept the consequences of our actions, and what I value most in life is the honour of a thing!'

He spoke gravely and almost gently; the accent of sarcasm had dropped out of his tone. It had a gravity which checked his wife's quick emotion; the resolution with which she had entered the room found itself caught in a mesh of fine threads. His last words were not a command, they constituted a kind of appeal; and, though she felt that any expression of respect on his part could only be a refinement of egotism, they represented something transcendent and absolute, like the sign of the cross or the flag of one's country. He spoke in the name of something sacred and precious – the observance of a magnificent form. They were as perfectly apart in feeling as two disillusioned lovers had ever been; but they had never yet separated in act. Isabel had not changed; her old passion for justice still abode within her; and now, in the very thick of her sense of her husband's blasphemous sophistry, it began to throb to a tune which for a moment promised him the victory. It came over her that in his wish to preserve appearances he was after all sincere, and that this, as far as it went, was a merit. Ten minutes before she had felt all the joy of irreflective action – a joy to which she had so long been a stranger; but action had been suddenly changed to slow renunciation, transformed by the blight of Osmond's touch. If she must renounce, however, she would let him know she was a victim rather than a dupe. I know you're a master of the art of mockery,' she said. 'How can you speak of an indissoluble union – how can you speak of your being contented? Where's our union when you accuse me of falsity? Where's your contentment when you have nothing but hideous suspicion in your heart?'

'It is in our living decently together, in spite of such drawbacks.'

'We don't live decently together!' cried Isabel.

'Indeed we don't if you go to England.'

'That's very little; that's nothing. I might do much more.'

He raised his eyebrows and even his shoulders a little: he had lived long enough in Italy to catch this trick. 'Ah, if you've come to threaten me I prefer my drawing.' And he walked back to his table, where he took up the sheet of paper on which he had been working and stood studying it.

'I suppose that if I go you'll not expect me to come back,' said Isabel.

He turned quickly round, and she could see this movement at least was not designed. He looked at her a little and then, 'Are you out of your mind?' he inquired.

'How can it be anything but a rupture?' she went on; 'especially if all you say is true?' She was unable to see how it could be anything but a rupture; she sincerely wished to know what else it might be.

He sat down before his table. 'I really can't argue with you on the hypothesis of your defying me,' he said. And he took up one of his little brushes again.

She lingered but a moment longer; long enough to embrace with her eye his whole deliberately indifferent yet most expressive figure; after which she quickly left the room. Her faculties, her energy, her passion, were all dispersed again; she felt as if a cold, dark mist had suddenly encompassed her. Osmond possessed in a supreme degree the art of eliciting any weakness. On her way back to her room she found the Countess Gemini standing in the open doorway of a little parlour in which a small collection of heterogeneous books had been arranged. The Countess had an open volume in her hand; she appeared to have been glancing down a page which failed to strike her as interesting. At the sound of Isabel's step she raised her head.

'Ah my dear,' she said, 'you, who are so literary, do tell me some amusing book to read! Everything here's of a dreariness – ! Do you think this would do me any good?'

Isabel glanced at the title of the volume she held out, but without reading or understanding it. 'I'm afraid I can't advise you. I've had bad news. My cousin, Ralph Touchett, is dying.'

The Countess threw down her book. 'Ah, he was so *simpatico*. I'm awfully sorry for you.'

'You would be sorrier still if you knew.'

'What is there to know? You look very badly,' the Countess added. 'You must have been with Osmond.'

Half an hour before Isabel would have listened very coldly to an intimation that she should ever feel a desire for the sympathy of her sister-in-law, and there can be no better proof of her present embarrassment than the fact that she almost clutched at this lady's fluttering attention. 'I've been with Osmond,' she said, while the Countess's bright eyes glittered at her.

'I'm sure then he has been odious!' the Countess cried. 'Did he say he was glad poor Mr Touchett's dying?'

'He said it's impossible I should go to England.'

The Countess's mind, when her interests were concerned, was agile; she already foresaw the extinction of any further brightness in her visit to Rome. Ralph Touchett would die. Isabel would go into mourning, and then there would be no more dinner-parties. Such a prospect produced for a moment in her countenance an expressive grimace; but this rapid, picturesque play of feature was her only tribute to disappointment. After all, she reflected, the game was almost played out; she had already overstayed her invitation. And then she cared enough for Isabel's trouble to forget her own, and she saw that Isabel's trouble was deep. It seemed deeper than the mere death of a cousin, and the Countess had no hesitation in connecting her exasperating brother with the expression of her sister-in-law's eyes. Her heart beat with an almost joyous expectation, for if she had wished to see Osmond overtopped the conditions looked favourable now. Of course if Isabel should go to England she herself would immediately leave Palazzo Roccanera; nothing would induce her to remain there with Osmond. Nevertheless she felt an immense desire to hear that Isabel would go to England. 'Nothing's impossible for you, my dear,' she said caressingly. 'Why else are you rich and clever and good?'

'Why indeed? I feel stupidly weak.'

'Why does Osmond say it's impossible?' the Countess asked in a tone which sufficiently declared that she couldn't imagine.

From the moment she thus began to question her, however, Isabel drew back; she disengaged her hand, which the Countess had affectionately taken. But she answered this inquiry with frank bitterness. 'Because we're so happy together that we can't separate even for a fortnight.'

'Ah,' cried the Countess while Isabel turned away, 'When I want to make a journey my husband simply tells me I can have no money!'

Isabel went to her room, where she walked up and down for an hour. It may appear to some readers that she gave herself much trouble, and it is certain that for a woman of a high spirit she had allowed herself easily to be arrested. It seemed to her that only now she fully measured the great undertaking of matrimony. Marriage meant that in such a case as this, when one had to choose, one chose as a matter of course for one's husband. 'I'm afraid – yes, I'm afraid,' she said to herself more than once, stopping short in her walk. But what she was afraid of was not her husband – his displeasure, his hatred, his revenge; it was not even her own later judgement of her conduct – a consideration which had often held her in check; it was simply the violence there would be in going when Osmond wished her to remain. A gulf of difference had opened between them, but nevertheless it was his desire that she should stay, it was a horror to him that she should go. She knew the nervous fineness with which he could feel an objection. What he thought of her she knew, what he was capable of saying to her she had felt; yet they were married, for all that, and marriage meant that a woman should cleave to the man with whom, uttering tremendous vows, she had stood at the altar. She sank down on her sofa at last and buried her head in a pile of cushions.

When she raised her head again the Countess Gemini hovered before her. She had come in all unperceived; she had a strange smile on her thin lips and her whole face had grown in an hour a shining intimation. She lived assuredly, it might be said, at the window of her spirit, but now she was leaning far out. 'I knocked,' she began, 'but you didn't answer me. So I ventured in. I've been looking at you for the last five minutes. You're very unhappy.'

'Yes; but I don't think you can comfort me.'

'Will you give me leave to try?' And the Countess sat down on the sofa beside her. She continued to smile, and there was something communicative and exultant in her expression. She appeared to have a deal to say, and it occurred to Isabel for the first time that her sister-in-law might say something really human. She made play with her glittering eyes, in which there was an unpleasant fascination. 'After all,' she soon resumed, 'I must tell you, to begin with, that I don't understand your state of mind. You seem to have so many scruples, so many reasons, so many ties. When I discovered, ten years ago, that my husband's dearest wish was to make me miserable – of late he has simply let me alone – ah, it was a wonderful simplification! My poor Isabel, you're not simple enough.'

'There's something I want you to know,' the Countess declared – 'because I think you ought to know it. Perhaps you do; perhaps you've guessed it. But if you have, all I can say is that I understand still less why you shouldn't do as you like.'

'What do you wish me to know?' Isabel felt a foreboding that made her heart beat faster. The Countess was about to justify herself, and this alone was portentous.

But she was nevertheless disposed to play a little with her subject. 'In your place I should have guessed it ages ago. Have you never really suspected?'

'I've guessed nothing. What should I have suspected? I don't know what you mean.'

'That's because you've such a beastly pure mind. I never saw a woman with such a pure mind!' cried the Countess.

Isabel slowly got up. 'You're going to tell me something horrible.'

'You can call it by whatever name you will!' And the Countess rose also, while her gathered perversity grew vivid and dreadful. She stood a moment in a sort of glare of intention and, as seemed to Isabel even then, of ugliness; after which she said: 'My first sister-in-law had no children.'

Isabel stared back at her; the announcement was an anticlimax. 'Your first sister-in-law?'

'I suppose you know at least, if one may mention it, that Osmond has been married before! I've never spoken to you of his wife; I thought it mightn't be decent or respectful. But others, less particular, must have done so. The poor little woman lived hardly three years and died childless. It wasn't till after her death that Pansy arrived.'

Isabel's brow had contracted to a frown; her lips were parted in pale, vague wonder. She was trying to follow; there seemed so much more to follow than she could see. 'Pansy's not my husband's child then?'

'Your husband's – in perfection! But no one else's husband's. Someone else's wife's. Ah, my good Isabel,' cried the Countess, 'with you one must dot one's i's!'

'I don't understand. Whose wife's?' Isabel asked.

'The wife of a horrid little Swiss who died – how long? – a dozen, more than fifteen, years ago. He never recognized Miss Pansy, nor, knowing what he was about, would have anything to say to her; and there was no reason why he should. Osmond did, and that was better; though he had to fit on afterwards the whole rigmarole of his own wife's having died in childbirth, and of his having, in grief and horror, banished the little girl from his sight for as long as possible before taking her home from nurse. His wife had really died, you know, of quite another matter and in quite another place: in the Piedmontese mountains, where they had gone, one August, because her health appeared to require the air, but where she was suddenly taken worse – fatally ill. The story passed, sufficiently; it was covered by the appearances so long as nobody heeded, as nobody cared to look into it. But of course *I* knew – without researches,' the Countess lucidly proceeded; 'as also, you'll understand, without a word said between us – I mean between Osmond and me. Don't you see him looking at me, in silence, that way, to settle it? – that is to settle *me* if I should say anything. I said nothing, right or left – never a word to a creature, if you can believe that of me: on my honour, my dear, I speak of the thing to you now, after all this time, as I've never, never spoken. It was to be enough for me, from the first, that the child was my niece – from the moment she was my brother's daughter. As for her veritable mother – !' But with this Pansy's wonderful aunt dropped – as, involuntarily, from the impression of her sister-in-law's face, out of which more eyes might have seemed to look at her than she had ever had to meet.

She had spoken no name, yet Isabel could but check, on her own lips, an echo of the unspoken. She sank to her seat again, hanging her head. 'Why have you told me this?' she asked in a voice the Countess hardly recognized.

'Because I've been so bored with your not knowing. I've been bored, frankly, my dear, with not having told you as if, stupidly, all this time I couldn't have managed! *Ça me dépasse*, if you don't mind my saying so, the things, all round you, that you've appeared to succeed in not knowing. It's a sort of assistance – aid to innocent ignorance – that I've always been a bad hand at rendering; and in this connexion, that of keeping quiet for my brother, my virtue has at any rate finally found itself exhausted. It's not a black lie, moreover, you know,' the Countess inimitably added. 'The facts are exactly what I tell you.'

'I had no idea,' said Isabel presently; and looked up at her in a manner that doubtless matched the apparent witlessness of this confession.

'So I believed – though it was hard to believe. Had it never occurred to you that he was for six or seven years her lover?'

'I don't know. Things *have* occurred to me, and perhaps that was what they all meant.'

'She has been wonderfully clever, she has been magnificent, about Pansy!' the Countess, before all this view of it, cried.

'Oh, no idea, for me,' Isabel went on 'ever *definitely* took that form.' She appeared to be making out to herself what had been and what hadn't. 'And as it is – I don't understand.'

She spoke as one troubled and puzzled, yet the poor Countess seemed to have seen her revelation fall below its possibilities of effect. She had expected to kindle some responsive blaze, but had barely extracted a spark. Isabel showed as scarce more impressed than she might have been, as a young woman of approved imagination, with some fine sinister passage of public history. 'Don't you recognize how the child could never pass for *her* husband's? – that is with M. Merle himself,' her companion resumed. 'They had been separated too long for that, and he had gone to some far country – I think to South America. If she had ever had children – which I'm not sure of – she had lost them. The conditions happened to make it workable, under stress (I mean at so awkward a pinch), that Osmond should acknowledge the little girl. His wife was dead – very true; but she had not been dead too long to put a certain accommodation of dates out of the question – from the moment, I mean, that suspicion wasn't started; which was what they had to take care of. What was more natural than that poor Mrs Osmond, at a distance and for a world not troubling about trifles, should have left behind her, *poverina*, the pledge of her brief happiness that had cost her her life? With the aid of a change of residence – Osmond had been living with her at Naples at the time of their stay in the Alps, and he in due course left it for ever – the whole history was successfully set going. My poor sister-in-law, in her grave, couldn't help herself, and the real mother, to save *her* skin, renounced all visible property in the child.'

'Ah, poor, poor woman!' cried Isabel, who herewith burst into tears. It was a long time since she had shed any: she had suffered a high reaction from weeping. But now they flowed with an abundance in which the Countess Gemini found only another discomfiture.

'It's very kind of you to pity her!' she discordantly laughed. 'Yes indeed, you have a way of your own—!'

'He must have been false to his wife – and so very soon!' said Isabel with a sudden check.

'That's all that's wanting – that you should take up *her* cause!' the Countess went on. 'I quite agree with you, however, that it was much too soon.'

'But to me, to me—?' And Isabel hesitated as if she had not heard; as if her question – though it was sufficiently there in her eyes – were all for herself.

'To you he has been faithful. When he married you he was no longer the lover of another woman – *such* a lover as he had been, *cara mia*, between their risks and their precautions, while the thing lasted! That state of affairs had passed away; the lady had repented, or at all events, for reasons of her own, drawn back: she had always had too, a worship of appearances so intense that even Osmond himself had got bored with it. You may therefore imagine what it was – when he couldn't patch it on conveniently to *any* of those he goes in for! But the whole past was between them.'

'Yes,' Isabel mechanically echoed, 'the whole past is between them.'

'Ah, this later past is nothing. But for six or seven years, as I say, they had kept it up.'

She was silent a little. 'Why then did she want him to marry me?'

'Ah my dear, that's her superiority! Because you had money; and because she believed you would be good to Pansy.'

'Poor woman – and Pansy who doesn't like her!' cried Isabel.

'That's the reason she wanted someone whom Pansy would like. She knows it; she knows everything.'

'Will she know that you've told me this?'

'That will depend upon whether you tell her. She's prepared for it, and do you know what she counts upon for her defence? On your believing that I lie. Perhaps you do; don't make yourself uncomfortable to hide it. Only, as it happens this time, I don't. I've told plenty of little idiotic fibs, but they've never hurt anyone but myself.'

Isabel sat staring at her companion's story as at a bale of fantastic wares some strolling gypsy might have unpacked on the carpet at her feet. 'Why did Osmond never marry her?' she finally asked.

'Because she had no money.' The Countess had an answer for everything, and if she lied she lied well. 'No one knows, no one has ever known, what she lives on, or how she has got all those beautiful things. I don't believe Osmond himself knows. Besides, she wouldn't have married him.'

'How can she have loved him then?'

'She doesn't love him in that way. She did at first, and then, I suppose, she would have married him; but at that time her husband was living. By the time M. Merle had rejoined – I won't say his ancestors, because he never had any – her relations with Osmond had changed, and she had grown more ambitious. Besides, she has never had, about him,' the Countess went on, leaving Isabel to wince for it so tragically afterwards – 'she *had* never had, what you might call any illusions of *intelligence*. She hoped she might marry a great man; that has always been her idea. She has waited and watched and plotted and prayed; but she has never succeeded. I don't know what she may accomplish yet, but at present she has very little to show. The only tangible result she has ever achieved – except, of course, getting to know everyone and staying with them free of expense – has been her bringing you and Osmond together. Oh, she did that, my dear; you needn't look as if you doubted it. I've watched them for years; I know everything – everything. I'm thought a great scatterbrain, but I've had enough application of mind to follow up those two. She hates me, and her way of showing it is to pretend to be for ever defending me. When people say I've had fifteen lovers she looks horrified and declares that quite half of them were never proved. She has been afraid of me for years, and she has taken great comfort in the vile, false things people have said about me. She has been afraid I'd expose her, and she threatened me one day when Osmond began to pay his court to you. It was at his house in Florence; do you remember that afternoon when she brought you there and we had tea in the garden? She let me know then that if I should tell tales two could play at that game. She pretends there's a good deal more to tell about me than about her. It would be an interesting comparison! I don't care a fig what she may say, simply because I know *you* don't care a fig. You can't trouble your head about me less than you do already. So she may take her revenge as she chooses; I don't think she'll frighten you very much. Her great idea has been to be tremendously irreproachable – a kind of full-blown lily – the incarnation of propriety. She has always worshipped that god. There should be no scandal about Caesar's wife, you know; and, as I say, she has always hoped to marry Caesar. That was one reason she wouldn't marry Osmond; the fear that on seeing her with Pansy people would put things together – would even see a resemblance. She has had a terror lest the mother should betray herself. She has been awfully careful; the mother has never done so.'

'Yes, yes, the mother has done so,' said Isabel, who had listened to all this with a face more and more wan. 'She betrayed herself to me the other day, though I didn't recognize her. There appeared to have been a chance of Pansy's making a great marriage, and in her disappointment at its not coming off she almost dropped the mask.'

'Ah, that's where she'd dish herself!' cried the Countess. 'She has failed so dreadfully that she's determined her daughter shall make it up.'

Isabel started at the words 'her daughter', which her guest threw off so familiarly. 'It seems very wonderful,' she murmured; and in this bewildering impression she had almost lost her sense of being personally touched by the story.

'Now don't go and turn against the poor innocent child!' the Countess went on. 'She's very nice, in spite of her deplorable origin. I myself have liked Pansy; not, naturally, because she was *hers*, but because she had become yours.'

'Yes, she has become mine. And how the poor woman must have suffered at seeing me—!' Isabel exclaimed while she flushed at the thought.

'I don't believe she has suffered; on the contrary, she has enjoyed. Osmond's marriage has given his daughter a great little lift. Before that she lived in a hole. And do you know what the mother thought? That you might take such a fancy to the child that you'd do something for her. Osmond of course could never give her a portion. Osmond was really extremely poor; but of course you know all about that. Ah, my dear,' cried the Countess, 'why did you ever inherit money?' She stopped a moment as if she saw something singular in Isabel's face. 'Don't tell me now that you'll give her a *dot*. You're capable of that, but I would refuse to believe it. Don't try to be too good. Be a little easy and natural and nasty; feel a little wicked, for the comfort of it, once in your life!'

'It's very strange. I suppose I ought to know, but I'm sorry,' Isabel said. 'I'm much obliged to you.'

'Yes, you seem to be!' cried the Countess with a mocking laugh. 'Perhaps you are – perhaps you're not. You don't take it as I should have thought.'

'How should I take it?' Isabel asked.

'Well, I should say as a woman who has been made use of.' Isabel made no answer to this; she only listened, and the Countess went on. 'They've always been bound to each other; they remained so even after she broke off – or *he* did. But he has always been more for her than she has been for him. When their little carnival was over they made a bargain that each should give the other complete liberty, but that each should also do everything possible to help the other on. You may ask me how I know such a thing as that. I know it by the way they've behaved. Now see how much better women are than men! She has found a wife for Osmond, but Osmond has never lifted a little finger for *her*. She has worked for him, plotted for him, suffered for him; she has even more than once found money for him; and the end of it is that he's tired of her. She's an old habit; there are moments when he needs her, but on the whole he wouldn't miss her if she were removed.

And, what's more, today she knows it. So you needn't be jealous!' the Countess added humorously.

Isabel rose from her sofa again; she felt bruised and scant of breath; her head was humming with new knowledge. 'I'm much obliged to you,' she repeated. And then she added abruptly, in quite a different tone: 'How do you know all this?'

This inquiry appeared to ruffle the Countess more than Isabel's expression of gratitude pleased her. She gave her companion a bold stare, with which, 'Let us assume that I've invented it!' she cried. She too, however, suddenly changed her tone and, laying her hand on Isabel's arm, said with the penetration of her sharp bright smile: 'Now will you give up your journey?'

Isabel started a little; she turned away. But she felt weak and in a moment had to lay her arm upon the mantelshelf for support. She stood a minute so, and then upon her arm she dropped her dizzy head, with closed eyes and pale lips.

'I've done wrong to speak – I've made you ill!' the Countess cried.

'Ah, I must see Ralph!' Isabel wailed; not in resentment, not in the quick passion her companion had looked for; but in a tone of far-reaching, infinite sadness.

Chapter Fifty-two

There was a train for Turin and Paris that evening; and after the Countess had left her Isabel had a rapid and decisive conference with her maid, who was discreet, devoted, and active. After this she thought (except of her journey) only of one thing. She must go and see Pansy; from her she couldn't turn away. She had not seen her yet, as Osmond had given her to understand that it was too soon to begin. She drove at five o'clock to a high door in a narrow street in the quarter of the Piazza Navona, and was admitted by the portress of the convent, a genial and obsequious person. Isabel had been at this institution before; she had come with Pansy to see the sisters. She knew they were good women, and she saw that the large rooms were clean and cheerful and that the well-used garden had sun for winter and shade for spring. But she disliked the place, which affronted and almost frightened her; not for the world would she have spent a night there. It produced today more than before the impression of a well-appointed prison; for it was not possible to pretend Pansy was free to leave it. This innocent creature had been presented to her in a new and violent light, but the secondary effect of the revelation was to make her reach out a hand.

The portress left her to wait in the parlour of the convent while she went to make it known that there was a visitor for the dear young lady. The parlour was a vast, cold apartment, with new-looking furniture; a large clean stove of white porcelain, unlighted, a collection of wax flowers under glass and a series of engravings from religious pictures on the walls. On the other occasion Isabel had thought it less like Rome than like Philadelphia, but today she made no reflections; the apartment only seemed to her very empty and very soundless. The portress returned at the end of some five minutes, ushering in another person. Isabel got up, expecting to see one of the ladies of the sisterhood, but to her extreme surprise found herself confronted with Madame Merle. The effect was strange, for Madame Merle was already so present to her vision that her appearance in the flesh was like suddenly, and rather awfully, seeing a painted picture move. Isabel had been thinking all day of her falsity, her audacity, her ability, her probable suffering; and these dark things seemed to flash with a sudden light as she entered the room. Her being there at all had the character of ugly evidence, of handwritings, of profaned relics, of grim things produced in court. It made Isabel feel faint; if it had been necessary to speak on the spot she would have been quite unable. But no such necessity was distinct to her; it seemed to her indeed that she had absolutely nothing to say to Madame Merle. In one's relations with this lady, however, there were never any absolute necessities; she had a manner which carried off not only her own deficiencies but those of other people. But she was different from usual; she came in slowly, behind the portress, and Isabel instantly perceived that she was not likely to depend upon her habitual resources. For her too the occasion was exceptional, and she had undertaken to treat it by the light of the moment. This gave her a peculiar gravity; she pretended not even to smile, and though Isabel saw that she was more than ever playing a part it seemed to her that on the whole the wonderful woman had never been so natural. She looked at her young friend from head to foot, but not harshly nor defiantly; with a cold gentleness rather, and an absence of any air of allusion to their last meeting. It was as if she had wished to mark a distinction. She had been irritated then, she was reconciled now.

'You can leave us alone,' she said to the portress; 'in five minutes this lady will ring for you.' And then she turned to Isabel, who, after noting what has just been mentioned, had ceased to notice and had let her eyes wander as far as the limits of the room would allow. She wished never to look at Madame Merle again. 'You're surprised to find me here, and I'm afraid you're not pleased,' this lady went on. 'You don't see why I should have come; it's as if I had anticipated you. I confess I've been rather indiscreet – I ought to have asked your permission.' There was none of the oblique movement of irony in this; it was said simply and mildly; but Isabel, far afloat on a sea of wonder and pain, could not have told herself with what intention it was uttered. 'But I've not been sitting long,' Madame Merle continued; 'that is I've not been long with Pansy. I came to see her because it occurred to me this afternoon that she must be rather lonely and perhaps even a little miserable. It may be good for a small girl; I know so little about small girls; I can't tell. At any rate it's a little dismal. Therefore I came – on the chance. I knew of course that you'd come, and her father as well; still, I had not been told other visitors were forbidden. The good woman – what's her name? Madame Catherine – made no objection whatever. I stayed twenty minutes with Pansy; she has a charming little room, not in the least conventual, with a piano and flowers. She has arranged it delightfully; she has so much taste. Of course it's all none of my business, but I feel happier since I've seen her. She may even have a maid if she likes; but of course she has no occasion to dress. She wears a little black frock; she looks so charming. I went afterwards to see Mother Catherine, who has a very good room too; I assure you I don't find the poor sisters at all monastic. Mother Catherine has a most coquettish little toilet-table, with something that looked uncommonly like a bottle of eau-de-Cologne. She speaks delightfully of Pansy; says it's a great happiness for them to have her. She's a little saint of heaven and a model to the oldest of them. Just as I was leaving Madame Catherine the portress came to say to her that there was a lady for the signorina. Of course I knew it must be you, and I asked her to let me go and receive you in her place. She demurred greatly – I must tell you that – and said it was her duty to notify the Mother Superior: it was of such high importance that you should be treated with respect. I requested her to let the Mother Superior alone and asked her how she supposed I would treat you!'

So Madame Merle went on, with much of the brilliancy of a woman who had long been a mistress of the art of conversation. But there were phases and gradations in her speech, not one of which was lost upon Isabel's ear, though her eyes were absent from her companion's face. She had not proceeded far before Isabel noted a sudden break in her voice, a lapse in her continuity, which was in itself a complete drama. This subtle modulation marked a momentous discovery – the perception of an entirely new attitude on the part of her listener. Madame Merle had guessed in the space of an instant that everything was at an end between them, and in the space of another instant she had guessed the reason why. The person who stood there was not the same one she had seen hitherto, but was a very different person – a person who knew her secret. This discovery was tremendous, and from the moment she made it the most accomplished of women faltered and lost her courage. But only for that moment. Then the conscious stream of her perfect manner gathered itself again and flowed on as smoothly as might be to the end. But it was only because she had the end in view that she was able to proceed. She had been touched with a point that made her quiver, and she needed all the alertness of her will to repress her agitation. Her only safety was in her not betraying herself. She resisted this, but the startled quality of her voice refused to improve – she couldn't help it – while she heard herself say she hardly knew what. The tide of her confidence ebbed, and she was able only just to glide into port, faintly grazing the bottom.

Isabel saw it all as distinctly as if it had been reflected in a large clear glass. It might have been a great moment for her, for it might have been a moment of triumph. That Madame Merle had lost her pluck and saw before her the phantom of exposure – this in itself was a revenge, this in itself was almost the promise of a brighter day. And for a moment during which she stood apparently looking out of the window, with her back half-turned, Isabel enjoyed that knowledge. On the other side of the window lay the garden of the convent; but this is not what she saw; she saw nothing of the budding plants and the glowing afternoon. She saw, in the crude light of that revelation which had already become a part of experience and to which the very frailty of the vessel in which it had been offered her only gave an intrinsic price, the dry staring fact that she had been an applied handled hung-up tool, as senseless and convenient as mere shaped wood and iron. All the bitterness of this knowledge surged into her soul again; it was as if she felt on her lips the taste of dishonour. There was a moment during which, if she had turned and spoken, she would have said something that would hiss like a lash. But she closed her eyes, and then the hideous vision dropped. What remained was the cleverest woman in the world standing there within a few feet of her and knowing as little what to think as the meanest. Isabel's only revenge was to be silent still – to leave Madame Merle in this unprecedented situation. She left her there for a period that must have seemed long to this lady, who at last seated herself with a movement which was in itself a confession of helplessness. Then Isabel turned slow eyes, looking down at her. Madame Merle was very pale; her own eyes covered Isabel's face. She might see what she would, but her danger was over. Isabel would never accuse her, never reproach her; perhaps because she never would give her the opportunity to defend herself.

'I'm come to bid Pansy good-bye,' our young woman said at last. 'I go to England tonight.'

'Go to England tonight!' Madame Merle repeated sitting there and looking up at her.

'I'm going to Gardencourt. Ralph Touchett's dying.'

'Ah, you'll feel that.' Madame Merle recovered herself; she had a chance to express sympathy. 'Do you go alone?'

'Yes; without my husband.'

Madame Merle gave a low vague murmur; a sort of recognition of the general sadness of things. 'Mr Touchett never liked me, but I'm sorry he's dying. Shall you see his mother?'

'Yes; she has returned from America.'

'She used to be very kind to me; but she has changed. Others too have changed,' said Madame Merle with a quiet noble pathos. She paused a moment, then added: 'And you'll see dear old Gardencourt again!'

'I shall not enjoy it much,' Isabel answered.

'Naturally – in your grief. But it's on the whole, of all the houses I know, and I know many, the one I should have liked best to live in. I don't venture to send a message to the people,' Madame Merle added; 'but I should like to give my love to the place.'

Isabel turned away, 'I had better go to Pansy. I've not much time.'

While she looked about her for the proper egress, the door opened and admitted one of the ladies of the house, who advanced with a discreet smile, gently rubbing under her long loose sleeves, a pair of plump white hands. Isabel recognized Madame Catherine, whose acquaintance she had already made, and begged that she would immediately let her see Miss Osmond. Madame Catherine looked doubly discreet, but smiled very blandly and said: 'It will be good for her to see you. I'll take you to her myself.' Then she directed her pleased guarded vision to Madame Merle.

'Will you let me remain a little?' this lady asked. 'It's so good to be here.'

'You may remain always if you like!' And the good sister gave a knowing laugh.

She led Isabel out of the room, through several corridors, and up a long staircase. All these departments were solid and bare, light and clean; so, thought Isabel, are the great penal establishments. Madame Catherine gently pushed open the door of Pansy's room and ushered in the visitor; then stood smiling with folded hands while the two others met and embraced.

'She's glad to see you,' she repeated; 'it will do her good.' And she placed the best chair carefully for Isabel. But she made no movement to seat herself; she seemed ready to retire. 'How does this dear child look?' she asked of Isabel, lingering a moment.

'She looks paled,' Isabel answered.

'That's the pleasure of seeing you. She's very happy. *Elle éclaire la maison*,' said the good sister.

Pansy wore, as Madame Merle had said, a little black dress; it was perhaps this that made her look pale. 'They're very good to me – they think of everything!' she exclaimed with all her customary eagerness to accommodate.

'We think of you always – you're a precious charge,' Madame Catherine remarked in the tone of a woman with whom benevolence was a habit and whose conception of duty was the acceptance of every care. It fell with a leaden weight on Isabel's ears; it seemed to represent the surrender of a personality, the authority of the Church.

When Madame Catherine had left them together Pansy kneeled down and hid her head in her stepmother's lap. So she remained some moments, while Isabel gently stroked her hair. Then she got up, averting her face and looking about the room. 'Don't you think I've arranged it well? I've everything I have at home.'

'It's very pretty; you're very comfortable,' Isabel scarcely knew what she could say to her. On the one hand she couldn't let her think she had come to pity her, and on the other it would be a dull mockery to pretend to rejoice with her. So she simply added after a moment: 'I've come to bid you good-bye. I'm going to England.'

Pansy's white little face turned red. 'To England! Not to come back?'

'I don't know when I shall come back.'

'Ah, I'm sorry,' Pansy breathed with faintness. She spoke as if she had no right to criticize; but her tone expressed a depth of disappointment.

'My cousin, Mr Touchett, is very ill; he'll probably die. I wish to see him,' Isabel said.

'Ah yes; you told me he would die. Of course you must go. And will papa go?'

'No; I shall go alone.'

For a moment the girl said nothing. Isabel had often wondered what she thought of the apparent relations of her father with his wife; but never by a glance, by an intimation, had she let it be seen that she deemed them deficient in an air of intimacy. She made her reflections, Isabel was sure; and she must have had a conviction that there were husbands and wives who were more intimate than that. But Pansy was not indiscreet even in thought; she would as little have ventured to judge her gentle stepmother as to criticize her magnificent father. Her heart may have stood almost as still as it would have done had she seen two of the saints in the great picture in the convent-chapel turn their painted heads and shake them at each other. But as in this latter case she would (for very solemnity's sake) never have mentioned the awful phenomenon, so she put away all knowledge of the secrets of larger lives than her own. 'You'll be very far away,' she presently went on.

'Yes; I shall be far away. But it will scarcely matter,' Isabel explained; 'since so long as you're here I can't be called near you.'

'Yes, but you can come and see me; though you've not come very often.'

'I've not come because your father forbade it. Today I bring nothing with me. I can't amuse you.'

'I'm not to be amused. That's not what papa wishes.'

'Then it hardly matters whether I'm in Rome or in England.'

'You're not happy, Mrs Osmond,' said Pansy.

'Not very. But it doesn't matter.'

'That's what I say to myself. What does it matter? But I should like to come out.'

'I wish indeed you might.'

'Don't leave me here,' Pansy went on gently.

Isabel said nothing for a minute; her heart beat fast. 'Will you come away with me now?' she asked.

Pansy looked at her pleadingly. 'Did papa tell you to bring me?'

'No; it's my own proposal.'

'I think I had better wait then. Did papa send me no message?'

'I don't think he knew I was coming.'

'He thinks I've not had enough,' said Pansy. 'But I have. The ladies are very kind to me and the little girls come to see me. There are some very little ones – such charming children. Then my room – you can see for yourself. All that's very delightful. But I've had enough. Papa wished me to think a little – and I've thought a great deal.'

'What have you thought?'

'Well, that I must never displease papa.'

'You knew that before.'

'Yes; but I know it better. I'll do anything – I'll do anything,' said Pansy. Then, as she heard her own words, a deep, pure blush came into her face. Isabel read the meaning of it; she saw the poor girl had been vanquished. It was well that Mr Edward Rosier had kept his enamels! Isabel looked into her eyes and saw there mainly a prayer to be treated easily. She laid her hand on Pansy's as if to let her know that her look conveyed no diminution of esteem; for the collapse of the girl's momentary resistance (mute and modest though it had been) seemed only her tribute to the truth of things. She didn't presume to judge others, but she had judged herself; she had seen the reality. She had no vocation for struggling with combinations; in the solemnity of sequestration there was something that overwhelmed her. She bowed her pretty head to authority and only asked of authority to be merciful. Yes, it was very well that Edward Rosier had reserved a few articles!

Isabel got up; her time was rapidly shortening. 'Good-bye then. I leave Rome tonight.'

Pansy took hold of her dress; there was a sudden change in the child's face. 'You look strange; you frighten me.'

'Oh, I'm harmless,' said Isabel.

'Perhaps you won't come back?'

'Perhaps not. I can't tell.'

'Ah, Mrs Osmond, you won't leave me!'

Isabel now saw she had guessed everything. 'My dear child, what can I do for you?' she asked.

'I don't know – but I'm happier when I think of you.'

'You can always think of me.'

'Not when you're so far. I'm a little afraid,' said Pansy.

'What are you afraid of?'

'Of papa – a little. And of Madame Merle. She has just been to see me.'

'You must not say that,' Isabel observed.

'Oh, I'll do everything they want. Only if you're here I shall do it more easily.'

Isabel considered. 'I won't desert you,' she said at last. 'Good-bye, my child.'

Then they held each other a moment in a silent embrace, like two sisters; and afterwards Pansy walked along the corridor with her visitor to the top of the staircase. 'Madame Merle has been here,' she remarked as they went; and as Isabel answered nothing she added abruptly: 'I don't like Madame Merle!'

Isabel hesitated, then stopped. 'You must never say that – that you don't like Madame Merle.'

Pansy looked at her in wonder; but wonder with Pansy had never been a reason for non-compliance. 'I never will again,' she said with exquisite gentleness. At the top of the staircase they had to separate, as it appeared to be part of the mild but very definite discipline under which Pansy lived that she should not go down. Isabel descended, and when she reached the bottom the girl was standing above. 'You'll come back?' she called out in a voice that Isabel remembered afterwards.

'Yes – I'll come back.'

Madame Catherine met Mrs Osmond below and conducted her to the door of the parlour, outside of which the two stood talking a minute. 'I won't go in,' said the good sister. 'Madame Merle's waiting for you.'

At this announcement Isabel stiffened; she was on the point of asking if there were no other egress from the convent. But a moment's reflection assured her that she would do well not to betray to the worthy nun her desire to avoid Pansy's other friend. Her companion grasped her arm very gently and, fixing her a moment with wise, benevolent eyes, said in French and almost familiarly: '*Eh bien, chère Madame, qu'en pensez-vous*?'

'About my stepdaughter? Oh, it would take long to tell you.'

'We think it's enough,' Madame Catherine distinctly observed. And she pushed open the door of the parlour.

Madame Merle was sitting just as Isabel had left her, like a woman so absorbed in thought that she had not moved a little finger. As Madame Catherine closed the door she got up, and Isabel saw that she had been thinking to some purpose. She had recovered her balance; she was in full possession of her resources. 'I found I wished to wait for you,' she said urbanely. 'But it's not to talk about Pansy.'

Isabel wondered what it could be to talk about, and in spite of Madame Merle's declaration she answered after a moment: 'Madame Catherine says it's enough.'

'Yes; it also seems to me enough. I wanted to ask you another word about poor Mr Touchett,' Madame Merle added. 'Have you reason to believe that he's really at his last?'

'I've no information but a telegram. Unfortunately it only confirms a probability.'

'I'm going to ask you a strange question,' said Madame Merle. 'Are you very fond of your cousin?' And she gave a smile as strange as her utterance.

'Yes, I'm very fond of him. But I don't understand you.'

She just hung fire. 'It's rather hard to explain. Something has occurred to me which may not have occurred to you, and I give you the benefit of my idea. Your cousin did you once a great service. Have you never guessed it?'

'He has done me many services.'

'Yes; but one was much above the rest. He made you a rich woman.'

'*He* made me—?'

Madame Merle appearing to see herself successful, she went on more triumphantly: 'He imparted to you that extra lustre which was required to make you a brilliant match. At bottom it's him you've to thank.' She stopped; there was something in Isabel's eyes.

'I don't understand you. It was my uncle's money.'

'Yes; it was you uncle's money, but it was your cousin's idea. He brought his father over to it. Ah, my dear, the sum was large!'

Isabel stood staring; she seemed today to live in a world illuminated by lurid flashes. 'I don't know why you say such things. I don't know what you know.'

'I know nothing but what I've guessed. But I've guessed that.'

Isabel went to the door and, when she had opened it, stood a moment with her hand on the latch. Then she said – it was her only revenge: 'I believed it was you I had to thank!'

Madame Merle dropped her eyes; she stood there in a kind of proud penance. 'You're very unhappy, I know. But I'm more so.'

'Yes; I can believe that. I think I should like never to see you again.'

Madame Merle raised her eyes. 'I shall go to America,' she quietly remarked while Isabel passed out.

Chapter Fifty-three

It was not with surprise, it was with a feeling which in other circumstances would have had much of the effect of joy, that as Isabel descended from the Paris Mail at Charing Cross she stepped into the arms, as it were – or at any rate into the hands – of Henrietta Stackpole. She had telegraphed to her friend from Turin, and though she had not definitely said to herself that Henrietta would meet her, she had felt her telegram would produce some helpful result. On her long journey from Rome her mind had been given up to vagueness; she was unable to question the future. She performed this journey with sightless eyes and took little pleasure in the countries she traversed, decked out though they were in the richest freshness of spring. Her thoughts followed their course through other countries – strange-looking, dimly lighted, pathless lands, in which there was no change of seasons, but only, as it seemed, a perpetual dreariness of winter. She had plenty to think about; but it was neither reflection nor conscious purpose that filled her mind. Disconnected visions passed through it, and sudden dull gleams of memory, of expectation. The past and the future came and went at their will, but she saw them only in fitful images, which rose and fell by a logic of their own. It was extraordinary the things she remembered. Now that she was in the secret, now that she knew something that so much concerned her and the eclipse of which had made life resemble an attempt to play whist with an imperfect pack of cards, the truth of things, their mutual relations, their meaning, and for the most part their horror, rose before her with a kind of architectural vastness. She remembered a thousand trifles; they started to life with the spontaneity of a shiver. She had thought them trifles at the time; now she saw that they had been weighted with lead. Yet even now they were trifles after all, for what use was it to her to understand them? Nothing seemed of use to her today. All purpose, all intention, was suspended; all desire too save the single desire to reach her much-embracing refuge. Gardencourt had been her starting-point, and to those muffled chambers it was at least a temporary solution to return. She had gone forth in her strength; she would come back in her weakness, and if the place had been a rest to her before, it would be a sanctuary now. She envied Ralph his dying, for if one were thinking of rest that was the most perfect of all. To cease utterly, to give it all up and not know anything more – this idea was as sweet as the vision of a cool bath in a marble tank, in a darkened chamber, in a hot land.

She had moments indeed in her journey from Rome which were almost as good as being dead. She sat in her corner, so motionless, so passive, simply with the sense of being carried, so detached from hope and regret, that she recalled to herself one of those Etruscan figures couched upon the receptacle of their ashes. There was nothing to regret now – that was all over. Not only the time of her folly, but the time of her repentance was far. The only thing to regret was that Madame Merle had been so – well, so unimaginable. Just here her intelligence dropped, from literal inability to say what it was that Madame Merle had been. Whatever it was it was for Madame Merle herself to regret it; and doubtless she would do so in America, where she had announced she was going. It concerned Isabel no more; she only had an impression that she should never again see Madame Merle. This impression carried her into the future, of which from time to time she had a mutilated glimpse. She saw herself, in the distant years, still in the attitude of a woman who had her life to live, and these intimations contradicted the spirit of the present hour. It might be desirable to get quite away, really away, farther away than little grey-green England, but this privilege was evidently to be denied her. Deep in her soul – deeper than any appetite for renunciation – was the sense that life would be her business for a long time to come. And at moments there was something inspiring, almost enlivening, in the conviction. It was a proof of strength – it was a proof she should some day be happy again. It couldn't be she was to live only to suffer; she was still young, after all, and a great many things might happen to her yet. To live only to suffer – only to feel the injury of life repeated and enlarged – it seemed to her she was too valuable, too capable, for that. Then she wondered if it were vain and stupid to think so well of herself? Wasn't all history full of the destruction of precious things? Wasn't it much more probable that if one were fine one would suffer? It involved then perhaps an admission that one had a certain grossness; but Isabel recognized, as it passed before her eyes, the quick vague shadow of a long future. She should never escape; she should last to the end. Then the middle years wrapped her about again and the grey curtain of her indifference closed her in.

Henrietta kissed her, as Henrietta usually kissed, as if she were afraid she should be caught doing it; and then Isabel stood there in the crowd, looking about her, looking for her servant. She asked nothing; she wished to wait. She had a sudden perception that she should be helped. She rejoiced Henrietta had come; there was something terrible in an arrival in London. The dusky, smoky, far-arching vault of the station, the strange, livid light, the dense, dark, pushing crowd, filled her with a nervous fear and made her put her arm into her friend's. She remembered she had once liked these things; they seemed part of a mighty spectacle in which there was something that touched her. She remembered how she walked away from Euston, in the winter dusk, in the crowded streets, five years before. She could not have done that today, and the incident came before her as the deed of another person.

'It's too beautiful that you should have come,' said Henrietta, looking at her as if she thought Isabel might be prepared to challenge the proposition. 'If you hadn't – if you hadn't; well, I don't know,' remarked Miss Stackpole, hinting ominously at her powers of disapproval.

Isabel looked about without seeing her maid. Her eyes rested on another figure, however, which she felt she had seen before; and in a moment she recognized the genial countenance of Mr Bantling. He stood a little apart, and it was not in the power of the multitude that pressed about him to make him yield an inch of the ground he had taken – that of abstracting himself discreetly while the two ladies performed their embraces.

'There's Mr Bantling,' said Isabel, gently, irrelevantly, scarcely caring much now whether she should find her maid or not.

'Oh yes, he goes everywhere with me. Come here, Mr Bantling!' Henrietta exclaimed. Whereupon the gallant bachelor advanced with a smile – a smile tempered, however, by the gravity of the occasion. 'Isn't it lovely she has come?' Henrietta asked. 'He knows all about it,' she added; 'we had quite a discussion. He said you wouldn't, I said you would.'

'I thought you always agreed,' Isabel smiled in return. She felt she could smile now; she had seen in an instant, in Mr Bantling's brave eyes, that he had good news for her. They seemed to say he wished her to remember he was an old friend of her cousin – that he understood, that it was all right. Isabel gave him her hand; she thought of him, extravagantly, as a beautiful blameless knight.

'Oh, I always agree,' said Mr Bantling. 'But she doesn't, you know.'

'Didn't I tell you that a maid was a nuisance?' Henrietta inquired. 'Your young lady has probably remained at Calais.'

'I don't care,' said Isabel, looking at Mr Bantling, whom she had never found so interesting.

'Stay with her while I go and see,' Henrietta commanded, leaving the two for a moment together.

They stood there at first in silence, and then Mr Bantling asked Isabel how it had been on the Channel.

'Very fine. No, I believe it was very rough,' she said, to her companion's obvious surprise. After which she added: 'You've been to Gardencourt, I know.'

'Now how do you know that?'

'I can't tell you – except that you look like a person who has been to Gardencourt.'

'Do you think I look awfully sad? It's awfully sad there, you know.'

'I don't believe you ever look awfully sad. You look awfully kind,' said Isabel with a breadth that cost her no effort. It seemed to her she should never again feel a superficial embarrassment.

Poor Mr Bantling, however, was still in this inferior stage. He blushed a good deal and laughed, he assured her that he was often very blue, and that when he was blue he was awfully fierce. 'You can ask Miss Stackpole, you know. I was at Gardencourt two days ago.'

'Did you see my cousin?'

'Only for a little. But he had been seeing people; Warburton had been there the day before. Ralph was just the same as usual, except that he was in bed and that he looks tremendously ill and that he can't speak,' Mr Bantling pursued. 'He was awfully jolly and funny all the same. He was just as clever as ever. It's awfully wretched.'

Even in the crowded, noisy station this simple picture was vivid. 'Was that late in the day?'

'Yes; I went on purpose. We thought you'd like to know.'

'I'm greatly obliged to you. Can I go down tonight?'

'Ah, I don't think *she'll* let you go,' said Mr Bantling. 'She wants you to stop with her. I made Touchett's man promise to telegraph me today, and I found the telegram an hour ago at my club. "Quiet and easy", that's what it says, and it's dated two o'clock. So you see you can wait till tomorrow. You must be awfully tired.'

'Yes, I'm awfully tired. And I thank you again.'

'Oh,' said Mr Bantling, 'we were certain you would like the last news.' On which Isabel vaguely noted that he and Henrietta seemed after all to agree. Miss Stackpole came back with Isabel's maid, whom she had caught in the act of proving her utility. This excellent person, instead of losing herself in the crowd, had simply attended to her mistress's luggage, so that the latter was now at liberty to leave the station. 'You know you're not to think of going to the country tonight,' Henrietta remarked to her. 'It doesn't matter whether there's a train or not. You're to come straight to me in Wimpole Street. There isn't a corner to be had in London, but I've got you one all the same. It isn't a Roman palace, but it will do for a night.'

'I'll do whatever you wish,' Isabel said.

'You'll come and answer a few questions; that's what I wish.'

'She doesn't say anything about dinner, does she, Mrs Osmond?' Mr Bantling inquired jocosely.

Henrietta fixed him a moment with her speculative gaze. 'I see you're in a great hurry to get your own. You'll be at the Paddington Station tomorrow morning at ten.'

'Don't come for my sake, Mr Bantling,' said Isabel.

'He'll come for mine,' Henrietta declared as she ushered her friend into a cab. And later, in a large dusky parlour in Wimpole Street – to do her justice there had been dinner enough – she asked those questions to which she had alluded at the station. 'Did your husband make you a scene about your coming?' That was Miss Stackpole's first inquiry.

'No; I can't say he made a scene.'

'He didn't object then?'

'Yes, he objected very much. But it was not what you'd call a scene.'

'What was it then?'

'It was a very quiet conversation.'

Henrietta for a moment regarded her guest. 'It must have been hellish,' she then remarked. And Isabel didn't deny that it had been hellish. But she confined herself to answering Henrietta's questions, which was easy, as they were tolerably definite. For the present she offered her no new information. 'Well,' said Miss Stackpole at last, 'I've only one criticism to make. I don't see why you promised little Miss Osmond to go back.'

'I'm not sure I myself see now,' Isabel replied. 'But I did then.'

'If you've forgotten your reason perhaps you won't return.'

Isabel waited a moment. 'Perhaps I shall find another.'

'You'll certainly never find a good one.'

'In default of a better my having promised will do,' Isabel suggested.

'Yes; that's why I hate it.'

'Don't speak of it now. I've a little time. Coming away was a complication, but what will going back be?'

'You must remember, after all, that he won't make you a scene!' said Henrietta with much intention.

'He will, though,' Isabel answered gravely. 'It won't be the scene of a moment; it will be a scene of the rest of my life.'

For some minutes the two women sat and considered this remainder, and then Miss Stackpole, to change the subject, as Isabel had requested, announced abruptly: 'I've been to stay with Lady Pensil!'

'Ah, the invitation came at last!'

'Yes; it took five years. But this time she wanted to see me.'

'Naturally enough.'

'It was more natural than I think you know,' said Henrietta, who fixed her eyes on a distant point. And then she added, turning suddenly: 'Isabel Archer, I beg your pardon. You don't know why? Because I criticized you, and yet I've gone farther than you. Mr Osmond, at least, was born on the other side!'

It was a moment before Isabel grasped her meaning; this sense was so modestly, or at least so ingeniously, veiled. Isabel's mind was not possessed at present with the comicality of things; but she greeted with a quick laugh the image that her companion had raised. She immediately recovered herself, however, and with the right excess of intensity, 'Henrietta Stackpole,' she asked, 'are you going to give up your country?'

'Yes, my poor Isabel, I am. I won't pretend to deny it; I look the fact in the face. I'm going to marry Mr Bantling and locate right here in London.'

'It seems very strange,' said Isabel, smiling now.

'Well yes, I suppose it does. I've come to it little by little. I think I know what I'm doing; but I don't know as I can explain.'

'One can't explain one's marriage,' Isabel answered. 'And yours doesn't need to be explained. Mr Bantling isn't a riddle.'

'No, he isn't a bad pun – or even a high flight of American humour. He has a beautiful nature,' Henrietta went on. 'I've studied him for many years and I see right through him. He's as clear as the style of a good prospectus. He's not intellectual, but he appreciates intellect. On the other hand he doesn't exaggerate its claims. I sometimes think we do in the United States.'

'Ah,' said Isabel, 'you're changed indeed! It's the first time I've ever heard you say anything against your native land.'

'I only say that we're too infatuated with mere brainpower; that, after all, isn't a vulgar fault. But I *am* changed; a woman has to change a good deal to marry.'

'I hope you'll be very happy. You will at last – over here – see something of the inner life.'

Henrietta gave a little significant sigh. 'That's the key to the mystery, I believe. I couldn't endure to be kept off. Now I've as good a right as anyone!' she added with artless elation.

Isabel was duly diverted, but there was a certain melancholy in her view. Henrietta, after all, had confessed herself human and feminine, Henrietta whom she had hitherto regarded as a light keen flame, a disembodied voice. It was a disappointment to find she had personal susceptibilities, that she was subject to common passions, and that her intimacy with Mr Bantling had not been completely original. There was a want of originality in her marrying him – there was even a kind of stupidity; and for a moment, to Isabel's sense, the dreariness of the world took on a deeper tinge. A little later indeed she reflected that Mr Bantling himself at least was original. But she didn't see how Henrietta could give up her country. She herself had relaxed her hold of it, but it had never been her country as it had been Henrietta's. She presently asked her if she had enjoyed her visit to Lady Pensil.

'Oh yes,' said Henrietta, 'she didn't know what to make of me.'

'And was that very enjoyable?'

'Very much so, because she's supposed to be a master mind. She thinks she knows everything; but she doesn't understand a woman of my modern type. It would be so much easier for her if I were only a little better or a little worse. She's so puzzled; I believe she thinks it's my duty to go and do something immoral. She thinks it's immoral that I should marry her brother; but, after all, that isn't immoral enough. And she'll never understand my mixture – never!'

'She's not so intelligent as her brother then,' said Isabel. 'He appears to have understood.'

'Oh no, he hasn't!' cried Miss Stackpole with decision. 'I really believe that's what he wants to marry me for – just to find out the mystery and the proportions of it. That's a fixed idea – a kind of fascination.'

'It's very good in you to humour it.'

'Oh well,' said Henrietta, 'I've something to find out too!' And Isabel saw that she had not renounced an allegiance, but planned an attack. She was at last about to grapple in earnest with England.

Isabel also perceived however, on the morrow, at the Paddington Station, where she found herself, at ten o'clock, in the company both of Miss Stackpole and Mr Bantling, that the gentleman bore his perplexities lightly. If he had not found out everything he had found out at least the great point

– that Miss Stackpole would not be wanting in initiative. It was evident that in the selection of a wife he had been on his guard against this deficiency.

'Henrietta has told me, and I'm very glad,' Isabel said as she gave him her hand.

'I dare say you think it awfully odd,' Mr Bantling replied, resting on his neat umbrella.

'Yes, I think it awfully odd.'

'You can't think it so awfully odd as I do. But I've always rather liked striking out a line,' said Mr Bantling serenely.

Chapter Fifty-four

Isabel's arrival at Gardencourt on this second occasion was even quieter than it had been on the first. Ralph Touchett kept but a small household, and to the new servants Mrs Osmond was a stranger; so that instead of being conducted to her own apartment she was coldly shown into the drawing-room and left to wait while her name was carried up to her aunt. She waited a long time; Mrs Touchett appeared in no hurry to come to her. She grew impatient at last; she grew nervous and scared – as scared as if the objects about her had begun to show for conscious things, watching her trouble with grotesque grimaces. The day was dark and cold; the dusk was thick in the corners of the wide brown rooms. The house was perfectly still – with a stillness that Isabel remembered; it had filled all the place for days before the death of her uncle. She left the drawing-room and wandered about – strolled into the library and along the gallery of pictures, where, in the deep silence, her footstep made an echo. Nothing was changed; she recognized everything she had seen years before; it might have been only yesterday she had stood there. She envied the security of valuable 'pieces' which change by no hair's breadth, only grow in value, while their owners lose inch by inch youth, happiness, beauty; and she became aware that she was walking about as her aunt had done on the day she had come to see her in Albany. She was changed enough since then – that had been the beginning. It suddenly struck her that if her Aunt Lydia had not come that day in just that way and found her alone, everything might have been different. She might have had another life and she might have been a woman more blest. She stopped in the gallery in front of a small picture – a charming and precious Bonington – upon which her eyes rested a long time. But she was not looking at the picture; she was wondering whether if her aunt had not come that day in Albany she would have married Caspar Goodwood.

Mrs Touchett appeared at last, just after Isabel had returned to the big uninhabited drawing-room. She looked a good deal older, but her eye was as bright as ever and her head as erect; her thin lips seemed a repository of latent meanings. She wore a little grey dress of the most undecorated fashion, and Isabel wondered, as she had wondered the first time, if her remarkable kinswoman resembled more a queen-regent or the matron of a gaol. Her lips felt very thin indeed on Isabel's hot cheek.

'I've kept you waiting because I've been sitting with Ralph,' Mrs Touchett said. 'The nurse had gone to luncheon and I had taken her place. He has a man who's supposed to look after him, but the man's good for nothing; he's always looking out of the window – as if there were anything to see! I didn't wish to move, because Ralph seemed to be sleeping and I was afraid the sound would disturb him. I waited till the nurse came back; I remembered you knew the house.'

'I find I know it better even than I thought; I've been walking everywhere,' Isabel answered. And then she asked if Ralph slept much.

'He lies with his eyes closed; he doesn't move. But I'm not sure that it's always sleep.'

'Will he see me? Can he speak to me?'

Mrs Touchett declined the office of saying. 'You can try him,' was the limit of her extravagance. And then she offered to conduct Isabel to her room. 'I thought they had taken you there; but it's not my house, it's Ralph's; and I don't know what they do. They must at least have taken your luggage; I don't suppose you've brought much. Not that I care, however. I believe they've given you the same room you had before; when Ralph heard you were coming he said you must have that one.'

'Did he say anything else?'

'Ah, my dear, he doesn't chatter as he used!' cried Mrs Touchett as she preceded her niece up the staircase.

It was the same room, and something told Isabel it had not been slept in since she occupied it. Her luggage was there and was not voluminous; Mrs Touchett sat down a moment with her eyes upon it. 'Is there really no hope?' our young woman asked as she stood before her.

'None whatever. There never has been. It has not been a successful life.'

'No – it has only been a beautiful one.' Isabel found herself already contradicting her aunt; she was irritated by her dryness.

'I don't know what you mean by that; there's no beauty without health. That is a very odd dress to travel in.'

Isabel glanced at her garment. 'I left Rome at an hour's notice; I took the first that came.'

'Your sisters, in America, wished to know how you dress. That seemed to be their principal interest. I wasn't able to tell them – but they seemed to have the right idea: that you never wear anything less than black brocade.'

'They think I'm more brilliant than I am; I'm afraid to tell them the truth,' said Isabel. 'Lily wrote me you had dined with her.'

'She invited me four times, and I went once. After the second time she should have let me alone. The dinner was very good; it must have been expensive. Her husband has a very bad manner. Did I enjoy my visit to America? Why should I have enjoyed it? I didn't go for my pleasure.'

These were interesting items, but Mrs Touchett soon left her niece, whom she was to meet in half an hour at the midday meal. For this repast the two ladies faced each other at an abbreviated table in the melancholy dining-room. Here, after a little, Isabel saw her aunt not to be so dry as she appeared, and her old pity for the poor woman's inexpressiveness, her want of regret, of disappointment, came back to her. Unmistakably she would have found it a blessing today to be able to feel a defeat, a mistake, even a shame or two. She wondered if she were not even missing those enrichments of consciousness and privately trying – reaching out for some aftertaste of life, dregs of the banquet; the testimony of pain or the cold recreation of remorse. On the other hand perhaps she was afraid; if she should begin to know remorse at all it might take her too far. Isabel could perceive, however, how it had come over her dimly that she had failed of something, that she saw herself in the future as an old woman without memories. Her little sharp face looked tragical. She told her niece that Ralph had as yet not moved, but that he probably would be able to see her before dinner. And then in a moment she added that he had seen Lord Warburton the day before; an announcement which startled Isabel a little, as it seemed an intimation that this personage was in the neighbourhood and that an accident might bring them together. Such an accident would not be happy; she had not come to England to struggle again with Lord Warburton. She none the less presently said to her aunt that he had been very kind to Ralph; she had seen something of that in Rome.

'He has something else to think of now,' Mrs Touchett returned. And she paused with a gaze like a gimlet.

Isabel saw she meant something, and instantly guessed what she meant. But her reply concealed her guess; her heart beat faster and she wished to gain a moment. 'Ah yes – the House of Lords and all that.'

'He's not thinking of the Lords; he's thinking of the ladies. At least he's thinking of one of them; he told Ralph he's engaged to be married.'

'Ah, to be married!' Isabel mildly exclaimed.

'Unless he breaks it off. He seemed to think Ralph would like to know. Poor Ralph can't go to the wedding, though I believe it's to take place very soon.'

'And who's the young lady?'

'A member of the aristocracy; Lady Flora, Lady Felicia – something of that sort.'

'I'm very glad,' Isabel said. 'It must be a sudden decision.'

'Sudden enough, I believe; a courtship of three weeks. It has only just been made public.'

'I'm very glad,' Isabel repeated with a larger emphasis. She knew her aunt was watching her – looking for the signs of some imputed soreness, and the desire to prevent her companion from seeing anything of this kind enabled her to speak in the tone of quick satisfaction, the tone almost of relief. Mrs Touchett of course followed the tradition that ladies, even married ones, regard the marriage of their old lovers as an offence to themselves. Isabel's first care therefore was to show that however that might be in general she was not offended now. But meanwhile, as I say, her heart beat faster; and if she sat for some moments thoughtful – she presently forgot Mrs Touchett's observation – it was not because she had lost an admirer. Her imagination had traversed half Europe; it halted, panting, and even trembling a little, in the city of Rome. She figured herself announcing to her husband that Lord Warburton was to lead a bride to the altar, and she was of course not aware how extremely wan she must have looked while she made this intellectual effort. But at last she collected herself and said to her aunt: 'He was sure to do it some time or other.'

Mrs Touchett was silent; then she gave a sharp little shake of the head. 'Ah, my dear, you're beyond me!' she cried suddenly. They went on with their luncheon in silence; Isabel felt as if she had heard of Lord Warburton's death. She had known him only as a suitor, and now that was all over. He was dead for poor Pansy; by Pansy he might have lived. A servant had been hovering about; at last Mrs Touchett requested him to leave them alone. She had finished her meal; she sat with her hands folded on the edge of the table. 'I should like to ask you three questions,' she observed when the servant had gone.

'Three are a great many.'

'I can't do with less; I've been thinking. They're all very good ones.'

'That's what I'm afraid of. The best questions are the worst,' Isabel answered. Mrs Touchett had pushed back her chair, and as her niece left the table and walked, rather consciously, to one of the deep windows, she felt herself followed by her eyes.

'Have you ever been sorry you didn't marry Lord Warburton?' Mrs Touchett inquired.

Isabel shook her head slowly, but not heavily. 'No, dear aunt.'

'Good. I ought to tell you that I propose to believe what you say.'

'Your believing me's an immense temptation,' she declared, smiling still.

'A temptation to lie? I don't recommend you to do that, for when I'm misinformed I'm as dangerous as a poisoned rat. I don't mean to crow over you.'

'It's my husband who doesn't get on with me,' said Isabel.

'I could have told him he wouldn't. I don't call that crowing over *you*,' Mrs Touchett added. 'Do you still like Serena Merle?' she went on.

'Not as I once did. But it doesn't matter, for she's going to America.'

'To America? She must have done something very bad.'

'Yes – very bad.'

'May I ask what it is?'

'She made a convenience of me.'

'Ah,' cried Mrs Touchett, 'so she did of me! She does of everyone.'

'She'll make a convenience of America,' said Isabel, smiling again and glad that her aunt's questions were over.

It was not till the evening that she was able to see Ralph. He had been dozing all day; at least he had been lying unconscious. The doctor was there, but after a while went away – the local doctor, who had attended his father and whom Ralph liked. He came three or four times a day; he was deeply interested in his patient. Ralph had had Sir Matthew Hope, but he had got tired of this celebrated man, to whom he had asked his mother to send word he was now dead and was therefore without further need of medical advice. Mrs Touchett had simply written to Sir Matthew that her son disliked him. On the day of Isabel's arrival Ralph gave no sign, as I have related, for many hours; but towards evening he raised himself and said he knew that she had come. How he knew was not apparent, inasmuch as for fear of exciting him no one had offered the information. Isabel came in and sat by his bed in the dim light; there was only a shaded candle in a corner of the room. She told the nurse she might go – she herself would sit with him for the rest of the evening. He had opened his eyes and recognized her, and had moved his hand, which lay helpless beside him, so that she might take it. But he was unable to speak; he closed his eyes again and remained perfectly still, only keeping her hand in his own. She sat with him a long time – till the nurse came back; but he gave no further sign. He might have passed away while she looked at him; he was already the figure and pattern of death. She had thought him far gone in Rome, and this was worse; there was but one change possible now. There was a strange tranquillity in his face; it was as still as the lid of a box. With this he was a mere lattice of bones; when he opened his eyes to greet her it was as if she were looking into immeasurable space. It was not till midnight that the nurse came back; but the hours, to Isabel, had not seemed long; it was exactly what she had come for. If she had come simply to wait she found ample occasion, for he lay three days in a kind of grateful silence. He recognized her and at moments seemed to wish to speak; but he found no voice. Then he closed his eyes again, as if he too were waiting for something – for something that certainly would come. He was so absolutely quiet that it seemed to her what was coming had already arrived; and yet she never lost the sense that they were still together. But they were not always together; there were other hours that she passed in wandering through the empty house and listening for a voice that was not poor Ralph's. She had a constant fear; she thought it possible her husband would write to her. But he remained silent, and she only got a letter from Florence and from the Countess Gemini. Ralph, however, spoke at last – on the evening of the third day.

'I feel better tonight,' he murmured, abruptly, in the soundless dimness of her vigil; 'I think I can say something.' She sank upon her knees beside his pillow; took his thin hand in her own; begged him not to make an effort – not to tire himself. His face was of necessity serious – it was incapable of the muscular play of a smile; but its owner apparently had not lost a perception of incongruities. 'What does it matter if I'm tired when I've all eternity to rest? There's no harm in making an effort when it's the very last of all. Don't people always feel better just before the end? I've often heard of that; it's what I was waiting for. Ever since you've been here I thought it would come. I tried two or three times; I was afraid you'd get tired of sitting there.' He spoke slowly, with painful breaks and long pauses; his voice seemed to come from a distance. When he ceased he lay with his face turned to Isabel and his large unwinking eyes open into her own. 'It was very good of you to come,' he went on. 'I thought you would; but I wasn't sure.'

'I was not sure either till I came,' said Isabel.

'You've been like an angel beside my bed. You know they talk about the angel of death. It's the most beautiful of all. You've been like that; as if you were waiting for me.'

'I was not waiting for your death; I was waiting for – for this. This is not death, dear Ralph.'

'Not for you – no. There's nothing makes us feel so much alive as to see others die. That's the sensation of life – the sense that we remain. I've had it – even I. But now I'm of no use but to give it to others. With me it's all over.' And then he paused. Isabel bowed her head farther, till it rested on the two hands that were clasped upon his own. She couldn't see him now;

but his far-away voice was close to her ear. 'Isabel,' he went on suddenly, 'I wish it were over for you.' She answered nothing; she had burst into sobs; she remained so, with her buried face. He lay silent, listening to her sobs; at last he gave a long groan. 'Ah, what is it you have done for me?'

'What is it you did for me?' she cried, her now extreme agitation half smothered by her attitude. She had lost all her shame, all wish to hide things. Now he must know; she wished him to know, for it brought them supremely together, and he was beyond the reach of pain. 'You did something once – you know it. O Ralph, you've been everything! What have I done for you – what can I do today? I would die if you could live. But I don't wish you to live; I would die myself, not to lose you.' Her voice was as broken as his own and full of tears and anguish.

'You won't lose me – you'll keep me. Keep me in your heart; I shall be nearer to you than I've ever been. Dear Isabel, life is better; for in life there's love. Death is good – but there's no love.'

'I never thanked you – I never spoke – I never was what I should be!' Isabel went on. She felt a passionate need to cry out and accuse herself, to let her sorrow possess her. All her troubles, for the moment, became single and melted together into this present pain. 'What must you have thought of me? Yet how could I know? I never knew, and I only know today because there are people less stupid than I.'

'Don't mind people,' said Ralph. 'I think I'm glad to leave people.'

She raised her head and her clasped hands; she seemed for a moment to pray to him. 'Is it true – is it true?' she asked.

'True that you've been stupid? Oh no,' said Ralph with a sensible intention of wit.

'That you made me rich – that all I have is yours?'

He turned away his head, and for some time said nothing. Then at last: 'Ah, don't speak of that – that was not happy.' Slowly he moved his face towards her again, and they once more saw each other. 'But for that – but for that—!' And he paused. 'I believe I ruined you,' he wailed.

She was full of the sense that he was beyond the reach of pain; he seemed already so little of this world. But even if she had not had it she would still have spoken, for nothing mattered now but the only knowledge that was not pure anguish – the knowledge that they were looking at the truth together. 'He married me for the money,' she said. She wished to say everything; she was afraid he might die before she had done so.

He gazed at her a little, and for the first time his fixed eyes lowered their lids. But he raised them in a moment and then, 'He was greatly in love with you,' he answered.

'Yes, he was in love with me. But he wouldn't have married me if I had been poor. I don't hurt you in saying that. How can I? I only want you to understand. I always tried to keep you from understanding; but that's all over.'

'I always understood,' said Ralph.

'I thought you did, and I didn't like it. But now I like it.'

'You don't hurt me – you make me very happy.' And as Ralph said this there was an extraordinary gladness in his voice. She bent her head again, and pressed her lips to the back of his hand. 'I always understood,' he continued, 'though it was so strange – so pitiful. You wanted to look at life for yourself – but you were not allowed; you were punished for your wish. You were ground in the very mill of the conventional!'

'Oh yes, I've been punished,' Isabel sobbed.

He listened to her a little, and then continued: 'Was he very bad about your coming?'

'He made it very hard for me. But I don't care.'

'It is all over then between you?'

'Oh no; I don't think anything's over.'

'Are you going back to him?' Ralph gasped.

'I don't know – I can't tell. I shall stay here as long as I may. I don't want to think – needn't think. I don't care for anything but you, and that's enough for the present. It will last a little yet. Here on my knees, with you dying in my arms, I'm happier than I have been for a long time. And I want you to be happy – not to think of anything sad; only to feel that I'm near you and I love you. Why should there be pain? In such hours as this what have we to do with pain? That's not the deepest thing; there's something deeper.'

Ralph evidently found from moment to moment greater difficulty in speaking; he had to wait longer to collect himself. At first he appeared to make no response to these last words; he let a long time elapse. Then he murmured simply: 'You must stay here.'

'I should like to stay – as long as seems right.'

'As seems right – as seems right?' He repeated her words. 'Yes, you think a great deal about that.'

'Of course one must. You're very tired,' said Isabel.

'I'm very tired. You said just now that pain's not the deepest thing. No – no. But it's very deep. If I could stay—'

'For me you'll always be here,' she softly interrupted. It was easy to interrupt him.

But he went on, after a moment: 'It passes, after all; it's passing now. But love remains. I don't know why we should suffer so much. Perhaps I shall find out. There are many things in life. You're very young.'

'I feel very old,' said Isabel.

'You'll grow young again. That's how I see you. I don't believe – I don't believe—' But he stopped again; his strength failed him.

She begged him to be quiet now. 'We needn't speak to understand each other,' she said.

'I don't believe that such a generous mistake as yours can hurt you for more than a little.'

'Oh Ralph, I'm very happy now,' she cried through her tears.

'And remember this,' he continued, 'that if you've been hated you've also been loved. Ah but, Isabel – *adored*!' he just audibly and lingeringly breathed.

'Oh my brother!' she cried with a movement of still deeper prostration.

Chapter Fifty-five

He had told her, the first evening she ever spent at Gardencourt, that if she should live to suffer enough she might some day see the ghost with which the old house was duly provided. She apparently had fulfilled the necessary condition; for the next morning, in the cold, faint dawn, she knew that a spirit was standing by her bed. She had lain down without undressing, it being her belief Ralph would not outlast the night. She had no inclination to sleep; she was waiting, and such waiting was wakeful. But she closed her eyes; she believed that as the night wore on she should hear a knock at her door. She heard no knock, but at the time the darkness began vaguely to grow grey she started up from her pillow as abruptly as if she had received a summons. It seemed to her for an instant that he was standing there – a vague, hovering figure in the vagueness of the room. She stared a moment; she saw his white face – his kind eyes; then she saw there was nothing. She was not afraid; she was only sure. She quitted the place and in her certainty passed through dark corridors and down a flight of oaken steps that shone in the vague light of a hall window. Outside Ralph's door she stopped a moment, listening, but she seemed to hear only the hush that filled it. She opened the door with a hand as gentle as if she were lifting a veil from the face of the dead, and saw Mrs Touchett sitting motionless and upright beside the couch of her son, with one of his hands in her own. The doctor was on the other side, with poor Ralph's farther wrist resting in his professional fingers. The two nurses were at the foot between them. Mrs Touchett took no notice of Isabel, but the doctor looked at her very hard; then he gently placed Ralph's hand in a proper position, close beside him. The nurse looked at her very hard too, and no one said a word; but Isabel only looked at what she had come to see. It was fairer than Ralph had ever been in life, and there was a strange resemblance to the face of his father, which, six years before, she had seen lying on the same pillow. She went to her aunt and put her arm around her; and Mrs Touchett, who as a general thing neither invited nor enjoyed caresses, submitted for a moment to this one, rising, as might be, to take it. But she was stiff and dry-eyed; her acute white face was terrible.

'Dear Aunt Lydia,' Isabel murmured.

'Go and thank God you've no child,' said Mrs Touchett, disengaging herself.

Three days after this a considerable number of people found time, at the height of the London 'season', to take a morning train down to a quiet station in Berkshire and spend half an hour in a small grey church which stood within an easy walk. It was in the green burial-place of this edifice that Mrs Touchett consigned her son to earth. She stood herself at the edge of the grave, and Isabel stood beside her; the sexton himself had not a more practical interest in the scene than Mrs Touchett. It was a solemn occasion, but neither a harsh nor a heavy one; there was a certain geniality in the appearance of things. The weather had changed to fair; the day, one of the last of the treacherous May-time, was warm and windless, and the air had the brightness of the hawthorn and the blackbird. If it was sad to think of poor Touchett, it was not too sad since death, for him, had had no violence. He had been dying so long; he was so ready; everything had been so expected and prepared. There were tears in Isabel's eyes, but they were not tears that blinded. She looked through them at the beauty of the day, the splendour of nature, the sweetness of the old English churchyard, the bowed heads of good friends. Lord Warburton was there, and a group of gentlemen all unknown to her, several of whom, as she afterwards learned, were connected with the bank; and there were others whom she knew. Miss Stackpole was among the first, with honest Mr Bantling beside her; and Caspar Goodwood, lifting his head higher than the rest – bowing it rather less. During much of the time Isabel was conscious of Mr Goodwood's gaze; he looked at her somewhat harder than he usually looked in public, while the others had fixed their eyes upon the churchyard turf. But she never let him see that she saw him; she thought of him only to wonder that he was still in England. She found she had taken for granted that after accompanying Ralph to Gardencourt he had gone away; she remembered how little it was a country that pleased him. He was there, however, very distinctly there; and something in his attitude seemed to say that he was there with a complex intention. She wouldn't meet his eyes, though there was doubtless sympathy in them; he made her rather uneasy. With the dispersal of the little group he disappeared, and the only person who came to speak to her – though several spoke to Mrs Touchett – was Henrietta Stackpole. Henrietta had been crying.

Ralph had said to Isabel that he hoped she would remain at Gardencourt, and she made no immediate motion to leave the place. She said to herself that it was but common charity to stay a little with her aunt. It was fortunate she had so good a formula; otherwise she might have been greatly in want of one. Her errand was over; she had done what she had left her husband to do. She had a husband in a foreign city, counting the hours of her absence; in such a case one needed an excellent motive. He was not one of the best husbands, but that didn't alter the case. Certain obligations were involved in the very fact of marriage and were quite independent of the quantity of enjoyment extracted from it. Isabel thought of her husband as little as might be; but now that she was at a distance, beyond its spell, she thought with a kind of spiritual shudder of Rome. There was a penetrating chill in the image, and she drew back into the deepest shade of Gardencourt. She lived from day to day, postponing, closing her eyes, trying not to think. She knew she must decide, but she decided nothing; her coming itself had not been a decision. On that occasion she had simply started. Osmond gave no sound and now evidently would give none; he would leave it all to her. From Pansy she heard nothing, but that was very simple: her father had told her not to write.

Mrs Touchett accepted Isabel's company, but offered her no assistance; she appeared to be absorbed in considering, without enthusiasm but with perfect lucidity, the new conveniences of her own situation. Mrs Touchett was not an optimist, but even from painful occurrences she managed to extract a certain utility. This consisted in the reflection that, after all, such things happened to other people and not to herself. Death was disagreeable, but in this case it was her son's death, not her own; she had never flattered herself that her own would be disagreeable to anyone but Mrs Touchett. She was better off than poor Ralph, who had left all the commodities of life behind him, and indeed all the security; since the worst of dying was, to Mrs Touchett's mind, that it exposed one to be taken advantage of. For herself she was on the spot; there was nothing so good as that. She made known to Isabel very punctually – it was the evening her son was buried – several of Ralph's testamentary arrangements. He had told her everything, had consulted her about everything. He left her no money; of course she had no need of money. He left her the furniture of Gardencourt, exclusive of the pictures and books and the use of the place for a year; after which it was to be sold. The money produced by the sale was to constitute an endowment for a hospital for poor persons suffering from the malady of which he died; and of this portion of the will Lord Warburton was appointed executor. The rest of his property, which was to be withdrawn from the bank, was disposed of in various bequests, several of them to those cousins in Vermont to whom his father had already been so bountiful. Then there were a number of small legacies.

'Some of them are extremely peculiar,' said Mrs Touchett; 'he has left considerable sums to persons I never heard of. He gave me a list, and I asked then who some of them were, and he told me they were people who at various times had seemed to like him. Apparently he thought you didn't like him, for he hasn't left you a penny. It was his opinion that you had been handsomely treated by his father, which I'm bound to say I think you were – though I don't mean that I ever heard him complain of it. The pictures are to be dispersed; he has distributed them about, one by one, as little keepsakes. The most valuable of the collection goes to Lord Warburton. And what do you think he has done with his library? It sounds like a practical joke. He has left it to your friend Miss Stackpole – "in recognition of her services to literature". Does he mean her following him up from Rome? Was that a service to literature? It contains a great many rare and valuable books, and as she can't carry it about the world in her trunk he recommends her to sell it at auction. She will sell it of course at Christie's, and with the proceeds she'll set up a newspaper. Will that be a service to literature?'

This question Isabel forbore to answer, as it exceeded the little interrogatory to which she had deemed it necessary to submit on her arrival. Besides, she had never been less interested in literature than today, as she found when she occasionally took down from the shelf one of the rare and valuable volumes of which Mrs Touchett had spoken. She was quite unable to read; her attention had never been so little at her command. One afternoon, in the library, about a week after the ceremony in the church-yard, she was trying to fix it for an hour; but her eyes often wandered from the book in her hand to the open window, which looked down the long avenue. It was in this way that she saw a modest vehicle approach the door and perceived Lord Warburton sitting, in rather an uncomfortable attitude, in a corner of it. He had always had a high standard of courtesy, and it was therefore not remarkable, under the circumstances, that he should have taken the trouble to come down from London to call on Mrs Touchett. It was of course Mrs Touchett he had come to see, and not Mrs Osmond; and to prove to herself the validity of this thesis Isabel presently stepped out of the house and wandered away into the park. Since her arrival at Gardencourt she had been but little out of doors, the weather being unfavourable for visiting the grounds. This evening, however, was fine, and at first it struck her as a happy thought to have come out. The theory I have just mentioned was plausible enough, but it brought her little rest, and if you had seen her pacing about you would have said she had a bad conscience. She was not pacified when at the end of a quarter of an hour, finding herself in view of the house, she saw Mrs Touchett emerge from the portico accompanied by her visitor. Her aunt had evidently proposed to Lord Warburton that they should come in search of her. She was in no humour for visitors and, if she had had a chance, would have drawn back behind one of the great trees. But she saw she had been seen and that nothing was left her but to advance. As the lawn at Gardencourt was a vast expanse this took some time; during which she observed that, as he walked beside his hostess, Lord Warburton kept his hands rather stiffly behind him and his eyes upon the ground. Both persons apparently were silent; but Mrs Touchett's thin little glance, as she directed it towards Isabel, had even at a distance an expression. It seemed to say with cutting sharpness: 'Here's the eminently amenable nobleman you might have married!' When Lord Warburton lifted his own eyes, however, that was not what they said. They only said 'This is rather awkward, you know, and I depend upon you to help me.' He was very grave, very proper and, for the first time since Isabel had known him, greeted her without a smile. Even in his days of distress he had always begun with a smile. He looked extremely self-conscious.

'Lord Warburton has been so good as to come out to see me,' said Mrs Touchett. 'He tells me he didn't know you were still here. I know he's an old friend of yours, and as I was told you were not in the house I brought him out to see for himself.'

'Oh, I saw there was a good train at 6.40, that would get me back in time for dinner,' Mrs Touchett's companion rather irrelevantly explained. 'I'm so glad to find you've not gone.'

'I'm not here for long, you know,' Isabel said with a certain eagerness.

'I suppose not; but I hope it's for some weeks. You came to England sooner than – a – than you thought?'

'Yes, I came very suddenly.'

Mrs Touchett turned away as if she were looking at the condition of the grounds, which indeed was not what it should be, while Lord Warburton hesitated a little. Isabel fancied he had been on the point of asking about her husband – rather confusedly – and then had checked himself. He continued immitigably grave, either because he thought it becoming in a place over which death had just passed, or for more personal reasons. If he was conscious of personal reasons it was very fortunate that he had the cover of the former motive; he could make the most of that. Isabel thought of all this. It was not that his face was sad, for that was another matter; but it was strangely inexpressive.

'My sisters would have been so glad to come if they had known you were still here – if they had thought you would see them,' Lord Warburton went on. 'Do kindly let them see you before you leave England.'

'It would give me great pleasure; I have such a friendly recollection of them.'

'I don't know whether you would come to Lockleigh for a day or two? You know there's always that old promise.' And his lordship coloured a little as he made this suggestion, which gave his face a somewhat more familiar air. 'Perhaps I'm not right in saying that just now; of course you're not thinking of visiting. But I meant what would hardly be a visit. My sisters are to be at Lockleigh at Whitsuntide for five days; and if you could come then – as you say you're not to be very long in England – I would see that there should be literally no one else.'

Isabel wondered if not even the young lady he was to marry would be there with her mamma; but she did not express this idea. 'Thank you extremely,' she contented herself with saying; 'I'm afraid I hardly know about Whitsuntide.'

'But I have your promise – haven't I? – for some other time.'

There was an interrogation in this; but Isabel let it pass. She looked at her interlocutor a moment, and the result of her observation was that – as had happened before – she felt sorry for him. 'Take care you don't miss your train,' she said. And then she added: 'I wish you every happiness.'

He blushed again, more than before, and he looked at his watch. 'Ah yes, 6.40; I haven't much time, but I've a fly at the door. Thank you very much.' It was not apparent whether the thanks applied to her having reminded him of his train or to the more sentimental remark. 'Good-bye, Mrs Osmond; good-bye.' He shook hands with her, without meeting her eyes, and then he turned to Mrs Touchett, who had wandered back to them. With her his parting was equally brief; and in a moment the two ladies saw him move with long steps across the lawn.

'Are you very sure he's to be married?' Isabel asked of her aunt.

'I can't be surer than he; but he seems sure. I congratulated him, and he accepted it.'

'Ah,' said Isabel, 'I give it up!' – while her aunt returned to the house and to those avocations which the visitor had interrupted.

She gave it up, but she still thought of it – thought of it while she strolled again under the great oaks whose shadows were long upon the acres of turf. At the end of a few minutes she found herself near a rustic bench, which, a moment after she had looked at it, struck her as an object recognized. It was not simply that she had seen it before, nor even that she had sat upon it; it was that on this spot something important had happened to her – that the place had an air of association. Then she remembered that she had been sitting there, six years before, when a servant brought her from the house the letter in which Caspar Goodwood informed her that he had followed her to Europe; and that when she had read the letter she looked up to hear Lord Warburton announcing that he should like to marry her. It was indeed an historical, an interesting, bench; she stood and looked at it as if it might have something to say to her. She wouldn't sit down on it now – she felt rather afraid of it. She only stood before it, and while she stood the past came back to her in one of those rushing waves of emotion by which persons of sensibility are visited at odd hours. The effect of this agitation was a sudden sense of being very tired, under the influence of which she overcame her scruples and sank into the rustic seat. I have said that she was restless and unable to occupy herself; and whether or no, if you had seen her there, you would have admired the justice of the former epithet, you would at least have allowed that at this moment she was the image of a victim of idleness. Her attitude had a singular absence of purpose; her hands, hanging at her sides, lost themselves in the folds of her black dress; her eyes gazed vaguely before her. There was nothing to recall her to the house; the two ladies in their seclusion, dined early and had tea at an indefinite hour. How long she had sat in this position she could not have told you; but the twilight had grown thick when she became aware that she was not alone. She quickly straightened herself, glancing about, and then saw what had become of her solitude. She was sharing it with Caspar Goodwood, who stood looking at her, a few yards off, and whose footfalls on the unresonant turf, as he came near, she had not heard. It occurred to her in the midst of this that it was just so Lord Warburton had surprised her of old.

She instantly rose, and as soon as Goodwood saw he was seen he started forward. She had had time only to rise when, with a motion that looked like violence, but felt like – she knew not what, he grasped her by the wrist and made her sink again into the seat. She closed her eyes; he had not hurt her; it was only a touch, which she had obeyed. But there was something in his face that she wished not to see. That was the way he had looked at her the other day in the churchyard; only at present it was worse. He said nothing at first; she only felt him close to her – beside her on the bench and pressingly turned to her. It almost seemed to her that no one had ever been so close to her as that. All this, however, took but an instant, at the end of which she had disengaged her wrist, turning her eyes upon her visitant. 'You've frightened me,' she said.

'I didn't mean to,' he answered, 'but if I did a little, no matter. I came from London a while ago by the train, but I couldn't come here directly. There was a man at the station who got ahead of me. He took a fly that was there, and I heard him give the order to drive here. I don't know who he was, but I didn't want to come with him; I wanted to see you alone. So I've been waiting and walking about. I've walked all over, and I was just coming to the house when I saw you here. There was a keeper, or someone, who met me; but that was all right, because I had made his acquaintance when I came here with your cousin. Is that gentleman gone? Are you really alone? I want to speak to you.' Goodwood spoke very fast; he was as excited as when they had parted in Rome. Isabel had hoped that condition would subside; and she shrank into herself as she perceived that, on the contrary, he had only let out sail. She had a new sensation; he had never produced it before; it was a feeling of danger. There was indeed something really formidable in his resolution. She gazed straight before her; he, with a hand on each knee, leaned forward, looking deeply into her face. The twilight seemed to darken round them. 'I want to speak to you,' he repeated; 'I've something particular to say. I don't want to trouble you – as I did the other day in Rome. That was of no use; it only distressed you. I couldn't help it; I knew I was wrong. But I'm not wrong now; please don't think I am,' he went on with his hard, deep voice melting a moment into entreaty. 'I came here today for a purpose. It's very different. It was vain for me to speak to you then; but now I can help you.'

She couldn't have told you whether it was because she was afraid, or because such a voice in the darkness seemed of necessity a boon; but she listened to him as she had never listened before; his words dropped deep into her soul. They produced a sort of stillness in all her being; and it was with an effort, in a moment, that she answered him. 'How can you help me?' she asked in a low tone, as if she were taking what he had said seriously enough to make the inquiry in confidence.

'By inducing you to trust me. Now I know – today I know. Do you remember what I asked you in Rome? Then I was quite in the dark. But today I know on good authority; everything's clear to me today. It was a good thing when you made me come away with your cousin. He was a good man, a fine man, one of the best; he told me how the case stands for you. He explained everything; he guessed my sentiments. He was a member of your family and he left you – so long as you should be in England – to my care,' said Goodwood as if he were making a great point. 'Do you know what he said to me the last time I saw him – as he lay there where he died? He said. "Do everything you can for her; do everything she'll let you."'

Isabel suddenly got up. 'You had no business to talk about me!'

'Why not – why not, when we talked in that way?' he demanded, following her fast. 'And he was dying – when a man's dying it's different.' She checked the movement she had made to leave him; she was listening more than ever; it was true that he was not the same as that last time. That had been aimless, fruitless passion, but at present he had an idea, which she scented in all her being. 'But it doesn't matter!' he exclaimed, pressing her still harder, though now without touching a hem of her garment. 'If Touchett had never opened his mouth I should have known all the same. I had only to look at you at your cousin's funeral to see what's the matter with you. You can't deceive me any more; for God's sake be honest with a man who's so honest with you. You're the most unhappy of women, and your husband's the deadliest of fiends.'

She turned on him as if he had struck her. 'Are you mad?' she cried.

'I've never been so sane; I see the whole thing. Don't think it's necessary to defend him. But I won't say another word against him; I'll speak only of you,' Goodwood added quickly. 'How can you pretend you're not heart-broken? You don't know what to do – you don't know where to turn. It's too late to play a part; didn't you leave all that behind you in Rome? Touchett knew all about it, and I knew it too – what it would cost you to come here. It will have cost you your life? Say it will' – and he flared almost into anger: 'give me one word of truth! When I know such a horror as that, how can I keep myself from wishing to save you? What would you think of me if I should stand still and see you go back to your reward? "It's awful, what she'll have to pay for it!" – that's what Touchett said to me. I may tell you that, mayn't I? He was such a near relation!' cried Goodwood, making his queer grim point again. 'I'd sooner have been shot than let another man say those things to me; but he was different; he seemed to me to have the right. It was after he got home – when he saw he was dying, and when I saw it too. I understand all about it: you're afraid to go back. You're perfectly alone; you don't know where to turn. You can't turn anywhere; you know that perfectly. Now it is therefore that I want you to think of *me.*

'To think of "you"?' Isabel said, standing before him in the dusk. The idea of which she had caught a glimpse a few moments before now loomed large. She threw back her head a little; she stared at it as if it had been a comet in the sky.

'You don't know where to turn. Turn straight to *me.* I want to persuade you to trust me,' Goodwood repeated. And then he paused with his shining eyes. 'Why should you go back – why should you go through that ghastly form?'

'To get away from *you*!' she answered. But this expressed only a little of what she felt. The rest was that she had never been loved before. She had believed it, but this was different; this was the hot wind of the desert, at the approach of which the others dropped dead, like mere sweet airs of the garden. It wrapped her about; it lifted her off her feet, while the very taste of it, as of something potent, acrid, and strange, forced open her set teeth.

At first, in rejoinder to what she had said, it seemed to her that he would break out into greater violence. But after an instant he was perfectly quiet; he wished to prove he was sane, that he had reasoned it all out. 'I want to prevent that, and I think I may, if you'll only for once listen to me. It's too monstrous of you to think of sinking back into that misery, of going to open your mouth to that poisoned air. It's you that are out of your mind. Trust me as if I had the care of you. Why shouldn't we be happy – when it's here before us, when it's so easy? I'm yours for ever – for ever and ever. Here I stand; I'm as firm as a rock. What have you to care about? You've no children; that perhaps would be an obstacle. As it is you've nothing to consider. You must save what you can of your life; you mustn't lose it all simply because you've lost a part. It would be an insult to you to assume that you care for the look of the thing, for what people will say, for the bottomless idiocy of the world. We've nothing to do with all that; we're quite out of it; we look at things as they are. You took the great step in coming away; the next is nothing; it's the natural one. I swear, as I stand here, that a woman deliberately made to suffer is justified in anything in life – in going down into the streets if that will help her! I know how you suffer, and that's why I'm here. We can do absolutely as we please; to whom under the sun do we owe anything? What is it that holds us, what is it that has the smallest right to interfere in such a question as this? Such a question is between ourselves – and to say that is to settle it! Were we born to rot in our misery – were we born to be afraid? I never knew *you* afraid! If you'll only trust me, how little you will be disappointed! The world's all before us – and the world's very big. I know something about that.'

Isabel gave a long murmur, like a creature in pain; it was as if he were pressing something that hurt her. 'The world's very small,' she said at random; she had an immense desire to appear to resist. She said it at random, to hear herself say something; but it was not what she meant. The world, in truth, had never seemed so large; it seemed to open out, all round her, to take the form of a mighty sea, where she floated in fathomless waters. She had wanted help, and here was help; it had come in a rushing torrent. I know not whether she believed everything he said; but she believed just then that to let him take her in his arms would be the next best thing to her dying. This belief, for a moment, was a kind of rapture, in which she felt herself sink and sink. In the movement she seemed to beat with her feet, in order to catch herself, to feel something to rest on.

'Ah, be mine as I'm yours!' she heard her companion cry. He had suddenly given up argument, and his voice seemed to come, harsh and terrible, through a confusion of vaguer sounds.

This however, of course, was but a subjective fact, as the metaphysicians say; the confusion, the noise of waters, all the rest of it, were in her own swimming head. In an instant she became aware of this. 'Do me the greatest kindness of all,' she panted. 'I beseech you to go away!'

'Ah, don't say that. Don't kill me!' he cried.

She clasped her hands; her eyes were streaming with tears. 'As you love me, as you pity me, leave me alone!'

He glared at her a moment through the dusk, and the next instant she felt his arms about her and his lips on her own lips. His kiss was like white lightning, a flash that spread, and spread again, and stayed; and it was extraordinarily as if, while she took it, she felt each thing in his hard manhood that had least pleased her, each aggressive fact of his face, his figure, his presence, justified of its intense identity and made one with this act of possession. So had she heard of those wrecked and under water following a train of images before they sink. But when darkness returned she was free. She never looked about her; she only darted from the spot. There were lights in the windows of the house; they shone far across the lawn. In an extraordinarily short time – for the distance was considerable – she had moved through the darkness (for she saw nothing) and reached the door. Here only she paused. She looked all about her; she listened a little; then she put her hand on the latch. She had not known where to turn; but she knew now. There was a very straight path.

Two days afterwards Caspar Goodwood knocked at the door of the house in Wimpole Street in which Henrietta Stackpole occupied furnished lodgings. He had hardly removed his hand from the knocker when the door was opened and Miss Stackpole herself stood before him. She had on her hat and jacket; she was on the point of going out. 'Oh, good morning,' he said, 'I was in hopes I should find Mrs Osmond.'

Henrietta kept him waiting a moment for her reply; but there was a good deal of expression about Miss Stackpole even when she was silent. 'Pray what led you to suppose she was here?'

'I went down to Gardencourt this morning, and the servant told me she had come to London. He believed she was to come to you.'

Again Miss Stackpole held him – with an intention of perfect kindness – in suspense. 'She came here yesterday, and spent the night. But this morning she started for Rome.'

Caspar Goodwood was not looking at her; his eyes were fastened on the doorstep. 'Oh, she started—?' he stammered. And without finishing his phrase or looking up he stiffly averted himself. But he couldn't otherwise move.

Henrietta had come out, closing the door behind her, and now she put out her hand and grasped his arm. 'Look here, Mr Goodwood,' she said; 'just you wait!'

On which he looked up at her – but only to guess, from her face, with a revulsion, that she simply meant he was young. She stood shining at him with that cheap comfort, and it added, on the spot, thirty years to his life. She walked him away with her, however, as if she had given him now the key to patience.

TITLES IN THIS SERIES

Eric Ambler
The Mask of Dimitrios
Passage of Arms
The Schirmer Inheritance
Journey into Fear
The Light of Day
Judgement on Deltchev

John le Carré
The Spy Who Came in from the Cold
Call for the Dead
A Murder of Quality
The Looking-Glass War
A Small Town in Germany

Raymond Chandler*
Farewell My Lovely
The Lady in the Lake
Playback
The Long Goodbye
The High Window
The Big Sleep

Joseph Conrad
Lord Jim
The Nigger of the 'Narcissus'
Typhoon
Nostromo
The Secret Agent

Catherine Cookson
The Round Tower
The Fifteen Streets
Feathers in the Fire
A Grand Man
The Blind Miller

Catherine Cookson
The Mallen Streak
The Girl
The Gambling Man
The Cinder Path
The Invisible Cord

Monica Dickens
One Pair of Hands
The Happy Prisoner
Mariana
Kate and Emma
One Pair of Feet

Gerald Durrell
My Family and Other Animals
The Bafut Beagles
The Drunken Forest
Encounters with Animals
The Whispering Land
Menagerie Manor
A Zoo in My Luggage

F. Scott Fitzgerald*
The Great Gatsby
Tender is the Night
This Side of Paradise
The Beautiful and Damned
The Last Tycoon

Ian Fleming
Dr. No
Thunderball
Goldfinger
On Her Majesty's Secret Service
Moonraker
From Russia, With Love

C. S. Forester
The Ship
Mr Midshipman Hornblower
The Captain from Connecticut
The General
The Earthly Paradise
The African Queen

E. M. Forster
Where Angels Fear to Tread
The Longest Journey
A Room with a View
Howards End
A Passage to India

Fourteen Great Plays*

John Galsworthy
The Forsyte Saga:
The Man of Property
In Chancery
To Let
A Modern Comedy:
The White Monkey
The Silver Spoon
Swan Song

Erle Stanley Gardner
Perry Mason in the Case of
 the Gilded Lily
The Daring Decoy
The Fiery Fingers
The Lucky Loser
The Calendar Girl
The Deadly Toy
The Mischievous Doll
The Amorous Aunt

Richard Gordon
Doctor in the House
Doctor at Sea
Doctor at Large
Doctor in Love
Doctor in Clover
The Facemaker
The Medical Witness

Graham Greene
The Heart of the Matter
Stamboul Train
A Burnt-out Case
The Third Man
Loser Takes All
The Quiet American
The Power and the Glory

Graham Greene
Brighton Rock
The End of the Affair
It's a Battlefield
England Made Me
The Ministry of Fear
Our Man in Havana

Ernest Hemingway*
For Whom the Bell Tolls
The Snows of Kilimanjaro
Fiesta
The Short Happy Life of Francis Macomber
Across the River and into the Trees
The Old Man and the Sea

Georgette Heyer
These Old Shades
Sprig Muslin
Sylvester
The Corinthian
The Convenient Marriage

Henry James
The Europeans
Daisy Miller
Washington Square
The Aspern Papers
The Turn of the Screw
The Portrait of a Lady

Franz Kafka*
The Trial
America
In the Penal Settlement
Metamorphosis
The Castle
The Great Wall of China
Investigations of a Dog
Letter to his Father
The Diaries 1910-1923

Rudyard Kipling
The Jungle Book
The Second Jungle Book
Just So Stories
Puck of Pook's Hill
Stalky and Co.
Kim

Norah Lofts
Jassy
Bless This House
Scent of Cloves
How Far to Bethlehem?

D. H. Lawrence
Sons and Lovers
St. Mawr
The Fox
The White Peacock
Love among the Haystacks
The Virgin and the Gipsy
Lady Chatterley's Lover

D. H. Lawrence
Women in Love
The Ladybird
The Man Who Died
The Captain's Doll
The Rainbow

Robert Ludlum*
The Scarlatti Inheritance
The Osterman Weekend
The Matlock Paper
The Gemini Contenders

Thomas Mann*
Death in Venice
Tristan
Tonio Kröger
Doctor Faustus
Mario and the Magician
A Man and His Dog
The Black Swan
Confessions of Felix Krull, Confidence Man

W. Somerset Maugham
Cakes and Ale
The Painted Veil
Liza of Lambeth
The Razor's Edge
Theatre
The Moon and Sixpence

W. Somerset Maugham
Sixty-five Short Stories

Ed McBain*
Cop Hater
Give the Boys a Great Big Hand
Doll
Eighty Million Eyes
Hail, Hail, the Gang's All Here!
Sadie When She Died
Let's Hear it for the Deaf Man

James A. Michener*
The Source
The Bridges at Toko-Ri
Caravans
Sayonara

George Orwell
Animal Farm
Burmese Days
A Clergyman's Daughter
Coming up for Air
Keep the Aspidistra Flying
Nineteen Eighty-Four

George Orwell
Down and Out in Paris & London
Homage to Catalonia
Selections from Essays and Journalism: 1931-1949
The Road to Wigan Pier

Jean Plaidy
St. Thomas's Eve
Royal Road to Fotheringay
The Goldsmith's Wife
Perdita's Prince

Nevil Shute
A Town Like Alice
Pied Piper
The Far Country
The Chequer Board
No Highway

Georges Simenon
Ten Maigret Stories

Wilbur Smith
When the Lion Feeds
The Diamond Hunters
Eagle in the Sky
Gold Mine
Shout at the Devil

Wilbur Smith
Hungry as the Sea
The Sound of Thunder
The Eye of the Tiger

John Steinbeck*
The Grapes of Wrath
The Moon is Down
Cannery Row
East of Eden
Of Mice and Men

Mary Stewart
The Crystal Cave
The Hollow Hills
Wildfire at Midnight
Airs Above the Ground

Evelyn Waugh
Decline and Fall
Black Mischief
A Handful of Dust
Scoop
Put Out More Flags
Brideshead Revisited

H. G. Wells
The Time Machine
The Island of Dr. Moreau
The Invisible Man
The First Men in the Moon
The Food of the Gods
In the Days of the Comet
The War of the Worlds

Morris West
The Devil's Advocate
The Second Victory
Daughter of Silence
The Salamander
The Shoes of the Fisherman

Dennis Wheatley
The Devil Rides Out
The Haunting of Toby Jugg
Gateway to Hell
To the Devil—A Daughter

John Wyndham
The Day of the Triffids
The Kraken Wakes
The Chrysalids
The Seeds of Time
Trouble With Lichen
The Midwich Cuckoos

***Not currently available in Canada for copyright reasons**